Moontide and Magic Rise

DAW Books by Sean Russell:

MOONTIDE AND MAGIC RISE

WORLD WITHOUT END
SEA WITHOUT A SHORE

SEAN RUSSELL

DAW BOOKS, INC.

DONALD A. WOLLHEIM, FOUNDER

375 Hudson Street, New York, NY 10014

ELIZABETH R. WOLLHEIM
SHEILA E. GILBERT
PUBLISHERS

www.dawbooks.com

First Printing, May 2018

1 2 3 4 5 6 7 8 9

DAW TRADEMARK REGISTERED
U.S. PAT. OFF AND FOREIGN COUNTRIES
—MARCA REGISTRADA
HECHO EN U.S.A.

PRINTED IN THE U.S.A.

Author's Introduction

Books sometimes have odd inspirations. Fantasy novels don't usually start with science, but *World Without End* did . . . in a way. I have long been fascinated by Charles Darwin and his world-changing Theory of Natural Selection. We tend to forget today that the idea of species evolving was around long before Darwin. Lucretius wrote about it in *De Rerum Natura* around 60 BC, even suggesting something like Darwin's theory. Darwin's own grandfather, who was a distinguished physician, author, inventor, and member of the Royal Society, believed in evolution, he just didn't understand the engine that made it work. Darwin and a gentleman named Alfred Russel Wallace managed to come up with a theory of how evolution might work at roughly the same time—though technically Darwin had developed it first, he had only revealed it to a few trusted friends.

World Without End had a simple premise, though one that was somewhat original for its time. What if a young naturalist, like Charles Darwin, was sent on a long voyage to distant parts of the earth, but instead of discovering a foundational theory of biological science, discovered that magic existed? Like William Bligh on *HMS Bounty*, our young scientist—Tristam Flattery—was sent seeking a specific plant, though in this case one that was being used for mysterious purposes.

Anyone interested in history soon comes to the conclusion that a belief in science and scientific method superseded earlier belief systems, like magic, and even to some degree religion. What I posited was a world in which rationalism and scientific belief did not just destroy people's faith in magic, they destroyed magic itself. The power of magic was being eroded because people no longer believed. One of the comforting things about science is it does not require a leap of faith. Scientific theories can be tested. Magical and religious beliefs . . . not so much.

With those ideas as the foundation, I set out to write what became two books—*World Without End* and *Sea Without a Shore*. And then came two more books set in an earlier time period of the same world: *Beneath the Vaulted Hills* and *Compass of the Soul*.

Along with these ideas, I wanted to write about man's perennial efforts to extend human life, and perhaps one day make us all immortal. Our hunger for more time, more life—and the cost that might exact.

And here, all these years later, these books appear again. Although I was a younger writer when I began these books, I think they combined elements of science fiction, fantasy, and history in a way that hadn't been done—or if it had, it hadn't been done often. So I'm glad to see them being published again, like ideas that first appeared among the Romans, and then wove their way through various traditions, to appear again in the time of Darwin. World without end.

—Sean Russell
2018

WORLD WITHOUT END:
For Karen.

SEA WITHOUT A SHORE:
For Michael Moravec, Don Deese, and John Higgenbotham—
through thick and thin.

Owl's song on whispered shores
Where the silvered sea dies
Along the wake of a running moon,
Moontide and magic rise.

* * *

Note to Readers:

Scientific Names, originally in Old Farr, have been rendered in equivalent or near-equivalent Latin.

World Without End

Would it be too bold to imagine, that in the great length of time, since the earth began to exist, perhaps millions of ages before the commencement of the history of mankind, would it be too bold to imagine, that all warm-blooded animals have arisen from one living filament which the Great First Cause endued with animality . . . and thus possessing the faculty of continuing to improve by its own inherent activity, and of delivering down those improvements by generation to its posterity . . . world without end!

—Erasmus Darwin,
"Zoonomia" (1794)

One of the two horns of my dilemma.

—Laurence Sterne,
"The Life and Opinions of Tristram Shandy" (1760)

⌒ One

The drama unfolding in the field below seemed so improbable that it could have been nothing more than two groups of players preparing a performance—the duel that would bring down the curtain on the first act.

"I've forgotten my field glass. Hawkins? Can you see what they're doing?"

The driver had been pacing, almost silently, back and forth between his team and the door to the carriage, but he stopped now and shielded his eyes with a callused hand. "It is not yet clear, sir. They remain standing in their separate groups, and no one is stepping forward." The driver stayed in his place for a few seconds and when it appeared that his employer would have no further questions, at least for a moment, he returned to whispering to the gray mare and gelding.

The man who watched shifted on the seat of his carriage and realized he was gripping his cane so tightly that the joints in his fingers had begun to ache. The gestural language of the theater was well known to him, and what he saw transpiring on the field bore the unmistakable signs of unfolding tragedy. Signs he had seen often these past months. The emotions that a pending tragedy engendered were also very familiar: the overwhelming sense of helplessness; the firm knowledge that the small justice of men was of little consequence on the larger stage; and then the growing horror.

He gazed out over the field where the curious whispered among themselves, as people did before the curtain rose. Somewhere a physician stood by with his bag of dressings and instruments.

The man who had come to witness this renewal of the art of the duel was not one of the idly curious. Unlike most of those who stood about the field, he had fought a duel, though it had been long ago. That was one memory that did not fade. He knew what it felt like to turn away from one's second and come suddenly to a full understanding that this was no longer the practice floor. These could be the final moments of one's life. He had hefted a blade to test its balance and felt that second sharp stab of knowledge: what he held in his hand was an implement to end life.

He had been fortunate and never killed a man. True gentlemen did not demand another's life to assuage their pride, for pride was invariably at the center of these affairs—not honor. The man in the carriage had long ago seen past that particular myth.

On the field, too far off for him to discern detail, a tall, angular man had removed his frock coat—snow white linen against the green. The Baron Ipsword. Never graceful of movement, the baron appeared puppetlike now, moving jerkily on the stage. And he stayed near to his supporters; too close, in fact. They were all afraid.

The forces that had animated this puppet for so many years had fled. The aggressive pride, the jealousy, and outright malice had been replaced by overpowering terror. The baron was not, it appeared, a courageous man—which might have explained why he was so vicious in attacking others. But a quick tongue would not shield him today.

Beyond the site of the duel a thin covering of ground-mist still resisted the sun. It hung over the river, obscuring the boles of poplars, like the vapor one would imagine rising from molten gold. A summer morning so still the sky seemed to hold its breath. Then came the quick flick of a horse's tail and the impatient shaking of harness.

The second swordsman could be seen now, stepping away from his fellows. This would be the Viscount Elsworth, as tall as his opponent but athletic and graceful. Even with poor vision, the man who watched could see these qualities. If Ipsword was a puppet, this man was an acrobat, a tumbler—nimble, flexible, and strong. He cut the air three times quickly with his blade, testing the balance of the weapon, and then pivoted, flexing one knee. Satisfied, he strode forward a few paces and stopped, staring expectantly at the party huddled under the elms.

A good actor could express a great deal at a distance, even to those sitting at the furthest extremes of a theater, but no actor could ever convey the complexity of emotion that Ipsword displayed as he walked forward to duel; terrified, enraged, sullen, meek, almost ready to beg, prepared to do murder. Only enough pride and arrogance remained to carry him to this place.

It was common, the man in the carriage thought, that the actors could not see the signs of impending tragedy. "*Poor fool*," the man whispered. "*It has almost nothing to do with him.*" He shifted again on the seat, the leather squeaking. If he was right in what he guessed, then first-blood would not end this affair. Ipsword might have been carried here by the remains of his pride, but Elsworth was likely concerned with neither pride nor honor.

"Pray that I am wrong," the man who watched said aloud.

The two swordsmen saluted with their rapiers and then stepped to the guard position, one so tentatively that it seemed he might break and run. A third man raised aloft a white handkerchief, like a flag of peace . . . and then released it.

The man in the carriage thought afterward that he must have blinked, for he did not see the thrust. Only Elsworth bent forward over a flexed knee, poised like a dancer, sliding his blade from the chest of the collapsing baron.

"*Flames!*" the man in the carriage whispered.

The viscount stood for a moment, looking at the fallen man, and then he turned and handed his blade to another. His second spoke to him and then went slowly over to the men gathered around the injured baron. He hovered on the edge of this scene for a moment—the faithful gathered around the fallen hero—perhaps he spoke, and then crossed back to the viscount, who stood now with a coat draped about his shoulders. They nodded to each other, like men of business at the end of the day, and then went directly to a large carriage drawn up under the elms.

The man watching realized he had raised his hands in horror and half covered his face. He took hold of himself as best he could. "Hawkins?" he said, leaning out to speak to his driver, his voice trembling. "Will you go down?"

The driver nodded stiffly and set off, picking his way hurriedly among the brambles down the slope to the open field. The man sat back in his carriage, breathing in short gasps, and then banged his cane hard on the floorboards. He had *so* hoped that he was wrong.

It was only a few moments until a gentle tap sounded on the carriage door. "Hawkins?"

"It would appear to be a thrust to the heart, sir." A pause. A breath roughly drawn. "I think he still lives but can't continue much longer."

"No, I'm sure he can't." The man looked out at the field once again. The retreating carriage. The small group bearing up their dying companion. He could almost see the horror on their faces. None of them had expected this—an accidental injury, perhaps, but not this.

"Shall I take you back, sir?" the driver asked quietly.

The old man shook his head. "No. We go on. You must have me in Merton by nightfall."

ᔐ Two

What are the beliefs of this "Man of Reason?" That the application of reason to all areas of life will lead mankind into a golden age of peace, knowledge, and prosperity. That religion and nationalism are merely guises of tribalism—manifestations of base passions unbridled by reason—and all lead us away from the "reasonable world" into ignorance and endless cycles of violence.

Beaumont: The Man of Reason

The sloop of war that carried Tristam Flattery to Avonel was named *Mysterious*, and he saw irony in that. He stood at the ship's rail watching the eastern shore of the sound creep past, listening to the slap of small waves against the hull.

"We will certainly make harbor this evening, Mr. Flattery." It was Hawksmoor, a minion of the King's Man—the one who pried.

"So perhaps now you can tell me the reason I have been summoned?" Tristam did not turn to look at the man. The ship moved slowly through the long shadow of the western shore, and Tristam found he did not want to take his eyes from the area still bathed in sunlight.

"I cannot, Mr. Flattery. In fact, I don't know myself. I was told to be sure you were the Flattery who assisted Professor Dandish with Baron Trevelyan's collection. No more. You may draw whatever conclusions you might from that."

"I have misclassified some rare flower and shall be sent to the tower for my sins?"

Even the man's laugh was artificial. "For such a crime a beheading is usual. A Royal Summons, Mr. Flattery. A chance to serve the King. People dream their entire lives of such an opportunity. You should be glad of it."

Tristam felt his shoulders shrug. In truth he was very pleased by the prospect of serving the King—but this "*man of the King's Man*," as Hawksmoor liked to name himself, was irritating beyond reason. Tristam was sure Hawksmoor knew full well why Tristam had been summoned—but kept it secret because it allowed him to feel some small sense of being in control of the situation. Tristam had seen this characteristic in men before. He would be willing to wager that Hawksmoor was used to being dealt with in this same manner. Pettiness begetting pettiness.

"The anchor will be down an hour after dark, Mr. Flattery. We should be ready to disembark immediately." Without awaiting a response Hawksmoor was gone, leaving Tristam standing at the rail, shaking his head gently. There must be something about the King's Service that shriveled a man's spirit, Tristam thought, for the pettiness of bureaucrats was unparalleled.

Tristam had not been to Avonel in two years and he realized some of his sour mood was due to this return. The place called forth his particular ghosts and no amount of time appeared to alter that.

"The studding sails are set and drawing, Mr. Flattery," came a voice at his side. Tristam glanced over at young Jack Beacham, midshipman in the King's Navy and Tristam's self-appointed mentor in things nautical.

"I can't tell you what pleasure they give me," Tristam said, hiding a smile as he looked up. The maintop, as the upper mast was named, was still in sunlight, the weathered canvas appearing stark in contrast to shadow and the evening-blue sky. Tristam often found himself teasing this good-natured young sailor, for it was obvious that the midshipman believed the sailing ship was, without question, man's greatest accomplishment.

"They are a beautiful sight, sir," Beacham said, almost wistfully. He continued to stare up at the filling sails for a moment and then seemed to remember his obligations as tutor. "Unfortunately, Mr. Flattery, these are light air sails, and it means the wind's dropping and the master expects it to fall lighter yet."

Tristam raised his eyebrows as though impressed with the master's great insight.

Beacham was a stocky youth, in his middle teens, perhaps. An officer in training, and well suited to the calling, Tristam thought, for the boy viewed life on land the way some feared prolonged illness. Tristam had not known the word "*landsman*" could be spoken with such heartfelt disdain.

The young sailor pointed a callused hand toward the shore. "But there's a wind line there or my name isn't Jack. Every evening about this time, if there isn't a gale to interfere, a breeze comes down off the hills. Cooling air, some have it . . . though you'd know more about that than myself, I'm sure."

Beacham, whose name certainly wasn't Jack (it was the name given to every new sailor, though Beacham seemed overly pleased with it), was mightily impressed with Tristam's education and became even more so when he discovered that Tristam knew as much, or more, about the geometrics of the sphere and the theory of weather as the officers aboard.

The two young men stood, staring off toward the eastern shore as the ship moved slowly through calm water. Across this narrow arm of the Entide Sea the crags rose up, supporting rolling fields which spread out toward hills, faded and distant under the summer sky. The land seemed fair to Tristam, and appeared very firm and secure, no matter what the young midshipman might think.

Hedgerows crisscrossed the downs, laid out according to no apparent design or discernable logic, they traced the contours of the land, standing out from their long shadows in the evening light. To Tristam they looked like the supporting framework of the countryside, forming an infinitely complex web of branchings and intersections, dividing one field neatly from the next, the holdings of one family from those of their neighbor. Though no two fields were alike in shape or size, Tristam saw a comforting order displayed on the downs which was almost restful to his spirit. It also said much about life in the Kingdom of Farrland.

"Excuse my manners, Mr. Flattery," Beacham said, still staring up, "it is not my meaning to pry, but are you any relation to Admiral Flattery who had command of the Blue Squadron at Cape Locke?"

"Oh, very distantly, I'm told. All landsmen in my more immediate family, I'm afraid."

"Well, sir, there have been many fine landsmen," Beacham said quietly, an obvious concession on the young sailor's part.

"Kind of you to say." This time Tristam hid his smile by shading his eyes to look aloft. Silence returned and Tristam waited for Beacham to screw up his nerve enough to ask the question that was no doubt gnawing away at him. It took some little while.

"We were wondering, my messmates and me," the lad began, "if you might be kin to Erasmus Flattery, then . . . ?"

Tristam lowered his shading hand but kept his attention fixed on the uppermost sails. "My late great-uncle," he said with some resignation.

"Ah." Beacham nodded as though he had been proven right. Apparently unaware of the sour note in Tristam's voice, the midshipman plunged ahead. "Was it true, then, that your uncle was apprentice to Lord Eldrich? It's often said that he was."

Tristam nodded, keeping his eyes on the men working the ship, coiling the myriad lines, going about their business without a word. "He never spoke of it to me, but apparently he served in Lord Eldrich's house for some short time. Eldrich must have been very old, and my uncle very young."

"Do you think it was true, then, that Lord Eldrich was a mage, as everyone said?" Youthful curiosity and enthusiasm overcame all other considerations.

Tristam heard himself release a hollow laugh. "To be honest, Mr. Beacham, I probably know less about Eldrich than you do yourself. Certainly my uncle was the most ordinary of men—except for his intellect and an impressive variety of eccentricities. There was nothing in his life that would make one believe he had abilities we poor mortals lack."

"I have never had the pleasure myself, Mr. Flattery, but those that have tasted them say the wines made from the Erasmus Grape have a bit of magic in them."

Tristam smiled. "A magic you could learn yourself. Breeding a new varietal and a structured inquiry into the process of fermentation. The magic of knowledge, Mr. Beacham, no more. Though that is magic enough for me."

Tristam never learned what the lad intended to say next, for the voice of the ship's master cut him off just as he opened his mouth to speak.

"Mr. Beacham. Would you be so good as to find me the ship's carpenter."

"By your leave," Beacham almost whispered, giving Tristam a nod and setting off at a trot looking for the drunk who, apparently, was also referred to as the ship's carpenter—the kindest appellation Tristam had heard thus far.

A small alcid surfaced alongside and then dove at the sight of the great, looming ship. Tristam stared down into the dark waters for a moment, trying to see if the bird swam using its wings as some said it did. Too dark.

Something faint and milky-white, almost apparitional, appeared in the water and it took Tristam a second to realize that this was not in the depths but a reflection. The city of Avonel, still aglow in the last light of the day, had chosen that moment to appear over the shoulder of a hill.

Tristam looked up to the rising towers and sloping slate roofs, not sure if he felt ambivalence or real animosity. *Why*, he asked himself, *can't I bury all my*

past associations with this place and see it anew? He squinted a little as though
it might help him with this exercise. Perhaps the city was too familiar, for the
shift he looked for did not occur. It remained as it had for two centuries, a
lovely city spread out beneath a graceful skyline—and greatly unaffected by
Tristam's feelings toward it.

There were, even Tristam had to admit, a few things about Avonel which
were undeniably admirable. The whitestone from which it had been built was
a naturalist's dream—riddled with the fossilized life of ages long past. Almost
every stone appeared to have carved upon it the shapes of sea shells, of crusta-
ceans and all manner of marine life, some of it quite unknown today and
steeped in mystery. Tristam, like many of his fellow scholars at Merton, often
wondered what had befallen these creatures.

Avonel was also unique in all the cities surrounding the Entide Sea, for it
had not grown haphazardly over the centuries, one period of architecture
thrown half atop that of another. The city of Avonel was the result of the vision
of one man, Prince Kirstom, who had been given the responsibility of rebuilding the city after it was razed by the armies of Entonne in the Winter War. The
intervening two hundred years had added much to the great designer's work.
The color of the stone grew warmer with age, trees and gardens matured, and
ivy, wisteria, and columbine draped the walls and eaves.

In the fading light Avonel began, finally, to change character, elements disappearing into shadow until the scene became unfamiliar, foreign. Tristam
could now easily imagine that he was approaching an unknown city, seeing a
new land from the deck of a ship fresh from the open sea.

As the very last hint of light disappeared, Avonel looked like the ruin of an
empty city, mysteriously abandoned. And then a streetlight flickered into being, and then another.

This nineteenth day of June, 1559.

*Arrived in Avonel late this day and am installed in a suite of rooms at
the Queen Anne—I feel rather like a gentleman of means. No one has yet
bothered to tell me why I have been summoned to the palace and my curiosity is swollen to near bursting. I shall hardly sleep this night.*

*I'm grateful that the Queen Anne does not afford me a view of the old
theater site. Martyr's flames, how I wish they would erect a building there!
Dandish always told me that if all men felt shame for the follies of their
fathers, every man in the country would live in constant disgrace. Good
advice, I'm sure, but from someone whose father did not, to my knowledge, have any great failure attached to his good name—let alone a failure
of vast proportion and infamy. And to suffer this ruin over something so*

frivolous as a theater! Why couldn't my father have failed in a nobler cause at least? And why must I always come back to this same matter? I am like a compass—turn me as you will, but I seek my one true direction. It is the anxiety of this strange summons that has led me into these too familiar paths of thought. Once I am actually employed in my task, whatever it might be, I'm sure these feelings will come under control again . . . for a while, at least.

∾ Three

Sir:

It would appear that Mr. Tristam Flattery is a man of great interest to us, though his connection with Erasmus is still troubling.

Briefly: Mr. Flattery is, at the time of this writing, twenty and three years of age and has recently left an appointment at Merton College: the same institution from which he graduated some three years past.

The sad tale of Mr. Flattery's father, the Honorable Morton Flattery, is well known; his marriage, against the wishes of his family, to an actress of vastly inferior social status; and then the final folly of the Grand Avonel Theater. The collapse of this endeavor led Morton Flattery to self-murder at the age of twenty-nine, and then, the following year, his wife was carried away in the terrible influenza epidemic. The child was then aged eight years. Subsequently, Tristam Flattery was raised by the senior member of the Flattery family, the well known Erasmus, though the uncle seemed to take small interest in his charge—his attentions being focused elsewhere, as might be imagined.

The child was an excellent student at Edington School, where he lived until graduation. There is little more to say of those years except that, unlike many of studious nature, Tristam Flattery proved himself a gifted athlete, showing skill with the bow, riding, fencing, rowing, and, due to instruction by his great uncle Erasmus, he also swam.

As one would expect, Mr. Flattery went on to Merton College. Here he came under the influence of Professor Sanfield Dandish, the celebrated botanist, and discovered the empiricists, joining the ranks of the, so-called, "men of reason": those who believe, among much else, that one should be of good character because it is sensible! For two years after graduation he assisted Professor Dandish in the taxonomic classification of Baron Trevelyan's great collection.

On the surface it would appear that he is a normal enough young man—perhaps a cut above the average in intellect and other gifts—but I discovered two incidents from his years at Merton that set him apart most distinctly. The first took place in a class exploring the arithmetical relationships of chance. I do not know the precise details, but no doubt it was a lesson much like we have all attended; discussion of rations and odds, etcetera. The salient detail is that Mr. Flattery was able to predict the outcome of a coin toss more than twenty times without mistake! (I have this on good authority, as there were a dozen students in attendance as well as the instructor.)

Being the most conventional of young men, and refusing to take risks (the lesson of his father) he will neither dice nor play at cards so it cannot be known how frequently Mr. Flattery might be able to perform feats of this nature. I do not need to say how great are the odds against such a thing!

The second incident concerned the so-called "ghost boy of Merton," the apparition that is said to have been wandering the town since the days of the first true plague—some two hundred years. I will not go into the details and history of the story for I am sure you are aware of them. Today's "men of reason" do not believe in this apparition, of course, and several pranksters have been caught with younger brothers dressed up in the appropriate costume which has discredited the story even further. In his second year at Merton Mr. Flattery encountered a small boy, dressed for the part, who actually approached him as though to speak, but, as this took place on the edge of a central common, several other scholars witnessed the meeting and gave chase to the "ghost." The boy ran into the common and around a tree but, true to all tales, was not to be found when the scholars arrived in hot pursuit. Nor had this child climbed up into the branches. A concerted search revealed no clue as to the child's disappearance. The scholars believed (and still believe, apparently) that Tristam Flattery had practiced upon them in a most clever way, though, for his part, young Flattery claims he was the victim of the prank. From the little I have seen I would venture that such a stunt would not be in keeping with the character of Tristam Flattery.

Perhaps here is our lodestone at last! Certainly he is as promising as any I have known.

If the opinion is that Tristam Flattery is a man of interest to us (and I would argue strongly that this is so) then it would seem prudent to find some way to shift his residence to Avonel.

I remain your servant,
E. D. H.

Sir Roderick Palle folded the letter and sat watching the ballet of flames in the hearth. Quiet moments were few in his life and found usually late at night—the price one paid for being the King's Man. A book he had been trying to finish for several months lay on the small table beside the chair, but—like most nights—the real world would not allow him escape.

He raised a glass of wine, taking great pleasure from the play of firelight in its dark ruby center, as beautiful as any gem to his eye. Knowing the history of the grape could not spoil that—at least not entirely.

He looked back at the letter he had laid on the table. There had been too many blind ends over the years for Palle to allow his hopes to rise. Keep the mind on the task at hand, that was his creed.

In the midst of savoring his wine a soft knock sounded—as though delivered by a hand lacking bones.

"Drayton?"

His man servant appeared, solemn as always. "Sir Benjamin, sir," he said, using the tones usually heard at funerals.

"Please bring him up. And Drayton? A second glass."

Benjamin Rawdon appeared, his handsome face seeming a little careworn.

"You are up late, Benjamin. Seeing to your patient, I presume?"

"The dreams again. I think they are almost unbearable sometimes." The physician, too, kept his voice low, as though afraid of waking the rest of the palace. He sat opposite Sir Roderick, accepting wine with some relief, his host thought. "I left Teiho Ruau singing—songs from his own land. Very haunting and beautiful."

"Music to soothe the troubled soul." Roderick raised his glass. "The King's health."

They each drank and then sat without speaking. There was something on the Royal Physician's mind, Palle was sure. Rawdon was not one to seek out the comfort of another man's company—the physician was of the type who could only be truly at ease in the company of women.

Palle decided not to ask what the problem was. He knew this was a little perverse, forcing the doctor to bring it up himself, but the man's reticence could be a bit annoying sometimes. The silence soon began to unsettle Rawdon.

"You have not had a reoccurrence of the pain in your legs?"

"No, I've been perfectly hale. Kind of you to ask."

Rawdon sipped his wine, nodding in response just as the glass touched his lips.

Sir Roderick continued to stare at the doctor. He had often been told that his gaze unsettled people, and at times he found this ability useful. Rawdon had interrupted this little bit of time alone and the King's Man realized he was making the doctor pay for that small offense. *Petty*, he told himself but kept his gaze fixed on the doctor.

After another moment of awkward silence he relented. "I take it there is something on your mind, Doctor." He made his tone kindly. Foolish to act this way toward Rawdon, as though the man had not had enough troubles of late.

The Royal Physician nodded. "Yes." He looked out the window. "Some of the others are concerned about this young Flattery."

"Are you speaking for them? Expressing your own concerns? Or are you merely keeping me informed of the mood of our colleagues?"

"I—I speak for no one else."

"Then you are concerned yourself?"

"Yes. . . ." He looked down into his wineglass. "Yes, I am. It is this family connection. . . . Doesn't it worry you?"

The King's Man held his wine out toward the physician as though it were, in itself, an answer to the question. "The great nephew and heir of Erasmus?" He paused, looking into the fire. "I understand why you are reticent, but I think it is not really such a risk. And the prince would like to see greater efforts made. . . . I want to have a careful look at this young man in any case. I showed you this?" He indicated the letter he had been rereading earlier.

The physician leaned over to look and then nodded.

"Even with his connection to Erasmus, we cannot ignore this." Sir Roderick laid his head back, suddenly tired. He closed his eyes and felt that slight acidic burning of exhaustion—a sign he habitually ignored. "We know so little of Erasmus . . . and his intentions." Roderick opened his eyes and looked over at his visitor. "The man laid down so many false trails. As I have come to the end of each, invariably I have had this feeling that it amused him to lead me on." He held up his glass again. "The finest grape in the known world. It is a measure of his genius for revenge. I taste it daily."

The physician's nod was so distracted that Roderick wondered if he listened at all.

"Well, I am glad it's you, Roderick, who will have young Flattery in hand."

This brought a silence in which both sipped at their wine. The flavor was complex, Roderick felt, the bitterness undetectable to most.

"Do you not worry, Roderick, that we might have miscalculated?" Rawdon asked, the tone of his voice admitting that this was his real concern. "We have made such crucial decisions based on so little knowledge."

Roderick did not hesitate before answering. "And what other choice can you see? We have the Entonne to consider, as always. And I am confident that much good will come of our efforts—as you should be, Benjamin. You of all people." The King's Man looked over at his companion. "Your life has been most difficult these past months, fraught with ill luck: at such times it becomes easy to believe a pattern has been cast. But be of good heart, Benjamin. Your wife is recovered. The King is hale. And our own endeavors proceed apace. Do not let pessimism and melancholia take hold of you, Benjamin. Once they have sent their tendrils into your heart, it is most difficult to free yourself again. And they have only found purchase because of your recent troubles—none of them of your own making."

The man forced a tight-lipped smile, though his eyes did not quite agree. "I'm sure you're right. I am easily unbalanced by things these days." He sipped his wine, without proper appreciation, Roderick thought. "You heard of this bloody duel?"

Roderick nodded. "Yes. No accident, I am told."

"Completely intentional! I spoke with the physician who attended. Has the word *gentleman* lost all meaning?"

"Yes, in fact, I fear it has—for many, at least. Though it is good to remember that Elsworth takes his instructions from a lady. Unfortunate the fools did not run each other through so we could be rid of them both."

"That is harsh judgment," the physician said quietly. "I thought Ipsword a fool—but nothing more."

Roderick laughed softly. "Is it harsh? Yes, I suppose. And I know folly is not the exclusive domain of the foolish. Look at this young Flattery's father. No fool, no matter what people say. Wed to ill luck, that was all—betrothed at birth. We who have fortune smiling upon us must not lose sight of that. One can too easily focus on only the bad. It is a tendency one should be wary of."

"I tell my patients as much," the physician said, displaying the mildest surprise, as though he had never considered this advice to be anything but words.

"And you are telling them true, Benjamin." Sir Roderick lifted his glass again. "Long life, sir."

"Yes. Long life."

↪ Four

The dream never varied. Tristam would become conscious in the dark, but he could not move, even to open his eyes. And then he would realize that he was aware within a dream—unable to wake. No amount of effort would allow him to move even a finger, to open his mouth to scream. It was like being buried alive. And then, finally, he would awake, gasping for air, his heart pounding. After that, sleep came with difficulty, or not at all, for, if he did sleep, sometimes the dream returned.

*   *   *

Tristam woke to the sound of carriages passing beneath his window. A sudden fear that one of these might bring the King's Man propelled him half out of bed where he stopped, staring dumbly at the clock face. After a few "ticks" the position of the hands registered. Half-six. There was time yet.

Tristam fell back into the bed and let his eyes close. Even before anxiety about the day could begin, he felt the emotion left by the dream still clinging to him. It had been a few months since the dream had haunted him, for that was how he thought of it—*haunting*.

It is brought on by anxiety, Tristam told himself. *My coming appointment at the palace.*

Sleep, always elusive in Tristam's world, was not going to return, so he forced himself up.

As he stropped his razor, Tristam tried to shake off the emotion the nightmare left behind like a residue. He tried to force his mind into the day and out of this state of enervation—neither awake nor asleep.

Dreams plagued him, and often, try as he might, he could not remember what they had been about. They would hover on the edge of consciousness, like a face just at the periphery of one's vision. Tristam often wondered if his nightmares were part of the cause of his insomnolence, for he was plagued by that as well—an inability to find sleep. Certainly he did not really like the dream state; to his mind the reoccurring dream was proof of that.

He stared at himself in the mirror. *Try to appear more in control*, he told himself. With his green eyes set too wide apart, Tristam thought he always looked as though he had just been startled—a man constantly surprised by the world in which he found himself. He was sure this was one of the several reasons that women did not throw themselves at him as they did at his blue-eyed cousin, Jaimy. The reflection in the mirror was less than he'd hoped, in fact. Nose not large but not finely formed either; mouth acceptably shaped, lower lip protruding marginally too far. Only his high broad forehead was admirable, and perhaps his hair—thick, dark blond, and given to curls. Still, his would never be a portrait that inspired women to sighs, he was sure of that.

His mind returned to the coming appointment. Despite the look that he believed was written large on his face, Tristam was not a person who liked surprises. This secrecy surrounding his summons was driving him a little mad.

Not much longer, he told himself, though it didn't seem to help.

Unwilling to wait for hot water, Tristam suffered a cold water shave, and nicked himself twice for his lack of prudence. He proceeded to dress with extreme care—a knight donning armor could not have been more thorough—as though the slightest flaw in his attire might leave an opening through which a blade might slip. His conduct and appearance seemed the only things, in his present circumstances, over which he could exercise any control, so he put his energies there.

Tristam emerged from his rooms looking like the scion of an important family. Nervousness, he hoped, remained hidden behind the costume. He locked his door with a decoratively cast key and set out in search of the dining room, wondering if his stomach would tolerate food.

Although Tristam would normally have chosen to break his fast in one of the establishments that represented the latest fashion in Avonel, a coffee house, he was afraid to stray far from the Queen Anne for fear of missing the arrival of Roderick Palle. This despite the fact that the appointed hour was still some time off.

A servant led him into a sunny courtyard to a table set beneath the boughs of an ancient butternut tree. Finches sang among the leaves, and kinglets flitted through the curtain of ivy that covered the courtyard walls. It should have been a perfect morning.

Anxiety be damned, Tristam thought, *I cannot begin such a day without coffee.*

When food came, Tristam registered on some level that it was very good, but even so he was not able to enjoy it to any degree. Instead he sat sipping coffee, musing on his coming appointment and occasionally trying to turn his mind elsewhere. The gardens provided some relief, for Tristam was not only a botanist by training but a gardener on no small scale at his own home. This was the influence of Dandish, though Tristam's great-uncle Erasmus had made a contribution as well, leaving behind a beautiful mature garden, which Tristam had done much to improve.

"Mr. Flattery?"

Tristam looked up to find a gentleman of round features looking down at him.

"Roderick Palle," the man offered.

Tristam almost jumped to his feet, only barely remembering to make a leg. "Sir Roderick. Have I mistaken the time of our meeting?"

"No, I believe, by some near-miracle, my driver has brought me early." He gestured to a second chair. "May I?"

The King's Man took the seat, looked around the courtyard briefly, and then produced a beautifully made pocket watch. "We have some few moments yet. Just time for a draught of their fine west island *coffea*." He offered Tristam a stiff smile as though this was something he did infrequently. "It is healthful, I'm convinced. My own physician recommends coffee highly. 'Drink in the morning until there is a slight tremor in the hands, and then the same at supper.' It sets one up marvelously, don't you find?"

"I'm sure there's nothing quite like it." Sir Roderick Palle did not fit Tristam's image as one of Farrland's most influential men. Portly, soft featured, eyes perpetually half-closed. The man dressed in the most conventional manner and colors. Tristam had seldom met anyone who more suited the part of gentleman's gentleman.

What does this man want from me? Tristam wondered, all traces of appetite gone.

Sir Roderick's coffee arrived and as he tasted it an almost imperceptible easing of tightness around the eyes might have been an indication of satisfaction, though Tristam could not be sure.

"I have the pleasure of being acquainted with several members of your family, Mr. Flattery: your uncle, the duke, and the good duchess also; the Earl of Tyne, though not so well." He hesitated and Tristam felt his own face grow warm. "I did not know Erasmus Flattery, though he is something of a hero to me." He held up his cup. "I would find a morning without coffee difficult, but I am in thrall to the Erasmus Grape. Your great-uncle shall have my undying gratitude for his efforts in viniculture."

Tristam managed a smile, relieved the man had not brought up his father.

"I understand you are the heir of Erasmus? Do you pursue his interests?"

Tristam shook his head. "No. Viniculture was my uncle's special province, Sir Roderick. I shall not attempt to compete with him there."

"I wish I had known him, but it was always said that Erasmus was not a social man."

Tristam was used to this by now. Those who knew of his uncle at all were usually a little fascinated by his life. "The truth is, I hardly knew him myself. Deeply and incurably reclusive is how I would describe my uncle. I always lived at school."

"As I did myself. Which was a great blessing—my parents were famous bores." He tried the smile again to only marginally better effect. "And what lies ahead for you, Mr. Flattery? Finished at the university, I collect. Have you considered the service of the King?"

Although Tristam had dedicated some time to imagining the possible conversations he might have with the King's Man, this was not one that he had considered. He was a little taken aback. "To be honest, Sir Roderick, the thought had never occurred to me."

Roderick nodded. "But you should allow it to occur to you, Mr. Flattery. There is much work to be done and too few to do it. Too few of ability, that is." Roderick's tone and manner would suggest he spoke half in jest, yet Tristam had the strongest feeling that he was completely serious. The younger man found himself looking quickly around as though he might need to bolt. His journey with the detestable Hawksmoor came back to him. Not for him, the life of a bureaucrat.

"I often encourage young gentlemen of conspicuous ability to consider the King's service. We cannot all live at our ease, Mr. Flattery; someone must shoulder the burden. At times I feel as though I am a dike holding back a vast sea of foolhardiness." All the while he spoke, Tristam noted that the man's tone did not alter, always remaining carefully neutral. Tristam suspected it would remain so even in a fit of rage. "There are any number of well-meaning fools who would bring Farrland to ruin in a trice. Without stopping to think, they would undermine our strength and have us, in the end, little more than a province of Entonne. And do not think our neighbor would not pounce on any opportunity. . . ." The color had begun to rise in the knight's face, but as quickly as it appeared the man seemed to gain control. He took a sip of his coffee. "It would raise my spirits to know that another had joined my colleagues and myself in our efforts. Young shoulders, Mr. Flattery; there is no substitute. Wisdom may come with age but, alas, the energies flag."

Tristam did not know how to respond. There was little doubt in his mind that to tell Sir Roderick the truth in this—that he would consider *prison* preferable—would damage the man's opinion of him irreparably. "It is such a new thought, Sir Roderick, I shall have to take time to consider."

Roderick looked down at his coffee, perhaps disappointed by Tristam's answer. "No doubt you have set a course of your own—graduating first of your year, and your family is not without influence."

Tristam felt his face grow warm again. Palle knew more than a little about Tristam, apparently. "Medicine," and then he added, more truthfully, "perhaps."

Roderick smiled, a little brittlely. "And would that be your choice if you were not trying to win the favor of a young woman? One whose father might look kindly upon the suit of a physician?"

Tristam's cup stopped halfway to his mouth. Roderick was showing terrible manners bringing up such a thing—but then he was the King's Man, after all. He would be sure to know a great deal about any person he brought into the King's palace.

"Am I being too familiar, Mr. Flattery?"

"Not at all. I was just framing a reply. As you say, the physician's calling might not be my principal interest, but it is a noble pursuit and one helpful to all. . . ."

"But not where your true interests would carry you?"

Tristam realized he hesitated. "Perhaps not."

"And your true inclination is . . . ?"

Tristam expected Sir Roderick knew the answer to the question already. "I would continue my study of the natural world," Tristam said as though admitting a great flaw of character.

"A worthy endeavor, but I will tell you; not a few men have served their

King in great capacity and contributed much in other fields as well. Such men do not lie awake at night worried that they have wasted the day." Roderick consulted his pocket watch suddenly. "Shall we . . . ?"

As they set out in Roderick's carriage Tristam had a sudden fear that they would pass by the ruin of the Grand Theater of Avonel, and found himself staring at the passing scene registering little. Roderick would certainly know the story of Tristam's father; all of Avonel did. Tristam had developed his own defense in this. Mention the Avonel theater and he would make the most disparaging remarks about his father. And then, afterward, he would feel cruel and disloyal. He forced himself to look at the street, consciously reading the shop signs, almost reciting them mentally.

He glanced over at Roderick, who remained absorbed in his own thoughts. For a second Tristam feared that he had already so disappointed the King's Man that Roderick could no longer bother to make conversation. The younger man tried to think of something to say, if only to gauge his companion's response.

You are just nervous, Tristam told himself. *No doubt this is what it's like to begin in a new position.* Never having known employment for wages, he could only guess.

All the while, Tristam paid close attention to their progress and was relieved when they turned away from the city's center.

Although the coaches of the wealthy were a common sight in the streets of Avonel, Tristam could not shake the feeling that he was an object of attention traveling in Sir Roderick's beautiful phaeton. Opposite him the King's Man lounged, a look of complete distraction on his face.

I am the country cousin, Tristam thought. Even though his uncles—his father's elder brothers—were the Duke of Blackwater and Earl of Tyne, respectively, Tristam had always lived on the edge of the charmed circle of his near-relatives. He had shared rooms with Cousin Jaimy at the university (Cousin Jaimy was the heir to the Blackwater title, and therefore addressed as "Lord Jaimas," though to Tristam he was "Jaimy" or even "J") and had often been a guest in his uncles' homes, though he had never felt completely at ease there.

It was the tradition in Farrland that orphans were raised by the eldest member of the family—an odd tradition, Tristam often thought. In his case it had meant being raised by a series of reserved, often uninterested, instructors. Tristam felt himself warm a bit toward the King's Man when he realized that Sir Roderick had endured the same fate.

Although Tristam had felt some jealousy of classmates who went home to families, he had been allowed a freedom that was the cause of great envy among his fellows. Tristam knew quite well that the adult world had felt some measure of pity for him—fatherless and motherless as he was—but Tristam had wasted little time on self-pity in this regard. The truth was his parents, when alive, had not had much time for him anyway. After his mother's death, Tristam had missed certain of the servants more than either of his parents.

The great "tragedy" of being orphaned, in Tristam's view, had merely served to make him extremely independent while still very young. "Loneliness," as other people described it, was something that Tristam had not experienced since he was very young.

If Tristam had any true "family," it was his cousin Jaimy, who was like a brother to him. Later there had been Dandish, of course, but he had been a mentor and a friend. Tristam did not subscribe to the commonly held belief that orphans sought out surrogate parents for the rest of their lives. Certainly he hadn't wasted his time in that endeavor.

The street they passed along was thronged now with carriages and wagons and men on horseback, and the walkways streamed with pedestrians. It was a street that wound its way up the side of the low hill over which the city of Avonel spread. The gray granite paving stones were so smooth and finely fitted that the well-sprung coach rode as comfortably as a boat on calm water.

Off to the south Tristam caught a glimpse of billowing white clouds on the horizon. An afternoon rain shower was likely, a common occurrence in this season.

The carriage passed a queue of people outside a small temple and Tristam saw Sir Roderick fix his gaze there for a few seconds, his countenance unreadable. Over the wide doors spread a relief of the Martyr upon the pyre.

We have a barbarous history, Tristam thought.

"Are you too much a man of reason to be a follower of Farrelle, Mr. Flattery?" Sir Roderick asked, much to Tristam's relief.

"I am a trained empiricist, sir. Superstition is not compatible with my pursuits."

"Ah, I wondered." Genuine amusement shone in Roderick's smile. "And I have been trained a pragmatist. Too much so to follow the path of the Entonne Martyr. You might say that religion is not compatible with my pursuits, as well." He tilted his head toward the line of believers. "Waiting to pay their tithes, no doubt. Money that could provide their children with educations is sent off to Entonne. Their own children! Ah, well, Lord Skye said, 'There is no other occupation in which idleness can be turned to such profit.' He knew something of priests, apparently—and perhaps *prophets* as well." Roderick rubbed absently at the palm of his hand. "They have become a nuisance, these priests of Farrelle; petitioning the government, stirring up their parishioners. Five hundred years since their power was broken and still they cannot accept that the church shall have no part in governing. Even the mages realized that government should be left to kings and their ministers."

The conversation ended there and Tristam decided to keep his thoughts on these matters to himself. There was nothing to be gained in arguing. It had been sixty years since the last war with Entonne, but many—and Roderick was obviously one of these—believed the long history of hostilities with this nation was not yet done. For these people, the Farrellite church was just another Entonne institution aimed at subverting Farr independence.

Like most of the students at the university, Tristam was an admirer of Entonne culture. War, he believed, was unlikely unless brought about by Farrland. Not something he could say to the King's Man.

There were fewer carriages on the road, and almost no pedestrians. A wide gateway led into an area of open lawns and carefully designed gardens: the famous parklands that surrounded the palace proper. But Sir Roderick's driver passed the gate by, paralleling the high, surrounding wall until he found a lesser gate, this one closed and locked. Two men, who were clearly not palace guards, appeared from the gatehouse and allowed the carriage to pass.

Roderick was alert now, looking about as they went. The driver took them along a narrow drive between closely planted trees and hedges—a path for the use of gardeners, Tristam was sure.

A cuckoo disappeared into a hedge, catching Tristam's attention for a second, and then the driver brought the carriage to a halt, footmen jumping down to open doors and lower the steps.

"I hope you don't mind a short walk, Mr. Flattery?"

"Not at all." Tristam stepped down and immediately the King's Man set off along a narrow, gravel walkway lined with flower beds and small trees.

The King's senior minister is trying to enter the palace secretly, Tristam realized. It was the last thing in the world that he would have expected. *He is attempting to spirit me into the palace unnoticed. But unnoticed by whom?*

Through branches moving in the breeze, the palace appeared, like an island in the waves, a rose colored cliff rising from a sea of green. The Farr flag rustled in the breeze; bands of blue, white, and deep crimson, the King's gold and black crest in the center.

The Tellaman Palace was the principal residence of the Royal House of Farrland, a family that had known as much tragedy as glory in the centuries of their reign. Tristam had never before been inside the walls and found now that he did not want that to change. His home in Locfal suddenly seemed a place of great peace and security.

Unlike the rest of the city, the Tellaman Palace was constructed of granite. Tristam had often hunted beetles in one of the quarries, so he felt an odd connection between that great scar on the land and the King's palace. Stone of both rose and gray had been used for the exterior and the roofs were of copper, weathered to green-blue. It was generally a low building, seldom more than three stories, four at the most, not given to soaring towers or high walls or other structures common to castle architecture.

The basic floor plan was in the shape of an "H" and, onto the main building, wings had been added, carefully maintaining the style if not the symmetry. Onto these wings other additions had appeared every few decades.

The door Roderick led Tristam to was not large but, as at the gate, two men awaited them. Both bowed to Roderick who did not bother to acknowledge them.

The "*young shoulders*" Sir Roderick had spoken of. The King's service looked even less appealing than he had previously imagined.

They were soon in a long hall lined with busts of the sovereigns who had reigned over Farrland since the restoration. Both Kings and Queens watched with equanimity as the two men passed. And there among them the child-King, Birchard, seemed to meet Tristam's eye with a look of infinite sadness. For a second Tristam felt that sadness, as though he were marching off . . . to what? To war perhaps, or something even more tragic, for Birchard's story was not a happy one.

Then Alecka the Fair, the childless Queen, looked down upon him, her face saintly, at peace, and though the sadness did not pass, Tristam felt as though Queen Alecka had just granted him silent forgiveness, for what crimes or sins Tristam did not know.

This hall was well known in Farrland, for it was often used in Royal ceremonies; to be raised to the peerage, for instance, one must pass down this hall. Perhaps a new baronet must gain the approval of all the royal ghosts. But this morning only Tristam and Sir Roderick represented the living here.

They turned into a narrower hallway where guards saluted them through high doors into a long, bright gallery, lined on one side by leaded windows. Pale marble floors reflected the sun and lit the opposite wall, which supported massive canvases depicting the sea battles that had played such an important part in the shaping of the world over the last two centuries. After a hundred ships had slipped beneath the waves, they came to the hall's end where purple-uniformed Royal Guards let them through more doors.

Farrland was a wealthy country and the Tellaman Palace reflected that. The ceilings in this hall were thirty feet overhead and ornate, painted with scenes of wood nymphs and fantastic animals. Floors were of marble, with pillars of different stones. Tall windows at the hall's end cast a long rectangle of soft light, as though it fell through the boughs of a summer forest.

Into this setting a woman's laughter floated, like the first notes of an aria—borne up by promise. Tristam saw two women rise from a bench half-hidden by a column. They stepped out so that the soft sunlight bathed them in gold and illuminated their hair like halos of soft flame. Tristam was almost transfixed, certain that this must be Princess Joelle, wife of the Prince Royal, for one woman appeared tall and regal.

To his great surprise Tristam heard Sir Roderick curse under his breath, and then suddenly the King's Man reached out, taking hold of Tristam's elbow and bringing him to a halt.

The two women continued to walk toward them, one a servant, Tristam realized, and the other dressed in a gown of pale green and gold. Even at a distance of twenty paces, Tristam could see that the gown highlighted the woman's long, copper-gold hair perfectly.

"*The Duchess of Morland*," Roderick said, bending his head somewhat.

Realizing that he was staring, Tristam immediately cast his gaze down. The dowager duchess was a favorite, perhaps *the* favorite, of the King.

When only three paces separated them, Sir Roderick bowed, and Tristam did the same.

"Roderick, what a pleasant surprise, and unaccompanied by your gaggle of secretaries and ministers." Her smile, Tristam saw, would melt the coldest of hearts. "I cannot say what led us to walk here, but I count myself fortunate." She nodded to Tristam and he thought her gaze, which rested on him for the briefest second, took in a great deal. Her manner was a little triumphant. This, clearly, was the person Roderick had hoped to avoid.

Before the King's Man could speak, she extended her hand to Tristam. "Elorin, Duchess of Morland."

Tristam self-consciously touched his lips to her hand, thinking as he did so that he had just kissed the woman said to be the most beautiful in Farrland. He hoped his discomfiture didn't show.

"Duchess," Roderick said quickly, his voice perhaps a little tight. "May I introduce Mr. Tristam Flattery."

"Certainly, Mr. Flattery, you are the colleague of the renowned Dandish?"

Ah, someone who did not immediately connect him to the Grand Theater! Tristam could hardly believe that the Duchess of Morland had heard of Dandish, let alone Tristam Flattery. His opinion of her went up immeasurably.

"I was his student and later assistant, Your Grace."

"You are being modest, I think." She smiled again and Tristam felt her reputation was well deserved.

The duchess then turned to Sir Roderick. "You are on your way to the arboretum, Roderick. I shall accompany you."

Roderick bobbed his head, saying nothing.

The duchess dismissed her servant and the three set out along the hall. Tristam noted that the green of the duchess' gown set off the green of her eyes perfectly and the subtle use of gold, in her gown and jewelry, was reflected in the gilt used in the hallway decoration.

The realization struck Tristam suddenly. Her entry had been staged; the exact place chosen, the light perfect, the timing of her beautiful laughter precise. Tristam, of all people, should have seen that immediately. His mother, after all, had been an actress.

"You are in Avonel for some time, Mr. Flattery?"

"I am not yet certain, Your Grace."

"At your leisure, I see. I have many friends whose interests are not so different from your own, Mr. Flattery. Perhaps you would enjoy an evening at my home . . . ?"

Tristam did not know how to respond. Clearly there was animosity between the duchess and Sir Roderick—but how could one refuse the Duchess of Morland?

"I am honored that Your Grace would ask," Tristam said, hoping it was a neutral enough response to offend no one.

She laughed. "No need to be so formal, Mr. Flattery. I have known your aunt, the Duchess of Blackwater, for many years, and the duke as well." She turned to him, her look coy, though it was clearly not to be taken seriously. "You needn't worry that we have only just met."

"I would be honored to spend an evening at your home, Your Grace."

"And bring yourself along as well, Roderick. The company of people whose opinions vary would do you good." A beautiful smile appeared on her face as she said this, as though she teased a dear friend.

Roderick's face pulled into a tight smile. He bobbed his head again. Apparently even the King's Man must bare his breast to the barbs of the King's favorite, and try to smile into the bargain.

What is it that these courtiers want of me? Tristam asked himself again.

Sir Roderick used a key to let them through a large door. Inside was a small antechamber with a tiled floor. Unremarkable, perhaps, but Tristam's nostrils were assailed by the dank odor of rich soils and vegetation. The air itself was quite moist and the temperature seemed to rise immediately upon the doors' closing: the arboretum mentioned by the duchess.

Tristam knew that the palace had a collection of the flora of Oceana that rivaled that of the university. Professor Dandish had spoken of it and had made several journeys there to compare specimens.

Tristam felt his excitement growing. The obvious animosity that existed between the two courtiers was forgotten. After all, involvement in petty rivalries was considered one of a courtier's vital signs.

Sir Roderick turned to Tristam. "I realize, Mr. Flattery, that you have been inconvenienced. Brought here without even knowing a reason. Soon, I hope to make it clear why this was so." He glanced over at the duchess, and then back to Tristam, who was surprised to hear anything approaching an apology from the King's Man. "Before I begin, I must tell you that I am about to speak of matters of great sensitivity. No part of this may be repeated. . . ." He seemed to be waiting for a reply from Tristam.

"Of course."

"Professor Dandish has always been our advisor in matters concerning the palace arboretum. It is a collection dear to our sovereign's heart, for, as you know, Gregory was much admired by the King."

They passed through an arch and into the arboretum proper. Tristam stopped involuntarily. Under a sky of curving glass the dense green of a tropical jungle thrust upward, life seeking the air and water and light without regard for the artificiality of its surroundings. Tristam recognized the nut palm and the crest palm immediately. And there the hotu and a *Plumeria*, a frangipani, no doubt; flora he had spent so much time classifying that he knew them as well as he knew the trees and flowers of his own garden.

Suddenly, Tristam realized that Roderick had stopped in the midst of his explanation.

"Pardon me, sir."

"As I was saying, Professor Dandish has always been our advisor. But, as you know, the good professor has not been well, nor is he any longer a young man. Fortunately, however, he is not the only empiricist in Farrland with knowledge of the flora of Oceana. Your monographs on the collection of Baron Trevelyan have been widely appreciated, Mr. Flattery."

They proceeded along a brick walkway that snaked through the jungle. Despite the distractions, the gravity of Sir Roderick's tone kept Tristam's attention. They turned off a side walkway past flowering frangipani, then made their way through several turnings to stop before a brass-bound, wooden door.

Taking a key from the pocket of his waistcoat, Sir Roderick turned the lock and pushed the door open. "Please." He held the door for the duchess and Tristam and then locked it once they had passed inside.

They were in a gardener's shed, or so it would have been were it not part of a palace. Wheelbarrows leaned against the wall and gardening tools hung in their proper places. A mound of dark soil covered a square of burlap on a potting table and terra cotta pots were stacked to one side.

"*Tumney?*" Sir Roderick raised his voice to call. "He does not hear so well as he did, our good gardener. He can't be far."

Another door at the end of the workroom let into a smaller arboretum, and this was planted with neat rows of a single species; one that Tristam did not immediately recognize.

"This," Sir Roderick said, his voice almost solemn, "is Kingfoil, or so Captain Gregory translated the islanders' name for it." He reached out and very gently touched the waxy leaves.

Tristam realized that this was a species new to him. His eyes ran over the branches almost of their own will, looking for the taxonomist's clues. The leaves would be classed as orbicular in shape, or perhaps reniform, but were divided into narrow pinnate segments at right angles to the central stalk, somewhat like feather palms, but these leaves were barely larger than a man's hand. The branches were covered in a brown-orange bark, plated and appearing thick.

"I'm not familiar with this shrub," Tristam said, "though perhaps its family is *Verbenaceae?*"

"I believe that is true," Roderick said, and Tristam saw the duchess nod.

"The genus," she interrupted, "is *Spuriverna*, and it is represented by only this single species, improperly rendered as *regis.*" She was clearly intruding on Roderick's office here, and Tristam was sure that the King's Man was not pleased, though Roderick's face remained unreadable. "As can be seen, it is an ordinary enough bush by the standards of Oceana. But this plant is of grave importance, Mr. Flattery. Kingfoil produces a seed from which a physic can be made, a physic with healthful properties unknown to us before the voyages of Captain Gregory." The duchess spoke even more solemnly than had the King's Man. "*Regis* produces few seeds, most of which are infertile—they produce no seedlings. These, and a few plants in the next chamber, are all the Kingfoil in our land. For this, and other reasons, this plant is kept a secret of the palace, explaining why you did not encounter it in your study. The physic made from the rare seeds is necessary to treat an affliction suffered by our King." She met Tristam's eye. "I will tell you in all frankness, Mr. Flattery, that without this physic King Wilam will certainly die." The duchess' green eyes began to glisten with forming tears, but she blinked them back and no droplet appeared on her cheek.

Tristam felt suddenly overly warm and longed to shed his coat and loosen his neck cloth. He also felt his own throat tighten at the duchess' obvious show of emotion.

What have I fallen into? he thought. He had come expecting to act as a tutor to a royal brat and found, suddenly, that it was the life of the King set on the balance. He dreaded what would be said next as much as an accused man feared the judge's pronouncement.

"*Regis* bears male and female flowers on different plants," Roderick said, grasping the opportunity, as the duchess recovered her equanimity. "There is a word for this...."

"Dioecious," Tristam managed through a dry mouth.

"Exactly. Kingfoil is dioecious. But recently the few seeds that germinate produce exclusively male plants and the females that remain produce fewer and fewer seeds. We do not understand why this is occurring, Mr. Flattery, but it is obvious what the result will be. Soon there will be no seeds to make the physic required by our King. Mr. Tumney, our worthy gardener, is not a man of education, Mr. Flattery. It is our hope that the methodology of a trained empiricist might provide some insight into this dilemma—perhaps solve it."

Both the duchess and Roderick were staring at Tristam in silence, trying to read his reaction, he realized. They wanted to be told that their problem would be solved. They wanted to hear confidence in his voice.

"I must begin by speaking with your gardener," Tristam said mildly. "Is there no monograph dealing with *regis*? Perhaps Lord Trevelyan . . . ?"

Roderick shook his head. Tristam had not spoken to give them hope or to deny it entirely, and this had been duly noted. "Only Captain Gregory had knowledge of *regis*. There is a brief monograph by Professor Dandish, but it is not based on information collected *in situ*. All of his observations took place within these walls and were combined with information from Gregory's unpublished writings." Roderick paused and met Tristam's eye; the bright awareness Tristam had now seen appear and disappear shone strongly. "Do you think there's hope, then, Mr. Flattery?"

"I think it would be premature to say such a thing, as much as I would like to. My inquiries may take several weeks, perhaps a few months."

"Indeed," he said quietly. Roderick caught Tristam's eye and held it. "Mr. Flattery, I feel it is necessary to say again that all information pertaining to Kingfoil is to be kept in the strictest confidence. The health of the King, as you must know, is a source of constant speculation. Even rumors can have disastrous effects on affairs of state—our present treaty negotiations with Entonne are but one example. I charge you to speak of this matter to no one not already involved: the duchess," he said; clearly a concession, "myself, Tumney, and Professor Dandish. Any lapse shall be dealt with without regard to your intentions, loyalties, or family. I hope that is clear?"

"Completely, sir."

He glanced at the duchess, hesitating. "I will locate our gardener." Nodding to her, he was gone without further formality.

Alone with the Duchess of Morland, Tristam suddenly felt awkward. He turned his attention to the Kingfoil, reaching out and touching a leaf, though his mind raced so that it registered almost nothing of the foliage.

"Mr. Flattery?" The duchess' tone was quiet, almost intimate.

"Your Grace." It was impolite to look away while being addressed and Tristam turned and looked into the duchess' striking eyes.

"Roderick has been known to have titles and estates granted to those in his circle for accomplishing nothing more than constant agreement with his opinions, but those he has not befriended could save the kingdom and hardly receive a note of thanks. It is the way of the court and courtiers. But not everyone is so blind. Please indulge my forthrightness for a moment. If you find a way to make the Kingfoil bear seeds again or grow female plants that bear fruit . . . the gratitude of the King will be great, as will be the gratitude of those who know of Kingfoil and its value to our sovereign. A title and the favor of the King, Mr. Flattery, would aid you in any endeavor you could wish to pursue."

Tristam really did not know what to say. "I . . . I am overwhelmed, Your Grace."

She favored him with a radiant smile and touched his sleeve. "You may call me Duchess, if you will."

Not knowing what to say, Tristam bowed his head.

"I will leave you to your important task, Mr. Flattery. Sir Roderick has instructions to assist you in all things, but if this arrangement should not prove completely satisfactory. . . ." She pressed a calling card into his hand. "And I have not forgotten your promise to attend an evening at my home. A world of luck to you, Tristam Flattery." With a swish of her skirts, the Duchess of Morland turned and disappeared back the way she had come.

Tristam was alone in the arboretum, but the tension between the two courtiers remained behind, still vibrating along his nerves. A sudden need to sit came over him, but he could see nothing that would serve his purpose. Unable to continue standing, he crouched down as though he would examine the *regis*, but his brain registered nothing. The life of the King was suddenly in his hands, yet he was no physician experienced in maintaining his equilibrium in such situations. *The life of the King!*

He pressed his hands to his eyes for a second. Certainly, if he succeeded, the rewards would be great. . . .

"Mr. Flattery, sir?"

Tristam removed his hands from his eyes and looked up to find an old man gazing down at him with some concern, turning a hat nervously in his hands as he did so.

"Are you well, sir?"

Tristam rose to his feet quickly. He tried to remember the name Sir Roderick had called out, but it was gone. "Perfectly well. And you are . . . ?"

"Tumney, sir. King's Gardener, and your servant, Mr. Flattery."

Tristam smiled to cover his search for some appropriate phrases. "Well, Tumney, it appears we have a task laid out for us. Sir Roderick mentioned a monograph written by Professor Dandish?"

"Sir Roderick asked me to say that he would have it sent around directly. The knight also sends apologies—called away on the King's business." Tumney shrugged. "The King's Man, you see."

As they spoke, Tristam realized that he towered over the King's Gardener. Tumney was a very small man, though well formed. His brown hair had thinned on top and he grew it long on one side and combed it across, trying to hide the expanse of bare skin. A wig was not an appropriate accoutrement for a gardener—even a King's gardener. The man's dress was what you might expect of his trade, though he wore a surprisingly elegant waistcoat beneath his jacket, jade green just visible where the last button closed. Clean shaven though not terribly wrinkled, Tristam would guess Tumney was seventy if he was a day.

Tristam reached out and brushed the leaf of a nearby bush. "You tend the Kingfoil. Tell me, Tumney, when was it first noticed? The lack of female seedlings?"

Tumney stopped turning his hat and reached up and patted the hair combed over his pate: it was an unconscious gesture. "Well, Mr. Flattery, it was very gradual so as to make a beginning hard to tell for sure. You see, she has played such tricks on me before. Seven years past, I would think, this same trick to the letter. Fewer and fewer seeds from each plant. Each planting had more boys and fewer girls until there were no girl children at all. She only lives about ten years in all, the Kingfoil, and bears scarce few seeds the first year or two, so I keep a nursery always full of children, you see. These ones here," he waved a hand at the planting, "they are all three to seven. The prime years for making seeds. Or so it always has been." He looked more than a little troubled as he said this.

"But this time is different, Mr. Flattery. When she played this trick before, it lasted long enough—near to seven months. But this has been going on longer than that. Almost a year to the day, sir."

"When this happened before, was it the same season?"

"No, sir, of that I'm sure. It was winter, but she will still flower here in our own little piece of Oceana, no matter what the season. Midm'nth was when I first took notice, Mr. Flattery, Midm'nth in the last year. I scratched it in my almanac, where I keep my record of planting and flowering and such."

"You have a record, then, of how this whole business began?"

Tumney gave a crooked grin, baring very even teeth. "Yes, sir. Everything is writ down just as Professor Dandish wanted it. Dates and numbers of seeds taken from each plant. I give every plant a name and that's marked on a plan of the beds, sir."

"You give me hope." Tristam felt his anxiety subside a little. If Dandish had prescribed the method of keeping records, it would be flawless and detailed. "Your almanac will save us a great deal of work. There are other plantings beside these?"

"There's a nursery, Mr. Flattery. I can show you if you like."

"That is exactly what I would like."

Tumney led Tristam down an aisle that ran along the side of the planting.

The old gardener walked with a stoop and an obvious stiffness in one leg, but his pace was not slow and he did not seem to labor to walk so. He was probably hardier than he looked, this man. Tristam had seen the type before.

They passed through a heavy wooden door and came into another small arboretum, this one less elaborate, as though it had been built in a rush. Here there were carefully spaced rows of Kingfoil, each row a different age, no doubt, from seedlings to plants two-thirds the size of the adults they had just left.

Many of the plants displayed small but elegant white blossoms. Tristam bent down to look at one of these closely. A pretty five-petaled bell with broadly curving petals, tinged in purple, and with a lengthened pistil. They were not large, the size of a new gold crown.

"There are no female plants in flower, Mr. Flattery," Tumney said quietly. "Nor have there been for some months. They grow well. They look perfectly healthy both in leaf and root, yet they produce no flowers." He removed his hat and patted his head again, then began turning his hat as he had before.

"I have no doubt that what you say is true," Tristam said, "but I'm obliged to examine them, leaf and root, as you say."

"Nothing would please me more, sir. Not one bit more. I'm a gardener by trade, Mr. Flattery. Prenticed under Hawthorne who was King's Gardener for thirty-odd years. But I've never stepped inside the gates of a university and I never had no one like Professor Dandish to steer me straight. I hope that you find old Tumney has missed the obvious—a mite or a blight I've never heard tell of. Nothing would please me more. No, sir; not one bit."

A ringing bell interrupted them and Tumney gave a quick bob. "That will be the good professor's monograph, I should think. Excuse me, sir. I'll return directly."

Tristam was alone again. Genus *Spuriverna*. Family *Verbenaceae*. There were several plants in the family with known medicinal properties—or at least thought so by the islanders of Oceana. Healing burns came to mind. The Old Farr name meant "sacred herb." The genus name was a bit odd—more common in a plant found in northern latitudes—for it would be rendered as "false spring."

Against one wall stood a table set with a wooden frame divided into small, closely spaced boxes. Tristam walked over to examine them, for they were probably planted with the seeds of the Kingfoil. He made a quick count and found one hundred and twenty boxes. Of these only six showed signs of a tiny closed fan of green pushing up through the dark earth.

"There will be a few more yet, Mr. Flattery. Perhaps ten in all, if things continue as they have. And there is no guarantee of that."

Tristam turned to find Tumney approaching, a quarto portfolio in vivid blue tucked under his arm.

"It isn't just that there are drastically fewer females: general fertility is decreasing, as well?"

Tumney stopped and scratched behind his ear, thinking. "That would appear to be the case, though the Kingfoil has never been a good bearer. From a hundred seeds planted I would expect to see twelve children, perhaps fifteen." He proffered the portfolio. "I'm sure Professor Dandish has recorded these things all in good order, sir. Much better than I could tell it."

Tristam took the slim portfolio from the gardener. "You haven't read this?"

"No, sir," he spoke a bit defiantly and Tristam suspected that it injured his pride to say it.

Tristam considered the warning of Sir Roderick and remembered that Tumney's name had been mentioned among those he could trust. "Would you care to see it when I have finished?"

The old man shrugged. "Well, I wouldn't mind, sir, if you think it would be all right." Tristam could see this small gesture of confidence pleased the man.

"I can't imagine why it wouldn't be. Is there a place where I might sit to read?"

"Follow me, Mr. Flattery. We're not entirely without comforts here."

They passed back into the larger arboretum and Tumney led the way to a corner, hidden away behind the tallest Kingfoil, and here there were a chair, a small table, and a lamp. There were one or two other comforts as well; a pipe stand and a tobacco humidor of the very finest craftsmanship, as well as a silver tea service, also very well made.

"There you are, sir, as homely as you could like, I should think." Tumney gestured to the chair and then stood with his hat in his hand again. He looked slightly embarrassed. "That humidor, Mr. Flattery, was a present from the King. Sent it to me on my fiftieth birthday with as nice a note as you can imagine—in the King's own hand, mind you." He flushed a bit with pride.

"And well deserved, I'm sure."

"I like to think so. The tea service is from the Duchess of Morland. And though some would speak ill of the duchess, to my mind there is not a more gracious woman in the Kingdom. Often the duchess looks in on my work and always has a good word. Even now, when the Kingfoil is not acting according to hopes, not a word of blame. As gracious as, as. . . . Well, I don't know, sir, but as gracious as a queen, I should think."

"You can't say fairer than that, Tumney." Tristam made a show of untying the ribbon that bound the portfolio.

"I have my morning tea at this time, Mr. Flattery. Could I bring you a cup?"

"That would be very kind of you, Tumney, very kind indeed."

The old gardener retrieved the tea set from the table, with some reverence, Tristam thought, and disappeared down the aisle between the rows of Kingfoil.

Inside the portfolio Tristam found his teacher's familiar hand on a title page.

The Life History of Verbenaceae Spuriverna regis, with
Instructions for
Cultivation in Northern Regions.
Illustrations by the Author
1542

Tristam turned to the next page and read

The species regis *is the only known example of the genus* Spuriverna, *though its family is known to comprise approximately forty different species, virtually all of these within the genus* Medicus. *Regis, also called Kingfoil, is indigenous to the southwestern region of Oceana and is found almost exclusively on the island called Varua by its inhabitants (named New Blanshford by Captain Gregory and so noted on naval charts). Its existence on other islands of the New Blanshford group is largely conjectural and based on stories told to Captain Gregory on his first visit. These may have been apocryphal and Captain Gregory himself states that his understanding of the language was imperfect.*

In its native environment regis *will grow anywhere there is loamy soil and some shade (for it does not grow out in the open) up to about three thousand feet in elevation. Despite* regis' *simple requirements, it is surprisingly rare. The people of Oceana value it extremely and, in their culture of taboos and prerogatives, all plants found are considered to be the property of the King.*

Regis seldom exceeds four feet in height and occasionally mature plants do not reach more than two feet eight or nine. Branches begin at about one quarter of its height and the main trunk often splits into two or three main branches not much above this, and each of these secondary trunks will support several branchings, often as close as every four inches.

A detailed description of Kingfoil's appearance followed, and Tristam was able to compare this directly with a mature plant not four feet away. As he expected, it was precisely correct in every detail. Dandish did not have his reputation without reason. At this point Tumney arrived with tea. Tristam buried his head in his reading and the gardener took the hint and went back to his own duties.

The King of Varua, who gave Captain Gregory the seeds of regis *as a gift to our own King, told the captain that it was possessed by a spirit that delighted in the playing of tricks. Often the spirit would cause the plant to stop producing seeds and it would then become barren; sometimes for several years or even forever after. Naturally occurring plots of regis, where the plant had grown for years, would suddenly die out and this would precipitate a search for other plots, with great rewards to the man or woman who found one. Several annual ceremonies on the island were apparently performed for the express purpose of supplicating this spirit.*

The islanders do not attempt to cultivate regis, or did not at the time of Gregory's visit, but rely on finding places where it occurs naturally. Gregory was told that regis invariably grew in stands and single plants were never found.

Without doubt, much more could have been learned of regis during Gregory's stay if his able ship's naturalist, Mr. Trevelyan, had known of the plant's existence and had been allowed to apply his considerable powers of observation to regis growing in its native environment.

We are left with Captain Gregory's account of the Varuan King's words, for the captain states clearly that, at no time, did he see regis growing.

The cultivation of Kingfoil in more northerly regions must be practiced in sheltered gardens, preferably within an arboretum especially constructed for the purpose. Such a building must have provisions to block some portion of the summer sun, for regis prefers to grow in shade. Temperatures must be maintained strictly and never allowed to fall below sixty-five (and even that for short periods only). An average of eighty degrees would create an environment much like its own. Whether one can create temperatures too hot for regis is perhaps moot, for it is difficult to maintain temperatures over ninety-five in our latitude and regis will be unaffected by such heat.

A prospective grower of Kingfoil must pay strict attention to the soils used. Regis grows only in soils of decaying vegetable matter (commonly found in the jungles of Oceana) that are not overly acidic. Therefore, soils made of decaying needles of pine (pinaceae), cedar (cupresaceae) or related gymnosperms should be avoided assiduously.

There followed a treatise on soils and their makeup. Though not new to Tristam, he read it carefully in case there was information that would bear directly on the growing of *regis*. Meticulous in detail—that was the creed he had learned from Dandish, and he had come to believe it as fervently as his former teacher.

Tristam looked up from Dandish's monograph and wondered how his life could have changed so much in so short a time. Only a few days ago he had been a gentleman of leisure with nothing that could even be seriously thought of as responsibility, and now the life of the King was dependent on his work. It did not seem possible. Not he, Tristam Flattery. Even for someone used to facing life alone, this was far too much all at once.

He glanced down at the monograph again and thought immediately, *I must write to Dandish.* The monograph had raised innumerable questions. The realization that his old professor was only a day's journey away took some of the weight off Tristam's chest and allowed him to breathe. Dandish might be old and of nervous disposition, but Tristam had never known his brilliance to fail. If nothing else, there was that to reassure him.

ᔐ Five

The fluttering of wings called Tristam out of the warmth of a deep sleep. He rolled over and raised his head, confused, unsure of where he was. The room was dark, but a sound on the balcony drew his attention. Wings beating and a movement of white in the pale light of the moon. "*Pigeon*," Tristam told himself. He let his head drop back to the pillow and continued to fall, into darkness and warmth . . . and then light.

A warm wind blew, and the fluttering of wings had not abated. There, out on the water. A bird Tristam had never seen, white as the distant line of surf. Two long tail feathers, elegant and exotic. The bird beat its wings, hovering over the turquoise lagoon, for that is where he was, standing on the white sand edge of a broad lagoon. The wind rustled the palms behind him; a sound he'd never heard though it was familiar in his dream.

Below the hovering bird a flower lay on the water, water so clear that the blossom, too, seemed to float in the air.

Hands appeared from below the surface, rising up, cupping the flower as though it were a treasure, an offering, lifting the blossom into the air. Perfectly formed hands—a young woman's hands. Tristam felt himself take a step forward into the warm lagoon.

A woman emerged from the water then, face and shoulders glistening wet in the sun, though, impossibly, her hair remained dry. Long black hair floating on the surface around her, blowing in the fair wind. With great care she placed the flower behind her ear and then she looked up and saw Tristam for the first time. A smile of delight lit her beautiful face.

She knows me, Tristam realized, though he had never seen her before.

Her dark eyes met his without shyness and she began to walk toward the shore. As she moved her beauty was revealed slowly, glistening skin that held no secrets from the sun. In water barely above her knees, the woman stopped.

She embraced him then, her wet skin warm against his own. He felt her lips touch his, touch his neck, and he kissed her shoulder—unimaginably soft. She pressed herself to him and Tristam felt a sharp, involuntary intake of salt air. He kissed a small breast and felt himself falling, back into water that caught them, surrounded them with soft warmth, supported them.

Without intending to he felt himself enter her, and they were moved by a slow, pulsing rhythm from the surf breaking on the distant reef. The flower fell from her hair and tumbled into the water. A swirl and a flash of white and the flower was gone, whisked down into the depths.

Tristam heard a moan and awoke to the sound of his own voice. He was tangled in the coverlets of his bed, blood pounding in his ears like drumming. It was dark and still. He lay trying to calm his heart, to catch his breath. Part of him reached out to hold fast to the emotion of the dream, but already the feeling was dissipating, like a spent wave. Ebbing back down the sloping sands—lost to him.

Tristam became conscious of light, of sounds. His attempt to seek his island woman back through the realms of sleep had been futile. If he had dreamed again, he recalled nothing.

It was his fifth day in Avonel and things were not proceeding as he hoped. The truth was Tumney had already performed virtually all of the procedures Tristam would have attempted. Despite Sir Roderick's reservations about the man, the gardener knew his trade. The inquiries that Tristam had begun were not yielding results of any significance, leaving him struggling against a feeling of failure which he knew was affecting his analytic abilities. It was, he decided, time to swallow his pride and seek assistance. He would write to Dandish again over breakfast.

He had sent a note off to the professor immediately after his visit to the palace, but that hadn't been a call for help—merely a few questions. Tristam hadn't understood the difficulty of the problem then.

Why entire stands of regis *have periods of infertility or suddenly become barren altogether is unknown and requires much further study. It is most likely to be part of an extended natural cycle and therefore can be best avoided by keeping seeds from the earliest plantings and using these to regenerate the plots.*

So Dandish had written. A simple paragraph suggesting a simple solution. But the professor had been wrong. Tumney had long since tried the obvious, to no avail.

The servants knew Tristam's routine now, and hot water arrived seconds after he rose. Even so he bathed and shaved without pleasure.

He had also written to Jenny, the young woman he courted back in Locfal; a letter which, he was embarrassed to admit, made his situation sound more glamorous than it truly was. Jenny, after all, did not share Tristam's interests. She would want to hear about balls and the theater and the doings of the Royal Family.

There had been at least two social functions at the palace since his arrival and Tristam had attended neither. There was only the hinted-at invitation to the home of the Duchess of Morland—an invitation that had not yet materialized and looked less likely every day. Tristam had found himself occasionally taking out the duchess' calling card to assure himself that the meeting had not been imagined. Upon his return to Locfal, Tristam would have little to tell.

The truth was he had dug in the soil quite a bit. Examined roots and seeds, dissected flowers, devised complicated planting schedules, searched for mites, blights, rusts, and numerous other parasites and diseases—all to no avail. He had taken regular temperature readings of both soil and air, proving nothing. It was quite clear that unless one of his plantings revealed a clue to the mystery, no less than a miracle would be required to have the Kingfoil bearing seeds again. He closed his eyes.

It was a bit embarrassing to be brought all the way from Locfal with great expectations, and then prove to know nothing more than one very elderly gardener. So much for his years at the university.

Dandish. He hoped the professor was well enough to offer some advice.

A zephyr of the feeling from his dream encounter touched him. Jenny suddenly seemed an annoyance, his letter to her embarrassing. The truth was he had barely thought of her in five days. Hardly a mad passion, but then he was looking for a wife—someone who would be his companion and supporter over the years. A sensible mother to their children. At least that was what he told himself.

His mind returned to the problem of the arboretum. "Another Flattery fails spectacularly in Avonel," Tristam said ruefully. But at least his failing was not public. Something to be thankful for.

What exactly would he say to Dandish? The worthy professor would not think less of him for asking assistance. Not one bit. Dandish was the ideal empiricist. Pushing back the borders of ignorance, that was his only reason for living. Other empiricists might suffer jealousies and defend themselves and their work with an aggressiveness that would not be out of place among bulls, but not Dandish. The professor could not bear criticism himself and so would not inflict it on others in anything but the mildest terms. He hardly even noticed that Lord Trevelyan gave him little credit for his years of work on the classification of his great collection. No, he would not criticize or judge his former student. Only Tristam felt that he had failed—Tristam and the King's Man, and perhaps the beautiful Duchess.

He crawled out of the bath and began to dry himself, the warm breeze coming in through the open window reminding him again of his dream—lack of sleep making it harder to manage the transition into complete wakefulness.

A knock on the door.

"Yes?"

"Mr. Flattery," came a muffled voice. "Your breakfast and a letter, sir." It was an old servant named Benjamin.

"Leave it on my desk, will you?"

"As you wish, sir."

A letter from Dandish. Tristam's spirits rose perceptibly.

He dressed slowly, in no hurry to rush to the palace as he had been only a few days earlier—his opportunity for glory was quickly beginning to look like the field of his defeat.

As he entered the sitting room, the smell of coffee assailed his nostrils and provided him with something approaching pleasure. He tilted the silver pot, splashed the steaming liquid into a cup, and raised it to his lips. He was holding back intentionally, preparing himself to not be disappointed if Dandish's letter contained no revelations. He lifted the envelope and found the seal of the university pressed into wax.

The letter turned out to be from Cecil Emin, Dean of Merton College, a man who had been a friend of his father, and a friend to Tristam as well.

Dear Tristam:

It is my sad duty to inform you of the death of our colleague, Professor Sanfield Dandish. I know you will mourn his passing as much as I. The good professor passed away in his sleep last night. A great loss to us all.

I was fortunate to have visited Professor Dandish but two days ago, and he mentioned that you were engaged in some matter in the Royal Arboretum. I hope this letter finds you still in Avonel. As you may know, I am the Executor of Professor Dandish's estate, but I don't think you can be aware that you are mentioned in his will: no fortune, I'm afraid, but some of the professor's personal effects that may bring you comfort.

It would be a great favor to me if you could spare a few days to help in the formidable task of putting the professor's effects in order. I don't think there is anyone better qualified for this task than yourself as you were so often at Dandish's home and knew his study in the college better than he did himself. Of course, the King's business may not allow this and, if so, I certainly will manage. Please do let me know your decision.

Your servant,
Cecil Emin, Dean

Tristam sat down hard in a chair. He felt suddenly dizzy, disoriented. Something was very odd. He heard the muffled sound of someone sobbing, far off. *Farrelle's blood*, he thought, *is that me? Am I weeping?*

Sir Roderick was extremely kind and solicitous upon hearing Tristam's news. Of course, he had known Dandish himself and such things always made a difference. Once assured that Tumney could look after the plantings and gather all necessary information, the King's Man had been only too willing to release Tristam for a few days. At the same time Tristam had confessed that there was, as yet, no indication of what was causing the problem with *regis*. Roderick had only nodded and looked down at his desk.

To Tristam's surprise the knight had insisted on providing Tristam with a carriage and driver, refusing to let him post up to Merton on the public coach—an act of kindness that Tristam found quite touching. Perhaps there was a heart beating in Roderick's chest, after all.

It appeared that the King's Man had a weakness for fine carriages—the *Bronam* that he lent to Tristam was not only the latest fashion but it was a paradigm of the carriage maker's art.

So Tristam's journey to Merton, the location of the university, passed in relative physical comfort. Ironically, or so it seemed to Tristam, the day was perfect and the green countryside rolled past in ordered tranquillity, the death of a single man having shockingly little impact on the larger world.

The journey was familiar to Tristam, as he had made it often enough as a student. He watched the miles roll by, memories of his years at Merton surfacing, Dandish playing a part in many of these.

At a slough by the roadside he asked the driver to stop so that he could take his glass and search the shores and pools—a practice he had followed for years. He went and stood on the edge where the irises grew, their ornate purples and highlights of yellow seemed so exotic they might have been the creation of an artist. The flowers reminded Tristam of Dandish, whom he could hardly keep out of his thoughts anyway. Among all his interests the professor had a soft spot for flowers, and cultivated them with all the love another man might have lavished on wife and children. The pond seemed a sad and lonely place today.

An evening egret was Tristam's chief find and he was gratified to see it nesting so far from their common range. The slough had its usual complement of ducks and waders, and passeriformes—perching birds—of the sort that preferred the wet lands to the dry. As Tristam moved his glass slowly across the scene, all singing ceased and the smaller birds disappeared into thickets. Tristam lowered his glass in time to see a winter falcon float over the water above the level of the surrounding willows. It disappeared behind the branches of a tree, and though Tristam searched the area with his glass, it was to no avail. The bird did not reappear.

Better than an egret, he thought, for winter falcons were not commonly seen in this season, at least not so far south. But Tristam was sure of what he had seen. His uncle had been a falconer. When Erasmus had died, Tristam had released all of his birds; but one, a winter falcon, was still seen occasionally, sitting in a tree in the garden. Tristam had begun to think that his late uncle, the alleged mage, had put his falcon to watching his errant nephew. But it was a beautiful bird and Tristam never tired of watching it in return.

Dusk was on the horizon as Tristam arrived in the town of Merton on Wedgewater. He took a room at the Ivy, an old establishment, covered, as the name suggested, in *Hedera helix*, the inside paneled in dark polished wood. A place suited to aging servants and hushed voices. Tristam requested supper in his rooms and ate by a window overlooking the inn's small park. A large elm grew nearby and the branches came close to Tristam's second floor window so that he felt he had moved into a tree house—and this idea pleased him as much as anything could that day.

As usual, sleep eluded Tristam, perhaps even more so that night. When it did find him, it was not sound. Again he was wakened by strange dreams several times, though in the morning he could recall nothing of them.

ᑌ Six

Before breaking fast his first morning in Merton, Tristam sent his card around to Dean Emin asking if he could call at eleven, and before long, a reply came saying that he would be expected.

Merton on Wedgewater was so small that Tristam elected to walk the short distance to the dean's. The town changed little over the years and Tristam half expected to meet his classmates on the street. It was the nature and part of the charm of Merton that scholars who had lived there even fifty years earlier felt the place virtually unaltered when they visited. A town that defied time, in its own small way.

Merton was "of a piece," the town's people liked to say. The architecture of the houses was generally a reflection of the university and, in any given street, one house was much like another, the principle differentiation applied was "old home" as opposed to "new." Old homes were built of uncut fieldstone and new of rough hewn. Of course, new homes were often two centuries old or more.

Eighteen Northmoor Road was a "new" house in a row of almost identical dwellings built hard up against one another. Their front steps emptied directly onto the walkway and if not for the evenly spaced chestnut trees growing before them, the houses would have shown a particularly bland facade to the world. Fortunately, as Tristam well knew, they were more than comfortable inside. In fact, the dean's home could be described as rather genteel. His late wife had seen to that, and Dean Emin did not attempt to improve upon her work.

The row of houses on Northmoor overlooked a common, and as he crossed the lawn, Tristam could see the dean standing in his study window looking out toward the spires of the university. Having been acquainted with Dean Emin for many years, Tristam knew that the man's eyes would be focused on some point in the impossible distance and he would be slowly turning his pocket watch over and over, his thoughts as far off as the point he gazed toward.

Barnes, the dean's gentleman's gentleman, answered Tristam's knock and escorted him up the stairs where he tapped lightly on the study door.

"Yes?" The dean's voice sounded surprisingly frail to Tristam.

"Mr. Flattery, sir."

"Show him in, Barnes. Thank you."

The servant opened the door and, as Tristam passed, said softly, "Good to see you, sir."

Dean Emin turned from the window and attempted a smile of welcome, though he was clearly too saddened to manage it. "So kind of you to come, Tristam."

"I only wish we met under more pleasant circumstances, Dean Emin."

"That's the way of humans, I sometimes believe. We wait until there is a tragedy to bring us together. Unfortunate." He waved at one of two ancient leather chairs and both men sat down. Tristam had not seen the dean for more than two years and he thought the don had aged more in that time than in the previous decade. His white hair and mustache did not seem so thick and lustrous and, like many scholars, Emin showed signs of his sedentary profession, for he was somewhat given to portliness. Thick lips and a small chin both seemed out of place on the man's round face, and his skin was so smooth and delicate it appeared never to have been out in the sun. But it also seemed to be stretched too thin, the veins showing purple at the temples. His eyes, once a vivid blue, were drained of their color and had lately become very pale. The old man kept glancing at Tristam with a look that verged on pity.

They sat in awkward silence for a few seconds and Tristam, unable to meet the dean's gaze, examined the room.

The study had walls built of bookcases, apparently a small fireplace, the dean's desk, the two easy chairs now in use, and a small table bearing a chess board. There was no art on the walls, for the bookshelves left no room. The floor was bird's-eye maple, the planks all of ten inches in width, and in the center of this was a faded rug that had once been a work of some beauty. The only window to the study was taller than a man, for the ceiling followed the contours of the roof and Tristam estimated it to be at least eleven feet. It was the room of a don, there was no question; a scholar's retreat, insulated from the world of the everyday by walls lined with the works of great minds.

Unlike most studies Tristam was familiar with, this one lacked the bittersweet smell of pipe tobacco, for the dean's wife had forbidden him to smoke indoors and though she had now been dead almost as long as Tristam had been alive, the dean still would not go against her wishes.

"Well, it is a sad day for us both, I'm afraid," the old man began at last. "Sanfield Dandish was certainly of the very first rank. A scholar and an empiricist to be admired and, I dare say, emulated. He was a great example to our young scholars, and quite a number of graduates from his classes have become names to be reckoned with. And that is living praise for the man, to be sure." He leaned over and touched Tristam's arm, an unusual gesture for the old man. "Could you use a brandy as much as I?"

Though it was far too early for Tristam to feel such a need, he could not refuse a gesture of affection from Emin, knowing how hard such things came to the old man. "Yes, I think I could."

The dean patted his arm awkwardly and then rose and went to call Barnes. He returned to his chair immediately, as though age or exhaustion had left him too weak to stand for long.

"I am loath to speak of practical matters at such a time, Tristam, but I must be at the college shortly and I will be unable to get free until this evening. Do you mind?"

"No, by all means. It's why I've come. Or at least part of the reason."

Barnes arrived with two brandy snifters on a tray. He retreated as silently as he had come.

"Well, the memorial service will take place the evening after next, the twenty-seventh, in Merton Hall. Will you want to speak?"

Tristam hesitated for a second. "I—I think not."

"It's a difficult thing to do and no one will think less of you if you don't. I'm expected to, of course, so I must do my best." The dean sipped his brandy and the awkward silence settled around them like a winter evening. Both men's thoughts returned to their friend, so recently gone. "He rallied a little at the end," the dean said. "I thought he might pull through. But then, the last two weeks. . . ." The old scholar pursed his lips tight together and closed his eyes. Tristam expected to see his shoulders begin to shake, but they did not. The dean glanced over at Tristam and attempted a weak smile, but it was so fleeting it appeared more a look of resignation and grief. "It is one of the most terrible aspects of growing old, Tristam; you begin to lose your friends. Men and women you've known for thirty and forty years—and more." He put a hand up to his face, and Tristam heard him sniff quietly.

To see this kind old man so grief stricken and dispirited affected Tristam. He wanted to reach out and touch him, just lay a hand on his arm, but he didn't want to add to the old man's embarrassment.

"The will reading can't take place before the memorial," Dean Emin went on, forcing himself to speak of the practical things, almost clinging to them—avoiding any words that reflected what he thought or felt. Only the tone of his voice and the barely contained grief spoke any truth. He paused to take a long breath. "Dandish and I shared a barrister. We'll meet in his office." His voice gained some strength now, as the dean mastered his emotions. "I'll let you know. He . . . Dandish, left virtually all of his estate to his sister. A sad story really." The Dean cleared his throat. "She's mad, you see . . . but this will provide her with some comforts she doesn't have where she is. I only hope she will be aware of them. His library, papers, and collections he left to the university, of course, with a few exceptions—and these exceptions he stipulated should go to you, Tristam. Things I believe you expressed admiration for at one time or another. His instruments also will be yours."

Tristam shook his head. He tried to find some appropriate words, but this faculty deserted him at that moment.

The dean went on, apparently wishing to have everything said. "Sanfield had no children, and though his students took the place of family for him, you, Tristam, were the favored son. He said as much to me on more than one occasion. Dandish had the highest opinion of your abilities . . . as do many others."

Tristam took a drink of his brandy and discovered that his hand trembled.

Perhaps to save them both embarrassment, the dean rose and went over to his desk. From a drawer he removed a ring of keys. For a second he stood looking down at Tristam, care written on his face. He smiled, not the smile of happiness, but the soft gesture of concern and affection. "Could you use more brandy?" he asked awkwardly.

It almost made Tristam smile. "No, no thank you, Dean Emin. I am not overwhelmed. Please go on."

The old professor looked at him for a moment, as though trusting his own assessment more than Tristam's words. "These are to the professor's house and rooms at college," he said, lowering himself slowly into the chair and proffering the keys to Tristam. "I'm not sure which is which, but I'm sure you will work it out. My barrister, who is a sensible man, does not expect a full inventory of the professor's effects. The will is not so complicated and there aren't several parties vying for advantage, you see." He raised his glass thoughtfully, but then pulled his focus back. "Don't concern yourself with the extraneous. The books, monographs, correspondence; these are really our concern, Tristam. No one else will be able to discern their importance."

Tristam looked down at the keys in his hand, a ring he had often seen the professor produce from his coat pocket. "I'll do everything I can."

"I have no doubt. It won't be a small task, though. It might take several days. Then there are Dandish's rooms in college. Perhaps the two of us should tackle that tomorrow? Or better the day after? You'll let me know how you get on."

Tristam nodded. "When it comes to the professor's rooms at Merton, the more of us the better. Despite his great interest in the order of things, the professor managed to bring little of it to his own life. His rooms will be in a state of chaos, I fear."

The dean smiled. "It was a small flaw in a great spirit. . . . I'm sure you feel the same." He held up his brandy snifter. "To Sanfield Dandish. May his labors bear fruit for a thousand years."

Tristam raised his glass in silent salute.

Sanfield Dandish had remained a bachelor all his life but, even so, he had lived in a largish house, well-suited to a family, set in a country-style garden. The house would not have stood out in Merton except that Dandish had designed a stone tower that was attached rather arbitrarily to one end of the structure. To a passerby this tower might have contained nothing more than a stairwell, but its upper story was actually a water tower. The water was pumped from a well up into the cistern by a wind-driven mechanism—another innovation of the professor's. Dandish's home boasted water piped into the water closets and the scullery as well. Tristam knew full well that the convenience of this had been of no consequence to Dandish—it was merely the delight in the design and execution that had led the professor to spend considerable energies in this project.

Tristam lifted the latch on the gate and stepped into the professor's world. The old man had done much of his own gardening, when he was able, and had closely overseen the rest. Several new varieties of rose had come from this very garden as well as variations on both ornamental and food plants.

"*Look at what has been done to the breeds through animal husbandry! And in the world of horticulture,*" Tristam remembered Dandish saying, "*entire new varieties! If man can do such things in living memory, what could nature accomplish in a few million years?*" Which brought the professor down squarely on the side of *Constant Change* in the species debate, a debate that still raged. This belief in the transmutation of species had made the old pedagogue somewhat of a radical in his youth, and, though the tide was beginning to turn on that issue, it marked the professor as a man who stood by his convictions. As long as Tristam had known him, Dandish had never been afraid to entertain ideas that others scorned. Unlike many, age had not cast his mind into rigid patterns.

Tristam had often thought the professor more flexible than his students. Certainly less sure that he knew the truth. Perhaps this had been what had made him so susceptible to criticism.

Tristam walked down a narrow gravel path between rows of exotic irises of different hues. Dandish had been a complex man. He had been quite surprised at his students' commitment to finding "the truth." "*In empirical studies,*" he once said, "*we formulate succeeding hypotheses to explain phenomena, each hypothesis fitted to our facts a little more closely. But ultimately, Tristam, I do not think we will arrive at truth. I think we shall arrive at a great mystery.*"

For some time afterward Tristam had suspected the professor of being a secret mystic, a transcendentalist perhaps, but Dandish had been as fixated on developing hypotheses as any empiricist Tristam knew. He had also said, "*A great hypothesis is like a great poem, as long as it explains something central to the human mind, it will stand. When it no longer fulfills this promise something else takes its place. But we all remember the name of Maritain even if we no longer read his poems. And if not for Maritain, there would never have followed Bartram and Northrop. A poet's greatness is not just measured by how long his poetry is read.*"

Despite all, Dandish had been as concerned with "immortality" as any of his colleagues. Tristam hoped the professor's work was substantive enough to assure it.

When Tristam had first come to know Dandish, he had been confused by the professor's penchant for talking about empiricism in terms of art and poetry, but over the years the student had slowly come to understanding. Dandish held the "fact collectors," as he called them, in disdain. The collection of information, to Dandish's manner of thinking, had one purpose—to support a hypothesis. Reason must be applied to guide the search for information and to interpret the findings.

To Tristam it seemed a statement of the obvious, but in the great debate between the "rationalists"—those who believed that everything could be understood by mere application of the mind, and the pure empiricists, those who believed understanding grew from one's experience of the world—Dandish had been attacked by both sides. Too much "rationalism" for the fact collectors and too interested in collecting facts for the rationalists. But this debate, too, was slipping into silence—the very word "empiricism" was changing in meaning, and the school of thought championed by Dandish and some of his colleagues was winning the field. Unfortunately, the personal cost to the hypersensitive Dandish had been immense.

Tristam strolled through the garden, partly to avoid entering the house, though he was not sure why. He was surprised to discover wet soil in the beds: someone had thought to come and water.

Although the professor had not been a large part of Tristam's life for the

past two years, they had spent many many hours together during the classification of Trevelyan's collection. Dandish had been a reserved, distant man, not
given to displays of affection or to discussing personal matters—Tristam had
not known of the sister, for instance. Theirs had been an odd, unspoken friendship, more important to the professor than Tristam had realized.

To think that he remembered me in his will, Tristam mused. *I wish now that
I had realized. I should have made the effort to visit. Had I only known he was so
ill. . . .*

He knew that he would harbor some regret over this. Of course, Dandish
may have preferred things that way. Friendship unacknowledged, unspoken. It
might have been easier for him, for it did not seem uncommon in the reserved,
rather cool, world of the Merton dons.

Tristam stopped and surveyed the garden. Thick hedges and stone walls,
shaded from too much sun by ancient trees. It was the town of Merton writ
small. Set off alone, a backwater into which drifted a certain type of man. Tristam had decided, years ago, that there must be more to life. There was a whole
world beyond Merton, after all. Did not empiricism mean to experience?

So Tristam had left Merton and returned to Locfal, disappointing Dandish,
perhaps, but the life of a Merton don was not for Tristam. It wasn't that he did
not share their interests. Certainly he did, and he was not about to give them
up. But he had realized that it was not a full life. It was *the life of the mind*, and
there were other parts to Tristam—uncharted territory, nearly. Of course, he
had not yet been able to decide what form his life beyond Merton would take.
That was the real struggle.

Occasionally, he feared that he had taken up with Jenny in hopes that the
relationship would provide an answer. Now he feared it would not—and was
not quite sure what to do about it. This line of thought always unsettled him,
so he turned away from it and approached the house.

He tried the most likely looking key and the front door creaked open. The
odor of stale tobacco smoke wafted out from the entry hall. Leaving the door
ajar, Tristam walked quietly into the house as though afraid to awaken the
occupants.

I believe in ghosts even less than I believe in magic, Tristam told himself,
despite pranks played to convince me otherwise. Still, he felt uncomfortable
alone in the house where a man had died so recently. He went into the dining
room and opened the windows. On the table, at the professor's accustomed
place, there was a book lying open. Closing it gently, Tristam saw it was Lord
Trevelyan's *Propagation in Tropical Angiosperms*.

He passed through the spotless kitchen, seldom used except for the production of tea and coffee. It was the professor's custom to take his meals in the
college dining hall or at an inn.

Tristam looked into all the ground floor rooms, opening doors and windows as he went, and a profound melancholy began to grow in him. The realization that all of the professor's mundane belongings easily outlived him, Tristam found very sad.

There was a narrow, back stairway to what would have been the servant's room, and Tristam followed it up to the next floor.

He avoided the door to Dandish's sleeping chamber—the room where the professor had died—and went directly to the library. Though he had never spoken of it, Dandish must have had some family money, for his library contained over three thousand volumes, and books were expensive things. A man on a professor's salary could hardly afford so many and such a capacious house as well. Most of the books were on the subjects dearest to the professor's heart: natural history, taxonomy in particular; all branches of natural philosophy; mechanics; and engineering. The breadth of the professor's interests was striking, for there were also many volumes of philosophy, poetry, linguistics, and history. He had even possessed a few novels.

The walls supported floor-to-ceiling bookshelves except for a bow window on one wall and a fireplace on another. Over the hearth hung an artist's study for a painting of sea lions in the surf. It was by a painter of some fame and Tristam knew it was one of Dandish's most prized possessions.

A complete collection of the *Annals of the Empiricist's Society* caught Tristam's eye and he found himself wondering if this set might be one of the things left to him. There were quite a number of gaps in the bookshelves and Tristam knew he would find the missing volumes lying around the house. Dandish typically read several books at once and he would leave them in different places around the house—some by his bed, some in the dining room, one or two in the morning room, more by each chair in the parlor. The library, of course, had books on the tables and desk. Even the drawing room would have its opened volumes.

On the desk lay another of the professor's innovations—a copying machine, the frame bearing a mechanical pencil that reproduced every stroke made by a pen, allowing Dandish to make two of any letter or document he wished.

Tristam looked about, not quite sure where to begin, but then he removed his jacket and laid it over a chair, opened his neck cloth, and chose a corner of the room. Work would be the cure for this sudden outbreak of emotion.

It was a slow process, for the professor's books were poorly organized—astonishing he had ever found what he wanted. But, oh, there were some treasures!

Tristam stopped occasionally to admire a volume; many were first editions, some very rare, and often inscribed by the author. In a long life Dandish had met most of the eminent men in his field. He had also been a member of the Empiricists' Society for more than twenty years and that had provided innumerable contacts.

It was always Tristam's dream that the professor would one day put his name forward for fellowship. That would never be, now, and Tristam had yet to do the work that would qualify him for a place in that august company.

Midday arrived and Tristam, nowhere near halfway through his task, was suddenly stricken by hunger. Locking the door behind him he made a brief foray to a nearby shop and returned with bread and cheese and a flagon of perfectly serviceable ale. There was a bower in the garden where Dandish often sat and here were two wicker chairs and a small table. He set his luncheon there and slipped back in the kitchen door to find a book and a mug.

Stepping into the hall he almost ran down an old woman and gave her such a start that she shrieked, scaring Tristam almost as much as herself. The two stepped back, eyeing each other warily.

"Mrs. Ebish?"

"And who might you be?"

"Tristam Flattery. I'm sure you don't remember. I was a student of the professor's." He smiled, he hoped reassuringly. This was the cleaning woman Dandish had employed. Tristam had met her once or twice and was astonished to have remembered her name.

"And what cause have you to be sneaking around here?" she asked, her voice sullen.

"Dean Emin, who is the executor of the professor's estate, asked me to come and itemize the books and papers. He gave me a key." Tristam removed the ring from his pocket and held it out as proof.

"Quite a fright you gave me," she said, obviously still not recovered and somewhat annoyed.

"Unintentional, I assure you. May I ask what you're doing here yourself?"

She looked a bit defensive. "I've been watering the plants," she said defiantly. "Someone's got to. Your Dean Emin never thought of that, I see. This morning I did the garden, but I had no time to tend to the house." She gestured to the battered watering can she held, much as Tristam had done with his keys.

"That is most thoughtful of you, Mrs. Ebish." He wondered how much of the professor's silverware she might have in her apron and immediately felt mean-spirited.

"I haven't watered the plants in the upstairs drawing room. The professor always kept that locked and tended to it himself. I suspect the plants in there are as limp as old rags by now." She nodded to the keys Tristam held in his hand. "Have you one for that room as well?"

He looked down at the keys. He hadn't yet looked into the upstairs drawing room. "I confess I don't know."

"It would be a shame to let the plants die. They were a special study, he told me, and seemed very dear to him."

"Well, perhaps we should have a look," Tristam said and motioned for the old woman to lead the way.

She was not spry, but she kept a steady pace as she mounted the stairs, clutching the rail strongly. Tristam seemed to remember Dandish saying she had cleaned his house for thirty-some years.

"It will be quite a change for you, Mrs. Ebish, without the professor to look after."

"I dare say it will. Though I must admit, my old bones could do with a bit of rest. It was me that found him, you know." She was suddenly embarrassed. "I'll say no more than that."

They walked along the landing to a large oak door and here the woman stopped and stepped back to let Tristam try the lock. He thought she was doing a poor job of hiding her anticipation: she actually licked her lips. The third key drew the bolt. As the door swung inward, Tristam caught a whiff of something familiar—dank, organic.

He pushed the door wide, revealing a large, formal room. All the furniture was stacked to one side and covered with sheets to leave space for the professor's "special study." There, before the broad windows, stood neat rows of copper-lined planting boxes, each filled with soil but empty of any flower or shrub. They lay like coffins in the squares of sunlight falling through the glass.

Tristam looked back at the cleaning woman and saw a clear look of disappointment.

"Well," she muttered. "Well."

"Not what you expected, I collect?"

She smiled, wanly. "I've often wondered. I thought there would be some beautiful flower that he was keeping so secret." She gave a short laugh. "Well. He must have finished with his study. Just like the professor to say nothing."

"Yes . . . exactly like him." Tristam turned back to empty boxes. There had clearly been something in them, for at regular intervals there was a depression in the dirt where it appeared some plant had been removed.

"Well, I won't have to worry about water here." She laughed, but it did not seem quite natural. "Good day to you, Mr. Flattery, and I wish you luck with your work. I can't say as I envy you; the professor's effects will be in a fine muddle, I'll warrant. Never a thought to the practical things, the good professor—rest his soul." Tristam listened to the woman's slow progress down the stair—the measured sounds of her step, the occasional squeak of her hand sliding along the railing.

Obviously, Dandish's secrecy had piqued her curiosity.

Tristam crossed the room and walked among the long copper-lined boxes. He sniffed the air, turning his head like a hound. A hint of a familiar scent lingered.

He dug in the soil and turned up roots that had been broken off, and though he could not say from such little evidence to what plant the roots had belonged, he was certain he had seen others quite like them. It was clear the plants that had grown here had been removed by main force—torn out of the soil—not carefully dug out to be moved elsewhere.

Tristam went to the window and looked down into the garden. Yes, it was still there—a small enclosure of brick for burning refuse. He glanced down at the empty planting boxes. "It is only a coincidence," he whispered. Locking the door after him, he went back into the garden.

The trash burner contained only fine ashes, but a subsequent search of the property gave Tristam the answer to his question. Caught in the branches of a laurel hedge he found a single leaf, curled and desiccated, singed on one edge, but it was unquestionably Kingfoil.

He stood, turning the paper-dry leaf over and over in his hand, trying to devise another explanation for its presence. He looked up at the empty windows of the drawing room and shook his head. There could be no doubt. The professor had been growing Kingfoil, and had destroyed it. Or someone else had.

A breeze brushed through the garden, an almost articulate whispering. He gazed up at the windows of the drawing room again and thought that the reflections of the surrounding trees could almost have been the leaves of *regis* pressed against the glass.

Clearly, Sir Roderick knew nothing of this or the King's Man would have said something to Tristam before he set out. This entire matter was taken so seriously by Palle that Tristam was sure it could not have merely slipped his mind. Roderick hadn't risen to such heights by letting things slip.

"There must be a perfectly reasonable explanation for this," he said aloud.

Tristam returned indoors and went resolutely up to the door of Dandish's sleeping chamber. Here he paused with his fingers on the handle, gathered his resolve, and pushed open the door.

The odor still lingered. Not unfamiliar to Tristam, who had studied mammal taxonomy, but this he found unbearable. He held his breath and pulled aside the curtains, then threw open the windows. He leaned out for a second, taking a number of deep breaths. Here Dandish had died alone, Tristam thought, and this chilled him completely. Taking a last deep breath he went directly to the night table beside the bed. The drawer was locked but the smallest key on the ring fit perfectly and within Tristam found what he expected—

three identical, leather-bound books. The professor's most recent journals. Locking the drawer, he retreated quickly from the room.

Back in the garden, he took up one of the journals. The first entry was April, two years earlier, and contained plans for work in the garden as well as a detailed description of a spider uncovered in the woodpile.

Tristam found himself reading whole passages, comforted to know about the small events of Dandish's days. He could imagine the words spoken in the professor's slow manner, each word chosen with particular precision. Tristam could feel Dandish's delight at the first blossoms of spring, at a small discovery at the university.

Almost gently he turned the pages, looking for the last entry, and found instead a page over which ink had been spilled so that the entire leaf had been blackened. The ink had soaked through to the next page, though the blot was not so large; then to the next, the mark smaller again, until on the fifth page it was a stain no larger than a coin . . . And then Tristam turned the page and the mark was gone.

It was the point at which Tristam's mind finally grappled with the reality of his mentor's death. For the next hour he walked among the shrubs and flowers, gaining no comfort from their transitory beauty. It took some time for him to master this dark mood, but finally the discipline that Tristam had developed in all the years he had spent alone allowed him to turn his attention away from Dandish and his loss.

He returned to his chair wondering if poor Dandish had become so ill that he had spilled ink into his journal. Or had the professor intentionally blotted out some pages? Tristam shook his head. If Dandish had wanted to erase something, far more effective to cut out the pages and burn them, as he apparently had done with the Kingfoil. If he had been able to.

He flipped back through the pages, reading randomly. Notes on meetings at the college. Inquiries the professor was conducting. Criticism of writings from several journals. References to correspondence posted and received.

A brief entry that described perfectly one of the scourges of Dandish's existence.

Ipsword has attacked me for the second time in a week. Not my work, but me personally! I cannot shake his maliciousness out of my mind and have barely slept or worked for seven days. I should not let myself be affected so, for the man is no empiricist at all. He is nothing but a blackguard!

Poor fragile Dandish. The entries for the days before this were all concerned with the same matter. What might the professor have accomplished if he had heard only praise? In truth, Dandish had not needed criticism from others—he had managed that well enough on his own.

Into the previous year Tristam finally found what he sought—a reference to *regis.*

I cannot understand why my regis *is suffering the same deficiency as the planting at the palace! My seeds came from the second crop, yet they are acting identically to plants grown from the later generations. Why??*

Dandish knew of the fertility problem before Tumney . . . and had kept it to himself!

An envelope slipped out of the back of the journal and Tristam pulled it free to find Dandish's writing across the face. It was clearly addressed to the Duchess of Morland.

Tristam felt his hands fall to his lap. He need not even open the letter. In a way he had known since discovering the empty planting boxes: the staged meeting at the palace; the duchess' interest in Tristam, completely out of proportion to his supposed accomplishments. Dandish had been growing Kingfoil for the Duchess.

Why?

A physic that kept the King alive.

Fierce competition among the courtiers for the favor of the King. Or at least between the duchess and Sir Roderick Palle. And somehow she had enlisted Dandish to her cause. Almost gingerly he pushed the letter back into the pages of the journal as though he could make it disappear.

Tristam looked around the garden as though it were not the home of his old professor, but some place he had never been. Try as he might, Tristam could not imagine a person less likely to be involved in the intrigues of the court. *And I thought I knew him.*

He stared off at the far border of the lawn where a stone wall stood guard between Dandish's world and the greater world beyond. Tristam had always believed that there was little commerce between the two worlds.

With a noise like a wing fluttering, the letter slipped from the leaves of the book again, and Tristam stared at it for a few seconds, as though fascinated by the texture of the fine paper. It seemed the most innocent of objects.

It is a letter addressed to the favorite of the King, Tristam reminded himself, and pushed it yet again into the book.

A few seconds of hesitation while Tristam struggled inwardly, but a sudden compulsion to know about this secret life Dandish had been living overcame all other considerations. No one could know of the letter's existence but Dandish and Tristam, that seemed certain. And Tristam wanted to know why Dandish had become engaged in this matter behind the back of Sir Roderick Palle. It made Tristam wonder about the motives of the King's Man.

That was all the justification Tristam required. He took a small clasp knife from his pocket and cut the letter open with some precision.

Your Grace:

> *It is with deep regret that I write to inform you that I am unable to continue the inquiry I had undertaken. My health has grown worse and I will be forced to give up most of my activities, including my position at the university. Even so, I believe I can say at this point that there is no answer to the problem.*
>
> *I say this with complete awareness that I have failed Your Grace in a matter of great importance: an unworthy return for your confidence in me as well as all of your kind attentions.*
>
> *It has been the greatest pleasure and honor to serve Your Grace in this matter and I only regret that I cannot, in return, do more.*
>
> *I have taken the liberty of destroying the plants in my possession as I am sure they are of no value to further study.*
>
> > *Your servant,*
> > *Sanfield Dandish*

It was clear which side Dandish had chosen in court politics.

Once more Tristam turned the pages, looking for what, he did not know. He came upon the last entry dated the twenty-first—Dandish had died sometime the next night. He began to read down the page.

> *Visit from Dean Emin. There is no denying the gravity of my situation. The look on that poor man's face; as though he had found a ghost propped up in my bed.*
>
> *My heart is not at peace this day, arrhythmic and fluttering, and my breath does not come easily. I must somehow find the strength to write Tristam, but not today. How deeply I regret his involvement!*

A sudden roll of thunder pulled Tristam back into the world. A blast of wind rustled the leaves in the garden like a hiss, and then there was a profound stillness. A summer storm had swept down upon Merton, and rain suddenly lashed the earth with the violence of a great battle of men.

After rushing about closing doors and windows, Tristam flung himself down in a chair in the parlor to catch his breath. Outside, the trees swayed and leaves tore free of their branches to disappear on the wind.

Unable to return to his task in the library Tristam found himself drawn back into Dandish's diary and near the end of the final volume he found a brief entry he had not seen. It had been written some four weeks past.

I am not quite the old fool the Duchess takes me for.
I shall get a letter off to Valary tomorrow.

Tristam looked up from his reading. *Valary?*

"Well, here is one mystery easily solved," Tristam thought aloud. Returning to the library he went to a stack of wooden boxes in one corner. These contained, in some semblance of order, the professor's voluminous correspondence—some four hundred letters a year. As a widely recognized authority in several disciplines, Dandish kept up a correspondence with innumerable empiricists in both Farrland and beyond and, to keep his memory fresh, followed the common practice of making a fair copy of each of his own letters before committing them to the post.

Two hours of searching produced no letters either from Dandish to Valary or the other way about. Nor was there a sign of a correspondence with the duchess.

A sudden blast of wind shook the house and a loud banging caused Tristam to start. When he went to investigate, he found someone was pounding on the front door. It seemed impossible to believe that Dean Emin was capable of such violence, and, a bit warily, Tristam opened the door.

Before him stood the drenched and dripping figure of his cousin, who measured Tristam with a concerned gaze.

"Jaimy?" Tristam said dumbly.

"Ah, you do recognize me. Thank goodness." Jaimy tried a smile, though it was still touched with concern. "Will you invite me in or shall we converse while I shower?"

Tristam heard himself laugh; a great relief. He reached out and drew his cousin bodily into the hall. "What on earth are you doing in Merton in the summer?" Tristam was overjoyed to find his cousin—his ally in so many things.

"Visiting Flinders, of course. He's a junior lecturer now, or some such thing. With typical bad manners he has abandoned me to my own devises for the evening as he is out courting. Our friend Flinders has gone all to pieces over a winsome lass—or so he says—I can't vouch for the girl's alleged winsomeness." Jaimy's attempt at joviality faded suddenly. "Dean Emin told me I would find you here. I am sorry to hear about poor Dandish, Tristam, I know he was a particular friend to you." He paused. "Is there anything at all that I might do?"

Tristam's throat was suddenly tight again. "I'm touched by your concern, J, but you needn't worry. I say quite honestly that I am well with it. He was an old man and lived a full life in his own terms." He looked at his cousin and shrugged. What could be said in such circumstances? "Dean Emin asked me to come down to go through the professor's papers. The will hasn't been read yet, but it seems that the kind professor mentioned me—some books I expect."

"He held you in high regard, Tristam." Jaimy glanced about. "I thought you might need to break from this. Shall we go find a meal? It might cheer you. And then I will offer you all the help I can in your task."

"It might fortify me, which I feel I need more than cheering. One moment." Tristam went in search of his frock coat and then bundled up Dandish's journals, careful to put the letter to the duchess into the pocket of his coat so that it didn't slip out, as it appeared to have a tendency to do. It was then that he realized the burnt Kingfoil leaf was still in the garden. He rushed to the door and could see through the glass that the leaf was gone, probably swept away on the wind. For a second he felt a rush of fear, but then he realized that no one would ever notice—just another leaf on the ground. It seemed appropriate somehow.

Returning to the entry hall, Tristam found Jaimy standing before the shelves upon which Dandish displayed many curios of his trade.

"What on the round earth is this?" Jaimy was looking down at a roughhewn bust of wood. It appeared to be hollow and had a hinged jaw and rather too-human lips shaped of leather. The sculptor had carved only the suggestion of a nose and the eye sockets had been left eerily blank.

"You've never seen this? It was the talk of Merton and the Empiricist's Society twenty years ago. Even the King asked for a demonstration. Here, pump this." Tristam directed Jaimy to a bellows attached to the back. "There is a mechanism inside made of ribbons of the thinnest copper." Tristam took hold of the controls, trying to remember what Dandish had shown him.

When he judged that there was sufficient "breath" being created, he moved the controls.

"*Ma'am*," the head hissed in a breathy, childish tone.

Jaimy stopped pumping in surprise. "What in . . . ?"

"It was an attempt to reproduce the mechanism of human speech—or perhaps I should say approximate it. Of course, it is very primitive, but ingenious all the same. There was some debate about the origin of human utterances and Dandish concocted this to prove a point. It makes three or four other sounds, but I can't recall how they're managed."

Jaimy gave a shiver, as though suddenly chilled from his drenching. "It is a little macabre. I don't think that I would choose it as an ornament for my entry. And this?"

He pointed to a device of wood and metal set on its own narrow shelf.

"Rover," Tristam said, almost laughing at the memory. "A gift from someone or other. A barometric dog, so called. Changes in atmospheric pressure cause it to flex, and creep along the shelf. Even with great plunges of the barometer, its movement is painfully slow—a slug would appear a regular racehorse in comparison—but it works."

There were a dozen other devices, but the rain had fallen to a drizzle, so they took the opportunity to set out, first for the Ivy. Tristam felt a great relief at finding himself so suddenly in the company of his cousin, for truly Jaimy was his closest friend. They had survived the rivalries and petty squabbles of their youth and had forged a friendship of great importance to them both. No doubt part of the reason for the success of this friendship was their "fit," for more often than not where Tristam was strong Jaimy was less so, and vice versa. It was also true that the two could never be rivals, for Jaimy was the heir to both title and fortune and was socially successful in the extreme, while Tristam's accomplishments as a scholar and empiricist, both knew, Jaimy could never hope to equal.

They were alike enough in coloring and size to be brothers, and were often mistaken for such. Jaimy's eyes were blue, rather than green, and the bone structure of his face was perhaps a bit stronger, but there could be little doubt that much the same blood flowed in their veins.

Upon first meeting, many thought Jaimy to be the older brother, for he was confident and well versed in the social graces of his class, but those who knew the cousins better believed Tristam to be the older of the two.

They stopped only briefly at the Ivy where Tristam lent Jaimy some dry clothes, and at the same time, though he could not say why, he buried the professor's journals under his luggage inside a wardrobe.

At Jaimy's suggestion they set out for one of their old haunts. The proprietor recognized Lord Jaimas immediately and led them to a good table by a window.

Over dinner Jaimy steered the conversation with great consideration for his cousin's mood—neither allowing it to become frivolous nor too serious. No further mention was made of Professor Dandish, and though Tristam dearly wanted to speak with his cousin about the discoveries he had made, Sir Roderick's warning could not be forgotten. Better not to involve Jaimy, no matter how strongly Tristam desired his council. Dandish had almost certainly broken laws and his ally appeared to be a very well placed lady. So Tristam held his peace, and though Jaimy could normally guess when something was troubling his cousin, the death of Tristam's friend seemed a likely explanation for his mood.

The summons to the palace was another matter, for Tristam could not very well give no reason for his presence this far from Locfal, so he explained it as a mission to heal an ailing shrub and made it sound absurd—another example of the foolishness of courtiers.

Midway through the meal, Tristam thought he might ask a few innocent-sounding questions of his cousin, for Jaimy's knowledge of the workings of Farr society greatly exceeded his own. "J? Have you ever met the Duchess of Morland?"

"Once or twice. Why do you ask?"

"I met her at the palace. briefly. I was in the company of Sir Roderick Palle and got the distinct impression that they were cool to each other."

"I should say! Palle is the confidant of Prince Kori, and the duchess is not popular with the princess. She is too close to His Majesty for the liking of Palle, you can be sure, and promotes the interests of her friends with great success." He flashed a smile. "The duchess is a great beauty. . . . Did you happen to notice? Watch yourself there," his cousin teased. "It is said the duchess enjoys the company of younger men."

Further questions were impossible, for Jaimy began to talk about his recent travels and was as entertaining as always, actually managing to distract Tristam from his troubles. The world began to look normal. The entire issue of Kingfoil and Dandish and the duchess began to seem rather impossible. Certainly impossible that Tristam could be involved in any such thing. Tristam Flattery of sleepy Locfal. The more ale he drank, the more it seemed that he must simply have blown matters all out of proportion—suffered temporary delusion.

Jaimy, it came out, had lost his heart to a young woman—the real reason he was in Merton—and was feeling very dejected because his suit was apparently not succeeding. Tristam was sympathetic, but a little surprised as well. Merton was not known to be the home of Farrland's aristocrats. "How in the world have you found a woman here?" he asked at last.

"Do you remember Professor Somers?" Jaimy said, still a little defensive, as though he expected to be laughed at.

"Of course. I even recall that he had daughters. Two, I believe."

"Four, in fact." Jaimy stopped to gather his thoughts. "Somers has carried out the most noble experiment, Tristam. He has educated his daughters. I mean truly educated them. Not just taught them to perform pleasingly on the pianum, or to fill in a silence in the conversation with a few words carefully chosen to ruffle no one." His eyes sparkled now and he leaned forward as he spoke. "They have read Lord Skye and Trevelyan; yes, and Halden, too. They know more about the significance of our treaties with Entonne than they do of the latest Entonne fashions. Why, just the other day in their garden, Alissa identified a beetle I could not name. The word education has a meaning in the Somers' home that it does not elsewhere."

Tristam was forced to remember that his Jenny played Brimm badly. "Alissa, is she not still a child?"

"Seventeen."

"Ah."

"Don't be tiresome, Tristam, her age is not the issue. Alissa is mature beyond her years. Beyond my years, I sometimes think. And she seems to care for me more than a little."

"And what of the good professor? How does he look upon this?"

Jaimy stared down into his brandy glass and then said quietly, "He thinks I'm a rogue, I suspect."

"Ah, cousin. This is most difficult."

"My father knows nothing of this, so you needn't ask."

"You don't think the duke would look upon this favorably?"

The young lord shrugged. "You know him as well as I."

"Not nearly as well, but I take your point." Tristam was having trouble maintaining his composure. "Well, cousin, you are about to be indebted to me eternally—that is, if you are truly serious about this young woman. Professor Somers is one of my great supporters. In second year I made a small contribution in his area of study and since that day, in the good professor's eyes, I can do no wrong. Leave this to me. I shall resurrect your reputation in the house of Somers, and all I ask in return is that you slave in Dandish's library like the most devoted of clerks."

☞ Seven

After parting from Jaimy, Tristam found that he was not drawn back to his bed at the Ivy. Not that he didn't feel the weight of fatigue in his body, but even so he knew that sleep did not wait for him in his rooms. He wandered down the streets of Merton, stopping to lean over the rail of the bridge and listen to the flowing river.

The air was soft with dew and the earlier rain, and into this renewed atmosphere summer seemed to have released all of her perfume. Small breezes pursuing the mother storm sighed in the darkness, bending the cat-tails by the river edge and swaying the robes of the willows. High over the towers of the university Tristam could see the moon in its first quarter, floating among stars that appeared suspended in liquid, for around the largest faint haloes glowed.

A bell in the university tower sounded the night's middle hour, and the echoes answered, then faded until the whisper of flowing Wedgewater was the only voice.

Despite his clear awareness that he was not well versed in the ways of the human heart, Tristam had a sense of what he felt, for he had known it before. It wasn't just the loss of his friend, it was the sudden awareness of one's own mortality that such losses invariably produced. The sudden shift in one's view, as though a death opened a window that normally was kept shut and shuttered. Most of everyday life's great issues looked trivial when seen through that window.

What were these foolish courtiers up to and why had they entangled Dandish in their schemes? All this so one very old man would look upon them with favor and forget to smile on their rivals. Oh, Wilam was not a bad king. Tristam did not wish him ill. But Wilam had had his own follies—most prominently, the last war with Entonne. If he passed on, the greater world would not likely be torn apart—but the lives of some courtiers would change irrevocably. So anything to keep him alive.

Tristam pushed himself away from the rail and walked on. Jenny had often hinted that Tristam was without emotion, always cool and detached. He was never quite sure what it was she expected of him. Her own beliefs in such matters were somehow different from his, but different in what way, he could not explain—nor could Jenny, it seemed. It was rather ironic considering that he had left Merton because he thought the life of the mind inadequate.

Tristam had come to believe that a life should be conducted in the light of reason. Love and passion had their place, certainly, but they should not rule. The idea seemed so eminently sensible that he could not see how anyone could argue against it. He wondered again about the course he had chosen. Tried to imagine life with this young woman who neither understood nor shared his interests.

He looked up at the stars, feeling again the stab of loss. If Jenny believed he was without feelings, then she should see him now. It struck him as rather sad that he could even consider that Dandish's death should serve to prove the existence of Tristam's emotions.

He turned into another street, lined with high elms.

I cannot sleep, he realized, *and there is no profit in this line of thought.* Picking up his pace, he set out for Dandish's home. Damn the intrigues of courtiers. Damn sentimentality. Let the flames take even love, for the moment. He would go and apply himself to the task he had been given. Three hours of real work would drive out these demons.

He had some trouble finding the right key by moonlight, but then the lock turned and the door swung open, the familiar smell of stale tobacco smoke wafting out into the pure night, followed by a thump quickly muffled. Tristam stopped on the threshold, suddenly alert. He stood listening, holding his breath so that he might hear even the slightest sound. Nothing.

He almost laughed. Perhaps he had not closed a window properly and it had been found by a breeze. Somehow Tristam did not think Dandish was a likely candidate to return and haunt his old home. Not that the professor didn't have secrets, as Tristam was learning, but still, Dandish had been a largely benign presence in the world. Tristam cleared his throat audibly if only to prove that he could control his fears.

He would have to find the implements to strike a lamp, but he was sure such things must lie by the fireplace. Slowly he began to feel his way toward the sitting room, his eyes adjusting quickly. There was a little light from moon and stars filtering through the windows and Tristam began to distinguish objects; a chair here, a small table.

For no reason that he could name, Tristam regretted clearing his throat. *Be reasonable*, he told himself, *you are not afraid of the dark.*

As he was about to step through the door into the sitting room, he heard a sudden curse and someone large shot through the doorway, the collision propelling Tristam back into the stair rail. His head struck the oak with such force that he collapsed into a heap, his ears ringing, the wind knocked from his lungs. The front door banged open and Tristam heard boots on the gravel path, running.

"*Farrelle's flames*," he heard himself whisper, despite lack of air. He tried to rise, afraid he was in danger, but he could only manage to sit, gasping. "Blood and flames," he said. His head spun from the effort of moving and his eyes closed of their own will. The room seemed to tilt, first one way and then another. Tristam fought to remain conscious, as though the darkness that tried to overwhelm him was death itself. He focused all of his will on that one act, opening his eyes just enough to see moonlight, to know that the world was not fading.

It took a second for the image to coalesce and register in his brain, but not three feet away, in the shadows and pale light, a small, frightened child crouched, his gaze fixed on Tristam. And then the room began to whirl again and he felt himself falling.

Tristam was sure he regained his awareness in only a few seconds. For some time he lay still, like an animal trusting to darkness and lack of movement for protection. From his position by the stairs Tristam could see no one—neither men nor small boys. An urge to rise and run out the front door came over him, but then he remembered that the nocturnal visitor had gone that way. The house, Tristam reasoned, was almost certainly empty now.

He raised a hand to his head and assured himself that there was no great flow of blood. The skin had been broken, but barely, and a welt was rapidly rising.

"I am whole," he said aloud. Very slowly Tristam pushed himself up onto moderately steady legs and held onto the stair rail, taking stock. He would do.

Not without some trepidation, Tristam passed into the sitting room, his eyes darting about as he went, searching the shadows. In one corner of the room Tristam saw a thin line glowing orange and he stopped in horror. And then he laughed aloud, crossing toward the dull light. As he thought, it was a storm lantern, light leaking from the crack on one side of the door.

He managed to open the lantern without burning himself and the soft, familiar glow of lamplight flowed out like a sigh, pushing back the pale light of stars and moon, pushing back the shadows. Tristam eased himself down into a chair for a moment.

Housebreakers. He had interrupted housebreakers. Here, in Merton. Think as he might, Tristam could not recall ever hearing of such a thing before. It unsettled him completely.

I should wake Jaimy, Tristam thought. It would be good to have a companion in this situation. But then he remembered again that the housebreakers were outside, somewhere, and decided that staying in the house might be the most intelligent course. After all, if he left the house and anyone was watching, they might come back to finish the job. Whatever it was they intended.

Realizing the door was still open, Tristam scooped up the lamp and forced himself up. Beside the entrance to the sitting room he found a fireplace poker lying on the floor and picked it up, hefting it. He was completely sure it had lain by the fire earlier that day. The small lump he had on his head would be nothing compared to what this would have done.

Tristam bolted the door and decided that he would hunker down here for the night, with his lamp and fire poker. Kindle a blaze in the fireplace. Light more lamps. It was unlikely he would sleep, but he would keep the house—and himself—from harm.

When the dull pewter of impending morning spread into the eastern sky, Tristam could keep awake no longer. He slept lightly for perhaps two hours and awoke to early morning, the garden alive with the songs of birds, sun bright, and lamps guttering in the sitting room. After lying for a moment, almost unwilling to face the day, Tristam roused himself and blew out the lamps.

Immediately he noticed that one of the double doors opening onto the garden had a shattered pane, and shards of glass were scattered across the floor. Why, if this was the door used to gain entrance, had the vandal run Tristam down to get out the front? It made no sense.

Taking up his poker again, Tristam went from room to room and everywhere met the same sight. The house had been ransacked. Cabinet doors hung open and the contents of drawers and closets were strewn across the floors. In the scullery a bowl lay shattered on the bureau, the pattern of yellow roses fragmented over the sheet-copper. He may have interrupted the housebreakers in their work, but they appeared to have been nearly finished anyway. The house was in ruins.

On the landing he found that the door to the drawing room had been forced, causing some damage to both door and frame. There was no harm to the room, however. The covering sheets had been pulled off the furniture, but all else remained untouched. Tristam continued his search and found the guest rooms had been given a thorough going over.

It was not until he entered the library that Tristam felt real dismay. Books lay everywhere, many torn and damaged, their covers hanging by a few threads or gone altogether. The drawers of the desk had been dumped out onto the floor and mixed with Dandish's correspondence. All of Tristam's careful work had been undone. The artist's study still hung in its place—not entirely a surprise— even though it was valuable and housebreakers usually knew their business.

The professor's sleeping chamber had been treated like all the others, though here the mattress and pillows had been slit. As he stood looking at the room, covered in a fine snowfall of down, a sharp rap caused Tristam to raise his poker in defense before he realized it was the brass knocker in the main entry.

Jaimy stood waiting on the steps, his most charming smile in place.

"Your clerk has arrived." The young lord looked down at the poker in Tristam's hand and then more closely at his cousin's face. "What is it?"

With some relief Tristam pushed the door wide. "I've just been searching the house. I came back last night and interrupted housebreakers, if you can believe it." Tristam bent to show his scalp to his cousin. "I received this when I collided with a vandal in the dark."

Jaimy carefully parted Tristam's hair. "Not too serious, I think. You will have quite a lump though. You are all right? Not light-headed? Not feeling ill? Your vision is unchanged?"

"I am perfectly whole. More than we can say for the house."

Jaimy looked around as though he suspected criminals to still be lurking. Tristam took his cousin to tour some of the wreckage.

"Is much missing?" Jaimy ventured.

Tristam shook his head. "I wish I knew. I had begun to inventory the library, but I was nowhere near finished. The house keeper might know, I suppose."

"If it wasn't her sons that did the deed."

"Mrs. Ebish? No, she will be quite innocent. 'Salt of the earth' is how you would describe Mrs. Ebish." Tristam picked up a piece of the shattered bowl, for they had wandered as far as the scullery. "I need to let Dean Emin know what's happened here. Would you watch the house for a while?"

"Of course, but it makes more sense for me to find the dean and you to stay here. You might begin to make some sense of this and I wouldn't know where to start."

Tristam looked around at the wreckage. "Yes, that would be best. The dean should be at the college, but if not he'll likely be at his home. Eighteen North-moor Road. Do you know it?"

Tristam watched his cousin go, sensing how troubled Jaimy was by the set of his shoulders alone. *And he cannot imagine what this truly means*, Tristam thought.

Not knowing where to begin, Tristam returned to the library and started in on the chaos. He had not toiled long when he heard a frail voice wafting up from the garden. It sang a children's song.

> *Posies, posies, a-singing to the rosies*
> *A-courting gladiolies*
> *A-dancing with the snow lilies.*

There were more verses but she, for it was Mrs. Ebish, repeated this one again and again as though it were an incantation, a spell used to conjure lost youth.

Tristam went to the window and saw the old woman at work in the garden. She was stooped over and apparently evicting weeds from a flower bed. For a moment Tristam watched and felt a sadness come over him that he could not explain. There was something pathetic in the scene—the bent old woman weeding in a dead man's garden—as though her life had been pared away until only routine remained.

Tristam cleared his throat loudly; when that did not catch her attention, he called out, "Mrs. Ebish! *Hel-lo*."

The old woman stood up sharply, looking around, a hand pressed to her heart.

"It's me, Mrs. Ebish. Tristam Flattery."

She saw him now and gave a small laugh. "Must you always sneak up on a body, Mr. Flattery? My old heart is a-pounding like a great drum." She laughed again, obviously relieved in some way. "I thought it was the professor's ghost calling out and that I was about to cross over myself."

The mention of ghosts did not cheer Tristam.

"I am sorry. I hope you'll forgive me. You see, a terrible thing has happened. Someone has robbed the professor's home. I was hoping you might help me determine what has been taken."

"Well!" she said. "My word! The poor professor."

*   *   *

The dean and Jaimy arrived as Tristam and Mrs. Ebish were trying to make some sense of the mess in the lower rooms.

"What a terrible thing," the dean said, as he surveyed the ruins. "You are unhurt Tristam? Did they attack you?"

"No, I was merely run down in the dark by some blackguard who was making good his escape. It seemed that I surprised him—or them—and they got away with little, perhaps even nothing at all." Tristam was not sure if he should alert the dean to his suspicions.

The dean nodded stiffly. The skin of his face appeared to have a layer of deep purple beneath it. "May I have a word with you, Tristam?"

The two stepped out onto the terrace, the dean pacing for a moment before turning to Tristam. "I was at the college this morning and there was an awful row going on. Dandish's rooms have been . . . *sacked* is the only word I can conceive to describe their state. And now his home, too. I can't remember such a thing ever happening before. Dandish was not a wealthy man, nor was there reason for others to think that he could have been. And, as you have said, things of value have not been taken. There is something very odd in all of this, Tristam, you mark my words. Can you think of anything that would explain it?"

Tristam looked down at the bricks of the terrace, shaking his head. "I can't say that I can, Dean Emin." There was a second's silence and Tristam could feel the don staring at him.

"Tristam," the old man said softly. "If I may be completely candid, you are the poorest liar. Lack of experience, no doubt—which is to your credit. But all the same, you are not telling me everything you know. Is that not so?"

Tristam looked up and met the old man's pale eyes. He felt shame burning on his cheeks. He nodded his head.

"But you are not inclined to speak further?"

"I'm not."

The dean looked out over the garden and took his watch from his pocket and turned it slowly, over and over. "I can't imagine either Dandish or yourself involved in something of questionable legality."

"Nothing of the sort, sir."

The dean nodded. "Well, I am relieved to know that, at least. This has something to do with the palace arboretum, I collect?"

Tristam hesitated. "I have been sworn to secrecy by the King's Man, Dean Emin."

The dean slipped his watch back into his pocket. If he was surprised by what he had just heard, he did not show it. "Say nothing more, then. I'm sorry to have pressed you."

"And I'm sorry to have lied to you, sir."

The dean reached out and put his hand on Tristam's shoulder. "I as much as made you do it, Tristam. Do not apologize. Let us go back inside."

Dean Emin soon left—called by his duties at Merton College—and Tristam, Jaimy, and Mrs. Ebish continued with the restoration of order to the professor's house. It was well past midday when hunger finally drove the young men out in search of food. Mrs. Ebish went off to perform some errand or other and they locked the house, wedging the back door as best they could. Tristam thought it was unlikely the house would be bothered in broad daylight, and besides, whoever was interested in Dandish had likely already finished searching for whatever it was they wanted. Whether or not they had found it was the question in Tristam's mind. Although he tried to keep up a front before the others, Tristam was deeply disturbed, and not just by this assault on Dandish's home.

The Ivy was not far off, so Tristam suggested they stop there for a meal. In truth, he wanted to check on the diaries in his room, for he was almost certain that the night visitors had been seeking Dandish's writings—anything he might have recorded about Kingfoil.

Excusing himself momentarily, Tristam went up to his room and was relieved to find the professor's papers still tucked away where he had left them. He was about to return to the dining room when there came a knock on the door and Tristam found a servant he had come to know standing in the hall.

"Pardon the interruption, Mr. Flattery. I saw you going up the stairs. There were two gentlemen here asking after you this morning, sir, and neither felt inclined to leave so much as a calling card. I thought you should like to know, sir."

Recent events had taken their toll and Tristam felt immediately suspicious. "You can describe them?"

"I believe so. The first was a young man, sir, about your age, I should think, and not unlike you to look at. I thought he might be kin to you, Mr. Flattery."

"He likely was. And the other?"

"A bit older, sir. A gentleman. Dark hair, the finest dress. Came in a good-sized carriage with footmen; very close on the heels of the first gentleman, as well. Handsome man, too, I should think."

Tristam racked his brain. There was no one he could think of in Merton who would fit such a description and certainly no one who would be traveling in such style. "Well, I can't imagine who it was."

"He asked after you in such a way as to give the impression of friendship, sir, and when told you were out said not to worry. I thought he knew where you must be. I gathered he was off to find you directly."

"Well," Tristam said, trying to pass it off as unimportant. "No doubt he will catch up with me yet. Thoughtful of you to remember."

"Not at all, Mr. Flattery."

Tristam had a sudden thought. "There is something you could do for me, if you will. I need to wrap a small parcel, about like so. . . ." He measured with his hands. "Could you find me some heavy paper, or oilcloth, and string?"

Tristam took Dandish's diaries from the wardrobe, and when the servant returned he wrapped them carefully and passed them into the man's care.

"Will you post this for me?" Tristam thought quickly. He did not like the sound of unknown gentlemen asking after him at his lodgings. "To Tumney, Tumney . . . what was his given name? Never mind: to myself, Tristam Flattery, care of Mr. Tumney, King's Gardener, the Tellaman Palace. Can it go off today?"

"By the evening coach, sir." The man showed not the slightest sign that he thought this an odd request.

Tristam locked his door, checking it with more care than usual, and hurried down to join his cousin.

"J?" Tristam said as soon as he was seated. "Did you call here this morning?"

"I did. I thought I should catch up with you before you left. Why?" Jaimy was already working on a mug of ale and wiped a mustache of foam off his lip.

"A servant just told me two men came by after I left for the professor's. I don't know who the second would have been."

Jaimy nodded. "Did your man say anything about your caller's appearance?"

"Tall, I think. Well dressed gentleman. Came in a good-sized coach with footmen."

Jaimy nodded, his brow furrowing as it did when he was truly worried. "As I was coming out of the inn, I saw such a coach stop outside. I didn't see the man who emerged, close to, but I was quite sure he was the Viscount Elsworth."

Tristam shrugged.

"*The brother of the Duchess of Morland, Tristam,*" Jaimy said, a little exasperated.

"Ah," Tristam drank from his own mug, hoping his hand would remain steady.

"You must remember that business a few weeks ago . . . ? The viscount killed Baron Ipsword in a duel. Surely you heard?"

"Yes. Yes, I did hear something about it. Rather barbaric business, I thought. Though it could hardly have happened to a more deserving individual." Baron Ipsword had been one of Dandish's greatest detractors and a man who spent much time promoting himself and his "theories."

Jaimy looked hard at his cousin. "The duel was over an insult, I was told—a fine world it would be if we fall back on murder every time a man feels he has been paid an insult. I thought that foolishness had been left behind."

"Despite this blot on his character, the viscount remains, if not a central player, at least a member of the Royal Troupe. His sister, the Duchess of Morland, the lady you met, is the leading actress; center stage in the charmed circle.

They have the King's favor and travel with the artistic crowd. Entonnophiles: far worse than any of our fellows here at Merton."

Tristam's mind went back to Dandish's diaries. Ipsword was a great opponent of transmutation. Over the years he had attacked Dandish savagely several times—never intelligently—but he had injured the highly-strung Dandish all the same, grievously on more than one occasion.

Impossible, Tristam almost said it aloud. Dandish was growing *regis* for the viscount's sister. . . . No, there could be no connection. It was too evil to even be considered.

"Tristam? Are you well? Let me look again at your wound. You are as white as a ghost."

"No, I am perfectly well." Tristam's mind was in a whirl. "Lack of sleep, I think. And I am famished as well."

A servant appeared at that moment, diverting attention away from Tristam. The subject was changed, but Jaimy did not lose his look of great concern and many awkward silences punctuated the meal—unusual for two who were so easy in each other's company.

As they walked back toward Dandish's home, Jaimy suddenly turned on his cousin, something verging on anger coming to the surface. "Shall I continue to act as though I'm too obtuse to notice, or will you condescend to tell me what it is you've involved yourself in?"

Tristam looked off, unable to meet his cousin's gaze, but even so he felt Jaimy staring at him.

"It isn't that I don't want to tell you, Jaimy. It isn't that. I. . . . To be honest I have been sworn to secrecy by someone of importance."

"This 'someone' would be Roderick Palle, I assume?"

Tristam looked over at his cousin. He should not have been surprised. Despite his easy-going manner, Jaimy was no fool of an aristocrat.

"Well, perhaps you should not speak, then," Jaimy said. "I cannot guarantee that I would bear up under torture." It was a jest but said without trace of humor.

Tristam remained silent, though with great difficulty. There was only one person he wanted to speak with more than Jaimy, and that was Dandish.

"Precisely how important a secret can a shrub be, Tristam?" Jaimy said after a moment, obviously not willing to let it go.

"More than you would think. Certainly more than I ever imagined."

"Well, if you have the Viscount Elsworth asking after you, perhaps you do not exaggerate." Jaimy reached out and took hold of Tristam's shoulder. "I should remind you, cousin, that I have kept every secret you have ever entrusted to me, going back to our childhood. If you are involved in something as peculiar as I think you are, you know I shall never talk. And even Sir Roderick Palle does not bully the son of the Duke of Blackwater. Besides," he said,

"You will need me. You probably didn't know who Sir Roderick Palle was before he summoned you to court."

They had arrived at the back gate to the professor's home and Tristam stopped, struck by the look of concern and determination on his cousin's face. "I do not jest, Jaimy, when I say you cannot repeat a word," Tristam said quietly.

"Not a syllable," Jaimy answered, the tiniest sign of relief in his tone.

They went into the garden and sat in the arbor. Tristam began with the arrival of a member of Roderick Palle's staff to his home in Locfal. Years of difficult study had sharpened Tristam's memory and he related the entire tale in great detail. For the most part Jaimy merely nodded, listening intently. Very occasionally he stopped Tristam to clarify some point, but the two knew each other so well that this was seldom necessary.

When Tristam finished, Jaimy rose and excused himself, leaving his cousin sitting in the sun-drenched garden. In a moment the young lord returned bearing two mugs of Tristam's ale, warm but welcome.

"Would you like to hear what I think?"

Tristam threw up his hands. "No. I have broken my oath to the King's Man merely that I might have company in prison."

Jaimy stirred at the head on his ale for second, as though he wrote something there. "To begin: this man Hawksmoor is Sir Roderick's most trusted minion—a man who would place himself in the way of a cannon ball if it would serve his master. Palle sends Hawksmoor on only the most sensitive errands. So why was it so important that he fetch you?" Tristam hoped that this question was not merely rhetorical, but after a moment of thought Jaimy went on without proposing an answer.

"Palle tries to convince you that your future success lies in service to the King," Jaimy said, his mouth turning up in a hint of a smile, "proving that Hawksmoor learned almost nothing about you on your voyage. Then, the Duchess of Morland offers you a title and whatever else you might desire if you can but make this recalcitrant plant bear seed. She even allows you, a comparative nobody, if you will excuse me for saying so, to address her as 'Duchess.' Quite suddenly, Tristam, you are the object of attention of two of the most powerful people in all Farrland. And despite their perfect manners and impeccable conduct, these are two people whom one never wants to cross." Jaimy leaned over and touched his cousin's arm. "I cannot stress this point enough. This incident with the viscount and Baron Ipsword is a perfect example. Trust that the late baron had run afoul of the duchess in some way. All this noise about him insulting the viscount was utter fabrication. Ipsword was a fool by any man's measure, and capable of offense, surely, when criticizing other empiricists, but he was not stupid enough to insult someone of Elsworth's reputation. Ipsword's only weapon was a razor-sharp tongue and an uncanny precision in its application, but he was no swordsman. I can't even imagine how he would have met the viscount."

Tristam looked away, Jaimy's words striking him like blows. "I think even you have missed the point," Tristam whispered, almost afraid to mouth the words, as though they were a spell with the power to create truth. "The late baron was an enemy of Dandish . . . Drove the professor into fits of despair and melancholia with his vicious attacks. After such assaults Dandish would be unable to work . . . for weeks sometimes. Unable to work on this study he undertook for the duchess. . . ."

The croak of a rook somewhere nearby. Then quiet.

"*Blood and flames,*" Jaimy said almost under his breath. "You can't seriously believe he killed Ipsword because the man . . . criticized Dandish?"

"Because Ipsword affected Dandish's ability to pursue the duchess' inquiry."

Jaimy put a hand to his face. "Tristam, that cannot be. . . . It is more than monstrous. There would have been a dozen ways to deal with Ipsword short of murder."

"Yes, I'm sure there were."

Jaimy rose and paced across the arbor, overcome with agitation. For a few moments he said nothing, only staring down at the ground and combing his fingers into his hair. Finally he turned to his cousin, his distress clear. "*Tristam. What on this round earth have you gotten yourself into?*"

The two sat for a long time pursuing their private thoughts, trying to make some sense of what little they knew. It was Jaimy who finally broke the silence.

"Let us consider this logically, as you are prone to saying. The duchess and Sir Roderick are clearly at odds over this seed that produces the physic. Palle involves you in hopes of solving the problem. The duchess, however, has had Dandish attempting to solve the problem for some time—over a year, you say?"

"As much as three, I suspect."

"Yet you claim that the King's own gardener did not recognize the problem until recently." Jaimy put the tips of his fingers together and touched them to his chin—a posture almost of prayer. "How intelligent do you think the duchess is?"

Tristam shifted in his chair and cast a look over his shoulder as though suddenly afraid they were not alone. "It isn't a question of intelligence, really. It's training. The duchess could be a natural genius and still not see what needed to be seen. I have looked carefully at Tumney's records and, assuming they are accurate, I would say that it would have been impossible to recognize the existence of the problem before Tumney did so himself. Plants do not always bear consistently year to year. You know this—one year there are more apples than can be eaten, the next there is hardly one to be found. Even in a controlled garden such as the arboretum there are cycles. Two years in which seed production declines does not necessarily have meaning, if you see what I'm saying. I suspect this problem has been increasing slowly for three years now and still that is not necessarily significant. The Kingfoil could produce a bumper crop next year. Although I, personally, do not expect it to happen. But you see my point."

"I have not read Dandish's journals. Is it possible that he had begun by merely growing Kingfoil for the duchess and then recognized the problem later?"

Tristam looked up at his cousin. "I can hardly imagine that Dandish would be involved in such a venture. Even someone as unaware of politics as the professor must have realized that this would not be strictly aboveboard?"

"The duchess is a persuasive woman, Tristam. Who knows how she would couch such a request. Here we have an herb that will cure a disease, apparently. Dandish was a good man, concerned with human suffering. . . . Or it is possible that the duchess made it appear a request of the King—to be kept secret, even from Roderick Palle?" Jaimy shrugged as though to say such a thing could be easily managed, and Tristam had to admit he was right.

"The Duchess of Morland is an animal of the court, Tristam. One would be foolish to presume to understand her motives. There is more than self-interest at work here, I think, but she is involved in so many machinations with such varied alliances that one could hardly imagine her intentions. The favor the King shows toward her makes the duchess much caressed wherever she goes. She need only speak a few words on someone's behalf and this person will find himself borne up—invited everywhere, feted—whatever you can imagine. The duchess' offers to you were not vain—granting such favors would be easy for her." Jaimy paused, looking off at the sky for a moment. "Despite all, the duchess must be getting rather nervous, for ultimately her strength is dependent upon a king who has lived well beyond his time. One would have to say that her ascendancy is near to its end. But, for the moment, if you are in some way a guarantor of His Majesty's health, well, the duchess will see that you are kept very happy, let me assure you." Jaimy paused, as though considering what he had just said.

"But there is something more here. It is almost as if the two factions in the court were vying for control of this seed. Is the King so weakened that he has allowed this to occur? The Prince Royal, of course, is close to Palle." He shook his head. "I can't quite force it to make sense."

"A hypothesis to fit the information," Tristam said.

"What?"

"We are looking for a hypothesis to fit the information. Some elegant explanation for everything we believe we know. Not so easy when it is human beings that we are dealing with. The courtiers are involved in a struggle over a seed that keeps the King alive. . . . Obviously the Prince Royal would gain the throne if the King were to die, and the duchess, as you have said, would lose her place at court. That fits most of what we know. Add to it the fact that Dandish clearly chose to support the duchess rather than Palle."

"You are suggesting that the King's Man, the sovereign's chief minister, is in league with the heir to 'dethrone' the King?" There was a little scorn in Jaimy's voice.

"It fits what we know," Tristam said, defensively.

"Flaming martyrs," Jaimy said, quietly. He finished his ale and looked reproachfully at the empty mug. "But why would Palle bring you to court? If he is trying to do away with King Wilam, it would be in his interest to have the Kingfoil never bear again."

"Hypotheses are built like this. A fact that does not fit must either be wrong or the hypothesis altered. And the truth is I do not know why Palle brought me. Perhaps he thinks me so incompetent as to be no threat." Tristam rose to fetch more ale from the house. A thought struck him as he walked.

"Jaimy," he said when he returned, "there is this entry in the journal about Valary. Do you know that name?"

"Another empiricist, I would guess. I'll make some discreet enquiries around the university tomorrow. Flinders might even know, or perhaps Dean Emin."

Yes—or no one might know. There was much that Tristam suspected was beyond conventional knowledge. The man he had collided with had been truly terrified, and it had not been Tristam who had inspired that.

I struck my head, Tristam told himself. *The child was merely a fabrication of light and shadow and blurred vision. Nothing more.*

It was late by the time Tristam finally stumbled into his rooms at the Ivy. When the servant who lit the lamps had gone, Tristam pulled off his shoes and collapsed in a chair. Outside his window a breeze rustled the leaves of the old elm—a sound Tristam found almost hypnotic. He awoke with a start as his chin hit his chest and he forced himself up, looking around the room quickly to be sure no small boys lurked in the shadows.

Out of habit he went to the desk to keep his journal, but it was not where he'd left it. Nor was it in the drawer. Tristam came fully awake then and mounted a concerted search, but the journal was not to be found. He sat thinking for a moment, but there was no doubt in his mind—he hadn't taken it from the room since his arrival in Merton.

The briefest sense of vertigo unbalanced him. He checked the pocket of his frock coat and found it empty. It was then he realized that he had changed coats that day. He went to his wardrobe where his fears were confirmed: Dandish's letter to the duchess was gone.

∽ Eight

"I'm not quite sure how you did it, Tristam, but I really will be in your debt forever." A jubilant Jaimy sat across from Tristam in the dining room of the Ivy. They had spent the previous night at the Somers' home, and it had been agreed that Tristam and Jaimy would come up to the lake country late in the season to assist Professor Somers with his fossil quarry. A fortnight near the object of Jaimy's affections!

Tristam, however, was not feeling jubilant. Sir Roderick's coach was being readied for the return to Avonel, and Tristam was filled with apprehension. Someone possessed the letter Dandish had written to the Duchess of Morland and if that someone was Roderick Palle, then Tristam's situation was . . . confusing, to say the least.

"You still think it was the duchess' brother who took the letter?"

Jaimy tilted his head and tried a half-smile. "You can't let this go, can you?"

"Nor could you if you were soon to be speaking with Sir Roderick Palle. And what am I to say? If he has possession of the letter, then he is now fully aware of Dandish's inquiry—and realizes that I know as well. If I choose to say nothing, then I am hiding things from the King's Man. If I speak, I will be incrimination the King's favorite as well as Dandish. And, as we have said, it might be the duchess who has the King's interests in mind."

Jaimy's manner turned serious. "It was also likely the duchess who had a man murdered for the crime of being an annoyance. Take no sides in this matter, Tristam. For my money, it was the viscount who took the letter and your journal. So say nothing to Roderick. Say nothing to anyone. Go about your task at the palace and then get free of this situation as quickly as you can. Let these courtiers have their battle without you. And, Tristam, don't let the duchess persuade you to take up where Dandish left off. Whatever you do, avoid that trap."

They finished their meal and walked out to find Tristam's carriage, but before they came within earshot of the driver, Jaimy pulled Tristam up short. "If you need me to, I will come to Avonel, but I caution you, Tristam—and I am not being melodramatic—trust nothing sensitive to the mails. Merely invite me to come visit you, or some such thing, but don't commit a word of this matter to paper."

"I can't thank you enough, J. I don't know what I would have done without your help."

Jaimy broke into a huge grin. "I have been paid back and double, Tristam, for I will have a fortnight in the lake country near my sweet Alissa. I am in your debt. Safe journey. Speak not to strangers."

As Sir Roderick's coach carried Tristam off toward the city of Avonel, the young naturalist began to suffer extreme trepidation. Any thought of his inevitable meeting with the King's Man caused his palms to sweat and his stomach to churn.

With some effort he turned his mind back to the occurrences of the last days and found himself wondering again why Dandish had been growing *regis* before the fertility problem had been recognized. Perhaps Jaimy was right and the professor's original intention had not been to solve the problem at all, even though it became his focus.

So the journey went by with Tristam's fertile mind creating one hypothesis and knocking it down, then creating another. There seemed to be no grand scheme that explained everything and this did not make him happy. When he faced Roderick Palle, as he was sure he must do, he wanted to be quite certain that he understood what was going on. Unfortunately, this did not seem very likely.

Some hours into the journey the driver stopped, jarring Tristam out of his whirling thoughts. He looked out the window and found they had come to the slough where they had paused on the way to Merton. The carriage bobbed as the driver stepped down to the ground.

"Thought you might like to have a look, sir," he said. "Or should I drive on?"

"No. Thank you. I shall look." One of the instruments Dandish had left to Tristam was his Fromme field glass. Tristam dug it out of a trunk and set out along the short path to the pond.

The Fromme glass was a relatively new invention—a field glass made up of three bronze tubes that collapsed one into the other so that it compressed to only a third its extended length. Far more convenient than the rigid glasses that had been made previously. But it was not just that innovation that made the Fromme instruments so coveted; it was the incomparable lenses as well. There was no glass so perfect, none with such ideal resolution. Tristam hefted it in his hand and then extended it for use. Inscribed on the inner tube he found the words:

For the use of Professor Sanfield Dandish, with thanks, R.M. Fromme.

Well, yes; the professor had many admirers. More than Tristam knew, it seemed.

He lifted the glass to survey the pool, and to his surprise found he could see nothing. Tristam shook the glass gently and thought he heard something move inside. A part of the instrument had come loose, apparently.

With great care he unscrewed the lens and tilted the glass to see if anything would slide out into his hand. The edge of a wad of paper protruded.

"What in . . . ?" Tristam breathed.

He tugged at the paper and pulled it free, fumbling to unroll it—a single sheet torn raggedly in half and awkwardly stuffed into the tube. Slough and Fromme glass were forgotten. Here was Dandish's writing, though firmer than usual, beginning in mid-sentence.

> stronger those few days, and my arrhythmia was all but gone. I have used the last of the physic, and learn that to desist ravages both body and mind terribly. Do these people truly understand what they have discovered? I must assume they do. At least now their desperation to produce more seed can be understood—I'm sorely tempted to do so myself. But I will resist. The planting must be destroyed. Pray no one else discovers the solution.

Tristam looked up from the page. *Dandish had solved the* regis *problem.* Solved it and told no one. Then he destroyed the plants, all his notes but this fragment, and wrote the duchess saying a solution was not possible.

"He was too ill to write me," Tristam said aloud, realizing suddenly what this hidden message meant. Here were the last words of Dandish—to Tristam at least. And perfectly clear, except for what was left unsaid. Dandish had tried the seed; made the physic and experimented on himself. Infinitely curious Dandish—and not nearly so naive in the ways of the world as Tristam had believed.

He could almost hear the old man's voice. "*Do not attempt to solve this problem, Tristam.*" That message at least could not be mistaken.

Tristam looked up and addressed his words to the infinite depths of blue. *But why?* was his first thought. Dandish had clearly not wanted to tell more. Good, unselfish, noble Dandish.

"I must trust someone," he said quietly, still addressing the sky. "And I'm sure you had your reasons, Professor, though I wish you had seen fit to tell me more."

He sat for a while, staring out at the dragonflies weaving their intricate patterns over the slough, like courtiers in a dance. Then he took the lens from Dandish's field glass and used it to focus the rays of the sun, setting fire to the professor's final message. The ashes he committed to the breeze, watching them scatter across the still surface of the pond like wind-borne seed.

∽ Nine

A letter had been awaiting Tristam for several days at the Queen Anne, but his immediate hope that it came from Dandish was quickly dashed. It was addressed in an unfamiliar hand. Tristam perched on the arm of a chair and read.

My dear Tristam:

I have only just learned the reason for your journey to Merton. This is the saddest news. Although I did not know Professor Dandish as well as you did yourself, I counted him a friend and admired his accomplishments, as any educated person must. Do accept my heartfelt condolences.

The King himself expressed grief at the loss, though His Majesty was reassured by my confidence in your skills.

If you return to Avonel by the last day of the month, and feel up to it, I will have an evening at my home that you might enjoy. Please do attend.

Yours,
Elorin, Duchess of Morland

Well, here would be the attempt to enlist Tristam in Dandish's place. Or had the duchess some other motive that Tristam and Jaimy had not even begun to guess?

A knock interrupted the pursuit of these thoughts and at the door Tristam found a liveried footman.

"From Sir Roderick Palle, Mr. Flattery." The man proffered a sealed envelope—the second in a span measured in minutes. "Sir Roderick awaits your reply."

"Sir Roderick is . . . here?"

The man nodded. "In the lobby, sir."

Tristam's heart sank as he read standing in the open door.

My dear Mr. Flattery:

I realize you have just returned from your duties in Merton, but, even so, I thought you might care to join me for a Society gathering this evening. There will be an interesting paper, I think, and, as always, the best conversation in Avonel. I await your reply.

Yours,
Roderick Palle

"Flames," Tristam said under his breath. Indecision kept him standing half out in the hall.

Neither faction was wasting even a moment, though he was still not sure what anyone wanted of him. The bait being offered—an evening at the Society—was certainly perfectly chosen to lure Tristam, but even that could not overcome his trepidation about speaking with Palle. Of course, he could not avoid the King's Man forever, nor would it be wise to snub him: best to have it over with than live with the constant anxiety about what might come.

"Would you thank Sir Roderick for his kind invitation and say that I shall be down directly?"

"Certainly, sir."

Closing the door, Tristam began a desperate search for suitable clothing.

It seemed a shame that he would finally achieve one of his dreams—attending a meeting of the Empiricists' Society—and have the experience virtually ruined by his fears of the coming interview. He had always hoped Dandish would take him to a gathering of the Society, but Dandish almost never attended himself—too much opportunity for conflict for the poor professor. The meeting notes in the quarterly *Society Annals* were a fascination of Tristam's, and he pored over them with a mixture of envy and vicarious pleasure.

Tristam was surprised to learn that Sir Roderick attended meetings of the Society. Was he a fellow, Tristam wondered? Certainly, to invite a guest, he must be.

Not fifteen minutes later he was flying down the stairs, three to a stride, making a most undignified entrance into the Queen Anne's lobby.

Sir Roderick rose from a chair, a half-suppressed smile enlivening his usually expressionless face. "Not to rush, Mr. Flattery. It is better to arrive with both legs intact. My driver informed me of your return. I realize you have had barely a moment to get settled, but I thought you might not want to miss the Society meeting."

Tristam nodded his agreement.

"We have time yet," Sir Roderick said. "I thought we might find something to eat—if you have not already supped?"

"I'm famished, actually."

"I am as well. Allow me to take you to an establishment I know. You will not have reason to disapprove, I think."

They found yet another of Sir Roderick's beautiful carriages outside and set off to the knight's promised meal. It was not quite dark—the lamplighters had just appeared—and Tristam caught glimpses of a vivid sunset here and there between buildings. The unhurried *clip-clop* of hoofs echoed in the quiet streets, preceding the carriage like a tired crier.

They passed into a neighborhood of fine homes where the driver turned out of the street and the carriage rolled slowly up a short drive, lamp-lit and garden lined. Tristam had not noticed any sign or device at the gate to mark the entrance as belonging to anything but a private residence.

"Is this a club?" Tristam asked.

"Of sorts. Though it has no official name or even a list of members. But I suppose it is a club as much as anything."

Servants appeared under the large carriage entrance and Sir Roderick greeted the steward by name. They were ushered inside a beautiful mansion dating, Tristam believed, from a century after the rebuilding of Avonel. It had that certain lightness, both in color and form, created by high ceilings in combination with carefully proportioned columns and openings.

There was little about the residence to indicate it was not a private home—though a wealthy family's home, to be sure. A servant led the way past the partially opened doors of a ballroom and from within issued the purest tenor voice Tristam had ever heard. Involuntarily, he stopped. The song was familiar, an aria composed by Ramsay for his great unfinished opera, and more moving for the knowledge that it had been the composer's last work. But it could have been anything; the voice was so sure, so devoid of artifice, so effortlessly powerful that it pierced the listener's heart.

The music ended to a riotous ovation, and both Tristam and Sir Roderick stopped in the hall and applauded as well. People began to stream from the room then, many greeting Sir Roderick with obvious pleasure.

The knight touched Tristam's elbow and they moved on.

"Teiho Ruau," Roderick said, quietly.

"So I expected. The descriptions I have heard were not exaggerated in the least. What an instrument that voice is!"

Ruau was an islander brought back from Oceana by Gregory. He was famous in all the lands surrounding the Entide Sea, and much caressed by the nobility. Even the King was known to be an admirer, often enjoying private performances.

"It almost makes one believe in gods and their gifts," Roderick said. "That was not a voice you heard; it was a miracle."

Just then the crowd parted and a young man, dark of complexion and round of features, came through the doors. He was smiling broadly, and nodding to admirers on both sides. Tristam could not help but notice that he dressed as a dandy, his clothing of the most exotic fabrics and colors, and under his arm he carried an elaborate, white-plumed hat. It must have been the naturalist in him, for Tristam's eye was drawn to the man's belt, which appeared to be made from the skin of a snake, but before he could be sure the man was lost in the crowd.

The people leaving the ballroom were flushed with apparent excitement and, to Tristam's dismay, he noticed they wore formal clothing.

"I feel I am not properly attired for the occasion," Tristam ventured.

"Not at all. We will take our meal in a private room. Had we come to the ball, that would be another matter. But for our supper and the Society later, we are both more than adequately attired. We do not all have to dress like our friend Ruau." He gave a gentle laugh and shook his head.

"You know him?"

"Oh, yes. Certainly. He is in the palace often. We share a tailor, though you would hardly know it." He indicated his own clothing which, though finely made, was quite conservative in style.

"Did I see a snakeskin belt?" Tristam asked.

Roderick laughed. "You did indeed. He can't be parted from it. You see, a bit of the savage remains, despite all of our efforts. Here we are."

They were led into a private room and there attended by servants of great skill and discretion.

"I see you are still wondering where I have brought you," Roderick said, alarming Tristam a little with his perception. "You have attended evenings dedicated to the appreciation of things Entonne?"

"At the university such things were common."

"I have no doubt. Well, in this place one can always find a celebration of things Farr—though celebration is perhaps not the correct word. Those of us who come here believe in the value of Farrland: her traditions, her culture, and art. You will never hear a word of Entonne spoken in these rooms, nor will you hear Entonne culture lauded at the expense of our own. We are not mad nationalists, by any definition, but we are a balance to this mania which promotes the worship of anything and everything Entonne. Does that set your mind at ease?"

"I was curious." So here was the center of the anti-Entonne movement in Farrland, Tristam thought. How was he to decline when he was invited to join, as he was certain he would be?

"You needn't look so concerned, Mr. Flattery. I brought you here only to find a private place to talk." Roderick smiled and lifted his glass in a toast. "I am aware of the feelings of our recent graduates toward overt patriotism of the sentimental variety. So let us drink to those things which are of value in all cultures." They toasted—Tristam sure his relief showed—and Roderick took a moment to examine his wine by the lamplight. It was, Tristam realized, excellent wine.

"You have traveled abroad, Mr. Flattery? You have journeyed to Entonne?"

"Yes, there and to Doorn as well one summer. Most pleasant." He could hardly be more non-committal than that.

"Do you share the Entonne fascination with the mages, then?"

Tristam realized he would never be able to predict where a conversation with Roderick Palle might be going, and though this sounded like nothing more than small talk, Tristam thought it would be wise never to assume innocence in anything this man did or said.

"No, though I find it a most curious thing. I have come to believe that the Entonne are more capable of embracing contradictions than we are ourselves. Something in the character. But they are in awe of the charismatic and I sometimes think their interest in the mages is related to this. Or so it would seem to me." There: some criticism of Entonne that he could make in good conscience. Perhaps that would prove he was a true citizen of Farrland.

"Yes, I would agree. How else do you explain this near-worship of Count Previsse? There was never a more despicable human being born of woman. And they think him a great poet and a painter as well as a statesman! It is beyond belief."

Tristam nodded. His classmates at Merton had all admired Previsse, for the high adventure of his life if for nothing else. A servant entered to pour more wine and his exit seemed like a signal for the conversation to change.

"I hope your journey to Merton did not leave you too out of sorts. It was a sad business."

Tristam nodded. "Yes. I will miss the good professor. He was a very kind and patient teacher to me, and I fear I was not the perfect receptacle for his vast knowledge."

"Let time judge that, Mr. Flattery. No man of the first rank is ever satisfied with his accomplishments, no matter what others make of them."

Tristam immediately thought of poor Dandish. "Well, that was true of Sanfield Dandish. If doubting the value of one's work is a measure of its importance, he approached greatness." *How in the world had such a man become involved in growing Kingfoil for the duchess?* Had he merely fallen victim to her charms? There was the note in Dandish's journal suggesting the duchess believed she was playing him for a fool. But he had played along, apparently, for reasons Tristam could not guess. And why had Dandish not allied himself with Sir Roderick Palle?

Jaimy was right, Tristam thought. It was best to stay out of this struggle between the courtiers at all costs. *I can't begin to see which side has intentions of which I would approve.* Tristam found himself looking at Roderick with even greater suspicion.

"Yes," Roderick said, "the professor was truly as modest as most gentlemen claim to be—though seldom are."

There was a moment of silence. Tristam felt a slow growing panic seize him. He could not think of what to say or how to begin describing what he had found in Dandish's drawing room. He was beginning to think that fear would not allow him to broach the subject at all.

"I have heard a rumor, Mr. Flattery," Roderick said very softly, "that Dandish's journals were not to be found. Perhaps stolen, in fact." This was said in the most matter-of-fact tone, but the King's Man fixed Tristam with his unfathomable gaze and did not look away.

Tristam nodded. He began to take a sip of his wine to steel his nerve, but his hand betrayed him and trembled so that he returned the glass quickly to the table. "Stolen is what I expect myself. I know that there were many volumes—perhaps fifty—yet they were nowhere to be found. Both Dandish's rooms at Merton and his home were broken into and ransacked, yet nothing of worth appeared to be missing."

Roderick nodded as though Tristam were merely verifying information from other sources, which disconcerted Tristam even more.

"An empiricist's journals are valuable, without question, but they are not valuable in gold and silver. What do you make of it?"

Tristam feared that he was betraying much. His mouth was dry and he clasped his hands together lest their trembling be noticed. Roderick stared at him and Tristam wondered what the knight knew already. The King's Man had resources that Tristam could only imagine and was proving himself perceptive in the extreme.

The best lies, Tristam thought, are made of half-truths.

"I fear, Sir Roderick, that Dandish's involvement in the palace arboretum has drawn the interest of others. I can hardly imagine anything else that would lead to such a thing."

Roderick considered his words and then nodded. "I shall send Mr. Hawksmoor to Merton directly. He will get to the bottom of things."

Tristam felt his heart sink. It would not take a genius to guess what had been planted in the professor's drawing room. Half the truth, he reminded himself.

"One thing he will find is a number of planting boxes—their plants gone—kept in a locked room in Dandish's home."

This produced a reaction in the placid facade of the King's Man. The knight looked as though he had just received the worst possible news, but his response was not grief—it was anger. He pushed back from the table, opened his mouth as if to curse, and then it passed, like a strange fit. Only a darkness remained, as though Sir Roderick exerted himself to mask pain.

"You think the professor was growing Kingfoil." It was not a question.

Tristam nodded, almost afraid to speak now.

Although his eyes were fixed on Tristam, it was clear that Sir Roderick's focus was on something else. "*I should have known*," he said, so quietly that he was obviously speaking to himself. To Tristam it sounded like self-accusation. "*Dandish*," Palle said as though naming a betrayer.

And in Tristam's mind echoed this same word. *Dandish*, the most guileless of gentlemen.

Roderick's reaction was so genuine that Tristam was now all but sure that the duchess' letter could not be in his hands.

"Do you have any evidence beyond the empty planting boxes and the coincidence of the journals being stolen?"

There was no moisture in Tristam's throat, but he tried not to swallow hard. "The corner of a burnt Kingfoil leaf," he managed.

"Which could have come from the palace arboretum?" Roderick said.

Tristam shrugged. "Perhaps."

"Who do you think removed the plants?" Roderick asked suddenly, obviously not believing his own objection.

"Professor Dandish, I suspect. The room was locked when I first arrived there—the door had not been forced. I suppose it could have been done by someone else—between the professor's death and my arrival. . . ." Tristam had trouble forcing out the lies. It was not his nature to prevaricate and this man who sat looking at him spent all his days sifting words for truth. "I can't tell you how difficult it is for me to inform you of this, Sir Roderick. Professor Dandish was my mentor and friend. . . ."

"You knew him well?"

"So I would have said." Tristam heard some small distress in his voice.

Roderick stared down into his glass, swirling the wine gently in the bowl, as though his anger had been replaced by sadness. "Do you think he could have found the solution to our problem?" he asked, then glanced up at Tristam.

Tristam found that speech had deserted him altogether, as though he had reached the end of his capacity to lie.

Roderick continued to stare, mild surprise registering in the instant before Tristam looked away.

"I don't know, Sir Roderick."

"You seem unsure, Mr. Flattery. Do you think there's some chance that he did?"

Tristam felt his shoulders shrug. "I can't answer either way. His notes were not to be found—destroyed with the plants, I suspect." Tristam had a sudden wild fear that the diaries he had sent to Tumney had been brought to Roderick's attention.

"I don't think he solved the problem," Sir Roderick said firmly, surprising Tristam. "And do you know why, Mr. Flattery? Because it cannot be solved. That is my belief. Teiho Ruau is convinced the plants will never bear again. '*Spirits*,' he claims. Once the Kingfoil stops bearing, the islanders say, it will never produce seeds again." He smiled suddenly. "Unless the spirit can be appeased by ritual. Tumney has not solved the problem. Dandish could not solve it. Nor will you, I fear, Mr. Flattery. And that is no reflection on your abilities."

Servants arrived with food, interrupting the conversation. Neither man touched his supper. Roderick lifted his cutlery but stopped. "The circumstances of the professor's death were not unusual in any way?"

"Why, not that. . . ." Tristam felt real distress at this suggestion. "You have taken me aback, sir. Could there have been someone so desperate to have *regis* that they would commit murder?" He thought immediately of the death of Baron Ipsword.

"The life of the King. . . ." Roderick left the sentence unfinished and began to eat, almost mechanically, for he had obviously lost his interest in food. "One wonders what the man was thinking." Roderick shrugged and appeared to pull himself away from whatever thoughts he pursued. His equanimity returned as well, as though he had not just said, in effect, that the King would now die. "Unless you can say more, Mr. Flattery, I believe we should leave this subject for now."

Tristam nodded. "There is one other thing, sir."

Roderick looked up.

"My journal disappeared from my room in Merton."

"Had you written about Kingfoil in it?"

"Not a word, sir. I have kept all my notes in the arboretum."

"Very wise of you, Mr. Flattery. It is still a loss, of course. I hold little hope of these missing journals coming to light, I'm sorry to say." And that was all he offered on the subject.

Conversation turned elsewhere, to Tristam's great surprise. That was all? Somehow he could not believe his lies had been accepted that easily. Even Dean Emin had seen through Tristam immediately. But Sir Roderick gave no indication that he did not believe everything he had heard. And, undoubtedly, he did not need Tristam to tell him for whom Dandish grew the Kingfoil.

It is how the game is played, Tristam told himself. *If Roderick believed there would be some advantage in exposing me in my own lies, he would no doubt do so—and easily, too.*

But Roderick appeared to have no intention of doing so. It was as though the conversation had never occurred, and Roderick's manner changed so completely—he became positively amiable—that Tristam almost began to wonder himself.

Another aspect of the King's Man was now revealed, for Roderick proved himself to be knowledgeable in many areas of natural history and natural philosophy, as well as a falconer and breeder of some real skill. The knight engaged Tristam in conversation, pulling him away from his own thoughts and fears so that in the end he gave in and allowed himself to pretend the situation was real.

Supper over, the two men took to Roderick's carriage again. Their conversation, which had flowed so freely over wine and food, dried up altogether. Tristam found himself considering the King's Man, trying to remember what he knew of Sir Roderick Palle. Jaimy would have been able to go on at length on the subject, but Tristam did not have a memory for such things. In fact, he was usually not interested in the "who's who" of the Farr court. Something that was changing rapidly.

If Tristam's memory was not totally faulty, Sir Roderick was of a good family—cousin to the Earl of Mindon. He had risen through the army quickly, for his organizational abilities were superb, and was taken into the service of the King by a high ranking officer who was briefly a minster. Even when his patron was gone, Roderick Palle had continued his climb, having exchanged his rank as officer for a series of new offices.

It had been a quick ascent. Certainly, Sir Roderick Palle was now, and for many years past, the most powerful man in the kingdom, after the sovereign and his heir, for the King's Man was the link between the ministers of the government and the crown.

Despite this, Roderick had refused all rank but the knighthood he had won for his service in the military—an uncharacteristic flouting of convention. Sir Roderick Palle was the first untitled gentleman to hold the position of King's Man . . . ever.

Tristam was absolutely sure that Roderick did nothing without purpose, but he had no idea what was achieved by this refusal of rank. It was possible that Palle garnered a certain popularity with the common people by refusing a title, but somehow Tristam did not think Roderick the type to care about what the people thought.

Roderick Palle was quiet, almost unassuming considering his position, but he was more powerful than any of the nobles in Farrland, no matter their title or connections or wealth. Tristam wondered if his continued refusal of titles unsettled the aristocratic families. Despite his birth, Palle had made himself almost an outsider by his refusal to acknowledge that most significant indicator of a man's importance—a peerage—and he did not seem to care about that either.

The King's Man was, as far as Tristam could tell, an enigma—not just to Tristam but to everyone. And here he sat, across from Tristam, appearing for all the world like a distracted scholar chewing on a problem. A man without an apparent sense of self-importance, and without noticeable manifestations of imagination as well. *What a facade he has created*, Tristam thought. *As impenetrable as the ocean depths.*

They arrived at the mansion that was home to the Empiricists' Society—part museum, part clubhouse—and the object of many of Tristam's dearest fantasies. He felt his excitement grow as the carriage pulled up before the doors.

The young naturalist was almost sure he had entered a dream, he even seemed to be floating, his mind registering things in a haze. The entrance hall was a marvel of pale veined marble—columns, floor, a sweeping stairway, and a high, domed ceiling—lit by a great chandelier so that the stone took on an aspect of almost liquid translucence.

A life-sized sculpture of Boran stood upon a low plinth in the hall's center, the father of empiricism holding out his arm in a sweeping gesture as though indicating the wonders of the world.

In a large niche in one wall the reconstructed skeleton of a dinosaur, *dracosaurus*, dwarfed everything and everyone in the room. Nearby, the imposing shell of *Tridacna gigas*, the giant clam of Oceana, sat upon a small pedestal.

Tristam realized suddenly that Roderick was watching him, gauging his reaction, perhaps.

"I must ask your indulgence for a moment, Mr. Flattery. I need to say a few words to Beall." He nodded toward a group of men gathered across the hall, absorbed in conversation.

"By all means. There is no lack of things for me to see."

Tristam was left alone and found himself wandering toward the side of the hall, as though he felt too conspicuous standing out in the center. A large canvas hung there and so disoriented was Tristam that he took a moment to realize it was the painting based on the artist's study he had inherited from Dandish. For some time he stood, lost in a close examination.

"A Hobbson," a voice said beside him.

Tristam turned to find an avuncular looking gentleman dressed in a style popular before Tristam's birth, including knee-high boots and a powdered wig.

"Averil Kent," the man said, offering Tristam his hand to clasp.

"Your servant, sir. Tristam Flattery." The man's name was familiar, but Tristam could not think why.

"It is a beautiful work, is it not? Hobbson was a master, I think."

"I could not agree more. I have the artist's study for this very canvas." Tristam said this with more surprise at his good fortune than from an intention to impress. But even so, the man turned to him with wide eyes.

"Do you indeed! Signed? What a treasure! How fortunate. Does it differ greatly from the final work?"

Martyr's blood, thought Tristam, *of course!* This was *Averil Kent*—a painter of great fame in his own right. He tried to gather his wits to answer the man's question. "Well. The study is very small, of course, so in detail it is far less complex. The composition is identical, to my eye," he added. "The palette here is generally more subtle, though this sunset is extremely vivid, perhaps creating greater contrast." Tristam looked over at the old man's kind face as he stared at the painting.

"I am intrigued, Mr. Flattery. To gain some insight into the inner process of Hobbson—that is the opportunity that such studies provide."

"I should be most happy to show it to you, if you would like," Tristam said, aware that it was most likely the man was merely being polite and did not really care to see the study at all.

"I should like nothing better!" Kent said warmly. "Do you live in Avonel? I collect you are a son of the Duke of Blackwater?"

"Nephew, in fact. I make my home in Locfal, but I'm in the city for a few days—at the Queen Anne. Perhaps we could sup together?" Tristam was gratified that the man's interest seemed genuine and he had not put him in a difficult position.

"How I wish I could, but my evenings are filled. If an afternoon could be made to suit, that I could arrange."

They agreed to meet for tea the next day and the artist continued his rounds, leaving Tristam feeling somewhat more welcomed and less like he had walked into a dream.

"I see you have met Kent." It was Roderick, returned.

"Yes. What a kind gentleman."

"There is no better sort. If he takes a liking to you, he will introduce you to every empiricist in the charted world. He has been a fellow forty years or more. Knows everyone." A servant came to the door of the hall at that moment and, as softly as one could, blew a clear note on a conch shell—the tradition in this place.

"Shall we go in? I am told this should be an interesting gathering, though I must warn you—there will be a moment for poor Dandish. I hope you won't mind?"

"Not at all," Tristam said, hoping he told the truth.

They entered a sizable hall and found a place among the rows of chairs. The room filled quickly and the Speaker took the podium—none other than Kent, whom Tristam had just met.

"The pleasures of the evening to you, gentlemen." Kent surveyed the hall with a look of such apparent affection that Tristam had the impression the artist was looking out over his own, much beloved, family. "Before we begin with this evening's lectures and discussion it is my duty to report the sad passing of our colleague, Sanfield Dandish, Layel Professor at Merton College."

Kent had obviously prepared carefully, for he spoke with great knowledge of the professor's accomplishments and with some feeling about Dandish, the man, neither overlooking his shortcomings nor exaggerating his many fine qualities. It was a balanced and fair summary of the professor's life and work. The famous *Book of Fellows* was brought forward and a final date was entered after the signature of Sanfield Dandish—something many present found very affecting, for there was more than one throat cleared with difficulty.

In the moment's silence that followed, Tristam found himself thinking that in this very book Lord Skye had written his name, and Boran and Thayer ... and his friend and mentor, Professor Sanfield Dandish. What honored company the professor kept! There could not be a better indication of a life well spent.

It made the professor's recent activities seem even more incongruous.

"If there are no pressing matters requiring our attention," Kent said quietly, breaking the spell, "I shall begin. . . ."

"Mr. Speaker." A voice familiar to Tristam punctuated the somber mood.

As Tristam turned to find the source of the voice, Roderick muttered, "Somers."

And indeed it was. The father of Jaimy's current passion.

"I have spoken before on the subject of female fellows and though I disagree utterly with the decision of my colleagues in this matter, I bow to the will of the majority." He bobbed his head. "Though we honor a female empiricist here in our own home with the dedication of the Marsfield Library for her contribution to medicine and human anatomy, still we do not allow ladies beyond our sacred doors. I would put it to my honored fellows that female guests—properly escorted, of course—should be allowed to attend our lectures. I know, myself, several women who read our annals with great interest and understanding and their presence here could only add to the discussion."

Somers was about to go on when Averil Kent took the opportunity to slip in between sentences. "Professor Somers, no doubt what you suggest should be given our most serious consideration, but this is not a properly constituted, voting assemblage. All matters pertaining to rules of fellowship etcetera must be put to the annual constitutional review board. I do thank you for bringing this matter to our attention and urge you to raise the issue again at the proper time."

Somers swayed on his feet for a second, then, with a nod, returned to his seat. Tristam heard the man directly behind him mutter, "Oddest notions, our Somers."

Kent turned back to his audience. "Before we begin, I would like to welcome our guests this evening. Count Massenet, Entonne Ambassador to the Farr court, and Doctor Paul Varese, distinguished empiricist and author." These gentlemen rose with an easy grace, bowing to the restrained applause.

Tristam had never heard of the ambassador, but Varese was certainly the Entonne champion of the Farrellite version of geological history—they denied

Layel's hypothesis that the earth was immeasurably old, perhaps hundreds of millions of years. *How Dandish will love to hear of this*, Tristam thought immediately, as people often do of those recently gone—and then felt the loss heavily.

"We also have in our company this evening," Kent went on, "Mr. Tristam Flattery, colleague of Professor Sanfield Dandish and co-author of several widely admired papers on the collection of Baron Trevelyan."

Roderick touched Tristam's arm; he rose and bowed, feeling slight embarrassment. So that is why Roderick had excused himself earlier, he realized. The thought disappeared in the rush of emotion though. He was being applauded by the most accomplished empiricists in the land. Even without introductions he recognized some of them from portraits he had seen. He sat again, feeling a small rush of pride.

The first lecturer was introduced. His paper was entitled; *Predator Identification in Bivalvia*. A rather graphic demonstration preceded the actual reading, delighting the audience and making them very receptive to any subsequent claims. In a shallow, copper pan, partially filled with salt water, the lecturer placed a dozen *Pectinidae*, commonly called "swimming scallops." He then held up a starfish, the deep purple rays curling slowly. The instant the man placed the starfish into the water with the scallops the entire pan began to shake, water splashed out on the table and then the scallops began to shoot out of the pan until they all lay on the now sopping cloth, and the starfish was left alone. An explanation and discussion followed—all rather polite and low key.

But all the while Tristam could feel a tension growing in the room. It was as though a storm was about to throw itself upon the building and everyone hushed to hear its approach. Mr. Varese was apparently to speak next.

A brave man, Tristam thought.

Varese was of average height, a bit emaciated looking as though he had been ill or was simply too preoccupied to remember to eat, for he had that look about him as well. He went reluctantly to the lectern, it seemed, though he did not appear nervous about his coming encounter.

The Entonne took a moment to settle an oddly shaped pair of spectacles on his nose, looked down at the papers he had spread out on the lectern and then began.

"I speak, gentlemen, of a subject dear to all of our hearts," he said, his voice strong. "Dear to our hearts but hitherto unaddressed."

Varese's manner was not conducive to gaining the sympathy of an audience, Tristam thought. The man's Farr was very good, but his manner would have been appropriate to a schoolmaster who addressed a group of boys too stupid to appreciate what he had to offer. Tristam was not sure this was actually the man's attitude—he suspected by the choice of words that it was not—but it was obviously his common manner of speech and it seemed that Varese was too socially obtuse to realize the effect it had on others.

"It is the accepted conception of history that empiricism came into being the day Wilam Tomas Boran first published his great book, *The Role of Experience in the Study of Natural Philosophy, or An Inquiry into Methodology*. Of course the interpretation of this great text led to the schism between the 'empirics' and the 'empiricists' as defined by Noam and Jaspers. In recent years this split in approaches to natural philosophy has largely been healed by the all but universal acceptance of the Jaspers' interpretation of empiricism—observations interpreted by reason. Few, if any, ideas have had such impact on the lives of men.

"Like many another young scholar, I became enamored of Boran's book and to this day I continue to follow the basic tenets that Boran set down some seventy-five years ago." He looked up then, regarding the audience over his spectacles. "But I have discovered that this accepted version of history is no more true than any nation's official account of its wars. Boran did not formulate the ideas of empiricism first and it is possible that he was aware of the ideas from his reading of another."

The dramatic pause could not have been better timed. Boran was worshiped in these halls. To say that he did not have primacy in the creation of the empiricist creed was sacrilege. To suggest that he *stole* these ideas from another was blasphemy. And to judge by the reaction of the men around him, some were ready to kindle the cleansing pyres.

At least two men stormed noisily out of the hall. Others muttered among themselves or merely to themselves. No one looked pleased. Finally, the voice of Averil Kent was heard.

"Gentlemen, please. Doctor Varese has not yet finished. Can we not accord him the courtesy which all are due here, in this hall where new ideas have always been welcomed?"

Varese nodded to Kent and then looked back at his audience. "I do not make such a claim brashly. Boran, as I have said, is one of my true heroes. Nonetheless, I do say it. Over the course of my researches I found, in the correspondence of the Marquis of Reme, three letters written sometime between the years 1430 and 1450. All of them were signed with nothing but a very elaborate letter 'L.' The signature, as I'm sure you are all aware, of Lucklow." He stopped to drink, and refer again to his notes. At the mention of the mage, Roderick had suddenly moved forward in his chair as though straining to not miss a word.

"I have made every effort to compare the handwriting of these letters with other samples known to be the mage's, and I am convinced of the authenticity. It is, unfortunately, unclear to whom these letters were addressed, for the name of the recipient was certainly a diminutive. Due to the nature of this diminutive and the tone of the writing I suspect these letters were written to a woman in the house of the Marquis of Reme: likely the marchioness, the marquis' second wife. One immediately wonders about the nature of this, hitherto unknown, friendship. I will only say that these letters did not lie unread for over a century for no reason. This was an intimate alliance kept carefully secret. The fact that these letters were not destroyed is fortunate in the extreme, for there are indications that there existed a larger correspondence—no more of which has been found among the family papers. I shall also add at this point that the Marquis of Reme was briefly the patron of Wilam Boran during the years 1457 and 58.

"Much of what is said in these letters, written in Old Farr, is in the common nature of such letters, even if somewhat veiled: the inhabitants of one time expressing much the same sentiments as those of another. There are, however, a few paragraphs dealing with other matters: politics of the time; gossip; and a single paragraph that I shall now read to you." The man paused to drink again, for effect, Tristam was sure.

Tristam took that opportunity to glance around. The hall was as silent now as it had been noisy moments ago. Sir Roderick was not the only man straining forward in his seat. The Entonne Ambassador had actually half-risen and then returned to his chair, his face contorted in what appeared to be great distress.

"Here, gentlemen, are the words of Lucklow." He cleared his throat. "'To suggest that one can deduce the workings of the world through sheer mental effort is a continuing fallacy that I cannot fathom. Haldbraith claimed the number of teeth possessed by a horse to be twenty, though he had never made the extreme effort of actually looking into the mouth of the beast. If one would know the number of teeth possessed by any animal, one must take the trouble to enumerate them, as one must do for the petals on a flower or the number of bones in the finger. Who could possibly believe that the exploration of the natural world was somehow akin to the study of abstract formulae, to be comprehended by mere logic?! In fact, to know the number of teeth possessed by a horse, one must count the teeth of one hundred horses to eliminate the possibility that some have been lost to accident and so on. Until such a numerative and empirical approach is taken up by our natural philosophers, they shall continue to fill book after book with facts created out of nothing but their own ignorance. Even the most illiterate shepherd will count his flock upon his fingers to see how many sheep he possesses. Only a philosopher would think to deduce the number according to some principle of logic.'"

There was a moment's stunned silence as the impact of Varese's claims wore off a little and then the room erupted. Questions came from all corners and not a few of them were outright accusations. Voices began to rise as everyone struggled to be heard. Averil Kent reached the lectern at the same time as the Entonne ambassador and as Kent held up his hands, attempting to gain a respite, the ambassador leaned over and spoke in the ear of his countryman. Without further adieu, Count Massenet ushered his compatriot out the nearby door, bringing the gathered voices to a crescendo in both volume and indignation.

The meeting broke up then, the discussion fragmenting as the fellows retreated in groups. Some made their way to the smoking room, others to the library and still others to various rooms around the old mansion.

Roderick led Tristam to a large drawing room where groups were forming and the discussion was already animated if not heated. Surprisingly, not all the talk was of Varese and his sudden departure—proving the old saw that the Entonne would make their exits without taking proper leave—for many named him a fraud and a crank and put his claims aside.

Nearby, three men were arguing about the age of the earth, while not far off another group debated the feasibility and merits of connecting Wrightfield and Kuldern with a canal. It was a lively company.

Tristam was introduced around by Sir Roderick, and the young empiricist was thrilled to find himself in the company of several of Farrland's most eminent thinkers: Beall, whom Roderick had mentioned before; the great engineer, Wells; and Noyes who had designed Bolingbroke Palace as well as written a landmark book on the new agricultural methods. Tristam received a warm welcome, for it seemed everyone was familiar with the work done by Dandish and Flattery.

The group fell immediately into discussion, as though there were not enough time in the evening to waste more than a moment on pleasantries.

"How did you like that, Mr. Flattery?" Beall asked. "A fine introduction to the Society! It is not every night we have someone attack the reputation of one of our most eminent thinkers and run off without so much as a 'by your leave.'"

"Did you see the way Massenet whisked him off?" Noyes said, laughing. "I'm sure the count feared he was creating an international incident!" He laughed again. "The ambassador should have thought of that sooner."

"But he did not know!" It was Beall again. "I spoke with the count earlier and asked what Varese intended. 'Something to do with methodology,' he told me. Well, I should say so!"

The entire group laughed, though Tristam caught Roderick sharing a glance with Wells that did not seem humorous in nature.

"Enough of that," Beall said, as though making a pronouncement. "Now, Sir Roderick," he began, acting as spokesman for the others, Tristam suspected. "You are far too close on these matters you have been pursuing and we are all wondering when you will see fit to tell us, your friends and associates, what you have discovered or invented, if that is the case."

Roderick laughed a little as though slightly embarrassed, but it was, Tristam suspected, only more of his act. "But, gentlemen, my endeavors, compared to your own great works, are so modest that I hardly wish to waste your time."

"We will be the judges of that," Beall responded and the other added their voices in support.

"I see that I may keep my small efforts to myself no longer. If you must know, I have been writing a paper on the nature of artesian wells and I think I have explained this phenomenon at last. There, now, is that not an exciting subject?" Taking a mechanical pencil from a pocket and calling for paper, the King's Man began a drawing depicting stratification in the earth. It was a short but very clear thesis that Roderick proposed and Tristam could see the others thought it ingenious. When this was complete and the others had given this hypothesis some small criticism, Roderick then began a second drawing of the workings of a carriage. "I have seen over the years that the greatest cause of carriages tipping, and all of the subsequent injuries to man, machine, and beast—loss of both teeth and spokes, much to the confusion of those who study such things—is the loss of stability caused when the front axle is turned." He had drawn a rough T shape. "The entire axle pivots on this central point, of course, and in an extreme turn . . ."—he drew the axle to illustrate this—"the support of the carriage in the front is made so narrow and the direction of the pull caused by the team is such that the carriage is often overset." The knight began a second drawing. "Here you see what I am proposing—in fact, I have made a successful model and am about to have a full-sized carriage so modified. The wheels pivot on their own individual points on either side so that the stability is not compromised. At first I thought they must each turn to the same degree, but this did not prove practical, for the wheels, as I should have realized, describe circles of different radii. Do you see? The circle scribed on the ground by the inner wheel is smaller than the outer? This, then, had been the difficulty. The geometrics I worked out easily like this. . . ." He drew a line through the rear axle and marked a point on this that became the center of the circles that the front wheels would scribe. "But to have the wheels somehow turn differently when the horses went off at an angle to the carriage, that was the problem. Can you think how I managed it?" he asked, a bit like a school boy impressed with his own cleverness.

The gentlemen present clearly loved a puzzle and in a moment suggestions began to come as they all bent over the drawing. After a few moments Sir Roderick, pleased that no one had seen the solution immediately, set his hand to the drawing again, showing how he had connected the two wheels and the draw bar by an ingenious series of rods and levers. "There, you see? Mr. Wells was coming close to the mark. If I have engineered the thing so that it will take the punishment from our roads, I think, gentlemen, that we shall have a much improved carriage." He was obviously quite pleased by the ingenuity of the design and Tristam was a bit in awe. No wonder Palle had said that he knew of men who served the King and made contributions to other fields as well!

At first Tristam was too intimidated to speak, but after a while he was asked his opinion on a particular point and he could see that those around him felt he acquitted himself well in his answer. After that he joined in, circumspectly, and was gratified to find that his opinions were not thought foolish by any means.

During the discussion Tristam looked up at one time to find Kent staring at him from across the room, a look of some concern on his face, but when Tristam met his eye the artist looked away.

After hearing Tristam's explanation of the movement of flower parts in carnivorous plants, Noyes turned to the King's Man.

"Well, Sir Roderick, when will this young man's name be put forward? He has a head on his shoulders, to be sure."

"We shall see." Sir Roderick nodded, as though considering. "Soon enough, I think."

Roderick was called away to give his opinion on the practicality of building the canal and Tristam excused himself briefly to find the water closet. On his return to the drawing room, he came upon Professor Somers and a young man in the hall. It was difficult to tell who was more startled, the professor or his companion. Both quickly hid their reactions but the professor only nodded as Tristam stopped to speak, leaving the young naturalist standing in the hall feeling a little foolish. *Well*, he thought, as he continued on his way, *Lord Jaimas has rather quickly worn thin his welcome at the Somers' home.* And Tristam had only left his cousin that morning!

He gazed around at the knots of fellows scattered about the drawing room, and realized for the first time that here was a gathering of the very species he was trying not to become. Despite all of his fantasies about the Society, what Tristam saw before him was a gathering of dry intellectual men—almost any one of them could easily pass for a Merton professor. Not that they were all like that, surely, but even so, Tristam had spent his life among instructors and had a pretty good eye for the type. *There is more to life*, he told himself and wondered, if he looked in a mirror if he would see a young don in the making.

His own group had dispersed and could be seen engaged in other conversations about the room. The students he had known at Merton would die to be in his place, Tristam realized, for it was a particularly august company in attendance that evening. No one from his year had yet been made a fellow of the Society and it occurred to Tristam that he could still be the first. He did not know if this thought pleased or frightened him.

Certainly one can be an empiricist and escape the mold, he thought.

An enormously large man sitting alone and leaning heavily on a cane nodded his mane of silver hair to Tristam and then motioned for the young man to join him.

"Baron Trevelyan," the man said quietly as Tristam approached. He nodded to a chair.

"Your servant, sir. Tristam Flattery." Tristam took the chair, feeling suddenly awkward. This was the naturalist who had accompanied Gregory on his first two voyages! "This is a great honor, sir. I was Professor Dandish's assistant when he toiled classifying Lord Trevelyan's magnificent collection."

The baron nodded shyly and spoke, his voice so soft and reticent that one had the impression of being addressed by a small child. "Yes. Poor Dandish. All that effort must have killed him. Glad I didn't do it myself." He looked away almost coyly.

Tristam was taken completely aback.

"Mr. Flattery. . . . You are the son of Erasmus, I should think. How unfortunate for you." He leaned toward Tristam and then whispered. "They will be after your blood, sir. I advise you to flee before you are entangled." The baron tilted his head to the room, and moved his eyes as though indicating the men standing nearby. "It happens without you knowing, sir. It happens as you sleep. Eat nothing they offer, drink only spring water." He nodded, as though acknowledging the wisdom of his own prescription. He motioned with his hand to have Tristam lean closer. Not sure what to do, Tristam bent forward as little as possible. "I knew Lord Eldrich," the old man said, his voice so low Tristam strained to hear. "Erasmus, too, but it was Eldrich brought the great evil. Skye. Oh, I knew them both. Trust no one, drink only water from the purest spring. Collect it at sunrise." He looked at Tristam imploringly, as though terrified his advice might not be heeded.

Tristam realized that several fellows kept glancing his way, some amused and others showing what appeared to be pity. Clearly, the baron was not entirely well.

Suddenly, Trevelyan banged his cane on the floor with such force that Tristam jumped. "Look at them," he hissed, his voice rising in both volume and pitch. "They will open the doors to darkness. To naked women and children. Bastard son of a bastard son. Cross-pollination—shouldn't be done, I tell you, Flattery. I told your father as well but Erasmus heard only his own voice. His visions and his voice. Poor fool. Our world wasn't ready. Still isn't." He looked about him then, his face red with rage and then, suddenly, the anger was gone and he spoke in his pitifully childish voice. "I would like some tea, I think. Wouldn't you?" He said this with such lack of confidence—as though Tristam would refuse him this small request—that Tristam felt a wave of pity. This man was . . . had been one of the great empiricists of their time. A great man in every sense.

"The pleasures of the evening, Lord Trevelyan." It was Roderick, performing a graceful leg.

"Pleasures? Yes," he said squinting up at Sir Roderick as if not sure that he knew this man. "That's the dark secret in our hearts."

"Would you mind if I took Mr. Flattery away for a moment?"

"Mr. Flattery? Ahh, yes. He knew Eldrich, you know. We have just been talking with him."

"I'm sure. Excuse us, Lord Trevelyan, if you will."

"How's the old fossil in the palace?"

Roderick took Tristam's arm, drawing him to his feet. "Ah. The palace fossils are well, Lord Trevelyan. Kind of you to ask."

Trevelyan looked up at Sir Roderick, his face set into the look of an earnest child. "Tell him . . . tell him no one lives forever. Even a young wife can't gift you that. Even . . . even a princess." He waved a finger at Tristam. "Only spring water. Never forget."

Roderick led Tristam away as two other fellows approached the baron, speaking in soothing voices as though they addressed a child.

"My word!" Tristam said as they left the room.

"It is very sad. The baron will get quite out of sorts if he's allowed to go on. That was a mild outburst compared to others I've seen. Very sad. Yet he still comes out. Strangely, he can be quite lucid at times. I've witnessed it. As though he were perfectly well. You haven't met him at his best, I'm afraid."

The evening came to an end, far too quickly in Tristam's view. As they left the brightly lit mansion, he felt he was being cast into the outer darkness. He stood waiting for Sir Roderick's coach, and turned to look back at the columned entrance, the light pouring out of the open doors into the dark night, which Tristam thought an appropriate metaphor. It was the efforts of the men who walked, and who once walked, these halls that had pushed back the darkness of ignorance.

Just then Baron Trevelyan appeared in the doorway flanked by two men who supported and guided him, for he seemed to have lost his way and kept turning as though he would return indoors.

They ushered him down the few stairs toward a waiting carriage, and as they came closer Tristam could hear them speaking.

"But I must warn him. . . ."

"There, there, Lord Trevelyan. I'm sure he understood you perfectly well. Here is your carriage, sir."

"But, no," his eyes suddenly fixed on Tristam and he struggled to stop. "Mr. Flattery!" He waved his cane. "Flee! Flee while you may!" The two men tightened their grip and began to move the old man forward again. With surprising strength the baron brought his cane down sharply across one man's shin. "It is your blood! They will have your blood, sir!" Two other men stepped up and helped push the baron into his carriage. The last sight Tristam had was of the old man's face in the window, struggling to lean out, his eyes still riveted upon Tristam. And then the carriage was gone, its lamps disappearing down the drive, flickering through the trees like fireflies.

Sir Roderick stood shaking his head, looking off toward the gardens. "I can hardly bear to see it," he said with some feeling. "That such a great mind should give way so completely. . . . It is the cruelest thing I can imagine."

Sir Roderick's carriage stopped before them and they quickly climbed in, as though to escape the air of embarrassment that was left in the baron's wake.

The drive through the night city passed in silence. Roderick stared fixedly ahead and Tristam thought the man so distressed by their encounter with Baron Trevelyan that he did not know what to say.

Tristam also was disturbed by his meeting with the baron, but he could not help but dwell upon his good fortune. *He had attended a meeting of the Society!* Lest in time he forget, Tristam tried to recall every word he had heard, attempting to etch them into his memory.

The silence lasted until the carriage rolled to a halt before the Queen Anne.

Tristam turned as his foot touched the paving stones. "I can't thank you enough, Sir Roderick," he said with genuine feeling.

"It was my pleasure, Mr. Flattery." Roderick paused. "I fear we shall require your services no longer." He tilted his head slightly to one side as though saying, "you understand." "I shall have Mr. Hawksmoor settle our affairs. It was kind of you to come so far. The pleasures of the evening, Mr. Flattery."

And Tristam stood watching the beautiful carriage disappear down the dimly lit street. What in Farrelle's name?! They had brought him this distance to dismiss him so quickly? What had Roderick guessed from their conversation that Tristam did not see? Had he realized that Dandish had found a solution? And, if so, how did he intend to pursue it without Tristam's help?

He does not intend to pursue it, Tristam realized. *It is the last thing he wants.* And, strangely, it had also been the last thing that Dandish had wanted.

ᕗ Ten

Roderick Palle stood before a table in his study, rolling the model of a carriage back and forth, his mind running over the details of the design and then turning to the events of the evening and their ramifications, and then back to the model. A knock on the door sounded so softly it hardly deserved to be called a knock at all.

"Sir Benjamin has arrived, sir," came the low voice of his man servant.

"Good." He rolled the carriage forward once more, observing closely the wheels, then turned away at the sound of footsteps. "Benjamin. Kind of you to come so quickly."

The Royal Physician stood beside the door looking, as he invariably did, like a man who had not enjoyed a full night's sleep in a very long time. He nodded, but said nothing, as though he could not muster the energy at that moment.

"You have heard about the Society meeting?"

He nodded again. "Thirdhand," he managed to say.

"Well, let us sit and compare tales—first and third-hand versions." The two men took chairs in the alcove overlooking the Royal Gardens. Night may have hidden their splendor, but the perfume was carried into the room on the smallest breeze.

Rawdon sat stiffly, his look slightly dazed—if such a regal looking man could appear dazed.

"No doubt you were told about Varese and his claims?"

Benjamin nodded. "I cannot believe Count Massenet could be caught so unaware."

"Nor could I, but I saw it myself. Beall had spoken to Massenet earlier and asked him what Varese intended. 'Oh, something about methodology,' was his answer. I'm sure the man has never felt such a fool in all his life!"

"You think this letter is real, then?"

Roderick considered a moment. "Wells would have to see it to be sure. But, whether it is or not, we'll hear from Count Massenet in a few days; 'the letters need to be authenticated by other scholars of this field,' he'll begin. In a week's time there will be 'grave doubts.' By next month they will be nothing but 'brilliant forgeries'—and such forgeries might even be produced as proof. All the while there will be a concerted search to be sure that there are no other letters to the marchioness left lying about in some relation's attic. Varese, of course, will suffer embarrassment, but he will be called a 'victim of some other man's fraud.' The Entonne King will grant him a knighthood and perhaps even a sizable pension for his other noteworthy accomplishments. And in years to come all that will remain is a story of the night this Entonne doctor appeared before the Society and cast aspersions on the memory and reputation of Wilam Tomas Boran." He paused for a second. "It will certainly not be remembered as the evening we mourned the passing of Sanfield Dandish." Sir Roderick told the physician of his dinner conversation with Tristam Flattery.

This jolted Rawdon back to his senses. "And we thought the murder of Ipsword a fool's argument." Rawdon looked out the window, seeming suddenly fragile, his movements those of a sick man. "I will tell you, Roderick, I would never have imagined betrayal by Dandish."

"No," Roderick said quietly. "Nor would I. It is a lesson we learn again and again: we must never underestimate the charms of our duchess."

Rawdon rolled his eyes. "No, if she so much as sneezes, His Majesty will have me attending to her at all hours—sitting outside her bedchamber in case she coughs. But then, I will confess, even I have enjoyed her company on occasion— her dinner conversation is full of wit, and the duchess is the most graceful dancer in Avonel. Her charm is genuine, even if it is designed to beguile."

"Benjamin, you should never confess such a weakness to me. Have you not heard that I suspect everyone?"

"Why else would I make such a confession? Anyone foolish enough to speak against himself must certainly have the most innocent intentions."

Roderick smiled. It was good to hear Benjamin even attempt a jest—he had been too long a victim of melancholia. It had been more than worrisome.

"Lady Rawdon is well, I trust?"

"Perfectly well," he said quickly.

"I am glad to hear it, Benjamin. The duchess may have her superficial charms, but there is not a more noble soul in all of Farrland than your fair wife, and this past year has proven that beyond a doubt."

The doctor nodded, looking down at his hands in his lap and then out into the darkened garden.

"You will be glad to hear, Benjamin, that I have decided to send young Flattery back to Locfal. No doubt he will have his use yet, but for now I think we should keep him out of harm's way."

Rawdon brightened a little at hearing this. "I'm sure you know best."

The King's Man nodded. "You will see to the baron?"

"First thing in the morning."

✑ Eleven

Averil Kent appeared at the door of Tristam's suite precisely on time. The leather of his high boots squeaked as he crossed the threshold and the scent of his freshly powdered wig wafted in behind him. He cut such a figure in his old-fashioned dress that Tristam thought it unfortunate that the wearing of swords had gone out of fashion, for a rapier swinging at the painter's side would have made the picture complete. Despite his odd notions of style, Kent did not for a minute appear foolish. If anything, he seemed like an historical figure come to life. One immediately treated him with deference.

"I have not been in the old Queen Anne for many a year," Kent said, looking about. "I used to lodge here often, years ago. I believe I have let these very rooms." He smiled at Tristam and took the offered chair.

Tristam had placed the Hobbson study up on a bureau so that it would receive the most pleasing light and then arranged the chairs so that it could be best appreciated.

"Ah!" Kent removed a pair of spectacles from his jacket and, adjusting them carefully, leaned forward, his entire attention given to the painting. After several moments of silent examination, the man sat back, removed his spectacles, and briefly held a hand to his brow, half-covering his eyes, which were pressed tightly closed as though he were overcome with emotion. Tristam found that this display of feeling moved him as well.

"I will tell you," Kent said, slowly easing back in his chair as though he had suddenly aged, "I have spent almost my entire life trying to capture something so elusive, so damnably inexplicable and with so little success as to make a man mad . . . and here. . . ." He waved a hand at the painting. "In little more than a sketch Hobbson has managed it better than I in all of my work." He shook his head half in sadness, half in awe. "It is a beautiful little piece, Mr. Flattery. I give you joy of it."

Tristam hardly knew what to say, and he found himself looking at the painting as though he had not seen it before. Suddenly he became self-conscious and turned away to pour the tea.

"How in the round world did you ever come by it?" Kent asked as he took up his cup.

"It was left to me by Professor Dandish."

"I see. Yes, of course. I knew Dandish—though not as well as I would have liked—and I esteemed him greatly. I dare say you shall think of him every time you look at this painting. What finer memento could there be?"

"None, I'm sure. The professor could not have been more generous. He kindly left me a dozen books—a first edition of Boran's great work—and all of his instruments, including a new Fromme field glass."

"I have a Boran as well, but there are not more than a thousand of the first printing in all of Farrland. Almost national treasures. Do not hide it away in some dark library, but preserve it from the dampness." Kent shifted in his chair, musing. "The Fromme glass will serve you well. I have been in line for one nearly three years now—Fromme makes so few." Kent sipped tea from the dainty cup. "Do you have it here?"

Tristam nodded. "I do. I'll fetch it." He excused himself and went to the other room. When he returned, he found Kent standing at the open double doors looking down into the street.

"Ah. And there it is! Now here is a different type of beauty. May I?" He took the glass from Tristam with some reverence. He extended the tubes and began to scan the street. "This is a noble instrument, Mr. Flattery. Why, I can almost read the words in that man's book. Have a look." He handed Tristam the glass and pointed out a man sitting on a bench opposite the hotel, as though Tristam had never looked through the glass before.

Tristam did as he was told and to his surprise found that he was looking at Sir Roderick's driver. The man who had taken him to Merton and back. Tristam realized that he had lowered the glass and stood staring somewhat slack-jawed.

Kent did not seem to notice but relieved Tristam of the glass and swept the horizon like a captain aboard his ship. Tristam thought the man's mood had changed, though; as though the glass had revealed something unpleasant.

They returned to their tea and then, after a difficult start, the conversation flowed again. The painter spoke like others Tristam had met who had lived full and satisfying lives—there seemed a sense of sadness that such a life could be drawing to its end, but this was mixed with a realization that, having experienced such good fortune, one could hardly ask for more.

As Sir Roderick had said, Kent knew everyone and he spoke of famous empiricists, both living and dead, in the most familiar terms. "Hobbson was very kind to me. I was so young when I met him and he was very encouraging. When I look back, I can't imagine why. My early work showed little that would indicate talent." He laughed. "I was not a protegé by any means." His attention was taken by the painting again.

"You speak Entonne, Mr. Flattery?" he said after a moment. "You know the word *isollae?* 'Loneliness in the face of beauty' is how it is sometimes explained, though it has many shadings. It is a word much loved by the Entonne. 'Melancholy' it is sometimes translated. Or sadness. Estrangement. Or 'isolated', for it derives from the same root. But loneliness in the face of beauty strikes closest to the mark, I think.

"Evoking this emotion, *isollae*, is Hobbson's great skill. The empiricists praise him for his dedication to presenting nature accurately, but that is something that can be learned through careful application. *Isollae* is far more elusive." The painter took out a square of cloth and began to clean his spectacles—an unconscious habit, Tristam was certain.

"I look at this simple sketch, Mr. Flattery, and I am suddenly *caught*, for here is a perfect moment of our world, as beautiful as any, and I know it passed almost before Hobbson could mix his paint. And I feel that loneliness—the sense that our existence is so brief and the world so large and filled with moments as beautiful and fleeting as this one captured here.

"The Entonne poets say that *isollae* is the beginning of wisdom." He looked at Tristam as though he suddenly wondered if he were talking sense. Seeing that Tristam listened raptly, he went on. "Isn't it odd that the painter most admired by the empiricists was actually trying to capture something that our pragmatism and 'reason' seem not to recognize? A sense of wonder and awe."

He sipped his tea and gazed at the painting again. Tristam did not dare speak for fear that he would shatter the mood.

"During the era of the mages, I believe wonder and enchantment were the order of the time. But now we see the world as a specimen to be examined under a magnification instrument, to be dissected, and ultimately understood according to laws which are rational and logical. How our view has changed: from seeing the world as a place of wonder and enchantment, where a tree was alive and sentient in the same way that we are alive and sentient; to our present view where the tree has become a member of a lower order that one day will be understood in all of its parts—how it takes sustenance from the soil and air and sunlight, how it passes on life through a seed. How it can be rendered 'useful.'" He held Tristam's gaze for a second.

"The rational mind does not admit *isollae*, Mr. Flattery, and we are in danger of losing much because of it." He fell silent, staring at the painting.

"I believe the transcendentalists say many similar things, sir," Tristam said quietly, touched in some way by the artist's words.

Kent laughed gently. "Oh, yes, they do. And much else that is less sensible to my way of thinking. But in this I am forced to say I agree with them. And for all that, I am an empiricist as well. As fascinated by the workings of the world as any fellow of the Society. Perhaps I am just growing old and beginning to ask other questions as well. Or perhaps *isollae* is only experienced by esoteric Entonne poets . . . and painters who've grown long in the tooth."

Tristam looked at the painting, at the sea lions playing in the surf as they had likely done in that very spot for thousands of years. "I suspect it is just that most of us are not aware of its value . . . but I know the emotion of which you speak. I feel it when I look at the world sometimes, but I quickly forget or turn my focus elsewhere." Tristam ran out of words.

"Well, perhaps you have begun your journey toward wisdom, Mr. Flattery," Kent said seriously. "We have such a short time and the journey is so terribly long. One cannot begin too soon."

Once Kent had gone, Tristam went to the window again and focused his glass on the man reading on the bench. There was no doubt: this was Sir Roderick's driver. The feeling of relief that Tristam had experienced since his discussion with Sir Roderick suddenly disappeared. And there was more than that. He was not sure that Kent had pointed the man out to him merely by accident. Kent?

A knock on the door drew him away and as he crossed the room he realized he felt a certain sense of dread. "Blood and flames!" he exclaimed. "I will become mad if I start to worry about who is at my door."

Whomever it was Tristam feared, he found only an old servant standing in
the hall bearing a simple envelope with nothing more than Tristam's name on
it. No post mark—nothing to indicate from where it had come.

Tristam slit the letter open and inside found a short note in a precise hand.

My Dear Mr. Flattery:

*I feel I must make an apology for last night. I was, as you saw, not well.
Please do not judge me by this one meeting. I have long wanted to make
your acquaintance and to thank you for the difficult labor you undertook
with Professor Dandish in classifying my collection. Is it possible that we
could meet today? Would four o'clock suit? I am not always able to have
visitors, but today I seem to be myself. Please come if you are able. No
need to send word, but only arrive.*

Your servant,
Baron Trevelyan

The letter was obviously the effort of a sensible mind, Tristam thought. Had
not Sir Roderick said that the baron could be quite lucid at times? Tristam
pulled his watch from his pocket. There was time.

Well if nothing else, he thought, *I shall be able to say I made the acquaintance
of Averil Kent and the great Trevelyan.* They were not names that would impress
Jenny, perhaps, or many in Locfal, but they were men that Tristam was proud
to know.

As he locked the door to his room, Tristam thought again of Sir Roderick's
driver sitting across the street. *Yes*, he thought, *and the man was in Merton all
that time. There when Dandish's home and rooms at college were broken into.*

Checking the door twice, Tristam set out along the hall.

When he left the Queen Anne, Tristam made very certain that he did not
look toward Roderick's driver, but set out leisurely along the street. After half a
block he stopped to peer in the window of a shop and then risked a glance
back. The man had not gone into the hotel as Tristam had half-expected but
had risen and walked in the same direction as Tristam, though along the avenue's opposite side.

Tristam set out again and in a few minutes was quite sure that the man
followed him.

How long has this been going on! he wondered. *Well, if I have been the fool
until now, that is about to change.* How had Kent known? Or had it been mere
coincidence?

Tristam turned into the courtyard of a hotel and quickly exited through a second gate onto the side street. Here he increased his pace for a moment and then started up a narrow flight of steps leading left. No one was on the stair, so Tristam ran to the top and stopped on the landing where a vine hid him from the street. A moment later Palle's driver passed, obviously looking about anxiously.

That will do, Tristam thought, somewhat satisfied, and he set out quickly for the home of the baron, though not without many a backward glance.

It was almost an hour's walk, but Tristam elected not to hire a hack as he wanted the ability to easily watch behind him and to slip up stairways and down alleys if necessary. He wondered what had led Sir Roderick to have his activities monitored and realized there were several answers. It might well have been agents of the King's Man who had broken into Dandish's home, as well as stealing Tristam's journal and the letter written to the duchess. This would mean that the knight knew Tristam had not told him everything and thought it prudent to monitor Tristam's actions. The other possibility was that Tristam had been entrusted with state secrets and Sir Roderick had been watching him all along—which made Tristam deeply regret his conversations with Jaimy.

The entire affair seemed to be running down tracks that Tristam did not understand, and he felt more and more that he was floundering—like a man waking suddenly to find himself being swept out to sea in darkness, unable to know even which direction could lead to safety. He stopped and examined the leaf of a tree, checking behind him.

It was quite a relief to find the baron's street empty of all traffic. He had managed to arrive here without being followed; though he felt some satisfaction at this feat, he was not sure precisely what purpose it served. So what if Roderick knew he visited the baron? The knight himself spoke of the old man with some affection. All the same, Tristam felt better to think that his actions were known only to him.

The house of Baron Trevelyan was set well back off the street behind tall oaks and willows and weeping birch. Letting himself through the iron gate, Tristam was immediately struck by how ill-kept the grounds were; gardens grown over, the underwood flourishing. It seemed as lacking in order as the poor baron's mind. Birds were everywhere in the trees and under the bushes. Squirrels flowed among the branches, and then, across the gravel path, a fox appeared. It stopped for the briefest second to stare at the intruder, and then disappeared into the dense brush.

"This is no accident," Tristam whispered. The baron had given the grounds back to nature, the object of his lifelong passion.

The house had been constructed of the same white-stone that had been used in the building of the city, and though it was well covered in curtains of ivy, the whirls and skeletal markings of the fossils stood out like the work of some unbalanced sculptor: a thought Tristam did not like.

A brass-handled bellpull was set into the frame of the door. Tristam sounded it and waited, not knowing what to expect, for the character of the place was so peculiar that one hardly anticipated the door to be opened by one of Avonel's typical somber domestics.

And it was not. A handsome gentleman answered the ring and stood appraising the caller for some seconds before he spoke. "Sir?"

"Tristam Flattery. I have an appointment to see Lord Trevelyan." The man was so well turned out and so regal looking that Tristam found himself suddenly a bit intimidated. Dark, dark hair, thick and perfectly groomed, graying at the temples. Eyebrows so heavy and black they would have dominated the man's face had not his eyes been even darker.

"Ah, Mr. Flattery. I wish I had known, sir. I would have saved you the trouble. Benjamin Rawdon; Lord Trevelyan's physician," he said but did not offer Tristam his hand to shake. "The Baron is indisposed this day, I regret to say. You are aware that Lord Trevelyan is not well?"

"Yes. Yes, I am. I'm terribly sorry to hear he is beset by . . . troubles today. I received such a kind invitation that I had hoped. . . . Well, may I leave a note to say that I called?"

"You may, or I will gladly convey your regrets. Whichever you prefer." The man stood blocking the half-opened door as though he felt it necessary to doubly convey the message that Tristam's presence was unwelcome. He made no move to invite Tristam into the hall or even to find him writing utensils.

"Please say I called and thank Lord Trevelyan for inviting me. I should certainly come again if it were ever possible."

The man nodded, a slight bow, and backed away half a step as though ready to close the door. "I'm sure Lord Trevelyan will be very sorry to have missed you, sir. The pleasures of the day."

"And to you, sir."

Tristam turned and started back toward the street, certain the man would have shut the door in his face had he continued to stand there. It was not common to meet a gentleman of such poor manners in hyper-polite Avonel.

Very odd, he thought. The note had seemed perfectly lucid.

The physician was not the city's most gracious resident, that was certain. But it seemed even more odd than that.

He shook his head. *Look how this goes*, he thought. *I discover I'm being watched and suddenly everything appears suspicious, everyone's motives questionable. I will become as mad as the baron if I am not careful. I'll be drinking only spring water . . . collected at first light.*

ᥱ Twelve

The carriage, Tristam realized, was becoming the metaphor for this period of his life: he neither owned, drove, nor directed one in any way but was simply carried along. And here he was yet again—riding in a coach driven by a man whose name he did not even know.

Jaimy would call me a fool.

This particular carriage belonged to the Duchess of Morland. When he'd returned from the baron's, a note awaited, informing him that a carriage would call at half-seven to carry him to the home of the duchess. Tristam knew he should have answered immediately with polite excuses, but he hadn't done so. And he could not say why.

Curiosity, he told himself, dragging out that old excuse. He wanted to know why Dandish had been growing *regis* for the duchess while at the same time telling Sir Roderick that he was too ill to labor in the king's arboretum. Why the professor had later written to the duchess to lie about his success with Kingfoil. *Tristam wanted to know what in Farrelle's name was going on.*

No doubt this was true . . . but why couldn't he erase the vision of the Duchess of Morland rising from behind a column into soft light, melodious laughter preceding her like a delicate overture? This image unbalanced him. Every time he thought of the duchess, he felt as though he were losing his balance and had to exert himself to take control.

Vertigo, he thought, *a condition without known cure.*

Frightening to those who walked through life as carefully as Tristam Flattery.

Jaimy would think him doubly a fool for doing this. A rather vicious and petty baron had died beneath the famous elms beyond Avonel for running afoul of this duchess.

A more critical condition yet: desire heightened by a sense of danger.

Perhaps the real reason Tristam had accepted this invitation was even more tawdry. The Duchess of Morland was widely considered to be the most desirable woman in all of Farrland—and she wanted something from Tristam. He simply could not return to Locfal and wonder for the rest of his days what it was she wanted, and how sweet the rest of the overture might be.

Tristam could hear a bell sounding deep inside the mansion in response to his hand on the tasseled pull, but it hardly compared to the jangle of his own nerves.

A moment later a servant ushered Tristam through the doors that all aspirants to fashionable Farr society hoped one day to pass. According to the judgment of many, Tristam Flattery had arrived.

He followed the elderly manservant into the temple of the charmed circle. Everywhere Tristam's eyes came to rest, he found evidence of the sophistication of the Duchess of Morland, and the contrast between her elegant and carefully planned rooms and his own rather rough and well-worn home caused him a little embarrassment.

Nowhere in his uncle's home could one find anything to compare: the careful matching of pale colors, the creation of atmosphere—here an alcove arranged for intimate conversation, here a morning room to bring light into one's very soul. Every object had its purpose in the composition and yet nothing seemed contrived. Tristam knew that he was quite ignorant of current fashions in interior arrangements, but even so this home struck him as being an enormously detailed and successful work of art.

A door opened and the duchess appeared, her face lighting up in a smile of welcome. It was then that Tristam first realized that it was this smile—showing just a bit too much of the upper gum to be perfect—that he found irresistible. How could a man not be charmed by that open, innocent smile in contrast with those green eyes that challenged and mocked and claimed knowledge of what lay hidden in one's heart?

In her dress and bearing the duchess was a study in contrasts; at once a girl in the blush of youth and at the same time the duchess of a great house, dignified and gracious. The tiniest change in her face or the movement of a hand would transform her from one to the other more quickly than the eye could follow. With skin that would be the envy of a debutante, and tresses thick and lustrous, the duchess could play either part as she chose.

"My dear Tristam," she said in Entonne. "You cannot imagine what pleasure you give me." She smiled and flickered into youth before his eyes.

The duchess held out her hand to be kissed, and Tristam touched the soft skin with his lips. He was sure his nervousness must show.

"The pleasure, Duchess, is mine," he managed, and no more.

The woman took his arm and walked close beside him down the hallway. "I am so glad you felt able to accept my invitation. After your recent loss, I'm quite sure you need an evening of diversion." She squeezed his arm gently. "Banish all cares this night, Tristam Flattery. You have passed through a portal into the private realm of the Duchess of Morland. Wearing the current fashions is not enough to gain you entrance here. It is a world of the individual—we live by the strictures of no land. Convention is cast aside and we find our own way with only our true hearts as guides."

She turned her green eyes on Tristam, and he felt himself nod, approving of what, he did not know. The pressure of her hand on his arm and, indeed, her closeness had taken his voice away. In the presence of the Duchess of Morland, any sense that he had achieved worldliness evaporated and he felt awkward and young.

"I hope you will come to see me often," she said softly, and these words were enough to cause Tristam's balance to waver.

"I should like nothing more, Duchess, but my appointment at the palace is at an end."

The duchess stopped him, taking one of his hands between both of hers. "Do you say that Roderick has released you? We are to give up all hope?" Tristam could hear genuine distress in her voice.

He nodded but said no more.

The duchess looked down at his hand, apparently, and bit her lip delicately. "Why has he done this? Did you learn something on your journey?"

Tristam hesitated before he spoke. "Sir Roderick seems convinced there is no solution to the *regis* problem. He told me so himself."

"So suddenly? Why has he decided this?"

She looked up and Tristam could see no mockery in her eyes now, only sadness and concern. He was not sure how to answer. He searched among the possible lies and none seemed adequate. The truth—*I told him Dandish had been growing Kingfoil and likely found no solution*—would hardly endear him to the duchess.

Applause caused them both to look up toward a door at the hall's end.

"We must return to my guests, Tristam. May we speak of this later? I am greatly disturbed by what you say."

Tristam nodded his head, hoping an answer would suggest itself in the interim.

As they walked toward the room from which Tristam could now hear music emanating, he stopped before a portrait.

"Who is this?" he asked.

"The Countess of Chilton," the duchess said, nodding at the woman in the portrait as though their eyes had just met across a room. "In her day she was the most celebrated woman in all of Farrland and beyond."

If the portrait was an indication Tristam could believe this was true: an astonishing cascade of black hair framing a heart-shaped face and a full mouth. Dark eyes that appeared to be focused on Tristam. Something told him that the artist had been under the woman's spell, for the painting had a quality that could not be explained otherwise.

"My uncle kept a portrait of this same woman in his home. I remember it well. I always wondered who she was, and what became of it."

"This is Erasmus Flattery you speak of?"

Tristam nodded.

"I'm surprised," the duchess said. "But then the countess was admired by everyone—certainly every man, at least. I was presented to the countess once when I was a child. I thought she was a goddess, more beautiful than the painting by far. She is a recluse now, and must be very old. It is said that the countess wishes to be remembered as she was. None but her servants have seen her these past thirty years. But the Countess of Chilton reigned over Farr society for almost two decades." She made a half curtsy to the dark-haired woman. "Let me introduce you to my other guests."

The sound of a pianum came from beyond a door though Tristam had not registered it before. The duchess let them into the room with care, as though a child slept within. Two gentlemen and three women were revealed, their backs to Tristam, obviously entranced by the virtuosity of a young man seated before the pianum.

Pushing the door closed with the same exaggerated care, the duchess nodded to a divan out of everyone's line of view. Tristam took his place beside her, closer than he felt was proper, but the seat was small. The duchess did not indicate by even the smallest sign that she was aware of how near they sat.

The young musician was completely absorbed in his playing. His expressive face changed as fluidly as the melody, reflecting the music as though it flowed out of his heart more naturally than tears or laughter. Tristam was not overly knowledgeable when it came to music, but he could see that this man exercised astonishing control of his instrument. The subtle shadings of expression, the nuances of time—lingering on a note, hurrying over others. Here was a player of some genius, Tristam suspected.

The composition was long and, when done, the player seemed to collapse where he sat. The others leaped to their feet and rushed over, one man pumping the musician's limp hands, the women caressing his shoulders and neck and showering kisses on his brow and cheeks. All the while they cried praises in the language of Entonne.

"Duchess," one of the women said, "is he not a marvel? A genius? A master of the pianum?"

"He is, Lucin, all that and more. Let me introduce my particular friend, Mr. Tristam Flattery of Locfal," and then she smiled at him, "and Avonel, we hope."

The three women and one man, Tristam learned, were all members of the cast of an Entonne opera preparing a performance for the citizens of the capital. The musician, however, was Charl Bertillon, a man of such wide repute that even Tristam recognized his name.

It was not a surprise when the last man was introduced as Julian Burne-Johns, the Viscount Elsworth; the duchess' brother. Tristam took his hand with some misgivings, though he hoped it did not show, and felt a little nausea when he released it. The hand that had murdered Ipsword had been offered so casually.

The gathering repaired to a dining room where the table was set with fine crystal and silver and porcelain that picked up the colors of the room and would, no doubt, reflect some element of the view if it had been daylight. This was not one of the endless tables at which Tristam had often been seated but a small affair set for an intimate gathering of friends.

The company was high-spirited, but Tristam thought the duchess did not fully participate. Her gaze kept clouding over, and he would occasionally see her lose track of the conversation only to recover with enormous grace and ease.

The finest foods and wines seemed almost to wash over the table in apparently endless courses, like waves on a beach. At one point the gentleman from the opera troupe stood and literally sang the praises of the table. He was definitely in his cups, but amusingly so, and the wine had not spoiled his voice.

Although everyone was welcoming, Tristam still did not feel very comfortable. Most of the talk was of art and music and the latest plays and books, things he paid some attention to, though he certainly was not nearly as well informed as the present company. Jenny had often told him he was too much the dedicated empiricist, and a gathering such as this made him think she was right.

It was not that he couldn't enjoy himself entirely in this setting, but a discussion of Skye's laws of motion or recent theories about elliptical and circular planetary orbits would make him more comfortable. One of the young women, Lucin, sat to his right and she kept calling him *my pet* and *my peach*, common endearments in her own language, but a little absurd to Tristam's ear.

"Listen to Tristam's Entonne," she ordered at one point, stopping the conversation. "Our voice instructor would delight in such a student." She turned to Tristam. "Say . . ." and she asked him to pronounce one of the several words that those not raised to the language of Entonne found virtually impossible.

Tristam did as he was instructed, and she clapped her hands and bussed his cheek. "He has the heart of an Entonne, Duchess. What charming friends you have."

Bertillon loved to hear himself speak and held forth at length, obviously used to being surrounded by devoted admirers. Fortunately, unlike many who insisted on dominating the conversation, he was not a bore, and often made people laugh, mimicking the accents and mannerisms of a host of public figures. The women present obviously delighted in his company.

But to Tristam's utter surprise, they were clearly quite taken with Julian Burne-Johns as well. Judging by the posture of the Viscount Elsworth, his hand was in the lap of Monay, the woman to his right, and she was having trouble maintaining her composure—her face quite red, and not entirely from drink.

The Viscount Elsworth was a large man—just taller than Tristam but broader of frame—in his early thirties, perhaps, and though dark-haired, handsome enough to have come from the same stock as the duchess. Despite his size the viscount had surprisingly delicate hands—hands one would have expected of Bertillon (though the musician's were actually unremarkable)—and the dark brooding eyes of a young poet.

Burne-Johns seemed as out of his depth in this conversation as Tristam, but the viscount did not seem to care in the least. He laughed at every joke—a great uninhibited laugh, full of his own pleasure—and partook of wine and food with great relish. It was difficult to imagine that a man possessed of such an easy nature could bring himself to kill another.

As a skilled hostess, the duchess occasionally steered the conversation this way and that, attempting to include everyone.

"This wine," the duchess said, holding up her glass, "is made from the famous Erasmus Grape, developed by one of Tristam's many illustrious relations. Are you not his heir, Tristam?"

He admitted that he was.

Upon hearing this news, the viscount showed surprise. "But is not Locfal rather far north for the grape to grow? Erasmus must have truly been a mage to accomplish that."

"My uncle had a small estate on the island of Farrow, Lord Elsworth. The Erasmus Grape, as it is now called, came from his years there."

"You possess an estate on Farrow, then? A winery?" the musician asked.

"Not a winery now. A vineyard. The harvest is sold to certain wineries and they are responsible for this." He held up his glass. "An art, perhaps not equal to yours, Mr. Bertillon, but an art in its own right."

Too used to compliments, Bertillon hardly acknowledged this one. "I have always wanted to travel to Farrow. You have seen the famous Ruin?"

"No. Unfortunately, no. Though I own a property on Farrow, I have never made the journey there myself. I plan to do so."

"Perhaps we could go together," Bertillon said. "I would find it fascinating, I think."

"Tristam," the duchess said, falling into the Entonne custom of using first names, "is also an empiricist of growing reputation."

Lucin made appreciative sounds.

Expected to continue, Tristam described the demonstration he had witnessed at the Society.

"All of them, out of the pan?" the viscount asked, a little incredulous. "Amazing! I should have liked to have seen that."

"I spoke with someone who was there, as well," Bertillon said quietly. "He told me that a man named Varese made a very bad impression by attacking the illustrious Boran."

Tristam nodded. "Yes. Yes, he did. Provoked quite a response."

Bertillon raised his eyebrows. "What did you think, Tristam? Is it possible that Boran could have borrowed his method from Lucklow?"

"I don't know. It all hinges on this letter he claims to have found." Tristam quickly told the others what had happened. "If it is authentic, it will shake Boran's great reputation, that is certain."

"But mages were not empiricists," Bertillon went on. "They were practitioners of dark arts, it is said. Not even natural philosophers. *The dark arts.* The antithesis of empirical studies, it would seem."

"*Dark arts,*" the duchess laughed. "Really, Charl. Lord Eldrich certainly expressed interest in geology, astronomy, and much else as well. Even music. What do we really know of mages? Perhaps they *were* natural philosophers. There are some who say that all the 'magic' of the mages was contrived by ingenious engines and chemistry."

The musician smiled and shrugged, conceding quickly to his hostess. "And perhaps they are right." He raised a glass. "To the arts—dark, light and all tones between."

The people present were prepared to toast almost anything, especially, Tristam suspected, if it would get them back to the topics that they found of interest.

Servants refilled glasses and Bertillon leaned forward, speaking low. "They say wine will kill you slowly." He nodded his head solemnly. "But that's all right, we're in no hurry."

Everyone laughed.

"Are you a fellow of the Society, my peach?" Lucin asked.

"I was the guest of a fellow," Tristam admitted. He realized he had hoped no one would ask and simply assume that he was.

"Soon enough, my dear Tristam," the duchess said, saving him an awkward moment. "I have it on good authority."

"To Tristam's pending fellowship, then," Viscount Elsworth offered, holding up his glass in his free hand. The toast was enthusiastic and Tristam realized how much he had drunk when he felt no embarrassment.

The musician leaned forward and stared carefully at Tristam in such an odd way that the others began to titter. "You see the high, strong forehead?" He nodded toward Tristam after a moment. "It is the mark of a superior mind, an intellectual's mind. One could know Tristam as a formidable thinker without exchanging a word." He tapped his own forehead. "The mark is unmistakable." And then his face split in a smile; Tristam had been a little afraid the man was serious.

"Like Jons'," the woman beside the viscount interjected, making everyone laugh, including Jons, who was without question the quietest and most inebriated person at the table. His forehead was unremarkable as far as Tristam could tell.

This theory that related the shape of the head to characteristics of the mind was currently in vogue, though given little credence by true empiricists.

The musician continued. "Lucin has a strong forehead, as well. There is no doubt."

The third woman, Tenil, leaned toward Lucin. Tenil was the youngest of the singers, and generally quiet, but Tristam had seen indications that she was possessed of the sharpest wit. "Ah, poor Lucin," she said, "such a neckline . . . and gentlemen remark on your forehead."

There was much laughter at this, for Lucin wore the most revealing gown of all—which was an accomplishment in this company.

"Now for all of those present who do not believe in the dark arts." Bertillon nodded to the duchess as he said this, but he was smiling. "I shall make a demonstration. Are we finished with this glorious meal? Then we must have the table cleared."

Servants did as requested and at the musician's instructions also brought him eight fresh candles set in holders. These he passed around the table so that each person had a lit candle. A single yellow rose in a narrow glass vase was moved to the table's center, and this Bertillon proceeded to douse in fine brandy, until a layer of the liquor floated upon the water.

"If you intend to turn this rose into a beautiful princess, Charl," Tenil said, "at least Her Highness shall be as soaked in spirits as the rest of us."

"I would like to speak with spirits," Lucin said a little breathlessly. "Someone famous and wicked."

The other lamps and candles were removed or put out so that only the eight candles remained. This still left quite a bit of light though, too bright really to create the needed atmosphere, Tristam thought. He had been involved in such things before. Some of them merely larks where nothing happened and others where elaborate hoaxes had been prepared. This had all the earmarks of a lark, he thought.

"Now," Bertillon began, making his voice low and solemn, "we must all join hands to form a chain, of course."

Tristam took the hands of the duchess and Lucin, feeling the softest pressure from the duchess.

"I will perform the incantation, so you must all be silent. Stare into the heart of your candles until you have fixed the image in your mind. Now, for a moment only, we must close our eyes. Clear your brain of everything but the image of the flame."

The table shifted suddenly making someone squeal.

"*Lord Elsworth!*" Monay said, as though addressing a naughty child. "He does this with his knee."

"This will never work if we do not cooperate," Bertillon said, his voice more serious. "Close your eyes again."

Tristam did as he was told, conscious of the contact with the two women.

"*Curre d' Efeu*," Bertillon began, his voice strong. "*Vere viteur aupel e' lo-scure. Vau d' Efeu. Ivanté! Pard' embou vere fant!*"

The tittering stopped while Bertillon spoke these words, if words they were. Tristam had never heard this language before, but if it was mere nonsense, it was convincingly done. To his ear it sounded like very archaic Entonne. Given time, he might work it out.

"Now, in turn, we must each blow gently on the flame of our candle. Not so hard as to put it out, but enough to bend the flame away from you. We begin with the duchess and then myself."

Extending her neck so that she was level with the candle, the duchess blew gently, making the flame waver.

"A bit harder, Duchess," Bertillon whispered.

The duchess increased her effort and the flame licked out toward the rose, perhaps an inch, and then snuffed out, a ribbon of smoke spiraling upward in the light of the remaining candles.

"I am next," Bertillon said softly. Like the duchess he began gently, and the flame flickered in response. With great control he kept it up until the flame lay over, wavering so quickly it almost pulsed, and then it, too, was gone, the pungent aroma of the smoke filling the air.

"Ah," someone whispered, disappointed, perhaps.

Each went in turn, with varied success—for no one really understood what they were trying to accomplish. Jons blew his candle out immediately. Tristam had half expected the man's breath to burst into flame.

Lucin followed the others, the room almost dark now. The mood was changing as the room fell into shadow, as though everyone feared the blackness suddenly.

Tristam followed Lucin—the last to go and glad to see the end near. He blew with the same exaggerated care Bertillon had exhibited and watched his flame quiver, trembling like a crimson leaf in the wind. And then the flame began to elongate, not much but longer than the duchess had managed. And then it flared and was gone. At the same instant, the rose burst into blue flame, with a sound like an exhalation of breath long held.

Everyone started back, eyes wide, and then began to laugh, a release of tension. Everyone but Bertillon, who seemed to have been thrown back, asprawl in his chair, his eyes fixed on Tristam, the cold-burning rose between them.

Tristam focused on the ghostly flames as the alcohol-saturated blossom began to darken and curl. The duchess squeezed his hand gently and then released it, but Lucin clutched his hand like a frightened child. She giggled nervously.

"Now what is the trick, Charl?" the viscount asked, his matter-of-fact tones breaking the mood.

Bertillon sat up in his chair, pushing his charming smile back into place. "Trick? Tristam is the empiricist, Lord Elsworth, perhaps he will tell us."

"Dark arts, Lord Elsworth," Tristam said, but the laughter this brought was weak.

"Does it take a moment for the fumes to accumulate?" the duchess asked, anticipating Tristam's explanation.

"Perhaps," Bertillon said. "I don't actually know. Often it doesn't work at all. Not a very reliable parlor trick, but exciting when it succeeds."

"And the incantation?" Tristam asked.

"Part of a children's nonsense rhyme. You hadn't heard it before?"

No one had, apparently.

"There is quite a bit more, but I can't recall it now. Lost with my youth." Bertillon smiled again, moving his shoulders as though to loosen the muscles.

Servants returned to replenish everyone's glass and the duchess rose, composing herself like someone upon a stage. "And now, for your continuing pleasure, gentlemen and ladies all, certain of my gracious guests have kindly offered to display," she pronounced the words with conscious precision, "their arts."

The gathered guests rose unsteadily to their feet, and while Tristam, the viscount, Monay, Jons, and Bertillon followed the duchess back into the room where the pianum awaited, the others left by a different door, making rough sallies about their "arts."

"Do make yourselves comfortable," the duchess said as the gentlemen found chairs, in Tristam's case quite thankfully. "Charl has kindly offered to perform the accompaniment to our little entertainment." She reached out and touched the musician's arm, holding his gaze for just a second too long.

Tristam felt the sting of jealousy. Clearly it was not Tristam the duchess was trying to impress, and this realization caused some private embarrassment. He turned away from the two, taking a glass of brandy from a servant.

The room was lit only by candles now and the furniture had been rearranged so that the focus of attention was no longer the pianum but one wall. The servants were suddenly gone.

Tristam found that if he closed his eyes his head spun a little. He took hold of the arms of the massive chair, realizing that his wits were more addled with drink than he had thought.

A door opened a crack and Tristam saw Bertillon nod. He began a slow, almost folklike melody, deceptively simple but very evocative.

Tenil, of the well-sharpened wit, appeared, dressed as a girl of the country, with a long, full skirt and a peasant's open-necked blouse.

Reaching up, she began to unbind her hair so that it fell in strands that shone in the candlelight. Tristam had not previously appreciated how lovely Tenil was. And then she began to sing, a sad air, her voice rich and filled with the tones of a woman reaching out, singing from her heart. And this ability seemed so alien to Tristam's nature, that he could hardly bear to hear it, yet he could not have left if he had wanted to.

She sang in the language of Entonne—about a love, distant and uncertain— and after a moment a second voice joined her from the back of the room. Lucin appeared in the light of the few candles that lit the scene. Sisters, they sang to console one another for the lovers who were in a distant war.

The two women, their hair unbound, told the tales, in song, of each first meeting their lover when peace had ruled the land.

It was an opera Tristam knew by reputation, though he had never actually seen it performed. Two sisters in their room at night preparing for bed. The opera had all but scandalized the people of Farrland when it had first been introduced some years earlier. For the women would step behind a screen to disrobe, appearing again in their sleeping gowns having actually undressed on the stage, though all but out of sight.

Here there was no screen, and to Tristam's utter surprise that did not seem to matter to the singers. As she sang, Tenil continued to undress.

Tristam moved a little uncomfortably in his chair, embarrassed by his own response. He did look away for a second and discovered that the viscount and Monay were entangled on a divan in the corner, her skirt pushed up so that one long leg draped over the back of the viscount's thigh—a white petal against dark wood.

Jons was passed out in a chair and the duchess stood behind it, her hands resting on the back. She moved her head, swaying slightly, in time to the music, her eyes bright and following the movements of the singers.

Lucin was singing now as she crossed the room, blowing out candles as she passed. Tristam wished now that he had not drunk so much, for his mind was unable to grapple with the situation. What was expected here? How was he to act to not look the fool?

He found his breath coming with some difficulty and he could feel himself responding to the erotic charge in the room.

Lucin glided past his chair, draping her blouse over the arm as she passed, and caressing his neck. There was only a single candle left now, burning on the pianum for Bertillon. Tristam realized that Tenil was singing to him, coming toward him with her hands outstretched. She was clad now in only an under-shift, very sheer, her long hair falling in a cascade about her lovely face, the fabric of her robe moving and clinging as she walked.

She took his hands and gently tugged him to his feet to lead him up near to the pianum. There was no music now but for the voices of the two women as they came to the end of their song. The last candle was blown out as they held their final notes. And then there was darkness and silence.

Tristam felt the young singer press herself to him, kissing his neck and then seeking his lips. A long sweet kiss. She stepped back from him, squeezing both his hands—then she was gone.

Tristam stood wavering in the dark, feeling abandoned and foolish. He reached out and found the cool edge of the pianum and then lowered himself onto the empty bench, accidentally setting his hand on the keys.

In the darkness he heard the rustling of fabric, a soft moan. Harsher breathing and bodies meeting in rhythm on the divan in the corner. Whispers. A laugh of delight.

Well, here you are, Tristam thought. *The evening you dreamed of through so many lectures and you are left sitting alone in a room where there are four women and only three conscious men.* He touched the keyboard a second time—an accidental trill.

"I thought I'd lost you," came a voice speaking Entonne.

Tenil! She had not abandoned him after all. Or perhaps the partner of her choice was already occupied. A vision of Bertillon entwined with the duchess and Lucin came to mind.

A sharply indrawn breath that became a moan of pleasure. Clothing slipping to the floor.

Hands found him. A woman, her breath sweet with wine, kissed his face, her hair brushing his cheeks and neck. Tristam found himself stumbling as he was led through the dark, out a door into the next room, as black as the one he had just left.

A thought of Jenny came to him, but was lost in a long kiss as the woman turned and embraced him. Tenil, Tristam thought, was very beautiful and at the moment only her presence mattered. He was awash in her perfume and the darkness of the room, blind to whatever lay beyond.

She stepped away, and Tristam heard the sounds of fabric rustling and then she pressed against him again. His head spun from drink and growing passion. He ran his hands up her naked back as she pulled his shirt open. They kissed and touched with more urgency.

Tristam was led again, a few steps this time, and he heard Tenil settle on a divan beneath a dark rectangle of window. He shed the rest of his clothing and joined her. Although Tristam's experiences with women were limited, he had drunk enough that he did not care. His passion was leading him and he had no time for doubts.

Tenil stroked his chest and his back, and he could feel her excitement grow as she touched him.

"What a beautiful boy you are," she whispered in his ear in Entonne. "You have skin like a baby, like silk, so smooth, so smooth," she cooed. Her fingers combed into his hair and he felt the ribbon tugged free so that his hair fell about his face.

In his other encounters Tristam had never felt such urgency in a woman, yet there was also a concern for his own pleasure, a desire to please him. Her kisses were both soft and demanding, and her hands were never still. "Oh, my pet—oh, my child," she whispered into his ear.

Reaching down, she guided him into her and Tristam was swept up on a wave of pleasure, his senses and those of Tenil entwined so that part of the fabric of his pleasure was her own. It seemed that the limit of his senses—of both their senses—was the boundary of their world. Nothing lay beyond.

"Oh, my gorgeous one." Her whisper became a cry. Suddenly she spoke in perfect Farr. "*Oh, my pet. Oh, Charl, Charl! Ohh!*"

Tristam's head spun. *The woman beneath him was the Duchess of Morland, and she believed he was Bertillon!*

He was frozen in place, unsure of what to do. She stroked his back tenderly. "It is not just the pianum you play so well, my sweet. You have many skills." She gave a small laugh of pleasure.

Tristam said nothing. He felt himself begin to shrivel, which produced a sound of disappointment from the duchess. He rolled to one side gently and heard her sigh.

She sat up slowly. "Oh, my. Such good wine, and so much of it." She found his face and kissed him gently. "Do not disappear, my gorgeous child. Your devoted Elorin will return immediately."

Tristam heard the rustle of clothing and then a door opened. "Find a candle, my pet," she whispered and then disappeared. Tristam sat up quickly and was rewarded for this imprudence with a spell of dizziness that had him holding onto the divan. He found his clothes and began furiously to pull them on. He must be gone when she returned.

Blood and martyrs, Tristam thought, *what have I done?* He knocked over a chair searching for the door. In the next room the evening was not over, it seemed. The sounds of love and laughter emanated from the darkness and the air was musty and thick.

Tristam stumbled into a piece of furniture and regained his balance by pushing on some very soft flesh. A woman shrieked in surprise and then laughed. A doorknob came to hand and he let himself into an unlit hall, reeling as though he'd found himself aboard a darkened ship in a gale, the hallway rocking and plunging.

Tristam could not remember how he got out of the house, but he found himself leaning against a lamppost in the drive. Looking back, he saw the duchess standing at a dimly lit, upper window, a look of great concern on her lovely face. Ever so slowly, she ran her fingers over her cheek, as though exploring a bruise.

Tristam forced himself to move and staggered into the darkened avenue. A wave of nausea drove him to his knees. He vomited wretchedly and knelt for a long time breathing hard, the acid taste of bile burning his mouth and throat. Finally he rose to his feet unsteadily and attempted to clean himself with his handkerchief. It was only then that he realized he wore no shoes.

Unsure of where he was, Tristam became lost in the twisting streets, but overall he was sure he made his way down toward the Queen Anne. Occasionally he sat and struggled against a wave of nausea, breaking out in a cold sweat and gasping. The moon floated high, two days from full, hidden now and then by great forests of cloud.

It seemed to be hours before Tristam arrived at the entrance to his lodgings. He was forced to ring the bell to gain entrance and felt the sting of humiliation at his state, which, upon looking into a mirror, he realized was far worse than he'd imagined. Even his hair was clotted with gorge.

He stripped himself and washed in cold water as best he could, thinking all the while. *What have I done?* It was almost a rape. *The duchess believed me to be someone else. . . . But I acted in all innocence,* he told himself again and again. *I did not know.*

He cursed the red-eyed reflection in the mirror. "What a terrible thing you've done." It occurred to him that either the viscount or Bertillon might demand satisfaction. This sent a shiver through him as he pulled on a clean shirt. Bertillon was probably far less adept with a blade than Tristam, but the viscount. . . . It was time for Tristam to leave Avonel.

Even as these thoughts went through his head, there was a part of him, a part he did not want to acknowledge, that whispered, *You have made love to the Duchess of Morland! The most desired woman in all of Farrland lay beneath you and shuddered and moaned with pleasure. What a night to remember!*

The day was no longer new when Tristam fought his way back to consciousness. He called for bath water and coffee. *Wretched* was the word that best described how he felt. Wretched and at a slight remove from the world. Dull pain coursed through his head at each beat of his heart, and his neck and back felt as though they would snap unless he moved with considerable care. The state of his stomach could not be made worse by the drinking of a vial of acid, and his hands trembled whenever asked to perform—and that did not complete the catalog of his ailments.

The previous night was half a blur. Tristam was not sure that his memory was accurate. Perhaps nothing had occurred the way he remembered. He could hope.

After a bath and a shave, he donned fresh clothing and realized he felt only marginally better. His malaise was more than physical, he realized. The events of the previous night weighed on him. *There'll be no more drinking like that in the future*, he told himself.

Packing was also on his mind. Packing and leaving the city with haste. What would happen to the health of the king he did not know. There was a public coach going north late in the day and Tristam decided that he would be aboard it. He would leave Avonel behind and return to the familiar world of Locfal. *It is a good place for me*, he thought. *I am not meant for the court and its intrigues.*

The act of preparing for the journey hardly lifted his spirits though the thought of leaving a most awkward situation behind brought some relief. Before an hour had passed, Tristam had convinced himself that everyone had drunk so much the night before that what had occurred would never be known—even by the duchess. It began to seem a bit funny, in fact.

"*I had love with the Duchess of Morland*," he whispered. "And she will likely never know." His feelings were in such conflict that one moment he almost laughed and the next he felt the deepest shame.

A knock took him away from his task and he found Benjamin at the door. The old servant passed a note to Tristam.

My dearest Tristam:

> *Excuse my manners, but I believe I am in possession of some of your belongings? Do you have a moment to spare me? I will come up, if so.*

> *Elorin, Duchess of Morland*

"This is from the Duchess of Morland," Tristam said stupidly.

"The lady did not identify herself, sir."

"The duchess is downstairs?"

"The lady who wrote the note is certainly there, sir."

"Blood and flames!" Tristam quickly dashed off a reply and went looking for a neck cloth and frock coat.

The duchess arrived moments later, accompanied by a footman she left outside the door.

To Tristam's great relief, she said pleasantly, "You look a little white, my dear Tristam. I hope the evening's entertainment did not disagree with you?"

"I think I may be a victim of my own grape. The wine was perhaps too good, Duchess, and I overindulged. A terrible weakness, but the flaw is mine entirely."

She gave a tiny smile. "Yes. I dare say there are others not at their best this morning."

As far as Tristam could tell, the duchess would not be among these: she looked as ravishing as always.

"May I sit?" she asked pointedly.

"Excuse me. I am addled. May I offer coffee or tea?"

"Kind of you. I can't stay long, however." She reached into an embroidered bag and removed a pair of shoes—Tristam's shoes. She raised her eyebrows.

"Ahem. Yes, I do seem to have misplaced a pair quite like them."

She stared at him in reproach for a moment and then broke into a delightful laugh. Tristam could not help himself and laughed as well.

"Your stockings must be a sight," she said.

"I ordered them burned."

"No doubt." The duchess fixed him with a look that he could not fathom, but he was sure it held no anger or resentment.

She does not know, Tristam thought, *though I wish that she did, and looked at me so kindly.*

"Tristam," she said, suddenly serious. "May I speak to you of your friend, Professor Dandish? Will it be painful for you?"

"No . . . it won't. Please, say on." He hoped he told the truth.

The duchess reached down and ran her thumb across a pulled loop in the bag's embroidery, then looked up and met Tristam's eye. "Do you have his missing diaries, Tristam?"

Tristam had wondered if this would eventually come up though it was Roderick he had expected would ask. He watched the duchess carefully as he answered, wondering all the while: *but are they not in your possession, Duchess?*

"They were taken from his rooms at Merton, I believe."

The duchess stared at him for a moment. "I think you owe me better than that, Tristam." She reached into the bag again and removed a blue velvet ribbon—the one that had been used to tie his hair the previous evening. A memory of her pulling it free came to him. She held it out as though it were evidence of his offense—proof of his indebtedness. Tristam took a long breath. "It was dark, Duchess, I did not realize . . ." he whispered. "I can apologize, but it will change nothing."

"You could tell me what I want to know. Is it really such a difficult question?"

"I was sworn to silence . . . the King's Man. . . ."

"The King's Man!" Her voice was sharp. "Do you really believe that knight in his armor of self-righteousness cares more for the interests of the King than I?"

Tristam shook his head.

"I think you understand my concerns, Tristam. Do not play the fool. It is beneath you, and I won't believe it."

Tristam looked down at his hands for a moment. "Sir Roderick knows nothing of . . . the matter that concerns the duchess. If that is a comfort."

"I care less for what Roderick thinks than I care for the health of our King. Dandish's notes, his diaries? Where are they?"

"All but the last three volumes did truly disappear."

"Thank you, Tristam. You have these three volumes here?"

He shook his head. "I did not feel they would be safe here." He looked up and met her eyes. "They contain no references useful to our area of concern, Duchess."

"What do you honestly think, Tristam?" she said with great familiarity, as though they knew each other well. "Did Dandish solve the problem? Did he find a way to make the plants bear seed?"

Why did Dandish lie to this woman after he had taken on the task of growing Kingfoil? Tristam was not sure, but it was all the information he had to go on— that and his warnings from Jaimy.

The room swayed, just perceptibly, like an after-shock from his night's drinking. Or it might have been the presence of the duchess, who always un-balanced him. There was a part of Tristam that wanted to please this woman, to gain her favor. The memory of her beneath him in the dark came to him strongly. The air stuck in his lungs for a second.

"I . . . I am not certain what went on at Dandish's. I found empty planting boxes. And then someone broke into the house, looking for what I am not sure. I searched through the three volumes of his journal, but he had erased some entries. Only one escaped his notice, and that gave no indication of his success. In fact, it would indicate he was not succeeding, though it had been written over a year ago. Why was Dandish growing Kingfoil for you, Duchess, out of Sir Roderick's sight?"

She gazed at him for a second. "Roderick has his own designs. If preserving the life of the King was part of them, would he be sending you back to Locfal?" The duchess fell silent.

Though he never expected to be able to tell what this woman was thinking, there could be no mistaking her reaction to Tristam's words. She actually looked away, trying to hide her disappointment. "Tristam," she almost whis-pered, "you are telling me the truth now, aren't you, my dear?"

"I am, Duchess."

She shook her head and gave him a wry smile, her recovery almost complete. "I must have time to think." She looked at Tristam then, as though making an assessment of his well-being. "Tristam, I may need your help in this matter yet. It is the life of the King I speak of. Do you understand?"

Tristam nodded.

"May I count on you in this?"

"I am the duchess' servant," Tristam said very quietly, hoping that he would never have to live by these words but unable to stop himself from uttering them.

She reached over and took his hand, her eyes on his, and what remained unspoken in this gesture plunged Tristam into confusion. Perhaps he had meant every word of his claim of servitude.

"Thank you, Tristam," she said, and then withdrew her hand, sitting back in her chair. "Poor Sanfield. He was not young when he took this on. I'm sure he tried everything."

"I believe he did."

The duchess pulled the bag into her lap as though she would rise—but stopped. "Although it hardly matters. . . . There may be certain . . . references in those journals that would be better expurgated. Do you take my meaning?"

"It shall be done, Duchess. And please trust that I shall show them to no one."

"Roderick has not seen them?"

Tristam shook his head.

"Why, Tristam. . . . Did you think you were protecting me?" She reached out and squeezed his hand again.

Despite her obvious haste, she rose gracefully. "I am to meet the King, Tristam, so I cannot tarry . . . as much as I would like to," she added, almost stopping Tristam as he began to rise.

Exercising great control to maintain his balance, Tristam accompanied the duchess to the door, her suggestion that she would prefer to stay echoing in his mind.

At the same time Tristam was relieved that there would be no enraged gentlemen sending their seconds to call. As his hand touched the handle, the duchess stopped and met his eye again.

"It was a lovely evening, was it not?"

"I am certain that I shall never know another like it," Tristam said, believing every word.

"You are sweet." She leaned forward and kissed his cheek.

The duchess was gone, leaving Tristam afloat in an eddy of perfume, the sensation of a soft kiss rapidly fading to imperfect memory.

Tristam stood by the door for some time, lost in thought, and then he shook his head and went back into the room. His eye was drawn to the blue ribbon. Did Bertillon not have straight hair?

*   *   *

Tristam could not imagine that he would ever see the inside of the Tellaman Palace again so, on this last visit, he was attempting to fix the details in his mind as he passed through the corridors. There were only three errands remaining to be dispatched; say good-bye to Tumney, return the key for the arboretum, and retrieve Dandish's journals. These last were hidden in Tumney's work-room, a place Tristam thought unlikely to be searched, and, even so, the room was such a clutter of flotsam and jetsam that Tristam was sure his treasure would not be found.

The bronze key Tumney had provided turned the lock to the *regis* arbore-tum and Tristam entered the arena of his greatest failure—not without com-plete awareness of that very fact.

The air here was something Tristam was sure he would never forget, the dampness, the odor of rich soil, and the distinctive scent of the Kingfoil blos-soms, like a hint of an exotic spice.

After listening for a moment to be sure he was alone, Tristam uncovered his bundle and put the journals into a small carrying bag he had brought for the purpose.

Tumney could not be found, which was not surprising. His role as King's Gardener took him all over the palace grounds, though Tristam had the im-pression that the old gardener had able assistants and his supervision was more for the sake of form than of necessity. *Regis* had been Tumney's only real charge for many years.

Tristam paused for a moment to look at the Kingfoil planting and muse on the matter he had been unable to solve. The Varuan King's story of the spirit that inhabited *regis* came back to him and magnified his sense of failure. What had Dandish discovered? It was a question that he knew would plague him forever.

Tristam suffered a near desperate restlessness that morning and decided to go in search of Tumney rather than wait for the old gardener to appear. Lock-ing the heavy door behind him, Tristam immediately encountered one of Tumney's gardeners, who directed the naturalist through doors into another inclosed arboretum—one which Tristam had not been aware of previously.

Calling out Tumney's name was as useful as shouting the name of a tree and expecting it to uproot and walk—the man was deafer than most realized—so Tristam went in, searching.

There was more of the flora of Oceana here and Tristam found himself progressing slowly as he paused to examine various specimens. As he bent to look more closely at a complex flower, a butterfly appeared at the edge of his vision: wings of delicately veined white, a flash of deep red. The insect alighted on a leaf within Tristam's reach but, as the naturalist turned his head for a bet-ter view, it took to flight.

"Flaming martyrs," Tristam whispered. "A crimson tip." It was a species from Oceana, he was quite certain. The pale wings appeared among the dark foliage again, and without hesitation Tristam stepped off the path and into the artificial jungle, careful as he went, but determined to have proof of what he'd seen.

The flora had been planted to represent some zone of Oceanic vegetation; a particularly rich and dense zone. Another glimpse of the gossamer wings fanning the air drove him on and in a few paces he came out onto a walkway. Much to his disappointment, the crimson tip had disappeared. Moving as slowly and carefully as possible, Tristam searched his surroundings. Just as he was about to give up, he saw the pale wings move. There! It was perched on the frame of an open transom window set above a wooden door.

He took a step; ever so slow, and then another. There was no doubt; the tip of the forewing was blood red. Halfway through a third step, the insect spread its wings and disappeared through the opening.

"Damn!" Tristam said aloud. He rushed forward and tried the handle, but the door was locked. "It is the worst luck," he whispered. "That would have been an addition to my collection, to be sure." But how had it come here? He had heard nothing of a butterfly enclosure in the palace.

Perhaps he could find Tumney and beg entrance to whatever hall this was. Immediately he was reminded of his errand and, on impulse, removed the key and tried it in the lock. The bolt turned soundlessly. Tristam looked around, a bit of guilt surfacing at making so free of the King's palace. *No one will care*, he told himself, *I've already been granted access to the greatest secret in the gardens.*

He pushed the door open, careful to turn the lock again as he passed. The butterfly was not to be seen and Tristam ascended a short flight of steps, regretting his lack of a proper net. At the top of the stairs a pathway of fine sand wound into the foliage of yet another entrapped Oceana. *It is like a puzzle*, he thought, *one inside another, inside another yet.* He stopped after each stride to search for the crimson tip. The sounds of a fountain bubbled through the dense trees and bushes. He almost expected to hear the wind in the palms as he had in the dream.

Overhead an intricately supported dome of glass showed a sky rapidly filling with clouds. Something moved. A glimpse of white in the dark green of the jungle. Tristam stepped off the path. The undergrowth was not so thick this time, and he moved more easily and more quietly. In the voice of the fountain Tristam could almost imagine a trill of laughter.

Again—white wings like a lady's scarf snatched away on the breeze. He began to make out the far side of the structure in glimpses through the flora— gray-stone, he thought. The sound of laughter came again, and Tristam was almost sure it was not the voice of the fountain. And then he saw water falling. Two more careful steps and he realized that there was no fountain at all; this was a waterfall cascading over rock into a clear pool. A natural composition from Oceana had been reproduced with enormous care.

The laughter came again and this time Tristam knew it was no auditory trick. It was a woman's laugh, though bitter and lacking joy.

"I despair, Your Majesty, of ever seeing our way through this," Tristam believed the woman said, though the falling water made hearing difficult. Even so the voice was known to him—a voice he had heard cry out in passion—the Duchess of Morland and, by the form of address, she could only be speaking to the King.

The young naturalist began to take a step back when a flash of white called his attention. The duchess' gown, and then the duchess herself, appeared through the leaves. Tristam sank to his knees. He could see the woman plainly now. She paced to the edge of the pool and stared into the falling water. This might be the duchess, but Tristam had not imagined her like this. She looked tired, defeated, overwhelmed by sadness. After a moment, she turned away and disappeared behind foliage.

How do I get myself into such situations? Tristam wondered. *Martyr's blood.* He started to retreat, but the duchess appeared again, preventing his withdrawal.

She stood at the edge of the pool, speaking over her shoulder as though she could not bear to face the man she addressed. "If you cannot bear up, how will I?" she asked quietly, but there was no answer. "The thought of what they might do. . . ." She shook her head as though this idea were too painful.

There was a long silence and the duchess moved back out of Tristam's view. He retreated a step, then another. A window opened in the foliage, and he could see the duchess again. She appeared to kneel in the sand. Tristam froze in place.

"I don't know where we shall find the strength," the duchess began and then her voice, pleading, fell so low he could not hear it. Then she spoke plainly again. "These last thirty years—they have been a golden age in Farr history. Without your wisdom, Wilam," she said, using the King's name as though she were a sovereign queen herself, "there would have been endless war. And now this." The melancholy in her voice touched Tristam.

She reached out and Tristam saw her take the dark spotted hands of a figure seated before her, a figure hidden by the jungle.

"*Yes. Nothing but old men standing between sanity and chaos,*" a voice said and the sound rocked Tristam. He had never heard such a voice! It was not a man's voice at all but an echo of a voice—distant and distorted as though it came from infinite depths and distances, funneled up an endless well.

"*Do not cry, child. I have passed my time, passed my golden age by far. I cannot continue. The dreams . . . nay, nightmares have begun to haunt my days as well as my nights. If I let my mind wander for an instant, they are upon me like howling wolves. The wolves of madness—Farrelle protect me. If only I could leave my throne to you, Elorin, I would pass on in peace at last. But there is no peace for me. I know now that one can outlive one's time on earth. My entire generation is gone. You cannot know what terrible loneliness that brings. You are all the joy that is left to me."* He paused and Tristam saw the duchess pulled gently forward, disappearing into the King's embrace.

"*Elorin, I am sorry,*" the awful voice went on. "*I grow selfish and difficult. I do not mean to hurt you, child—you, of all people. I will not give up, just yet. Farrelle forgive me, but I will continue a little longer.*"

Tristam slipped back several paces on hands and knees and then turned and fled as though he himself were hunted by wolves.

⮌ Thirteen

Tristam was walking on the hill above Highloft Manor, a canvas shoulder bag bouncing against his thigh, his ash-plant punching the soft ground at every other step. A wide-brimmed hat protected his face from the maturing sun, but even so his arms and neck were the nut-brown of a haymaker's.

A flicker of yellow in a holly had Tristam pulling Dandish's Fromme glass out of the shoulder bag—but even that instrument could not entice a bird to appear if it were disinclined to cooperate. A half-hour's wait produced nothing, and Tristam gave it up and passed on. Usually he would take such a thing as a challenge, but today he did not feel his usual self—nor had he for some time.

A long month had passed since his return from Avonel, and Tristam had become progressively more downcast and enervated with each day. It was not at all like him, he knew, but he could not shake himself out of this funk. High summer had come and gone and the season hovered now on the cusp of late summer. A stay in the lake country with Jaimy was looming. Tristam was not looking forward to it at all and had begun to consider possible excuses.

He sat down on a stone perched on the roll of the hill and opened his water flask. Below him the Tithy ran, its narrow course tucked under the hill's curving shoulder. Tristam surveyed his world: the old manor house with its various roof lines sloping off, each with its own idea of "level"; his uncle's eccentric gardens defying the laws of taste in both design and color; dilapidated outbuildings, each original only in its progress toward utter ruin. The pasture land, divided by a web of drystone walls and hedgerows, ranged outward to the surrounding hills crowned with nodding green woods. Today it did not seem the wonderful gift it once had.

Nothing had gone well since his return to Locfal. Jenny and her infernally pragmatic father had welcomed him home as the returning hero, but Tristam had not responded as he thought he would to this turn of events. In fact, he had become more and more distant, and this had caused a cooling in return. He could not help but think Jenny was a little relieved at this. They were not a match, he had realized.

His lack of success at the royal palace was weighing heavily on him—not that he had been given half a chance—but even so he had begun to feel that this had been a blessing in disguise. It saved him from having to fail in everyone else's eyes. Allowed to continue, he was now convinced, he would not have discovered the solution—Dandish's solution.

Something else to add to his growing melancholia.

Tristam had once thought that his estate would provide him with a lifetime of study in natural history, but recently it merely looked small and somewhat run-down. The journey to Avonel, he realized, had brought about a change in his perception . . . but it was a change he did not yet understand.

He told himself over and over that his encounter with the Duchess of Morland had no bearing on his present state. She was, after all, coldhearted and manipulative. Someone better kept at a distance. But the truth was, his thoughts never strayed from the duchess for long. Nor did they stray far from the last, overheard, conversation.

More than anything, Tristam felt as though he had been swept into a whirl-pool, spun about several times, and then suddenly ejected into a sleepy back-water. His time away had left him in utter confusion, and the more time elapsed the less certain he was of the few things he thought were clear.

What in the round world was so important about *regis*?

"It is all a muddle," Tristam thought aloud. "A puzzle within a maze."

At least he had discovered the identity of Valary, or, thought he had. An eccentric historian—more highly regarded by Entonne scholars than he was in his own land. Tristam had written the man, hoping he was the Valary mentioned by Dandish, but so far he had received no letter in return. In his present state, Tristam had even begun to think this was somehow his fault.

Dandish's journals had been the subject of endless scrutiny this past month. Every word mulled over. Any sentence the slightest bit obscure analyzed for hidden meaning. This had led to such flights of fancy that Tristam had begun to doubt the soundness of his own mind and had put the books away.

And then there was the fragment hidden in the field glass. A warning Tristam still believed. Well, Dandish would be pleased by one thing. Tristam was as far from this matter as one could be and still remain in Farrland. If only he could shake it out of his mind.

Tristam had spent many a sleepless night wondering how Dandish had solved the *regis* problem. He had spent almost as much time in this as he had reliving his brief evening of love with the Duchess of Morland. Had she really thought he was Bertillon?

He pushed his hair back from his face, letting out an involuntary sigh. More than anything, he had begun to feel that he needed to get away. Escape for a few months. He had even considered a trip to his vineyard on the island of Farrow. At least he would be engaged in something.

Tristam's aging retriever came panting up the hill and threw itself down at his feet. He reached out automatically and scratched behind its ears.

"Well, should we go down and find you some supper? Eh?"

The dog managed three beats with its tail, the normal response to being addressed on matters not completely clear. Man and beast followed a well-worn track down the hill, the ash-plant punctuating the sounds of their passing with perfect regularity.

Tristam hung his bag on a hook in the hall, tossed his walking stick into a corner, and proceeded into his uncle's comfortable old home. His housekeeper, Mrs. Cowper, was dusting in the parlor and, without being noticed, Tristam scooped the day's post off a stand and made a quick retreat out onto the small terrace.

He collapsed into the best of several decrepit chairs and examined his mail. The first was a letter from Jaimy and he tore this open immediately.

My dear cousin:

> *I apologize for not writing sooner; I have been terribly busy helping the Somers' household prepare for a stay in the lake country.*
>
> *It shan't be long now! I'm looking forward to our idyll with an enthusiasm that you may only begin to imagine; not least for the opportunity to see you again and to smash away at some promising rocks as well. I do intend to help and not spend every minute with my sweet Alissa, as much as I would like to (note: I said idyll not idle).*
>
> *Now. . . . I have an answer to your inquiry. No, Professor Somers has not soured on either of us (quite the contrary, I think). I will tell you why he was so cool to you at the Society meeting but you cannot, you must not, breathe a word of it.*
>
> *You may or may not remember that the good professor was accompanied by a young man? Perhaps you didn't notice. All the same, it was hardly a lad at all, for it was my own Alissa (with her beautiful curls tucked up under a wig) dressed as a young gentleman!*
>
> *It says much for the powers of observation of our most skilled empiricists that not one of them noticed—including yourself, Tristam. Of course*

that is why Somers avoided you; he thought you might recognize Alissa and give the game away—though I am sure you wouldn't have done so intentionally.

Now you are a party to the secret and I trust you will not say a word. Alissa gave me a full account of the evening, which you must have enjoyed. Professor Somers assures me your name has been bandied about as a Fellow-to-be. You need only produce a substantial piece of work and the ring is yours!

I must run. Write if you get a chance.

Yours in haste,
Jaimas

PS: I have thought a great deal about various matters and look forward to discussing these with you again. All my preparations are complete. How go your own?

Tristam dropped the letter onto a bench and stared off across the garden. Jaimy's overflowing happiness made him feel even more desolate. He was jealous, he realized. Not that he begrudged happiness to his cousin, whom Tristam felt was a deserving individual indeed. It was merely the contrast between their states that struck him.

"Well, good for J," Tristam muttered. As he said this, he noticed, in the shadowed branches of an ancient hornbeam, the pale shape of his uncle's falcon. "My familiar," Tristam said. And then to the raptor, "He is gone forever, you foolish bird. Be off."

"Who is there?!" Mrs. Cowper's voice came from inside the open doors.

"Tristam, Mrs. C." Tristam called out.

The grandmotherly housekeeper appeared in the doorway, wiping her hands on her apron. "Oh, there you are, Mr. Flattery. I am deafer by the day, I didn't hear you come in." She looked around. "Were you speaking to someone just now?"

"Just a bird."

"Oh . . . I thought I'd heard something. Well, do excuse me." She turned back to her chores but stopped. "I've almost forgotten." She began fumbling in the pockets of her apron, and finally produced an envelope. "I had meant to give this to you straight off when you came in—had I heard."

Tristam took the envelope. It was postmarked from Avonel.

"I hope it's something to cheer you, sir, and not. . . ." She trailed off.

"Thank you, Mrs. Cowper." Tristam tore at the flap and then realized the housekeeper stood looking on. "*Thank you, Mrs. Cowper.*"

She reluctantly disappeared back into the house and Tristam removed the single sheet of paper, a slight tremor in his hand. A letter from the duchess was what he hoped for, but a note from Tumney was what he expected; not what the envelope, in fact, contained—a brief note from Sir Roderick Palle.

Dear Mr. Flattery:

I write trusting that you will treat everything said in the strictest confidence. As we hold no hope of our Kingfoil ever bearing seeds, His Majesty's government has issued instructions to the Admiralty for the preparation of a voyage to Oceana. The purpose of this voyage will be to procure fertile seeds or plants of the regis variety. As this purpose is to be known only to the senior officer and to a naturalist, your name immediately came to mind. It is the greatest good fortune that you are both qualified and already aware of our plight. I must say your reputation, and the high regard of several of your professors, have also been a factor.

Therefore, I am offering the position of naturalist on said voyage to you. Due to the gravity of the matter, a ship will be made ready with all haste to sail before summer's end. I require your decision in the return post. This gives you little time to consider, I realize, but it cannot be avoided.

I would say, if I may write candidly, that, though such endeavors are not without risk, similar voyages have made the reputations of our most eminent empiricists. There is also the possibility of finding some clue as to the fate of Gregory, not to mention performing an invaluable service to the King.

I await your reply,
Sir Roderick Palle

Tristam looked up, his gaze climbing over the nearby hills. In the sky beyond he could see clouds borne up on a distant wind. He realized that if he had prayed, this letter would be the answer to that prayer.

Fourteen

The vessel in question was built at Crouch by Fishborn and Daly, her present age three years seven months. She is full built, single bottom with galleried stern and comes nearest the tonnage mentioned in your warrant and is not so old by 15 months. She is 90 feet in length of upper deck; of extreme breadth 24 feet 4 inches; in draught 11 feet fully laden. Her burthen in tons 290 71/94. I cannot conceive of a more fitting vessel for service in remote parts. The survey indicates a refit necessary as her use has been hard, though she is sound in all her parts. Swallow could certainly be made ready for sea by the date required.

"So that is your ship, Mr. Flattery," Sir Roderick said, "though we may hope that not all the claims prove as false as that in the last line."

"She is ready for sea now, though?" Tristam sat in Sir Roderick's office looking at a letter from the Surveyor's Office of the Navy Board to the Admiralty.

"Yes . . . well, there are some special arrangements required to accommodate her officers and passengers. But they should be all but complete now." Roderick stood, leafing through a pile of papers on his desk.

Tristam turned and gazed out the window that overlooked the grounds of the Tellaman Palace. Trees were showing hints of the colors they would soon wear in full glory. The autumn migration was well advanced.

Roderick sat down and looked directly at Tristam. "It has come about that you will have another aboard whose concern is the *regis* plant." The King's Man paused. "The Duchess of Morland is determined to make this voyage and, remarkably, the King has allowed it."

Tristam could not quite believe that he had heard correctly. "The *duchess . . . ?*" he said stupidly.

Roderick nodded.

Tristam shifted in his chair. His thought processes seemed to have paused. The conversation he had overheard months ago in this very building came back to mind, but suggested no explanation.

"I was against it, as you might imagine. And the Admiralty refused—initially." The knight shook his head. "But we have orders from the King . . . so the duchess will be aboard when the *Swallow* weighs."

But I have signed aboard this ship to escape, Tristam thought. *Escape from this woman among a hundred other things.*

Tristam had hoped this would be a curative voyage, ridding him of his mild obsession with the duchess, restoring his spirits. And now she would be aboard the same vessel.

To his chagrin he felt his hopes rise at this news as well.

"The Duchess," Roderick began, interrupting the younger man's thoughts, "has not undertaken this voyage for her health. You understand, Mr. Flattery, that any Kingfoil or seed procured is the express property of the King of Farrland? To treat it in any other way would be treason."

What had Palle just said?

"I . . . understand completely, Sir Roderick."

Palle managed a thin smile, almost a facial tick. "You will find the captain a solid man; not *all sail and no ballast*, as the saying goes. Captain Stern, by name. He was not given command of this voyage without reason, Tristam. I can say with assurance that Captain Stern will not be swayed from his duty, no matter what occurs.

"He was senior lieutenant on Gregory's first voyage and would have sailed with the great navigator again if he had not been appointed to his own command. An amateur natural philosopher of some knowledge: Gregory's influence, no doubt. I'm sure you will find much in common." Roderick appeared to consider for a moment as though there were something to remember. "Stern is much like his mentor Gregory in other ways as well, Mr. Flattery. He is very concerned that officers aboard his ship conduct themselves in a gentlemanly fashion. Not that I think you would ever do otherwise, mind you, but much of the irreverence that is common among university men would be . . . misunderstood by Stern."

"I take your meaning, sir. I shall be on my guard." Tristam paused, then offered. "Stern seems a doubly likely name for a ship's captain." How could he find humor in anything at this moment?

Roderick was leafing through his papers again and did not smile. "I dare say."

Obviously much had been going on in the court in the past months. He gathered his nerve for a few seconds. "Sir Roderick? If I may ask; what has inclined the duchess to undertake this voyage? It shall not be a comfortable outing, by all accounts."

Roderick leaned back in his chair and sighed. Exasperation was not something the King's Man displayed often. "Mr. Flattery, what the Duchess of Morland intends at any given time is one of the great mysteries of our age. But the King is under her spell. . . ." He looked at Tristam and raised his eyebrows. "This herb, Tristam; it keeps the King alive. Never forget that. It has caused no end of folly among those who know of its existence. Consider what you yourself discovered about Professor Dandish. . . . I wish you good fortune, Mr. Flattery."

⌒ Fifteen

The fountains before the Tellaman Palace were known throughout all the lands of the Entide Sea for both their artistry and their technical ingenuity. The bronze sculptures were leafed in gold: ancient gods and goddesses; characters from mythology; historical figures; and fantastic creatures of land, sea, air, and combinations thereof. Water jets would suddenly erupt, rise to the height of the palace, and then subside or disappear altogether. At times, thirty-some different fountains would spout simultaneously.

Roderick stared out over the pool to the island on which the main fountains stood. An ancient god rode a giant seahorse that sprayed a fan of water from its mouth, while porpoises leaped around them, water spouting from their blowholes. Roderick had often wondered why the sculptor had chosen to portray this god of the sea as he had—a strong, handsome face contorted in anguish. There was no myth that Palle knew that would explain it. The knight had come to believe that this anguish was the emotion of the artist who had designed and built the fountain—completing it just before his own death.

Alone among the other figures this one seemed to be of the real world, Roderick thought: a god learning that he was mortal after all.

Hawksmoor interrupted the knight's contemplation of the fountains.

"There is little to tell, Sir Roderick. The Entonne are showing Varese's letters to no one, though I expect there will be some forgeries produced before long. I have, however, learned one thing of interest. When Varese first found them, he took the letters to a man named Valary to have them authenticated. This would have been some months ago."

Roderick nodded. He had not expected even Hawksmoor to be able to get access to these letters, for they were undoubtedly in the hands of Count Massenet. "Valary? Should I know this name?"

Hawksmoor looked down at the ground for a moment. "No, I don't think so, Sir Roderick." He paused again. Unlike the man to be reticent.

"Out with it, Mr. Hawksmoor."

The man cleared his throat. "Well, the man is an historian—something of a rival to our Mr. Wells, it would seem. Mr. Wells maintains the man is a fraud. . . ."

"And . . . ?"

"I am afraid that professional jealousy can occasionally cloud anyone's judgment, Sir Roderick."

Roderick used his foot to brush a small pebble into the water.

The two stood on the edge of the pool, backed by an area of open lawn. Not the best point from which to observe the fountain but a perfect place to speak privately. The day was warm, autumn—the flowers now outdone by the vivid colors of the trees.

"This man Valary wrote a book about the mages—translated and published only in Entonne—which would explain how Varese knew of him. It would seem that Valary is highly regarded by our friends across the water."

"And we have not seen this book?"

Hawksmoor hesitated. "No, sir," he answered quietly.

"Find me a copy, Mr. Hawksmoor, and we need to know more of Valary. He dwells in Entonne?"

"No, sir. Though I believe he travels there often."

"Well, I do not like the sound of a Farrlander being regarded as an authority on mages by the Entonne."

"No, sir."

Roderick moved a few paces down the stone walk and then stopped, Hawksmoor keeping pace, moving almost silently, the knight realized.

"I believe there has been no contact between Mr. Flattery and the duchess, Sir Roderick, if that is of any comfort."

Roderick shrugged. "That is about to end. He didn't seem to be suffering from melancholia when I met him. . . ."

"No," Hawksmoor said. "I think the prospect of this voyage has lifted his spirits. Which is a good thing—I was afraid young Flattery might follow the example of his father."

"A concern of mine, as well," Roderick said. He glanced out at the sea god astride his mount. "I do hope he does nothing so rash. We may have need of Mr. Flattery."

"Not for two years, I hope. Our efforts go well, I trust?"

Roderick tilted his head from side to side. "Well enough." Roderick looked out again at the anguished god half lost in the mist. "What of Massenet?"

"If he were not the most social man in Avonel—and the most popular—I would be able to tell more of his purpose. As it is. . . ." Hawksmoor stopped, thinking. He never offered more than he actually knew, no matter what, and that was one of the many reasons Palle valued him. "The count is so skilled, sir. I will tell you truthfully that I have some admiration for the man."

"His weakness is the ladies of Avonel. Realizing his country will not soon conquer us in the field, I think this count has decided to make his conquest of Farrland in the bedchamber. That is where Massenet will make his mistake."

"I'm sure you're right, Sir Roderick, but he has not done so yet."

"Never fear, Mr. Hawksmoor, men are betrayed by their appetites." Roderick turned back toward the palace, but stopped. "Valary—everything that can be learned about him. I will deal with Wells."

"Immediately, Sir Roderick."

The King's Man nodded, and set off briskly toward the palace, the anguish of the god forgotten for the time being.

～ Sixteen

"Flames, I wish you had spoken to me before agreeing to this voyage, Tristam," Jaimy said. "I think it is a terrible error."

They had been over this before. Tristam tried not to show annoyance. "My answer was required by return post, Jaimas. I am not the only trained naturalist in Farrland. Hesitation was not possible."

Tristam and his cousin sat in the window of an ale house overlooking the harbor of Avonel. Out among the many ships they could make out the bark, *Swallow*, lying at anchor, her decks and rigging teeming with sailors who appeared to be running in all directions simultaneously.

Tristam's mind was in a similar confusion, for preparations had been lengthy and complex. At the last moment, the Society had requested that he perform a number of tasks for various fellows and, though Tristam had been delighted to oblige, it had not made things easier.

But there was something he had meant to tell Jaimy. . . .

"I had a letter from this man Valary, at last."

Jaimy's expression changed immediately—interest kindled.

"It was lucky he replied when he did or his letter would have lain unread until my return." Tristam reached into an inner pocket of his coat and retrieved an envelope, his name and address across the face in an odd, irregular hand. "I'm afraid you will have a time deciphering it, the man's writing is abominable." He handed the letter to his cousin, anxious to hear Jaimy's response.

My dear Mr. Flattery:

> *I am sorry to have taken so long to reply, but I have been abroad these last months and your letters lay in a mountain of others awaiting my return. I am greatly sorry to hear of the passing of Professor Dandish, for, though I never had the honor of making his acquaintance, I had great respect for his work. It was very considerate of you to write and inform me of his passing.*
>
> *In answer to your question: yes, I did correspond with the professor, though one letter only. I am not certain what bearing, if any, it might have upon this inquiry of the professor's that you attempt to complete, but I will*

write you out a copy and send it along. The letter was not of a personal nature and I'm sure the professor would not mind. Interestingly, I had cause to mention Erasmus Flattery in this letter, whom I assume to be a relation of yours?

Good luck to you, sir. Do not hesitate to call upon me at any time. I am always willing to offer any assistance to a colleague of the professor's.

Your servant,
F. T. Valary

My dear Professor Dandish:

I cannot tell you my delight at receiving a letter from a gentleman I have so long admired! I will confess that I felt some pride that a man of such learning would approach me for information. But I fear I shall not provide answers that you will find satisfactory, for, in my pursuit, things are not easily measured or verified.

As the professor is no doubt aware, the mages were enormously secretive about their arts. I fear the result of this has been endless conjecture over some fifteen hundreds of years. Sifting this, looking for "truth" is a pursuit with few rewards, though occasionally one strikes a rich vein. Several of the matters you refer to are likely not verifiable and, in my opinion, not accurate. They had their root in an odd little book written by a man named Decker, who served in the house of Lucklow. The man was a servant and upon Lucklow's death thought he could earn some money from an account of his years with the mage. I suspect a true account would have held little of interest for the reading public at large, so much was fabricated (perhaps by the book's publisher, as is their wont).

As to the longevity: I think there can be no question. Certainly Lord Eldrich, whose birth and death were carefully recorded, lived to be one hundred, seventeen years. And I am quite sure that Dunsenay could not have been less than one hundred, thirty-three—and perhaps several years older. Most men in the time of Dunsenay could not have expected spans of more than fifty-some years. I will say, categorically, that Pylf did not see two hundred, twenty years, or even anything like it. This is a popular myth, I'm afraid, but typically the mages lived many years more than their contemporaries and there is no evidence that any succumbed to the common ailments or even to the terrible epidemics of their own ages. I often think that most people's fascination with the mages is inspired by curiosity about this great longevity and nothing else. Of course their longevity is, in most cases, quite beyond dispute whereas so many other things attributed to them are difficult, if not impossible to verify. Magic, people have come to doubt, but to live to twice, or even thrice, man's common span—that is too tempting to disbelieve!

Herb-lore, as you say, was the province of the mages, and it surprises me that gentlemen of your pursuit have not paid more attention to this. Certainly they knew much of healing, and some of this knowledge they did not hoard so carefully. I could, if it would be of use to you, trace a good number of common herbal remedies that had their origin with one or other of the mages. But if they were free with some knowledge, they were extremely close with far more, and, like all of their arts, this one has passed from knowledge. I spoke at length to the late Erasmus Flattery about this and though that worthy gentleman said a great deal, when I reflected upon his words, I could find little to profit me. Rather like the writings of students I'm sure you have had occasion to see, where the author hopes to hide lack of inspiration behind a wall of well-wrought prose. Now Erasmus Flattery was a man of some substance, I am well aware, but whatever he learned from his three years in the house of Eldrich he took to his grave.

I remember well that this worthy gentleman questioned me much about my own work, which flattered me more than a little at the time. Later, I had cause to reflect that Mr. Flattery's interest was as keen as my own, and I suspected he had not been so free with his knowledge as I had been with mine. But he did tell me, and I think he let this slip, that Eldrich had once intentionally infected himself with the yellow fever merely to observe the effects! And then, in a matter of days, grew well again! I do not think it possible that he observed this himself but more likely was told it by someone else in the house.

Specifically, was there a link between some course of herbal physic and longevity? I cannot answer with any certainty. Certainly there is evidence that this might be the case, but equally there is evidence that this great age was achieved through other, more arcane, methods. Holderlin, who developed a great friendship with Queen Vaill, wrote many letters to Her Majesty and I think he dearly enjoyed dropping hints about matters "magical." In one such letter he wrote: "It is true, Your Majesty, that to extend the life of a great ruler would benefit everyone in Farrland, and perhaps beyond, but long life is not a gift a mage can offer. To live to the age that some have, one must follow the art with an unwavering, iron discipline, else one would pay a terrible price."

He said nothing more that I am aware of on this subject, but this (rather dark) hint was quite uncharacteristic of the mages. One is left with the impression that, whatever the mechanism by which they extended *their lives, it was part of the larger discipline, perhaps a result of practicing the art as a whole.*

Now, to your final question: do I believe, myself? Well, sir, to answer in the affirmative would open me to the ridicule of my peers and would also cast my own objectivity into question. This particular area of scholarship has suffered such raillery over the years that I am loath to endanger any respectability my studies have finally achieved.

Have I danced enough? Let me simply say this. Men of obvious power, the nature of which is difficult to explain by currently accepted methods, lived among us until quite recently. I am convinced that at least some of the feats attributed to them actually did occur—how they were achieved, again, I cannot say. Are there still mages among us—hidden? No, I don't think so. I believe Eldrich was the last, and it would appear that he was not even a particularly powerful practitioner of the art. I believe their time had passed, for reasons that we do not understand. Perhaps even the mages did not understand themselves. And they were very careful to take their knowledge with them—a fact which is more suggestive of their intentions at the end than anything else we know. Except perhaps this: Eldrich is buried in the grounds of his family home and no one is allowed near the grave—but I have been told by someone who is in a position to know that the inscription on the headstone reads:

The last to begin
The journey out of darkness
Takes but a lifetime

As cryptic as anything that can, with any certainty, be attributed to a mage (and not helped by the lack of punctuation), but, "the last to begin" would appear to mean the last of the mages. Or so I surmise.

I hope, sir, that this has been of some use to you. Please do not hesitate to write again if I may be of further service. I have information about herb-lore that I believe you would find of interest.

Your servant,
F. T. Valary

Jaimy looked up. "Flaming martyrs," he managed.

"Not what you were expecting?"

"I. . . . No! What in the round world does this mean?"

Tristam had been pondering that very question day and night for the past week. "It is quite clear what it means, I think. That isn't the problem. The difficulty is accepting the implications." Tristam glanced out the window and then back at his cousin. "Dandish must have believed this herb had something to do with longevity—the King, after all, is very old, past his centenary now—and connected it somehow with the only other group known to have achieved this much-sought-after lengthening of years: the mages. It would seem that, for reasons unstated, Dandish saw some danger in this and destroyed his planting and the notes of his inquiry. I can't think of another explanation."

"But, Tristam, the Kingfoil was first brought from Oceana by Gregory— only some thirty years past. It cannot have any connection with mages, the last of whom died near to half a century ago."

"The logic of that is impeccable, cousin."

"And this talk of our Uncle Erasmus. . . . Well, we both know that it is completely absurd. Erasmus was no more 'magical' than this mug of ale." He shoved his glass toward Tristam. "Dandish didn't believe this, did he?"

Tristam pressed fingers into the corners of his eyes. He was tired and struggling to make his brain function. "Perhaps. . . . Perhaps not. But what if he thought others believed? I think we are too young to really understand what it means to age. But it has driven people to mad desperation often enough. Think of the number of people who have been duped by charlatans who promised a return of youth? Some of our earliest voyages of exploration were motivated by rulers who sought rejuvenation. The 'apples of immortality' is not just a phrase in a hundred bad poems—people once believed these apples existed. Fountains with enchanted waters. Elixirs. Potions. It was not so long ago that men sought the secret of turning lead into gold. Turning old age into youth—it is an irresistible myth, as Valary says.

"If some people believe, it would explain a great deal, I think. It might even explain why the professor destroyed his planting. He was an old man himself— he probably understood the lengths others might go to."

Stronger those few days and my arrhythmia was all but gone. The phrase surfaced unbidden.

"Blood and flames, Tristam. You think these people are seeking some elixir of youth?" He gave a short laugh, almost a snort. "Courtiers have always been notoriously foolish, but this is beyond all. Roderick Palle? He is not a foolish man, Tristam; I have met him." Jaimy took a drink of his ale, his focus inward. "Who is this man Valary, anyway?"

"That I can answer, at least somewhat. He is an historian of some note. Well respected in his own area. But apparently he has as a hobby the study of mages. He has even written a book, a history, though he could not find a publisher in Farrland, for the book is apparently not very sensational—an academic study, in fact. It has been translated and published in Entonne, however. You might find a copy of it while I'm away."

"But he is a crank, wouldn't you say?"

Tristam shrugged. "You read the letter. Was it the work of a crank?"

Jaimy picked up the letter and stared at it for a moment. "I know what you mean, but the most successful charlatans are those who seem the most reasonable."

"Whether he is sincere hardly matters, Jaimas. My guess now is that at least some believe this herb we seek has the property of extending one's years—the King's great age, you see. Pathetic really, for I'm sure this will turn out to be no more substantial than the 'apples of immortality': the King is old, but not yet unnaturally so." As he said this, he remembered the voice he had heard in the arboretum—hardly natural. "If even one person is desperate enough to believe, what would he not do?"

"*Ipsword,*" Jaimy said, as though it were a word with intrinsic meaning.

"Exactly. The professor must have heard of the man's death. Dandish was no fool. He would have realized immediately what this meant."

Jaimy looked out over the harbor and then quickly turned back to his cousin. "It isn't too late to give up this voyage, Tristam."

"No, it is too late." Tristam looked down at the table, unable to bear the concern in his cousin's eyes. "No, I will go on. To bring us back some answers if for no other reason." He shrugged, offering up his hands as though they bore an explanation. "It is the opportunity of a lifetime, Jaimy, as you realize. A chance to make my name in my field. I can't give it up because of the foolish beliefs of some courtiers. And it seems likely that this seed does have some medicinal purpose: it keeps the King in health. That much seems true, and for that reason alone it is an endeavor worth pursuing. I will go, J. I seem meant to go, really. I was Dandish's protégé. I worked on Baron Trevelyan's collection. This task is for me to complete, I'm sure."

Jaimy nodded, the concern not leaving his face. "I should be going with you," he said quietly.

"Your fiancée would not approve." Mention of Alissa gained a small smile. "I told you that Viscount Elsworth is coming as well?"

"You did. Seldom has one of His Majesty's survey ships had such an esteemed company," Jaimy said dryly. "A duchess and a murderer. One hand of velvet and one of iron. I would imagine the duchess must consider missing an opening night at the theater an intolerable hardship, and yet she takes on this. . . ." Jaimy eyed his cousin. "She can't possibly believe she can maintain her youth? The duchess is certainly not that foolish," Jaimy said, and then almost smiled. "Her decision has the cream of Farr society in a whirl of constant speculation."

Tristam tried to smile in return. "Well, I will let you in on the real truth: a race of talented milliners and dressmakers has been discovered dwelling in the great southern ocean. You know what lengths some will go to for fashion."

One of Sir Roderick's footmen came rushing into the room at that moment and, seeing Tristam, made a beeline to his table.

"Excuse me, Mr. Flattery, but some sailors have taken all your baggage. I couldn't stop them."

Tristam bolted out of his chair. "Blood and flames! Were they drunk?"

"Not so's I could tell, sir. I was told to say it was Jack Beechnut transported your things to the *Swallow*." The poor man was obviously wretched. "I am sorry, sir, I know you charged me to let no one touch them."

"About this tall?" Tristam held up his hand. "Curly, almost-blond hair?" The footman nodded, and Tristam burst out laughing.

"You know him, sir?"

"If his name was Beacham and not Beechnut, I do indeed." He sat down again.

"It might have been Beacham, sir. I didn't take proper notice, I'm afraid. Is there anything I should do, sir?"

"I think my baggage is in good hands. Please take Sir Roderick this note, with my regards and thanks. He has been most helpful, as you have yourself." Tristam quickly wrote a note for the footman and gave the man a coin.

When they were alone again, the two young men sat in silence for a few moments and then Jaimy turned to his cousin, his face serious. "You be careful, Tristam Flattery. Watch that bloody-handed viscount. You're the only cousin whose company I can bear for more than half of an hour. I should not want to lose you."

"And I don't want to be lost. I shall be on my guard at all times." *And drink only spring water, gathered at sunrise.*

The Admiralty was housed in an ancient building that stared down, many-eyed, upon the harbor of Avonel. It was here that decisions were made to send ships out to explore the globe, to blockade harbors, or to bring war to an enemy. Here was the brain of the great beast that was spreading over the oceans of the globe.

Inside the Admiralty, oak floors, which appeared to have been heaved by frost, creaked loudly as men set foot upon them, in stark contrast to the somber voices, the hushed conversations. Captain Josiah Stern had been in the building before, but this was his first visit to the fifth floor. It was here that the Sea Lord and the senior admirals had their offices. It was on this floor that the war room lay, waiting patiently, its massive charts changed every fortnight as new information was received from merchant ships, surveying vessels, and ships of war—the mysteries of the world being revealed inexorably.

A "midshipman" led Captain Stern along a corridor, the floor marking their passage with groans and creaks, as though they were the protests of a living thing. Despite his uniform and rank, the young man who escorted Stern was merely an office lackey, but this was the Navy and every man in it held a rank, whether or not he had set foot aboard a ship. This lad had not, Stern was quite certain. And in ten years he would be deciding the fates of seamen, like Stern himself. The captain felt a surge of resentment toward this boy—a mere teenager, and not overly impressed by the captain who accompanied him, that was obvious.

At least the men who held the high offices had once been sailors. The present First Lord of the Navy had spent a life at sea: Admiral Sir Jonathan Gage, a man Stern had once glimpsed as he passed in a carriage. The distance between a mere post captain and the Sea Lord was far greater than the few floors that commonly separated them would suggest.

The midshipman turned Stern over to Admiral Gage's secretary, an efficient middle-aged man in a post captain's uniform, but a bureaucrat nonetheless.

Seated to await the Sea Lord's pleasure, Stern was given a cup of tea and time to ponder. It was highly unusual for the captain of a survey vessel to be called to the office of the highest ranking officer in the service. Unheard of, might be more accurate. Of course, not every survey ship had members of the king's court aboard—and one a woman, at that. He sipped his tea and looked over at the secretary who was busily arranging papers on a massive desk.

Stern wondered what in the name of Farrelle had brought the Duchess of Morland aboard his cramped little ship. When he had first been told, he had not asked: one did not question orders. Not if one wanted to advance. No matter what kind of fool's errand a man was sent on, he did not think to question its value or even its practicality. The naval officers took pride in their dedication to duty. Every one of them would sail their command into certain destruction if ordered to do so. And the men before the masts of five hundred other ships would sing a sad song of it—sad and proud.

But this did not stop a man from wondering, in the privacy of his own thoughts, of course. The Duchess of Morland?

Stern was not a well connected officer. He had come up through the ranks— the son of a mildly successful banker. His patron in the service, Sir Josiah Fitsch, had died years earlier leaving Stern "orphaned," as the saying went. But Stern had managed to rise on merit alone—although slowly. Sailing as first officer to Gregory had been a boost. Then he had made his post. But he was forty-four now, an age when many another led squadrons, flew the pennant of a Rear Admiral, or even more. Such was the nature of the service. Not that the incompetent necessarily rose simply because of their family or connections— but even the skilled officer needed support from someone within this building. And the sons of mildly successful bankers did not hobnob with the right crowd to find that support.

The death of Fitsch (a man married to an aunt of Stern's mother) had been more than the loss of a mentor, a friend, and a good officer. It had likely been the death of Stern's career as well.

For that reason, Stern was more than a little surprised to find himself here. He could not help but hope this might be an indication of some change—a sea change.

"Captain Stern?"

The secretary stood before him, his head bent a little, like a manservant. Stern had obviously been lost in his thoughts.

"Sir?"

"The admiral will see you now."

Stern set his cup back onto the silver tray and stood, taking up his tricorn and tucking it awkwardly under his arm. He wished he had a glass in which to check his uniform.

The large doors to the Sea Lord's office were opened and as Stern was about to enter, the secretary whispered, "Sir Jonathan:" the admiral's preferred form of address—something known by every man in the navy, Stern was sure. Decidedly nervous, Captain Josiah Stern put one foot before the other rather stiffly and went to see what the future might hold.

The admiral sat at a desk so large that it immediately brought to mind the deck of a ship of war. It even had a miniature cannon positioned on one corner. Admiral Gage was a man of about seventy years, his skin and hair giving the appearance of having had the pigment bleached out of them until they were as white and clear as sun-melted soap.

The man bent over a stack of papers on his desk, his face so close to the page that his long nose could almost have come away with ink on its tip. Although the admiral was a man of normal size, behind this desk he appeared to be as small as a child.

Hearing the door close, he sat up, a look of slight confusion on his face. Stern quickly made a leg.

"Ah, Burns. . . ." The Sea Lord said, and waved a hand at a chair. "Please, be comfortable."

"Captain Josiah Stern, Sir Jonathan."

"Stern, yes, of course."

It was a clear day, sunlight streaming in the huge window with such strength that Stern half-expected to see some of it filtering through the admiral—but there was a shadow on his desk. Gage looked back to his papers, signed something with a quick scrawl, and then turned his attention to his visitor.

"So, we have you going back to the Great Ocean?" he smiled, his almost colorless lips pursing.

Stern nodded.

"Well, I'm sure you will perform your duties with competence, as usual." The man rose a little stiffly, steadying himself with a hand on the back of his chair. He stretched his back, clearly with some pain, and then walked to the window where he stood peering down at the harbor, his hands clasped behind him. To the admiral's right a large telescope stood mounted on a bronze tripod, its glass eye pointed toward the ships anchored in the harbor.

"We are both busy men," the admiral said suddenly, turning away from the window, his face a little troubled, perhaps, "so let us not waste time in needless pleasantries. You have read your orders?"

"I have, sir." These had not been the type to be opened only when the ship was safely at sea.

"This young man, Flattery; he is well versed in the botany of Oceana, so there should be no trouble there. The situation, however, is more complicated. This herb the palace wants us to find—it is sacred to the Varuans. A level of diplomacy will be required to procure it."

Stern nodded.

"You have had good luck with these islanders before, Captain. I'm sure you will get on without troubles. Of course it is all a bit pointless, really," the admiral said suddenly, looking Stern directly in the eye.

Stern felt his eyebrows raise as though he asked why.

The admiral returned to his desk and picked up a mechanical pencil made of gold. "This herb, it alleviates the suffering of the King. . . . His Majesty is not entirely well, you understand. But the King is *very* old." He shook his head. "It is sad, really, for it is beyond imagining that His Majesty will. . . . Well, let us just say that two years has an entirely different meaning to those of advanced years." He raised his hands a little. "Even so, we must send out a ship—the palace has requested it. But Captain . . . do not waste the opportunity entirely. There is much that can be done: past discoveries that have not yet been properly charted, and you will have this naturalist along as well. Quite skilled by all accounts. Do what you can as you go. Any addition to our charts might save lives one day. Yes?"

The admiral set aside the paper he had signed and glanced at the one beneath. "Now, as to this matter of the Duchess of Morland, and Lord Elsworth." He kept his eyes on the papers before him. "It is a complicated business—the court, you know. . . . One faction vying with another. They would let the country go to ruin rather than give up the slightest advantage. I cannot fathom what drives such people. And within the palace there are some who do not trust us to do our duty, Captain." He said this with a little indignation. "And the duchess. . . . Well, what advantage will be gained if she returns to find that King Wilam has finally gone to his much deserved rest? Though I pray this will not be so, of course."

He looked up from the desk then. "Be certain, when you return from Oceana, that this herb is in your possession, Captain Burns. Otherwise you shall receive scant credit for your efforts. Do you take my meaning? Good." He looked back to the page, raising a corner to see what lay beneath. "It is a voyage for which you will get little enough recognition as it is. You understand that you must not speak of this herb? Yes?

"But rest assured that I will not forget you, Captain, even if the palace does not take great notice." He smiled at Stern, who was not terribly reassured—the admiral clearly did not know his name to begin with. "Now, the duchess. . . . I realize the situation shall be difficult for you. This is a woman well used to having her way. But command of the voyage is yours, Captain. I am relying on you to treat the duchess as someone of her station deserves, and yet discharge your obligations with alacrity. Not an enviable position you will be in, but I have complete faith in you. Perhaps all these damned delays will work in your favor. It is much more likely that you will get a good blow between here and Farrow at this late date. That might be all it takes to dissuade the duchess and her retinue." He smiled at this thought. "We can only hope. Good fortune to you, Captain."

ᔇ Seventeen

It was dusk before the *Swallow*'s deck was cleared of enough debris that Tristam was allowed aboard. The yawl boat bumped gently against the dark hull and Tristam was directed to the rungs of a crude ladder. This he climbed by touch alone and pulled himself over the bulwark onto the deck of the small bark.

"Mr. Flattery, is it?"

"Why, Jack Beacham! The pleasures of the evening to you."

"And to you, sir." The young midshipman appeared in the light of the stern lamps. "I must say that your prediction has not come true, Mr. Flattery."

"I should give up making predictions. They never work out. Remind me— what was the nature of this one?"

"When last we parted, I expressed the wish that we might sail together again and you said I would likely be an officer before such a thing would come to pass."

Tristam laughed. "Well, I am sorry to hear my prediction failed you, but I am glad that you will be aboard. It's good to have a true sailor around to keep the landsmen out of harm's way."

"Well, sir, I will do everything I can. Perhaps we can make an arrangement. I will teach you the ways of a ship if you might be so kind as to set me straight with weather and the geometrics. The geometrics of the sphere do seem to have me flustered, Mr. Flattery." In the poor light Tristam could see the lad shake his head, and his tone was one of concern.

"Well, I'm sure we can steer our way among the shoals of spherical geometrics, Mr. Beacham, and the channels and capes of weather can be even more easily navigated—though, of course, nothing is so sure in that particular study."

Beacham looked somewhat relieved by this. "I would be in your debt, Mr. Flattery. I took the liberty of bringing your baggage aboard, sir, but I should present you to the ship's master before we see to it. The captain and first lieutenant have gone ashore but Mr. Hobbes, the master, will wish to make your acquaintance. Can't have strangers walking around on the decks of His Majesty's ship. You could be an Entonne agent."

Tristam responded with a few words of his best Entonne.

"You speak it, then?"

"After a fashion."

"I wish I had your education, Mr. Flattery," Beacham said with great sincerity. "Knowledge is a wonderful thing."

"Do not be too impressed by my own, Jack Beacham; it is as thin as an old copper . . . and of similar value."

Beacham found the ship's master and the boatswain crammed into a small cabin, poring over records of stores. Mr. Hobbes, the master, was a tall-built man, very angular—all of his features large. One of those men whose frame was so big that there did not seem to be enough flesh to cover it properly, yet he appeared very strong. Tristam had never seen a man whose appearance was more uniformly gray: iron gray hair, stiff as wire; pale skin with a dull cast. Even the man's eyes suggested gray; they were such a pale blue. His callused hand enveloped Tristam's in a firm clasp and the naturalist was surprised at the gentleness of the man's tone and manner.

In contrast, Mr. Pickersgill, the boatswain, was a small round man with a joyous smile and an ease of manner that must have won him many friends. He winked at Tristam as though they shared a private jest and Tristam could not help but smile in return.

"So that's the famous Mr. Hobbes," Beacham said as soon as they were out of earshot, and making their way through the poor light below decks. "He sailed with Gregory as did our captain." Beacham said this in a near whisper, as though the statement filled him entirely with awe. "Not a man will need be pressed to make up his crew. Every man Jack of them knows our master and captain will bring the ship back whole, and the crew as well."

"Pickersgill seemed a pleasant sort," Tristam said.

"I should say, though as great a blackguard as any boatswain in the King's Navy, I shouldn't doubt. 'Mr. Handy,' he is called."

"Really?" Tristam was taken aback by Beacham's response. He had thought the lad so open of nature as to be incapable of criticism.

"It's the way of them, sir. Sell the sails out of the lifeboats. Sell the provisions if they could. Farrland needs a special prison just for boatswains, if you ask me." The thought of provisions appeared to cheer Beacham. "Did you know, Mr. Flattery, we have tinned victuals aboard! Can you imagine? They say it will last years and the tins are proof against weevils and the like, though you have to paint them to keep away the rust."

"Paint the weevils?"

Beacham laughed at this weak jest. "Paint the tins, sir."

Tristam followed Beacham forward to see his cabin, although the term *closet* might have been more accurate.

The cabin appeared to be square and wedged tight up against the curve of the hull. Inside the door there was a tiny open area less than two feet square, to the right a tall locker, to the left a type of desk, and against the hull a cabinet with doors and drawers. Tristam saw no bed, or berth, if that is what such things were called aboard ship. Air and presumably light, if it had not been dark, would come from a tiny, bronze port set into the break in the deck, for Tristam's cabin was built against the forward end of the quarterdeck.

Beacham apparently read the look of confusion on Tristam's face. "There is a hammock here, Mr. Flattery." The midshipman dug into a corner the lamplight did not penetrate and unrolled a contrivance of fishnet and canvas. This was stretched corner to corner cross the cabin and tied into an iron ring-bolt. Beacham hopped up with an enviable grace and swung into the hammock to demonstrate the proper method of boarding and sleeping in such a contrivance.

"You'll soon get used to it, Mr. Flattery. Far more comfortable than a bunk and leeboard. A hammock swings with the ship—which is to say the ship swings and the hammock maintains its position relative to the earth—more or less. Have a try." Beacham rolled out, landing easily on his feet.

The young sailor did not hide his glee well and Tristam knew there must be more to it than there appeared. He contrived to copy Beacham's movements as closely as possible and in this his greater height was an advantage. He launched himself into the contraption and, to Beacham's disappointment, managed the thing without mishap.

"Why, that's it, sir! You've the way of a sailor, to be sure."

Tristam managed the exit almost as well, only banging his elbow a little. "About my baggage?"

"I commandeered a corner of the 'tween decks mess and piled your things there with threats to all should anything untoward befall them. It seemed that piling them in your cabin would leave no room to work at stowing them away."

Tristam followed the ever-resourceful (or so he was beginning to believe) midshipman into the 'tween decks mess. Two other young midshipmen were there and Tristam was quickly introduced. He got the impression that Beacham may have been talking him up a bit, for the young gentlemen were very respectful, even a bit nervous.

Tristam stared at the massive pile of his equipment and clothes and various stores. "Where in the world will I put all of this?"

"In your cabin, Mr. Flattery. Why, I could fit twice this in and still leave room for a hornpipe. You'll see."

The two worked away at the task of stowing Tristam's baggage and Beacham kept up a flow of conversation the entire time. He related the history of the ship and assured Tristam that she was a "lucky" vessel, and he talked of the ship's crew, some of whom he had sailed with and others whom he knew by "scuttlebutt." The midshipman showed great surprise when Tristam confessed he had never heard tell of "the famous" Mr. Hobbes before their recent introduction.

"I thought all of Farrland knew of Mr. Hobbes, sir." Beacham stopped emptying a crate of instruments. "Nothing else was spoken of for months on the docks and in the ale houses. You did not hear of the decision of the Navy Board?"

Tristam had only recently heard of the Navy Board.

"Well, Mr. Flattery, I can tell you justice was never so poorly served in all of history." He said this with utter conviction. "You see, Mr. Hobbes was once a lieutenant, one step away from being made post captain, or so everyone says, and I believe it. He was given command of a rotting little scow called the *Briss*, which is Doorn for 'breeze,' though I'm sure you know that," he added quickly. "A surveyor by training, Mr. Hobbes and his command were sent to survey in the Archipelago above fifty—fifty degrees that is. Well, like every good officer Mr. Hobbes began by surveying his own vessel and discovered that she was not as fit for sea as the Navy Yard had made out—too much of the money for her refit had gone into the refitting of gentlemen's pockets, if you take my meaning, sir. Well, Mr. Hobbes wrote to the Navy Board with his complaints and the upshot was that he was ordered to sea, if you can believe it, in a vessel that was near to sinking at the wharf! You can see what would happen.

"Somehow the *Briss* made it through the summer months without disaster, but on their return voyage to Farrland they were set upon by a great blow of an autumn storm, sir, and the boat foundered." Beacham banged his fist on the door, clearly outraged. "The company, or most of it, got into the ship's boats, for survey vessels often carry three boats, Mr. Flattery: a yawl-boat, a cutter, and a long boat as well. The long boat, commanded by Mr. Hobbes, made the crossing with great hardship, losing only one man—almost one hundred twenty leagues! Near to two thousand miles! And at a terrible time of year as well. The other two boats. . . . Well, they were never seen again, Mr. Flattery, unless it is while haunting the nights of certain gentlemen." He took a long breath before continuing his story. "But was Mr. Hobbes thought a hero? Was he given his post, as well, and a pension from the King? No, sir! He was taken before the Navy Board and broken of his rank! That is how they rewarded him for preserving twenty-six lives! The letter Mr. Hobbes had written was 'lost' and he was charged with setting to sea in a vessel he knew unseaworthy. That is the truth of it, sir, I'm sorry to say. And the gentlemen who lined their pockets with the monies meant to refit the *Briss* . . . why, Mr. Flattery, they pay for their servants with that money. They pay for fine carriages, too!"

"I see what you mean," Tristam said quietly.

"Since Admiral Gage was made Sea Lord things have changed, but poor Mr. Hobbes will never pass beyond the rank of master even though he sailed with Gregory and Pankhurst and is one of the most respected seamen in the navy. He has the love of the Jacks, though, I'll tell you that. When they were crossing the Gray Ocean in the early winter, and in an open boat too, often as not he gave his ration to the weakest man. And without so much as a compass, he sailed to Farrland by the stars, making as fair a landfall as a ship of war. Sailed in the entrance to Wickham Harbor in the fog, sir! Sailed in as though it weren't impossible. There is not a Jack in the navy that wouldn't put himself in the way of a cannonball for Mr. Hobbes. You will see, Mr. Flattery. You will see."

After this outburst, they worked on in silence for some time.

True to his word, when everything was stowed away, there was room for a hornpipe, albeit danced by a dwarf. Through casual questioning as they worked, Beacham learned that Tristam was lacking certain articles that would make his life aboard easier; when Tristam went ashore, he had a list of things to purchase before the *Swallow* sailed, as well as instructions as to where such articles could be found and what price should be paid for them. Beacham was a thorough young man and Tristam had the impression that he did not think a landsman could be trusted to shave himself in anything but a flat calm.

As soon as his mind was free of his task aboard, it returned to his real concern. This voyage would not provide escape from the intrigues of the court, nor would it give him the time to heal as Tristam had hoped. But far worse: how was he to live, for two years, only a few yards from the Duchess of Morland? What if she were to find a lover among the officers? Once they passed through the archipelago, there would be no hope of leaving the ship. No escape at all.

⌐ Eighteen

Having now circled the globe entire, and having looked upon strange and foreign lands perhaps more often than any man alive, I have come to realize that this great endeavor of "discovery" is vastly misnamed. Almost without exception we have found men living in these distant lands, and in those places thought uninhabited we have often found evidence that humankind once made homes there. The true age of exploration and "discovery" took place long ago; unheralded, unrecorded, and with great hardship I am sure, but in ages before our own civilization came into being. When one considers this lost history, the world seems endless indeed.

Gregory: Voyages

The fifteenth day of October dawned clear and autumn-warm, a fresh breeze sweeping down from the hills, spreading the scent of land out over the sea. Gulls searched frantically among the great ships at anchor, filling the air with their forlorn cries. And high above the bay an osprey hunted, as stationary as a kite on a string, as patient as a mage.

Tristam stood at the stern rail, out of harm's way, as the crew and officers prepared to make sail. He tried not to let his glance stray to the Duchess of Morland, who was plying the officers with her considerable charms. Although Tristam knew that meeting the duchess again would not be easy for him, he had underestimated his reaction substantially. The cries of the gulls were like echoes of his own anguish.

Orders were given to weigh anchor when an officer noted a cutter, flying the flag of the Admiral of the Fleet, sailing quickly toward the *Swallow*. As it drew alongside, an officer stood up in the stern and called out, "The compliments of His Majesty, to the Duchess of Morland, Lord Elsworth, Captain, and crew, wishing a safe voyage for all." And then, to everyone's delight, Teiho Ruau, the Varuan, rose in the bow and began to sing.

It was the same unworldly tenor that Tristam had heard with Sir Roderick, but it was a song from Oceana, soft and haunting—words that Tristam did not understand but which affected him nonetheless. A song of farewell, Tristam realized, though he could not understand a single word. The entire crew stopped their work and stood silently along the rail, listening. Even the most hardened-looking Jacks appeared to be moved by the music, and unembarrassed to be so.

A voice to pacify the brutal soul, Tristam thought. Interesting that Ruau, from a race whose culture did not compare with that of Farrland, appeared more civilized than the poor Jacks of the *Swallow*. Yet even as he thought this, Tristam saw the islander was wearing his belt of snakeskin—a talisman of some sort.

His song done, the Varuan doffed his white plumed hat in a sweeping bow, and the cutter pushed off and was soon lost among the other ships.

Immediately, the boatswain blew his pipes, breaking the mood, and the capstan began to turn from the efforts of men at the bars. The chain cable rattled slowly through the hawsehole, and finally, after great effort, the laboring Jacks stumbled forward a step as the anchor broke free of the harbor bottom. Sails were loosed by the crewmen aloft and the survey vessel, *Swallow,* turned her bow toward the open sea.

As the ship left the harbor Tristam found that his gaze was drawn back, not forward. He wanted to linger on the sight of land rather than gaze out toward the empty horizon.

The great cabin of the bark *Swallow* spanned the ship's entire beam, making it the only civilized accommodation aboard. Light and air were provided by an arc of transom windows and a skylight set among the heavy beams that supported the quarterdeck. Even on this late evening the cabin remained bright, for the overhead was painted white as was much of the other woodwork.

Captain Josiah Stern stood near the table, the brass buttons of his jacket reflecting in the polished surface. He was apparently unaware of the motion of the ship, for his large workman's hands hung easily at his sides, clearly not poised to make a desperate grab for a handhold. In this he differed noticeably from the others present.

The captain, Tristam guessed, was in his middle forties and appeared to have the build of a bricklayer, a fact which was at odds with the man's careful dignity, for Stern appeared to do everything with great deliberation, as though he thought every action through at length. Tristam suspected the man of being somewhat like the great ships he commanded—slow to get underway but, once moving, very difficult to stop.

In his habits of dress, Stern was obviously fastidious, his uniform carefully tailored and impeccably clean. "*He likes to think himself a gentleman,*" Beacham had noted, "*but he will not brook dissent, Mr. Flattery.*" Beacham had lowered his voice at this. "*The most pleasant officer afloat, sir. But he is not to be argued with. Not our Captain Stern, for he will change as quick as the sea beneath a squall.*"

Tristam sat on the sill of an opened transom window, bracing himself by spreading his feet wide and pressing his back into the hard wood of the window casing—one hand grasped the sill and the other occasionally twitched in his lap as the ship lurched. He had chosen this position, for it afforded him a good view of everyone in the room, especially the Duchess of Morland.

The duchess perched in a chair that had been removed by several feet from the table end, so that she would not have to look up too abruptly at the captain. As always, she seemed utterly composed, waiting with, if not a smile, a look of pleasant expectation on her face. A few errant strands of golden hair had come free of her combs and Tristam thought the wind had given her face the most innocent blush. The naturalist forced himself to look away, thinking that her brother might feel that he stared.

When she had arrived aboard, the duchess had greeted Tristam like a long lost cousin, kissing him on both cheeks, making great show of her affection for him. Not a word for months, and then she responded as though she had missed him every second they had been apart—and said almost as much. He was sure that he had been the envy of every man on the deck—her intention, undoubt- edly. And this had left Tristam in the grip of such confusion—resentful, de- lighted, hopeful, even a bit proud that such a woman would offer this public statement of her affection for him. He carried that confusion around with him now, like a chronic ache in his chest.

"I thought it important," Captain Stern began, interrupting Tristam's thoughts, "that we have a word before our wake has stretched too thin." He tilted his head slightly toward the duchess as he spoke. Some form of acknowl- edgment, Tristam thought.

The viscount sat in a second chair, which he had braced against the leeward of the cabin's two berths so that the slight heel of the ship held him firmly in place. He propped an ankle up on the opposite knee, and leaned back in his chair, smiling like an amiable drunk. Tristam was struck again by the size of the man—as large as any of the Jacks who worked the forecastle, and they were the most powerful of the sailors.

Tristam glanced over his shoulder at the ship's wake stretching out astern toward the hills of Farrland, floating dusky purple on the horizon like an exotic island. A gull, borne upon a current of air made by the passing ship, kept cock- ing its head reproachfully at Tristam, as though he were expected to throw something edible into the sea.

"Although I have had peers aboard ships of my command in the past," Stern went on, "they were always admirals or members of the Admiralty. Men who knew the sea, as well as the service and her ways."

The emphasis, Tristam noted, had been on the word "men." Stern put one hand behind his back—a rather courtly gesture.

"Even when I have had an admiral, a gentleman of title, aboard my ship, there has never been any confusion about who was to command—who was to give the orders to officers and men. It is a long tradition of the navy. A ship can have only one commander, or she will soon be torn apart. A vessel cannot follow two courses; and the Jacks . . . well, they must have a consistent routine and fair but strict discipline.

"The Admiralty has seen fit to give me command of both this ship *and* this expedition." He paused, meeting the eyes of each person in turn. "I hope that is perfectly clear?"

Tristam nodded quickly, but the duchess' only response was a slight tightening of the lips—not really a smile. The viscount's look of vacant foolishness did not change.

Chain of command, Tristam thought. *It is the litany of the navy men—their central belief.* He had been wondering how Stern intended to deal with the duchess aboard.

"Two years or more on a small ship . . . this takes greater effort on the part of everyone aboard than most realize. The smallest annoyances, things we should hardly notice ashore, have led men to violence after months at sea. But if a strong captain, known to be just, sets the tone of the voyage—clearly marks the boundaries of acceptable action, and sticks to these with an iron will—then life aboard can be perfectly pleasant, if not as comfortable as some are used to. Discord is a disease and I shall not hesitate to wield my scalpel to cut it out." Again he met each person's eyes in turn. "In this I require your unwavering support. Aboard every ship there are those who are less than satisfied with their lot in life, and, instead of exerting their efforts to improve that lot, they channel their energies into disruption. It takes very little to encourage them in their natural ways. If they find one or two others of like mind among the Jacks, that can be cause enough for mischief. But if they believe there is support for their disaffection from officers or others aboard. . . ." The captain motioned up toward the deck, raising his heavy eyebrows. "I shall ask you to speak no ill of the navy, nor of the officers aboard, no matter what your opinion. Even in private be circumspect, for I will warn you also that privacy aboard ship is illusory—hardly more than a convention we have all agreed upon."

Stern looked down at the table, rubbing one hand across the smooth surface. As he did so, the captain turned just enough that Tristam could see the hand behind his back was knotted into a tight fist.

"At the various naval stations, you will often find that the officers have their families with them—wives and children. And these ladies have traveled out aboard His Majesty's ships. It is, therefore, not unheard of to have ladies aboard. It is, however, uncommon for women to travel on a voyage of such length." He glanced up, a bit embarrassed, Tristam thought, though he sailed on. "I anticipate no problems in this regard. The Jacks know full well that to offend the duchess or her maidservant in any way would elicit the harshest possible response from me. But if you would not mind speaking to your servant, Duchess, and suggest that she should, at all times, comport herself most circumspectly so that her actions could never be interpreted as encouragement. . . ." He raised his eyebrows, looking at the duchess, but she refused to reach out her hand to the drowning man. Tristam hid a smile. The captain had a great deal to learn about the Duchess of Morland.

Stern looked down at the table again, perhaps hiding his annoyance at the woman's response. "I'm sure you take my meaning. We are fortunate to have a good crew aboard. No man was pressed. The stories of Oceana brought volunteers enough to man five ships or more. Hobbes and I chose among them with some care. The First Lieutenant, Mr. Osler, is but a step away from his own command, and an officer I trust implicitly. And Mr. Hobbes . . ." He glanced up at those present and Tristam thought the man's look a bit defiant. "No matter what you may have heard, Mr. Hobbes is the finest noncommissioned officer in the navy. It is my opinion that he should be a post-captain today if not for. . . ." Stern caught himself, stopping awkwardly.

Tristam was not sure if the others present knew the story of Mr. Hobbes, which Tristam felt might not have come to him from the most disinterested source. But obviously Stern's view was similar to Beacham's.

"They are fine officers," Stern said quietly, "gentlemen all." He looked up again, this time fixing his seablue eyes on Tristam. "And I use the word to describe a man's way of going through the world—his manners and actions—not the circumstances of his birth. I am sure I can rely on you gentlemen to treat my officers as they deserve. It shall make all of our lives easier over the next two years."

Tristam nodded immediately. Lieutenant Osler had come from a situation not unlike Tristam's own—the young seaman's grandfather had been the Earl of Firthe—and as for the famous Mr. Hobbes. . . . Well, Tristam thought of himself as being above the prejudices of his class anyway, but he was prepared to treat Mr. Hobbes with deference, and especially so if the man's story proved to be true.

"You will not find me a difficult man to sail with," Stern went on. "I am not one of those martinets whose only purpose is to subjugate everyone aboard to his will. No, I think you will find me a reasonable man. My creed is simple: duty to King and service; a gentleman always, to both friend and foe; tread upon no one else to raise one's self higher, but progress only according one's own merit. Old-fashioned, you will no doubt say, but those are my beliefs, and I have yet to meet a man who could find fault with them."

Tristam thought of the warning he had received from Beacham about not gainsaying the captain. It was no wonder Stern's beliefs had not been challenged. They could probably be far more objectionable than these banal homilies and Stern would never hear a word of criticism.

The officer brushed his hand across the table again as though attempting to erase the reflection of his gleaming buttons. "I will tell you honestly that there were those in the Admiralty that were against the duchess taking ship," Stern said, glancing up from the table.

Tristam could almost feel how tight the captain's fist was now. The man spoke as if he were straining to lift a heavy weight.

"And I will be perfectly candid, Duchess, Lord Elsworth—I feel that the task I have been given is well within my powers." He nodded toward Tristam. "With Mr. Flattery's skills and my own, I am sure that we shall succeed. And, despite what many seem to think, I am not the minion of any minister or courtier. I serve the King." His voice almost trembled as he said this. "It will be a long, arduous voyage, and not, I must tell you, without dangers. There will be an opportunity to reconsider when we reach Farrow and again at the Queen Anne Station.

"The Duchess, of course, is welcome aboard my ship," he added quickly. "And yourself, Lord Elsworth. Please do not misunderstand me. I only wish to offer assurances that my interests are those of Farrland and her sovereign. I have never yet failed to fulfill my orders."

"And what are those orders, Captain Stern?" the duchess asked evenly, her voice almost sweet. She fixed the officer with the same gaze she had turned on Tristam in the past, and the naturalist wondered if it unsettled Stern as much.

"I hope the Duchess will forgive me. Orders from the Admiralty are not to be discussed." He looked very grave as he said this, but Tristam thought he detected a certain amount of satisfaction in making this pronouncement.

"Have you other orders, other tasks, besides the one that concerns us all, Captain Stern?"

"Again, Duchess, forgive me, but I may not speak of this."

The duchess was not so easily put off. "I am not asking that you reveal the specifics of your orders, Captain, but only to tell me if there are other tasks assigned to this voyage. I am sure you cannot be accused of treason for revealing that?"

"I do apologize, Duchess, and to you gentlemen as well, but I am unable to discuss my orders. Even my officers have only the most general understanding of what we intend—and they know nothing of this . . . other matter," he added, leaning forward and almost whispering. "They know that we are a survey vessel and that we have been sent out equipped to perform that function. We sail to Oceana, west-about, and shall carry a chain of measurements as we go. That is, Duchess, what my officers have been told and it is true enough." He smiled as he finished, as though he had just made an enormous concession to "getting along."

"Well, Captain Stern," the duchess responded, obviously not appreciative of these crumbs of information, "I only hope these tasks you allude to will not interfere with our true purpose. That is, you should know, one of my deepest concerns. For my part, and I think I may speak for Lord Elsworth in this, we intend to cooperate to the greatest extent of our abilities. You shall not find us interfering in the running of the ship or in the routines and discipline of shipboard life. We are out of our depth here and place ourselves entirely in your hands, deferring to your great experience and judgment. As to this other matter . . . I am aboard your ship for one reason and one reason alone, Captain, and that is to see that the intrigues of the court have not stowed away aboard, secretly. Like you, I, too, serve the King. That is why I have inquired about the exact nature of your orders. I would not think to challenge your knowledge of the sea, Captain Stern, but I have my area of knowledge. Your orders, despite their appearance, might not be in the best interests of the King, but instead might reflect the interests of others within the court. It would not be the first time."

Stern placed his other hand behind his back and stood very erect. "Allow me to assure the Duchess that this is not the case."

The duchess did not respond, but she and the captain had locked eyes and neither looked away. No doubt, Stern, who did not care to be gainsaid, was not used to being so confronted aboard his own command—and by a woman at that. There would be nothing in the seaman's vocabulary of responses that would suit the conditions. This woman was the favorite of the King of Farrland, after all.

"It is a more complex situation than most realize," the duchess said, giving not an inch.

Stern considered this a moment and then said, evenly, "I may be only an uneducated sea captain, Duchess, but I am not a fool."

"And I would never suggest that you were, Captain. Let us say that, for the moment, I am reassured." The duchess smiled suddenly, and Tristam saw that this affected even Stern. Threw him off balance, as though he had misunderstood the entire interchange—had taken it far too seriously—making the man wonder if he had just looked like a pompous fool. The captain reached up and took hold of the beam close overhead.

Yes, Tristam thought, *welcome to the world of the Duchess of Morland, Captain.*

"I hope you might all join me for supper this evening?" the duchess went on sweetly, looking around at each man in turn. "You do not all have other social engagements? Your calendars are not too chock full?" She smiled again, transforming herself in that way Tristam had seen. Despite himself, he felt a smile appear in response.

"You are all very kind." She turned then to Stern, her manner still animated.

"Do not concern yourself, Captain. We shall make every effort not to disrupt the sacred routine of the King's Navy or to upset the delicate balance of this vessel."

Stern smiled in return, bowing his head slightly, as though he had just received a compliment from a queen.

It must have hurt Stern immeasurably to give up his accommodations to the Duchess of Morland, Tristam thought, looking around the great cabin. There was no other cabin aboard that compared—certainly not the cubbyhole the captain was in now, hardly bigger than Tristam's own. Stern, more than many others, must know what it would mean on a two-year voyage.

Tristam sat on the sill of the transom window, watching the Duchess' Entonne maid putting the final touches on the table, set for eight, though it would have been crowded to seat six. The duchess stood looking on and giving the maid and the captain's steward last minute instructions. For a woman used to a staff that would number in the twenties, she seemed remarkably calm.

The steward tried twice to interrupt—something about how tables were to be set in the navy—but the duchess would have none of this. They may be aboard a ship, but her table would be set according to the standards of Avonel, or as near as could be managed under the circumstances.

Tristam glanced out at the water bubbling out from beneath the stern. Five knots he had been told they were traveling, but if one looked directly down into the water, it seemed much faster. The swirls and bubbles of white, whirling off astern, were lost in the waves and the frothing wake. He felt a rush of joy at this sight, joy in the movement and the power of a ship under a sail. Rising on each swell, surging forward as she passed the crest, then settling into the trough, the sound of swift flowing water changing tone as the ship slowed, only to lift and surge forward again. Relentless rising and falling on the heaving breast of the great ocean.

Tristam was beginning to think that he might just survive this proximity to the duchess after all. He felt much relieved now that the ice had been broken. Her manner toward him was very kind. One would have thought Tristam was an old and dear friend. He still felt the incredible physical draw toward her, found it difficult to keep his eyes off her when they were together, but perhaps that would pass.

Below, the sea foamed and rushed.

"You are not ill, are you Tristam?"

Tristam turned away from the sight of the passing sea and forced a smile on his lips. "Not in the slightest."

The duchess looked at him, a bit concerned, it seemed. Tristam thought she was about to speak when a precise knock sounded on the cabin door.

"Your guests, Duchess," Jacel said.

Captain Stern made way for Doctor Llewellyn, a physician who accompanied the duchess, for the King had insisted she not sail without one, and then the captain entered followed by the navy men, scrubbed and fresh-shaven, their uniform buttons gleaming.

Tristam thought it possible that Osler, the first lieutenant, was not a total stranger to society, but certainly none of the navy men had ever been invited to dine with anyone of the duchess' station. The duchess, however, set about banishing their discomfort immediately. She greeted them all by name, her demeanor indicating she could not have been more delighted with her guests if they had been members of the Royal Family. Of course, they were all men, and the duchess was utterly confident in her affect on men, nor was she wrong in this.

In the babble of greetings and beginnings of conversation there was suddenly the most awkward pause, broken only by the voice of the physician who seemed unaware of the silence. Tristam had risen to greet the guests, but he stopped, surprised by the reaction. The navy men stood for a second, gazing at the table, and then they all looked immediately to the captain.

The duchess put a hand on the physician's shoulder to silence him and turned to the others.

"I fear I have committed some breach of etiquette, Captain Stern?" she said quietly.

Stern tried to smile. "It is just an old superstition, Duchess. The first night at sea the table should be made up of seven. It slipped my mind in the confusion of setting out: I apologize for not bringing it to the Duchess' attention."

"Well, we are all people of education," the physician interjected. "Not superstitious old shepherds. I will sit at a table of eight—or thirteen, for that matter."

The navy men all kept their eyes fixed on neutral points in the cabin, their features frozen—clearly horrified by the doctor's suggestion.

"Will you forgive me, Your Grace," young Osler said, trying not to appear awkward. "I should see to the running of the ship."

"Now, Mr. Osler . . ." Stern began, but did not finish, obviously as distressed as the others.

"I hope, Mr. Osler," the duchess said warmly, "that this doesn't mean you will not join me another evening?"

"I would be honored, Your Grace," he said, bowing slightly.

"Then I shall allow you to reduce our numbers at table appropriately. Thank you, Mr. Osler." The duchess curtsied to the lieutenant, having turned him into the sacrificing hero. Tristam felt a flash of jealousy and realized that perhaps life around the duchess would not prove so easy after all.

Before Osler could back from the room, the captain's steward pounced on the offending place setting, collecting it up as quickly as his hands would move.

From the forced manner of the sailors, Tristam guessed that, despite Osler's retreat, they believed the damage had already been done—the offense already noted by whichever sea god monitored such crimes.

The remaining dinner guests were seated, and a rather forced conversation began. Tristam, who was not feeling in the least social, found his mind wandering, and his gaze drawn again and again to the duchess, who was the focus of everyone's attention anyway. Tristam could not imagine that nature had ever created a more perfectly formed woman. If he closed his eyes for a second, even the sound of her voice enchanted him.

He wondered now if he would have escaped the duchess even if she had not come on the voyage.

Tristam tried to concentrate on the men seated around the table—an exercise he undertook halfheartedly. Stern, with his impeccable uniform and his close-cropped beard that could easily have been modeled on the beard worn by Jaimy's father, the Duke of Blackwater. A man displaced from his position as axis around which life aboard would turn. He was doing the best he could to appear unaffected, but even Tristam, who did not know the man, could see it was an effort.

Taine, the ship's surgeon, in contrast to his captain, was a little shabbily turned out, grime apparent on his cuffs and collar, a cheap scent masking his lack of a recent bath. The man must be feeling more than a little displaced himself, for it was commonly the surgeon who acted as the ship's naturalist, or at least made what collections he could. And here was poor Taine aboard a ship with a trained naturalist and a real physician, too—a physician who had apparently once served the Royal Household.

This physician, Norrish Llewellyn, was an odd man. Too talkative and completely insensitive of the fact—his manner condescending, which Tristam could not bear. The doctor had a small mocking laugh, which was often released when he was asked a question, as though foolish queries brought him some amusement.

"Do the Varuans suffer from the scurvy?" the duchess had asked, and this had triggered Llewellyn's mocking laugh.

"No, Your Grace, the scurvy is a disease brought on by improper diet, as Gregory proved, and the Varuans have a healthful diet. Nor will scurvy touch a soul aboard this ship, for we have all the tried and true antiscorbutics aboard. Limes and sour-cabbage and beer brewed from the spruce." He looked up at the duchess, his lips twitching into a small smile of amusement. "You have Llewellyn aboard—a physician of the Royal College. It will not be disease that brings this voyage into danger, that I assure you."

Tristam was not sure who was more enraged: the duchess, who could not bear condescension; the surgeon, who was a graduate of the lowly Naval College; or the officers, who did not like to have it implied that the only danger that existed was mismanagement of the voyage. Somehow Llewellyn had missed offending Tristam. And the physician was unaware that anyone could find this insulting—he was, after all, only speaking the truth.

It was immediately apparent, though, that the doctor was a scholar of some real knowledge—as he made sure everyone knew—for he spoke several languages, and was a good amateur naturalist. But to Tristam's eye, Llewellyn had all the signs of a man who, though he knew much, had lived little. Fifteen minutes of conversation had not been needed for the physician to alienate almost everyone at the table, and the poor ship's surgeon most of all. Llewellyn corrected the man twice, before everyone, as though Taine were a lowly apprentice. He then made several mocking comments about the superstitious, as though he would, by such ill contrived "instruction," change the beliefs of the sailors present.

Tristam had seen teachers do the same in his school days—always the instructors most hated by the students, and least effective in the practice of their profession.

Even the duchess did not find it easy to wrest control of the conversation from the irrepressible doctor, for he did not notice hints, even of the less subtle nature. In turn, she gave everyone at the table permission to address her as 'Duchess,' with the exception of Llewellyn, and even this took a moment to make an impression on the man. But finally he fell silent, perhaps realizing that even the lowly surgeon had been granted a favor that he had not. He was to remain in his place as her employee and address the duchess as "Your Grace."

"Captain Stern," the duchess said, rather solicitously, for she was obviously aware of the captain's loss of social standing that her presence had caused. "I wish to propose a toast but do not wish to compound my earlier error. Is there a tradition in this as well?"

Tristam thought that Stern noted her sensitivity to his position and seemed genuinely affected by this. "There are only a few areas one should beware of, Duchess. One never whistles aboard ship, for it is believed to bring storms. Likewise we never toast, 'fair winds' or words to that effect—which can leave one becalmed for weeks, or so it is believed. It is considered bad luck to give voice to specific kinds of fears, such as saying that one hopes we do not founder. All things supernatural are feared by the common sailors and not spoken of. It is bad luck to leave port on Friday." He laughed suddenly as he realized how quickly the catalog grew. "At its outset, we commonly toast the success of the voyage, Duchess, and at each meal we drink a glass to the health of the King."

"To the success of the voyage then, gentlemen," the duchess said, "and to the King's health."

Tristam saw the tightening around the eyes as she said this, as though the thought disturbed her. Perhaps the duchess had superstitions of her own.

"This is very fine wine," Llewellyn said, and Tristam was not sure if he intended this compliment to make amends for his earlier offense or whether this was merely another opportunity to display his store of knowledge.

"It is from the grape developed by Erasmus Flattery," the duchess interrupted quickly, "whose heir graces our table."

"You are the son of Erasmus Flattery," Stern asked, his glass stopping in midair.

"He was my great-uncle, Captain."

"Well, you should keep that information to yourself, Mr. Flattery," Stern said, shifting in his chair. Then he looked around the table. "We should all keep it quiet. I'm sure there is no truth to it, Mr. Flattery, but the rumors that connect your great uncle to Lord Eldrich are well known. The men before the mast, the common Jacks, they would be genuinely frightened to know the heir of Erasmus Flattery sailed with us."

Stern attempted a reassuring smile, but it failed to do its duty. Tristam felt a flush of anger, coupled with a mild fear. Something else he did not seem able to escape.

The conversation went off in various directions after that, but Tristam hardly followed it. The duchess made great efforts to include everyone, but she obviously concentrated her charms on the ship's master, Mr. Hobbes. The master may well have suffered at the hands of the lords in the Admiralty, but it was clear he was ready to absolve the duchess of any connection to this group. It was a rather astute and totally cold-blooded strategy on the duchess' part. Hobbes was worshipped by the Jacks. Winning his approval would assure the duchess' acceptance by the crew.

Tristam took a deep drink of his wine—a private, unspoken toast to her genius. Stern might be so committed to duty that he could not be influenced by the duchess, but Tristam was willing to wager that no one else aboard would offer the same resistance. No, the *Swallow* would be the first ship in Farr history to surrender without the crew even being aware that they had done so.

Tristam watched the stars, picking out the constellations he knew, focusing his glass now and then on a familiar point only to find the many more suns that lay behind—the infinite number of stars wavering in his lens. It was the night of the new moon and there was not a better time for viewing the heavens. Tristam felt as though he had slipped away into his own element. Dinner had not been easy.

Running away to sea was not proving very successful.

And his simple life as ship's naturalist was now complicated as well: court intrigue proving as difficult to elude as the duchess.

And yet there was a part of him that could not believe his good fortune. Two years aboard a ship with the most desired woman in all of Farrland! And it did not seem likely that he had a rival here. Had she not seemed genuinely delighted to see him when they met?

She is a dozen years your senior, he told himself, *of the very highest strata of Farr society, the favorite of the King, and a woman famous for her ability to manipulate—especially men.* Jaimy would think him a proper fool, Tristam realized. He knew what the word "obsession" implied.

But when I am with the duchess, Tristam thought, *I feel as though my entire being has been engaged—intellect, heart, desire. It is like suddenly waking. Unlike my days with Jenny*, he realized.

Do not be a fool, Tristam Flattery, he told himself. *The Duchess of Morland is not interested in a relatively poor naturalist from Locfal—beyond his, possibly useful, botanical skills.*

Of course it would be easier to conquer his feelings if he had not once felt the duchess beneath him crying out in pleasure—not that it was his name she had been crying!

"There you are, Tristam," the duchess' voice came out of the dark behind him. He felt his eyes close involuntarily.

"I had hoped you would stay a while and keep me company."

She came to the rail beside him, wrapped in a dark shawl, the starlight playing in her uncovered hair.

"Are you communing with nature? Is that what naturalists do?" she asked, her manner teasing but her voice quiet, perhaps remembering Stern's warning about privacy aboard ships.

"I was thinking of a conversation I had with Averil Kent," Tristam lied. "Do you know him?"

"Anyone who travels in society in Avonel knows Kent."

"He spoke to me at length one day about art, and about the Entonne word *isollae*. 'Loneliness in the face of beauty,' he translated it. I wonder if it describes what I am feeling."

The duchess did not answer, but he heard her stir beside him, the soft rustle of wool moving over her gown. They stood silently looking out into the depths of the sky and at the surface of the sea, faintly illuminated by starlight. A wave rolled by beneath them with a sound like a long exhalation.

"There is more to you than meets the eye, Tristam Flattery," the duchess said. "But does the word not also mean 'isolated'? I hope that is not what you feel."

Always, Tristam thought. "No, of course not."

The tips of three fingers touched his shoulder. He could feel them even through his coat. "Listen to me, Tristam. As much as I wanted to write you these past months, I could not. I could not draw attention to you and to us. But we are together in this matter. . . ." She paused; Tristam could sense her thinking. The pressure of her hand disappeared from his back. "Allow me to give you some small piece of information, Tristam. That is what empiricists seek, is it not?" She paused again, wrapping her shawl more tightly about her shoulders. "I knew your father, or perhaps it would be more accurate to say I observed him. I have always had an interest in the theater, the opera, even when I was young, so our circles were not so different despite our disparate ages. Your father was caught up in the cult of sensibility that swept through Farr society fifteen years ago, and has now, mercifully, all but disappeared. But I felt even then that the cult of sensibility gave your father an opportunity to express something that was true in himself. I am not telling you anything new to say that Morton Flattery experienced all his emotions in extreme. When he felt joy he was in ecstasy; when he felt passion it was near to madness; and when he knew despair. . . ." The duchess turned to Tristam, staring up into his face so that he could not look away. "But you are not like him, Tristam, not like him at all. You need not live in fear that your course in life follows his. It does not. You need not deny so much of yourself. To open some small corner of your heart will not bring you to ruin. Do you understand what I'm saying?"

Tristam felt his hand gripping the rail as though afraid he would lose his balance and pitch into the night sea. It was as though she had known his thoughts. He could not find words to answer, but nodded his head, feeling that the eyes searching his held as many mysteries as the night sky.

She turned back to the rail. "I hope you do."

"All those around me, as long as I can remember, have engaged only my intellect, Duchess." A long succession of instructors who smelled of pipe smoke and closed rooms. "There has never been anyone to speak to my heart."

She glanced up as though surprised. "Do not look to me for this, Tristam," she said, softly, almost imploring him. "Please. Hearts have never been safe with me. I say this only because I care for you." She reached out and laid her hand on his arm. "We must not start the crew gossiping. The pleasures of the evening to you, Tristam Flattery."

He listened to her footsteps as they crossed the deck. The night seemed to have grown a little cooler suddenly, as though the breeze had risen. The ship lifted on a crest and then settled slowly into the trough, making sounds of disappointment. A sheet stretched in its block, releasing a long, indescribable vowel that seemed almost an animal expression of sympathy.

"*Isollae*," Tristam whispered.

When he finally went down to his cabin, Tristam discovered an envelope tucked under his door. He opened it by lamplight and found a note scrawled across the top of more neatly written text. *This is the letter I wrote and should have sent*, it said, and was dated the thirtieth day of July.

My dearest Tristam:

I hope this letter reaches you before you hear from Roderick Palle. In this past month there has been a struggle in the court such as I have not seen in some years. But in the end His Majesty's government has ordered a voyage to Oceana to seek the elusive herb. I have made every effort to influence the selection of the members of this voyage. I can claim only partial success—but I have managed to have you, Tristam, named the prime candidate for the position of ship's naturalist.

I am sure you will feel some reservations about involving yourself in this venture, given what you have experienced of court intrigue, but the herb must be found, and quickly. There is no one in all of Farrland more qualified for this position than yourself, nor is there anyone more likely to succeed. So much is at stake in this matter—I hope some day to be able to tell you exactly how much.

Please, please, give this appointment your most serious consideration. I shall not know a moment's rest until you have said yes. And if you do consent, I shall be more grateful than you can imagine.

I realize that such an undertaking has its dangers, and not only shall I miss your company for the duration but I will worry constantly. I should never choose to send you off if it were not so crucial. Please write to me immediately, and, if you can, come to Avonel so that we may discuss it at length.

Yours,
Elorin

Tristam lay in his hammock, listening to the sea gurgle and splash as it passed over the hull outside his cabin. So varied was the vocabulary that he almost found himself trying to understand, listening for words, attempting to sense the mood of this discourse.

◯ Nineteen

The carriage tilted abruptly to the right and then jolted back upright. Kent grasped tight to the leather hand-loop, but when the road ran on more or less smoothly for a hundred feet, he loosed his grip and returned the gloved hand to the head of his cane. Despite lack of moon and stars, the branches of trees could just be seen, swaying erratically as though they tried to shake free of the wind that pressed them down. The last leaves of the year fluttered, batlike, around the carriage. Occasionally, one flattened itself to the carriage window like sodden paper. Now and then the wind seemed to find a tunnel through the forest and the entire carriage would sway and rock like a boat on the sea.

It was not much farther, he was sure, though at the pace they traveled, it would still take a precious half of the hour.

"*What a fool I have been,*" he said under his breath, and not for the first time. He had been mumbling the same litany for several days now, and thought it might be some time before he stopped—if ever.

"*An old fool,*" the painter whispered bitterly.

A sudden lurch of the carriage had him reach out and take hold of the loop again. They were turning. It must be the gate.

"*Fool,*" he said, as though getting in one last blow.

The driver gentled his team to a halt beneath a covered carriage entrance, which allowed Kent to disembark—something he no longer managed so spryly—and still remain dry. On either side of the doors of the old mansion flickering stormlamps appeared to be standing in challenge to the elements, the circle of their light swaying and contracting as the wind swept beneath the eaves, moaning as though the voice of an ill earth.

Logs burned in the fireplace of an entry hall decorated in the "old style," and the painter was not sure which warmed him more. The same servant he had seen here for he could not remember how long took his hat, coat, and cane, and led him to the familiar sitting room. Here a fire burned, as well, and on the table beside a chair by the hearth stood a decanter of brandy, a cut-glass snifter, and a warmer, already lit. This would be his chair for the interview, or perhaps "audience" would have been a more appropriate term.

He poured the brandy and slowly turned the glass over the blue flame of the warmer, taking in the exquisite smell of the liquor.

There was not a single lamp in the room, so it was difficult to tell if the room had been altered; somehow he was quite sure that it had not. The weak light from the fire didn't penetrate many shadows. Here he could see part of one wall, there a well-used chair, and before him a painted screen.

A door opened, and that was followed by the unmistakable swish of a gown, sounds that always made his heart respond.

"I am so happy to see you, Averil." The voice had not changed either. Not cold but unexpressive, almost without inflection.

The countess took her seat in the chair beside the screen, arranged perfectly so that the light from the fire could not illuminate her face. She sat, as always, in shadow.

"And I am delighted to be in your company, Lady Chilton."

Her gown was deep blue, almost black, with white lace at the neck, he was sure. White lace at the sleeve cuffs covered her hands, though not completely, and these she clasped in her lap. He knew as the evening wore on, the hands would move more and occasionally even extend out into the dim light of the fire—and this was all he would see of the woman once thought to be the most beautiful in all the countries surrounding the Entide Sea.

"You are well?"

"I am. And I hope Lady Chilton can say the same?"

The head nodded. His eye was adjusting to the dark now—the trick was not to look at the fire, keep the pupil open. Her hair must be dyed. More likely, it was a wig, for he could see long dark tresses, even against the deep blue of her gown.

"Your letter has caused me great concern, Averil. Shall we speak of this?"

"Yes, certainly." Kent stared at the hands lying so still. "I fear I have made a grave error."

A nod, the dark coils of hair moving ever so slightly.

"They have sent young Flattery off on a ship bound for Oceana."

"We thought they might."

"Yes, but it never occurred to us that the Duchess of Morland and her brother would go as well," he said, as gently as he could, as though relating the death of a loved one.

The hands pulled back into the darkness. He followed the white of the lace. She pressed her hands to her face, he thought.

"*Elorin*," she said softly, with almost a hint of affection. "Tell me what you have learned, Averil."

Kent took a long breath. "I have . . . made mistakes, I fear." He paused again, the rehearsed speech suddenly forgotten. "Professor Dandish, I'm quite sure, was growing the blossom in his home. I had not realized it. I . . . I thought he was merely engaged to oversee the planting at the palace. Stupid of me. Once I became certain that he was not involved with our friends, I spoke to him. Told him just enough to alert him to the dangers, or so I thought. He wrote to Valary. At least, I predicted something correctly. Valary responded with just the right letter and the professor burned his Kingfoil almost immediately. I think no harm was done."

The hands returned to the lap where one scribed a small circle on the dark satin. "Certainly Dandish did not grow the plant for himself?"

"No. I think . . . I'm quite sure he grew it for the Duchess of Morland."

The hands found each other, and then became suddenly still. "The duel with Ipsword," she whispered.

"Yes. . . . And to think, she cites the Lady Chilton as her model." He paused, suddenly realizing that this might wound the woman sitting in the shadows. He forged on. "Flattery . . . that is Tristam Flattery, has become a great interest for them."

"They seem surer, now. Do you feel that as well?"

Kent nodded. Yes. They were more sure. "I still have fears that Eldrich did not, or could not, destroy all of his writings. Or perhaps Erasmus did manage to spirit something away, though how I can't imagine. They are more sure. As though they have a rough translation of some significant text. I can't believe they have gone beyond that, and none of them have talent, that is certain."

The hands moved into the darkness again, perhaps pressed to the heart. "And this young man. What do you make of him?"

"Well, I have met him." Kent thought a moment of the serious young man he had found wandering at the Society evening. "I think he is not one of them, though I'm sure they have hopes. He believes himself to be, like most of today's educated gentlemen, a man of reason. I sounded him quite thoroughly. He would laugh if we told him our fears. No, that is not true. He is far too polite to laugh, but he would certainly think us unbalanced or at least, irrational—which means he would react the same if he were approached by others. Despite this, I would say he is intelligent. Well educated, certainly, and not just as an empiricist. I'm told he speaks Entonne like a native, and knows something about art as well."

The head shook slightly.

"He is naive, and terribly so. Certainly completely unaware of what he is involved in. I would also say he is by nature a good man. Too trusting, and a little . . . romantic, I think."

"I did not think empiricists were romantic."

"No? Listen to them rhapsodize about the perfect world that reason will build. . . ." Kent poured himself more brandy.

"Do you think he is the one they are looking for?" Dread . . . she hid it well, with her flat tones, but still, Kent could hear it.

He turned his snifter slowly over the flame, watched the steam condense on the glass. "I fear that it is so. I waited far too long. I wrote you about the coin toss and the encounter with the ghost boy?"

The head nodded.

"And we can see now how his involvement has grown. Merton College. Dandish's prize student. Botany. Trevelyan's collection. Like a salmon nosing up a stream. Then he is called to the palace. Kingfoil." Kent stopped, dismayed for a second by his own catalog of "coincidences." "The night Sir Roderick brought him to the Society Trevelyan was there, if you can believe it. Another strike. And the Baron tried to warn him! Tried to warn Flattery! Everyone thinks him quite mad, fortunately, for you would not have believed what was said. And then there was this Entonne doctor, Varese, with his letters from Lucklow. You see how it goes? Tristam Flattery has no more awareness of what he is doing than the poor brute of a salmon, but he is in the stream. He senses the current and he is tracing it toward the source." Kent took his glass from the burner and cupped it in his hands. He found it too hot but held it all the same—penance. "I was a fool, Lady Chilton. I did not realize they had progressed so far."

"But you say he is intelligent, Averil. How long can it be before he will realize what occurs around him? Certainly even a man of reason cannot rationalize these things as coincidence forever."

"No," Kent admitted. "Even a reasonable man will be forced to see, eventually. What he will do when he realizes . . . I do not know. He will be in the company of the duchess when he finally wakens . . . the Duchess and whomever Palle has placed aboard. My fear is that Flattery will have performed the task needed of him . . . and then, even if he rejects the aims of the others, well, they can find another with talent—eventually. Tristam Flattery will not be necessary then."

"You are sure that it was not this very Tristam Flattery who found the book you say his uncle stole?"

"*Might* have stolen, Lady Chilton. Might have. One would have to meet the young man," Kent said, sure of this one thing at least. "Flattery would have to be the greatest actor in Avonel to put forth such a facade of sincerity—such genuineness. No. Tristam is what he seems, I am sure. Too thoughtful. Views himself as a man of the intellect, but his nature is broader than he realizes." Kent drank the hot brandy, coughing lightly from the fumes. "I have not told you of the bird?"

The hands opened.

"I have seen it myself now, and others have noted it on several occasions. A winter falcon, Lady Chilton."

"I think you know I have not studied ornithology."

"Excuse me. It is a large falcon that makes its natural home in the north, but it is much prized by falconers. Erasmus had such a bird, and now there is one that follows the nephew. Blood and flames, it is almost a familiar!"

The countess' reaction made Kent wonder if this was less significant than he had believed, in which case he had just looked the fool. She raised one hand to her mouth and seemed to consider.

"That is not necessarily a bad omen." The head shook. "It is difficult to say." A pause, then the flat voice again. "What will you do now?"

"Where to begin?" He fell silent though he felt he must speak to hide his fears, his growing panic. "We are not yet strong, Lady Chilton. We must move so slowly, like a man standing before a viper—we are invisible when still. A word to the wrong person and we are lost. I must be so very careful. I did not dare speak to young Flattery, even though I was so sure. . . ." *Was that my mistake?* Kent wondered. "I have made arrangements, though hurried and makeshift. I have also sent a message ahead to Farrow with a ship of war. We will wait and see what we hear."

"*Farrow.*" The hands clenched into small fists.

"Oh, yes. As I have said, he is the salmon in the stream," Kent affirmed. "The hound on the scent."

The countess shook her head. A pure white finger raised. "It is like life, Averil. Do you see? Seeking only to live. Seeking to be born anew." The finger disappeared and the white lace sleeves appeared to hang loose, like a doll's. "Is there anything else I should know?" she asked, her voice even more devoid of expression, if that were possible.

"Dandish was not as careful as he thought. Several parties know of his planting."

"But it was destroyed?"

"Yes. But still, they know." Kent hesitated before he spoke again. "I am also beginning to believe that all of the activity of Entonne agents in Avonel is not due to the treaty presently under negotiation." There, it was said.

"Palle is a fool!" she spat out, her voice suddenly coming to life with anger.

"No," Kent responded softly. "He is no fool. Ignorant of what he has begun, yes. Obsessed with the 'Entonne threat.' But no fool." He looked into the flames in the hearth, forgetting that he had intended not to. "Curiosity. It is our nature. The search for knowledge is presently enshrined almost as a first principle for the men of reason. Though others have learned that some knowledge should never be sought."

"The past," she said, her voice quavering just a little, "it always haunts us."

They did not speak for some time. Kent noted that the storm still assailed the world outside, and he did not look forward to leaving the warmth of the fire.

"You have been very busy, Averil," the countess said. "I am always impressed that the most innocent seeming gentlemen should be so cunning."

Kent gave a short laugh. "But I have survived as an artist all of my life, Lady

Chilton, and done rather well. There is no courtier half so cunning as an artist, I will tell you."

The countess laughed, and it was like some part of her youth emerging, unbidden. Kent had never forgotten that laugh. Even an echo of it cut into his heart like a lash.

How have we grown so old? he thought, and realized he had pressed a hand to his eyes.

"Averil? Are you well?"

He pulled his hand away and nodded.

"There is nothing more, then?"

He almost dropped his glass as he set it on the table. "Just this," he managed and reached into the pocket of his coat to remove a small leather bag. He worked free the knot and pulled out a neatly folded handkerchief. This he unfolded with some care, laying it open to reveal three small seeds, one half-decomposed. He leaned forward and held these out to the woman in the shadows, looking down at the floor as he did so, despite his true desires.

The square of linen was lifted from his hands, and he sat up. There in the shadow he could see the countess peering into the folds of the fabric. Kent could hear her breath coming in short little gasps. Unexpectedly, she leaned forward into the light, but her hair fell in such a way as to hide her face.

"I dug them from the boxes Dandish had used for his planting," Kent said, hiding his disappointment, he hoped.

She leaned back, her head resting against the chair. He could almost make out a profile—white skin against raven black hair. "There is so much we don't know." He saw the head roll back and forth. But then she forced herself upright, sitting with the seeds cradled in her hands. "I have taken a precaution, Averil, in case something untoward occurs. I have written out the little I know regarding these matters. Don't worry, it is well hidden. You will receive this document if. . . . Well, you understand. There is much at risk."

He nodded, almost raising his hands to stop this line of conversation, but instead he reached out and lifted his glass again. He peered down at the burning logs. For some moments they did not speak, and he became lost in the maze of questions that he pondered through virtually all his waking hours. For the briefest second, the idea of being left the countess' document thrilled him, but then his saner self took hold. No, no. Better to remain ignorant. Far better. And the countess . . . he could not bear the idea that she would be gone.

"I think you must have spent some considerable sum of money in this endeavor, Averil." The voice was expressionless again except that it had become soft.

The painter looked up and then quickly down again. He nodded.

"I have meant to say that I feel very strongly that I paid far too little for the last painting I purchased. It is a work of some considerable merit and gives me constant pleasure. You are too kind to your friends, Averil. Too generous. We take advantage of you. I absolutely must make amends. No. Do not protest. I will not hear it."

◁ Twenty

After two days at sea Tristam had adjusted to the constant motion of the ship and it was unusual for him to need to put out a steadying hand—something he took a little pride in. If he was to spend two years on this voyage, it would be best to adapt to the conditions as completely as possible.

The lieutenant, Mr. Osler, had allowed him to climb aloft, though Tristam had only gone as high as the lower yard—the "main top," this small platform was called—but even there the motion was much greater than on deck. Even so, Tristam had wanted to stay, high in the branches of this strange tree, with its massive trunk and tracery of supporting vines. The swaying of this tree in the wind was almost hypnotic and the feeling that he stared out over a vast, empty plain Tristam found strange and compelling.

Glancing down, he noticed the duchess shading her eyes, looking up at him. She waved and that smile appeared. Tristam raised a hand in return. He felt a pull, as though gravity tugged at him, but he resisted. *But it is inevitable*, he admitted. *I will go down. My resistance will crumble.*

He had spent most of a sleepless night mulling over the conversation with the Duchess of Morland. *"But you are not like him, Tristam. Not like him at all."* It had seemed such a genuine expression of concern. . . . And somehow Tristam felt that the duchess had believed what she said. Even her warning against trusting his emotions to her had seemed to come from the heart. A warning he knew he should heed.

The contradictions were too great, and so Tristam remained at the crosstrees, hoping the wind would eventually clear his mind enough that all contradictions would find resolution like the image in a glass as it was brought into focus.

One moment he found himself questioning his earlier cynicism about the duchess, and the next, some remembered incident would prove the feeling reasonable. The murder of Ipsword kept coming to mind, like a whispered warning. The viscount followed the orders of the duchess, or so Jaimy claimed, and Tristam thought it unlikely that his cousin was wrong. *Ipsword.* The name had taken on its own meaning, like an incident of history—a tragic incident. *Ipsword.*

All so confusing. Even the fresh sea wind did not clear his mind sufficiently that he could see his way through the maze of other people's motivations.

For several hours he stayed, sweeping the ocean with his glass, hoping to see whales or the low skimming albatross, trying to force his mind away from his problems—and from the duchess.

There was something purifying about sitting up on the crosstrees among the swelling sails, anointed by the wind. If it did not help him solve the mysteries surrounding this voyage, Tristam felt that at least he gained some peace of mind from the experience.

When hunger finally drove him back down to the deck, he felt a sense of inner calm, as though the machinations of men were short lived and of small import when compared to the timeless grandeur of the sea.

As he descended the companionway, Tristam was met by the duchess' maid who addressed him in Entonne, perhaps happy to hear her own language. The duchess, she said, had invited him to tea. His return to the real world was going to be abrupt.

Jacel was petite, red-blond, and pretty in a day-to-day fashion—she did not possess the regal beauty of the duchess, and her movements all seemed small, controlled, fearful of offering offense—but there was some part of Tristam that appreciated her more for that. Jacel dimpled when she smiled, and Tristam found immediately that he would make small jests with her in an attempt to cause these dimples to appear. She had told Tristam that she suffered from the sickness of the sea and he thought she looked a little desolate—as though she dearly wished her mistress had not chosen to make this terrible voyage.

Tristam slipped into his cabin and put his Fromme glass away, dug out a neck cloth, and proceeded to the door of the great cabin. He found the duchess, wrapped in a heavy woolen shawl, playing a solitary card game. She looked up as Tristam came in and greeted him in the language of Doorn—a common practice of the Farr aristocracy: to speak a language not accessible to their servants.

"Do you know, Tristam, I have already read an entire novel since we set out. I fear now that I have not brought nearly enough books. I hope we shall be able to exchange . . . ? Stern and Osler, it turns out, are both readers as well, so we might hope their interests are not too . . . seamanlike."

"I have brought, almost exclusively, the reference books of my trade, Duchess, space being so limited, and have only a handful of other things. But if you want to read botany, ornithology, marine biology, geology, I have sufficient numbers of these texts to last this voyage and more."

The duchess laughed, transforming herself into a charming innocent girl. "I should not even have asked. But I will not make fun. In a few months even geology might seem fascinating."

Tea was offered, for the afternoon wore on, and Tristam took a seat at the table.

"Do you think we may speak privately like this?" the duchess asked, glancing up at the deck.

"Sailors travel, Duchess. Doorn is visited often. We should take no chances."

"Then move closer, Tristam, for I want to hear your thoughts."

For the first time that day Tristam reached out to steady himself, moving his chair so that it was near to the duchess, gripping the table as he did so. Her knee pressed against the side of his thigh, and when she did not immediately move away, Tristam felt his body respond to this closeness.

"I wanted to talk to you about Professor Dandish," she whispered. "I have thought much about him." She paused to stare directly into Tristam's eyes, as though she were gauging whether or not he could be trusted. He was not sure what she decided. "It seems to me, now, that the professor gave up too soon. Does that not seem true to you?"

Tristam felt his anger ignite, surprising him completely. Whatever his thoughts had been of the duchess over these past hours, his sympathy was suddenly erased. Why had she drawn poor Dandish into this?

She must believe me a terrible fool, he thought. This suggestion of intimacy was obviously designed to have him open his heart to her, to tell her the things he might have hidden in the past. After the genuineness of their discussion the previous night, this caused Tristam some pain. He made an effort to keep his voice neutral. "I am not sure how long Dandish was engaged in this inquiry, Duchess, but it is my belief that the professor knew his health was precarious and destroyed his study so that it would not be discovered."

"You think that's it, then?" Those searching eyes held his, causing the anger to soften a little but not erasing the pain.

He shrugged. "It seems likely."

"There is no chance that the professor solved the problem?"

"Nothing is impossible, Duchess."

"Perhaps your explanation makes sense, but there is just something . . . I cannot explain it, but it seems like the professor acted so rashly. He was not rash by nature, Tristam, or so I thought."

"Perhaps it was something else, then?" Tristam said it with difficulty, led on by his resentment.

"What do you mean?"

What had Dandish written? "*I am not quite the old fool the duchess takes me for.*" *Nor am I the young fool*, he thought, *and she might as well know it.* "The destruction of the planting, Duchess, it took place immediately after the death of Baron Ipsword." He heard himself inhale as though strongly in need of air.

Her mouth lost all of its soft beauty. She turned away and nodded, as though saying, *Yes, it was only a matter of time.*

He expected her to explode in sudden anger, or to plead ignorance of what he implied, but instead she spoke very softly.

"Tristam, it was never my intention that the baron would be harmed." She stopped, closing her eyes for a second. When she looked up again, a tear had streaked her cheek, like the ocean's spray on clear glass. "Julian. . . ." She looked away, touching delicate fingers to the bridge of her nose for a second. "He swears it was not intentional. Others . . . others say differently, I realize. I was not there. But I never intended anything more than to have Ipsword leave poor Dandish alone. He tortured him, you know that. Dandish had no defense against this irrational hatred. Ipsword's attacks—merely jealousy—caused the professor terrible anguish. I did what you probably wished to do yourself." She formed a fist and beat time on the table to the next words. "I wanted Ipsword to leave the professor in peace. That was all. But Julian. . . ." Her voice caught as she said this, her fist opened and spread flat on the dark wood. "I swear, Tristam, that no such thing will happen again. I could not bear it." Again the duchess looked away, turning in her chair to stare out the transom windows. "Some need protectors," she said so quietly that Tristam was not sure he had heard correctly.

Standing at the rail, watching the sun set, Tristam felt the cold of the sea air. The master stood at the opposite rail, waiting with his sextant to shoot the first stars to appear—something that normally would have interested Tristam. But not this evening. Even the sunset, which was spectacular, barely drew his attention.

A litany of questions repeated themselves over and over, all to do with the true nature of the Duchess of Morland and her intentions—and with his own nature as well. Was it true that the viscount had not followed her instructions? Somehow Tristam could not imagine the duchess issuing an order to have a man murdered. She was not a criminal. Tristam thought of the viscount and felt a shiver course through him. He seemed like the most amiable of men. . . .

I am being buffeted about like a feather on the winds, Tristam thought. He wondered if his character really did differ fundamentally from his father's? He wondered if it was possible for someone to be coldly self-interested, manipulative in the extreme, and still have a heart? Human beings seemed capable of embracing such contradictions.

❧ Twenty-One

A gale found them on the fifth day beyond sight of land. It was not a bad gale as such things went, or so the sailors said, but it was enough to lay the green hands and passengers low with the sickness of the sea and keep them in a state of constant fear. Even Tristam suffered, though he managed to eat and retain the bit of food he forced down.

On the second day of foul weather he tumbled out of his hammock and struggled into the oilskins Jack Beacham had urged him to purchase. Although Tristam had found the sounds of the gale frightening from the comparative protection of his swinging hammock—the thunder of waves reverberating through the hull with such force that he was almost certain the ship would not stand it—he was truly alarmed when he made his way up through the hatch. The sounds of the seas pounding the hull were not as pronounced, but the wind in the rigging produced a chorus of screaming and wailing that he realized had been much muffled below. It was quite unnerving. And the seas appeared truly monstrous.

The deck was wet and slick from spray and the crests that broke over the forward quarter. They foamed down the lee deck and filled the scuppers so the bulwark looked to be a short wall standing in the midst of a chaotic sea. Tristam braced his feet against the hatch cover and grasped the lifeline that had been rigged at the onset of bad weather.

The rain had abated, but clouds flew low overhead, their gray presence threatening the deluge. Topsails whipped and cracked each time the ship labored to the top of a green crest and the wind howled in the rigging, changing pitch with the gusts: a most disconcerting chorus.

The *Swallow* was "lying to," which Beacham had explained meant riding to reefed topsails, and she made no headway, or movement forward, but only held her own against the head winds, making half a knot of leeway—the term used to describe the ship's sliding to one side. Tristam watched the spectacle for a long while, until the little ship's rise to every wave began to inspire a semblance of confidence. Once he felt his fear begin to subside, the naturalist in him began to observe, for he had only experienced such weather upon the land. Each time the ship rose and shook off the water that had crashed aboard, Tristam felt a little triumphant. On top of each wave he gazed down the long, reptilian spine of the crest, thinking how much it looked like a living thing. And then it passed beneath, shrugging the ship aside, the crests tumbling and blowing off in white spume.

"Your first gale at sea, Mr. Flattery?" a voice shouted above the tumult.

Tristam turned to find Captain Stern calling out from down the quarterdeck. Tristam nodded and forced a smile. He made his way, hand over hand, along the lifeline and joined the captain at the binnacle. Behind him two sailors tended the helm, one steering and one standing by to assist.

The captain grinned at Tristam. "We've weathered the worst of it. I think we will be under way again before dark. The wind is abating. Can you feel it?"

Tristam could not, but he held up a hand as he'd seen sailors do and nodded to the captain, hoping he did not look completely foolish.

"Already it's veered a point or more. Not much of a gale, really, just enough to ruin our two days' run and test the green hands. You seem to be recovering quickly? Have your sea legs now, eh?"

Tristam nodded, hoping this was true.

"You might look in on Doctor Llewellyn, Mr. Flattery. The poor man has become the physician who can't cure himself. Mr. Taine has been trying to tend him, but he has two seamen who slid across the deck and have real injuries. Nearly lost them over the side." The captain shook his head, alarmed even at the idea.

"I'll see to him immediately."

Tristam climbed back down the companionway and into the dim bowels of the ship, where all the hatches had been closed against the weather. Below it was more difficult to keep one's balance, for there was no horizon to fix on, and Tristam was relieved to find that his nausea did not return immediately.

Passing forward through the ship, Tristam knocked at the door to the doctor's cabin. When there was no response, he became alarmed and tried the door, which was not locked.

"Doctor Llewellyn?" The cabin seemed even darker and more airless than the rest of the ship. Something shifted in the shadows.

"Mr. Taine?" came a hoarse whisper.

"It is Tristam Flattery, Doctor. The captain asked me to inquire after your health."

"Ah, Mr. Flattery," the doctor rasped. "I am as wretched as a man can be. The ship still swims?"

"Sir?" Tristam realized suddenly what the doctor meant. "Oh, yes. The gale is blowing itself out and the ship is riding like a duck. Captain Stern says we shall make sail before sunset."

"Thank Farrelle for that," the man said with real feeling. "How fares the duchess?"

"I don't know, Doctor; I have only just found my sea legs, as they say. Shall I look in for you?"

"Would you, Mr. Flattery? I have been poor help."

"I shall be glad to." Tristam closed the door and left the man to his misery. The young naturalist found himself smirking. There was, Tristam had to admit, some satisfaction in seeing a man convinced of his own superiority reduced to a condition of utter humility. And the good doctor was thanking *Farrelle!* Tristam laughed aloud. Some "man of reason."

In the poor light Tristam found the door to the great cabin and knocked.

"Yes?" came the voice of the duchess. It did not seem to be greatly affected by the gale.

"It is Tristam, Duchess."

"Do come in," the woman called over the sounds of the wind and sea.

Tristam pushed the door open and found the duchess sitting on a low stool wedged into a leeward corner of the cabin. She held a steaming cup in her hands and leaned over a berth rigged with a lee board. It appeared that the duchess wore her warmest possible clothing and was wrapped as well in several woolen blankets. The effect was incongruous, for she looked like a wealthy beggar, a vagabond duchess, if such a thing were possible. On the berth beside her lay a motionless form, apparently much reduced by the ravages of her condition. Poor Jacel.

"I am glad to see that at least one landsman has survived," she said, her voice hale and spirit apparently as strong as ever.

"I seem to have found my sea legs," Tristam said. There was something irresistible about the sailors' language to Tristam and he used it whenever opportunity presented itself. "The Duchess is well?"

"Yes . . . though I'm supposed to be a delicate flower, Tristam, in truth, I have the constitution of a mule. Poor Jacel has not done nearly so well." She turned to the inert form and said in Entonne, "Have you, my pet?" There was no response.

The duchess sipped from the cup. "I am grateful to cook who brought me this broth. I would be a block of ice without it—almost am, in fact. I never thought such wretched fare could be so welcome." She sniffed the cup and wrinkled up her perfect nose. "I didn't realize that they poisoned the crew thrice daily. It is a miracle they survive."

Tristam laughed, half from mere relief.

At that moment the maid rolled toward the edge of the bed and the duchess deftly scooped up a bucket. Tristam backed from the room at a nod from the duchess but not before he had glimpsed the strangest of sights: the Duchess of Morland holding a bucket into which her maid was terribly ill. And odder yet, the duchess seemed amused by this as well.

Tristam went looking for his mentor in the ways of the sea, Jack Beacham, but when he could not find the boy in the 'tweendecks mess or the midshipmen's berth, Tristam climbed out onto the deck once more. He was not sure, but the winds seemed to be falling—and the seas, though still large, did not break so regularly.

Hobbes stood at the rail, a glass trained out to sea on the starboard quarter. Stern stood at his side, gazing in the same direction.

"The *Raven*, I would say, Captain."

Stern nodded. "Nash has had her this past year. Their destination will be the same as ours, though look how they come! See how they are pushing their ship!"

Tristam moved a little closer. He scanned the waves off in the direction in which the officers stared. There did seem to be a small dot of white that did not appear and disappear the way the crests did.

"Ah, Mr. Flattery," Stern said, noticing Tristam. "Here is a sight to chill your heart. Fortunately, she is one of ours." He handed Tristam a well-used field glass. "There. A ship of war," he said, his voice filled with admiration. "Now there's beauty for you!"

Tristam took the heavy naval glass and, after a moment, found the ship—appreciating all the more his gift from Dandish. The black hull was throwing spray as she pounded into each sea. After Stern's words Tristam did find the sight ominous. "I am glad she is ours, Captain Stern."

"And for good reason, Mr. Flattery. The *Raven* would make short work of our little *Swallow*. But not to worry, even if we are wrong and she is not the *Raven*, there are no unfriendly ships in these waters." The captain took a watch from his pocket. "She will overhaul us before dark, Mr. Hobbes. Have the signal man stand by."

Tristam stayed at the rail for some time watching the great ship of war as she bowled along in a headlong rush over the dark ocean. Poor undermanned, under-canvased *Swallow* must lay to in such conditions, Tristam thought, and uncomfortable she was, too, but the great frigate, he could see, had reefs only in her top gallants, though her royal masts had been housed or sent down, Tristam could not tell which.

Under the oppressive gray of the passing gale, the black ship came abreast, though she stood off a quarter mile. *Raven* only luffed her sail a bit, slowing like a great horse, rolling its bit and dancing in place. A hoist of signals appeared, causing Stern and his officers some consternation, Tristam thought, though he could not hear what was being said. This was navy business and not for the landsman to know.

Stern had his signal man answer, and then the *Raven* dipped her ensign, trimmed sail, and gathered way again. In only a few moments she was throwing spray thirty yards off her bow. Tristam watched her go, her great galleried stern bobbing over the waves.

It was time, too, for *Swallow* to be off. Reefs were being shaken out of the topsails by the topmen and upper staysails were being set. Tristam watched the procedure, or "evolution" as it was called, as the men fought the wet canvas and the motion of the ship. It took a long hour, for the *Swallow*'s crew was small compared to a ship of war, and the master did not call all hands unless it was truly necessary, preferring to let the watch below have their rest.

It was dusk when the Jacks scrambled down the ratlines and most disappeared below for their supper, only a few remaining on deck to coil lines and to stand ready to do the deck officer's bidding. Tristam noticed the captain had gone below, to his own meal, no doubt, in the tiny wardroom that served the senior officers.

Overhead the cloud cover was finally breaking and there would be a quarter-moon that night, or so Tristam estimated. He moved to the rail and peered out into the growing darkness, certain he had seen the shape of an albatross sweep by close above the rolling sea. For some time Tristam stood staring out into the dark on an almost deserted deck. It was eerie, hearing the great sweep of the seas left by the passing gale, feeling their power even as it diminished. Again Tristam had that sense of loneliness in the face of the great ocean's strength, which made him think of Kent.

Suddenly there was a fluttering before him and he started back, thinking a piece of the rigging had torn free. But it was not so; a white bird hovered before Tristam, beating the air with its wings, and even in the darkness he was sure it was a falcon.

"Begone!" Tristam said, waving his hands. *We are hundreds and hundreds of miles from any shore!* But the falcon would not go. It hovered before him, reaching with its talons as though expecting him to hold out a falconer's glove. Tristam pulled a belaying pin from a pinrail and thrust it at the bird. "Begone!" he exclaimed. But the bird would do nothing of the sort. It grasped the pin and Tristam found himself supporting the bird as it tried to adjust to the ship's motion.

A noise behind caused Tristam to turn, and there in the main hatch stood a Jack, eyes wide. He made a warding sign and hurried below. Tristam pushed the belaying pin out into the darkness, letting it fall into the sea, and the bird took to wing and disappeared.

"Blood and flames!" Tristam whispered. "We are hundreds of miles out to sea. This isn't possible."

Tristam had slept fitfully, not uncommon for him, his dreams disturbing but only half-remembered—gone entirely by morning. The motion of the ship had eased considerably during the night and was very near to normal now. There was also sun, Tristam could tell by the light in his tiny port, even though he had hung a cloth over it for privacy. Footsteps descended the companionway ladder, not far outside the door of Tristam's cabin. These footsteps came from leather shoes, so this was a midshipman or officer—not a barefoot Jack—and the owner of these shoes was in a considerable hurry. Jack Beacham or midshipman Chilsey.

A knock sounded on Tristam's door.

"Yes?"

"It is Jack Beacham, Mr. Flattery," an anxious voice said. "I think you should come on deck, sir."

Tristam was not sure what this was about, but he rolled out of his hammock immediately. "I'll be along directly."

Tristam threw his clothes on and thumped up the ladder to the deck. Beacham waited at the stairs descending into the ship's waist. There was a gathering at the mainmast where Tristam could see the tall gray form of the ship's master standing out among the others.

As he approached, Tristam realized there was something on the mast that had drawn everyone's attention. His first thought was that it was a bird or something else of interest to an empiricist, but then the unnatural silence struck him. When the Jacks saw him, they all stepped back, their eyes fixed on him in a manner that was not friendly.

"Do you recognize this, Mr. Flattery?" Hobbes asked, pointing to an opened book pinned to the mast by a knife driven through its spine—like a dead butterfly tacked to a board. It even fluttered a bit in the breeze.

Tristam found himself unable to answer but managed to nod, adding to the silence.

"Take it down, Mr. Hobbes," came the captain's voice. "May I speak with you, please, Mr. Flattery?"

"I realize it is difficult to take such things seriously, Mr. Flattery, but it is one of the central superstitions of the Jacks." Stern looked a little ill, Tristam thought. "To drive a knife into the mast will bring winds, usually a full storm—a hurricane, as you call it on land. But it is believed that men caught for weeks in the doldrums have done it out of desperation: usually with calamitous results. That is the root of it. But to take something that belongs to a man and spike it to the mast with a knife is to bring calamity upon the man himself."

Stern sat at the table in the small wardroom the officers used for their meals. Tristam was not sure if the captain was this subdued because he was embarrassed by the actions of his own crew or whether this ominous calm had some other cause. To the captain's right stood Mr. Osler. The officer's manner gave Tristam his only hint. Osler was almost rigidly still, spoke only when addressed, and then quietly and with deference. Tristam found that he was unconsciously imitating the lieutenant's manner—like two truant school boys.

"Now tell me, Mr. Flattery: we are seven hundred and fifty nautical miles from land. *Fifty leagues.*" Stern paused, looking up into Tristam's face. "Is it possible that this hawk could fly so far?"

Tristam suppressed the response that came first to mind. ("How else do you think it came there, Captain? Magic?") The truth was that though land birds were sometimes seen far from land—blown out to sea by storms, some thought—Tristam knew of no sighting of a large powerful hawk so far out to sea.

"I don't know, Captain Stern," Tristam offered in a small voice. "It seems unlikely but . . ."

"How do you explain it, then?" Stern said, not so quietly, his voice clearly accusatory—an attitude that the naturalist did not like.

"I cannot, sir, though I think it was a trained falcon, for it seemed to want me to give it my wrist upon which to land."

"Captain Stern?" The physician's face appeared in the open doorway. "If I may, sir?" Llewellyn was still pale and weak but showed signs of returning to his normal manner.

Stern glanced up at Osler quickly, but the young officer did not meet his captain's eyes. Llewellyn should not have been interrupting. But then Stern shrugged.

"Yes, Doctor?"

"As a naturalist myself, I thought I could shed some light on this matter." Llewellyn pushed the door open and entered, taking a chair, though it was not offered. Obviously, the man had been listening from beyond the door. "It would seem likely that this was a falconer's bird, escaped, no doubt, from a passing ship. Coming upon the *Swallow,* it tried to land. In its exhaustion and confusion at finding itself at sea, the bird took to the first man it saw, as it would to its own master. I do not doubt that the bird would have responded thus to myself, or to yourself, sir, had we been the first it saw. There can be no other explanation."

The captain looked at his lieutenant, who nodded. "Well, that does make some sense," he conceded. "Though it will take more than a cogent argument to convince the Jacks, damn their superstitious ways!"

The captain fixed Tristam with the look he no doubt used to reduce sailors to the consistency of jellyfish. "Had I known you were the heir of Erasmus Flattery, I tell you honestly, I would have thought twice before having you aboard."

Tristam felt his timidity passing and his own anger beginning to stir. "I am his heir, Captain, but I hardly knew the man. I am not his direct descendant, nor am I his protegé in any way. I am almost as closely related to Admiral Flattery who had control of the Blue Squadron at Cape Locke." This was not strictly true, but Tristam was grasping at anything that might keep him afloat.

The captain considered this for a moment, tugging at his close-trimmed beard with long fingers. His voice softened just perceptibly. "Well, no doubt what you say is true, Mr. Flattery. And I believe none of this mage business myself, mind you. It is only the poor ignorant men before the mast who I am in consideration of. Foolish and ignorant though they be, they are necessary to the success of this voyage and if the Jacks think you are the heir of a necromancer . . . well, they are a superstitious lot and there's no telling what they might do."

"Do you mean that Mr. Flattery might be in danger, Captain Stern?" the doctor was clearly shocked.

"Oh, now, Doctor Llewellyn, I would not say that. No indeed. But their beliefs and fears will affect their service. I have seen it before. There will be no violence against an individual on a ship that I command, you can be sure of that. But the Jacks may not make Mr, Flattery welcome, and that is a hard thing when you are on a small vessel for two years."

The physician straightened in his chair. "Well, the lack of understanding; nay, the jealousy of the uneducated is not something we are all strangers to, Captain. Be of stout heart, Mr. Flattery, the approbation of the ignorant is a worthless coin, I can tell you."

Tristam did not know how to respond. He felt like he was on trial here, when he had done absolutely nothing wrong. He had known the navy men were superstitious, but he did not imagine it could be taken to such absurd lengths.

The captain turned to his senior officer. "We will have to try to control the damage that this incident has caused. Fother the hole, as it were. Mr. Osler, you will spread the word that this was a domesticated hawk—a falconer's bird escaped from a passing ship—that happened to find Mr. Flattery on deck when it looked for a place to light. Speak to Mr. Hobbes . . . you know how the Jacks hang upon his every word. If he were to say he once saw such a thing when he sailed with Gregory . . . well, the men would be touching Mr. Flattery for luck. Though I don't imagine Hobbes would agree to lie. Still, if he does not give credence to this mage business, it will help immeasurably." The captain turned back to Tristam and tried to smile reassuringly. "Don't be too concerned, Mr. Flattery. I'm sure this will pass. Just carry on as though nothing has happened. It is always the best course."

The naturalist nodded. "Yes, sir," he said and went out of the wardroom toward the companionway, feeling as though he had just been before the headmaster—something he thought was well past in his life.

Tristam emerged on deck into bright sunlight. There was no sign of the gale that had halted their progress, and *Swallow* was bowling along with a fair wind over a blue sea. Jack Beacham was loitering by the rail, and when he saw Tristam, he crossed over to the naturalist immediately.

The young man examined Tristam's face as though looking for damage. "A word, Mr. Flattery," Beacham said, and then cast a worried look along the deck. "A Jack named Kreel. A big man with a scar over his right eye. Dark hair and complexion. It would be wise to stay clear of him, sir." Beacham broke into a sudden smile as though they shared a jest. "Pleasures of the day to you, Mr. Flattery." And the lad was gone.

Tristam did not know the code of the sailors, but he was quite sure that Jack Beacham had just breached it—or perhaps officers in training stayed aloof from such things.

Tristam had this sudden impulse to go talk sense to the Jacks—even to this man Kreel. But he knew that Captain Stern had believed the explanation of the tame falcon because it fit into his beliefs. The Jacks would believe their own explanation—that Tristam was somehow the spawn of a mage—because it fit theirs. Though what they thought this meant, other than bad luck, Tristam was not sure.

Sweeping his gaze the length of the ship, Tristam found the duchess perched on a bench the carpenter had built so that the two women could sit in relative comfort on deck, with their backs to the rail. She clutched a book in her hands and stared up, shading her eyes with a gloved hand.

Needing the company of someone who did not think him supernatural, Tristam crossed the deck to the duchess.

"Tristam! The pleasures of the day to you." She smiled and Tristam noticed that the sun had given her face a very appealing blush.

"And to the Duchess. It is a fine day."

"Indeed, it is." She pulled her skirt closer and motioned for Tristam to take a seat beside her.

"What is it you read?" Tristam asked, for he could not bring himself to broach the subject that concerned him. He realized then that he missed having a true friend—someone like Jaimy—in whom he could confide.

She held up a clothbound book so that he might read the title. It was Bedwell's *A Young Seaman's Manual*. "I'm quite tired of not understanding the half—nay, far more than half—of what is spoken aboard this ship. I have set out to learn my ropes, as they say. I thought it would pass the time as well."

Tristam found himself smiling at the idea of the Duchess of Morland learning to speak like a sailor.

"You needn't look so amused, Tristam, I am just as capable of learning such things as any half-educated farmer's son. Now," she waved the book at the ship, "perhaps you can clarify a few matters for me, since you have become such a seaman yourself. What area, precisely, is referred to by the word 'focs'le'? I hear it spoken of constantly, yet I cannot find reference to it in this little book."

"The seamen say, 'focs'le', Duchess, but it is properly written 'forecastle'. No doubt you have found it spelled so in your book."

"Ah, that is the way of it."

"There are a number of terms compressed in this same manner." Tristam pointed to the rigging. "These lines the Jacks use to climb aloft . . ."

"The ratlines."

"Precisely. They are referred to as 'ratl'nes'. Just as the word inscribed as 'gunwale' is pronounced 'gunnel'. 'Boatswain' is said 'bosun'. 'Studdingsails' are 'stuns'les.'"

"I begin to see." The duchess waved the book again. "And this mast—the small one at the back—it is the mizzen?"

"It is, indeed, though one should properly say 'aft.'"

"Aft it is. The large one in the center is, quite logically, the main mast, and the smallish one on the forecastle," she pronounced the word correctly, "is the foremast?"

"Correct in every detail."

"Now perhaps you can help with this cloud of sails. There seem to be so many . . ."

All of Tristam's reservation about the duchess disappeared in the next hour, as they tended to do in her presence—when she was not obviously manipulating him to some end. Tristam realized that she had sensed how alienated the incident with the Jacks had left him feeling and she focused all of her charm and wit in an effort to combat this. It was, Tristam thought, like finding oneself suddenly in a shaft of warm sunlight after the cold and rain. His mind was taken completely away from recent troubles and Tristam found himself actually able to laugh.

He was also impressed with the pace of her learning and realized that in no time she would be able to talk ships and sail in a manner which would no doubt set all the officers' hearts aquiver.

The watch changed, and the seaman who came to the wheel nodded graciously to the duchess but conspicuously ignored Tristam.

The men detailed to stream the log acted in the same manner.

The duchess touched Tristam's arm. "This foolishness about your uncle has become tiresome, has it not? Do these Jacks think you will turn them into toads?"

Tristam shook his head. "I do not understand it myself. I wish that I could perform magic. I would live a different life, that is certain."

"Well," the duchess said very quietly, "I have often wondered if you once took on the appearance of an Entonne musician?"

The change in Tristam's face must have been extreme, for the duchess patted his hand. "I jest, dear Tristam. I try to cheer you. It was dark, everyone had consumed too much of the Erasmus Grape. . . ." She looked at him slyly. "Do such things often happen when you drink the Erasmus Grape?"

"Duchess, I am at your mercy in this, as you well know. I—I do not know how to make amends for what occurred. Tell me what you would have me do and I will gladly do it."

"Such an offer, Mr. Flattery! I must consider this seriously. Perhaps . . . well, no. Let me think a while."

She was, Tristam knew, taking the greatest pleasure from his discomfiture.

The duchess' attention was drawn away. "Tell me, when they heave the log; that is to tell the depth of the sea?"

The change of subject was abrupt, and Tristam almost shook his head to get his wits clear. "They 'stream' the log, I believe, and 'heave' or 'swing' the lead. The log is a device to measure the ship's speed through the water, something that must be known for accurate navigation. They stream the log aft—it is a device that will stay more or less still in the water—and they count the number of knots on the streaming line that pass in a measured period of time. Thus the nautical term 'knots.' We are making five knots.

"The lead, or lead line, is a weight on a graduated line that is lowered to measure the depth to the bottom. Beacham let me heave it once in the harbor of Avonel. I was surprised to find that one can really feel when it contacts the earth. There could be no mistake.

"The sailors sometimes put tallow into a depression in the bottom of the lead and material from the sea bottom will stick to this and indicate something about the nature of the ocean floor. Quite ingenious."

"I see. Stream the log, heave the lead."

Hobbes, the ship's master, came up then, speaking to them kindly and jesting with Tristam in a way that would indicate friendship between them. Tristam knew the old sailor was doing it at the order of his captain, but, still, he felt tremendously grateful, for even the man at the wheel nodded to him when the master had gone off to his duties.

The duchess decided she had been too long in the sun and excused herself, and Tristam went below to his closet, suddenly afraid that a falcon would appear, as impossible as that was so far out to sea.

They were seven days to their next landfall, the island of Farrow. The place where Tristam owned a vineyard. During that week Tristam tried not to constantly scan the skies for white birds, but lost himself in his duties. He dragged a net behind, four times a day, and spent hours examining what was caught under his magnification instrument—plankton, largely. Sometimes the physician would come to look into Tristam's instrument and discuss what had been found, and sometimes Beacham or the duchess would drop in to see what had been caught in his net. The microscopic world was fascinating to most, Tristam found, and even those with no previous interest in natural history, such as the cook and boatswain, took their turn peering into the lens. Jack Beacham was by to peer into the instrument so often he was almost an annoyance, though he was too good-natured to be truly a bother.

All the while Tristam kept careful journals of what he saw, of weather and sea conditions, birds and sea life. The master and his mate used a *deep line*, a lead line used for measuring the ocean depth, and carried a set of measurements across an area of sea that had not formerly been investigated. Tristam examined every sample they brought up from the bottom and was rewarded with two species of *Onuphis* he was sure had not been previously recorded, and at unheard of depths—which made Tristam wonder if they were not some other genus that displayed similar characteristics. The complexities of taxonomy aside, the problem of finding an appropriate name for his first discovered species was rather pleasant. He would have liked to name a new species for the duchess, but a sea worm did not seem appropriate.

He spent some time each day with the duchess, often talking about natural history, for she had such a lively mind she seemed interested in everything. Tristam spent even more time than usual wondering about her own feeling for him, but as life aboard ship offered them little privacy, there were no awkward situations as a result.

The duchess was always kindness itself to him, but she also treated him like a favorite younger cousin, not a potential suitor. But just when Tristam convinced himself that her feelings to him were purely innocent in nature, she would do something to set him wondering—lay her hand on his arm in a most familiar manner and hold his eye just a little longer than was proper. One night, as he left her company, she leaned against him so that he felt the swell of her breast, and then she kissed him tenderly on the corner of his mouth. Of course, aboard ship people often lost their balance, but Tristam did not think that was the explanation. At lease he preferred not to think that.

During those days Tristam seemed to swing between feelings of joy and utter desolation depending on what occurred between him and the duchess—or it might have been more accurate to say, according to his current interpretation of what occurred between them.

On the morning of the sixteenth day at sea they raised the island of Farrow. It floated on the horizon under a pile of white cloud, as islands often do: two graceful purple hills rising out of the blue sea.

Twenty-Two

As the *Swallow* drew closer to Farrow, Tristam realized that not all the cloud hanging over the island was composed of water vapor. Some of it was certainly smoke.

"I have not seen that in twenty years," Stern said as he lowered his glass.

Tristam kept his own instrument trained on the lip of the volcano. There was smoke, to be sure, but very little.

"Mount Forwood has done this off and on since the discovery," the captain mused. "I can't think why it would stop now."

"*Sail, Mr. Osler! Two points off the larboard bow,*" came a cry from aloft.

Tristam swept the area off to larboard.

"The mail ship, sir," the lookout called down.

There was a general moan among the crew and officers alike.

"That is bad luck," Stern said. "It will be two weeks before our letters go off now."

"Shall we try to signal them, Captain?" Hobbes stood shading his eyes and looking off at the distant ship. Tristam got the impression the old mariner did not need a glass to see so little distance; his eyes were not like those of mere humans.

The captain considered for a moment, perhaps measuring the distance. "They cannot have seen us, or they would heave to and take our mail. Try a gun to larboard with a flasher. Have the signal man stand by if that draws any attention."

Tristam watched as one of the bronze three-pounders was uncovered, primed, and run out for firing. The speed and precision Tristam expected did not occur and he realized that this was not a ship of war which exercised her guns several times a week. It was the first time a gun had been unhoused since they had set sail.

"There shall be a prodigious cloud of smoke, Duchess," Stern said, "and an alarming crash. Would you prefer to go below?"

The duchess tore her eyes from the preparations, which she had been following as raptly as the cabin boys. "I have heard so much about the skills of the navy's gunners, Captain, and this terrible invention of Lord Skye. Why, I would not miss it for the world."

A moment later the air exploded in the most almighty crash, and the ship was enveloped in a thick, choking smoke. The breeze took this cloud off to leeward and amidst the coughing Tristam heard the look-out call down.

"*She's holding her course, Captain.*"

Stern nodded. "Stand in to the harbor, Mr. Hobbes."

A fair wind and a slack tide welcomed the *Swallow* into the anchorage. Stern wanted to put on a display of seamanship for the other ships and those watching from shore. He intended to enter the harbor under full sail. "*We may be an undermanned survey vessel,*" he had said, "*but that doesn't mean we don't know our business. Call all hands.*"

The boatswain's pipe shrilled and the sound of feet pounding the deck as men took their stations reverberated through the hull like a beaten drum. Almost every able-bodied man in the crew was given a place and Tristam volunteered to haul with those squaring the fore topgallant yard.

"Clap on to the bitter end, Mr. Flattery," Beacham instructed, his color higher than usual. "We'll show these fancy frigate men that we know what we're about."

A silence fell then and Tristam could tell that every man was anxious that he not let down his mates and embarrass captain and ship. Looking along the deck, Tristam could hardly believe his eyes, but there, on the foredeck, was Viscount Elsworth, stripped to shirt and breeches and hardly looking out of place among the huge forecastlemen.

Garvey, the master's mate, took the wheel, for he was acknowledged to be the most able helmsman aboard, and the captain stood by speaking quietly to his officers. As the ship passed between the two stone towers that guarded the harbor entrance, the ship's number was run up and the identifying codes were sent aloft as well. The flag dipped above the ramparts and four guns were fired to acknowledge a friendly ship.

The breeze was affected by the land formations, and suddenly the *Swallow* surged forward across the flat water of the bay. The staysails came down at a quiet order, but the ship slowed only marginally.

"We do seem to be moving rather fast," Tristam ventured, trying to sound calm.

Beacham put a finger to his lips and then must have realized that Tristam was exempt from normal ship's discipline—maintaining silence during evolutions was expected. "We'll round up into the wind and back the topsails," Beacham whispered. "You'll be surprised how quickly she will lose way."

The ship continued her headlong rush into the harbor, passing the stern of an anchored ship, which gave the impression of even greater speed. Tristam could not count the anchored ships, but there seemed a good number for such a small bay, though he kept his peace on this point, not wanting to get Beacham into trouble. The ripple of the *Swallow* passing through the water and the Jack standing in the chains heaving the lead and calling the depths were all that was heard.

The master's mate put the helm over at an order from the lieutenant, and

Tristam missed the rest of the maneuver for Beacham whispered, "Haul away, brightly." And Tristam put his weight into the work, feeling the coarse hemp, pulled tight, resist their efforts, but then give way a little each time they heaved. When the yard was squared, Tristam jumped to another line, but the Jacks did not make room for him there and Tristam was left standing, realizing that the foolishness of the Jacks was not going to pass as quickly as he hoped.

"*Let go stock and fluke*," someone called and then Tristam heard the slow rattle of chain running out as the ship settled back onto her anchor. Tristam stepped clear of the Jacks working. Those around him seemed to feel some euphoria at their success and their safe arrival, but Tristam didn't feel part of this.

"Make the ship secure, Lieutenant." The captain's voice was quiet and calm. "Mr. Hobbes . . . hoist out the cutter. A tot for the men should be in order, Mr. Osler."

"The island of Farrow," the duchess said at Tristam's elbow. "You have not visited here before either?"

Tristam shook his head, his eye drawn to the shore. Although the island of Farrow consisted of two volcanoes thrusting up from the sea, they were very ancient volcanoes. Layel had written a monograph on the geology of the island, and Tristam remembered that the last eruption had certainly not been in the present millennium. From the harbor only one of the two cones could be seen, Mount Forwood, sloping gently down to a flatter plain a hundred feet above the sea, and then plunging more steeply to the shore.

The island was green and fertile with a climate that many thought ideal. A warm ocean current kept the winters at bay and the almost constant breeze ensured that summers were never unbearably hot. For much of the year there was sun, though rain fell in quantities enough to sustain a productive agriculture. The south-eastern slopes of both cones were given to vineyards, as these were protected from the westerly winds, and it was upon this crop that the people depended for most of their livelihood.

Terra-cotta roofs dotted the open green landscape and the roads and hedges and fields all seemed miniature versions of the real articles, made to the scale of the island.

"It is charming!" the duchess said suddenly. "I expect the people to be the size of children, and draft horses the size of ponies." She laughed.

Stern turned from saluting an officer on another ship. "We must go ashore and pay our respects to the governor. I'm sure the worthy gentleman will wish to make your acquaintance, Duchess, and Lord Elsworth's as well."

"I shall be ready in a trice," she said cheerfully.

"And, Mr. Flattery, you are a landowner here, I collect?"

"That is so, though I have never seen my vineyard." He thought of his small home in Locfal. "It might be a sad affair, I fear."

"Never mind, sir. You must come along as well. Here you will not be looked upon askance, for the name of Flattery is well loved on this island. The Erasmus Grape has greatly increased the fortunes of the islanders."

In the end Doctor Llewellyn joined the shore party also, making the cutter a crowded vessel. The cox-swain and six oarsmen dressed alike in white trousers and blue jackets and, with their varnished straw hats bearing the ship's name, Tristam thought they must make a very nautical sight crossing the harbor—the captain sitting in the stern, the ship's guests in the bow. The day was warm and the contrast with the temperatures they had experienced at sea—even five minutes out of the harbor—was great.

I will have to record some temperatures here and as we sail off, Tristam thought.

Rather than coming to the quay or to a dock, the boat fetched up on a section of pebble beach, where the men disembarked, and the cutter was shifted up onto the land so that the viscount and captain could assist the duchess ashore.

"My, what is this?" she said as she found her feet. "The island is swaying as much as the *Swallow*. It must have slipped its mooring, Captain."

Stern laughed. "The feeling will pass directly, Duchess. One must adjust to the movement of the ship and then, once that is accomplished, to the stillness of the land again. But it does not make a friendly port less welcome, I find."

They walked the few paces up the beach and were met by the governor and his party.

Sir Stedman Galton had been the governor of Farrow for twenty years or more and was almost as much a Farrower as those born to the island. Most in the King's service felt the small island to be a posting on the edge of nowhere—and leading to the same place in the King's service—but it seemed to suit Galton. And the islanders were happy to have him stay. He was a fair man and known to promote their interests well.

"The pleasures of the day to you, Lord Governor," Stern said warmly. "It has been too long. It is my great pleasure to present the Duchess of Morland."

Introductions were made, and the governor's delight at the coming of such company was obvious. He was perhaps sixty years in age, Tristam judged, with hair that was a mixture of white and faded blond, for wigs were not fashionable on Farrow. His girth was great and Tristam noticed that he seemed perpetually out of breath, perhaps a congenital condition, and his color was high.

"Mr. Flattery." The governor looked at the naturalist with great interest. "Welcome to Farrow. The word quickly spread that the heir of our own Erasmus Flattery was to pay a visit. You will be more welcome here than you can imagine. Your uncle is something of a hero to the people of Farrow." He waved them toward a waiting carriage. "Lady Galton sends her apologies, for she is not well today. I hope she will be recovered for the ball this evening. Would you come to tea?"

And so they went to tea at the home of the governor of Farrow. It was a spacious house built in the style of the island—plaster over light-brown stone, for the underlying structure could be seen where the plaster had cracked. The roof was tiled, like all the others Tristam had seen, and there were covered porches and tiled terraces. The house overlooked the harbor and was nestled among olive and tall, elegant cedar trees. The party sat on a shaded porch and looked out over the Gray Ocean, which belied its name for it was certainly very blue in this area.

"Captain Nash of the *Raven* gave us news of your coming. Of course, Sir Roderick had written weeks ago, but we were unsure of your time of arrival. Nash was in here like a hurricane chased him. Watered and provisioned his ship and was off, making all possible sail." The governor shook his head.

"Nash is an able commander," Stern mused. "A man who can fight a ship. I have no doubt that he will see the thing done."

The thing, which could not be discussed before mere citizens, even Tristam could guess the nature of: corsairs were making themselves known in the archipelago again. Nash had undoubtedly been dispatched to strengthen the station there.

"It will have nothing to do with your business, I am sure," the governor hurried to add. He smiled reassuringly at the duchess, then turned to Stern. "I hope you will stay longer than Captain Nash?"

"Several days, perhaps a week. I have a small crew so we must rig, if not merchant-fashion, at least in a manner that will allow us to work our ship and not diminish the crew. It is a long way to Oceana."

This was something that Beacham had explained to Tristam, and which seemed like the worst foolishness. Survey ships, like the *Swallow*, came out of the Navy Yard rigged to navy standards, yet typically carried crews too small to make the best use of such a rig. Even though it was well known that these survey vessels altered their rig at first opportunity, the navy persisted in following regulations and continued to turn out survey ships with "proper" navy rig. It was bureaucracy run mad, Tristam thought.

"A week," Galton said, perhaps a bit disappointed. "Well . . . that is good news. Lady Galton will be so glad to hear it. There is much to do and see on this island, far more than its size would indicate. And perhaps you saw that Mount Forwood has taken to smoke again? Why, Mr. Flattery—and yourself, Doctor Llewellyn—such eminent empiricists will not want to miss such a natural wonder. There is a carriageway more than halfway to the crater rim and from the end it is a short walk to the Ruin and then a brisk tramp to the top." The governor spoke with the excitement of one who wishes others to love his home as he does. Tristam wondered if his seeming respiratory ailment stemmed from this propensity to talk without taking a breath.

"And, Duchess, the Ruin can be easily reached and is not to be missed. Still a mystery, as you know. Who built it, no one can say. Even the famous Erasmus Flattery spent some time in an inquiry, though if he learned anything, he did not tell it. There are strange letters, or runes, carved into stone that no one has yet deciphered. It is the most wondrous thing you can imagine."

"Why, Sir Stedman," the duchess declared, "you make me want to set out straight away. We must arrange an outing."

Tristam agreed immediately, for he had hoped to have time to visit the Ruin. It was every bit as mysterious as the governor claimed.

"And the wineries . . . you shall not want to miss those. And our absurd cranes that live in the crater lake in Mount Sedgel. They make a sound like a child's trumpet and aren't the least bit distrustful of people. And there will be a ball. You will not be bored, I can tell you. . . ."

To Tristam's great relief, the governor insisted that Tristam, the duchess, Viscount Elsworth, and the physician stay with him and his wife while the ship was being rerigged. A week away from those superstitious Jack-fools, Tristam thought, and his spirits lifted immediately.

Captain Stern begged leave to remain on the *Swallow*, citing duty, which the governor could not argue with. After tea, Tristam was shown to a room, and servants were sent off to gather up a list of his belongings that would be wanted for a week ashore. He also wrote a note to the proprietor of his uncle's vineyard, for so he still thought of it, and the governor had it delivered.

Tristam felt both excitement and apprehension about this property. Oh, he wanted to see it, there was no doubt of that, but he was curiously afraid that he would be disappointed.

"Absurd," Tristam said to the room. "It is only a bit of land and some buildings. One would think it were a woman."

There was, Tristam realized, more to this than a bit of land and a few buildings. Despite the fact that Erasmus Flattery had dwelt at Highloft all his life, and the house was obviously well lived in, there was little there that revealed anything of significance about the man himself. Tristam's claim that he had hardly known his uncle was not an exaggeration. In the years after his parents died, Tristam had lived only parts of three summers at Highloft; the rest of his time was spent at boarding school or visiting relatives.

At Highloft, though his uncle had not been unkind, he had never been very attentive, leaving Tristam much to himself. The only exception occurred when Tristam had nearly drowned himself in a nearby pond and then his uncle had spent several days teaching his nephew to swim, an activity the old man did almost every morning that weather allowed. It was just another eccentricity of his uncle's, for almost no one in Farrland swam, including sailors and fishermen. It was said to be injurious to one's health, especially to the respiration.

Erasmus Flattery passed on, not apparently as a result of swimming, leaving no journals or letters. His monographs on various herbs and other plants went to the university; and that was all the writing that Tristam had ever discovered. So now he found himself hoping there was some key that would unlock the enigma of Erasmus Flattery at his estate here on the island of Farrow. Thus Tristam's contradictory feelings. If he found nothing, the secret of who Erasmus Flattery had been would never be revealed. That was his dread; this was the last and only chance he would ever have.

Tristam walked out onto his own low balcony. "Why does it matter?" he asked the trees. But no one knew the answer to that question, least of all Tristam. It was important. That was all he knew.

The ball that night drew all of Farrow society, such as it was. To say it was a small affair by the standards of Avonel would have been speaking kindly: it was even small by the standards of Locfal. Despite this, Tristam enjoyed himself, for the islanders were friendly people and decency seemed to be their most common trait. The orchestra was passable, and one violinist was very good indeed.

The Duchess of Morland was treated like a queen and Tristam heard any number of residents note that, "*the duchess does seem to be enjoying our little affair.*" There was a certain tone of relief when they said this—and perhaps a little pride. Lady Galton did make an appearance and spent much of her evening talking to Doctor Llewellyn, who spent much of his evening looking professionally solicitous and the rest holding forth on subjects that Tristam could only guess at. He avoided that corner of the room.

Though the island of Farrow seemed well endowed with comely young women, Tristam realized that their attentions meant little to him. He often found himself searching among the faces for a glimpse of the duchess.

A niece of Lady Galton was visiting from Farrland and she was clearly not interested in the many suitors from the island and so spent some part of the evening speaking to Tristam. Later he saw her dancing and laughing with a young lieutenant from one of the ships of war and discovered that, though he was not interested in her in the slightest, his pride was wounded a little all the same.

"Don't stare, Tristam, it is unbecoming." The duchess had come up behind him and spoke quietly near his ear. Tristam turned a little red.

"Any woman foolish enough to consider a naval officer is not worth a moment of concern. Imagine marrying a man who came home once every two years to make a child on you, pat his latest progeny on the head, and then go out to drink and gamble with sharpers. You can find a brighter woman than that. You do want a woman who has a mind, don't you, my dear?"

"And a heart as well, Duchess."

The sounds of music and laughter were not louder than the duchess' silence. "I see," she said rather coolly.

Tristam felt immediately ashamed of his remark, and not sure why he had made it. "Please . . . I meant nothing by it, Duchess."

"Nothing, Mr. Flattery? I am confused. You want a heartless woman, then? There are some, I think, but they usually marry for money and rank." She reached out and tugged Tristam's arm. "Now here is a tune that one can actually dance to. Come, Tristam, you have not been paying attention to me as you should."

They took the floor, Tristam certain his remark still hung in the air between them. They did not speak for several minutes, but danced on.

"Why, Tristam!" the duchess said suddenly, her voice filled with its normal warmth. "You play the country squire so convincingly that I am often fooled. But you are the finest dancer here, by far, and would be among the best in Avonel. Wherever did you learn?"

Tristam hoped this was a sign that he had been forgiven. "At school. It is one of the arts taught to young gentlemen. We were forced to dance with our classmates, something very few enjoyed."

The duchess laughed her delightful laugh, youth appearing like a blossom. "Well, I have danced with many a graduate of your school and none stepped so fairly as you."

"The Duchess is very kind, and certainly the finest dancer I have had the pleasure to meet."

"Better than your classmates, even? I see why you were named flattery." The duchess met his eye. "Oh, my. I see you have heard this before. And I thought it so original." She looked at him slyly. "Though I'm sure it would pass as wit here." She laughed at Tristam's look. "Now I *have* said the wrong thing."

They spun at the end of the dance floor and, for the briefest second, she pressed herself closer to him than was strictly proper. Tristam almost missed a step.

"You have partaken of the Erasmus Grape, I assume?" The duchess did not wait for a reply. "I have been watching you but see no signs that you have begun to shape-shift. You are a bit redder than usual, but that might mean nothing. I will certainly look carefully at all my partners this evening, though."

The music came to an end, and the duchess took Tristam's arm. "I must have some air. I believe it is one of the arts of young gentlemen to escort ladies onto the terrace."

The moon was just past full, and that was all the light the terrace required. A group of men gathered at the leeward end, smoking pipes, and a few couples stood speaking quietly by the balustrade, ostensibly enjoying the moon. The duchess led Tristam there, keeping a distance from the others.

She looked out at the moonlight on the sea. "I like Farrow more than I could have expected, even if it is rather sleepy."

Tristam nodded. It seemed appropriate, somehow, that the duchess would make her decision so quickly. "It does have a charm, as you observed when we arrived."

"We have Sir Stedman and Lady Galton to thank for that. Have you spoken to Lady Galton?"

"Just to meet her."

"Well, do better than that. It is she who looks after the interests of this island and its people, for which she is well loved. Lady Galton is a cousin to Princess Joelle, you know."

"I did not know." Tristam was surprised. The Princess Joelle was the wife of the Prince Kori, the heir to the throne. "And she stays here?"

"Yes, it is her health, and Galton's as well. You have noticed his breathing? They must have the climate. But they seem very happy prisoners, to my mind. Farrow has become their cause, in a way. You no doubt remember the passing of the Daye Laws a few years ago?"

"I'm afraid not."

"Tristam, really!" She gave him a searching look, as though discovering a case of mistaken identity. "It affected your fortunes, without doubt. Previously, the wineries of Farrow could not sell their wines to foreign countries but must sell them only to Farr companies who had been granted a charter, oh, two generations ago at least. It was rather a good thing for the Farr companies, for selling the wines took no effort and it was profitable in the extreme. But the Daye Laws allowed the wineries of Farrow to form their own company and trade their wines abroad. It was a difficult thing, for the men affected were not without influence; yet the Galtons managed it. She is a woman of parts, our Lady of Farrow. You would do well to know her better."

Tristam felt his face burning a little. He had known nothing of this. "You are well informed, Duchess."

"Aren't I? You would do well to be so yourself, Tristam. There is more to life than herbs and birds, or birds and bees, for that matter." She turned her head as the orchestra began another melody. "That will be the last dance, and I certainly must have it with the governor." The duchess looked around quickly and then gently pulled Tristam behind a column. To his surprise, she proceeded to give him a long kiss of such sweetness that he was left breathless. She stepped out from behind the column and curtsied primly. "Good night to you, Mr. Flattery. I enjoyed our dance." She swept up her skirts and disappeared back into the ball.

The evening drew rather quickly to a close, for Tristam learned that, unlike Avonel, on Farrow such affairs ended when the music stopped.

Upon returning to his room he found a soft breeze wafting through the balcony doors; welcome after the heat of the ball. He shed his coat, neck cloth, and shoes and walked in stocking feet out onto the balcony. There was a hammock here, not the narrow shipboard type but one with a wooden spreader at each end. He swung himself into this device and stared out over the garden. The duchess' kiss brought back memories of a night in Avonel. And this disturbed him in two distinctly different ways.

The duchess was a bewitching woman. She seemed to both encourage and discourage him, and he was so confused by this that he was not always sure it was true. Tristam found himself drawn to her in a manner he could not explain even though he knew that she manipulated him as easily as she released her lovely laughter. Part of him resented this quite profoundly and another part of him was thankful for even that attention. "Pathetic," he said to himself. "She is cold-hearted and manipulative, and you would do well not to forget it."

He lay in the hammock a moment longer and then went inside and prepared for bed. If sleep sought him, it was spectacularly unsuccessful. After an hour he stripped the coverlets from the bed, took a pillow, and arranged himself in the hammock.

The balcony was low, for his room was on the ground floor, and he had a view across a stretch of lawn to a row of lemon trees. A sound drew his attention and he saw one of the Farrow deer, a tiny species that had been found upon the island's discovery, though certainly not native. It had been introduced, no doubt, by the same race that had left the Ruin on Mount Forwood.

He closed his eyes and slipped into a dream.

Something brushed his shoulder. His hammock continued to rock gently to the motion of the sea. Something soft caressed his cheek, and he awoke with a start. His hammock was indeed swinging.

"Shh."

He twisted around to find a woman standing by his head, her hand resting upon the netting, rocking him gently. Even in the dim light he knew it was the duchess. Tristam was so used to waking in his dreams that he was not sure for a moment if he waked or slept. The duchess looked down at him with what appeared to be genuine affection.

"How pretty you look in your sleep," she whispered.

Her fingers combed into his hair. Unbound, her curls fell about bare shoulders. She was wearing only a sleeping gown of pure white and truly seemed an apparition—but Tristam realized now that she was not.

Taking his face between her hands, she bent so close that her breath caressed him. "*It is so far to Oceana.*" Saying this she kissed him, though not so tenderly as earlier. There was desire in the kiss, and Tristam was swept up in his own response.

Taking him by the hand the duchess led him inside. "Draw the curtains," she instructed.

Tristam did as he was told, pulling the light curtains to, where they were easily wafted by the breeze. He turned to find the duchess' gown gliding to the floor, and he joined her in the bed.

Almost immediately he realized how dulled his senses had been in their previous encounter, for every nerve in his body seemed doubly alive now. The duchess touched him and stroked him and kissed him, and he could feel this excited her as much as his own attentions.

"What a gorgeous child you are, Tristam," she whispered in Entonne. "You have not a hair on your perfect chest. As smooth as a child's." She ran her cheek from his shoulder to his stomach and then kissed his navel.

Despite her passion, the duchess was in no hurry to have it slaked, and Tristam discovered what a truly skilled lover was.

Morning was not far off when he lay, spent, and more confused than ever. The duchess sat staring down at him, twisting a lock of his hair around a delicate finger. He had realized something as they made love; more than anything it was his youth that excited her. It was obvious, when his wits were not addled by drink.

"My poor Tristam. You look entirely out of sorts." She smiled sadly. "Caught between reason and passion. . . . I wonder which you will choose? It seems that you love me a little, and hate me a little, and are angry at yourself for feeling like this." She caressed his cheek with the backs of her fingers. "Do you really think I am a . . . cold-hearted manipulator?" She laughed at the look on his face.

"It is a lesson that awaits us all. So many years of schooling provide so little education." She took her hand away and hugged her knees to her like a girl.

She took her eyes from him and gazed at the wall. "You have no notion of my life, Tristam Flattery, none at all. I lost my duke . . . many years ago now." She paused, but he could not read the look on her face. "I am thirty-seven years old . . . and this face that I have been gifted will last, perhaps, another five years." She took his hand and pressed it to her breast. "This skin will wrinkle and sag and . . ." She met his eyes. "Do you know that Lady Galton was once a great beauty?

"You think I am a manipulator, and I will not deny it. When Sir Roderick waves his hand and changes your life, you do not feel anger and resentment as you do toward me. But he has his power and I have mine. Men are not resented for being strong, for being cunning, for being leaders. Yet these powers allow them to manipulate others. The difference is less than you think.

"I have an excellent mind, you know, but I am a woman and can never be the King's Man. . . . My husband is gone. And my protector has grown so very old.

"You wonder what has led this pampered duchess to take ship to Oceana? It should be obvious that when the King dies I will move to an estate in the country and quickly fade from people's memories. I keep the portrait of the Countess Chilton in my hall to remind me. That is reason enough. So His Majesty's health is of great concern to me. Selfish, you think? Cold-hearted? Everyone at court is scurrying to protect themselves against the day the new King takes the throne: not least among them, Roderick Palle. He has ingratiated himself into the favor of the heir, something I will never do, for the Princess Joelle disapproves of me as much as you would like to." The duchess gave a short laugh.

"Am I cold-hearted?" She shrugged. "I care for the King, though many do not believe it. And there are others. . . . I told you of the Daye Laws. It was your clever duchess who convinced the King that they were unfair. His Majesty spoke to the Prince Kori, whose wife had been applying her own pressure on behalf of her cousin—our Lady Galton. So Princess Joelle—who would go to some lengths to thwart me—assisted in this matter, though I'm quite sure she was unaware of my part . . . at the time. Friends of Roderick's lost their lucrative monopoly." She laughed aloud. "*Gentlemen who value things Farr*, or so they style themselves. Lady Galton is in my debt over this. And Roderick would like to wring my neck." She shrugged and caressed his chest.

"So you see, that is the way of it. I do what I must. . . . And I must keep the King alive. His Majesty requires his physic. But I am certain Roderick has not given Stern instructions to find *regis* at all costs. The captain believes it is a minor task on a voyage of surveying and discovery. He does not understand the true importance. Only you, and I, and Lord Elsworth realize what hangs in the balance. Only we three can preserve the life of the King."

"But Duchess," Tristam whispered, "the King is so very old. What if . . . ?" He could not finish. One did not suggest the King might die—especially to one who cared for him.

"The King will not die," she said firmly, "unless we are unable to return with the seed in two years' time." She nodded her perfect chin. "*He will not die*," she said, though quietly as if reassuring herself.

The duchess fell silent again, stroking Tristam softly. Her gaze met his in the darkened room. "And so I come to you," she said, "my ally, I hope." Reaching out, she took his face between her hands and stared into his eyes. Then let him go, stroking back his hair. "I prey upon you, don't I, Tristam Flattery? But I do try to give something in return." Saying so, she bent and took him in her mouth, something no woman had done before.

Tristam's surprised intake of breath turned into a moan. The soft warmth of her mouth and the caress of her hands quickly brought him to a climax and he lay trying to catch his breath.

Without a word the duchess slipped off the bed, gathered up her gown, and disappeared through the wafting curtains. Tristam sat up, looking after her, his mind and heart in such turmoil that he felt tears sting his cheeks.

↜ Twenty-Three

The governor's carriage rolled slowly up the slope of Mount Forwood bearing the Duchess of Morland, her brother, Viscount Elsworth, Governor Galton, Tristam, Lady Galton's niece, and Doctor Llewellyn. A wagon overfilled with servants came behind, and they seemed to be laughing and enjoying themselves every bit as much as the august company they followed.

The carriageway described a complete circle around the cone of the ancient volcano, rising gradually with each mile, and generally provided an excellent view of the island, though here and there stands of trees interfered. The day was sunny and the wind—ten knots, west-north-west Tristam estimated—was brisk, though not too cool. A shadow, from cloud that seemed to be perpetually forming over the island, would overtake them from time to time, but then the wind would tear a ribbon free and sweep it off toward the horizon, and they would again enjoy the sun.

As the party gained elevation, the smoke from the crater became more apparent, its tinge of yellow more obvious against the pure white clouds. Tristam gazed up at the crater rim and felt an odd chill. To think that molten lava had once spewed forth and run down these slopes, like a tide into a steaming sea. It was difficult to imagine on such a fine day.

"So this road, Sir Stedman, was built by the same race?" the duchess asked, and the sound of her voice called Tristam's attention.

Doctor Llewellyn answered before the governor could take a preparatory breath. "It does not appear as it once did, but certainly it was here at the time of the discovery, or perhaps we should say *rediscovery*." Knowing they would stop at Farrow, the doctor had spent some time reading about the history of the island. "There is a section, Your Grace, not far off, I shouldn't wonder, where some of the original stone that once paved the road can still be seen."

"I was about to say," Galton managed, showing only the slightest crack in his shell of overwhelming good humor, "that one can see the old paving stones just beyond these trees."

Tristam sat quietly pretending to listen to the conversation, though it was of little interest. He had made an effort to inform himself about Farrow's history and geology years previous and nothing new was being offered this day. His thoughts were entirely of the duchess.

It was the second day since the ball and Tristam had barely shared two words with the duchess since she had disappeared out through the curtains of his room. The subsequent night had not brought a visit, as Tristam had hoped. The idea of going to her chambers had began to obsess him, but he was quite sure that the duchess would not relinquish control over the timing of their assignations. It was entirely possible, he believed, that she might never allow such intimacy again.

The duchess continued to treat him as one might treat a cousin or friend of the family—as she had led the ship's company to believe she was—with some affection and familiarity, but not a single indication of attraction or intimacy.

Tristam tried to take his mind off the matter and back to the conversation. He also tried to take his eyes off the duchess—not an easy thing, for she seemed very beautiful to him that day. And no less so for seeming out of reach.

Sir Stedman was managing to hold the field. "We do not know how long ago the early inhabitants lived on Farrow. The other ruins found have been well buried and only discovered by the sheerest chance. There is even a ruin on Tristam's estate. The remains of a good sized building, it would seem. And when I say ruin, we must differentiate. The 'Ruin of Farrow,' as it is called, is not really a ruin at all. It is quite intact, as you shall see."

"They did not leave because of the volcano, I collect?" Galton's niece asked.

"It seems unlikely, for there is no sign that the ruins we have found were devastated by lava. No, they dwelled here long after the volcano became dormant. Here's the spot where the old road can best be seen."

Everyone climbed down from the carriage to look at the ancient paving stones. They were impressively large blocks, two yards square, worn and smooth, though seldom broken. Trees offered good shade here, and Tristam thought there must have been a spring nearby, for moss outlined each pale block as though it had been laid into a setting of green velvet. In some places hardy saplings had squeezed up through the cracks.

"You can see the ruts, worn no doubt by the wheels of carriages or wagons," the physician pointed out the smooth furrows, where water ran when it rained.

"No one has ever found evidence that horses inhabited Farrow," Tristam interjected, "though there were many other species introduced before our own history began here." He found the physician so annoying that Tristam could not help but dispute with the man on occasion, though he always felt childish afterward.

"But that does not mean horses were never here, my dear Tristam," the doctor said, as though addressing a child. "Not at all. But even so, it is possible that there were wagons. Drawn, perhaps, by other beasts, or by slaves for that matter." He stood in the center of one of the paving stones, beaming, surrounded by his listeners; the world obviously as it should be, according to Llewellyn.

Tristam shrugged and bent to look more closely at a stone. He was annoyed that the physician had begun to use his familiar name—not an issue that Tristam usually had particularly strong feelings about. The fellow was maddening in the truest sense of the word.

"It is not far now," Galton said. "Fifteen minutes will see us at the Ruin."

Tristam let everyone board ahead of him and then said, "I must stretch my legs. Go ahead, I shall not be far behind."

"Are you sure, Mr. Flattery?" Galton asked. "The way is steep, or at least I find it so." He smiled and waved Tristam on. "But no doubt your young legs will not notice. We'll wait at the end of the carriageway."

Suddenly, the duchess stretched out her hand and said, "I will accompany you, Tristam, if you don't mind. I have been sitting long enough as well. No, no, Doctor Llewellyn, keep the governor company, please."

Tristam handed the duchess down, and the carriage and wagon rolled on to the creak of leather and the squeaking of springs. The second they were out of hearing the duchess released a theatrical sigh.

"My word, a carriage is far worse than a ship," she said. "There is no escape at all. I do hope I don't become ill. Can you imagine being trapped in a sick bed by that man? Or trapped in any bed at all. It is no wonder he has never married." The duchess looked up at Tristam from beneath her bonnet and laughed. "I am wicked, aren't I?"

Tristam said nothing, for he wanted dearly to resist the duchess' charm. It seemed to lead him only to confusion and something near to despair.

"Do not complain, Tristam. If I were not so wicked, you would not adore me as you do." She laughed and took Tristam's arm. "You have not yet paid a visit to your estate?"

"Tomorrow," he said, trying to ignore the soft caress of her hand on his arm. "Such as it is."

"Such as it is?" She looked up at him and smiled, her green eyes catching the sun in a most disturbing manner. "Why Tristam, did not Galton say it has its own ruin? The ancients dwelled in your very garden, perhaps. As our good governor would say, *'It is the most wondrous thing you can imagine.'* "

Tristam laughed in spite of himself.

"That is better," she said, taking her skirt in her free hand and swishing it in the breeze, one of those entirely unconscious, childlike acts that Tristam found so endearing. "I am your friend, you know, despite all that you think. On this journey a friend may be more important than wealth or even an uncle at court. So do not spurn me."

"You can't possibly think I spurn you."

"Well, you do keep fixing me with the oddest looks. One would think I had done you some irreparable harm. Did you not have the fullest pleasure of me this two nights' past?" She looked up at him as she said this, meeting his eye with no sign of embarrassment.

Tristam had never had a woman speak to him so candidly and found himself unable to respond. He felt his resistance melting as well. Perhaps she cared for him more than he realized, and he was simply acting like a petulant child because she had not chased after him like a lovesick girl. She was the Duchess of Morland, after all.

"Tristam?"

"I—I can't think what to say. Certainly I have hardly thought of anything else since. Why, it was . . . perfect in every way."

She rested her head against his shoulder for a second. "And though I will confess that I took pleasure from you as well—great pleasure, I might say—I thought it freely given . . . ?"

"Yes, certainly."

"Good. We do not have a misunderstanding, then." She waved off toward the sea. "Look. We have come full circle. I believe I can see the good bark *Swallow* lying in the harbor."

Tristam found it difficult to keep pace with the change in conversation, though he was relieved to have it stray into more familiar terrain. "So it is," he managed. "I am, sometimes, more than a little amazed to find myself on such a journey." It seemed an appropriate response to Tristam, a slight confession, but not too intimate.

"Those who cease to be amazed, Tristam, have placed one foot firmly in the grave, I believe. One should be wary of it." She pressed his arm close to her for a second. "I am so glad you are on this voyage. I should be mad without your company." She smiled at him, her lovely eyes holding his for a few seconds. She turned her attention back to the path again. "But, of course, naturalists have often gone on voyages of discovery, while I am certainly the first duchess to undertake such an enterprise. Imagine how strange I find my predicament."

Tristam found this small attention from the duchess had improved his mood remarkably. "What you say is true, but perhaps it will become customary, just as taking a naturalist is today. In the future we will hear great speculation:

'Who do you think will be the duchess on the next voyage to remote parts?' they will say. 'Perhaps the Duchess of Armond?' 'No, I don't think she's duchess enough to get the thing done.'"

The duchess dissolved into delighted laughter and kissed his cheek. "You make sport of me, Tristam Flattery." And then, " 'Ship's Duchess' has connotations that I do not care to consider."

They strolled on, talking of very little, and Tristam realized again that his normal resentment toward the duchess very quickly drained away in her presence. It simply could not stand up to her considerable charm. *So fell Dandish,* Tristam reminded himself, but to no avail.

The carriage and wagon came into view, wheels blocked, their teams led away to graze or drink. Lady Galton's niece waved a parasol, and the duchess swept off her bonnet and signaled in return.

"We might truly be on a picnic," Tristam said quietly, "rather than on the King's business."

The duchess pulled back and gave him a look of apparent amusement. "But we *are* on a picnic, Tristam. Do try to enjoy yourself. Why, one of the serving girls has an eye for you. You might have her to bed, if you wish." With that the duchess released his arm, waved her bonnet again, and strode ahead.

As Galton had promised, it was not far to the Ruin, and it was just as well, for it was all the man could manage. He was terribly out of breath the entire distance, short as it was. Tristam and the viscount got a little ahead of the others on a stair and waited at the top.

"This is rather crude stonework," the viscount observed. "I thought these ancient engineers were said to be unsurpassed?"

Tristam ran his hand along the low wall. "This was done by our own Farrowers. The stone in the Ruin is unlike this—not even from the island. It was brought from some yet undiscovered quarries."

"Is that true?" the aristocrat obviously knew nothing of the Ruin, for it was hardly a secret. "No wonder this is thought such a mystery. A race that has disappeared. Stone transported across how many leagues of ocean. Writing that no one can read. Worth the few days of bad weather and worse victuals to view such a site." The viscount stared down at the harbor. "What is our present height, do you think?"

Tristam dug into his fine memory. "The Ruin is at three thousand, five hundred feet. The peak of the crater is four thousand two, I believe."

"How do you know that?" the man asked, more impressed than Tristam would have expected.

"I believe I read it somewhere, Lord Elsworth. Barometric measurements were performed here several years ago."

"Ah, barometric measurements." He nodded. "That would answer." He looked back at the group following for a second and then turned to Tristam suddenly. "Would you call me Julian, Tristam?"

"I would be very pleased to," Tristam heard himself say, wondering if his tone sounded as false to the viscount as it did to him. *And while we're at it*, he thought, *precisely why did you murder Ipsword?* This viscount, Tristam had come to realize, was a complete cipher. A bit like a beast in the wild, apparently at peace but unpredictable and potentially deadly.

The viscount smiled at him. "You do have a prodigious knowledge, Tristam. I am in constant amazement. The duchess has the highest opinion of you, as well, and the duchess is a difficult woman to impress."

"Very kind of you to say." Tristam gave a small bow of the head. "In many of life's important fields, however, I'm just finding my feet, I'm afraid."

The viscount chuckled, a warm laugh much like his sister's. "Are you all right there?" he called down to the others.

"Perfectly fine. Don't wait for us," the duchess called back.

Tristam could see that they had stopped to allow Galton to catch his breath. The old man was redder than usual despite the fact that he was supported by two servants. Beside him, the duchess looked very concerned and the niece seemed not to know what to do. A few stairs farther down, Doctor Llewellyn was leaning heavily against the stonework, two of the servant girls hovering by, obviously anxious. Despite the condition of the two gentlemen, Tristam found himself wondering which of the servant girls was so interested in him, and then chided himself. *Don't be a fool; the duchess said that to keep you off balance, as she loves to do.*

Realizing that the two older gentlemen were in such straits, Tristam hesitated to go on.

"Well, let's be off," Lord Elsworth said, obviously not concerned. "I am eager to see this thing now." He set out immediately but had not gone four paces when he realized Tristam wasn't following, and turned, his look expectant. "They will be all right, I'm sure. The duchess is there with a gaggle of strong servants. They can carry the gentlemen up if need be. There is nothing for us to do."

Tristam's own curiosity overcame his feeling that he should wait for the others.

They set off at a good pace up the last slope to the Ruin. They were above the level of trees here and the grass was a bit thin, rock more prominent. Three hundred feet above them was the boundary of true vegetation; beyond that, flora existed only in small pockets.

Suddenly, quite close, the top of the Ruin came into view—a gray stone lintel bridging the gap between a column of light color and one of rose. Tristam felt a strange vertigo, as though he had passed through a portal into antiquity, for here lay the distant past, still living. The lintel, a simple piece of stone, appeared to be imbued with some mysterious quality that the naturalist could not name. Tristam had seen other objects that affected him thus. Lord Skye's pen and inkstand, though the most ordinary of objects, had more impact on Tristam then any religious relic ever could. Skye had written his great laws of motion with these very instruments!

The angle of their ascent revealed nothing further for a few moments and then they topped the rise and there stood the Ruin of Farrow.

Across a grassy common the columns rose up above a stone platform that was reached by a broad flight of stairs. Both men stopped to stare, for it was indeed the strangest sight, this artifact of stone rising out of the most pastoral landscape. But for Tristam it seemed more than that. Suddenly, he wanted to go no farther. He felt a wave of anxiety wash through him and realized he had broken into a sweat. The Ruin did not appear so innocent, but seemed to be a device imbued with terrible intent, like a guillotine or an implement of torture.

This is foolishness, Tristam told himself, and started forward again, though reluctantly. He was not sure if he was more unsettled by his response to the Ruin or by the knowledge that he could have such a reaction, for it clearly had no basis.

Upon the terrace columns had been placed to describe a half-circle and the slope behind had been cut back to create a wall which formed the other half. The ruin was truly incongruous in this setting, and the fact that it didn't resemble any known form of architecture made it appear even more alien.

As they walked, they could not take their eyes from the sight, and neither felt inclined to speak.

The stair had once been a graceful affair of white marble, wider at the bottom, curving toward the top like a perspective drawing, giving the impression that the stairway was almost infinitely long. The carved rail was shattered and several of the stairs were cracked and had been pushed askew.

Tristam forced himself to place a hand on the rail and once he had done this his anxiety seemed to evaporate as quickly and completely as a bead of water in the sun. He was not sure what he had expected—it was only stone, after all. Stone warmed by a mild Farrow day.

The two men mounted the stair slowly, almost reverently, as though they were believers entering a temple. Tristam almost felt they should remove their shoes.

At the stair's head they walked out upon a flat terrace, perhaps forty feet in breadth, bordered on the ocean side by seven tall columns joined by a gray stone lintel carved with the runes referred to by Galton. A section of the lintel lay broken on the terrace, and here the strange writing could be examined closely.

Tristam walked over to the first column and ran his hand over the off-white marble. It was not fluted as he expected, but its smooth surface was decorated by runes and carvings in relief. There were seven such columns, the two farthest out of white marble; the next two, on either side, of rose colored granite; the next pair were green marble; and the single center column shone black in the sunlight.

The terrace itself was patterned like a fan with lines running from the base of each column to the small fount that was built in a half-circle against the wall. This was fed by a flow of water that issued from the carved beak of a raptor, though the head of the great hawk sat upon the shoulders of a man as though it were a mask. Above this, perhaps twelve feet up the stone wall, the unclothed forms of a man and woman appeared to bear a small platform upon their shoulders—a platform one could climb to by a narrow stairway that followed the curve of the wall. The countenance of both figures was hidden, for each had an arm raised to their face as though in great sorrow.

Tristam walked back toward the wall and gazed for a moment into the gently bubbling fountain, and then up at the two forlorn figures above. Although he could not even guess at the purpose of this place, the figures shielding their eyes would indicate its intent was not entirely innocent.

To either side, flat tablets had been chiseled into the wall and upon these, within an elaborate floral border, more of the strange writing could be seen.

There was a low stone bench opposite the stairway and Tristam went and sat there where he could take in all the wonder in silence until the others arrived.

It was not long until the voices of his party could be heard, and then their footsteps sounded on the marble stair. But the laughter and the buzz of conversation stopped as they reached the terrace and Tristam watched their faces transform. The group that had set out on a day's idyll was suddenly transformed into an assemblage of earnest converts.

Only Galton and the doctor did not seem so affected and as they collapsed on the bench, gasping, Tristam rose quickly to allow the women a seat as well. No one spoke for a time, and then the duchess turned to Tristam.

"Do you know the significance of these columns, Tristam? They are all carved with the most wonderful things."

Tristam hated to usurp Galton's place, for the man so loved to talk of his adopted home, but it seemed likely that Llewellyn would regain his breath first, and Tristam could not bear to have the man take charge here.

"I'm certain that Sir Stedman can tell you much more than I, Duchess, but I have read something of the subject and shall be glad to relate what I can remember." He turned and cast his eye around the Ruin, looking for a place to begin. "The outermost columns, the white ones, indicate astronomical relations." Tristam walked over and began to point at the various figures. "The sun and the moon are obvious, of course, but some of the constellations are less so, for whoever created this place—and we by no means understand its purpose— saw the heavens differently than we do." Tristam borrowed a walking stick from the governor and used it as pointer. "These spheres would seem to be planets, indicating the builders knew something of our own corner of the heavens. This, I believe is the Great Mare, though joined by these lines it appears different than our own characterization. It is even possible that this constellation was seen as a letter of their written language. If you look at this." Tristam indicated the figure of a man set within a circle, his arms straight out at his side, legs spread. Tristam searched the characters that covered the lintel from end to end. "Here it is. Layel's brilliant contribution to solving the mystery was his realiza- tion that this human figure and this character were the same. Or perhaps it would be more accurate to say that the written characters are based on the human forms you can see carved here, though greatly abstracted. Look, here is another." This one was a woman in profile, arms up together, knees bent. "And over here you have the written character. You see; here the arms, the bent knee, et cetera. Though stylized and more elegant, you soon begin to see the way of it. And this first character is similar to the lines joining the stars in our Great Mare. So the builders may have found their writing in the heavens, so to speak."

"Yes, I see two alike," the duchess said, "the man and woman together above your head and that character—third along. Most extraordinary."

Tristam looked and found, as he expected, that the duchess was right. Her quickness of mind never ceased to impress him. "Of course, despite Layel's great insight, we are hardly closer today to being able to read this script. We do not even know if these characters represent sounds or if they might signify entire words. We cannot tell. It is thought that these two columns represent the sky on a certain day of a certain year, but all attempts to prove this have, as yet, giving us nothing. It is difficult, even with what we know today, to accurately picture the sky at a given time in the distant past."

Tristam moved to the next column, which was of beautiful polished granite of the palest rose. "There are, as you can see, a pair of these—one to either side. These granite columns seem to represent things geographical. It would almost be safe to say this is a stylized map or chart, though of a very different type than our own.

"You see here an island with two peaks—that is thought to be Farrow. Is that not so, Lord Governor?" Galton nodded. His breathing was still terribly labored and his eyes bulged from his efforts. Glancing at the physician, Tristam realized he had only a minute or two more before the man would be trying to wrest control of the situation.

"There are two other islands, here and here, which you can see should be nearby, though neither island exists. This was the cause of much debate at one time, and had many doubting the veracity of the ancients' geography, but recent soundings have shown that there are two sea mounts where you would expect these islands to lie. Many now think they were volcanic islands, like Farrow, that erupted and broke apart, disappearing back under the sea—though they are still comparatively close to the surface.

"This curving line is, without question, the coast of the Entide Sea, proving that the race that lived here knew of our own land. The harbor of Avonel would be somewhere here."

"But, Tristam . . ." the physician broke in, though he was still fighting for each breath.

"Now, Doctor Llewellyn," the duchess said, patting the man's hand. "You must save your breath. In a moment you shall have your chance. Do go on, Tristam. I am fascinated." She leaned forward as though not wanting to miss a syllable of what was said, which Tristam could see caused the doctor much frustration.

"If one stands atop that platform," Tristam pointed to the place supported by the two carved figures. "One can sight across the top of columns five and seven precisely toward the positions where the islands are thought to have existed. This may tell us something of the ruin's purpose. But it is also known that, on the summer equinox, the sun rises and sets in line with columns one and seven. And, at noon, is behind the black central column. At that point the sun's height can be measured as the angle between this intersection in the pattern and the top of the column. So the ruin appears to have served an astronomical purpose as well.

"The green columns are the most cryptic, for they are inscribed only with the written characters and the odd figures that seem to be the basis of this writing. Perhaps they are of a religious nature, or are directions to wondrous lands the ancients knew of. All guesses are equally valid, I should think. Poetry. A table of laws." Tristam threw up his hands.

"But what of the final column? The black one," asked Lady Galton's niece.

"Yes, Tristam, what is that material? I don't think I have seen its like before." The duchess continued to give Tristam her undivided attention, hanging on his every word, and Tristam was sure she did this to torture Llewellyn.

"It is obsidian. Glass, really. This is a natural column created, somehow, by volcanic means. Obsidian is the volcanic outpouring cooled so quickly that it does not form a crystalline structure. In a sense it is hardened liquid: glass. How this was formed so perfectly is a mystery. A natural wonder never seen before."

"It was not carved, then? Not polished?" the viscount asked.

Tristam shrugged. "Unlikely that it was carved, Lord Elsworth. Imagine carving glass. Polished? Possibly, though naturally formed obsidian often appears so. The plinth," Tristam tapped the column's base, "is polished basalt—or was polished long ago. One can see the difference. A crystalline rock formed from the volcanic outpouring but cooled more slowly."

Tristam turned toward the rock wall. "Now the fount is something else altogether. It is fed from a pool not far up the slope and drains through a waterway under the terrace. The stone is marble; white and variegated, as you can see. Its purpose remains unknown, if it had a purpose beyond the aesthetic. The man-bird form is not shown anywhere else in the carvings, and its significance is a mystery as well. The water is said to be quite palatable." Tristam dipped a hand in and tasted the water. It was warm but unremarkable.

Tristam felt he had lectured long enough. A fear of becoming like Llewellyn—in love with the sound of his own voice—haunted him.

"I'm sure Sir Stedman will have more to say, for I think our modest governor has been studying this site for many years and has theories of his own."

As Tristam finished, the others began a closer examination of the ruin, each drawn to some different facet. Galton's niece went to the fount and then cast a quick glance at the figures above. When she realized Tristam had seen her actions, she blushed furiously and went immediately to examine one of the columns.

A picnic was spread by the servants, who laid rugs and cushions on the marble terrace. Galton and the physician both regained their voices, and though the doctor tried his best to dominate the conversation, he had to give way to Galton's very real expertise on the subject.

The governor spoke as he ate, wiping his mouth constantly, for the acts of eating, speaking, and breathing together resulted in a certain amount of spittle escaping onto his chin. "From the platform, as Mr. Flattery called it, one can indeed sight toward the sunken islands. Imagine that somewhere under the ocean lie ruins such as this. But there are other lines scribed into the top of the lintel as well and if one extends them back to the platform, or sighting balcony as it is also called, they converge on a central position. It is conjectured that these indicate geographic locations significant to the race that dwelt here. We do not yet know enough of the geography of this great globe to prove this yea or nay." The governor wiped his mouth and chin seemingly unembarrassed, perhaps even unaware, that everyone looked away. "One can climb to the sighting balcony easily. I've done it many times myself. The stair is narrow and the balcony does suffer from the lack of a balustrade, but if one is not too adversely affected by the fear of heights it is a most wondrous experience."

After the meal Tristam and Lord Elsworth decided to climb up to the balcony but, as the stair was so narrow and the platform so small, Tristam insisted the viscount have the honor of ascending first, for it would not take them both.

"Do be careful," the duchess called out as her brother set foot to the stairs.

Though he was a large man, the viscount was quite nimble and went up quickly, his back pressed hard to the wall. The platform was set at a height to allow a man to crouch, or kneel, and sight across at the top of the lintel.

"I see the marks you mention, Sir Stedman," the viscount called down. "Quite clear." He peered out to sea, shading his eyes. "I can't quite make out what it is they point to. I believe the one on the left might intersect the ale house by the bay."

The mood of the party seemed to be lighter now and this jest brought more laughter than it perhaps deserved.

Tristam ascended in his turn. The stair was only a foot and a half wide at the most and the wall, though surely vertical, seemed to overhang the stair slightly. Tristam immediately understood why the viscount had pressed his back to the wall, and did the same.

From a position crouched on the balcony Tristam could see the lines scribed across the lintel blocks. He stared out to sea and tried to imagine what distant, mysterious lands these lines indicated. Cloud on the horizon could have been snow covered mountains at the limit of vision, or a distant land thrown up above the horizon by some optical phenomenon. His own destination seemed suddenly unbearably far away. Months off yet. Thousands of leagues across open ocean.

Soon enough, he thought.

To Tristam's surprise, as he alighted, the Duchess of Morland insisted on ascending the stair herself—against the protests of both the physician and Galton. Her brother, wisely, Tristam thought, said nothing.

"I'm certain I can manage, Doctor, Sir Stedman. I will simply shed these shoes, imperfect for the climbing of cliffs, and proceed in my stocking feet. I must hitch up my skirt in a most unladylike manner, I fear. I trust that no gentleman will take unfair advantage, for my ankles will be most terribly exposed."

The duchess went up the stair easily and with no sign of fear, though her brother did walk below to break her fall should she suffer a slip. On the balcony Tristam thought she looked like a figure that had been made by the ancient carvers, for, if anything, she was more perfect in form than the figures chiseled out of the stone.

The duchess laughed with delight as she stood looking out over the Ruin and the island below. "Why, it is the oddest feeling. Imagine that someone from an ancient race stood in this very spot to view the sunrise of the winter equinox. It makes one feel all out of place. If you were not, all of you, here, I would feel I had been magicked back into ancient times."

She came down, to everyone's relief, much elated.

Tristam wanted very much to look into the volcano, as he had never before had the opportunity to examine one that was at all close to being active. The climb was not steep or difficult and was quite short. "Easily managed," Galton had said, in two or three hours—both up and back. The rest of the party seemed content to spend this amount of time poking about the ruin, so it was decided that Tristam would make a foray up to the crater rim. Viscount Elsworth expressed a desire to see it as well.

At some length, Dr. Llewellyn expressed his regrets that he could not accompany the young gentlemen, and then explained in detail what it was they were likely to see. The young gentlemen made their escape as quickly as possible.

The day had grown warmer, so jackets and neck cloths were left behind, and Tristam carried his canvas satchel with his Fromme glass, notebook, and other tools of his trade. Above the ruin they stopped to look at the lie of the land and fix upon their best course, though the slope was nowhere steep. A plume of yellowish smoke wafted over the edge and swirled in an eddy just below the rim, so it was decided to stay south of this. They set off diagonally upward and soon settled into a comfortable pace.

"I must say, Tristam, that I'm most glad the doctor is not so able physically as verbally. It means I could accompany you on your botanizing forays and escape the man, at least for a time. That is, if you don't mind."

"Nothing would suit me better," Tristam lied, then ventured, "He does seem to be an odd choice for this voyage. Where in the round world did the Duchess find him, Julian?"

"I think he found the Duchess, is the truth of it. When Sir Benjamin Rawdon's wife was so very ill, Llewellyn replaced him for a few months as the King's Physician. Say what you will about the man, he is reputed to be an excellent physician—and that is not just his opinion. It was the King who insisted that the duchess engage a proper medical man for the voyage and Llewellyn was informed of this by Sir Benjamin. So he put himself forward, as you can imagine. On paper, as they say, he seemed the perfect choice. No family," the viscount grinned, "perhaps no friends as well. A physician of note—tended the King. An amateur naturalist of some skill, I gather. And a linguist into the bargain. Llewellyn was very keen to go—wants to write a book, apparently."

Benjamin Rawdon? The man who had intercepted Tristam at the home of Baron Trevelyan. The man of the dark, noble features, and terrible manners. "He . . . he does not lack talents, to be sure, but I am a bit surprised that His Majesty did not mention the good doctor's . . . unusual manner in social situations."

The viscount nodded and walked a few paces before he answered. "Not to criticize the King of course, but I think even Doctor Llewellyn does not speak out of turn in His Majesty's presence."

"No doubt that is it," Tristam nodded. "Rawdon. I think I met him once. Dark-featured fellow. . . ."

"Yes, that would be him. Kindest gentleman in all of Farrland. Would have to be to be a friend of Llewellyn's." The viscount laughed.

The King's Physician had been treating Baron Trevelyan. . . . Of course, the baron was a man of note in Farr society, Tristam knew. Certainly the most famous empiricist in the land—well known to the King, without doubt. Still. . . .

A tangy smell assailed his nostrils.

"Can you make out that odd odor? Sulfur, from the vents in the crater."

They continued on, clambering over bare rock now, vegetation confined to ledges. Tristam wondered again if the viscount had taken his journal and Dandish's letter from his room in the Ivy. It seemed the most likely hypothesis—the viscount or someone acting for him. And yet here they were climbing a volcano together in the midst of the Gray Ocean and speaking in the most congenial manner. Jaimy had said the viscount would not act without the knowledge of the duchess.

Blood and flames, Tristam thought, *what a despicable situation! Is there no one aboard this entire ship whom I might trust?*

"Tristam?"

The naturalist had stopped unintentionally. "An odd bird . . . far over the shoulder of the hill. It's gone now." Tristam pushed on. They passed above a small pool, shaded by a scrub of bush.

They stopped two hundred feet below the rim so that Tristam could hammer free a piece of the rock for his collection. He also wanted to give the viscount a chance to catch his breath, for although the man was young and strong, he obviously had not spent his years tramping overland as Tristam had.

The naturalist held up the piece of rock he had broken lose.

"Lava?" panted the viscount. He wiped his face and neck with a handkerchief.

"Basalt. Lava cooled slowly, thereby taking on a crystalline structure. Like the base of the black column." Tristam hefted it in his hand. "All to be worn away one day."

"Did you feel that?" the viscount asked suddenly. He placed both hands flat on the rock as though to brace himself. The ground seemed to have trembled beneath them.

"I'm not sure." Tristam dared not move.

They both remained very still for a moment, straining to sense any sound or vibration. But there was nothing.

"Are they firing the guns at the fortress?" the viscount asked.

Tristam could see no smoke there. "I think we would hear them from this distance. Wouldn't you?"

"I don't suppose this volcano could be about to erupt?"

Tristam shook his head. "Volcanoes inactive as long as this one seldom erupt without warning."

They remained still a moment longer and then they both laughed.

As the two men set off, a cloud enveloped them in a mist so thin that it appeared to be illuminated by sunshine. Only the sound of the wind and the scrape of their boots on the stone broke the silence.

"The top can't be far," the viscount offered, as though he thought Tristam needed encouragement.

The sulfur was suddenly quite strong, making Tristam's eyes burn and water. To his right, the viscount covered his nose and mouth with a handkerchief.

Through a spasm of coughing Tristam managed, "We should . . . make our way more to the left."

They began to traverse but did not emerge from the smoke as they expected; it seemed to cling to them and followed as they went. Suddenly, they both stopped as the earth vibrated beneath them.

"No mistaking *that!*" the viscount said. The man's eyes were watering so profusely that he appeared to be in tears.

Both men held their positions for a moment and when nothing else occurred, began moving laterally across the slope.

Not a dozen paces farther on, the earth shook again, violently and without accompanying sound. Both men lost their footing and slid, then tumbled a dozen feet, the mountain beneath them vibrating as though determined to throw them off.

In seconds it was over; they rolled to their feet and began an immediate retreat down the slope. In a hundred feet they came out into bright sunlight and fifty feet farther down they collapsed on the ground, coughing uncontrollably.

Tristam recovered first, pushing himself up into a sitting position. He wiped his eyes on his sleeve, having lost his own handkerchief. Around him the day remained perfectly calm; the prevailing wind blew, a sparrow sang nearby. The island appeared unaffected.

The viscount lay on his back on the slope, his arm cast over his eyes to protect them from the sunlight. Tristam was so reminded of the figure carved into the wall of the ruin that he could do nothing but stare for a moment.

"Flaming martyrs . . ." Tristam managed, though, beyond that, he didn't know what he had begun to say. "Bloody flaming martyrs," he heard his voice mutter again.

Shaking himself out of his trance, he produced his water flask and offered it to his companion. In his turn Tristam tilted the flask, the warm water spreading through his dry mouth and throat like a priceless elixir.

He passed the flask back to the viscount, who had struggled up to his elbows. "Finish it, Julian. There is a spring on our way. We should go back down to the others immediately, though I'm sure no one would have been hurt."

Julian nodded, then tilted the flask back and drained it, still breathing too hard to speak.

Anxious about their companions, they set off, though at a much reduced pace.

"Do you think we're in danger?" the viscount managed finally, looking over his shoulder at the crater rim.

"No. I think that was an earth tremor, unrelated to the volcano. There is no cause for concern here, though tremors can be followed by massive waves."

The Ruin came into view and Tristam took out his glass. "It seems there is no need for concern," he said, focusing on the columned terrace. "Nothing has toppled, everyone seems intact. There are no signs of people rushing about in panic. They seem rather unaffected, in fact."

"Well, I'm glad to hear it. If there were such a wave, Tristam, when would it appear?"

Tristam considered what he had read about such waves. "I don't know if it's possible to say. Our understanding of the relationship between the two phenomena is imperfect."

Water from the spring refreshed them and they covered the last section to the Ruin in good time. As they appeared on the stairs, no one seemed at all concerned about their safety and were greatly surprised to see their torn and dirty clothing.

Distress immediately appeared on the duchess' face and Tristam felt a sense of warmth toward her. "Whatever has happened?" she asked.

"Did you not feel the tremors?" Tristam asked. "There were at least two and perhaps a third."

Galton came up showing much concern for his guests. "We were not sure. Some thought they felt something and others not . . . but the horses were terribly spooked suddenly and the drivers barely managed to control them. You aren't injured, I hope?"

"Not at all," the viscount answered. "Barely a scrape or two."

"We had the oddest thing happen." The governor stopped in mid-sentence as though to catch his breath but, to Tristam, he looked out of sorts, as though he were trying to hide great alarm. "Just seconds before some of us thought we felt the . . . tremor, the strangest sounds were emitted, apparently out of the opening from which the water comes." He gestured toward the fount. "At the risk of seeming a bit mad, it sounded like the voice of some giant being speaking from the very depths of the earth. I've never heard anything like it in my life. Nor have I heard tell of such a thing happening here before."

Tristam found himself staring at the source of the fount's water, the man-bird carved out of marble. "I wish I had heard it myself."

"We had quite an adventure of our own," the viscount said. "Or it seemed so to me." He released his hearty laugh, partly from relief, Tristam thought, and partly from the sheer pleasure of adventure. "First we were lost in clouds, then the most foul smoke you can imagine drove us back just as we reached the rim. And then the whole mountain began to rattle as though trying to shake us off. Sent us skidding down the rocks." He laughed again. "Once that stopped, Tristam and I lit out like hares until we came into clear air. We were nearly suffocated, I should imagine."

Dr. Llewellyn saw this as his opportunity to take control and insisted the two gentlemen sit down while he listened to them breathe, took their heart rates, and percussed their chests. Pronouncing both of them sound was taken as a signal by the entire party and everyone began making their way back to the carriage and wagon. Tristam found himself supporting Sir Stedman as they descended the longer stair, though going down did not seem to tax the old man as ascending had. They were the last at the base where Tristam stopped to allow the governor to find his breath. Finally Galton nodded to him, but just as they set off, he drew the naturalist back, staring at him oddly. "Tristam, did you drink from the fount before you ascended the crater?"

"Why, yes. I believe I did."

Galton nodded once and walked on.

ᓚ Twenty-Four

Tristam was surprised to find himself sore and bruised the day after his climb to the crater's rim, for at the time the tumble down the slope had not seemed to cause much harm. He lay in the bath contemplating the excursion to the Ruin, the odd conversation with the duchess (*"Did you not have the fullest pleasure of me this two nights past?"*), his strange reaction to the sight of the Ruin itself, and finally the earth tremor and the macabre "voice" that the others had heard.

"Where to begin?" he whispered to the empty room. The duchess. . . . There was no understanding the duchess. *"I am so glad you are on this voyage, Tristam. I should be mad without you."* Perhaps, but she had not visited him that night as he thought she might. One could predict the moods of the sea more readily than the actions and moods of the duchess. *"To open some small part of your heart will not bring you to ruin."*

Then why did he feel so wretched this morning? There might be more to life than the purely intellectual world of Tristam's past, but the world of the heart seemed to be composed of constantly shifting ground. It was almost impossible to keep one's feet.

With an effort Tristam tore his thoughts away from the duchess (knowing they would return soon enough). He still wondered about his reaction to the ruin; it had been such a physical response, as though his body had felt a fear his mind could not recognize. Like the feeling one had when awakened from sleep by a clap of thunder—terrified but unsure of the cause.

Perhaps traveling would always bring up unexpected thoughts and sentiments as new things were encountered and assimilated. Nothing to worry about, he told himself, you are not suddenly losing your grip.

Now the "voice," well. . . . As he thought of the group's experiences, the strange feeling that the Ruin was an object of horrible intent crept over him, as though the bath water had suddenly turned cold. This propelled him out of the tub and he began to rub himself down vigorously, as though he could erase any unwanted feelings.

It is possible to think too much, he told himself, and realized no irony in this.

Another fine Farrow day was just beginning as he left his rooms, for he had risen earlier than usual that morning. It was his intention to ride the twelve miles to his uncle's estate that day.

A servant informed him that the morning meal had been set out in the garden and Tristam arrived there to find Lady Galton sipping coffee. The duchess was not in sight.

"The pleasures of the morning to you, Tristam," she said, a look of distraction disappearing immediately. "I hope you don't mind me calling you Tristam?"

"Not at all, Lady Galton." Tristam made a leg. "And the pleasures of the day to you, as well." He took the chair offered and Lady Galton served him coffee. Tristam noticed that her hands trembled as she poured.

Lady Galton was proof of the old saw that married couples grew to resemble each other over the years, for Tristam thought she could have easily been mistaken for Sir Stedman's sister. There was some quality about her—perhaps the look that at most times a remark of some wit was being considered, though almost never spoken—that reminded Tristam of the governor, and certainly her coloring was much the same, though her eyes were more hazel than blue and her hair tended more toward silver.

If Lady Galton had once been a great beauty, as the duchess had said, then age had slowly overcome that beauty until it was, in its entirety, concentrated in her eyes, still large and alive and bordered by dark lashes. Tristam could see hints that the woman's great natural poise was slowly being eroded by the ravages of age, but it was too strong, too much the habit of a lifetime, to surrender without a struggle.

"Our earth tremor does not seem to have precipitated a terrible wave, as we feared," Lady Galton said, though she did not sound relieved. "And that is something to be thankful for."

"It certainly is," Tristam answered, as prepared as anyone of his class to make small talk, especially with his hostess. "As the tremor was not felt even in the town, I should think it too small to cause such a wave. Still, we don't truly understand how one affects the other yet. So I will record this as another small bit of evidence."

Lady Galton sipped her coffee and gazed at Tristam thoughtfully. She opened her mouth to speak, and Tristam saw that she changed her mind and chose a different tack. "Sir Stedman has studied that ruin the entire time we have lived on Farrow, and the other ruins as well. It is his greatest interest, after the good of the island's people—almost an obsession, really. Yet the noises heard yesterday have never been reported before. He is beside himself with excitement. I think he shall have a camp erected there again as he did in the old days." A smile of great affection flitted across her face. "Though I don't suppose such a thing happens twice in a hundred years.

"Stedman is convinced that the 'voice,' as he calls it, is the reason the Ruin was built in the first place, or at least part of the reason. He has not given up on his theory that Farrow lies at the intersection of geological lines of stress—or perhaps 'force' would be a better word—but this voice has certainly caused him to consider the thing anew."

Tristam buttered a pastry as he thought. When he looked up, Lady Galton's gaze flitted away as though she had been caught out in some way.

There is something she wants to say to me, Tristam realized.

"It is difficult to know, Lady Galton, why such an artifact was created—what it meant to the ancient builders. I suppose if they believed the noises being emitted from the vent were coming from a subterranean being—perhaps a god—well, that would be reason enough. If we could only plumb the mystery of the written language, we would probably have many, if not all, of our answers."

Lady Galton nodded and Tristam saw the tremor again, this time in the motion of her head. She touched her cup to her cheek as if in thought, and any sign of trembling was thus masked. "Your uncle was fascinated by the written language, as well. He and the governor spoke of it for hours on end."

"Really? I did not realize you knew my uncle."

"Oh, yes." She smiled again, as much with her beautiful eyes as with her mouth. "He visited us often and, of course, Stedman had his camp at the Ruin in those days, so they could not help but meet. They were both very keen on the same things. It was Stedman that set your uncle off in search of the new varietal and into his study of oenology. Not that we take any credit, mind you. The Erasmus Grape was the product of your uncle's very substantial genius, but the governor did plant the seed, so to speak."

Lady Galton looked around the small arbor. "I had hoped to see the duchess this morning. We have had so little time together." She looked closely at Tristam. "The duchess is a remarkable woman, is she not?"

"I believe she is." Tristam concentrated on dissecting an orange.

"This voyage has piqued my curiosity, Tristam, as you might imagine. Why do you think the Duchess of Morland would suddenly take this notion to join a survey expedition? It must be the talk of Farrland."

Tristam tried to keep his tone offhand. "I'm sure that it is. I believe the duchess has developed an interest in natural history, Lady Galton, as well as a great curiosity about the world itself. A sense of adventure cannot be limited to men alone. As you have said, the duchess is a remarkable woman."

"Yess. . . ." She stretched the syllable out tentatively. Tristam felt her lovely eyes on him. "I have known Elorin many years now—since she was a girl. And yet this took me by surprise. At first I could not believe His Majesty would allow her to go. In a way she is what keeps the King alive, I think. And she chooses to go off now, for as much as two years. I cannot understand what would possess her."

Tristam decided it would be best to evade the question, if possible. "Have you spoken to the duchess about this, Lady Galton?"

"We have barely spoken two words," she said, and Tristam could not tell if she was hurt or merely frustrated by this. "I have not been myself, of course, and I am sure the Duchess does not want to impose." She sipped her coffee, but Tristam thought he saw a hint of something—perhaps regret—on her aging face. "Or perhaps some matter has taken up her attentions entirely." She gazed at Tristam as she said this, her face purposely set to reveal nothing.

"Perhaps." Afraid he might give away more than he meant to if they kept speaking of the duchess, Tristam took this as an opportunity to change the subject. "I must say, Lady Galton, that you and Sir Stedman have been most kind and hospitable. I am forever in your debt." As he was speaking pleasantries, Tristam was pondering what Lady Galton had said. It seemed impossible to him that someone of the duchess' sensitivity would not spend the requisite time with her hostess on such a visit. It was a terrible snub to both Lady Galton and the governor.

She smiled briefly. "It has been a great pleasure indeed. We get so few visitors and even fewer such as yourself—why, you seem to have become the object of interest of some of Farrland's most noted citizens. Sir Roderick wrote of you to the governor in the most flattering terms. And I have had the most charming note from Averil Kent who spoke of you as well." She smiled again, her eyes probing his. "I should have realized that you would know Kent."

"I only just met the gentleman in the summer, at an evening of the Society. I don't think there is a kinder man in all of Farrland."

Lady Galton nodded, her face suddenly troubled. "And Sir Roderick Palle?" she said very quietly. "What do you think of him?"

It was such an odd question, so disconnected to the conversation and so . . . bluntly asked as to be impolite, that Tristam was taken aback for a second.

"I am not sure what you mean, Lady Galton."

She looked up, something coming alive in her eyes—defiance, Tristam thought—as though she had made a sudden decision to cast aside caution, in a society where caution was as ingrained as the language.

"Don't you? Then I will try to be even more candid. I have come to distrust Roderick Palle, myself. What of you, Tristam? What of your own dealings with the King's Man?"

"He has been most kind to me, Lady Galton," Tristam answered evenly.

"Yes, that is the polite answer. But I am not being polite, as you can see. I think Palle has become involved in matters that . . . that are a danger to everyone." Her head trembled now, and she made no effort to disguise it. "I believe you are a man of principles, Tristam Flattery. Look carefully at what you are being asked to do. You are a man of reason, I have heard you say it. Why would you align yourself with those who seek to undo the efforts of reason?"

Tristam was so utterly surprised by this outburst that he pulled away from the lady before him, actually shifted his chair back.

"Lady Galton. I am a ship's naturalist engaged upon a voyage of discovery in the service of the King. I have no intentions other than to fulfill my duties to the best of my abilities. I was appointed to this position by Roderick Palle, yes, but I know nothing of any. . . ." He stumbled to a stop. "I don't know what it is you suggest. I am innocent of the politics of the court. Sir Roderick hardly seems the man to be involved in something . . . nefarious."

She reached out and put her hand on his arm, though gently. "You see, that is the myth, Tristam; 'evil deeds are done by evil men.' But it is not the truth. Evil deeds are done by those who mean only well or at least do not mean to do evil. Look at our history and you will see." She paused. "Good intentions, Tristam, as are your own, I am sure. That is why I have chosen to speak with you, because I believe, in your heart, you wish to accomplish only good."

She sat back slightly in her chair, removing her hand from his arm, and searched his face—looking for what, Tristam was not sure. He felt as though she were forming some judgment and he did not know how to react.

"If you are in league with Palle," she said suddenly, "then he will know that I stand against him. But if you are not, you need to understand that others have plans that you know nothing of or that you may only suspect." She leaned for-ward, speaking quietly, her voice wavering slightly. "*Do not bring this terrible bloom back to our world. Do not pass it into the hands of those who cannot un-derstand its purpose.*" She settled back in her chair as if this warning had sapped her vital energies. Her face had turned chalk-white.

She knew! Lady Galton knew of Kingfoil.

"Why?" Tristam heard himself say. "Why should I not? What is it that this . . . bloom will do?"

He thought her eyes widened a little as though she had been surprised. "Do you support Roderick Palle?" she countered.

"I do not know what you mean, Lady Galton. Certainly it was Sir Roderick who engaged me in this position, as I have told you."

She sat and regarded him for some time and when she spoke again she had recovered somewhat. "Your loyalties, Tristam, are unclear. Therefore, I shall not say more. I will not be so easily convinced to reveal what it is that I know. But consider what it is you do, Tristam. If you know as little as you claim, trust that this is no innocent errand you have been sent upon."

Tristam heard the sound of someone clearing his throat and looked up to see a servant standing down the path through the trees. Lady Galton nodded in return and then smiled at Tristam before lifting her cup to drink, her entire manner changed, all signs of distress carefully masked.

For a second Tristam thought it would be the duchess arriving, but it was Lady Galton's niece.

She kissed her aunt and curtsied to Tristam, taking a chair that would keep her pale skin from the sun.

"We have just been speaking of the Ruin, my dear," Lady Galton said and the conversation trailed off into the pleasantries that seemed to make up much of the social discourse.

Tristam found his mind wandering immediately. What in this round world had just occurred? In truth, Lady Galton seemed quite sane, yet she had just gone on about . . . what? It was not entirely clear, but one thing was certain; Lady Galton believed deeply in the warning she had spoken.

He realized that he had been addressed and had no idea how to respond. Something about the Ruin. "It is the oddest thing, isn't it?" he tried. Then, groping. "I . . . I was surprised to hear my uncle was interested in it as well." This, at least, was true. Erasmus, as far as Tristam knew, had always been com-pletely reclusive, and the amiable Sir Stedman hardly seemed to be the type of companion his uncle would choose, or so Tristam would have thought.

Lady Galton nodded, smiling vaguely, alerting Tristam that he had been caught not listening. "You should really talk to Stedman, Tristam. He and Eras-mus spent so much time together up there. I never go up myself—just the once soon after we came here. I do not care for the feel of the place. I'm like the native Farrowers in that." She hunched her shoulders slightly as if fighting a shudder. "It does give some an odd feeling. Have you ever been in a house said to be haunted?"

Lady Galton's niece had not, apparently. Tristam smiled. "No. Though I was told I met a ghost once in Merton."

The women looked puzzled for a second and then Lady Galton's eyes smiled. "Oh, yes. The ghost boy, was it?" She laughed, but it seemed forced. "Well, there you are. No doubt, it was similar. But if you want to know about the Ruin, you must talk to Stedman. The governor has been working on his own book on the subject." She gave a soft laugh, genuine this time. "Though I think it shall never be done. It has been written over and over these past ten years and is no nearer completion than it was after year three. And now this 'voice' . . . why, that will set him back, who knows how long." She laughed again, a laugh full of affection. "It is rather like that old jest: do you know it? About the man who wrote the syllabus to be used in the education of his son— but the writing lagged always behind the growth of the child and so the boy never benefited from a single lesson. I fear Stedman's book is going the same way. Though we learn nothing new about the ruin for years on end, our increase in knowledge still outstrips his speed of writing."

Tristam laughed as well, but his curiosity was fired by this news. "I should like very much to see this book, Lady Galton, if the governor could be so persuaded."

"Perhaps he can. I shall ask. I know he did not speak of it to Doctor Llewellyn. Stedman will not show it to just anybody . . . but he likes you, Tristam. And you are the heir of Erasmus, after all. I shall ask."

Tristam poured more coffee for all of them. He was anxious to be off so that he could think—and for other reasons as well. Now that the decision had been made and the time set to visit his uncle's estate, he wanted to get on with it, but Lady Galton was his hostess . . . and he found also that his curiosity would not let him go. If only the niece would take her leave, he might find some answers— though Lady Galton may well have said all she meant to say.

"Do you know, there is an odd cult associated with the Ruin, or so it is said on Farrow. A secret society, I collect. No one knows truly what they do, but there are several of our islanders reputedly involved—as well as outsiders from all four nations, not just Farrland." Lady Galton lowered her voice as though she spoke dark secrets, but her eyes laughed. "It is said that the members of this society have had the secrets of the Ruin revealed to them . . . in dreams." She laughed. "They make it up, I expect. But they are rumored to go up there, on specific nights of the year, and perform rituals. Do you think it would be human sacrifice? I do hope they will leave our poor Farrow virgins in peace—they are in such short supply as it is."

The niece turned slightly pink at this, but Tristam laughed. "There appears to be no sacrificial altar, Lady Galton. I should not lose sleep over your virgins."

"Well, I hope you are right. You are off to see Erasmus' estate, I collect?"

"Yes, such as it is."

"Oh, Seabright is very comfortable. You will not be disappointed. Of course, it is not large, but then, this is Farrow, and there are no holdings of scale here. No, Erasmus' property is very good, and some of the noblest grapes are grown there, as should be. Seabright is quite fine, you shall see. And very well kept. The Borrows family have managed there since your uncle came by the place, and they treat it like their own. They are the best sort, I would not hesitate to say. No, Tristam, it is altogether a solid estate. I should send along some gooseberry jam to the Borrows. Cook makes the finest on Farrow. Have you tried it?"

And so Tristam was sent off bearing gooseberry jam, his mind set to spinning like the wheels of a racing carriage by the events of the morning. Lady Galton . . . of all people. It was difficult to believe that this gentle, aging woman was somehow involved in court politics, but the duchess had intimated as much. Was Lady Galton not a cousin of Princess Joelle, a woman who lived in the very center of Farr politics?

But what did Lady Galton know of Kingfoil? *This terrible bloom*, she had called it. What else could she be referring to? And Palle. . . . She spoke of him as though he were about to accidentally start a cataclysm. "*Evil deeds are done by those who mean only well. . . .*" she had said.

"Blood and flames," Tristam muttered. "I am set off around the world on an errand, the significance of which it seems only I do not understand." *I can leave this ship*, he thought, *abandon the voyage. It is still possible.*

"That will save you from having to make any real decision in this matter," he said to himself. And then what would happen? He would return to his life in Locfal, a thought that he found did not cheer him. And something would occur in the larger world. Some event over which he would exercise no control. And he would be leaving the duchess, an idea he did not relish.

"I will go on," Tristam said to the wind. "But if I find *regis*, I will not consent to return it to Farrland until the duchess answers all of my questions."

He realized there was some advantage to being thought naive—if one were not. Roderick had his facade and the duchess hers. Tristam could hide behind the belief, firmly established he was sure, that he was innocent of people's motives.

Tristam brought Galton's gentle little mare to the cliff top and tethered her to a tree where she might graze. He stood looking out to sea for a moment and then pulled his notebook from his bag and sat down in the grass.

Taking out a mechanical pencil he began.

One: Valary's letter seemed to indicate that there might have been an herb that had something to do with the mages and their great age. Dandish destroyed his plants immediately as well as every note he had made except the one he had left to me in the field glass. (Had the professor not written: "Do these people understand what they have found? I must assume they do."?) Dandish had been growing Kingfoil for the duchess.

Two: Roderick did not allow me to attempt to solve the regis problem (which Dandish apparently did solve). Why? Why would he not want regis seeds, and yet send me out on this voyage to collect this very plant?

Three: The duchess is Roderick's opponent at court. Lady Galton just warned me against Roderick. Yet the duchess does not seem to be aligned with Lady Galton.

Four: Who else seemed to be involved in this matter? Trevelyan? (Or was he merely mad?) Rawdon, who kept me from seeing the baron (and who is apparently a friend of Llewellyn as well as the King's physician!)? Lady Galton (and by extension, Princess Joelle?). Prince Kori? The King. Kent (mentioned by Lady Galton)?!

For an hour Tristam sat and mulled this over; at the end of this he wrote:

Mages. Erasmus. Regis. Rejuvenation. Struggle within the court.
Roderick . . . Prince Kori. Farrlander faction.
Duchess . . . King Wilam. Entonne sympathies?

It was a workable hypothesis. And if Tristam had not had breakfast with Lady Galton, he might have believed it. The horror he had heard in her voice did not support anything so common. Not that the possibility of war was not horrifying—especially to those who had seen war—but somehow Lady Galton's concerns were not so simple. War she would not have hesitated to speak of, Tristam was sure.

Tearing the page from his notebook, he set it afire and then mounted his borrowed horse and set off, the words of Lady Galton still echoing in his mind: *"Evil deeds are done by those who mean only well. . . ."*

The day was unfolding in what Tristam had come to think of as the Farrow pattern: eight knots of wind out of the northwest, a smattering of small clouds over the sea, a warm sun. The ever-present cloud that hung over the peaks of Farrow appeared to be wafting ribbons of rain over the highlands, feeding the numerous tiny streams and pools that kept the island green.

Occasionally wagons would pass, bearing precarious mountains of hay, for the islanders were at work taking off their last crop of the season. Winter, if it could be called such, slowed the growth enough that it was not worth harvesting again until spring—though, if properly managed, there was pasture all year. Everyone spoke to Tristam as he passed; many knew his name, in fact. No one was in such a hurry—even while making hay!—that they could not say hello or stop and gossip for a moment. If his morning had not been so disconcerting, he would have found this aspect of island life quite charming.

It had been Tristam's intention to see some of the island as he went and to make some notes in his journal, and he forced himself to continue this plan as a tonic against the tide of questions and fears that attempted to overwhelm him.

He left the road after a short while and crossed the open fields to ride along the cliff top. Several species of pelagic birds made their nests here in the spring, and many were still to be seen—northern gannets in particular were new to him.

The cliff ran down to the beach after a mile and here Tristam stopped and let his mare graze. He shed his boots and waded into some of the tide pools, losing himself until hunger, and the advancing tide, drove him up onto the rocks to eat. Here he spread his specimens to be examined more closely, deciding which would be preserved and which returned to the sea.

As was too often the case, Tristam found his thoughts turning to the duchess. His discussion with Lady Galton that morning had set him to wondering again why the duchess was aboard the *Swallow*. The duchess' own explanation did not seem as logical now as it had when she perched, unclothed, on the edge of his bed. Certainly the King might need his physic, as the duchess claimed, but Wilam VII was over one hundred years old! Did she really believe the *regis* physic would keep the King from aging? When considered objectively, her explanation made little sense. It was no wonder the duchess was avoiding Lady Galton—her charms would not so easily muddle that good woman's brain.

But now Lady Galton had made Tristam question what little he had been told about Kingfoil. What could it be that she believed the seed did that she would speak of it in such dire terms? Obviously, not something so innocent as the control of a disease.

Tristam shook his head. What a business! Valary's letter to Dandish. Mages. *Mages. . . . I seem to have been connected to them through my uncle*, Tristam thought, and this disturbed him more than a little. His uncle. Whose home lay not far off. Thinking this, he collected up his specimens and returned them to the sea, then set out resolutely toward the home of his mysterious relative.

The lane which led to Seabright lay at the bottom of a tunnel formed of high-branched poplar trees. Leaves rustled and sighed with the sounds of deep summer, despite the lateness of the season, and smears of afternoon sunlight painted the lane bright and dark. The red dirt of the path blew off in small clouds where Tristam's mare landed her dainty hooves, for there had been no rain on the lower slopes for several days.

A low stone wall paralleled the lane—a highroad for squirrels, Tristam noticed—and, on the opposite side, a defeated old laurel hedge bordered the lane with faded greens and yellows. Past a bend in the lane a stone bridge crossed a running stream and into the pillar to either side a letter was chiseled— "E" to the left, "F" to the right. It was the only sign Tristam had ever seen to mark his uncle's passing through this world. Even the man's grave had, by his own request, been left without a headstone. Tristam stopped his horse for a moment and looked down at the two simple letters carved into stone.

If a man's deeds do not outlive him, of what value is a mark in stone? Halden, but it was a phrase that could have been spoken by his uncle. Tristam spurred his horse forward, trying to ignore the nagging anxiety he felt growing.

Come along, lad, Tristam chided himself, *this will certainly be the most tame adventure on such a voyage. Get on with it.*

A rhythmic squeaking became audible as he made his way along the drive, and then the sounds of a woman humming a tune he did not recognize. As he passed through an opening in a hedge, both sounds stopped abruptly and he found a large woman lifting a full bucket from a well. She did this one-handed, locking the crank-handle that raised the bucket in the other.

Tristam's mare whickered and the woman turned, a smile already forming as though she never had visitors who were not welcome. The whiteness of the woman's smile contrasted greatly with the dark tan on her round face, and brown eyes took Tristam in without a hint of suspicion. He found himself liking her immediately.

"Mr. Flattery?"

He doffed the hat he wore against the sun. "Tristam Flattery."

The woman curtsied, smiling as though she found his formality odd, but a bit charming all the same. "Welcome to Seabright. I am Elizabeth Borrows-Linn. Willis Borrows is my father. We have been looking forward to your coming, Mr. Flattery, for everyone who has had the pleasure to make your acquaintance has spoken very highly of you."

Tristam smiled. As he had been told, Farrow was very small. If there were a secret society centered on the Ruin, then Tristam would guess it was no secret . . . except perhaps to outsiders.

"And I have had only the kindest things said of the Borrows family. It is a pleasure to meet you at last." Tristam dismounted.

"I'm so sorry my father isn't here to meet you, but everyone is off to the Rowes'. The hay making, you know." She poured the water from the well-bucket into another, and then lifted a bucket in each hand, as though they weighed nothing at all, and set out, refusing Tristam's offers of help. She was not as tall as he, by five inches, Tristam guessed, but she would not be much lighter. Tristam was slight of build compared to this woman.

She passed through a garden gate and returned almost immediately, at a trot, to take Tristam's mare in hand. The horse went into a covered stall and was fed and watered in a manner that indicated Elizabeth handled stock often.

"No doubt you'll want to see your property, Mr. Flattery, but would you care to refresh yourself before or later?"

"I have a terrible thirst, but beyond that I am ready to tour the grounds, if you have time. Curiosity has the better of me."

"Father said to take you around if that was your desire. The others likely won't return until long after dark. There will be a bit of merry making if they get all the hay in. Father will be sorry not to have shown you about himself." She grinned as though she were playing a trick on the old man. "The house we just passed is the manager's house, the 'Grange' it's called, where the Borrows and our various in-laws dwell. It's a big old place and not uncomfortable."

Tristam could see little of the house above the garden hedge and surrounding trees, but it did seem to be a big old place and ramshackle as well, with wings and rooms added to no apparent design. The main roof had a distinct bow, indicating that the house was very old, probably built not long after the discovery some four hundred years ago. Stone houses with tile roofs lasted a long time in such mild climates.

"Your uncle's house is in the copse off there," she pointed down a long row of poplars and at the end he could just make out a terra cotta tile roof among a stand of amber beech and tall cedars. The house would enjoy a view down to the sea, Tristam noted.

"I left some ale there this morning, as we knew you were coming. Would you like to start there or in the vineyard?"

"The house and the ale seem to be calling to me, Mrs. Borrows-Linn. Do you mind?"

"Not one bit." Her brown face wrinkled up in a smile. "Though you must call me Beth, or no one will have the slightest idea who you are speaking to—least of all me."

They set off down the lane, Elizabeth setting a no-nonsense pace. Tristam was wondering how old this woman might be. Early thirties was his guess, so she would have been a child when Erasmus Flattery was a resident here.

"You knew my uncle, I collect?"

"Well, I was only a girl at the time, so I could hardly say I knew him, but I saw him often and spoke with him occasionally. I had strict instructions not to bother Mr. Flattery for he was always deep in thought. Your uncle was very kind to me, though—to all the Borrows children, in fact." She laughed as though at a memory. "My older cousins teased us—my sisters and brothers—with tales that Erasmus Flattery was a mage. We were all struck dumb in his presence, terrified that he would practice some enchantment upon us. In truth, we always hoped to see some magic, but of course we never did." She laughed again. "Children do love to believe such things."

Yes, Tristam thought, *children and sailors.*

They passed through a gate into a surprisingly well kept garden, still awash with bright colors. The house was at least as large as Tristam's home in Locfal, the stone showing through in places where the plaster had cracked.

"It is an old home, by Farrow standards," Elizabeth said when she saw Tristam's eye drawn to the broken plaster; but it was merely a statement of fact, not an apology.

She pushed open the main door, which was not only unlocked but appeared to have no mechanism to secure it beyond a latch. As Lady Galton had said, it was a comfortable home: Tristam liked it immediately. Though it appeared a bit uncared for on the outside, Tristam realized that this was not true of the interior. The walls were plastered and painted in pale shades, and the rooms trimmed in a dark wood Tristam did not recognize. Floors were polished wood or tile and, like other homes on Farrow, there were covered terraces and double doors with many-paned windows. The view was over fields to the sea and a small island not a quarter mile off shore. Tristam could see the tile roofs of several other buildings in their settings of green trees, and out on the blue ocean the sails of fishing boats were like a scattering of petals on a pond.

Elizabeth fetched ale for the two of them, and they sat in comfortable chairs on the main terrace. Off to the right, stretching up the gradual slope, were the vineyards, their vines cut back now as they must be each autumn. They looked like dark, twisted letters and brought to Tristam's mind the written characters he had seen at the ruin.

"We hope you will stop with us for a while, Mr. Flattery. I know Father is anxious to discuss the estate with you." She hesitated a moment, the wrinkles around her eyes pulling tight. "To be honest, we are all curious to know if you have plans for Seabright that we should consider." She was watching Tristam carefully as she said this.

"No, Beth, it is my hope that your family will continue to manage the vineyard, which you have done so ably. I hope to learn more of the business, one day, though that will have to wait for another visit, I'm afraid. I must return to the governor's tomorrow, for the ship will be ready to leave sooner than expected and I have much to do."

She smiled and Tristam could see a sense of relief there. "Well, I'm sorry to hear we will lose you so soon." She looked out over the vineyard and Tristam thought there was a sense of ownership in that look. Pride and ownership.

Just then Tristam heard a door thump open and the sounds of running feet. A girl, not more than twelve years, appeared. "Oh, Beth," she wailed, "come, come! Justy has swallowed a whole spoon!"

The woman leaped up. "Farrelle save us! Is he choking? Did you see him do it?"

"No, but it's gone. I turned my back and it's gone." The girl burst into tears.

Beth took her hand. "Well, I can't think he could swallow a spoon and not choke. But let's along and see." She turned to Tristam. "Do excuse me, Mr. Flattery."

Tristam sat on the terrace a while longer, admiring the view and considering the difference in this landscape and that of Locfal. *A painter*, Tristam thought, *would say the palette is cooler and the light warmer. I cannot quite describe it, but it is striking and very beautiful.*

Curiosity, as usual, called to him and he rose and went to explore the house even though he had the feeling he was sneaking around someone else's home.

Although it was much smaller than the Galton's mansion, Erasmus Flattery's abode was similar in style, as Tristam was beginning to suspect all homes on Farrow were. It was well appointed and showed signs of having been built by accomplished craftsmen. The first floor consisted of a small parlor, a morning room, library, drawing room of good size, a formal dining room and a breakfast nook as well. The kitchen, scullery, and pantry were a half-floor down, with high windows and stone floors.

Tristam was disappointed to find the shelves of the library almost entirely bare, though the few books there all related to the island of Farrow: its history; flora; fauna; agriculture, and even architecture. Three books dealt specifically with the Ruin of Farrow and its builders, but Tristam had read them all at one time or another.

A large desk was set before a window that looked out over the sea and, after a moment of hesitation, Tristam began to go through the drawers. Nothing out of the ordinary: bottles of dried up ink; pens of older design, though good workmanship; folders of yellowed paper; blotters. A small leather-bound notebook excited him for a moment, but he found its pages blank. It was, however, exactly the kind of book that empiricists favored for their journals and gave Tristam a bit of hope. Perhaps his uncle had kept a journal after all. But what had happened to all the volumes, if that was true?

He pushed the last drawer to and stared out the window. "Well," Tristam said aloud, resisting his disappointment. "I should have expected as much."

He wandered into the hallway, lost in thought, and then made himself mount the stair to the next floor.

There were six sleeping chambers—one obviously a nursery—with sitting rooms attached to the two largest. A covered balcony off one room offered a view and, from it, stairs led down to a terrace on the roof of the kitchen wing. Tristam realized that if he had not hoped to find some key to his uncle's character he would have been well pleased with the house, for it was comfortable and inviting. Looking out into the garden, he resolved to come and live here at some time in the future. "At least one could escape the winter," he said flatly, but the prospect did not seem to excite him.

As he descended the stairs to the terrace above the kitchen, Tristam heard someone call out.

"*Hello,*" Tristam responded, not sure of the sound's source.

"*Mr. Flattery?*" It was a man's voice.

"*On the terrace.*"

The sound of slow steps and a cane on stone was heard, and then an older man appeared on the stairway to the garden.

"Ah, Mr. Flattery. There you are." The man smiled, and Tristam knew immediately that this was Beth's father. Thick hair, white as snow, fell to the man's shoulders, a contrast to his thinning crown. Here a darkly tanned scalp showed through. Across the freckled forehead the man's skin appeared to have been stretched thin and taut. Heavy white eyebrows and an impressive white mustache, waxed to fine points, created a contrast to dark eyes. And in those eyes Tristam saw enough laughter to suggest that the exotic mustache was partly in jest. "You haven't been left on your own, I hope?" the man said, his concern apparently quite genuine.

"Only for a moment. A domestic emergency called Beth away."

The man laughed. "Well, we have only two hundred of those a day . . . each one a crisis. Willis Borrows, your servant, sir."

"I am most pleased to make your acquaintance, Mr. Borrows. I have heard nothing but good spoken of you since I came ashore."

The man looked pleased at this. "Well, I'm sure you have met only the most generous souls. Wait a bit yet."

Tristam laughed.

"You have had a look about the house?"

"I have, and a fine house it is. I could not be more pleased with it."

Borrows gazed up at an ivy covered wall. "Your uncle was always very fond of this place, the garden in particular, and we have done our best to keep it much as it was. I believe there is a decent ale in the pantry, if you would care for a sip."

Tristam followed the old man, who was hindered by a serious limp, as he descended the stairs into the garden and from there into the kitchens.

"I came as soon as I heard you'd arrived. They don't really need me to make hay anymore." He tapped his leg with his cane. "I drive one of the teams, so someone quicker can work in the field or on the mow. But there are always more than enough able hands these days."

Ale was poured, and the two men walked back out into the garden where Borrows led the way to a wooden bench set in the shade of an ancient oak tree. They sipped their ale and talked of Farrow in general and Seabright in particular. Tristam was again surprised at how little interest the islanders took in Farrland, almost never asking, and, when they did, giving the impression that they were really just being polite. Farrow was an insulated little world.

Willis Borrows was obviously relieved to know that the new owner had not come to put the estate up for sale or replace the Borrows as stewards. Tristam felt a little odd holding the future of this family hostage to his whim, for the Borrows had managed Seabright since before Tristam's birth and, in a way, he felt it was far more theirs than his.

A tour of the vineyards followed and, finding in Tristam a willing and able student, Borrows explained viticulture and the managing of the business in perfect detail. Always a glutton for knowledge, Tristam was completely taken by this dissertation, and his excellent memory and training in horticulture impressed the old man.

The afternoon was well past when Borrows completed his lectures; by then he had led Tristam across the fields to the neighbor's where, in the wake of the haying, a massive supper had been laid out under the trees. Tristam was welcomed like an old friend and brought into the discussion as though he'd merely been abroad for a short time.

A dance followed the meal, two fiddlers, a whistle player, and a frame-drummer providing the accompaniment. Tristam found himself in great demand as a partner, for rumors of his skill had arrived before him. In this way the day and a good part of the evening passed without Tristam thinking of the true troubles that beset him.

It was late when he finally found his way back to his uncle's house, and he was gratified to find lamps lit in the hall. Though mortally tired, he went out to the terrace where he collapsed in a chair and stared out over the sea. The moon was a few days past full, and its distorted globe glittered on the waves. A warm zephyr curled about the house, its source undetectable.

After all the activity of the day, Tristam felt terribly let down. It seemed that Erasmus Flattery had managed his escape into the past as completely as yesterday's sunset. Only the imperfect memories of the few who had known the man remained. And even they would fade soon.

Part of Tristam's disappointment, he realized, was due to his growing hope that there would be some clue here that would reflect on his own troubles. It had been the letter from Valary. An unjustifiable feeling was growing in him that his uncle's time in the house of Lord Eldrich was somehow the catalyst that had begun his involvement in all of this. "Ridiculous," Tristam said without conviction. He could not shake the feeling though, and now, if he was to articulate what he felt coming here, it was. "*You got me into this, Uncle. Now give me a clue as to the way out, please.*"

"Ridiculous," he said again.

Perhaps the truth is, Tristam thought, *that I love knowledge more than property and, though I am grateful for my material comfort, I would rather have whatever knowledge my uncle gathered over his long life. I am his heir in the physical sense but not in . . .* Tristam groped for a word . . . *not in spirit. I continue none of his work. Pursue none of his passions except by chance. If we had never met, I would know almost as much about him.* He thought of the letter from Valary. But what in this round world was the man involved in?

Thinking this, he fell asleep where he sat.

The dream began as so many did. Tristam became conscious in half-darkness, a muted, unearthly light illuminating the stairs he climbed. The silence was so complete he might have been deaf. Each step was an effort, managed so slowly, as though he struggled against an invisible current. On the landing, Tristam came to a door which required all his strength to open. Beyond the door was a bower, and beneath the trees, in full summer leaf, falling snow filled the air so completely that Tristam could barely make out the scene.

Erasmus Flattery sat bent over a desk, snow covering his shoulders and hair. He was writing with a quill, a long white feather, and Tristam could see that the ink, too, was white. And instead of words appearing on the page as the pen flowed, they disappeared—disappeared into the eerie silence. As Erasmus came to the bottom of a page, it seemed to explode into white fragments, like fine down or ash, which floated slowly to the ground. Tristam realized the "snow" was to his waist and rising and he could not move. Another explosion of white. Snow rose to his shoulders. He fell somehow and was held by the impossible weight bearing down on him—drowning.

I must wake up, he thought. *I must wake.*

Tristam awoke gasping for air, his heart pounding. He was in the chair on the terrace, but up and pacing immediately. Agitated. Terrified.

"*Blood and flames,*" he exclaimed. "Bloody blood and flames!"

It was morning, and his neck was so stiff he could not turn his head. He tried to calm his pounding heart and clear his head, which throbbed with each beat of his heart.

"Martyr's blood," he breathed.

He began to walk toward the sea, trying to shake off the dream. *Do dreams haunt others this way?* he wondered. He broke into a trot, as though he could leave the dream behind.

The beach of pebbles and broken shells crunched gratifyingly underfoot, unlike the deep silence of his dream. Tristam stood for a moment, hesitating, then stripped off his clothing and plunged into the ocean. He came easily to the surface, breathing the welcome sea air. Twenty minutes later, he rose dripping from the sea, nearly restored to the waking world.

Willis Borrows was waiting in the garden when Tristam returned. Beth arrived moments later, supervising two younger women who bore coffee and food. Tristam was glad of company just then—the presence of others always helped him shake free of his dreams.

"You swim mornings, Mr. Flattery," Borrows said. "Just like your uncle."

Tristam stopped dead in his tracks. And then nodded, casting about for something to say. "You lost neither spoon nor child, I hope?" Tristam said to Beth.

"Sir? Oh, no. The spoon was found under a chair. It's the usual thing." She laughed, her brown eyes crinkling up in a manner Tristam found quite delightful.

Breakfast was substantial fare, food for those who did much labor, no doubt, but Tristam found his appetite was whole. Borrows was cheerful. And the day, now that he took a moment to look, was very fine.

Details of the business were harder to digest, but Tristam did his best to listen and remember what the old man was saying, for this estate accounted for a not insignificant part of his livelihood. He approved of everything Borrows planned for the coming three years and negotiated a slightly larger portion of the profit for the manager—well-deserved, Tristam was sure. That concluded, Tristam found himself wondering what best to do with the rest of the morning; he would not need to start back to the governor's until after dinner.

"You must have spoken often with my uncle?" Tristam ventured.

"Yes indeed." Borrows showed obvious signs of relief at having the business done. "Viticulture was dear Mr. Flattery's obsession, there was no doubt. We talked of it by the hour, and awfully knowledgeable your uncle was, too."

"Was he not often up at the Ruin, then?"

"Perhaps he went there, most visitors do. Farrowers don't go up often." He laughed. "Superstition I guess. Botanizing; your uncle was often off botanizing."

"Really. Sir Stedman told me he regularly saw my uncle up at the Ruin."

"Truly?" the man shrugged. "Well, I'm sure the governor knows what he's saying. Never spoke of it to me, though. Grapes and wine, that was all I ever heard." He lifted his stick suddenly and waved it like a lecturer. "And now, this talk has reminded me, I have something for you. Your good uncle wrote the year he passed on and asked that I give this to you when you came to Farrow. . . . And here you are."

The feeling from the dream washed over Tristam for the briefest second. "You have something for me? From my uncle?"

"Indeed I do. Come along up to the Grange and I shall give it to you at last, and a few other things as well."

"But what is it?"

The old man got slowly to his feet, hobbled by his bad leg. "Now, as we say on Farrow, Mr. Flattery, one should never ask after a gift—and right enough, too. It won't take us five minutes to walk up to the Grange."

It took ten minutes—Tristam was certain. They entered one of the attached sheds and here Tristam saw his first locked door. The old man located a key above the frame and drew the bolt, and then remembered they must have a lantern. Tristam insisted he could find one and rushed off, locating Beth hanging clothes in the garden. She was not in the same hurry as he was and Tristam realized impatience had him bristling even at her sunny disposition.

At last he returned to the shed where Borrows was sitting on the top step of a stairway that had been locked behind the heavy door. The old man looked rather frail seated there, hunched over his walking stick, looking down into the darkness.

"Mr. Borrows?"

"Ah, there you are, sir. Perhaps you should lead with the lamp, if you don't mind. Careful as you go. It's a steep old stair and twists off to the left."

Tristam began down the flight of stone steps, catching spider webs in his hair. He was careful to keep his pace slow and hold the lantern so as to light the steps for Borrows as well as himself. It was a difficult descent for the old man with his bad leg. Tristam could hear it in his breathing, sharply inhaled and then held, let out in a sigh, but Borrows did not utter a word of complaint.

The air was refreshingly cool and not as damp as Tristam expected, at least not by the standards of cellars in Locfal. There was an odd odor, not unpleasant, like good loam just turned by the plough. A rough stone wall on either hand allowed no view of what lay below.

They stepped down onto a floor of packed earth and Borrows sighed again, stopping with his hand against the wall for a moment. Tristam held the lamp high, chasing shadows into the corners. Before him stretched a cellar with walls lined by long racks filled with wine bottles.

The old man looked up as if to gauge Tristam's reaction.

"It is a fair sight, is it not?"

"I should say it is!" Tristam answered. His first thought was: *Jaimy would believe he had passed into a sort of paradise if he saw this.*

Borrows nodded, with great satisfaction. "Yes, there are some very fine wines here. We always take some of our payment in wine and it is a good practice. This is as fine a cellar as you will find on Farrow, though perhaps the governor's might boast to be the best. All the same, we have done quite well. See for yourself."

Tristam hung the lantern on a hook in the center of the cellar and began to explore. He was only moderately knowledgeable in the area of wines, but even his summary knowledge told him that this cellar would be the envy of . . . well, the Duchess of Morland.

After he had examined the labels of perhaps thirty bottles, he began to realize that his estate manager had understated the quality of this collection quite substantially. "My word, Mr. Borrows, you have a cellar fit for a duke."

"But, Mr. Flattery, it is yourself that has a cellar fit for a duke. Each and every bottle here is your own." The old man could contain himself no longer. He hobbled over to the nearest rack. "Look at this. A *Delisle Estate* red, from the grape of thirty-five. There can't be a hundred bottles like it in the known world. And here: a *Five Oaks*, twenty-nine. Even the King of Farrland can't boast such a wine! It is more rare than white crows, I'm sure." The old man could not stop himself. He went on enumerating treasure after treasure for a good hour. Tristam realized long before they were done that Willis Borrows was an oenophile of the first order.

"So this is my uncle's surprise," Tristam said when he had a chance.

"Ah, I'd almost forgotten." The old man curled his mustache unconsciously. "Now . . . it will be over here." He limped to a corner the lamp did not light. Stooping awkwardly, he slid a plain, wooden box from a low shelf. "Hah. There we are." Borrows cradled the box in one arm so that he might still use his cane and made his way to a small table set near the lamp. "Now here is something I'll warrant you have not seen before."

The box was hinged with leather straps and closed by a green brass clasp. Tristam realized he had gone rigid with anticipation.

"Yeess . . ." the old man said as he opened the lid. Inside was a wine bottle of such dark green glass it was almost black. "The only surviving bottle. Our own wine from the days when Seabright was a winery, made from the original crop of the true Erasmus grape." He removed the bottle carefully from the straw that protected it, bringing it into the light.

Tristam read the label: Seabright, *Regis, 1239.*

Regis!

Borrows held out the bottle to Tristam reverently. "It is the only bottle left, and there were few enough to begin with. A collector, like Roderick Palle, would pay a king's ransom for such a treasure." The old man watched him expectantly. "Mr. Flattery?"

Tristam tore his eyes away from the bottle and tried to smile. He searched for something to say, but his brain would not help him. *Regis?* The word meant king in Old Farr and was common enough, but the coincidence was still unsettling.

His eyes went back to the bottle, to the label in particular. An ornate border surrounded the lettering, vines and other flora intertwined—he knew it, he was certain. It was the same motif that bordered the text on the wall of the ruin. But it was the upper corners of the motif that caught his eye. At first glance he had thought them grapes and vine leaves, but now he realized that this was not so. They were not clearly drawn, but they bore a striking resemblance to the leaves of the *regis* plant he had seen in the King's palace.

ᕲ Twenty-Five

Kent felt that this task he had undertaken had been meant for a younger man. Too much travel, far too many nights passing without anything like his necessary sleep. He was sore from being battered about aboard the ship that had brought him down the coast, and now he was forced to stand in the cold and rain and wait for his carriage.

And yet, despite all of it, he was certain that he had not felt so alive in a very long time—more years than he could remember. Oh, yes—he was exhausted, but he felt vital! It was almost as if his youth were struggling to return, if only his body would awaken and welcome it as the rest of his being had.

He shook his head, spraying rain from the brim of his hat. It is the great temptation, he told himself.

But he had had his youth and very satisfactory it had been, too. He was not like some who had nothing but regrets for all that they might have done or might have seen. Averil Kent had so few regrets that he could enumerate them on one hand. More than enough, he felt.

Even as a boy Kent had felt driven to live every hour to the fullest, as if he thought he would die young and must make the best use of his time. But he had not died young, nor even in middle age. And now he was getting quite old indeed.

But here he was involved in an adventure. Oh, it was no lark, that was certain. No, he did not make that mistake. This was the most serious matter he had touched upon in his long life. Deadly serious. There were too many nights when he awoke in the grip of cold fear. But, blood and flames, he felt vital!

It is having a purpose, he told himself. Not that he had ever truly lacked purpose, but this was different. Much depended upon him. More than almost anyone realized. But it would be easier if he were younger. This journey was a perfect example. He needed to visit Valary more often—the debacle with Varese could have been avoided. Fortunately, no real harm was done. In fact, it had been a little comical. Massenet and Palle caught like amateurs!

A carriage came around the corner of a darkened building and bobbed along the rough stone quay. The old painter raised his cane and waved, hoping he would be seen in the darkness.

Blessedly, it was dry inside the carriage. Not far, he reminded himself. At least Valary did not have quite the fondness for solitude that the Countess Chilton displayed. Or perhaps it just was easier to achieve in this area of Farrland. Of course Valary had never been celebrated in four lands and, therefore, had no real need to protect his privacy. He was a historian of some reputation, that was true, but the countess. . . . Men had traveled across the Entide Sea for a glimpse of her—just one glimpse. And this was no exaggeration; Kent had met such men.

For a moment he fell into a memory of the countess on a certain evening many years ago. With his painter's recall of detail he could create a picture of her that was so complete, so near to real—why, he could see the individual lashes around her magnificent eyes. It had been the evening she had made a choice that had all but shattered Averil Kent.

So, in fact, he did have regrets—at least one that time could not dull. He would never become philosophical about that.

He thought of the woman hidden in the shadow of the screen. Occasionally, he felt some resentment toward her. How in the round world could she have hidden herself away for so long? *Farrelle's flames*, he almost said aloud, *the rest of us are bearing up. We parade our selves, faded and failing, before the world. What of it?*

But it was no use. Anger served no purpose—one of the lessons of age. The countess had made her choice, and some part of him understood. It was not merely an excess of vanity, as some believed. The countess had not been merely a beautiful woman, she had been an entire age's ideal brought to life. Gentlemen she had never even seen fought duels with complete strangers over her. It had been a madness, really.

Kent could remember the effect of her entering a room—the sound of every person, young, old, gentleman, or lady, catching their breath. Conversation stumbling to a halt. The arrival of a member of the royal family did not compare. He laughed aloud. Well, it was all past now. Done and past. And not since those days had Kent felt so vibrant.

"Just let me live until this task is done," he whispered to no god in particular.

It was late and Valary had made them a second pot of strong coffee, for the night would be long yet. Kent stood with his back to the fire, sipping from a very dainty cup the historian had given him, some family heirloom, Kent suspected, for the cup was terribly old.

"Imagine that several hundred years ago a house was torn down," Valary said. He looked at some papers he had spread on a massive table that was all but hidden under piles of books and manuscripts and still more papers. Some part of his hair had escaped the ribbon which supposedly held it tame, and it had sprung up like long, gray wool from one side of his face. This rather comic touch contrasted with the seriousness of the man's manner. "Imagine that it had been demolished and all of its materials, every stone and brick and tile, every stick of wood, spread across the four countries, and even further, for some has reached as far as Farrow. Some parts are used again in other houses, while other elements have been hewn into headstones or now make up parts of roads. Much of it simply was thrown into the bush to rot away, which it has done most effectively. Other parts went into foundations, which were then carefully buried; the tiles are on six dozen stables spread over a thousand miles; and still other parts were lost at sea while being transported." He looked up, peering over small spectacles. "Do you see? That is how difficult my task is. And I am trying to rebuild this house without even a sketch to begin with. Oh, I know where there is a depression in the ground where it is said the house once stood, but others say there was never a house there at all. That is the life of a mage-scholar. I put together scraps of conversations, perhaps inaccurately recorded; bits of letters; the scribblings of illiterate servants; glean some few half-truths from five hundred badly written books, all purporting to be true. That is why there are so few of us. So few who apply exacting standards, that is. There are any number of people who claim to know the secrets of the mages."

He turned back to his papers again, looking for something. The man had such a distracted manner that Kent wondered if he even remembered what he searched for.

"Ah, here it is." He held up a large sheet of paper, and smiled. "In the summer of 1407, three mages met at the castle of Locmeade." He looked up. "Three that we can be sure of—but there is anecdotal evidence that there were more. At least three more. Now Tenbaum always had a weakness for the ladies, and he almost certainly visited the Duke and Duchess of Ariss at their country home in Downe. A certain singer was a guest there at the time. Downe is a mere six miles from Locmeade Castle." He tossed the paper back onto the table; it had obviously jogged his memory enough. "Make of it what you will, but after this I have three separate references, two by Tenbaum in letters, and one by Lucklow in conversation with the Marquis of Reme, that all make reference to their 'great endeavor.'" He held up both his hands. "Now in another area of study, I realize this would be considered slim evidence indeed, but in the study of mages—well, it is a contribution that would make a man's reputation. So,

Kent, that was the beginning, you see. For over one hundred years—and Medawar said in a letter to Lady Henslow that he had been involved in a single pursuit for one hundred twenty years—they pursued some common goal. Do you see? Over a century, mind you. And with one exception these six were the last mages. Eldrich was not of their time, really, for he was merely in the service of Lucklow. And he was the last."

He crossed to the chair he had been in and out of over the last hour and picked up his cup of coffee; setting it down almost immediately without taking a sip. "The 'great endeavor.' And then . . . for no reason that we know, they stopped passing on their knowledge. Gave up the practice of . . . well, we don't know how long—but centuries, certainly. Every word, gone. Destroyed, it is said, and I think it is true. But Eldrich. . . . Why was he allowed to complete his training?"

Kent shrugged. Certainly it was a question he had asked many times.

"He was left to complete something, but not their 'great endeavor.' No. Eldrich was left to be sure that all the knowledge of the mages died with them. That was his task, I am sure. He intimated this to Flattery. Almost said it aloud."

"But did he manage it?"

Valary stood toying with one of the remaining buttons of his ancient waistcoat. Then he reached up and removed his spectacles, pressing his fingers to his eyes for a second. "I would have said yes. Unquestionably, yes. Eldrich was a thorough man." He replaced his spectacles. "But now. . . ."

The man lowered himself into his chair where he sat looking up at Kent, his face set into hard lines, the exhaustion he no doubt felt finally showing.

"You mentioned a language," Kent said softly.

"Yes." He raised his hand and waved a finger like a lecturer, as indeed he had once been. He was on his feet again, pacing, as though his passion for the subject animated him. "Now, as everyone knows, the four languages of the Entide Sea are all related. That is, they all descended from one common language. So long ago that the single root produced branches as different as separate species of trees. But still, to the philologist, there can be no question. I'm sure we can both cite a hundred examples to prove this. But there are other languages even more ancient, and if they are distant relatives of the tongues of our time . . . well, we know so little of them that in truth we cannot say. But the vowel shift! You see, the vowel shift is often consistent. This young man named Littel. Egar Littel. In a flash of great brilliance he realized that if the vowel shift was consistent, or nearly so, he could postulate words. Postulate whole languages, in theory. Now, of course, he is thought a charlatan, but I am quite sure he is anything but. I have applied some of his principles myself, and the results are impressive. Look. Look. I will show you."

There followed a half hour of Valary tracing words back into ancient tongues and Kent was impressed, for the historian then showed how he had translated an ancient fragment of a poem, and the result made perfect sense.

"So you see, we are closer. What I have done is comparatively simple, of course, and the language not so different from Old Farr. But there is no doubt that the mages spoke a language, or perhaps several related languages, that are unknown today, and certainly were unknown to all but them in ages past. Dunsenay was heard to call out in an unknown tongue at the Battle of the Midden Vale. But if they were related, even very distantly, to our root languages . . . You see?

"So, yes, if we had a text in this mage-language, and if—and I say *if*—it is related to the root language, we could, perhaps, begin to make sense of it. Of course the mage-language was recorded with its own script, I am sure, but even so. . . ."

Kent paced across the wide hearth. A sudden blast of wind caused a downdraft and Kent stepped away as a small cloud of smoke escaped the fireplace. "My fear is this." He looked up at the historian. "If we believe the mages practiced an art. . . . Well, Valary, if I were told that my own paintings would somehow cause inconceivable harm in the world, flaming martyrs, there are few pieces that I would be loath to destroy. We are talking about my life's work— their life's work. Could I not convince myself that just one piece, one small painting that bore my signature, could do no harm? Damn it all, Valary, they were men, just like you and me. Could you stand to have every word you put on paper destroyed?"

Valary seemed to consider this for a moment and then he shook his head, looking down at the fingers of one hand.

"A single text," Kent said. "Just one. That is all it might take. Erasmus Flattery. I will tell you true, I admired that man as few others but if he did this deed. . . ."

They both fell to musing. Another winter storm blew outside, and the house sat close enough to the sea that there was little protection. It almost shuddered with each blast of wind. Valary began the ritual of filling and lighting a pipe.

"I do not like this news of his nephew," Valary said, his excitement gone.

Kent shook his head, scowling. "No. It is not good. Though I am sure he is a man of principles, or at least he is not bad. It is difficult to believe, having met the young man, that he has talent."

"But you spoke highly of him." Valary puffed his pipe to light and blew out a long stream of smoke with obvious satisfaction.

"Oh, yes. He could become an empiricist of some stature. There is almost no question. But he seems . . . very much of this world. There is no mystery to him."

"That does not matter, I think. It is unlikely that we could recognize this talent. But it is in some people just as the ability to sing is there. You cannot look at a man and tell that he has a voice." He drew on his pipe for a moment. "Imagine that this power lies in the earth the way oil sits in the bowl of a lamp. Certain things are needed to make that oil give light. A wick must draw the oil up to the air, and, once there, a spark is needed to start the flame. Do you see? Those with talent are wicks, Averil. Like young Flattery; the power comes up through him, but what is lacking is the spark. The spark, I think, comes from ritual, and the ritual is dependent on language . . . and elements we are only beginning to understand. But even now he draws the power up. At least that is their hope. And if it is true, well, strange things will begin to happen around him. Virtually every mage had some affinity with the animal world. This falcon. It was the first sign."

"I was a fool," Kent said bitterly.

"No, no. Do not whip yourself, Averil. You could not have known."

Kent shook his head, taking no comfort from Valary's words. "Do you know I am worried about the boy, as well. I know he is the focus of this blind madness, but he is not part of it—at least not yet. What will become of him? Precisely what do the others aboard the ship intend?"

"It is a worry," Valary said quietly. "You can see it throughout our history. Those who showed any signs of talent too often were victims of ignorance and superstition. Stoned to death or cleansed with fire before a mage could discover them or before the talent had truly taken form. But once the power is manifest, it will begin to protect its possessor—though to preserve itself, not Tristam Flattery."

⌒ Twenty-Six

Tristam Flattery leaned heavily against a post on the balcony of his room and gazed out over the darkened garden. A warm wind, fickle in its attentions, swept across the lawns, rustling the leaves, first of this tree, then of that. It leaped down to play among the flowers, swaying the gladioli and foxglove in quick, circular patterns.

The moon, in its last quarter, floated clear of the trees, marking the hour— later than Tristam had realized. A farewell dinner had gone on longer than Tristam expected; the governor and Lady Galton were clearly unwilling to let their guests depart. The *Swallow's* officers and passengers had been joined by the senior officers of the other Farr ships in harbor, and it had made for a lively evening. Among so many nearly identical dress uniforms the duchess had stood forth like a single blossom in a field, vivacious and witty and, Tristam felt, not a little flirtatious, surrounded by so many gentlemen. There had been something in her manner that had brought back memories of the night of the governor's ball, and Tristam found himself hoping that events would repeat themselves.

He swung himself easily into the hammock so that he could look out over the garden but found he could not remain still. The drop to the garden was not two feet and Tristam stepped out onto the lawn. He was not at all sure which window belonged to the chamber of the Duchess of Morland, but he walked out across the grass and, once he had reached the shadow of a tree, turned, hoping to find the familiar silhouette.

Nothing.

A few more paces took him to a bench which afforded a view of his own balcony—he did not want the duchess to arrive at his chambers and find him gone. The yearning he felt was stronger than he would ever want to admit. *I am lost*, he thought. *Though the Jacks think I am supernatural, it is I who am the victim of enchantment.* Tristam dropped his head into his hands and rubbed his eyes as though he could wipe away the vision of the duchess over dinner. She had the glow and demeanor of a woman recently in love—irresistible, Tristam thought.

A sound came to him above the whispering of the wind—a woman's laughter. Tristam turned around, listening. It came again, less clear but unmistakable. Immediately he feared the worst, and he felt his heart sink.

You are far gone, Tristam Flattery, he chided himself. This will be one of the Galton's maids and some young officer—the very men the duchess had disparaged the night of the ball.

The laughter came again and this time it propelled Tristam to his feet. Mixed into the wind it reminded him of the laughter he had heard in the arboretum when he had come upon the duchess and the King. Very quietly he moved forward, against his will it seemed, certainly against his better judgment. *You would be better not to know*, he told himself. But his feet kept moving, one before the other.

Not far into the copse he was stopped by the sound, very near now and he began to search the shadows. There, upon a square of darkness . . . movement. Tristam stood letting his eyes adjust and slowly the scene was revealed to him. Certainly he was at least half-right—the gleam of gold buttons could be seen on a jacket, tossed aside. The dark square was a blanket.

He could hear the harsh sounds of the lovers' breathing, the occasional half-smothered moan. *What am I doing?* Tristam asked himself: *if I am caught, embarrassment will be the least of my worries.* As quietly as he could he stepped back, one pace, then two. The couple before him rolled over out of the darkest of shadows and Tristam saw it was the very officer who had been courting Galton's niece when the duchess had given Tristam her little lecture about the unsuitability of navy men. And the woman lost in pleasure beneath him was surely the Duchess of Morland. Tristam stopped, against his will.

This is what your obsession with the duchess will lead to, always. He stood, staring, as though he must imprint this image in his mind, record the pain, like a child forced to look at the ruin he has made of some object. If he looked long enough, perhaps the memory would help him escape.

The man appeared to be in rut. Tristam could see white buttocks thrusting in a near frenzy. Strangely, it struck him that here was a man with no thought for anyone but himself. And the duchess, a woman who had revealed herself as a tender lover, seemed as lost in her pleasure as the young bull who mounted her.

Tristam tore his eyes away, took three silent steps back, and then fled. At the edge of the trees he lost his balance somehow and sprawled headlong on the dew-wet grass. He lay for a moment, suddenly out of breath. He tried to rise, but the ground seemed to shift beneath him. Struggling, Tristam heaved himself to his feet and discovered that he staggered like a drunk. He could almost hear the duchess' words: *"Hearts have never been safe with me."*

ᔐ Twenty-Seven

My Dear Jaimas:

We sail from Farrow this very day, so I must dash this note off to you. The position of ship's naturalist does not seem too far beyond my meager talents, and it is intriguing work and promises to become more so. One could do worse.

I have been to see our late uncle's estate; a small affair typical of the island, it seems. Not unsuitable for an eccentric bachelor, which is rather what I expect to become.

Life aboard our tiny ship is a bit claustrophobic, as you might imagine, but then one always has the machinations of the duchess to keep one amused. I have shipped you a second small wedding present which I hope will arrive intact. Remember me to all, especially your blushing bride-to-be.

Yours in haste,
Tristam

The motion of the open ocean had once again established its ascendancy over life aboard the *Swallow* when the peaks of the island of Farrow blended into a bank of cloud and were gone.

A light drizzle and cooling breeze had driven Tristam below into the confines of his tiny cabin, a rude shock after his room in the governor's mansion, but it at least offered some privacy—some safety. Having claimed that he felt a bit under the weather, Tristam hoped that he would be left alone. He was avoiding the duchess. The memory of her, lost in pleasure beneath her sailor, seemed to dance before his eyes like the image of a candle flame after it has been snuffed. The pain this image brought to Tristam verged on the physical.

Did she not warn you? he asked himself. *She made you no promises, Tristam Flattery.* But logic had no impact on what he felt—complete and utter betrayal. If the duchess had been his innocent young bride, he could not have felt this more strongly. Nor could he have felt more a fool. How could he have thought for a moment that this woman cared for him? Obviously, she cared only for herself.

It was also painful to realize that she must have found him entirely inadequate as a lover. And even worse, she had gone to a young bull of a naval officer: a man so dense and insensitive that even Galton's niece had lost interest in him.

Why am I responding like this, Tristam asked himself? *Do I think I feel love for the duchess?* No. No, he was fairly certain that this was not so. *I am obsessed*, he told himself. *I am in the grip of a self-inflicted madness, as though an enchantment had been cast over me—but it is of my own making.*

Oh, certainly the duchess had done much to promote this madness; it had not come entirely from Tristam's desires and imagination. She had, after all, come to him in the night.

"*Did you not have the fullest pleasure of me this two nights' past?*" she had asked. "*Good, then we don't have a misunderstanding.*"

Apparently only Tristam had a misunderstanding. The sheltered existence of an academic had not prepared him for the Duchess of Morland, that was certain.

He could understand why so many of the dons of Merton spent their lives behind the protective walls of the university, living their priestly, asexual existences, aloof from desire. The life of the mind—the life that Tristam had decided was inadequate.

Well, here is where that gets you, he thought. His tiny cabin seemed positively claustrophobic at that moment—a reflection of his life. There was no escape but to have stayed on Farrow.

And why didn't I stay?

He was not sure, but he feared that, even after what had occurred, he still followed in the wake of the duchess, like a magnet drawn to iron.

I cannot stay in my cabin forever. But perhaps a day or two of feigned illness will allow me time to regroup, at least enough that I can put a face on it. Unfortunate I did not inherit the craft of my mother.

A knock brought Tristam back to the world. His first thought was that it was the duchess, come to check on his condition.

"Yes?"

"Flattery? It is Osler."

The lieutenant had spent one year at Merton and had immediately taken up the common practice among the young scholars of addressing others by their family names. Tristam suspected that Osler felt some loss of his university career—though he was certainly an exemplary naval officer—and saw having Tristam aboard as a way of recapturing some of that life.

At a call from Tristam, Osler opened the door, a half-smile that spoke both amusement and concern appearing on his pock-marked face.

"Landsman's fever, is it?" he asked.

"I fear so, though it is not so bad. I'm sure I will be better in short order."

"No doubt. Odd that you were not troubled by it when we set out from Avonel—but then it is a mysterious ailment. I suffered it once for a terrible hour after I had been at sea for three years. I'd thought I was well over that." He smiled.

Tristam realized that he no longer really registered Osler's scarring—the result of the harbor pox—though he was quite sure the young officer never lost his awareness of it.

"Well, there is some news to cheer you, Flattery. You will have a great opportunity to see some sea birds in a fortnight. The captain is going to try to fix the position of Bird Island once and for all. It is presently charted in three different locations—surprisingly far apart. But apparently, as the name suggests, it is the home of some thousands of birds."

This kindled Tristam's curiosity, at least a little, but then a second thought occurred to him.

"This can't be on the common route to the Archipelago, surely?"

Osler shook his head. "No—farther north—but ships pass through the area often enough that the rock is quite a hazard."

"Ah. And we'll take how long to find it, do you think?"

Osler shrugged, leaning against the door frame, at ease on the rolling sea. "A week, perhaps. A fortnight at the outside."

Tristam nodded. He wondered immediately if the duchess knew of this. For a second he thought he should rush to her with the news, as though a threat to their common cause might rekindle the intimacy that Tristam had thought—or perhaps imagined—had been growing between them. But then he decided he had made a fool of himself over this woman often enough.

"Does the duchess know of this?"

"I don't think so," Osler answered, and then he brightened a little. "Do you think I should tell her?"

Tristam knew that both Hobbes and Osler looked for excuses to speak with the duchess.

"I'm sure that would be appreciated."

"I hope you're back on your feet again soon," Osler said, anxious now to leave. "The pleasures of the day to you, Flattery."

The door closed. Tristam laid back in his hammock, a bit jealous. Why had he done that? To see someone else look like a fool over the duchess; that was why. Tristam was not alone in being affected by this woman—though perhaps the others were not obsessed in quite the same way.

Tristam closed his eyes for a moment, but the image of the duchess beneath her lover came immediately to mind and Tristam could not bear that.

He must soon master this madness or he would be lost. The duchess would do this to him again and again if he let her.

A few moments later a second knock sounded on Tristam's door, this one gentle and tentative.

"Excuse me, Mr. Flattery. It is Jacel."

Tristam rolled out of his hammock and opened his door to find the duchess' maid clinging to the door frame, looking truly ill.

"Jacel, you should be lying down." Tristam felt his own fakery seemed absurd, suddenly.

"No, I feel no better. I must try to keep my mind on something else." She paused to breathe, barely controlling her illness. "Would you have a moment to speak with Her Grace?"

Tristam nodded. It was a very small victory—illusory really—but at least the duchess had called for him and he had not given in and found some excuse to go to her. Not that it would be any easier.

"I shall be along directly."

Tristam passed back through the empty wardroom and knocked at the door to the cabin of the Duchess of Morland.

This is what comes of having no escape, he told himself even as he waited for the door to be answered.

Jacel answered his knock, her pretty face still an unbecoming shade. It was difficult for Tristam to believe that the woman had chosen to continue the voyage, and though he had heard some citing the maid's devotion to her mistress as the reason, Tristam was quite sure it was the young Entonne's attachment to her mistress' brother that had led her back to sea. And he thought his obsession was fraught with trouble.

"Is that Tristam?" a voice called from within. "Bring him in, please, Jacel."

In the bright cabin beyond, Tristam found the duchess propped up on her berth, a book in hand, her legs covered by a heavy wool blanket. She smiled as Tristam entered, but he could see that she searched his face, reading him, he guessed, with little more difficulty than the book she held.

She pulled her legs up, making room at the foot of her berth. "You look all out of sorts, my dear Tristam. Do sit, and tell me what troubles you."

And here we are, Tristam said to himself, suddenly she is kindness itself. One would think that the smallest inconvenience to me caused her great distress.

Seeing that Tristam hesitated to speak, she turned to her maid. "Jacel? Would you mind."

The maid bent a knee and bobbed her head—a ship-board curtsy—and went out, closing the door silently.

The duchess set her book aside, and leaned forward, hugging her knees as she had that night in Tristam's room. He could not bear it, he realized, and looked away. He did not see her nod, and then bite her lip.

"Tristam? It was a great risk for us to spend the night together in Galton's house. I should have told you." She reached out and tugged at his arm, forcing him to look around at her. She smiled at him as though there were nothing out of place in the world. "I dearly wanted to visit you again, but. . . ." She paused, gazing into his eyes for a few seconds, reading how much, Tristam could not guess.

She pushed the blanket aside and rose gracefully in the swaying cabin, crossing to the small desk where she removed an envelope from a locked drawer. "The King's Man," she said in the language of Doorn, "has unlikely allies."

She slipped a letter from the envelope and handed it to Tristam without a word. He unfolded it and read:

My Dear Roderick:

> *Tomorrow (the sixth day of November) the duchess and her entourage will set out again, but what an interesting visit we have had! I have experienced something so overwhelming, so utterly unexpected that I fear I have not recovered yet.*
>
> *I carried a party up to the Ruin, the duchess, Lord Elsworth, Tristam Flattery, and others, and gave the usual speech for visitors. Afterward the Viscount Elsworth and Flattery made shift to climb to the rim of the volcano. As they were about to reach their goal, a small tremor gripped the mountain and, in the gentlemen's own words, "attempted to shake them off!"*
>
> *To us at the Ruin this was barely felt, but, along with a distinct emission of sulfurous gases, an eerie sound spewed forth from the mouth of the*

bird-man. A deep, rumbling, string of vowellike sonants that seemed for all the world an attempt at vocalization. We were all so shocked that every person there stood, staring at the sculpture, struck completely dumb.

I think that no one, not even the duchess, suspected what this might mean, for you see, I had noted that young Flattery drank from the fount earlier. And here he was, living under my own roof! Surely he is the candidate we have sought for so long. I tell you, Roderick, I am impressed with the young man, and not simply because of this unprecedented incident. We must make no mistakes. And I will say candidly, I question the wisdom of sending Flattery off on this voyage. Yes, I know the argument . . . but still, we should take no risks. Who knows how long it will be until we find his like again?

The duchess works her charm on him, I fear, though in the end this may not matter. Time will tell, and I am sure you have taken all precautions.

𐤧 𐤨 𐤩 𐤪 𐤫 𐤬 𐤭 𐤮

Your servant,
Stedman Galton

Tristam stared at the page, unable to tear his gaze away, not sure what it was that disturbed him most: Galton's words or the single neat row of characters. *Runes!* Galton had written in runes! Was it a jest?

"Is this truly a letter to Sir Roderick?" Tristam was embarrassed by the incredulity in his voice.

"It is an exact copy. Including the runes at the bottom. Similar to the writing on the Farrow Ruin, it seems."

Tristam nodded. "How in the world did you come to possess it?"

The duchess made the tiniest motion, almost a shrug, a slight twist of her head. "I made the acquaintance of an officer aboard the ship which carried the government dispatches," she said simply.

The naturalist looked away to hid his reaction.

"Do you see? I realized my privacy might not be treated with proper discretion." Having returned to her former place, the duchess leaned forward suddenly and kissed the lobe of Tristam's ear. "I have not worked my charms on you as much as I would like, that is certain." She released her melodious laugh, taking Tristam back to the time he had first set eyes on her. *She cannot know that I saw her with another. It was her, wasn't it? The night was dark, after all.*

"Did you not warn me, Duchess, not to trust my heart to you?"

He heard her release a long breath, though he did not turn to face her.

She slipped closer to him, resting her forehead against his shoulder, taking his arm in both her hands. "You could have said no. I would have been hurt, but I would have survived. I have certainly suffered worse." She raised her head, and forced him to meet her eye. "And so will you, Tristam, unless you manage to run the gauntlet of human affairs differently than everyone else. It cannot be done without risk. Without some damage. And many suffer far more. My warning? I offered it in good faith. You chose to disregard it. *You* chose." She paused. "You may change your mind, however. But only once. Is that what you wish?"

Tristam could not think with those green eyes looking into his. *Vertigo*, he thought. He felt his head shake.

The duchess brightened a little, her seriousness disappearing like years. "I am glad." She leaned forward and kissed him softly. Then put her forehead to his, running her fingers into the hair at the base of his neck. Tristam heard her breath catch, and just that increased his pulse.

"We must not start rumors," she said, pulling free of their embrace, her face a bit flushed, he thought. She smiled as though teasing. "I have my good name to think of, after all."

She put her hand over his, tilting the letter so that she might read.

"Whatever does it mean?" Tristam asked, hoping words might disguise his state.

The duchess looked at him with a gaze devoid of emotion. "I had hoped, Tristam Flattery, that you might have some ideas. It is you that Galton calls '*the candidate we have sought for so long.*'"

"I haven't a clue." Lady Galton came suddenly to mind. She had spoken of Palle with some disdain—but this letter was supposedly from her husband to Sir Roderick!

"I think it is time we talked of your uncle, Tristam," the duchess said, her voice soft but so firm Tristam could not mistake the determination. She paused, waiting.

"I can't imagine what you would want to hear." Tristam felt a surge of unexplainable fear which almost immediately gave way to growing anger. "The truth is, I hardly knew the man, though it seems no one is inclined to believe me. I spent almost all my years in boarding schools," he said, some bitterness slipping into his tone. "Parts of three summers I lived at my uncle's home, and during those visits I was almost completely ignored. In my third year at Merton my uncle passed on and left me his worldly possessions, though this inheritance did not include a single written word. That is what I know of Erasmus Flattery. Less, I would guess, than many another." Tristam paused to catch his breath. "What did my uncle have to do with this?" He waved the letter.

The duchess, in her maddening way, shrugged, never taking her eyes from his.

Neither spoke for a long moment, and Tristam looked down at the letter again. His mind was in such turmoil that the entire letter might well have been runes—the words seemed to convey no meaning.

The duchess smiled suddenly. Then laughed aloud. "You have every right to such resentment, my dear Tristam. Why, you have been buffeted about, lied to by the King's Man. Sent on an errand that Roderick hopes will not succeed or at least not succeed in time. It is a wonder you have not exploded like a primed cannon." She reached out and caressed his shoulder. "You do not, I take it, understand what Galton thinks you are a candidate for?"

"I have not the slightest idea!"

She nodded, then leaned her forehead against his shoulder again. They stayed like that for some minutes, Tristam so entirely confused by the situation that he could not move.

"They have plans for you, Tristam Flattery," she said softly, causing him to tense up even more.

He felt resistance rise up in him like a rage. "Madness," Tristam spat out. "What kind of insanity has possessed these men I cannot imagine."

Nothing. She said nothing. Desperately Tristam wanted to hear her agree.

"But do you see, Tristam, what great significance Galton attaches to this *voice?*"

"Blood and flames," Tristam growled. "Foolishness, I tell you. Obviously a vent from the crater lies behind the figure of the bird-man. All that was heard were escaping gases."

"A belch, you say?"

Tristam thought he heard a smile in this question. He nodded and the duchess said nothing for a moment, then: "An empiricist's answer."

"Meaning?"

"Nothing more than said, I assure you."

Tristam's mind raced. "These runes? Have they deciphered them? Was this merely a jest?"

"Roderick seldom jests. Galton? Perhaps. But there is far more to our good governor than his . . . jovial manner would suggest. Do not be deceived."

No, Tristam was tired of being deceived and he was beginning to think that it was everyone's intention—to deceive him for their own ends. *A candidate for what?* Tristam wondered.

"I doubt that I will persuade Stern to give up this search for his missing island," the duchess said, matter-of-factly. "You know how he responds when resisted." She still leaned against Tristam's shoulder. "A few days should not matter, but if this becomes the pattern of our voyage . . . something will have to be done. We cannot well afford to waste months or even weeks. I can count on you in this, can't I, Tristam?"

Tristam could not answer for a second, then he heard his voice whisper, "Yes."

The duchess pulled away from him, sitting up as though she required some distance to think. "You see how cunning Roderick actually is? I realize now that Stern is not one of Roderick's minions. Our good captain is that rarest of species—a man of principle. An officer who will not be swayed from his duty. And if he believes that his duty is to carry on with the surveying of Oceana or the Archipelago, or to search for lost islands in the Gray Ocean, well, he will do it if he is at all able." She swung her legs off the berth and put the rug aside. "You see? Far better to send an . . . honorable man. Someone who truly believes in the concept of 'gentlemanly conduct,' rather than merely dressing himself in the proper clothing and manners." She shook her head. "A man less formidable than Roderick would have sent someone he believed to be his creature—a man to whom he had promised wealth and titles. But I would guess Stern has been promised almost nothing: oh, perhaps a small promotion has been dangled before him, though maybe not even that." She looked at Tristam, her large eyes wide, as though to say, "Do you see?"

"And this too-earnest dedication to 'gentlemanly conduct' and bull-headed devotion to duty—these are far more difficult to deal with than simple corruption." She shook her head, though Tristam thought this gesture indicated some admiration. "Stern is in a terrible position. If he returns from Varua with the seed . . . no one will know but Roderick and a few others. And Palle is notoriously ungrateful to those outside his own circle—something Stern may or may not be aware of. And within the navy this voyage might well hurt Stern's career. Returning without even having charted some new territory will give the appearance of having mismanaged his voyage. With no patron in the Admiralty or within the court, Stern has likely reached the height of his career—and I do not think he is unambitious." Tristam thought she was speaking her thoughts now.

"I could offer him whatever his ambition might desire—but you heard what he said about rising according to his own merit. I think he might actually believe that—and look where it has got him! If he believes the King's health cannot hold until we return, then any promises made by the Duchess of Morland will be a worthless coin." Her mouth tightened in mild anger.

She turned to Tristam. "But we must find a way to bring our good captain to his senses. It shall not be an easy task."

"If anyone can accomplish this, I believe the duchess shall manage it."

She tilted her head, looking at him as though wondering if he teased. Apparently she decided he was sincere. "You may call me Elorin, when we are alone. But do not do so in public, please, Tristam. It would not look right."

He bowed his head as though he had just been knighted.

He felt a kiss of the utmost tenderness on his cheek. "You are dear to me," the duchess whispered into his ear and then her arms encircled him and she held him close. "You must go before there is talk. Ships are such small places. Perhaps we can arrange a night ashore when we reach the Queen Anne Station: that is, if you are not tired of an aging woman?"

Tristam closed his eyes tightly—trying not to see a vision of the duchess beneath her lover in the dark. "I think you are the most desirable woman I have ever known."

Soft lips brushed his cheek again. "You are sweet. But you must be gone or I must call in Jacel. Take the letter, if you wish to puzzle over it, but whatever you do, keep it safe. Who knows who might be Roderick's agents aboard this ship."

Tristam had returned to the comfort of his swaying hammock and lay there, lost in thought. Within him a battle seemed to be in progress—the memory of the duchess and her lover at odds with the words she had just spoken to him, with the affection she had shown and with the promises made.

Yes, she had warned him and, yes, he had chosen to ignore that warning—though it had hardly felt like a choice at the time. More a compulsion.

The duchess had slept with someone else, but then she had made no promises of fidelity—nor was she likely to. But had she lain beneath that bloody officer so that she might get hold of Galton's letter? Tristam did not know if this idea brought relief or whether he felt some distaste. His image of her did not allow such a common act. How desperate was the duchess to get her hands on this seed?

Given the other implications of Galton's letter, Tristam was surprised that things with the duchess seemed so much more important. What in Farrelle's name had Galton meant? A candidate? For what? Considering the warning of Lady Galton and her husband's letter together there was mounting evidence that some believed there was more to *regis* than its healthful properties or even the promise that it might extend one's years. This led Tristam into the area he did not wish to acknowledge. The dream of his uncle came back to him. *I am being drowned by the things he did not speak of.*

Deciding that he must make some effort to turn his thoughts elsewhere, Tristam pulled out the two packages he had been given by the Galtons upon leaving Farrow.

As he cut the twine from the first bundle, Tristam realized that his discussion with the duchess, despite the fact that neither had mentioned her encounter with the officer, had taken away some of his despair. She had raised his hopes again. *Or perhaps*, Tristam thought, *I have raised them myself.*

He pulled the paper off the first package. And it was a manuscript—Sir Stedman's perennially unfinished book about the Ruin.

"Well, well," Tristam said to his cabin. A letter from Galton lay atop the bundle and Tristam took it up.

My Dear Mr. Flattery:

I have a more recent fair-copy of my book, but Lady Galton insists it is identical to this one but for the placement of the commas; I fear she is not far wrong. I hope you find it of some interest for I am only a dabbler in the discipline of archaeology, as you know. Let me say again that it was a great pleasure meeting you and I do hope we will have the pleasure of your company again. Farrow has a way of getting into a person's blood: I dare say you will find it so. Good fortune to you on your adventures.

Your servant,
Sir Stedman Galton

Tristam began to leaf through the book; Sir Stedman's shaky hand covered page after page. Some rather plain but serviceable drawings of the Ruin accompanied the text as well as a complete compilation of all the runes carved into the ancient stone.

Tristam dug into a locker and removed the bottle of wine Borrows had given him. Galton's drawings were not so exact that Tristam could say for certain, but surely the pattern in the label was modeled from the border of the text on the Ruin. But did it represent *regis?* Without actually taking the bottle up to the Ruin, he could not say with certainty.

Tristam read bits here and there as he leafed through the loose pages. Though Galton's writing may have been stiff and formal, the work itself appeared to be exhaustive, something any trained empiricist would have been proud to have done.

Turning back to the first page Tristam began to read, but he realized that the words did not register meaning, almost as if they came from a language unknown to him. Images of the duchess kept appearing in his mind and with each of these his emotions would take a sudden turn—delight, arousal, despair, frustration.

"I *am* in a state," he whispered. At least the man she had been with was not an officer aboard the *Swallow.* That would be intolerable.

He forced his mind away from the duchess again though it took some effort of will. Thinking the second package might contain something that would draw his attentions more, he cut the string surrounding it. Inside he found a thick cloth-bound book, its title in Entonne: *A History of the Mages by F.T. Valary.* Valary's book!

He opened it quickly and discovered an inscription.

For Tristam:

"Colder than starlight on midwinter's night,
Dark, dark. My thoughts eclipse the sun.
The silence comes, stealing, o'er the heart.
But hear in the distance, the sea's tumble and run."

Lady Galton

The lines were vaguely familiar though Tristam could not name the poet—a translation, he thought. Gently he put the book aside, almost afraid to go further. He felt that Lady Galton had somehow looked into his soul that morning as they had broken their fast in the garden. Did she know about his involvement with the duchess? Yes, he realized, it was likely that she did. Those beautiful eyes suffered no loss of sight—nor insight, it seemed. He hoped she was right about the healing power of the sea. Valary's book?!

But it is not coincidence. There is a pattern here. I feel that I am part of it, too much a part of it in fact—I can't step back far enough to see the design. He puzzled over the problem for some time, getting nowhere, as usual.

Tristam returned his attentions to Galton's manuscript, with only marginally better luck at first, but then his curiosity was awakened and he lost himself to it. Two hours found the last page and Tristam was pleasantly surprised by the text, for it was a work of some merit indeed. There was not, to Tristam's knowledge, a more complete work on the subject. Galton had done much to clarify the history of the Ruin's discovery, making some sense of the many stories that had long muddied the truth. The description and drawings were the most complete, if not the most artistic, he had seen.

Galton's careful observations on the other ruins on Farrow and how deeply they were buried were extremely well documented and raised the question again of how old the Ruin of Farrow was, compared to other remains found on the island.

Unquestionably the greatest original contribution of the monograph was the section that dealt with the shards of pottery found about the island. After Galton's years of collection and careful work, there seemed little doubt that much of the pottery was decorated with a written script that differed in fundamental ways from that found on the Ruin. Interesting indeed.

There was only one thing missing from Galton's work; a glaring oversight it would have seemed a day earlier, but now Tristam did not view it that way. Galton spent no time on the runes—they were barely mentioned in fact—only a paragraph saying they remained undeciphered.

⤳ Twenty-Eight

In certain respects Averil Kent did not have the proper disposition to be a painter. The pursuit required long periods of solitude in which one focused on nothing but one's art, and Averil Kent had been born a most social man. The companionship of others was, to him, as necessary as air, and the more convivial the company the better. He savored the art of conversation as much as he loved the art for which he had become famous—perhaps even more.

The company of intelligent women, banter with men of good spirit, weighty discussion of matters most grave, wicked mockery of the pretentious—all of these delighted him in ways that solitude—his own company—did not. Oh, he loved to paint, there was no doubt of that. For most of his life it had been his other grand passion. But the time alone. . . . That was another matter. The irony in all of this was that Kent absolutely had to sequester himself away when he painted. There was no other way for him to make contact with his muse, whom he thought of as a jealous lover, unwilling to share him with anyone else.

So Kent was forced to alternate between periods alone at his country home, where he fought despondency and melancholia the entire time, and spells of travel or at his home in Avonel. Of course, when he was living the social life, he always felt a nagging sense that he was frittering away his time—something he no longer possessed in abundance—so after a few weeks this feeling would drive him back to work in the country . . . and growing melancholia.

Sometimes Kent felt that he was a man whose needs would always be at war. Even that brief period when a canvas sat on its easel, complete, no longer produced a feeling of peace, for he believed, for some years now, that his work grew progressively less vital as well as less original.

The few months that he had been caught up in this . . . *matter* had been an odd hiatus for the painter. For the first time that he could remember, Kent felt completely justified in abandoning his painting. Oh, he did experience the occasional twinge—the odd feeling that he should be standing before an easel, but these feelings were not overwhelming nor even that frequent. More a mere emotional habit, he thought.

Not that this was a holiday he had embarked upon. Not by any means. But all the same, he did feel a sense of freedom that was unique in his life. "*The muse,*" he told himself, "*is as difficult a mistress as any in this round world.*"

This day he had come to his club, largely to see what he could learn of events that passed in both Avonel society and in the court. At such times he felt a bit like an insect, his antennae testing the air around him, delicately sensing the currents, ready to dart beneath a leaf.

He was well known here, as he was in most of Avonel and beyond for that matter, and the staff treated him with great respect and affection—"like a favorite uncle," a friend had once said, and he thought it was not far from the truth.

"The most innocent seeming of men," the countess had called him. Perhaps not a sobriquet that most men would choose, but it suited Kent's purpose admirably—his more recent purpose anyway.

The Brixham Club was not overly full at that time of day, but Kent wanted a chance to establish himself in a place where others would realize he was present, but he would still have enough privacy to carry on conversations—should this be required.

The squeaking of leather from his great boots accompanied Kent up the marble stair. The staff nodded politely as they passed, moving at a pace that never seemed so hurried as to be bothersome to anyone yet propelled them along at a surprising rate. A skill Kent would like to master in his life—never appear to rush yet be moving much faster than anyone realized.

The dark polished paneling, the finest eastern black walnut, gave the club a peaceful hushed atmosphere, yet the upper walls and high ceilings the color of new-cut ivory would allow no feeling of oppression to settle in. The place reminded Kent, in a small way, of his own home in Avonel.

Entering a large common room, Kent went to the periodical stand. Here he selected something to read and went up to the next level and took a table in a large bow window. It was the most private place in the great open room, and the most visible as well.

"Coffee, Mr. Kent?" came the soft tones of a servant whom Kent had known twenty-some years—perhaps it was even thirty.

"I know I should break my habits and dare something different. . . . But what would I enjoy so well? And at my age I have tried everything. Coffee; yes, thank you."

Opening the first pages of the city news, Kent realized he felt a bit of excitement, like a barely perceptible vibration somewhere in his center. It was not just this task he was so caught up in, it was the social life—or its potential—that caused this inner hum.

Kent had innumerable sources of information in the great city of Avonel. Something about his fame, his profession, and his personality led people to trust him with the most sensitive information. Everyone needed a confidant and who better than a man completely outside their sphere of activity? An artist, a man who had no involvement in the court or in business. A true innocent. And, even better, an intelligent and sympathetic listener. A person who invariably could see one's point of view, and—astonishing, considering his pursuits—give remarkably sensible advise. And this proved especially valuable when it pertained to other personalities. Kent, after all, knew everyone. Was liked by everyone.

And here he sat in the window of his club, occasionally glancing out at the street and the harbor below, though out of the corner of his eye he kept track of who came and went in the room, and who arrived at the front entrance.

It was the height of the season in Avonel, soon to culminate with the anniversary celebration of the King's coronation, and everyone who was anyone had repaired to their city residences. The theaters offered their most elaborate productions, the major orchestras played almost every evening, and the small chamber ensembles were continually engaged. It was a time of year that Kent never missed, though this season he had other things on his mind.

A tiny, handsome man entered the room and nodded to Kent, his face showing the kindest look, and Kent bent his neck in turn. Lord Harrington, Chancellor of the Exchequer. A close associate of Roderick Palle and a man with quite a considerable mind. Kent was sure that no one would ever know the true amount of the monies Lord Harrington had put aside over the years. The man must be rich beyond imagining, Kent was sure. The chancellor took a seat at a small table near to one of the hearths—his customary place—and, like Kent, he began to pore over the periodicals.

A large carriage pulled to a rather hurried stop outside and from it appeared the Entonne Ambassador, Count Massenet: late for an appointment with the chancellor, Kent assumed by the way the man rushed. If only Kent could put an ear to the wall and hear what these two would say. It might have no bearing on the matter that interested him, but all the same, there were hardly two more central players in the great theater of politics. And formidable men! Kent would hardly want to run afoul of either. Wills as hard and sharp-edged as tempered steel.

The count appeared, stopping for the merest second in the doorway. A tall man, handsome, his appearance, Kent thought, as precise as his mind. Dark colored with a look not unlike the King's Physician, Rawdon, but leaner, stronger. He dressed in Entonne fashion, his clothing black and embroidered in silver thread. A silver sash ran from shoulder to hip and on his right breast he wore a jeweled medallion worth more, perhaps, than Kent would see in all his life. If there was one man in all of Avonel whose charms the ladies seemed unable to resist, it was this Entonne aristocrat.

As expected, the count crossed immediately to Lord Harrington, and though Kent was intently interested in what would be said between these two, it was certainly unacceptable to gape at men of such stature.

Reluctantly he went back to his reading, glancing out the window occasionally. A break in the cloud illuminated sails against a black squall and the drama of this caught Kent's eye.

"Mr. Kent?"

It was a very slightly accented voice. Kent looked up to find the Entonne Ambassador standing one step down, but still seeming tall. The man had the bearing of a military officer, Kent realized, but not stiff or overly formal.

The painter rose quickly, making a leg. "Count Massenet," he said, using the Entonne address. In Farrland an earl, the equivalent rank, would be addressed as "*Lord*." "The pleasures of the day to you."

"And to you, Mr. Kent. It has been such a long time since we have spoken. I trust you are well?"

"I am most certainly well, and I hope the count can say the same?"

"Life treats me more kindly than I deserve, I assure you. If you do not await someone . . . ?" He made the slightest motion toward the empty chair.

"Do join me, please. Excuse my terrible manners. I thought you had come to meet the chancellor." Kent looked up and realized that the Farr minister had gone.

"Lord Harrington? No. A chance meeting, that is all." The count took the offered chair and a servant arrived almost silently. "I would join Mr. Kent in coffee, though make mine Entonne fashion, please." He turned back to Kent, smiling warmly.

"You are taking a well-deserved rest from your labors, Mr. Kent?"

"It is the season . . . I can't resist," Kent admitted, surprised that he felt a bit of embarrassment.

The count nodded. "I understand completely. Have you been to the opera? No? It is truly superb! And I do not say this because it is Entonne. No, it is a performance of the kind we might witness once in a decade. Not to be missed."

The servant arrived with coffee, obviously readied the moment the count appeared. Like Kent, perhaps, a man of habit.

"And your own affairs, Count? They go well?"

The man made an odd face. "Well enough. We continue to negotiate the treaty, endlessly apparently, to everyone's continuing loss." He smiled wryly. "You know how such things go. We no longer debate to gain real advantage but to come away from the table having created the perception that we have some-how won. 'Politics,' this is called. In truth, the losses in trade while this goes on more than erase any advantage. I confess, I am getting a bit bored with it all. Our interests do not exist in such opposition as some imagine." He raised his eyebrows, his look clearly saying that true gentlemen, such as he and Kent, were above such foolishness.

Kent found he smiled in return, honored to find himself momentarily a peer of Count Massenet.

It occurred to Kent that the count had probably never truly been bored in his life. His station would take care of that, even if his character had been capable of boredom—something Kent seriously doubted. Men of imagination were seldom bored and the treaty was only one of the man's responsibilities.

"Perhaps it is a function of age, Mr. Kent, but other matters seem more important to me lately. . . ." He glanced up from his coffee and met the painter's eye.

Kent said nothing. A man of Massenet's brilliance and position did not normally choose a Farrlander for a confidant. If he had anything to say to Kent that was not of the purest social intent, then the man had another purpose. Kent found himself leaning forward a little.

"Do you know a young man by the name of Flattery? A nephew to the great duke, I think?"

Kent nodded, feeling for a moment as though gravity had released its hold of him. Instinctively his hand clutched the table. "He is an empiricist of some potential."

"So I am told. And an intimate of the Duchess of Morland, as well." The count took a second to examine his fingernails on one hand. "Mr. Flattery is an acquaintance of one of my dearest friends, a musician and composer. I understand he is off on a voyage to the Great Ocean?"

It was hardly a secret of the crown but Kent found himself hesitating to confirm this. "I believe that is true."

"In the company of the Duchess of Morland and her savage brother."

One of the few men Kent could imagine who would have no fear of insulting the Viscount Elsworth. The count's skill with a blade had kept many a husband and father from calling him out.

"Yes. As all of Farr society have noted."

The count sipped his coffee. "I think there are strange things going on in your fair city, Mr. Kent. The favorite of the King—a woman—takes passage on a ship of the King's Navy and sets out on a voyage to the very ends of the earth. A nephew of the great Erasmus makes a journey to visit the Ruin of Farrow and then beyond with this same duchess. Certain members of the court have taken more than a passing interest in the doings of the mages."

Kent almost shut his eyes to hide the fear. What did this suave count want of him? What did the Entonne government want?

"Of course that is hardly new. Others have had this same fascination, even in Entonne. But this is not the same, I think." He glanced around the room and then back to Kent. He leaned forward so that the medal on his chest swung free. "You need say nothing, Mr. Kent. I do not ask that you confirm or deny—only that you hear me out, please." The man took Kent's lack of response as permission and went on. "These men have hopes of rediscovering knowledge long lost—and better lost, too, as we both realize. The people who are involved in this—they are not eccentric scholars or bored aristocrats desperate to amuse themselves. They are formidable men." He leaned back, touching his fingertips together—almost a feminine gesture; it was so gently done. "Do you know what concerns me most about these gentlemen? Oh, not what you might think. I do not believe them bad. They are not even particularly greedy or selfish, for men in their station. No, what concerns me is the narrowness of their vision. It is a problem with men driven by the need to accomplish. They focus on the task at hand to the exclusion of all else—and it is an absolute necessity for them to do so. They walk a narrow road, and because the road itself is treacherous, they do not raise their heads to look to either side or into the distance—even to the next bend. *Never* do they turn their gaze back." For a second he paused. " 'Gentlemen who appreciate things Farr.' " A shrug and then he looked closely at Kent again, assessing the impact of his words, sensitive, no doubt, to the smallest facial tic. "Have you been to the famous linen factory of Hogarth? He is a great friend of your King's Man."

Kent nodded.

"Is it not a wonder? So many ingenious machines laboring incessantly and producing . . . well, I have forgotten the exact figure but an impressive yardage of fabric of the highest quality. Great profits for all involved, without question. That is what these gentlemen see. They do not look to either side—not for a moment. Self-doubt is not a quality that will assist a man in rising to the heights that these gentlemen have reached. Do you see? No one appears to have noted that the Wye River, once a beautiful waterway and aswim with fish, now flows like a rainbow stained with the colors of a hundred different dyes and bleaches. The fish are gone and the fishermen with them. A great wheel powered by the river current drives the factory and only a tenth the number of workers are needed to make the linen." He looked out the window for a second, as though to shake off the vision of the Wye Valley. "Many things are ignored when they paint their picture of this bright future, and it is their vision that all of Farrland—all the countries around the Entide Sea—will echo with the clatter of these precious machines. *To do a thing.* The mere act of accomplishing it. . . . That is everything there is to these gentlemen.

"Given a few new mechanical principles and look what these men do. Imagine if they were to possess a power greater than any of them can yet imagine? And not for a moment do I suggest they would set out to do evil. Oh, no, but all the same, those who serve them are not always so mindful, so eager are they to rise in the esteem of their masters. And those same masters may gain great advantage by turning their eyes away at critical moments. Of the world's great canvas they perceive only a corner—and even that is chosen with great care. A dangerous thing, I think."

The count leaned back into his chair, shaking his head gently. "The anniversary of the King's coronation is not far off. My own sovereign has sent a most generous gift, though this gift of long life can hardly be matched. Almost unnatural, wouldn't you say, in a family not known for longevity?"

Kent held his peace, afraid to hear what the man might say next, but the count did not speak. Unable to bear the silence, Kent heard himself fill the void. "These things happen, Count Massenet."

The count nodded, still staring at the old painter's face. "Yes. But if that knowledge can be recovered, what will be next?"

The painter shook his head. "I'm sorry, I do not take your meaning." Kent reached into his pocket and found his time piece.

"Mr. Kent," the man said, reaching out to stay Kent's hand, his voice both warm and vulnerable, like someone asking a great favor. "You are a man of enormous gifts. No one in all of Farrland is respected as well or trusted by so many. Even more, I know something of your activities, of your concerns. You will excuse me," he said, bobbing his head in a bow, "it is my function." He fell silent for a second, gauging Kent's reaction to his admission. "As fate would have it, my own concerns are not so different. I believe that we might be of some assistance to one another, Mr. Kent, and thus perform a greater service for all."

Kent felt his head nodding but not in agreement. *Yes, now I see.* "Our nations are at peace, Count Massenet," Kent said, "but that situation might change. I have seen it do so, and quickly, too."

The man nodded. "Yes. I can't deny it. But I do not ask that you enter into an alliance with my country against your own. This concern that we share. . . . If those involved were not well placed in the court, you would be less hesitant, I think. It is a question of perception. To oppose gentlemen so highly placed could appear . . . well, almost treasonous." He leaned forward again. "But do you not oppose them even now? They are not, after all, pursuing the policies of your government in this. Is not *their* treason the greater?"

Kent tore his gaze free of the count's, looking out the window for a moment. Danger. The wrong words could bring an end to everything he worked toward. Count Massenet would likely not hesitate to use whatever means were necessary to achieve his ends. Coercion would be nothing to him.

"I know what you are thinking, Mr. Kent, or I believe I do," the man said gently. "To ally yourself with a servant of the Entonne government. . . . Well, you are a man of honor and loyal to the land of your birth—qualities that I appreciate deeply—but it is possible that, if these gentlemen go too far, my own government will have no choice but to become involved. You remember what happened when Farrland had the cannon and Entonne did not. Mr. Kent, you could help avert this disaster." He raised his eyebrows as though asking, *Do you see?*

"Allow me to say only one thing more. I am not sure how much knowledge you have—a considerable quantity, I suspect, or I would not have taken this risk myself. Let me give you one piece of information—freely offered with no expectation of return. This will prove my sincerity, I hope, and convince you that an '*exchange*' between us would. . . ." The count pushed back in his chair suddenly and laughed. "I believe, Mr. Kent, that the ladies of Avonel must think you terribly wicked." He looked to his left. "Ah, Lord Harrington. You know Mr. Kent, of course."

Mr. Kent tried to keep his wits about him, rising to make a leg. Later he realized he hardly remembered a word of what was said. Social pleasantries, no more, and the chancellor had not appeared at all surprised that Kent spoke with the ambassador.

And then Kent was alone, left to his own devices by both men. For a moment he sat in something of a daze, unable to find his bearings. *You are in your club*, a small voice whispered. *You are perfectly well.*

A servant appeared.

"Ah. Yes. I believe I shall have dinner, and perhaps a bottle of wine. Do you have any of the Southern Estate 1251 left in your cellar? Excellent! And the sea bass, the way I always have it. Thank you."

Kent stared out at the open sea. Great towering clouds grew on the horizon, billowing upward and blossoming at the top. If one focused, he was sure, one could actually see the clouds change and spread. Change. Change happening so subtly and continually that one must not allow one's gaze to wander for a second. One could not even blink.

Well, it was not an entire surprise. Kent had suspected for some time that the agents of the count had interests other than the treaty and the other maneuvering of the Farr government. There had been signs. But that they were aware of him! After he had taken such pains to remain in the shadows. It was more than unnerving. Kent felt a rush of fear like a blast of winter wind. Oh, it was not his own life he feared for—at least not entirely—but it was his task, and the others he had involved.

Wine came and Kent dashed off a glass, which seemed to have no effect at all. Who else might know of his efforts? Suddenly Kent felt completely exposed sitting in the window, as though someone involved in the matters he pursued should never be out in broad daylight. Taking a grip on his nerves, he forced himself through his meal—not hurrying too much—and then made as jovial an exit as he could manage though he felt as if he were merely doing a poor imitation of Averil Kent.

At the Club's entrance his carriage waited by the curb. He nodded to his driver and climbed aboard.

As the door closed behind him, Kent realized there was a package, wrapped in silver fabric, sitting on the seat. A calling card was tucked into the fold, and

Kent took out his spectacles to find the letters "AK" written on the card's back in a large, strong hand. The painter removed this and, turning it over, found, as he expected, that it was the calling card of the Entonne Ambassador.

Curiosity—the damned passion that had drawn him into all of this in the beginning—took hold of Kent and he lifted the small package, hardly longer than his hand and twice as thick. In a second he had the wrapping off. Inside was a finely made rosewood box, hinged and closed with a bronze clasp. This he opened and inside found a folded letter.

My Dear Sir:

May you accept this as a token of my esteem for you. In my country, after all, artists have fine avenues named for them and the most accomplished women vie for their attentions; which is as it should be. The letter that I have enclosed is very old, and it is the original. Please take your time in verifying its authenticity. Perhaps you know an historian who could assist you with this?

I remain, sir, your servant.

There was no signature. Kent removed an envelope from the box. For a second he paused with the paper in his hands as though it were some binding document and opening it would commit him to a course that he did not clearly understand or perhaps approve. The painter stayed like that a moment, even letting his gaze wander to the passing scene. A street in Avonel, the sounds of carriages and people talking. Familiar. Not a strange road at all but something he had known all his life.

He opened the envelope and from within removed a scrap of yellowed paper, as thin as an onion skin, almost transparent. Careful to cause no damage, he laid it on his open hand. He was surprised to find the language was not Entonne but Farr, and of a slightly antiquated nature as well. He began to read and realized that this was only a fragment, beginning in the middle.

I have been a witness to this horror and can tell you that our colleague exaggerated nothing. Children armed with fearsome weapons roam the streets as brigands, killing man or woman for little gain—often enough for none at all. Sky choked with a yellowish pall, noxious and unwholesome to the lung, it blots out the blue by day and the stars by night. The poor starve on the paving stones, and citizens shut themselves up in homes that have casements barred and doors of iron. In our darkest times we have not known such calamity, and this is the common day in

*this benighted land! At all costs we must end this fool's endeavor! We are
tainted enough as it is.*

In place of a signature Kent found only an elaborate letter "L."

"*Lucklow*," he whispered. Valary would have to verify it, but certainly that
was the mage's manner of signing. He remembered the Entonne doctor at the
society meeting. Varese had been his name. A man known to Valary. Had they
found more correspondence after all? *Lucklow.*

Kent put his fingers to his forehead as though testing for fever. What a day
this had turned out to be! His eye was drawn back to the box again as though
hoping there would be some explanation there, but all he found was a small
brocade purse, closed with a silver cord. Uncertain of what other revelation the
count might have prepared for him, Kent picked it up gingerly as though it
might burn his fingers. Working open the string, he tipped the contents out
into his hand. A fine silver chain bearing a clear, cut stone the size of his thumb-
nail. Kent turned it over in his hand feeling the weight, watching the light refract through the facets and break into a rainbow on his palm. It was a diamond,
he was quite sure. A gem of such size and perfection that its worth could hardly
be imagined. All the monies Kent would make if he lived to be the age of the
King would not buy it.

"*Flames,*" he whispered. Was he now in the pay of the Entonne? Did they
believe they had bought Averil Kent? He bent over the stone, half shielding it
from view as though someone might see and know immediately his guilt. A
delicate silver setting held the gem to its chain—filigree of leaves and branches.

He thought again of the fragment, part of a letter it would seem. If it had
truly been written by Lucklow, Valary would not even notice the diamond were
they laid side by side.

ᕫ Twenty-Nine

It was a perfect day to be at sea. From his position at the upper trestletrees
Tristam surveyed this new world. The wind was consistent, and had been now
for several days, blowing from the same quarter and creating seas that resembled each other so completely that they appeared to be merely an endless reoccurrence of the same wave.

And the world around him was blue. Dark blue of the deep ocean, and the
sky a soft aquamarine around the horizon changing hue as one's eyes lifted. The
graduation of aquamarine to the hard diamond blue of the sky overhead was
so subtle that one could not mark a point where the changes occurred.

Blue. Aquamarine, azure, turquoise, cyan, ultramarine, lapis, indigo. Blue. At some time during the day every shade or hue appeared, if only for a moment, in the ever-changing sky.

Clouds, like the fluff from cottonwoods, tumbled slowly in the air, wool-white, and, high overhead, the mares' tales curled against the very dome of the heavens.

Tristam drank in the air—pungent, salty. *It is a beautiful world,* the ocean, he thought, *its essence so permeated with blue that one begins to think of even the air as blue. One almost expects to taste the color with each breath.*

He looked down at the deck far below. Things with the Jacks were not good, apparently, though they did nothing more than ignore him. At worst, he occasionally found someone staring with something like disdain. But his renewed intimacy with the duchess more than compensated. Tristam was sure he was the envy of every man aboard—something that might not be helping his position with the Jacks. The duchess continued to treat Tristam as she always had. There was no hint of impropriety, and of course there had not been any to speak of. Stolen kisses. Promises of what was to come when they reached the Naval Station—a fairly civilized place, by all accounts. An actual town.

Tristam wished they would find this damned rock and get on with the voyage. He realized his keyed up desires were beginning to make him a bit mad.

An indistinct, dark line blotted the horizon to the north. Tristam focused his Fromme glass for a moment and then cupped his hands to his mouth. "Squall to starboard, Mr. Hobbes," Tristam called down to the deck. The Jack supposedly acting as lookout on the other mast would not be pleased. *Farrelle take him,* Tristam thought. They did nothing to make Tristam's life easier; he was damned if he would do anything to help them.

So the days passed. Tristam was not easily bored and had enough to keep him busy, so the time did not weigh on him. Lord Elsworth, on the other hand, had gone through a phase of pacing the deck like a caged animal, his look a bit wild with frustration. Now he seemed to have fallen into somnolence—hibernating, apparently.

Tristam descended before the Jacks came aloft in case sail would need to be reduced. He went down to his cabin to keep his journal.

It would have been considered an insignificant mass of rock had it not been the only piece of dry land within fifty leagues. There was no point of the island that could claim an elevation of forty feet above spring tides, and, on the entire four acres, there was not to be found a single tree or shrub.

Without a spring, or even a brackish pool, to slack a man's thirst, *Bird Island* was of almost no worth to mariners. Eggs of the innumerable birds that made their nests there could provide some sustenance, no doubt, but few ships strayed into this corner of the ocean without proper stores.

The island's only true consequence to the navy was as a hazard to navigation, and for that reason the *Swallow* had swept the ocean for two interminable weeks.

"Martyr's blood, Lieutenant," Tristam said to the ship's first officer. "No worth at all? Why, just look! It is the cradle of nigh on a dozen pelagic species. Thousands of birds, sir. Thousands! Why, it is a paradise."

The thickness of the navy men, even the officers, sometimes astonished Tristam. He leaned back to watch a species of fulmar pass close above the masts. He could feel his pulse racing with excitement—the King and his physic were not matters of concern at that moment. Even the duchess was not foremost in his thoughts.

"*She holds, sir,*" the ship's master called along the deck.

"Clear away the starboard cutter," Osler called out. He leaned over the rail as he spoke and looked down at the heaving waters. Tristam could hear him muttering before he turned to oversee the hoisting out of the cutter.

Viscount Elsworth stood at the rail, almost itching to have some involvement. Action! Excitement. The man only came to life when there was something going on.

Jack Beacham appeared at the naturalist's side, looking uncharacteristically grave. "This is as poor an anchorage as I have ever known, Mr. Flattery. There is nothing but a stone bottom beneath our keel and not a whit of protection. What the anchor has bitten into is a mystery to every man aboard."

"It is a wonder." Tristam hardly registered the midshipman's comments. The clamor of the bird colonies could be heard each time a sea hissed by, a shrill crying and shrieking—eerie here in the middle of the lonely ocean. These were sounds that Tristam was certain could not have been heard by men more than a half-dozen times in all of geological time—millions upon millions of years. To Tristam it was a siren's call, compelling, irresistible.

"*Walk back the falls! Lower away!*" came the call and the cutter dropped onto a wave as it crested alongside.

"Mind yourself, Mr. Flattery," Beacham said. "There is a mean swell running." The midshipman relieved Tristam of his shoulder bag and dropped it into the hands of one of the Jacks in the cutter. "Now, sir, brightly."

Tristam slipped over the side to meet the rising cutter but, but just as he let go, a breaking crest grabbed the cutter's bow and opened a gap between boat and ship. Tristam flailed at the ship's side but only succeeded in twisting himself around. A resounding *crack* against the back of his head and he felt himself plunge into the cold ocean. Dark . . . darkness rocking him, taking him in its soft arms and carrying him down, to safety he was certain, to the island girl of his dream. To warmth. Light.

"We almost lost young Beacham, as well, who took a dive after him. I don't know what possessed the boy," Stern said gravely. "He can't swim a stroke."

The Duchess of Morland stood in her cabin, both hands pressed to her face. Stern was certain she would cry and he did not know what he would do; call her brother or perhaps her physician.

"Tristam, gone!" the duchess managed. "It is *impossible*. I don't believe it! I. . . . He can swim. He told me so himself."

"He hit his head on the cutter's gunwale, Duchess." Stern spoke as softly as he was able, as though this would ease the blow. "It was a terrible misfortune."

He had seen this before; people unable to accept another's death. She was an old friend of the Flattery family—had known the young man for years. Poor woman.

But grief did not seem to be what the duchess was feeling at that moment. She fixed him with such a hard gaze—an irrational fury, without doubt. "It is impossible, I tell you! *Impossible!* It is not. . . ." She stopped, confusion coming over her now. "We will search for him," she said as though speaking to a servant.

Stern took a long breath. "Search? However will we do that? I am more sorry than you know, for I was very fond of our young friend. But the ocean has carried him off, Duchess, and will not give him up now."

There was a thumping alongside as the cutter returned from the rock. Osler had completed his sights.

"*Bring the physician!*" came a cry from the deck. "*Call Doctor Llewellyn. They've found him.*"

Stern was physically thrust aside and was hard-pressed to keep pace as the duchess dashed up the ladder. Rain was lashing the sea, making the heaving deck slick, but the duchess rattled down the steps into the waist without breaking stride. Stern came to the rail to find the cutter scraping alongside, the drenched oarsmen all standing, looking down at the form of Tristam Flattery, laying in a heap in the boat's bilge water, his face white as a fish belly.

Taine, the ship's surgeon, was bending over him, feeling for a pulse. The surgeon stared up suddenly, his look deadly serious. "*He lives,*" he said, the certainty that this could not be true clear in his tone. "I don't know how, but he breathes."

"We found him on a scrap of beach," Osler said to the captain, his tone as full of awe as that of the surgeon.

One of the Jacks in the boat turned to his fellows. "I saw a flash of something white in the sea, I tell you—as he fell." His tone was filled with awe and fear. "Like the wings of a great ray. It carried him ashore." The man stepped away from the prostrate Tristam as though afraid.

"Enough of that!" Stern bellowed. "Rig a tackle and boatswain's chair and we will swing him aboard.

"There you are, doctor," he said as Llewellyn appeared at his side. "We will have your patient aboard in a trice."

"Captain Stern, sir," came the voice of Beacham, filled with urgency. "To larboard, sir."

"What?" Stern turned to look out to sea. "*Squall to larboard! Make sail!* Mr. Hobbes, buoy the cable and let it run. We will return for it. Mr. Osler! Get that man aboard and take the cutter in tow."

Apparently from nowhere, Viscount Elsworth dropped like a cat into the bobbing cutter, swept Tristam over his shoulder, and came up the ladder one-handed. The others swarmed up behind him.

"Take him to my cabin," the duchess ordered, and she and Llewellyn followed the viscount down the companionway, chaos breaking out on the deck as all hands were called.

Tristam regained consciousness to the smell of drying wool and the sounds of the ship plunging into a whole gale. Opening his eyes did not seem a good idea just then, so he lay, still as death, listening, trying to remember. It was not morning, he was sure of that. A voice registered, though it seemed distant.

"By every regulation of the navy I should have you flogged, Mr. Beacham. You abandoned ship, sir! Now how do you account for that?"

Beacham, Tristam thought, he was in some trouble, it seemed. Snitching pies, no doubt.

"But I could not let him go down, Captain. He is not a sailor, sir, but a landsman in our charge, as it were. And no one else made shift to catch him, sir."

"But you can't swim a stroke!" Stern roared.

"I did not rightly think what it was I did, sir," Beacham said so quietly Tristam could barely make out the words. The wardroom—they were in the wardroom outside the great cabin, where Stern conducted all such interviews.

A long silence followed and Tristam began to think it was only a dream he had just wakened from.

"Mr. Osler. Let the record show that Mr. Beacham slipped over the side while grabbing for a man who had the misfortune to fall overboard, and was then rescued by the men in the cutter who were standing by at the time. It is my considered opinion that he abandoned neither ship nor duty.

"Be sure in the future that you keep your foolish head aboard this ship, Mr. Beacham. Now return to your duty."

Tristam lay in the warmth and softness, floating slowly to the surface of consciousness. A hand rested on his forehead and then he felt blankets being tucked in around his neck. He sank down into warmth again, where a small child watched over him—a sullen boy, frightened and furtive.

Murmuring. Voices whispering above the sounds of a raging sea.

"I cannot give it credence with such little proof, Duchess. Certainly the sea pulled the bow of the cutter out and away: whether the men aboard did all they could to hold it is difficult to know. I was not there to see. Nor was the Duchess."

"But, Captain Stern. They managed to save Beacham, and yet no man made even an attempt to reach Tristam. There are several witnesses who say the same thing. And it was this man Kreel who held the line. You know he is the one instigating this persecution of Tristam."

"I do not deny it, Duchess. I do not deny it. But there are too many explanations of their actions. They were thrown off balance when the boat lurched. They were surprised initially and then recovered. You must put yourself in my position. Men will accept discipline from an officer they know to be fair. But this . . . ? Well, the Admiralty would certainly not uphold any ruling I make on such paltry evidence. And it is such a serious charge!"

"That is your answer, then? You will let an attempted murder take place under your command and do nothing? I might remind you that Tristam Flattery is the nephew of the Duke of Blackwater and the Earl of Tyne. I have heard the King speak of him on more than one occasion, Captain—and I would hazard that the King does not know the name Stern. And I do not even mention this matter we are to keep so secret. But I will say that without Tristam we will not accomplish it. Be sure of that."

"Duchess, I have the highest opinion of our naturalist, and am well aware that he is of a good family. I had a note from the duke before we sailed asking me especially to watch over his nephew. I shall bring him home unharmed. You may be sure of that. I give you my word as a gentleman. Nothing will befall Mr. Flattery while I command this ship."

"I dearly hope you are right, Captain Stern. For if you are not, there will not be a ship in all the known world upon which you will sail."

Silence. Stern had just been threatened aboard his own command.

"If the Duchess will excuse me." Very polite, entirely cold.

"There is still the matter we discussed earlier, Captain."

"And I have no more to say of it!" He flared up, anger showing. But then, calmer. "I have had my orders from the Admiralty."

"And a private conversation with Roderick Palle, no doubt."

"I am called by duties, Duchess. The pleasures of the evening to you."

A door closed softly. Tristam felt the cold sea envelop him again, but he could not move his limbs to seek the surface.

Footsteps crossed the cabin in no regular rhythm, for Tristam could feel the gale pounding the ship, tossing it like a toy. He opened his eyes to find the duchess standing over him in a swaying cabin.

"I thought I heard your breathing change. Are you whole? Shall I call the doctor?"

"I believe I am here entire, though I have only the vaguest memory of what occurred."

She smiled down at him, not quite hiding a look of concern. Lamplight glinted in her hair and Tristam realized it was night. "You fell over the side as you boarded the ship's boat. You don't remember?"

"Ah. Did I hit my head, then? I have a powerful sharp pain in the back of my skull."

"Yes, you did. I shall wake Llewellyn."

"No, no. I am able to see perfectly well, I feel no nausea and I think the hurt in my head is in my skull only. No more than one would expect. Someone pulled me out, I collect. Who was it?"

The duchess put a hand gently on his shoulder. "I believe you owe thanks to some propitious tide or current—or so the captain thinks—for you were found a few moments after your mishap, washed up on a narrow little ledge. Something of a miracle. . . ." The look on the duchess' face did not convince Tristam that she believed her own words.

"I see." Tristam said nothing for a moment. "And what have the Jacks to say of that, I wonder?"

The duchess shrugged. "I think the poor crew are at sixes and sevens now, for Lieutenant Osler tells me that a man granted his life by the sea is thought to be charmed. You have given them something to ponder and fit into their way of thinking about the workings of the world." She forced a laugh. "I shouldn't worry."

"I missed the birds, then?"

The duchess laughed again, relief showing. "I see you are returning to your natural self. But, Tristam, are you shivering?"

"It does seem suddenly very chill. Is there another blanket, perhaps?"

"A blanket will be of no avail against a fever," she said feeling his forehead for the second time. Stepping back she shed her shawl and gown, and thus clad in her undershift the duchess lifted the blankets and slipped into the narrow berth beside her patient. Her soft arms encircled him and Tristam felt the warmth of her body as she pressed close to him.

"You are a block of ice, Tristam. Perhaps I should call Llewellyn, though he is none too well himself with this sea running."

"Wait a bit, I'm certain this shall pass." And he fell back into a troubled sleep.

Some unknown time later the wailing of the gale in the rigging brought Tristam awake. He felt neither cold nor hot and surmised that his fever had broken. Beside him the duchess breathed evenly, close against him. He brushed her hair gently back from his face and felt her stir.

"Mmmm." She pushed tighter to him. "You are recovered, I think," she said, feeling his desire rising. The duchess began to kiss his neck. "Now here is a feat that will test our cunning," she whispered as the ship lurched, pressing them against the lee board, and then tossing them the other way. "Though I can cry out with utter abandon, I'm sure, for who could ever hear?"

Tristam spent part of the next day in the care of the duchess and then returned to his normal shipboard life. The gale had blown itself out by morning; when Tristam ventured onto the deck in the early afternoon, the sea was looking decidedly less threatening, though overhead dark clouds still hung heavily above a gray ocean.

The first lieutenant, Osler, nodded to him and smiled. Overhead, the Jacks were setting more sail, the master trying to make the most of a fair breeze, for they had encountered more than their share of head winds since leaving the island of Farrow.

The duchess and her maid were taking the air at the stern rail, but as Doctor Llewellyn accompanied them, Tristam descended into the waist of the ship, planning to perch on the spare spars. As usual, the duchess' manner toward him was completely opaque, and Tristam had to admire her skills as an actress—though these same skills made him wonder sometimes how genuine her affection might be.

He levered himself up onto the spar and leaned his back against the bow of the cutter. A panorama of a rolling, empty ocean stretched out before him. He closed his eyes and leaned his head back against the planking, wincing as his injury touched hard wood.

If I keep hitting my head like this it shall surely be weakened, I have not so much wit that I can afford to have it diminished. He felt more than a little exposed sitting there, out in the open. The Jacks working on the deck no longer seemed just ignorant and superstitious. But why in the world would the Jacks try to drown him? So they believed his uncle had been a mage. . . . So what? Why would this lead them to murder?

Somehow Tristam couldn't believe it would, but there was a part of him that kept whispering, "You can't afford to disbelieve it."

It seemed most likely that the act had not been planned in advance, but when he fell, no one had moved to save him. Not an act of murder so much as murder by inaction.

"Mr. Flattery, sir?"

Tristam opened his eyes and found Pim, the youngest Jack aboard, standing with a steaming mug in his hand and looking decidedly nervous. He proffered it and Tristam caught the odor of coffee.

"Cook's compliments, sir."

Tristam noticed that several Jacks stood about the deck, watching. There did not seem to be animosity in their eyes but expectation.

Was it a peace offering? Tristam wondered. He reached out immediately and took the cup.

"My thanks to you, Pim, and to cook as well."

The lad bobbed in an awkward bow, already out of words, apparently. The others had gone back to their duties.

"With your leave, sir," he said, looking as though he would bolt.

Tristam smiled and the boy was off at a trot. The coffee was strong, unsweetened, bitter. The naturalist closed his eyes and sipped quietly. Pim had never been unfriendly to him. Just a shy boy, eager to please and very intimidated by the high-born passengers.

"Ah, Mr. Flattery, it is good to see you up, sir." Tristam opened his eyes again and found a happy-seeming Jack Beacham. "The pleasures of the day to you."

"And to you as well, Mr. Beacham. I am equally happy to see you whole, for I have heard that you plunged into the sea after me. And though I applaud your bravery, this was a foolish endeavor for a man who swims as well as the best of stones."

Beacham broke into a smile. "I did not think what it was I did, Mr. Flattery, until the cold ocean cleared my head. I could not reach you, but good fortune had a Jack hit me with a lead line. I have a prodigious bruise on my buttocks but grabbed the line and am here, as you see. They say I am the strangest sample they have ever brought up on the lead, sir, and I'm afraid I will be called 'Bottom Beacham' from now until I am truly dead."

Tristam laughed. "Well, I thank you for taking such a chance. Perhaps, when circumstances allow, I shall teach you the fine art of staying afloat and even making headway. It may stand you in good stead if such acts of heroism become common to you."

"I should like nothing better, sir, for I do not believe for a moment that it reduces one's constitution. I have been out in the coldest rain many times and soaked through until my skin wrinkled up, and I was never once sick afterward. It is a misguided belief, I think, and after all, I for one would rather reduce my health somewhat, if that were the case, than drown altogether."

"Well there is some sense in what you say. I am sure of that." An awkward moment when neither spoke. "Tell me true, Jack Beacham . . . are the Jacks set on doing me harm?"

Beacham looked around, suddenly more uncomfortable than Tristam had ever seen him. He took a step closer. "The hands are split, sir. There are those that think this has gone too far. They think the men in the cutter could have made shift to catch you, Mr. Flattery. And there is the undeniable truth that the sea has granted you your life. . . . There is a split in the forecastle that I have seldom seen, though fewer and fewer side with. . . ." He gave the slightest motion with his head toward the bow.

Tristam nodded, closing his eyes again. His wound had begun to throb. Kreel was a forecastleman.

Tristam felt a sudden chill as though his fever returned. *Blood and flames,* he thought, *they tried to murder me!*

"But, Mr. Flattery, with such luck as you have just shown I should not worry about anyone doing you harm. I have never heard of such a thing happening and there are a thousand stories of men saved from their end in the sea."

Tristam did not open his eyes. The tone in the boy's words was perfectly clear.

"It was a stroke of luck, Jack Beacham," Tristam said weakly, "nothing more."

Silence. Tristam knew Beacham would not answer because he would not gainsay him, but clearly he did not believe. As superstitious as the Jacks, Tristam thought.

"Now set me straight in a matter of ornithology, Mr. Flattery," Beacham said quietly, changing the subject. Tristam opened his eyes to discover a Jack had begun working nearby. "I have made an observation that perhaps should go into your journal." The boy was making an effort to cast aside the seriousness of the moment. "Or perhaps it is nothing at all." He smiled, a bit embarrassed.

Beacham had taken an intense interest in natural history, questioning Tristam constantly. The midshipman had discovered that one did not have to be a fellow to get one's name into the *Society Annals* for a contribution, and he was hoping that Tristam would credit him for some yet undiscovered species or phenomenon.

"Yesterday, not long before we both plunged into the Gray Ocean, I saw, off in the distance, a bird dive out of the sky and strike another in the air, sir. Even at the distance I saw feathers fly and the bird, the diving one, took the other off. I don't know where, for there were such a prodigious number of birds in the sky that I lost sight of it. I have looked in the books, but I can't make sense of it at all."

"Have I pointed out a jaeger to you?"

"As we left Farrow? The one that chased the others for their catch? Too lazy to fish for itself?"

"Exactly. It is likely what you saw. A jaeger would not *take* a bird, that is *kill it*, but it might seem to have done so at a distance."

"Well, I did not have a field glass at hand, but it did seem so at the time. A white bird . . . just folded up its wings and dropped like a stone." Beacham demonstrated with his arms, "Though, as you say, it was not near enough to be certain. I'm sure a jaeger is what it was, though, I confess, I had hoped it might be a species never before recorded."

"White you say? And diving?"

"That's right, sir. Just like this." He again demonstrated the bird folding up its wings and plummeting out of the sky. It was a good imitation of a hawk or falcon, there was no question.

"Well, that doesn't seem like any jaeger I know. There could not be raptors so far out to sea. Unless there is some larger island nearby that is undiscovered. I shall mention it to Captain Stern."

Impossible, Tristam thought.

↶ Thirty

Another gale was blowing when Tristam woke, though he was sure it was not the storm sounds that had called him from sleep. He lay still in the darkness, mentally measuring the arc of his hammock as it swung in the confined cabin, and he listened. Hadn't there been a call? Perhaps a knock? He strained to hear above the din. The pounding of seas upon the bow and the creak of stretching cordage . . . but no sound of his name being repeated.

A dream, Tristam thought, and adjusted his position hoping to return to sleep. After this long at sea, gales did not really wake him fully. They merely registered in his mind, no more threatening than the storms outside his home in Locfal. He decided that his sleeping position was not the right one and tried turning on his other side, careful not to end up being pitched out of his swaying bed.

The wind moaning in the rigging brought back a memory of the gale during which he had made love to the duchess—the fever of the storm at sea like an echo. It was not a memory that would help him sleep, so he tried to push it from his mind. Part of the problem was lack of air, for the ship had been closed up against the weather.

Tristam decided he needed a breath of air. He rolled carefully out of his hammock and balanced in the dark. The cabin was so small and so well organized, that almost everything was within reach. In a moment he was pulling on oilskins over breaches and shirt.

Bootless, he crept out of his cabin into the glow of a shuttered lantern. Up the companionway stair, and then out beneath canvas weather-cloths.

Immediately the cool wind lashed him and driven spray was dashed in his face leaving the taste of salt. Tristam almost laughed. On occasion the great absurdity of his life aboard ship struck him strongly. It was not quite the way he had lived in county Locfal.

So far the gale was not proving a bad one. He knew this more from the sound of wind in the rigging and the motion of the ship, for he could not see twenty feet—could barely make out the helmsmen in the light of the binnacle.

Tristam realized how accustomed to life aboard he had become. Only a few weeks earlier such a gale would have reduced him to sickness and to huddling in his cabin in real fear. But now the great seas, heard and sensed more than seen, did not seem the black monsters they once had.

The ship was lying to under reefed topsails, making no headway but holding her own handily. With such a small crew Stern often employed this tactic in bad weather as it allowed him to rest his crew and keep them fresh. The watches were small and frequently all but the helmsmen and one man on deck-watch would stay below ready to be called if needed.

Tristam stood, face into the wind, though it blew spray under his storm hat and cold tendrils of water felt their way down his neck and onto his chest and back. A distant flash of lightning illuminated an area of cloud and the crests of seas. For the briefest second Tristam could see the ship, bow high as it rode over a sea, and then it was utterly dark again.

He realized that if this were a larger storm, truly threatening to the small ship and crew, it would provide one benefit: it would drive all other thoughts, all other concerns and anxieties out of his rather overactive mind. Crises were cleansing in that way.

A sudden dull thumping up forward drew Tristam's attention—two hollow reports of impact on timber. Some piece of gear had probably come loose, and he set out quickly along the heaving deck. His growing competence in things nautical saw him taking such actions more and more often and he was surprised at the satisfaction there was to be gained from such simple tasks: belaying a loose line, tightening a gasket around a flapping sail.

In the darkness Tristam went hand over hand along a lifeline that had been rigged against the weather. Crests tumbling over the bow would occasionally wash past his bare feet, ankle deep, the sea here still cool, and feeling colder on such a night.

A larger sea rolled the ship until she all but buried her rail; Tristam was forced to halt his progress just to keep to his feet. He slid several feet toward the leeward bulwark, feeling the rope stretch. There was a precarious moment where the ship hesitated before beginning to right herself, and Tristam made ready to grab for the rigging if his lifeline parted, which it seemed ready to do.

He heard the hiss of a crest breaking, washing over the forecastle and then sweeping along the deck. Water, thigh-deep, struck him with force, trying to tear his hands free of the sodden line he clung to with all his will. A series of thumps not a yard away warned Tristam that whatever had come loose was being swept his way, and he tried to pull himself up the slope of the deck.

A man, or perhaps men, blundered into him as they were washed, struggling, past. Tristam released one hand and made a grab in the dark but only tore away part of a shirt. He heard spluttering and coughing not two yards off as the water ran off the deck around him.

"*Blood and flames!*" Tristam spat out. "Are you there?" He made his way along the line, waving one hand before him as he went. There was a terrible thump of flesh on wood almost underfoot.

"*Helmsman!*" Tristam bellowed, hardly hoping to be heard over the moan of the wind.

Another flash of lightning, far off, and there was someone kneeling over the figure of Kreel, hands to his throat and the giant seaman struggling to pull those hands free. Before he could move or speak, Tristam saw Kreel's head lifted and driven down hard on the deck. And then darkness returned.

"*Who called?*" came a shout from the quarterdeck.

Tristam stood riveted in place for a second.

"*Speak up, forward.*"

Tristam jumped forward, guessing in the darkness, and threw his weight against Kreel's attacker. A massive arm swung around and sent Tristam skidding across the deck. He crashed hard against the bulwark.

Above the noise of the sea Tristam heard the ring of the bell which called the watch. A wave washed around him and he felt himself rising in a panic, coughing up salt water.

Dark. Too dark. He could make out nothing. A groan and the sounds of something dragging over wood. Tristam staggered along the deck, clinging to the rail for balance. He collided with someone, catching the person off balance as the ship heaved upright. In the darkness Tristam grabbed the limp form of Kreel and fell back from the rail. He hit the deck with the huge weight of the Jack half on top of him.

Sounds of men coming out the hatch.

"*Here!*" Tristam called out. He rolled the Jack onto the deck, clutching tight to his arms lest he be washed away in the dark. "To starboard."

A flash of lightning revealed the men coming, hand over hand, along the lifeline.

"He's not conscious."

"Call Mr. Taine," he heard someone shout. Strong hands suddenly lifted Tristam to his feet and others grabbed the inert form of Kreel.

"Flames, what's done for him?" a Jack hissed, looking suspiciously at the naturalist.

"I don't know. . . ." Tristam heard himself stammer. "I–I came out on deck for some air and I heard a thumping forward. Thought it was something come loose. I found him instead. Another few seconds and he'd have been washed clear over the side."

There was no time for talk. The men gathered their fellow seaman up and made their way, staggering, toward the hatch.

Alone on the deck, the naturalist stood clinging to the lifeline, his breath coming in deep gasps.

Flaming martyrs, Tristam thought, *I stopped a murder!* He hadn't seen the attacker's face, but he could think of no one powerful enough to take on Kreel, except for the Viscount Elsworth.

"Flaming martyrs," he said again. "Murder."

Stern was seated at the small table with the ship's log open before him. To his right sat Osler, pen in hand and paper ready. Hobbes stood to his captain's left, and Tristam thought both seamen looked very grave indeed. Even Osler did not offer Tristam the slightest indication of a comforting smile.

"Mr. Flattery," Stern began, his voice at once tired and yet full of tightly controlled outrage. "This is a very serious matter, I must tell you. We are here," he glanced at Osler, "to take your statement and though this is not a hearing in the proper sense, nor is it a court of law . . . still, everything you say will be recorded and duly reported to the Admiralty and the Navy Board. There is a possibility that, upon our return to Farrland, you will be asked to corroborate or to speak further on this matter. Do you understand what I'm saying, sir?"

Tristam nodded. "I do, Captain."

"Well, then begin by telling us what it was that you saw last night and why you were on the deck at such a late hour in weather so foul."

Tristam swallowed, not too obviously he hoped. "I could not sleep, Captain Stern. It is not uncommon for me, as almost anyone aboard can tell you. When I found that sleep would not come, I thought it might be due to the closed state of the ship—everything being so close and airless. I dressed and went up onto the quarter deck. Perhaps the helmsman saw me emerge?"

A nod from Hobbes.

Tristam looked down at Stern who stared up at him with a very cool and distant look. "As I stood taking in great breaths I heard a noise forward—a thumping—so I thought, as the crew were below, I would see if it was something come loose that I could easily tend to. I went down into the waist, and along the lifeline. Almost at the forward deck I was stopped when the *Swallow* took a great roll and shipped a large sea. As I stood, bracing myself, and clinging to the line, something, that I realized immediately was a man, washed past me and I made a grab for him." Tristam paused to look at the others, feeling, somehow, that his words did not sound truthful. There was sweat on his brow. What to say now? Did he tell them his suspicion?

"I came up empty-handed, but a flash of lightning revealed two men struggling, Captain, one whose face I could not see and the other was Mr. Kreel. I called out to the men at the wheel and they rang up the watch, who took Mr. Kreel below." Tristam paused, pretending to search his memory. "I can't think what else there is to tell, Captain Stern."

Stern looked down at his log for a moment, as though checking Tristam's story against another written there, and then he looked up. "You saw no one else? Or heard no one?"

"Not a soul, sir." Tristam felt a small surge of panic. "Though it was very dark."

"And you cannot identify this other man? Think, Mr. Flattery. Anything at all. Color of hair. A distinctive bit of clothing?"

Tristam shook his head.

Stern looked away, obviously unhappy with the answer.

Tristam tried to regularize his breathing.

"It is the damndest thing," Stern said, almost to himself. "Well, I will tell you Mr. Flattery—and I will have this go no further—there were others about last night. Oh, hidden by the darkness I'm sure. But there were others. One of the men at the helm thought he saw three men by a flash of lightning, though the other helmsman is not so sure. I will say this; Kreel did not receive such wounds from an accident—as he claims. The man was near throttled and the marks on his throat are plain to see. It is a wonder he lived." Stern slapped his hand down toward the log, but at the last second he pulled it back so that it landed softly.

"Mr. Kreel says it was an accident?" Tristam asked.

"Yes; the worst foolishness. The man will tell us nothing. Not a word. You are not a navy man, Mr. Flattery, so you have not seen this before. But I have seen whole crews split and turn on themselves. Turn murderous, too. And if the officers cannot get to the bottom of it. . . ." Stern thumped the log hard this time, but it was only punctuation—his temper was still in check.

"Despite the fact that it appears Kreel is the victim of this attack, I may have to flog the man and throw him in chains because he will not say who his attackers were. And that is a breach of the war articles, clear and simple. You see, Mr. Flattery, the Jacks have their own code, benighted as it may be. Kreel must deal with this himself or be thought a lolly-Jack by all the men before the mast. Bloody foolishness." It was the second time the man had sworn and knowing

Stern's disapproval of such things made Tristam realize how deeply this attack affected the captain.

Tristam thought of Kreel and could still hardly believe that even the viscount could best such a man. Whoever it was had tossed Tristam across the deck with almost no effort.

"I can't think who the man could be who would dare face Kreel," Tristam said quietly.

"It was not one man," Stern asserted again. "You can count on that. The man took a savage beating. Kreel is a good and able seaman, but a great bully at times, and there are some who have had their fill of it, I would say. No, his own messmates, or some of them, took the man on in the dark, though there is not one among them who does not claim to have been elsewhere. If not for you, Mr. Flattery, Kreel would be sinking still. He has you to thank for that."

✑ Thirty-One

The Northeast Trades proved to be elusive winds that season and the Variables, the band of winds that lay between the Westerlies and the Trades, seemed to stretch on forever. As their name suggested, the Variables were unreliable in both strength and direction and at times disappeared altogether, leaving the *Swallow* wallowing on a windless sea.

Tristam lay in his hammock, the only position of comfort in his cabin, Valary's book open in his hands, but his mind elsewhere.

The past week had seen only fickle winds and little progress, and Tristam could feel the growing frustration of the crew and officers. Both Hobbes and Osler labored to keep the Jacks employed, for idle hands soon found their own endeavors and these were not always to the good of the ship. Tristam had made an effort to stay clear of the Jacks, not sure what the response to Kreel's attack might be, but the animosity the Jacks had harbored toward Tristam seemed to be diffusing. According to the code of the Jacks, Kreel was now in Tristam's debt, and this seemed to have brought an end to the enmity. Beacham had hinted that there was some relief among the Jacks over this.

Tristam had pumped the midshipman for information, trying to learn the scuttlebutt that passed before the mast. According to Beacham, Kreel, released from sick bay some days, would say nothing, leaving the Jacks at a loss; no one seemed to know who the guilty party was. An unheard of situation. If there was a feud aboard ship, Beacham assured Tristam, the Jacks would know who was set against whom.

But Kreel would say nothing, and Tristam assumed that no one thought of Julian. The man was a lord. Peers did not engage in anything so common as a brawl.

Someone had suggested that Tristam was responsible and this joke had been popular for a few days. Tristam the giant killer.

The viscount had not so much as hinted at the matter in any conversation with Tristam, of which there had been several.

"*The viscount is the trained falcon of the Duchess of Morland,*" Jaimy had said, "*and she carries him about on her wrist to be sure that all know it.*"

And she had guaranteed that Julian would never act in such a manner again. And Tristam had believed her—though he wondered. Had the duchess only asked Julian to see that Kreel left Tristam in peace? And then things had gotten out of hand?

Was the viscount merely murderous? Some men were, it was said. Tristam found this a chilling thought—but then Ipsword's death had been utterly cold-blooded, monstrous really, or so Jaimy had claimed.

Beacham was shocked by the attempt at murder. "*Kreel would not be the first Jack murdered by one of his mates,*" the midshipman had said, "*but it is more commonly done in the midst of a fight, Mr. Flattery. An accident, really: done while the blood is hot. But this attack on Kreel . . . everyone believes it was coolly planned.*"

But planned by whom? The truth was, Tristam could not positively identify the attacker. He had not seen the man's face.

He turned his attention back to his reading.

Contemporary accounts are in general agreement on the essential facts of the battle, unfortunately they tend to such a high-dramatic style (the style of the time) that they are often not credited. Here is an example written by an observer, one Brenton Lace, scribe to the Earl of Highgate.

The army of Farrelle came upon the field to the trumpeting of horns and the waving of banners, for their pride was such that each house should be marked and none go unnoticed on this great day. The Prelate Anjou made a fire to his god and burned upon it the leaves of holyoak so that all his soldiers might breathe the blessed smoke.

Upon the Midden Hill the gathered mages looked down from their tower and knew despair, for they could boast but one warrior for every ten of Farrelle. But Lord Dunsenay went out of the tower upon his gray steed and rode most brazenly across the crest of the hill. Waving his spear at the sky as he crossed one way and then the other, stopping only to beat on his shield, great crashing blows that unnerved the enemy in the vale below. And as he rode he called out in ancient tongues, words that no one had ever heard. In the valley the Farrellites stopped up their ears for fear of bewilderment.

In midday the green sea-light formed around Dunsenay, wrapping him in an unearthly green fire as he stood upon the Midden crest and at this the forces of the Prince of Delgarthy withdrew from the field.

A great cloud came out of the west, then, as gray as Dunsenay's steed, and the thunder shook the Midden Vale.

The Prelate Anjou stood before his host and called upon Farrelle to bring down the lightning upon the tower of the mages. And as he called out the thunder rolled and the lightning lanced into the midst of the Army of Farrelle and they turned and ran from that unholy place, crushing their own in their terror.

Although the man does not seem to clear on the priority of lightning over thunder his account agrees in all salient points with that of another observer—or participant in this case.

Tristam closed the book and lay his head back. Children's tales.

His hammock hung almost motionless across the small cabin, for the ship only moved slowly up and down as though it rested on the breast of some sleeping giant. It was warm, though not unbearably so, but the lack of a breeze soon had the small ship stuffy and noisome.

The sound of someone pounding down the ladder outside Tristam's cabin came through the thin plank door and then the door itself reverberated to an ungentle knocking.

"Mr. Flattery, sir. The captain bids you come on deck, sir. Double time or they will be gone."

The man ran off. Tristam rolled out of his hammock and took up his Fromme glass—he had learned not to answer such a summons without it. Over the last few days there had been several species of whales about in numbers and the officers called Tristam whenever one was observed.

In unshod feet he mounted the companionway stair and came out onto the deck at a trot.

"Ah, Mr. Flattery!" The captain stood at the stern rail with several others. He motioned to the north where Tristam could see a dark squall, like a moving shadow, passing over the lead-gray sea.

Stern lifted his glass as Tristam came up. "They will certainly come this way, Mr. Osler. Do you see, Mr. Flattery? Waterspouts. A natural phenomenon I thought might be new to you." The seaman swept his glass across the horizon, missing very little, Tristam suspected. "There is a good breeze of wind beneath that cloud. Mr. Hobbes; call all hands. We should be ready to reduce sail."

Tristam searched the shadow bearing down on them and immediately found the spouts. Three: no, four of them, like elongated funnels spinning up into the dark mass of cloud.

A rustle of skirts told him the duchess had arrived and, like all the other gentlemen present, Tristam lowered his glass to make a leg.

In her hands the duchess carried one of Tristam's spare field glasses and she raised it, now obviously quite familiar with its use.

"Why, there they are!" she sang out. "Do you see three, Tristam? I can't quite make them out."

"Four, I think, though it is difficult to tell."

"They will be close very soon," Stern offered. "Perhaps closer than we might hope."

"Are they dangerous, Captain?" the duchess asked, not lowering her glass. Only aboard a ship would such an action not be considered impolite.

"No need for concern, Duchess, the *Swallow* is a stout vessel. But if such a spout comes aboard . . . well, look to our sails. It will tear them to rags in a trice. I have heard tell of spars coming down, but I believe they must not have been sound or their standing rigging was in a weakened state.

"Here is some wind now," Stern said, raising his hand. "We will have steerage way in a moment and move clear."

Tristam heard Hobbes giving orders to the helmsman and felt the ship slowly begin to make way, the *thuddle* of the steering tackles vibrating up the stern-post and into the deck.

"The tip of a wind vortex, Your Grace." The physician had arrived on deck. "They funnel water up from the surface of the sea. It is said that a cannon ball through the spout will cause it to collapse."

The duchess lowered her heavy glass. "Is this true, Captain?"

Stern seemed almost to grimace, Tristam thought, for he found the physician as annoying as Tristam did himself. "So it is said, Duchess, though I have not witnessed this myself nor have I known anyone who has seen it done—no one whose word was a steady wind, that is."

The duchess raised her glass in the ensuing silence, and Tristam tried not to grin.

"There is a whale spout, I think!" the duchess said, giving a little jump of excitement. "Do you see, Tristam? Halfway to the squall and to the right?"

"You have a knack for observation, Duchess. Whales they are."

This compliment pleased her more than Tristam would ever have thought, and he could hear it in her voice. "I have missed my calling, I think. Do you see them, Doctor? The great leviathan. What variety would they be, Tristam?"

Tristam made an effort to hold his glass still. "It is difficult to say at such a distance, Duchess. Baleen whales, I think, though I cannot say which species."

"Sperm whales," Llewellyn said firmly, contradicting Tristam, as was his usual practice. "*Physeter catodon*. Easily told by the shape of their spout, Your Grace."

"The squall is blowing the spouts off too quickly for my poor eye to tell," Tristam said, and then added, "though of course, the doctor might be right." Tristam was making an effort not to argue with Llewellyn; it was a great waste of one's mental energies, he had decided.

The squall overtook the whales and they disappeared into the darkness without any sign of concern. Perhaps, Tristam thought, they took pleasure from the rain upon their great backs, as other beasts seemed to take pleasure from the sun.

Although the *Swallow* had been nearly stripped of canvas, she began to make good speed, the burble of her hull moving through the water lifting the spirits of everyone aboard. Despite the ship's speed, the squall bore down on them quickly. As the gap became smaller, Tristam could see that there were more waterspouts than he had originally thought, half a dozen, at least, and these rose like strange columns upholding a maelstrom-dome.

A blast of wind struck the ship, almost rolling the lee gunwale under. Tristam grabbed the rail and at the same time steadied the duchess—almost losing his Fromme glass in the process.

He followed the duchess and the physician below, but once Tristam had secured the portlight in his cabin and returned his glass to its locker, he rushed back on deck wrapped only in a cotton square, and clutching soap in hand. Though they were in the midst of some chaos he stood by the stern rail and washed himself in the falling fresh water—a precious commodity aboard ship.

The *Swallow* ran steadily before the wind now and the waterspouts Tristam had seen were gone. A sail came free with a *crack* and the foretopmen were sent aloft to tame it—a dangerous endeavor, for a wet sail flogging in the wind might as well have been made of iron.

"Making the best of it, are you, Mr. Flattery?" Stern grinned at Tristam from beneath his storm hat. The captain was wrapped in his oilskins and may not have been much dryer than Tristam.

A great blast of wind threw the ship on her beam ends and Tristam slid half the width of the quarterdeck before his slippery hands managed to find purchase on the rail. Out of the corner of his eye he saw a shadow plummet from the upper yards.

"*Man overboard!*" Stern bellowed, his cry all but lost in the wind.

Tristam saw a flash of dark blue in the frothing sea. "I have him!"

"*Mr. Flattery! No!*" But it was too late. Tristam plunged headlong over the rail. He hit the cool ocean two yards from the sinking Jack, and, not a fathom under, grabbed the flailing seaman by his hair. The air was so full of spray and rain that Tristam could hardly be sure if they reached the surface.

"Don't let me go, sir. I don't swim."

Tristam realized that it was Pim he braced under the arms—one of the greenest hands aboard.

"I shan't let you go. But don't struggle so! Lay back and kick your feet."

"Oh, Farrelle save us, Mr. Flattery. The *Swallow* is gone! They'll never find us. Oh, Farrelle." The boy was quivering with fear.

Tristam shook him, shouting over the wind. "Think what you're saying! They'll run free of the squall in ten minutes and about-ship right away. In less time than you can think, you'll be back aboard. Why, we won't even be properly clean. But we must save our strength. . . ."

Whatever Tristam intended to say was lost in the most horrifying roaring he had ever heard. It was caused by the wind, no doubt, but Pim's hair stood completely on end.

"Flaming martyrs!" Tristam whispered, for a waterspout spun toward them not thirty feet away. Both men were frozen by fear and it was only a mouthful of saltwater that had Tristam kicking to keep them afloat.

The waterspout roared toward them, its black, whirling mass tearing the surface off the water and sucking it into the vortex as though by dark attraction. Tristam heard Pim rapidly mumbling a prayer as though he raced to get through it before he was swallowed whole, but the waterspout passed them by.

"Well," Tristam heard himself say, surprised by the calmness in his voice. "I shall be able to boast the closest observation of a waterspout—by any man who lived to tell about it, at least—I'm sure of that." The terrified Jack looked at him as though he had gone mad, but Tristam could not help it. The encounter with the waterspout seemed to have exhausted his fear. In fact, he felt remarkably calm, almost lighthearted. "Don't look so downcast, Pim, the squall is passing and I think there shall be sun, which will make us easier to find."

The squall moved off to the south, hiding any sight of the *Swallow*. Tristam hoped she wouldn't be carried too far off. Pim would drain him quickly.

The sun fell upon them suddenly and Tristam realized the squall had left the same conditions in its wake as had existed before—a windless calm—though the squall had whipped the sea into a short, confused chop, forcing Tristam to use a great deal of his strength to keep them afloat.

"Well, I think we should have a look while we are here," Tristam said, forcing confidence into his voice. Taking note of the sun's position, Tristam began to side-stroke after the *Swallow*, towing Pim with one hand. "Kick your feet and do not struggle to keep your whole head out of water. You will wear me out. That's better."

I am fortunate, Tristam thought, *that he is too terrified to panic. For the moment he will do anything I ask.*

They made slow progress against the steep little seas, but Tristam could not bear to stay in one place and wait. Sharks would become a real danger in a short time, for it had often been observed that they would appear not long after a man was in the water—even here in the open ocean. *What senses they must have*, he thought!

Pim was growing calmer, and making more of an effort to kick his feet. He even moved his arms a bit. He was a strong boy, there was no doubt of that. It was unfortunate, Tristam thought, that it was not Pim's strength they were relying on to keep them alive.

With some effort he bobbed up to search the sea, and there he thought he saw the *Swallow*, almost hull-down on the horizon. The squall had carried them farther than he had estimated. *Well, this may not be as easy as I hoped. They will launch boats, but even so it could be some time. And I criticized Beacham for diving in after me. This was just as ill-considered. Though how could I have done otherwise?*

Towing Pim was already beginning to seem an effort, which caused Tristam's first real feeling of fear. He knew they would have to stay afloat a good length of time, for they could not expect to be found immediately . . . if they could hope to be found at all.

I shall not look until I have counted to three—no—five thousand, Tristam decided. And with each stroke he counted one.

"Mr. Flattery?"

"One thousand, six. Yes?"

"I am sorry you . . . that is, I. . . ."

"Now you've made me lose count." Tristam swam a few stokes more. He could feel his companion was kicking less. "Don't worry, Pim. The ocean gave me back my life once. I can't think it means for me to drown: nor you. But paddle, lad! I can't keep you afloat if you won't help."

A renewed effort resulted. Tristam began to count again but lost patience at two thousand and bobbed up to look. He could not find the ship. Although it took great effort, he tried again. Yes! There she was! And perhaps he had seen a dot on the ocean as well. A boat, he hoped.

"The cutter has been launched," he reported, hoping to raise the boy's spirits.

"Farrelle be praised. I have been praying, sir. Praying as never before."

"That's good, Pim, so long as it doesn't take away from your kicking."

Row, you bastards! Tristam thought.

On the count of two thousand Tristam would look again. Keeping the leaden Pim afloat for any time was beginning to look impossible. The human body is almost naturally buoyant, Tristam told himself. It takes only a few pounds of floatation to keep the average-sized man on the surface. It should not require so much effort!

One thousand, nine hundred, ninety nine. He pushed himself up.

"Damn!"

"What is it, sir?"

"There are two boats and they are making for the wrong part of the ocean. We must swim." Tristam set a course he hoped would intersect with the searchers. Pim waved his legs ineffectually. "Come on, damn you! Pim, we'll drown if you don't do better than that."

The terrified seaman improved his efforts again, but Tristam could not count on that happening forever. The cold water was sapping their strength.

Tristam lost count yet again. It was all he could do to keep his limbs moving as they should. After a suitable time he popped up. There was a boat, but it was going to pass them by! *Damn this sea*, Tristam thought.

The squall had been uncommonly strong and the short little sea it left behind would make them hard to spot, especially from the low vantage of the cutter. The sun had slipped behind a cloud and that wouldn't help either.

"Could you see them, Mr. Flattery?"

"Yes, we are on a collision course. Don't let off kicking."

If I can keep this up for ten minutes, it will be a miracle.

Pim went suddenly rigid. "What was that?"

Turbulence! Something moving in the water nearby. A great explosion of breath, followed by an inhalation that echoed in a massive chest. The smell of rotten fish oil.

"A whale," Tristam said, almost laughing with relief.

Suddenly they felt a tugging from the water as though a current pulled at them from beneath the waves. The whale had sounded directly under them.

Pim turned in a blind panic and tried to climb out of the water onto Tristam's shoulders. The naturalist went under and received a heavy blow on the forehead from the sailor's knee. He let himself sink a few feet more and then pushed himself away. The whale, he was sure, would not harm them intentionally, but Pim could drown them both.

Tristam stroked to the surface five feet from the frantic Jack. Pim was flailing about and barely keeping his mouth above water.

"Oh, Farrelle save me. Mr. Flattery. He'll eat us both."

"It means us no harm, you bloody fool! I can't keep you afloat if you're going to drown me."

Pim was reaching out for him but Tristam kept just out of range. "I'm drowning. Oh! I'm drowning."

"Yes, you will, too, unless you take hold of yourself."

The whale surfaced once more, its glistening back rolling to the surface not fifteen feet away. Again the unmistakable explosion of massive breath. It was a baleen whale, Tristam was glad to see, and not a toothed variety. At least they could not appear edible to this giant.

"Mr. Flattery!"

Against his better judgment he reached out and took Pim's hand, and to his relief the boy did not try to climb onto his shoulders again.

The whale stayed on the surface and circled them slowly, blowing at irregular intervals. Tristam found himself making mental notes—a habit he would take to his grave, apparently. Small dorsal fin set in an area of mottled gray-white. Otherwise it was a black back. Length was hard to guess, strangely enough, for it was too close, but it was large.

A shout. Then another. Tristam bobbed up, almost at the end of his reserves. His tussle with Pim had drained the last of his strength.

The cutter was making directly for them, someone standing in the bow. The whale blew once more and then sounded, disappearing into the mysterious depths of the vast ocean.

Tristam and Pim lay in a heap at the coxswain's feet, so relieved to find themselves rescued that both had tears in their eyes.

"Praise be, praise be," Pim kept saying over and over, though whether it was a prayer or simply an indication of how addled the boy was, Tristam could not be sure.

Lieutenant Osler sat on the gunwale above them, almost as joyous as the two castaways. He had given Tristam his jacket so that he might cover his nakedness.

"It was Mr. Hobbes saw you, Mr. Flattery." Osler nodded to the ship's master in the bow. "The whale spout drew his attention and then he caught sight of you with his glass. Blood and flames, but it was a near thing. If not for Hobbes' leviathan, you would be swimming yet."

Tristam shook his head. "I don't think we could have lasted another minute. We were at our end." It was all he could manage. The naturalist had never felt so entirely drained in his life.

Both seamen and officers alike clapped Tristam on the back as he came over the rail, wearing Osler's jacket tied around his waist like an odd skirt.

"I will tell you, Mr. Flattery," the captain said, pumping Tristam's hand, "I despaired of ever seeing you again. It was a nobly foolish act of bravery, sir. There is no doubt." He waved at the gathered crew. "Let him through, now. Let the man find his clothes."

The duchess stood by as well, clutching the rail for balance, it seemed. There was no mistaking the relief on her face. She put a hand on Tristam's naked shoulder for part of a second but took it away quickly.

Tristam tried to smile at her but had so little energy he could not manage it. Shaking as he went, he slipped below and into his cabin where he collapsed on the tiny square of cabin sole. A few minutes later, a knock roused him.

"Tristam? Are you whole?" It was the duchess.

"A moment." He managed to pull on breeches and a shirt before opening the door.

Distress was obvious on the duchess' face. She looked quickly behind her, where Osler stood at the bottom of the companionway ladder. The lieutenant discreetly exited.

Reaching out as though she would embrace him, the duchess took hold of his shirt front, then pushed his soaking hair back from his face. "How could you have been so foolish?" she demanded. "You risked everything for the life of a cabin boy."

ᔕ Thirty-Two

Although he understood the principles of optics perfectly well, Tristam still found that he was attempting to see his entire six foot frame in a looking glass not five inches square. It made him laugh. With a great show of impatience he smoothed his coat as best he could and brushed haphazardly at his sleeves. It would have to do. The ship's officers, he was well aware, would arrive dressed impeccably, as usual—but they had stewards and other servants to look after their uniforms. Tristam had Tristam.

"And a miserable gentleman's gentleman you make, too," he whispered to his reflection in the looking glass.

It had been some three weeks since Tristam's act of heroic-foolhardiness— jumping into the ocean after a drowning Jack—and despite the considerable passage of time, the *Swallow* had not yet reached the pass that would take them through the Archipelago.

Those wholly honest, unfailingly steady winds that Beacham had sung praises to, the peerless Northeast Trades, had materialized only intermittently— a few precious days of fair breezes between complete calms, and gales which brought unyielding head winds. Even now Tristam could hear the sails slatting about in their gear, for the *Swallow* was becalmed again and had been since just after noon—the day's run a paltry twenty-five nautical miles.

The lack of progress was not only frustrating to all aboard, but seemed to turn everyone's thoughts to the worst purpose. It had become obvious to the Jacks, and perhaps the officers, as well, that Kreel studiously avoided the viscount, almost as though he were afraid—or at least so the man acted. Tristam believed the Jack was making a silent accusation, though clear enough to anyone who was not blind.

Tristam hoped that Julian—if it actually had been Julian—was not still planning to finish the job. He didn't want any responsibility for Kreel's death, for Tristam was sure the viscount had been acting either to protect him or out of vengeance. But there was nothing he could do. He had not seen the attacker's face.

I have done enough for Kreel already, Tristam told himself. *I saved his life. One attempt at murder paid back by another. The accounts are balanced.*

But what would the Jacks do if they believed the viscount had tried to kill their messmate? It was hard to say. Kreel, the naturalist had come to realize, was not generally popular beyond his own small group of followers—feared, yes, but not liked. Most of the crew were probably happy to see him get his own back. For any of the Jacks to harm the viscount was almost unthinkable. Stern would have to hang someone for that—he would have no choice. But then, the hands had impressed Tristam several times with their inability to foresee the results of their actions. Some of them were little more than children in that regard. Julian should bear that in mind.

Over the past weeks Tristam felt he had been accepted by the majority of the crew. Beacham said the Jacks had begun referring to Tristam as "the professor," and that it was not meant unkindly. A good sign, apparently.

He pulled his frock coat down in the back in an attempt to straighten the shoulders. It would have to do. A sudden crack of canvas overhead stopped Tristam with his hand on the door to his cabin, but it was just the sails slatting as the ship rolled, not wind as he hoped.

In his search for fair winds Stern had been forced farther south than he thought ideal. As a result, the *Swallow* was far off her course. The bands of wind might be boldly marked on the Admirality charts, but, in truth, they shifted—not only from season to season but year to year as well.

Even so, this foray into the south had not improved their situation in regard to winds. As things stood, they would have to make up some distance to the north to reach the Queen Anne Passage.

Stern kept joking that at least there was no fear of meeting corsairs, and that was likely true, for the marauders tended to patrol the sea lanes as close to the pass as they dared, hoping to catch one of the rich prizes coming from Farrland's silver mines.

Tristam heard little about the situation there and often wondered what had occurred for the Admiralty to send the *Raven* out to the station at such a pace.

He checked his pocket watch. Mustn't keep the duchess waiting. Meals had become less and less appetizing as the voyage stretched on, and had acquired an air of ritual. The most banal food would be served in the duchess' cabin upon silver and fine porcelain, the guests commenting upon this terrible fare as though it had come from the most noted kitchen in Avonel. Tristam knew that the duchess found this amusing, but he suspected that the navy men did not see any humor in it at all. They were too inured to life aboard. So much so that they believed this new tinned food to be "dietetically salutary"—an opinion the duchess made great sport of in private.

Tristam passed through the tiny wardroom that lay between his "closet" and the duchess' cabin and met Stern and Lieutenant Osler arriving at the same time, brass buttons gleaming, not a speck of lint in evidence. They entered to find the viscount and the physician, drinking port and perched on the ledge of the gallery windows, which had been opened to catch any breath of wind that might happen along. When they greeted the viscount, neither Stern nor Osler showed the slightest sign that they had sensed the mood of the Jacks or knew who it was they had come to suspect in Kreel's attack.

For his part, the viscount appeared his usual jovial self, perhaps a bit tipsy, but happy to see everyone.

With the skylight and stern windows open, the great cabin was a welcome change from Tristam's stifling accommodation. Even so the duchess suggested that they not stand upon ceremony and insisted all the gentlemen remove their jackets, which Tristam found a great relief, for they were far to the south now and winter was but a vague memory.

The duchess, Tristam noted, did not appear to be affected by the heat. In a white gown she seemed as fresh as anyone sitting in the shade in a breezy garden. A look of heightened excitement, as though she were newly in love, was something the duchess seemed to be able to achieve at will. Tristam found it very alluring and so did other men, he realized. Her glow of not-so-secret love had no apparent focus—she had no lover to anyone's knowledge—and perhaps subconsciously this fed everyone's fantasies, doubling the effect.

Tristam looked around the room at the present company: who was there who stood a chance against this woman? Not Tristam, certainly. He might be able to muster some resentment toward the duchess when she was not present (after all, she did manipulate him terribly), but he was beginning to concede that she could sweep the feeling aside with little more than a smile and a toss of her lovely curls.

With the exception of Stern, the others showed no more resistance.

Sunset began to prepare its spectacle just as dinner was served, casting a warm glow into the cabin—perfect light for a woman with the duchess' coloring, Tristam noted.

The salt pork and tinned peas arrived on silver chafing dishes. "Lovely," the duchess cooed, and cast a conspiratorial glance at Tristam. Fortunately wine kept well, and this at least was worthy of its serving vessel and cut-glass stemware.

"There is a rumor, Lieutenant Osler," the duchess began, "that just over the horizon lies the Archipelago, and that if the mainmast were only a bit higher we would be able to see islands from the maintop." The duchess said this with complete ease, the nautical language as much a part of her common speech now as the social discourse of the drawing room.

Tristam had noticed that the duchess had launched a new campaign; she had begun to focus her charm on the ship's officers, devoting noticeably less of her attention to Captain Stern. It was difficult to guess what she hoped to gain from her actions, but it was clear that the officers had become as devoted to the duchess as they could be to any sovereign. Stern tried to maintain his pose of gentlemanly dignity, but Tristam thought the captain might not bear up much longer. Here was a man used to being both in command and the person who set the tone of whatever social life existed aboard. The navy was the only life Stern knew and suddenly he must feel he was losing his place in it. The man was adrift. More and more it looked like he was merely in the employ of the duchess, around whom life aboard now centered.

"We certainly are close, Duchess," Osler said, obviously pleased to have her attention, "though perhaps not as close as rumors have it. But with any wind at all we could raise the Archipelago in a good day's sail."

The duchess smiled at Osler as though he had just said something that pleased her immeasurably. "Well, I will be glad to see it. There is some possibility of fresh food, I have been told."

"Well . . ." Osler glanced at his commander, a bit sheepishly, Tristam thought. "If the captain chooses to land a party. . . . We have much northing to make up and may well find a shore breeze to take us on our way."

"What say you, Captain?" Llewellyn asked, unaware, as usual, of the undercurrents flowing around him.

Stern feigned slight surprise at actually being asked for his opinion. "I would not gainsay the lieutenant, Doctor," he said, more peevishly than he meant, Tristam guessed. "We have much time to make up. But we will see. If the ship is becalmed near a likely landing place, we might put a party ashore. There is only one protected bay charted between here and the Queen Anne Station—it is a treacherous stretch of coast—so we cannot count on getting fresh victuals. But our crew is hale and we are not in real need."

An actress of the duchess' ability could speak to her audience with little more than a gesture, and she smiled, raising her eyebrows as though saying to the others, "Could we not have guessed?" Without a word she managed to make it seem that Stern had said something foolish . . . yet again. Tristam felt a bit sorry for the man.

What precisely she hoped to achieve by isolating Stern, Tristam could not imagine. There was certainly tension around the table. Was she merely angry with the man? Unlikely, Tristam realized. The duchess was far too calculating.

"How much longer until we reach the island—Varua, that is?" Llewellyn addressed this question to the table, apparently, for he did not look up as he spoke. Tristam thought the man looked a little under the weather, and he seemed to have reacquired the cough he had suffered from on Farrow.

A second's silence and then the captain answered. "If the winds in the Ocean Beyond are as fickle as those we have experienced so far, I would not wish to speculate, Doctor. Certainly the crossing is commonly thirty-some days at this time of year. There is, however, valuable work we might do along the way, for the Palle Island group, discovered by Pankhurst and our own Hobbes, has never been properly surveyed. A month and a half there, or perhaps a bit longer, would see a significant addition to our hydrographical knowledge. Not to mention what could be learned in the way of botany and the other disciplines." He nodded at Tristam.

"A month and a half?" Llewellyn looked up at this, his face registering the most remarkable change—like a patient who had received the worst possible news. Life aboard ship did not agree with the good doctor. "It . . . it seems an awfully long time, Captain."

Stern shrugged. "It is our business, Doctor Llewellyn. But once you are ashore in the Palle group, you will find much to interest you, for they are said to be beautiful islands with a wholesome climate. Uninhabited, too, though perhaps we shall find evidence that this has not always been so."

"Beautiful, but not on our course to Varua, I am told," the duchess said, looking at Stern over the rim of her wine glass.

Stern's color began to rise. He was not made to live with this situation, that was certain. Tristam expected an outburst, but Stern forced good humor into his voice, looking around the table as though he would cajole the company. "Come, come. We have an opportunity not granted to one citizen in a hundred thousand—or even fewer. We are seeing the new world! A world we have only begun to explore. If we can carry the lines of the globe's charts a bit farther into the areas presently marked *unknown*, we shall be taking part in history." He turned to the downcast-looking Llewellyn. "Consider, Doctor, if we continue the practice of previous surveyors, and I have every intention of doing so, then there will be a notable feature of the world's geography named for each and every one of us. Your name will not be inscribed on some bit of stone

to be lost amongst the numberless others—it will be writ upon the world itself! There for all men to see, down through the ages. You can't ask for more
than that, sir."

Llewellyn managed a weak nod and then returned his gaze to the table—
unwell, Tristam was sure, for certainly such a suggestion should appeal to a
man as vain as the physician.

"Yes," the duchess said dryly, "won't that be lovely."

Into the ensuing silence a call from the masthead dropped like a rat onto
the table. "Sail, Mr. Hobbes! To larboard, forward quarter."

The two officers erupted out of their seats and bolted out the door, the
sound of their boots stomping up the companionway stair echoing back to the
diners.

"Well, so much for our dinner party," the duchess said, tossing her napkin
onto the table. She regarded her food with obvious distaste. "Shall we have a
look, as well?"

At a more dignified pace, the others proceeded to the deck. The captain was
perched on the stem, clutching a forestay, gazing off to larboard with his glass.
In the failing light Tristam could make out the sails of another ship.

"Mr. Flattery," Stern said as Tristam mounted the forecastle, "would you be
so kind as to lend me your Fromme glass? Tell Mr. Hobbes to have a midshipman carry it up to the masthead." Stern turned and walked back to the shrouds
of the mainmast.

Tristam bolted down to his cabin, returning with his field glass. Shedding
his shoes and stockings, he grasped the ratlines and climbed up after the captain, determined to deliver the instrument himself so that he might have some
idea of the other ship's identity. All the sailors aboard had become very grim-
faced and Tristam did not like that in the least.

Pulling himself up onto the crosstrees, Tristam found Stern and Osler sitting astride the main topsail yard.

"Ah, kind of you, Mr. Flattery." Stern turned Tristam's glass on the distant
ship. The naturalist waited for a pronouncement, watching Stern's face for a
hint, but the captain suddenly handed the glass to his lieutenant, without saying a word.

"It is a Farr flag, to be sure," Osler said, no hint of tension in his voice.

"That does not surprise me," the captain answered. "Give the glass to Mr.
Flattery. He has keen sight."

Tristam quickly focused on the ship. Very distant, a dark hull under a pale
cloud of sail.

"Is it bow toward us, Mr. Flattery?" Stern asked.

"Yes, I believe it is, Captain. Or nearly so."

"Wind in its sails?"

"They are flapping, sir."

"It is hard to tell from this angle, I know, but does the stern seem unnaturally high and broad? Look carefully now."

"Well, the light is not good, sir," Tristam said, understating the case, "but it does seem to have a greater sheer than the *Swallow*. In fact, I am quite convinced of it."

"Lieutenant?"

"I'm afraid I agree, sir."

"It is the damnedest luck," Stern said quietly.

"But why would they be down here, sir?"

"Perhaps Nash or some other has chased them down. Or they might be seeking wind as we do." Stern took the glass again and had a last look before the darkness closed in completely. He swore an oath under his breath and then handed the glass back to Tristam.

"No lanterns tonight, Mr. Osler. We will keep the ship dark. Hoist out a boat and tow our head around to the north, and keep it there. If there is a wind, we must make the best of it. Perhaps by morning we will be far from here . . . and from them." He cocked his head toward the distant ship. "We can only hope."

"Shall we clear for action, sir?" Osler asked this terrible question in a calm voice.

"No, they will not close with us this night. If they are still within view, we will exercise the guns at first light." He made a move to go, but stopped. "Not a word of this to anyone, Mr. Flattery."

Tristam's cabin seemed particularly close and airless that evening and he rolled in his motionless hammock so frequently that he was sure he would wear a hole through. He wondered if others were suffering in the same way. For some reason he dearly longed for the company of the duchess—not as he normally wished but merely her presence. They could be a comfort to each other.

Corsairs.

It was difficult to believe. They were only an under-gunned survey ship with nothing of true value aboard—except, of course, the Duchess of Morland. No doubt, the King would pay any price to have her returned safely, though it was impossible for Tristam to believe she would be returned completely unharmed—and it could be much worse than that.

Tristam rolled over again, striking his ankle against some hard corner, reminding him of the box in which his uncle's rare wine lay hidden. Worth a small fortune he had been told. . . . Exactly how small? He rolled the other way, without further bruising.

Stern was a clever officer and had met corsairs before. There was every chance he would keep them at bay, at least until the Naval Station could be reached. The idea of running the *Swallow* in under the safety of the guns at Queen Anne Station gave the naturalist a moment's comfort. But it did not last. What if the enemy ship had found wind? Tristam knew it was possible. He had often seen the ripple of a breeze on the water not a mile off while the *Swallow* bobbed in a dead calm.

"This will never do," Tristam said aloud. Rising as silently as possible, he dressed and went barefooted up to the quarterdeck. It had become his practice, upon reaching the deck, to go immediately to the stern rail and look for any sign of a wake, and that night his hopes were higher than usual.

Without lanterns only starlight illuminated the deck, for they were just a day past the new moon. The *thirteenth moon*, the Jacks had noted. A year of thirteen moons was believed to be a time of ill omen, and the coming full would bring the most dreaded days of the cycle. Tristam, however, had not been infected with the superstition of the sailors.

He nodded to the helmsman, neither man speaking, for they were directly above the cabin of the duchess.

Tristam was surprised to find a man bent almost double over the stern rail as though ill—ailing in a flat calm. Taken unawares by Tristam's nearly silent approach, the man turned with a start. And it was Hobbes! A sailor who could not have known a day of seasickness these past thirty-five years—and his face twisted in fury.

Tristam was stopped in his tracks by the master's reaction, but the look on Hobbes face changed immediately, deep embarrassment or chagrin replacing the rage. With a perfunctory nod he left Tristam at the rail and made his way quickly forward.

Hobbes was so even-tempered that Tristam stood in some shock, wondering what could possibly have caused such a reaction. And then he heard the voice of the duchess not three feet below him. She whispered in Entonne, but Tristam could make out her words perfectly.

"It is most maddening, Julian. If Stern realized what miracle lay waiting in Varua, he would drive this ship as he has never driven a ship before. There would be no more talk of 'contributing to the hydrographical knowledge of the sphere,' that is certain. I would take the man into our confidence if I thought for a moment he would believe me."

"He would not believe." Lord Elsworth said. "It is maddening, though; I agree." Silence.

What miracle, Tristam wondered?

"At least we have managed to keep Flattery out of their hands," the viscount said, causing Tristam to spread his hands on the rail as though needing support. "Though I must tell you, I am none too comfortable in the man's company. Farrelle's oath, I am glad I was not there when the whale came. Is it not remarkable?"

"Yes," the duchess shook her head distractedly, Tristam was sure. "One cannot alter one's view of the world overnight. Time. It will take time." The duchess paused. Tristam could almost see her nibbling her lip delicately as she did when deep in thought.

He felt a sense of dread, growing inside him like a tumor.

"We have no choice, Julian. We follow Tristam's course, now—blindly. You must stay close to him, as close as you can."

"Yes, I understand. But, in truth, we have greater concerns at the moment."

Tristam had come to know the duchess so well that he almost heard the sigh the silence masked. "Yes." A second's hesitation. "I almost hope they are corsairs. We are not such a great prize to them, so they should not be so difficult to discourage. The alternative is far worse."

A small ripple of water—a sea creature surfacing.

"Perhaps, but even marauders should not be taken lightly. This is not a ship of war. Stern has few men, fewer guns, and a slow ship. You should not have such faith in old tales." Silence for a moment, making Tristam wonder if they had become aware of his presence. "I must sleep," the viscount said. "We will need our wits about us these next days."

The noise of people moving below. Tristam turned and silently made his way forward, not looking at the helmsman as he passed.

What had he just heard? "We follow Tristam's course, now."

He went down into the ship's waist and slumped against the bulwark.

Keep him out of whose hands?

The duchess had spoken of him as though he were charmed—or cursed. He covered his eyes. To hear her speak of him so coolly, so objectively. . . . "Farrelle's flames," he muttered.

What did these people want of him? They were as foolish as the superstitious Jacks! But Tristam knew the duchess was no fool.

ᕰ Thirty-Three

The journal of Tristam Flattery:
this fourteenth day of December, 1559.

There is no sleep for me this night, and not simply because we have been discovered by marauders. What in this round world have I heard? Each time I believe I gain some understanding of the machinations that occur around me something new happens and I am thrown off the scent completely, find that I have been in the wrong track. What is it these people expect of me? How is it possible that they have come to regard me as having some role in their designs? This idea is so misguided as to verge on lunacy. Whatever the function of this seed that I seek I have come to regard it with some dread. I am of half a mind to say nothing even if I do find it—as Lady Galton suggested. I cannot imagine what has come over these people . . . whoever they are.

The eastern sky showed no signs of the approaching dawn, yet most of the *Swallow*'s people were on deck, peering silently into the darkness. A small breeze had reached out from the Archipelago during the night and Stern had taken the advantage to move north, hoping to sail beyond the corsairs, who lay between the *Swallow* and the Queen Anne Station. But the breeze had raised their hopes for only two brief hours. What the marauder had chosen to do under cover of darkness was the question that had brought so many on deck so early.

Tristam had been sent aloft as a lookout and perched, with Lieutenant Osler, on the topmast trestletrees. Below them the sails hung limp, wafting only to the roll of the ship, while overhead the fainter stars were beginning to disappear, hinting at daylight. Both Osler and Tristam scanned the dark ocean, looking for a light or the white of sails.

"There seems to be a dark line to the west," Tristam said, his voice hushed, for there was something very solemn about their situation.

The young officer kept his glass trained to the east. "I wouldn't be surprised. There is a strange current here that has set ships to the northwest in the past, and we sailed north and somewhat west during the night. That will be your Archipelago, Mr. Flattery. Wait a bit until there is no doubt and then you may call 'land-ho.' It may lift the spirits of a few."

As there were no signs of a ship in that direction, Tristam overcame his curiosity about the islands and turned his glass out to sea. There was a grayness in the eastern sky now, without question.

"Mr. Osler?"

"Sir?"

"Almost directly abeam to starboard . . . perhaps forward of that." Pale, ghostly, far out on the rolling ocean.

Osler turned his glass to starboard, searching carefully. "You have found our corsairs, Flattery, damn their eyes." He cupped a hand to his mouth and called down to the deck. "Sail, Captain. Two points and a half off the starboard bow."

There was a shuffling on the deck as everyone moved to a better vantage.

"We cannot make them out, Lieutenant," Stern called up after a moment. "There is no doubt?"

"None, sir. And there is land on the western horizon, as well."

The growing daylight illuminated the distant sails for all to see, and the peaks of the far islands, for only the peaks could be seen catching the light of the rising sun. In those few moments of the morning's twilight the island tops had little definition, an irregular line of deep purple spanning the western horizon, appearing to Tristam like an illustration of mountains in a child's book— unreal, naive, the details sketched in by imagination alone. Irrational though it was, Tristam felt these storybook islands seemed a haven from the distressing reality of the corsairs' ship to the east. The truth was, however, the *Swallow* was trapped against an impenetrable maze of shoals and channels.

Osler stared at the distant ship as though he would sink it with the intensity of his gaze.

"Is it the same ship, then?" Tristam asked quietly.

Osler apparently did not hear, but, as if in answer to Tristam's question, the Jacks began to uncover and un-house the *Swallow*'s guns. Of the distant ship Tristam could make out little, though it appeared an ominous sight in the empty ocean, reminding him of the *Raven* bearing down on them as they sailed toward Farrow. Where was the *Raven* now, he wondered?

"Is this a fast ship, our friend out there?" Tristam asked, raising his voice a little.

"Fast? No, but she has a longer waterline and with the wind free she will have the advantage over our little *Swallow*. And the corsair's captain can set more sail as well—right up to royals and sky sails. She is a bird of prey, if I might borrow from your discipline, Mr. Flattery, and she has her eye trained on us.

"That ship was once an Entonne merchantman: perhaps one hundred thirty feet in length of deck and deep in the hold. If properly strengthened, she could carry two decks of guns—ten- or twelve-pounders—in opposition to our few four- and six-pounders." He paused as if to consider more. Tristam was impressed with the man's calm detachment.

"But it is not all dark, Flattery, for the *Swallow* will certainly be faster going to weather, more maneuverable, and shallow water may be our greatest ally. You can be sure that Mr. Hobbes is searching the charts as we speak. An area of reefs or shallows will protect us better than a deck of twelve-pounders—especially with our crew. Hardly a man among them has been in an action, but for the Master and Captain Stern."

"You have not been in a battle?" Tristam was surprised. "You seem awfully calm. I wish I could say the same for myself."

"Not a fleet action, no, but several single ship actions. I have met corsairs before, perhaps even this very captain who chases us. Do not be concerned, Flattery, we carry no silver, as they well know. If we make the taking of us difficult enough, they will be discouraged—especially if chasing us draws them farther from the common sea lanes. It is bullion they seek, not a naturalist's collection." He smiled as he spoke but kept his glass trained on the far ship.

"Look carefully, Flattery, and tell me . . . does our sea hawk appear to have wind under her wings?"

Tristam turned his glass on the dark hull of the other ship. The sails did not seem to flutter and the ship heeled steadily. "I think so. There are waves cresting around it as well." Tristam felt his heart sink. "They seem to have found the trade."

"Not the trade, I think," Osler said. "Look how they go. That is wind from the southeast, I'm sure. Perhaps we will see the trades yet today, but until then this southeaster will have to do. It will reach us by and by."

"But this black ship will be borne on its wings."

"They can't sail swifter than the wind, or even nearly as fast. They will close the gap some, but we will be on our way soon enough." There was a shout from the deck. "We are called down, Mr. Flattery."

Tristam slowly descended by way of the ratlines as the Jacks scrambled past him on their way up to loose sail. Osler slid down a backstay, arriving at the deck in seconds and making Tristam vow to do the same at his next opportunity—if he was not to be captive of corsairs.

Mounting the quarterdeck, Tristam found Captain Stern standing alone at the after rail and the duchess leaning on the bulwark near the break in the deck. Tristam was surprised to find that the duchess did not show the slightest signs of fright or of having spent a sleepless night.

"The pleasures of the day to you, Tristam," she said, as though they were not being pursued by men whose reputations must be deeply unsettling to a woman.

Tristam found himself unable to take his gaze from her face—the overheard conversation still echoing. Only the threat of corsairs kept his questions at bay.

A breeze rustled the duchess' hair and then a small gust filled the sails, causing the ship to heel and the rigging to creak loudly. The southeast wind Osler had predicted. There was an audible sigh from the crew.

"Wear ship as soon as we have steerage-way, Mr. Hobbes," Stern said quietly. Tristam knew it was a captain's responsibility to exhibit confidence no matter what the circumstances, but even so, he was struck by Stern's manner. The naturalist felt an easing of his anxiety.

Along the deck the Jacks jumped to their duties without any goading from the officers, and the ship answered her helm like a well-mannered saddle horse. The yards were braced around and *Swallow* spread her wings and began to fly from her pursuer.

Tristam watched as Stern stood looking aloft, then staring back over the rail toward the black ship, then to windward. He appeared, for all the world, like a gambler weighing his hand, deciding whether he would stay or ask for cards.

"May I look, Tristam?" The duchess nodded to his glass and he passed it to her.

"They seem almost to be on a different course from our own. Do you see? Almost parallel to our own way of going."

Lieutenant Osler stood nearby, watching the final stages of the evolution. "Though they are to windward of us, Duchess," the young man said, "they cannot sail directly to us for we shall move on, if you take my meaning. You will see that we are hard on the wind as we go, yet they have the wind on their beam—their course not so parallel as it appears. The captain of that marauder is steering to intersect our course, Duchess, and to keep his advantage of the 'weather gauge,' as we say. As we sail now, they cannot close with us much before midafternoon, I shouldn't think."

"Mr. Osler!" Stern said sharply, surprising Tristam for the captain's idea of gentlemanly deportment did not allow hollering at his officers—gentlemen themselves.

"Sir?" The young officer jumped to a rigid attention.

"See to your duty, sir," Stern said more quietly, perhaps surprised by his outburst. "We will exercise the guns."

Osler was off at a run, without looking back at Tristam and the duchess.

Garvey, the master's mate, appeared from below just then, a rolled chart under his arm, and joined Hobbes and the captain at the rail. Tristam and the duchess moved a pace closer, almost without thinking, but still could not hear what the navy men were saying. Tristam thought Hobbes' manner to him was a bit cool that morning, though under the circumstances it was difficult to judge. No one was acting normally.

Stern pressed his finger to the chart, nodding and occasionally asking questions. Glancing down the deck at the men preparing the guns, the captain noticed the duchess and Tristam watching, and appeared to take pity on them. He bowed his head to the duchess in invitation, and she and Tristam almost rushed to the rail.

"You can see, Duchess, that our position is not impossible. We are not so far from the naval station that the coast has not been well surveyed. We may thank good fortune for that. The *Swallow* is here and our corsairs' ship would be hereabouts. You can see this cross. . . ." He gestured to a mark on the chart. "As things stand now, that is where the two ships shall converge—later in the day. Of course, much could change between now and then, and almost any change would be to our advantage. The arrival of our trade would put the naval station to windward, and we can certainly work our way to weather more handily than our marauder." He glanced off at the distant ship.

The duchess pointed to a pass into the islands. "Can we not go through there, Captain Stern, and hope to lose our pursuer in the profusion of straits and narrows?"

The area the duchess indicated, Tristam could not help but notice, was surveyed less than a mile in from the ocean shore. Beyond that the Archipelago was represented on the chart by a vast blank area marked "*Unknown.*"

"Many of the passes are difficult to enter, Duchess, for the tides, though not great at this latitude, still create substantial flows in the narrows. Beyond such passes lies an area of extreme danger to ships. Or we might sail into a blind pass—a bay, for all purposes—where we would be trapped. I would enter the Archipelago only if no other course were possible."

"Captain Stern." It was Osler reporting in a most uncommonly clipped manner—still stinging, Tristam realized, from Stern's earlier rebuke. Tristam had never heard the captain speak harshly to his officers before and he wondered if the black ship affected Stern more than Tristam had suspected, or whether the duchess' attention to the younger officers was beginning to tell.

"We are ready, sir."

In the waist of the ship Tristam could see the gun crews of the larboard watch standing by their bronze machines of war. The men did not appear confident.

Stern spoke more kindly to his lieutenant. "The bow and stern chasers are still housed, Mr. Osler."

"I can man them only at cost to sailing the ship, sir. Shall I do so?"

"No . . . no. Our chief hope is in flight. We dare not reduce the efficiency of the ship. Press every available man." Stern turned to Tristam. "Mr. Flattery, I hope you will not object to joining in our defense?"

"I am yours to command, Captain."

"Good. And Lord Elsworth, and even the boatswain and carpenter, as long as we can spare them. Leave only the surgeon and Doctor Llewellyn to their specific duties."

"I am a competent archer, sir," Tristam offered, wondering what part he could play in such a situation.

"I hope we will not come so close, Mr. Flattery. Place Beacham in command of the larboard quarterdeck gun. He fancies himself quite a gunner. Mr. Flattery, you may assist Beacham though I will not have you swabbing or ramming powder."

A few moments later Tristam found himself under the command of Jack Beacham, who was himself under the watchful eye of the captain. The bow and stern chasers, as they were called, were small guns, throwing only a four-pound ball. Their range was not great, but for short distances they could be fired quite accurately by an experienced crew. They would not shatter a strongly built hull, yet they could do substantial damage if they struck the rigging—not to mention men.

"*Lord Skye's terrible invention,*" the duchess had called the cannon, and it was so, Tristam knew, for the naval gun had turned the tide of a war, winning great sea battles over the formidable Entonne navy, until the enemy had managed to forge their own cannon—though how they had managed it was still a great mystery.

The next two hours were spent in going through the drill of running guns in and out, swabbing, and priming. After these operations had become reasonably smooth, the guns were primed and fired, an operation that Tristam found surprisingly satisfying. Beacham had served aboard a ship of war and seemed to Tristam to know his business—incongruous in one so young and pleasant of manner.

The carpenter, a great bear of man named Tobias Shuk, had been sent to work the aft gun as well, and though he did not stint in his efforts, it was clear to Tristam that the man was greatly shaken by the entire enterprise. A landsman, like Tristam, the man had been a ship builder, lured into this voyage by the stories of Varua. When the gun was finally discharged, and Tristam watched the ball throw up a column of spray, he turned to find the carpenter near to tears. Tristam thought it was because of the clouds of sulfurous smoke, but then he heard the man speak.

"What a great evil Skye brought into this world," he muttered, his voice taut with emotion, and then bent down to his labor and hid his face from the others.

Tristam looked back at the marauder just then and saw it enveloped in a shroud of smoke. Then a prodigious explosion rolled across the ocean, freezing every man to his place.

"It is an old trick, gentlemen," Stern's voice fell into the silence that followed. "They try to unnerve us, but they cannot enlist us to their cause so easily. Carry on."

And they did. The *Swallow* had only limited supplies of powder and shot, but they used what Stern felt they could spare and by midday they began to resemble a fighting ship, at least to Tristam's uncritical eye.

The black ship of the corsairs had come much closer and Tristam could easily see now that it was a substantially larger vessel. If it did not have the appearance of deadly efficiency the *Raven* had displayed, it certainly bore all the threat of a large man—unswift, perhaps even clumsy, but still immensely strong.

Tristam stood at the rail, drinking from a flask Beacham had given him, when the duchess came and stood at his side. Tristam nodded, too tired to make a leg, and then realized she was dressed in the uniform of an officer.

"Do not stare, Tristam. Stern ordered Jacel and me below, not wanting these marauders to see a woman aboard, but I could not stand it. Lieutenant Osler was good enough to lend me these clothes and Stern relented his earlier decision." She raised a glass and focused on the black ship. "They have come up quickly, haven't they?" The duchess turned to look to leeward. "Well, there is our Archipelago, Tristam. I had hoped to be more pleased to see it. I understand it will soon be what is called a 'lee shore'?"

A long line of low hills could be easily seen. Behind them, rugged peaks thrust up into the sky running both north and south like a range of distant mountains, for that is what the Archipelago was—an immensely long mountain range half-risen from the sea.

"A lee shore, yes, but not for a while, yet." Tristam tried to measure their angle to the distant land and decided they still sailed almost parallel to it. Even so, they had drawn much closer over the course of the morning—ships had a tendency to slide a little sideways as they made their way forward, "leeway" the sailors called it. If the coast bent outward to the east, even a little, they would no longer be able to stay clear on their present course, which would be a disaster. They would be forced to tack out toward the enemy.

Borrowing the duchess' glass, Tristam followed the coastline south and to his great relief there did not seem to be much deviation. If anything, the shore bent a little to the southwest.

The watch was piped to its dinner, and Tristam and the duchess stood on the deck watching the massive black ship slowly close the gap.

"Duchess, Mr. Flattery. . . ." It was Stern emerging from below, his manner kindly, Tristam thought. "You would do well to set yourself some task. Watching this ship will not bolster your courage, I can assure you."

The master and the midshipmen came on deck to shoot the noon sight and Tristam was enlisted to work the mathematics with the midshipmen.

This did not take long, for the midshipmen had benefited much from Tristam's earlier instruction and there was little deviation in the sights shot—which is to say they were all close to that of Mr. Hobbes. A cross was placed on the chart and Tristam could not help but notice it was uncomfortably close to the cross which marked the spot where the two ships were estimated to meet.

Returning to the deck, Tristam found the carpenter hard at work with his mate and several Jacks cutting gaping holes in the larboard bulwark and setting strong iron rings into the frame heads.

"What is this?" Tristam asked Beacham.

"I don't know, sir, but if I was forced to guess, I would conjecture that the starboard guns will be moved over beside their mates, doubling the weight of our broadside, so to speak. We might pray the ship will take the strain."

Tristam walked back to the aft rail where the captain stood talking quietly to Hobbes as though a ship full of corsairs was not bearing down on them.

"There will be scant room to fight the guns, sir," Hobbes was saying.

"No matter, we shall not stay to fire a second time, Mr. Hobbes: it would be the end of us. We will pump most of our water over the side as soon as the carpenter is done. The guns themselves may follow. If we can get to weather of them, we have a chance, but we may have to lighten ship considerably." He swept his gaze across the horizon. "These winds cannot be relied upon." The captain fixed on the enemy ship for a few seconds, and then he shook his head. "I see what you say. They are hardly the ragged band I had expected." He paused. "But I cannot think that war has been declared in our absence."

The two men stood watching the corsairs. Tristam could make out individuals on the deck now, especially on the quarter deck where there were fewer men, and certainly these men did not look the part of corsairs. What was Stern suggesting? Had war come to the nations of the Entide Sea?

The two rows of open gun ports, each framing a gaping mouth, made his stomach turn over.

"It will be a near thing. If this does not answer, are we prepared to wear and run in close?" Stern kept his eyes fixed on the marauder.

"We are, sir. Let's hope this barge is as unhandy as the rest of her kind."

The afternoon crept by. Tristam helped move the three six-pounders from the starboard side to their new positions to larboard, more difficult than one would think, for the ship rolled and pitched unmercifully. As Mr. Hobbes had suggested, there was scant room left to work the guns, but it could not be helped. To the surprise of the naturalist, half the guns were loaded with lengths of chain rather than with balls. Beacham explained that with such small guns they could do little damage to a ship's hull, but chain would wreak havoc in the rigging.

The bow and stern chasers were housed and their crews moved to the larger guns in the waist. Beacham assured Tristam that these guns were identical to the gun they had drilled with that morning, except for their larger size, but Tristam still felt some apprehension at firing a weapon he had no experience with.

By the time the *Swallow* had been cleared for action, the sun had cast the eastern shore of the Archipelago into shadow, stripping away all sense of depth and again giving the impression of a children's drawing. Tristam stood by his gun, watching. He dearly wanted his glass but had left it below out of harm's way. A soft rain misted his back, and he looked up to find Jacks out on the footropes, wetting down the sails and rigging—a precaution against fire.

At a quiet order from the captain, the master's mate put the helm over and the *Swallow* turned two points toward land, putting the wind just aft of the beam. A bubbling and rushing along the hull spoke of the increase in speed. The Jacks braced the yards and sheeted sails without a word, no shanties accompanying the heaving of lines.

The corsairs turned as well, falling into line almost astern.

"I would venture to stay that the captain knows his business better than the marauder who commands that forsaken vessel to windward." Beacham had appeared at his side. "Do you see? They have fallen in behind us as we hoped. Impatience and so many more guns have caught them out."

"*Stand by your guns*," came the order.

The cannon that Beacham and Tristam manned was farthest aft, at the foot of the stairs to the quarter deck, and Tristam could still hear some of what was being said by the officers. The duchess was sent below and Tristam saw her nod to the viscount, who was stationed at a gun forward. He thought for a moment that he had been forgotten, but she paused and tried to smile at him—which meant more to him than he realized.

Tristam could see Julian, standing a head above the Jacks around him, intent on his duty, and then his view was blocked by another, equally large. Kreel was stationed at the gun next to the viscount's.

Better that they were farther apart, Tristam thought, but at least Kreel was far from him.

Stepping up onto the second stair, Tristam could just make out the masts of their pursuer. With each second he was certain he could see them drawing closer and this set his nerves to jangling.

"Take your place, if you please, Mr. Flattery." Lieutenant Osler smiled as though in apology for giving Tristam an order.

Stern came to the break in the deck then and addressed the men. "Do not fire before the command. We shall only have one opportunity and cannot afford to waste it. If we are fortunate, gentlemen, we shall be out of this within the hour. Let each man do his duty."

The men gave three cheers, in which Tristam joined self-consciously. He, for one, was decidedly frightened and wondered if it showed, for he could not even force a smile and felt his face drawn and tight. Worse, his bowels were in a tangle, complaining loudly on occasion.

An explosion sounded in the distance. To Tristam's great surprise he saw a cannon ball skip across the top of the waves not a hundred feet off.

"Just getting the range," Beacham whispered. "That will be their bow chaser—a little six-pounder."

The others laughed and Osler hushed them into silence with a stare. Tristam could feel the tension on the ship as they waited. Unlike the others around him, the naturalist had no real understanding of what Stern was about to attempt. Certainly if the captain let this great ship within range, one broadside would destroy the poor *Swallow*. Yet he could see the corsair ranging up behind them. There was no need to stand on a step for a view now.

"There she goes," one of the Jacks whispered, nodding to the other ship. "Making leeway like a log."

Tristam looked back and could see that the man was right, the corsair was having to trim her sails and steer a higher course lest she lose the advantage of the weather gauge.

A second explosion and Tristam found himself half crouching. Nothing happened, but then there was a loud slatting overhead and Tristam looked up to see the mizzen topsail crashing about in its gear and a ragged hole torn in the canvas.

Beacham turned to Tristam. "Acceptable. They should find wood next time."

The helmsman began to work the ship up closer to the wind, and the Jacks trimmed sail accordingly. The sounds of the hull moving through the water had changed now and Tristam looked up to see their ensign was not fluttering as it had. The wind was falling light just as the sun began its final plunge toward the far mountains.

Beacham held out his hand and measured the distance between the sun and the horizon. "Half of an hour, no more," he said, and Tristam felt hopes rise at the statement. Darkness would hide them.

"*Run out your guns,*" came the command suddenly, and Tristam strained on the tackles with the others, running the gun out against the heel of the ship. The carriage thumped up against the bulwark and Beacham put the firing cord into Tristam's hand.

"Not before I say, Mr. Flattery. Make no mistake." The midshipman took his fid and stood by to elevate the gun.

The men were utterly silent, every ear straining for the commands of their officers.

"Luff and touch her, Mr. Garvey," Tristam heard, and the *Swallow* swung suddenly to windward so that they were broadside to the corsair, broadside and on the marauder's forward quarter. Tristam had a clear view now and could see the corsair's yawing gun ports, and her men standing by their guns, as intent as Tristam himself.

The captain of the black ship ordered his own helmsman to put his ship up, to bring her massive broadside to bear, but she did not respond as the agile *Swallow* did.

Beacham pried the gun up quickly.

"*On the roll!*" came the order.

The *Swallow* crested a wave and as she did, Beacham gave the gun a last pry. "Stand clear, Mr. Flattery. . . ." He held up his hand, staring off at the enemy ship. "*Fire!*"

There was a great explosion as the *Swallow*'s guns roared and Tristam was blinded by a thick, choking pall. He felt the ship fall off and begin to sail again. A hand found him in the smoke and pulled him down. "Lie flat on the deck," the carpenter said, and Tristam did not wait to be told a second time.

With his face pressed hard against the rough planks, Tristam waited for the answering roar of the corsair's guns. And then he heard a cheer. Around him, men began to jump to their feet and he did the same. In the clearing smoke he saw the corsair was turning downwind, away from the *Swallow*.

"She has lost her fore topmast!" Beacham shouted over the cheering. "She is turning downwind lest she lose the mast entire."

The *Swallow* was gathering way, making a course to windward—her one superior point of sail. Men were clapping each other on the back and shaking each other by the hand. Osler led the men in a cheer for Captain Stern, in which, Tristam was sure, the Jacks shouted themselves hoarse. And then, abruptly, the deck was silent. Something had changed. Tristam looked around wondering what it was, wondering why the men's faces had suddenly fallen so completely grim. And then it struck him so powerfully, he almost felt the air jarred from his lungs. *The wind had died.*

Like everyone else aboard Tristam turned immediately to the quarter deck, staring at the captain who was appearing out of the cloud, standing as rigid as Gregory's statue, Tristam thought, staring off at the enemy vessel. Both ships were rapidly losing way, but Tristam knew their great momentum would slowly pull them farther and farther apart—a condition which he applauded. The ships now viewed each other stern to stern.

The captain turned to Osler and in the hush his voice carried forward.

"Reload. And hoist out the boats. We will tow ourselves out of range if we must."

Before the lieutenant could come to the rail and give his orders, the Jacks were in a fury of motion. The guns were spaced so closely that their crews were on top of each other. Jumping to haul on a tackle, Tristam knocked one of the Jacks from the next gun crew flat on the deck.

As they finished loading, the first boat lifted off the skids, Tristam could hear Hobbes calling orders over the tumult, his voice loud but devoid of panic. Beacham leaped up onto the bulwark, grasping the boarding net.

"They are all a-scramble to stay the foremast, lads. We shot the forestays clean away and some of the shrouds as well, I think. Blood and flames, but we could rake them stern to stem if we could fire now! I'll wager we could smash their rudder to flinders."

"The lieutenant," one of the Jacks said quietly.

Beacham jumped down to his place again. As he did so, the port beneath the steps to the quarterdeck opened and the voice of the Duchess of Morland issued out into the growing darkness.

"Is that you, Tristam? Please tell us what has happened. We are mad with ignorance below, and no one will let me into my cabin where I might have a view."

Tristam crouched down to where he could just make out the anxious face of the duchess in the gloom. "We have almost toppled the corsair's foremast, Duchess, and were about to make good our escape when the wind fell flat. Boats are being readied to haul us out of cannon range."

"Has anyone been hurt? Lord Elsworth is still standing?"

"I don't know if there were injuries, Duchess." Tristam popped up to look along the deck and could make out the viscount by his gun, a huge grin on his face. "Julian is unharmed—in fact, I believe he's enjoying himself."

The duchess shook her head. "He would. A sea battle is, no doubt, a dream come true. Will we escape them in the dark?"

The very question that was causing Tristam to despair. "It is very likely," he said as confidently as he could.

"Mr. Flattery," Beacham whispered and Tristam returned to his place, standing by, ready to fire. To his great surprise, he realized he dearly wanted another shot at the corsairs. His earlier dread and terror had been replaced by a great excitement.

The ship was beginning to roll, broadside to the waves, and Tristam could see the helmsman spinning the wheel to no effect. "We have lost steerage-way," he heard someone say.

The first boat crashed into the rail as it dropped over the side, eliciting a string of oaths from the ship's master. But the cutter had barely scraped down the topsides when the second boat swung into the air, as poorly controlled as the first. The small crew was being stretched too thin, Tristam realized—not enough hands to perform any task properly.

The carpenter and boatswain were called away to rig tow-lines at the bow.

"The corsairs have launched boats," a man at the next gun whispered and it was obvious the news had come down the line from one gun crew to the next.

"Dakin caught it," someone else whispered, "got in the way when the gun reared back. Cracked his skull. It is a lucky thing there is a proper physician aboard, I say. You can't saw off a man's head!"

This brought a despairing laugh and the remark was repeated down the line. Tristam heard the distinctive sound of a knotted rope lashing into a man's flesh, and there was quiet again among the gunners.

Twilight was quickly settling, as though the light had been borne off on the disappearing breeze. There was a sudden murmuring along the deck and Tristam could see the officers huddled at the after rail.

"A white flag," someone whispered. "Their boat bears a white flag."

Too used to having the run of the ship, Tristam was going mad having to stand by his gun. Suddenly he was reduced to the level of the poor Jacks, not privy to any of the discussion that decided their fate. One of the *Swallow*'s boats was hailed and ranged alongside and Stern went quickly over the rail. No one could miss the fact that he bore a short standard and white flag.

"What kind of parlay can be held with corsairs?" Tristam whispered to Beacham, unable to stay silent, but the midshipman only shrugged.

The absence of wind was like the lull in a couple's conversation of impending divorce—a silence so full of desperation one could almost touch it. Only the regular noises of the ship lifting and falling on the swell. Along the deck Tristam could see the tense faces, all signs of elation gone, everyone wondering.

How does one parlay with a corsair? Tristam asked himself again. What could they possibly offer? He could think of only one answer. They knew about the duchess. Word had reached them through some agent in Avonel or Farrow—or worse yet; from the Queen Anne Station. Tristam was almost certain this was the answer. The marauder would let the *Swallow* and her people go if Stern would release the duchess into their hands. Ransom. A queen's ransom. That was their goal, and only a small survey vessel to fight to gain such a treasure. What foolishness had led the duchess aboard!

Darkness fell while the boats from the two ships met. Tristam had just a glance as the *Swallow* turned somewhat on a wave. The two white hulled boats out on a dark, windless sea, their oars dipping and backing as they held position a cable apart.

The thirty minutes Stern was gone from the ship passed so slowly Tristam was sure the hands of the ship's clock must appear nailed in place. And then a call and the boat thumped alongside. Tristam could just make out Stern as he came over the side. The man did not hesitate but went directly to the quarter deck, spoke briefly with his officers and then disappeared below, his manner so stiff and determined that Tristam could sense the anger.

"That does not bode well," one of the men whispered.

Osler crossed to the head of the quarterdeck stair.

"The Captain would see you, Mr. Flattery," he said quietly, and turned immediately back to his duties.

Tristam cast a look at Beacham, who offered nothing but a lift of his eyebrows. Quickly the naturalist mounted the stairs to the quarterdeck and descended into half-obscured lamplight below.

Tristam was utterly mystified as to why he had been called, but hoped he might at least learn some part of what was going on.

Stern was not seated at the table in the wardroom, as Tristam expected but instead paced back and forth before the door to the duchess' cabin. He rubbed his short-cropped beard with one hand as though he searched for some lump or disfigurement hidden beneath, and his other hand was fisted upon his hip where his long navy coat had been thrown back. When he saw Tristam, he stopped his pacing and knocked on the duchess' door without so much as a nod to the naturalist.

Jacel answered and stepped outside, curtsying to the gentlemen, obviously not intending to follow them in, but Stern beckoned her.

The duchess no doubt understood from Stern's manner that his meeting with the corsairs had disturbed and angered him deeply but she stood with her arms crossed. If not looking completely defiant, she at least did not look as intimidated as everyone else aboard when the captain was in one of his moods.

As soon as the door was closed, Stern turned on Tristam, his face unreadable in the unlit cabin. "I have just been promised safe passage for my ship and crew if I will but hand over one of my passengers to these Entonne marauders." Though the words were spoken quietly, there was no mistaking the passion in the seaman's voice. He looked around the group standing mute before him, then back to Tristam. "Tell me, Mr. Flattery. . . . What is it they want with you?"

"*Me!*" Tristam looked desperately at the duchess but in the failing light he could not tell if she showed any signs of surprise.

"Yes, *you*, sir," Stern answered, Tristam's response adding fuel to the slow blaze of his anger. The man slammed his fist on the table. "I will have some answers here. What is it that I have not been told? Are you so valuable to someone in Farrland that these marauders would take you to ransom before they would take the Duchess of Morland? For they know the Duchess is aboard as well."

"It is not ransom they seek," the duchess said quietly. "They will do Tristam harm."

This stopped the officer for barely a second. "And why would they wish to do such a thing, Duchess?"

The woman looked down at the cabin sole, and perhaps shook her head,

Tristam could not be sure. "Because they are as foolish and superstitious as your Jacks, I fear."

"That is not an answer that I can comprehend, Duchess," Stern said quietly.

She looked up. "Nor is there likely to be a better one, Captain Stern, for I know no more than that. Roderick has kept you in great ignorance, I fear."

Stern stood, hands on hips, glaring at the duchess for a moment, but she did not give way at all. Tristam would have thought she was completely unaware of the captain's rage, or if she was aware, thought it unimportant. Stern was so accustomed to having everyone at the mercy of his moods that he clearly was thrown off balance. This was the Duchess of Morland he faced—the favorite of the King.

The captain turned on Jacel suddenly. "There were two Entonne ships in the harbor on Farrow. Did you take the opportunity to speak with those of your own nation?"

Tristam could see the poor maid stiffen. Her mouth worked, but no words came. Here was someone properly cowed. She looked over to the duchess and then back to Stern. She managed to nod—Tristam could just make it out in the dark.

"And did you speak of the other passengers—Mr. Flattery and the duchess?"

Again she nodded. Tristam could sense her fear growing—fear and understanding. "But, Captain Stern," she said, her voice quavering. "It was no secret. All of Avonel knew, I am quite certain."

"Yes," Stern said, deadly quiet, "one thing that was not a secret." He continued to glare at the young woman for a moment and then turned back to Tristam. "My ship and every soul aboard are in danger, because of you, Mr. Flattery. Why is that? I will have an answer, or, by Farrelle, I shall give serious consideration to granting this marauder's request."

Tristam thought of Lady Galton: *Do not bring this terrible bloom back into our world.* "I do not know, Captain Stern, though I dearly wish that I did." He wanted to look over at the duchess, certain that she had the answer that Stern wanted—that Tristam wanted.

Stern raised his fist as though he would shake it in Tristam's face.

"He speaks the truth," the duchess said, her voice still calm. "Threats will gain you nothing." She turned to her maid. "Jacel, that will be all."

The maid gave the quickest curtsy and fled from the cabin.

Turning away, the duchess walked to the gallery windows and looked out into the dark night. Stars were clear above the horizon, but no other ship could be seen.

"Think, Captain; other nations have objectives and intentions we know nothing of." She turned back to the two men. "The life of our King depends upon the success of this voyage." Tristam could tell that she searched the shadows, trying to see the captain's face, to meet his eye. "I do not know what Roderick has told you, but I fear you don't understand the importance of this quest. This Entonne ship—for though it plays the part of a marauder, surely you have realized the truth—this emissary of the Entonne government can lose nothing by negotiating. After all, if you give them Tristam, we would almost certainly fail to find the seed. But once they have Tristam, they will still do everything within their power to destroy the *Swallow*. War is being risked here. They will have no witnesses."

Stern looked down at his hand gripping the table and he released his hold, splaying fingers almost gently on the polished surface. "This is madness," he said, so quietly Tristam barely heard. Distracted, Stern turned away, lost in his thoughts. Then he looked up at the duchess, his anger gone—displaced by the realization that the intrigues of ministers and governments had found them in the trackless ocean. And he was only a sea captain, not privy to the policies of his government. "The oarsmen all claimed to not understand Entonne," he said, his tone subdued, "so perhaps the Entonne captain's demands will not be known. I have sworn the boatmen to silence on pain of being charged with treason, but we can only hope the Jacks don't guess the truth." He looked over at Tristam, his anger gone but the questions still present. "Perhaps we will get free of them in darkness, though they are likely not alone. There will be other ships abroad with the same purpose. It is a vast ocean." And then, shaking his head, he left.

The duchess stood looking at the closed door as though her gaze had followed Stern to the last second, trying desperately to see something.

"Why do the Entonne want me, Duchess?" Tristam asked quietly.

In the gray light Tristam thought she looked over at him, as though she had not quite heard the question, for her thoughts had been elsewhere.

"Want you? Because you will keep the King alive."

No, Tristam thought, that was a lie.

We follow Tristam's course, now.

There was nothing Tristam could say. The duchess would admit to nothing.

"I have a gun to tend."

Beacham smiled at the naturalist as he returned and Tristam felt an immediate, all pervasive guilt.

Everyone here is endangered by my presence.

It was no wonder Stern had threatened the boatman with a charge of treason. Was it possible that none of them spoke Entonne? Sailors traveled widely and saw many ports. But most harbors that took the coin of seamen were prepared to accommodate—the people spoke the languages of the Jacks. Perhaps the Entonne request would go unknown. Even if they had spoken Tristam's name, it might not have mattered: *Flattery* spoken with the accent of Entonne was almost unrecognizable.

Darkness was now so complete that Tristam could not see his own gun-mates. The shifting of men, a half-muffled cough—that was all there was to indicate the presence of the crew.

Tristam wondered what would happen to the *Swallow* if no wind came to rescue them. The waves would set them slowly toward shore, some five miles off, he surmised. There might also be a current here, though the charts did not show it.

He waited. Hunger began to replace excitement. But to Tristam's horror, the anxiety returned. Every creak of the rigging, every splash of an oar from the towing boats had Tristam straining to hear, fearing their position had been revealed to the marauder. Smells became more pronounced, as they often did when he was hungry; the caustic sulfur, and the sweat of the gun crews, mixed with the ever present smell of tar and the salt and decomposing matter that characterized the ocean.

Fear that the corsairs would suddenly appear alongside kept everyone on their feet, starting at every sound, imagining shapes in the darkness. A bucket of precious water came down the line, the captain's own steward rationing it carefully, for much of the water had been pumped over the side to lighten ship.

Along with all the agonies he shared with everyone aboard, Tristam kept coming back to the fact that the marauders wanted him. But why?

Sometime after midnight a breeze from the west began to rustle the ship's pennant and the yards were braced around as silently as possible. The *Swallow* was heading south and Stern elected to continue in that same direction, per-haps afraid to go too far from shore now that their water was low, or perhaps he felt there was always a chance here that his ship's ability to beat to weather would stand him in good stead close to a lee shore. A dangerous gamble, Tris-tam knew, but they had little choice.

It was most likely that the corsairs would assume the *Swallow* had turned north, hoping to reach the safety of the naval station. In which case the corsairs would use this same breeze to carry them north, hoping to find their prey still within sight come daylight.

There was great relief among the Jacks to feel the ship moving. Osler came along and divided the gun crews in half, letting one group lie down on the deck and sleep. Tristam drew the second watch and so leaned against the bulwark, spellbound by the swirls of phosphorescence streaming outward as the ship passed. *Phytoplankton*, he knew, caused to luminesce by the disturbance of the passing hull.

"Mr. Flattery?"

A whisper, but still a voice Tristam should know. *Kreel!*

The massive Jack appeared in the starlight, stepping near to Tristam. Reflexively, the naturalist drew back.

"Tell him I mean you no harm," the man said, so quietly Tristam could barely hear. "We are quits, thee and me." What was this he heard in the man's voice? Fear? "He did for Dakin in the smoke, thinking it was me. You have to tell him." Tristam felt a hand grip his shoulder strongly, but it was a pleading, not threatening, gesture. "He's mad, you know, but he'll listen to you. Tell him. . . . Tell him you saved me. We're quits for all time." The pressure of the hand was gone and the man faded into the darkness.

Martyr's blood, Tristam thought. *Dakin? Julian tried to kill Kreel and got Dakin?*

The naturalist stood by the rail in great turmoil, wondering what he could say to the viscount—if he could even find the man. A sudden fear that terrible things might be happening in the darkness made Tristam feel ill. Did Kreel speak the truth? Surely the duchess must realize who had tried to murder Kreel that night. Mustn't she?

If Kreel died now, murdered in the dark or in the heat of battle, Tristam would bear some responsibility. He left his place as silently as he could, up to the quarterdeck and down into the darkness below. There was a shuttered light at the base of the companionway, but Tristam found only darkness as he passed into the wardroom.

Feeling his way as silently as he could, Tristam came to the duchess' door and opened it without knocking. There were too many people lying awake this night, listening, Tristam was sure.

"Elorin?" he whispered crossing toward her berth. He heard coverlets move.

"Who is it?"

"Tristam." He took three more paces and then dropped to his knees beside the berth. "It is Kreel. He swears that Julian tried to kill him in the smoke. The man says we are quits—Kreel that is—he will do me no harm. He was frightened when he came to me. I don't know if what he says is true, but if it is even remotely possible. . . ." Tristam hesitated.

He felt a hand reach out and find him in the dark and he clasped it tightly. The pressure was fear.

The duchess threw her covers aside. "Where is he?"

"Julian? He is at the forward gun, or should be."

The sounds of someone groping, clothing hurriedly arranged.

"Take me there."

Her fingers found him again, squeezing his hand once, and then Tristam led her across the dark cabin.

They came up onto the deck into starlight, faint shadows of rigging like a net thrown across the deck. At the forward gun the viscount was not among those sleeping or standing watch. Tristam paused, bewildered for a second, his heart pounding, thinking they were too late.

Kreel did not seem to be sprawled near to his gun, either.

I should not have hesitated, Tristam thought.

Someone materialized out of the shadow. "Mr. Flattery?" whispered Beacham. "They're on the foredeck." And then, just as stealthily, he was gone.

The duchess had heard Beacham and they both rushed to the steps, the slap of bare feet loud in Tristam's ear.

There. Two silhouettes on the bowsprit. Tristam could make out someone, clutching a forestay, brandishing a belaying pin, and then another dark form, crouched two yards away.

"*Martyr's blood!*" Tristam hissed. "*Julian!*"

He jumped onto the spar and started out along it, balancing precariously in his rush.

"Tristam! Stay back from him!" It was the duchess, whispering urgently from behind. "Julian. That is enough! Let him be."

Tristam realized it was the viscount before him, and holding something in his hand, though Tristam could not tell what. The viscount turned quickly to look at Tristam, shifting his position as though Tristam were a threat. The naturalist stopped so quickly he almost slipped into the sea. Kreel had retreated to the very end of the jibboom where he clung to a stay, swaying with the movement of the ship.

The breeze was so light Tristam could hear the viscount breathing raggedly, as though with pent up rage.

"Tristam." It was the duchess. "Come back." She scrambled, on hands and knees, up onto the base of the bowsprit. "Julian, it is Tristam. Be careful what you do. Calm yourself."

The viscount made a slight movement back toward the ship and Tristam sprang back a step, his hands out as though to ward the man off. Flames! Someone was going to see this, despite almost total darkness. There were too many about.

Tristam could not make out the viscount's face, but he could see the man moving, his head weaving back and forth as though he struggled with the fire in his blood. He kept casting glances at Kreel, like the Jack was some prey snatched from his grasp. And Tristam felt this strongly—the creature before him was not quite human.

The viscount took a step in toward the ship.

"Back up, Tristam!" the duchess said sharply.

The naturalist did as he was told. He came up against the duchess and the two clung to each other, moving backward off the spar. Julian hesitated. Tristam thought that the man would make a rush out toward Kreel, but then he shook his head, and moved toward the ship. He sprang past Tristam and the duchess, landing easily on the deck, the shadow-net falling over him—and then he disappeared into the darkness.

Tristam heard himself let out a long sigh. He handed the duchess down off the sprit, where she pressed herself against him for a moment, her shoulders shaking briefly.

"I must find Julian," she whispered close to his ear. "You deal with Kreel. He must speak of this to no one. I will guarantee his safety, now—and more if necessary. Offer him silver. Anything." She embraced Tristam and then went after her brother.

For a moment Tristam stood calming his heart. She assumed he would do as asked: protect her murderous brother. Had he really hit Dakin?

Kreel had slipped in along the sprit, still hefting his belaying pin.

"I heard Her Grace," the man whispered, hunkering down into shadow. "No word from me. Just keep that monster away from me and my mates. That's all we ask."

Tristam returned to his gun, and found Beacham standing in his place.

"How in the world did you get involved in that?" Tristam asked.

The midshipman's face was invisible in the darkness. "I couldn't sleep. I was lying awake nearby when Kreel spoke to you. I just sensed trouble, sir."

"Well, bless your sense, Jack Beacham," Tristam whispered.

"Things have been put to right, then?"

The question gave Tristam the feeling that Beacham knew quite a bit more than he'd realized. "I hope so, yes."

He saw Beacham's head nod. "It's my watch, sir. You should lie down and try to sleep."

Tristam did as suggested, though sleep was impossible. He wondered how many men had heard what went on. Flames, the ship seemed small to him suddenly. Dakin. Tristam barely knew the man to see him, but Farrelle save him. . . . The man had done nothing. *Should I go to Stern with this? I have no proof myself.* And Kreel would not be a witness, he was sure of that.

Tristam lay with his ear on the planks of the deck, listening to the small voices of a ship wallowing on a windless sea.

Fewer people stood watching at first light that second day; most were exhausted by a night of fitful sleep. The atmosphere aboard was hard to discern, for only speech necessary to handling the ship was allowed. Even so Tristam could see the crew was decidedly surly and somewhat frightened.

Forward, the viscount stood at his gun, Kreel not a dozen feet away, both men apparently intent on their duties. If any of the other Jacks had heard what had transpired in the night, they were not letting on.

To his great relief Tristam was sent aloft with Osler to stand lookout, a welcome change from gun duty, and it also seemed a small escape—the best that could be managed aboard ship.

"I will wager, Flattery, that they have gone north on the same wind that carried us south." Osler was not looking so unruffled today. Lack of sleep and the tension of his position were leaving marks. His eyes were red, and his smile wooden.

"I don't think I'll take your wager. I'm sure you're right." Tristam answered, staring out to sea. "Were I Captain Stern, certainly I would have set my course to the north and off shore."

"Yes, and you might have sailed directly into the marauder in the dark of night. Still, it is the likeliest course. What captain wouldn't run for the protection of the naval station?" They were trying to convince themselves that all was well, Tristam knew. Both men continued to scan their section of the ocean, hoping not to find the white of sails in the slowly increasing light.

"Do you feel that?" Osler asked suddenly. "That will be our trade arriving, pushed along before the sun."

A pennant at the masthead began a slow dance and then streamed northwest—the anomalous southeast wind had arrived again. But the direction did not seem to matter to the crew, it was wind and the master had the Jacks on the run to take full advantage.

"But which direction are we to sail?" Osler asked, scanning the ocean. Without knowing the enemy ship's position they could set sail toward them.

To leeward the denser shadow against the gray sky was the shore. *How close are we?* Tristam wondered. Above the sounds of the breeze and luffing sail, Tristam thought he heard a slow rhythmical hiss.

"Do you hear surf, Mr. Osler? Far off, I think."

The officer leaped up, grasping the futtock shrouds, as though the increased height would enhance his ability to hear. Turning his head delicately from side to side, he looked like a seer attempting to gaze beyond his own time.

"Farrelle be damned! Keep the sharpest watch you can." Osler swung his glass over his back, grasped the backstay, and shot down to the deck at such speed that Tristam was certain he had flayed his hands to ruin.

The naturalist searched to leeward, struggling both to see through the darkness and to contain his imagination, which created reefs out of every patch of gray. But soon he was certain there was white, and then suddenly there was no question. A line of surf materialized out of the gloom, undulating like a dying snake. It was not an unbroken line, Tristam was sure, but nearly so.

The face of midshipman Chilsey appeared just at the height of the trestletrees, and below him, spaced a few feet apart, a line of men progressed down the ratlines to the deck.

"We've formed a whisper line, Mr. Flattery, direct to the captain. Tell us what you see."

"There is a reef to leeward, about two miles off and barely breaking the surface. I cannot make out its extent, but it stretches away to both south and north."

The midshipman ducked his head and muttered to the man below. Quickly Tristam scanned the ocean to the east where the light was growing, but still there were no sails. The ship heeled abruptly to an accompanying chorus of creaking and stretching in the rig. Tristam reached out and steadied himself on a shroud.

"She's just sighing, Mr. Flattery," Chilsey whispered. "Stretching like a man fresh out of his hammock."

Osler pulled himself onto the topmast head at that moment. "We'll continue as we are, Mr. Flattery. Watch the larboard and aft."

Under the influence of a freshening breeze the *Swallow* began to spread a wake astern. Five knots, Tristam estimated, and not done yet. The sky was changing its hue and Tristam could no longer say if it was black or the deepest of blues as the night transformed itself into day.

There was no question in Tristam's mind now that if one stared into the semidarkness long enough one would find whatever one sought. What the eye could not locate the mind would manufacture. But there was a spot of lighter gray, he was certain . . . almost. Tristam hesitated a moment longer.

"Lieutenant? Would you look to windward." Tristam pointed "About four miles, I should think, and a little aft of abeam."

Osler searched for a moment and then lowered his glass. "There will be no need for silence now," he said, his face conveying the distress his voice tried to hide. "They're not on top of us." He leaned out and called down. "Sail, Captain! Half a point aft the larboard beam."

There was a groan from the men on deck as they moved about to catch a glimpse of the ship—all hoping it might be a ship from the naval station.

Osler checked the reef again and then turned back to the distant ship. "He outguessed us, Mr. Flattery. A damned skilled seaman even if he is a marauder and deserves to be thrown over the side with a fathom of rusted chain for a neck cloth." Osler looked back to his reef and then forward.

John Chilsey arrived at the masthead for the second time, a glass slung across his back. "Captain bids you gentleman to come down, Mr. Osler."

"Well, stay awake, Chilsey," Osler said, swinging off the trestletrees to the shrouds. And then as an afterthought, "And don't go falling off. You are wet enough behind the ears as it is and Mr. Flattery cannot be expected to go aswimming after every Jack-fool aboard."

He disappeared before the midshipman could find a reply. Tristam followed the officer, impressed that anyone could make a jest under their present circumstances.

On the quarterdeck Tristam found the duchess dressed in her uniform again, listening to Stern and the ship's master, hands clasped behind her back as though she were imitating an officer. Tristam was almost certain he had seen such a thing at the theater.

Stern was waiting for Tristam and Osler.

"There was no end to this reef that you could see?"

"None, sir, though it does not seem to go on without interruption. There are many gaps in the line of surf, Captain, some quite wide."

Stern glanced at Hobbes and then at Tristam. "Our chart shows three rocks in a line—no more. And such efforts are called a survey! Damn the . . ." He stiffened suddenly.

As if to hide his embarrassment over this outburst before the duchess, Stern trained his glass on the corsairs' ship. After a moment he turned back to his officers.

"They will not let us make fools of them twice. If they can trap us against this infernal reef, they will pound us until we surrender, which will take no time at all. We will be lucky not to end up on the rocks." He cast a glance over his shoulder at the black ship and then turned back, his moment of indecision over. "We'll find the likeliest looking break in this reef—I shall go to the masthead myself—then heave to and lower a boat to sound the pass. Lieutenant Osler, you are in charge of the cutter. Have it ready. There can be no mistakes. May I have your glass again, Mr. Flattery?"

Tristam accompanied Stern to the trestletrees, sending young Chilsey down. The sun had floated free of the horizon and the blue of the southern sky was spotted with the small clouds identified with the trades, though they had abandoned their parent wind and sailed on the southeaster that continued to blow. The depth of the ocean must not have been great, for the seas were higher and closer together, causing the ship to roll sharply. Every so often she would all but put her gunwale under. Tristam wedged his back against the mast and pushed his legs through the trestletrees, hooking his feet into the futtock shrouds, but, even so, he was forced to clap onto a line with his hands regularly. The motion up the mast was much greater than on deck.

Despite the extreme movement, coffee was delivered to both Stern and Tristam and the two men examined the reef the *Swallow* paralleled, paying special attention to changes in the color of the water in the irregular breaks in the line of surf.

Stern did not take his eyes from the reef for a second, even to speak. "We have little time before we are brought to by this marauder, Mr. Flattery. A hole in this reef must be found. If by some stroke of ill fortune we do not find such a pass, I will put the duchess, Lord Elsworth, and yourself into a boat, together with such men as I think appropriate—Mr. Hobbes, most likely, and Beacham as well. It is likely you can escape into the Archipelago and make your way north to the Queen Anne Station." Stern paused, leaning out as though to see over the side.

"Though we are not done yet. Not by any means." Stern kept sweeping his glass along the length of the reef. "It is time, Mr. Flattery, that we had a candid conversation." He kept searching among the breaking seas.

The naturalist wondered what was coming. *Dakin*, he thought. *Farrelle rest him.*

"I will tell you in all honesty, Mr. Flattery, that this has been the damnedest voyage I have ever conducted." He shook his head slightly, and then fixed on a single point for a few seconds. The ship heeled more than usual and Tristam grabbed the shroud. "You see, the Admiralty gave me to understand that this was a bit of a futile endeavor—undertaken to keep peace with the palace, but hardly expected to succeed in time. Do you understand what I'm saying? And then the duchess insists on becoming part of the voyage, apparently to be sure all haste is made to complete the task. I find you are the nephew of Erasmus Flattery, something bound to cause difficulties with the Jacks. Then a falcon comes to you fifty leagues from land. I hear tales of your trip to the Ruin—a 'voice' never heard before your visit. No one knows how you came to be lying on the rocks of Bird Island. The sea itself seems to have saved you. And then a whale rises out of the great ocean and circles you until your rescuers' attention is drawn. Most fortunate. And the list goes on. The duchess is utterly convinced that the Jacks attempted your murder, though she was not there to see. Someone tries to kill Kreel, the man who the duchess believes caused your plunge into the sea. Hardly a coincidence, I would say. Though you stopped that murder, didn't you?" A pause. "And now an Entonne marauder is out to sink us because you are aboard my ship—risking possible war. Or perhaps they will not sink us—perhaps you are too important for that. . . . All of this has one focus." Stern turned his gaze on Tristam. "You, Mr. Flattery. Perhaps you would like to tell me why that is?"

Tristam found he could not meet Stern's eye, and looked out over the foaming reef.

"I am waiting, Mr. Flattery."

"I wish I had an answer for you, Captain Stern, but I will tell you truthfully that I am as much in the dark as you." Tristam shook his head, looking down to the deck. His earlier explanation—that some people believed Kingfoil would extend their years—seemed foolishly inadequate now. The catalog that Stern had just recited did not even include the other things that Tristam had experienced: Dandish, and all the events around the professor's home; Ipsword; the letter from Galton to Sir Roderick; the warning of Lady Galton; perhaps even the events at the Society evening. Tristam closed his eyes tightly.

"My ship, Mr. Flattery, is in danger—and I do not even understand why. I think I am entitled to an explanation."

"As do I, Captain Stern, but I have not yet found one. I will tell you, though, that I did not know my presence, or more likely our purpose, would bring your crew into danger. Sir Roderick gave no indication of it to me. I am not sure what he might have said to you."

Stern looked back to the reef. "I have never met the man."

The statement rang completely true, Tristam was certain. The duchess had been wrong.

Stern leaned forward suddenly, cupping a hand to his mouth. "Heave to, Mr. Hobbes. Hoist out the boat."

Stern handed Tristam his glass, a look of complete distraction on his face. The naturalist could see the man fighting to marshal his thoughts. "I shall bring you through this, Mr. Flattery." He swung himself around the futtock shrouds, the wind catching his coat and shaking it like a luffing sail. "But I would dearly like to know why I am endangering every soul aboard. Two years we shall be on this voyage. I do not intend to continue sailing onward, like a fool, unable to take proper precautions because I am kept in ignorance. You have a considerable intellect, Mr. Flattery. Even if you do not know all the reasons, I am sure you've spent many hours in thought. I will hear your thoughts before we go another league or I shall heave the ship to and wait." Stern looked down at the deck for a second, then back to Tristam, his determination unmistakable. A perfunctory nod of the head and then Stern disappeared.

Tristam sat for a moment, watching the officer descend to the deck, and then took the tin cup he had wedged between his knees and sipped at his cold coffee. A sudden lurch of the ship caused him to grab for purchase and he watched his cup hurl out over the waves, spinning as it fell, until it disappeared, its splash unseen in the chaos of the sea.

*   *   *

True to Stern's prediction the captain of the black ship was not so easily confounded. As soon as the *Swallow* hove to, the marauder altered course, driving straight toward its prey, setting every sail it could. Tristam stayed at the masthead, his gaze riveted to the charging ship. As she ran down on them, the corsair threw great arcs of white spray from her bows and these would occasionally refract the sunlight, breaking it into a rainbow. A most incongruous sight.

Whatever damage the *Swallow*'s guns had inflicted the previous day had been repaired during the night, for Tristam was sure she would not have been able to drive on so otherwise.

To leeward the cutter was hoisting its sails and striking out for the break in the reef. Occasionally a trough in the seas would be deeper than the others and Tristam would be allowed a glimpse of the glistening rock hidden beneath the confused surf. Stern was taking a chance heaving to so close to the reef, Tristam realized. He had learned enough of the handling of ships to know that one did not sail so close to windward of an obvious peril—and heaving to was even more dangerous. The captain was counting on the handiness of his ship and the skill of his crew—and he was desperate as well. If a squall should catch them in this position.... He did not like to think of it, for there had been squalls enough this past week.

Tristam turned his gaze back to the corsairs. Through his glass the men aboard were still only tiny automatons, their movements barely connected to any result that Tristam could perceive, as though the basic laws of cause and effect were breaking down before his very eyes.

The cutter appeared only through the gaps in the sails, now. One moment it was riding over the heaving seas, heeled to the rising wind, and the next it was surging into the foaming gap, picked up on a wave and racing ahead until it slipped behind a sail. How they would sound moving like that he did not know.

Turning back to the corsair, he realized that such haste was their only hope. The crew of the marauder could be made out now, even the men on the quarterdeck could be distinguished—officers standing out in uniform reminding Tristam that this was not truly a marauder but a well managed ship of a great nation. They had opened their gun ports and Tristam could see the gleaming bronze of the cannon, their mouths agape, ready to speak fire.

Suddenly the *Swallow* was sailing again, moving south, passing the break in the rocks. Tristam got a glimpse of the cutter, beyond the reef and sailing hard in the same direction as the *Swallow*.

"Mr. Flattery!"

Tristam looked down and saw Hobbes waving him to the deck. The men were mustering at the larboard guns. Tristam collapsed his glass and slung it over his back. Leaning out, he grasped the backstay, hesitated a moment to gather his resolve, and then sprang out, taking the cable into his embrace as he had seen the Jacks do. A bit jerkily he slid down the cable to the rail, Beacham giving him a nod of approval as he jumped down onto the deck.

"You have a moment, Mr. Flattery," Beacham said, his tone even but his face giving the lie to his voice, "if you would care to put your fine glass below. The captain would be at a loss without it."

Tristam vaulted up to the quarterdeck and almost fell down the hatch. He threw open the door to his cabin and it struck something soft and heavy. *Something has come loose*, was his first thought. In a terrible rush, Tristam jammed the door back with all his strength, not caring what he damaged.

Poking his head in through the narrow opening, Tristam hit the back of his skull as he drew back in surprise, for he had Doctor Llewellyn pinned against the locker. Tristam's first reaction was to apologize, thinking there must be a perfectly justifiable reason for the doctor's presence in his cabin—after all, their situation was extraordinary—but then he noticed the man held a sheet of letter paper in his hand and other papers lay on the tiny bureau.

Tristam pushed the door open, crushing the cringing physician even further, then, reaching down, he hauled the man to his feet.

"Tristam," the man spluttered. "This is not what you think. . . ." Immediately he began to gasp for breath.

Tristam pressed himself through the narrow gap and into the cabin, banging the door closed behind him. "You mean my eyes deceive me, sir? That is not my personal correspondence you hold in your hand?"

Tristam reached out and jerked the letter out of Llewellyn's grasp. "Get out, sir! I shall take this up with the captain and the duchess. Gentlemen don't read one another's correspondence! Or had you forgotten?" Tristam opened the door and helped the doctor out with a hand under his arm. For a moment he stood, lost in confusion, and then he remembered his purpose and yanked open a locker and installed his glass. Quickly he gathered up the papers spread about and shoveled them into a drawer, but before he pushed the drawer closed, he was stopped by the realization of what Llewellyn had been reading— it was the copy of the letter Galton had sent to Roderick. *Gentlemen don't read one another's correspondence.*

A noise on the deck reminded him of his duty and he set out running for the companionway.

"They are almost within range," Beacham said as Tristam took his place. The black ship had drawn much closer. "For their twelve-pounders, that is," he added.

Tristam turned to leeward, searching for the cutter, for the opening that would be their salvation. Still there was the undulating line of surf breaking on the reef, much closer now—too close, Tristam thought. The cutter rose and fell on the seas, heeled so far that on the crests Tristam was sure he could see her keel. They were pressing their boat toward the next break in the reef.

"They need to take a reef in that sail," one of the Jacks observed, quietly, sounding utterly absurd to Tristam in their present situation.

"Stand to," Beacham said, his voice sounding much older and more grim than Tristam would have believed possible. "They are bearing up."

Off to the east the great black ship was indeed altering course to parallel the *Swallow,* bringing her two decks of guns to bear.

"Hold your fire." It was Stern standing at the rail. "If you see smoke from their guns, lie flat on the deck."

A hoist of signals shot up to the *Swallow's* mast head.

"We are surrendering," one of the Jacks whispered. "Farrelle save us. We are done for."

"It is only to buy us time. To confound the bastards," Beacham hissed.

A blossom of smoke appeared at the corsair's side, and like many others Tristam dropped to the deck. When he looked up and realized most of the experienced men remained on their feet, Tristam scrambled up immediately.

"They have laid in a shot across our bow," Beacham said. "If the captain does not bring us to, the next shot will be in earnest."

"But will we not go on the reef?" Tristam asked.

"If we are damaged as we should be," Beacham looked at Tristam. "Unfortunate that you did not have the opportunity to instruct me in the art of staying afloat. . . ."

He said no more for all around them men fell to the deck and Beacham and Tristam did the same. The blast of the corsair's guns unnerved Tristam completely. He heard a voice whimpering and wondered if it was his own.

"*Oh-please, oh-please,*" someone near him said over and over as though it were a chant. "*Ohplease.*"

The sound of wood splitting and shattering drowned every sound. Something struck Tristam's back, but he dared not move to survey the damage. Silence, and then a rending sound overhead.

"*Topmast coming down!*" A crash somewhere behind him. The "thwung" of taut rigging parting.

"*Up, lads! Fire as she bears.*"

Tristam scrambled to his feet. The sound of men crying out and moaning pierced his ears. A Jack from his own gun crew lay crumpled on the planks, unmoving.

Beacham was prying the barrel of their gun up, his hand covered in red. "Stand clear, Mr. Flattery," he said, his voice conveying no hope at all.

"*Fire!*"

The *Swallow's* ragged broadside boomed across the waves and Tristam held his breath, waiting for the smoke to clear. A moment later the corsair appeared out of the haze—some of her sails were shaking in the wind but otherwise she was apparently unharmed.

"*Reload!*"

Tristam took the shot given to him by the captain's steward and passed it to a Jack, then stood by a tackle, ready to run the gun out. Two Jacks carried a man past, his head split wide open, eyes rolled back to pure whites.

The men were going about their business, but Tristam could tell the fight had been knocked out of them. The next broadside would do for the *Swallow*, and all aboard knew it. Tristam felt a hollowness inside—fear seemed to have been replaced by numbness.

As he waited for the order to run the gun out, Tristam searched for the cutter and found it attempting to beat into a narrow gap in the reef, a man standing in the bow ready to heave the lead. In the pass Tristam could see a tight ball of gulls, hovering and diving. He could even hear their cries. And then, into their midst, fell a hawk, scattering them like feathers before the wind—*a winter falcon*. It did not give chase to its prey but spun about, hovering in the sunlight.

"We have to go through the pass," Tristam heard himself mutter. Without a further thought he vaulted up the steps to the quarterdeck and crossed to Stern, who stood beside the helmsman, a glass focused on the opening in the surf.

"Captain! We must go through," Tristam said.

Stern looked up, his face twisted in anger. "Mr. Flattery! Take your place, sir!"

"The corsairs have run out their guns," someone called.

Tristam grabbed the man's arm and stepped close, staring into his eyes. He was not sure what he would say—whatever was necessary. "You asked why they pursue me. . . . My uncle was a mage. The falcon. The falcon that came to me at sea." He pointed, but the bird was gone. He turned back to Stern, desperate. "It hovered in the pass—a sign. We must go through."

The gap was almost abeam. Stern hesitated.

Tristam was certain he must sound like a madman, unhinged by the sight of battle—raving. The captain shrugged off Tristam's arm and turned to windward to stare at the great ship as it prepared to fire. Calm, the man seemed desperately calm.

"Take us through, Mr. Garvey," the captain said quietly. "Mr. Hobbes, trim to run before it." Having made his decision, the captain turned his back on Tristam, on the black ship, and focused on the opening in the rocks.

Tristam stood by the wheel, bracing himself against the roll of the ship. They came around slowly. To windward he could see that the corsairs were passing on now, their captain caught off guard. He did not expect Stern would put his ship through the pass before the cutter had sounded for bottom.

The ship came around until the fresh wind was on the larboard quarter, and then she lifted on the swell and was carried forward by the sea, only to settle in the trough as though resting before her next effort.

As they rose again, the corsair fired. Despite their great exposure to the enemy guns, not a single man on the quarterdeck did more than flinch. No one crouched and Tristam stood among them, waiting to be blown to pieces, but the corsair had fired hurriedly as they turned to follow their prey and the shot had fallen harmlessly into the waves.

The seas piled up before the reef, their crests building until, too high, they tumbled into foam. The cutter had beat into the gap now and the Jack with the lead was sounding furiously. Suddenly, a black flag went to the masthead of the cutter and the men in the boat all turned and stared at the ship bearing down on them.

"What is it?" Tristam said. "What does it mean?"

Stern stared at him for a second, his look unreadable, and then he turned back to the pass. "There is not enough depth for the *Swallow* to pass, Mr. Flattery. Hold your course, Mr. Garvey, we have no choice now but to go on."

Another sea lifted them, carrying them in its powerful grasp. The ship began to rush down the face of the sea, and then this wave, too, passed beneath them, rushing forward to hurl itself upon the rocks. The motion was extreme now and Tristam reached for the binnacle to steady himself.

"Mr. Flattery!" the helmsman grunted. "Take hold!"

Tristam did not wait but grasped the spokes of the wheel.

"To me," the man said, his voice strained. "We'll broach to."

Tristam wrestled with the wheel, putting every bit of his strength into it, feeling the resistance, the spokes cutting into his hands as the ship began to yaw to larboard. Slowly they forced the helm over and the ship answered.

"Back the other way, now—brightly," the man said and Tristam helped him spin the wheel back as the strain came off.

Again a breaking sea overtook them and again they fought the wheel, struggling to keep the ship on course. Even as he worked to steer the ship, Tristam watched them sweep into the narrow pass, the seas so great that foam ran in through the scuppers as the ship rose. To either side waves broke in confusion.

"*Clap on!*" Hobbes yelled. "*Brace yourselves!*" Both the master and captain took hold of the shrouds, and Tristam waited for the ship to smash down upon the rocks lying below.

The sea rolled out from beneath and the ship settled her great weight down into the trough, searching for the bottom. *But they were through*, carried on a crest!

Each and every man aboard stood, so surprised at their good fortune that none had voice to speak.

"Mr. Hobbes, is it possible for us to heave to?" Stern asked, apparently un-affected by their near ruin.

Tristam saw the gray old master look up at the rigging. "Not without losing our foretopmast and perhaps the whole of it, Captain."

Stern looked back over the rail. "Then we shall have to hope they cannot follow."

The master looked back at the corsair following now in the wake of the *Swallow*. "We could rake them from stem to sternpost if we could heave to, but I fear it would leave us unable to control our vessel."

Stern nodded. "Carry on as you are, Mr. Garvey. Where is our cutter? Who can see?"

"They are on our beam, sir," Garvey reported, "and giving her everything they have."

"Signal Mr. Osler to follow us. We certainly cannot stop to pick them up until we see what course our black friend chooses."

Tristam went to the stern rail and stood with the captain and Hobbes. The duchess appeared beside him and if Stern noticed he said nothing.

The corsair's ship, with the wind free, was charging down on the foaming gap in the rocks. Tristam could see men standing on the forecastle, apparently benumbed by the crashing of the waves, and the swirling, foaming eddies in the pass.

"They must draught more than we," Tristam said.

"Substantially," Stern answered. "We are about to see a marauder go up on the rocks, with very great loss of life, too." There was no hint of pity in his voice. "How long until our foremast is stayed, Mr. Hobbes?"

"We are running cables now, sir. Half of this hour will see us able to heave to. An hour will put us mostly to rights." Hobbes waved a hand at their pursuer. "I think they have lost their nerve. See the Jacks all a-scurry to shift their yards."

"Tristam!" the duchess said suddenly. "You are hurt." Tristam felt her pull his shirt away where it stuck to his back. Fingers probed the muscles, and he winced involuntarily. "You will live, I think. Take off your shirt and I will bind this." Tristam did as he was told and the duchess bound the garment about his middle.

The two ships were not more than half a mile apart, Tristam guessed, and he could easily see crew standing by to shift the yards, but still they held their course.

Stern spread his hands on the rail like a man stretching days of strain out of his limbs. "They will not come through," Stern said with obvious satisfaction. "We shall be away. Shape our course north, Mr. Hobbes. Heave to and take in the cutter as soon as we are able."

Hobbes began to turn toward the man at the wheel but stopped. The corsairs had not altered course, though the men stood at their stations prepared to do so. For a moment no one spoke. With no change in her great speed the corsairs' ship plunged on toward the passage.

"The captain is a fool," Stern spat out. "They have no choice now."

The marauder yawed suddenly and Tristam thought they would broach to but their helmsmen won the struggle and the ship lifted on a wave and swept into the gap between the rocks. Tristam held his breath and the duchess reached out and grasped his arm.

The massive ship seemed to hang in the chaos between the rocks and then it slipped into the trough. For the briefest second it appeared to stumble and plunge its bow, but then rose again, gathered way and sailed into clear waters in the *Swallow*'s wake.

The captain smashed his fists down upon the rail. "Will we never be shut of them?" Stern cried out, but his outburst was lost among the anguished cries of the crew. "A chart, Mr. Hobbes."

The master was off at a run. Stern turned to Tristam. "You might work some magic for us, now, Mr. Flattery. It is our only hope, I fear."

Tristam said nothing, for he could not tell if the officer spoke out of despair and grim humor or if he was truly hopeful.

What madness possessed me? Tristam wondered. But the falcon. . . . How could it have been a coincidence?

A chart appeared and Hobbes and the captain bent over it. "I had hoped we should not be forced to this," Stern said quietly.

Hobbes put a long finger to the chart, his manner equally grave. "We might trap ourselves into a false channel or a bay. There is no way of knowing."

Stern looked up, regarding the pursuing ship, and then went back to the chart. "Set course for the narrows, Mr. Hobbes. It looks like we might fight a small tide in, but with any luck the wind will follow us. Signal Mr. Osler. They must come aboard as we go. We will tow the cutter or lose it, if we must. The bow and stern chasers are to go over the side. Lighten ship, Mr. Hobbes, lighten ship. Once into the narrows, I will turn our broadside out to sea, then we shall know how badly this marauder wants to take us. They shall have only their bow chasers and we will rake them three times over as they come." He clapped Hobbes on the arm. "But we cannot be caught out here or all is lost. Nothing is more certain than that."

Tristam was enlisted to help heave the small stern guns over the side. Despite their size, they were not light and the few men set to the task were almost not equal to it. Inside the reef the seas were smaller, but still there was a surge, rising and falling, and they struggled to accomplish their task upon a rolling deck.

Despite all, the guns went over the side with only minor injuries sustained, and Tristam found that he was now truly mad with thirst. Immediately he went to haul lines with the Jacks and was surprised to find himself sending the studdingsails aloft with the Duchess of Morland. When the studdingsails were drawing and the lines coiled, the duchess looked up to find Tristam staring at her.

"If you dare call me 'Jack,' I shall belay you sharply with that pin," she said, nodding to the pin rail.

"I believe the term is, 'lay one out with a belaying pin,' Duchess." He bowed.

She tried to smile, but her gaze slipped off over Tristam's shoulder and he turned to see the corsair bearing down on them. Each time the *Swallow*'s bow rose on a wave, the marauder appeared to those standing in the ship's waist—and at each revelation the black ship grew larger.

"If we had a topmast . . ." Tristam heard a Jack say, but they did not and that meant the main topgallant could not be set as well as at least one staysail, and the ship's speed suffered for it.

Tristam realized that one of the officers standing on the quarterdeck, staring astern, was Osler, and then, in the ship's wake, the cutter appeared, crewless, lifting on the waves and slewing off the crests, its helm swinging free. Somehow the cutter's crew had come aboard while Tristam's attention was elsewhere.

Forward, the Archipelago lay closer than Tristam expected. The dense green of the shore was resolving into identifiable trees, bluejack oak and cedar, but even so the distance was too great. Tristam could see that. The corsair might not beat them to the shore, but certainly the marauder would pull within easy gun range any moment. The duchess mounted the stairs to the quarterdeck and Tristam was about to follow when the gunners were piped to their stations.

Beacham mustered his gun crew, still one man short. "What of Telman?" the carpenter asked.

"He folded up his cards, lads," Beacham said, "it sorrows me to tell."

One of the Jacks made a sign to Farrelle, a hand splayed flat on his breast, head bowed.

"That's two," Beacham said. "Dakin and Telman." He bent over and examined the flintlock, blowing into the mechanism. When he rose, he looked out to sea and then up at the yards—his interest feigned, Tristam was quite sure.

Dakin had died—murdered, perhaps, by mistake. Tristam could not bear to look at the men around him. Beacham had overheard Kreel. Had anyone else? *I am protecting a murderer*, Tristam thought.

"No one else, I hope?" Tristam asked, and got a shake of the head to ease his conscience.

"They're luffing!" someone hissed.

The corsair was indeed, though not quite head to wind they were turning out to sea and their sails began to luff and slat about.

Osler hurried the duchess down the companionway. The *Swallow's* stern lifted and Hobbes yelled out. *"Down on the deck!"*

Tristam did as he was bid, glad of the break in the deck, which afforded him great protection from the coming broadside. The deafening crash of the corsairs' guns reached them and then the crash of steel smashing wood. The mizzen topsail yard swung wildly, creaking and squealing, battering the lee shrouds, its windward end broken off into a jagged butt, the sail trailing off to leeward and shaking so violently the rigging vibrated.

Around him men were rising and Tristam did the same. Smoke swept down on them from the corsair, though it was only a thin film. Something black shot across the deck as the ship rolled and Tristam saw men leap clear as it thundered into the bulwark. Two men pounced on the object and raised it aloft triumphantly.

"There's a good view of the twelve pound ball," Beacham actually laughed. "I've heard tell of the favor being returned, so to speak."

"Firing it back?" Tristam said.

"Right back, yes." Beacham slapped the breach of the gun. "Ours're too small, though."

"I would like to do that!" one of the Jacks said. "Return the favor." He laughed.

"Silence there!" Hobbes shouted. "This is no bloody frolic."

The men fell quiet. Astern the corsair had fallen into their wake again, unable to reload before the *Swallow* was out of range. Not far off Tristam could see a line of breaking surf and beyond that a long, sandy beach. No opening could be seen, but there was a place where hills seemed to run down and meet. In the chains a Jack swung the lead, letting it fly with all his strength, and calling out the depths. Overhead the hands had already bowsed the swinging yard to the shrouds and were running a cable to the shattered end to act as a brace.

Suddenly Hobbes was off the quarterdeck. *"All hands to shorten sail! House those guns and bowse them tight!"*

"Martyr's blood!" Beacham spun around. "What . . . ?"

"Let go the lee sheets and slack the topgallant and topsail halyards!"

One of the Jacks pointed aft and there Tristam saw a mass of cloud or perhaps a whirling fog—opaque, lit brightly by the sun yet dense to its center with scud breaking away around its edges. It was passing over the line of surf that marked the reef, tearing the crests off waves and churning the sea to spume and foam.

"A white squall," Beacham said and jumped to his station to shorten sail.

Tristam and the carpenter were left to bowse the gun up to the rail, and if the man had not been so powerful, Tristam was sure they would not have managed it.

"They do not see it . . . the corsairs," the carpenter breathed. "Look."

Tristam ran up the steps to the quarterdeck and realized that Tobias' assertion might have been true, but it was true no longer. The corsairs had been so intent on catching their prey that they had not kept watch astern, but the sight of the *Swallow* shortening sail alerted them, for they were in a mad scramble to pull down canvas.

Tristam was called to help brail in the mizzen, taking hold of a sheet that tore at his hands. Before the squall hit, Tristam had a view of the corsair, thrown onto her beam ends, enveloped by roaring white. . . .

A gust caught the mizzen sail and it broke free, lifting Tristam and Tobias off the deck and throwing them hard against the shrouds. The sheet ran through Tristam's hands as he fell and, immediately, the sail began to flog itself to pieces.

Blinding rain hit just then, driven before a powerful wind, the drops pelting them like grape-shot. The *Swallow* ran toward the pass as the squall struck, wind shrieking in the rigging, waves breaking on either side, and then the pass, too, disappeared in white.

"Steer your course, man!" Tristam heard Stern yell and then saw the captain jump to the wheel, tearing it from the tired hands of Garvey who had tended it all that long day.

Tristam grasped the shrouds and stood, back to the wind, battered by hard rain, almost blinded by the fury of the squall. Suddenly he was thrown forward, his hands almost torn from the shrouds. The *Swallow* seemed to hesitate, as though she stuck, and then she slid slowly free and continued.

No corsair will follow us here, Tristam realized, *that was the earth we just touched.*

The sea was suddenly calm, and above them the sun began to break through the white. The downpour slacked to a pleasant rainfall and Tristam tilted back his head and opened his mouth, feeling it soft on his face, wet on his tongue. The squall rushed on, and out of the cloud the new world appeared, green and fresh. It was as though they had passed through a portal and left the black ship, in all of its cruel reality, behind.

◈ Thirty-Five

Tristam became aware that something was not right. He opened his eyes, glancing quickly around. He was in his cabin and it was daylight. But there was a quiet, a stillness, that whispered of lack of motion. No surge of the ship pushing her bow into the seas. No gurgle of water passing along the hull. No wind sounds or creak of cordage. His hammock hung still, like the pendant of a clock that had run down.

We are in the Archipelago, Tristam remembered; *safe.*

Unless the ship had been moved while he slept, the *Swallow* lay in a protected bay not far from the mouth of a stream of sweet water. Stern had found
his way in here the previous evening, his ship battered, his crew suffering from
lack of hydration, want of fresh food, and from the strains and pressures of
battle. The corsairs had not followed. When a boat was sent to the mouth of the
pass, they saw no sign of the marauder: both a comfort and a source of anxiety.
Where were they now?

They were after me, he remembered suddenly!

Tristam continued to rock in his hammock. He had no emotional response
to this realization, as though his mind were unable to consider the implications. But that was not true—his mind seemed particularly clear that morning—
filled with an odd silence.

My emotions have been swept away by battle, Tristam thought. And he lay
exploring this, attempting to find words to describe his state. *Hollow. Calm.
Silent. Still.*

In some corner of his mind Tristam expected to find a few embers of emotion that he could prod back to life. He tried turning his thoughts to matters
that he knew affected him deeply. The image of the duchess beneath her brute
of an officer—no response. The duchess leaning forward to kiss Tristam
softly—the touch of her lips. Nothing.

Empty. Motionless. Drained. Becalmed.

If he had only felt half-alive in the past, now he felt less than that.

*Perhaps I should have stayed at Merton and become a professor like Dandish
and Emin*, he thought.

But this thought, too, created no emotional resonance.

It occurred to Tristam that this state was the opposite of his father's. Where
Morton Flattery had responded to all events, all matters, with extreme emotion, Tristam now had no response at all. Neutral to everything—even to his
loss of feelings. For the first time he thought he had some small understanding
of what had controlled his father's life.

Perhaps there is merely a sluice gate within each of us, Tristam reasoned,
*controlling the flow of emotion, and some are born with it opened wide. And
others are born like me—with it closed off but for a trickle.*

It was only a reaction to battle, Tristam told himself again, to surviving a
surfeit of emotion. It would pass.

He closed his eyes and imagined he was floating beneath the surface of a
cold clear pool—or had it been a dream?—animated only by the smallest eddies and currents. No sound. Just thoughts as clear as crystal, appearing in his
mind without weight, utterly free of any emotional gravity.

No irony, no sadness, no humor, no warmth.

I am an automaton, Tristam thought. *Perhaps this is what occurs inside the viscount at all times.* But then he remembered the beast in the darkness; the man did not seem to lack passion, as perverted as it might be. An emotional compass that deviated, attracted to something darker.

And right now my own compass spins as though there were no magnetic field at all.

In his present state, the events that carried him along did not seem disturbing. He could even contemplate, quite dispassionately, the string of strange happenings that had brought him here. The Entonne ship had been after him. Galton's letter to Roderick came to mind. These people had some very strange ideas about Tristam. But instead of immediate denial, he began to explore. He remembered Stern on the crosstrees reciting his list—a list Tristam could easily add to. Not so disconcerting, really, if looked at coolly.

Assuming the duchess was correct, then the Entonne marauder was no marauder at all but under orders from the Entonne government. If it was their intention to stop Farrland from acquiring more Kingfoil, then they would need to do more than take the ship's naturalist. It was Tristam whom the Entonne had wanted to keep from Oceana. They did not want *Tristam* to find the seed.

We follow Tristam's course, now.

These words would not stop echoing in his mind. The duchess, at least, did not think Tristam was without an internal compass.

Again he thought of Stern on the masthead—the determination in the man's voice. The captain was tired of being kept in the dark, as though he were a fool. Oh, Stern would carry out a voyage for the Admiralty understanding absolutely nothing of its purpose, Tristam was sure, but to have his ship and crew endangered without even having been warned—and to be sure that the civilians he carried knew the reason. . . . Poor Stern could not bear that. Even a career naval officer must get tired of being used eventually. Especially when this unquestioning loyalty had clearly brought him almost no recognition.

I do not want to end up like Stern, Tristam thought: the dutiful servant, silently chewing his resentment, hoping, pitifully, that his sacrifice would one day be rewarded.

This thought seemed to ignite a flicker of warmth, a small glow of feeling. It appeared somewhere near his core. Resentment, perhaps. He reached down inside himself and fanned the coals, realizing that this emotion could burn away inside him until one day there would be nothing but emptiness—as was happening to Stern.

I will not allow that, he vowed. *Let me use these coals to forge something else: iron determination.* That would be his compass. He was not going blindly to Varua to fulfil someone else's purpose. He was damned if he would do that.

A rhythmic scraping began in the stillness, vibrating through the very bones of the ship, resonating in the great drum of her hull. It sounded to Tristam like the heartbeat of a massive beast and it seemed such an affront to his present state that he could hardly bear it. An attempt to stop his ears with his pillow did nothing more than lower the sound's register.

It was no use. He realized he would have to rise, and swung stiffly from his hammock. He fumbled through the pockets of a waistcoat until the smooth metal of his watch came to hand. *Half-two!* He had been in his hammock some sixteen hours. Lack of sleep, thirst, exertion, and, yes, fear, had consumed all of his reserves.

The scraping grew suddenly louder, carried on the breeze into his open port like irritating insects come in to buzz about his ears. A curl of wood shaving tumbled in the port and lit in Tristam's hair.

A clean shirt did not exist, so he settled for one "less dirty," which did not seem to matter to him—Tristam the fastidious.

Searching through the lockers for clothing reminded him of the encounter with Doctor Llewellyn, and he dreaded the idea of going to the man to have his injury examined, though a quick probe with his fingers indicated that he was probably not badly hurt.

Another puzzle. Llewellyn? What had he been looking for? Tristam realized he had no idea. He would have to bring it up with the duchess.

I must stop keeping other people's correspondence, he thought; *it leads to nothing but trouble.*

Tristam went in search of food, locking his cabin as he left—a practice he intended to keep up in the future.

Coming into the bright light of day, Tristam saw Tobias, the carpenter, and his mate shaping a new topgallant yard from one of the spare spars. The two men worked in the ship's waist, using adze and draw-knife, tapering the spar toward either end.

"The pleasures of the day to you, Flattery."

Tristam turned to find Osler, shading his hand and looking at the naturalist, a bemused smile on his face.

"And to you, Mr. Osler. You are undamaged, I assume?"

"Yes, thank Farrelle. Though I think fatigue has crept right into my soul. I feel . . . odd. As though removed a step from the real world." The lieutenant shrugged.

"I thought it might just be me," Tristam said, relieved to hear he was not alone. He noticed the cutter, heavily laden with men, setting out across the bay, a white bundle amidships.

"Dakin, and Telman, Farrelle rest them. They'll lay them to rest above the high tide line on that small island. Can't have a pyre when we don't know what has happened to our marauders."

Tristam watched the oars dip and lift as the boat passed over still water, the reflection of its white hull following, cloudlike, on the surface.

> *"And they laid him in a small boat*
> *Beside his helmet and sword*
> *And set it aflame as it took to the waves,*
> *Fire and sea carrying off their lord."*

Tristam and Osler turned to find the carpenter standing below them, a draw-knife in his hands, his eyes fixed on the distant boat, and then he went back to his work.

The younger men shared a look.

Osler bent his head toward the stern rail and Tristam followed him there, his eye drawn back to the funeral boat.

"Do you know any reason why the captain and duchess would have a row, Tristam?" the lieutenant asked quietly, using the naturalist's first name.

A row? "Not that I can think of. What has happened?"

Osler shrugged, his eye turning to the boat now.

"I don't know for sure. It happened ashore, well away from everyone. I just happened to be out in one of the boats and saw, at a distance. There is no mistaking the captain in a rage, even if one can't hear his voice. I just wondered what might have caused it. We will be two years aboard, as you know. . . ."

Tristam shook his head. "I was dead to the world myself. I hope it was resolved." Had Stern gotten wind of the viscount's attempt on Kreel? When had that been? The previous night? Or had suspicions developed about the death of Dakin? He would ask the duchess.

Tristam turned to look at the nearby shore. If he were not in this strange, emotionless state, he would be beside himself with excitement. The new world.

"Would you like to go ashore, Flattery? We will likely be here a few days. The captain wants to rest the crew, and then we will water the ship, hunt food, cut some firewood. You will have an opportunity to practice your trade."

"Yes. Yes, I'd like nothing better. But first I must find something for my stomach. I feel like I have not eaten in a week."

The boat ground up onto a beach of fine gravel and sand and Tristam set foot on the new land. The beach was a scene of great activity—Stern obviously had a peculiar idea of resting his crew. Jacks were drying fish on lashed-together racks while others butchered a small deer. Beyond this the captain's observatory tent was being erected, indicating they would stay a few days, for Stern was going to establish the accuracy of his chronometers by the method of lunar sights—*lunars*—an exacting process that required some time. Trees were being felled along the beach and sawn into firewood, and water was being ferried by the barrel out to the ship.

Not too far in the distance, on a grassy rise over the bay, the duchess and her maid sat on chairs under a sail cloth awning. But Tristam's emotionless state persisted, and he found he had no interest in the company of his own species—even the Duchess of Morland. Tristam was also afraid that he might find the viscount there, and not be able to escape the man afterward—a terrible thought.

No, he would go alone, to wander in this place where perhaps no man had ever walked before. The sound of a gentle breeze through the trees would be a welcome change from the howl of wind in the rigging.

Tristam set off along the strand, his unstrung bow in hand, and a battered canvas bag over his shoulder. Thayer's swallow-tailed kite passed overhead, low to the seagrape trees, and Tristam took out his glass to watch. It was, without a doubt, the most graceful raptor the naturalist had ever seen. Rather than riding on the breeze, and subject to its vagaries, the kite seemed to be borne upon its own currents, sailing where it chose with only the occasional beat of its long wings. Tristam watched, noting how the deeply veed tail flared and cocked, steering constantly.

What a clumsy thing a ship is, he thought, *when compared to such a miracle of design. Sailing upon the winds more easily than a cloud.*

The kite disappeared and Tristam walked on, stopping at the stream to drink.

"There is a pool at the next stream, Mr. Flattery," said one of the Jacks, waving down the strand, "not far back from the beach."

Tristam took the man at his word and followed the small stream, not more than a long stride in breadth, up into the green forest. There was no path, but the underwood was not dense, and Tristam easily made his way. All around him stood trees unlike any he had seen and yet he knew them from his studies; *seagrape* and the *bluejack oak, tallowwood, strangler fig*, and something Tristam thought was called a *doveplum*, though not really a plum at all but a member of *Polygonaceae*. And there, beneath an awning of swaying branches, held aloft by the trunks of gracefully curving trees, he found a shallow pool. The water was clear, as though untouched by man and his works.

Shedding his clothes onto a carpet of moss, Tristam slipped into the water, cool enough to wash away his lethargy but not so cold as to drive him quickly out. The image of floating beneath the surface came to him, causing a second of uneasiness—perhaps his emotions were beginning to come back to life, to surface again.

He lay on his back and looked up at the trees, full of small birds and squirrels, and listened to the music of the place—the delicate melody of the birdsong mixed with the gurgle of the stream over stones and the whispering and sighing of the breeze in the trees.

Here I will stay, Tristam thought suddenly, *give up this foolish voyage, and build a home. I will become a true part of the world I study, making my living from the forest and the sea.* He closed his eyes and saw the kite drift across the sky again.

The falcon, he thought. *I saw it, among the gulls . . . thousands of miles from its native range. But how?* Perhaps, he reasoned, it was only a light-colored hawk of the new world. Without doubt there were many species not yet noted by man.

But in his heart Tristam did not believe this explanation. He turned his thoughts away from this subject—something for which he could contrive no rational explanation.

Soap and articles for his toilet had not been included in Tristam's necessities for a trek ashore, so he washed as best he could and combed out his tangles with his fingers. He stretched out upon a rock to dry in the sun and breeze and had the good fortune to capture a strangely marked beetle which was so cooperative as to walk onto the palm of his hand.

As he dressed, Tristam heard the sounds of movement in the bush and paused to listen, thinking it was some large beast. The rhythm of the movement convinced him this animal was bipedal—a member of the crew or a member of a hitherto unreported native race. A flash of sudden fear—emotion—what if this were men from the Entonne marauder?

A branch swept aside and Doctor Llewellyn appeared, puffing terribly, his face scarlet. It was the only time Tristam could remember being happy to see the man.

"Tristam. Ah ha. We need. . . ." He wavered as he stood. "I must . . . sit," he managed. He lowered himself partway to the ground and then collapsed the rest of the way, to sprawl, gasping for breath so desperately that Tristam was tempted to run for the ship's surgeon.

"Are you all right, Doctor? Shall I get help?"

The man raised a hand. "A moment. . . ."

It was several moments, but the physician slowly gained control of his breathing. Tristam found himself edging away from the wheezing man even though he knew the doctor could not be consumptive—the entire crew would have been infected long before now.

Llewellyn fumbled at his neck cloth, pulling it open, and then wiped a square of linen over his face, for he was sweating profusely.

"I am better, I think."

Tristam sat on a stone where he looked down upon the doctor.

"Mr. Flattery, I realize that I have done a contemptible thing, but when I have explained myself I hope you will at least understand what has driven me, even if you cannot bring yourself to excuse my actions." He searched Tristam's face for a second as though assessing the impact of his words. As usual the doctor's tone rang false, overly obsequious, and insincere.

"I have, no doubt, mentioned that I served as the Royal Physician briefly during the absence of Sir Benjamin Rawdon. Benjamin and I studied together and he has always been a friend to me, even when Llewellyn was perhaps the least popular student at Merton." The man paused to take several long breaths.

Rawdon, Tristam thought, the man who intercepted me on my visit to Baron Trevelyan.

"Benjamin's wife fell very ill," the physician went on, "and he asked me to examine her to corroborate his diagnoses. Lady Rawdon had a form of the cancer, Tristam. I shall not go into the details but suffice it to say that I thought she would not live out the year. I was most disconsolate, both for the gracious lady and for my friend and colleague, for his devotion to Lady Rawdon has always been unwavering. When Benjamin asked me to take his place in Tellaman Palace, I agreed immediately and made arrangements for my own practice.

"During the next few months I had only two brief letters from Benjamin. In the first he said Lady Rawdon was 'getting on very well' and in the second he wrote that she was almost completely recovered. I remember hoping, for both their sakes, that he was not deluding himself, as people in such situations are apt to do: physicians are not immune to such folly.

"During this brief time I had occasion to serve the King only twice—minor complaints from which His Majesty recovered extremely quickly. The King, as you no doubt know, is astonishingly well preserved . . . for a man who has passed his centenary by more than a decade. In fact I would venture to say he is physiologically no different from a very healthy man in his late sixties, which is truly remarkable.

"My consultations with the King were very brief and His Majesty never spoke to me directly but rather whispered to an old servant who then related the King's words to me. I marked this as very odd, but then the sovereigns of Farrland have had stranger eccentricities.

"During my second attendance upon the King, I had opportunity to make a small jest, such as physicians do to put their patients at ease, and this amused the King enough that His Majesty laughed. I cannot describe this laughter to you but it was of such an odd character that I asked leave to look into His Majesty's throat. The King would not allow this, which worried me somewhat. Later, Benjamin assured me that there was no cause for concern. That is the sum service required in my time as acting Royal Physician.

"A month later Sir Benjamin and Lady Rawdon returned to Avonel from their country seat and, to all appearances, the lady's remission was complete. I did not examine her, mind you, but a physician can tell much from signs others do not mark. Such recoveries are not unknown, though I have never seen one so swift or complete from so serious an illness. When I asked Rawdon to tell me of his course of treatment, he said that nature had effected his wife's cure, and would add nothing else." Llewellyn looked off as though he were seeing some part of the story he told. "Now I have known Benjamin Rawdon for thirty-some years. In fact, I think there are few who know him so well. There was something out of place in his response, I had not the slightest doubt. He was not lying to me—Benjamin is almost incapable of such a thing—but he was avoiding telling me much.

"I flatter myself that I did not perform my duties at court too poorly, for some months later Llewellyn was again requested to act as physician to the King—Rawdon and his wife travelled to Uppcounty for the marriage of their middle son." Llewellyn stopped his tale at this point and looked down at the ground for a moment.

In his new state of disinterest, Tristam could almost see where the story was leading.

"It shames me to admit what next occurred." The doctor began to work the sleeve of his jacket between thumb and finger. "I had seen two rather remarkable recoveries while in the service of the King, and though the King's own ailment was not of a serious nature, even trifling diseases can be most devastating to the very old, and yet the King recovered more quickly than a man a third his age. Llewellyn's natural curiosity—a trait that you share, I think—was aroused. I had access to Sir Benjamin's office and I confess I began to poke through it, looking for what, I did not know. I found nothing obvious, but rather than leaving the affair to rest I began to feel a strong fascination, almost an obsession. One day I forced access to Benjamin's locked drawers and cabinets." The man pushed out his lip, a small gesture of defiance, Tristam thought.

"I came upon a monograph concerning Lady Rawdon's recovery. Sir Benjamin had treated her with an herb, Tristam, and noted in careful detail how his good wife responded. Although one could hardly consider this to be empirical evidence—her recovery could have been coincidental—Rawdon, a careful professional man, did not even consider this a possibility. It had not been nature that had managed her recovery: Lady Rawdon had been cured of a disease hitherto invariably fatal. *Rawdon had a cure for the cancer and he was not shouting it to the world!* In all of his notes there was but one sentence that threw light on this: 'It is the saddest thing to think that the Kingfoil is so rare, even in its native Oceana, that there will never be sufficient quantities of the physic to do general good'.

"So wrote Rawdon. Sir Benjamin returned and a year passed. I thought much of this matter, Tristam, I can tell you. My imagination was afire. Everyone in the palace knows of the locked arboretum, though none, I think, suspect what I do. I had begun to wonder if it was this physic that kept the King in such good health for so unnatural a span of years. So often the old are broken by one illness coming upon another—minor afflictions to the young, but to the aged each one is like a heavy blow driving them ever down until they are beaten into the grave itself. But the King . . . the King recovers from each affliction as though he were a man of youth and vigor—or so I conjecture.

"I pondered this long and most often late at night, for I was driven to insomnia by my thoughts. And then one night I had a fever and the sweats. And then the next as well. 'Nothing,' I thought but it did not abate and then I began to feel this. . . ." He placed a hand on his breast and then rubbed it as though trying to assuage pain. "It is not the consumption, as you might think. It is the *black lung*—a form of the cancer, some think—here in my left lung to start and now spreading in the right as well. But for a miracle, I knew I would be dead in a few months . . . a terrible wasting death, too: I have seen it. But, Tristam, I knew of a miracle." He looked around suddenly as though it occurred to him that someone could be listening. Reassured by the quiet, he continued.

"I went to Rawdon and confessed what I had done—that I had read his notes. I told him what I suspected of the King. He denied it and said his wife's recovery was a miracle of nature." Llewellyn put a hand over his eyes for a second. "I called him a liar and a false friend. . . . I named him my murderer. I begged. I wept. And he wept as well, saying finally, 'Llewellyn, I should do anything for you. But this one thing I cannot do.' He admitted that he had possessed some small quantity of the herb for his wife—granted to him by the King—but that he had no more, and that the King would soon have none as well, for the plant had ceased to bear the seed that was the healthful part. I believed him now, for I could see he had opened his heart to me and was greatly distressed by my condition. I allowed myself to be sworn to secrecy." He looked up at Tristam. "But I began to read everything ever written about Oceana. I learned the language. I traveled far just to look at obscure documents and journals. I learned nothing of this plant I so desperately sought.

"My condition deteriorated, not so quickly as I feared, but still it was not so slow that one could begin to have hope. And I had no hope. I considered writing a pamphlet telling what I had learned—letting all of Farrland know what the King kept in his palace. But this was only spite and anger and would accomplish nothing. I confess as well, though I know you scoff, I found comfort in the Church of Farrelle." He shrugged.

"And then I heard of this voyage. Again I went to my friend Rawdon and begged him to help me find a position on this ship, for it could only have one purpose—to find more of the plant that bears the miraculous seed. Benjamin took pity on me, and through his influence the King was convinced that the duchess should not make such a voyage without a proper physician—a position which I obtained. And so I have come here, through great trials—I dare to say through greater suffering than any soul aboard.

"But I would suffer ten times as much to find this seed, Tristam. Not just for myself but for all of mankind. A cure for the cancer and what else we do not know!" He looked oddly at Tristam. "Or perhaps we do know. . . .

"You are the ship's naturalist. A trained botanist, expert in the flora of Oceana. I knew you were the one sent to find this herb. And so I took an opportunity to search your cabin, Tristam. A shameful act, but I am a desperate man, as you see. I would venture to say that nearness to death will rob most of their dignity and honor . . . and Llewellyn is dying—a little more each day. Foolishly, I hoped I might find some of this seed." He shook his head sadly. "And in my search I found the letter from Galton to Roderick Palle. How is it, Tristam, that you came to possess such a document?"

"I feel no need to explain my possessions to another, Doctor."

"And quite rightly," Llewellyn said quickly. "I only asked because of the runes, you see. I could not help myself. Can Palle and Galton read them, then? Have they broken the cipher and told no one?"

Tristam stared at the man, wondering if his emotionless state was reflected on his face. "This seed, Doctor Llewellyn, you say it is a cure for several diseases, and protects its user from the ordinary death by common ailments?"

"Yes, exactly. It somehow strengthens the body's natural defenses against disease—at least that is what Rawdon thinks."

"So why has the duchess come?"

"I do not know for certain." Llewellyn shook his head, and looked down as though considering the question again. "Loyalty to the King. Fear that other factions at court have influenced the voyage. The King is very well preserved—it might lead one to believe the seed had other effects. The duchess would give much to preserve her youth."

We follow Tristam's course, now.

Llewellyn appeared to have arrived at the same conclusions that Tristam had once reached—before he overheard the duchess' conversation with her brother.

"You may be greatly disappointed when we reach Varua, Doctor. Sir Roderick Palle told me that any Kingfoil found was the property of the King."

"But, Tristam!" the man cried. "I need only the most paltry amount. So little, surely, that no one could miss it. Rawdon cured his wife with less seed than would fill the bowl of a wine glass. From all the plants in all of Oceana I require so little. Could you truly possess this and watch me die?"

Tristam looked down at the man, so pathetically sprawled on the ground, and knew that, normally, he pitied the man somewhat. *I could not stand by and watch Pim drown*, Tristam remembered. He had already decided that he would not surrender Kingfoil to anyone before he understood their purpose. He had already decided to risk treason.

"Doctor Llewellyn . . . this seed is more rare than you realize and what little is found by the islanders is the property of their own king. It is very possible that we will return with nothing. . . ."

Llewellyn did not wait for Tristam to finish. "But, Tristam, I can help you," he cried out, his anguish apparent. "I speak the islanders' tongue and I am a trained empiricist, as are you." He looked up, and Tristam could see tears glistening in his eyes. "We are brothers in our quest to press back the borders of ignorance and bring forth the age of understanding. A world where disease and poverty and ignorance will be banished. A world where you and I will be recognized for what we are and what we have contributed . . . and what a contribution we can make, Tristam! To overcome the cancer and who knows what other scourges. Our names will live on with Skye and Marsfield and Boran. And to overcome such disease will mean the lengthening of our short lives. As empirical medicine has added a decade to those lives, so we shall do again—perhaps more. . . ."

Tristam was afraid the man would begin to sob.

"A handful of seeds, Tristam." He was begging now. "The smallest handful. That is all I ask."

Tristam hefted his canvas bag onto his shoulder and went and offered his hand to the physician. "Allow me, Doctor," he said quietly. "I was trying to say that I will give you what help I can. But it may be less than you hope for—the plant is difficult to find."

The man looked up in surprise, almost afraid to believe what he had heard, but then he took Tristam's offered hand and struggled awkwardly to his feet.

"I—I thank you with all my heart Tristam. . . ." and it was the first time Tristam had heard sincerity in the man's words.

ᕔ Thirty-Six

The naturalist stepped out from under the green canopy of the forest and stopped to survey the cove. A smaller island nestled up to a larger one formed the bay—roughly rectangular, a quarter mile in width by three quarters long with a narrow entrance at either end. Stern had chosen it mainly for that reason—if the corsairs found their way into the Archipelago and discovered the *Swallow*, they could not bottle the Farrlanders up, for prevailing eastern winds would allow escape through either entrance. It was as safe a location as could be found.

Tristam lowered his shoulder bag gently to the beach, mindful of the specimens waiting to be preserved. He had spent the afternoon botanizing, suspended in the strange state of inner calm. His emotions were still absent. Tristam had also spent the afternoon in thought, an odd experience when one's thoughts engendered no feelings.

And to think I used to worry that I was without emotion. This *is what it's like to be without emotion.*

Swallow lay at anchor on the calm water, sails furled, her ensign wafting in the breeze, the crew at work on her rig. There were still gaping holes in the larboard gunwale where they had set the guns and signs of the enemy's marksmanship on the hull, but she floated, proudly, Tristam thought. "*A game little ship,*" Stern had called her with great affection, and that seemed an apt description to the naturalist.

There was talk of careening the ship, for her copper was beginning to foul, long tendrils of weed growing on her hull, but the tidal range was so small that it would have been a difficult task, if not impossible. There was also a fear that the corsairs would appear and catch the *Swallow* heaved down on the beach.

On the rise of the point Tristam could see the duchess under her awning, shading her eyes and waving.

It is time, he thought.

He raised an arm in return. Hefting his bag to his shoulder Tristam set off along the strand, passing among the Jacks who worked on the beach. They nodded as he passed; no sign of animosity now.

The abandoned cutter had been found that morning, cast up on the sand not too far outside the narrows and miraculously only in need of small repairs. For all her lack of a helmsman she had come through the surf intact. Tobias Shuk had taken the boat in hand and had her blocked up on the sand where he was in the process of replacing a section of her gunwale and a broken frame.

"The pleasures of the day to you, Mr. Shuk," Tristam greeted the man.

"And to you, friend Flattery." The man was a member of the society of friends: a transcendentalist. He had joined the voyage to Oceana so that he might see man living in his "unspoiled natural state."

The carpenter leaned over and put his bearded face close to the cutter's rail and sighted along its top. "Built by men who knew their business," he pronounced with satisfaction. "She'd never have survived being tossed up on the beach otherwise." He took up a carefully shaped piece of hardwood and flexed it into place, showing his great strength. "That will do," he muttered.

"I believe it will more than do," Tristam said. "I could not make out a seam where the ends butted. How do you do that?"

The man smiled, almost shyly, Tristam thought. "Well, friend, I have been at joinery since I was little more than a boy." He paused and looked at the strake in his hands. "And I understand the wood. Now, that will be my secret—if I have one. Wood is a gift from the world of nature to we undeserving men." He nodded down the beach to the Jacks sawing firewood beside a great pile of branches, their leaves wilting in the sun. "One should be thankful for such gifts, take no more than we need, and waste none of that."

Tristam nodded. He wondered what Tobias would say about the bag of specimens he carried.

"Do you know if we will begin to survey here? Is that the captain's plan?"

Tristam shrugged. "I don't know the captain's mind, and I have heard nothing."

Tobias nodded. Picking up a small plane, he addressed his beloved wood with a few tender strokes. "I wondered, for I will have to build the longboat if we are to begin the survey in earnest."

"Build a boat? Here?" Tristam looked around at the shore and the edge of the wild forest.

Tobias grinned pleasantly at this reaction. "Well, not out of the forest. We carry a longboat in parts stored in the hold. It is a large boat and awkward to have on deck for long passages. That is why we wait and do not build it until we are at our destination. I had thought it would wait until we were in Oceana. Then we would leave the boat there—a gift to the King. Though the Varuans have their own shipwrights." Tobias looked up at Tristam. "Did you know the shipwrights in Oceana are priests—or very near? Building a boat is thought to be a spiritual act, a creative act, like writing a poem, only more so. There is as much ritual as craft goes into each boat, for the boat itself has a spirit passed down from the tree, which is thought a great living being in itself."

Tristam nodded. "Perhaps the Varuans will set you up for a god, Mr. Shuk, when they see what a skilled shipwright you are."

The carpenter turned back to his work. "I am only repeating what Doctor Llewellyn told me, friend Flattery," he said quietly.

"I jest, sir," Tristam said, a bit ashamed at baiting the man, who was good-hearted in the extreme, despite his odd ideas. "I'm sure the Varuan practice is as it should be. Craftsmen do not get their proper due in our world—and I say that quite honestly."

Tobias gave him a half-smile. "Kind of you to say, Mr. Flattery." Tobias took a worn oilstone and began to sharpen a plane iron. "What do you make of the doctor, Mr. Flattery?" he asked overly casually.

The carpenter's manner was always so genuine, so lacking in guile, that Tristam was immediately aware of the change. "What do you mean, exactly?"

The carpenter hesitated for a moment. "He is a learned man, or so he appears to one as ignorant as myself. But do you think he is . . . 'well found,' if you take my meaning?"

Tristam felt his mouth go dry. "What has he been saying to you, Mr. Shuk, that you would ask?"

The man shrugged his heavy shoulders, looking a bit alarmed by Tristam's sudden seriousness. "We have talked much of Varua and the islanders, for friend Llewellyn has read more about the islands than any man living, I think. I should venture that he knows more about the islands than Hobbes, and the master has *been* there.

"The doctor has been kind enough to instruct me in the language, and has shown great patience, I might add. I was never the best of students, though I venture to say that I read as well, and as frequently, as most educated men. In return, I have promised to help the doctor find some herbs and shrubs that the Varuans use for healing—I believe he wants to write a monograph on the subject."

Bloody fool! Tristam thought, but it made sense. The doctor was enlisting the assistance of the most serious and able man who was not an officer. "Something seems amiss to you . . . ?"

"Well, I cannot be sure." He reassembled the plane without looking, his skills residing as much in his hands as his head. "But you know the good doctor has the cough and the shortness of breath. . . . I may be out in my thinking, but it is my belief that he has fixed his hopes on finding a cure in the islands." He looked up and said quickly, "Now I believe that much is known by people who live closer to the mysteries of the earth—for they healed their people long before empirical medicine came to be—but I think the doctor has his hopes set very high, though he tries not to show it. Just as he tries to hide the seriousness of his illness, friend Flattery. This sickness. . . ." Tobias looked up at Tristam, compassion clear in his eyes. "I have seen the doctor spit blood. It is a terrible thing, I know. I saw a man—a strong, good man—taken with the black lung. A ship builder such as myself. He did not last the half-year." The carpenter paused for a second, his normally serious nature suddenly even more grave. "It seems cruel to us, but it is the way of nature." He met Tristam's gaze. "I fear that friend Llewellyn may not have strength enough to sustain him until we reach our destination—or he will be so reduced when we arrive that nothing can be done. And I will be left seeking some herb that I know nothing of, for the doctor does not think the good islanders will share their healing skills readily with strangers, and he knows much of their ways." The man took a long breath, picking up his piece of wood again as though its feel reassured him.

"I am much concerned, Mr. Flattery." He looked up at Tristam. "Have you knowledge of these herbs? Will I be able to help our good doctor? I should hate to have his death on my hands."

Tristam almost said, *but it is the way of nature.* He stopped himself for he could see great concern on the man's face. "There are many herbs on the islands, Mr. Shuk. I have books that can tell us much. But I am concerned, too, now that I have heard you out. The doctor may have been driven by desperation to wild hopes." Tristam toyed with the buckle on his bag. "Perhaps we should not speak of this to others; the doctor's dignity . . ." He did not finish, but the carpenter nodded.

"I think that would be wise. The doctor has suffered much at the hands of others, for he is one of those who can never be easy in the company of his fellow men. Though I warrant he is no worse than the rest of us when you come to know him."

"I am sure you are right." Tristam walked around the boat slowly, his eye caught by the skill of Tobias' work. "I shall look forward to watching you build a boat entire, Mr. Shuk, for I am almost as in awe of such skills as the Varuans are said to be."

Tristam set off down the beach, barely watching where he walked, the conversation with the carpenter almost ringing in his ears. Llewellyn was a desperate man. Desperate men bore watching.

The duchess came a few paces down the knoll to meet him, her smile broad. "We have survived," she said. "Most of us anyway. How are you, Tristam?" She reached out and took his hands as a woman might her brother's. "Your injury is not too serious."

"It is nothing." Tristam thought she looked a little tired—a relief to know that there was something that might distress the duchess enough that some ill effects could be seen. "And the Duchess?"

"Oh, I'm undamaged." She looked down at Tristam's bag. "But you have been botanizing. . . . I am most curious to know what you have found in this new world. Have you made any great discoveries? Is your name already made?" Her teasing had an air of artificiality, as though the duchess tried to imitate her usual manner.

Tristam set his bag down and began pulling at the buckles. With great care he unwrapped a small package and from it took three identical blossoms of such beauty—exotic in both shape and color—and as unlike the domestic flowers of Farrland as to be almost fey.

"*Orchidaceae cattleya Elorinae*, if you will allow me to name it for you. An epiphyte I believe previously unknown."

"Why, how very presumptuous of you," she said, obviously pleased, and took the blossoms from him with great gentleness. "I will allow it this once." She leaned forward as though she would kiss his cheek, then caught herself. "But I shall have to thank you properly another time. And what other treasures have you collected?"

Tristam crouched down and began removing his booty from the bag. Several bird skins came to light, a dozen and a half insects, rock samples, fossils, nine different mosses, thirty or so leaves of various trees, seed pods, bark; and finally, carefully rolled into Tristam's handkerchief, the intricately patterned skin of a snake.

The duchess almost took a step back, revealing the normal response to reptiles. "My, what is that?"

"A type of adder, I believe. I had such a time killing it. I thought it was going to bite me before I did for it. But I finally managed to catch it on the skull with my staff." Tristam broke into a grin. "It convulsed and turned belly up and then fell still. Fortunately, I had read of this subterfuge before and turned it over with my stick. And what did it do? It turned back belly upward, for it was only practicing upon me! Had I picked it up, it would have bitten me. But such snakes believe that, to appear dead, they must lie on their backs, and so they will always roll back to that position when turned." Tristam laughed. "What a time I had, for I didn't want to damage his fine skin."

The duchess put her hand to her mouth. "You could have been bitten."

"Oh, unlikely." Tristam held up the head, opening the mouth to reveal the fangs. He went to test the sharpness with his finger, but the duchess jerked his hand away and then laughed at her own reaction. Tristam realized that the snake was unsettling to her.

"Shall we call it *Viperidae pallei*, Duchess?" he asked, trying to lighten the mood.

She laughed, a bit too loudly. "That may not be wise—though not inappropriate, of course."

She fixed Tristam with her searching gaze, making Tristam wonder if she sensed his state. Perhaps she felt something similar herself. Osler had admitted to not being himself earlier.

"Shall we walk along the beach?" the duchess asked. "It feels so good to stretch one's legs."

Duchess and naturalist set out along the edge of the bay. They held their silence as they went, only stopping to view a pod of porpoises through Tristam's glass.

When they were far enough down the beach that no one would be able to guess even the tone of their conversation, they sat on the trunk of a fallen tree. They watched a flock of terns feeding over the calm water, crying out and diving, then leaping nimbly back to wing.

The silence did not bother Tristam, who still felt nothing—not even the things he would expect to feel when alone with the duchess.

"I know you are upset about what happened with Julian. I am myself." The duchess broke the silence, trying to guess what was on Tristam's mind. As she spoke, she watched his eyes carefully, as though she was ready to change what she would say, adjust the emotional tone, depending on his reaction. "Tristam,

I want you to know I did not give Julian instructions to harm Kreel. I just wanted to be sure you were safe. The man tried to murder you at Bird Island; do not doubt it. And Julian claims it was Kreel tried to kill *him* in the heat of battle. He showed me the most gruesome bruise on his shoulder—another man would have had shattered bones." She reached out and squeezed his arm. "But we stopped the worst from happening."

"No," Tristam said, surprised by how flat his voice came out. "The worst happened anyway. Dakin. Kreel swears that, in the smoke, Julian killed Dakin, mistaking him for Kreel."

The duchess put her hands over her mouth. "Do we know he's telling the truth?"

Tristam shrugged. "No. Kreel's word, only. But Dakin's skull was crushed by a severe blow. The Jacks think he got in the way of the gun when it reared back." Tristam paused for a second. "If I question them more closely, they will certainly wonder why. They may be uneducated, but they're not all fools."

"*Say nothing, please*," she almost whispered. The duchess turned her gaze away from Tristam, staring out over the bay. Her anguish was genuine, Tristam was sure. And for the first time that day he felt a trace of human emotion—compassion.

For several moments they sat silently together, Tristam feeling that vast gulf that sometimes opened between two people, like a fault in the earth.

The duchess reached out and took his hand again. "What you saw in the dark—he struggles against his nature, Tristam." She whispered now, her voice pleading. "Kreel *must* have provoked him. The damage to Julian's shoulder is very real. He . . ." Her eyes closed tight. Tristam watched; the odd sense of being removed from the world began to dissolve slowly.

"Surely you can see, Elorin, that he is unnatural?"

"Yes," she said emphatically. "And you have no idea the anguish this brings him. Separated from us, always. He knows he is not like us, that if people knew his true nature. . . . That is why he has learned to control it. He would give anything to be like us. Like you, Tristam. You see how he has created this persona: the good-natured fool. It intimidates no one. He can move freely through society. He is terribly handsome and women are drawn to him. They sense he is hiding something—some secret. It is part of his allure. If ever they find out what it is . . . they are gone, terrified. But he is not without feeling, Tristam. These women hurt him. His situation is agonizing. He hunts often, knowing that much of his need is dissipated in that.

"He did not set out to injure Ipsword, Tristam. Yes, I know what everyone said. It *was* less than an accident—but less than intentional, as well. His nature . . . it is complex."

Tristam never thought he could feel sorry for this woman, so strong and so vibrantly alive, but he felt sorry for her now. Clearly she allowed Julian an occasional lapse—an expression of his "true nature"—as long as it was someone like Ipsword or Kreel . . . or Dakin. Someone of little consequence, in her scheme of things. Had she not called him a fool for risking his life to save Pim? Tristam felt a little ill.

She squeezed his hand.

I don't want to be drawn into this, he realized, *watching out for her unnatural brother.*

Already he had become too involved, not telling Stern about Kreel's claim—about Dakin. *An accident of battle,* the duchess clearly thought, Kreel more responsible than her precious brother.

She looked so very fragile, suddenly, clinging to his hand as though afraid he might abandon her—now that he knew. He had only the word of Kreel. . . .

"Men are killed in battles," Tristam heard himself saying, his pity for the duchess winning out. "Kreel is no saint. He would have no reason to tell me the truth."

The duchess nodded quickly. For a second she moved closer to him, resting her forehead against his shoulder, caressing his back. But then she pulled away, afraid they might be seen.

Tristam looked for some change of subject. "Did Stern give you a difficult time this morning?"

"Does everyone know?"

"By now? Probably. Osler told me."

She raised her eyebrows and forced a smile. "It was much the same conversation that took place after his parley with the marauders. But he was more adamant this time. He is determined not to move the ship an inch farther until he knows why the Entonne were after you." She looked at Tristam now, her anguish passing, the vivacity quickly returning. "My previous explanation does not seem to have satisfied him. I believe Stern thinks *you* unnatural, Tristam."

Receiving the same description as the viscount would normally have unsettled Tristam, but not that day. "But I am unnatural; don't you know? My uncle was a mage. Governor Galton believes I caused the voice at the Ruin. A whale rose out of the sea and offered to take me on its back. A falcon marked the break in the reef—the same bird that came to me at sea. And it is a longer list than that. You believe it as well, don't you, Elorin?"

Stern has made his attempt, Tristam thought, *so I will add to the pressure.* He still felt that the world around him was devoid of its normal emotional resonance. He could think and say things that he would usually not even contemplate.

"This is no time to jest, Tristam," the duchess said, but Tristam could see the change in her face. She looked at him oddly—apprehensive, perhaps.

"'We follow Tristam's course, now'" he said quietly, watching for her reaction. This did not give her pause, as he expected.

"You have taken to listening at my door?"

"No. I came upon Hobbes bent over the stern rail one night. Embarrassed him terribly, for he was listening to your conversation. I heard my name. You know how it is when you hear others speaking of you." He shrugged.

The duchess stood and walked to the edge of the bay, her gaze cast down. She crouched, pulling back her sleeve, and retrieved a shell from the water's edge, shaking it and her hand dry as she returned. She held it up to Tristam.

"*Terebra maculata*," Tristam said. "The spotted borer."

The duchess turned the shell over in her hands. "Nature usually achieves such perfection," she almost whispered, and then she looked out over the bay.

"You said, a moment ago, that my brother was unnatural—and you were right. But if even my dearest friend had suggested that to me years ago, I would have slapped their face. I would have shouted them into silence. Of course they would have been as right as you, but I was not ready to hear the truth then.

"Despite the empiricists' vaunted objectivity I don't think you would have listened to me before now." She turned to see how Tristam had taken her words. "I showed you the letter from Galton. I am not certain what Palle and Galton and their group are doing. Obviously, they have another use for *regis*, or believe they have. It has something to do with your great-uncle and Eldrich, and the Ruin on Farrow—as surprising as *that* may seem. Galton called you 'the candidate we have sought for so long' but I understand they have another name for you as well. They call you their 'lodestone,' Tristam, and have sent you on this voyage to seek out something they want. *Regis* is part of this, but I think there is more. They believe you are 'charmed' in some way, and I am beginning to agree. Even Stern suspects this." She fell silent, watching Tristam, her beautiful green eyes revealing nothing now.

"Why were the Entonne after me?"

"Because you set a rose afire in my dining room," she said without hesitation. "I am to blame, Tristam. I never would have suspected Bertillon. Massenet, you see, has agents everywhere. If I had realized what Bertillon was up to. . . ." She shook her head. "It was a test, I believe. Did you recognize that language? The nonsense rhyme?"

Tristam shook his head.

"Neither did I. I fear the Entonne know more than perhaps even Palle and his group."

"Flames," Tristam heard himself mutter.

"Exactly. But you see, Tristam, that is why I was forced to come. His Majesty's needs are of little importance to Palle. He has other concerns. And, I say this honestly, I was worried about you. I don't know what they expect of you, but I fear it." She looked around the quiet bay as though it were not the place of refuge it had been named. "I have become suspicious of any coincidence—especially where you are concerned. I have begun to suspect even the winds. I wonder how the Entonne found us on so large an ocean. I wonder why we have come to this place. I fear where we might go. We must proceed with such care. I don't know what Roderick wants of you, but I am afraid that you might accomplish it and we would not even know." She looked over at Tristam, concern clear on her face. "Keep the viscount close, Tristam. Please."

She must have sensed his revulsion.

"You are safe from him. Julian would lay down his life for you, Tristam."

"Why would he do that?" Tristam found the thought appalling.

"Because I have asked him to protect you. And because he does not value his life, overly. And because he admires you, Tristam. He knows you are good and honorable, and intelligent, and that you have an open heart. All of the things he would choose for himself—had he been able to choose.

"Your good nature has even won over the superstitious Jacks, who think, now, that you are their good luck charm and that no harm can befall the ship while you are aboard."

"They don't know that the marauder was after no one but me," Tristam said, a little bitterly.

The duchess shrugged. "Even if they did, they would likely justify it somehow. Resent the Entonne for trying to steal their good luck, or some such thing. Once people have truly taken an individual to their heart, that individual can do no wrong. Look at the terrible rulers who have been adored by their subjects."

Yes, Tristam thought, *and look at your own relations with your brother, Duchess.*

"But what about Stern?" Tristam asked suddenly.

"I am not sure." She fell into contemplation for a moment. "He is not ready for the truth—so far as we know it. I tried to tell him about Bertillon and the rose but he thought that I mocked him. He would have none of it." She shook her head—an admission of error. "Stern is not old enough to have fought in the last war, but, even so, the navy men consider the Entonne their natural enemy. This incident with the marauder has unsettled him deeply. I tried to use that to convince him that our voyage is of more importance than he was led to believe. I am not sure what he will do." She looked up at Tristam. "Although an officer, and a man of some education, Stern is, in his way, as superstitious as the Jacks. He has half a mind to leave you at the Queen Anne Station, just to have you off his ship. But at the same time I think he is afraid that this action might bring him bad luck.

"I tried to convince him that without a trained naturalist we could never hope to find Kingfoil. He is sure there are things I am not telling him—despite the fact that when I tried to tell him what I knew he would not listen. He is not ready. I think he will spend a few days here, stalling, hoping that one of us will tell him a 'truth' he can accept. He knows that this is the one area where he has leverage: I want the voyage to proceed as quickly as possible, and he has it in his power to thwart me. He might do it simply out of frustration, or resentment."

What explanation would Stern have believed, Tristam wondered? The man had almost accused Tristam of being . . . unnatural. And yet he refused to believe the duchess' story. Did Stern know something that Tristam did not?

Tristam realized that *he* did not believe that what the duchess had just told him was the truth—or perhaps she had told him the best lie: half the truth. There were things she was keeping back, yet. But she would not tell more now, he was certain of that.

The duchess seemed to rouse from her thoughts for a second. "I am not sure what to do about Hobbes." She shook her head as though rejecting some idea. Silence again. The distant sound of the Jacks calling out—the long rending crack of a tree falling, its final crash to the beach, branches breaking.

So marks the arrival of men to paradise, Tristam observed.

"I had an odd conversation with Llewellyn," he said quietly. "Something else you should know." He told the story of finding the doctor in his cabin and then of their conversation earlier in the day. The duchess turned her shell over and over in her hand as she listened, and when he was done she flung the shell into the bay.

"That explains some things," she said, and no more. Picking up the orchids Tristam had given her, the duchess went to the water's edge. She crouched down suddenly on the narrow strip of wet beach that followed the ebbing tide. Very deliberately, she set the blossoms on the surface, like a child would do—to see if they would float—and when they did not sink, she let them go and, gently, the current drew them away. She stood to watch them go, standing very still for many minutes, all of her attention taken up by the flower's voyage.

"Such perfection," she said quietly, but without resignation.

The journal of Tristam Flattery:
This seventeenth day of December, 1559.

> *It has been a day of strange conversations and experiences. My emotionless state seems to be slowly giving way and the return of "feeling" brings me great relief.*
>
> *I do not know which I found more strange, the duchess comparing me to her brother, or her admission that she believes we have not come to this place—to any place, in fact—by accident.*
>
> *If I am indeed a "lodestone," what is it that I seek? I would turn aside, but I'm now afraid that any course I take will be the one predestined. I am*

almost afraid to take a step. This area of the Archipelago no longer seems the pristine and innocent new world, but has begun to seem ominous, forbidding, full of secrets. I wish we had not come here. I wish I had not taken ship at all.

✑ Thirty-Seven

Stern showed no signs of moving the *Swallow* from Refuge Bay, and on the third day he sent out the boats to begin a survey of the area. As ship's naturalist, Tristam went along and was left on one island or another so that he might determine something of the geology and add to his rapidly growing collection.

Names were given to prominent features of geography as they were added to the chart and Tristam soon had an island named for him *(Flattery Island)*, as well as a headland *(Professor's Point)*; the latter he thought would give visitors pause for as long as the name persisted.

When he could not manage to avoid it, Tristam was burdened with the company of the viscount on these outings and it was all he could do not to show his discomfort. Not that Julian acted any differently—he remained utterly good-natured—and he was eager to assist, carrying large loads without complaint. Tristam soon found that he could not accomplish nearly as much without the man. But Tristam could not forget what he had seen that night on the bowsprit, nor could he stop wondering about the fate of Dakin.

On the third day the *Swallow* lay to her anchor in Refuge Bay the lookouts spotted a sail out on the Gray Ocean. It was well beyond the reef and to the north, so distant that they could not say with assurance that it was the marauder; though no one seemed to think it could be another. And this meant Stern would definitely not move to go north.

The evening of the third day—a day when the naturalist had managed to get away without the viscount—Tristam returned to the ship late. While the others went to find their hammocks, Tristam spread the result of his day's effort on the afterdeck in the dull light of the ship's lanterns. He, too, was in a frenzy of assigning names, and so far had named a particularly beautiful flowering bush for Jaimy's fiancée, a bird for his uncle (the Blackwater finch), a new species of willow for Dandish, and this was barely a beginning. This day's haul had been particularly rich. In the poor light he entered his findings in a notebook beside the date, location, and a brief description of the habitat.

Since the day after the battle the state of Tristam's emotions had continued to be odd. The feeling of numbness persisted, but then he would have waves of intense feeling—anger, joy, despair—and these were completely beyond his control. They would last minutes sometimes, hours occasionally. And then the strange emotional silence would return. He felt his emotions ebbed and flowed like tides, but were not subject to the regulation of sun or moon.

Tristam tried to keep his mind on his work, hiding his state as best he could, hoping he would wake one day with his equilibrium restored. Tales of men returning from the wars and acting strangely for years, going mad sometimes, began to haunt him.

A faint shadow fell over Tristam's notebook as he wrote and he looked up to find the Viscount Elsworth standing above him.

"From the duchess," the man said, proffering a small envelope.

The viscount did not leave after he had made his delivery, as Tristam expected, and a second of awkwardness ensued. The lamplight flickered orange on the viscount's face, giving it a garish cast, and causing it to change and vary. It was an eerie effect.

"I missed you this morning," Tristam offered, trying to sound at ease. "I'm not sure where you got to."

The viscount nodded. A longer silence. "Do you know the true difference between you and me, Tristam?" he asked quietly, his voice completely natural.

The naturalist found that he shook his head, not quite sure he had heard correctly. *What?*

"I am more in control of where I go and what I do. It is not *you* that should fear my company." Saying this he nodded, stepping back out of the lamplight, and then disappeared below.

Tristam stood, looking after the viscount. "Blood and flames," he whispered. "The man is a ghoul." He felt a quick flaring of intense resentment. *Unnatural.*

Farrelle save me, Tristam thought, *look who I have become brother to!*

Remembering the letter, he tore open the envelope as though it offered an escape from the viscount.

My Dearest Tristam:

I have moved ashore into a commodious new abode—a tent—for the duration of our stay in this place. Although the stern captain has set sentries to watch over me, I don't think they are as devoted to their duty as one might expect. I'm certain that any man who could swim and made his way to my tent by the western approach would never be seen—a situation of great concern to me. Might I have a visit from you soon? Your explorations are of great interest to me.

Yours,
Elorin

Tristam hesitated for only a second, and then he began throwing his specimens into a bag. Morning would be soon enough to deal with these. In a moment he had stored the bag in his cabin, locked the door, and was back on deck.

Slipping past the anchor watch was not difficult, and Tristam went quietly over the side and into the cutter. He paused there to look down at the opaque surface of the bay. Stars hung, suspended in the calm waters, a mirror to the depths of the heavens. Thoughts of what might swim in those waters caused not the slightest ripple of fear and Tristam slipped, seal-like, among the stars.

The bay was surprisingly warm, the water seeming dense to him, as though it were some other liquid with a different viscosity. As silently as possible, he began to paddle toward the shore. He felt the depths below him as something tangible, like a presence. The increased coolness of the water at the low point of his kick seemed, in its way, like the heat one felt from another body in the darkness—there was much life below. A thought of the great whale swimming near him in the ocean caused Tristam to suddenly pull his limbs in as though the fetal position would protect him.

He almost turned back to the ship in a panic. *Why is this happening to me?*

With an act of will he forced himself to swim on. *I will be afraid of the dark next*, he thought. *But how can I control this ebb and flow of emotion?*

The shore couldn't be far. The coals of a fire glowed on the beach and a jagged line of blackness cut off the stars at the edge of the forest. Tristam focused on the dark area of the knoll and thought of being in the duchess' arms, which did not excite him as he thought it should.

If anything can reawaken my emotions, Tristam told himself, *it is the duchess.*

He kept this focus for perhaps a hundred feet, then he felt turbulence beneath him.

"*Blood and flames!*" Tristam cried aloud. He spun about searching the surface for some movement, but there was nothing. Steeling his will he forced himself on, his belly and genitals feeling suddenly very exposed.

A few more strokes and he heard the sound of voices—the Jacks camped on the beach—a comforting moment of laughter.

Turbulence again. Something broke the surface a yard behind, causing him to spin around.

"*Blood and . . . !*" Tristam spat out. A dolphin released its breath into the air, accompanied by a squeal. Another surfaced a few feet away, and then another. The air was full of the rank smell of rancid fish oil and the squeals and squawks of the dolphin tongue. They began to gambol around him, splashing water into his face and brushing by him so closely he felt the occasional rub of soft skin. Tristam could sense their excitement, like children greeting a loved one.

A man! A man among us in the dark waters!

Glowing green trails of phosphorescence marked the dolphins' passing, and these would swirl into confusion and then fade away, only for another to appear, and then another.

He controlled his breath and swam on, his heart banging inside his ribs, beating against the water's pressure on his chest. The beasts swam about him at such speed in the dark waters that he was afraid they would strike him—but remarkably they did not.

A few more strokes and he was close enough to shore to stand. The dolphins continued to play around him, swarming about his legs, their motions more frenetic now, their voices more insistent.

Do not go yet! You have just arrived.

But I cannot live among the race of dolphins, Tristam thought, stood a moment and walked into the shallows, leaving the gamboling mammals behind. For a second he stopped and turned back, looking for them in the dark, but it only seemed to take a second for them to forget him, and they were away.

He stepped up onto the beach and collapsed for a moment, catching his breath, calming his beating heart. Then, dripping, he hurried along the sand. The rocks and moss of the knoll passed underfoot, first coarse and brittle, then soft and yielding. The white of a tent appeared in the dark, its shape blurred, apparitional.

Tristam paused, looking for the sentry, listening for sounds, but heard nothing. The man would be on the knoll's opposite side where there was some chance of a drunken sailor coming from the camp on the beach. Such men would not venture into the forest at night for fear of the unknown, and they did not swim, so guarding the beach was all that was required.

Sure that no one stirred, Tristam went toward the white haze of the tent, which seemed to float on the rise of land. The door was only a flap and after a few seconds of exploration Tristam was able to pull it aside. Inside was utter darkness. He listened but could hear no sound of breathing.

"*Friend or foe?*" came a whisper.

"It is Tristam." In the darkness he could not see her, but the rustle of coverlets led him.

The duchess had risen to greet him and she giggled when she touched his skin. "You are sopping! Have you swum the fierce Bosapool for me, my love?" she teased.

Tristam was feeling decidedly chilled now for he wore only his soaking breaches. He was about to ask for a square of cotton when the duchess pressed herself close to him, stroking him almost fervently. She kissed his chest and then peeled off his breaches—and drew him further into the darkness.

At first Tristam was afraid he had made a terrible mistake, for he did not seem to react to the duchess' attentions, and then suddenly something awakened in him, but not the feelings Tristam associated with his heart. His breath came hard, and he felt that mysterious force take hold of him—desire. It washed through him and he felt as though he were in the surf, in the soft clutches of something overwhelming. It lifted him and he tumbled and turned, disoriented, losing his sense of time.

It might have been the middle of the night, Tristam did not know. The duchess lay beside him and they spoke in whispers. It was the first time Tristam felt that they were lovers, lying close, sharing their thoughts, making absurd jests, stifling their laughter. He hoped morning was not near.

The duchess nestled her head into his neck, hair tickling Tristam's face. "Is it difficult? To swim, I mean?"

"Not difficult. The human body is buoyant. Boran estimated that less than fifteen pounds of floatation would keep the average man aswim. So it takes a little effort to stay on the surface and some small amount more to move forward. Easily learned once the fear is conquered. Did I say that I swam among the dolphins on my way from the ship?"

"You did not!" She pulled back a little as though to look at him, but darkness was too complete. "You're not teasing me?"

"Not at all. They came and played about me as I swam, so close that I felt them brush against me on occasion. They had no fear at all and wear the softest skin you can imagine."

"You have the softest skin I can imagine. It must have been a feeling like no other."

"It was too dark to see much. I couldn't even tell the species, let alone make any useful observations, though it was remarkable how quickly they swam and how close they came and yet not once did we collide. What eyesight do they have that would allow this?" He would have fallen to musing, but the duchess interrupted his thoughts.

"You are a hopeless empiricist," she chided him. "You have such an experience and it sets you wondering about their senses! Are you always like this, Tristam? Do you make mental notes as we have love? Will you publish your findings? *An Inquiry into Copulation in the Human Species* by Tristam Flattery, Esquire." She bussed his cheek. "You are no poet, Tristam Flattery, I will tell you that much.

"You do me an injustice," he whispered close to her ear. "I am transported when we have love. My mind has room for nothing else."

"Ah, Tristam, occasionally you do say what a woman wants to hear." She kissed him tenderly.

An owl hooted and in the silence Tristam was sure he could hear the *"pooshh"* of a small whale blowing in the bay. It came to Tristam that he could not have moments like this with the duchess without the burden of her brother: one did not come without the other.

"Julian gave you my note, I suppose?" she asked, suddenly, as though she had sensed his thoughts. "Did he tell you about today's discoveries?"

"No."

"There is some debate, I understand—I think only you will be able to say one way or the other—but they found what might be stone work on a point of land."

"Stone work?"

"Yes. Though Osler thinks it is a natural formation of some kind—and that would seem most likely."

Tristam thought for a moment. "The Archipelago is largely unexplored, but in the known sections we have found no signs of men. It is likely nothing." Tristam felt a tug of anxiety. What had brought him to this place? A marauder. A falcon. A white squall.

"I'm sure you're right. The other discovery will interest you more, for I'm sure it's real. There is apparently a smoking volcano a few miles off. That might reveal something significant of the islands' geology."

"Now that is news." Tristam felt his interest kindle. "All I have seen is stratified rock raised up out of the sea. Today I found fossils in stone at three thousand feet—fossils of sea creatures. A volcano I will have to see."

The duchess began to kiss his neck, and then his ear. She pressed herself to him, running a finger along the curve of his neck. "I thought that young men on voyages were said to be insatiable when they finally reached land. . . ."

"Absolutely true. I was only acting out of consideration for the Duchess' dignity and years."

She grabbed hold of his hair close to the scalp and shook his head gently. "I'll show you how advanced I am in years, you insolent wretch."

The journal of Tristam Flattery:
This twentieth day of December, 1559.

The islands are yielding up their secrets: a new and noble species of Quercus (which I have been all but forced to name the Elsworth oak: Quercus elsworthi). (If I find a new beech I shall name it for Beacham! The Beacham beech!) A vole, I believe (I shall have to get some more expert opinions in classification in some areas. Oh how I miss Professor Dandish.) A variant of the peregrin falcon: not a new species I am sure, though lighter in color and smaller in size. Some striking butterflies and another beetle. Only just missed a snake of the most lurid green: too quick for me, especially as I did not know if it would prove a poisonous variety. All in all a grand day.

I want to have a look at this stone formation the survey party found, though I'm sure it will amount to nothing. Still, it would be the find of the decade if it was the work of men. I am subject to the emotional tides even yet. Three days now. I hope it will not last much longer. Had an evening like no other, this night. Daylight is not far off now, but I don't want to sleep—don't want to let this feeling escape.

⌒ Thirty-Eight

Alissa Somers had never felt so entirely divided in her life. Her mind told her that she was managing perfectly and that only someone who knew her well could guess the truth—but inside she was quaking. She felt so completely out of place. Reminding herself that these were merely people, far less accomplished than many of her father's guests, did no good. In the company of famous empiricists and scholars she was at home—in the midst of aristocrats she felt her confidence evaporate like spilled preserving spirits. And this left her with a tiny echo of a question: had her confidence always been so illusory?

I should not care so that they approve of me, she chided herself. But these were Jaimy's people and she found she did care, though her father would be appalled to hear her say such a thing.

Alissa had been left in the company of three of Jaimy's female cousins her own age—nieces of the duchess, Jaimy's mother—and though Alissa was certain this had been done to make her feel more at ease, the plan was not working. It was difficult for her to believe these . . . *girls* could, in fact, be her own age. She was certain that she had never been so . . . well, *girlish,* so concerned with trivial things. It was almost impossible to keep her attention on the conversation and she found herself scanning the crowd, praying for Jaimy's return. Suddenly she brightened.

"Oh, please do excuse me. There is an old friend of my father's. I must say hello." And with a perfect curtsy she swept off, leaving the "girls" to discuss her in her absence she was sure.

"Mr. Kent?"

The man in the old style wig turned around and his kindly face took on a look of the greatest joy. "Miss Alissa, I have been so looking forward to giving you my congratulations in person! I will say that this young lord is more fortunate than he deserves by a great deal. Does he have any idea how lucky he is?"

Alissa was surprised at how soft his lips were when he kissed her hand, holding it with obvious affection. Kent actually was a close friend of her father's, and in years past had been often at their home.

"I believe I am the fortunate one, Mr. Kent," she said, believing every word. "And even more fortunate now, for I have found you and we can have a real conversation." She cast a look over at the gossiping nieces, glad to have made good her escape.

The Duke and Duchess of Blackwater, Jaimy's parents, were having their annual celebration of the duchess' birthday—no small affair—and everyone with claims to being anyone in Farr society was in attendance, including the Prince Kori and the Princess Joelle, though they had made their appearance and already departed—their visit being brief, not out of disrespect for the duke and duchess, but because the members of the Royal Family were aware that their presence had an inhibiting effect on such gatherings and took the focus away from the person in whose honor the celebration was planned.

"You can have a real conversation here, if you are determined and know precisely whom to approach." Kent waved a wrinkled hand toward a man by the windows. "The Marquis of Sennet is one of the four most skilled ornithologists in Farrland, and a fine and interesting man as well. Ask him about his study of the nesting habits of *Falconiformes* and you shall have all the 'real' talk you can possibly manage.

"Or if you would rather talk politics and the affairs of nations, there are any number of people present, foremost among them Sir Roderick Palle, of course, and the Chancellor of the Exchequer." He nodded toward the King's Man, who stood by the fireplace, gesturing with a wineglass to a very small man. "But then I think it is *bivalvia* that is your particular interest, if I am not mistaken?"

Alissa wondered what he could possibly mean and then she realized—the Society meeting.

Kent went on quickly. "Oh, do not look so concerned. Your secret is safe with me." He lowered his voice. "But surely you did not think you could hide such charms from everyone? I pray you take care with such adventures, Miss Alissa. I am in complete sympathy with your father's and no doubt your own, position. I should like nothing better than to open attendance at Society gatherings. But do be careful, there are others almost as aware of small details as painters. A small curl escaping from beneath a wig will eventually alert someone." And then, as though her surprise were enormously gratifying, he laughed quite heartily. He had caught her out and was quite pleased with himself. Alissa's relief was great, and his mirth so genuine and fully felt, that she found herself laughing as well—sharing the jest.

"There," the painter said wiping a tear from the corner of his eye, "now you look less like a frightened fawn and more yourself." Motioning with his head toward the room in general he went on. "An impressive company, is it not? The Earl of Mandbridge and his countess. . . ." He stood taller, casting his gaze around the room. "And his mistress—the plump woman over there. The one with too much rouge and the ghastly jewelry. Of course they are near paupers you know—they've spent everything. Only the largesse of relations stands between the earl and the gutter. And they are not the only ones here in that situation. Do you see that very lovely young woman over there? The one looking around, rather sadly? She searches for her husband, who has disappeared with the wife of the drunken gentleman by the window."

He bent his head slightly toward her so that Alissa could smell the powder in his wig. "Never," he said firmly, "be intimidated by a person because of the size of house in which they were born." He nodded at her, as though confirming this advice.

Alissa felt a wash of warmth toward the old man. He had sensed her state and was making a valiant effort to make her feel more comfortable. Alissa had known Kent so long that she had learned his tricks over the years; his appearance of being a little inept in this effort to put her at ease was part of the design, part of the charm of the man. People were often deeply touched by his apparently simple and open manner. Even Alissa, who had long been aware of his subterfuge, had enormous affection for him. He always meant the best.

"Mr. Kent, I am sure you are the kindest gentleman in all of Farrland," she said.

"You have no idea how much gentlemen dread hearing those words from the mouths of young women. It is like a sentence. 'Old, old.' And I have been hearing them now for some considerable sum of years." He shook his head, but she could see that he still smiled.

Alissa drew herself up primly. "But, Mr. Kent, I am engaged to be married. I have my reputation to think of. Put yourself in my place, sir."

This made him chuckle, and she was glad.

"Why, Miss Somers, you are the kindest betrothed woman in all of Farrland, and beyond I think." He cast his eye around the room for a second with that look of great affection he almost always wore. A man at peace with his world, she thought.

"But of course if it is real conversation that you want, I should not send you elsewhere and lose the opportunity myself." He looked down at her, the wrinkles appearing around his eyes as he smiled. Wrinkles from a life of joy, Alissa thought, not from care.

"I will tell you something of great interest," Kent began, and the change in his manner suggested that he was no longer merely playing—this *was* a matter of real interest. "Have you read Chatterton's journals?"

Alissa had not, though she was dying to do so. Chatterton had been the great novelist and pamphleteer of the older generation—Kent's generation—and now, more than ten years after his death, his sister was overseeing the publication of his journals and letters. It was the type of event that delighted the educated of Farrland. Editions would be snapped up faster than the printer could create new ones.

"Well, I have read the first volume," Kent stopped, his look distant, "and I can tell you that Chatterton's writings have been expurgated . . . sanitized."

"You knew him," Alissa said flatly, not meaning it as a jest. Kent knew everyone.

"Oh, yes. I knew him well, I think. Well enough that he occasionally read me excerpts from his works in progress and from his journals. Brilliant, irreverent, scathing toward pretension. The man really was a genius." Kent stopped, looking down at the shine on his boots. "But his sister, Mrs. Hidde, has taken her own pen to his works. It is a crime. The efforts of his lifetime—a life of thought and insight . . . gone."

Alissa could see genuine anger taking hold of the man. She had not thought Kent could be anything but pleasant, but then she understood his resentment—it was a terrible thing.

"And the great man's thoughts have been replaced by the woman's own . . . insipid maunderings! Do you believe it? She has taken her brother's journals and used them as a stage for her own empty ideas. Now there's a heresy for you. She should be thrown on the pyre herself."

Alissa felt her own anger begin to flow. Injustice was something a Somers could not bear. "What has been done with his actual writings, do you think? Has Mrs. Hidde destroyed them?"

"I pray not, but nothing she did would surprise me now." Kent took hold of himself, pushing his sudden anger down. "Can you imagine a worse travesty?"

At that very moment Alissa could not. "I believe the works of great minds belong to every thinking person, Mr. Kent. They should never be shut up, altered, denied. It is like cutting out a man's tongue, and worse, for Mr. Chatterton is dead and cannot defend himself."

Kent nodded, casting his glance around the room as though checking on his children. "And it is not the only case, not at all. I know of others. Too many, in fact."

The painter fixed his gaze on her, though not unkindly, searching her face. "I may even know of a similar incident very close to home. Could you, Miss Alissa, be enlisted in the undoing of such an injustice? 'The works of great minds belong to every thinking person,' you said. Do you have the courage of your convictions?"

Alissa found herself looking around, feeling more uncomfortable than she had all night. People stood so close by that she wondered if they could be overheard. Exactly how close to home did Kent mean? And whose home, exactly?

"I must hear more," she said, almost too quietly.

Kent cast his gaze around the room again, his look of great warmth cooling a little. "Of course I would never ask that you compromise your principles in any way." He must have sensed the source of her discomfort. But then he hesitated, too long, as though afraid to speak his request—making Alissa fear what it might be.

"I must ask that you treat what I say in confidence, whether you choose to answer yea or nay."

She smoothed a seam on her gown. "That, at least, I can agree to."

Kent nodded, approval not acknowledgment, she thought. "It begins with Erasmus Flattery. . . . I knew him somewhat." The painter wet his lips, speaking now very softly. "He told me, not long before his death, that he was engaged in a project of great significance, yet, according to his nephew, the duke, Erasmus left no notes or writings beyond a few monographs. It is my belief that the duke might not understand the importance or significance of his uncle's work. Oh, certainly the duke is a fine man, but not an empiricist, not a scholar. Families have hidden many things that they did not understand—novels written by wayward sons, important works of philosophy thought to be blasphemous texts. Many works suppressed by families for many reasons—most misguided." He looked around again, forcing a smile back onto his lips. "I think it is possible that the works of Erasmus did not simply disappear." He paused, catching her eye. Alissa could feel his yearning, but still he asked nothing specific of her.

She had hoped it would be a far more innocent request—some research at Merton College, perhaps. Something only her father might have access to. But this was Jaimy's family he was talking about.

Were there really extant works of the great Erasmus? This thought was almost spoken in her mind—as though her curiosity had its own voice.

She realized that Kent had considered carefully before choosing her. If it had not been Jaimy's family. . . .

"What you ask, Mr. Kent. . . ." She paused, knowing she must refuse. "It is more than a little presumptuous. I. . . ." She felt a wavering, confusion. She was a Somers at heart, and would remain so no matter what family she married into. "I will give it some consideration," her voice said quickly. "I can promise no more than that."

Kent nodded, showing no disappointment. "But we will keep each other's secret?"

"Torture could not drag it from my lips," she said, mock sincere.

The old man looked a bit alarmed. "I hope it will not come to that," he said softly.

Kent stood watching Alissa—as she made her escape. Was this a foolish risk? He had known Alissa Somers for most of her life and thought highly of her.

And this request he had made. . . . It was merely a hunch and would likely come to nothing. He also tried to comfort himself that, though she did not know it, Alissa was already caught up in this matter.

Kent stared at the walls, hung with overly-flattering family portraits. Ministers, admirals, King's Men, ladies of letters, but no Erasmus Flattery. It was telling.

She will help me, he thought.

A young couple greeted him as they passed.

She will help me and come to no harm, I'm sure. Not that he could afford to let his feelings about acquaintances get in the way of what must be done. Not now.

Sir Roderick caught his eye from across the room. The King's Man nodded, his smile tight-lipped but amiable.

I am quite sure I know your purpose here, Kent thought, *but are you equally aware of mine?* He could not say how dearly he hoped the King's Man still thought him, to quote a friend, "the kindest gentleman in all of Farrland."

Now where was this young lord? Not too far from his betrothed, Kent was certain. He should like a word with the young man before Roderick found him.

The painter discovered Lord Jaimas Flattery in conversation with the Marquis of Sennet. The two men were wedged into a corner of the library, where most of the well known empiricists and writers had gathered among their admirers. It was a sign of the times that these gentlemen and ladies had been invited to such an occasion.

"Mr. Kent," the marquis said, "we were just speaking of falcons, if you can believe it." The man beamed at the painter. Kent had always liked the way the ornithologist made mild mockery of himself and his own obsessions.

"You must know Lord Jaimas."

"I do indeed, Lord Sennet, and I have come to offer my sincere congratulations, for Lord Jaimas is about to marry a young woman I esteem very highly. Almost a niece, in fact."

Jaimas gave a slight bow, a smile spreading across his face. He looked more like his cousin than Kent had remembered.

"And I shall be proud to call you uncle, Mr. Kent, for anyone who thinks so highly of Alissa is as dear to me as a member of my own family."

Kent wondered exactly how great the similarity was between this young man and Tristam Flattery. Did Sennet say they were discussing falcons? He would have to corner the marquis later and find out just what had been said.

"And I have congratulations to offer, as well," the marquis said, lowering his voice, "though I must tell you, it is not yet official. But Sir Roderick assures me that you are to be raised up, Kent, granted a baronetcy by His Majesty. And more than well deserved, I might say. *Sir Averil Kent*. Does it not sound completely natural, Lord Jaimas?"

Kent was sure that the blood drained from his face. It seemed that Roderick Palle was more aware of him than he had hoped.

ᕯ Thirty-Nine

"Well?" Osler asked, impatient for a verdict.

Tristam bent over the rock formation, scraping away lichen. He shrugged, hoping that would be answer enough for a few moments.

Flames, Tristam thought. *Look at this!* The tide of his emotions had turned again and the hollowness was, at least for now, replaced by an irrational and rising sense of dread. The naturalist could not shake the feeling that the incoming tide of emotion flowed out of this jumble of stone and into his heart.

Ridiculous.

But so strong was this feeling that he feared it would soon overwhelm his reason altogether. It was all he could do to keep his mind focused on his efforts.

But look at it!

"Mr. Flattery?" It was Osler, his voice sounding odd.

Tristam realized that he had rocked back on his heels and crouched there, doing nothing but staring.

"Just thinking." Tristam did not move. "I will tell you one thing, Mr. Osler, the surrounding rock is altered volcanic, and this is very old marble."

Marble once hewn by men.

Tristam was of half a mind to lie. Tell them it was a natural formation after all. Get them out of here. Get *him* out of here.

All along he had thought the battle and close brush with death had affected his emotions but now he realized that this was not so: *it was this place.*

He looked around, hardly aware of the others staring at him. The islands of the archipelago spread around the horizon like the work of a great artist, their sweeping silhouettes and wavering reflections creating a composition of great beauty, Tristam was sure—but the scene did not seem beautiful to him. It was this place. . . . If Tristam was Palle's lodestone then the iron that drew him was buried here—or very nearby—he could feel it, somehow.

They had come here that morning, leaving the ship at first light, winding their way westward through the hidden channels of the Archipelago, and had slipped silently between islands until the cone of the volcano had appeared. That thin shroud of smoke had seemed terribly ominous to Tristam. And then they had landed here on this point and scrambled up to this jumble of rock . . . this unnatural formation.

A streak of sweat ran coolly down Tristam's neck. He looked up to find Osler standing over him silently, touching his lip with a finger as though exploring a sore—not looking at Tristam.

I am behaving oddly, Tristam realized—unsettling the others. The naturalist forced himself to stand, brushing hair back from his face.

"Who has the spade?" he asked, forcing his voice to sound normal—almost succeeding. But this place unnerved him completely.

Tristam pushed the blade into the soft earth, gingerly, stopping as soon as he felt resistance. In half an hour he handed this work over to a Jack who proceeded as Tristam had and the naturalist stepped back, crouching again; watching, feeling the dread still growing inside him. Each time the spade revealed more of the stone Tristam felt a bit more of his own facade was stripped away, exposing something unknown beneath. Revealing the creature who had been drawn to this place.

I am their lodestone. But what have I been led to?

More marble was revealed and Tristam shifted uncomfortably. He forced himself up again. Struggling against this incoming tide of feeling. Struggling to stay on its surface. He heard himself breathing raggedly.

Using his hands Tristam began to work at exposing rock. Everyone joined in as they could, even the most uneducated Jack a little in awe of the possibilities. They worked silently for the better part of two hours and it became more and more obvious to everyone that there was a regular shape to this formation.

"Well, Mr. Osler," Tristam said, finally. "Do you still think this natural?"

Osler stood for a second, looking down at the rock, his serious face suddenly a little sad. He shook his head. "No. Though what it is the remains of I cannot begin to guess."

Tristam nodded agreement. "It is very ancient, I think. Far older than our oldest cities." As he spoke he used a square of cotton to wipe the grime from a small white shard he had unearthed. He held this out in his hand, turning it in the sunlight. "Do you see this?" Tristam pushed the object on Osler. "It is a fragment of pottery. Do you see how fine it is? The ridges indicate that it was turned on a wheel. Those are the marks of the potter's hands." He found he shuddered as he said this, as though he had been touched by someone long dead.

A ghost.

Tristam looked around at the faces of the men present. They were as silent as mourners, unable to find words for something so momentous. Men had been here before them.

But why have I been led here? Tristam asked. *What is it Roderick wants me to find? Could there be Kingfoil in this place? Or is it something else altogether? Something perhaps even Roderick and his followers do not suspect?*

"If this were Farrland," Jack Beacham said quietly, "we would put a navigation beacon on such a point."

A few men gave half a laugh, but no more. Did they feel some of what Tristam felt?

Tristam tried to smile but could not. "It is as good a guess as any, Beacham."

He remembered the strange feeling that had almost overwhelmed him as the Ruin of Farrow had come into view. Turning, he tried to look off through the trees. The cone of a volcano lurked somewhere not far off—as on Farrow.

Osler set the fragment of pottery down on the stone work, suddenly. "We have our survey to continue. You will want to be left here, I should imagine, to continue searching. Meet you here two hours before sunset?"

Here. Yes, here. The feeling of dread surged in him like a sudden dark wave, but Tristam felt himself nod to the lieutenant. "Two hours before sunset."

I should go with Osler, he thought. *Run from this place.*

But some part of Tristam knew this would not work. His presence here had a sense of inevitability about it. If he went to some other island that would be the place he was meant to have gone.

Tristam realized suddenly that he was not afraid. Fear was not what was growing in him. He felt *dread,* which he had not realized was so different. Fear could make a man turn and run or not allow him to continue, but this feeling Tristam experienced was made up in large part of acceptance. Deep apprehension of what was to come, yes, but coupled with a knowledge that it could not be avoided. Roderick had set him off, searching, and he had been drawn to this point. To this island. Perhaps even on this very day. There was nothing that he could do.

The Jacks began to collect up their tools, quietly as though they had unearthed a sacred place. Or perhaps they were observing silence for Tristam and his companions who were to be left behind.

As they began to pick their way down the rock to the boat Tristam thought they resembled nothing so much as a burial party, armed with implements of their trade, respectfully silent.

"Mr. Flattery?"

Tristam turned to find Beacham staring at him.

"Are you well, sir?"

Tristam nodded, bending to lift the worn bag to his shoulder, and then set off to forestall further questions. Beacham had managed to have himself detailed to assist the ship's naturalist that day, so Tristam had a boy and a murderer for bearers—and he wondered if that was inevitable as well.

My faithful servant, Beacham . . . and this dark brother—both of us unnatural.

Tristam felt as though his movements were no longer managed by his own will but proscribed, the scene unfolding like history. The mountain, smoking vaguely at the island's center, did not help. It was like a presence, casting a shadow that followed them as they went.

What has happened to me, he wondered suddenly. Very recently I was an empiricist, struggling against ignorance and superstition. And now . . . ?

Am I sinking into madness? Is that what befell my father?

"It would be easier going along the beach, Mr. Flattery," Beacham offered. "Or do you plan to set a course inland?"

"The beach," Tristam said, knowing it did not matter.

They scrambled down the rocks of the headland onto a curving margin of sand that formed a wide bight in the island's flank. Here they trudged on, three abreast, Beacham stopping to retrieve shells and other bits of flotsam from the tide line. They made their way slowly, the midshipman bringing Tristam his finds like a faithful retriever.

At Beacham's insistence they stopped to wade in the shallows and cast a net. Tristam sat in the shade of a tree and stared at nothing, uninterested in the practice of his profession. Occasionally he glanced over to the midshipman and the viscount. Their activities seemed so normal that Tristam could not quite understand why he no longer felt like a ship's naturalist. It was as though these strange changes in his emotions had swept away the core that was Tristam. But who was emerging?

Finishing with their net Beacham and the viscount came and sat for awhile, eating in the shade of this previously-unknown species of tree, and then they set out again along the sand.

Thoughts of his night with the duchess began coming back to Tristam like fragments of a dream or long forgotten memories. He clung to these like a sailor grasping at the shrouds in a gale. Had he had love with the duchess only the night before? It seemed an age ago.

"Who is it has the cough?" the viscount asked, suddenly. "I thought he should hack his lungs up. I believe he kept me awake half the night. Have we taken aboard some new world consumption?"

Beacham kept his eye fixed on their surroundings, taking his duties seriously. "It is the physician, Lord Elsworth. Now that we are quietly in port his coughing can be easily heard. He has an illness of the lung, as I'm sure you've noticed. It strikes him down and then lets him be for a time. Last night was the worst I've heard." He was quiet for a few seconds. "Though it is the good doctor's nightmares that most often wake me. I have never known a man for nightmares like Doctor Llewellyn." He pointed off toward the crown of a nearby island. "Is that a kite, Mr. Flattery?"

Tristam studied the bird for a moment, little more than a black dot against the pale blue—a bit of animated punctuation that had taken wing from a page and was making its escape heavenward. A raptor, perhaps. A falcon?

"Only a gull, Mr. Beacham."

They walked on, Tristam separating himself from his companions so that he could have silence.

A headland rose up in front of them and they scrambled over the rock and into bush, climbing a short section of cliff. Here Tristam left his companions behind briefly, so convinced was he of the inevitability of the day that he could not believe he was meant to fall to injury. He had scaled the rock like a man who believed he could fly.

Beyond the headland they found another beach circling a shallow bay. It was some hours past noon, Tristam judged by the sun, for he had come away from the ship without his timepiece. The sun was passing into the west and the nearby islands were falling into shadow with only the highest points catching the direct light, creating subtle patterns in green and gray. The afternoon was perhaps more advanced than he had thought. The hour of their meeting with Osler was not so far off.

I will escape this place, Tristam thought suddenly. *Osler will come and take us away and nothing out of the ordinary will have happened.* But this thought did not alleviate the feelings he had borne all that day.

The songs of unknown birds filled the air and the wind spoke among the trees, a mysterious tongue. Small waves lapping the shore added to the discussion.

Along the beach, trees pressed close together, branches spreading in ways both familiar and slightly alien. New world trees filling niches similar to those at home.

Black willow, bayberry, and a species he did not know, stood near at hand. Bluejack oak spread its hardy branches in several places along the shore, and *Planera aquatica* grew near to a stream mouth. Tristam forced himself to name these as he went, like a litany. The litany of a man of reason. But they seemed only words—perhaps not even words but just sounds—arbitrary and a little absurd. Their meaning draining away at each repetition, as though it were dissipating like old magic.

They came to a stream, and Beacham dipped a finger in and tasted—apparently approved—and cupped his hands for a longer drink. The others did the same, for it was a warm day.

Crouching by the stream's edge Tristam's gaze followed the flowing water back into the trees where it descended a slope in small, regular steps. And there, perched on a branch, was a small owl looking down at him with large, dark eyes set within multiple rings; one black, one white, the next the color of dried blood. The body was whitish, and flecked in brown, almost rufous. Brown eyes stared back at Tristam sadly, blinking occasionally as though struggling against tears.

Beacham followed Tristam's gaze, and seeing the owl he stood suddenly, setting the bird to wing. It disappeared silently into the dark shadows of the wood.

The midshipman shuddered. "We had no need of *that.*"

"That was a new species," Tristam said, expecting to see the midshipman's face light up.

"New or old makes no matter, sir," Beacham said, his tone uncommonly serious. "It is terrible bad luck. Owls are often augurs of death, Mr. Flattery. There is no surer sign."

"Not even the cessation of breathing?" the viscount asked, but neither Tristam nor Beacham laughed.

Tristam began walking up the stream's edge, looking at the rock formation over which the water ran.

"Look at what regular steps this waterfall takes," Beacham said suddenly.

Unnatural.

Tristam stood staring up into the dark forest, listening to the ancient song of water running over stone. His companions joined him, all three gazing up the watercourse, which fell in even steps, each just less than a foot. The stream itself lay between stone banks, the low, steep bank on either side so covered in moss and fern that they seemed solid walls of vegetation.

Beacham stepped into the flow and mounted the first steps but Tristam found himself watching with a growing horror, and it wasn't fear that the boy would slip. The viscount moved away, examining the corner of the cliff, which was covered in mosses and fern. He pulled away a clump of green from a ledge and stood back.

"It is a slick stair," Beacham called out, "but it can be climbed."

Tristam turned away, suddenly feeling as though the incoming tide was winning. In a moment there would be no air to breathe.

Can I not refuse to go, he thought. Can I not stop what is unfolding?

The viscount swept away more vegetation, pulling free the clinging vines. Several ancient roots defied him but bare stone was appearing.

"What have I found, Tristam?" the viscount asked, his words jarring the naturalist. A root broke away suddenly and the viscount staggered back.

Beacham had stopped on the stair and was looking back down to his companions. "Surely this is not the work of nature," he said.

Tristam wanted to cover his ears, wanted to dive into the sea and swim away from this place, from these men who did not understand what they were doing. But he stood, fixed to that place, no more able to turn away than to take to the air.

Beacham came down from the falls and stood looking on. "Well, Lord Elsworth, you shall have your name in the history books yet. Do you see? There is an eye. And here would be its brow."

Tristam stepped back while the two cleared away more of the covering vegetation. He felt ill, suddenly, and sat heavily on the sand. He glanced up the waterstair, for he knew that's what it was—a stairway carved by the hands of men.

Why have I been led here?

As he sat there he felt the numbness begin to creep back in, as though the water flowing down the stair trickled into his soul.

Beacham and the viscount stopped to look at what their efforts had revealed. "Is it an animal?" the viscount asked.

"*Avifaunal*," Tristam answered. He did not even need to look. "A hawk. *Raptor. Ravisher. Plunderer*. And that is what befell this." He waved a hand at the rock. "It has been smashed by men." He turned away and gazed at the watercourse. It led up into the shadows of the primeval forest, into the heart of this mystery.

'*We follow Tristam's course, now.*'

"What does it lead to?" Beacham asked, his voice subdued.

The inevitable, Tristam thought.

"I don't know," Tristam said softly. "Let us follow your owl and see."

Water running over stone like an ancient song, the rock so worn now that the song had almost returned to its natural form. Still, there were vestiges of the regularity that the even steps had imposed but this was in the background now, a quiet harmony.

Tristam was reminded of the dream from his uncle's house on Farrow—pushing up a stair against an invisible current.

The three men went slowly up, concentrating on their footing, not speaking, their breath soon coming hard. The constant sound of water running and the wind in the trees were like whispers and sighs.

Tristam slipped and the viscount grabbed his arm, pulling him upright with that massive strength. Perhaps the man was here for that sole purpose.

In places the stairs had been eroded to mere irregularities and here the climbers were forced to drag themselves along the walls using rock or root or vine.

The stair continued up, its angle of ascent unvarying as far as Tristam could tell, for perhaps two hundred and fifty feet, making a slip potentially disastrous. Occasionally they halted their progress and examined sections of wall that were exposed through the covering of green. Once these surfaces had been richly carved, though time had effaced them.

A gust of wind moved the branches overhead causing patterns of sunlight to dart in a mad array across the stream and the underwood, and at the same time a haunting tone, like a deep note from a massive woodwind, sounded somewhere in the forest above. All three of them cringed as though this sound presaged some calamity, but the note ended in a dying fall, leaving only the sounds of water and breeze.

"Martyr's blood!" the viscount said. "I did not like the sound of that!"

They stood, rooted, for some minutes but when the sound was not repeated they worked up their nerve and went on. Beacham fell and slid several feet before he managed to catch himself, coming up wet and bruised and a little unnerved. He progressed more slowly after that, testing his footing with care.

Finally they came to a place where they could no longer see the stair ascending above them and Tristam felt as though a cold stone had grown in his stomach.

But when they reached what they took to be the stairhead it proved to be only a landing—thirty feet of level stone covered in water, and then the stair went up again, disappearing into the green of the forest.

Not far above this they found a natural arch of rock spanning the stair, and in this they could see a number of holes, natural or manmade they could not tell, but here could be heard an eerie breathy drone. They stood waiting and catching their breath for some time but there was no long note such as they had heard earlier and they pressed on.

Not thirty steps further the wind came up suddenly and, after a moment of vibration on the edge of audibility, the strange wail sounded again, causing them all to stop, jarred by the power of the sound so close to its source. Tristam had felt the note in his chest.

"I should not like to hear that on a dark night," Beacham muttered. "Why, it would stop the heart of a man thirty years at sea. Freeze the saltwater in his veins."

They pushed on and found that the rock wall had fallen away in one place, choking the stair with debris, and constricting the flow of water so that it rushed through a narrow gap, growing deep and swift. They wedged their way through this, dragging themselves over stone, afraid all the time that the rock would shift and the whole dam give way.

Around them a strange world was slowly being revealed. Massive ferns, twenty feet in circumference and taller than a man, sent out a hundred elegantly curving fronds. Unknown vines and flowers crept up trees, twisting about the trunks and branches like mad lovers intent on suffocation. Thick beards of moss hung from branches and spread in carpets over much of the ground. The sun fell in shafts through the dense canopy overhead, illuminating tiny portions of the forest as though nature were drawing attention to itself. *'Look. Do you see the perfection? Can you recognize the miracle?'*

The burble of water flowing down the giant stair drowned most other sounds so that the wind or the calls of birds seemed eerie and distant, marking their ascent with another note of strangeness.

As they went they surprised a water snake, which slipped silently into a crack in the wall, its long tail whipping once as it disappeared into the earth. After that they kept to the stair's center, proceeding in single file.

Under the arch of trees that overhung the great stair there appeared a crescent of sky, raising the hopes of the explorers.

"I hope it is not just another resting place," Beacham said, laboring in the rear. "Not that I couldn't use a resting place. . . ."

The naturalist should have felt the same—his legs were burning with the strain—but something forced him on now. It was as though he longed to get whatever was going to happen over with. He found he had taken the lead.

The final arch of trees was only yards away. Tristam glanced back and saw that his companions had stopped, bent double, gasping for breath. Tristam looked up at the blue sky framed in the portal.

He had been in the chill water so long that the cold seemed to have crept into his bloodstream. Tristam felt a certain detachment, as though he watched himself calmly from a safe distance.

I might not go on otherwise, he thought.

Best to have it done. He forced himself up the last steps, as though it were the finish of a race.

A blast of wind funneled up the stair, stirring the ferns and the branches overhead, sounding the long moaning note. A bird fluttered out of the trees above and Tristam thought he caught another glimpse of the owl—Beacham's owl.

With a final burst of energy Tristam stood upon the stairhead looking out over a topography of jumbled white stone and tangled forest. *A ruin*, he realized. *A lost city.*

Someone heaved himself up onto the stair at his side and cursed under his breath. Tristam realized that the viscount stepped away from him, his gaze fixed on Tristam, not the wonder before them. Unable to bear the accusation in the man's eyes, Tristam turned away.

What appeared to be a plaza opened up before them: paved in marble, utterly overgrown to either side with dense forest. A shallow stream ran from the plaza's opposite side where water fell between two stairways half-smothered in vines and mosses and tanglewood.

Beacham arrived at the stair head. "Well, sir," he said, his voice subdued by awe, "we shall be known all our lives for this discovery. I never dreamed. . . ." But he could not finish.

I dreamed, Tristam thought, *up a stair against an invisible current and then into an arbor. . . . I have come, Sir Roderick, but to what purpose?*

Before him spread the ruins of an alien city, overwhelmed by the forest, which sent columns of vines and roots twisting out onto the small remaining area of barren stone. Here they trapped soil carried by the wind and the rains and anchored this with scrub grasses and ground cover, patiently collecting enough soil for the trees—like courtiers preparing the way for their king's return. But beyond this small area the forest had pushed far into the city's borders in its relentless campaign to reclaim a lost kingdom.

There were no sounds of men, here; only the whisperings of the world of nature, which men often called silence. Tristam imagined he heard the language of the forest itself. *Have men returned? Are all our efforts to be undone?*

Around the small plaza the ruins of shattered buildings lay covered in a carpet of green, reminding Tristam of objects buried in snow, their true shapes disguised, in time to be lost entirely. But in places sections of stone wall could be distinguished—a window casement from which trailed a wild vine covered in exotic crimson blooms. The remnants of a high portico could be seen, tapering columns supporting a lintel and a roof of curling branches. Even the pale marble had begun to take on the colors of the forest, stained to pale shades of green and dusky brown.

Further on Tristam could see the city rising up to a second level and here the tumbledown ruins of truly massive structures stood, though they were now so covered in undergrowth they seemed almost natural outcroppings, part of the strange landscape.

Above the double stair, the top of an enormous building could be seen in the distance—higher than any other, almost a pyramid, flat-topped and stepped, crowned with a swaying tree, branches waving like a conqueror's banner. The triumph of the ancient wood over this abode of men.

Wind came up the water-stair again, voicing strange words—chanting an eerie tonal scale, and all three men moved away from the stairhead.

Areas of exposed stone lay to either side of the flowing stream—the result of regular flooding, Tristam surmised, swept clean by water—and they were glad to feel hot stone under foot. The gentlemen stooped to pull footwear from their bags but Jack Beacham was content to go barefoot.

Crouched down, pulling on his boots, the viscount could not take his eyes from the decaying city. "How long do you think it has been lying so?" he asked. "Abandoned."

Tristam ran his hand across the weathered paving stones, and looked around at the height of the trees, the overlying layer of soil. He shrugged. "Centuries? I don't know."

Here? To an ancient, abandoned city. Why?

The feeling of dread seemed to crest like a wave, and Tristam found himself walking on, nearly unaware of the movements of his body.

They skirted along the stream heading toward the double stair and the next level—what appeared to be the city proper—Tristam choosing this course without discussion, the others following. The sound of their boots on the stone did not echo but was muffled by the surrounding forest. Even so, Tristam could not help but feel the sound was terribly out of place, intrusive. The city did not seem merely empty and abandoned, but ominously so.

Beacham stopped before the half-hidden sculpture of a woman, which leaned out from the corner of a building, held from falling by dense vines. The three gazed up at the headless figure, her one remaining arm reaching out from among the sinuous vines and leaves like the last sight of one drowning. A spray of white flowers could have been wave crests.

The hand was perfectly rendered, and expressing such forlorn need that Tristam wanted to reach out and rescue the woman from the overwhelming forest. But they were too late—she had drowned long ago.

They went on.

Avenues branching off to either side were now choked with forest, the pale boles of curving trunks appearing here and there in the dense tangle of branches and leaves. These ancient streets curved back into the darkness of the wood like canals of vegetation flowing into an ocean of unbroken green. Streams that led into a mystery so old, and so well buried that men could no longer pass inside. Glints of stone appeared in places where the sun penetrated the canopy of green, and in some of these surfaces were shattered openings that Tristam found so disconcerting he could hardly bear to look at them, as though something would be revealed to him that he did not want to see.

He forced his attention back to the remains of the vast city that had once thrived here, to the scraps the forest had not claimed as its own. What race had dwelt here? What had been their commerce, their arts, their science?

He had been led to what might prove to be the greatest mystery known to man. He, Tristam Flattery. But why?

At length they came to a pool, perhaps thirty feet across, that lay at the base of the double stair, fed by a falls between the steps. Here, at least, the mystery of the water-stair was solved, for the pool was broken and choked with rock and gravel and debris from the forest.

"The water once fell into the pool and was likely carried off beneath the plaza by a conduit," Tristam said. "Our stairway was dry in the past." He waved at the ruin of the pool, water flowing through the broken rim out into the plaza. "Unless it was flooded intentionally for defense."

They stood for a moment looking back down the broad avenue with its shallow stream, the fallen buildings beneath their carpet of green to either side. Tristam did not know how his companions reacted, but his own feelings were torn between complete awe at such a discovery and this terrible sense of dread that had sent its tendrils into his heart the way the forest overwhelmed the ancient city.

At the stairhead lay a massive tapered pillar of black stone, broken in three. The width of the column was fully eight feet, two feet taller than Tristam as it lay, and in length perhaps fifty feet. Tristam ran his hand along the worn stone.

"Do you see?" he said, feeling he should break the silence. He sighted down the length. "A single piece of stone. Black marble. And once richly carved." What Tristam said was no doubt true, but whatever design had been etched into this stone was now all but lost to time.

The points where the column had been broken were now polished smooth by wind and rain. Tristam began to think that the city might have been lying abandoned far longer than he had imagined. Beacham wedged himself into the gap and climbed quickly up to the column's top where he scraped off some of the grasses and thin covering of detritus.

"It is not so different from the columns we saw at the Ruin on Farrow," the viscount said as he too pulled himself up onto the stone. "Though far greater in size."

"Yes," Tristam said, "but round columns can be found in our own antiquities. The shape is too obvious to confirm a link between the ruins."

Farrow. Races of men had preceded Tristam's own by centuries, perhaps millennia. He thought of the bottle of wine Borrows had given him. Were the vines carved on the Farrow Ruin depictions of Kingfoil?

Tristam went over to examine the base where the column had once stood. It was six sided, perhaps four feet in height and a dozen feet across. Each side had a sculpture in relief but they were all but gone now, and not just from the wearing of the years. Tristam was sure that men had made an effort to obliterate what had been carved here.

On one side he thought he found a constellation represented, and on another what might have been oddly shaped sails, doubly pointed at their peak.

He turned and stared out over the plaza. To either side, fifty yards apart, lay the ruins of two massive structures. A row of weathered columns stood before one, the lintel long since fallen and consumed by the forest. Neither structure was now more than three stories, Tristam thought, but their bases were enormous. Here and there green hummocks jutted above the trees suggesting that once the buildings had boasted towers. Other than that it was almost impossible to guess at the original shapes and styles of these structures. The forest had smothered them completely. Tristam thought it would take years of excavation to lay bare the stone work but it was possible that some of it that lay buried might in fact have been given better protection from the elements. Under the layer of green some parts of the city might reveal much more than what still stood above ground.

Behind these mounds of stone and greenery the forest had swallowed any other signs of the structures, but Tristam had the impression that the city was not small. The builders had chosen a site in the draw between the cone of the volcano—which seemed to hang over the city like a dark being—and a lower hill. The city could easily step up either side of the valley some distance; there was no way to tell but to explore.

Directly before them, across the terrace, lay another double stair and Tristam could see water falling between these as well. Behind that, on the next level, the central pyramid rose grandly above the surrounding forest.

"I don't know where to start," the viscount said, looking around, bewildered.

Tristam turned in a circle, like the needle of a compass. There. He pointed at the far pyramid. "From there we will have a view." *Up*, he thought; *up into the air*.

In the center of the plaza Beacham was crouched, examining the paving stones, brushing his hair out of his face as the wind whipped it like a flag.

"What is it, Mr. Beacham?" the viscount called out. "Have you found your likeness there?"

"Not quite, sir. But I have found something." Still staring intently down, Beacham stood and moved slowly to one side.

Tristam realized that there was a pattern in the plaza floor here, made up of marble and basalt, the darker rock running like striations across the plaza.

"This will bring joy to the captain's heart!" Tristam said as he came and stood beside Beacham. "If it is what I think."

"I believe it is a chart, sir. Though I'm sure Mr. Hobbes would name it more properly a map. The scale is not true, I would say, and . . . I don't know how to say it, sir. . . . All the islands have been rounded off, so to speak. The roughness of the shores is gone. But nonetheless it is a chart and of the Archipelago, or at least this part of it."

The three men all bent over the plaza floor, searching the pattern. Five yards further on Beacham stamped his feet on the stone.

"And here we are, gentlemen, or my name isn't Jack Beacham." His face lit in a grin, and turned a deeper red so that his freckles seemed to grow larger. He was pointing at piece of basalt set into the marble. It was badly scarred and cracked.

"Are you sure?" the viscount asked.

"As sure as sure, Lord Elsworth. Here is the narrows we passed through earlier." He began tracing their route as though he were a ship. "Here is where the *Swallow* lies to her anchor, and here is the pass we followed into the Archipelago from the Gray Ocean." He paused, studying the chart intently. "It is not properly scaled, but look. . . ." He crossed to the west. "Here are the hidden channels between the islands. And the Great Ocean beyond! The captain will be the happiest man in the King's Navy when he sees this."

Immediately the midshipman began to plot a path through the archipelago.

"This chart would save us from many a wrong turning, Mr. Flattery. Do you see?" He tapped his toe on a blind passage to illustrate.

Already the viscount was bored, wandering away. He walked twenty feet and stopped to survey their find. "What area does your chart include, Beacham?"

The sailor jogged off toward the distant stair but stopped long before the stair was reached. "It might be two hundred miles, sir. Certainly no more and I should not be surprised to find it less."

"Their kingdom," Tristam said, "if kings they had." Tristam bent down and looked at the small crater where the city would be situated. "This. . . . It was caused by man, not nature. I would say this city was not abandoned—but sacked and defaced."

Beacham had stopped fifteen feet away. "Do you see, sir? There was another stone here."

Tristam went to look and found a small cavity in the basalt—a shard of blue still to be seen in its bottom. He bent and blew some sand from the hole. "*Lapis lazuli*," he said. "It marked something of significance. Perhaps another city." He shook his head. "Perhaps we have found an ancient nation. What became of it, I wonder?"

"There are no fortifications to be seen," the viscount said, turning in a circle. "Perhaps war found a people who did not practice its arts." He shrugged his shoulders as though to say that speculation was not in his nature.

The viscount kept looking at Tristam oddly and though the man did not stray far from Tristam's side, the naturalist got the impression that Julian tried to keep a few feet between them.

"Let's climb up," the viscount said, "and see what is to be seen."

The pool at the base of the next stair was not so damaged, but it was filled to its upper rim and they could see that debris from the forest lay thick in the bottom.

"The rain this morning would have caused an overflow," Tristam said, looking out over the plaza. "That is what keeps your chart so clean, Mr. Beacham."

A stream of water fell into this pool from the next terrace, a height of perhaps twenty feet. The decorations on this pool were not so damaged, though they had not escaped the wearing of the elements. Tristam was sure there had been a motif of vines and leaves encircling this fount. Columns had been toppled to either side of each stair and these, too, once bore a similar design. The left hand stair was much broken by the incursion of roots that lay among the jumble of blocks like thick curving fingers. From somewhere in the forest came the lonely notes of a hermit thrush, a muffled echo sounding along the abandoned avenues.

As they ascended the intact stair, Tristam looked up at the sun and realized they would have to push on if they were to return to the beach that day.

The third plaza was over three hundred feet across, ending at the foot of the pyramid that dominated the city. Tristam stood looking a moment, trying to understand what this view might have meant to one of the original inhabitants. Was this a seat of government he looked at? A temple?

From the pyramid's base a narrow canal flowed straight across the plaza and Tristam realized now that the face of the structure was dominated by two long stairways reaching to the top. Between the stairs water ran down a steep flume, feeding the canal. The plaza stepped up to both right and left, Tristam thought, but the forest hid anything else that may once have completed this plaza. A series of evenly spaced columns lay on the edge of the trees to either side, some lying on the ground, others still keeping their vigil.

A sense of purpose seemed to have taken hold of the explorers now and more than just wandering at whim, they pushed on toward the structure before them. Tristam looked into the canal as they went and found it less than a yard in depth and only twice that across. The sides were worn and smooth, and fluted by the countless years of erosion. Over the centuries the water had slowly eaten away the rock until the paving stones were undercut by almost two feet, another sign of the age of this place.

"How is it, do you think, that the water flows down from the pyramid?" the viscount asked suddenly.

Tristam was surprised that he had not noted this immediately. He scanned his surroundings. "I cannot say from where the water comes, Julian, but certainly the source must be a lake or pool higher up the slope."

The viscount nodded. "The engineers who built this city knew their business."

They were hurrying now, Beacham almost breaking into a trot. To find a vantage to view it all was what spurred them on. Tristam turned his attention to the plaza floor, for in places the stones were cracked and broken and subsiding or were being lifted by some unknown force beneath, making treacherous footing. A faint tang of sulfur pulled Tristam's gaze up to the peak. He remembered his retreat from the volcano on Farrow, how the mountain had seemed intent on shaking them off and this reinforced his feeling of disquiet.

Perhaps this is the source of the fear that nags me, he thought. *This is too much like our day at the ruin: mysterious structures, a smoking cone above. . . . Enough to unsettle the mind*. That would explain some of this anxiety. The brain, Tristam knew, had its own, more primitive, memory of past experiences.

The edge of a block caught Tristam's sole and he stumbled forward but recovered and went on. As they came to the foot of the long stair, they slowed for no apparent reason, then each looked to the others, wondering who would lead.

Tristam's course, the naturalist thought.

To both left and right of the stairs there were broken fragments of stone from sculpture but the stairs themselves appeared to have been attacked only by the slow assault of the ages.

Tristam put his foot to the first tread as though testing to see if it would bear his weight. He looked up at the steep pattern of lines formed by the rounded edges of steps, resettled the bag on his shoulder, and began to climb.

The treads of this stair were not wide, and Tristam did not look forward to descending. As it was, traversing back and forth as they went would almost have been easier, for the original inhabitants must have been created with feet smaller than Tristam's. They rose up to the level of the tree tops and here the trade wind blew freely, catching at Tristam's hair and luffing his shirt like a poorly trimmed sail.

"There is wind up here, sir," Beacham said, catching his breath. "That is why the clouds can outsail our poor *Swallow*."

The pyramid itself stepped up in seven tiers, the little stone that could be seen closely set and perfectly shaped. Here on the walls, some of the carvings were undamaged by whatever tragedy had befallen the city. Tristam could make out a horizontal motif of the natural world—vines and leaves and the great bowls of trees. And on the next level, stylized fish and whales and perhaps the heads and wings of birds. A great cat crept across one section of wall and above this lay a mountain with a cloud at its peak, no doubt a portrait of the smoking cone above. But there was no representation of people, leaving of the inhabitants a mystery.

The narrow steps were too treacherous to allow one's attention to wander, so the climbers did not spend much time examining the structure. Later there would be time to admire carvings and speculate about the meaning of symbols . . . perhaps.

The viscount collapsed to a stair for a moment to catch his breath and Tristam stopped to wait, taking the opportunity to look out over the city. He suffered a moment of vertigo and lowered one knee to the stone. The strange instrument on the water-stair howled and the trade wind whipped at Tristam's clothes and shoulder bag.

They were just high enough now that the shape of the ancient city was beginning to appear, towers and turrets of green standing up above the forest: the suggestion of a pattern being revealed. A cloud floated across the sun, chasing a shadow which flowed over the ruins with surprising speed.

In a distant strait between islands Tristam could see one of the ship's boats, heeled to a breeze of wind. The sight reduced his anxiety until he realized how very far away the boat must be. What did this city look like from a distance? Had he looked up here himself and not realized?

Lord Elsworth nodded to Tristam and rose to go on. Beacham had become terribly silent and Tristam caught a glimpse of the boy's face as they set out. *Yes,* Tristam thought, *how large and strange the world turns out to be.*

Again the head of a stairway drew near and Tristam was half-prepared for it to prove another false end to the climb.

What was it the inhabitants of this city placed so high?

His legs were still responding to his urgings, but not willingly and he feared that he might fall if he could not rest soon. Suddenly he could see over the rim of the pyramid's top and he realized that the black slope must rise higher, making the front appear cut away. Here, raised only a step, was a half-circle of smooth stone, like a terrace, set between polished columns—the two farthest out made of white stone, the next two of rose, the next of green, and the single column before Tristam shone black in the sunlight.

All three men stood there, fighting to fill their lungs with air, staring at this strange apparition.

"*So,*" Tristam heard himself mutter. "*So.*"

Why am I not shocked? Why am I not horrified? Because I am on a track cut into the globe that leads me to its own ends. Here, clearly. Perhaps beyond. But here.

"You wanted to see the ruin of Farrow, Beacham?" Tristam asked softly. "Well here it lies."

The viscount had shut his eyes tightly—tendons stood out on his wrists and his hands appeared to have spasmed into claws. Tristam heard his own breath coming in gasps, felt himself swaying where he stood.

Dread.

Twice now he had been brought to this same artifact though he had not the slightest understanding of its significance. What did Galton know? What had his uncle learned?

Tristam wondered if Roderick had known that this was where his journey would lead. 'Their lodestone' they called him. But to what had he led them?

The viscount looked around as though there might be some threat, something of which to be wary. Tristam stepped away from the man, turning his attention back to the artifact—the seven columns joined by a gray lintel.

Had the builders of the Farrow Ruin lived in this city?

Beyond the smooth pattern of marble, water bubbled into a small fount and above that perched a tiny platform that appeared to be braced upon the limbs of a tree carved out of the stone.

Tristam felt himself walking forward, dazed, then stepping up onto the marble terrace. Something on the floor moved with the wind, and Tristam's eyes darted down to find white feathers, stuck in dried gore. Some animal had made a meal here, it seemed. Some raptor, Tristam feared.

As though it might burn him, Beacham reached out and touched a column. "*Stone*," he said, as though he had expected it to disappear at his touch.

The fount caught Tristam's eye, for it was formed from the stone coils of a massive snake that raised its head up behind the fount—but instead of the viper's jaws Tristam expected, the snake's body ended in the head of a raptor. And from its curving bill flowed clear water.

"It is not precisely the same," he said, certain he sounded a fool. Somehow this did not seem the place for fools.

Along the lintel, characters were marked, and these, too, bore a resemblance to those on Farrow, but were not identical. Nor were the columns decorated the same. It was as though the Ruin of Farrow had been recreated by a slightly different sensibility, or the plans had not been entirely precise.

Which is the copy, Tristam wondered?

He followed Beacham's example, touching a column gingerly. Sun and moon were recognizable on one, and the constellation of the Great Mare as well, but on the same column—one dedicated exclusively to the heavens in the Farrow ruin—there was a fine filigree of vine work that twisted about its base and then wound lightly upward, joining the stars and planets.

But is it Kingfoil? Tristam asked himself. It was impossible to say. Perhaps.

"This place appears completely undamaged," Lord Elsworth observed, his voice sounding calm—much to Tristam's relief.

"Only the elements and time have been at work here," Tristam said, "and even they seem to have had little effect. As though it has been preserved somehow." He looked up at the characters spanning the lintel. "I should never have thought to find such a thing had I. . . ." He shook his head. "It is beyond imagining."

The naturalist felt a sudden need to sit, and walked over and perched on the rim of the fount. The viscount continued to examine the columns, running his fingers over the black pillar.

"What is this, Tristam? It is certainly not the same material we saw on Farrow."

"Marble. Black marble, like the great column we found lying broken below. But you are right, the central column on Farrow was obsidian, and featureless." He would need the drawings in Galton's book to compare, but this artifact differed, and the black column in the center—on it was carved a horseshoe shape, like a gate, or so it appeared. An arch, carved with stars, the supporting pillars shaped like twisted horns, and between these a gate carved with the same runes that could be seen above.

A gate.

I have come, Tristam thought, as though announcing his presence. *But I do not know my purpose.*

Beacham had mounted the stair to the balcony and went up gingerly, for this stair was even narrower than the one on Farrow.

Tristam dipped a finger into the water and put it to his lips. Cool, unremarkable. He cupped his hands and drank, thinking of Galton.

The columns were casting long shadows across the terrace as the sun descended toward the western horizon. The day was quickly disappearing. Tristam did not think they could make it down the water-stair in darkness and the thought of spending the night in the dark city was terrifying.

We arrived here late, he thought, *we are meant to stay.*

"Can you see if there are sighting lines, Beacham?" the viscount asked.

"Not yet, sir."

Although Beacham would ascend to the main tops without the slightest hesitation, this narrow stair and drop of twelve feet had slowed him considerably—the strangeness of the place had shaken his confidence.

"Mr. Flattery?" Beacham had reached the balcony and the tone of his voice indicated some surprise.

"Beacham?"

"I believe there was a man at the head of the water-stair just now." He spoke quietly and calmly just as Tristam had heard men do immediately after they had sustained grievous injury, as though maintaining an appearance of normality would somehow help—'*Everything is all right, do you see? I'm really undamaged.*'

"It is Mr. Osler come after us," Tristam said.

"I don't think so, sir."

Tristam and Lord Elsworth went to the head of the stair and looked down over the city.

"Are you certain, Beacham?" the viscount said. "I see no one."

Beacham was scrambling down from the balcony, slipped and half-jumped, half-fell the last five feet. "It was not a trick of the light, Lord Elsworth. A man, just at the stairhead." Beacham peeked over the rim as though he did not want to be seen.

"Well, let us wait a moment and see," Tristam said.

"Could it be the corsairs?" Beacham asked.

Do they seek me yet? Tristam wondered.

The viscount stepped back from the edge suddenly and turned back to the Ruin as though searching for something. "The wind often drops at night," he said. "If we crouch back against the wall, we shall have some protection. I, for one, will feel better about going down at first light. Here, at least, it would be difficult to approach us without one of us knowing. We have food. Shall we make a supper as we can?"

Tristam could not eat. He sat in the fading light, wrapped in his jacket as the day quickly cooled, and listened to his heart racing.

Martyr's blood, he thought. *Why did I come here?*

Across the western horizon, above the peaks of the Archipelago, the sunset lit the sky in gold and red, setting a long snake of cloud aflame.

"It is an eerie place, is it not, Mr. Flattery?" Beacham huddled over his meal, his collar up to the wind, looking for all the world like an old man. "What did they use such a place for, I ask myself. And this snake-hawk? It makes my blood cold, that's for sure."

Tristam shrugged. He was expending effort to control his breathing. *What will happen to me*, he thought. *What will happen to us all?*

"Is it not strange that we have been to the Ruin on Farrow and now we find ourselves here? Like a pattern, don't you think?" Beacham ventured.

"Coincidence," Tristam said reflexively, not believing for a second.

"Well," Beacham said, almost to himself, "Mr. Shuk claims there is no such thing as a coincidence in this world."

"Yes," Tristam said, his voice heavy with sarcasm, "carpenters know all about such things." That stifled the conversation, to Tristam's relief.

Light faded quickly once the sun was down, and as the light went, the city below fell into shadow as though the forest spread silently at night.

In time the conversation resumed, though it fell to near whispers. The wind almost died away and a moon, waxing toward full, floated in the eastern sky, casting the palest light on the distant water. *The thirteenth moon*, Tristam remembered. *Flames!*

They took turns going to the edge to gaze down the dark stairway, but each time one of them returned, there would be a shake of the head and the conversation would be picked up again.

Tristam remained silent, lost in the labyrinth of questions. He worried that he had brought his companions into danger. But had there been any choice?

Against the stars, smoke curled out of the volcano, tinged with a dull orange glow, which Tristam was certain came from within the volcano itself.

Lord Elsworth surprised Tristam by talking easily and earnestly with Beacham, and despite what the midshipman knew of the viscount he responded in the same manner.

As the night wore on conversation was punctuated with silences of increasing length. Even with the wind reduced it was a cool evening and the explorers huddled into their jackets, trying to find comfortable positions—impossible in their present situation.

"Perhaps here we shall have an opportunity to look into a volcano," was the last thing Tristam heard the viscount say before the man began to snore softly.

*   *   *

"Are you sleeping, sir?" Tristam heard Beacham whisper. Perhaps he had been. Either that or he had been in a different world—where a hawk battled a fiery snake in the air.

"What is it?"

"A light, Mr. Flattery. Well, not properly a light, but a glow, I think. You should come see, sir."

Tristam rose stiffly, pulling cold hands from his sleeves. He shivered. The moon was gone.

"Have you been awake all this time, Beacham?"

The midshipman nodded. Tristam stopped by Beacham's side and stared where he indicated. It took a moment for him to decide, but he agreed—there was a glow.

"That is the water-stair," Tristam said. He could pick out the arch of trees at the stair's head. And the glow seemed to flicker almost imperceptibly. "Fire."

Beacham nodded.

"I hope it is our own people," Tristam said. "Wake Lord Elsworth."

Beacham disappeared, leaving Tristam staring into the dark. The glow was growing brighter, he was sure. Branches were beginning to take shape and the line of the stairhead appeared straight and clearly defined.

"*Mr. Flattery!*" Beacham said, his voice full of fear. "*He will not wake. . . . Sir?!*"

A single flame flickered into being below the arch of trees, and then another. Torches.

Tristam swore and tore himself away. He had not gone two steps when he heard the midshipman cry out.

"*Flames! My hand!*"

Tristam ran. In the starlight he could just make out Beacham, kneeling over the viscount, holding his hand up before his face.

"What. . . ." Tristam couldn't finish for there was a sharp pain in his cheek and jaw. He stopped, stunned. With his tongue he could feel a shaft in his mouth—through the cheek and hard into his gum. And then his tongue went numb.

He wrenched a dart from his mouth as he sank to his knees. A noise above him.

"Sir?" Beacham whimpered, and then was silent.

Tristam tried to rise and felt himself float free of the earth. Movement to his right. . . . The soft hiss of a snake in the darkness.

↬ Forty

Lieutenant Osler and midshipman Chilsey stood atop the water-stair gazing at the ruins of the city. Osler was a bit ashamed to admit not insignificant jealousy: he dearly wished he had come upon it first—even if he had argued against men in the Archipelago. He cupped his hands to his mouth, hesitated and then shouted.

"*Hel-lo, Mr. Flattery! Hel-lo!*"

There was nothing, then a small cry in answer: the last syllable of the naturalist's name—an echo. Both men stood in silence a moment, straining to hear, and then moved out of the water onto the dry stone of the lower plaza.

Osler looked up at the sky. Local noon, he would guess. They had found the stair while looking for their companions that morning. Obviously Tristam and his companions had come up—probably the previous day—so Osler had sent the cutter off to carry news of the find to the captain and he and Chilsey had climbed up to find the others—and to see for themselves what lay above.

"I wonder where they are, sir?" Chilsey asked. "I hope they've found a treasury full of gold and silver and are rolling around in the stuff as we speak."

Osler smiled. The lad was pretending to joke, but Osler could tell he was more than half-serious. Myths of lost cities usually involved riches. A university man might hope for artifacts and lost knowledge when he considered such a find, but the uneducated thought immediately of gold and silver.

He was also becoming a little worried, probably unwarranted, but concern was growing all the same. The strange arch that moaned and cried when the trade wind blew had set his nerves on edge and ever since then he felt a disquiet that he could not explain. But no doubt he would find them, tramping about like excited children, not only unharmed but without a care in the world.

He finished pulling on his boots and looked up at the city. There had been a civilization of great sophistication here. A city not much smaller than Avonel, it seemed. And that long stair carved through solid rock. . . . It must have taken a hundred years! "Where shall we start, do you think?" Chilsey asked.

"The open areas first."

Chilsey nodded his head in quick agreement with this plan. "I hope they're not in the forest," he said. "Did you see that viper Mr. Flattery killed?"

"Yes. Bloody mean looking." It seemed they were of one mind in that matter. Stay out of snake terrain if at all possible.

They set off toward a distant stair beside a shallow stream that flowed across the plaza.

*   *   *

The Duchess of Morland braced herself against the cutter's heel just ahead of the helmsman and across from Captain Stern. Though wrapped in a sailor's oilskin she was still getting wet from spray and certainly her hair must be a sight. The instant word had arrived that a stairway had been found, Stern had readied a boat to go see this wonder for himself. The thought that an important artifact might have been discovered by his voyage had cheered him quite considerably, though the duchess could see that he tried to protect himself from disappointment yet. "It is likely nothing," he had said when he spoke to the duchess, "but I must look into it. Would the Duchess care to accompany me?"

So here they were, beating into the now consistent trade wind, headed toward a smoking mountain. She worried about the missing men—out through the night. *It is likely nothing*, she told herself. But if that was true, why did she feel like an over-wound watch spring?

A wave caught them smartly on the forward quarter and a sheet of water came over the rail. She pulled her head inside the oilskin and felt the water hit her like a hard slap. She emerged cautiously.

The coxswain, an impertinent young man, grinned broadly, water dripping from the end of his nose. "It isn't getting hit by water that we mind, Your Grace, it's the fish."

Stern gave the young man a withering stare, and the boy went back to steering intently, his color suddenly a bit gray.

Poor lad, the duchess thought, smiling despite Stern. *The fish: ha!*

They were drawing near to an island and she dearly hoped it would be their destination. Of course, one could never tell, for sailing boats often went off at the oddest tangents from their true destinations. She checked the wind. They had been tacking since rounding the tip of a long low island. But certainly this must be the volcanic island, for there was the smoking cone above.

In the bow the duchess could see Llewellyn doubled over, soaked through no doubt, and miserable from the sea sickness—but the man would not be left behind. As an empiricist he simply must be present at such a discovery—thinking of his reputation, no doubt. She shook her head; if this stair had more than a dozen steps, the physician would never be able to ascend and would have suffered in vain.

When told of Llewellyn's search of Tristam's cabin, she had initially been tempted to confront the doctor, but something had stopped her. Better to have him wonder what she knew. To observe him. Even better to have the physician think Tristam had kept his secret. She stared intently at the man, hunched over in the bow. Ever since Llewellyn had been maneuvered aboard she wondered whose interests he served—though she was fairly certain she knew.

Palle, she thought, *you would follow me to the ends of the world.*

She looked back over the blue sea. Certainly the cutter was making for the beach.

She regretted every second they spent among these islands—every second that was not used to carry them forward—but to find signs of a civilization here. . . . It was the stuff of dreams. No sign of inhabitants on the beach, apparently. Gone—she wondered where.

A memory of history: Avonel being razed and rebuilt. If the King had ordered Avonel to be located elsewhere, the ruins of the city would have been left to the elements, to be buried eventually. Such thoughts made her own civilization suddenly seem a tentative arrangement. A shiver ran through her and it was not just from being wet in the wind.

The foresail was lowered suddenly, and the boat glided in toward the shore. A gust of wind caught the sail as it came down, shaking it quickly, and a deep, sonorous moan sounded in the forest—like a great horn.

"What on the round earth is that?" she heard a voice ask.

Stern caught her eye, the same question clear on his face.

The cutter ground to a gentle halt on the sand beach and the Jacks jumped over the side to pull it up another few feet. She could see the look of relief on Llewellyn's face. He had bent over the rail twice during their sail and wore that terrible look of desperation which those who suffered the sickness of the sea quickly acquired. She almost felt sorry for him.

The captain and coxswain helped her ashore and she shed the oilskin, for it was suddenly quite warm now that they had some shelter from the wind. It appeared to be a beach like many others, the thick green of the forest leaning out over the sand as though the wood were so crowded the trees along the marge were being pushed out.

One of the Jacks shouted from the edge of the trees and everyone converged on the spot where the stream disappeared into the rising forest.

Even the physician managed to cross the few feet of sand, but he stood looking up at the flooded stairway and the duchess heard him mutter, "What a tragedy. I shall never have the wind to climb such a slope."

The duchess was seized by panic as she stood, staring up into the wood. She thought immediately of the Ruin on Farrow. Tristam's course led here. Here. And she did not know if that boded good or evil.

Osler stood looking up the steep stairway of the pyramid, wondering if it was the best course of action. Certainly there had been no response to their repeated calls. Flattery and his companions might be inside one of the ruins, he reasoned, and unable to hear.

"It will give us the best vantage," Chilsey offered.

The lieutenant hesitated a second more. "I think you are right. Let us go up and set a watch. They will have to appear in time."

The two men mounted the stair, glad of the cooling breeze, for all this climbing was proving hot work. They stopped to catch their breath after a few moments, and Osler looked out over the ruined buildings, thinking what a great city it had once been. Plazas as large as any he had seen in the countries surrounding the Entide Sea. And here it lay for who knew how long, mysteriously emptied of its people. It would fire the imagination of the dullest mind.

Jon Chilsey looked over at him and forced a smile. Life aboard ship did not build up the lungs and both men were short of wind. Strands of the lad's dark hair were plastered to his forehead with sweat, and his face, though deeply tanned, was red from his efforts.

"Ready?" he asked gamely.

"A moment more," Osler said, wanting to give the midshipman a chance to find his breath.

He looked up the rise of stairs. They had completed perhaps half.

Stern left the impertinent coxswain on the beach to watch both the boat and Dr. Llewellyn, but everyone else, six sailors and the duchess, accompanied the captain up the water-stair.

The Jacks led the way out of consideration of the duchess' modesty, for she was forced to hike her skirts up to her knees or they would have been sodden. Stern accompanied her, giving her his arm and carefully averting his eyes. It made the duchess smile, for Stern took his dedication to gentlemanly conduct more seriously than many lords and princes. She suspected he was a prude—a sad state for a man on a voyage to Varua where the maidens were said to be both comely and unhindered by the mores of sophisticated societies. The place, perhaps, where she should have been born.

They had discovered that the loud moaning noises came from what appeared to be natural wind-pipes in a stone arch that spanned the stair. The trade wind would gust and the deep sound would begin, echoing up the stairway in the strangest manner. It reminded her of wind blowing across the mouth of an empty bottle.

The stair was long and treacherous and in one place partially blocked, but she was not about to turn around because of a little water and dirt. Who knew what lay ahead, after all, and if she was not the first one there, she was at least directly on the discoverers' heels, and that was something. If she had not felt a growing sense of anxiety, she would have been truly elated by her situation.

*   *   *

They would have collapsed on the top step if Jon Chilsey had not cried out, for there was Jack Beacham, half-hidden by a pillar, stretched out on the shining stone of a strange terrace.

Both sailors stumbled forward and found Tristam Flattery and Lord Elsworth there as well. All three lay in a scattering of white petals, though over Flattery, who lay along the central meridian, a down of white and dark red plumules mixed among the petals.

Their faces were painted a reddish brown that Osler suddenly realized was blood. He found himself stepping back and looking around, his heart acting oddly.

"Are they dead?" Chilsey whispered, horrified.

Osler forced himself to go to Flattery's side and kneel. For a moment he was almost afraid to touch the man, so cold and still did he appear. The naturalist had been stripped to the waist, his face smeared with blood, now dry, and delicate shells laid over his eyes. The fingers of his left hand curled around his field glass, which had been placed on his chest, and the right hand pressed to his heart, a coil of red tattoo winding around the wrist.

Chilsey came and stood beside him, looking down, his breathing ragged. Osler thought the lad mumbled a prayer.

Putting his hand near Flattery's mouth and nose, Osler could feel no breath, nor did the chest seem to rise and fall. Gently he moved Flattery's hand from his breast and discovered the wrist had been gashed and was red and swollen, the entire hand appearing bruised.

"He is not cold," he said. A sudden moan from the distant stair caused him to start back, but then he put his ear to the naturalist's chest. "It beats, I think— quick but faint."

He examined the other two in the same way and found them not so badly off. There were no cuts upon them and their hearts beat more strongly and regularly.

Chilsey half-crouched, looking around them constantly, hovering near to his friend, Beacham. "Who did this?" he asked. "Flames and blood: I feel as though I am being watched. My heart is a-pounding worse than it did in any action." He touched Beacham's arm tentatively. "Jack," he pleaded, "wake from this."

When Beacham did not stir, Osler thought the lad would sob.

"What has been done to them?" Chilsey cried out. "They are so near to death. . . ." He fell into a frightened silence.

Osler felt sorry for the terrified midshipman but could not think what to say. Nothing he had learned in the King's Navy had prepared him for this. He looked around at the terrace. There was no question of what it resembled—the Ruin on Farrow. He found this almost as disconcerting as the three men who lay stretched out so carefully on the meridians etched into the floor.

*   *   *

"Did you hear that?" Stern asked. He cupped his hand to his ear and turned his head. The sound echoed again. A shout, certainly, but the words were unclear, distorted. He could not discern their origin.

"Captain!" One of the Jacks pointed. "Atop that . . . great pile of stone, sir."

Someone was waving an article of clothing from the top of the pyramid.

"It is Julian, I think," the duchess said, relief in her tone.

Stern took off his hat and waved it in reply. He had been sure there was no cause for worry. Flattery and his party had simply come upon this place late in the day and made a camp for the night. He was a bit annoyed that they had not made shift to inform him of their find earlier, but it was almost understandable.

Stopping only to put on shoes, Stern and the duchess set out in the wake of the barefooted Jacks who walked close together, silent, their eyes wide, tripping over each other as their gazes flitted from this to that, never having imagined in their lives that they would find themselves in such a place.

They had mounted the second set of stairs before realizing the man calling from the top of the pyramid was Lieutenant Osler and that he was shouting for help.

Stern started off at a brisk walk but soon realized he was leaving the duchess behind in this strange place and slowed his pace. The duchess hurried as best she could but was hardly dressed for an expedition. Damned nuisance, Stern thought, why hadn't she waited down on the beach, or at the ship? Or in Avonel!

Glancing down, the captain almost tripped. He stopped so suddenly one of the Jacks ran into him.

"What is . . . ?" The duchess stopped in mid-sentence. "Is it a chart?"

"Yes, of sorts."

Osler cried out again, having seen them stop, perhaps, and Stern pulled his gaze away. Farrelle's flames! It was a map of the Archipelago, or at least some part of it. He forced himself to hurry on, conscious of the shapes of islands and narrows and sounds passing beneath his feet.

By the time they had reached the base of the pyramid, she and Stern were both forced to sit for a moment, and the water running in the channel was most welcome. He moistened his handkerchief and gave it to the duchess to wipe her face and neck.

They could hear Osler now, shouting to them. "We'll need help to get them down."

"What has happened?" Stern called back. "Is someone hurt?"

"They have all been rendered . . . unconscious, sir. They cannot be stirred from it. We must bear them down. Do you have a rope?"

They did. Stern had brought one from the cutter thinking to use it as a kind of lifeline if the stair proved too slick underfoot.

After a moment the duchess rose, ready to go on. She looked sick at heart but, if nothing else, Stern had to admire her courage; nothing seemed to stop her.

"Unconscious?" she muttered. "Whatever could he mean?"

It was a difficult climb, with no handholds the entire way. The poor duchess had to hold up her skirts lest they trip her. Stern saw her look back once, and then she reached out and grasped his arm to maintain her balance.

"Don't look down," he said, repeating the instructions given to green sailors going aloft.

The captain felt a certain dread creeping over him as they pushed their way up the stair. Unconscious? All three of them? Flattery might claim to be no spawn of a mage, but Stern was not so certain. The captain had been at sea many years and had never known a man around whom strange things occurred so regularly.

The duchess swayed again as they reached the stairhead and, once he was sure she had her feet beneath her, Stern looked up and almost reeled himself. Before him lay the Ruin of Farrow in barely altered form!

The sight of her brother lying upon the cold stone jolted the duchess into motion.

"They are alive, but we cannot rouse them," Osler said, almost apologetic. Stern was surprised by the lieutenant's manner. Osler was not a man easily rattled.

"We have seen no one else, Captain," the lieutenant managed. "We found them lying thus, but there is no sign of who might have done such a thing."

The duchess knelt beside her brother. Stern could not see her face for blowing hair, but her motions were slow, tentative. Tenderly she wiped at what appeared to be blood caked on Lord Elsworth's face.

"Where is that fool of a physician when he is needed?" she muttered coldly.

Stern took a few moments to ascertain that Osler was correct in what he said. All three men were sunk in a deep torpor, Tristam worse than the others. He was no medical man to know the best course, and the doctor could certainly never make it to this place under his own power, but it might prove foolish to move these men in their present conditions. He just did not know.

Stern looked up at the sky, gauging the hour and the likely weather. Hesitation, he knew from long experience, could often prove as calamitous as any other course. There was no help for these three to be found here.

"We will make litters and bear them down," he said. There were nine men and the duchess; it could be done. The viscount was a large man, but both Tristam and Beacham were of only average weight. It could be done, though it would take the rest of the day.

"Lieutenant. We will want some stout poles. Our jackets and shirts will be needed as well. Be quick. By the time we have sent for help, we can have them on the beach—if we set our wills to it. Mr. Flattery leaped into the ocean to bear a man up, and we can make no less effort here. Let no man say we have shirked our duty to our shipmates."

It was near dusk when the exhausted Jacks finally brought the unconscious men down to the beach. They set their litters on the sand and collapsed where they stood—strong men drained of all reserves. The great fear that had beset the Jacks as they made their way through the city and down the stair had also taken its toll, for the sailors were almost sure that they would be attacked and treated like the men they carried. And for men as superstitious as the Jacks that was a terrifying prospect.

Whatever ritual had been performed in the ruined city—for ritual it obviously had been—had unnerved the common sailors.

Only Stern's strong will had carried them through. The duchess thought each one of them a hero, for they had performed their labor without faltering or complaint. The captain had taken his turn bearing the litters and proved more powerful than she would have ever expected—resolute and strong. She had helped as she could, but these were men who did hard labor every day of their lives and were toughened by it in a way that she had never fully understood.

When they arrived at the beach, Llewellyn, as she had seen before, went through a transformation; from ineffectual little man to confident physician.

Each man in turn was carefully examined, but it was over Tristam that he lingered. Finally he turned to Stern and the duchess and spoke quietly and calmly.

"Lord Elsworth and the young Jack are in no danger, I am sure. Each has a mark, the smallest puncture, in their skin. They have been struck by a bolt or a dart tipped with a substance, perhaps derived from some relative of the genus *Strychnos*. They will recover fully, I believe." He glanced over his shoulder at the three prostrate men. "But I am in fear for Mr. Flattery. The radial artery has been slit and he has lost much blood. His pulse is weak and rapid, and his color pale. The laceration has already grown septic. Putrefaction will spread its miasma into the blood. Already he is burning with a fever. We must take him to the ship immediately."

The duchess saw Stern look around as he did when sensing wind upon his face and neck. He shook his head. "The trade is falling. We might be forced to man the oars." He cast a look of concern toward his crew. "And they are all in as it is." He shook his head again, then caught the duchess gazing at him. "I swore I would bring this young man back unharmed and I will." He went to the cutter and took out the tin box of victuals and set it on the beach where his crew sprawled. Opening the box he began to distribute food.

"We are not finished yet, lads," he said, his voice more touched with kindness than the duchess had ever thought to hear. "We must use what wind there is, so we cannot tarry or take time to rest. These men are terribly ill and must be carried to the ship without delay."

It was near to morning, though still dark, the stars bright outside the windows of the great cabin. The sounds of a ship at anchor—the working of timbers and the creaking of the rig, the muffled sounds of the rudder moving to the current deep below—all had become as familiar to the duchess as the sounds of a sleeping lover.

Llewellyn had left to rest and the duchess took the watch over Tristam, exhausted herself, but worry would not let her sleep. Gently she wiped the naturalist's brow with a damp cloth. His condition was deteriorating, she was certain. Julian and Beacham were mending quickly and though they were yet unable to speak they had regained consciousness and some small control of their limbs. But Tristam was burning up and had barely moved since Osler had found him on that alien pyramid. And she was frantic with fear.

As quietly as possible she paced across the cabin sole. The ship was so small and the walls between the cabins so thin that almost any noise was transmitted some distance—a lesson she should have learned earlier.

She perched on the ledge of an open gallery window and looked out at the dark night. An owl hooted somewhere on the shore and the sounds of some large mammal breathing on the surface came to her.

"He has more place in my heart than I knew," she said to the night.

If Tristam died, she was quite certain the voyage would end in failure. She could not hope to succeed without him—no one else realized that as she did. For no reason other than that she knew he must be saved, no matter what the cost.

She pulled the cord that summoned her maid. Poor Jacel. Julian's illness had driven her to anguish. Fool of a girl.

The maid appeared almost immediately. Obviously she had been awake and fully dressed.

"Your Grace?" she said quietly.

"Llewellyn," the duchess said, and the young woman curtsied and ran off.

"*At any cost*," the duchess whispered.

In a few moments the physician arrived, rubbing his eyes, the neck of his shirt open.

"Your Grace," he said, crossing toward Tristam.

"His condition is unchanged, Doctor Llewellyn."

"Oh?" The man pulled up short, trying to show no annoyance at being wakened to no purpose.

"There is a matter we should speak of, Doctor." She thought she saw signs of apprehension in his face. He continued to stand dumbly in the middle of the cabin, the light from the shaded lamp casting odd shadows around him.

"I have often wondered," she said quietly, "why Roderick Palle was so determined to maneuver you aboard the *Swallow*." She fixed him with her gaze as he started to speak. "I would prefer you did not insult my intelligence with denials, Doctor. I know your friends, perhaps better than you do yourself. Wells, Rawdon, Noyes. They are not so hidden as they think, nor are their intentions so artfully disguised." She stepped near to Llewellyn so that her height might be felt and so that her voice could be used to greater effect. "I'm certain no one else has glimpsed the actor behind the character, Doctor, but I for one do not believe this pose. You are neither bungler nor fool." She held his eye for a second. "What did you find in Tristam's cabin besides Galton's letter?"

The man did not answer for a few seconds, but stared at the duchess as though he were making a careful assessment.

"I have asked you a question, Doctor," she said, making her voice so cold it hurt her throat. "Be assured I will have an answer. I am more resourceful than you know."

He shook his head. "Nothing but the treasures of a naturalist."

"No *regis* seeds?"

He hesitated for a second and then cast his gaze down.

"So you have only what Rawdon gave you?"

He looked up in surprise but then shook his head. "I don't know to what Your Grace refers."

"Doctor, let me assure you . . . I have no use for you. You are more than an annoyance, you threaten my purpose. I have twice decided to rid myself of your presence; once in Farrow and once since. You do know of my brother's reputation?"

He said nothing, but his posture answered her question.

"But twice I have decided to wait and see what time would reveal. And look what such prudence has brought? I suddenly find I have a use for you, after all. You will save the life of Mr. Flattery. You have *regis* seeds. Do not deny it. I have seen you begin to sink beneath the burden of your illness and then rise like a martyr from the flames, renewed in health and vigor. I have more intimate experience of the effects of the seed than anyone in Farrland—save one. You will use it to save Tristam, Doctor Llewellyn, or I will have no use for you at all."

Llewellyn rubbed a hand across his cheek, as though he had been struck there. For a long moment he said nothing. He looked up as though in silent appeal and finally he managed to speak. "But Your Grace does not understand. Without the seed, I will certainly die. What choice have you given me? The death of the black lung or a death by . . . drowning, will it be? It seems that Llewellyn sinks either way . . . and the sailors say drowning is not accompanied by pain." He shrugged.

The duchess walked across the cabin slowly, considering. She had known he was not a fool, but she had also been certain he was a coward. When the corsairs had chased them, she had seen it—he was more than terrified. Gently she pressed her hand to Tristam's brow. He was on fire.

"What is it that you want, Doctor?"

"I have been reduced to that most basic of animal desires, Your Grace. I want to live."

She continued to look down at Tristam, his beautiful young face glistening in the lamplight, his color high, as though he glowed from the fire blazing in his veins.

"You are telling me you don't have enough seed to save Tristam and to keep yourself alive until we reach Oceana."

Another long pause, then a rasping whisper. "We do not know how long it will take to find the seed, Your Grace, nor do we know when we shall arrive. I fear I will die before we find this island." A pause. "There is also a possibility, Your Grace, that the seed will not be the physic that Tristam requires."

"Yes," she heard her voice come out in a flat whisper, "I know." She wiped Tristam's face. Held her hand briefly over his heart and then went and rang the bell for her maid.

"If I do not have coffee, I shall expire. Will you join me, Doctor?"

Llewellyn looked up in surprise, and then shook his head.

"*Captain Stern*," she whispered in Jacel's ear, and sent her out with a hand upon her arm.

"He will not live, will he?" she said when the maid closed the door.

Llewellyn looked over at the naturalist and she thought she saw some compassion there, but only a little: Llewellyn did not care for the human species. He shook his head a little distractedly, far more concerned with his own situation.

She reached out and placed her hand on Tristam's shoulder, thinking that her heart might break—for the first time in many years. "What did they do to him?" she whispered.

"They took his blood," Llewellyn answered flatly.

And the duchess shut her eyes, so tight that no tear could escape.

Stern entered, his gaze flitting from the duchess to the doctor. And then he stopped in mid-stride—faltered, really. "We have lost him," he said, his voice filled with real regret. "I am so sorry, Duchess."

"He lives yet, Captain, though he cannot continue much longer. Tristam's cure, however, is within the power of Doctor Llewellyn, for he has stolen from Benjamin Rawdon some of the Kingfoil seed that sustains our King."

Stern's look of compassion turned immediately to suspicion: his natural response to the duchess. "Doctor Llewellyn?"

Llewellyn, she could see, was frightened now. His face was ashen. She thought he would have to sit, for he wavered where he stood.

At any cost, she reminded herself.

"I assure you that a search of his cabin will prove me right, Captain."

"What say you, Doctor Llewellyn?"

The physician lowered himself awkwardly into a chair. For a moment he did not speak and the duchess could see that his mind raced to find a way out of this trap. In the end, he looked up, appeal on his face. "But what of my life?" he whispered. "It sustains me." He nodded to the duchess. "She would have me die, Captain. I would do anything to save this young man, but you cannot ask me to give my own life."

"Llewellyn has the black lung, Captain. He has enough seed to keep him alive—until we reach Varua, at least. It is his hope to find more when we arrive, enough to cure his disease entire. Ask him yourself. You might ask him as well if the King will live until we return from this voyage, for the good doctor knows far more than you might guess."

Stern said nothing but turned his gaze on the doctor who supported himself on the table, even though he sat.

He waved his head from side to side, eyes pressed closed. "There is not enough for us both. Not enough, I tell you."

"How is it you have come by this seed, Doctor?" Stern asked.

Llewellyn glanced angrily at the duchess. "I am no thief, Captain. It was given me freely. I tell this as the truth."

"By Sir Benjamin?"

The little man shook his head. "I cannot say, Captain."

"Doctor Llewellyn," Stern said, his anger coming to the fore, "aboard ship I am King's Barrister, judge, and jury, all. I shall have answers to my questions, sir."

The look on the physician's face seemed to say; *here it is again: persecuted, humiliated, robbed.* "Sir Benjamin Rawdon took pity upon me, Captain Stern," he whispered.

"The King knows of this, then?" Stern reached up and grasped a beam as though to steady himself.

Llewellyn hesitated a moment and then shook his head.

Stern cast a glimpse at the duchess.

"Then this seed you have is the property of the King of Farrland?"

"Captain," the duchess said in real alarm. "Let me remind you that without Mr. Flattery we are unlikely to accomplish our purpose. Dr. Llewellyn is certainly incapable of searching for the plant himself, which would leave us dependent upon the generosity of the Varuan king. You have found your lost city, and a passage through the Archipelago as well. That is accomplishment enough for one voyage. But return without the seed, and the King will die. Llewellyn will tell you this is true. Whatever your orders, the truth is that speed is our greatest need. If we return too late, even if we bring the seed, you will pay the price for the King's death. Count on it. No one in the Admiralty will shoulder the blame, as you well know."

Stern wavered. He did not trust her, the duchess knew this, but he was not a fool—and Stern was well acquainted with the workings of the Admiralty. "But, Duchess, would you have me condemn Doctor Llewellyn to death?" Stern fixed her with a gaze like an accusation.

She felt her anger rise and she spoke very carefully. "And when we reach Varua, will you give him the seed that is, as you have just said yourself, the property of the King? Will you ignore your orders to save his life? Or will you bring every seed back with you, and watch the doctor die?"

Stern glared at the duchess, but she met his gaze without blinking. She would not be intimidated like some midshipman.

Finally, quietly, he said. "What would you have me do?"

"It is possible you might save them both. Treat Tristam with the *regis* physic and sail on with all haste. Drive your ship across the Ocean Beyond. Time is what will kill Doctor Llewellyn. He must have the seed, but so must Tristam. And Tristam must have it now." She turned to Llewellyn. "You are a physician, sworn to sustain life. Will you not take this risk, Doctor? I will tell you true, without Tristam you won't find your cure in Varua."

Both Llewellyn and Stern fell into silence and indecision. It was a moment balanced like a goblet on an edge. If she reached for it now, it might upset, but if she hesitated, all could be lost.

"What say you, Llewellyn?" the captain asked.

The doctor closed his eyes and she could almost hear his thoughts: *persecuted, put upon, robbed—it was always the same.* She was certain he valued his life more than anything: more than honor, good character, love. . . . More than the regard of his fellow men. It was the only thing he truly cared for. *Does he not see that without Tristam his hopes are dashed?*

He nodded suddenly. "I will use my few seeds to treat Mr. Flattery's condition if the good captain will agree to carry me with all haste to Varua." He paused as though summoning courage. "And allow me the seed to effect my cure."

Stern turned away to look out the great windows of the cabin: the captain's cabin. Over the bay the sky was no longer black, casting shades of gray into the cabin. "You ask a great deal." He glanced at them both. "I have never gone against the orders of the Admiralty. Never forsaken my duty."

The duchess could not hold her peace. "Let me make a shrewd guess, Captain Stern. Your orders instruct you to sail to Varua and return with the seed. That is what has been committed to paper. But what has been said to you is somewhat different. Survey as you go. Haste is not required. But if you return too late . . . only what is written on paper will be brought forward—as evidence of your incompetence. And if you let die the only naturalist aboard, you may not even find the seed." She turned to Llewellyn, then back to Stern. "Have either of you even seen this plant we seek?"

Both men looked down. She crossed to Tristam again and felt his brow. For a second she thought he did not breathe, but she could just feel a hint of it upon her fingers.

"Consider much longer and the decision will be made for you!" she said angrily.

"Doctor," Stern said, his confidence shaken, she could tell, "you attended the King. Will His Majesty live until we return? Is this possible?"

Llewellyn looked up, confusion on his face. The duchess suddenly realized that he might not know the truth. Did he have the wit to understand there could be only one answer here?

"It is as Her Grace has said," the physician managed.

Stern shook his head. "Then use your arts to save our naturalist. I shall carry you to Varua without further delay, and if we are able to find this herb we seek, I will spare what, in good conscience, I can. I promise no more than that."

Llewellyn looked at the duchess, a look of the greatest relief on his face.

"Your patient, Doctor," she said.

He took Tristam's pulse, and then went quickly out.

The duchess and Stern regarded each other for a moment. They had many thousand leagues to sail together yet, she reminded herself.

"I thank you, Captain. I am sure you have made the wisest decision in a difficult situation."

He nodded as though any compliment from the duchess was of dubious value. "There is one other matter, Duchess, now that you have achieved your ends."

"Sir?"

The next words came with some difficulty. "I would have my officers back."

She almost smiled and was forced to hide it by dipping her head in a mock bow. "Captain Stern," she said with all the grace she could summon, "they are yours."

⌒ Forty-One

After endless struggle Tristam awoke to the sounds of a ship at sea. *Had he found his way back, then?*

A gentle breeze funneled down from above and cooled his face, but he was warm, tucked into a bunk under a weight of blankets.

Do I dream, Tristam wondered, *or have I wakened into another world?*

The ghost boy . . . he had been following the ghost boy, had been almost a ghost himself, thought and feeling so ephemeral they seemed to drift off, like smoke on the wind, leaving only the smallest scent behind. An endless dark maze of alleys and tunnels, and shattered, ancient stairs. Where had he been?

Nowhere. Lost.

And through that endless night he had clung to his awareness of self lest it drift away with his thoughts. *I am Tristam*, he chanted to himself. *Tristam*. And at the worst of times; *I am me. I am me. I am me.*

Following the boy who slipped silently along in a silent world, squeezing through holes so small that Tristam thought he would never follow. And then overhead the viper battled the white bird.

Tristam would echo this battle inside, as though his heart were a hollow drum, reverberating to an outside will. A thought drifted into Tristam's mind; *my blood is on fire and that is the battle to quench it.*

Follow the ghost child, slinking furtively along a darkened, dead street. Afraid, always afraid. Looking for springs to quench their thirst—just a few drops of blackened water, like blood dripping from a wound.

And then light, and soaring strength. Tristam would lift on great wings, stretching into the sky, looking. Searching for the viper, and the battle would be engaged among the clouds.

And then he would plummet, twisting within the coils of the biting snake, crash back to earth where a small boy waited, leading Tristam away from the fire.

A sound of a man laughing foolishly, like a returning memory. *I am a naturalist on a voyage of discovery*. Or was that a dream also?

The creaking of the deck overhead as footsteps passed. Water gurgling close to his ear. A ship at sea.

I have wakened into that other world, he thought. *I am alive in that world of light and air and men and women. And I am Tristam. I walked up an endless stair and passed through the gate. . . . And now, I have returned, somehow. Led by a small child.*

Water, I must have water.

Opening his eyes he found the glare of light on the white beams overhead too dazzling and pressed his lids closed again. *Water*. He felt as though the dryness began in his mouth and spread to every corner of his being, as though the snake biting him had drawn out all of his life fluids—as spiders did of their prey.

An attempt to move brought on a wave of dizziness, near blackness.

"Tristam?"

Yes . . . I am Tristam.

It was a warm voice—one that he knew, or had known long ago. A hand touched his forehead.

"Do you wake?"

His mouth was too dry to speak, but he nodded, which caused more vertigo.

The hand was removed to his chest and he felt a soft kiss upon his brow. "Perhaps I shall begin to believe in gods," the voice said, and he could hear a change in its timbre, spoken through a constricted throat.

"Duchess?" he managed. A memory from that world of light.

"Elorin."

"I must have drink."

"Yes, of course."

A moment later a hand slipped behind his head and raised him up and the wet rim of a cup touched his lips. *Glorious water.* He felt it run cool down his throat. He thought it should hiss when it reached his stomach.

"That is enough for a moment. I believe too much at once will not be good. Oh, Tristam, I am relieved beyond imagining. I have been frightened nigh on to death myself. But you are well, aren't you? Your fever is broken?" She shook him gently. "You frightened me, you frightened me! You have been raving and muttering and lost in delirium."

"Lost . . . yes. How did I come here? I have been battling the bird-viper for night upon night. I can't think how I have survived." He opened his eyes to slits and suffered the pain of adjusting to daylight.

The duchess bent over him, running her hand gently through his matted hair. "Llewellyn," she said, almost a whisper. "He had some of the seed. It saved your life, I'm sure. Terrible nightmares are one of its less salutary qualities. But you are out of danger now."

Tristam closed his eyes. *Out of danger?* Regis. *They had given him* regis. Drinking the water, dark as blood, and then soaring up into light. *I should never have taken the* regis *seed,* he realized. *Never.*

He felt his body had been invaded—had become a host, like a body into which parasites burrowed. He felt ill and hollow and corrupted. And something else. A yearning more powerful than he had ever imagined. The *regis.* . . . Dandish had become addicted.

"You should have let me die," he whispered.

"Tristam?" Distress at his words. Confusion.

"I should never have taken the seed. Not me." Horror. Despair. But why? Why did he know this?

Silence. Thinking. A sharp mind hovering over him. A hand took his own, gently. The softness of it, the warmth, reduced Tristam to tears. He did not know why.

"Tristam . . ." His name, spoken with such tenderness. "What happened up there?"

Up there? He tried to order his thoughts. The city. He had gone up into the abandoned city with. . . .

"The others?"

"They are well, Tristam, do not be concerned. They did not suffer the same injuries as yourself."

Injuries? A memory so horrible he turned his mind away. "*They slit me open . . .*" he said, mouth dry. "Farrelle save me, Elorin. They let my spirit bleed out and tried to make it take another form. . . . But I escaped into the air. And the child led me. Through the streets of the ruined city and through the city that lays beneath."

A hand on his brow. Fingers wiped a tear off his cheek.

"You have had terrible dreams, Tristam," she said, voice wavering. "The fever from the wound on your wrist. And the physic."

She took his right hand out from under the cover and touched his wrist as gently as she could, her fingers cool. "I will tell you true that we thought you would not keep this hand for the putrefaction was terrible."

Tristam opened his eyes and saw that a tattoo encircled his wrist, winding out of an ugly wound—red and tender but closed, already healing.

"It is where the snake . . . the bird struck me," he said.

"In your dream."

Dream?

The duchess shook her head, her curls catching the light. "The King suffers horrific nightmares as well," she whispered. "So powerful they seem more real than . . . reality. But they are dreams. Nothing more."

Tristam flexed his fingers and the snake tattoo appeared to squirm. He felt a wave of nausea and shut his eyes.

"You have no memory of what they did to you, Tristam? What was the purpose of this?" She touched his wound.

"I can't separate the dreams from memory, I think. But do you see, it is the bird-viper from the pool atop the pyramid. There is an artifact, like the Ruin on Farrow. . . ." He opened his eyes and stopped, seeing that she knew. "You have seen it?"

She nodded. "Yes, we brought you down. I think better of Stern for it. He took his place among the Jacks to bear you down the flooded stair. They are a coarse lot, the hands, but their hearts are true. You would be there still without their efforts."

She caressed his chest and shoulder. "I have orders not to tire you when you wake, Tristam. Drink some more and I shall try to find a broth that will not endanger your life."

He drank again. Sleep was calling to him, but he feared slipping back into that netherworld. This one was so light, so warm. "Tell me where we are."

The duchess' face lit in a smile. "Can you turn your head a bit?"

With her help Tristam managed to look out the stern windows and there, on the horizon, mountaintops glistened white in the sunlight. "Do we sail back to Farrland?"

"No, Tristam, we are in the Great Ocean Beyond. We have passed through the Archipelago by a new route and we point our bow to the west. You cannot see, but we sail in the company of small clouds, a fleet of them spread across the blue sky, traveling, as are we, toward Oceana. And the western horizon seems vastly far away, as though we can see a hundred leagues and all is blue and empty, the sea running up into the sky."

Tristam lay his head down and his eyes closed of their own volition. He felt a kiss on his brow—so soft and full of tenderness that it was almost a word. And then another on his cheek, and then, even more softly, on his lips. Three words.

Tristam felt himself drifting away again—not into darkness and fear—but into a warm dream of rocking on the ocean, embraced by a soft breeze that was the love of this woman named Elorin.

Outside the stern windows a bird cried and Tristam let go completely, slipping into a fair dream: a white bird sailing in the ship's wind, looking down upon him from an empty sky.

Sea Without a Shore

We will now discuss in a little more detail the Struggle for Existence.

—Charles Darwin

The Origin of Species (1859)

⌐ One

Tristam lay in his gently swinging hammock listening to the burble and pulse of the ocean passing over the *Swallow*'s hull—like the sounds of the womb, he was sure. He did not open his eyes, but lay sensing the now familiar movement of the ship and exploring his own capacity for health.

Llewellyn's *regis* had stemmed the spread of infection, but the body was slow to replace the blood of which it had been robbed. As a result, the naturalist suffered continual exhaustion, dizziness, and lack of strength and vigor. He also suffered from his desire for the physic: nausea, pain in all of his joints, trembling, and headaches so violent that they could not be described.

And then there were the dreams—nightmares, in fact. Tristam tried not to think of these. He remembered the King describing his own dreams as *devouring wolves,* but this did not begin to describe it. Repeatedly he dreamed of a great battle on a darkened field. It was so strewn with the corpses of the fallen that it filled Tristam with horror.

Tristam felt as though he had been tainted. That letting the *regis* into his blood had changed him irrevocably.

He opened his eyes for a second to find that the open port had let in a small lens of sunlight, which swung wildly across his cabin and appeared to be searching with the same frantic desperation that Tristam's body yearned for the *regis* physic. It was worse than a hunger, worse than starving, Tristam was sure. The disk of light flowed across the surfaces of his cabin, back and forth with mad determination.

I would not take it now if it was freely offered, Tristam vowed. *I would not.* He shut his eyes and struggled against the images that tried to form in his mind. The *regis,* he knew, would stop these nightmares, stop the feelings of anxiety and melancholia, restore his vitality and usual optimism. It would do all of these things . . . temporarily.

Time, he almost whispered. *Time will restore me, and I will not be in thrall to the seed. Like Llewellyn. . . .*

The doctor may have convinced Stern that he needed only the smallest handful of *regis* seed, but Tristam knew better. Unless Llewellyn had a strength of will like no other, there was little chance that the doctor would ever give up the physic willingly. Not after so many months of servitude.

Who else had become enslaved by the physic, Tristam wondered? Benjamin Rawdon's wife, or was that story entirely fabricated? Trevelyan, Tristam was now sure, or at least the baron had once been enslaved. Now he might be free . . . and quite mad. Not a comforting thought.

Tristam pressed his eyes closed, feeling ill and fragile. Two weeks he had lain in this state, improving so slowly that it was impossible for him to see a difference day to day. His mind had been affected as well, unable to focus, to follow a train of thought, to draw on his hitherto excellent memory.

And there were other changes that were equally disconcerting. *Of all people, I should never have taken the seed,* Tristam thought. He had begun to realize that he was aware of things that he could not possibly know—or at least there was an illusion of knowledge. Like Trevelyan's habituation to *regis*—it seemed perfectly obvious to him now (how could he have not seen before?). Or Llewellyn's inability to break free of the seed. He knew also that Llewellyn was something else altogether. Knew it as though the man had told him.

Tristam wondered, for the thousandth time, if he were going mad.

With his new insight he saw that even Beacham was not quite what he appeared, as astonishing as that seemed. Only the duchess eluded him. Only the duchess kept her secrets, though he was not sure how. She had some talent of her own, he thought, though she made efforts to hide it. That night at her home she had not let Bertillon suspect. Unlike Tristam who had blundered on like a fool . . . bringing an Entonne marauder after them.

Too much knowledge, Tristam thought. *I can barely hold a thought for two minutes. Can I trust these insights?* But somehow they were undeniable. *Perhaps the delusional always feel this.*

The most frightening realizations had to do with himself. Tristam realized now that to become a mage was not to learn a difficult art—though it was that, too—but more than anything, it was a transformation. A transformation that Tristam had begun; perhaps when he had first touched the leaf of a *regis* plant, but certainly when he drank from the fount at the Farrow Ruin, and then climbed up to look into the volcano. And then he had been led to the Lost City, and the remains of a people who still performed arcane rituals. . . . But for what purpose?

To regain lost power.

This thought seemed to come from no knowledge that Tristam possessed— as though it were spoken into his mind.

But what use had they made of him? That he did not know, nor did he want to. They had been after his blood, just as Trevelyan had warned; that much he knew, and that was enough.

He remembered the endless trek with the ghost boy, who was drawn to Tristam in the same way that Tristam was being drawn along his own particular course. Thoughts of the boy pushed Tristam toward the strange dream state that the *regis* physic engendered.

He opened his eyes quickly, relieved to see the disk of light still searching his cabin. He felt suddenly that he could trap it by opening a drawer in its path and then pushing it quickly closed. Trap it as he had been caught, on this voyage he could not escape.

The effects of the physic were wearing off—not all of them and not all together—but there was a noticeable change.

I may never be entirely free of it, Tristam thought, *but I will be as free as I can. I will regain as much of myself as is possible. I am Tristam. Tristam.*

"He is recovering as I would expect, Your Grace. There is no reason for concern. The body cannot make so much blood overnight. In a month he will begin to seem himself, and then another few weeks to regain the strength he has lost. Tristam is young and hale. In two months there will be no signs that he was ever ill."

The duchess perched on the sill of the stern window looking at the doctor who sat, leaning on the table. Llewellyn was lying to her—oh, not about Tristam's medical condition; that was no doubt true—but he was lying about other things. It was a difficult situation.

"Tell me, Doctor, why do you think Tristam was treated in this way? You seemed quite certain that his attackers had wanted his blood."

Llewellyn worried the cuff of his shirt for a few seconds, then opened his mouth to speak, apparently thought better of what he was about to say, and finally nodded his head to some inner decision. "I said that only because it was clear from the nature of his injuries. The radial artery had been slit with surgical precision. Whoever did that wanted to take as much blood as possible—or so I assumed. Why? You know as much as I, Your Grace. Tristam . . ." he looked out the stern window, "is the focus for strange occurrences. There is no denying it."

"But why is he such a focus, do you think?"

Llewellyn shrugged. "I don't know. . . ."

The duchess fixed him with her most piercing look. "But I think you do, Doctor Llewellyn. In fact I'm quite sure of it. Roderick would never have sent you otherwise."

Llewellyn turned in his seat as though he would rise and leave—an action he did not quite dare to take. He was in the presence of the Duchess of Morland, who was also his employer. He turned to the duchess, meeting her gaze steadily, something he almost never managed.

"I will tell you this, Your Grace," a bit of resentment coming to the surface, "you will need me to sustain this young man. Perhaps you think that your own knowledge of *regis* and its effects will be enough—but it won't. Without me, Tristam Flattery will not survive what is to come. I beg you remember this when next you consider threatening me with your dear brother." Llewellyn did rise then, stiff with some long contained rage. "Your Grace will excuse me; I have a patient to see." He bowed quickly and went out, leaving the duchess alone with her surprise.

"Well," she said. That, at least, was the truth—or so the doctor believed—there was no doubt of that.

"Come in Doctor," Tristam called out.

Llewellyn pushed his bulk through the narrow door. "And how are you today, Tristam?" Llewellyn asked, his tone professionally solicitous.

"Well enough."

Llewellyn nodded and smiled as though to encourage improvement, but his attention was focused on taking Tristam's pulse as the hammock swung.

"Still dizzy when you rise? Headaches?"

Tristam nodded.

"It will take time." Llewellyn turned Tristam's hand over, as though examining the color, but it was the fading tattoo that was of real interest, Tristam knew. "And these terrible nightmares?"

"They have begun to abate a little. How go your own, Doctor Llewellyn?"

Llewellyn lowered Tristam's hand. "It is you I am concerned about, Tristam." The man hesitated. "And you feel no . . . *need* of the physic?" He wet his lips gently as he asked the question.

Tristam brought his hand close to him, almost hiding it. "I feel the need, Doctor, but it grows weaker. Weaker as I grow stronger."

Llewellyn said nothing.

"What did you imagine, Doctor? That I would fall into madness like poor Trevelyan?"

Llewellyn searched blindly behind him for the door handle, but Tristam tried to hold the man a little longer.

"I know that you lied to Stern, Doctor Llewellyn. The tiny quantity of seed you require to cure your 'disease' will not be enough. There will never be enough, will there? Stern can never grant you all that you need. Or has Sir Roderick already promised that? Perhaps you have so much already in your possession that it does not matter?"

Llewellyn turned the knob, but didn't open the door. "One of the sad effects of the physic, Tristam, is it can make you believe that you are persecuted, plotted against. You should guard against this. I am your physician. Your well-being is my paramount concern." He managed a tight-lipped smile, trying to make a dignified escape.

Tristam lay thinking for a moment, watching the lens of sunlight tear about his cabin, searching. He held up his right hand, turning it slowly. The snake seemed to be fading from its head toward its tail, as though it were retreating into the wound on his wrist. Slipping back into the vein.

Quickly he lowered the hand to his heart, feeling it beat softly but surely.

↪ Two

False springs were not unknown to Averil Kent. He strolled in his February garden, basking like a newly awakened flower in the warmth of an unseasonal sun. For a moment he stopped to survey the garden in its entirety, gazing down the south-facing slope toward the nearby river. A scene of tired winter greens and grays and browns, relieved in places by bright berries of red and a few plants that would flower in Farrland's mild winter.

Come spring all this would change, but spring had not yet arrived—not really.

He went on, prodding the earth here and there with his walking stick. He had come to his country house to think in peace, but this was not yielding the results he wanted.

The air was cool but calm, and the sun so uncommonly warm, that the day seemed positively balmy. *False spring. Spuriverna.*

Kent had too much on his mind. Count Massenet's overture had disturbed him more than he liked to admit. He had been so cautious! Too cautious, he had sometimes thought. It had been Varese approaching Valary that had set the wheels in motion: there could be no other explanation. Obviously, Kent had not been conscious enough of the Entonne. Unlike the Farrlanders they realized the seriousness of Valary's work.

Valary.

He continued down a path of crushed gravel, the soles of his boots making a harsh grinding sound at each step.

Massenet was careful, of course, and he was unbelievably social. Over the years Kent had spoken to him fairly often. It would hardly raise suspicion—unless Palle and his cabal began looking toward Valary themselves. . . . A real concern. It was fortunate, Kent thought, that he had been so circumspect, telling Valary no more than necessary. It had been his habit with everyone he involved. No one was aware of all the strands of the web—except for Kent . . . and the Countess. And now he was keeping something from her: his contact with Massenet.

"May they never find their way to the countess," he whispered.

He moved on, his focus wandering as his anxiety returned.

I have come to live a life of anxiety, he thought. And it was beginning to show. It sapped his energies, whittled away at him, both waking and sleeping. He felt like a wounded hart, escaping into the underwood, fleet of foot to begin, but the slow loss of blood from the unstopped wound. . . . It sucked his life away, and Averil Kent knew he could ill afford that. Not at his age.

But he was not down yet. Massenet had caught him unawares, but there was still some strength in his aged legs—enough for one last run.

Kent looked out across his garden. Forty years of effort.

"You see how you have squandered your days, Averil," he chided himself. No wife, no children to carry on. Everything that was in his heart had gone onto canvas and here, into this garden—almost everything. He stepped down three steps beneath the pergola, the tangle of wisteria vine twisting like strange braid around the faded wood.

Forty years. Kent had spent so much time in this garden that he believed he knew its every stone, every branch on each tree. Yet it was a garden, and each season it came forth from the earth, like magic, almost mockingly familiar, but never twice the same. An ever-changing canvas, no single day ever to be repeated. One could plan a garden in infinite detail, but what blossomed forth from the earth was only an approximation of the vision. And in this way, too, it was like a painting, or like a man's life, for that matter. One could never predict what the magic of the earth would produce.

False spring.

If too many flowers blossomed now and there was frost. . . .

He shook his head and walked on.

Massenet, Massenet, Massenet. He was a damnably unfathomable man. Charming, brilliant, deceptively kind, deceptive, gifted with great strength of character, and not lacking courage. Not lacking anything that Kent could think of: certainly not lacking women.

The Duchess of Morland—that was whom Kent was reminded of when he thought of Massenet. Oh, their personalities were differently formed, certainly, but they were more alike than dissimilar. Like two species of rose—different in color and structure, but both beautiful, resulting from endless effort, both concealing a thorn.

In many things Kent would be glad—more than glad—to have Massenet as an ally, there was no doubt of that. But Massenet was, first and foremost, Entonne: an emissary of His Holy Entonne Majesty. Thwarting Palle and his supporters was Kent's desperate hope, but to do so and betray Farrland to the Entonne. . . . Better, perhaps, to take his chances with Palle.

But was that true? He thought back to his conversation with Massenet. Either the wily count had taken Kent's exact measure, or Massenet and Averil Kent were of one mind on many of life's essential truths. And the fragment . . . ! Valary assured him that it was authentic. Not in his wildest dreams. . . . The painter paused for a moment, as though he had forgotten where he was and where he was going.

Yes. . . . Massenet. Valary. He shook his head and walked on, a sudden dull throbbing in his hip forcing him to put weight on his cane—something he had carried only for reasons of fashion all these years.

At the edge of the pond Kent took a seat on a stone bench. He closed his eyes and felt the warmth of the sun on his face, the cool breath of the softest breeze. He thought of the countess. Her life of seclusion had become almost macabre. The thought caused him pain. How distant she was, and yet he knew she was not without a heart. He knew.

How fortunate Jaimas Flattery was to have found a young woman like Alissa Somers. Warm of nature, and sweet of spirit—and with such an intellect! Not driven to sacrifice a part of her life upon any altar.

Not like the Countess of Chilton, who had taken on her role like a consumptive artist driven to finish one great work before the end. Sacrificing everything to this passion.

Passion. A word that was becoming frail. A spell that lost its power with age—but never all of its power.

The bare branches of a willow swayed, the sound vaguely skeletal. Kent opened his eyes to see a tiny cat's paw ripple across the pond, disturbing the water lilies on their moorings.

The *Swallow* had not reached Queen Anne Station, not at last report anyway. Foolish to begin worrying about that as well; they had not been a month overdue when he had heard. Not entirely out of order.

The world is vast and its problems endless, Kent told himself. *I cannot worry about them all, especially those so entirely out of my control.*

Thinking this, he raised himself up on his cane and continued along the path that skirted the pond's border. Water iris would begin to blossom here by mid May, dabs of yellow on curving lines of green, their forms reflected among the clouds on the surface of the pond. Beside these, a rare blue daylily, would sway delicately in the breeze. A trellis of climbing roses, in coral and pink, brought back from Doorn. Peonies, and to the path's left, hydrangea—multicolored and oddly foreign looking. Arrowhead and sweet coltsfoot.

Come spring the garden would rush into blossom, wave after wave of flowers, color and texture. They would wash across the garden like a succession of floods: life in all of its exuberance and mad rush toward existence. And then winter. A brief rest for flowers and gardeners. A brief rest.

Kent turned down another path crossing over a stone footbridge that he had designed himself, decades ago now. It should be. . . . Yes. Here. A variety of cherry and, as he had been told, it was coming into blossom; the silver-pink flowers half-opening as though uncertain of their decision.

Kent pulled a branch down to eye level, admiring the cluster of small blossoms, the perfect petals and delicate yellow-headed stamens.

False spring. He feared that they would be disappointed in their endeavor.
There would be no bees to carry pollen. This tree would be barren that season.
As barren as the King's *regis.*

Kent made his way back through his treasured garden, wondering, as he often
had these past years, if this would be the last season he would witness its miracle. He had been told that Halden, in his eightieth year, had ordered the removal of the cherry tree outside his study window. Everyone thought it odd for
a man who so loved nature, but Kent understood perfectly. That spectacular
blaze, the blossoming cherry, stripped bare by the first wind. Life was short
enough, the old did not need such pointed reminders.

As he approached the house in the fading light of a short winter day, Kent
heard music. Someone was playing his pianum, though who in the world
would be so presumptuous he could not imagine.

Kent did not go into the hall but went straight to the doors opening into the
drawing room. As he stepped over the threshold, he stopped in surprise. He
hadn't recognized the sheer virtuosity of the playing. His old pianum had never
known such mastery!

On the bench a slender man bent over the keys, his lank hair falling free
and hiding his features. As he played, the man contorted continually, almost
spasming, as though the music inside fought to escape by any means it could
and only supreme effort channeled it into the hands.

The man looked up, registered Kent, and the music died away, like petals
taken on the wind.

The man's lean face split into a sad smile.

"Mr. Kent. Charl Bertillon, at your service."

Ah, the famous Entonne.

"I do hope you don't mind." He nodded to the pianum as he stood. "Your
man put me in here to wait, and, well . . . I could not help myself."

"When the muse calls, Mr. Bertillon, one must respond. Certainly my poor
pianum has never had such a master at its keyboard. I'm sure it will never be
satisfied with my poor efforts again."

The young man crossed the room and took Kent's hands warmly.

"I hope you have time for a visit, Mr. Bertillon. I'm sure supper cannot be
too far off . . . ?" Kent, who saved all of his socializing for Avonel, wondered
what this young musician could want with him. Was he an admirer? An art
collector? Kent usually knew of such people—those of stature, at least. But then
many were fired with a sudden need to acquire art, some for more genuine
reasons than others.

"I do not want to interrupt your contemplations and your work, Mr. Kent.
You see, I am really just a messenger for another."

Kent stopped. Perhaps his eyebrows lifted.

"My good friend, Count Massenet, asked me to look in on you."

"Ah. And how is the ambassador?" Kent pulled light gloves off his fingers, gratified to see how still they remained.

"Well. I have never known the count to be less than well." Bertillon smiled. "It is his diet, I think."

Kent did not smile at this sally.

"I dare say. Shall I let the servants know there will be another for dinner?"

Despite the day's hints of spring, the night was clear and cool and Kent was glad of the fire. The two gentlemen sat at the table, cleared now of most of its dinnerware. By the light of the fire and candles Kent thought his Entonne visitor had a wraithlike quality. The man obviously cultivated the appearance of a sensitive artist, something Kent had always avoided. But then Bertillon's fine bone structure and light complexion lent themselves to it.

Kent looked down at the letter the young man had carried with him. It was couched in the terms of a letter of introduction, though it did ask Kent if he would return the "book" with Bertillon, and also stated that Massenet trusted Bertillon completely. Its meaning was clear. Kent was certain it was no forgery.

"I must apologize, Mr. Bertillon. The book in question is in the hands of a scholar of my acquaintance."

"That would be the able Mr. Valary, I assume," Bertillon said quietly.

Kent did not respond.

"Not to worry. I was to return it only if convenient to you, Mr. Kent," Bertillon said in Entonne. He shifted in his chair and reached for his glass. Like many another man of slight stature that Kent had known, Bertillon seemed to have enormous capacity for liquor. He had not stinted, before, during, or after dinner, and he didn't show the slightest effect. It was a myth that only large men could hold their drink, that was certain.

"May I make a small suggestion, Mr. Kent?"

"By all means."

"We should speak candidly. We are both aware of how important this matter is and how little time we might have."

Kent nodded, glancing at the letter again. He held it loosely in his hand, as though he could hardly bear to touch it, but neither could he bring himself to set it down.

Bertillon did not look the type to be an agent of Count Massenet, which, of course, made sense. And certainly the man had entrance everywhere. He had probably played for the King. In fact, Kent seemed to remember that he had. Perhaps Sir Roderick had even attended!

"It is our hope that you have considered the count's proposal and will agree to mutual assistance?"

Kent reached forward and with some effort placed the letter on the table, and then hooked his thumb into a pocket in his waistcoat. The diamond remained there, awaiting the right moment to be returned. Kent was not about to take money, in any form, from the Entonne. He looked into the dancing flames in the fire for a moment, thinking of his meetings with the countess—one did not want to look directly into the flames. It left one blind in the darkness.

"I cannot remember, in all my years, being offered such a difficult choice," Kent said. He was glad they spoke Entonne, a language none of his servants knew well.

Bertillon nodded, saying nothing until certain Kent was not about to speak. He must have realized that the painter had not made a decision.

"Perhaps, Mr. Kent, you could tell me what you would require to feel more inclined toward such an alliance?"

"Require? Oh, that is easy, Mr. Bertillon. What is difficult is finding a way to arrange for my requirements." Again a silence while Kent considered. "It has often been the experience of those who, for reasons of conscience, cooperated with foreign governments, that they would then find themselves unable to withdraw their services. They had, after all, committed a terrible crime— treason, punishable by death—and were henceforth easily coerced." He thought of making his point by returning the diamond, but he hesitated and the moment passed.

"You might respond that Count Massenet is a man of honor, Mr. Bertillon. And that this matter is far too momentous to even weigh such paltry concerns. But, as you have said, we must be candid here. Count Massenet has dealt with men in just this manner in the past. Do not protest. I know more of what goes on in Avonel than most—perhaps even more than Count Massenet—or you would not be here this night. The suicide of Lord Kastler I have never thought to be such a great mystery."

He looked up at Bertillon. *This is not an old fool you see before you.*

Bertillon rubbed a finger along his cheek. He nodded but offered no other response.

Kent's eye was drawn back to the flame, and he reached into his pocket to retrieve the diamond.

"Would it be reassuring to know," Bertillon began, staying Kent's hand, "that, if somehow the worst did occur in Farrland, you would be made welcome in my country? You are already famous there—famous in a land that venerates artists."

"I will have to tell you, Mr. Bertillon, that it is small comfort, for if I am forced to accept this offer, it will mean that I am perceived as a betrayer in my own country. I am not prepared to accept that. Call it pride, but I will not be known to history as a traitor."

Bertillon raised his eyebrows, perhaps a little impatient. "If Palle and his group manage to accomplish this thing, Mr. Kent. . . . Well, they cannot be allowed to get so far." Bertillon leaned forward in his chair. "I do not say this as a threat, but you must realize what this could lead to. My government cannot allow Palle, of all people, to gain such power. You know the man, Mr. Kent, you must realize what he would do. Entonne . . . it is his obsession. And the matter is larger than that. Farrland would be in terrible danger as well."

Kent thought that Bertillon would reach out and grasp his arm for emphasis, but the man held himself in check, only gazing up at the painter with those intense eyes. *War*. He was speaking of war.

Kent wondered if he were making a mistake. Perhaps the matter *was* too large to worry about the judgment of history.

Bertillon sat back in his chair, not taking his eyes from the painter. He let out a long breath, almost a sigh. "What if you were privy to information that would almost certainly guarantee your safety from Palle and would at the same time ruin the count—at least make it impossible for him to be of further use to the Entonne government?"

Kent shifted his position, his shoulders aching—from tension, he realized. "I can't imagine what this could be, Mr. Bertillon." *What in this round world?*

Bertillon considered a moment longer and then, motioning with his hand, he leaned forward, not speaking until he was close to Kent's ear.

The painter almost rose out of his chair at what he heard. "That is not possible!" he protested. "I know her!"

"I'm afraid it is more than possible, Mr. Kent," Bertillon said quietly. He reached into his frock coat and removed an envelope which he passed to Kent. "We trust you will keep this safe. Much depends on it."

Kent took the letter reluctantly. Would he be allowed to keep no illusions? Was no one beyond corruption? He opened the letter and read, feeling warm suddenly, perhaps his face flushed. When finished, he shut his eyes for a moment.

"Is it true," Bertillon said softly, "that the *Swallow* has not reached the Queen Anne Station?"

Kent felt his head nod, though with great effort. He did not look up.

"And what, do you think, are the intentions of the Duchess of Morland?"

Kent took a long breath, forcing his gaze toward the fire, into the center of the dancing flames. "It is a great mystery, Mr. Bertillon. I am not sure. There are so many rumors in the palace—there is no lack of information; but what is true . . . ? I cannot say."

"She wishes to extend her youth?"

"At the very least."

"We assume you have someone reliable aboard the *Swallow*?"

Kent nodded. "I have someone, yes. How reliable remains to be seen."

Bertillon paused for a second, as though recalling the list of questions he had, no doubt, been given. "This man; Professor Dandish. We are not clear about what happened there. He was the advisor for the palace arboretum, we know, but. . . ."

"He was secretly growing *regis* for the Duchess of Morland," Kent said, and then rose and moved to the fire.

Bertillon released a breath, almost a whistle. Massenet, apparently, did not know everything.

"And the cabal, Mr. Kent. Are our lists the same? Palle, Wells, Beall, Rawdon, Noyes, Hawksmoor, of course."

"Sir Stedman Galton. Prince Kori."

Bertillon looked up, hesitating, then he looked away. "Yes, though we have hopes that His Highness will see the folly of this course." Bertillon caught Kent's eye. "Who is unraveling this mystery for them?"

"Wells, primarily. Galton, too. And now a young man named Egar Littel— a complete innocent. He has no idea of their intentions."

Bertillon nodded. "The innocent," he said quietly.

"And who do *you* have unraveling this mystery?" Kent said, a bit of resentment coming through in his tone. When Bertillon showed surprise, Kent went on. "An exchange of information was what I agreed to."

Bertillon nodded. "A woman—I should not say. . . ." The young musician looked up and perhaps read the look on Kent's face. "Miss Simoe Dewitt. She is the daughter of Dewitt, the linguist. And now Varese—you were witness to our folly there. We had hoped for Valary, but someone was too quick for us." He smiled.

Silence. The two men regarding each other, like duelists. Like brothers.

"What do you think they will do, Mr. Kent?" Bertillon asked at last.

Kent paced across the hearth and then back.

"It is not easy to say. Their intentions, I'm sure, you have guessed. They are too fascinated by knowledge to stop—believing themselves wiser than the mages." He looked up at the painting above the mantel. The Countess of Chilton. One of several Kent had done. "So much depends on the nature of the text," he said almost to himself and then glanced over at his guest, hoping.

Bertillon shook his head. "We know no more than you, there."

"Even if they manage the translation, there is more, or so Valary says. They need the *regis* seed. They need time to learn—perhaps a great deal of time, we don't know. And they need someone with talent. Without that they are lost."

"Flattery?"

"You tell me, Mr. Bertillon. Did you not test him yourself?"

Bertillon nodded, no longer showing surprise at what Kent knew. "There is no one else?"

"Well, I have a fear. . . ."

Bertillon raised his eyebrows.

"Tristam Flattery has a cousin. Lord Jaimas."

"Is he one of them?"

"No. No. Not at this time, at least. And unlikely that he would become so. His father, the duke, has always been wary of Palle, and Lord Jaimas is no fool. It is only a hunch, anyway. But I watch him, all the same." Kent stopped his pacing. "And you, Mr. Bertillon; how far along are you?"

"Not far. Not as far as Palle and his friends, that is certain."

"But you yourself—you have talent? You could not have performed the test otherwise."

Bertillon reached out and brushed a crumb from the table. "Yes, though I have it in small degree only, Mr. Kent. Nothing like your young friend Tristam Flattery. Just learning that single test . . . by comparison, learning to play the pianum was child's play."

"Worth it, though. Invaluable, I would say."

Bertillon nodded. "Perhaps I should meet this young lord. I could answer your question once and for all."

"I'm not sure how we would arrange such a thing, but I will consider it." A moment while both men thought.

"If Prince Kori cannot be swayed in his path, Mr. Kent. . . . Well, there is concern in Entonne about the succession."

Kent felt great alarm at Bertillon's words, and stopped himself from pacing in agitation. This was a foreign agent making such a statement. A foreign agent in Kent's house!

"It would be unwise to meddle in this matter, Mr. Bertillon."

The musician looked up. "Unwise?" He shook his head. "Many people are involved in matters that are unwise. It forces us to consider desperate measures, Mr. Kent. Unwise? I agree. But what else can we do? You know what is at stake here."

A log shifted in the fire, sending a spray of sparks up the chimney. Kent felt nothing but discomfort now, regretting having said a word to this man. His gaze came to rest on the letter lying on the table and he motioned to it. "You realize that I could do great damage with this letter, and not just send the count back to Entonne."

"Perhaps." Bertillon flexed his fingers as though preparing to play. "Count Massenet is a man of honor, Mr. Kent, he would not endanger the lady. He trusts you will not use this information unless absolutely necessary."

Kent shook his head. "Strange conception of honor," he muttered.

"He has the lady's permission, Mr. Kent," Bertillon said evenly, showing no sign that his friend had just been insulted.

This brought Kent up short. "Really?"

Bertillon nodded.

"Blood and flames," the painter said.

Kent still stood before the fire—more out of habit than necessity. Bertillon had taken a candlestick from the table, increasing the shadows and darkening the colors in the room, and retreated to the drawing room, from which now emanated the most extraordinary music. A minor key, richly melancholic, darkly melodious. Kent did not recognize the piece, but it was a powerful composition. Bertillon must have been afraid he had not driven his message home with ever-unreliable words, and so resorted to his true medium of expression. The piece was unquestionably a requiem.

The painter patted his waistcoat pocket, realizing that he had forgotten the diamond, but he made no move, now, to return it.

Kent looked up at the portrait of the countess, those imperious blue eyes staring coolly down at him. *"Isollae,"* he whispered.

⤷ Three

The scent of flowers drifted in the open port and this perfume was so out of place that it roused Tristam from his sleep as surely as a touch or a sound—a bell to his olfactory senses. He inhaled the fragrance, the pungent cinnamon of sun-warmed soil blended with . . . with what? Sweet pollens, honey, lavender, lilac and plum: all of the sweetest fragrances he could conjure up did not compare. This perfume had even sweetened his dreams, for he had been dreaming . . . what? Something comforting and languorous, vaguely sensual. After weeks in the confines of the *Swallow* this smell was like a glimpse of light to an unsighted man.

Tristam realized that the ship was not moving forward through the seas, as he had come to expect, but was lying to, her motion eased. Rocked only by the whispered sigh of waves as they lifted the ship and passed beneath.

Varua, Tristam thought; *we are lying off Varua.* He rolled from his hammock and searched the darkness for his clothes.

By the time Tristam emerged onto the deck, a soft trade was blowing, sweeping the perfume of flowers back toward the island. Tristam paused at the top of the stairs and realized he wasn't alone. Not only was the entire watch on deck, but there were others as well. A quiet anticipation almost charged the air. *Land.* And not just land, but the fabled island of Varua. The voyage out was over.

Gregory had said that the Varuans were the most contented people in the known world, and he had called the island group the Happy Isles. Even Tristam, who believed the reports of the islands were exaggerated, felt his imagination fire.

A party of Jacks sprawled on the forecastle, singing low—a sad song that was much loved by them. The words drifted back to Tristam:

"Bury me deep, fifty fathoms or more,
Beyond all sight of land-o.
And if I have a son,
By the sea's tumble and run,
May he stay upon the strand-o."

Tristam moved away from the hatch, going to the rail. To the west he was sure the stars on the horizon were interrupted over a small area: the darkened peaks of the island. There might even be a sound of surf—the endless succession of waves that had crossed the Great Ocean before the trades to end weeks of travel by casting themselves upon the reef. It was like a doomed migration—salmon struggling up the river.

"My pay I cast upon the quay
For it'd been six months or more-o.
And an ancient whore with a heart of stone
Took me for her boy-o.

So bury me deep . . ."

"I had begun to think we should never arrive." The duchess appeared at Tristam's side and for a second she pressed his hand on the rail, but then she seemed to remember his injury and pulled her hand away as though she had touched heat in the darkness.

Tristam turned to look at her. In the faint, cool light of the stars the duchess' face was a mask—planes of pale light and shadow—and Tristam immediately thought of the theater and wondered which character would wear this mask. Not the ingenue, certainly; the duchess was neither innocent nor naive. Not the dutiful wife, never the harridan. Elorin, Duchess of Morland, was only herself; the beautiful widow, with more intelligence than Farr women were supposed to reveal; all the strength of a King's Minister; and somewhere behind the mask, a heart that truly longed for lost love—or so Tristam had come to believe. A heart the character only revealed by the pains she took never to let it be seen.

"I have often looked at the great globe of our world in Merton College," Tristam said, "and yet I never conceived of the size of the Ocean Beyond. There are things that cannot be comprehended with the intellect alone."

"I thought I should never hear such an admission pass your lips, Tristam Flattery." In the poor light he thought he saw the mask smile, teasing but not cruel.

A shooting star blazed briefly across the sky, and he found himself making a wish, not sure which embarrassed him more: the urge to wish or the wish itself—something to do with the woman standing beside him.

"I have a confession as well," she whispered.

There had been no opportunity on the voyage for them to spend a night together and Tristam found the intimacy suggested by Elorin's whisper was enough to set his blood coursing, though he was sure she meant to suggest no such thing.

"I cannot quite believe it, but I have some regrets that our voyage nears its conclusion," she said, her breath sweet as the scent of flowers. "How insular a ship is, and though one is cut off from many of the amusements one loves, all of the affairs that one detests are equally held at bay. No secretaries can reach you, there is no post, no unwanted guest, no intrigues, no plotting among courtiers, no gossip mongers, no surprises arriving at one's gate. We have been on a moving island, isolated, untouched by all the blather that goes with our positions in the world." She smiled in the darkness—Tristam saw the mask change. "Of course, the ship itself could bear some improvement, but it has carried us over the great ocean, and that has been an experience I shall not soon forget. I feel the entire pulse of my life has slowed. Most of my anxieties have fallen away—for what can a body do about them aboard a ship? Not a thing. The pulse of my own existence has begun to follow the rise and fall of the ship on the trade wind seas. A languid lifting and falling, regular in the extreme, and though strong, gentle in nature." She stopped, her speech tapering off like a ship's wake. "I have not the wit to tell what it is I mean."

"Nor has anyone, I think," Tristam said. "But I believe I understand all the same. The sailors call it an evolution—what happens after some time on the open ocean. A 'sea change,' they say."

The duchess might have nodded, shifting the light on the mask. Neither of them spoke, but they stared off toward the dark area on the horizon, the deep voices of the Jacks carrying off into the night.

"There is no place for a sailor boy
Where his heart can wonder free-o,
So I left the land, with its heart of stone,
And set once more to sea.

Oh, bury me deep . . ."

It was the next afternoon before the survey vessel *Swallow* entered the pass into the lagoon, for navigation among the coral reefs must be done with the sun at one's back or the dangers in the water would be hidden by reflection on the surface.

Varua rose up out of the deep ocean, the peaks of her green mountains awash in cloud and cleansed by dark curtains of silken rain that wafted, skein-like, over the high valleys and sheer cliffs. Tropical sun illuminated the swaying fronds and leaves that, Tristam thought, looked like cilia—the green slopes the flank of one great organism.

This contrast of light and dark—brilliant green and the shadows of cloud and falling rain—brought much drama to the scene, as did the slow powerful rhythm of the surf with its crests and foam of snow: the graveyard of the white-maned seas.

The sun did not appear to be the same star that illuminated the countries surrounding the Entide Sea. The light it cast infused colors with an astonishing vibrancy, and did not muddy the air but was at once clear and warm. For some reason Tristam thought this light was pure, unsullied by the deeds of men.

From his perch at the masthead, Tristam could see deep into the waters of the lagoon where the *Swallow*'s shadow swept across the bottom before them, like the passing of a great bird.

"Take a turn of this around your waist," Osler said, holding out the end of a line. "If we run onto a coral head, we would be thrown to the deck. A fate, perhaps, preferable to the rage of the captain."

Tristam took the salt-stiffened line and tied it loosely around his middle. A shoal of fish darted away from the approaching shadow, like bright autumn leaves plucked up by a sudden wind.

The two men were aloft, "conning" the ship through the intricacies of the lagoon, which, in places, was a maze of coral heads, some quite near to the surface. Fortunately, these dangers could be clearly seen on such a day, and the light colored waters, sandy brown and palest turquoise, were easily avoided, the ship staying to the darker blues and greens—Osler calling instructions down to the helmsman.

Below them, Tristam could see the duchess standing at the rail with Doctor

Llewellyn and her maid. Her summer dress appeared from beneath a yellow parasol as she moved, talking to those around her, pointing excitedly. Occasionally she peeked out from under the arc of her parasol and, catching Tristam's, eye, she grinned—as delighted as a child—the whiteness of her teeth bright against the coloring of the sun in her face.

Across the lagoon Tristam could see the gracefully curving trunks of palms along the shore, their shaggy heads swaying in the fall winds that swept down from the highlands above. There was no sign of habitation here. No smoke from cooking fires. The islanders preferred to live on the eastern shores where the trade blew and kept at bay such insects as there were. Parties would occasionally come to the western side to harvest coconuts and other fruits and to fish and dive for shells in the lagoon, but otherwise this shore was left to the hermit or holy man who required solitude—a difficult thing to find among the social Varuans.

The clarity of the water seemed impossible to Tristam, as though it were merely air, and the *Swallow* had truly taken wing. As if to prove this true, a skate soared languidly through the air-clear waters, looking as though the lazy beat of its wings could carry it up through the invisible surface until it took its place among the birds. All around the ship, terns cried and dove, splashing into the lagoon, proving there was, after all, a boundary between sky and water—between the two worlds.

The ship was closer to the island now, and Tristam focused his glass there for a moment, picking out the trees and flowering bushes that he knew; though the small white flower he sought could not be seen—to his relief. The trees admired by the islanders grew in profusion, breadfruit, coconut palm, and banana: the trees that provided so much of their sustenance.

For the past week he had swung between great excitement and anticipation, and utter dread. Arrival in Varua would bring many things to the surface that had lain dormant aboard ship.

He glanced down and saw the doctor staring through his field glass. Llewellyn, who had spirited the seed aboard this ship. Llewellyn, who had rescued Tristam with the physic that he should never have taken, and then had told the duchess that only he could preserve Tristam in the days to come. The naturalist brushed his wrist against his leg, pulling down the shirt cuff to mask the scar.

Over the past weeks Tristam had spent much time trying to acquire a little of the islanders' language, and in this endeavor the doctor had been a great help, for Llewellyn had an astonishing grasp of the language for a man who had never been to Oceana. But it had become clear to Tristam that either there was a significant gap in Llewellyn's knowledge, or there was an area he was not ready to share, for Tristam could learn little about the language surrounding the islanders' religion—which all but governed their lives. The doctor would only shrug when questioned, that condescending smile appearing. "Perhaps, Tristam, you will be able to fill in that particular area of linguistic study. Llewellyn must admit ignorance there."

Unlikely, Tristam thought. There were things that Llewellyn was not telling. Why, Tristam did not know. His dislike of the man had intensified greatly. Even the pity he felt for the doctor's condition was disappearing. The man was hiding things from him.

Osler pointed suddenly, sighting along his hand as though it were an arrow. "Islanders!"

Tristam raised his glass and on a not-too-distant headland he saw a dozen figures, all women, scrambling easily out over the broken rock, their tanned sturdy legs flashing in the sunlight. Shining black hair wafted in the breeze, and Tristam could see dusky cinnamon skin barely covered by brightly patterned fabric wrapped about the waist. Flowers took the place of jewelry, and the women wore them in their hair and around their necks in chains. Tristam felt a stirring, remembering his dream from the first night in Avonel.

"I think the master would feel more confident if your attention was focused on the lagoon," Osler said quietly.

Tristam glanced down quickly and saw Hobbes looking up at him, hands on his hips. The naturalist went back to his duty—which was not his duty, really, for he was not a member of the ship's regular company.

Gusts of wind drove the ship in bursts and she seemed to lurch closer to the point until a glass was no longer needed to appreciate the beauty of the women. The officers prowled the deck and the sound of a knotted rope punctuated the soft sounds of the day and sent the love-starved sailors back to their tasks.

When the ship drew near enough, the women began to sing, their song drifting over the lagoon, the surf beating out its pulsing rhythm. To this music they danced slowly and gracefully, motioning with their hands and arms. It was an enticing song, almost an enchantment, and Tristam could feel the bite of the rope around his middle as he leaned out to catch a last glimpse of the singers disappearing behind a sail. Several of the women stripped off their pareus and plunged into the lagoon, as at home there as seals.

"Well," Osler said, "it would seem that some things about Varua have not been exaggerated. I don't think one could mistake their meaning."

"Should we alter course to larboard?" Tristam asked suddenly.

"*A point to larboard!*" Osler shouted down to the deck.

In the lee of the island the mountains blocked the trade, and as the afternoon wore on to evening, the fallwinds coming down from the high valleys became less frequent. Stern decided to anchor for the night off a stretch of beach before the quick-falling tropical night made navigation dangerous.

In the brief twilight Tristam went ashore with a boat sent to retrieve palm leaves—a symbol of peace to the Varuans. While the men under the command of Osler went about their task, Tristam set out along the sand in search of something like solitude. He had never before realized how much he valued time alone. Living aboard ship was like returning to boarding school where privacy was almost unknown, but worse, for the ship was so small.

He felt the fine sand, flourlike and cooling, on the soles of his feet and between his toes. How very far he had come—halfway round the world—to this verdant green island floating in an endless sea, with its necklace of surf breaking on the reef. Part of him could hardly believe it.

He climbed slowly up a hand of rock, his limbs not yet back to strength, and sat at the top looking out at the quickly fading sunset, the broad turquoise lagoon, and the ship lying still at anchor.

Tristam ran his hand over the smooth stone—altered volcanic rock—and thought of the Varuans. No one among them did anything but the most basic crafting of stone, yet there was a great deal of stonework on the island, and Trevelyan suggested that there might be far more hidden beneath the luxuriant vegetation. It was believed that the Varuan culture was layered over another earlier society, the way streams laid down layers of silt, eventually to become rock. An earlier culture that understood some principles of engineering and knew how to shape and build with stone.

Darkness came swiftly at that latitude, flowing out from among the shadows as though the sun's setting was a signal, breaking the spell of light. A planet floated above the horizon, its disk almost apparent to the unaided eye. Lanterns appeared on the deck of the *Swallow,* the small flickering flames of men who feared the dark. Even Tristam, who loved the night, felt a bit uncomfortable alone with the dark, tropical jungle at his back.

He turned to look over his shoulder suddenly, as though he felt he were being watched, and was sure he saw eyes staring at him. Eyes that almost shone in a dark face and beneath a mass of tangled hair. And then this apparition was gone, with only the sound of branches swept aside and the quieter fall of a foot to assure Tristam that this had not been merely a figment of his imagination. It had been a man, dressed in strange, ragged clothing.

For a moment Tristam stared into the shadows, holding his breath, and then suddenly he leaped to his feet and made his way back to the beach and the small comfort of his shipmates.

ᠵ **Four**

The country home of the Duke and Duchess of Blackwater had twenty-three sleeping chambers—a fact that kept popping into Alissa Somers' mind as she wandered through the maze of halls and rooms. In the winter season much of the old mansion was closed off, unheated, and largely ignored by both staff and family, and it was through one of these wings that Alissa explored. An explorer was how she felt, too, for the place was so vast, so labyrinthine that she truly believed she could be lost for days, and had brought no crumbs to leave a trail.

"A map would be appropriate here," she mumbled. The hall she walked seemed to be used for the display of family portraits thought to be of so little worth that they were not even given the protection of heat in winter months. One serious-looking youth appeared to be her own Jaimy, but when she stopped to look she discovered, in fact, that it was a painting of Erasmus Flattery, aged seven. This reminded her of her purpose and she walked on, the tap of her shoes on the wooden floor echoing in the cold hall.

She remembered how, as a child, her family home in Merton had seemed such a vast holding, full of secret places where children could play, far, far away from the adult world. The closet beneath the stairs. The hollow tree at the end of the garden. The tunnel into the ancient hedge. And best of all, the attic! How she had both loved and dreaded that attic! But the truth was her childhood home could be housed many times over in one wing of the Flattery family mansion.

She stopped to look at another portrait—her soon-to-be father-in-law. Not as handsome as his son, nor nearly as happy, judging by his countenance, but still a man of imposing bearing. She had begun to feel some affection for the old duke, for he obviously had taken a great liking to this commoner who had lost her heart to his son—and the duke's response surprised her.

Well, I am not a social climber, and though I am sure there are many who could never be convinced of this, I do not think the duke to be one of them.

No, the Duke of Blackwater was not a poor judge of people, that was certain, and this astuteness concerned her a little. Unsure of what she had done to gain the duke's approval, she now feared that, through some equally unconscious action, she would just as easily alienate him. And here she was involved in this endeavor—trying to find out if the duke had hidden the writings of his famed uncle.

How Mr. Kent had drawn her into this she still did not know. The artist had appealed to some sense of justice that was strong within her, stronger than she had realized, perhaps. And then there was Kent's sincerity—one could not doubt that he was a man of honor—honor in the old style. Much like her own Jaimas and his cousin, who had intervened with her father on Jaimy's behalf and then set off on a voyage of discovery.

Of course, she had not taken on this task without spending some hours justifying her actions—if only to herself. The truth, she had decided, was that she was merely proving Mr. Kent's notions to be false. Thus she would perform a service to an old family friend, and do no harm to Jaimy's family in the process. Perfectly acceptable.

Perfectly acceptable until she had begun her detecting. She had befriended one of the servants—a girl close to her own age. There was a bond there almost immediately, no doubt because Alissa was not of the nobility herself. Over a number of conversations Alissa had learned that there was gossip among the servants about the estate of Erasmus Flattery. Much had been removed from the man's house under the direction of the duke and his secretary, or so it was claimed. Those involved had been sworn to keep silence on this matter—as though life below the stairs had suddenly changed its character and allowed secrets to be kept.

There was, Alissa knew, usually at least a kernel of truth in the whisperings of servants: enough that she had begun to wonder if Averil Kent's suspicions could actually have some basis. Enough that Alissa Somers could no longer be sure of the principle she served. If she was not clearing the reputation of Jaimy's family, at least in the eyes of Mr. Kent, then what in this round world was she doing?

She turned a corner into another hallway, dimly lit by bars of late afternoon light that fell through shutter slats, closed over tall windows at the hall's end. Somewhere here she should find the door she was looking for. The members of the Flattery family were born with such an all-consuming curiosity that they had, over several generations, accumulated a vast collection of books, monographs, periodicals, and pamphlets. The lovely library on the mansion's central courtyard could not begin to hold all the volumes that had accumulated over the years and Alissa had discovered that a second library had been created— not so elegant as the one she knew—to hold the overflow.

Alissa realized it was unlikely that, having taken the trouble to whisk away the writings of Erasmus Flattery, the duke would then simply store them in an unlocked library for all to read. But she knew no other way to begin than by eliminating the obvious.

Having assured herself that there was no copy of Dennis' *Moonlight at Winter's End* in the main library, Alissa then stated loudly at breakfast how very much she had always wanted to read this book. *"Might there be a copy somewhere in the house?"* The duke had immediately offered to have a servant search the closed library, but Alissa had insisted that this would deprive her of one of her chief pleasures in life—poking through shelves of books. The duke was far too much of a gentleman to deprive her one of life's greatest pleasures—as she had suspected. So here she was—feeling a bit clever, too.

She stopped before a pair of doors that were all of ten feet in height. If she had understood the directions correctly, this should be the library.

Pushing one heavy door open, Alissa found a scene she did not expect. Lamps blazed, lighting the white edges of shelves so that they framed staggered rows of book spines like the darkened pigments of ancient paintings. A walkway at the height of the second floor allowed access to the walls of books and, before her, a fire crackled in a carved hearth.

She paused for a moment, surprised by the light and warmth in a room she had expected to be empty and unused, but clearly the duke or the duchess had sent a servant ahead to make her visit pleasant. This made her smile, for the family were continually doing such things—to make her feel welcome she was sure.

Alissa pulled the door to, cutting off the cold breeze from the hallway beyond. At the sound of the door closing, a man, hidden behind a wingback chair, leaned forward.

"Alissa?"

She let go of the door handle she had grabbed, so surprised that she was prepared to bolt. "Duke . . . ? You startled me."

"I do apologize, but you must rest assured that you could never come to harm within our walls, Alissa. You are too much of a treasure to us all."

The duke rose from his chair, a tall, well proportioned man, dark in coloring and handsome in his years. Gesturing to another chair, he said, "Come, sit by the fire. It is dreadfully cold, is it not?"

She pulled her shawl closer around her shoulders and nodded. Despite all his kindness Alissa remained somewhat intimidated by this man. He had been born to the highest rung of Farr society and had succeeded brilliantly—a man respected throughout the Kingdom.

Alissa was glad of the warmth as she felt herself perch, somewhat woodenly, on the offered chair. The duke took a moment to place another log on the fire, banking the coals expertly. And she could watch him, seeking the characteristics that he had contributed to his son. Certainly the duke's face was more strongly formed, and sharper featured, though that might be merely a result of age. In size and shape they were much alike, not that she was to notice such things, of course. The duke's hair was tightly curled and his beard he kept trimmed short, in the style of gentlemen. Despite this rather strong, masculine appearance, the duke moved with surprising grace, using his hands most expressively, and Alissa liked this contrast, this softening of his image.

Suddenly Alissa realized that this meeting was no accident, and the belated realization made her feel even more a country girl. Her lack of dowry suddenly loomed up, large, at least in her mind, for its embarrassment. How her father would lecture if he could read her thoughts! Wealth and titles were of no value in his scheme of things.

The duke returned to his chair, crossed his legs, and smiled in a manner she was certain was intended to reassure, though it did not have that effect.

"You have come down the 'hallway of unlikenesses'?" he asked, waving a long finger at the door, his mouth taking on the same near-smile that her own Jaimy affected when he thought he was being a wit.

She nodded, smiling to show she did not miss the humor.

"My family has a tradition of supporting failed painters." He shook his head a little. "And that is not said entirely in jest."

Jaimy took after his mother in coloring, but father and son had many mannerisms in common, and though their eyes were not the same in either color or shape, they both had a manner of crinkling them up, as though about to laugh, that Alissa found very endearing. Of course, the duke had many more and deeper lines than her Jaimy, though one day, no doubt, his face would be etched in a similar way. She would not mind.

"Of course," he seemed pressed to add, "there are many paintings in the house that are very fine. There is no doubt of that. Occasionally my forebears did engage the services of someone with actual talent, though I think these instances were far too few and a result of a certain amount of luck." He shrugged. "We shall have to have you sit for someone of talent after the wedding. A future Duchess of Blackwater, and one so lovely, should certainly grace the walls of our home." He leaned forward slightly. "And we shall not relegate your likeness to a cold hallway, be assured of that." He turned his attention to the fire for a moment, propping his elbow on the chair's arm and placing a long finger alongside his eye, just as Jaimy did when lost in thought. "Certainly, if you have an artist that you would prefer . . . I believe you have an interest in artists." He turned back to her, his face slightly more serious—the crinkles gone from around his eyes. "Did I not see you in the company of Averil Kent at the birthday celebration?"

She hesitated—a moment of guilt—but then hurried to answer. "Mr. Kent, yes. He is a friend of my father's. Why, I think I have known him all my life."

"No doubt. It is unfortunate he does no portraits." He nodded, as though agreeing with this statement. "He is a man of some interest, our Averil Kent . . . though he does have some very odd notions." The duke looked off toward the windows where the last light of day was absorbed by gray mist and rain. This view seemed to hold his attention for a moment and then he spoke suddenly. "Kent once questioned me about my uncle, Erasmus Flattery. . . . do you know to whom I refer?"

Alissa nodded. No educated person could claim ignorance of the great Erasmus, but she felt she was admitting to more than just knowledge of his existence. Her perch on the edge of the chair felt suddenly precarious.

"Yes? Well, *'question'* is not truly what I mean. He virtually accused me of hiding Uncle Erasmus' papers after his death. I was the executor of the estate, you see." He shook his head. "I must say, if not for the man's great age and the esteem in which he is held by the entire nation. . . ." He left the sentence unfinished. "Of course, he is a friend of your family, and a good man, I realize, but . . ." He raised his eyebrows and she could see a bit of tension in the muscles of his jaw. "As though I would steal from my own nephew, who was Erasmus' heir." He fell silent again, staring down at the pattern in the carpet.

Alissa wondered if the hairs on her neck could truly stand on end. Her mouth was completely dry, and she was quite sure the duke expected her to make some comment, though she was too frightened to speak.

Then the duke went on, to her relief. "Well, I suppose there were many who felt great disappointment that Erasmus destroyed all his work before the end. I confess, I was saddened by his decision myself. A lifetime of effort, and such a brilliant, even if erratic, mind. Terribly sad."

She could hear the rain on the window now, a soft sound that usually brought her comfort.

The duke looked up and smiled at her. "Individuals are viewed so differently by others." He waved a hand at the doors, and the hallway beyond, and his eyes crinkled at the corners. "Look at the portraits of anyone, even Erasmus himself. Each artist saw a different person. And it is often the case that one portrait is pilloried by friends and relations as being entirely false, while others, equally close to the subject, say the likeness is exact, even uncannily so." He laughed. "Different eyes see different things, apparently, and some people are less easily defined than others, I suspect. Erasmus Flattery was one of these. A man of infinite complexity and an equivalent number of moods. What painter could hope to understand all of that?"

Alissa smiled, she hoped agreeably: *what painter, indeed.* Deciding that she could not bear her perch a second longer, she rose to stand before the blaze. It would have been unforgivably impolite to turn her back on the duke, though she longed to do so. To hide her reaction. His eyes, though not unkind, seemed bent on looking into her innermost thoughts. Clearly she had not been as clever in her questioning of the maid as she had believed. *Idiot,* she thought. The Flattery family were obviously taking careful measure of their interloper. Undoubtedly the friendly maid had been sent Alissa's way. She felt a flash of anger—but then had she not been false to them? Was she not, in fact, here with a secret purpose? *Idiot,* she thought again.

Alissa looked off at the fading light, invisible rain spattering softly against the glass. "I—I am certain that many empiricists were hoping to learn much of the mysterious Erasmus Flattery from his writings, Duke. There were so many rumors about Mr. Flattery—his connection with Lord Eldrich, I am sure. . . ."

The duke nodded. "Exactly so. Rumors. Often begun by people who should have known better, as well. Poor Kent, I fear his disappointment was so great that it led him to speak rashly." He shrugged. "But that was some years ago now, and, of course, we are on the best of terms again. I don't mean to speak out against an old friend of your family, and not someone as good-hearted as our Mr. Kent." He reached to the small table beside him and lifted the cover of a book, tilting his head to read the cover page. Then he looked up as though remembering his point. "The duchess and I would very much like to engage an artist of reputation for your portrait, Alissa. You will be one of us soon—'Lady Alissa'—if you don't mind me saying so, for we do not mean to take you from the bosom of your own family. Not at all. Let the Somers and the Flatterys have great commerce between them. That is my hope, and the hope of the duchess as well." His eyes crinkled up as he smiled at her. "I dare say we could use the addition of a bit of substance. Too many generations of coddled aristocrats." He shook his head. "Bad for the blood."

Alissa nodded, tight-lipped. *Do you think me a brood mare, then?* she wondered.

"I shall leave you to your searching of the shelves, though it is my fear that you shall not find what you seek here." The duke rose from his chair and bent to kiss her hand.

A cool draft wafted in from the "hall of unlikenesses" as the duke left, making Alissa press closer to the fire. She turned so that she might more easily warm her hands and found herself staring at the portrait of a woman that hung over the mantel.

It may have been true that the Flatterys engaged some poor artists, but that was not the case here, though Alissa could see no signature. A woman of surpassing beauty seated on a divan, a cascade of dark curls framing a heart-shaped face. If this was a past Duchess of Blackwater, then Alissa would be embarrassed to have her own likeness hanging in the same house.

But then the discussion of portraits had not been the true purpose of the conversation, she reminded herself. The purpose had been to warn her not to pursue Mr. Kent's suspicions. A gentle rebuff.

Alissa tore her eyes from the portrait and stared down into the flames. She felt her cheeks burning. *"Clumsy fool,"* she hissed. Jaimy's father would never trust her again. Not that he had placed any trust in her before, clearly. *Farrelle's blood,* she thought, *I allowed myself to be outwitted by a servant girl!*

Her eye was drawn again to the painting above the mantel. Whoever this woman was, or had been, she did not look the type to make a fool of herself in such a situation. For the briefest second Alissa found herself thinking that it would have been better if she and Jaimy had never met. Everything would have been so much simpler, and she would never have been involved in this scheme of Kent's. Her anger veered suddenly and fixed on the avuncular painter—but that could not last. She knew the decision had been her own.

Nothing to be done now but to carry on, to act in good faith with herself, and not get drawn into foolish schemes that Jaimy's family would not approve.

She turned her eye on the bookshelves. No doubt there was a scheme of order—she would have to learn the rules.

An hour had passed and the only light in the room came from the oil lamps and the glow from the fire. Winter's darkness had descended on Deptford County like a black rain. Alissa had long since found the volume she sought but continued to search the shelves for the mere pleasure of it. Now here was something that would cause even her father to feel envy. This room, which apparently was largely ignored, was as full of jewels as the King's treasury— though jewels of literature, to be sure. The Flatterys were gifted in languages and the library reflected that—philosophy, novels, and poetry could be found in all the tongues of the Entide Sea, though, unlike her own home, the literature of empiricism was not so well represented.

Alissa had mounted one of the sets of steps that rolled along the shelves and was examining books, convinced now that life was far too short, for she could spend one lifetime reading in this library alone.

The sound of a door opening caused her to start, and she grabbed the steps lest she lose her balance.

"Alissa?"

It was Jaimy. She felt her face grow warm.

"Is that you, my darling Alfred?" she called, choosing a name at random.

"No. No, it is your poor fiancé. Alfred was detained elsewhere."

"Oh, well. You'll just have to do." She scrambled down the ladder, fearing that, in her haste, this was done in a less than ladylike fashion.

Jaimy stepped through the tall doors. He had been out to hunt with the neighbors that morning and was now, clearly, fresh from a bath. He had, no doubt, been sent to remind her of dinner, which would give them as much as half of the hour alone. One of the greatest pleasures of being engaged—they could spend some small amount of time together without the burden of a chaperon.

Jaimy took both her hands and kissed her, once gently on each cheek, and then on the lips. They embraced, far more closely than any chaperon would have thought proper, and she could feel the longing they carried within them, both by night and by day.

Not long now, she told herself, though she did not quite believe it. They had decided on a traditional spring wedding—some two months off yet. Mere weeks . . . but when had the week grown to such length?

Jaimy pulled back enough that he could see her face. His eyes crinkled at the corners but then he turned serious. "Is something wrong? You look as though you've seen a ghost."

Ah, yes, the other issue. In taking up with Mr. Kent's intentions she had not been honest to her betrothed—not that she had lied to Jaimy, of course, but still, honesty required that she speak of all things of import. Or so she believed.

She pushed her face into his chest for a moment. "Come and sit by the fire," she said, pulling back to meet his now concerned eyes. "I have a small confession. Nothing to cause you worry, so do not look so. Come." Alissa took him by the hand and led him to the two chairs that stood by the fire. As she had before, she perched on the edge of the nearer chair and Jaimy unknowingly took his father's place, though he did not look nearly so forbidding.

She gazed into the fire for a moment and then up at the imposing woman who stared down at her from above the mantel. "I had the oddest conversation with Mr. Averil Kent." She glanced over at Jaimy, who nodded, apparently acknowledging that he knew Kent. "This was at the birthday celebration for the duchess." She bit her lip and then plunged on. "Do you know, Mr. Kent is of the opinion that the papers of your great-uncle Erasmus might have been . . . hidden away." Her gaze was pulled back into the flames. Suddenly she felt she had really betrayed Jaimy—saying nothing to him until now. "I should have told you," she said, her voice coming out as a whisper.

Jaimy continued to stare at her, his face unreadable she realized, and that struck her like a blow. Did she not truly know him?

She found herself staring down at the carpet—reds and soft greens, an unfamiliar pattern. "I confess, I asked among the servants about this. There is gossip, as there always is, of course." Her voice evaporated for a few seconds, and when she looked up to speak again, she felt tears clinging to her lashes, about to run over. "The duke heard of my inquiries and spoke to me about them. Not harshly, but. . . ." She could say no more but only shrugged, stupidly, she thought.

Jaimy rose from his chair and crouched before her, taking her hands. He brushed a strand of hair back from her face and caressed her cheek.

"You have no need of tears, my dear Alissa, or embarrassment. The duke will have forgotten the incident by now. That is his way." Jaimy stopped, staring into her eyes and attempting a smile. "I have my own confession, far longer and more tangled than your own. Perhaps we can make sense of this together." He brought her hands to his lips and kissed each finger in turn. "It began in Merton last summer . . . my chance encounter with Tristam. He was there to help

Dean Emin with Dandish's estate, as you no doubt remember. I sensed something odd when Tristam and I first met there, though I attributed it to grief at the time. I don't know if I told you that Dandish's house had been broken into, or perhaps you had heard through your father?"

Jaimy sat at her feet, staring into the fire, and as he told his story, she ran her hand gently through his hair. Jaimy tended to be serious so infrequently that she found this sudden change in his manner most unsettling, as though he had suddenly become ill. And the story was so very strange: a physic that kept the King alive; intrigue in the court; Professor Dandish, of all people, involved in a venture that was likely treason; the theft of the professor's journals; a correspondence with Valary the mage-scholar in which the name of Erasmus Flattery emerged. It went on and on, becoming more and more tangled and peculiar as it unfolded.

"I do wish you had not allowed Tristam to go off on this voyage," she said when Jaimy paused.

He squeezed her hand. "I fear that I was mistaken in that as well. I pray he will come to no harm." He took a watch from his pocket and checked the time. "We must go along to dinner in a moment," Jaimy said; sadly, she thought. "But I must tell you about Kent before we go. The same day that he spoke to you, Mr. Kent rather rudely interrupted a conversation I had just begun with Sir Roderick Palle, who had taken me aside for a word. Not that Kent was rude in his manner. Obtuse is more the word I want. Interrupted our conversation as though he could not see we were intending to speak privately. Dragged Sir Roderick off to meet someone, too. Now Kent is very old, but he has the most genteel manners and a carefully cultivated sensitivity. Clearly he intended to keep Sir Roderick and me apart." He fell silent, and Alissa could feel the muscles in his neck had become hard.

"Now as to your own concern," Jaimy said. "I have listened to the servants' talk as well. I am quite sure that some things *were* removed from my great-uncle's home before Tristam came into possession. Perhaps the works that Kent seeks, but other things as well." He gestured up at the painting over the mantelpiece. "This canvas certainly hung in Highloft Manor in the days of Erasmus," he said quietly. "I know that for a fact. The Countess of Chilton. You know of her, of course?"

Alissa nodded, looking up at that too-beautiful face. So that's who this woman was.

"There was some scandal. Perhaps scandal is the wrong word, but some . . . *involvement.* I can learn nothing for certain, but something occurred between my great-uncle Erasmus, Lady Chilton, Lord Skye, and, I have begun to suspect, Averil Kent." He paused again. "And there is more. This portrait has some significance to my father as well. He keeps a fire in this room, to protect the books, he says, and he comes here often. And this is a room my mother never ventures into."

"When I spoke to Kent . . ." Alissa began, but Jaimy hushed her with a finger to her lips and, as quickly, seated himself in the chair opposite. A soft knock on the door, and then it opened a crack, though no face appeared.

"I am sent to bid you to dinner, m'lord Jaimas. Lady Alissa." It was an underbutler, performing his duty with a little embarrassment, no doubt.

Alissa and Jaimy smiled at each other. She felt like a child caught breaking rules, though the use of the honorific—strictly premature—caused a second of confusion. As though she had been mistaken for someone else—someone far grander.

"We shall be along directly. Thank you."

The door closed.

Jaimy made no move to go but sat gazing at her; his face, usually so animated and full of life, appeared careworn and older than his years. "There is a part of me that would like to ignore all of this. I often tell myself that I have taken some small incidents and blown them all out of proportion, but my better half tells me that this is not true. And then there is Tristam, off risking much in this cause. Somehow I cannot abandon him. Farrelle knows whatever happens in Farrland will have no bearing on events halfway around the globe, but still. . . . If Tristam returns with several pieces of the puzzle, I shall feel I have let him down if I have done nothing. Do you see?"

Alissa saw completely. She crossed to Jaimy and kissed him tenderly. He could not imagine the relief she felt. Her deepest fear had been that her charming fiancé was not a man who would ever choose the difficult course, for comfort was too available to a man born into his world.

As she took his hands and drew him up, she felt a tear streak down her cheek like rain on glass, but she was not in the least sad.

⌒ Five

The road at least was reasonably well kept up even if it did wind and twist along the valley floor. Kent stared out at the stark, silvered-gray branches passing by, and beyond them a leaf-strewn bank rising steeply up toward sunlight and the blue he could almost sense somewhere above. On the narrow valley floor subtle shades of gray and brown and deep, living green must pass for color in a place where direct sunlight would not be seen all the long months of winter.

Glacial movement had formed this series of near parallel valleys between high ridges; or so Layel had conjectured, and that was all that Kent really knew. Geology was not the painter's great passion, nor, in truth, was painting—at least not in recent months.

Valary's letter had been so insistent, the tone so urgent.

Come immediately to Tremont Abbey. Waste not a moment! You must see with your own eyes what I have found.

Written as though whatever Valary had discovered was in imminent danger of disappearing; and perhaps it was, Kent did not know. The letter had hardly been effusive, but he and Valary were in this together, and though he was well aware that the old scholar was an eccentric of the highest order, Kent did not think the man would drag him halfway across the country without good reason—at least that was his hope.

He bent so that he might look up toward the ridge above. Yes, that might be the ruins through the trees, as though perched on a branch staring down, Kent thought, silhouetted against a chaotic sky. Another blast of wind shook the carriage on its springs, and Kent sat up to brace himself.

It couldn't be far now. He only hoped that there was a passable track up to the old abbey ruins. The prospect of climbing up out of this valley by his own efforts had no appeal. For the thousandth time he wished this matter had arisen when he was young.

To the road's left a narrow river swept along its twisted course, swift to carry away the winter rains, its surface scarred by ripples and eddy lines, and darkly pigmented with silt.

Deep in the valley, periods of utter calm were punctuated by fallwinds plunging down the valley walls, stirring the trees, and moaning horribly. Moss and dead leaves and broken branches would batter driver and team, rocking the carriage like a ship at sea.

It was the ragged end of another snowless February gale sweeping in off the open sea, some dozen miles to the east. Kent pulled his greatcoat closer about his neck. It was far worse for poor Hawkins, he realized, and did not indulge in self-pity. But this journey could not have been undertaken at a worse time of year—nor could it have been put off. Valary had discovered something. Something Kent desperately hoped would help them in this endeavor he despaired would ever come out right.

"*Let it be worth the effort,*" he prayed, and as if in answer the horses slowed and then stopped. Kent threw open the window so that he might put his head out to see what went on. To the right, massive gate stones towered over the road, their gates long missing. Each stone stood at its own angle to the earth, leaving the impression that, over the ages, they had been pushed askew by the wind.

With some effort Hawkins began to work the four-horse team around the sharp bend and then up the sloping track. It was a difficult climb as the old carriageway was rutted and slick with moss and wet leaves. Kent braced himself in his seat, wondering in the end, if he would not have been better off on foot. But finally they came up into the full daylight and the harsh wind of the sea, and here, above the trees, the ancient abbey kept vigil, like some mysterious standing stone. Its empty-eyed openings stared off toward the gray sea, waiting for what, Kent could not imagine.

The driver drew the carriage to a halt and Averil Kent, pressing his tricorn down onto his head against the efforts of the wind, stepped to the ground. He held on to the door for a moment, though the wind tried to tear it from his grasp, and stood with his cane in one hand, his coat blowing around him like the branches of a great cedar.

"What a foul wind, sir," Hawkins called as he climbed stiffly down from his high-seat.

The painter nodded, moving his hand to his hat as a gust struck. Closing the door, he stood away from the carriage and stared up at the remains of Tremont Abbey, the ancient stone covered in lichen and vines and the hardy flora that could bear up to the winter storms.

It was a pre-Farrellite abbey, Kent knew, though he could remember little more than that. There were signs that it had been torn down by the hands of men—though the job had never been finished—and here and there the stone was blackened as if the structure had once been fired. It was an eerie, forbidding place, and not helped by the day.

Kent turned and stared off over the downs toward the distant sea, but his eye was drawn to the racing clouds that chased the patches of sunlight across both land and water. Great towering clouds, flayed to ribbons by the sea wind, went scurrying inland as though in pursuit of the parent storm that had left them behind.

"Shall I look about for your friend, sir?" the driver offered, though not terribly enthusiastically. The poor man was undoubtedly frozen near to death.

"No. No, find shelter for yourself and the team." Kent looked up to find the position of the sun. "It will be dark in three hours. I don't know where we shall stay the night, but let me only find Mr. Valary and perhaps I shall have an answer."

Kent set off immediately toward the ruin, thinking he would circle it once and see what there was to be seen.

"*Hel-lo!*" he called, but it seemed to him that the wind took his voice and stretched the words thin, drawing them up into the sky to chase off after the scurrying clouds. Even so he persisted, calling every ten steps or so. Stopping occasionally to listen. Where in the world could the man be?

The ruin appeared to be half-sunk into the ground, though Kent knew it was the ground that, over the centuries, had risen up. No doubt this ferocious wind deposited soil daily against the walls. It was a wonder the abbey could be seen at all.

The stonework was very fine, better than he expected, the openings all curving up to graceful peaks, and he could see that they had once been divided by fine stone traceries. In the structure's corners the walls ran off, curving down to the ground like ramps, though these features had been badly damaged. Kent climbed up a six-pace rise of soft ground and noticed fresh boot prints pressed into the dark earth. Valary must not be far off.

He bore on, around the far end of the abbey, where he found some protection from the wind, and then he heard, quite clearly, the unmistakable sound of metal scraping stone. The sound was not loud, but its sharpness echoed up among the shattered walls like a bell through fog.

Kent stepped into the protection of a doorway and stood listening. When there was a break in the work, the painter called out again and in a few seconds heard footsteps growing louder.

"Ah, Kent!" The head of Valary appeared through a hole in the floor some forty feet away. His hair was awry, like a skein of wool caught in the gale, his face smudged with dirt and red from wind or exertion, but all the same the old scholar looked well pleased with his lot. He continued his ascent—up a stairway apparently—and with each step Valary appeared more unkempt, more covered in grime. He wore a short coat of heavy oiled-cotton such as workmen favored, and, beneath this, hunter's heavy wool breeches. High leather boots completed this outfit—very sensibly, Kent thought.

The aging historian crossed to Kent, who had not moved from the doorway, and clasped the painter's hand tightly, as though unaware of how dirty his own hand was.

"Kent, you cannot begin to imagine how pleased I am to see you!" He broke into an awkward smile, so out of character for the serious scholar that Kent felt a smile appear despite his utter discomfort. "Or is it yet Sir Averil?"

The painter shook his head, sorry to be reminded of this.

"Well, either way, you cannot begin to imagine what I have found!" Valary stopped and peered at Kent closely, as though searching for the marks of some disease, but then his smile returned. "Oh, you needn't look so. I haven't taken leave of my senses, entire. Not in the least. No, my dear Kent, when you see what it is I have unearthed. . . ." Taking the painter's arm, he drew him into the abbey, into the excitement of his discovery. "Why, you will count your journey as easy coin for such a return, I can assure you."

Without further explanation he crossed the floor of the ancient building, now covered in grasses and stunted broom, and started back down the stairway. "Mind your step. The stone has been too long exposed to the elements and is much degraded. This one especially—it rocks badly. Place your foot squarely."

Kent braced himself against the wall as he descended, tapping each stone with his cane as though by sound alone he could test its potential for treachery.

The chamber below was small, though one wall had been partially broken down and opened into some larger area; too dark to tell how great. A vaulted ceiling was supported by pillars and solid responds that had once been much carved but were now broken and worn, though Kent, with his painter's eye for form, felt that he might be able to make out the design if only allowed enough time.

Valary fetched a storm lantern left sitting on the floor and led the way through a low door into a dank passage, so small that Kent was forced to hunch over, soiling both hat and coat on wet stone. At a turn in the passage a rough square of stones had been removed, and Valary pressed through this opening. Almost immediately they were in a second stairway that wound down as though it burrowed deep into the hill.

The sound of scraping or digging came clearly up the well and grew louder as they went. Perhaps fifty feet down Kent followed Valary through a second opening broken into the wall, leaving the stair to continue its downward spiral. They picked through a rubble of dirt and rock, crouching to clear the ceiling, and then they slipped down from this into the chamber proper.

"You remember Laud?" Valary said, distractedly.

The scholar's driver, gardener, and sometime houseman tipped his hat to Kent, who had never actually heard the man speak.

"Of course." He nodded in return.

Valary stood and looked at him expectantly, the light of several lanterns turning his skin to darkened gold. Kent resisted the urge to wipe at the dirt he had acquired in his climb down, and instead turned slowly, gazing about the room. It was not large, less than fifty feet square. There was an open area obviously under excavation, and the gaunt Laud stood in its center; the walls were of smooth stone, not easily seen in the poor light. This ceiling, too, was vaulted, the supporting pillars six-sided and plain. Here and there Kent could find signs that the parts of the chamber had once been richly carved. Nothing extraordinary. Nothing worth rushing half the length of the Kingdom for.

Sensing Kent's disappointment, Valary spoke. "Do you not see it?"

Kent immediately felt a bit foolish, and a mild surge of annoyance as well.

"Look." Valary took him by the arm. "It is all around us." He dragged the painter into the excavation and across a stone floor half caked in dirt. "Look carefully at this wall." He grabbed one of the lanterns and held it aloft.

The wall the scholar indicated was a mass of broken and missing stones—

astonishing really that it had not crumbled completely. Kent found himself looking up at the ceiling for signs of stress-cracking.

Valary took a step closer and held the lantern near to one of the sections where the blocks were missing entirely. "Here. The defacement was done in some hurry, I think."

Because the rows of blocks were staggered, Kent could see that some parts of a carved pattern remained on every second stone: a design that had run vertically up both sides of the area.

"It is floral," Kent said, pulling out his spectacles and having a closer look.

"It was indeed . . . once." He waved at the wall six feet away. "And there, another like it."

"Yes," Kent said, still not sure what it was Valary had found, though clearly the man was excited to the point of foolishness.

Between the two areas of missing blocks the wall had been shattered and broken so that it was impossible to tell what, if anything, had existed there. A trickle of water dribbled from the shattered stone and disappeared through one of the holes in the floor. At the foot of the wall the floor had been torn up and obviously Valary had been excavating here, for there was an opening going down some number of feet—difficult to measure in the dull light available.

The historian stood gazing at him, a look of expectation on his face.

"Well, what is it?" Kent burst out in frustration.

Valary took little notice. "Now, I will give you one more clue and then I suppose I shall have to tell you."

Kent shook his head. *Farrelle's flames,* he thought, *tell me and be done with it!*

But the old scholar was not about to let Kent off so easily. Valary had solved this puzzle himself, and he wanted to be sure Kent had that same experience. He crossed back over the dirt-covered paving stones and held his lantern over a spot on the floor where again the stones had been removed. He looked up at Kent, who shook his head, though he felt himself drawn into the mystery again—his frustration replaced by a vague sense of what was perhaps familiarity.

A few paces to the right Valary showed him another such spot, and then another.

Kent suddenly stopped, drawing himself up in surprise. *"Blood and flames!"* he whispered.

He looked at Valary, who beamed, no doubt enjoying the shock written on the painter's face.

"Is it an approximation of the Ruin on Farrow, but writ small . . . ?" He said it in a whisper, as though the discovery were so momentous that it should not even be spoken aloud.

Valary nodded; quick, jerky motions of his head. "Yes. Yes. That is it exactly."

"How in the world . . . ?"

"Endless searching and a stroke of sublime luck." The man almost pranced, he was so delighted. "Oh, I have a tale to tell you, Kent. But first I must show you one last thing and then we will retire to better lodgings."

Suddenly showing signs of fatigue, Valary trudged back to the hole through which they had entered. As before, he held up his lantern and Kent could see that on this side of the thick wall there had been a proper doorway, with a richly carved lintel stone.

"Now, you are a naturalist, Mr. Kent. What do you make of this?"

The damaged carving of a bird in flight was positioned centrally over the opening, but despite its ruined state there could be no mistake. "A falcon," Kent said, and Valary nodded thoughtfully in response.

His elation had gone now and the exhaustion of long hours of effort drained off his animation. "Yes, and see this bit of the design left here?" He waved his hand vaguely. "It is mirrored to the right, but a different section has been left."

"A flower. A rose, perhaps."

"A vale rose, to be precise, or so I conjecture." Valary cast a glance at Kent and then back at the carvings above the door. "Let us go up," he said quietly.

Just over the crown of the ridge Valary had established himself in partial comfort in a small cottage that had been built out of the path of the winter winds.

Kent sat at a table pulled up before the hearth where a kettle heated over a freshly banked fire. He was still cold and knew he would remain so for some time yet—age cooling the body's furnace. It was a brutal place, he thought, as the wind moaned over the hilltop.

Valary, somewhat washed and in cleaner clothes, stood at the table's head pouring boiling water into a teapot he had not bothered to warm. Unable to hold himself back any longer, Kent reached out and snatched up the man's smudged spectacles and, taking out his own linen handkerchief, began carefully to clean them. Valary did not notice.

"It was like so many things in my work, Kent. If you just keep digging. Follow every possibility, no matter how slim." He glanced up from his preparations. Even though he looked somewhat refreshed now, Kent was sure that Valary had lost weight—not that he was exactly thin, but he had obviously been pressing his inquiry very hard. Following every possibility, no doubt.

"I received a visit from an old colleague—Dolfield. Perhaps you know him?"

Only by name, Kent thought, but did not interrupt now that Valary had begun.

"The purpose of his visit, it came out, was to question me at length about some obscure events of the remote past. Not unusual, really. But Dolfield is the present expert on the abbey, and eventually the conversation came around to that, and what he had found up here in his recent explorations. Well, Kent, I tell you, I nearly fell out of my chair when he described that chamber. It was all I could do not to run out the door in the middle of the conversation, I so wanted to see what he described with my own eyes." Valary replaced the steaming kettle on its hook, not interrupting his story, and Kent took this moment of distraction to return the spectacles to their place. Laud came in quietly with a pail of water from the well, fussed about in the corner, and went out again.

"Not quite able to believe what he had told me, I set out with Laud to see for myself, not wanting to trouble you until I had some more substantial evidence." The old scholar took a seat, propping his feet up on a low wooden stool by the fire.

"Do you know, I am quite sure that Dolfield does not realize what he has found." He looked over at Kent, his eyebrows arcing up almost comically. "It is one of the great discoveries of our time, in his field at least, and he has not yet seen it. Why, this was only one of a dozen things he spoke of, none of them even remotely as significant, but he just does not see—the tree for the forest, as it were." The old man shook his head, causing the woolly hair to bob. "Of course, there are still a thousand unanswered questions. I don't begin to understand what it all means." He looked over at Kent. "And that is where you come in, my dear Kent."

The painter tilted his head to one side, an odd motion he was unaware of. "In many things, Valary, I look to you for my answers. Mage-lore is your province—more than any man I can name, that is certain."

Valary looked up from his tea and raised a finger. "Any man, yes, I would agree. But there is one other who might add greatly to our knowledge."

Kent was taken unaware for a second until the words struck home.

Valary went on, apparently unaware of Kent's reaction. "I have long suspected that the Countess of Chilton might tell us much if she chose to. Not that there's much chance of that."

Kent sipped his own tea, not looking up. "The countess? This surprises me."

"Oh, yes. The countess may have a great store of knowledge, actually." He dropped his feet from the stool and turned so that he faced Kent, placing his elbows firmly on the table. "Did you not know that she had an . . . *involvement* with Skye? And Skye, of course, was well known to Erasmus Flattery and perhaps to Eldrich as well. Now the countess corresponded with Eldrich, I know that for a fact, though of course one cannot hope for access to either set of letters. A terrible shame. There was some difficulty among this group. The countess, no doubt, or more to the point, the gentlemen around her. It needs looking into, I dare say. I do know that Erasmus Flattery kept a portrait of the countess in his home at Locfal. And not to stray too far from the point, also kept a residence on Farrow—near to the famous ruin. Do you see? It all fits so neatly together."

"Most intriguing." Kent shifted in his chair so that he almost faced the fire. "This man Dolfield . . . what did he tell you?"

Valary was apparently easily drawn off the scent, for he responded to this immediately. "Dolfield, yes. Well, much that he said was not new to me. The abbey was built on the site of an earlier structure, for this has long been considered a holy place. The Oriston Monks, who disappeared before the birth of Farrelle, are believed to have constructed the abbey we see here—at least the part that is above ground. That is Dolfield's opinion, though what you and I have seen today could alter that considerably. The ridge was fortified at different times; pre-Farrelle and after as well.

"We know almost nothing of the monks—the followers of Farrelle were so damnably successful in eradicating our history!" He said this with the anger that only an historian could feel. "They traveled widely, though we do not know why, for their influence did not spread much beyond Kerhal, what is now Locfal, and perhaps half of Kerdowne. Barely a decent duchy, really. It isn't likely that they ever numbered more than a few hundred strong. Perhaps not even so many. Of their beliefs we know virtually nothing, though we do know from the journal of Aiden, the Farrellite Bishop, that it took some effort to 'cleanse' certain beliefs among segments of the population, though the monks had disappeared hundreds of years before Farrelle's birth. We also know that the Farrellites thought it important to occupy this site—making this a monastery of their own for some hundreds of years.

"Now, I cannot prove this, but it is very likely that they took the abbey from a mage—Helfing being the most likely candidate. There is no doubt that the Farrellites had to fight to gain control of the abbey, though if this was recorded in their history, it has been lost. Certainly the mages drove the Farrellites from this place late in the tenth century—one can easily dig up artifacts from the later battles and there are remains of those fortifications all around. Unmistakable." He looked off into the middle distance, his habit when drawing upon his prodigious memory. "But at least fifteen hundred years before that, the Oriston Monks dwelt here. Scholarly, prone to superstition, practitioners of the lesser arts, some say. And then gone." He snapped his fingers and turned his palm up as though he had performed slight of hand.

"Not much of a story, really . . . except for the *Lay of Brenoth*. Do you know it?"

"Just what every second-year man knows. It is only a fragment, I seem to remember, and the translation is rather . . . disputed."

"Yes, that's it. At least that is what we are told in the halls of Merton."

Kent could see that, despite his exhaustion, Valary's eyes had come back to life. He had a tale to tell, obviously, and was determined not to rush the telling. "You remember when last we met, I spoke of this young man, Egar Littel? Well, he applied some of his abundant intelligence to the *Lay of Brenoth* and the results were interesting. Not what we have thought for many years, that is certain. And not what the fine fellows at Merton and other such institutions wanted to hear either. All the same, Kent, I think it a work of interest to us. The *Lay* has long been thought a simple story of the heroic type, more valued for what it revealed of the ways of the Oriston Monks than for its literary merit." Valary considered a moment.

"An ancient sage of the Oriston Order is writing a scroll of unprecedented wisdom and clarity, but unfortunately his health is rapidly failing because of his great age. His followers are distressed beyond words, and send a young monk to seek an herb that will keep the ancient sage alive. A distant kingdom, said to lie beyond a range of impassable mountains, is the one place in the world where the herb grows, and one can find it only by passing through an immense, labyrinthine cavern. A cavern where strange things occur and nothing is as it seems. This kingdom, situated in a high valley, is always fair and green, untouched by the harsh mountain winters, for in this valley there is a power. The young monk, not the ideal choice for the job, it goes without saying, is sent off on his quest through all manner of difficulties until he finds the kingdom. Of course, this being the type of tale that it is, the real test is to leave this kingdom once it has been found, for the place is seductive, fair. No one is ever ill, or appears to age. And perhaps time does not run true there as well. The sage may be many years dead after only a few days there. You know the rest, I am sure."

"That story differs in significant details from the tale I remember," Kent managed, trying to dredge up the threads of the *Lay* from a time more decades off than he cared to consider. *Sent to look for an herb. . . .* He felt a strong urge to hurry to the countess with this. Did Valary know of Kent's involvement with the countess, then? He had not been careful enough. Kent felt a sudden surge of guilt at how often he had gone to visit her using this matter they pursued as an excuse.

"No, indeed. But is it not too perfect? Can you imagine? It has always been thought that the monk went in search of the 'plums of immortality,' but Littel's translation hinges on a few select words differently rendered. And through a cavern! That is different, as well. He believes. . . ."

"But, Valary," Kent hurried to interrupt, "who do you think built this chamber you have shown me?"

"Ah, now that is the question." The man rose from his seat and paced across the small room, hands clasped behind his back, head bowed. "Now, everything I have to say is only speculation—hunches, really—though what I am about to tell fills in an entire piece of a design I have been working on virtually my entire life." He stopped and turned to Kent. "I have developed a sense for these things, Averil. . . . I know this is hardly empirical, but even so. . . ." He moved to the fire and stood with his back to the heat. "In the years that I have pursued my vocation I have, on occasion, found references to a secret society. Now we are talking some good time in the past, mind you; the middle of the tenth century, I should think—five hundred years ago. *'That is hardly uncommon,'* you will say, but this society had an interesting purpose, or so I believe. Their intention was to learn the arts of the mages, and to that end, I fear, they had few scruples." Valary turned and sat on the stool on which he had so recently propped his feet. Clearly not yet warmed from his hours beneath the cold floors of the abbey, he rubbed his hands together before the flames. "Of course, this was not the first nor likely the last group to have such an aim, I'm sure, but this one was formed by Teller, a man who likely served at least part of the lengthy apprenticeship with Lapin, a mage of note in the history of mages." Valary rose from the stool with effort, as though he had grown stiff as he sat. "It has always been that the few who undertook true apprenticeships with mages did not leave their master's service—another reason to believe that Erasmus Flattery did not apprentice with Eldrich. We are not sure if this was due to the effectiveness of the selection process—the mages simply did not choose anyone who would not suit the task—or whether some more arcane persuasion was used to assure loyalty. Either way, those who began apprenticeships did not stray from the course set by their teachers. Teller, however, is an exception, and I am not sure why. It seems most probable that Lapin died before Teller had completed his studies." Valary looked down at Kent as though he had just realized something as he spoke. "I think it most unlikely that the mages had no arrangement to deal with situations such as this. But somehow Teller slipped through the cracks, as it were. The mages had their own troubles at the time, of course, and the explanation may be no more mysterious than that. It is possible that Teller briefly fell into the hands of the Farrellites; an intriguing possibility. Think of it. How did the Farrellites battle the mages with such success? And I am talking about their true success, not their own false claims. They must have had methods of at least partially countering the powers of the mages. What other explanation can there be?

"In any event, there is no doubt that a society existed with the aim of learning the mages' arts and it is likely that this began with Teller, who must somehow have escaped the clutches of the church. Not too difficult, I would imagine, in light of what befell the Farrellites." Valary moved away from the fire, returning to his seat at the table, where his fingers began to prepare his pipe slowly and apparently of their own accord. "Like almost everything in my field, little can be said with certainty about Teller's society. The Count of Joulle, the great Entonne historian, believed the society was destroyed by the mages prior to the Winter War, so sometime about 1415." Valary looked up and met Kent's eyes.

The painter blew out a long breath. "Destroyed? That says a great deal, Valary. The mages would hardly have bothered to do such a thing if this society had not . . . offended them in some way. Farrelle's flames! They must have learned something."

The historian nodded. "Yes, and though the mages were not incapable of mistakes, it is unlikely that they made any in such matters." Valary rose again, lighting a taper from the fire, which he then used to puff his pipe to light. "Perhaps the only thing I know with any certainty is that Teller's society used as their token three vale roses."

"And the falcon?"

Valary stopped in mid-draw, clenching his pipe stem between his teeth. "I still don't know. A familiar, I suspect, though whose I cannot say. Many of the mages kept such creatures, though what significance they had, if any, is a matter of speculation only. Despite all the popular beliefs, we do not know the purpose of familiars, let me assure you."

It was Kent's turn to become agitated and he pushed himself up, using the table in place of a cane, and took up Valary's place, warming his back by the fire, his shadow wavering across the table. There was no need to say anything of the falcon which appeared to follow Tristam Flattery. "The missing stones in the abbey . . . do you assume they were text of some sort?"

Valary nodded. "I think so, though, of course, only our knowledge of the Farrow Ruin would lead us to that assumption." The old man leaned back in his chair and rubbed a hand gently across his somewhat reduced belly as though he suffered some upset of the stomach. "If not text, then I don't even know where to begin speculating. Nothing we have found so far would give any indication, though I will say we have hardly begun to do the work that is needed. I intend to press on with it for some time yet. Poor Dolfield—I can't imagine what he will say when he returns to find someone has been busy in his own personal quarry. It will not be appreciated, and, of course, I would never have done such a thing if not for the gravity of the situation."

Kent found that his brain would not tackle all this new information in a useful fashion—it was like attempting to grasp a hot poker; try as one might, the hand would not close upon such heat. "But if this is some . . . *cognate* of the Farrow Ruin, what does it mean? You still have not told me which tenant of the abbey would build such a thing?"

Valary put his smoking pipe on the table, thinking for a moment. "The island of Farrow was discovered four hundred years ago," he began, his voice slipping into the measured tones of a lecturer. "Teller may still have been alive, though I have no evidence of that. It would seem possible, though, that Teller or his followers did the work here. Several of the mages had a great interest in the Ruin on Farrow. It meant something to them, more than a mere curiosity, you may be sure of that—though for the life of me I do not know more." The old scholar tested his tea but found it cold and pushed it aside. "Could what we have found been built during the occupation of the abbey by the mages? Before the discovery of Farrow? With the little we now know I don't think we can rule this out. Is there a chance that it is even older yet? Created by the Oriston Monks? Or even someone who preceded them? By the same people who built the Ruin on Farrow, perhaps?

"This site. . . . it has long been important to the peoples who lived by the Entide Sea. Delve into the ground hereabout and there is no end to what can be brought to light. Men have been performing rituals in this place for longer than most imagine. And this hallowed ground was the object of bitter disputes since long before our own coming. One can find arrowheads of flint lodged in the earth here. *Flint!* And broken swords made of bronze. Helmets of strange design." He shook his head almost sadly.

"In truth, I do not know who built this artifact, Averil. I do not know. But if I was forced to guess, I would say that it is old. Older than our history, that is certain. Ancient. As old as the Ruin on Farrow. Perhaps even more ancient yet." He paused, pushing the tips of his fingers together and staring intently at Kent. "And Erasmus Flattery knew of it—years before Dolfield—of that at least I'm sure. Dolfield believes he was the first to find the chamber you saw, for it was carefully closed when he discovered it."

Kent leaned forward, his question unspoken, and in response Valary reached into the pocket of his waistcoat, removing some small object. He paused with this hidden in his hand, like a conjurer not willing to give away the secret before its time. "I found this two days ago, after I had sent word to you." He reached out his hand, still closed, and then slowly opened his fingers, revealing a small clasp knife, its bronze case scratched and worn but with a sheen like old gold. Turning it with a finger, Valary revealed two letters set into the opposite side in silver. The metal had worn thin, but the letters remained perfectly clear: *E* and *F*.

"I feel I place my foot into the boot marks of Erasmus at every turn," Kent said, his voice suddenly weary. "It is almost as though the man were still alive, and pursuing the same thread as we, but a few steps ahead."

Valary nodded. "A few steps, in a historian's view of the world . . . but Erasmus was here some forty years ago, I think. In the matter we pursue, Averil, that is too long. We are lagging far behind, I fear."

⤜ Six

Gregory Bay lay in the ring of an ancient volcano, which had been largely destroyed by a massive eruption some ages past. Arriving at yet another volcanic island was disturbing to Tristam, and reminding himself that this volcano had been dormant for thousands of years did little to alleviate his anxiety.

My course, he thought. *We can sail no other.*

In some age past, one wall of the crater had collapsed, allowing the waters of the lagoon to flow in on either side of a small, high-sided island that stood like a sentinel in the center of the pass. The volcano's rim had crumbled and natural erosion created a narrow, low-lying plain, backed by tusks of gray stone. The islanders called the bay *vaha nea:* the 'eel's mouth'—not terribly romantic, by Farr standards, but then the creatures that dwelt in the sea had a greater significance to the Varuans.

As the *Swallow* sailed into the bay in the early afternoon sunlight, Tristam stood at the crosstrees, enthralled by what lay before him. A lapis lazuli set in a ring of living, moving green, surrounded by jagged gray spires.

Beaches spread in a great circle, the honey-colored sands stretched taut against a backdrop of tall coconut palms, and above this stood Mount Wilam, the high peak of Varua, attached to the cloud by fine threads of drifting rain. Waterfalls of startling white twisted down the steep cliffs, looking like the fabric of clouds torn into ribbons.

Everywhere Tristam could see flowers: the exotic *frangipani* and the *tiara Varua* most obvious by their numbers, but innumerable other species displayed their colors as well. The warm trade stirred the scents of these in the great bowl of the volcano, creating a perfume of exquisite fragrance. A fragrance that Tristam imagined was worn by all the women of this beautiful island.

Osler stood beside Tristam, as silent as the naturalist, for there seemed to be no words for such an experience, no words for what they felt.

Halfway around the globe, Tristam thought.

The trade found its way into the bay as a soft breeze, where it rippled the water into fish scales and pushed the tall palms to and fro. A pair of double-hulled sailing canoes, with their strange twin-peaked sails, went skimming across the surface, like water spiders caught by a gust, their wake barely a scratch on the surface of the bay.

As the ship stood in from the outer lagoon, the islanders in the canoes suddenly put their helms over and came beating up against the trade, both men and women moving excitedly on the decks.

Immediately, people began to gather on the beach before the village at the end of the bay. With his glass Tristam could see the fales, the tall houses with their corner pillars of stone and roofs of sun-grayed thatch—the houses of the common people. Separated from the village by a stand of breadfruit trees, a marae stood in the shadows of towering trees, a stone platform, intricately carved with stylized animals. This was the stone work that so mystified the Farrlanders, for the present day Varuans did only the most crude masonry. *"Left by the servants of the gods,"* the islanders claimed, and that was all they felt needed to be said.

Above the lower village stood the City of the Gods, an almost flat stone plain three hundred yards across, the core of a secondary volcanic cone. Here stood the great house of the King as well as the larger marai used in important rituals. This City of the Gods had caused much speculation on the part of the Farrlanders. Who had built it?

When Tristam had questioned Stern about this place—not coming out and asking if it bore a resemblance to the Lost City—the captain had guessed his concern immediately. Stern had laughed kindly. "Do not be concerned, Mr. Flattery. This so-called City of the Gods must have been home to the most rustic gods. No great towers or edifices. Nothing even remotely resembling the Farrow Ruin. Thatched houses typical of the rest of the island, though greater in size. A few remains of older structures, but these were not grand. No, the City of the Gods is largely a natural feature, though highly unusual, I must say. Only the stair leading to it is really of interest. Carved into a vein of basalt, I think, which stands proud from the softer rock around it. Lord Trevelyan believed it was made by a race that inhabited this island long ago. But who can say? Perhaps the Varuans have merely forgotten this craft."

Tristam had been much relieved by Stern's kind words, but even so he felt some anxiety coming here.

"There is no such thing as a coincidence in this world," Beacham had said that night on the pyramid. Tristam looked up, trying to catch a glimpse of this mysterious stairway, but it was hidden in the overwhelming green.

The Varuans believed the place was the work of gods and their servants who had dwelled there long ago. Gods who had left their home to a single servant who had remained to keep their houses, awaiting their return. Descendants of the servants of the gods, that was the claim of the Varuan Kings, and it was not so different than the claims of Kings in Tristam's own world.

The tropical day evolved beneath the floating sun, hot, languorous—sensual, Tristam thought. He fixed his glass on the shore again and saw the islanders pointing, children prancing across the sand, and others pushing outrigger canoes into the water.

Stern had ordered all the ship's colors flown, a gaudy, unnautical display, but designed for the eyes of the islanders. As the ship reached the center of the bay, two guns on either side were fired, and the great crash caromed off the crumbling walls of the ancient volcano, the echo taking an impossible length to die away. For a moment the islanders stopped, listening to this slow-dying report, but then they realized its purpose and laughed.

The Jack at the wheel put his helm down and the ship rounded slowly into the gentle trade, her sails backing, and as she lost way and began to slip aft, the anchor was let go into the glass-clear water where it could be seen to turn over and bury a fluke in the golden sand. The *Swallow* fell back onto her anchor cable, and hovered above her shadow like a kite.

Before the ship's boats could be lowered, the first canoe came alongside and the agile islanders climbed easily over the rail, as animated as excited children.

Osler slid down the backstay, but Tristam stayed where he was, immobilized by his disbelief. *Varua.* They had arrived. So much had been written about this island, and so idealized were men's descriptions, that it had become a place in a book—not real at all. Yet here it was, and more beautiful than any man's ability to express.

Swimmers began to reach the ship, which was now at the center of a raft of canoes, filled with smiling, chattering islanders. They delighted Tristam with their ease of manner, and the joy that shone in their beautiful round faces. Almost everyone that came aboard, even the swimmers, brought soft fruit or coconuts, flowers or shells. Soon the Jacks below had both faces and hands dripping with the sweet nectars of these gifts as they gorged themselves on the exotic fruits of the fabled land.

Tristam could see the duchess and Jacel hemmed in by both men and women, for the islanders had never seen a light-skinned woman before and always wondered why the Farrlanders sailed with only men aboard their ships. The duchess was trying to smile and retain some semblance of dignity; difficult, as the press around her was great, and so many hands reached out to touch and pinch her. Tristam could not help but smile.

A trill of laughter caused Tristam to turn, and there, perched on the yard behind him, sat two young women, dripping wet, though their luxuriant long hair (kept in a tight knot as they swam) was perfectly dry and drifted about their slim forms like fine grass moved by the wind. Around their hips they wore pareus patterned in rich reds and blues and yellows, and about their necks and in their hair they had arranged flowers in flattering colors, their sense of style as refined as any woman of Entonne. But for these pareus they wore nothing, and their soft cinnamon skin, beaded still with jewels of water, glistened in the sunlight.

They eyed Tristam with good humor and spoke to each other in their melodious tongue, laughing and smiling at him as though he were a child too young to understand.

Self-consciously, he greeted them in their language and at this they laughed again, looking at each other in some amazement and then back to Tristam.

He went to move toward them but was stopped abruptly, and it was only then that Tristam realized he still kept a line tied around his middle.

It was a strange assortment of gifts for the sovereign of such a tiny kingdom: a chest of overly-ornate silverware bearing the crest of the Farr Royal Family; a dozen parasols in shades of yellow, pink, and peach; a stock of canned foods (this in a place where food, both fresh and healthful, could be easily picked from the trees!); twenty bolts of cloth in colors not commonly seen on this island; feathers of the more exotic varieties (especially red ones); a looking glass; several books of engravings displaying the architecture of Avonel; two enormous rugs and many smaller ones; a box of combs, earrings, hair pins, rings, and other woman's jewelry; a leatherbound copy of the *Books of the Martyr* (a request of the Farrellite Church, but no one here could read it); various hand tools and sharpening implements, including hatchets, adzes, spoke-shaves, saws, and caulking tools; and, atop everything else, an equestrian portrait of King Wilam before the fountains of the Tellaman Palace.

It was this last gift which drew Tristam's attention, not only because the scene depicted seemed so alien here, but because it showed the King at, perhaps, fifty years: half the monarch's actual age. All Tristam had seen of the King in the arboretum had been his hands, and the naturalist had been so afraid of discovery that he had hardly noted how aged those hands had seemed.

Since their arrival, the Farrlanders had learned that King Sala still ruled, and though he must be well past his centenary, Tristam was not at all surprised—nor were several others aboard, he was sure.

The great pile of booty had been ferried ashore and carefully arranged on the beach, like goods in the market. The Varuans stood about in awe, driven to silence by such an abundance of riches. To Tristam's surprise this scene caused him some distress—for these "gifts" were not a hundred-thousandth part of the wealth of King Wilam, and yet here they struck the population dumb with wonder. It was beyond their imagining that even an entire island should possess such abundance. And Tristam knew that Stern kept more goods in reserve in case this did not achieve the desired result.

There were other gifts as well, for the lesser chiefs and the "Old Men," the *kenaturaga;* the Varuan shamans who held great power on the islands.

"But where is the King?" the duchess asked. She had, more or less, recovered from the affront of being misused by the curious Varuans, and Stern had granted her an honor guard of four large Jacks. The islanders were keeping a distance from the duchess now, but they were not shy about staring openly. From the little Tristam knew of their culture (from the little any Farrlander really knew), they might now think the duchess was *"tapu,"* for Varuan culture seemed to function within a complex system of prerogatives and tapu. Tristam did not know if such things applied to people.

The Farrlanders had been standing on the beach before their offering for some time now, and it was not clear where the Varuan sovereign was. "Hobbes said something about a ritual," Tristam offered.

Something was not right; even the Varuans had begun to look uncomfortable. They had recognized Stern and Hobbes immediately and had greeted the two seamen with obvious affection, but now they stood about, staring at the pile of gifts, speaking quietly among themselves and making the Farrlanders wonder if they had broken some tapu of which they were unaware.

Hobbes was endeavoring to discover the cause of this coolness, but he seemed to be having little luck, and Stern was capable of only a few rudimentary phrases of greeting and politeness. Llewellyn was by far the most fluent of them all, but Stern had told the doctor in no uncertain terms that he was not to speak unless asked. Stern, Tristam guessed, was concerned that Llewellyn's need for the *regis* seed not undermine his own purpose. Tristam could see that the doctor was almost twitching with his desire to use his command of the language.

"Mr. Hobbes?" A voice speaking perfect Farr came from somewhere in back of the crowd. *"Is it Mr. Hobbes?"*

The crowd of Varuans parted, and down the corridor they formed, strode a gangling Farrlander of middle years, incongruously dressed in a calf-length pareu and a ragged shirt. He was smiling such an enormous smile that Tristam thought his tanned face was in danger of actually tearing. He had seldom beheld such a look of delight.

"Mr. Wallis!" Hobbes said, jumping forward to grasp the man by hand and shoulder. "I thought I should never lay eyes upon you again in this lifetime!"

The man's grin widened as he took the master's large hand between both his own. "And I thought never to see another in this lifetime, as well, for all I could be sure of when the *Southern Star* sailed off was that I should die far from my own land." Perceiving the change in Hobbes' face, he hastened to add. "But I have not the slightest doubt in my mind that Captain Pankhurst did the right thing. There is no question but that I would have died on the return voyage, and who knows how many others with me? No, Mr. Hobbes, do not feel badly for a moment. It was the right decision in every way, and I would likely not be here otherwise." He smiled at the Farrlanders, as though absolving them of any sin.

"Excuse my manners, sir," Hobbes hesitated, glancing at the duchess, and then gave a slight bow to his captain. "Captain Stern, commander of His Majesty's Survey Vessel, *Swallow.* I would give you Mr. Wallis, ship's artist on Captain Pankhurst's voyage."

"Madison Wallis, at your service, Captain." The man wrung Stern's hand as though he had just discovered a long lost cousin.

"Your servant, sir," Stern answered. "May I present you to the Duchess of Morland."

Wallis looked suddenly very awkward, glancing down at his clothing. "It is a great honor, Your Grace. Please, pardon my . . . poor showing."

The duchess took a step forward and took the man's hand, meeting his eyes with complete openness. "Make no apologies, Mr. Wallis, it is a miracle that you are here. You could not be a more welcome sight if you were dressed as a member of the royal court."

Wallis actually blushed at this, red competing with the deep color the sun had burnished his skin.

The duchess half-turned to Tristam. "And let me introduce my particular friend, Mr. Tristam Flattery, ship's naturalist."

"Your servant, Mr. Flattery. I cannot tell you all how quickly I have run to come to you." He laughed, and Tristam realized the man did look flushed. "Why, I have come half a league since first light, and on my own legs, too, for I was up in the high valley. Farrelle be praised, how good it is to feel my own language on my tongue and to hear it spoken true." He laughed again, apparently from sheer delight at finding people of his own land.

"I'm sure you have a tale to tell us, Mr. Wallis," Stern said, "but first, do you know why we have been received so coolly? We have not had so much as a message from the King. Is he not well?"

"Ah, you don't know?" and seeing the looks of the men before him he nodded. "The *mata maoeā* has begun." Seeing the incomprehension on the Farrlanders' faces, he went on. "A ritual of cleansing and purification. Began at sunrise yesterday. It is one of the great rituals of the Varuans, employed only in the times of greatest need. The King and many of the Old Men shall be taken up with it for a fortnight, at least."

"A fortnight. . . ." Stern did not hide his deep disappointment at this news.

Wallis nodded. "While the Old Men and the King are engaged in rituals, it is difficult to tell who is left in charge. Varuan society is not ordered in the same way as ours. The King here is jealous of his prerogatives, and, officially, no one is allowed to stand in for him." Wallis pointed out into the bay beyond the *Swallow,* anchored with her broadside aimed toward the village.

"Perhaps here will be the answer to your questions. Anua. Did you meet her on your previous visits? No? She is presently the King's most influential wife— not eldest, mind you, but her family have become very strong this past year."

A large, double-hulled sailing craft came gliding swiftly over the bay, sailors in their short pareus moving surely on the deck, and children peering from the bows.

The sailing canoe passed by the *Swallow,* and in contrast the islanders' craft looked like a water insect, light on the surface, quick of movement, with long spindly arms and steering oars like antennae. The double hulls came to a gentle halt a few feet from shore and the crew quickly slid a narrow plank out and into the shallows.

A woman of great dignity and indeterminate age, perhaps in her late thirties, led a small child down the plank, walking as though it were a grand staircase. This was the first woman Tristam had seen wearing the loose, sleeveless cloak of the Varuan nobility and the almost ankle-length pareu that showed her rank.

The Varuan equivalent of the peasants wore their pareus short, not touching the knee, and there seemed to be any number of intermediate steps.

Some of the islanders went forward to greet her, wearers of longer garments themselves, and there was much joy in this reunion. Tristam was sure, by their looks, that they spoke of the Farrlanders. After a few moments, the woman and child came toward Stern and Hobbes.

She spoke her own tongue, and then said, "I welcome you," in softly accented Farr. She gestured to Wallis, and the castaway came to greet her, only slightly less awkward than he had been before the duchess. Like everyone else, he treated her with great deference, but also with affection. She spoke quietly to Wallis, smiling all the while, the child at her side staring wide-eyed at the strangers before him.

"Anua says that, no doubt, the King will be sorry he was not here to greet you. Most of the Old Men and the chiefs are either involved in the maoeā in the city of the gods or they are performing private rituals before their own. . . ." Wallis paused. "I think shrines would be our nearest word." The tall artist waved a hand at the mountain of gifts. "If these are for the King and the chiefs, then you must wait for the ritual to end before you can present them." Wallis looked a bit uncomfortable. "It would be unwise, Captain Stern, to give out any gifts before the King has returned." Tristam got the impression this was Wallis speaking, not translating for the Varuan noblewoman. "If you are in great need of stores, perhaps you might trade for them, but to open trade proper before the King has come would cause uncounted troubles. Things that could take months to work out."

Stern nodded quickly. "We will take your advice in this, Mr. Wallis, as no doubt we will in much else. I will have everything returned to the ship immediately. Please thank Anua for her kindness and say we did not know it was maoeā and hope we shall not upset the ritual in any way. If there are any special tapu in place for the duration, please tell us and we will obey them."

Wallis spoke to Anua, who did not seem perceptibly reassured by Stern's words. "Anua says that it is important that you not upset the balance of the community. No one should enter the City of the Gods—one must be properly purified to do so during maoeā—and your men must stay away from the marai, the stone platforms. They are used for the ritual and have been specially prepared." He glanced at the woman and then quickly back to the Farrlanders. "If I may say so, Captain, this ritual . . . imagine that it is like our own Days of Atonement. Even those not directly involved in the central rite make their own offerings, and the atmosphere of the island is generally subdued."

As Wallis stopped, the noblewoman spoke again briefly.

"Anua would like to introduce the Someday King—the Prince Royal, Ra'i Auahi. Her grandson."

The small child at her side was pushed gently forward, though he did not take his hand from her pareu nor did he remove his fingers from his mouth. Hobbes greeted him in his soft voice, and the child looked up at Anua in great surprise, making everyone laugh.

"Ra'i Auahi is shy, yet," Wallis said, smiling down at the boy.

Wallis then introduced the other Farrlanders, and it seemed that, like the other Varuans, Anua was most curious about the duchess and her maid. They spoke at some length through the efforts of Wallis, Anua asking many questions.

Tristam was introduced as well, and he made his best efforts to greet her properly in Varuan, which he saw pleased her.

Llewellyn took the opportunity offered by his introduction to speak the language of the islanders, feeling, no doubt, that this freed him of the strictures imposed by the captain. Wallis stood by ready to translate, but realized quickly that this would be unnecessary, and he began speaking with his old friend, Hobbes. Tristam listened carefully to everything that was said, trying to tease out words or phrases he knew, attempting to create meaning. At one point the smiles on the faces of the Varuans listening to Llewellyn disappeared, and the islanders looked at each other, obviously uncomfortable. He thought they shrank away from the physician.

But what on earth did he say, Tristam wondered?

"I can't remember everything of my first days after the *Southern Star* sailed, for I was in a terrible fever." Wallis paused to think for a second, and the joy that seemed always apparent on his face passed.

They sat in the duchess' cabin, listening to the story of Wallis' time among the islanders. Stern had brought the artist new clothing, but he would take only the shirts, fearing that he might insult the Varuans by abandoning the pareu. Llewellyn had asked about his remarkable recovery, for Wallis had been left for dead when Captain Pankhurst ordered his ship to sea.

The castaway stretched his lanky frame out over a chair, as though he had lost the knack of using furniture. To Tristam, Wallis seemed a man reduced—as though his disease had left him thin and drawn. There was not an ounce of surplus flesh on his thin frame. Even the man's hair was lanky and sparse, bleached of its color by the sun, and his skin had been bronzed like dried leather.

"The Old Men tended to me, for the King himself had promised Captain Pankhurst that I should not be abandoned. They fed me and gave me the pounded roots and herbs and such that they use for physic here, and they chanted and sang over me. If I described some of the pagan rituals that were performed, well, you should think I had been in a terrible delirium . . . though, in truth, at times I was."

The duchess glanced quickly at Tristam.

"I grew stronger," Wallis said quietly, simple words to describe the near-impossible. He looked at each of his listeners in turn, as though gauging their cynicism, and then went on. "At first I believed it was a miracle. Few survive the stillwater fever, though it is said some do. But now that I have lived among the islanders for a time I believe the Old Men cured me. They have herbs for mending, and ways that would seem strange to the medical men of our own land, but. . . ." He looked at Llewellyn and shrugged apologetically. "They can accomplish much with them."

Stern glanced at Tristam as though to be sure the naturalist had marked this as he had, but nothing was lost on Tristam, not even the reaction of Hobbes, who stared down and became suddenly very still, as though afraid any movement would reveal what he was thinking.

"And so, I lived. But here I was among a strange people, speaking then only a few words of the language. At first I thanked Farrelle hourly for delivering me, I was so grateful to find myself alive. But then I began to falter, for I knew it could be some time before a Farr ship returned. Years perhaps. I began to imagine all kinds of things going on at home. War, plague, death of the King and change of government—anything that could delay a ship being sent to Oceana." He sipped from the mug of ale he had been given. "I had no family—no wife that is—but even so I was desperately lonesome for home. The Varuans would have none of that. They have a saying that does not translate perfectly. Perhaps; 'To wait for life is the pathway to death.'" He smiled. "They seem so childlike in their happiness and carefree ways that we cannot conceive of them being wise, but often they are.

"I was made one of the islanders. Taken in by a clan. Given the pareu; below the knee, too, if you please. A fale was raised for me, and a wife was found—or perhaps she found me." He laughed at this as though it were a private jest, and the look on his face changed, like the sun rising on a calm sea. "And, for good measure, we were given loan of a child, for the islanders could not believe we would be happy without children." He laughed at this, as well. "Some of their ways are terrible strange to our own way of going. I was granted a Varuan name: *Yawa Yanu*. 'Who knows distant islands.' For they cannot conceive that

Farrland is not an island, you see, and there is no point in trying to convince them otherwise. I have a strange place among the Varuans, for I am thought wise in many things, and yet I do not have the most common knowledge; knowledge that children have about the fish that dwell in the lagoon, which fruits grow in various seasons. A bit like an old don who knows all the works of Boran and Halden and speaks Old Farr like a man of the past, but cannot perform the simplest day-to-day tasks." He smiled, not embarrassed by the admission. "I am a sage and a fool, and an artist as well, for I was left all my belongings. Most I gave away to those who helped me, but I kept my paint box. I have taught our language to some—the King's eldest son, Anua, and others. They are not the best students, for they do not have the habit of sitting and applying themselves to their studies as we do, but despite that, a few have learned rudimentary, but quite passable, Farr." He looked up at them, suddenly a bit embarrassed by what he was saying. "So, I have made a life here, and not unhappily, for some six years. I have painted much, and recorded all that I could of the language and the ways of the people and everything that I could learn of their own beliefs and history, though these are apt to be a little fanciful—in the way of tales, really."

He fell into silence looking down at the ale mug in his hand, realizing, perhaps, what the *Swallow*'s arrival meant. Tristam wondered what Stern would do. Could he leave Wallis here, against all orders? Tristam thought it unlikely, and felt some compassion for the man.

"But what of the islanders?" Stern asked softly. "Did they not contract your sickness?"

Wallis looked up, confusion crossing his features, as though he was not sure how he had come to be upon a Farr ship. "I was kept apart from the people. Captain Pankhurst had made that clear. As to those who tended me; they did not acquire the disease, nor did they spread it to others. You may rest at ease, Captain Stern, we did not visit a terrible plague upon them, as has been done in the past."

Stern nodded, a little relieved, Tristam thought. "Well, we must be thankful for that. You cannot imagine what a relief it was to find you, Mr. Wallis. And I'm sure you have learned much that will smooth our way here, so that there are no misunderstandings, as there have been in the past." Stern did not complete this thought. Everyone knew that once the guns of a Farr ship had been turned on this village.

Wallis nodded. He looked up at the doctor suddenly. "I must tell you, Doctor Llewellyn, although the Old Men of Varua are healers, it is not quite correct to give yourself their title. It means more than 'healer.' A great deal more."

Both Stern and the duchess turned accusatory glares upon the physician.

"I . . . I did not realize," Llewellyn said, shifting in his chair. "I had no idea."

*   *   *

The company for dinner had been carefully selected; the duchess, Tristam, Viscount Elsworth, Stern, and Wallis. To his consternation, Llewellyn was not invited. Stern had also taken the precaution of having Osler keep the quarterdeck clear. It would be as private a conversation as could be had aboard ship.

Wallis was a bit surprised not to find his friend and former shipmate, Hobbes, in attendance, but sensing the reaction of the captain when he mentioned this, Wallis fell to making stilted conversation. The man was no fool, Tristam realized. He knew something was afoot.

"Tell us about this ritual, Mr. Wallis," the duchess said, motioning to her brother to pour the castaway more wine.

Wallis did not lift his replenished glass, but stared into its ruby center as though it were a seeing crystal. "In matters of religion, Your Grace, it is always difficult for an outsider to discern exactly what the Varuans are doing. At times the religion seems little more than an expedient for maintaining the fortunes of certain groups. But at other times, I'm sure, it is meant to be quite sincere. An outsider, of course, cannot afford to flout the islanders' religion, no matter what we perceive to be its goals. But in this case I believe its intent is genuine." He interlaced his long fingers before him.

"There have been a number of strange incidents, here, that were taken as omens by the Varuans. Perhaps a month and a half ago, seven large whales somehow became stranded on the beach. There is not much tide at this latitude, so I can't explain how this occurred. The Varuans, as you likely know, view the whale as sacred. They are believed to carry the moon back into the east after it falls into the ocean in the west. This was cause for many sacrifices and the performances of rites, but the islanders, especially the Old Men, were obviously disturbed by this."

Stern looked a little askance at this information. "Mr. Flattery might owe his life to one of these sacred whales," he said suddenly, a hint of a smile appearing. "He bravely went swimming after a man who had fallen overboard, and we found them only because a curious whale circled around them, drawing the attention of Mr. Hobbes."

Wallis looked over at Tristam, oddly impressed by this information, and then went on. "Perhaps a fortnight after the whales were stranded, on a perfectly clear day, a series of great waves crossed over the lagoon. They were not catastrophic, but seven children who had been swimming, were lost. A terrible tragedy, for the people here love children above all else. And there was some damage, even here in Gregory Bay, especially to the canoes, and canoes are of astonishing importance to the islanders. The Varuans say there were seven waves, though, in truth, I think this might be a bit fanciful. Their superstitions will allow them to believe things without much critical thought. They also claimed seven canoes were destroyed, but it seemed to me there were several boats they did not really try to repair, thus reaching the magic number." He shook his head, clearly remembering the tragedy. "Again rites and sacrifices were performed, and ever since the King and the Old Men have been troubled. They began to practice augury, trying to see what might lay in the future, and several made journeys into the night world—a kind of trance where they're said to walk in the world of the spirits. Those who journeyed returned deeply disturbed, saying that the gods had turned their back on the people. Then, suddenly, a white bird—a raptor appeared on the island. And seven days later, the white-sailed *Swallow* hove into the bay. So you see, they do not really believe in coincidence, as we do." He glanced around the table, wondering how the others were reacting to this information, but no one seemed amused by the superstitions of the islanders.

"The Varuans have come to believe that the gods are displeased in some way—hence the maoeā, to appease the gods." He glanced up at Tristam, a bit unsettled, the naturalist could see. "This whale, Mr. Flattery, it actually circled about you?"

Tristam found himself shrugging, as though he had been asked for an explanation he did not have. "It appeared to, yes, though as you pointed out, one cannot rule out coincidence. But even if it was curious—well, certainly animals show curiosity often enough. I have often been followed by seals as I rowed a small boat on the coast, and anyone who has done so will have had the same experience. But I will say, it was a bit unnerving having a beast of such size so close, even though I was certain it meant us no harm."

For a moment silence smothered the conversation, each person appearing to take some interest in their food or their drink.

"Tell me, Mr. Wallis," the duchess said, sounding like the polite hostess, "how have you managed, so far away from your own people, and immersed in such a strange culture?"

Wallis made an effort to shrug off his own seriousness—this was a social dinner after all. "I have managed very well, in fact, Duchess. The truth is that after a few years on Varua, some aspects of Farr culture have begun to look a bit strange to me." He laughed at this. "But your way of seeing things changes when you live here. Back in Farrland you spend most of your time dealing with the world of men. Pursuing your vocation, paying the rent, the taxes, going to the theater, to the butcher shop, and the baker, answering your post. It is an endless succession of duties, but most of them contrived by men. Here, on Varua, you seem to deal directly with the world itself—or, perhaps, directly with life. A more elemental life. You harvest food from the trees and the earth, fish in the lagoon, repair your roof after a storm, gather firewood, raise children, help your neighbor. It seems more genuine, somehow, and the world contrived by men seems very distant, and strange, and artificial. Oh, not that this life is all easy and good. I'm not a foolish romantic. I have lived here, after all, and can tell you it takes some work. And there are comforts you come to miss: books, a soft bed." He held up his wine glass as further evidence. "But, on balance, the things gained outweigh those lost. You cannot imagine how carefree and joyous the people are; and there cannot be a more beautiful place on this globe, of that I am sure." Wallis looked around as though challenging those present to name a place.

"I have no doubt what you say is true," Stern responded, clearly uninterested in the artist's philosophical insights. "Perhaps, with the knowledge you have gained in your time here, Mr. Wallis, you can answer a question. There is a botanical matter that concerns us," Stern said, broaching the subject at last. "There is an herb. . . . What is the islanders' name for it, Mr. Flattery?"

"Hei upo'o ari'i."

Wallis nodded his head like a man hearing long-expected bad news. *"King's crown or king's leaf."*

"Do you know it?" the duchess asked.

Wallis nodded his head again in the same sad manner. "Yes. Yes, I know of it. It is not a secret here." He reached forward, and took a drink of his wine, as though it would fortify him. "I will tell you, Captain Stern, there are no stronger tapu on the islands than those surrounding this herb. It is the property of the King and the King alone. To even touch it is to incur a penalty of death. Even members of the royal family have faced this penalty in times past. It is the most sacred object on this island. You would be wise not to even speak its name, here."

"But Captain Gregory was given some of the seed by King Sala to be carried to our own King. It was given freely."

Wallis' face twisted as though a sudden pain had announced itself. "King Wilam has it?"

"Yes," Stern said. "Has had it these many years."

"Farrelle preserve us," Wallis muttered, setting his glass down too hard, and slopping wine onto his plate. "The Varuans believe, above all else, that king's leaf is cursed. It is the duty of the Varuan King, and the Old Men, to bear this curse for the people. Oh, king's leaf is said to give power, too—it is needed for much of the religious ritual—but it bears a curse which can never be entirely obviated, even by the strictest adherence to form and ritual. *'The curse of strength,'* it is called." The artist looked desperately around the table. "Don't you see? This was not a gift. It is a scourge, a blight. Far worse than anything we have ever done to the Varuans. It was revenge!"

Stern sipped at his brandy, clearly shaken by the conversation with Wallis, and since the castaway had left, he kept repeating the same phrases; "The man has gone a bit strange. His near-brush with death . . . and then living so far from his own people. Yes. A bit strange."

If the captain was shaken, the duchess was stunned, saying nothing. Perhaps it was Tristam's newfound insight, but her face seemed easily read to him. The way she shook her head so minutely: *denial*. She would smooth her skirt, and press her beautiful full lips together, her eyebrows moving as she considered what the artist said in relation to everything else that she knew.

Tristam, however, was not even surprised. It had almost seemed to the naturalist that he had heard Wallis' warning before, but had temporarily forgotten. And look how many bore this curse now . . . ! In Varua it was just the King and Old Men. But in Farrland. . . . Even aboard the ship there were two—himself and Llewellyn. *Cursed.*

ᔕ Seven

Five elaborately dressed palace guards escorted Averil Kent along a cold hallway devoid of functionaries. If he closed his eyes for a second, he could imagine that he was escorted only by sounds: heavy boots beating in time, the harsh strike of iron-shod heels followed by the squeak of leather soles. The hiss of fabric moving as arms swung through the air, and scabbards slapping thighs in perfect time. They were not comforting sounds.

An ancient suit of armor, wired together to give the appearance of a guard at his post, stood in the hall. The long coat of chain mail, the massive battle ax, and the blank emptiness of the eyes brought to mind a guard of the underworld, causing Kent to shiver as he passed.

The escort turned into a corridor lined with the busts of Farrland's sovereigns and before each bust the leader of the procession dipped his standard while the others clashed their sword hilts with metal gauntlets.

Obeisance to the dead, Kent thought, and felt like they were passing into the underworld indeed. He wondered at the lack of compassion he saw in the stone faces. Was it a trait of the Royal Family or was this supposed to be a regal attitude? There was not much to reassure him there either.

At the hall's end they stamped to a halt before a guarded set of doors.

"Who would pass into the palace?" a guard captain sang out in an expressionless voice which, nonetheless, echoed impressively in the near-empty hall.

"Mr. Averil Kent, escorted by the King's own guard."

"Is Mr. Averil Kent a peer or a freeman?"

"Mr. Averil Kent is this day, by the grace of His Majesty, Wilam VII, to become a Peer of the Realm."

"Then let Mr. Kent pass in."

A horn was sounded, loud in the hall, and the doors creaked slightly as they parted, a small day-to-day sound that seemed to stand against the solemnity of the occasion. Beyond the doors, the Honor Guard wheeled right and entered the Hall of Banners, tall and festooned with flags and standards, most old and torn, some stained by smoke and even the rust of ancient blood. These were the flags that had been carried into Farrland's most terrible battles, the pennants taken at great cost from enemy ships, and the colors won in the field or brought down from distant towers.

It was a somber hall, lit from dark leaded panes high up, the faded reds and blues and golds and greens hanging limp overhead, though in his mind Kent could see them all waving proudly in the breeze, colors untainted. For each tattered banner, how many lives had been exchanged? And how many of those had been completely forgotten, never to be honored, mourned only by a few? No knighthoods for their great sacrifice. Each banner, Kent was sure, represented a thousand sad tales, despite the claims of courage and glory.

With some relief he passed out of the Hall of Banners and mounted a wide stone stairway that progressed from landing to landing, turning abruptly at each, until they had gone up three levels. It was brighter here, the hallway lined with a row of tall, mullioned windows. Every fifty feet a hearth kept the winter chill at bay and guards in purple snapped to attention, saluting smartly as the escort passed.

The trek through the palace was almost finished and Kent was glad of it. Had they waited another few years to honor him in this way, he would have had to suffer the ignominy of being carried to his own knighting. Not the first to be so treated, but it was an indignity he was relieved to have been spared.

Of course Kent was not convinced that this baronetcy had anything to do with his supposed accomplishments, though he would readily admit that others who had done less had been accorded far greater honors. But Palle had been the one insisting that Kent be raised up—and the painter was more than a little disturbed by Sir Roderick's support. Palle did favors for no one outside of his own circle.

Kent shook his head. Perhaps this honor was nothing more than it seemed. If Palle wanted to let Kent know that he was aware of his activities, why have him knighted? Absurd. But even so, he found the day disturbing.

With a precise stamping of feet the guard halted before a set of nondescript doors, which appeared to open of their own accord. Immediately the guard marched forward again, entering a small paneled chamber, not sixty feet long. Here, two simple thrones sat on a dais raised perhaps half a foot. Two fires burned in large hearths, and windows reached from floor to ceiling along one wall, letting in a thin light from the north. The carpets, Kent noticed, were very old though they showed hardly a sign of wear. It was a room that saw little use.

The honor guard escorted Kent to his place, seven paces before the thrones, and stepped back, arranging themselves behind him. This was one of many cues, and doors to either side of the dais opened and people filed in. Kent immediately recognized Sir Roderick Palle, two Gentlemen of the Bedchamber, an Official of Ceremony, a Chancellor, and several senior Ministers of the government. Each of these took up a position in relation to the thrones and stood, hands clasped before them, no one so much as nodding at the painter, as was proper. A page, standing just inside the door, announced in a clear youthful voice, "His Royal Highness, the Prince Kori. Her Royal Highness, the Princess Joelle. His Royal Highness, Prince Wilam."

All three members of the Royal Family entered, the young Prince Wilam giving the painter a quick wink, for they had met before and the young man dabbled with a brush himself.

The prince and princess took their places upon the thrones and everyone in the room bowed, Kent sweeping off his plumed hat, which a guard then took away.

The Official of Ceremony stepped forward. "Your Highness," he began, the singular encompassing all members of the Royal Family thus addressed, "Gentlemen. By the will of His Royal Majesty, King Wilam VII, Mr. Averil Josiah Kent, Esquire, in recognition of his great contribution to the arts and to empirical studies, is this day, the fifteenth day of March, 1560, to be raised up to the rank of *Baronet* of the peerage of Farrland."

A guard entered from either side of the dais, one bearing a low kneeler, the other a sword. Prince Kori took the sword and stood before his throne, looking once at the princess, who smiled pleasantly, first at her husband and then at Kent.

The heir to the throne was not tall or of impressive bearing, as Kent had often noted before. He was, in fact, a nondescript man, having neither wise nor piercing eyes, nor indeed any other characteristic that people loved to associate with sovereigns. With the exception of one thing: it was very clear that Prince Kori knew his place well, and although not a pompous man, the prince expected all those around to defer accordingly. He was the heir to the throne of Farrland, at the moment the most powerful Kingdom in the known world, and he expected to be treated accordingly.

Kent, of course, knew much of the prince; knew his judgment was respected by those who governed the nations around the Entide Sea. Kent also knew that the man had almost no interest in art, but enjoyed music, often attending concerts in Avonel, and occasionally he was seen at the theater. Though the prince did not appear to be someone who could harbor great appetites, Kent knew that the prince had a mistress: a stunningly beautiful woman, who was said to be installed in a vast mansion at the city's edge. Kent often wondered if the princess knew of this arrangement.

The Official of Ceremony nodded to Kent, who stepped forward, bowed to the prince, and placed one knee on the kneeler. The elaborately embroidered coat of arms cushioned his knee, and Kent found himself staring at the silver-buckled shoes of the future King of Farrland. He could, in fact, see his own reflection there, and, though distorted by the buckle's curve, the faces of most of those present as well. In this instant Kent felt as though he viewed the scene through a flawed glass, the men present standing over him, their bodies curving up unnaturally to macabre, nightmarish faces. And his own countenance seemed no less strange—overcome with fear as though this were a beheading.

The curved blade of the sword swept up and hovered above him for an instant, and then descended, crisply tapping one padded shoulder of his frock coat, and then the other.

"*Arise, Sir Averil,*" came the prince's ordinary voice, and Kent looked up at the man's face, which was creased by the slightest of smiles.

He gazed around at those present, all of whom seemed to wear a similar benign look. The Official of Ceremony made the tiniest motion with his delicate hands, and Kent understood that he still knelt and pulled himself up with less dignity than he intended.

It was, he realized, one of life's unreal moments. One of those occasions when you felt as though you were not actually present but perhaps caught in a dream. Even as the moment unfolded it seemed like an imperfect memory.

Someone led him forward and he kissed the hand of the princess, who made some brief comment that did not register, and then he made a leg before the young prince. Congratulations and the shaking of hands all around.

Then he was before Roderick Palle, who held Kent's hand in his own soft grip. "So you see what all of your efforts have brought you to, Sir Averil?" the King's Man said, smiling, and those who heard laughed quietly.

"If you would, Sir Averil?" the Official of Ceremony said, taking charge of the situation. And Kent found himself walking behind his honor guard, through large doors and into a brightly lit hall filled with people. They gathered in two lines down which marched the guard, Kent reluctantly in tow. This was the simple ceremony he had been led to expect? To either side, people nodded to him and applauded politely, the tips of fingers slapping soft palms. Kent really felt as though he were in a dream now. The dream that you are the center of attention and everyone is staring at you expectantly, but you can't for the life of you think why.

In the sea of faces there were many that he knew, each passing like a wave: empiricists, fellow artists, scholars, actresses, players, a conductor, philosophers, aristocrats, and patrons. Kent's association was vast and well represented here. He continued to walk slowly down this avenue of admiration, his head bobbing to either side like a flower in the wind. Wondering if it was indeed a dream and at the end of this corridor he would find two hooded men waiting before a block, sharpening their axes.

He was halfway down the two rivers of faces when he almost stopped in surprise, for there, politely applauding, but unable to completely hide his look of distress, stood Valary.

Kent laid his elaborate frock coat over the back of a chair, and set his sword across the arms. A fire crackled in the hearth and a single lamp wavered on the table. He realized after a moment that he had simply stopped undressing, and stared off at nothing, like an old man whose memory had begun to fail.

But it was not his memory he feared, it was his intelligence. *"Fool,"* he said, but could not raise his customary bile.

A knock at the door jarred him out of this, and the face of his manservant appeared.

"A Mr. Valary to see you, Sir Averil. He is most insistent." The servant held out a calling card.

"I will speak with him, Smithers. Send him up."

Kent went to a sideboard and removed a decanter and two glasses. A moment later, Valary, his face flushed, hurried through the door.

"Will brandy be strong enough?" Kent asked, and the historian stopped in his tracks, unsure of the painter's mood.

"I felt there was little point in secrecy now. How in the world did they know of our association? I'm sure it wasn't me who let it out."

Kent waved a glass toward a chair. "Sit. Please. No, do not blame yourself, Valary. I don't know how Palle found us out, but do not for a moment blame yourself. It is far more likely the fault is mine." He poured two glasses of the amber liquor and took a second seat by the fire. "It is the damnedest thing," he said after a moment. "Before I saw you there, I was hoping, foolishly, that my knighthood had nothing to do with our interests." He shook his head. "I'm sorry now that I dragged you into this, Valary."

The historian waved his hand. "No apologies. We're far from being children. I entered into this with my eyes open." Despite his words the historian looked decidedly frightened, his jaw muscles taut and his complexion nearing gray.

Kent looked down at the fire, blinking like a man awakened from sleep. *"Benighted* is really the truth," he spat out suddenly. "Flames! How long has Palle been aware of us?"

Valary shook his head. "I . . . I hardly knew what to do. The Royal Invitation arrived only this three days past. I sent you a note upon its arrival, but. . . ."

"I'm sure it will be somewhere in the vast pile of letters of congratulations," Kent said. "There was nothing you could do. One can't refuse a Royal Invitation."

Valary sat stiffly in his chair, contemplating the worst, no doubt. Imagining the cells in Avonel's infamous tower, wondering if the horror stories of interrogations might be true. Kent had never expected the man to be brave—or at least he had hoped the scholar would never have to discover if this trait lay dormant inside him.

"It must have been my contact with Varese," Valary said suddenly. "Obviously Palle would have taken an interest in the Entonne after that night at the Society. I wish now that I had never spoken with the man."

Kent nodded. Likely, Valary was right. And Kent was more glad than ever that he had never mentioned the countess to Valary. Perhaps Palle did not know that connection—not yet, anyway.

"What about our other friend?" Valary almost whispered. "The one who gave you the fragment from Lucklow?"

Kent shook his head. "I don't know. Perhaps that connection is still hidden. I hope. But I must have that fragment back. Best to be rid of it quickly."

"I have it with me," Valary said, then sipped his brandy, maintaining his posture of injury. "Old men," Valary muttered.

"What?"

"Old men, Kent." The historian slumped down a little in his chair. "That's what we are. What hope do old men have in such a venture?"

"I don't know," Kent said, thinking how much he agreed. "But at least we're not in prison. Perhaps we can do something yet, though we will likely be under the eye of Palle's minions from this day forth. Still, I don't know how we can give up. I know no one as certain as you of the importance of our endeavor."

Valary reached over and hefted Kent's sword in its scabbard. "No, we can't give up. If you were not so famous, we likely wouldn't be free, but Palle can hardly throw the illustrious Averil Kent in prison. He has tried to frighten us off—two doddering old men, after all, how difficult could it be? He is trying to use me to threaten you. 'You, Kent, I may not touch, but your associates. . . .' But don't allow that to affect you. Without us, at the very least, there will be war with Entonne. And if Palle and his group manage to recover some of the arts that have so long been lost. . . . Well, prison might be a good place to be anyway."

Kent nodded. He knew Valary was making an effort to raise his spirits, to assuage some of the guilt he felt at involving others. Alissa Somers had been there! Was that merely coincidental?

Valary waved Kent's blade, and made a halfhearted effort at a riposte, as though laboring to recall a lesson many years in the past. But it was lost, and the riposte nothing but an awkward thrust, and then the sword slipped from his hands and rang on the floor. He looked up embarrassedly at Kent, his face strained by fear and determination.

And there they are, Kent thought, *the key elements of courage. But what use would courage be if they had not the strength and skill to carry the day?*

The lengthy celebration left Kent feeling a deep fatigue that sleep seemed to do little to erase—not that he had slept particularly well. He sat before the hearth in his small parlor, wearing a blanket like a shawl about his shoulders, his feet up, too tired to have even combed out his hair let alone donned a wig or neck-cloth.

It was at moments like this, after some particularly taxing effort, that Kent felt his age. For some strange reason the arches of his feet ached so that he could hardly bear to put weight on them, and a sharp, hot throbbing pierced into his lower back, and sometimes stabbed down his leg like the blade of a rapier. As if that were not enough, his muscles were overly sensitive and weakened, leaving him feeling vulnerable and fragile.

But worst of all, on such days, he felt the fatigue settle in his once good mind, like a thick fog in which his thoughts lost their way, unable to connect one to another. And somewhere in there his memories wandered as well and, search as he might, they could not be located.

He sipped the coffee he cupped in both hands and closed his eyes, feeling the warmth from the fire, trying to will it into his bones as though it were a power that could flow, hot into his veins, like returning youth. But it did not seem to work—as though the cold in his limbs were infinite, absorbing all heat to no effect.

"Damn you, Wilam," Kent muttered. "Damn you to Farrelle's own pit of flames." His anger toward the King and what he had done could not be suppressed on days such as this; the King had brought so much into danger in his maniacal quest to remain young. *Damn you.*

When his mind was so fogged with fatigue, Kent always found it strange that random recollections from his youth would come to him, although the feelings once attached to these were now long forgotten. He did know that he had spent entire nights lost in passion, untiring, like some fine animal bred for that one thing alone. Flaming martyrs, he could name a few young women he had loved then. What were their names . . . ? But, sadly, he realized that even these memories did not stir him now.

I am far gone, he thought. *Far gone indeed.*

It was difficult to believe these things had taken place such a very long time ago. The events seemed distant, as though he had only read about them and not experienced them at all. He knew that at this point his death was far closer, far more tangible. That was something he could almost touch. One could feel one's mortal form progressing slowly to ruin, like that old abbey—the signs were undeniable. Things went wrong inside a man and did not come right again. That was the truth that hung over one's head like a blade. Injuries and illnesses were no longer easily repaired. And as with some part of a painting that he could never get right, the great danger was to see nothing but what was wrong. The trap of age.

He drank more coffee. That morning he had ordered it very strong, as though he could shock mind and body into alertness and activity. It only seemed to sour his mood though, touching neither the fog in his brain nor the enervation in his limbs.

Footsteps creaked on the old stair: Smithers. The man had been with him so long that Kent could tell Smithers' mood from how quickly he ascended the stair, the fall of his footsteps on the treads. And today his mood was sullen. His master was very recalcitrant—and on this day that should be so full of happiness, too. After all, had his master not been raised up? Had the King not granted him some five hundred new gold coins? Were not commissions flooding in? Poor Smithers, he could not fathom his master's mood, that was certain.

"Sir Averil?" came the man's ancient growl, like a wave on a pebbled shore. "There is a Miss Alissa Somers here to see you, sir."

"Have I forgotten an appointment?"

"No, sir. She has come unannounced. Most irregular."

Kent looked around the room, and then at himself in a glass. His long white hair spread out around his shoulders, across the blanket that he used as a shawl. *I must look like her old grandmother,* he thought.

"Oh, send her up," he said, unable to bear the thought of even rising.

"Here, sir?"

"Yes, here. And brew some more coffee. Try to put some teeth in it this time."

Kent shut his eyes and let his head fall back against the chair. I might as well be seen for what I am. An ineffectual, feeble old man.

A moment later two sets of footsteps could be heard on the stair, one so light that the ancient, creaking treads hardly noted their passing.

"Miss Alissa Somers, Sir Averil," Smithers growled, and disappeared.

Kent saw her hesitate at her first step into the room and the smile falter, followed by a narrowing of her beautiful eyes.

"Are you unwell, Sir Averil? I—I fear I have come at the worst possible time...."

Kent tried to smile, though he feared he made a bad job of it. "No, I am perfectly intact. Only just worn out from all the excitement. A bit much for a man my age, I'm afraid. Do forgive me for not rising...." He waved a hand vaguely. "My feet seem unwilling to bear me this day. Like bad tempered horses."

She came farther into the room so that the soft light filtering in the windows from the overcast sky reached her. Youth seemed almost to radiate through her skin. He could not imagine a greater contrast: the ruin of an old man and this vibrant young woman.

She took the seat opposite him, setting a small hand-purse beside her. "Father suffers such pain in his feet and legs. I have often rubbed them for him with some oil but even just a rub can do wonders." She started to reach out tentatively. "If you think it might help . . . ?"

Kent did not quite know how to respond and she took this as acquiescence. Her hands were warm, the skin soft as only a young woman's skin could be, and her touch gentle. He felt his lungs take a sharp, involuntary breath.

Praise the god of old fools, he told himself, *I thought never to feel a young woman's touch again in this life. It is almost as if she actually wanted to touch me—my withered ancient frame.*

Now don't be a perfect old fool, he cautioned himself. He wanted to close his eyes and just feel these soft hands gliding over his skin, bringing the nerves to a life they had not known in so very long, but at the same time he stared at her in wonder. *Why in this round world would you ever be so kind to a wrinkled old man?*

"Is this all right? It doesn't pain you?"

"No, no. I am sure my poor old feet have not been so well treated in some time." He did close his eyes, if for only a few seconds, but in that brief interval something was restored to him. He could recall now some of the feelings that had coursed through him so strongly long ago. A name came back to him: Lauron. Immediately he forced his eyes open and tried to smile, as though afraid his thoughts might be read on his face.

My word, Kent, you are becoming a deviant, he chided himself. *Sir Averil, indeed! She is hardly more than a child.*

"I'm sure that has helped a great deal," he said suddenly, disentangling his foot from her grasp.

"But I have only just finished the one."

"But the other is fine as it is. Thank you, my dear Alissa. I think you may have the power to heal in those perfect small hands."

"Well, your feet are colder than snow, and almost as white. If you can't bear to wear slippers, then you should prop them closer to the fire and wrap them lightly in a blanket." Saying this, she shifted his footstool so that it was nearer to the blaze.

"I think that Smithers shall bring us some fresh coffee momentarily," he said, at a loss for words.

"That would be very welcome, though I must tell you this is not a visit of a purely social nature. Though of course I do wish you joy of this great honor His Majesty has bestowed. A gentleman more worthy I cannot conceive of, Sir Averil."

Given his recent thoughts, Kent could not even bring himself to acknowledge that she had spoken.

Alissa looked down at her hands, turning them over slowly as though wondering if he had spoken the truth about their power. "Yesterday, at the celebration, I was approached by Her Highness, the Princess Joelle. Her Highness seems to have taken something of an interest in Jaimas and myself." She flushed the tiniest bit at this statement. "The Duchess, Jaimas' mother, and Her Highness are more than passing acquaintances, I collect. It is the second time the princess has spoken to me. The first was at the party where I had the honor of your company as well."

"The duchess' birth celebration?"

"Exactly." She fixed Kent with a look, and for that second he saw the determined child he remembered. "Her Highness asked if I would do the favor of delivering a letter to you, which I agreed to immediately. The princess also requested that I tell no one of this, and, naturally, I agreed to this as well. Her Highness has a certain way about her. . . . I think one would do much for such a woman and ask neither questions nor favors in return."

Kent nodded. He understood precisely what she meant, having known the Countess of Chilton for so many years. "You brought this letter with you?"

She nodded, removing a plain gray envelope from her hand-purse.

Kent took it, and turned it over once. It bore no mark, no address. Not even his initials.

"Please, don't mind me. It might be something needing a reply, which I would gladly carry."

Kent reached for a bone letter opener from his side table and slit the envelope. Inside was a short note in a hand he did not recognize.

My Dear Sir Averil:

My warmest compliments. Your long efforts have only now truly begun to be recognized. And though no one deserves a rest so much, I do hope you do not intend to abandon your important work. Again, congratulations!

It was so good to see you at the palace, for you have not been to visit us nearly often enough, although we often hear about your doings: the manservant of your colleague the historian (I hope you will forgive me if I cannot remember his name) appears to have a friend in the palace.

I do hope to see you sometime before the season is over.

Respectfully,
J.

Valary's servant!? It was Valary's manservant who had betrayed them. Far-relle's flames, he must get a note to Valary immediately.

"Do you wish me to convey a reply?"

"I. . . . No. It is not necessary. Thank you, Alissa."

Kent stared at the paper a moment longer, not quite able to believe it. He wished that he could be alone to consider. Why in the world would the wife of Prince Kori send him such a note?

"Sir Averil?"

He looked up.

"Please excuse me, but there is one other matter I should discuss, if you don't mind?"

Of course. Erasmus' papers. "Please, say on."

"I am not quite sure where to begin. . . ." The way she avoided his eye made him fear the worst. He shifted in his chair, suddenly feeling warm for the first time in the day.

"To begin, I must say I broke my word to you, Mr. . . . Sir Averil. I would not have done so if I had not made promises to another before I made mine to you." She blinked, daring a brief glance at his face. "I can only say that I am sure that anything said to Jaimas, for that is to whom I spoke, will never be repeated." She smoothed her skirt carefully over her slim legs. "I made some queries among the servants of the Duke of Blackwater, in a manner I thought would not be noted, for little passes in a great house that the servants know nothing of. And this proved to be true, for there was a rumor that the duke and two servants had indeed re-moved some possessions from the house of Erasmus Flattery. But my inquiries went no farther than that." She shifted in her chair, and Kent could see a look of . . . what?—humiliation—pass across her face. "I suppose the Duke of Blackwater was . . . curious about this stranger who had stolen into their midst. My activities must have become known to him." She shook her head, a quick motion, and straightened in her seat. "Not that the duke reproached me directly. But he did make it known that he was aware of my interest in Erasmus." She paused, then looked at him directly. "Actually he told me that you had once all but accused him of hiding the work of his late uncle. And then he denied this allegation."

"I did nothing of the sort!" Kent blurted out before he could think, and then let himself sink back into the chair. He rearranged his shawl over his shoulders and stared for a moment into the flames. "I do apologize, my dear Alissa, for involving you in this matter which has, no doubt, caused you deep embarrass-ment. It was just that . . . my enthusiasm overcame my judgment. I am not sure now how I will make amends."

"Oh, Mr. Kent, you needn't concern yourself with that. It was my own fool-ishness that brought my efforts to the duke's attention. You can hardly be blamed for my clumsiness. No, no; don't concern yourself with it for a moment.

You see, after my conversation with the duke, I spoke to Jaimy. And do you know he told me that he had long suspected that some things *had* been removed from Highloft Manner—the home of Erasmus—before Tristam took ownership. He indicated a portrait of a woman—the Countess of Chilton, I believe—that he was sure had hung in Erasmus' house."

Kent feared he did not hide his reaction well. He jerked his leg back as though he would rise, and hot pain shot both up to his knee and down his thigh from his back. For a moment he stayed rigid and then slowly forced his muscles to relax, easing back into his chair. He felt Alissa's hand on his shoulder, for she had risen.

"Are you all right, Mr. Kent? Shall I call your man?"

"No, I'm. . . . Stupid of me to move so quickly." *Farrelle curse this worn out body!* He opened his eyes and forced a smile. "A portrait, you say. Did you see it?"

Alissa looked carefully into his eyes, gauging his well-being, and then she returned to her seat, though she perched on the edge as though ready to rise at any moment: to call for assistance, no doubt.

I must look near to death to her, Kent thought.

"I did see it. The canvas hangs in a room in the Flattery country house." She described it perfectly. "Do you know it, Sir Averil?"

He nodded, meeting her gaze as coolly as he was able. "Yes, perhaps. But Lord Jaimas . . . he is not aware of anything else from the house of Erasmus?"

She shook her head.

"Well, it is very odd," he mused aloud. And what had the duke said? That Kent had once accused him of hiding Erasmus' papers! He had done no such thing! Oh, certainly he had once asked the duke if he thought Erasmus' papers had been stolen, but it was not an accusation—nor had it been taken as such, he was quite sure. *Throwing dust in this poor girl's eyes,* he thought. *I did not mean to pit her against such a formidable man.*

He looked over at Alissa. One thing was perfectly clear: being caught out by the duke had only strengthened her resolve. He could see the determination there: never would she be so foolish again. These Somers women had great character, that was certain. He wondered if young Lord Jaimas would be a match for her.

"We are not done yet," Alissa said quietly. "Though I am not certain what we shall do if we find Erasmus' papers. What terrible embarrassment that would cause the duke."

"But you must do nothing," Kent said quickly. "Nothing until you have spoken with me. As you say, we do not want to embarrass the father of your fiancé. Certainly we must approach this most circumspectly. I should not want the Flattery name to suffer. No. If any papers are found, first we must search through them to see if they're of importance."

She paused to consider his words. "Well, we shall simply have to deal with that in its time." She smiled at Kent. "I fear I have imposed upon you quite enough, Sir Averil. Do forgive me. I shall leave you to your much deserved rest." She rose from her chair. "No, no. Do not even consider rising. I shall find my way down." Saying this she clasped his hand, tenderly, he thought, and kissed him lightly on the cheek before letting herself out.

Kent closed his eyes and lay back in his chair, letting the touch of her lips fade away, like wind ripples on a pond.

After a moment he tried to bring his thoughts back to his real problem, but his mind was unable to take in all that was new, so he turned again to the letter Alissa had delivered. Princess Joelle. It was so improbable. Lady Galton had never for a moment even hinted such a thing, though they were cousins, but even so. . . . Well, Kent had not told Valary about the countess. It was just too improbable. The wife of the heir!

Well, there was really only one answer to the question. He must contact Lady Galton—most secretly if possible. And Valary! Farrelle's flames, had the man mentioned the countess before this damned servant?

If what the princess appeared to be saying was true, then Palle and his associates did not really know what it was Kent was up to. There was no time to waste in self-pity. No time to worry about age—all vanity anyway, or largely so. No, he must press on. There was still time.

Kent forced himself up and discovered that he had not lied entirely, his feet did not pain him as they had. And then he sat down again, almost collapsing on his footstool, but not from some failure of his body. One of his portraits. It had been in the possession of Erasmus . . . ? For how long, Kent wondered? Many years, perhaps. And now it hung in the home of the Duke of Blackwater. Farrelle's flames. She wove a spell that would last a hundred years.

∾ Eight

It is strange to think that I, of all people, became a smith of the language, for my relations with human kind have always been marked by a fundamental lack of commonality, as though I came from a distant land and spoke an alien tongue. I have always looked at my countrymen and thought that they slept as they walked: a sleep without dreams.

HALDEN, "To Sleep without Dreams"

Across the eastern horizon, sunrise seared the sky in a narrow band, turning the clouds to molten copper, the sea to lava. Tristam stood alone on the beach, having escaped all and sundry, including his shadows, Julian and Beacham. Immediately he began walking, putting as much distance between himself and the party of Farrlanders that had come ashore as he could. He was not sure of the exact purpose of this escape, other than a desperate need to be alone.

He had brought his bag of naturalist's tools, but he no longer suffered under the illusion that he had come to this island to botanize: not since he had climbed up a flooded stair and discovered a Lost City. Though why he was here was still a mystery. He was no longer even sure the duchess knew—as he had long believed.

As he made his way along the beach, Tristam could see the islanders going out to tend their gardens, to gather fruit, and see to their livestock before the heat of the day descended. They were graceful silhouettes moving beneath the trees. After walking only a short way, Tristam decided that the Varuans were avoiding him. He turned back and could see the other Farrlanders were the center of joyful mobs of islanders—men, women and children. Was he to be an outcast here as well? Had the innocent islanders been infected by the superstitions of the Jacks? Flames! He would never escape those incidents.

Tristam took a path that wove its way up into the bush, hoping to meet no islanders, for he could not bear to be rebuffed again. He felt like a man accused, but never given a chance to defend himself. It disturbed him deeply.

He tried to turn his thoughts outward, and found himself alone in the jungle of Oceana, awash in its sounds and smells, like an island of Farr sensibility in this exotic world. Birds called in the trees, their songs unfamiliar, and the trade wind spoke its hissing language among the palms—which the Varuans believed signaled the presence of gods or the spirits of ancestors.

All around were the plants Tristam had studied with Dandish, and later found in the King's collection at the Tellaman Palace. While he had worked on Trevelyan's collection, Tristam often daydreamed of visiting this world, but he had never thought it would be anything more than that. Just a dream, not something that he would pursue. Tristam's life had never seemed the sort that could be planned—after being orphaned in childhood, plans seemed particularly suspect to him. Experience taught him that the future was uncertain and one could prepare for it only by learning indifference to disappointment and loss. It was, he sometimes thought, the defining characteristic of his personality.

The path slithered steeply up to the crest of the headland, and here, from a clifftop, he could look out over the aqua lagoon to the ring of breaking combers, and the shell-white crests of the trade wind seas.

He stood in the breeze, drinking in the rich aroma of the reef and lagoon, and the perfume of flowers. At that moment the world of Farrland seemed particularly distant and alien to him, as though he were no longer part of it, but a castaway on this pristine island, in the middle of an immense sea. A place where a man took his food from the trees and the lagoon, and never worried about the bill from his tailor. Even two days on Varua, and the contrived life that went with "civilization" as Farrlanders thought of it, seemed very removed from "reality." The words of Wallis seemed very wise at that moment.

Tristam laughed bitterly. It was all illusory, he was sure. Man, he suspected, had a particular genius for complicating things, for creating social hurdles that one must leap or be thought lacking. Wealth was clearly not evenly distributed on Varua—though to a Farrlander even a wealthy Varuan seemed to be living in poverty—and the poorer classes labored for the good of the chiefs and other nobility. Tristam knew it was not Farrland writ small, but he could also see that it was not the innocent paradise it had been painted either. In difficult times the Old Men were known to perform human sacrifice, and raids on neighboring islands saw the capture of slaves, who were the lowest caste on Varua. It was not quite paradise, though from his vantage it would be hard to believe otherwise.

For a while Tristam tried to botanize, identifying the plants and insects in the immediate vicinity, but he felt that he was only playing naturalist, the way one forced oneself to pursue the normal routine of life when tragedy struck. He was holding desperately to the familiar strands of his old life. *I am Tristam.*

He set out along the path again, following it down toward the beach. The conversation with Wallis the previous night kept coming back to him. The omens the artist spoke of did not seem so coincidental, for there was far too much coincidence in his life. Even a dedicated empiricist had to admit that after a while. The great waves Wallis spoke of almost coincided with the discovery of the Lost City—within a day either way, it seemed.

How can that be? the empiricist in him asked, but the voice was less strident, less sure.

A white flower caught his eye, but it wasn't Kingfoil. Tristam did not like the way his body responded to the mere thought of the seed—an immediate hunger as insistent as lust.

The craving had been much reduced, but it hadn't gone away entirely, and every so often it would return, as though it lay watching, waiting for a moment of weakness. He had begun to think that, as much as anything, it was his exposure to *regis* that had lost him control of his emotions. He still suffered from uncontrollable emotional tides: sudden anger, melancholia, great joy, and almost overpowering desire. There were times when he lay sweating in his cabin, his mind so full of the duchess' presence that he feared he was going mad. He imagined that he could see her in her cabin, undressing as she readied for the night.

It is the transformation, he thought, *but I will not give in to it.* With enormous effort he turned his mind elsewhere.

The forest thinned as he came down to the beach, and he walked through a stand of breadfruit trees.

As he came out on the beach, Tristam found a group of island maidens who had dropped their baskets of fruit and were staring up into the sky over his head. Tristam turned just in time to see a swift white form plunge into the trees.

"What?" he asked in his halting Varuan. "What was it?"

The girls began backing away from him immediately. One of the girls said something in Varuan. "Spirit bird," Tristam thought she said. And then they beat a quick retreat, clearly frightened.

Tristam found his field glass and began scanning the trees, almost afraid of what he would find. Among the foreign shapes and foliage, brightly colored kingfishers and lorikeets fled into shadows, as though something terrorized them. He kept sweeping his instrument back and forth slowly, and there, in the branch of a *mori* tree, half-hidden by leaves, he saw a patch of white feathers.

As silently as he could, Tristam moved forward, and then dropped to one knee, and raised his glass again. For a few seconds he thought the bird had fled, but then he found it, still partly obscured. Moving slowly, Tristam strung his bow, left his canvas bag on the sand, and taking his glass and two arrows, slipped forward.

The forest was so thick that he could not find an open view of his quarry, though a relatively clear shot at the patch of white might be possible.

It cannot be a falcon, Tristam told himself. *There is not a white falcon in Oceana*. But if it was a falcon, he was going to put an end to the question of its origin. If it was merely flesh and blood, an arrow would bring it down, and at the very least, he would add it to his collection of skins.

As he raised his bow and notched an arrow, his hand shook, and he tried to calm his breathing and pounding heart. Taking a long, slow breath, and thinking, *Pester me no more*, Tristam let the arrow fly into the jungle.

The sound of wings desperately beating the air came to him, and then silence. No cry. He was not sure his shaft had struck, and quickly he raised his glass to search. For only a second a white bird appeared above the trees, then plunged into the forest top.

An owl, Tristam was sure of it. A pale owl, hardly bigger than a songbird, with a heart-shaped face and golden eyes. An owl never seen before. An owl, he was sure, that would be unfamiliar even to the Varuans.

Tristam sank down on the sand, remembering the owl Beacham had seen as they ascended the water stair. What had it foretold? If this owl augured events even remotely as macabre, Tristam would almost rather die.

He looked out to the sea crashing on the reef. A fine mist filled the pure air, and this sight seemed like an escape, suddenly. If only the sea would take him, comfort him, as it had when he fell into its embrace at Bird Island. But he could not forget the outcome of that. The sea had refused, and returned him to his airy world—the world of living men.

An owl. Though he had been almost certain that the bird he glimpsed originally was larger, swifter, more powerful. A raptor.

Tristam took up his bag and trudged on, wanting only to escape. The moments of feeling a sense of release from this mad quest had been few. There was no escape.

The world around him was forgotten, and Tristam plunged back into a whirl of thought, like a man in the grip of melancholia. A relentless cycle, in which he went round and round, finding no escape, though becoming more and more desperate.

After a walk of indeterminate length, Tristam found himself at the mouth of a broad stream that spoke the peaceful language of brooks as it flowed joyfully into the lagoon. Here Tristam stopped to drink, trusting that the lack of fales in the vicinity would mean there was no one bathing or washing clothing upstream.

"There is a good place to make a bath, in the trees," said a voice behind him, and Tristam turned to find a young woman standing five paces away, twisting together the stems of bright flowers with barely a glance at her swiftly moving fingers.

"You speak Farr," Tristam said, surprised, though perhaps equally surprised that she did not run from him as did the others.

The girl shrugged her bare shoulders. "Wallis taught me. . . . Taught me?"

"Taught, yes."

Tristam was not sure of the girl's age, barely twenty he thought, perhaps younger, for girls became women early on Varua, having children when they would have still been considered children themselves, had they been born in Farrland. She had the friendly, pure white smile that all the Varuans seemed blessed with, and a face slightly less round, framed by thick, dark hair pulled into a knot at the back of her head. The young women seemed to compete over the length and beauty of their hair. Her pareu fell below the knee, though she wore no tunic, leaving her torso covered only by her hair and a necklace of flowers.

One of the qualities of the islanders that enchanted Tristam was their lack of self-consciousness, and this young woman stood before him, stripped to the waist, and regarded him with utter candor.

"Are you the son of a great chief?" she asked suddenly.

"I . . . No, not at all. My father is dead," he said, thinking immediately that this was a foolish answer.

The woman nodded, as though it were a sensible answer after all. "Wallis says that you . . . the *dausoko* who are clean and do no work, are the sons of great chiefs."

"Ah. Well, we don't have chiefs in the same way, but what Wallis says has some truth. My family are . . ." Tristam searched for a word, "influential." He saw that she did not understand. "They have some wealth." Still, he was not making himself understood. "My uncle is a great chief," he conceded.

She nodded at this. "My aunt is Anua. Do you know Anua?"

"Yes. Yes, we were introduced." Tristam searched for a phrase that could not be misconstrued. "She is very wise."

At this the woman nodded, clearly both understanding and agreeing. "Very wise. Yes."

"My name is Tristam."

She nodded.

"Can you tell me your name?"

"Faairi."

Tristam smiled. "It is similar to a word in our language."

"Yes. Wallis told me. A small person with magical powers, like a spirit. It makes me very sad that I am not a small person with magical powers." She continued to regard him, her expression hardly changing, as though he were some mildly interesting phenomena, or perhaps a beast she had never seen, and though she had been told it was harmless, was taking no chances.

She shifted her concentration to her work, suddenly, as she finished twisting the flowers together in a garland. This she held out before her for careful, if quick, examination, and then, with the first sign of anything resembling shyness, she proffered it to Tristam.

The naturalist was completely charmed. It was, of course, a modest gift, something which the islanders made in minutes, but it was the gesture that mattered, its spontaneity and lack of guile.

Tristam bent and let her slip the necklace over his head. Immediately he felt that he should give her something in return. Metal was much prized by the natives and iron spikes had become so common as the price of a woman's favors that Farr captains had made the removal of iron from the ship a crime almost as serious as mutiny. Otherwise the ships would fall to pieces in the lagoon from loss of structural integrity due to lack of fastenings. Somehow, despite what he knew of this practice among the islanders, Tristam thought it would be an insult to give this generous young woman a piece of iron. It would be construed as a suggestion, and though Tristam thought she was very beautiful, still he could not shake his Farr standards of conduct.

He opened his canvas bag and rummaged among the contents, looking for something he could part with that would not affect his ability to carry out his studies (another idea that he could not give up, despite circumstances), and finally realized that he had several small hand lenses. More than he could ever use, or lose, for that matter.

He produced a palm-sized leather case and held it out to her, not sure what the reaction would be. A great smile appeared on her face, and she met his eye with a quick look of such intensity that he felt a surge of desire. But then she hesitated, and he could almost see her suspicions forming by the changes on her face.

Thinking that she did not know what it was, Tristam opened the case, revealing the circle of glass inside. He raised up one of the blossoms from his necklace and looked through the glass at it, moving the lens until he found the point of focus. He turned the lens toward the woman and motioned for her to look. Tristam had the definite impression that curiosity overcame some reluctance. He moved the lens slowly up and down, hoping the flower would come into focus for her, and when it did she exclaimed; some Varuan word he did not know.

Tristam picked up a scrap of dried palm frond from the sand and focused the sun on it. Faairi stood close to him, watching intently, and the scent of the flowers and the oil Varuan women used for perfume caused Tristam to take long deep breaths, drinking in this aroma. Her bare arm touched him as she stood and Tristam caught himself before he moved away, as he would be expected to do in Farrland.

A small circle of the leaf began to blacken and a tiny feather of smoke appeared, presaging diminutive flames which sputtered in the breeze.

Faairi turned to him in great delight. "It is *makawa*," she said, and made no move to claim the offered gift.

"I don't understand?" Tristam said.

"Old Man's work," she tried.

"Ah," Tristam said, with a sinking feeling that she meant necromancy. "But it is just a piece of glass. Nothing magical or forbidden. I have several."

He still held it in his hand, not quite offering it to her again, afraid that there might be some tapu involved, but hoping she would take it, as it hung in the air between them. He thought she seemed overly impressed with this display of Farr technology—or white skin's magic.

"The day is very hot," she said, glancing toward the sun. "Will you come and bathe?"

How easily such a suggestion was made, Tristam thought. He tried to imagine Jenny saying such a thing. But then he remembered the evening he had spent at the duchess' and realized that there were places, even in overly-proper Farr society, where the rules and expectations were flouted. A foreign visitor would likely never see such things, and would come away with a completely different picture of life in Farrland.

Tristam followed Faairi up a narrow path that bordered the stream, her supple waist and the tight wrapping of her pareu around her buttocks drawing his eye. The contrast between this young woman and the duchess struck him as they walked. Her dress seemed almost a symbol of the difference between the two women—a simple piece of cloth made from the inner bark of the paper-mulberry, *Broussonetia papyrifera,* wrapped simply about the waist and held in place without fastenings. It seemed as though the layers of artifice that Farr culture required were peeled away with each layer of clothing. Tristam thought of the whalebone corsets that Farr women once used to squeeze their figure into the fashionable shape, and here was Faairi, who wore little more than a string of flowers. And she had spoken to him, not needing a "proper" introduction. Tristam realized he was shaking his head in disbelief.

Her strong back and square shoulders moved with such ease as she went, and Tristam found himself wondering what it would be like to kiss that perfect golden skin.

They found the pool, created by a dam of rocks—not a work of nature at all, Tristam was sure. Faairi laid her necklace carefully on the ground, and stripped off her pareu, laying it over the branch of a bush. Reaching back to free her hair raised her breasts in the most enticing manner, though she did not seem aware of this. She waded into the pool, casting a look over her shoulder at Tristam, as the water distorted her perfect legs.

He began pulling off his clothes, realizing that he had stood entranced, watching her. Tristam's clothing seemed absurdly complex and impractical, suddenly, and his life even more so. How he wished that he could peel away the layers of complexity, sloughing them off like old skins.

Before entering the water, he set the magnifying glass on the ground near Faairi's necklace of flowers, leaving her to take it or leave it, whichever she chose.

He plunged into the water, trying to hide his rising desire. The pond was just deep enough to swim and he struck out for a dozen strokes and then stopped, his feet finding the soft bottom.

"You swim," Faairi said, clearly pleased. "How is it that your sailors cannot?"

"Many people in my country believe swimming will make them ill," Tristam said, a bit embarrassed at the foolishness of his countrymen. "Of course, the water in our land is much colder than here."

Faairi smiled and shook her head, trying not to laugh, he thought. "Farr-landers believed many strange beliefs," she said. "There are only two women on your ship, and so many men. It must be very . . . lonely."

"Well, in the past there were no women at all," Tristam countered.

She nodded, her look unreadable, as though she considered this carefully. "These women . . . the old one is Stern's woman, and the other is whose?"

"The old one," Tristam tried not to laugh at this term, "the Duchess of Morland, is not Stern's woman. She is like a great chief herself—like Anua—a woman of wisdom who is much respected in Farrland, and who is also a great friend of our King. The young woman, Jacel, is her servant. Do you know 'servant'? Someone who does your work; brings your meals, cleans your clothing, heats the water for your bath."

She nodded, although heating water for baths seemed unlikely work here.

The slow current drifted Tristam down toward Faairi, and she held her place, watching him with that same look of odd detachment.

"When you walk in the dream world, have you come often to Varua?" she asked suddenly.

The words did not convey meaning to the Farr mind, but Tristam was afraid that he understood her only too well, though he was curiously reluctant to admit it. He nodded, saying nothing.

"Once I saw a woman in the lagoon."

"Who was she?"

Tristam shrugged. "I don't know."

"Did you . . ." she searched for a word, "have the love with her?"

Tristam laughed. "I confess, I did."

"Ah," she said, as though it were approval. "What did she look like?"

Tristam laughed aloud this time. "She had long black hair, brown eyes, skin the color of yours."

Faairi shook her head. "Wallis said that our people are much alike to your eye." She regarded Tristam. "Your people are not so much the same, I think. Taller, shorter, hair like sand, eyes that are green or the color of the sea." She cupped water in her hands and lifted them, letting the water run out in a glittering stream. "In the world of dreams I have walked in your land," she said, "though only one time."

"And what did you see?" Tristam asked quickly.

"A village of stone, and beasts like giant pigs that drew people in *wagons,* I think. Smoke rose out of the roofs, which were smooth and black. It was like the paintings that Wallis showed to me, but everything moved and I could hear the sounds and smell the smells." She wrinkled up her nose. "In your village the earth found its way through stone only in small places. The ground was very hard. As I walked, the sun set and I came upon a house that had fallen. Such a large house that it looked like a mountain of broken stone, and among the stone a small boy was hiding, though I think he was a *tamaroa mo'e.*"

"What does that mean? A boy? Some kind of boy?"

She shrugged. "One that cannot be reached. A boy who lives in the world beyond."

Tristam nodded. Wallis had shown her some illustrations of Farrland, apparently, but he guessed there was no ghost boy in them, nor would there likely be the ruin of his father's theater. Who was this woman and why had she, of all the Varuans, come to befriend him? "Do you have such dreams often?" he asked, instead of his real questions.

She shook her head. "My sister is a dream walker. She is lost in the dream world, now. They could not call her back to her body, and she is lost forever. But this cannot happen to me. Look." She stood taller in the water, pointing to a small blue tattoo between her breasts. It was all Tristam could manage to glance at anything beside the glistening dark nipples that seemed to bob on the surface. The tattoo was a small diamond shape, intersected with many lines.

"It is my star," she said, "so that I might always find the way home." She settled back into the water, to Tristam's disappointment.

"That would do it," he said, hoping as soon as the words were out that she would not take offense, but irony did not translate easily.

"I would like to regard your hand," she said, which made Tristam smile.

He raised his hand, dripping from the water.

"No. Another hand."

He hesitated. Had she seen his scar as he undressed? Reluctantly he raised "another hand."

She took hold of it softly, turning it over so that the scar was exposed. For a moment it was as though she had forgotten him; she stared so intently at his wrist—like a doctor examining a wound. Then she laid the palm of one hand gently over the scar, and though she raised her head, her eyes remained closed.

Tristam was not sure what she intended, but for some reason her touch seemed cool upon the wound, and the desire for *regis* seemed to diminish. He closed his own eyes, and breathed out slowly, unsure of what was happening— not certain it was anything but imagination.

Then he opened his eyes and found Faairi gazing at him, her look full of curiosity. Her grip had shifted so that she held only his fingers, and her manner was less grave. "You walked near to the burning gate and returned," she said. "So very few have done this thing. Were you not afraid?"

"I am not sure what happened," Tristam heard his voice whisper. *What am I saying? She is not making sense!*

She nodded. "Memories do not always return with us from the dream world."

Tristam said nothing, only shutting his eyes. What was she talking about? Did she really understand what had happened to him? He felt a hand touch his cheek.

"You must be careful to not let yourself slip away. If you turn your back on the world of the sun . . . I saw it happen to my sister. You must keep hold of this world, Tristam. Do not let it go." She squeezed his hand tightly as she said this, and then raised it to her breast, slipping close to him. He felt her legs wrap around his waist, and her arms encircle his neck. Desire took hold of him. It was like sinking into a *regis* dream. A feeling that he lost himself, or something else took control. He felt his own personality submerging, as though it were driven down into the depths. A cry sounded loud in his ear, and though he thought it was Faairi, it became the cry of a bird of prey.

Tristam woke to find himself lying on a bed of flowers and leaves on the edge of the pond. For a moment he felt a terrible vertigo and then this passed. He turned his head and saw Faairi stretched out on her back upon a rock, her soft belly arching, the muscles pulled taut, her small breasts flattened. She turned her head to him and smiled, though there was some concern there.

"Are you returned?" she asked.

"I think so, yes."

She rolled over and came near to him, laying a hand on his chest. "You must learn not to let the other master you," she said.

"What? What happened?"

"Shh," she said softly, and then moved to sit astride him. "You must not take your eyes from mine. We will go very slowly." She reached down and helped him into her, and he felt the warmth and softness embrace him. "So slowly. You are Tristam," she said, beginning the slowest rhythm. "Tristam. And we are here on Varua, in the world of the sun—the waking world. *Ohh.*" She closed her eyes for a second in pleasure, and then snapped them open. "Stay with me."

He reached up and touched her face, and she kissed his fingers. Again her eyes closed, and she moaned, but opened them again quickly. She moved his hand to her breast and he rolled the nipple in his fingers. Something stirred in him and Tristam recognized it as that force, the desire that had overwhelmed him. With some effort he struggled to keep control, feeling his hips rise to meet Faairi as she moved.

I am Tristam, he said to himself. *Tristam.* I am not a mage. No matter what they want, I will not become that. He kept his eyes fixed on the beautiful face above him, and then saw the tiny star tattooed between her breasts. She was his star at that moment. His point of contact with the world of the waking. He brushed his fingers over this mark, and she took his hand and kissed the scar on his wrist.

"*Tristam,*" she whispered, and then words in her own language that he did not understand, but which sounded soft and fair.

✑ Nine

Ceremonies for graduating scholars had taken place annually in Merton since the founding of the university some five centuries earlier, and, as things did in Farrland, the rituals had become quickly entrenched.

A member of the Royal House of Farrland did not necessarily graduate from the university even once in a generation, but even so, there were rituals to deal with this eventuality, too. Although there were no invitations sent, certain segments of Farr society were expected to turn out for the royal graduation—those of the right strata of society or of the correct association simply knew—while anyone appearing who should not would be marked for life for their presumption.

The graduation of Prince Wilam, the son of the Prince Royal, appeared to follow the expected course, flowing as predictably as the River Wedgewater, which had not overflowed its banks in living memory.

The official reception after the ceremony was held at the home of the University Chancellor, a man who had been born at a level in society that would have required his attendance on this day even if he had not been presiding over much of the ceremony.

Sir Averil Kent had twice put himself in the path of Roderick Palle, only to have the King's Man turn aside to greet another—not snubbing the painter openly, but Kent knew the man avoided him. Kent was not even sure why he was going out of his way to greet the King's Man, just some strange urge. A desire to let Palle know he was not intimidated—to leave the King's Man wondering why he seemed at ease. He wanted a little revenge on the man for the misery that his knighthood had caused. But Palle was not about to give him the opportunity, it seemed, and the painter decided it was time to stop being so childish, and continued on his rounds through the crowded rooms.

He had already stood in line to pay his respects to the Prince and Princess on the graduation of their son, and Kent was sure that, as the Princess took his hand, he had felt an almost imperceptible increase in pressure—a message. There had been no other sign, that was certain. The Princess was no more cordial with him than with anyone else who came before her, and Prince Kori was as amiable, and at the same time as distant, as always.

This small incident with the Princess, a minute caress of his hand, had left him feeling somewhat elated, even protected here, as though no evil could befall him—an illusion he knew, but even so, he felt it strongly, and this was a vast improvement over the gnawing anxiety he had known these past months.

Passing into a large ballroom Kent stopped for a moment to survey the crowd. It was an odd mixture of Merton dons, uncomfortable in their formal clothing, aristocrats, and scholars attended by their friends. The scholars wore robes of deep crimson trimmed in gold, and carried old fashioned tricorns tucked under their arms. They were flushed with elation, and in some cases drink, their clear pink complexions glowing, reminding Kent vividly of his own graduation, so many years ago.

Too many members of Kent's own year had passed on, too soon, he thought. He didn't like to count. A point would come when there would be more dead than remained alive, which Kent felt had some terrible significance—those remaining would be thought "survivors." But, Farrelle bless them, these young men and women he saw here had no fears of growing old and dying—an event that no doubt seemed impossibly far away.

Thoughts of mortality soured Kent's mood a little, for it always brought up the questions about *regis*—the great temptation that Valary had once spoken aloud; to use it themselves if they were ever to have such a chance. Valary was certain the physic would drive anyone who did not know the arts of the mages to madness, as it apparently had Trevelyan. Poor man. No, Kent knew he would have to grow old as gracefully as he could—there was no alternative for him.

"Sir Averil, is it?" a familiar voice said. "You haven't forgotten your old friends though, I hope."

Kent turned to find Professor Somers, Alissa's father, making his way through the press, smiling as he came. "Professor. Please, no need for the title. We both know, only too well, how these things are usually acquired, though mine was truly a surprise, I will say in my own defense."

"Which goes without saying. Titles *have* been awarded to deserving individuals occasionally, and I don't mind using the honorific; for you, of all people, have my respect." Somers took Kent's hand warmly. "My Alissa has said you have very kindly come to her rescue at various social functions, and I must thank you for that." His face changed then, a hint of worry appearing.

"Oh, hardly, hardly. She is perfectly able to carry these things off without help from me. But I congratulate you on Miss Alissa's coming marriage. I know your feelings about the aristocracy, Somers, but I will tell you, I think this young man is a fine gentleman and will do everything within his power to make your daughter happy. It is a good match, and she will rise to the social demands with ease, I'm sure. The Flattery family are people of substance, as you must have realized, and not caught up in the more superficial parts of the aristocratic life. The Duke of Blackwater is a man I esteem greatly, and his wife, though not well these past years, is a kindly, intelligent woman. You are not seeing her at her best, but let us hope you will."

Somers nodded, clearly glad to hear these words from an old friend. "I'm sure you're right, Kent. It was a bit of a shock, I will admit." He shook his head, and then a bemused smile appeared. "You have not the blessing of children, Sir Averil, but no matter that one thinks one knows them better than they know themselves, they will surprise you—force you to admit that they have lives of their own." He glanced quickly about the room, as most people did occasionally, looking for friends they had not seen in some time, or others they felt some social obligation to greet. "I must tell you, Kent, there are some I miss at times like this—Dandish most of all."

The painter nodded. "Yes, he was not a social man, but those of us who knew him realized his value."

Somers swept his gaze around the room again. "I pass his house occasionally and it always affects me. Whoever bought the old place, though, is tearing it to pieces; digging up all the gardens, ripping out the interior. Madness! It was a perfectly lovely home as it stood."

"Tearing up the garden?" Kent said, too quickly. "Who bought the place?"

Somers shrugged. "Dean Emin could tell you, I'm sure. Ah, there's my future son-in-law now." The professor nodded toward the far end of the room. "I have grown fond of him, I will admit, though I can't help but wish Alissa had fallen for the young lord's cousin. A solid young man and an empiricist of some promise. Do you know him? Tristam Flattery?"

Kent nodded, keeping his face carefully neutral. "I do indeed. Perhaps when he returns, he will capture the affections of another of your lovely daughters." Kent followed Somers' gaze, and there was Lord Jaimas talking to a group of young men about his own age.

"I would not be against it, though he does live rather far off, in Locfal. Do you mind, Kent? I should speak to Lord Jaimas for a moment. Come by if you can. The house is full of people, as you might imagine, but everyone would dearly love to see you."

Somers set out into the sea of faces, bumped and buffeted like a boat on the waves.

Tearing up the garden? Kent wondered how soon he could politely escape. Dandish's house seemed to be an object of continuing interest. But to whom?

Kent was about to turn and leave when he noticed a woman exiting by another door; the sight stopped him, like a bird striking glass. All he had seen was a cascade of shining black curls, but this had brought back a memory so powerful that for a moment he thought he had wakened from a dream of being old to the sight of the woman he cherished retreating from the room—retreating from his life.

"Flames," he whispered. Too many memories lurked in the depths, surfacing unexpectedly, some like old leaves, rising dark and shapeless from the bottom, others like blossoms, appearing, bejeweled in beads of water. His memories of the countess were of both types, some dark and despairing, others so full of light it hurt to recall them, though he often did, and bore the pain. He could not help it, the currents that brought memories to the surface were inconstant and mysterious.

As the Ambassador of His Imperial Entonne Majesty, Count Massenet had carried both gifts and expressions of his King's great respect to the Farr Royal Family, and he was now doing the two things he did best in the world, charming women and seeking information he was not supposed to be privy to. Lady Galton did not appear in Farrland very often, preferring her adopted home, the island of Farrow, and the count did not want to waste an opportunity to speak with her. There were two reasons for this: the lady admired him extremely (unfortunate that she was not still young and beautiful), and she was the cousin of the Princess Joelle.

"I have not had more than a moment to speak with the Princess. Her Highness is well, I hope?"

Lady Galton's eyes lost focus briefly, as though she were a little bored with questions about her royal cousin. "I believe Her Highness is well." Suddenly she looked sharply at the count. "Though I thought you should know better than I."

Massenet did not blink or hesitate. "I am at the palace often, it is true, but seldom do I see anyone of any interest or real charm. Ministers and officials and so on. I wonder sometimes whatever led me to take this position."

Lady Galton laughed softly. "Because intrigue is your nature, Count Massenet," she said, her smile remaining, her still-beautiful eyes laughing, "as it is a bird's nature to fly. When you were pushed from the nest, I believe you landed in the royal court. But am I being unfair? Perhaps you were not pushed, but jumped?"

Massenet bowed his head in surrender. How he loved intelligent women!

But Lady Galton was not done. "And intrigue offers such possibilities, for it comes in so many varieties; political, courtly, social, intrigues of commerce, intrigues of the bedchamber. Variations without end."

Yes, Massenet agreed silently, *like women.* "Though I hate to dispel any myths concerning my origin, I fear that ambassadors are not born, Lady Galton, but merely appointed. I understand that Farrow was graced this autumn by the Duchess of Morland. There is no end of speculation as to why the lady set out on this remarkable voyage."

"I thought everyone knew . . ." Lady Galton said ingenuously. "She seeks youth . . . in the form of a young empiricist. What was the young man's name?"

Massenet attempted something he found difficult—he tried to look foolish, as though he could not think who or what she meant, exactly.

"Well, that's my guess at least. It is a flaw some cannot overcome. They pursue youth." She waved a hand at a gathering of young women who kept glancing coyly toward the count. "They may not think that is their purpose but . . ." She shrugged. "But such pursuits end in tragedy, Count Massenet. We will all grow old, as I have, or die young. No artifice can change that." She reached out and touched his arm. "I am called away. It has been a great pleasure." She curtsied like a girl, no small effort for her, he was sure, and swept away in the wake of a Royal Page.

Youth. He glanced at the group of young women, but they had gone, and in their place was a single woman, who stared at him openly, her look amused as though she had heard the entire interchange and understood its undercurrents completely. And she was an astonishing beauty! She bent her long neck toward him as though in acknowledgment, a dark cascade of hair moving like something in nature, and then she went off in the same direction as Lady Galton. Massenet, to his surprise, merely stood and watched her go, watched everyone step aside as she passed, as though she were the Queen herself.

"You look as though you've seen a ghost."

Massenet turned to find the Marqeuss of Sennet staring in the same direction as he.

"But who was that woman?" Massenet asked, his voice coming out as though the wind had been knocked from his lungs.

"Well, if I am not mistaken, that is Angeline Christophe. Though I am surprised to see her here. Perhaps she knows someone who is graduating."

"Really." Angeline Christoph was the woman rumored to be Prince Kori's mistress. "Well, I should very much like to meet this young woman. Will you be so kind as to introduce me?"

Sennet smiled, perhaps enjoying the count's candor. "I have never had the pleasure myself. She is something of a recluse, I understand. I don't know a soul who claims to be her friend. So you shall have to be bold, Count Massenet. I dare say you are able."

Jaimy walked in the garden, listening intently to his companion, becoming more and more alarmed at what he heard.

"It was almost an impossible task to translate. They would allow me only a copy of the original text and this had been broken up into fragments and given to me in an order that would make it difficult to recognize as one piece. These men, Wells and Llewellyn, attached themselves to me as I worked and I began to realize, by their endless questions, that they must be attempting a translation of some sections of the thing themselves. But their attempts to hide the nature of the text were rather futile. Anyone would eventually realize what it was." Egar Littel looked around the garden as though suddenly afraid. "I insisted that I must come to Merton to search the library—told them I couldn't continue otherwise. I am still amazed that I managed to give them the slip." He stopped, clearly frightened. "You're sure we're safe here? There are any number of people coming and going." He looked back to the lights of the house. Dark shapes could be seen moving in the windows.

"Try not to worry, Egar. If any of your tormentors arrive, Alissa will alert us. But what will you do now?"

The young man began to pace again, staying to the shadows of the trees and hedges. "I don't know. I must get away. Out of the country if I can." Jaimy could tell the man was staring at him suddenly, trying to read his face in the darkness. "I shouldn't have come to the professor's house like this, but I really didn't know where else to go. The Somerses were always so kind to me in my time here."

"Don't apologize, you've done absolutely the right thing, though I think we should not bother the professor about this just now. I will tell you more once we have you out of Merton. We need to decide on a course of action, though." There were any number of places he could hide the young man. Even Tristam's home in Locfal. But out of the country might make the most sense. Entonne, probably. Egar's skill with languages was such that he could probably pass for a native. But there was more to it than that. Flames, he wished Tristam were back! Here was another piece of the puzzle, falling into his lap unexpectedly. But what did it mean exactly?

"This text, Egar, what did you make of it? Ancient, you say. But who wrote it, do you think?"

The young man put his hand to his forehead. "I can't give you a name, if that's what you mean. Its purpose isn't even perfectly clear. It's stranger than you can imagine, and, of course, I saw it all out of order with some crucial sections excised. It is both prose and verse, dissertation and syllabus, and it is not all in the same language, even. The subject is necromancy—I don't know what else to call it—though I don't know who could ever make sense of it. There are continual references to things—herbs and I don't know what else, like *belloc root,* and *kilsbreath,* and *kingsblood.* They do not translate into modern Farr, and what they are, we don't know. But the subject is definitely the arts of the mages, and written, I would say, by someone intimate with its practices."

"A mage."

"I would assume so."

They paused at the end of the garden for a moment and the young scholar lit a pipe with a coal from the smoldering incinerator. Jaimy could see the hands tremble in the hot glow of the pipe. He realized the young man could not bear up much longer.

"And the worst thing is," Littel said suddenly, clenching the pipe between his teeth, "these men—Wells and Hawksmoore and Noyes—they take this all so seriously. It is not just scholarly interest. They really believe they can rekindle the arts of the mages. In this day and age, if you can believe it!"

"Well, if they kept you half a prisoner, they must have some reason to think this. They aren't foolish men, Egar."

The scholar said nothing, but gave Jaimy a quick glance that almost spoke anger.

"Listen, Egar, there is someone else I wish to involve in this. Someone who knows more about these men and these matters than I can claim."

The young man nodded, his pipe bobbing like a ship's lantern in a seaway. "Who?"

"I hesitate to say until we have you safely away."

Littel stopped, removing the pipe from his mouth slowly. "I would like to know who you are involving. It is my safety in the balance."

"I understand." Jaimy looked up to find a star had appeared through a hole in the cloud. "Do you know Averil Kent?" he said quietly.

"The painter?"

Jaimy nodded.

"Only by reputation. He will help us? I thought he had just been knighted at Palle's insistence. Didn't I tell you that Palle was part of this?"

"You did, but I can assure you that Kent is no friend of the King's Man, despite appearances. I can explain further, but it will take time."

Littel walked a few more paces. "It seems very odd to me. You're sure of the man?"

"Quite sure," Jaimy said, though in truth it was only a hunch. "Kent's in Merton now, or was earlier today. I'm sure I can track him down, but we need to hide you away. I'm staying with Flinders. Do you know him? No? Good. I'll tell him you're an old friend and there isn't an inn with a free room in the town. He won't mind in the least. Flames, I wish Tristam were here. He would give anything to see this text. Unfortunate that you couldn't have spirited it away with you."

"But I did." The scholar looked quite surprised. "Don't you know? I can recall entire books without error. It is my memory—I seem to be unable to forget anything, no matter how trivial. It would take me a few hours, a day at most, but I can copy out this text, and my translation of it. Would that interest you?"

"Interest me!? Farrelle's blood, Egar, you can't begin to imagine what an unlooked for miracle you are."

Kent elected to walk the short distance from his inn to the house that had once belonged to Professor Sanfield Dandish. The streetlamps here were far apart and the night sky was half blinded by drifting cloud, so the streets were dark, and still damp from an afternoon rain. The small storm lantern Kent carried would have lit his way had he not chosen to keep it shuttered so that only the faintest glow escaped along with a feather of smoke.

It was a night of celebration in Merton; even the scholars who were not graduating used the occasion to justify their revels, but in this corner of the city things were relatively quiet. Kent found himself taking more and more care as he went. He did not put his cane down with the customary tap, and set his boots lightly, though the leather squeaked all the same. For some reason he thought that he was being watched or, more to the point, followed. Twice he turned quickly only to find a darkened street. His imagination tried to make something out of the shadows, but even with his imperfect eyesight he was almost certain he was alone. He heard nothing, and his hearing was not failing as quickly as his sight.

No light showed at the windows of Dandish's old residence, but Kent decided to circle the block and enter through the alley. The gate set into the hedge was not locked, and Kent stepped through it quickly to pause in the shadows, listening. Even in the poor light he could see the garden was in ruins, as though an excavation was underway. There were piles of dirt and rubble everywhere. Only the majestic trees had been spared, and they stood over this carnage, stretching their bare limbs up to the sky in silent lament. Kent could not help but think that this would break poor Dandish's heart.

After five minutes he was sure he was alone, and began to pick his way across the garden, using his walking stick to probe for open pits and to locate obstructions. Once he was forced to open his lantern, a brief appearance of light, like the moon emerging from behind a cloud, but then he closed it again, not wanting to draw anyone's attention. He was still not absolutely sure who was responsible for this travesty. He had sent a note off to Dean Emin but didn't expect a reply until morning.

The back doors to the house had been broken during the excavations and nailed hastily shut. Using his walking stick Kent had one ajar in a moment. He squeezed through the crack and opened his lantern to find that the house had been treated like the garden. Laths and plaster had been ripped from the walls and the flooring torn up, exposing the joists and beams. Inside, the house had been reduced to a skeleton. He could look between bare ceiling joists into the upstairs rooms.

Kent felt a need to sit. "What in Farrelle's name?" he said aloud. Someone had been desperately looking for . . . what? He stepped out gingerly onto some planks that had been laid across the joists, and could see down into the cellar bellow.

The entire house had been treated the same; only the main stairway was left intact. Kent went from room to room, remembering each as it had been when Dandish still lived—and on his last visit after the man had passed on. The professor's involvement with the court and *regis* was still causing ripples on the pond. Was this the work of Palle, trying to be sure that Dandish left no information, no trace of his efforts? Or was there someone else who Kent was not even aware of (one of his great fears)?

The painter made his way down the stairway, which seemed to stand almost unsupported, as though it were the spine of this skeletal house.

"Mr. Kent?"

Kent was so startled that he nearly missed the next step. A young man stood on the bottom tread, and for a moment Kent thought he was looking at Tristam Flattery.

"Lord Jaimas! What a start you gave me."

"I apologize, sir, I was surprised myself."

"What on earth are you doing here?" Kent came down to the young man's level and reached out to take his shoulder, as though reassuring himself that he was substantial.

"I went to Dean Emin to ask if he knew where you were lodging and he mentioned that he had a note from you inquiring about Dandish's house. When I could not find you at your inn, I thought I would come here, as it was so close by. Isn't it a crime? Look what they've done to poor Dandish's home!"

"But who did it, do you know?"

Jaimy shook his head. "I haven't the faintest notion." He looked around the entryway, then back at Kent, catching the man's eye. "Sir Averil, I have talked to Alissa about your request of her, as I think you know, and I believe that we have a common cause; you, and Alissa and I, and my cousin Tristam, as well as a few others. I do not want to say more, here."

Kent almost smiled. "Let us go out by the back," the painter said, holding up his lantern so that they could both see the way. They came out into the dark battlefield that had once been Dandish's precious garden, and as they stepped onto the brick terrace, a child bolted out from behind a pile of rubble and shot through the gate, though the gate was quite clearly firmly closed.

Kent sat before the fire in the drawing room of a friend of Lord Jaimas'—he had not caught the man's name—but, anyway, he was conveniently out. For a moment the painter closed his eyes, listening to the voices. His stomach had taken to burning as though he had swallowed mild acid, and the pain flared up now—a sign of his distress. Things were much worse than he had imagined. How he wished Valary were here!

"It is nothing like you imagine, Miss Alissa," Egar Littel was saying. "The text, even if perfectly translated, which we are not yet capable of, is so . . . arcane, so dense and convoluted." He paused, searching for words that would convey his meaning. "You would almost think it had not been written by a man at all but by some being from a nether world with an entirely different mind. It is in no place clear and logical or linear. It is as though the sentences were taken and randomly mixed."

"But did you not say they had given it to you in fragments, out of sequence so that you would not understand what it was you read? Could Wells and his group have merely mixed the sentences?"

"No," he said emphatically, and then stopped at the corner of the room to which he had paced. Kent watched the young man, could almost feel him thinking, with his thumb hitched in his waistcoat, his other hand to his forehead. He was surprisingly presentable for a scholar, the painter thought, attempting to make the most of his looks. To think that he had been telling Valary only weeks before that they must make an effort to find this young man, and here he was. Not out of the country at all, as they had been led to believe. Kent almost smiled. *You are too clever, Palle, but luck has favored me this time. Your genius escaped and came directly to me!*

"When I say it has no logic, that does not mean it has no pattern." Littel looked a bit ill at ease as he said this, as though stating this contradiction was like admitting he sometimes had the urge to do terrible things. "I cannot explain this, but there is some deeper pattern. I sense it more than see it, but I'm sure it's there. And I'm certain that Wells did not jumble the order of the sentences. You would have to see it yourself, but they follow, in their own strange way, from one to the next."

"I am dying to see it," Alissa said. "We will have to lock you in a room somewhere until you have reproduced it."

Littel drew himself up to his full height. "I have already been locked away in a room somewhere. I came to you to avoid that in the future."

"Oh, certainly, Egar," Alissa hurried to add. "It was just a figure of speech."

"Alissa is right, though," Kent said. "We must get you away, and you absolutely must reproduce that text. It is imperative that we know what Palle and his group possess. And Valary must see it." *And the countess,* Kent thought, bringing back a vision of the woman he had glimpsed earlier in the day. Had she really looked so much like the countess? Absurd, of course. If he had seen her face, the illusion would have been dispelled.

"I can give you some sense of what it is—at least my opinion. I believe it's a description of a ritual." Littel looked around at the others. "An incantation, a chant of warding, a procedure to create some kind of physic or elixir, and instructions for making an offering, perhaps even a sacrifice. That is what I think they possess."

Flaming martyrs! Kent thought. "What do Wells and the others think?" Kent realized suddenly that he was very tired. It would soon be light.

"They do not say, but I have come to believe they think it is a ritual that opens a portal or a gate."

"What gate?" Jaimy asked.

Littel shrugged. "I don't know."

"But what is behind the gate?" Alissa asked. "What is it they seek?"

Littel rubbed his eyes for a second, almost seeming to cover his face in horror. "I don't know that either, though whatever it is, they seek it desperately." He lowered his hands, and Kent thought his face suddenly looked quite pale. "Desperately enough that I fear what they might do if they find me. And I regret extremely my part in their scheme."

"I think we should get you away tonight," Kent said, his mind made up. "They must be seeking you even now. When I was young, there was a walking trail from Merton to Bothwell. Is it there, still?"

"Most certainly," Alissa said, almost jumping up. "I have walked it myself. Five brisk hours in the daylight."

"I can't stay in Bothwell," the scholar protested. "There aren't two hundred people there, all of whom know each other's business."

"No, you mustn't even enter the town, but I will meet you on the high road with my carriage and take you on. I have a place in mind. . . ."

A great thumping at the door stopped all conversation. Everyone looked to Kent, their alarm apparent. Littel stepped behind the back of a chair as though it would protect him.

"Your sight is better than mine, Lord Jaimas," Kent said quietly, forcing confidence into his tone. "Will you go to a window and see who it might be?"

The thumping came again, and everyone sat in silence but for Jaimy who sprinted up the stairs. In a moment he was down again, looking perplexed. "It's a man, alone apparently. It seems to be Prince Wilam."

Jaimy went and spoke through the door, then immediately threw it open, bowing quickly to the King's grandson.

"No time for that, Lord Jaimas," the prince said. "Palle and some others are on their way." The prince dropped a bag to the floor and then pulled off a heavy cloak. Beneath the cloak he still wore his graduation robes. "You're Littel, I collect?" he said matter-of-factly.

The scholar was so stunned he could not answer, but managed to nod.

"Put this on," the prince pulled crimson robes from his bag. "And you as well, Lord Jaimas." He bowed to Alissa. "I do apologize, Miss Alissa, but I have no costume for you." And then he turned to Kent. "I will leave you to see Miss Alissa home, Sir Averil. But we must meet later, though I'm not sure where to suggest."

Kent stood looking on, weighing this twist in events, gratified at how little it surprised him. It all fell neatly into place—made sense somehow. There was no choice but to trust the prince, if for no other reason than he was more his mother's son than his father's.

"At the Bayswater Bridge, before the track joins the high road to Avonel. I have a place to hide Mr. Littel."

"It will take us a few hours." The prince turned toward the others, dressed now as graduating scholars, and still young enough to be believable.

"Your Highness?"

The prince turned back to Kent.

"How close is Massenet on our heels?"

"Quite close."

"Then we should be on our way. Please, lead on."

∽ Ten

Kent had made his way through the streets crowded with revelers, delivering a somewhat worried Alissa Somers home, and then had gone back out into the fray, struggling on to his inn. He was surprised as he entered the lobby to find Dean Emin and Professor Somers waiting rather impatiently.

"Ah, Kent." Somers was out of his seat much more quickly than the aging dean. "I have lost a wager due to your timely arrival. But never mind. You can spare us a moment, I hope?"

Kent stopped in his tracks. He had no moments to spare. The thought of letting Littel fall back into the hands of Palle and his company was propelling him along at new found speed. Farrelle's blood, this young man knew what Palle and Wells were working on!

"A moment . . . ?" He looked at the worried faces of these two good men. "Can you come up?"

They ascended to the painter's rooms in cold silence.

"Won't you sit?" Kent said as a servant came in to light the lamps.

Dean Emin took a chair, but Somers stood, clearly agitated. "I prefer to stand, thank you," he said, a bit coolly, the painter thought.

As soon as the servant was gone, Somers raised a finger. "It is time we knew what is going on, Kent," he said emphatically. "Palle has been to my house asking after you and one of my former students, who showed up at my door earlier this evening looking like a man who'd just escaped the gallows. Lord Jaimas and my daughter took this young man off before I had a chance to find out what was going on, and now all three of them have disappeared. An hour ago Prince Wilam himself came by asking for Lord Jaimas. And your note to the dean would indicate that you have a continuing interest in Dandish and his doings. Perhaps you even know why his home has been destroyed." He paused, looking suddenly weary. "I am worried nigh on to death about Alissa, Kent."

"She is at your home, Professor, perfectly safe. I delivered her there myself not half the hour ago." Kent poured three brandies and passed two to his guests, though he was sure it was he who was in need. "Mr. Littel is safe as well, I hope. Which is to say he was not, when last seen, in the company of Palle."

Emin and Somers glanced at each other. "It seems that the King's Man has had a hand in much of this, Sir Averil," the dean said quietly, his manner subdued, as though he would make up for his companion. "Though Dandish's home was purchased through a barrister, it was this man, Hawksmoore, who had the house stripped to the bones. He was not so clever as he thought. I saw him there myself."

Kent paced across the floor. Too many knew too much already. "I wish I had an explanation . . ." Kent began, but could go no further. He desperately needed a moment to think. And even more desperately, he needed to get away!

"Was this flower that Dandish grew so very important?" Emin asked innocently.

Kent stopped abruptly, looking at his companions with surprise.

"So important that Palle would have his house torn to pieces . . . searching for what?" Somers said. "And was it the King's Man who took Dandish's journals?" Somers paced away suddenly, too upset to continue, it seemed.

"We would not be so worried, Sir Averil," Emin said, almost apologetically, "but the Flatterys are involved—relations of old Erasmus—one of whom is to marry Somers' daughter." Emin looked over at his colleague with some concern, and then went on. "Tristam Flattery was here last summer after Dandish died, and even then was involved in some affair that unsettled him greatly. Something to do with the palace arboretum, I realized, though he would not speak of it. And this young man, Littel, Somers tells me, has some tale of being held a near-prisoner while he translated an ancient text, which, if he is of sound mind, is quite an astonishing claim." Emin shook his head, saddened. "And Palle has been about Merton this evening, in a flap, asking after you and Littel. What in the name of sanity is going on here, Sir Averil?"

Kent slumped down into a chair as he looked at his two inquisitors. Good men, he had no doubt, but they would be better off knowing no more—better to know less than they already did, in fact.

"I should not tarry here with Palle looking for me, gentlemen. If you let me escape this night, I swear I will return when I can and tell you the whole long tale."

Somers stopped his pacing. "But what of my daughter, and Lord Jaimas? Are they involved in this madness in some way?"

Yes, Kent thought, *what of them*? "I will try to dissuade them from further involvement, Professor, though they are adults now and may not listen to me."

Somers stabbed his finger in the air. "Lord Jaimas may have reached the legal age of majority but that is not true of Alissa. I will not have her in danger, Kent! I will not."

Kent nodded, feeling a pang of guilt. Her involvement was his doing. "I understand, Professor. She is, I am sure, in no danger. Miss Alissa is one day to become a Duchess of Blackwater. Palle may be willing to bully a young scholar like Egar Littel, who is not well connected, but the daughter-in-law of the Duke of Blackwater he would bow to if she picked his pocket. You need not worry. Of that one thing, at least, I am sure."

The heavy thump of boots came from the hall, and then a solid knock at the door. All three men fell silent, not even daring to move. Kent took a long breath. "A moment!" he called. And then, quietly, to his guests. "I don't think there is any point in hiding."

As he crossed to the door, Kent realized that he had spoken with some degree of confidence, something that he did not feel. Was it only a few hours earlier that the Princess Joelle had squeezed his hand, imbuing him with a sudden feeling of invulnerability? What a delusion that had been! Flames, it might have been a warning!

His hopes that it would be some innocent caller were dashed the second he opened the door. Despite the fact that they were not in uniform, Kent was sure he confronted three Palace Guards in the hallway.

"Sir Averil Kent," one said, "you are to accompany us."

Kent looked at the men, all large and young enough to be strong, yet old enough to not be cowed. "And what reason would I have to do that? Are you officers of the peace? Have I been charged with some crime?"

Only a second of hesitation. "Sir Averil, I am to bring you by whatever means necessary," he glanced at his companions, who seemed eager to carry out such a threat, "and we will do that, if forced to."

Kent nodded, not surprised. It was the damndest luck that Somers and Emin had delayed him—but it had to happen in time. Foolish of him to have thought he could escape. "May I gather my things?"

"We'll see to those," the officer said.

"And my guests?"

"They are free to go."

Prisoner in my own carriage, Kent thought.

They were on the road back to Avonel, pressing the team cruelly. Poor Hawkins; he could not bear to see animals mistreated so, and here he was forced to do it himself. One guard rode before them and two behind. Kent could just make them out in their dark capes.

It had not happened quite the way Kent had imagined—and he had imagined his arrest over and over. He had expected to be taken quietly, without witnesses.

They let Emin and Somers go! But had they really, he wondered, shuddering at the thought that evil might have befallen his friends.

Palle was either desperate or supremely confident. There would be a hue and cry at Kent's "disappearance," that was certain. *Unless they intend to charge me with treason,* he thought suddenly. What in this round world had led him to have dealings with Massenet?

"*Fool,*" he whispered.

Leaning forward he peered out the window at the passing scene, trying to gauge their progress. A stand of beech trees glided by, barren of leaves, their silvered bark just visible from the coach lamps' glow. The bridge should lie just beyond. How he hoped that Lord Jaimas and Littel would not be recognized . . . if they had managed to get this far. Could they still be with Prince Wilam? Unlikely. But if so, Kent was sure that Palle would not dare to interfere with the prince—unless he had specific orders from Prince Kori.

Rain had begun to fall, yet Kent opened the carriage window, hoping to show himself to Lord Jaimas and Egar Littel. They wouldn't be foolish enough to shout to him? Kent decided he had to take the risk.

He clutched a glove in his hand into which he had stuffed a note he had written with difficulty in the moving carriage. The glove was almost black, but even so Kent feared that the riders behind might notice what he did. He looked back again and felt a little reassured. The road was wet, the riders were keeping their distance so that they were not covered in mud thrown up by the passing carriage. It was unlikely they would see the glove.

For a moment he considered jumping but decided something as large as a man would likely be seen, and he would undoubtedly be injured as well.

Ahead, at the roadside, Kent could make out a lantern, and then the shape of a large coach. The rider leading them slowed and Kent feared he would stop, but he spurred his horse again, and hurried on.

Kent could see only a driver down on the roadside, no one else, and then the carriage was alongside. But what if this isn't whom I think? He pushed down his doubts and threw the glove as best he could, hoping it would hit the driver or land near enough that he would be aware of it. And then they were crossing the bridge, the clatter of hooves on granite echoing like fireworks.

Despite utter exhaustion Kent could not sleep, and stayed awake watching the darkened miles slip by. A cruel drizzle fell for much of the trip, and the night was cold. The painter shivered under a heavy fur rug, aware that poor Hawkins hunched out in the cold and wet, driving his team on in a manner that must pain him terribly. Their ghostly outriders kept their stations. *My carriage to the netherworld,* Kent thought.

Perhaps three hours before sunrise they came to Avonel, and Kent forced himself to sit up and monitor their progress, wondering where he would be taken. Palle's home? Or some more neutral place. To his surprise the rider led them straight to the Tellaman Palace and stopped unexpectedly by a side gate.

Flames, he is bold, Kent thought. *What control he must feel he has to bring me here, to the center of all intrigue in the kingdom.*

Kent got stiffly down from his coach, casting a brief glimpse up into the tortured face of Hawkins. One of the riders came and supported Kent, taking his arm strongly and causing him to hurry more quickly than he was really able. How he did not fall in the dark was a wonder. Through a door, not lit with lanterns, and then into a hallway. A single dull candle far off. Through locked doors, and into the arboretum.

As exhausted as Kent was, he could not help but look around him. The famous arboretum. The place where the King grew his cursed *regis.* But the light was so poor, and his eyes so tired.

And then the sound of water running, and Kent was allowed to sit on a rough wooden bench, his guide standing silently at his back.

After a moment of slumping, eyes closed, overcome by fatigue and the pain of being thrown about and frozen for so many hours, Kent forced himself to look around. The scene was unreal, enchanting, as though he really had been transported to another world, but not a terrible place at all. He sat near to a waterfall and a small pool. Beneath his boots he could feel sand, and near at hand there was vegetation—exotic and aromatic. A shuttered lantern hung a dozen paces off, casting more shadows than light.

A sudden shuffling sound, accompanied by breath roughly drawn and muttered curses, came to the painter.

It can't be, Kent thought, and realized that he was suddenly sitting up straight.

Three men appeared, two guiding another who seemed to be blind. They took him to a chair set not far off. And then they stepped back, standing at attention. The seated man cursed and muttered again, struggling for breath.

"*Kent?*" came a terrible voice, ruined and guttural, almost unable to pronounce human sounds.

"Your Majesty." Kent bowed his head, unable to rise. The lantern was adjusted so that some light fell on Kent. Immediately he was reminded of his interviews with the countess. He could not see the man in the shadow.

"Flames, man, you are old. How long has it been?"

"Twenty-some years, sir."

Perhaps the head nodded. "Twenty years . . ." the voice said, as though testing these sounds for meaning. "I am lost, Kent, overwhelmed," the King said suddenly, as though remembering the purpose for this meeting. "Lost. Disappearing. And now that Elorin is gone . . . So many are gone."

Quiet. Kent could almost hear the man searching for the thread of his thought.

"If you are weak, it makes you mad eventually. Like Trevelyan. In the darkness I see . . ." Nothing. No sound. Just a man breathing. "The seed has grown scarce. Fallen to the frost, like all things. Too weak to resist. And I will follow." Kent could tell by the sound of these last words that the King looked directly at him. "Do you fear death?"

Kent was taken aback but hurried to recover. "Doesn't everyone?"

"Yes, but not all men will sacrifice everything because of it. These two behind me . . . they fear death; I'm sure of it, but they would die to keep me alive. Do you see? And I would let them do it, even if it was the death I deserved. That is the lesson." A wheezing that might have been a laugh . . . or a sob. "There is something that you must do, Kent. A last royal request. . . ."

"Anything Your Majesty could ask, I will do."

The waterfall continued to whisper, the endless pouring forth of water from the bones of the earth. One of the guards shifted his feet in the sand. Kent was sure he heard fingers snap.

"Though I cannot sit for you, you will paint my last portrait, Kent. Concentrate your mind, for you shall have only this one sight of me."

The lantern was carried forward. Kent prepared himself, ready to observe, fumbling with his spectacles. Without warning the light was cast upon the seated man. And Kent stopped, hearing his own gasp, barely muffled, then looked away. It was all he could bear.

"He was cadaverous, Valary!" Kent stood by his fire, swaying from fatigue. "Unimaginably ancient, and hideously so." He raised his hands to rub his eyes, but instead merely covered them in horror. "We have been wrong all along. Martyr's blood, but I expected him to be young! At least younger than his actual age. Every rumor we have ever had from the palace. . . ." He lowered his hands and stared at his companion, thinking that he was so tired and so overwhelmed that tears might come.

Valary looked down at the paper on which he had been writing, forcing Kent to recall every word that had been said. "You're sure the King said; 'And now the seed has grown scarce. Fallen to the frost, like everything. Too weak to resist. And I will follow.'?"

Kent nodded. "More or less; yes."

Valary puffed out his cheek and drummed the end of his pen against it. "What in this round earth did he mean?" the historian muttered.

It was morning, a gray light streaming into the room through swiftly moving clouds. Outside the door, footsteps squeaked on the stairs, and then came Barnes' familiar knock.

"Yes?"

"I have posted your letter to Merton, Sir Averil," the servant said, puffing to catch his breath. "Mr. Hawkins is in a hot bath, as you ordered, sir. Food and coffee will come directly."

"Excellent, Barnes. See that Hawkins doesn't nod off and drown, he must be beyond exhaustion. Put him to bed and have the doctor around this afternoon. It will be a wonder if he doesn't take sick from this. Double pneumonia, at the least."

Barnes nodded and retreated from the room. Kent raised a hand and rubbed his forehead gently. "That should stop Somers and Emin from raising the alarm, I hope. Now what were we saying?"

"I was puzzling over the King's words," Valary said, still staring at what he had written. "But perhaps he is no longer lucid. What did you think?"

"Well, it was a strange audience. . . ." Kent thought for a moment, remembering the meeting. "I did not get the impression that His Majesty was mad so much as unable to . . . focus his mind. Do you know what I mean? Like a man overly tired, as I am now, though more so. But, no, I can't say he was not in his right mind." He looked over at his companion. "The point is, Valary, King Wilam does not appear young. It has, all along, been one of our central assumptions. And if that is wrong, then in what else are we mistaken?"

Valary looked up at Kent as though he had finally registered what it was the man was saying. "Did I not quote Holderlin's letter to you? 'To live to the age that some have, one must follow the art with an unwavering, iron discipline, else one would pay a terrible price.'"

"What are you saying? That what I saw was a man who had paid that price?"

"So it would appear. The King is not, to the best of our knowledge, in possession of talent."

"But I have spoken with reliable people. They swore that, to all appearances, the King had not aged beyond sixty or at most sixty-five."

"And at the time they saw His Majesty I would conjecture that they spoke true, Kent. But that was some time ago—at least five years. Who knows what stages this habituation goes through? If one does not follow the larger art, perhaps the seed ceases to be effective after some time. There is certainly evidence that King Wilam has dramatically increased his use of the physic over the past two years. As it ceases to have the desired effect, perhaps the only answer is to take more. But how much can a body tolerate? Do you see? I think what you saw was undoubtedly true, but it does not negate what was observed by others. Not at all."

Kent went to a chair. He was so exhausted he could barely stand, but he could not sleep either.

"Let me read this back to you once more, Averil. Listen carefully, it could be very important." The historian read the conversation once again, slowly and clearly, like a school boy at his lessons, and in the middle of it, Kent fell deeply asleep.

The three young men piled out of the carriage, and watched the coach disappear across the bridge. "But that was Kent, I'm almost certain," Jaimy said. "Why did he not stop?"

Prince Wilam stood beside him staring down the now dark road. "Because he was accompanied by guards. I'm quite sure of it. Though they wore no uniforms, they were Palace Guards. Palle's people, I'm sorry to say."

The driver came up then, having calmed his team, which had been stirred up by the other animals racing past. "This glove was dropped from the carriage, Your Highness. Or more rightly, thrown, I think."

Littel almost snatched it from the man's hand. "Ah! Look at this!" he said. "There is a note stuffed into one finger." They took it forward to the carriage lamp and huddled over it.

"What species of hen scratched this?" Jaimy asked, for the note was barely readable.

Littel took a small magnifying lens from an inner pocket. After a moment he shook his head. "Well, it is signed with a 'K,' but it makes no sense to me. *'If you need refuge: the home of the lady who dwells with your looks.'* What in Farrelle's name?"

"That is helpful," the prince said, "we need a riddle right now. I suggest we move on before Palle or my own father comes along."

"I agree," Littel said, obviously still frightened. "Let us be on our way."

"Could it say 'books'?" Jaimy asked suddenly. "' . . . who dwells with your books'?"

"Yes, I suppose, and would mean just as much," Littel said, putting a foot on the step of the carriage.

"How in this round world would Kent know that?" Jaimy asked, addressing the night, it seemed.

"Never underestimate Averil Kent's knowledge," Prince Wilam said. "Do you have some idea what this means?"

"I know exactly what it means," Jaimy said incredulously, "though I should never have thought of it in twenty lifetimes. But I don't know how we shall travel there."

"It doesn't matter, get in," Littel urged. "We'll play thirteen questions as we go. Come on."

Kent could rouse himself only to semi-consciousness, just enough to recognize the two men responsible for waking him—Valary and Barnes.

". . . from Professor Somers, sir," Barnes was saying. "He's here in Avonel."

Kent realized he lay on the sofa in his sitting room, though he could not remember how he got there.

"I'm fully dressed?"

"Yes, sir," Barnes said solicitously.

"The duke requires a reply, and quickly, I think," Valary said.

"What duke?" Kent sat up, suddenly afraid that things of import had been occurring while he slept. It was daylight.

"The Duke of Blackwater, sir," Barnes said, obviously repeating himself. "The butcher boy just came with the meat and he also brought a note from the duke and Professor Somers."

"Ah, a note. Let me see it."

Barnes hesitated.

"It's in your hand, Averil," Valary said softly.

Kent realized that he did indeed hold a piece of paper. His servant handed him his spectacles and Kent read, trying to force his mind to awareness.

To the Manservant of Sir Averil Kent:

Sir:

> *I have come to Avonel with Professor Somers searching for your employer. Do you know Sir Averil's whereabouts? Please send an answer back with the boy who bears this note.*

> *Edward Flattery,*
> *Duke of Blackwater*

Kent looked up at his companions. "Apparently my letter did not reach Merton before they acted." He removed his spectacles, and gently pressed fingers to his eyelids. "A pen and paper, Barnes, please." He looked up at Valary. "They must believe Palle has set a watch on my home, and I'm sure they're not wrong." He tried to push some of the fog from his mind. "Have we had any word from Lord Jaimas?"

"None," Valary said. The historian was still dressed as he had been when Kent had roused him so early that morning. Was this the same day?

Taking paper from Barnes, Kent asked, "What is the day?"

"Sunday, Sir Averil. Sunday the sixth."

The date meant something, Kent was sure. "Are they not opening the iron bridge today?"

"They are, sir. The festivities must already have begun."

Kent wrote quickly.

I am perfectly hale, and flattered by your concern. Wise to stay away from my home, though. I will attend the iron bridge festivities, which will allow me to speak with everyone.

From where Kent's carriage stopped, the dark framing of the bridge looked like a section of web made by some monstrous spider of prehistory, cast across the gorge to snare the unwary. The painter could not tell if he was filled with admiration for its simple, functional beauty, or if he was disturbed by the image it brought to mind. The bridge, however, was not the work of some prehistoric monster, but of man. One man in particular, for it had been conceived and designed by the redoubtable Mr. Wells. The same man who had been working with Littel to translate the mysterious text. Apparently he did not lack intelligence—of a certain kind, at least.

Kent was still so tired he felt as though he remained half in the world of dreams, and so stiff that just getting down from his carriage seemed like the descent from a precipice.

Valary had accompanied him (and poor Hawkins had insisted on driving), and now the two gentlemen stood on a rise by the river, staring out over the gathered crowds, toward this "great monument to man's ingenuity," as it was being called. The day was blustery, but more spring-like than winter, and the sky was a riot of cloud, thrown hard up against the winter blue.

"*Sir Averil,*" called the Marquess of Sennet as he came along the cliff top. The man smiled giddily, and waved a field glass toward the bridge. "Is it not a wonder of the unnatural world?"

Kent introduced Valary, and the three men turned their attention back to the bridge.

"But why not a bridge of stone?" Valary asked in a small voice.

"I am told that this was done merely to prove the principles—hardly an essay in the craft. Much larger spans are possible, larger than have ever been managed with stone. This, Mr. Valary, is the bridge of the future—to the future, in a way. They say Wells is planning a great building on the same principles." The marquis searched the crowd with his field glass. "I think everyone but the King has come out," he said after a moment, and then added, in a tone far more serious than was common for him, "may Farrelle restore him."

"What's that?" Kent asked quickly, as alert as ever to the subtleties of conversation and tone.

"Surely you have heard the rumors, Sir Averil?"

Kent raised an eyebrow toward Valary. "Even I do not hear rumors before you, Lord Sennet."

The marquesss laughed with some delight at having surprised Kent. "It is said that the King has taken leave of his senses. I expect a regency to be declared by the senior ministers and the palace at any moment. Perhaps by week's end."

Kent leaned a little more heavily on his walking stick. The exhaustion of his night's drive came over him like a shroud. "And who will be named to the regency council?"

Sennet lifted his glass to his eye again. "That is the parlor game of the moment—guessing who will be named. Certainly Prince Kori." He stopped his searching. "Yes. There is the heir assumptive, now. You get no credit for guessing that correctly, of course. Then I would say this nondescript man I have in my glass now."

"Certainly not Palle?" Kent said. "He is the King's Man and should perform the same role to the council."

"Yes, it will be a break with tradition, but I will risk my money there." He moved his glass on. "And the third? Well, that is the hardest to predict. Every group is trying to have someone from their own faction appointed—even the reformers. I think I will not commit myself on this yet." He lowered his glass but continued to stare toward the bridge. "You are coming to the festivities at the Winter Garden, I assume?"

Kent nodded distractedly. The crowd before the bridge suddenly began to move, like a great army of ants, and the vanguard of this army set out onto the bridge, dark silhouettes, tiny at this distance. The first carriage rolled out onto the deck, and the sounds of the crowd moving swept down the river gorge like a torrent.

"I shall get back to my carriage," the marquess said, "for I don't want to miss my chance to cross over. Will you join me?"

Kent stared out at the great web and felt a chill run through him. Without even consulting Valary, he answered. "We will go back as we came."

Alissa Somers was fortunate to pick the correct entrance, and her patience paid well, for she was certainly the first person to find Kent. He almost hobbled in the door in company with a badly dressed man whose hair seemed to have been cruelly punished by the wind—a scholar, she was certain, and she was overly familiar with the type.

But poor Kent! The man looked like he might expire right on the spot. His face was bleached of all color, and she could see his neck tremble just to hold up his head. He looked infinitely worse than when they had last met, and she had been most concerned about him then.

"Sir Averil." She curtsied quickly, and then took his arm.

"Miss Alissa," Kent said, his voice barely audible in the din of the hall. "May I introduce Mr. Valary."

"A pleasure, Mr. Valary. Now, you, Sir Averil Kent, will come with me." His hand was so cold it did not seem to have life in it, which alarmed her terribly. "I know a quiet place where you may sit by a fire, and I shall see you are brought tea and hot food."

Kent seemed about to protest, but then acquiesced, having lost the strength to resist.

She led the two gentlemen into a hallway just as they had a glimpse of the main hall, and the crowd swarming about the model of the iron bridge.

Not too far along this hall the Duke of Blackwater had reserved a room for the use of his family, and Alissa found the door and eased the ailing painter in.

With Valary's help, she lowered Kent to a chair, and sent servants scurrying for food and drink.

"Oh, Mr. Kent," she said, no longer able to hide her distress. "I have no idea what you have been up to, but you will not stand another day of it, I am absolutely sure of it." Alissa realized that she was almost in tears seeing this dear man in such a state.

"This young woman is right, Kent, you need rest." Valary looked concerned as well.

Alissa pulled a chair up to the painter's. Leaning close, she spoke quietly, her voice full of concern. "And no one has heard from Jaimas since we parted last night. Do you know where he is? Is he safe?"

Kent lifted his hands in a gesture that seemed a little helpless. "I am not sure. He is almost certainly safe, for you know whose company he was in. We shall hear from him soon, I think."

Alissa was only slightly comforted by this. She did not like what was going on around Kent. She looked at the man again. He was so very frail. How in the world had he become caught in the center of Farr politics?

The door banged open, causing Alissa to jump.

"Father!"

Professor Somers closed the door quickly. "Alissa. Kent, how in the world did you get free? I was sure you were freezing in some prison cell." He stood shaking his head in both disbelief and admiration. "I don't know how you did it."

"I shall have to explain another time, Professor, it is a long tale."

Somers seemed to realize for the first time how frail Kent actually was. "Did they harm you, Kent? Do you need a physician?"

"No, I need rest, that is all. I travelled all night to Avonel, and nearly froze into the bargain. I shall be myself in a day or two."

Somers perched on the edge of a chair, looking solicitously at the painter. "It is unfortunate you are not well. There is a mad struggle over who will be appointed to the regency council. You've heard about the King?"

"It is not just a rumor, then?"

"Apparently not." Somers shook his head sadly. "The duke is at work as we speak. There must be someone on the council to balance the prince and Palle."

"Who is most likely, do you think?"

"Lord Harrington is the prince's choice, but there is a strong resistance to this. The duke supports Galton."

"Stedman Galton?" Kent asked. "But he is one of Palle's inner circle!"

Somers sat back in his chair, surprised. "Galton? But the duke is most adamant that he is the man for the job."

Kent made to rise from his chair, but found he could not, and felt a cold sweat seep from his pores. "Where is the duke? I must speak with him."

"Somewhere in the building. I might find him, I suppose." Somers did not seem inclined to do so, and looked at Kent oddly, as though the painter had ceased to make sense.

"Please, Somers do that. Warn him about Galton, and tell the duke the claims about the King are entirely false. His Majesty is perfectly coherent."

"What are you saying, Kent?" The professor seemed sure that Kent was not making sense, now.

"I was in His Majesty's presence this very morning. Spoke with him, in fact. Tell the duke that this is nothing more than a palace coup. Tell him, Somers."

⟿ Eleven

The feast was small, for the ritual of *maoeā* would allow only the most modest expressions of welcome, and to perform even these required appropriate rituals and sacrifices to be sure the gods would not be offended. Only the Farrlanders who had been to Varua on earlier voyages realized how subdued and modest this affair was. The others were so taken with their new surroundings, the beauty of the music, the vivacity of the women, and the exotic fare laid before them, that they thought they had made a landfall on paradise indeed.

Tristam sat on a plaited mat before the "table," long mats laid end to end and decorated with flowers and vines. The sun had set only moments before, beyond the high peak of Mount Wilam, and the moment of twilight was passing quickly. The trade continued to blow, warm from the lagoon, and the evening was perfumed with a thousand scents both exotic and familiar. The pungent odors of smoke, sand baked beneath the tropical sun, the perfume of flowers, and the smells of the salt lagoon. The Varuan women all wore flowers in their hair and about their necks, as well as scenting themselves with sweet oils that they kept in shells and applied occasionally. The breeze would blow, sweeping the air clear, like water cleansing the palate, and then would come some new treat for the senses. The smells of the freshly cooked food, fish and meats baked in the ovens in the ground, actually caused Tristam to salivate.

Fires offered only dull light, but the stars were quickly appearing. The moon, perhaps two days past the quarter, hung high overhead, its oddly unbalanced shape offering some cool light. Tristam had been told that this was the night of a ritual dance, and the visitors were extended the honor of witnessing this rite.

Each Farrlander seemed to have been adopted by a Varuan family who looked after them, making sure they were never without food, or sweet coconut milk to drink. Tristam's own hosts were a man and wife whose two daughters sat on either side of him and plied him with morsels, some of which he was expected to eat from their fingers, something he found very odd at first and then a bit erotic.

These young women flirted with him quite openly, and not only did their parents not mind, they seemed to encourage it. Often Tristam felt a bare breast press softly against his arm or his back, and hands brushed him suggestively. He thought he must be recovering his health, for despite his tryst with Faairi that morning, he felt a growing charge of desire.

He kept searching the faces in the crowd, hoping to find Faairi, though he was a little apprehensive about her reaction to his present situation. Although visitors to Varua always wrote that the islanders appeared to never suffer from jealousy, Tristam could not quite believe it.

Occasionally he caught the duchess gazing at him from across the mounds of food, and she appeared to be amused. *"Do not miss your opportunities among the young maidens out of some misplaced sense of obligation to me,"* she had said as they came to the feast, leaving Tristam wondering, as usual. But how would she respond if she knew of his afternoon's encounter?

The duchess is trying to rid herself of me, he thought suddenly. But then he wondered if that were true. It seemed more a statement of the nature of their involvement—he was not to expect matters to run in the normal course. This was not courtship leading to marriage, as one would expect in Farr society. But where was it leading? The true nature of their involvement was still a mystery to Tristam. If there were rules, then they were known only to the duchess.

Tristam realized that his morning of love with a complete stranger, rather than damping his desire, had increased it. He found himself wondering what the duchess would look like dressed as an island maiden. The thought excited him. The duchess displaying her charms with the utter candor of the island women—something Tristam was sure she could do easily, if not for the impact on her reputation. He suspected that the duchess, given the opportunity, would be as free with her favors as any island girl. It was part of the reason that he desired her so—because she would occasionally reveal this secret side of herself to him.

Tristam smiled at the women beside him in turn. What would Jaimy think if he could see Tristam now, seated between two beautiful young women who were bedecked in flowers and scented with oils, barely half-dressed, their hair caught by the breeze and teasing about him? It was a dream that many a student had nurtured, Tristam was sure.

Tall torches were lit as the sky faded and the smell of burning pitch was added to the evening's complex perfume. Shadows moved and flickered in the light, disturbing Tristam, who found the effect too much like his recurring dreams of wandering through darkened ruins. Despite the warm evening, he shivered, and wondered if the shadows were real or if they were merely a product of his own state.

He suffered waking dreams still—the dream world that Faairi had spoken of—though less frequently, but they were not unlike this, a feeling that his senses were overwhelmed and could no longer separate the myriad sights and sounds and smells.

He turned to one of the women at his side, hoping for reassurance, hoping there would be no signs of distortion. She smiled at him in the partial light, and this lifted his heart a little. Leaning forward she spoke close to his ear, her breath tickling his neck. She whispered in her musical language and Tristam only understood one word: *nehenehe,* which meant handsome, he thought, and hoped she meant him. The look she gave him afterward assured him that she did, and then a shadow crossed her face, though it was not real.

I am Tristam, the naturalist thought, unreality laying its cold hand on him.

Food was being cleared away and the crowd rearranged itself in a large circle. Shadows began to take on substance for Tristam, as though they were ribbons of smoke, spreading throughout the scene, painted across the people in irregular bands, like random applications of charcoal. But they moved. Tristam closed his eyes and felt himself floating, as though he had taken the *regis* physic.

He felt one of the young women put her hand on his back, almost tenderly, and she sighed, her breath catching. Even though the waking dream pulled at him, Tristam felt himself respond.

A sudden gust of wind hissed through the trees, like the night's whisper of desire, and drums began a slow rhythmic pounding in imitation of the surf.

Tristam tried to find the other Farrlanders in the crowd of faces, but the shadows moved like a stain floating on the surface of his eye, allowing him only glimpses. He could feel the excitement of the crowd more than he could see what occurred.

Into the circle came a dancer, a lithe young woman, not twenty he was sure, a small, white flower behind her ear.

"*Pōti'i mo'e,*" the woman near to him whispered, pressing herself closer.

What? Had she said 'lost girl,' or 'ghost girl?'

Tristam felt himself pulled further into dream, the ground beneath him less solid. The blossom behind the dancer's ear could have been *regis,* but in his present state he could not be certain. *Regis!*

The drums began to beat a more demanding rhythm. Tristam was no longer sure if it was the wind sighing in the trees or if he heard his own breathing.

One of the women ran her hand up to caress his neck just as the dancer began to twirl, her fine combed skirt of grasses fanning out, her neck arched back so that the long shadow of her hair seemed to spin outward, joining the darkness. Her hands and arms moved with such supple grace that they were almost tendrils. Shadow seemed to wrap itself about her like a web, but Tristam could not tear his eyes away.

She is being consumed by shadow, he thought suddenly. *I am falling into a* regis *dream. I have been given the seed.* But this knowledge did not move him. He stayed, fixed to his place, watching the dancer in the midst of the growing hallucination.

A male dancer in a long-beaked bird mask leaped into the circle, as though he had alighted from the sky. Across his shoulders and arms stretched a cloak of feathers creating the effect of wings. Wings that cast shadows upon the ground and the wall of faces.

Through some artifice the beak moved and produced a sharp clacking sound as it snapped shut. The two dancers continued their movements, separated by a dozen paces. Tristam felt a finger gently trace the curve of his ear. The trade wind combed through the palm fronds like a quickly indrawn breath.

Shadows flickered, painting the dancers and the open circle of ground with undulating bands. Suddenly the drumming stopped and the bird-man spread his wings, turning slowly. He had discovered the other dancer, who froze in mid-step.

And then the drums began again, the dancers moving swiftly about the circle, the bird-man in pursuit, clacking his bill. What Tristam saw being enacted was sexual pursuit, like animals courting. Aggressive display and posturing from the male, coy tempting from the woman.

But what did it mean? What myth or legend was being played out here? A ghost girl and a bird-man. Tristam's head whirled. The two women beside him pressed closer now, excited by the dance, by the pulsing beat of the drums and the sighing wind in the trees.

Tristam felt out of control. He reached to balance himself and touched soft skin. Someone whispered in his ear. Foreign words. And then a soft kiss.

The dancers had come closer now, not touching but their pelvises were only inches apart, their hips moving in a frenzy, driven, like copulation. He could see the sweat on their skin, on the woman's quick moving waist.

The drumming was fierce, reaching toward a crescendo. Tristam could see other couples touching, pressing near. And then, as the performance came to its climax, the bird-man stopped suddenly, turning about toward his audience, toward Tristam, and ever so slowly opened the great bill, and inside there was a second mask, half consumed by shadow—the face of a man, tattooed like the skin of a snake. The woman took the white flower from behind her ear and dropped it into the long beak, which clacked closed with finality.

Tristam was up then, pushing through the startled islanders. Staggering into the darkness, tripping as he went into the shadows. The two women were beside him, supporting him, guiding him, as though somehow they understood his panic.

"*Blood and flames,*" Tristam muttered. "What the hell was that?"

"Only a dance of transformation, Mr. Flattery." It was a man's voice. "Nothing more. Are you ill? Shall I call your Doctor Llewellyn?"

"No!" Tristam turned toward the voice. Wallis. It was Wallis, he was sure, though the man's form contorted in the dark like the stuff of nightmare. "No. I need only be alone for a few moments. Some water, and a place to lie down."

Wallis spoke a few words to the women, who did not answer, but Tristam felt himself guided suddenly to the left. "I know a place," Wallis said. "Leave it to me. Not forty paces."

Tristam realized they were in a glade of trees, walking along a twisting path. He was all but blind and let himself be led by the women, who seemed to have no trouble seeing in the dark.

Wallis spoke again, words Tristam did not catch, and suddenly he was being supported by the artist alone, the women gone. "Not far now," Wallis encouraged. "You can manage."

Flames appeared—a low-burning fire—and around it men hunched down into the moving shadows. Tristam tried to stop, but the gentle strength of the artist carried him forward. "Not to fear, Mr. Flattery. I have not brought you to harm. Please. . . . Sit quietly."

Tristam felt a hand on his shoulder, pressing downward. He sank to the sand, looking around him, trying to make out who these men were, but his vision was too clouded now. The nightmare was overwhelming him. The flames from the fire, thick with smoke, seemed to dance about him.

"These are *kenaturaga.* Old Men," Wallis said. "Do you know what I mean? Yes? They mean you no harm, but wish to ask you some questions."

Wallis had seated himself a few feet away from Tristam, as though disavowing any connection between them. The Old Men did not speak, but stared. Seven still figures, like carvings, Tristam thought, except that the shadows they sat in writhed. He could see little of their features, and he was not sure if the dark patterns on their faces were shadows or tattooing, but they seemed to swirl and undulate, as though resisting the firelight.

Finally one Old Man pointed with a carved stick and spoke.

"Show them your hand," Wallis said, just as Tristam realized he had understood some of the words.

"Why?" *Faairi.* She had betrayed him!

"Mr. Flattery, they mean you no harm, but they will not brook insubordination. These men are powerful, here. You must answer to them. It will prove the easier course, believe me."

But still Tristam held his hand close to his body, the sleeve pulled down, as he always kept it.

"Mr. Flattery. . . ." Wallis said, the warning in his tone compelling.

Tristam leaned toward the flame, reaching out his clenched fist.

The Old Man swung his stick aside as though to be sure it did not touch Tristam, and then moved forward to stare. He nodded to another who took hold of Tristam's elbow, jerking it forward until the naturalist could feel the hot breath of the flames. His shirt was yanked up, revealing the scar. Tristam tried to pull back, but the man was immensely strong.

"They're burning me!" Tristam appealed to Wallis.

"Hold still, Mr. Flattery. They will soon be done."

Tristam smelled the hair on his hand begin to singe.

"Martyr's blood, Wallis!"

"Be still. They are not patient."

The others moved forward, their gazes fixed on Tristam's hand. Suddenly one barked a single syllable and they all began to mutter.

Tristam looked down and then closed his eyes, trying desperately to pull his hand back. *The tattoo had reappeared!* It seemed to writhe across his wrist in the inconstant firelight and it *burned,* like a hot lash.

"Sweet Farrelle preserve us," Wallis intoned.

Suddenly Tristam's hand was released and he pulled it away from the flame, cradling it with his other arm. Holding it, throbbing with pain, near to his heart.

The Old Man who had held his arm leaned over the fire, extended his hands palm down, and passed them through the flames once, twice, and then a third time. He did not move quickly nor did his face display anything but concentration. He then went back to his place, and sat, not even glancing at his hands.

The Old Man with the stick addressed Wallis, speaking too quickly for Tristam, who was still absorbed in his pain—the pain of seeing the tattoo return.

"How did you come by this tattoo on your wrist, Mr. Flattery?"

How had they known about the tattoo at all? Faairi had seen only a scar. But then Wallis must have heard the story from the Jacks. Perhaps she had not betrayed him after all, he thought with some relief.

Tristam felt trapped, not knowing what it was these men wanted of him—if it would be prudent to lie, and if so, what lie to tell. Tristam felt the *regis* dream was sapping his energies, eroding his judgment. Certainly Wallis had heard much of the story already.

"When I said they were not patient, Mr. Flattery, I was quite serious," Wallis cautioned.

"I don't know where to begin . . ." Tristam said, his memories confused by *regis*, he was sure. "We were pursued . . . into the Archipelago by corsairs, as you must have heard." And he proceeded to tell the tale, his audience listening raptly to Wallis translate this story of the strange doings of men in a world far beyond the reef. When he finished, the Old Men spoke again among themselves.

There was a silence then; only the whisper of the trade in the trees, the far off roar of the surf, and the crackling of the fire. The singing had stopped at some point—Tristam only now noticed.

In this silence the Old Man who appeared to be in command, spoke in an ancient voice. Wallis listened attentively, his entire manner suggesting the demeanor of a retainer, making Tristam wonder where the man's loyalties lay.

"*Toata Po* asks why you have come to Varua," Wallis said.

"Certainly, Mr. Wallis, you have already told them our purpose."

"They want to know *your* purpose, Mr. Flattery, not the purpose of the voyage."

What to tell them? That, in truth, I am not sure? My course was chosen for me? I am drawn along, toward some end I cannot see?

"Mr. Flattery?"

"I serve the King, Mr. Wallis, and I mean no one harm. You may tell them that."

The artist seemed to consider this a moment, and then, with a show of reluctance, he translated for the Old Men, who spoke quietly among themselves again, for some minutes. Finally one addressed Wallis.

"Mr. Flattery? I assume as ship's naturalist you have been given the duty of searching for King's leaf. But you must not even consider attempting this. If you were to find this bush growing naturally—unlikely in the extreme—even to touch it would put everyone on your ship in peril. Do you understand what I'm saying?"

"But will the Varuan King not give some of this seed to us?" Tristam asked.

Wallis may have shrugged in the darkness. "The King is involved in the *maoeā*. Who knows what he will do when he returns? But I can assure you, you would be better to take none of it back. Farrland would be better without the fruit of this flower."

Wallis was interrupted then and he listened respectfully for a moment. "They want to know about Doctor Llewellyn. He claimed the title of 'Old Man' when he arrived here, and the Varuans can see the marks of the seed on him. What is his place? Is he your teacher?"

"My teacher?" The question seemed absurd. "You must tell them that Llewellyn is only a physician. An employee of the duchess. Nothing more."

"Mr. Flattery . . . it is obvious that he is something more. These men before you are wiser than you seem to realize."

Tristam tried to make his mind work. What to say? "Llewellyn is a minion of Sir Roderick Palle, but I don't know his purpose. There appears to be a struggle in the court. I understand little more that that."

Wallis was silent a moment and then he began his slow translation.

"What did you tell them?" Tristam asked suddenly.

"Only that Llewellyn supports a courtier of the King who has his own desire for power. On Varua the families of the King's wives vie for power through the succession. They are familiar with such things."

Tristam searched around the faces, thinking that perhaps the shadows were retreating a little—becoming merely absence of light. The feeling of nightmare was loosing its grip—a little.

Tristam thought he could feel the distant pounding of the surf transmitted through the earth. If he strained to listen, he could hear it, a din like a crowd where no single voice could be distinguished—no sound of individual waves, just the constant rumble. A force so consistent, so elemental that to Tristam it seemed geological—the rumble of the slow, incontestable movement of a landmass.

The youngest man present began carrying half-coconut shells around the circle, stopping before each Old Man, who would clap his hands loudly three times. The man who bore the cup would then speak a few words, and present the shell with both hands, the gesture oddly formal. One came to Tristam—a musky, pungent odor rising out of the dark bowl. He looked at it suspiciously.

"It is *kava*," Wallis whispered. "Made from a root. We drink it as one, all of it in a single draught. It is the custom."

A few words were spoken by one of the Old Men—half prayer, half-toast, Tristam thought—and he copied the others, lifting the shell in both hands and draining it completely. He almost gagged. A bitter taste of roots, spicy, warm, bits of sinuous pulp catching in his teeth.

One of the Old Men spoke quietly and the others nodded.

"I will guide you back, Mr. Flattery," Wallis said.

"That is all? Will you not explain why I have been brought?" He held out his right hand, shaking it in the firelight, causing looks of distress among the Old Men. "Will no one tell me what this means?"

Muttering all around now, men moving back from the fire, deeper into shadow.

Wallis pulled Tristam to his feet. "This is not the place." He almost pushed Tristam, placing himself between the naturalist and the others. "You will get no answers like this."

The artist was stronger than he looked, and Tristam found himself guided out into the dark beyond the fire where again he was without sight. He stumbled and Wallis bore him up. The ground tilted, first this way and then that. The fine sand of the beach came under foot, and Wallis stopped, balancing Tristam like a pole on end, testing to see if he could stand on his own.

The soft night wind swept across the lagoon and the stars hung in the sky, so clear that Tristam could feel the great depth of the heavens swaying above him. For a moment he felt a sense of vertigo, as though he could topple over into the stars, and then his rump hit the soft sand.

"You'll feel all right in a moment," Wallis said, gently. "It passes quickly." The man stood for some time, a moment—an hour—Tristam could not be sure. "Will you wait here, Mr. Flattery? Don't go wandering off without me."

Tristam made a noise that had been meant as words. His lips were numb, as was his tongue; thickened flesh in a dry mouth.

Wallis headed off down the beach and Tristam toppled backward so that he was lying, staring up at the moonless sky. Patterns of stars, moving, fading, then returning. A sound approaching. A large part of the sky turned to black and then Tristam realized a person stood over him. *Wallis,* he forced himself to remember the man's name. *Whatname Wallis.*

Cool hands touched his neck and forehead, and soft hair drifted over his chest.

Not Whatname, Tristam registered. Then a voice, speaking Farr.

"Is he all right?"

Wallis.

"Yes. I believe yes," A woman's voice, softly accented. He knew that voice. "He drank the *kava* for the first time?"

"Yes, but it is the *ari'i* he was given," and then he added something more in Varuan.

An indrawn breath. "He is not ready for this, I think."

Tristam felt a soft hand caress his face. *Faairi.*

"Best to keep him ashore until you are sure he has recovered. Will that cause trouble?"

"No. He is largely independent of ship's discipline. I'll see to him. I have a canoe."

The woman stood, said something in Varuan, and to Tristam's disappointment, was gone. He listened to her steps retreat across the beach, like the rhythm of his heart. From somewhere he heard singing.

"Mr. Flattery?" It was Wallis, his tone concerned, tinged with guilt, perhaps.

"I'm not quite ready to move." The stars were spinning and Tristam closed his eyes. "Tell me about the dance. The dance of transformation." He desperately needed to hear someone speaking.

He heard Wallis settle himself on the sand. "Well, that is easy enough." The words arched out toward Tristam like a lifeline. "It is an old legend of the islanders. In the ancient times they believe spirits took the form of animals. The dancer you saw tonight—the man—portrayed a bird now seldom seen, they say; a great sea eagle. It came to Varua long ago, where it saw a beautiful young maiden with the white flower behind her ear. Because the moon was not yet full, the spirit did not realize that the maiden was actually a ghost, wandering in the darkness. She is called the 'dream girl' sometimes, though it is not meant as we mean it.

"The spirit thought this maiden surpassingly fair and pursued her in the manner of his own people, the people of the sea and air, but he could never touch her. Determined to win her, the spirit transformed himself into a human man, only to realize then that the woman was a ghost and had no substance in this world. He could not reach her, nor could he transform himself back into an eagle. So he became the first Varuan man, named *Tetarakihiva*. The islanders say the ghost of the girl is still seen on occasion, and none can wear a white flower unless chosen to dance the part."

"But the face, the inner mask. It was tattooed like the skin of a snake."

"Was it? Well, it was very dark. Part of the drama is that you cannot quite see the man within. Can you rise?"

"Not yet. The white blossom. Was it *regis*?"

Wallis hesitated. "It was," he said softly.

Tristam looked up again at the stars, but they still would not remain still. "Tell me another legend—it will help me." Tristam needed the voice to anchor him.

"There are many. Surprisingly many. For a people without writing, they love tales. My favorite is the explanation for the moon rising and setting. Of course they know the world is a globe and floats in the heavens, and the moon circles round it. They even have the solar year, believe it or not—something we've had for only two centuries—so in some way the story is independent of that knowledge. I don't really understand.

"The Varuans say that the moon falls into the ocean at night where it is swallowed by a great whale, one of two whales who were once lovers. There are constellations named for them—one seen in the extreme east just after sunset, another in the west. One of the whales swallows the moon and swims under the waves across the ocean to the eastern horizon where it then blows the moon back into the sky with a great breath. When the moon is waning, the whales, who are very hungry from their labors, eat a piece each night. But when it is all gone and there is blackness—the new moon—they become so frightened that they make it again; regurgitating a bit more each night until it is whole. I think the moon is a great lump of ambergris." Wallis gave a small laugh of pleasure.

"While one swims east bearing the moon, the other sleeps, overcome with exhaustion from their labor. But when one arrives with the moon, the other must immediately set out to the west to be ready to catch the moon as it falls— they do it turn about. Because this great journey is so difficult they can never pause to speak as they pass but must rush past each other, only gliding close so their flukes touch. If you stand on the outer beach, just at moonrise, sometimes you will hear them touch—a soft sigh hard to distinguish from the sounds of the wind and waves, though the Varuans have no difficulty."

"What happens to the sun?"

"What? Oh, who swallows the sun and carries it into the east? I don't know, Mr. Flattery, but surely the sun is very hot. There will be another explanation for that. I will ask." Wallis chuckled. "Are you well enough to rise?"

"In a moment." Tristam opened his eyes and was relieved to see the stars hanging above him, clear and still. He wondered which cluster would be the whale.

"There was one other question that the Old Men asked, Mr. Flattery," Wallis said slowly, as though not quite sure he should say this. "I had difficulty explaining to them that the Viscount Elsworth was no relation to you. At first I simply thought they believed the duchess to be your wife and the viscount your in-law—brother-in-law, as it were. But it came out that they believed the viscount to be your brother, and I had trouble convincing them that this was not so. In truth, I'm not sure they believed me. You speak some Varuan; do you know the word *va'ere*? No? I think it is made up of parts of the words 'spirit' and 'dark.' Dark spirit." Wallis was silent a moment. "Let me tell you one last fable of the Varuans. Once there was a very powerful chief who had a beautiful daughter who was not happy among her people. No one knew why, for she had not been ill or unlucky in love. She was young and might still have babies, so no one understood her dissatisfaction. One day she disappeared and was nowhere to be found. Her father could not be consoled, but one night while he sat weeping on a rock by the lagoon, a dolphin came to the surface but a few feet away. 'Do not weep, father, for I am happy at last,' the dolphin said, and the man knew that his daughter had been transformed by some spirit, and now dwelt among the people of the sea. 'But daughter, I miss you, and I will never sleep for fear of what has befallen you. You live now in the world of the shark and barracuda.' The daughter blew a little fountain of water into the air. 'But, father, a shark is always a shark and barracuda always a barracuda. You know what they are and what they will do. But on land sharks and barracuda go about disguised as men. They are difficult to recognize and unpredictable in their cruelty.'" Wallis shifted on the sand. "Do you take my meaning, Mr. Flattery? The Varuans have ways of knowing these things. This Viscount Elsworth, he is a *va'ere*—something vicious dwells inside him."

Yes . . . and what dwells inside me? Tristam wondered. The viscount was another man transformed. The bird-man of the dance came back to mind, leaping high over the sitting audience to land in the circle. It made Tristam think of the bird-viper in the Lost City. The stars wavered, but Tristam forced himself to remain calm, breathing evenly. A dance of transformation. What had Wallis said? "You cannot quite see the man within."

A pounding in his ears brought Tristam out of sleep into a state of immediate reactive anger.

"Mr. Flattery?" came a demanding voice. "Captain wants you. In the duchess' cabin, double time, sir. He's in no mood to be kept waiting. Mr. Flattery?"

"Yes. Yes. I'll come along directly."

It was broadly light—late morning. He sat up, assessing his state. Something near to normal, he thought, and he was awake—fully awake.

Tumbling out of his hammock, Tristam stood for a moment, dazed. Yes, fresh clothing. He had fallen asleep in his clothes the night before. But how had he even come aboard? Wallis! Suddenly he remembered his meeting with the Old Men.

They had given him regis. *And his tattoo had reappeared.*

Tristam held up his hand and found the tattoo had almost faded to invisibility again, though not quite, and the hair on the back of his hand was singed short. It had not been a dream.

Fearing that he looked badly disheveled, and feeling some apprehension that he might have caused the voyage trouble, Tristam took himself out to meet the captain.

"Mr. Flattery," Stern said as Jacel let the naturalist in. "Be warned that we are at stations this morning."

"Stations . . . !" Tristam said. He looked over at the duchess, who seemed uncommonly subdued.

"Yes. We lost two men last night." He nodded to Wallis who sat by the table, clearly distraught.

The artist glanced up at Tristam, his eyes rimmed in red. "Two men were caught in the City of the Gods last night. They had entered the house of the most powerful Old Man, Toata Po, which they were searching. For King's leaf, it is claimed. They were executed on the spot."

"Flames!" Tristam said. "Who?"

"Garvey and midshipman Chilsey," Stern answered softly.

"Chilsey! But how could he even know?" Tristam blurted out, and then realized the answer. *Hobbes!* Garvey was the master's mate. Blood and bloody flames! Hobbes! Tristam could not help but look over at the duchess. She must realize as well. But the duchess would not meet his eye, looking down at a handkerchief she had twisted tightly around one hand.

"Sorry fools," Stern spat out. He looked up at Tristam. "You have not spoken of *regis* to anyone? To Beacham, perhaps?"

"Not a word, sir."

Stern shook his head and began to pace, his coat thrown back where he pressed a fist to his hip. "What do you think the Varuans will do, Mr. Wallis?" he said after a moment.

Tristam looked over at the painter, who seemed to hang over the table like a man exhausted by life. Stern obviously did not consider for a moment that the castaway's loyalties could be with the islanders—the people who had saved his life—not with those who had left him to die.

"I cannot say, Captain Stern. I suspect that nothing will be done until the King has completed the *maoeā*. I have tried to argue that these men were not acting on your orders, but if you demand reparation for their deaths. . . . That will indicate otherwise. You must make a public admission that their act was a crime."

Stern stopped abruptly, looking down at Wallis. "Are you suggesting that I allow these savages to murder two of my crew and simply let it pass?"

Wallis looked completely taken aback. "They broke two of the central *tapu*—laws—of this society, Captain. You must realize. . . ."

"And you must realize that I will not allow my men to be murdered without trial on the word of someone I have never even heard of! I cannot allow it. No, they should have been brought to me, and I would have dealt with them. Navy men meet navy discipline."

"But, Captain, if this were Entonne, you would not expect any of your crew who had committed serious crimes to be turned over to you. They would be subject to the justice of Entonne."

"Yes, justice! A trial at which they could be properly represented. Not summary execution for a crime they may or may not have committed. For martyr's sake, they might have been lost. They might have had an assignation and gone to the wrong fale. There might well have been an explanation, but we will never know."

"They had seed in their possession, Captain, taken from the Toata Po's fale. I had warned you about this seed, Captain Stern, and Anua asked that no one enter the upper city."

Stern did not answer. Tristam could see that the captain was in a rage. He also realized that the crew would expect him to respond.

"There is more to consider here, Captain Stern," the duchess said suddenly. "We have our obligations to King Wilam. Directly to King Wilam. His Majesty expects us to succeed."

Tristam remembered the duchess' reaction after he had saved Pim: *'You risked everything for the life of a cabin boy!'* It was not likely that she would worry much about the loss of the two seamen. Not where her own purpose was involved.

Garvey and Chilsey . . . had Hobbes put them up to this? Martyr's blood, Chilsey was hardly more than a boy. And his father was a captain in the navy, too. Someone Stern would know.

The thought of the captain turning the *Swallow*'s broadside, even as small as it was, on the village caused deep revulsion in Tristam. The Varuans had acted according to their own laws, their own interests. Tristam had seen the same thing the previous night when he had been taken before the high court of the Old Men.

"Is there no appeal to the Varuans under their own customs?" Tristam asked.

"They view their laws differently than we do ours, Mr Flattery. There are no mitigating circumstances, no trials in our sense. Whoever caught your men last night executed them on the spot—they did not go looking for higher authority. The laws are the laws. Not all laws affect all the people, that is true, but everyone is subject to the rules that govern their caste. Even the Royal Family. Even the Old Men live by specific laws."

"And exactly which of their laws govern us, Mr. Wallis?" Stern demanded.

"It is difficult to describe, Captain Stern, for it is still not perfectly clear. In laws of what you would call 'property,' you are largely exempt. The Jacks go about picking fruit without ever asking who might have rights to a tree. But in *tapu* of religion you are subject to the same laws as everyone but the Royal Clan, the chiefs, and the Old Men. They will not exempt you there, I fear. It is possible that you might be able to negotiate reparations for some other transgressions, just as we pay fines back home. But in religious matters, and certainly anything to do with King's leaf. . . . Well, I don't think Varuan customs would allow any exemption. You must realize they feel bound by their laws." Wallis slumped in his chair, lost in thought. "I don't know what to do, Captain

Stern. The Varuans are strange to our way of seeing things. They will have great regret over the deaths last night, and at the same time feel they were completely justified. Do you see?"

Stern paced the small cabin, like a man imprisoned. "The Jacks will expect me to exact some retribution for what they will see as murder; the laws of the Varuans seem foolish to them. We have that to think of. We cannot afford to alienate the crew, not this far from home."

"And I'm sure your only chance of acquiring King's leaf is through the goodwill of the Varuan King." Wallis stood up, ducking his head beneath the beams. "You will have to find a way to mollify your crew, Captain Stern, or you will sail home empty-handed."

Stern was taken aback and stood glaring at the cast-away with both surprise and anger. "Let me assure you, Mr. Wallis, that I have no intention of sailing home empty-handed. You might tell that to your Varuan friends."

ᕬ Twelve

Midday found Jaimy and Egar Littel riding cross-country with a cool wind at their backs. They had purchased riding horses and tack as well as more useful clothing, but were still underprepared for this journey. Jaimy thought it a blessing that it was not raining. Littel, it turned out, was a passable horseman and a good companion except for his overwhelming fear of being apprehended by Palle. *"I spent much effort in appearing so obtuse as to be no threat to anyone,"* he had said, *"but now they must realize I understood more than they thought. They will want me back."*

Jaimy was becoming slightly less worried about being apprehended as each mile passed. The real concern now was finding the place Kent had indicated, for Jaimy had only the vaguest idea of where the Countess of Chilton lived.

Egar glanced back over his shoulder as he had been doing periodically the whole morning.

"No army in pursuit, I hope?" Jaimas said, hoping to bring a smile to the worried scholar's face.

"I am not being foolish about this," Egar said, perhaps thinking Jaimy made fun of him. "I'm quite sure Roderick Palle sees my flight as betrayal, and men of his type do not accept disloyalty easily. They have absurdly misplaced importance on this text. They will make great effort to have me back. I tell you this for your safety as well as mine."

Jaimy nodded. "I did not mean to make light of what has happened to you,

Egar. I agree that we should take no chances, but speed you to safety, which is what we are doing. No, I understand your concerns."

It was partially a lie. Jaimy was now almost certain they had slipped away unnoticed, but it seldom paid to mock a man's fears.

This journey with Littel reminded Jaimy of his many rides with Tristam, which set him to wondering where his cousin was now. Was he on some exotic isle surrounded by beautiful maidens, indulging his passion for things natural in a new way?

They came to the crest of a hill where Jaimy pulled his horse to a halt. He surveyed the surrounding countryside—beautiful even in late winter when the trees were bare and the colors muted. "That will be Coombs to the east. You can see the smoke rising in the draw." He pointed. "We will want to give that a wide berth. There is an inn on the Postom Road, where we can likely stay quietly."

"Lord Jaimas," Littel said, his voice almost a whisper.

Jaimy turned to find his companion staring back the way they had come. There, passing across an open pasture between two small woods, a clutch of riders could be seen, looking at a distance like a many-legged beast scuttling across the landscape. And before this beast went smaller creatures, bounding and baying: *hounds.*

"Hunters, do you think?" Littel said.

"Yes," Jaimy said, standing up in his stirrups, "but they do not hunt the fox. We are their quarry, I fear. Come on, we must get off this hillside."

They rode quickly down, finding a path winding among ancient elms. They stopped before a low stone wall at the bottom, and Jaimy could see that Littel was desperate, casting his gaze from side to side, like a fox at bay.

"Which way?" Littel said. "Which?"

"Let me think."

"Think! There is not time!"

"Yes, there is time now. Later we may not have the luxury." Jaimy looked up the slope and tried to estimate how far ahead of their pursuers they might be. When they had left the town they had set out on a west-going road, and then doubled back overland, so that anyone asking after them would be thrown off. But it had not worked. Someone had likely seen them leave the road.

Jaimy tried to pull a map together in his mind. The River Whipple would not be far to the north, and could only be crossed at its bridges or fords. There were three towns of any size nearby, all best avoided now.

"Our horses will soon tire," Jaimy said, thinking aloud.

"They will not have a chance to tire if we stay here."

"We must stay on our course north as though we are making for the Wye

Bridge and Caulfield Town. Once it is dark we'll turn east and south, for Avonel. That's not what they'll expect."

"But what of their hounds? Dogs aren't likely to care for their master's expectations."

"No. We will have to throw them off somehow. But right now, we need to stay ahead of them. They're a larger party and will go more slowly if the land is not open, though our horses are hardly racers. I wish we were riding my best jumpers, we would quickly leave them far behind."

They cantered beside the wall until they found a gate, then set their horses to a good pace to cross the open meadow. Once they were in the shelter of pine trees, Jaimy dismounted and slunk back to see how close their pursuers were.

"Just starting down the rise," he said as he returned and mounted, spurring his horse on. They pushed their horses as much as they dared considering that they would not have fresh mounts for some hours—if at all. Jaimy hoped that their pursuers had found their mounts at the same inn as he and Littel, for they had taken the best horses there by far.

"Once they see we have begun to press our pace, they will realize we have seen them and guess their purpose," Jaimy called back over his shoulder. "We must try to keep this distance between them and ourselves." How he wished they had bows. He had never thought of shooting at a man, but it might come to that. Even a warning shot might have some effect. Were these men armed? If they were guards, they would likely have blades. More than he and Littel could claim.

At the far side of the wood they came out into the open and were faced with a fen, stretching on to a distant line of willows, lit by a shaft of sunlight so that the yellow of their drooping branches stood out against a dark cloud.

"Dare we cross?" Littel said.

Jaimy could see what he thought was fenberry growing, and in places, cattails. He wished that Tristam were here. Just by looking at the flora, the naturalist could usually tell how wet such a bog would be.

"I don't know, Egar. We'd better skirt the edge, I think. It looks shorter to go east-about."

They hurried in earnest now, spurring their horses on. Jaimy was certain that the dogs belonged to a local man, someone who would know the land well—know whether he could cross such a bog. Jaimy looked up to find the sun, judging the hours of daylight left. Two hours. They could not turn east yet, that was certain. He didn't want the hunters to know they were heading toward Avonel.

They would have to keep going north. Jaimy wished he were in country that he knew. Anywhere near his family's country home, he would give their pursuers the slip with ease. But what did these men plan? Would they take Egar prisoner, with the son of the Duke of Blackwater as witness? Certainly they would not dare to harm either of them. No, likely they would take Littel on some false charge, that would be their likeliest route.

The fen curved north now, and they pressed their horses to keep moving, feeling exposed here in the open, their eyes fixed on the line of trees ahead. An eerie call, like a badly sounded horn, was carried on the wind, and Jaimy knew that sound well. The baying of hounds. Their pursuers were closing in.

Without being told, Littel spurred his horse to a gallop, jumping a fallen tree as he went, landing badly but keeping his seat. They were almost past the bog now, the trees rearing up before them like a row of massive hairy beasts. As they slowed to push through the hanging branches, Jaimy turned and saw the hunters follow their hounds straight into the fen without pausing. They could have crossed, but had lost that time.

For the first time Jaimy felt truly frightened, wondering what these men intended.

Beyond the willows lay a narrow track running east-west, and they pulled up their mounts here, looking around as though searching for a place to hide. Beyond the road lay a small lake, perhaps a quarter of a mile across. Jaimy wheeled his horse east and called for his companion to follow. If they did have better horses, perhaps they could put them to advantage on the road.

The dull drumming of hooves on mud; and distant, the shouts of men and baying of hounds. The wind whipped at the drooping willow wands, which swayed out into the track like grasping tendrils, making the riders work their horses lest they shy.

So this is how the fox feels, Jaimy thought as he struggled to keep his horse moving and beneath him. He made a silent vow that he would never ride to the hounds again.

A mud farmyard appeared, and a cottage and ramshackle buildings. They barely slowed, scattering fowl before them. Then suddenly out onto a proper road. Jaimy did not hesitate to consider, but turned his horse north. He looked back at Littel, and realized that neither horse would go much farther at this pace.

"Off the road," Littel called. "We must get off the road."

Yes, but where? The underwood here was dense, and no paths could be seen opening into its inner halls. Jaimy didn't know what they should do. Ride on as long as their horses could stand. That was all they could do.

They galloped round a bend and came upon three men, two mounted and one standing by his horse. Before Jaimy could react, one man lifted a bow. He turned his horse then, and plunged blindly into the wood, staying low to the horse's neck, clinging to the mane, letting his mare find her way. Certain that at any moment a branch would crack his skull.

There were sounds of someone behind him and Jaimy hoped it was Littel and not one of their pursuers.

Someone had made to fire an arrow at him! And at that distance might have killed him easily. Killed him!

The bush thinned just perceptibly and Jaimy dared to raise his head. He could feel his horse laboring to breathe, her chest heaving beneath his knees. A quick glance behind and he saw that he had Egar in tow, his face set and grim.

The trees thinned again, and the underwood all but disappeared so that they were galloping over a soft cushion of decaying leaves. A low stone wall, almost buried in a thicket of vines, rose up before them and without thinking Jaimy made his horse jump, and heard a loud grunt as Littel landed behind him. Jaimy turned again and found his companion still in the saddle and flailing with his foot to retrieve a lost stirrup. They were in another wagon track, and turned again to follow, not knowing where they would go or what they would do. Only keep to the saddle and run their horses until they dropped. That was all they could do now.

Out of the bush ahead a fox suddenly appeared, some small rodent in its jaws. For the briefest second it paused on the road, staring at the riders bearing down on it, one dainty foot raised, and then it bolted into the bush to the left. Jaimy almost let out a whoop.

Hoping Egar would have the presence of mind to follow, he turned down the track of the fox, forcing his horse to keep her pace. Branches whipped him, tearing at his skin and clothing. His cheek was raked terribly, and he rode with one arm up before his face, barely able to stay in the saddle. Then the fox appeared again, and Jaimy swerved off, leaving it to go its own way.

At the bottom of a steep embankment he found a shallow stream and turned to follow it, his horse slipping and stumbling on the smooth stones. After half of an hour of this he stopped and his horse stood panting, fighting her bit to drink, which he dare not let her do.

Egar Littel came up beside him, gasping almost as hard as his mount. He had suffered worse than Jaimy and one eye was almost closed by a cruel welt.

Not far off, hounds bayed.

"We should not stop," Littel managed.

"No, listen. . . . They are going north, chasing our fox. With luck he will drop his prey and that will cause even more confusion. They are spoiled for chasing us now. The riders will take hours to pick up our trail again, and by then it will be dark."

Jaimy slipped out of his saddle and into water to his knees. Tired of struggling with his horse he scooped up some water in his cupped hands and let her take a little. "Come, we will walk them so that they don't cool too quickly. I think we must stay to the river a bit longer, though it can't be good for our poor mounts. We will go up the bank just at dark. I think we would be best to go east, and then north. I'm afraid to go toward Avonel now in case we meet reinforcements for the dogs." He waved off toward the baying hounds.

Littel almost fell from his saddle, splashing down into the stream bed. He looked hardly able to continue, despite his fear.

"Best we move, Egar," Jaimy said softly. "You saw them aim an arrow at me. I am not convinced they wouldn't have shot either."

"At you?!" Littel said, incredulous, and then turned his shoulder toward Jaimy. He pulled at his coat, displaying a ragged hole in the sleeve. "Did that arrow come this close to you?"

Jaimy stood, a bit stunned, as the realization made its way through the layers of fear and confusion. *They had tried to kill them! Tried to kill them rather than let them escape.*

⤷ Thirteen

Sir Roderick Palle was not at peace with the world. He stood on a balcony in the Winter Garden, looking out over the crowd gathered to celebrate the opening of Wells' bridge of iron, and something about the sight of the milling masses unsettled him. The people below seemed so . . . rudderless. So lacking in real purpose. They had been told that Wells' bridge was a marvel of the modern age and, dutifully, they had come out to celebrate this auspicious event. The King's Man suspected that not more than half a dozen people in this whole great building understood what it meant.

The hall, Sir Roderick believed, was filled with the benighted. Fashionable aristocrats who saw this as merely another social function, no different from the theater or opera. Perhaps there were even some softhearted transcendentalists and nature lovers staring up at the model of the iron bridge and shaking their heads in dismay, and for no reason other than this concept was new. Palle was sure that even many of the empiricists present did not fully comprehend what had happened right before their eyes.

We have broken away from stone, the King's Man thought, *weaned ourselves of the material of the ancients. Hundreds of years ago we delved down into the earth and wrested something new from her aged bones. We smelted and refined until we found the essence of the earth's strength. And now, through an act of creative genius, we have built a structure of this material. A structure that balances the forces and stresses in such a way that it supports itself. And it is only a beginning. We have broken away from stone.*

But Palle could see that these vacantly smiling faces, these mouths that spoke nothing but gossip, did not realize they stood at a crossroads of history. What would they say if they knew Wells was certain ships could be built of iron? Ships of iron that would not only float but repel cannon shot!

This lack of understanding made the King's Man uncomfortable. These people could misconstrue anything. Pledge unwavering support to the worst tyrant, vilify the most honorable minister. Even a man such as himself could fall victim to these people. All it took was some rabble rouser to stand up and convince them his lies were true. Never mind that Roderick Palle had given them over a decade of security and good government. They would march in the streets, chanting his name as though he were a demon in need of exorcism. He had seen it happen to others.

Oh, today the crowds had come to celebrate the iron bridge, but they might just as easily have come to tear it down as a symbol of their oppression . . . or some such thing. One could never be absolutely sure. And anyone who was, soon came to a bitter end.

He suddenly realized that he was beginning to think like Rawdon, and this caused him to shake his head. He was sure that the Royal Physician was actually superstitious and believed that if he never became overconfident, as long as he always believed that the worst could happen, then it would not. The King's Man smiled. Perhaps the doctor was right in this belief and was averting disaster with this regimen. In which case, it was good that the doctor laid awake at night looking out for their interests through his program of constant anxiety. Palle never lost sleep over his choices. Or very seldom anyway.

It was true that he had not slept soundly the previous night. But then who would have? Littel gone, and Averil Kent disappearing from Merton—hardly a coincidence, he was sure. Kent had something to do with Littel's disappearance, unquestionably, but he was not sure what he could do about it. Valary's manservant swore that there was no one staying in Kent's home but the two elderly gentlemen. So if Kent did not have Littel, where was he?

Kent was fortunate that Palle was a civilized man. In times past many of those designated as King's Man had not been so discreet, nor did they care much for the reactions of the people—which had brought many of them to their demise. Roderick knew; he had made careful study of these matters. As things stood he was not quite ready to weather the storm that would result from apprehending Sir Averil Kent. Oh, he wasn't really worried about what the people milling about below him might think. They would likely accept whatever explanation they were given, especially if it somehow fit their expectations. But there was a group who would not believe Palle's explanation, and that group concerned him. He couldn't afford to offend them. Not at this point anyway. And there *was* the unreliability of the crowd to consider. . . .

It was the problem with Farrland; the country was governed by compromise. Compromise between this group and that. Between the industrialists and the merchants, the landed gentry and the Farrellites. And now even the reformers were beginning to play a part! A development he looked upon as benignly as a surgeon looked upon gangrene.

He gazed out at the people gathered on the floor of the Winter Garden's great hall and thought that, except for small, temporary setbacks, things proceeded as they should. This very day would see the formation of the council of regents—in fact if not in name. Official announcements would come soon enough. Best to tidy up the loose ends first. He didn't want Egar Littel galloping about the countryside telling what he knew—not that it was likely that many would believe him. Still, there were some. . . .

Noyes appeared at his side, quietly, his tall somewhat comic form standing a head above the King's Man. There could be few men in all of Farrland whom high fashion suited less. It was unfortunate that a man with such an intellect should persist in looking so foolish.

"I think it is all but done, Sir Roderick," the empiricist said, smiling broadly.

"The duke has agreed?" Palle asked, betraying a bit of surprise, he realized.

Noyes nodded solemnly, although this solemnity did not erase his smile entirely. "Not only has he agreed, but Galton was one of the names the great duke put forward himself!"

"Do not laugh, Noyes," Palle said quickly. "Let no one see you laugh." Palle turned to look out over the hall, feeling a great easing of tension in his body, like a carriage spring relieved of its load. "I can't believe it came so easily," Palle whispered, almost speaking to himself.

"Nor can I, Sir Roderick. Nor can I." Noyes shifted on his feet, and spread his large hands out on the railing. "There is only one condition. The duke wishes an audience with His Majesty."

The King's Man nodded. "I'm sure Doctor Rawdon can arrange a meeting that will convince the duke our claims are true. At His Majesty's convenience, of course."

"I will inform the duke. Will you bear the news to Galton or shall I?"

Palle looked around and saw the governor seated near to his wife, speaking with a group of young nobles. "I shall inform him of his most recent honor."

For the briefest second Roderick felt suspicion take hold of him. The duke had put Galton forward? But then he smiled. All those years on Farrow had made Galton seem the most innocent of men. Clearly he had no greater ambition than to help the people of Farrow, which he had done in great measure—especially his efforts toward rescinding the Daye Laws, which apparently had a devastating effect on the economies of certain of Palle's friends.

Palle turned away from Galton. The good news could wait until the governor was alone; it would give the King's Man a few moments to savor it. Such moments were like fine wines, not to be rushed.

Noyes continued to stand at his side, saying nothing, perhaps enjoying the moment as Roderick did.

"Sir Roderick." It was one of his secretaries.

The King's Man turned.

"A messenger has come from Mr. Hawksmoor, sir."

"Yes."

"He will deliver his message to no one but you, Sir Roderick."

Roderick nodded. "Well, bring him along, then."

"Sir, he has been riding hard for several hours." The young man looked around, a bit apprehensively. "Perhaps you would prefer to meet him more privately?"

Roderick nodded, waving the man to go ahead, and taking Noyes in tow. Now what in Farrelle's name went on here? He did not have long to ponder this for Hawksmoor's messenger was waiting in a nearby alcove. Roderick's first thought was to commend his assistant for recommending that he meet this man in private. The messenger was covered in mud and grime, his clothing torn, and he looked entirely out of sorts, like a man who had, by good luck and hard riding, escaped highwaymen. He bowed quickly to Roderick and passed him a letter closed with Hawksmoor's seal.

Sir:

> *After a difficult chase, we caught up with Mr. Littel. I regret to say that Mr. Littel and his companion fought quite fiercely and, in the heat of the moment, both were killed. As Littel was last seen in the company of the son of the Duke of Blackwater, I fear the very worst may have occurred. I am hurrying now to the scene of this tragedy, and will relay more information as soon as is humanly possible.*

> *I remain your servant,*
> *E.D.H.*

Palle found he could not move, but stared at the note as though certain these words were somehow misarranged. It simply couldn't be true.

"Sir Roderick?" Noyes said quietly. "What is it?" The empiricist reached out toward the letter, and when Roderick did not respond, he took the sheet of paper from the man's limp fingers.

"We are undone," Noyes whispered. He lifted a hand toward his face but then let it fall.

Seeing the reaction of his companion, Roderick suppressed his own emotions. "Were you involved in this madness?" Palle asked the messenger.

The man nodded, apparently too frightened to speak.

"Did anyone know these men you captured?"

The man shook his head. "Two young gentlemen, sir." The man's voice was so hoarse he could barely be heard. "We had been pursuing them for the entire day. Hunting them with hounds, sir. Caught them just at dark. I was sent off to Mr. Hawksmoor immediately, and then he had me come here."

Palle turned away, taking the letter from Noyes as he did so, concealing it quickly in his coat, as though just being seen in its possession could bring calamity.

"Noyes," Palle said, turning to his confederate, speaking so no one else could hear. "You must take charge of this. At the gallop. If it is the young gentleman that Hawksmoor suggests, then you must take every step to be sure that no one—no one—will ever know." Palle reached out and took the man's forearm. "Do you understand? If the duke were ever to learn of this, it would not matter that too little evidence could be found to convict us in court. The entire nobility would be raised against us." Palle looked around quickly to be sure no one could hear. "Whatever steps necessary. Our survival depends on it."

Noyes nodded a bit tentatively.

"Mr. Hawksmoor will be there to carry out whatever measure you deem necessary, don't worry. Your own hands will stay clean." Palle turned and looked out toward the great hall. "If this proves to be true, then it would be best if we were to hunt down the boy's murderers ourselves. Hawksmoor will understand."

Roderick thought it best if he returned to the celebrations. He had good news for Galton. The other matter he would keep to himself, for now. Even his closest associates might lose their nerve if they heard about the duke's son.

Roderick wondered if the duke would expect him to pay his respects, but decided there would be nothing odd in his not doing so. Galton was acquainted with the nobleman, anyway, and would be better suited to expressing appreciation.

For a few seconds Palle felt pity for the duke. The poor man had lost his only son. That would be hard. Roderick wondered if it would ever be possible to trace the murder back to him. They needed to find out how Littel had escaped Merton. That was the key. He had been there, in the company of this young lord—this cousin of Tristam Flattery!—and then he had disappeared, and no one knew how.

Kent had been seen walking through the city, and then he, too, had slipped away. Palle had only this rumor of Kent seen, apparently alone, in his carriage heading for the Avonel Road. But this was just a rumor.

Roderick made an effort to calm himself. Panic stopped one from making intelligent decisions—he knew this well. He had made a reputation for coolness under fire, and was damned if he would falter now. He smiled at some passersby, not entirely confident that his face was not still betraying his recent shock.

Rawdon appeared out of the whirl of faces. Here would be a test. The physician knew him as well as anyone and would notice immediately if something was not right.

"Sir Roderick." Rawdon bobbed his handsome head.

Occasionally Palle felt jealous of Rawdon's appearance, having been born so plain himself. "Doctor. I thought you had been detained with your patient. Everything is well, I hope?"

"Well enough, I think." The doctor looked around, then bent his head closer to the King's Man. "Though I have a fear that something might have happened at the palace last night."

"Things happen at the palace all the time, Doctor. Speak more plainly."

Rawdon cast a look around. "The King went down to his waterfall very late in the night."

Roderick nodded. "Unusual, I agree, but not terribly so."

"I spoke with a chambermaid this morning who was in the garden last night, and said she saw someone being taken from the arboretum. Someone quite elderly, she thought."

Roderick was truly alarmed now. "The King is there still, is he not?"

"I attended His Majesty this morning. But, do you see, he might have met with someone. That is my suspicion."

"Well, it is slim evidence, Doctor, but I understand your concerns." *Kent?!* Could it have been Kent? "I'll look into it when we return. We'll speak to this chambermaid together. If she was about at such a late hour, then there must have been a young buck as well. Or an old one. And who assisted the King? He could not have gone so far on his own—not these days. We will soon get to the bottom of it."

The doctor looked so kind, and had suffered so many troubles of his own that Roderick found he wanted to confide the news about the duke's son. But he stopped himself, knowing what such news might do to the doctor's fragile mental state. He had suffered badly from melancholia this last year—ever since his wife had fallen ill.

"It is likely nothing, as you say," Rawdon conceded. "I worry overly, as you have often noted, Roderick."

At the extreme end of the great hall a drunk stepped up onto a chair and began to harangue the crowd, much to the amusement of many. Officials began to push through the gathering toward this man, but he did not seem to notice, or perhaps care, and carried on in a deep powerful voice. The noise in the hall began to drop as more and more became aware of the disturbance, and as the crowd fell quiet Roderick began to make out some of the man's theme.

". . . houses of iron, and iron ships with terrible weapons." The man slurred his words and stretched his vowels comically, but his tone was so full of dread even Roderick could feel it. "And iron nannies will care for your children, suckle them on molten metal until they grow souls like engines ticking inside them. Where will this bridge take us? Can you see that distant shore, darkened by a cloud of sickly smoke? Can you see yourself in chains of iron? Can you see your children?"

It was then that the officials reached the orator and hauled him down bodily, carrying him away, shouting and struggling. There was a moment like an indrawn breath, and then the chaos of several thousand people talking at once.

Rawdon looked over at Palle and shrugged, but the King's Man could see the doctor's face had gone white. He thought Rawdon might collapse where he stood.

"I think you should sit down, Benjamin," Palle said, taking him by the elbow and steering him toward a seat.

The doctor sat down, and laid his head back for a moment, closing his eyes. Roderick was afraid he'd lost consciousness, but then he roused himself and managed a weak smile.

"Forgive me, Roderick, I don't know what came over me."

"Far too many sleepless nights caring for your patient. It is unfortunate that we lost Llewellyn. I would prefer to see you with some reliable assistant."

"No," the doctor said with surprising firmness. "There are too many involved as it is." He took three deep breaths. "I am recovered. Don't be concerned." He made an effort to force off his normal manner of distraction. "Tell me how things proceed. We have worked out this problem with Mr. Littel?"

Roderick hesitated. "I'm not sure," he said evenly.

"Well, offer him more. A title. An estate. You have been too tightfisted with him, you will excuse me for saying, Roderick, but that's what I think. I realize he isn't one of us, but it hardly matters. We need him yet, or at least that is what Wells says. Our Mr. Wells may be the great polymath, but Littel is certainly unparalleled in his field. A genius, really."

"Perhaps you're right, Benjamin. I shall do what I can when next I see him."

Benjamin nodded, happy to have set the King's Man straight in this matter.

The Entonne Embassador had rushed through his official responsibilities as quickly as decorum would allow and now his attention could be devoted entirely to his latest interest. He had been, almost desperately, trying to meet Angeline Christophe, the mistress of Prince Kori—or so everyone said. Massenet was no stranger to blinding passions, but this one, he was quite aware, was even more misguided than usual.

She is the mistress of the prince, who is about to become the real head of the Farr government. He had repeated this to himself countless times in the past thirty-six hours, but it did not seem to have any effect on his behavior.

I just want to speak with the woman, he told himself, *to see if she is as beautiful as I first thought—which I'm sure she can't be.* The young woman he had seen was something of a goddess, he had thought.

But that look she had given him. . . . Just the memory of it had the most stunning effect—as though, when he drew a breath, it went right through his entire body, even right out to the ends of his limbs. Like breathing a draught of distilled life. It was remarkable.

Massenet, of course, was no young fool. He even thought that he had become somewhat jaded these past years. Not only had he become adept at predicting the behavior of others, but he could predict his own behavior just as well. He no longer surprised himself. It was one of the saddest things about aging.

The count was well aware that he took a particular pleasure from cuckolding husbands. He had admitted this, at least to himself, long ago. And the more accomplished and successful the man, the more Massenet enjoyed stealing his wife's affections (of course such men tended to have the most beautiful wives, as well).

It was not a particularly personal thing. Some of the husbands Massenet cuckolded were quite decent men; acquaintances whose society he enjoyed. He also made every effort to be sure they did not discover the truth. He did not, after all, wish them ill. He could enjoy his little triumphs quite privately.

And now he knew part of what was driving him was the desire to cuckold this fatuous little prince. She could not possibly desire the man! It was only his position. His power. Massenet had a great deal of information that made him quite sure of this.

She had looked at Massenet with such . . . interest. He knew that look. He had seen it, perhaps more often than any man in Farrland. He knew it.

"The pleasures of the day to you, Count Massenet," a voice said in perfect Entonne.

"Bertillon! Pleasures indeed." Massenet smiled warmly, though he kept glancing off, searching the crowd for those dark tresses. "I am surprised that a miracle of metal would interest you, Charl."

"It seems everyone assumes I have no interests but music and the arts, which is not true. I believe I might find clients in this mass of intelligent and cultured people."

Massenet smiled. "Money, then?"

"In a word. And you, my Count? Searching for the woman who will measure up to your ideal? What would this ideal maiden be like, if I may ask?" Bertillon, too, kept searching the crowd.

"I hate to disappoint you, Charl, but it is not anything so romantic. I am too old and jaded. Have you heard who will be named to the council?"

"Galton?"

Massenet laughed. "Foolish of me to think I could surprise you, Mr. Bertillon. Perhaps you know something about last night's events in Merton? Palle was searching the town. Kent was one of the people he sought, but he was not the only one. I confess I was unprepared. Hawksmoor is seeking someone still, I think."

"I will see what I can learn." Bertillon was about to leave but hesitated. "I have just learned the oddest thing. Not useful, I'm sure, but interesting. I just watched Princess Joelle very intentionally steer her son away from a young woman—the intended bride of Lord Jaimas Flattery—and the look on the young prince's face! He tried to hide it, but . . ." Charl shrugged.

"You think there is some involvement there?" Massenet asked, his interest suddenly piqued.

"No, in fact, I don't. I think there is youthful infatuation. Something to be marked. One might note the qualities of this young woman. They can't be so unique that we could not find another with similar charms. It is at least a possibility."

The count pondered this for a moment. "Perhaps the son will take after the father," he said after a moment. "Do you know this Angeline Christope?"

Bertillon shook his head. "She is hardly ever seen, apparently. I don't even know who her friends are, apart from the obvious, that is." Bertillon turned to his companion, his manner suddenly grave. "You will be careful there, Count Massenet. Whatever could be gained would be lost ten times over if your interest were discovered."

Massenet realized he had drawn himself up, and fixed Bertillon with his most imperious glare, but he managed to catch himself and soften his tone. "I'm sure you're right, Charl. I am merely making the most delicate investigation, that is all. Nothing to fear." Massenet looked around the hall. "I have not seen our favorite artist here. Would you speak with him? I would dearly love to know what went on in Merton."

Bertillon bowed and went off on his rounds, leaving the ambassador feeling somewhat chastened. The musician was right; he should forget about this woman. It was unfortunate that this was the one area in which Massenet's phenomenal will often could not be brought to bear.

Alissa sat near to her father in the Avonel residence of the Duke and Duchess of Blackwater. Despite the reassurances of Averil Kent, she was worried to near madness about her missing fiancé. And she could see that the duke was as concerned as she, which was even more worrying. This was not a man who revealed his concerns.

"If Kent gets himself in too much trouble, I'm not certain that I will be able to extricate him. What do you think he is up to, Professor?"

Somers shrugged. Alissa noted that her father was always a little uncomfortable in the duke's presence, which she had originally thought indicated that the professor was intimidated by the great man. She had come to realize, however, that her father was actually uncomfortable with his reaction to the duke. He liked the nobleman. Respected him, in fact. It was a difficult thing for a dedicated reformer like her father to discover that this wealthy aristocrat had concerns for others. Had thought deeply about the nation and its people, and had grave concerns about the unfolding future. Of course, her father was a mild reformer. He shuddered at the blood shed in the streets when the mobs marched. The deaths distressed him terribly.

"I don't quite know. Kent has managed to avoid telling me anything on two occasions now, and I am not sure I will ever learn more than that. I'm not even sure that Emin is telling me everything. I must say though, that Kent was distressed to hear what had been done to Dandish's home. I think he is afraid that Hawksmoor found something there. Some information about the inquiries that the professor pursued in private. Emin spoke with Dandish's old cleaning lady who told him that she and your nephew had opened a locked room in Dandish's home. Apparently, according to the woman, Dandish had been very secretive about this chamber. But all that was found inside were empty planting boxes. Nothing more." Somers' eyes looked off through a wall as though he imagined the room in Dandish's home, and perhaps might conjure up its past contents. "It is all very odd," he muttered.

Alissa looked away from her father to find the duke's penetrating gaze on her. She looked away immediately, and felt a slight flush on her cheeks. No doubt the duke was wondering about her involvement with Kent, and she cursed herself again for being caught like a fool.

She leaned forward and poured herself more tea, hoping to hide her reaction. A fear that the duke might know she acted as Princess Joelle's liaison with Kent was taking hold of her. *Don't be absurd,* she chided herself. *Even the duke cannot read thoughts.*

"Kent is adamant that he did not engineer the disappearance of Jaimas and this other young gentleman?" The duke addressed this question to no one in particular.

Alissa said nothing, hoping her father would answer. She did not want to lie, and now that she had not heard from Jaimy, she wanted to tell the duke the truth, hoping he might help. Afraid that if she kept her secret she might be endangering Jaimy. But Kent had been adamant. *No one must know of the prince's involvement.* And she understood the importance of that. She had worked up her nerve to approach the prince at the Winter Palace, but he had been surrounded by courtiers and other hangers on, and she could see no way for them to speak privately. The prince had noticed her, though. Their eyes had met, and she had felt the look a bit disturbing; she could not tell why. As though he were trying to tell her something. It had made her quite afraid.

"Apparently so," Somers said. "Alissa, you spoke with him."

"Sir Averil assured me he did not know their whereabouts."

"Palle would not dare to harm my son. . . . But I still wonder about this young man. Littel you called him?"

"Egar Littel. He used to come around the house to my Friday evenings. Something of a savant in linguistics, though I suspect his real reason for coming was Alissa's older sister."

The duke nodded, glancing again at Alissa.

"I promised the duchess that I would read to her this evening," she said, rising abruptly. "If you will excuse me, Father. Duke."

She could not help but feel the two men stared after her as she made her escape. It made her feel so stiff and awkward that she almost tried to draw her back in closer, as though protecting the area from a blow.

Once out into the hallway she sighed audibly. She went first to the chamber she was now becoming accustomed to sleeping in while visiting Avonel, and here she found a shawl and the book of poems she had taken from the library. Before leaving she stood looking around the room, which was vast by her standards. The maids had turned down the bed and lit the lamps for her, and there were fresh flowers from the greenhouse. Yellow winter roses in arrangements with a delicate fern. For the briefest second she longed for her small room in her family home, and the comfort of her sisters' warm laughter. Despite the fire, this room seemed awfully cold.

Squaring her shoulders Alissa set off for the chamber of the duchess.

A maid sat in a small antechamber. She let Alissa in immediately, smiling at her warmly. The staff were always so welcoming and kind—even the ones who weren't spying on her. The duchess lay beneath a heavy comforter of goose down, though the room was not cold. Her eyes were closed, but her face did not seem peaceful. Alissa looked at her, feeling sad and helpless. This woman had been so kind to her, and she seemed to be having her life drained away. It immediately made her fear that Jaimy would one day suffer the same fate—and it did not help that the woman's face on the pillow bore such a similarity to her son's. The duchess' hair was the color of Jaimy's, or had been before gray had begun to appear—silver locks among the gold. And she had the eyes almost exactly. Alissa so wanted to make her well.

"Duchess?" Alissa whispered, and those fine eyes flashed open. They were so rimmed in red that Alissa thought the duchess had been crying.

"Lady Alissa," the woman said, and her voice, though subdued, did not betray signs of recent tears. Her face brightened somewhat, and a smile appeared.

"I am not Lady Alissa yet, Duchess," Alissa said, and took the offered hand in her own. The duchess' fingers were so cold—like barren branches.

"Will you not indulge an old woman in her dreams? I have so wanted a daughter I could fuss over, and whose marriage I could ruin with constant meddling." She gave a small laugh. "You must not hesitate to remind me that you are mature enough to make your own decisions, and that I have grown old and meddlesome."

"The Duchess is neither old nor meddlesome. In truth I will accept all the guidance you would care to offer." It was true that the duchess was not old—not fifty years—but her constitution was so delicate, and she had been a near invalid for so long.

The duchess squeezed her hand, meeting her eye and holding it as she often did, her gaze not searching but filled with affection. It was no wonder the woman was adored by so many.

"There is no word from Jaimas?"

Alissa shook her head, not meeting the duchess' eye. She thought for a second that a tear might escape, but it did not. The duchess squeezed her hand again.

"No doubt he will turn up in the morning, and I shall upbraid him terribly for worrying you so. Such selfishness is not characteristic of him, I want you to know." The duchess looked off toward the fire for a moment. "You brought some poetry?" she said, her voice sounding utterly fatigued, suddenly.

"I must warn you, it is modern. . . ."

"It does not rhyme? I am scandalized." She settled back into her pillows and closed her eyes. "Read to me, Lady Alissa," she whispered.

Reluctantly Alissa released the cold hand of the duchess, just as it had begun to take on some of her own warmth. She opened the book, turned slightly so that the light fell on the page, and began.

> *"I lie down at the gnarled foot of an oak*
> *And watch the ants explore the vast desert*
> *Of my cast off cloak.*
> *What treasures might they mine from pockets*
> *To return, triumphant, to city and queen?*
> *High summer passes in Wicklow County.*

I spent my morning
Watching the salmon spend their too short lives
Against the rocks and falls of Wicklow River.
Battered and rotting, they skulk in shallow pools
Gathering strength in sullen silence.
I watched them brood, and hover,
An insolent flick of a still powerful tail.

Sailors return from the open sea
To die upon the grass,
And have their ashes spread
On the slow currents of rural streams.
One must wonder why, when they say
Men buried at sea are reborn
As dolphins.

I am caught in a back eddy,
Floating in the shallows of this field
Spinning slowly, beneath the summer sun,
Pockets emptied.
Who carried off the treasures of my life?
Once bright memories, fading.

Rest a moment, rest.
Soon we must begin,
The struggle again.
A last leap
Into the empty sky.

Alissa closed the book gently, her gaze coming to rest on the duchess' face.
"Lord Skye?" the duchess asked softly.
"Yes."
"He makes it sound so easy," the duchess murmured, not opening her eyes.
A tiny smile appeared on her still beautiful lips, and then her breathing became regular and the lips suddenly relaxed, drawing open a fraction. Alissa thought that all the skin on the duchess' face went slack, like a pavilion when the ropes were loosed, and this seemed a picture of death to her. She stared at the duchess for a moment, distressed, almost frightened, and then, carefully, she tucked the woman's cold hand beneath the covers, and pressed the comforter gently around her white throat, so that no currents of cold air might touch her.

ᕆ Fourteen

Tristam stood at the rail watching the tropic birds perform their mating flight over the clear lagoon. It was an astonishing display, these cloud-white birds, dark eyed and red billed, their two elongated tail feathers streaming like blood-red banners. They fanned the air with elegantly curved wings, cocked their tail to one side, and flew backward through the air.

Tristam had been watching carefully, and was quite sure past observers had not exaggerated; the birds actually propelled themselves backward. Tristam was not sure how impressive this was to a prospective mate, but it certainly astonished him.

Across the lagoon the village was still empty, though at this time of day it did not seem so strange, for during the heat of the afternoon the Varuans usually rested or slept, and the village could be very quiet. The people had fled to some hiding place in the interior, expecting the Farrlanders to turn their guns on their homes, as had been done once before. The abandoned village seemed both very picturesque and a bit forlorn, bringing up unexpected emotions in Tristam. It reminded him again of Kent and what the painter had said that afternoon they had met. *Isollae.* Loneliness in the face of beauty.

A Varuan rail emerged gingerly from behind an empty fale. These flightless birds did not commonly come near to dwellings of men, but here it was, tentatively exploring among the abandoned fales. It made Tristam realize, again, how quickly man's works went back to nature.

There was a call from the masthead lookout, and Tristam moved a little along the rail to get a better view. From the breadfruit trees behind the village, appeared two groups of islanders wearing crowns of green leaves and bracelets of white flowers. They walked close together, their steps measured and slow, and among them bore two burdens covered in red tapa cloth. Red, the color of prestige and wealth.

In the central common the two groups laid down their burdens—two bodies, Tristam was certain. The Jacks had gathered at the rail, and Tristam could hear them muttering ugly threats. The duchess suddenly appeared at his side.

"Farrelle rest them," she said softly. "Is it Garvey and Chilsey?"

"So I hope," Tristam answered, not thinking how odd this might sound. He was afraid that this might be two Varuans, sacrificed to mollify the Farrlanders. The Varuans did not sacrifice humans often, unlike the inhabitants of some other islands, but in desperate times even they would resort to this terrible practice.

The Varuans stood in rows on either side of the draped bodies, looking down at them silently. Then they clapped three times in perfect unison, and one man spoke, his voice loud, almost chanting. The man's speech was brief and the speaker too distant for Tristam to discern any words, and then they began to sing softly. Tristam was not sure, but it sounded almost like the song that Teiho Ruau had sung as the *Swallow* departed from Farrland, and this chilled him a little.

Wallis came up on Tristam's other side.

"What is this song, Mr. Wallis?" Tristam asked.

"It is sung at the outset of a voyage, Mr. Flattery, such as the islanders have made through all their history. Great voyages, as you know. It is a song of sadness, and of hope. They sing it as part of their funeral rite, as well, not so incongruous to them, for death is thought to be the beginning of a voyage to the sacred island—the 'Faraway Paradise,' they call it." Wallis listened for a moment, and then began to recite, slowly, as though he were translating what he heard.

> *"The mother wind carries us*
> *Into the distant west*
> *The great whale appears*
> *With the sun's last rays.*
> *And stars light to mark our way*
> *Like islands cast upon the sea.*
>
> *Gently sings the mother wind*
> *Across the lapping seas.*
> *Gently sings the mother wind*
> *Of islands far away.*
>
> *The whale appears to call its mate*
> *Lonely beneath the waves.*
> *And we follow passing moons*
> *Their sails bright in the sky.*
> *Slowly we're drawn, by moon and sun,*
> *Into the distant west.*
>
> *Gently sings the mother wind*
> *In our swelling sails.*
> *Gently sings the mother wind*
> *Of islands green and fair.*

May you find clear lagoons,
Protected from the storms
And may the maidens think you fair
And sing you welcome songs,
Across the seas you take our hearts,
To keep until we meet again.

Gently sings the mother wind,
Gently."

The painter fell silent. In the distant village the islanders finished their song and from baskets began to scatter something over the bodies. Again they stood looking on for a moment, then clapped their hands loudly, and turned and went back as they had come, in two lines, as though they still shared a burden among them.

"First murder them, and then honor them," the duchess said so that only Tristam might hear. "Though they would rather have life than honor, I think. How very sad."

Only the few animals that had been left behind wandered the village, a sow and her young rooting about in a taro patch, fowl waiting for their feed of coconut shards. The bright fabric of pareus left out to dry flapped lazily in the trade, large strange blossoms. The party from the *Swallow* went through the empty lanes and open areas between the houses with a sense of foreboding. Tristam couldn't help but think of the Lost City, abandoned as well, and these thoughts did not comfort him.

It was late afternoon, and the shadows of the palm trunks elongated impossibly across the sand, like crooked fingers pointing toward their fallen shipmates. Stern had sent a party ashore to retrieve the bodies and to make contact with the islanders if possible: Wallis, because he was half an islander himself; Hobbes, whom the islanders treated with affection and respect; Beacham, to add numbers and because he was level-headed; Tristam, because Stern thought the naturalist uncommonly lucky; and the viscount, because the duchess had insisted. Tristam's shadow, after all.

Hobbes walked a few paces ahead, keeping intentionally to himself. Since they had landed on the beach the ship's master had not spoken a word, though he was supposed to be in command of this party.

Stern hoped they might somehow reestablish relations with the Varuans, but the islanders were not to be seen. They were up in the hills, Wallis said, in secret caves used to hide women and children from invaders. Tristam wondered if they realized there were limits to the range of the ship's guns—they would have been safe just beyond the village.

Tristam wondered again what part Hobbes had played in the deaths of Garvey and Chilsey. Had the master schemed with the two and sent them to look for Kingfoil? Or had he merely been careless—talking too freely about the conversation he'd overheard—and the two sailors had taken it upon themselves to search for *regis*? Tristam could not decide, but one thing was certain—Hobbes bore a great burden of guilt over the deaths.

Tristam had never seen the ship's master so distracted. Didn't Stern realize Hobbes was presently unfit for command? But no doubt the captain thought Hobbes was affected by the death of Garvey, the master's mate, and a fine seaman. It would be expected. It would also be expected that an old sea dog like Hobbes would rise above his grief.

The entire party slowed as they came nearer the bodies, as though they were already part of a funeral procession. A sweet smell of blossoms came to Tristam and then the putrid smell of the dead, left out in the tropical day. Hobbes clapped a square of cotton over his mouth, and stopped six feet away. Tristam could almost see a panic in the master's eyes, as though he would not be able to face it—to face what he had done.

The others passed Hobbes by, and came and stood by the bodies, as the Varuans had earlier. Under patterned tapa cloth Tristam could see the forms of the men, like the geology of a land beneath a covering of vegetation. Tristam reached down and gently pulled the cloth away from one of the faces, and found Jon Chilsey, blood matted in his hair where his skull had been broken. Beacham sobbed, and turned away to hide his face.

Garvey had been treated the same. Delicate white shells had been laid over their eyes—the paper nautilus, Tristam noted automatically, *Argonauta argo*—and upon each cheek the Varuan symbol of the sun had been tattooed. Between the lips of the dead men the delicate petals of pale blossoms appeared, as though they had taken root in the sailor's souls.

The scene was so reminiscent of the ritual in the Lost City that Tristam was shaken. He knew the others must be thinking the same thing. And then the naturalist in him noticed the blossoms, and he almost snatched one up. They were *regis* flowers. Tristam removed the shells and the blossoms from the men's mouths, putting them into one of his pockets, as though the honor the Varuans offered these two men were an offense.

"Farrelle protect their souls," Wallis said. "These are Varuan funeral rites. The stone adze in the hand is for the making of boats and fales. These plants set by their feet are young breadfruit and coconuts to plant when they reach their destination, to sustain them in the life to come, as are the sacrificed fowl and pigs."

Hobbes had walked away some ten paces, turning his back on the scene. Tristam saw him press thumb and forefinger delicately to the bridge of his nose, and then realized that the man wept, absolutely silently, as though a lifetime aboard His Majesty's ships had taught him that skill as well.

The viscount had turned away from the bodies, and stood staring at Hobbes, as though the master were a specimen pinned to a board. Tristam looked away, unsettled by the viscount's apparent fascination with the master's grief.

Wallis continued, almost reciting, it seemed. "When people are laid out in this manner, beneath a coverlet of blossoms, they are being honored, not treated as enemies. There is regret over these deaths."

"Then why did they murder them?" Beacham asked angrily. He knelt near to the body of his fellow midshipman, so filled with anguish that he moved his limbs without focused control, puppetlike.

Wallis shrugged. He was near to tears himself, Tristam thought. "They broke the tapu, Mr. Beacham. A serious tapu. The islanders who did this would have felt that they had no choice in the matter."

"No amount of debate or anger will bring them back," Tristam said suddenly. "We must bear them down to the shore, so they can be taken for burial."

Beacham glared at Tristam, his anger suddenly fixed on the naturalist, but rather than speak, he jumped up and walked away twenty paces, where he began to pace back and forth like an agitated guard. Hobbes did nothing to marshal his party.

Tristam was left with Wallis, who crouched on the ground five paces from the dead men. He tucked the elbows of his spindly arms between his knees and twined his hands together. He looked down at the ground before him and then up at the dead, repeating this action again and again.

"I don't think you will find what you want here, Mr. Flattery," the castaway said suddenly, keeping his voice low, and not looking up at Tristam.

"What I want? I have lost any sense of what I want, Mr. Wallis. I wish only to perform my duty and return to my home."

"But that's what I mean, sir. I don't think the islanders will give you the seed. Even if it really is meant for your King, the Old Men would never give it to you."

"And why is that, Mr. Wallis?"

The castaway looked up, a bit of surprise registering. "Is it not obvious, Mr. Flattery? A series of omens the islanders find quite unsettling, and then you arrive with this strange tale of a Lost City. A whale saves you from being lost in the vast ocean." He nodded at Tristam's hand. "And this. . . . The islanders fear you, Mr. Flattery, they can't imagine what it is you want here. They have enough troubles without someone such as yourself appearing."

"Bloody foolishness!" Tristam spat out.

Wallis rocked back on his heels, dragging his fingertips along the ground.

wished he could take them out to examine them more carefully. But why? he asked himself. More and more he was convinced that he would be best to have nothing to do with *regis*. He should have thrown the blossoms away.

Looking out toward the ship he thought he saw a slim figure pacing in the great cabin, crossing and recrossing the small distance before the windows. The duchess. It was difficult to image that a woman with such poise could fret—it just did not seem in character, but he could almost feel her anxiety and worry from the way she moved. It was like finding an actress backstage—imperious before an audience but frightened and vulnerable behind the curtain. He felt his heart go out to her.

He closed his eyes for a moment and felt the flooding of his emotion, like a tide running through his being. How did one swim when the tide was inside?

"What?" he heard himself say. Beacham had been addressing him.

"Perhaps there will be time to teach me to swim," the midshipman said.

"Perhaps." Tristam looked out at the ship, though stare as he might the duchess could not now be seen. Had he fallen into a brief sleep?

The night sounds of Varua, unfamiliar and exotic, surrounded them: the constant voice of the trade, though softened after sunset, and the sounds of insects, as discordant as a tuning orchestra.

Something moved on the edge of the firelight, but when Tristam turned, he could make out nothing. *I must shake off this mood,* he thought. Fear of slipping back into the dream state induced by *regis* haunted him. He tried to call up Faairi's star, but it no longer seemed so clear.

"Tell me, Mr. Beacham, how did you come by the name Averil?" Tristam asked suddenly.

Beacham looked up, a bit surprised, perhaps even a little apprehensive. "You've found out my secret. I hope you won't let on, sir. I've suffered all my life for that bloody name. Life aboard would become very unpleasant if the others should find out. It is an old man's name."

Tristam took a long breath, and let it out under perfect control. "There are just the two of us here, Beacham. No one to hear. Averil Kent and his interests are known to me." He tried to say this last with confidence, for he was really not sure. In fact, for a moment he wondered if he sounded a little unbalanced—if he *was* a little unbalanced.

Beacham stared out over the bay for a moment, then turned to speak, faltered and went back to looking at the darkened water and the stars. "My father is an artist in the Admiralty, a cartographer, but a painter as well. Over the years he has been much encouraged by Mr. Kent, though he actually paints very little. Gifted with skill but not inspiration. Mr. Kent has always been something of an uncle to me. Thus the name. But I know nothing of Mr. Kent's . . . 'interests' as you call them—except for nature and art."

"That night when we were hunted by the corsairs. You knew what was going on with the viscount and Kreel. But you said nothing to the captain."

At the mention of the viscount, Beacham looked over his shoulder, obviously uncomfortable. "'Keep out of the business of your betters,' my father always told me, Mr. Flattery. I think it good advice."

Tristam looked out over the bay, to the small ship swinging to her anchor, the web that was her rigging just visible in starlight. "All right, Jack," he said with resignation. "Tell me only this. Do you have information about my situation? You were with me in the Lost City. You've seen what has happened around me—and to you, now." He held his hand out into the firelight, but the tattoo remained drawn back into the vein. "You were there when this happened. I'm struggling in the dark, Jack. I don't know what's happening to me." Tristam closed his eyes. "I don't know what's happening to me," he whispered.

A log shifted on the fire, sending up a spray of sparks like an offering to the stars. Beacham moved, almost squirming, took a breath as though to speak, and then said nothing. The silence stretched on. "I can tell you this," Beacham said after a long struggle. "There are rumors among the Jacks about this . . . herb. It is said to cure any illness, extend one's years, command a vast fortune for only a few seeds. The miraculous survival of Mr. Wallis has turned many who scoffed into believers."

"Farrelle's blood!" Tristam said. "How in the world . . . ?" but he hardly needed to finish.

Beacham shrugged. "Ships are small," he said, keeping his eyes fixed on the bay.

A land crab scuttled along the edge of the firelight, causing Tristam to start. The naturalist pulled his knees up and wrapped his arms around them, burying his face in the circle of his arms. Stern apparently did not know this. Blood and flames, the poor captain was out of his depth. Tristam looked out at the ship, half expecting a mutiny to break out as he watched.

But there was some truth in what the Jacks believed—that was the irony. The worth of the seed was almost incalculable. There were any number of Farr adventurers who would lay this island to waste to get their hands on something of such value—if they only knew.

What have we unleashed on these poor islanders? Tristam thought. It was no wonder the Varuans believed the seed was a curse.

"We have to tell Stern," Tristam said. "He will have a mutiny on his hands, and no warning."

The midshipman became utterly still for a moment. "You could tell him, Mr. Flattery . . . and leave me out of it."

Yes, the code of the sailors. Beacham could not tell—caught as he was between being a seaman and an officer. "All right, though it is likely he will guess where I've learned it. Blood and flames, what a situation. Already we've lost two men. That is enough. We should sail from this place. Set out tomorrow and forget this fool's quest."

Beacham nodded. "Yes. None of us knew what we were sailing into, and it has turned out to be strange territory." Beacham put his hands near to the fire as though he had grown cold.

"That night at the temple, Mr. Flattery, when we were poisoned, did you dream?" He said this with such unguarded concern that Tristam feared the worst.

"Yes. I dreamed. I dreamed until I finally regained the world, and even now dreams still haunt me. And you as well?"

Beacham nodded. "Yes," he almost whispered. "I dreamed that I was standing before the entrance to a cave, and inside a fire was burning. I could see the dance of the flames. Feel the heat, like hot breath. Although I was more afraid than I have ever been, I walked forward. I could not stop myself, Mr. Flattery. As I drew closer, I heard the hiss of the flames, as though the fire were alive. Against my will I went inside. But when I had passed in, it was to the outdoors. And I saw a city in flames, the people blackened, screaming silently, and toppling like burning trees." Beacham kept his eyes fixed on the horizon, his voice had become flat. "I thought it was the Lost City before me, but it wasn't—it was Avonel. And then I saw someone, someone who was afire. He walked toward me through the flames, and in his arms he carried a burden. A burned and burning man. A man who wore a crown that shone white in the red of the flames. Suddenly I could move, and I ran, into a tunnel. An endless tunnel. I was thirsty and weak, and lost and frightened. But finally I saw another—in the distance. It seemed to be a child, and I followed him into a small opening in a wall of solid stone, and when I emerged, I was swinging in a hammock, muttering something, looking up at the face of Llewellyn."

Tristam said nothing. He could not offer the common reassurance; *It was only a dream,* for he did not believe that. These were more than dreams.

He moved and felt the delicate shells and blossoms that rested in the pocket of his shirt—miracles of nature. Frightening miracles.

An urge to get up and walk along the beach whispered to Tristam, but he looked out into the darkness and realized he was afraid of what might wait in the night world of the islanders.

Hobbes crawled forward the last few feet to the cliff edge, and felt the salt wind on his face. Below he could see the pale, luminescent crests of breaking waves undulating along the base of the cliff some hundred feet below. His breath came with difficulty, and this was not due just to the hour's hard march.

"*Blood and flames,*" he said, "*you deserve such an end.*" His fingers curled over the edge of the damp rock and he stared down to the sea boiling among the rocks. A man might jump clear of that and into the deep water, where death would find him swiftly, painlessly. It was here that the Varuans sent captives of war to death—any escaping the rocks were said to be swept away by strong currents, where they fell easy victim to sharks.

"Let the sea take me," he said, barely able to catch his breath. "Flames, Chilsey was only a boy!" The ship's master felt the sting of tears, and not just from the wind on his face. "Not fit to command, nor fit to be master. And Garvey, a man with family." He wanted to scream, but instead fought to catch his breath. "What a ruin of a life . . . and it should never have been so. A curse on every desk captain in the Navy Board!"

He stared down, almost hypnotized by the flow and ebb of the pale crests in the starlight. *What an end,* he thought. *But all I deserve now.*

"Do you seek death, old man?" came a near-whisper, barely audible above the sounds of surf.

Hobbes turned his head, startled, sitting back quickly from the cliff. He recognized that voice: Elsworth.

"I know him," the voice continued. "Know how hard he can be to find. But I know a way."

Hobbes searched in the darkness, and now he could see the viscount, hunching down in shadow. He felt his skin crawl. It was the viscount, wasn't it?

"I can help you, Hobbes," the voice went on, oddly full of emotion and strangely like a priest. "Make it easy." He paused, drew a sharp breath. "Wrestle with me, Hobbes. One of us will fall. If it is me, you will know it's not your time." He heard the man shift, move closer. "You seek death, don't you?" he said, almost too quickly. "Atonement for those two who've gone before you— innocent as you believe they were. Let me help you. Or you might be spared, Hobbes, and he might take me. . . . But one of us can end our suffering. End it this night."

The viscount moved again—almost seemed to slither closer. Hobbes could hear him breathing, like a man overcome by passion. The breeze suddenly seemed chill, drying the sweat of his forced march. He moved back from the cliff involuntarily—the instinct for self-preservation strong.

"Don't show him fear, Hobbes! Not that. Do you feel him? Here, with us." Again the viscount slid closer, his form indefinite, like a shadow octopus.

"Come no nearer!" Hobbes said, suddenly, surprising himself.

"You have thought too long. Thought weakens the resolve, Hobbes," the viscount went on, as though he had not heard. "It will force you to live in growing misery, until he comes for you—which he will do in time. But you aren't afraid of death, Hobbes. I've seen you face him. Stand strong before him in the midst of battle. You were unwavering. Come—one of us can make an end." And then more quietly, "Perhaps me. Or perhaps I will escape . . . again. Come, let us see who he will choose this night, for my sins are as great as yours."

The viscount was close enough now that Hobbes could make him out, like a darker shadow, moving slowly through shadow. The master no longer tried to escape, but waited, terrified, relieved, fascinated—like some poor beast at bay before a predator.

Death. Was that not what he sought? And here it was, in the form of this mad viscount. Now it would not matter if his nerve failed. Elsworth would see to that.

"Push me off," he heard himself say, the words coming out in a whisper.

"No! Hobbes, wrestle with me. Let me feel his hand. His breath upon my face. Let me see if I am still his servant."

Hobbes felt a hand grasp his forearm in a bone-hard grip. He twitched, but then held himself in check.

"It will soon be over, Hobbes. See if he will absolve you of your sins, and take me. See if he will do that, Hobbes."

The hand on his arm loosened a little, held him almost tenderly, and then the man was upon him, immensely powerful, smelling of sweat and fear. Hobbes fought back, struggling under the man's weight. Rolling toward the edge.

Yes, he thought, *let us see who he will take.*

A hand so strong it could have been a machine wrenched an arm behind his back, twisting it painfully, an arm took him around the chest, crushing the air from his lungs. The viscount tried to shuffle him toward the cliff, to lift his feet off the ground, but Hobbes reached back and took hold of the man's hair, and kicked at him with desperate force, twisting free. They fell, landing hard on stone.

"Feel his breath," the viscount whispered. *"We are before him."* And the man grappled with him again.

A life at sea had toughened Hobbes far more than his appearance revealed. He met the man, head on, holding his ground. The viscount tried to knee him in the groin, but Hobbes twisted away, losing his balance so that they fell again.

And then the man's mouth close to his ear as they struggled. *"Pray he will reward us both,"* he said. *"Take us both from our misery."* He tried to pin Hobbes' arms to his sides, and the seaman dug his heels into the ground and pushed, only managing to move them along the stone. Where was the cliff edge?

Hobbes brought his knee up hard and then broke the circle of the man's arms. He tried to turn away, and the viscount grasped at his waist and then drove forward, tumbling Hobbes onto his side.

Age betrayed him then. Hobbes struggled for breath, and felt his strength beginning to fail. The sound of the surf came to him.

The viscount butted his head down, smashing his forehead into Hobbes' ear. He lunged ahead now, dragging Hobbes under him, and the master felt his hands scrabble desperately, seeking a hold on the stone, until his fingers curled around a hard edge.

Again the viscount tried to drive him forward, but the master's grip held.

"I am his servant," the viscount hissed. *"Let yourself go to him, Hobbes."*

The viscount tried to tear his hand free and Hobbes let go suddenly, driving his elbow back quickly into the man's forehead. Twisting around, he grabbed at the man's throat, and the viscount let out a scream of anguish such as Hobbes had never heard. And then he was writhing, twisting, pulling free, in the grip of madness. The viscount's strength seemed to grow while Hobbes' waned. Suddenly the viscount had the master by the throat, lifting his head and driving it back against the stone with such force that Hobbes was left limp, barely holding onto consciousness. And again.

It is over, the seaman thought, and felt himself sob.

Again the viscount raised his head, and then his hands slipped off and he toppled forward, burying Hobbes beneath his enormous weight. They both lay still, Hobbes fighting to breathe, to maintain consciousness, to live.

The weight came off slowly as the limp form of the viscount was dragged to one side. Hobbes lay gasping sweet salt air. He could see blurred lights—stars overhead. Someone else was there, standing over them in the darkness.

"You shall not go so easily," a ravaged voice said.

Death. Only death could have such a voice.

"Live with your misery, as I've lived with mine. And damn you for it!"

Gone. The thing was gone. He could hear it shuffle noisily into the bush like some drunken beast.

For a moment more Hobbes lay drinking in long draughts of air and then, almost desperately, he began to crawl back into the dark jungle.

ᕲ Fifteen

After forty-two years of marriage Lady Galton believed she could almost read her husband's thoughts—or at least read his mood and, with what she knew of events, predict what was on his mind. She watched him fuss about at his desk, pretending to be absorbed by work and avoiding her eye. But he was uncommonly agitated, and it was not very well disguised as concern over work. His breathing was quick and shallow, louder than usual, and he could not keep his hands still. There were other little betrayals of his true mood, around his eyes, and his jaw clenched stiffly shut, not noticeable to most in that round, fleshy face. He had learned something today that was upsetting him terribly.

Of course he had been named to the Regency Council, though not officially, and that had to be taken into account. But even beyond that, something was very wrong. So wrong that he could not discuss it, even with her.

Lady Galton turned the page of her book, no more reading than Sir Stedman was working. She would wait a bit and then ask. The time was not yet right. And there was always the chance that Stedman would broach the subject himself—which would be a relief, for it would mean that whatever had occurred was not so very terrible, but only blown out of proportion. Though she was afraid this was a vain hope.

Galton continued to fuss, periodically releasing a loud sigh, as though he struggled with some problem that frustrated his every effort. Once she saw, over the edge of her book, that he darted a glance her way, gauging the success of his charade. There was, perhaps, a little guilt in that look.

"It is cool here, isn't it?" she said after a moment.

"Shall I bank the fire for you, my dear?" the governor said quickly.

"No, no. It is fine here by the fire, Stedman. I was thinking more of you, over in that dark corner."

He smiled, affection showing on his round face. "You are so kind to an old man. Whatever did I do to deserve such a wife?"

She gave a tiny smile, and turned the page she had not read. "You were young, and charming, and quite handsome, I thought. But it was really the young Stedman's open heart that won me—open and trusting and a bit naive. As though he wanted so badly to believe in the good of his fellow men, that he would bare his breast to their blades. I could not refuse that."

Stedman Galton slumped just perceptibly in his chair.

"Do you think you might tell me, sometime, Stedman, what it is that is causing you such distress?" She still kept her attention on her book, but she could feel his eyes on her.

Galton sat for a moment and then he rose and very slowly came and settled on the end of the divan, not too close, and that presaged something bad. Lady Galton put her book aside and braced herself.

He took a moment to start, but she waited, almost holding her breath. "I found out today that this young scholar, Egar Littel, was being . . ." he paused, searched for a word, "coerced into translating the text."

That was bad enough, but there was worse, she realized. Something much worse. She nodded, encouraging him to speak.

"He contrived to escape just recently. Slipped away from the library at Merton College." Galton turned away, staring at the fire, his face stiff. He closed his eyes. "In their attempt to apprehend him, some of Palle's minions . . ." A long exhalation. "Farrelle preserve us, they *killed* the poor boy." These last words were barely sounded.

She drew in her breath quickly, her hand going involuntarily to her mouth as though she were trying to suppress her own response. And Stedman was not finished. There was something yet to come, something that was going to hurt her terribly—she could read all the signs.

"Littel had a companion," the governor gave way to his distress now, and his voice trembled, as he fought for breath. "Farrelle protect him, it appears to have been Lord Jaimas Flattery, the son . . ." But he did not finish, a muffled sob escaped Lady Galton.

Galton reached out to comfort his wife, but she brushed his hands away, standing quickly with her back to him. But she did not move further, only stood, sobbing quietly.

"Heartless scoundrels!" she managed after a moment. "Beasts!"

"You have been right all along, my heart," Galton said softly. "Sir Roderick has lost all sense of honor—of what is right. And I have gone down that road with him—too far. . . ." There was anguish in his voice as he said this.

"You are not like him, Stedman!" she said emphatically. "Nothing like him."

He shifted along the divan, closer to her, and she did not move away. He reached out, but checked himself, afraid to lay his hand on her lest she shake it off, which he could not bear a second time.

Neither of them spoke for many minutes and Galton found this excruciating, fearing that he had stepped beyond the distinct moral lines drawn by his wife. She was very rigid in this, and the thought that he had disappointed her pained him terribly. His great fear was that what he had done was irreparable.

"I have straddled the border long enough," he said firmly. "I must declare myself in this."

Lady Galton turned to him then, staring down at the man sitting in abject misery before her. If he had tried to justify what had happened. . . . But no, Stedman was too good for that. Too noble. He would always shoulder the burden of his mistakes. "You must not declare yourself to Palle, Stedman." She sat down facing him, and took his offered linen to dab at her still flowing tears. But they did not touch. "He must be stopped—stopped utterly—and I can see no other way. I am frightened by the risks, but you must conspire against him, without revealing your true allegiance. It is the only way to remove the taint of this murder." And then, "Do the duke and duchess know?"

He shook his head. "Everything is being done to hide the truth." Neither of them spoke for a moment, realizing what this could mean.

"I will speak with the princess, and then, perhaps, I will go to the duchess. We must be careful. If the duke accuses Palle of this murder, well, the time is not right for such a thing." She stopped to think and felt a hand take hers tentatively, tenderly, and she squeezed this, massaging the fingers gently.

"I was blinded by my passion for the Ruin, for the knowledge," Galton said.

"Yes," she whispered. "I know."

"I should never have ignored your counsel." He took her other hand.

"No, you shouldn't have."

"I will not be so foolish in the future."

"You are not foolish. You are many things, Stedman Galton, but never foolish. We will find our way through this. We owe it to those young men. Farrelle rest them. The poor duchess almost died to bring that child into this world, and now he is gone. She will never survive it, Stedman. Palle might as well have put a blade in her heart. I shall not forgive him this," she said, surprising her husband with the bitterness in her voice. It was as though Palle had just murdered the child they could never have.

⤿ Sixteen

The prince had always wanted a room in a tower, ever since he was a child, and his corner room, high up in the palace, had been made to feel as much like a tower as was possible. He sat in the alcove of a window, wiping condensation from the glass, gazing down into the darkness. A black fog had slipped, dripping, into the garden, and remained—like a part of the night that had begun to solidify. The prince could make out the shapes of trees, and rectangles of open lawn. Perhaps that line was the edge of a pond—or was it a hedgerow?

The shapes were so indistinct, almost varying shades of darkness, that it occurred to him that anyone unfamiliar with this view might imagine an entirely different scene. But after living in the palace all nineteen years of his life, he could not look at it with an outsider's eyes.

"Grays," he whispered. The world was composed of grays, with almost no white and even less black. As a king, he would one day be dependent on his ability to differentiate between the myriad, nearly identical shades of gray. The prince stared down into the garden with renewed focus.

If he leaned back from the grass a little, his reflection appeared, smeared with the beads and rivulets of condensation that streaked the glass. It was like looking at himself through tears, and he suddenly had a strong premonition—one day someone would look at him this way.

I will break a heart, he thought, though he could not imagine how. As much as he was aware, it was not someone else's heart that was in danger. He stared at his reflection, which seemed to float on the surface of a pool of darkness. What did Alissa see when she looked at him?

"*Had I only met her first,*" he said aloud, and then almost winced.

But he had not. He leaned forward again, his shadow obliterating his reflection. Perhaps she thought him young, though, in truth, he was two years her senior.

He didn't need to close his eyes to call up an image of Alissa—standing beside the Duchess of Blackwater at her birthday celebration. He hardly had eyes for anyone else, still . . . what a contrast that had been! Alissa seemed almost to be aglow with life and youth, while the duchess' fires had burned low; there was barely a flicker when she smiled.

And then they had spoken at the opening of the iron bridge. Prince Wilam felt a bit of embarrassment, even here in the privacy of his own rooms, at how quickly his mother had whisked him away. Anger flared in him for a second. He hoped Alissa had not suffered embarrassment over this. The fault was his. He was the one acting like a lovesick puppy. Alissa had never been less than ladylike.

She must think me an idiot.

What is it I want from her? he asked himself again. He was quite certain that she had not entered into her engagement with Lord Jaimas for any but the most genuine reasons. So what *did* he want?

He placed his forehead against the cool glass, and shut his eyes, Alissa appearing in his mind as he best remembered her. He had passed a note from his mother to be delivered to Averil Kent. For the briefest moment this young woman's forthright gaze had met his own. And he still felt that no one had ever looked at him like that. She had looked at *him.* Not at a prince of Farrland. Not at a future king. But at him. He could not imagine giving that up. Giving that up for a life of polite smiles and measuring gazes. Measuring gazes.

And what *did* he want? Only to tell this young woman what he felt. To tell her how much that had meant to him. He hoped that she might give him some indication, even the smallest sign, that she shared some of that feeling. Even if they both knew that her heart belonged elsewhere. That was what he desired— just a simple moment of clarity in this existence. A moment where every other consideration was stripped away, and two people revealed their hearts. A moment of truth to sustain him through all the years of lies that were to come.

He leaned back and stared at his reflection again, distressed to realize that his own gaze measured as coolly as any courtier's. Certainly that is what Alissa had seen. He couldn't change that, but it was his hope that he could explain and she would understand.

The gentle double tap on his door was so familiar that he knew immediately who called. He stared only a second more, and then swung off the window seat and crossed to the door.

"Princess," he said, bowing to his mother.

"Prince," she said, curtsying in return. "I thought you would be awake yet." She tilted her head toward the room. "May I?"

Prince Wilam stepped aside, and his mother came in. Normally she entered a room as though she owned it—no one had as much right to it as she—but tonight she clearly entered his room. Her manner was subdued. She took a seat by the fire, like a guest.

"You think I was rude to Miss Somers," the princess said, not allowing an awkward silence to take form between them nor resorting to meaningless pleasantries. She was always so forthright with him, at least since he had become an adult. It never failed to flatter him.

"I am to blame," he said quietly. "We should not embarrass Miss Somers for my foolishness."

She did not answer, neither agreeing nor disagreeing. For a moment she stared at her son, then took a long breath, turning to look toward the dark window. "She is charming." She shook her head. "No. That belittles her. She is more than charming. Alissa Somers is intelligent, poised, entirely genuine, charming, and quite lovely to behold. Everything a Farr princess should be." She turned back to her son. "Everything we would want in a future queen."

A small silence began to coalesce between them, but beyond it Wilam saw the compassion in her face. "There will be others, Wilam. I know that must seem impossible, now, but it is true. Alissa Somers could never sit on a Farr throne, nor do I think she'd want to. I am not saying that, if circumstances were different, she could not have feelings for you. But the reality of ruling Farrland requires that we choose our alliances with great care. I would never want you to marry against your will. I would not see you condemned to that life. But there are many eligible young women. It is not as though there were only three to choose among." She tried a smile. "The life of a queen requires a certain preparation, Wilam, preparation that begins almost at birth. You would not want your bride to live unhappily, surely?"

The prince shook his head. "No. I wouldn't," he said quietly, knowing it was the truth.

"Have I ever told you that you are noble in more than birth?" she asked, a slight quiver of pride in her voice. She smiled at him for a moment, and then her manner became more serious. "I wanted to speak of this before I told you what I had learned." She paused, drawing a breath. A look of great sadness spread across her face, the tiny lines of beginning middle age appearing around her eyes and at the corners of her mouth. "Although you did everything you could, Palle's minions caught Lord Jaimas and Mr. Littel." She looked up, meeting her son's eyes, tears forming. "They killed them both, Wilam. Murdered them rather than let them escape with what they knew."

Wilam felt a rush of hope—far less than noble in its origin. And then the realization, and the sadness. A thought of Lord Jaimas laughing—a young man he both liked and felt enormous jealousy toward. He imagined Alissa, suffering her loss, and felt his heart go out to her.

"You realize what this means, of course, and so will Alissa. The palace had her fiancé murdered. We did not sanction it, you or I. Even my pathetic husband would not have approved, I'm sure, but it does not matter. Your father's weakness allowed this to happen. *Your* father. And you appeared to rescue them, Wil, then sent them off to their destruction. Imagine how it looks." She reached out and grasped his hand, holding it tenderly, sharing the pain. "I want you to promise me—you will maintain your distance from Miss Somers. No matter what you feel, no matter what your instincts, you must stay away. There is no comfort to be had from a murderer's son. Promise me," she said squeezing his hand and forcing him to look at her. "Promise," she said but it came out as a whisper, her voice failing. Tears streaking down her face, like rain on glass.

He nodded.

She cleared her throat. "Whatever happened, Wil?" she asked, her voice small and full of despair. "He was not always like this. Not always. . . ." Words failed her altogether.

Wilam shook his head. The son did not understand the father, nor would he forgive. Not this.

A ribbon of starlight twisted slowly as it fell through the forest. Prince Wilam held a taper before him, and made his way slowly through the vegetation toward the pool. Overhead he could see the clouds had fled, and faint stars splashed their light on the wet glass overhead and the waterfall below.

He came to the edge of the forest just as Teiho Ruau began another song. The pure tenor seemed to belong to this place as much as the call of a bird or a breeze sighing among the trees. Prince Wilam stopped and listened, closing his eyes so that he might concentrate more fully on the music. But as soon as his eyes closed, the image of Jaimy Flattery appeared, lying in a field, staring up at the sky—and then Alissa, her sorrow hidden by a veil.

Close to the waterfall Wilam could see his grandfather seated on a bench in the near-darkness. The old King slumped like a sleeping drunk. Wilam knew his grandfather found the songs of Oceana comforting, but he often wondered if the King really heard them, if he actually listened. There was certainly no sign that this was so, lost as he was in the dreams brought on by the physic.

The scene suddenly seemed pathetic to him. Sad beyond measure. What a price this man had paid for his extra years. Had it been worth it? Certainly not now that no amount of physic kept the aging at bay.

For a moment Wilam struggled with his conflicting desires—he both wanted to stay, and wanted to turn away. But as the song ended he went forward.

"Grandfather?" he said, surprised at how youthful his voice sounded.

Silence. Wilam was sure he had not been heard. The dream state was like that. The King would be neither asleep nor awake, but absorbed in his dreams, eyes wide open, staring.

"*Wil?*" the King answered, something like tenderness in his ruined voice.

The prince smiled with relief. "I need to speak with you, Grandfather."

A longer silence this time. "I am not well, child. Wilam? Is that you?"

The prince reached out and laid a hand on his grandfather's arm. "It is me. I. . . . I need to speak with someone, Grandfather. It is important." He sat near to his grandfather on the bench.

"Ah. . . . Important." A dry hand found the prince's in the darkness—a touch like parchment, ancient and fragile. "I will try. Please, leave us," he said to his attendants and the singer.

Wilam leaned close. "They have killed Lord Jaimas Flattery," he said close to the old man's ear.

"Who has?"

"Hawksmoor's men."

"Palle?"

"Yes." Wilam could barely see his grandfather in the dark, but he could hear him fighting for every breath. Knew the look of confusion that appeared when he struggled to come back to this world—even for a few minutes. The prince closed his eyes. It hurt him to find his grandfather like this, enslaved to the seed, aging daily now.

"Wil?"

"I'm here, Grandfather."

"What? What did we just say?"

"Palle killed Lord Jaimas and Egar Littel."

"Yes." He paused. "But why have you come?"

Wilam swayed where he sat.

"There is something else. . . ." The prince wondered if they were making sense to each other at all. The King's concentration would not hold for a long explanation, as necessary as one might be. "I am in love with the woman who was to be Lord Jaimas' bride," he blurted out, realizing that this misrepresented his situation entirely.

The King nodded, as though he considered solemnly. "You can't have a man murdered and then marry his fiancée. Wouldn't look right."

"Grandfather . . . I didn't have anyone murdered."

The dry hand squeezed his. "I know, Wil. I know, but it was done by the palace, and you are to be King one day. Do you see? If she knew—if anyone . . . does the duke know it was Palle?"

Wilam hesitated. "I'm not sure."

"Let us pray he learns the truth," the King whispered. He seemed to look at his grandson for the first time. "Don't say a word, Wilam," he pleaded, and then began to wheeze. "I must have my physic. They will take it from me."

The prince put his hand on his grandfather's shoulder. "No one will take your physic, Grandfather. I promise you."

The King nodded, making an effort to calm himself. "Where is Ruau?" he said peevishly. "Where is my physic?"

Wilam rose, waving to one of the attendants he could see silhouetted in the starlight. "Ruau is coming, Grandfather. Calm yourself."

The dry hand took hold of his wrist suddenly, the grip surprisingly powerful. "When you are on the throne, Wil, see him gone. See his reign ended. But don't endanger my physic. There's a good boy."

The prince listened to him wheeze in the darkness, fighting for air, for one more breath. "Goodnight, Grandfather."

The hand released him, the King already slipping back into his waking dreams, drawn away from the world of men.

As the prince walked back into the forest he found Teiho Ruau, standing still and silent among the trees.

"Ruau," Wilam said nodding to the Varuan.

"My Prince," the islander said, his voice filled with music even when he spoke. They stopped, perhaps feeling it would be polite to speak, but neither knowing what to say. "He will have to pass through soon," the Varuan said suddenly.

"I don't understand."

"Mr. Ruau!" came the voice of an attendant.

"Soon," Ruau said, and set off toward the king, beginning to sing as he went.

Prince Kori looked with despair on the first few lines of the letter he had begun hours before. His hand was atrocious, he knew, but this was not a letter he could have his secretary copy. He began to read again, trying to put himself in the position of the woman he addressed, attempting to measure the impact of each word.

My Dear Angeline:

> *It has been such a long time now since we met and there have been so few letters. I wonder, often, about your well-being, and where you are. Recently, I was told that you had returned to Farrland, but I have missed seeing you. Are things so bad between us that you do not even send the prince a note?*

He crumpled the page, crushing it between his fingers. How despicable that the future King of Farrland was reduced to writing letters like a jilted school-boy. And he had so little skill with words—words of love, at least.

It seemed ironic that he was able to maneuver his own people onto the re-gency council—against powerful men who had spent their lives in politics! And yet here he was, reduced to the same circumstances as any man in Farrland—on bent knee before a woman who spurned him. Spurned him!

And she had seemed so . . . intrigued by him upon that first meeting. Three years past, now. The memory was so fresh. The midsummer costume ball. He had found her alone on the balcony, holding a mask in her hand, the white of her shoulders like snow against the blackness of her gown and the night. He could not remember feeling so nervous. And she had turned and smiled at him. Those beautiful lips parted, and she had smiled the way a kind woman will when she sees you are uncomfortable. He had felt like a school-boy, even then.

Later he had taken her to the arboretum, and they had talked for hours, sitting on a hard stone bench, walking along the narrow paths. And then she had allowed him to kiss her. Those perfect soft lips, the curve of her neck. He had felt like a man granted the greatest privilege in the kingdom. When he had placed a hand on her breast she had demurred, in the most charming way. And they had sat longer still, speaking quietly, and then, strangely, he had fallen asleep, waking later to find her by the waterfall, chatting with the King, as though they were old friends.

To the prince's surprise his father had said nothing of this night—not even a censorious look—which was very odd when one considered the great favor the King showed Princess Joelle. But then the King's own married life had not been beyond reproach.

Angeline had exhibited no surprise at the relative youthfulness of the King, and had laughed when he tried to swear her to secrecy. Kissing his cheek, she had agreed, her manner mockingly solemn, as though she were humoring a child. And then she had disappeared. Disappeared utterly. They had exchanged letters. He had even spoken of her to his friends—intimating that he had a mistress of surpassing beauty and charm—but they had not met again. She had gone abroad. Then returned to care for an ailing aunt in the country. And then the letters had stopped altogether.

The prince could not understand how she could be so indifferent to his position; as though he were just another man. He often wondered what he had done to chase her off. She had seemed so enamored of him at the time (and he had told his friends as much!). Every word that he could recall of their conver-sation had been analyzed over and over. In the end he decided that he had bored her. The prince knew that he was not a fascinating conversationalist, nor was he terribly attractive. At least his wife did not find him so. The princess had clearly been bored with him for years.

Prince Kori pressed the heels of his hands to his eyes and leaned back in his chair. Why he struggled with this world of women he did not know. It was not for him. He did not speak the language, and remained a foreigner, always, with all the attendant feelings of being in another culture. The awkwardness, the embarrassment, the feeling that you were never seen for what you were.

The prince took his watch from his pocket, remembering that he must meet with Sir Roderick. Casting his failed letter into the fire, Prince Kori went to the bookshelf and removed a volume, a vast tome of great reputation which he had never read. He opened it to a random page and tried unsuccessfully to read, but could not see beyond the image of that beautiful face looking at him with apparent adoration.

"I see Your Highness is enjoying Halden," Sir Roderick said when he arrived. "He always leaves me feeling so . . . inarticulate. It's his ability to look inside and express things I was convinced there were no words for, until I read Halden."

"I feel much the same," the prince said, closing the book and looking up at the King's Man. "You have the proclamation?"

Roderick waved a large, rolled document. "According to the letter of the law." They spread it open on the desk and went over every word together— comfortable words of law.

The prince nodded, reading through the text one last time. He dipped a pen in ink, and signed, aware of how poor his hand appeared. "Read it in the house tomorrow." He clapped Roderick on the shoulder. "We reign both in fact and in law. I had anticipated more of a struggle, but it was hardly even sport."

The King's Man blew on the wet ink, then rolled the proclamation, closing it with a purple ribbon. "Win often and handily enough, and your opponents learn the futility of opposition." The King's Man pursed his lips in what passed for a smile with him. "I have been to see Wells and Galton. They will soon have as complete a translation as is possible. We might have to act more quickly than we anticipated."

The prince placed the pen back in its stand. Any talk of this text brought up thoughts of the duke's son. The most unfortunate accident. What had the boy been doing, in the company of that traitor? It was very sad, but then the security of the nation sometimes required sacrifice. It had always been so, though the prince had great hopes for a period of security—a Farr peace that would encompass all the nations of the Entide Sea. "I thought we were still months away."

Roderick leaned back against the desk, an uncharacteristic act for an ex-military man. No doubt he was exhausted from his constant efforts. "Littel was in the company of the Duke of Blackwater's son. If what he knew was passed on to the duke. . . ." Roderick paused as though considering whether to continue. "I have learned something from Wells; something he did not immediately realize was important. Littel was more than a savant of language, the man had a genius of memory such as I have only read of. He forgot almost nothing. Although we are certain that he took no copy of the text on his flight, it is very likely that, given a few hours, he could have produced one. If that is true, it is possible that our enemies no longer have just vague suspicions about our activity.

"There were some that placed young Flattery in the company of Averil Kent the night that he and Littel fled Merton. All three of them disappeared for a time—Kent and Littel and Flattery. And then there is this servant who saw an old man being led from the palace—secretly. We still do not know who that was, though for my money it was Kent again." Palle put his hands on the desk as though to steady himself. "There are the Entonne to consider, as well. We still don't know what they plan, or even what they know. I think we must be prepared to act."

The prince realized he felt a certain sense of alarm. Like one might feel at the moment of declaring war. It was one thing to discuss the possibility, but to actually give the order. . . . The moment had always seemed so remote. Perhaps he had never believed it would arrive. "Well, better sooner than later," the prince said quickly. It was his role as regent and heir to the throne to be decisive, and he believed it was his skill as well.

The prince looked over at a painting on his wall. A hart staring out from the trees over an open field toward a village, half-shrouded in smoke—the world of man from the point of view of the animal. How bewildered that poor beast looked. "I have been wondering about Kent. Have you learned anything more?"

"He is harder to keep under one's eye than one would think, considering his age. But I have not lost sight of him altogether. I am almost certain that he is involved with Massenet, and I think we should not let that progress too far."

The prince raised a hand. "A few months abroad—Farrow, perhaps, or Doorn. But only if we absolutely must. He is old and if he were to die while in exile. . . . I have enough troubles without that." The prince shook his head. Kent was admired by every member of his family: the King, the princess, his son. Harm a hair of that man's head and he would hear howls from all over the kingdom, and from within the palace loudest of all. Never mind that Kent was almost certainly committing treason!

Palle considered this a moment. "I shall do everything in my power to see that he does not come to harm, but we both know what is at stake. I was far more willing to indulge *Sir Averil*," he spoke these words with some disdain, "before I realized that he had fallen under the influence of that Entonne. . . ." Words failed him.

"Perhaps a brief tour abroad would be best," the prince said, not liking

Palle's qualifications. "Something restful. Could the crown not gift him an estate on Farrow? And send him there to see it? He could stare at the Ruin then,
and consider the folly of his ways."

Palle raised his eyebrows. He was silent a moment longer. "But we would
be thought cruel in the extreme, sending such an old man to sea before the
storm season had passed. I have heard experienced captains complain of that
passage in winter." He seemed to notice the mood of the prince for the first
time. "But spring is not so distant. I could set things in motion, and hope Kent
does nothing foolish between now and then."

Left alone, the prince paced almost silently around the room, stopping to
look down into the fog-enshrouded grounds. He paused for a moment and
examined the painting of the hart, wondering what the animal saw. What did
the activity of men look like from a distance? He realized that he could not
imagine.

Returning to his chair, he hefted the book he had taken up earlier, though
he was not sure why; he no longer had Roderick to impress. Perhaps it was
merely because he felt he would not sleep easily that night.

This collection of Halden's essays was the most quoted book in Farr history, the prince was sure, yet he had never been able to sustain an interest in
the author's vague dissection of a human life. It said almost nothing about the
true arena of man's endeavors—statesmanship. The prince flipped through
thick chunks of pages, pausing to read a few lines wherever his eye fell, hoping
to find some way into this great tome—for in truth he felt a bit embarrassed
that he claimed to have read it. And then a line caught his eye and he began
to read:

> I sometimes rise late in the night beset by anxieties, thinking that my heart
> is about to stop beating; that robbers lurk outside, seeking entry; or a
> terrible storm is about to send lightning down upon me. I am convinced
> my talent has withered, and I have grown old and foolish; that women
> laugh cruelly when they speak of me; and all my careful investments have
> collapsed, leaving me a pauper. I imagine that a terrible war has begun
> that will sweep away all we know, and silent lines of soldiers pass by in the
> night. I worry that lack of rest will bring my health to ruin.
>
> And then, when I can bear it no more, the terrible, infinite depths of
> the night sky turn stone gray, and the sun rises again, lifting up above the
> horizon like a bright promise, and I realize the condition from which I
> suffer is but the human condition. Our solid lives are balanced on the edge
> of calamity, so much so that we do everything possible never to think of it,
> for contemplation drives one to despair. Despair that there is nothing we

can do except promote the illusion that all is well, though we live with the secret knowledge that this is not so.

We wake in the grip of terror, the night telling us that we are utterly alone, our safe lives nothing but dreams. And our greatest fear of all—that we will be released from this world of anxiety and terror. The sun will not rise on the morrow.

The prince let the book slip into his lap and gazed at the darkened window, imagining that silent companies marched by toward a distant city, shrouded in smoke, aflame at its center.

⤳ Seventeen

The guards sent Wallis on, and the painter continued through the darkness, up a narrow stair cut into stone. The tropical forest moved around him, the shadows stirring in the constant trade. Unlike the Varuans, Wallis was not uncomfortable in the darkness. He did not hear his ancestors whispering from the edge of the forest, or feel the presence of spirits—the coolness on the skin that announced their presence.

Of course, his years on Varua had done much to strip away his condescension toward the islanders' beliefs—he had certainly witnessed things that he could not explain, even if he was not always ready to accept the Varuan explanation. But fires wandering through the forest at night, burning nothing; the green sea light enveloping holy men; people cured of the most dire illnesses; these could not be ignored. Even so, the night did not frighten him.

Wallis slipped sideways through the narrow gap leading to the ledge before the caves—the "stone haven" as he translated the Varuan name.

"Anua," he said to the first person he recognized, and she pointed. As he walked, the castaway searched for his wife, looking for her friends and family, for that is where she would be. But he could not see her, nor could he hear her gentle laughter.

There were several fires burning low, the smells of cooking. He could sense the numbers of people around him, the entire village and more, huddled here in fear of the Farrlanders' vengeance. But despite the numbers in such a small place, Wallis knew that there would be no flaring tempers over space or supplies of food. The Varuans would not only remain at peace, but they would turn it into an outing, a picnic. Released from their normal routines, they would sing and have love, dance and laugh, talk, weave, cook, and eat.

Despite the crowding here, there was no terrible odor such as one would expect if the same number of his own people were equally confined. He thought of His Majesty's ships and their stench. Here a clear stream ran down from the mountain and a pool had been built where everyone managed to bathe at least once a day if not twice.

Anua, he found, had set up court in a comparatively quiet corner, beneath the branches of a small breadfruit tree. A group of young people were singing not far off, their sweet tones carrying softly through the encampment—*like the perfume of flowers,* Wallis thought.

The King's senior wife waved him forward. She sat with her sleeping grandson in her arms, rocking to the slow rhythm of the music.

"Wallis," she said in her own language. "I have been hoping that you would come."

"I could not get away sooner, Anua, I apologize."

"What are the *dausoko* doing?" she asked; a polite term meaning "sailor." "Are they going to set their great guns to fire on us again?" He could hear the concern in her voice even if he could not see it on her face.

"No. I don't think so. Though Stern has not decided on a course." Wallis shifted where he sat. "He is like a King who mustn't lose the respect of his chiefs and his people. His followers think we have committed murder, for their tapu are different than our own. The sailors, perhaps even some of the officers, think Stern should respond by pounding the village to ruin. But Stern, despite his anger, is a civilized man. He does not want innocent people to suffer. But he cannot afford to lose the regard of his men. Do you see?"

Anua nodded. "Yes. It is a hard choice. If it was a fleet of our canoes lying off a distant island, I'm not sure we would be more understanding. Leaders must not lose face." She fell silent, stroking her grandson's hair as she rocked. "But we cannot give up the men who killed the two thieves. They acted according to our laws—they acted correctly. If only the King were here." She shifted the boy's limp weight, but he did not stir. "What about this one, Flattery? What do you think now?"

Wallis thought for a moment, considering the quiet naturalist. He seemed to bear such a burden, this young Flattery. "I'm sure that he is in some way part of what was predicted. And I am even more certain that the date of his discovery of the Lost City and the day of the seven great waves were the same. The Old Men were not wrong about some things, that is certain."

"But what is his purpose, Wallis? Can you guess?"

Wallis picked up a small stick and began to draw in the dirt. "I don't yet know. Nor does he, I think. Certainly Tristam means no one harm—I'm sure of that. Though that is no guarantee, I realize. I am beginning to believe that he does not understand his own purpose—or perhaps is unaware of it." Wallis realized that he was sketching his own fale. He would be able to go to his wife and children soon—when Anua finished questioning him. The thought of his family caused Wallis a moment of distress. He had not realized how much he had come to take their presence for granted.

"This story that he told the Old Men. . . . I do not understand."

Wallis nodded. "The world beyond the lagoon has its own laws, Anua. In my land the stars in the sky are not the same stars we see here. What happened at this Lost City—it is not easily explained in our own terms. My view is that the power is the same, but the way men find it varies from place to place, as does their use of it and even their beliefs concerning this power. Here a tree is a being. A spirit, that exists in this world in the form of a tree. In Farrland people believe that trees have no spirit. They are cut down without ritual or concern, and used for any purpose without thought for the spirit's dignity. An ancient tree, many times older than our oldest village, might be made into fence rails. No one would think it the slightest bit odd. The world is strange."

"How could anyone not realize that a tree has a spirit?" Anua said with some disbelief.

Wallis shrugged. "They find our beliefs equally hard to comprehend."

"But certainly the trees that have been made into their great ships—the builders knew their names and blessed their spirits?"

Wallis shook his head.

"How is it that they sail so far? Have the Farrlanders' gods no care for their charges?"

"Different people, different gods, Anua."

She kissed the head of her grandson, and nuzzled his hair with her cheek. "Has the King misunderstood the signs?"

Wallis stopped his drawing, considering what to say. "I don't know. The Old Men did not see Tristam Flattery on their journeys. Only one warned us of the snake."

"Perhaps Flattery was able to hide himself from us?"

"Tristam has no such control. Not yet, anyway."

"I think it could still happen, Wallis. The spirit within might do it."

"Perhaps."

They were silent again, and Wallis listened to the music. He had often heard his wife sing this same air when she was happy and content—though, oddly, it was a sad song.

"Faairi tells me that Flattery cannot control the power within. It can overcome him."

Wallis stopped his drawing. "How does she know that?"

"She saw, Wallis. Faairi was there, with him, when he was overpowered."

"He'd taken the King's leaf?"

He saw Anua shake her head in the dark, as she kept rocking her child.

"I am worried," Wallis said suddenly.

"Yes. We are all frightened. But it is worse. This bird that came with the ship. . . ."

"The falcon."

"Yes. Flattery transformed it. Faairi saw, as did several others. He put his power into an arrow and shot it into the falcon. It burst into flames, they say, and out of the smoke came the spirit transformed into a ghost owl."

Without realizing, Wallis brushed his stick across his drawing. "But what does it mean?"

Anua brushed strands of hair back from her grandson's face, and looked out into the darkness. "The snake will come. As Vita'a said. And there will be nothing to stop it. Will not this *dausoko* who calls himself an Old Man teach the young one?"

"I don't know. I think he is not what he claims."

The singing continued, unaffected by Anua's pronouncements. Wallis sat very still and listened. A small gust of wind began a recitation in the trees, and this stopped even the singers. It died away after a moment, and a single voice picked up the tune again—one woman—but no one joined her for some time.

When finally the others began to sing again, Anua turned back to the castaway. "You must be anxious to see Hau and your children, Wallis. I have kept you too long."

"It is all right. I will go to them in a moment." He made no move to rise. "Have you thought more about . . . ?" He did not finish.

Anua looked into his face. "You must obey your chief, Wallis. If Captain Stern agrees, you may stay with us, but you must live by his word."

Wallis looked down at his half-erased drawing. It was the order of the King of Farrland that no man be left on the islands when the ship sailed.

Tristam lay staring up at the stars, thinking of the tattoo Faairi had shown him. The star by which she found her way back from the world of dreams. Part of him thought of this as the most primitive superstition, but to another part it made perfect sense. He wasn't sure he did not need such a talisman himself.

Tristam closed his eyes and saw the column at the ruin on Farrow and its particular view of the heavens. Did it represent a view from a specific place or a time? If it was a place, what did it signify? He had not made a careful examination of the sky while they were in the archipelago, but was it possible that he might have seen the view recorded on the Farrow Ruin?

He opened his eyes at a sound, but it was merely Beacham, muttering quietly in his sleep, troubled, perhaps, by the dreams that had started that night in the Lost City. Sitting up, Tristam cast his gaze in a circle. The fire had died to coals, and still there was no sign of their shipmates. He worried most about

Hobbes. Not only was the master out in the dark alone, with the mood of the Varuans unclear, but the viscount was out there as well. Tristam was sure that nothing would happen to Julian. The truly macabre seemed immune to misfortune—as though their twisted spirits were misfortune enough.

A sound behind caused Tristam to turn, staring into the darkness. There was someone there.

"*Tristam,*" came a whisper.

He rose to a crouch and froze. "Faairi?"

"I don't wish to be seen by your fellows," she said. "Can you come with me?"

Tristam hesitated, looking at the sleeping Beacham, and then out to the ship. And then he moved quietly into the darkness. He almost believed he could smell her perfume, the scent of her hair.

They found each other in the shadow of the trees, and clung together fiercely.

"I snucked away," she said, as pleased with herself as a truant. "No one is to be here but the watchers."

Tristam laughed, feeling great relief to be in her company.

She took his hand. "Come with me. I have something to show you."

He resisted the tug of her hands, looking back to the beach. "I am concerned about Beacham."

"He will be safe. The watchers will let nothing befall him."

"The watchers?"

"The men who watch the ship. They will keep him safe."

"But Faairi, what will happen now? Two of our crew have been killed. Your people hide in the forest."

Tristam could not see her, but he could sense her seriousness in the dark. She became very still. "It has not to do with us, Tristam. Your fellows defiled the fale of an Old Man and came into the Sacred City against the King's wishes. It was their fate. Your captain should see that."

Tristam stood, realizing that she did not know what her people planned, or would not say. Somehow he trusted her to tell him if he were in danger— though he did not know why. The insight the seed had given him, perhaps.

She led him surely through the trees in the utter darkness, onto a narrow path where Tristam stumbled occasionally. After a reasonably long climb he heard water running, and stars appeared overhead through a tear in the trees. They went on another fifty yards, or perhaps a hundred, Tristam could not be sure. She stopped several times and kissed him tenderly, promises of what was to come.

Finally they emerged into a clearing where Tristam could see something almost white, twisting like a ribbon in the darkness. This narrow fall of water seemed almost illuminated by the starlight, and for a second Tristam wondered if there could be some luminescent life that dwelt there.

"Do you see?" she said, clinging to him. Tristam could sense her excitement. The vapor cooled the air, and Tristam felt a refreshing mist reach out to him.

"It seems to glow in the darkness," *Ghostly,* Tristam thought, and shivered.

"It is the starlight," she said, her voice full of awe and pride, "it falls into a pool high up on the mountain and, on certain nights, spills over into the stream. It trips and falls and runs again, until it pours into this pool—the pool of fallen stars. From here it goes into the sea where you can see it glowing sometimes as the fish pass, or along the line of surf."

Luminescent phytoplankton, Tristam thought. But this. . . . He could not explain this. The falls did seem to be illuminated somehow. Faint moving threads of silver, as though the entire falls were crystal, and refracted some source of the whitest light.

"Sometimes the moonlight is caught in this same falls, spilling into the pool. I have seen it glow white, like the moon soon after it has risen, huge over the eastern sea."

She released him, suddenly, and left him standing, staring at the ribbon of falling water. He could almost believe it *was* starlight. A moment later she returned, a coconut in her hand. With Tristam's knife she opened it deftly, sharing the sweet milk with him. She scooped the soft flesh out, and they ate that as well, licking each other's fingers and laughing. Faairi had him strip off his clothes, and leaving her pareu on a branch, she led Tristam into the shallow pool.

Chanting something in Varuan, she began to fill the empty nut with water from the falls.

"Star water," she said.

"Good for many things, I'm sure," Tristam said, bending to kiss her neck. He felt the "other" stir within and he almost stepped back, struggling with a surge of fear.

Perhaps sensing what happened, she embraced him, repeating his name softly, over and over, like an incantation. She placed the coconut carefully on a rock and gently pushed Tristam back into the falling water. It rained down upon him, cool in the tropical night, like the weight of the sky. As though the falls were a column, upholding the dark dome of the star-scattered night.

The water seemed to glitter as it fell, twisting coils of silver disappearing into a luminous froth at his feet. Tristam realized that he was sobbing, though he did not know why—adding the salt of tears to the stream flowing out toward the moving sea.

He felt that the water flowed into him, and had done so for an endless time, like water wearing away the soft stone of the earth. Something was carried away, leaving him with a strange sadness, a hollowness that echoed with memories, though they were memories of dreams. His uncle sitting at a desk covered in snow. A woman rising from the water, lifting a white blossom in her perfect hands. Following a small boy through twisting, darkened streets. He opened his eyes and the world seemed to have shifted. Did he see the silhouettes of massive structures not far off? And was that a small boy scurrying along the water's edge? A clear tenor came to him, singing a sad air, and a young man clung to the hands of an old man.

"Tristam?" It was Faairi, but he could not see her.

"What has happened?" he heard himself say. "Where am I?"

"The world of the night," she answered. "The world of dreams."

"Why have you brought me here?" The water continued to fall—the ancient song of water running over stone.

"To help you find your way. What do you see?"

Tristam searched the darkness. Around him there was whispering, the scuttling of creatures. A snake's tail disappeared into a fissure of darkness. An owl's barren call. A woman walked at the edge of the pool, unaware of being watched. She swished her long skirts and her hair moved with the breeze. The duchess, he realized, but then a second woman appeared, younger, he thought, though they were far off. They stood facing each other, neither speaking nor moving. And then they reached out their hands as though to touch, but the hands passed through each other, causing them to search more frantically. Ghosts.

A bell rang, echoing down the stone streets of a great city and a single carriage, drawn by a gray horse, passed slowly through an empty square. Tristam could see no driver, and the passenger was hidden by a veil.

"Tristam?"

"Avonel. I see Avonel. A funeral."

He saw men climbing a long stair, bearing a living man laid out like a corpse. Stars appeared, as though he stood on the top of high hill. Stars like he had never seen, arrayed about him, almost close enough to touch. Below, a procession of carriages moved slowly along a valley floor, a twisting road following a twisting river. A ruin stood atop a long ridge that curved like the back of a giant beast.

"I am afraid," he said, but then a star rose above the hills, and he felt his spirits lift also. It floated high, increasing in brightness as it went.

He lifted on a breeze, following this star. Over water, which lay still and heavy, like mercury dyed the deep purple of dusk.

And then the island appeared below, and a white light like a star reflecting on a pond. Tristam was under water, trying to rise, but could not move. Nor could he breathe or call out.

Then the darkness gave way to indistinct points of light, which coalesced into stars. Someone's face hovered over him.

"Tristam?" It was Faairi, her voice full of concern.

He was lying on his back, staring up, his heart pounding and his breath coming in gasps.

"You are safe," she said, laying her hand on his cheek. "My star brought you back." She pressed his hand to her tattoo, holding his fingers there. She was warm and real. Then she bent and he felt her soft breasts press against him, and her arms gathered him and pulled him close to her. Her star had led him back, but from where?

ᔕ Eighteen

Whatever plans they made, though all makeshift, came to nothing. That was Jaimy's realization that morning. As though events conspired to limit their choices. To avoid the men who they were sure were seeking them, they had been forced to abandon any ideas they had of going to Avonel and instead had ridden around the countryside like men bewildered. Somehow they had avoided capture.

Although there were men about in numbers, at a certain point they seemed to stop searching. The hounds were called off. But, still, they kept seeing groups, or even single horsemen moving about. For the life of them they could not guess what transpired.

In the end they had been driven so far off their course they decided to return to the original plan and follow Kent's advice. They were so afraid of capture, however, that they stayed off the roads, going cross-country. On the second evening they stopped at the most isolated farmhouse they could find, and only because their horses could not go on. They purchased hay and grain and the farm wife made them a perfectly awful meal of rabbit and last summer's root crop.

They slept until two hours before dawn, and then continued slowly, riders and mounts still, exhausted. Finally they came to the county where the Countess of Chilton was said to live. Jaimy was afraid to go asking about after the countess for fear that they might still be pursued, but finally they broke down and asked a boy they found cutting peat on the edge of a bog. Everyone, it seemed, knew about the countess, though no one had seen her for decades. She lived on quite a sizable estate not five miles off.

In the end they walked on blistered feet the last few miles, leading dispirited horses, hungry and exhausted. The weather had not been perfectly cooperative, either, for they had been the victims of a fine drizzle most of that morning, which, finally, had mercifully stopped.

Littel was quiet and sullen, much affected by their suffering, which, in the larger scale of things, Jaimy thought was not really so great. He tried to imagine what a war would be like. Even Tristam, on his voyage, was no doubt suffering worse privations than this. He kept reminding himself that it was not really so bad. But such suggestions, he soon learned, were not appreciated by his companion.

They came across the fields of what they believed to be the countess' estate and, finally, by a small lake and wood, they discovered the manor house. They could see the stone walls and slate roofs above the naked branches of the surrounding trees.

Jaimy was suddenly beset by a fear that he had misread Kent's riddle. What if they had come all this way and he was wrong? What a fool he would feel. And Littel would never forgive him, that was certain—even though the scholar would certainly have been captured without Jaimy's help.

If the countess turned them away, Jaimy was not sure how they would proceed. It might be foolish to send Littel back to Avonel now. Better, perhaps, to spirit him out of the country, though with what he apparently knew, it might not be wise to send him to Entonne—hadn't Kent asked the prince about Count Massenet?

Tristam's home in Locfal was beginning to seem a good possibility. If they could buy fresh horses, it was only four to five days' ride. Jaimy would have to find a way to send a message to Avonel, or perhaps he should return and let Egar go on alone. It would almost be safer. Their pursuers were after two young gentlemen, not one. And if Jaimy turned up in Avonel, that would likely confuse things. They might try to murder him out on some lonely heath, but surely no one would be so foolish as to try it in Avonel. Littel, however, was another matter.

Each time they came out into the open, Littel would start glancing behind them. Jaimy could almost see the man fighting this urge, but then he would give in, snapping his head around as though afraid that a dozen mounted men with hounds had somehow snuck up behind them. It would normally have made Jaimy smile but he was too exhausted, and, now that they had almost certainly escaped, he bore a smoldering anger over what they had been put through. *How dare they?* he would find himself thinking. *How dare they? Hunt us like common criminals!*

"There is someone walking along the shore," Littel said, one of the few times he'd broken his silence all day.

Jaimy could make out a figure, dressed in black, moving slowly along the shore. "Let us speak with them."

The woman, for Jaimy was almost certain it had been a woman, disappeared behind some small pines, and they adjusted their course to intercept her. Though the clouds were beginning to break, Jaimy could not yet tell where the sun might be. There could be two hours of light left, not much more.

They came up to the stand of pines and picked their way over a bed of damp moss. So silent did this make their passage that when they emerged from the trees the woman was taken completely by surprise. She stopped on the gravel path that bordered the waters, and glared at them without the slightest sign of fear.

Before Jaimy could speak, she seemed to recover. "Well, I would take you for highwaymen if you rode better horses. So I must take you for fools, ruining those poor beasts, and then showing your faces here, where you certainly are not welcome."

Jaimy was almost unable to respond, guilty as he was over what they had been forced to do to their poor mounts. But there was more. He was certainly in the presence of the loveliest woman he had ever seen. Those eyes! The lashes were so lustrous and dark, and the eyebrows so perfectly arched. Her anger had heightened her complexion a little and Jaimy found this almost irresistible.

"Excuse our terrible manners," Jaimy said, gently. "We didn't mean to alarm you. We're looking for the estate of the Countess of Chilton."

"And who might you be, sir?"

"Lord Jaimas Flattery." He hesitated, not wanting to use Littel's name, though not sure why. "We have been sent by a friend of the countess."

"This friend, has she a name? For I know all of the countess' friends."

Jaimy was not sure how to proceed. He had this terrible feeling that to make an error here would send them back out into the fields, where hounds and men might find them yet. "Sir Averil Kent is his name."

"Kent . . ." she said, and he could see that this truly surprised her. "Why has he sent you here?"

"You will excuse me, Miss, but I am to speak of this only with the countess."

"Well, come along. I don't know if the countess will be able to receive you, but let us see."

It was well past dark, and Jaimy and Littel had not yet seen the countess. They had been given rooms in the vast old mansion, allowed to bathe, and then provided with clothing of the finest quality, though thirty years out of date and ill fitting, having once belonged to someone larger in both stature and girth. Jaimy thought they both looked a bit buffoonish.

"You don't think we've been betrayed, and are merely sitting here, comfortably, waiting for Palle's men to arrive?"

The thought had occurred to Jaimy as well. "I don't. Our choice is to wait out in the cold, prepared to leap into the saddle of our exhausted horses." Jaimy blew on a spoonful of soup. They sat in a cavernous dining hall before a tall hearth in which blazed a fire of good sized logs. It dated from a period when ancient castle architecture had been the rage. The room seemed extremely out of place in this elegant old manor house, but Jaimy found he liked it.

"I think I shall copy his room when Alissa and I find a house. It has a certain charm, don't you think? Perhaps it is just the ride that we have survived. Doesn't it seem fitting that we would end up here? If we only had a few horns of ale to quaff."

Littel looked up from his food, raising an eyebrow. "I don't know how you can jest. This has been the worst three days of my life. I've sometimes wondered if I wouldn't have been better off as Palle's prisoner. Yes, I know what you will say; men have gone to war throughout history and experienced things infinitely worse, but that was bad enough for me. I have saddle sores that will leave me scarred for life, I'm sure."

Jaimy laughed, though not mockingly. He felt somewhat relieved to be here, though he was not sure why. "I can't believe we did not ask her name," he said suddenly.

Littel shook his head, as though his companion had gone a bit mad. "You can't really be thinking of that!" he said reproachfully. "Especially in your betrothed state."

"Curiosity only," Jaimy said. "One has to wonder how a woman of such astonishing beauty could go unknown in Farrland. She must have lived the most sheltered life."

"She was something of a vision, I will grant you that," Littel said a bit wistfully. And then turned back to his meal with a distracted air.

"If we are certain this will be a haven for you, Egar, I think you should set straight to work on reproducing this text."

He looked back at Jaimy, and then registered what had been said, and he nodded quickly.

A servant came in to clear the table, and he bobbed his head to Jaimy. "When you are done, sir, Lady Chilton will see you."

Jaimy immediately rose. "We are quite done, aren't we Egar? Do lead on."

They were taken up to a small withdrawing room, lit only by a single lamp and the flames in the hearth. The servant was quite adamant about which chairs they should take, and before he left lit the burner beneath a warmer that stood beside a decanter of brandy and two snifters.

They sat silently for a moment, heating their glasses alternately.

"This seems very odd," Littel whispered. "What do you make of it?"

Jaimy looked around the room, at the chair just visible in the shadow cast by the screen. "The countess is a recluse—has not been seen in decades. I assume she is making certain that does not change."

Littel leaned a little nearer to his companion. "She is even more eccentric than your friend Kent."

"You think Kent eccentric . . . ?" but he did not finish, for the sound of a door opening hushed them both. The lightest step crossed the floor behind the screen and then a woman dressed in a black gown took the shadowed chair.

"I am not quite sure if I should bid you welcome, Lord Jaimas, Mr. Littel," came a flat voice, almost devoid of expression. "I do not care to have my solitude interrupted." She paused and Jaimy waited, not certain if he should speak. He found that he was uncharacteristically nervous.

"What reason did Kent have for sending you to me, and what message did you bring?"

Jaimy took a breath, and then another before he started. "We have only this note, thrown to us by Sir Averil as his carriage passed, escorted by three men we could not identify in the darkness." Jaimy took the scrap of paper from a pocket, but was not sure what to do. He did not feel he could approach this woman who made such effort to hide her face. Her hands almost reached out, he could see them covered in white lace.

"Would you read it?" she said.

"Yes, certainly," Jaimy held the note closer to the firelight, and realized, suddenly, how absurd it would sound. *If you require refuge: the home of the lady who dwells with your books.*

"That is it? On the strength of that you came to me?" There was just a little color in the voice now, and it was the crimson of anger. "Have you your books here, and I am unaware?"

"I believe Kent is referring to a portrait of Lady Chilton that hangs in our library. In fact, I am quite sure of it."

She was silent for a moment. Jaimy saw her hands, which had gestured in anger a second ago, fall to her lap. "The portrait that Erasmus kept," she said quietly.

Jaimy nodded.

She drew in a long breath. "You should begin your tale from the beginning, Lord Jaimas. Leave nothing out. I must hear every detail, even those you think too small to warrant mention. Perhaps, especially those."

Jaimy took a moment to marshal his thoughts, realizing that Egar was unaware of much of this. "It began last summer, Lady Chilton. I was in Merton . . . I confess I had lost my heart, and my suit was proving unsuccessful in the extreme. In the midst of this, my cousin Tristam Flattery appeared, completely unlooked for." The story was longer than he realized and much of it he had to dredge up from unclear memories. He had only seen the letter from Valary to Dandish that one time, for instance. He could not see the reaction of the countess, who sat perfectly still and asked no questions until Jaimy related how he had come by Kent's note, when the painter was escorted past by horsemen the prince was sure were palace guards. Here she raised a hand to her heart, as though it suddenly raced.

"Kent has been taken by Palle?" she said, not even her flat tones disguising her fear and concern.

"So we conjecture, Lady Chilton, but we have no evidence other than what I have just related."

"Please," she said, calming herself, the hand returning to her lap where it clasped the other tightly. "Continue."

The countess remained in that pose for the rest of the story, though, at each new revelation Littel became more agitated.

Jaimy thought he saw her long hair move, as though she shook her head, when he related the attempt on their lives, but he was not completely sure of that. Finally he came to the story's end. "And so we came to your estate, Lady Chilton, and so exhausted and beset with fears were we that we didn't ask the name of the kind woman who took us in."

The countess said nothing, but sat with one hand twisting a lock of ebony hair around her fingers, over and over. "This boy gave you directions to my home—tomorrow we must find him and see how many others might know of your arrival here." That said, she fell to thinking again. Jaimy had a terrible feeling that she would say nothing more, but rise and leave them, wondering.

"And the text," she said at last, "Lord Jaimas says you can duplicate it, Mr. Littel?"

"I can, Lady Chilton," he answered, with more deference in his voice than Jaimy would have expected from a reform sympathizer.

"Will you do that immediately? This night? It might be more important than we know." She thought a moment more. "I will find out what has happened to Averil Kent," she said softly. "Pray that he has come to no harm, for it has been a formidable task, and he is no longer young."

"Lady Chilton?" Jaimy said, a bit surprised at the meekness in his voice. "We do not understand what we have been caught up in. Do Palle and his group believe they can learn the arts of the mages? Is it possible?" Jaimy was sure that the shadow stared at him. Almost, he could see eyes in that darkness.

"It is the question we are all asking. I am anxious to see this text Mr. Littel has been translating. Though you have not yet finished, I collect?" she said to the scholar.

"No, not yet. It is a difficult task, and has become more so at each stage. I don't know if I shall ever render it exactly or completely." He shrugged.

"I hope you will not object to continuing, Mr. Littel. I realize you've been through a terrible experience and would like some peace."

"I. . . . If it will assist you, Lady Chilton, I will gladly do it, but I fear I must ask leave to sleep a little. I can barely keep my eyes open, I apologize for saying."

Jaimy thought she nodded assent. "Certainly. Sleep, but not too long," she said, warmth lighting her voice like a wick giving birth to flame.

*   *   *

Egar Littel had not exaggerated his exhaustion and went immediately to his chamber and bed. Jaimy, though hardly less affected by their flight, could not sleep and finally rose and dressed. He paced across the cold room, for despite the fire in the hearth the night wind seemed to penetrate the walls.

He did not light the lamp but measured the length of his floor, back and forth, by the light of his fire. Occasionally he crouched before the hearth and warmed his hands as though by a fire in the woods. He was concerned about his family and Alissa, who had not heard from him in three days, and it would take more than a day for a letter to reach them—if a letter was advisable. He would have to ask the countess.

What a strange audience that had been, almost a bit comic, though somehow the voice that came from the shadows did not inspire laughter. What terrible vanity, though. To hide oneself away for decades because one had lost the beauty of one's youth. It seemed so very odd, for Jaimy would expect such a person to be . . . well, strange. Some of that vanity would seep into the conversation, but the countess had seemed positively genuine, even modest. Not at all what he would have expected.

His thoughts returned to the woman they had encountered by the lake. The countess had not fallen for his ploy and supplied the woman's name. *You are engaged to be married to the most delightful young woman you have ever met,* he reminded himself. That did not mean he stopped feeling attraction for other women, however. He was, after all, not yet twenty-four. He couldn't stop himself from feeling admiration for someone's beauty, but it must not go beyond that.

He moved to the window ledge, pulling the curtain aside and feeling the cold through the glass. There were other lights still on, but only a few among the myriad blind openings. Bare branches twined around his window, clutching to the cold stone. Tristam would have named the vine, but Jaimy could not, and marveled again at how little he had managed to learn in his years at Merton.

Someone moved at a window, one floor higher and at such an angle that he could make out no more than a shadow—which seemed to be the way things went in this place. For a moment he waited, wondering what this person would do. Wondering if it was the countess or the young beauty, staring out into the night. A small bird sat on that window ledge, or so it seemed. It was so still it might have been only an ornament chiseled in stone. After a moment he felt as though he were imposing on someone's privacy and decided it was time to wake Egar. The work must begin.

A servant had been detailed to see to their needs, coffee being chief among them. They worked at the same table where they had eaten their dinner, side by side, their backs to the fire. Egar had turned a page on its side and ruled it neatly into thirds. The first column he began to fill with rows of odd characters, as unlike the script used by the people around the Entide Sea as Jaimy could imagine. The second column was direct transliteration of the characters into the common script, but the language was unknown. The third column was reserved for the translation.

Jaimy's task was to make a fair copy of the second and third column, for his hand was much finer than Egar's. The work did not progress quickly, but it seldom halted, Littel's memory being every bit as phenomenal as he had claimed. As the night wore on, the scholar did begin to falter, and at one point he laid his head down on his arm on the table and fell asleep for thirty minutes, like every student had done at some time or other.

There were still two hours of darkness left when they finished. Egar sprawled in a chair near to the fire and sipped a brandy, his eyes red and puffy, his jaw a little slack.

Jaimy tried to make his exhausted mind grapple with what he read. The text was long, almost twenty pages, and oddly cadenced and phrased. Most of it was in one of two languages, but there were bits of other unknown tongues as well. In places Littel had used Entonne to translate words or phrases, and in a few others he had used the language of Doorn. Sections, some quite large, were left untranslated, although a few of these bore notes suggesting what they *might* refer to.

"But what in Farrelle's name does this mean?" Jaimy exclaimed. "Who could make sense of this? It does not seem to have been written for men at all, but some other race whose perception of the world is not as ours."

"Exactly. That is how it seems. Did I not warn you?"

Jaimy nodded, his eye running down the page. "But listen to this:

> *"Lifesblood blossoms, bear up, blood white*
> *Spring snow. Gathered then, palely gathered.*
> *Rose thorns stab, heather heals*
> *Gather with the new moon's light.*
>
> *Snow bears moonlight.*
> *Starlight, in the winter rain,*
> *And clearly run to Terhelm Spring*
> *Where the singer awaits*
> *The secret song."*

Jaimy almost threw the page onto the table. "What is that supposed to mean?"

"But you've chosen one of the simplest passages. Merely a set of directions for gathering herbs or some such things. When it should be done, and where. It also tells that starlight and sunlight can be collected from a spring, for they are contained in snow and rain. And this is what Palle, and Wells, and even Kent and the countess seem to take so seriously. For this, someone attempted our murder!"

Jaimy picked up another page. "And you've used so much Entonne," he said.

"Yes, it is very odd. Some of it translates better into Farr, and, in other instances, the Entonne words are a much closer fit. Or so I imagine. It is almost translated more by intuition and inspiration than by pure scholarship. It might take years to do it properly, but Wells and his companions wanted something immediately. In many places I have translated the sense of it more than anything else. But it is shoddy scholarship, I am well aware."

"And listen to this," Jaimy said. "It wounds like a children's rhyme:

> *"Owl's song on whispered shores*
> *Where the silvered sea dies*
> *Along the wake of a running moon,*
> *Moontide and magic rise."*

"Yes, and there are four verses like that. All in what seems to be a different dialect. And that is not the only place I have encountered them. In the *Lay of Brenoth* one of those lines appears again, almost word for word: '*Beyond the wake of a running moon.*' Far too close to be accidental. And I think it was preserved elsewhere, in one of the songs of the Carey minstrels. And from there it found its way into a poem by an obscure Doornish poet. Who knows who will use it next."

Jaimy stared at his companion. "Flames, Egar, you are the Tristam Flattery of language!"

"What?"

"My cousin Tristam is like you, except his province is birds, and trees, and insects. He has a head stuffed with the most amazing facts. I am in awe of him, sometimes, as I am of you."

Littel shrugged and tried to smile at what he hoped was a compliment.

"But I can't make any sense of this," Jaimy said turning back to the text. "This is what everyone is struggling to possess and it is gibberish, as far as I can tell."

"To you, perhaps." The woman they had met by the lake was standing by the door. Jaimy had not heard her enter and had no idea how long she might have been listening. She smiled at the two of them, though there was no joy in this gesture, and she crossed to the table. Jaimy had not marked how gracefully she moved before, as though she were a virtuoso of that one act, had studied it for years.

"It is complete?" she asked looking down at the sheets spread over the table, but she did not move to touch them.

"As complete as I can make it at this time," Littel said, his voice changing in the presence of this woman. "I would need access to quite a library to go much farther."

She nodded, not taking her eyes from the pages. "This is the fair copy, without the characters?"

Egar nodded. "I will add the characters, though I am not sure I can do it tonight. I am all in, I fear."

She turned a genuine smile on them both then, with the result that they suddenly felt their energies return. "You have done more than can be asked: both of you." She pulled out a chair and sat. "I will fill in the third column. And I will be as meticulous as you would be yourself, Mr. Littel. You may review my work when you have rested. I do not think you will have cause to criticize."

As though they were the most fragile of ancient documents, she reached out and slid the pages toward her. And then she looked up at the two men staring at her. "Sleep, gentleman. You have completed your task, and difficult it was, too. Sleep, and when you have risen tomorrow, at your leisure, and broken your fast, I will have someone show you our library. Now, sleep well, and long. You are safe here."

The two gentlemen went reluctantly to the door, and as Littel passed through, Jaimy turned, almost leaning out from behind the door.

"I could sit with you a while. Perhaps there is something yet that I might do."

The woman looked up from the table, forcing a smile as she took up a pen. "Rest, Lord Jaimas. You must rest. We don't want you returning to your fiancée, and then hearing that we mistreated you. Sleep the sleep of the innocent and I shall see you on the morrow."

Jaimy nodded, and backed out the door closing it softly behind him. When he reached the foot of the stair, he realized he still did not know her name.

Back in his chamber, Jaimy resumed his pacing. For a few moments he lay down on the bed, staring up at the ceiling. What had she said? "Sleep the sleep of the innocent and I will see you on the morrow"? A phrase he had not heard in many years. His grandmother had used it. It was a sign of the life this woman led, shut up here with an old woman who hid herself from everyone's sight. What a life! He felt a wave of pity for her.

I am engaged to be married, he thought, *I should not be affected so.* But when he closed his eyes, he saw that extraordinary face looking at him. There was no sense of vagueness to this image—it was as sharp as if the woman stood before him. The nameless woman, with her high forehead and prominent cheek bones. Almost the same face that looked down from the mantel in his father's library. Almost. She wore her hair up, and that changed her look, but even so, the similarity was striking. He had been truly exhausted not to have seen that immediately. The countess' daughter, he thought, though she must have been born late.

He wondered if Alissa ever met men who had this same effect on her. Somehow he thought she would not let herself have these feelings, and his guilt increased. He rose after a while, stiff with cold, and went to the window, looking for signs of the morning light. Darkness still prevailed.

He began to undress, but instead of going to bed when he finished, he put on his own clothes that had been returned, clean and mended.

"I will look like a fool," Jaimy said aloud, but the idea of being thought foolish by a woman was a bit alien to him. It had happened so seldom.

The hallways were lit only by candles, spaced at some distance, but Jaimy made his way down the stairs, through the silent mansion. No light appeared below the door to the dining hall, and he almost did not go in. But then he turned the handle and stepped into the room. It was dark but for a dull glow from the coals in the hearth. He crossed to the table, placing his hand on the back of the chair where she had sat. He reached out and brushed the table, but his eyes were not wrong: the text was gone.

"It is safe with me," came a near whisper from behind, making Jaimy start.

"Lady Chilton?" Jaimy said, turning to the sound. The countess sat in a high-backed chair by the hearth, wrapped in a dark shawl or a blanket. In the slight glow from the fire he could see long curls, and it brought to mind sculptures he had seen. It brought to mind the portrait in their library that his father made pilgrimages to view.

"Yes."

She seemed to be huddled in the chair, drawing into herself, like someone left to die of the cold.

"Shall I rekindle the fire for you, Lady Chilton?"

"No. I am not bothered by the cold."

"You have read Egar's translation?" Jaimy asked, surprised at how softly these words came out.

"Every word," she said, her voice even more flat, if that were possible.

"What . . . what does it mean?"

She shifted in her chair; he could just make out her head turning toward the fire. "It means many things. It means that the mages failed in their last great endeavor. That is its central meaning. It also means that a way once denied at great cost, might now be opened again."

"Egar said it was a ritual—perhaps to open a gate."

She waved a sheaf of paper which he had not realized she held. "Oh, this will not do that. No, this is far simpler, though it is complicated enough. This . . ." she shook the papers slightly, "is merely the end of a string. What you will find when the string is drawn in, that is my fear."

"And what will we find?" Jaimy asked.

She shrugged, Jaimy was certain.

"Tell me about your cousin Tristam. Were you with him when he was approached by the ghost boy?"

"No," Jaimy said, disappointed that she had avoided his question. "No, I was not. And he does not like to speak of it." Jaimy stared into the barely glowing coals, which looked to him like cooling molten lava. "Kent thought he saw the ghost boy, though."

"You did not tell me *that*. When?"

"As we left Dandish's ruined house the night we made our escape. As we stepped out onto the terrace, a child bolted across the garden and out the gate. Kent was quite shaken, and certain that it was not a natural child."

"Poor thing," Jaimy thought she whispered. "Did this boy open the gate to pass through?"

Jaimy hesitated. "He did not appear to."

"But still, you do not believe?"

Jaimy said nothing.

"I must find out what has befallen Averil," she said, as though to herself. He thought her voice quavered just slightly as she said this. "If you would like to send a message to your family, I will have it delivered, but I fear you must stay here for a few days, at least, until we know more of what goes on beyond our gates. Write something quickly and I will have a servant collect it from your chamber, though say nothing of being here with me." She looked at him now, he could tell by the sound. "And then you must find rest, Lord Jaimas. We must all harbor our strength. I cannot predict what will be asked of us before this is over."

He did not move immediately, and a hand emerged from the shadow into the dull light, a graceful hand, and it waved him away as one might a child. He almost smiled, and for some reason thought the countess did, too.

The clatter in the courtyard below brought Jaimy to his window. He had written quick notes to both his mother and Alissa, with instructions that both could be delivered to either, and a servant had rushed off with them.

In the courtyard below he saw that a good-sized carriage had been pulled up before the door, and servants were bustling about with baggage. Four horsemen stood by their mounts, wearing capes against the weather, reminding Jaimy immediately of the riders who had accompanied Kent—poor Kent. Jaimy hoped that no harm had come to the man, but considering how casually his own murder had been attempted he held little hope for the painter.

The door to the entrance hall opened and someone emerged. Under the roof of the carriage entrance he could see only the hem of a dark coat, and a woman striding quickly the few paces to the carriage, which barely jiggled when she boarded. There was a moment's fuss while everyone found their places and then the carriage set out, preceded by two of the horsemen. He watched the carriage lamps disappear in the slight mist that hung beyond the courtyard, the sounds of horses coming up to him even through the cold glass.

ᥱᢖ Nineteen

Lady Galton did not look well that afternoon. Alissa had heard that the woman lived on Farrow because the island had the climate required for her health, and wondered if the poor woman had been away from her adopted home for too long. Her color was high and she seemed somewhat short of breath as they ascended the stairs to the duchess' private sitting room.

"The duchess is well, though? Her nerves not too frayed?" Lady Galton asked, as they paused on the landing.

"The duchess seems very well today, but perhaps Lady Galton knows how nervous excitement does affect her. They live very quietly here, and I fear the coming wedding has been more than enough excitement."

Lady Galton put her hand to her forehead as though she had a sudden pain.

"Are you well, Lady Galton?" Alissa asked, concerned. The older woman nodded, still not revealing her face, and when she did look up, her eyes were rimmed in red.

"You are such a sweet child," she said with greater feeling than their brief association would seem to support. They had met only once before.

They continued up the stairs, slowly, for Lady Galton seemed almost to be carrying a burden, something that weighed heavily upon her. Alissa thought the poor woman seemed overcome with sadness, and she wondered what had befallen her. Despite what Kent claimed about this woman's husband, Lady Galton seemed very kind and warm.

"It is not much farther," she said quietly, and Lady Galton nodded in response, keeping her eyes cast down.

They paused again at the head of the stairs, so that the older woman might catch her breath, and she tried to smile at Alissa, though it was a very weak smile. Finally she nodded, and they set off along the hallway. Never had the passageway seemed so long. With each step Lady Galton appeared to become more reluctant, and when they finally came to the door, she paused, straightening her posture, and took control of her breathing. Alissa got the impression that she was gathering her resolve.

They found the duchess sitting in a chair by the fire, reading by the fine sunlight that blessed them that day. Her pale face lit with a smile when Lady Galton appeared, and a decade of cares were erased in that instant. She rose to meet her old friend, and to Alissa's surprise the two women fell into each other's arms like schoolgirls, both of them shedding tears.

Alissa stood by, a bit embarrassed, a bit charmed by the scene, and she found her own eyes damp. Jaimas always teased her for crying so easily, though she knew he loved her for it.

Reluctantly the women released each other and sat, dabbing at their eyes and laughing a little at their show of emotion.

The duchess reached out and took Alissa's hand. "You have met Lady Alissa before? You see, Margel, I finally have a daughter, and I shall embarrass her by saying I could not be more pleased if I had brought her into the world myself. Bless her poor mother, gone now these many years."

This reference to Alissa's mother, for some odd reason, seemed to steal the joy of the reunion from Lady Galton's face, and a tear welled up in each eye, causing her to blink.

"I cannot bear this task I have been set!" she said suddenly, looking at the two women with such compassion. "I am the bearer of the worst news, for both of you." She leaned forward in her chair, reaching out and taking both women by the hands. She moved her mouth to form a word but no sound came, and Alissa suddenly felt a chill of fear.

"I have received news, I cannot begin to explain how, but your son, Anthia," and she cast a look of pity toward Alissa. "Your dear son, and his friend as well, were found . . . found dead in County Coombs." Her voice disappeared again, and then she managed. *"I am so sorry."*

The duchess put her hand to her heart, all color draining from her face. "But this can't be. When? When was this to have occurred?"

"Two days past."

The duchess let out a long sigh, and a tear slipped down her cheek. "But we have had word from Jaimas this very morning." She reached over and lifted a sheet of letter paper from her reading table. "Here it is, dated yesterday. And Alissa received a letter as well. There can be no doubt." Her face fell a little. "Unless there is a mistake in the date, or something has occurred since then."

Lady Galton hardly knew what to say. "No. No, it was two days past, I am quite sure. You are certain this is from Lord Jaimas?"

The duchess nodded, vigorously. "Absolutely. He has a very distinctive hand and manner of expression. No, there is no doubt." The duchess looked over to Alissa for confirmation, and she nodded quickly. Her own letter, she was a bit embarrassed to think, was tucked inside her bodice near to her heart. She dearly hoped she would not be asked to produce it!

Lady Galton sat back in her chair, though she did not release their hands.

She looked as if she would be the one needing comforting. "But how can this be?" she said to herself.

The duchess was obviously shaken by the news, and Alissa was certain that she would take to bed again for several days.

"I'm quite sure our letters were written yesterday," Alissa said firmly, "just as the dates indicate. Jaimy said explicitly in mine . . ." she felt her face color a little, "that he has missed me terribly these three days. That would be correct. I last saw them in Merton on Saturday, the fifth. Yesterday was the eighth, and that is the date on the letter. And you think something befell them on the sixth, Lady Galton?"

"Yes, the day the iron bridge was dedicated." Lady Galton appeared confused and upset that she may have borne this terrible news falsely, carrying doubts to these poor women.

"Then I think your information is not quite correct, Lady Galton," Alissa said, taking the duchess' hand, which remained limp.

"Alissa," the duchess said, a bit pitifully, "are you certain?"

"Absolutely. Jaimy would never mistake the date by two days. And he said that they had found refuge after some difficulty, and that he expected to return in a few days, perhaps at the week's end." Alissa turned on Lady Galton. "Perhaps, Lady Galton, you would explain what has led you to bring us this news."

The old woman looked as though she would expire on the spot from embarrassment and guilt. "I hardly know where to begin," she said.

Jaimy walked along the path that traced the lake's border. On the opposite shore, a hawk sat high in the bare branches of a tall tree and turned its head slowly, as though it stood vigil. Spring, that day, was a rumor whispered on the breeze. The sun, too, hinted at the coming season, and snowbells appeared, pixielike, in the grass and moss.

Jaimy kept scanning the edge of the lake, but the tall figure he hoped for could not be found. He went another forty feet, and stopped to survey the scene again, feeling a bit like the hawk across the waters.

The servants had told him the countess had gone away for a few days. *And the other woman?* She was indisposed at the moment; they would tell her he had inquired.

He had learned only one thing; the woman's name was Angeline, and the servants said she was the daughter of the countess' cousin. All that day Jaimy had spent in contemplation. He was surprised to find that he was glad to have an excuse to spend another day or two here, and this made him wonder if he was in fact the rogue that Professor Somers had initially taken him for.

Did he not love Alissa? Or did he not love her enough? How he wished Tristam were here so that he might speak of this with someone. Littel was cooped up in the mansion's impressive library, wallowing in books. Jaimy had always heard that the countess was known for her beauty and her wit, but had not realized that her interests were so broad. He thought of the woman who had questioned them that night—she did not seem the type to collect books merely to impress others. There appeared to be no others to impress.

He took a seat on a bench and stared out over the water, which held the sky and the trees of the other shore. He worried about Tristam, and every new thing he learned made this worse. What he most wanted was to gather everyone together; Kent and the countess, and this man Valary, and Littel—and find out what they all knew. It was like a children's treasure hunt, with clues buried all over the countryside. And he was getting frustrated from pursuing them. And now someone had attempted his murder. So casually attempted it!

A figure appeared across the small lake, causing him to sit up, but immediately he recognized the walk—Littel had torn himself away from the books. Jaimy smiled. One sight of the countess' library and the trials of the past days had been forgotten. To find such a library the scholar would have braved their cross-country chase without hesitation. Braved it daily! Now that Littel was recovering from his fright, Jaimy found he quite liked him—and not just because he reminded Jaimy of his cousin, whom he missed terribly.

It occurred to him suddenly that perhaps Angeline was more interested in Littel, for she seemed to be something of a scholar as well.

"You are acting the fool," he chastened himself. He wondered if Alissa was worried about him. If he were causing her distress. And yet he had no desire at the moment to rush to her, and this made him wonder exactly what kind of man Jaimas Flattery was.

ᑐ Twenty

Kent was still far from recovered, despite the fact that he had nearly slept the clock round, but he felt such a need to speak to others. As his actions were the subject of much scrutiny, the only way to do this was in public. Preferably some place where he could speak with as many people as possible, so he could bury the important conversations amongst fifty others that were of no import whatsoever.

The opera was almost perfect, for many of the people he really wanted to see would be there, and afterward anyone who was anyone would collect at a select few homes in the city—and Kent, of course, had standing invitations to all of these.

He surveyed the crowd from his box in the balcony, noting those he wished to see, and those who he might speak with to confuse anyone watching. There were certain people to be avoided—anyone who would try to monopolize him, certainly—but he knew how to steer through such situations. He also knew where most of the important people habitually gathered at intermission— everyone had their favored place.

He saw that Alissa Somers was present in the box of the Duke and Duchess of Blackwater, but she was accompanied only by Lady Galton. On the same level he saw Count Massenet in the company of two beautiful young women whom he did not recognize; one blonde and one dark.

The place glittered with jewelry (an Entonne passion adopted by the women of Farrland), and was as colorful as any summer garden. Kent delighted in the sight, considering how it could be represented on canvas, the rows of colors making random patterns, broken by the balustrades and gilt columns and balconies. But what could never be represented was the excitement. Even an old man could feel it. Everyone in their finery. Beautiful necks and shoulders, bared by the recent fad for low necklines. The pleasure he could see in the shining eyes. The feeling was so strong, it made the courting of spring birds seem subdued.

He turned his attention back to the stage where a young Entonne singer was exercising her magnificent soprano. And even here he could not escape it, for she wore the most revealing gown of all, he was sure. So low cut that he could have never raised his opera glass to look, despite his eyesight, lest others should see him. Instead he consulted his list of players, and found her name: Tenil Leconte.

At moments like this he thought it a cruel trick that his youth had fled. He could feel this tangible sexuality, but it was past for him—oh, not the feeling certainly, but his time. He was nothing but a ruin of an old man, not even a prize for an elderly lady.

For a moment he shut his eyes, unable to bear the beauty spread before him any longer. The singer's voice seemed to pierce him, cut through the facade he had built to protect himself, and the notes of her sad song seemed to be a requiem for his lost youth. It brought to mind his response when Alissa Somers had rubbed his aching feet—physical, beyond his control. It was like falling victim to a spell that one could hardly bear, it was so compelling and yet so painful. Like the obsessive, unrequited love he had experienced when he was young.

"Kent?" It was a whisper—a man's voice.

The painter turned to find Bertillon standing in the shadows at the back of the box.

"May I join you?"

Kent waved him forward, feeling a bit of embarrassment, as though afraid Bertillon would know what he had been thinking—or feeling, in fact.

Bertillon took a seat, and Kent leaned a bit toward him. "This girl is magnificent! Have you heard her before?"

"Heard her?" Bertillon smiled. "Indeed."

Kent turned away from this handsome young man, realizing that the woman was his lover, or had been at some time. He felt a moment of outrage, focused on Bertillon, but it was merely life he felt this anger toward. Outrage that this disease called age should befall him.

"Our friend would like to meet with you. It's very important."

Kent nodded. "As you must have realized, Palle is watching me. A meeting now would not be wise."

Bertillon nodded, and then began to applaud as the air ended. He leaned close to Kent's ear. "Five minutes of your time. No more. At the Earl of Milford's tonight." He stood, continuing to applaud, and much of the audience followed.

During intermission, Kent made his way out into the upper lobby, packed with tight knots of people, alive with the buzz of conversation—like putting one's ear to a hive and giving it a tap. The painter did not feel quite so tired, society was ever rejuvenating, and people greeted him with smiles rather than with looks of concern. He must not look as though he was about to expire, as he had since his return from Merton.

Picking his way carefully among the people, Kent finally found Sennet, who detached himself from his group at a nod from the painter.

"Sir Averil. I must say you are looking more hale tonight. I confess I was concerned."

Kent smiled and shrugged. "I cannot go without sleep as I did when I was young." Pleasantries were brief between the two. They had known each more decades than they cared to count, and were well aware of each other's interests.

"Would you have guessed the governor would be appointed to the council?" Kent asked, and Sennet, surprisingly, shook his head.

"Not at the time we last spoke. I was taken unawares." He laughed as though this gave him pleasure, as though the antics of court and government were not to be taken too seriously. "If all goes as planned, they shall announce the council tomorrow, though who will be surprised other than illiterate shepherds in northern Locfal, I can't say." He drew himself up in mock outrage, though it seemed he was ready to burst out laughing. "Many are predicting a long regency. Do you know some young wit had the effrontery to offer odds that the King would outlive *me*! And while I was present, too!"

Kent could not help himself; he laughed.

"Do not laugh, Kent," the marquis said seriously, "I got better odds than you," and then when he saw the look on the painter's face, he could contain his laughter no longer. "I tell you, Kent," he managed after a moment, "this younger generation, they will turn anything to profit."

They laughed a moment longer, and then Kent stopped, surveying the room. "The Duke has seen the King, then?"

"This very night," Sennet said.

Kent squinted. "Is that Lady Galton, by the stairs?"

Sennet raised himself up on his toes. "I believe it is, accompanying the young woman the prince is so taken with."

Kent must have revealed his surprise. "Alissa Somers?"

"You know her?"

"I should say so. Have known her many years. Her father has a chair at Merton. But she is engaged, you know, to Blackwater's son."

Sennet's smile was huge. "Lord Jaimas? Of course. Well, her fiancé should watch himself. Not, of course, that I doubt the intentions of Miss Somers. The daughter of a don, you say?" This seemed to please him immeasurably. "That would set Prince Kori and the princess into a spin!"

Kent felt a little horrified. He should never have told Sennet that this was Alissa. The man really was a terrible gossip. But he was so well connected, and far more shrewd than most realized.

Kent took his leave of the marquis, crossing the room at an opportune moment, wanting to speak with Lady Galton, but not wanting to share her with others.

"Sir Stedman has not accompanied you?" Kent asked after he had kissed Lady Galton's hand.

"No, he was called away by other matters," Lady Galton smiled with affection. "No doubt you've heard," she said, not meeting Kent's eye.

"Yes," he said quietly.

Lady Galton raised her head, her look a bit defiant, perhaps. "But Stedman seems to be over this strange condition that has plagued him these past few years—he has hardly been himself. But he is recovered, now."

"I am so glad to hear it," Kent said, perhaps not hiding his surprise as well as he should. "I can't tell you how I have worried about the governor." So the duke was right! Galton was no longer supporting Palle—and obviously Palle must not know.

Lady Galton reached out her hand and offered Kent a folded card—an invitation. "I don't think you will have a more interesting time anywhere else this evening," she said, just as the bell rang to call everyone back.

Kent returned to his box and, before the performance began, took out his spectacles and read his invitation. Inside there was an unfamiliar address, and the invitation also named Valary. The writing, however, was well known to him. It was the hand of the Countess of Chilton, though she had not signed her name. *The countess, in Avonel!* To the best of his knowledge she had not been in the capital for decades. He tried to imagine what had drawn her from her fortress, and found the thought ruined his ability to concentrate on the remaining performance.

Kent peered out the back of his carriage. There was no breeze that evening and the smoke from a thousand chimneys settled into the streets and alleys and commons. It seemed to grow thicker around the streetlamps, where it gathered like silt in a river's eddy. He could not be absolutely sure they were not followed.

"I'll have Hawkins let us out a few blocks away from our destination, Valary, and we will walk the last bit. Easier to see if we are unaccompanied."

"You are being rather mysterious, Kent," Valary said. He had been deep into his pursuit when Kent arrived, trying to convince himself that some long past event was merely a coincidence. "You have me a bit nervous. We're not going to meet the King, are we?"

Kent shook his head, still staring back into the smoke.

"The city is awful when it is like this, is it not?"

Valary realized his question had not registered. They went along in silence another block.

"Do you remember, Valary, the last time I visited, you said there was someone who might know more about the mages than you?"

Valary looked confused for a second. "The Countess of Chilton?" he said suddenly. "That isn't who we're going to meet?"

"Well, it is."

Valary touched the painter's shoulder. "How in the world did you arrange that?"

"It is a long story, Valary. I will try to explain later."

Kent had Hawkins stop, and the two men stepped out onto the wet cobbles. The driver went on, with instructions to return to this spot in one hour. They were not so far from Kent's own home that he did not know the area, and he took them into a darkened side street.

"Are you sure this is wise, Kent?" Valary almost whispered. "I should stay out in the light."

"I think it's a small risk only. We mustn't be followed. Better to be set upon by cutpurses than let anyone know our business tonight."

They stumbled up a flight of stairs where they surprised a group of young boys drinking sour smelling wine. The second the gentlemen appeared, they took to heel. At the stairhead they found themselves back on a lit circle, where a single carriage made its slow way around the central park, almost disappearing between streetlamps, its progress marked only by the sound of iron-shod hooves on stone. Kent and Valary stayed in the shadows, watching the coach pass, and then draw up before a house where a gentleman and two children got down, talking in hushed tones.

When the street was empty, the two men set out briskly along the walk until they found the address they sought. It was a three-story townhouse, with a broad stair to its entrance and an ornate iron fence protecting it from the street. They tugged on the bell pull and waited.

Kent found he was a little nervous. He also realized he did not want to share his privilege of visiting the countess with another. Did not want to spoil whatever intimacy there was in these meetings. He was also terribly anxious, simply from wondering what would bring the countess to Avonel.

The door opened, and to Kent's relief, a servant he recognized stood in the entryway.

The room was different from the one Kent was used to—this was a small library—and there was a single lamp, though well shaded and burning low, not casting even a shadow beyond the table on which it was all but hidden. The fire flickered, almost ready for a log. Not far from the hearth, a screen patterned with irises stood, and two chairs sat on either side of a table which held a pair of glasses, as well as brandy and a warmer.

"Will they not bring us another lamp?" Valary asked.

"No," Kent said. "I should have warned you, Valary. Lady Chilton does not allow herself to be seen. Please, indulge me in this, and do not rise from your chair. Your trouble will be amply rewarded, I can assure you."

The historian did not respond, but sat staring at the fire, his face set in concentration, as it was when he was seeking some bit of information from the vast storehouse that was his memory. Kent noticed that he rather furtively pushed his shirt cuffs into his jacket, and then tried to tame his unruly hair. Kent was so used to the man wearing frayed clothing and looking like a distracted don that the painter had become convinced the man never gave his appearance a second thought.

He is old enough to remember, Kent thought. When she withdrew from society, the countess was still the most beautiful woman anyone had ever seen. That was the image she had fixed in everyone's mind—he glanced at the screen—and she was not going to ruin that now.

Kent heated his brandy, turning it slowly over the blue flame until the aroma of it filled the room. It was comforting, familiar, a part of the ritual.

A door opened and he heard the light footfall, the swish of a gown, and she was sitting opposite them, dark in the shadows.

"Averil. Mr. Valary," came the flat voice. "I am so glad to meet you at last."

Valary bowed his head, unable to speak.

"And Averil, I received your gift. I hardly know what to say. . . . Wherever did you come by such a stone? It must be. . . . Well, it is overly generous, I think."

Kent waved off her protest. "Not at all, it was left to me by an admirer. What in the world was I to do with such a thing? No, I'm a bit ashamed to admit it cost me nothing. I hope you will accept it."

He could not see her reaction in the darkened room, but she seemed to hold him in her gaze a moment, and then she nodded, as though she had not the words to express her gratitude. Kent took a long breath of relief. It was out of his hands now, and he had profited by it not at all.

"Lord Jaimas managed to bring Mr. Littel through, Averil," the countess said, "though it was a near thing. I was more than a little surprised that you would send them to me, but when I saw the text Littel had been working on for Palle. . . . You certainly did the right thing, and as far as I can tell, no one realizes where they are."

"You have seen the text?" Valary blurted out.

Kent was sure she smiled. "I have, Mr. Valary. And if you agree, soon you shall see it as well. Though I warn you not to agree too quickly. Palle tried to kill Lord Jaimas and Littel so that no one else might possess it."

Kent was more than a little taken aback by this. Thank Farrelle they survived! He had assured Somers and Alissa that no one would dare harm the son of the Duke of Blackwater. He felt as though he had seated himself at a gaming table, and, too late, discovered the stakes were beyond his means. He gave voice to the fear that had been plaguing him. "Lady Chilton is certain they were not followed?"

Tentative. "Yes. . . . As sure as I can be."

"I will see this text, Lady Chilton," Valary said suddenly. "I will take the risk gladly."

"I thought you might, though I'm not quite convinced you understand what is involved, Mr. Valary." Kent saw the tips of her fingers come together. Her hands seemed so small. He did not think of her as frail. It was the illusion that he carried, as did many others, that she was still young. An ideal, after all, never changed.

"If you go to the table behind you, I have laid the text out there. The translation, as you will see, is not complete, and may never be. But it might be enough, or is very nearly so. I am interested in your response, Mr. Valary. Please," she said, gesturing with a lace-covered hand.

Valary seemed curiously reticent, now that he had been invited, but Kent put this down to mere anticipation. The man had spent so much of his life waiting for a moment like this, and now that it had come it would take on that unreal quality that Kent had felt when he was knighted. One felt no need to rush; time seemed to slow down in fact. For a second he wondered if they would be disappointed.

The two of them bent over the papers spread on the desk. "This is a copy only," Valary said, speaking to himself.

"That is true, Mr. Valary, but this young man Littel is possessed of the most remarkable memory. Nearly infallible, as far as I can tell."

Valary reached out and so very gently pressed down a corner of one page, his eyes darting back and forth as though he tried to take it all in at once.

Kent, too, stared at the text: a column of unfamiliar characters, what he took to be a transcription into the common script, and then a translation, though incomplete.

Valary let out a long sigh, as though he had been holding his breath. He glanced at Kent, excitement lighting up his face. "This is exactly what I tried to explain to you that night, Kent. Littel is a genius. Look at this! Assuming he's correct, this would have taken anyone else decades. I can't imagine how he did it." He turned to the countess. "Did Palle and Wells find a key, or some samples of an intermediate language?"

"No, this is the work of Mr. Littel, assisted by Wells . . . and Stedman Galton, I regret to say."

Galton, Kent thought. His wife claimed he was no longer with the King's Man, and she had carried the note from the countess. Pray she was right.

"Look at this," Valary said, pointing. "It is almost an incantation. And this is a description of a ritual, I would say. And here a verse fragment. Farrelle's flames, is it whole or is it several fragments thrown together?"

"That is what I hoped you would tell me, Mr. Valary. My own feeling is that it is whole. The mind of a mage was not the mind of a normal man, I can tell you that, nor did their ritual and cant follow anything like logic."

Valary picked up a page and held it closer to the light. Kent could see him shaking his head. "Forty years I have searched for something like this. Look, here, a warding chant. I knew such things existed, but never did I think to hold one in my hand."

Kent looked at the sheet Valary was holding. It was hardly more than gibberish to him. "But what would happen if this were . . . performed by a person with talent? What would result?"

"There is more to it than that, Averil," the countess said softly. She had risen from her chair and stood warming herself by the fire, though she kept her back turned to them.

From where Kent stood, she could be the same woman he had known so long ago. The thick dark hair, though shorter now, and dyed he was sure. The slim form, not what had been thought ideal before the countess had swept Farr society before her.

"There are many elements required, and even this text is not complete enough, I suspect." She returned to her chair, and Kent tore his gaze away, looking back at the text. Valary had pulled out a chair and sat poring over the first page.

"Here, a reference to the serpent and the hunter," he said, as though Kent would understand the significance.

"Yes," the countess said. "The falcon Averil saw."

"Tristam's falcon?" Kent said.

"Yes," she said sadly. "His hunter. His champion in the struggle to come."

"It *was* a familiar, then?" He could just make out her shrug in the darkened room.

"Familiar? We don't know exactly, but probably all of the mages had one. Sometimes it was a wild cat or a wolf. Some believed the emerging mage created the hunter unknowingly. Others said it was a natural creature, transformed as the mage was transformed. But it is all speculation."

The countess was revealing more than she had in the past, which surprised Kent. He thought she had opened the door to some memories kept hidden, and now that it was open they floated out like old ghosts.

"Eldrich had a wolf. Massive, beautiful, supremely wild. It followed him— almost haunted him—appearing at the oddest times. It even came into his home, prowling the hallways at night, as though it searched for something— like a mother seeking her cubs."

Kent could hardly believe his ears. In all the years he had known her, she had barely said two words about Eldrich. He sometimes believed it was only gossip that connected her to the mage.

"What think you, Mr. Valary?" she said quietly.

Valary adjusted his spectacles, and sat back in his chair, tearing his gaze from the text with some difficulty. For a moment he sat staring blankly. "I suppose we shall never see the original," he said wistfully, "but even so, my first impression is that the document is authentic. Of course there have been many hoaxes, but I doubt this is one, if for no other reason than it is so very . . . odd." He removed his spectacles and rubbed his eyes with the back of his wrist. "I am surprised to find more than one language here—two main ones, it seems. Once one has Littel's work in hand, one can begin to see the way of it. How words might have evolved into our own ancient tongues.

"There were, to the best of my knowledge, nine books of lore, although I believe they were really compilations, each devoted to some study or art. One to herb lore, for instance. Some of these were books of history, and were constantly added to, I believe. Others were books of ritual, or incantation, or what have you—the arts. But these were the nine disciplines of the mages. And all of their knowledge fit into one of these. Each book had a name, and I have discovered four of them, or so I think, though little good it does us, for they tell us nothing. *Owl Songs,* I believe, was one, and the book of herb lore, I am almost certain, was called *Gildroth.* I have puzzled over that word for years: I should like to hear Mr. Littel's thoughts on it. *Gild* would seem to be an early form of 'gilt,' ancient Farr for gold. But then *ildroth* itself might be a root word. There is a village called Eldrith not far from Tremont Abbey, oddly enough, and I think there was once a wood of the same name there, though centuries ago, for there are references to it in old songs. Tremont, is clearly from tree mount, as I'm sure the hill was once called. And Eldrith may resemble Eldrich only by coincidence, one cannot be sure. *'Golden wood?'* The north road passed through both wood and the town of Eldrith, and perhaps the road took the same name in that area. It was commonly so. 'Golden way?' 'Golden wood?' 'Golden Road?' Do you see all the possibilities? One can spend the night tracing these words toward their sources: like grasping the very top branch of a giant tree, the roots lie somewhere deep in the earth.

"Eldrith has an interesting possibility—'elder,' which has 'eld' as its root. *Ellaern* was the name of a small, white-flowered tree. We call it 'elder' now or even 'elderberry,' though I am not convinced it is the same tree at all. The name 'Elorin' is from the same source."

"The Duchess of Morland's given name," Kent said, and Valary nodded.

"Do not assume these names are mere coincidence," the countess said softly. Kent glanced over, but she was invisible in the shadow now that he had come into the lamplight.

Valary nodded agreement. "Be that as it may, I believe the book of herb lore was called *Gildroth,* probably meaning 'the golden wood' or even 'the golden tree.' There is a reference in here to this book, and it is almost like an instruction: 'Get this part from the book of *Gildroth,*' though it is not quite so plainly said. Very few would even know the word, so I can't think it is a forgery.

"And then there is a verse fragment that begins," he leaned over and picked up one page, "'*Owl's song on whispered shores.*' One book, as I said, was called *Owl Songs.* There may be more such references, I would need to spend much time searching." He studied the page a few seconds longer, then picked up another. "And this section near the beginning, Lady Chilton. It is a warding, or so I think. Done almost as a preamble to the longer ritual." His brows pushed tight together, and he thrust out his lower lip. "I need much more time. . . ."

"Time is the one thing that we do not have, Mr. Valary. Let me tell you what I think, and then you may have until morning to examine the text." The countess shifted in her chair, turning almost sideways, one lace-covered hand cupping her knee. "Erasmus Flattery believed there had been a struggle among the final generation of mages. Those who followed Lucklow, and believed their time was past—though Erasmus did not know why—and those who worked against this decision, though to all appearances agreeing. I do not know what the mages found or did or perhaps foresaw that led to their decision, but whatever it was must have seemed truly terrifying. I knew Eldrich—oh, not as well as some think, but I knew him. One of the few things I learned from this brief association was that mages were not known for self-sacrifice. They were willful, self-centered, arrogant, selfish, and less concerned with the affairs of men than many think. Much of what is thought to have been done for the benefit of humankind was really secondary to the benefits gained by the mages—or perhaps even one mage.

"This text that we have, it was somehow hidden away, left to be found, when all the mages were gone. And that was no easy thing, for every effort was made to guard against this. They left Eldrich behind, who was trusted. But this text, Averil, Mr. Valary, I fear it is like an island, just over the horizon. One performs the ritual and the next island in the string will appear, and then the next. At the end could lie anything. Even that which caused the mages to bring an end to their own kind."

The Duke of Blackwater visited his wife in her chamber every night, though their times of intimacy had become few due to the duchess' health, but the duke still yearned for her company and required her counsel. This evening he arrived late from his appointment and found her sleeping, the lamp turned low, and her pale, thin face ghostlike. For a moment he stood staring down at her, almost overcome by melancholy. Her face had become so thin that he could see the structure beneath, and though this was thought beautiful by many, to him it was a sign that she wasted away. He remembered how different she had been when they first met, gangly children then. Full of life and vital in the extreme. How unfair it was that she had fallen victim to this wasting condition that sapped her vital energies and caused her such pain at times.

Aging is like slow robbery, he thought. *All of the skills we spend so many years acquiring and perfecting are stolen from us one by one.*

The duchess stirred then, and he gently lowered himself to sit on the bed's edge. Her eyes opened, and for the briefest second he saw confusion and pain, and then a smile appeared—real for the most part, but also partly feigned, he knew: it was the mask she hid behind.

"Edward," she said, reaching out and finding his hand. He brushed his fingers across her cheek then bent and kissed her. In the warm lamplight her color appeared almost healthy, and he felt a stirring.

"And how is my love today?" he asked.

Gently, she put her hand on his heart. "My love is never the problem," she said, and smiled again. "In truth I have had an unusual day." She stopped then, examining his face as though she did not need to inquire about his own well-being, but only look for a moment. "Your meeting with the King has left you troubled, Edward."

He looked down at her hand, resting so lightly in his. "Yes," he said quietly. "Yes. I remember His Majesty, thirty years ago, when he was thought miraculously well preserved. . . . He had an impressive mind, which one cannot always say of kings. What I saw tonight . . . His majesty's once fine mind has been overwhelmed by a terrible dementia." He looked up and met his wife's eye. "It was like looking into our futures—your future, my future. Dementia and helplessness. He was once the most powerful man in the known world. . . ." He fell silent. "It doesn't matter. We suffer the same end as our gardener."

"Yes," the duchess whispered, taking his hand in both of hers, "but before that comes we are fortunate to live lives our gardener can only dream of. It is all the compensation that we have, but it is more than enough, I think. We should never complain."

He brushed hair back from her forehead. "You have made a religion of never complaining. I am not nearly so skilled in this area."

"I have never known you to complain . . . unless it is about this one thing. We will grow old and pass through. I like it no more than you." She reached back and plumped her pillow so that it lifted her head. "His Majesty is no longer competent: Palle is not lying?"

The duke shook his head. "The King is mad, there is no doubt. He did not even recognize me, though of course we have not met in many years. He called me Kent, of all things, and kept raging about his portrait. 'Where was his portrait? How did I expect him to go on without it?'" He looked over at the book lying on the night table. "The audience was very short, but I am satisfied, at least, that it is not a palace coup, though the result is much the same."

They were silent for a moment; almost awkward.

"Will you stay with me this night?" the duchess asked. "I wish to keep you near."

She sensed that he might be the one needing comforting, he realized. "Yes, give me but a moment."

When he returned the duchess seemed to be asleep, and he almost retreated, but then she opened her eyes, and stretched like a child, beckoning him. He slipped into the bed beside her and was shocked at how cold she was, here beneath this weight of down quilts. She wriggled close and nestled her head on his shoulder, so that her mouth was close to his ear.

"We must send someone north to County Coombs," she whispered so quietly he almost did not hear. "Two innocent young men have disappeared there—murdered, I fear. It is possible that Palle thought they were Jaimas and a young man named Littel, though our son and his friend are safe."

She felt him stiffen, and soothed him. "Shh. Jaimas is safe. Do not be concerned."

"How do you know this? Palle would never do anything so mad."

"Madness awaits us all, some sooner than others. Palle's madness is caused by a belief that he is smarter than all others. This friend of Jaimas' escaped from Palle with something the King's Man valued extremely."

"How did Jaimas get involved in this?"

"I am not certain, though I suspect Alissa may have some part in it."

"Alissa!"

"Shh. Yes. But I will deal with it. I forbid you to put servants to watch her again." She shook her head. "I absolutely forbid it!"

He did not argue. There was no point when she used that tone. He tried now to hide his growing rage. If what she said was true, Palle did not realize what an enemy he had made. *He tried to kill Jaimas!* No, he would not become angry until he knew more. He would send someone to Coombs in the morning.

"How did you learn this?"

"Galton has come over, as I told you he would."

He lay still for a few seconds, considering this news. His duchess was seldom wrong when it came to people. "You astonish me, my love," he whispered, but her breathing had become regular, and she slept.

Kent listened to the lonely sound of his team making its way through the dark city. It was now very late, and a fog crept in off the bay, compounding the effects of the smoke. Kent was now sure that he simply could not be followed, the pall was so dense that one could not see beyond the horses, who plodded on, gingerly, into the obscurity. Sounds seemed to come from all directions at once, and Kent was certain the only way he could be followed would be by someone holding on to the back of his carriage, and he had checked for that.

He had left Valary alone in the countess' library, looking over the ancient text, and gone off to keep his appointment with Massenet, though it was now so late he was sure the count would be gone. Even so, he thought it best to go. His conversation with the countess made him realize how desperately they needed to know the extent of the Entonne knowledge. He had been lulled by the fragment that Massenet had shown him, but there really was no reason to believe the Entonne did not want to recover the arts of the mages. Especially if they thought Palle and his followers were close to doing so. And there was Bertillon. . . . The countess and Valary had been more than a little shocked when he told them of the musician's trick with the flaming rose. It now seemed possible that Massenet had someone with talent, and—more than that—he had some knowledge of the mages' arts. These damn smooth Entonne! Bertillon had been so convincing when he denied possessing any real talent.

They needed to find out the extent of the Entonne knowledge. And they desperately needed to discover the origin of Palle's text. Could there be more? He prayed there was not.

Lights were still burning at the home of the Earl of Milford's, and carriages lined the curb, the drivers huddled round a charcoal brazier, shoulders hunched against the cold and damp, talking quietly.

He almost sent Hawkins over to ask if the ambassador was still inside, but decided against it. Drivers gossiped, and no one had more carriages and drivers than Palle. Better simply to go in.

The earl had come into his title and fortune early, and was now only in his late twenties. His home was the haunt of the more willful sons and daughters of some of Avonel's leading families. But Kent knew the earl was also a devotee of the theater and the opera, as well as a patron of the arts, so he could not fault the man entirely. The painter also remembered that he had spent many an evening at just such houses when he was younger, and did not seem to have suffered greatly for it.

Despite the hour, the house was nowhere near empty, laughter and conversation coming from every room. The aura of sensuality that he had sensed at the opera was even more tangible here. He sometimes wondered if humankind had another sense for these things.

He had not gone far into the mansion before realizing that, at this hour, he was by far the oldest person present, by quite some number of years, too. He hoped he could find Massenet and escape quickly, for he felt rather removed from these beautiful young women, and the dandies scattered among them. It was not the kind of gathering where one expected to find Averil Kent—and this concerned him.

The sound of a pianum drew him, and as he expected, he found Bertillon, surrounded by admirers, most of them women. Kent leaned against the door frame, and felt a wash of envy. He was so tired he could hardly think of anything but rest, and here was this young musician who, no doubt, had not even begun the exertions of his evening.

"Sir Averil Kent?"

He turned to find a young woman, her hands clasped together, her manner prim and timid, though her dress contradicted her manner most strongly.

"Yes?"

"I can't begin to tell you how much your paintings mean to me," she said, coloring a little. Her accent was Entonne. "I have dreams of walking in your garden—vivid dreams. I hope you will paint your garden again."

Kent smiled, and bowed his head. "You are very kind. I think you are right—I have not given my garden the attention it deserves. One or two paintings only, though I have perhaps a dozen studies. Wherever did you see my garden paintings?"

"Count Massenet owns one, and the other is here, in a room upstairs."

"Ah," Kent said, "I didn't realize the count possessed one of my paintings."

"He has three, I believe. Three in Avonel. His collection at home is said to be vast, so he could easily have more. But three paintings by Sir Averil Kent is treasure enough for one man." She paused, a bit awkward yet. Kent would soon have put her at ease—he was used to admirers, after all—but he hardly had the time. It was late, and he needed to find Massenet, if the man was still here.

"Did you enjoy our performance this evening? You were at the opera?" she said.

"I was, indeed, and I enjoyed it enormously. You are a singer? I confess I do not recognize you."

She gave a small laugh. "I was the heartbroken lover, but without the makeup I am very plain."

"That is not true at all," Kent said. "You are far more beautiful when playing only yourself."

She curtsied. "Be careful, sir, I admire you extremely, and even the slightest hint of compliment may raise my hopes."

Kent laughed. He realized Bertillon was watching, and the musician smiled, and inclined his head toward the singer, his meaning plain.

"May I accompany you, Sir Averil? I shall introduce you to anyone you might want to meet."

Kent held out his arm. "I cannot be properly introduced by someone who keeps her name from me."

"Oh. I am Tenil Leconte; and please call me Tenil."

"Well, Tenil, if I were blessed with grandchildren, I would want them all to be just like you. Even the boys."

They made their way through the mansion, Tenil making only occasional introductions. This was the younger set, but Kent had watched many of them grow up. He was always shocked at how adult these children had become in so short a span of time. They seemed to remain children for years, and then, in a matter of weeks, transformed into adults—young adults, certainly, but unquestionably no longer children.

The young woman who held his arm seemed to be quite pleased to be in his company, as though she was escorted by a new beau of whom she was particularly enamored. He had realized years before that there were young women in society who truly loved art, and held great admiration for those who produced it. Kent had known this kind of admiration before, but he no longer allowed himself to believe that such a young woman actually felt something for him. If he had not been a famous painter, she would have thought him just another feeble old man. It was his art she was enthralled with, though she might not distinguish the "singer from the song," as the saying went.

It was common, though. Many artists, or singers for that matter, were not particularly admirable human beings, in Kent's view, but they still had their followers. It was a bit perverse, he had always thought.

Tenil smiled up at him. She was not tall, or fine featured, but her roundish face was still very beautiful with the most striking dark eyes, and a mouth and smile that he thought perfect. Her revealing gown tugged at his eye, like a line in a painting, leading one irresistibly into the composition.

They made their way up the stairs, Kent following, assuming that Bertillon's nod meant she would take him to Massenet. She stopped and opened a door a crack, peeking in, and then opened it quickly, drawing Kent in behind her. It was a small, dimly lit sitting room, which had obviously been recently used, for there were wine glasses and bottles on a table by a divan that had been pulled up before the fire.

Laughter could be heard, and Kent was sure it came from behind a second door.

Tenil smiled. "I will interrupt him, as he so wants to speak with you." She squeezed his arm and left him standing in the middle of the room. The laughter stopped abruptly as Tenil rapped on the door.

"*Yes*," came a man's voice.

"It is Tenil. The count's guest has arrived."

Rustling followed by a footfall. A moment, and then the door opened, and the count appeared; behind him Kent could see a bed, and unbound hair, both blond and dark, and ivory bare arms, and there a leg.

The count had obviously thrown on his breeches and shirt, and stopped now to pull his hose quickly over white feet. He waved toward the door and Tenil went into the room he had just left, clearly to be sure no one tried to leave, or listen.

"My dear friend," he said quietly. "Just let me bolt the door."

Massenet came back from the door and took a seat on the divan, pulling his shirt into order as he did so. Kent looked at the man sitting near to him, his usually perfectly groomed hair mussed, a light in his eyes—that unmistakable light. There was also a poor attempt to hide the smugness. Kent wondered why he had come.

"There was a terrible fuss in Merton, just a few days ago," the count began, speaking low, leaning close to the painter. "What in Farrelle's name was going on?"

Kent said nothing for a moment, staring into the man's dark eyes. "How much more of the Lucklow correspondence have you uncovered?" he countered.

The count did not answer immediately. He rose and picked up a wine bottle, tilting it to measure its contents, and then he poured some of the liquid into a glass, chosen at random. He looked up at Kent. "I have no clean glasses, I apologize. Shall I call for wine?"

Kent shook his head. "I have not come for wine."

Massenet returned to the divan, lost in thought. "You have lost confidence in my intentions, Sir Averil," he said at last, almost as though this hurt him.

"Perhaps I need to be reassured," Kent said. "Answers to my questions might restore my faith."

Massenet nodded. "The letters Varese spoke of at the Society, which I believe your Mr. Valary has seen. Other than the revelation that Varese unleashed that evening, they contain very little but for a bit of insight into his sexual interests. We discovered a few entries in a diary kept by the marchioness, and the fragment you saw. Nothing more. The letters, by the way, are authentic, just as Valary no doubt has told you. Boran really might have been inspired by a mage, though his reputation is safe. I will destroy the letters soon enough."

"But Bertillon. . . . He performed a rite at the house of the Duchess of Morland. Where did he learn that? And how much talent does he possess?"

The count sipped his wine. "We have a fragment, about nine pages from one of the so-called books of lore. I suspect it is from the same source as the text I assume Palle possesses. You have heard of Teller? It is our belief that he managed to hide a few fragments of what he learned. Concealed them here and there, so that the mages could not trace them all. Or perhaps they were hidden by one of the mages. We don't really know." He looked up at Kent. "Our fear, Kent, is that there might be one fragment that is a key—leads to the others. Or perhaps each has that potential, if it can be unraveled. You cannot imagine how . . . arcane the text is. We have hardly begun to understand."

Kent was sure this was not true. "Bertillon performed a rite, Count Massenet."

The count nodded. "Yes. It is not really a rite of the mages, so much as an artifact of the lesser arts, as they are called. Healing, and augury, things of that nature. It was known to those who opposed the mages. One does not need to be a mage or even possess much talent to perform it. We have another who can do it just as well. You might be able to master it yourself, Sir Averil." Massenet tasted his wine once more, grimaced, and dashed it in the fire. "Does that satisfy you? I am not seeking to bring the arts back, but if Palle manages to do so . . . well, we must be prepared to defend ourselves. But answer my question now—what did happen at Merton?"

"I will merely be confirming your knowledge, Count Massenet. Littel did escape. He is safe at the moment."

"You have him?"

"He is safe. I can say no more, for his own safety, which I'm sure you can understand."

"But did he have the text? Have you seen it?"

Kent hesitated and feared this would tell the count more than a lie. "He did not carry it with him, so we have only what he can remember, and his own thoughts on its purpose."

"But is it a key? Flames, Kent, should we be sitting here talking so calmly?"

"Even if it is a key, Palle still lacks someone with talent."

"Are you sure? Have you a source in Palle's group? That is how you got this Littel away?"

Kent shook his head. "Littel managed his own escape. How I wish I had someone close to the King's Man."

"But the King's Man is about to become King—or at least a third part of a King. When will the regency be announced?"

"As soon as tomorrow. Not later than a few days from now." Massenet certainly knew this; he was using an old trick. Ask questions to which he knew the answers, and if he heard lies, then his source could not be trusted.

"They might find someone," the count said, almost to himself.

"Talent, I am assured, is very rare. The one man we know to possess it is on the other side of the world."

"Doing what?" Massenet said quickly. "It is a constant fear of mine. Why did they send this Tristam Flattery so far away?"

"I am not sure," Kent admitted. "Not because he is a promising empiricist, that is certain. They have something in mind."

"And that is why we must be allies, Kent. Palle is not pursuing this out of curiosity. We both know this knowledge should never see the light of day. We must take this matter into our own hands, and end it as it should have been ended, long ago."

Kent felt a bitter smile tug at his mouth. "And when we have this mage lore in our hands, how will we destroy it? Will you merely trust that I will put what we have to the flame? You will keep nothing back in case we are not acting honorably?"

The count cast a look back at the sleeping chamber door. "You have struck to the heart of the matter, Sir Averil. That is why I chose you. Someone who would understand what must be done. Someone I hope I can form a bond of trust with. If we cannot do this, Kent. . . ." He did not need to finish. "You should go," he said.

Kent nodded.

Massenet rose and stopped as he began to turn back to his bedchamber. "Tenil is your great admirer, Sir Averil. I'm sure you could entice her to accompany you home tonight, but I will tell you, if it is not already obvious, that she is an agent of the Entonne government. Take her into your house with that in mind. You see, I will try to be as forthcoming as I am able." With that he bowed, and went back to the door.

Kent sat staring at the empty wine bottles, the smeared goblets, a hair ribbon and a lace garter. He thought of it as a still life. *The Seduction*, he would call it.

Tenil reappeared, the awkwardness she had shown upon their meeting having returned. "I see the Count has been a terrible host, Sir Averil. Is there anything at all that I might bring you? Wine? Something to eat?"

Kent tried to smile but found he was too exhausted. *Sleep,* he thought. *I must have sleep.* But it was not possible. He must return to see how Valary was progressing. *If only I were younger,* he thought, looking up at the beautiful woman before him.

"You seem very tired," she said suddenly.

"Yes," he said, "I suppose I am."

She crossed over to him. "Stay a while more, Sir Averil. I will make you comfortable here. You can close your eyes, and let your worries fall away."

Kent could hardly answer; there was nothing he wanted more than to close his eyes and sleep, even for half of the hour.

"Put your feet up and lie back," Tenil said.

He struggled within. It would be folly to stay here. He looked up at the lovely face of the singer, filled with apparent concern for him. "But you must wake me in an hour," he said quietly.

"I promise." She removed his boots and fetched a light coverlet, and then banked the coals in the fire herself and put more wood to burn. She removed his wig with the expertise of someone who worked in the theater, and then lifted his head, but instead of a cushion, she slipped under herself, lowering Kent's head gently to her lap.

"In one hour I will wake you. There is a clock on the mantelpiece." She began to stroke his face tenderly, running her fingers through his thinning hair. "Sleep. . . . Sleep," she breathed, and then very softly she began to sing. And to his surprise, Kent began to drift off into a languid dream, her song echoing among the trees of an exquisite garden.

He awoke to the moans of a woman in the grip of pleasure. The lamp had burned out, and the room was lit only by the fire, burning low. He could feel Tenil's breathing, responding to the sounds from the next chamber, where Massenet lay with his two lovers.

The fingers of her right hand had taken hold of his shirt and they curled, almost quivering, as she listened to the other woman's orgasm.

She realized then that Kent was waking and released her grip, pressing his shirt flat against his chest. Coyly, she leaned over to look down into his eyes. "Your hour is yet ten minutes off, Sir Averil," she whispered, trying to control her breathing now.

Kent found that he, too, was excited by the sounds. How many years had passed since he had held a woman in his arms while she shuddered in pleasure and cried out like that?

"The sounds of love," Tenil said, a small laugh escaping. "We are like animals there. We hear them, even in our sleep, and our hearts respond." She laughed again and brushed a lock of hair back from his forehead, then kissed his brow. "The count has intimated that you might, in the near future, come to live in Entonne, which would be an honor for my country, not to mention what it would mean to your admirers."

Kent sat up abruptly, almost pushing her away, as though he were overcome by claustrophobia. "No," he said, shocking her with his response. "I will not."

The night was still windless, and the fog and smoke so thick that Kent wondered if they would even be able to tell when the sun rose, which could not be more than three hours off. Hawkins took a convoluted course through the city, stopping here and there to see if anyone would appear out of the murk behind them. Finally he dropped Kent near the countess' home and in twenty feet dissolved into the murk.

The city seemed deserted at this hour, abandoned and dreamlike. Perspective and depth were erased by the fog and darkness, and the street lamps illuminated nothing but the fog itself, like small moons behind thin clouds. Kent waited a few moments in shadow, until he was certain he was alone, and then set out for the countess'. His hour's sleep, and the sweet kiss that Tenil had given him as he left, had rejuvenated Kent more than he would have expected. There was almost a bit of spring in his step. But this was tempered by what she had let slip. There could be only one reason for Massenet believing Kent would take up residence in Entonne. He trusted the man even less, now.

He found Valary still studying the text, an untouched cup of coffee, now cold, balanced on the table's edge. A second lamp had been provided and both were turned bright, illuminating the room, including the countess' empty chair.

Valary looked up as Kent came in, confusion written on his face. "Kent?" he said, as though they had not seen each other in thirty years.

"What have you found, Valary?" Kent asked, pulling a chair up beside the scholar.

"What an astonishing document, Kent!" he said, his voice filled with awe. "I count myself blessed to have lived to see it. And this man Littel. . . . I don't know how he did it! I really don't know."

"Yes, but what is it? What is its purpose?"

Valary's enthusiasm waned a little. "Well, that is not so easily answered. I am not entirely sure I agree with the countess, you see. I'm not even convinced it is of a piece, though it is difficult to tell. There are four stanzas of verse, and each is like an epigraph to a section, but if you put the verses together in the order in which they are found they don't really flow smoothly, or at least that is my impression. They seem to go much better like this.

> *"Owl's song on whispered shores*
> *Where the silvered sea dies*
> *Along the wake of a running moon,*
> *Moontide and magic rise.*
>
> *Beyond the sea without a shore*
> *The choral stars in silvered verse,*
> *The white bird rides the sailor's wind*
> *O'er spoken sea, and silent curse.*
>
> *The ancient tongue of sea worn words*
> *Sighs along the brittle shore*
> *And broken stones speak naught to man*
> *Of ancient sites, forbidden lore.*
>
> *The journey out through darkened lands*
> *A way beneath the vaulted hill*
> *The tidal years sound elder bells,*
> *Though falcons cry and thrushes trill."*

"Does that not sound right?" Valary said looking up to Kent and raising his eyebrows so they arched over his spectacles.

"It does seem to flow more easily, but Valary, you know far more of these matters than I."

The countess' odd voice seemed to echo out of a shadow, though she did not appear from behind the screen. "I think you are right, Mr. Valary, and it might help our understanding substantially."

"It would mean the warding remains where it is, at the beginning, but the section that describes the collection of herbs is now second rather than last; although this same section appears to tell how to collect moonlight and starlight. I don't really know what this reordering signifies precisely, but do you see, Kent? At least we will be reading it in its proper order." Valary picked up a page and shook his head. "But this. . . . It is in a different style, with unusual phrasing. Much of it remains untranslated. I would dearly love to speak to this young man Littel about it." Valary looked up at Kent, and then over at the screen. "But if it leads to other similar documents. . . . I can't say. It could be the work of years to understand such a thing, not hours."

Kent saw the countess' gloved hand take gentle hold of the top of the screen.

"Would you consent to stay here for a few days, Mr. Valary? I have sent for Mr. Littel, and you could work with him here, uninterrupted."

Kent felt a flash of jealousy.

"Yes." Valary began bobbing his head quickly. "Yes, indeed."

"But I must warn you. Do not become too enamored of this task. This text must be destroyed, sooner rather than later. I am reticent enough to have anyone see it, but we must know more of its purpose. And there is one copy that I can't yet see a way to destroy, even though it must be done."

ᑌ Twenty-One

Galton sat staring at Sir Benjamin Rawdon, who looked more distressed than he could remember, and that was saying quite a bit. Rawdon might be the most celebrated physician in Farrland, but he was a man beset by melancholia, a man easily overwhelmed by life's hardships. "A poor swimmer," Lady Galton would call him, an odd term in a land where few swam at all. But Rawdon was a man who could barely keep his head above the tides and currents of human affairs.

Galton had known the doctor for many years now, had consulted him, in fact, and knew there was more to Benjamin Rawdon. In the company of Lady Rawdon, or several other women Galton knew of, the doctor was transformed. A poor swimmer returned to solid ground. From nowhere, a delightful wit appeared, self-deprecating, yes, but informed by great insight. In the company of women, the Royal Physician's conversation was filled with intelligent observation, even wisdom. He smiled often and laughed in all the right places. He was not this distracted, awkward man Galton saw before him. The governor could not begin to imagine why, but Rawdon could never be comfortable in the company of men.

"I am distressed beyond measure, Stedman. I can't begin to tell you." Rawdon shook his regal head. "These men. . . . What on this round earth were they thinking?"

Galton shook his head as well. "Thinking? Clearly, they took no time for that. The son of the Duke of Blackwater. They might as well have murdered the heir to the Entonne throne. If the duke ever learns who did this. . . ." He did not need to finish. That very day his wife had gone to see the poor duchess. Galton was not sure it had been wise, but had kept his own counsel. He'd been wrong often enough these past months. In the morning Lady Galton would return, and he would learn how the duchess was faring. Her only son, and she would never bear another.

Rawdon looked up, and managed a wan smile. "Sir Roderick assures me that nothing like this will ever happen again. But this man Hawksmoor. . . . I tell you, Stedman, I have never liked him. People talk of Elsworth as though he were some sort of monster, but Hawksmoor. . . . I'm convinced he would throttle me if he thought it would please Roderick." His mouth twisted in disgust.

Galton looked up at Rawdon, wondering if this was genuine disillusionment. "I know what you mean. I feel much the same. Our good Roderick is a little blind in this, but Hawksmoor's utter devotion to him must seem such a useful quality at times."

Neither man spoke for a moment. A slow measured dripping of rain could be heard leaking from the gutter pipe.

"How go things with Wells?" Rawdon asked, obviously changing to a less disturbing subject.

Galton shrugged. "Not as quickly as we hoped, I fear. We need Mr. Littel more than Wells ever admitted."

"I am not surprised to hear it." Rawdon shifted in his chair.

"Do you ever have reservations, Benjamin?" Galton asked suddenly, almost certain that this was a safe question under the circumstances. "Does your conviction waver?"

Rawdon raised his dark eyebrows. "Yes. And more strongly now, after what has happened. I don't care who their fathers were, these were worthy young gentlemen with bright futures ahead of them. It simply cannot be allowed to happen again."

"I agree. I will not condone it twice. Noyes is not pleased either. He had to deal with the situation, and now lives in terror that the duke will learn of it. He will not put himself in that position again, and has said as much to Roderick."

"I have expressed my concerns as well. Roderick is not a monster, Stedman. It was a terrible mistake—one cannot justify it—but it will not happen again. I have Roderick's solemn word on that."

Galton stared at his companion. Not a very strong ally, he thought. Probably not strong enough.

ᕬ Twenty-Two

Kent awoke in a darkened room. He felt uncommonly warm and pushed the coverlets away, trying to remember where he was.

"Averil? Are you awake?" It was the expressionless voice of the countess, quite close by.

He realized that she held one of his hands, and Kent turned his head, looking into the utter darkness of the room.

"How do you feel, Averil?"

"What happened?" he asked.

"You collapsed. Fell hard to the floor. You must tell me how you feel. Is there pain?"

"Pain? No." He stretched his limbs, searching for anything untoward. He realized that the duchess' hand was quite warm in his. "I seem to be whole."

She squeezed his hand and then released it. He heard her move away and realized there was a high-back chair set near to him. "I want you to sit up now."

Kent lay for a second, feeling there was something strange or out of place in this situation, though he could not say what. He felt completely odd, as though something were missing. He pushed himself up, and drew a quick breath.

"Averil?"

Kent turned his focus inward. "I seem to be . . . I feel perfectly hale . . . I feel vital." He looked up at the shadow before him. "What has happened?"

"It will not last long—a week, perhaps two—and then you will pay a price for it, Averil, I'm sorry. But we cannot fail in this. I realize that, more than ever, now." She fell silent, then found his hand again in the dark. *"I'm sorry,"* she whispered, and Kent felt that she was apologizing for something more. For all the mistakes of their long lives.

He could not answer. They clung to each other in the dark, her warm, still-soft hands in his. He could not remember the last time they had touched. So long ago that the time would be measured in decades.

"Have you given me the seed, then?" Kent said, dreading the answer.

"No! No, I should never do that. I. . . ." She did not finish.

"Eldrich," Kent said, the word coming out unbidden, like the name of an illness. *She had learned this from Eldrich! It was necromancy. Magic!*

They sat, holding each other's hands tightly. He thought he felt a slight trembling, as though her shoulders shook, as though she wept in the darkness, and the overwhelming sadness flowed down her arms into her hands and his.

Kent's carriage wound slowly through the mist filled streets of early morning. How different this fog looked in the silver morning! How different the world looked.

It is the enchantment, he thought, though it hardly dimmed his spirits. Kent had left the countess' home, all his questions unasked. He still did not dare to presume too much; there had been so many years without word from her. He could not bear that again, even if the years remaining to him were few.

And the truth was that he probably did not need his questions answered: he likely understood only too well. And this understanding left him with a feeling of such profound emptiness—as though her secrecy were a betrayal.

Eldrich had passed at least some of his knowledge on to the countess. There could be no other explanation. Despite the task that Eldrich had been sworn to complete, he had given up some of what he knew. In Kent's mind there could be only one explanation, and he was sure it was not merely jealousy.

The duchess had been the most beautiful woman Kent had ever seen. Eldrich may have been very old, but Kent knew that age didn't prevent a man from feeling desire—and apparently even ancient mages had ways of increasing their strength. If it had been within Kent's power, would he allow that beauty to fade? It had been like art, it was so perfect. In his own life he had watched so many things fade and decay. He knew, absolutely, that he would give his life for the countess. What might Eldrich have given?

Did she take the seed? Did she still appear youthful to the eye? Could that impossible beauty still live? Kent could hardly bear the thought of it. As though some part of his youth still existed, though out of reach.

Of course, at the moment, he too felt youthful—or at least middle-aged. He could not remember feeling so strong, and so at peace—that feeling in the body that one experienced after good strenuous exercise. And his desire had come back as well, rising at the thought of the countess. It was his one great regret, that they had never been lovers. Part of him wanted to go back and storm the walls of her resistance.

Could she really still appear as he remembered? Was that possible? Or, like the King, was she aged and decayed beyond her years? Had the seed betrayed her, too?

The carriage stopped before his house and Kent jumped down to the ground, and then looked around, wondering if he had been seen. Better to lean on his cane a little, though he wanted to vault up the stairs two at a time.

Smithers met him at the door. Despite the hour he had obviously been awake.

"There is a young woman here for you, sir. I could hardly turn her away. She has been waiting some time."

Alissa, Kent thought, and then cautioned himself—best not to let her rub his feet today! "Did she tell you her name?"

"Miss Leconte, Sir Averil."

Kent stopped as he went to hand Smithers his walking stick. "She came alone?"

"Yes, sir. She's in the library, sir. I've just served her tea and biscuits."

"Thank you, Smithers."

Kent paused at the door to the library, wondering how he looked after his near sleepless night, but then decided he did not care, and opened the door. Tenil rose as he came in, and stood with her hands clasped together as she had before. For a few awkward seconds, neither of them spoke.

"You understand my involvement with Count Massenet?"

"You are his agent?" Kent said.

She nodded. "The count believes that, because I am young, you will be easily influenced by me."

"He is not always subtle," Kent said, feeling her beauty so strongly that it almost touched him. "What do you expect of me?"

"To be honest, I expect you to send me away. And I will remind the count that not everyone suffers from his own weakness."

Kent stood gazing at her, the short curls that fell about her exquisite neck. Something like defiance in her manner. He felt the habits of decades struggling with the energy of his returned youth. "But would you not like to see a painting of my garden before you go?"

She brightened, then hesitated before answering. "You are being too kind."

Kent laughed. He could not help it. The situation seemed so absurd. "Miss Leconte, I could never be too kind to you, try as I might, it would be less than you deserve. Come with me. This house is awash in my paintings and sketches. The attic is so filled with things I am trying to forget that I cannot bear to go up there."

Kent took the young woman on a tour of his paintings and if her interest was feigned Kent thought she was a better actress, even, than singer—and she was a beautiful singer.

In the seldom-used studio, they went through the canvases stacked against the walls and she made the most appreciative sound.

"But this is a child," Tenil said, surprised. "I did not think you were interested in the human figure?" Tenil was still dressed in the clothes she had worn at the Earl's, and as she bent over the canvases the beautiful curve of her breast was revealed to the very edge of her nipple.

"Oh, but I am. She was the daughter of an old friend. It is a study only. But she was playing in my garden and I could not resist. Do you like it?"

"Like it? It is beautiful. Look at her face. She is an angel."

On impulse he said, "If you will sit for me, Miss Leconte, I will gift it to you."

Tenil straightened up, her look very serious. "But it would be an honor to model for you. I could not take this. It is a treasure."

"But I insist," Kent said taking her hand. "You must have it."

Her seriousness did not waver. "Then I will sit for you, in return." She rose up on her toes and kissed him on both cheeks, as the Entonne did. Kent felt such a surge of desire, it was all he could do not to reach out and take her in his arms, even knowing she was an agent of Massenet. And then Kent remembered the countess and his suspicions there.

"I must change and wash," he said. "Would you mind? Shall I have Smithers prepare you something? Are you hungry?"

"No. May I not stay here?" She waved a hand at the paintings yet unseen. "I shall be very, very careful."

Kent nodded.

He ran up the stairs, only realizing it at the top. It had been some years since he had done that. He called for water and washed quickly, setting aside his wig, ignoring strange looks from Smithers.

What on earth was he doing? He should send this girl off immediately. She might be truly an admirer of Averil Kent, but that would not likely affect her loyalty to Massenet. Women simply did not betray the count.

There was so much for Kent to do. He needed to speak with the Duke of Blackwater. He must find out what Palle was about now. Did the King's Man still believe that Littel was dead? How long would that last?

Kent emerged from his bathing room still rubbing his face with a towel, and there stood Tenil, wearing only her undershift.

"Where shall I stand? Or would you prefer I lie down?"

This was not quite what the countess had in mind when she imbued him with such vitality, he was sure. Unable to stop himself, Kent crossed to her. Without a word he took her in his arms. He did not care if she found his body beautiful, or that she was an agent of the Entonne government. Nor did it matter that this was a false spring, brought about by enchantment. He did not care if her admiration was genuine or if she despised his art. He did not even care if his heart gave out. Nothing mattered.

Kent was not sure how this enchantment the countess had laid upon him worked. He felt strong and vital and young, but he was not sure what the effects of strain might be on his bone and muscle, so he stopped himself from doing some things that came to mind. Even so, he had not had such pleasure in many years.

Her skin was soft and yet it had that tautness that only the young possessed. And she responded to him as Kent had thought a woman never would again. He thought her cries of passion were the most beautiful music he had ever heard—more beautiful than her singing by far. Her caresses seemed to bring his flesh to life—as though she were possessed of magic herself.

Kent's own climax seemed to surge through him like some strange force, like the crashing of waves on the shore. And when it was over he lay gasping, awash in such pleasure. What in the world had the countess done to him?

"You put young men to shame," Tenil whispered, squirming beneath him. "To think that earlier this night I thought you would fall where you stood."

It was like a slap reminding Kent of what his true task was. "Yes. Look what you've done for me. I feel like you have brought back my youth."

She raised up her head, looking at the clock, and then let it fall back. "I shall have to sit for you some other time, I'm sorry to say. The opera company calls." She giggled. "Though I would rather lie for you, if I have my choice."

*   *   *

When Tenil had gone—slipping out the back, for whatever good that might do—Kent stood at the window looking down into the street. He had slept only part of an hour that night, had love with a woman a third his age, and he felt well. Oh, he was tired, but not devastatingly so. And best of all, his mind felt clear, alert. What was Massenet's reason for sending this woman to him? What else did the count want from him? And why was he so sure that Kent would one day move to Entonne? Kent shook his head. His mind might feel clear, but he could not see the count's design—not yet.

A knock sounded at the door, and at a call Smithers appeared. Kent could not tell if it was disapproval or astonishment on the man's face. "You are awake, sir."

"Yes," Kent said. "I must break my fast, Smithers, bathe, and then sleep for two hours—not a minute more."

Kent turned back to the view as the servant left. A neighbor woman was walking her small dog along the walk, and she bent with each step, leaning heavily on her cane. Kent felt great pity for her, aged and frail as she was—and then he remembered that only a few hours earlier he had looked much the same. He realized that age had always felt like an illness to him—he always expected to recover and feel as he had—as he should. And now it had actually happened. *A week, perhaps, two,* the countess had said. Already that seemed like a sentence—life in the prison of his failing body.

Kent closed his eyes. What would he not do to have his youth returned? It was easier to say no before he had felt as he did now. He had forgotten what youth was like.

The countess must be near in years to this woman he watched make her slow way along the street. Had she betrayed him and taken the seed? Taken it perhaps for years? But where in the world would she have found it? Where did the mages find it?

Kent felt suddenly a little small for having love with Tenil, for despite the obvious reasons, he was sure his feelings of betrayal had pushed him into it. Young. Did the countess feel like he did now? Had she been so for all these years? And if so, how did she deal with the desires of youth? It was a painful thought, and unworthy, but Kent could not help himself. Of all the women he had known, only the countess brought up such feelings.

⌒ Twenty-Three

At sunrise Tristam emerged from the shadow of the trees onto the shore of the calm bay. Beacham paced back and forth along the water's edge, occasionally glancing out to the *Swallow,* which stood dark and angular against the blossoming sunrise. Tristam came slowly down the quiet beach, feeling tired and empty and oddly sad after his night journey.

"Ah, Mr. Flattery. Quite a fright you've given me," the midshipman said, obviously relieved and resentful at the same time.

"I'm sorry, Jack, I should have woken you." He realized he did not know what lie to tell, not knowing how long he had been missed. "Have you been awake long?"

"Long enough," Beacham said curtly, and then his gaze fixed on something down the beach. "Is it Mr. Hobbes?"

A lone individual was making his way along the water's edge, limping awkwardly, his shirt flapping lazily in the breeze. Tristam could see that the man staggered.

Without another word the two set out, almost trotting they were so concerned, and as they came closer, their concern grew. Hobbes appeared to have been savagely beaten, his face bruised and stained with blood. He cupped one elbow as though the arm and shoulder was injured, and walked with such a terrible limp that he looked as though he might not manage another step. His clothing was torn and soiled, and smeared in places with crimson.

"Who did this to you?" Beacham asked as they reached the ship's master.

"No one, Mr. Beacham," Hobbes said, his voice sounding dry and broken, like a man overcome by grief. "I went searching for our Varuan friends, hoping to meet some that I knew, and got myself foolishly lost in the dark. I fell— thrice, I fear—once down a steep ravine. Just an old fool, lost in the dark. Nothing more."

Tristam might have believed this had he not developed this strange insight that plagued him. "Did you encounter the viscount on your travels?" he asked quietly.

Hobbes looked at him sharply, but then turned his eyes away. "No, no. Is he not with you?"

"He went off into the dark just after yourself," Beacham said, offering the master his shoulder for support.

"Well, no doubt he will turn up, unless he is foolish enough to go up into the city."

A boat put out from the *Swallow* just then, oars flashing out in unison, and pulling the craft forward toward the trio hobbling along the beach.

"We'll have you aboard in a moment," Beacham said.

"Yes," Hobbes replied, his tone a little distracted, "let's get that over with."

The scene that met them as they scrambled over the bulwarks was not what Tristam had been expecting. Every soul aboard ship stood on the deck. The silence that met their arrival was disturbing. Tristam thought immediately that this reception was meant for them, but then he realized that all the officers and guests stood upon the quarterdeck, and the Jacks had gathered below in the waist—split into two groups that kept a distance from each other. Into the ten-foot gap between the Jacks and the quarter deck the men recently returned from their night on the island stopped, looking about in bewilderment. Beacham gave Tristam a gentle nudge toward the quarterdeck, and it was then that Tristam realized what was in the wind.

As he came to the top of the stairs, Osier unobtrusively put a blade in his hand. Stern looked at the ship's master for the briefest second, and then turned back to the gathered men on the deck. The silence persisted.

A hand touched Tristam's shoulder, and he turned to find himself looking into the eyes of the duchess, who was more alarmed than he ever expected to see her. Her lips formed words, but she dared not utter a sound: *"Where is Julian?"*

Tristam shook his head and shrugged, hoping that his look was sympathetic. *Take a look at Hobbes,* Tristam thought, *that should answer your question.* Had the master managed to do the monster in? Highly unlikely, Tristam thought. Monsters were never so easily vanquished.

"Go on, Mr. Kreel," Stern said, nodding to the large forecastleman who stood half a pace before his mates.

Kreel turned his straw hat carefully in his hands, uncharacteristically subdued. "If we were to find a treasure or take an enemy ship, sir, there'd be prize money for all. That is all we're saying. If this flower is half as valuable as is said . . . well, it should not be kept from us who've taken risks equal to the officers and guests. We're poor sailors, Captain Stern. We only want what's fair." He looked up and met Tristam's eye, perhaps by accident. "That's all."

Stern did not answer but raised his eyebrows as though acknowledging what had been said. "There's nothing more?" he said, his voice so quiet that even Tristam found it menacing.

"Well, there is Garvey and Chilsey, sir. Their murderers have not met justice. Not by a long stretch. These heathens had best not get to believing they can kill His Majesty's seamen, sir, or none of us will be safe. They sacrificed men before we Farrlanders came, and made a feast of them, too. And now they are murdering our shipmates, and keeping this flower for their own, as well. We may not be a sloop of war, Captain, but I reckon we can still show them the error of their ways, and should do it, too, before they forget what they're being punished for."

"Is there anything else, *Captain Kreel*, or does that complete your list of demands?"

Kreel looked up sharply. "I've just been picked to speak by the drawing of lots, Captain Stern. I am no more the leader than. . . ." Words escaped him. "I'm just speaking up so we might avoid trouble, sir."

Stern nodded. "I will take everything you have said under consideration," Stern said, addressing the entire gathering. "I will tell you true, though, that there is no special prize being offered for anyone on this voyage. I doubt I shall even make my post for such a voyage, and if things continue as they are . . ." he did not need to explain what that meant, "I may retire from the sea altogether." He raised a hand. "Be about your duties, and I shall give your requests my full consideration. But let me say this. Don't think for a moment that a ship of mutineers can find a place to hide where the women are comely and a man's livelihood can be picked from the trees. The Admiralty knows that if such a thing were allowed to happen once. . . . Well, let me just say that the world is not so large as you might imagine."

Stern stood his ground, staring down his crew, and slowly, in twos and threes, they went back to their duties, nothing being said, but many a look exchanged.

Stern turned immediately to Osler. "Keep a presence on the deck. No change in the duty or shore-leave rosters. No idle hands, Mr. Osler." He half-turned toward the ship's master. "I will begin with Mr. Hobbes," he said curtly, and then disappeared below, the old seaman in his wake, trying to hide his limp.

Tristam stood for a moment, still holding the sword that Osler had given him, suddenly feeling the endless leagues of ocean that separated them from Farrland. A terrible row broke out below, obviously muffled, but not nearly enough. Stern was taking the ship's master to task for dereliction of duty. Poor Stern. This was not the moment when he could afford to have his officers falter.

"Where has he gone?" the duchess whispered to Tristam.

"Julian?" He shrugged. "He and Hobbes disappeared just at dusk."

"He left you alone?!" she said, and Tristam could not tell if she was angered or terribly disturbed by this.

"I was with Beacham."

She turned away as though to hide her reaction. "I must find him," she said suddenly.

"I am not sure that Stern will let you ashore given the circumstances."

"I do not depend upon Stern to approve my decisions," she said angrily. "Look how he has mismanaged things thus far."

Tristam shrugged. "Though it was likely Hobbes overhearing your conversation that set this all in motion."

She looked up reproachfully, as though hurt that Tristam did not support her as she obviously believed he should. Her surprise was so great that she didn't respond for a moment. "Young Varuan maidens will not get you through what is to come, Tristam," she said suddenly. "Do not for a second doubt that." And she spun away quickly and went down the hatch without looking at him again.

Osler came up then, and took the sword from his hand. He raised his eyebrows at Tristam, obviously having witnessed, if not overheard, the exchange with the duchess.

"The favorite of the King," Osler said quietly.

"It must have slipped my mind," Tristam answered, the sarcasm not very well masked.

"The captain will want to speak with you soon, I imagine. What in the world happened to Hobbes? Did the Varuans attack him?"

Tristam shook his head. "I don't know. He claims he got lost in the dark and fell several times, once down a ravine."

"Hobbes, lost?" Osler said, clearly not believing for a second. "The man has a binnacle in his head. Have you never heard of his feat when his ship foundered? Sailed the ship's boat across the Gray Ocean and made his landfall at the very mouth of Wickham Harbor in the fog! Don't tell me he was lost."

"I am only repeating the master's own words," Tristam said, and then noticed the captain's steward motioning to him. "My audience, I think."

Stern was in the great cabin with Llewellyn and the duchess. The captain had taken up a place before the open transom windows, and stood with his coat thrown back and his fist on his hip, as he did when his temper was in ascendance.

"Our voyage is in great peril," he said, keeping his voice low so that he would not be heard on deck, but hiding none of his anger. "Two men dead, and every man in the crew demanding 'prize money' for this seed we seek. This secret seed. I, for one, let no word of this matter escape," he said, the accusation clear. He paced quickly across the small open space, then stopped and looked at each of the others in turn. "Landsmen believe discipline on His Majesty's ships is insured by dire punishments, but this has never been the truth. No, it is fairness and concern for the men's well-being—mixed with a just use of the lash, to be sure—that keeps a ship safe from the crew's worst impulses." He pointed a long finger forward. "Those men before the mast, they have not a hope for anything in this world but poverty and the succor of drink. Not one in a thousand will make the rank of master. And here they see a chance for some small sum—though a fortune to their eyes. They might buy their way out of the service and have a bit of land and a cottage, for there is commonly no prize money to be had on a voyage of discovery. And they feel it more on this voyage where the dangers they have met are not of the natural kind. Lost Cities, and strange peoples, necromancy, and death at the hands of 'friendly' natives. They feel the injustice of this. They feel they're owed something for standing brave before such madness, for any Jack would face a thousand battles before they'd choose to face anything deemed unnatural. And now what am I to do?" He glared at the others, obviously believing they were the cause of his problems, mere landsmen who did not have the least understanding of the ways of the navy.

"I cannot, by order, admit the existence of this seed. And even if I did, I can't, on my own authority, give them prize money for its procurement. Yet, have they not stood their ground in the face of the one thing that they fear most? Is there not some justice in their demands?" He turned and stared out over the lagoon, lost in his dilemma.

"I could offer to reward the crew at the voyage's end," the duchess said quietly. "Ten gold crowns for each man, or even twenty, from my own purse. I'm sure the King would approve."

Stern turned and eyed the duchess for a second, then shook his head. "I did not mean to suggest such a course. It is against regulations. If we begin offering bribes to every crew that threatens mutiny.... Well, the Admiralty would never allow it. I will keep discipline in my crew, though it shall not be an easy task now."

The duchess almost took a step toward the officer. "But, Captain Stern, you said yourself that the Jacks deserve something for what they've done, and I think you were right. It has been a disturbing voyage for them in many ways, with all their superstitions.... A few crowns at the end of it all would seem like a small return. And it would come from me personally, not from the Admiralty. A token of my appreciation, not something that others would expect from their captain. We dare not endanger the voyage ... for the King's sake."

Stern had gone terribly quiet, his anger apparently past. "No. Leave the crew to me. I will deal with them without resorting to bribery. I did not for a moment mean to suggest it." He looked down at his hand, suddenly, turning it over and flexing the fingers as though doubting their sureness or strength.

The duchess looked as if she would speak but chose to say nothing.

"Doctor Llewellyn," Stern said, "will you see to Mr. Hobbes, and then relate the conclusions from your examination back to me?"

The doctor nodded, obviously glad to be released. Stern thought briefly, then drew himself up to his full height. "I shall send a party ashore to find Lord Elsworth. Duchess. Mr. Flattery." He went quietly out, all of his bluster gone.

Tristam waited for the duchess to speak, but when she did not: "You did not press your offer of gold with much conviction, Elorin," Tristam said.

She moved to the seat by the transom window and drew her knees up so that she turned sideways and stared out over the lagoon, her beautiful chin propped on one hand. "Give me credit for knowing something of the ways of men, Tristam. Just the crew's knowledge of the existence of *regis* spells the death of Stern's career. And I'm sure you're right—it was not Stern who let this knowledge slip. But to stoop to having a woman bribe his crew to avoid a mutiny. . . . Well, the captain has some pride left. This might be the last voyage of his ill-fated career, but he will not have it said that he required a woman to bribe his crew so that he could make port. Poor Stern could not bear that. I'm not sure what we will do, for the men certainly do feel they have a right to some part of this treasure we seek—though of course they have no idea what is really taking place."

"And what is taking place?" Tristam said. "Why *are* we really here?"

She turned away from her view, examining Tristam with that disinterested look that she had perfected. "Will you go ashore with me, Tristam, and search for Julian? Did he do this to Hobbes? Is that what you think?"

Tristam shrugged, not much willing to cooperate when his question was so obviously ignored.

"What led to the two of them going off? Did they go together or did Julian follow?"

Tristam hesitated, but the duchess' real distress touched him. "Hobbes looked as though he were entirely overwhelmed at the deaths of Garvey and the young midshipman, which makes his involvement in what befell them almost certain. Once we had borne the bodies down to the shore, he disappeared into the forest. I didn't see Julian go, but I think he followed."

The duchess nodded, closing her eyes for a moment. "Do you think Hobbes could have intended to take his own life? Was his despair that great?"

"It is possible, I suppose."

She nodded. "It probably began innocently enough. He would have gone to watch Hobbes make his end."

"*That is your idea of innocence!?*" Tristam blurted out, his offense at the very idea obvious.

The duchess turned on him. "For Julian, yes. But it might have gone wrong, somehow. We absolutely must find him." She put her fingers to the ridges above her eyes, and tears appeared, though she made no sound.

"I will go with you," Tristam said quickly.

"*Thank you,*" she managed and then turned her head away, propping her chin on her hand, and staring out across the azure lagoon as though she watched the white terns awash in the wind.

Stern did not protest as Tristam expected him to, but then perhaps the captain was beginning to have his own suspicions about the viscount and would rather the duchess dealt with her brother. The duchess and Tristam went ashore with a party of reliable men, all armed. Beacham and Tobias Shuk and three stout Jacks who earlier had stood apart from their mates during the confrontation with the captain.

They did not go thirty paces into the village before they saw the viscount, sitting on the trunk of a felled tree, staring down at the ground like a man in a state of catatonia. He did not hear the others approach, and when they were fifty paces off, the duchess raised her hand.

"Lord Elsworth is sometimes subject to fits of melancholia," she said, as though revealing this secret to her closest friends. "Perhaps it would be better if we did not all approach him. Tristam? Would you accompany me?"

The naturalist followed the duchess, who made every effort to move silently. When they were a few paces away, she stopped Tristam with a hand on his arm, and went forward alone.

"Julian?" she said pleasantly, keeping her voice quiet and calm. "Julian. It is Elorin." The viscount did not move or show any sign that he had heard.

Tristam found that he had become quite tense, and gripped his walking staff with both hands, as though he would be forced to go to the duchess' aid at any second. How unpredictable was this man?

The duchess crouched down three paces before her brother, and smiled at him. "Julian?" she said softly. "It's all right. It's me. I've come to take you home."

Tristam realized that he felt a certain revulsion at this sight. How could she do it? The man was a ghoul.

Lord Elsworth raised his head a fraction, but Tristam could not see if his eyes were opened or closed.

"Nothing is amiss, my dear. Come along and we will find you a bath and a meal. No harm was done, Julian. Come along, now."

The viscount took a sharp breath, and shuddered as though he had been touched by a ghost of a breeze. "I'm no longer his servant, Elorin," he said as though he referred to a tragedy beyond imagining.

"Julian! You promised never to speak of this again," she said sharply.

"But he would not take me," he went on in the same voice. "Neither of us, worthy of him."

"*Let this go, Julian,*" she said, an edge of desperation in her words.

He raised his hands, which had been clasped between his thighs, hidden by the sleeves of his shirt. One hand was red with blood, and the other held a dagger.

"My word! Julian? What have you done?" The duchess moved forward instinctively, but the viscount's head snapped up and she froze in place.

"Put it down, Julian, I beg you. Put it down, please."

"I am cast out," he said, a note of desperation entering his voice, and then he began to sob, sob with the abandon of a child whose heart had been broken.

The duchess moved forward then. Prying the dagger from his fingers, she cast it away and tried to pull his hands from his face. "Help me, Tristam, please."

The naturalist went to her assistance with no enthusiasm. He could hardly bear to witness this scene, let alone become involved.

The duchess had pulled the viscount's bloody hand free, and tried to open it, searching for a wound. Wiping at it with Tristam's handkerchief, she revealed a hideous gash. The viscount had tried to incise the radial artery. And around the wrist circled the bloody form of a snake, carved raggedly into the skin with the point of a knife.

The duchess led her brother through the trees to one of the bathing pools the islanders used, and here Tristam helped her undress and bathe him, while the others discreetly disappeared. The viscount was like a man who had slipped half into catatonia, hardly aware of what was done. He clasped his hands together obsessively, as though he held something of immense importance there.

With her own hands, the duchess rinsed her brother's soiled and bloody clothing and spread it over the bushes to dry. The viscount sat in the shade, his hands still clenched, the only sign that he recovered was a loosening of the knotted muscles. Tristam gathered some fruit and opened a drinking nut, but the viscount could not be induced to take any sustenance.

"Let him be for a while," the duchess said. "He will come around on his own." She looked toward the trees. "Do you think the others can see us?"

"I'm sure they have no desire to witness what is done here," Tristam said, immediately worried that his honesty would not be appreciated, but the duchess just nodded distractedly.

She began to open her blouse, and in a moment had slipped out of all her clothing and went to the edge of the pool, tying her hair into a knot as she went. Tristam could not take his eyes from her. He thought immediately that she had lost weight from worry, for she seemed tall and willowy. For the life of him he could not imagine why such a woman was worried about the effects of age. She was so perfectly beautiful.

She waded slowly into the water, brushing her fingers across the surface and then settled down with the water just lapping about her shoulders. She turned back to Tristam, a tiny bit of her worry washed away by the immersion in water. "I am not entirely sure why Palle sent you, Tristam," she said suddenly, as though she had just registered his question now. "He clearly did not want you to find the seed for the King, but what his own purpose was, I cannot guess. Llewellyn must know but, of course, will never say. Although everyone thinks that I convinced His Majesty to allow me to come on this voyage, it was the King that sent me."

She moved her hands just beneath the surface, as if treading water, though Tristam knew her feet touched the earth. "As you heard me say, 'we follow

Tristam's course now." You are their lodestone, Tristam. Palle has sent you to begin some process. For a time I thought that the things that happened to you in the Lost City were the events they hoped for. Your part might be done. But Llewellyn, in a fit of anger, said something that made me think this was not so." She took two steps toward him, looking around as though her words might be overheard. Tristam could see her body through the clear water. It distorted slightly in the light slanting into the pool, as though part of her existed in another world—a world that had its own physical laws.

Tristam waited for her to tell him what Llewellyn had said. He leaned forward in expectation.

The duchess examined her brother, who sat unmoving on the bank. Then she turned back to Tristam. "If I can take the seed back to the King, I will, but I can't help but feel that this is not the reason we are here. History, Tristam, is like the web of a spider. Those who are ensnared never see it until too late. The web is ever-expanding, ever more complex, growing as history grows. Without our realizing, some strand, some event from the past, reaches out and wraps about us. Struggle against it as we might, we cannot escape. Why we are chosen is a mystery, but there is nothing we can do but try desperately to see the pattern in which we have been caught.

"This is what I think has happened, Tristam. Some strand of events from the past has wafted out on the breeze of time, and has us in its grip. Our own lives and intentions have become unimportant. History has chosen us, and there is no hiding, no shirking. We must somehow attach this strand to the future, though where in the web we choose to do this may have the most unexpected repercussions." She came up to the edge of the pool and reached out with her dripping hands to take hold of Tristam.

"But what is at the center?" Tristam asked. "What is the spider?"

She shook her head. "We are only human, Tristam. How can we know that?" She took his hand and kissed it. "The mages did not regard time as we do. They lived long, and began enterprises to be executed over generations. They are gone, but who knows what enterprise they might have left behind, unfinished, waiting for others to complete."

"That is what you think? We are fulfilling some plan initiated by a mage?" Tristam did not like even the sound of this. Already he felt that he walked a preordained line, that free will had been denied him.

The duchess shrugged. "I think there is more to all of this than anyone realizes. Consider what happened in the Lost City. Did it not seem that those people had been waiting for you? Think of it: the Ruin of Farrow perched atop a temple in an unknown part of the world. And we found our way there. Found our way to that one island in a chain of a hundred thousand such islands. Sir Roderick Palle is the most ordinary of men with the most ordinary aspirations.

He had not the slightest idea that such a thing could occur, let me assure you. Llewellyn was staggered by what happened. Absolutely staggered. I saw it."

"But the mage who set this all in motion . . . what did he intend?" Tristam said, his voice subdued and small.

The duchess rose up out of the water and embraced him, encircling him with her soft arms, dripping water on his face, pressing her wet body close to him. "I don't know, Tristam. That is why we must stay close together. Support each other, at all costs. We are caught in a mystery and need all of our wits and strength."

Tristam closed his eyes and felt this woman close to him, her wet skin cooling his like a refreshing breeze, even as he warmed from desire. "But why . . . ?" he whispered. "Why in this round world did Julian cut his wrist in imitation of mine?"

"He wants to be like you. Free of his demons. Free."

No, Tristam realized, filled with sudden insight. *He believes he has lost his master and seeks to draw mine.*

Tristam had escaped the glade of the bathing pool, leaving the duchess with her brother. As he came out into the village, Tristam found Tobias Shuk standing over the almost-completed hull of a canoe. The carpenter bent over, examining the craftsmanship, but he would not lay his hands on the wood.

"You have found your priest-builders, I see," Tristam said.

Tobias looked up. "Their work, at least. Abandoned when they fled our revenge."

Tristam looked down at the great hollowed tree, carved without proper tools. "Are you well pleased with your noble islanders?" Tristam asked.

Tobias squatted down on his haunches, as Tristam had seen the islanders' do. "I would be better pleased if they had left our shipmates alive. But, yes, they are much as I hoped. Not perfect, of course, and they have the same misguided idea of inherited worth: aristocracy. But do you see how genuine are their concerns and lives? Not taken up with the polish and scroll work. Their time is spent on the important things—food and shelter and spirit and children, singing and dance and. . . ."

"And love," Tristam said.

"And love, yes." Tobias turned back to the canoe, rising to sight along one gunwale. "Though I shall not fault their morality until I have some proof that it brings them harm. So far, it makes me question our own practices." He moved to the bow to examine the head carved there, an elaborate, long-necked sea creature. "This flower that everyone speaks of . . . is it the herb that friend Llewellyn needs to affect his cure?"

Tristam was not sure what to answer. The carpenter turned his large, sincere eyes on Tristam. "There is an herb the Varuans value above all else, Mr. Shuk. Only the King and his high priests may possess it. Any other who so much as touches it is put to death. Garvey and Chilsey did not know this. Do not seek it for Llewellyn. I am not sure the doctor is being entirely honest with us when he speaks of his condition. Do not risk your life for Llewellyn, Mr. Shuk, he may be less of a friend than you suppose. Do you take my meaning, sir?"

Tobias nodded. He opened his mouth as though he would speak, but a call cut him short.

"Mr. Flattery!"

They turned to find Wallis crossing what was almost a common in the center of the village.

"I hope you bring us good news, Mr. Wallis," Tristam said, realizing that the look on the man's face did not indicate that his mission had met with great success.

"Well, there are no signs that the islanders want anything but peace, that is certain, but they can conceive of no way in which that peace can be achieved but for your captain to admit that his men were in the wrong." Wallis looked a bit distressed. "The King might find a way around this, but he remains entirely taken up with his ceremonies."

"But how long can they stay up in the forest, Wallis? Certainly they must come down eventually."

"They are patient in ways that we are not, Mr. Flattery, and what would seem hardship to Farrlanders is hardly inconvenience to them."

"Can no one see that both sides are wrong?" Tobias said, his voice filled with sadness. "Garvey and Chilsey should never have broken the tapu, and the Varuans should not have killed them so needlessly. But now what do we do? The crew are calling for revenge for their mates, and the Varuans are unable to admit that their laws are arbitrary, and should not have been so callously applied to guests who did not understand the consequences of their actions."

Wallis sat down in the shade of a palm. "What you say has some truth to it, Mr. Shuk," he conceded. Clearly he understood both sides too well to be able to see a solution. "Anua asks that you make yourself available this evening, Mr. Flattery. I am to make this request of Captain Stern if necessary."

"What does Anua want of me?" Tristam asked, his suspicions rising.

"She would not say, but I am certain she means you no harm. After all it would be easy to send a party down to fetch you off the beach right now, if she wanted to take you against your will. Do not be afraid. Anua is a woman greatly honored by her people. You will be under her protection. She also asks that the viscount accompany you."

"The *va'ere?*"

Wallis looked up at him, clearly uncomfortable. "Yes."

∽ Twenty-Four

Bertillon did not like mornings. The light pained his eyes, his mood was never anything but sour. People seemed bent on tormenting him, asking him foolish questions, bringing him things he did not want. It was only after two terrible hours that he began to feel more himself. Women with whom he had spent the night said he was transformed in the morning—the kind of man they would never have consented to spend the night with, had they but known. Fortunately the world seemed to take its proper form by the time the sun was a little above the bell towers, or Bertillon would likely have slept alone for the rest of his years.

The morning was not that far advanced, unfortunately, and the musician wasn't happy to have been summoned at such an hour. Of course, Massenet didn't need to sleep, or so it often seemed to Bertillon—and the count was almost twice his age!

"Bloody fog," Bertillon said as he looked out the window of his carriage. In truth, it was beginning to clear, but he ignored that. Better to vent his anger on the fog than the count.

The musician wondered what had led to the hasty summons. Although he made no attempt to hide his connection to the ambassador, Bertillon was careful to disguise the nature of that connection. It was, after all, one of the ambassador's duties to promote Entonne culture in Farrland, and it was well known that Count Massenet was a lover of music—especially beautiful young singers. So it was not at all unusual for Bertillon and Massenet to meet often. But to call Bertillon to his home early in the morning—that was not necessarily wise. The musician did not like it. He was not a member of the embassy staff—which meant he had no diplomatic protection. A charge of spying would likely mean his death, unless his Imperial Entonne Majesty could be convinced to pay a substantial sum into the coffers of the Farr government. Something Bertillon dearly hoped the aging monarch would do.

The carriage pulled up sharply before Massenet's residence—no apartment in the embassy for this ambassador, who liked to keep many of his activities from the prying eyes of even his own people.

Bertillon found the count sitting at a table, all the news and magazines of Avonel spread out before him, coffee steaming in a bowl.

"Ah, Charl! You can't imagine what I have learned this morning." No apology for dragging the musician out so early, or for compromising his safety. The usual Massenet. Whatever he had learned seemed to delight him more than a little.

"Well, if I can't imagine, you will have to tell me."

The count poured his guest coffee. "You saw Kent last night at the opera?"

"And gave him your message, yes." Bertillon settled back in his chair, sipping his coffee, hoping the world would soon undergo its daily transformation and become a reasonable place once again.

"And how did he seem to you?"

"Exhausted beyond measure. I am concerned about him, in fact."

"And what would you say if I told you that not long before sunrise, after being out the entire night, this same Averil Kent had passionate love with a woman a third his age? Not just passionate, but prolonged."

Bertillon stopped with the cup at his lip. "Kent? But . . . the most accomplished actor in the world could not have been so convincing. The man had no hint of color in his face. He trembled to raise his opera glass."

"Exactly so. When I saw him, I thought our alliance would be brief, for he must surely expire within weeks. I can't believe such a thing could be feigned."

"Nor can I. He even appeared to be making an effort to *hide* his infirmity rather than convince others of it." Bertillon set his cup back on the table. He realized he must look a bit stunned. "Is he taking the seed, or is his infirmity an act? And if it is an act, why?"

Massenet rose from his chair, crossing the room slowly. The sun penetrated the fog then, casting its pure light through the large windows. The count appeared to examine his shadow, as though to be sure it really was his own. "I can only think that he has been careful to hide his vigor from us. That, or he came so near to collapse that he began to take the seed. Though I don't know when, or how long it takes to have an effect."

"It is a difficult thing to give up, once begun," Bertillon said. "Youth is a difficult enough habit to break."

Massenet looked up as though he thought he were being criticized, but he saw Bertillon lost in thought. "It does make me wonder about the intentions of our ally," Massenet said quietly.

Bertillon nodded. "But what a temptation. . . . Could you resist it?"

Massenet looked down at the musician, squinting in the sunlight. "I must," he said, "for I was not born with talent. But Kent has been giving in to temptation lately. He might begin by telling himself it is only so that he might complete his task, but it will not end there, I think. Don't forget that he took a large diamond as the price for his loyalty. Temptation. He is cooperating with a foreign government."

Bertillon looked up at Massenet, wondering if his utter shock was apparent. "I am quite sure Averil Kent is an honorable gentleman. He truly believes that Palle's intentions are a threat to everyone. Otherwise you would never have caught him in your snare, which I'm sure you know."

Massenet raised a finger. "But he did not return the stone."

Bertillon paused, and then said quietly, "Well, it is of enormous value. Such a thing might prove useful one day. After all, Kent may be forced to fly if things do not go as we hope." Bertillon looked down at the papers spread across the table. It was utterly like Massenet to perform a seduction and then think less of the person who had fallen to his overture. Not that he ever let anyone know. Bertillon was certain that Massenet was never less than polite to any woman who had shared his bed—he might act as though it had never happened, but he was charming about it.

And now Kent was being viewed in the same way. The painter had been taken in by Massenet's cunning, and how could the count maintain his regard for someone like that? It occurred to Bertillon at that moment that Massenet might view him the same way. How would he ever know? As long as he went on being useful, the count would treat Bertillon like a colleague of great value. As he would Kent.

"If you were Averil Kent, where would you hide Mr. Littel?"

Bertillon looked down at his cup. "I told you that Noyes was dispatched to County Coombs with some haste. From all I can learn, there has been some commotion there. Are you sure Mr. Littel really did escape? Kent is not lying in this?"

Massenet paced to the window, folding his hands at his back. "I can think of no reason for him to lie."

"Unless we have not taken his measure at all. What if he desires this knowledge for himself? After all, you think he might be taking the seed."

Massenet nodded. He did not answer Bertillon for a long moment, and then spoke almost to himself, his voice sad. "Why did he take my diamond?"

Littel had been anxious most of the journey. Only when they entered Avonel's city limits did he begin to relax. Jaimy decided not to tell the scholar that this was the part of their journey that caused him the greatest concern. He pulled the curtain back an inch and looked out. Lamplighters were setting their globes aglow, and dusk came over the city like a gray bird settling onto her clutch of glowing eggs.

"Not far now," Littel said.

"So I assume," Jaimy answered, though they had not been told their destination. They were joining the countess in Avonel—nothing more.

Now that they neared his home Jaimy had begun to feel some guilt about his attraction to Angeline. He had done nothing wrong, of course, but there was a nagging thought that undermined this justification somewhat. Had the opportunity arisen, he wasn't utterly convinced that he would have kept his vow to Alissa. Even now he hoped that he might see Angeline again.

There had been less conversation during the journey than Jaimy had expected. Littel had been fretting silently, and Jaimy had been thinking about women. Now the scholar stretched and his face lit with a smile.

"Do you think Palle and Wells will try to perform these rituals?"

"Rituals? Was there more than one?"

"I'm assuming the text Wells worked on was a ritual. He would not speak of it, but the questions he posed, the odd word or line he asked my opinion of—they led me to believe it was a ritual."

"I can't imagine what they're planning," Jaimy said.

"The countess, she seemed to take these matters as seriously as Wells and his group."

"You don't take it seriously?"

Littel seemed to consider for a moment. "I didn't really worry too much about that, to begin with. It was the most fascinating linguistic challenge I had ever encountered. I had never even dreamed of finding such a thing! And here it was, unknown to other scholars. I am not one to worry overly about recognition, but I have suffered more than my share of abuse from the conservative element of my profession. But this text! It would make my name. No one would be able to criticize my theories after this." He paused, perhaps going over events in his mind. "I thought I should talk them out of their intention of keeping it secret. They were intelligent men after all. But then, even before I talked to you, or met the countess, I had begun to have doubts. It was the text itself. . . ." A look of frustration crossed his face. "I can't really explain, but the longer I worked on it the more powerful it seemed. As though it started out a work of fiction and then began to take on substance. I began to see the world described, hear the characters' voices." He shrugged. "I was very slow to realize that they would not let me walk away, knowing what I know. They treated me well enough, chiding me, offering me money. Hinting at even greater rewards. But it was not until they tried to murder us on the road—murder us in cold blood— that I realized they were not merely eccentrics, deluding themselves about the mages. These were powerful men willing to do whatever was necessary to keep this knowledge secret. Even going so far as to murder the son of one of the kingdom's most powerful men. I woke up then. They did not do that without reason." Littel turned and looked at Jaimy. "I have to thank you, Lord Jaimas, for getting me through this ordeal. I didn't thank you properly before, but I realize, now, what you did. I was no friend in trouble, but a complete stranger. Though I hope that has changed now." He smiled.

Jaimy tried to smile as well. "Changed utterly, Egar. We are more than friends. We are fellow fugitives. Did you not play at being highwaymen when you were a child? Well, our lot is far worse than that, and I can't see how it is going to change."

*   *   *

"Believe us dead?" Jaimy sat in his chair looking toward the countess, who not only stayed in shadow but appeared to wear a veil. "How in the world did they come to believe that?"

The flat tones of the countess revealed little emotion. "They murdered some innocent young men, I fear. I am not sure who they were. It is a terrible thing, but it means they have given up searching for you—at least for now. No doubt these poor young men will be missed, and then. . . ."

Jaimy looked over at Littel, who sat with his eyes pressed shut.

"Do not lose sight of the truth, either of you. These deaths were none of your doing. Palle and his followers bear full responsibility. Do not forget that."

"And Mr. Kent?" Jaimy asked.

"He is well. You might see him soon. But I stress, you must stay hidden. I am not even sure you should return to your home, Lord Jaimas, despite your desire to see your family and fiancée."

Jaimy considered her words, but did not protest. Was Angeline here, in this house?

"There is someone else whose acquaintance you shall want to make." She rose gracefully from her chair. "Come," she said, gesturing for the others to go ahead.

They went through a door into the next room, almost as dimly lit as the first, though there were two shaded lamps set on a table, and someone hunched over there, working. At the sound of the door he looked up, his spectacles crooked on his nose, a skein of loose hair projecting out from the side of his face. Jaimy thought he had seldom seen anyone who looked so comic, but then the man's eyes suddenly focused, and his look was so serious, so intelligent, that Jaimy's smile disappeared.

"Mr. Valary," the countess said, lingering in the shadowed doorway. "May I introduce Lord Jaimas Flattery, and Mr. Egar Littel. I think you are aware of each other?"

The man named Valary almost bounced from his chair. "I have looked forward to this moment more than you can imagine." He actually shook hands with Egar first, clearly not much impressed by the son of a duke. "I have admired your work for years, sir. And this. . . ." He turned and gestured grandly toward the papers spread over the table. "It is a work of genius, I can tell you, and I know something of these matters."

"Mr. Valary is our resident authority on mage lore," the countess said. She had taken a seat away from the light.

Valary bowed toward the countess. "I am but one of two," he said with great courtesy.

"I had hoped the two of you might make some sense of all this. We need only Kent and we shall have all the pieces we have gathered in one place."

The countess gave Littel and Valary leave to examine the text together, which only their good manners prevented them from doing. The two huddled over the table, and Jaimy took a chair opposite them, pushing it back so that he did not exclude the countess who sat across the room, listening to the conversation.

Valary explained his reordering of the text, surprising Littel. The younger man pored over the pages, considering.

"I take your point, Mr. Valary. It does make more sense, if 'sense' is a word we can use in describing this." He brushed a hand over the pages.

"Did the others, Wells and company, have this exact translation?" the countess asked. "You made no progress of which they are unaware?"

"No. I'm afraid I hid nothing from them. Wells and this man Llewellyn were often at my side, and by the time I had decided to escape them, I had completed almost everything you see here."

"How capable is Wells, do you think?" Jaimy asked.

Littel stood for a moment considering. "Capable enough. At the risk of sounding vain, he learned much from me. But he is not intuitive. 'Plodding' is the word I would choose to describe him, but he will eventually get the job done. Of course, we do not know the length of the text he held back. It could be quite short. It would make sense that Wells kept the simplest sections to tackle alone." Littel considered a second. "My contribution to their endeavor was in the translation of the sections that were meant to be spoken—by far the most difficult parts for they were in a much older language. Wells and Llewellyn were not of one mind on the usefulness of this. Oh, certainly they wanted to know what was being said, but Dr. Llewellyn believed it was not strictly necessary to the performance of the ritual, for it was meant to be performed in that language, if you see what I mean. And he seemed quite certain that he knew the purpose of the ritual, though he never elaborated around me. But the sections in what they called the 'mage language'; I gave them those, I'm afraid."

Valary stood, looking around at the others. "If I may explain a bit more. . . . The text appears to be broken into a ritualistic chant—what is said by the person performing it—and description of physical aspects—the parts of the ritual that must be performed—and these are in vastly different languages, or so it appears." He looked over at the young scholar who nodded distractedly. "One language is not so different from our ancient tongues—once one sees some of it translated, it begins to make sense. Fortunately Mr. Littel is possessed of extraordinary recall, but normal men, like Wells and myself, must spend hours sifting through old books and manuscripts searching for words that might be descendants of the words in this text. Some have no descendants, so we must fill in around them and hope that, eventually, their meaning will become clear—difficult when a word is found only once or twice in the entire text. In a way it would be easier if we had more. If we had the piece Wells is working on, or some other text, it would pose more problems, but provide solutions to others."

Littel was nodding his head in agreement. "Though I wish it were true that I had no need of references. Unfortunately I'm almost as dependent upon them as the next scholar. There are any number of words here that I have not yet deciphered." He looked down at the text, a bit unsettled perhaps. "It is the greatest mystery," he said quietly. "The greatest mystery."

Kent had slept two hours that morning and arisen with a smile on his face, and no sense of exhaustion or nagging pain, as was usual. Two more hours were given over to a sketch of the King, while the memory was fresh, and then the artist had taken himself off to his club, hoping to find some of his compatriots and perhaps learn something about what went on in Avonel.

He took his usual table by the window and watched gentleman stream in. Talk, it seemed, centered on the just-declared Regency Council, and the state of the King's health—a subject of constant speculation.

The artist ate alone, trying to graciously deflect invitations from several tables. There were only certain individuals with whom he wished to speak. A grand coach arrived at the doors below, reminding Kent of his meeting here with Massenet. And this brought up thoughts of Tenil, which caused a strange sense of physical pleasure and euphoria to tide through his body. It was an effort to hide his vitality and sense of well being.

Although he half-expected Massenet to emerge, to Kent's surprise Sir Roderick Palle stepped down from the carriage, and only a moment later a servant approached his table.

"Sir Roderick is asking if he might join you, Sir Averil."

Kent tried to show no surprise. "Of course. It would be my pleasure."

Kent rose and made a leg to the new regent, and Palle waved him to his seat. There was a brief silence in the room as the gathered gentlemen witnessed the arrival of their new ruler—one of three, at least—and then the hum of conversation began again. Recent change of rank aside, Palle was not a new face here.

"You look well, Sir Averil," the King's Man offered. "You are one of the few people I know who appear to be getting younger. Massenet is another. But then I am told his youth is a gift from enchanting young singers."

Any hope that Kent had harbored of this being a chance meeting was dispelled.

A servant asked Roderick's pleasure, and the King's Man turned back to the painter. "I think it is time for us to speak candidly, Kent. If I may borrow an image from the natural world, for some time we have both been sitting like spiders at the center of our respective webs, our fingers on the strands, alert to every vibration. And we are not alone in this endeavor—our friend, the charming Count Massenet, has been similarly engaged." Wine arrived and the King's Man took a moment to taste it and have glasses poured for them both. "The

King's health," Palle said, raising his glass, and Kent joined him, dearly needing something to moisten his suddenly dry mouth.

Palle smoothed the tablecloth before him, not raising his eyes. "Within the palace walls, Mr. Kent, you have several admirers, which makes charging you with treason more than a little difficult. But not, I will tell you, entirely impossible." He looked up, meeting Kent's eyes, and it was all Kent could do not to look away. "It isn't a course of action I wish to take, of course. You are a national treasure, Sir Averil, and I am well aware of it. You are also acting from a misguided sense of honor. I despair to think that you trust my intentions less than those of Massenet." He looked down again, shaking his head sadly.

Kent glanced out the window, looking for the palace guards that would take him away. He felt his palms begin to sweat. *Treason.* They could behead a man for treason.

"Let me make one last effort, Sir Averil, and I do hope you will give what I say your most serious consideration. My loyalty is to Farrland, and to the royal court. My endeavors have no purpose but to protect those interests. Although I hardly expect to be believed when I say this; I am willing to give my life for my principles.

"I am not a terribly appealing man, I realize. Women have never found me fair. My conversation is not spiced with wit, and I was not born with a surfeit of personal charm. I am well aware that I cannot appreciate art as it should be appreciated. But I serve, Mr. Kent. I serve the interests of my nation. And in this it matters little what people think of me. Men like Massenet are able to turn others to their purpose by the sheer force of their personality. But Massenet is not to be trusted. I'm sure you are aware of the truth behind Lord Kastler's suicide? Our charming Entonne does not lay awake nights, suffering for his part in this tragedy, I can assure you."

Palle turned and stared out the window for a moment. He was like a man performing a task that he found terribly distressing. A bearer of the worst news. Then he turned back to Kent, looking suddenly tired. "I look at you, Sir Averil, a man suddenly restored to strength. No. Make no explanation. I have seen this before. I also know where it leads if one does not posses certain qualities and knowledge . . . and what happens when the physic is withheld. It is terrible, Kent. I should not like to see anyone suffer such a fate—especially one I esteem." The King's Man lifted his spoon unconsciously, staring at his reflection in its bowl, as though trying to see what it was that he lacked that he should be so mistrusted. "I shall make you an offer, Mr. Kent, in good faith. You may speak to Rawdon about it, or Wells, or any other who might reassure you of my sincerity." He looked up at Kent with his blank, unreadable stare. "I will offer you a place on our council, not the regency council, but the true cabinet. You shall have your say in all matters, and do not think that we are so united that you will never be heard. We are not of one mind, I will tell you. Whatever we learn in these matters that so concern you will be put to your judgment. I will even offer you the position of liaison with Massenet, so that he will be assured that we do not seek the domination of Entonne, which I tell you we do not. And finally, Kent, I will offer you your continued vitality, if that is within our power. You may live as you do now for some considerable span of years. Your art will be renewed. You might have all the young mistresses you desire, for you are much admired. Think of it, Sir Averil, double your span of years, perhaps. Like being granted a second life." He sat, staring at the artist, gauging the effect of his words.

"But how do you know I will cooperate? I might say 'yes' only for my own purposes, and to avoid this undeserved charge of treason."

Palle nodded. "I will need assurances, Sir Averil, though your word will be chief among them. It can be done."

"You will excuse me for bringing it up, Sir Roderick, but if I do not control the physic, I control nothing. Once habituated, a man must have his physic at all costs." *Why am I discussing this?* Kent asked himself. *Because I must. If I refuse, I will be in the tower by nightfall.*

Palle looked down at the spoon, as though the face he saw reflected there was unfamiliar. "When there is no trust, these things are always difficult. Obviously we must give you the plants and let you cultivate them yourself."

"But I have no talent. Will I not suffer as the King suffers?"

The hesitation this time was long. Finally Palle spoke. "I cannot guarantee it, but we think there might be a way past this," he said softly, as though admitting his blackest deed.

Kent's next words came out as a whisper. "But can you make the plant bear?"

Palle nodded his head with that same air of sadness.

"Then why . . . ? Why did you send Tristam Flattery to Oceana?"

Palle looked up. "I can tell you nothing more, Sir Averil, until I have been assured of your cooperation."

Kent nodded. "Of course," he said softly. He shut his eyes for a moment. Palle was offering him a second life! He could feel the way he did now for how long? Fifty years? Sixty? And offering him a place in his cabal, a say in their decisions. It was beyond imagining.

"You hesitate, Mr. Kent. . . ."

"I am being asked to betray those to whom I have given my trust."

"And thereby saving them much misery, Sir Averil. I will give you my word that none will come to harm. At the worst a comfortable life in the country. Excuse me for pointing this out, but it is your association with our Entonne friend that has endangered them."

Was Palle bluffing? Did he have enough evidence? Did he even need it?

Kent decided it was time to let the King's Man know that he had taken precautions against this very eventuality.

"You should know, Sir Roderick, that the Entonne government has a root that extends right to the heart of the palace. I can cause enough scandal to bring down your regency, and have not done so only to protect some who are dear to me."

Palle nodded, not meeting Kent's gaze. "Becalmed beyond cannon range. Is that the situation?" He looked up, his gaze still mild, frighteningly so, Kent thought. "So you refuse my offer?"

Kent did not answer immediately, and then he glanced out over the men sitting in the room. Did they wonder what this conversation was about? He suspected they could not imagine. Who would control the knowledge of the mages; that is what they bargained here. And Kent was being offered a part in that decision.

"Do you mind if I speak with Wells and Rawdon, and perhaps Galton?"

Palle made a tiny motion of his head, as though granting permission. "But quickly, Sir Averil. I find my faith in others is eroding as I grow older. Delay will make me suspicious, and I despair of losing my faith in mankind altogether."

"May I not be the cause of that," Kent said.

Palle raised his glass for a second time. "Long life," he said, and Kent raised his glass as well. He could not help himself.

It was late afternoon. The fog had retreated out to sea and gathered on the horizon where it swirled slowly like cream poured into a glass of coffee. Tongues of gray lapped at the sky and the almost calm sea. A few ships hovered on the edge of the fog, their sails barely drawing, their wake invisible at a distance.

Kent had intended to throw off the men who followed him and make his way to the home of the countess, but instead instructed his driver to go out to the headland that overlooked the sea at the harbor mouth. He sat in his carriage as it jogged along, gripping his cane as though it were his only hold on sanity.

The thought of his night with Tenil seemed so present, as though her body had left an imprint on his. He could smell her perfume. Imagining her voice caused him to catch his breath. He was being offered this. He could have his life back! His true life. The life he had been deprived of by this disease called age.

All the way out to the park Kent remained in terrible turmoil. What a temptation he was being offered. Had the countess kept her youth? Was it possible that they could still find a way to be together? It seemed as though fate were offering him a second chance. Would he not be a fool to refuse?

The carriage rolled to a halt and Kent stumbled down onto the grass, instructing his driver to wait. He walked out into the damp sea air. The sun had fallen to the horizon where it plunged into the moving mist, lighting it from within.

Was Palle speaking true to him? Were his intentions so honorable? His *intentions,* perhaps, but what of his actions? The King's Man had murdered two young gentlemen thinking they were Littel and Flattery. Murdered them rather than endanger his schemes.

Kent tried to square this with the man who had sat across from him in his club—a model of moderation and dedication to duty. *Overzealous underlings,* Kent told himself. Roderick would never have allowed these murders.

Kent came to the cliff top, and stopped, looking out over the still sea. The glowing fog bank stretched across the horizon, and the undersides of clouds turned to near-crimson. The sky to turquoise. It was a scene that seemed tranquil, yet was also powerful and strange. Kent was transfixed, memorizing every detail—the habit of a lifetime.

"How many more sunsets?" he said aloud. He had come to expect there would be few. Very soon a day would come when the sun would rise, though Averil Kent would not see it, nor any thereafter. "It is close," he whispered. "And I have it within my power to change that. To escape the grip of death, for a while, at least."

But he would betray the countess. A woman to whom he had been loyal his entire life, even when she had spurned him.

A gull cried, as though it had found itself soaring over a barren world.

But what had she been doing all these years? She had contacted Kent again after decades of silence and sent him on this quest to stop the recovery of the arts of the mages—and yet she practiced them herself! She let him age while she herself, he had begun to believe, remained young. She was letting him die, and preserving herself. Was her purpose even what she claimed?

A few days earlier Kent was sure he would give his life for the countess and her purpose. But now. . . .

"*She* betrayed *me,*" he said, looking up at the white bird floating overhead, "and chose another. And now betrays me again, letting me age and die, while she keeps the bloom of youth alive."

He sat down on a lichen-stained rock and watched the sunset burn to glory, and then fade to darkness. Stars appeared, giving faint light.

"It was not a betrayal," he whispered after a time. "She chose another. I had no promise from her, other than the one I hoped for, the one I imagined." He placed his elbows on his knees and felt his shoulders sag.

After an hour Kent rose and returned to his carriage, wondering to what lengths he would go to cheat death. One thing was certain; no matter what he did, he could not lie to himself about the decision—that *would* be a betrayal.

*   *   *

Jaimy sat quietly listening to the two men discuss the problems, trying to follow their speculation. The Flattery family were known for their gift with languages, so Jaimy did better than many might have, but he had not studied the ancient tongues, and they were most relevant here. His smattering of Old and Middle Farr was of little help. Whenever possible, he searched through books for the two scholars, seeking references they vaguely remembered, or perhaps merely hoped for. Littel had brought a trunk of books from the countess' library, but they were wishing for more before an hour was out.

Egar wrote out all that he could remember of the lines and words Wells had brought him from the secret text, and he and Valary pored over these.

"Did Wells bring them to you in this order, do you think?"

Littel nodded. "Yes, but I would not attach too much significance to that. You know how these things go: you work away at what you can, not necessarily from beginning to end."

Silence, as the two stared at the page. Jaimy rose to pour himself more coffee. A servant had stayed awake to provide for their needs. Taking up a sweet tart, Jaimy paced into the next room through the open door. Valary had come in here and slept for an hour earlier. The man looked so disheveled, clearly sleeping only when he could not go on, and paying no attention to the time of day or night. Jaimy was about to turn back to the other room, deciding he did not need to sleep yet, when he realized someone was sitting before the fire in one of the high-backed chairs.

"Lady Chilton?"

Angeline leaned out, her look serious. She put a finger to her lips. "I confess, I am listening, but did not want to disturb you in your work."

Jaimy took the other chair. "My work? I am hardly of any help at all," he confessed, and then laughed. "I pour the coffee."

She said nothing, looking down into the fire.

"How is it that I have not met you before?" Jaimy asked suddenly. "Do you never travel in Avonel society?"

She cocked her head to one side, exposing the lovely curve of her neck, causing her hair to move in the most delightful way. Jaimy wondered if everything this woman did appeared seductive.

"I have had enough of Avonel society, I fear. I prefer a quieter life."

"A scholar's life," Jaimy said. "Isn't it true that you understand what Littel and Valary are doing—far more than I can comprehend?"

She looked up at him, a bit surprised, but did not answer.

"Why do you hide your skill?"

"They are each more expert than I."

"But you have knowledge that they don't possess—isn't that so? From the countess. . . ."

She turned back to the fire. Jaimy could hardly take his eyes from her. She stood out in that somber room like a blossom in a shaft of sunlight. A single large emerald hung at her throat on a silver chain, complementing the green of her dress. He wished she would turn her eyes back to him—as dark as a night filled with soft rain.

"You mustn't do this," she said, looking at him, her eyes pleading. "It is futile even to begin. A young bride awaits you, and I will soon be gone." She rose suddenly, causing Jaimy to sit back in his chair, staring up at her. "It might be best if you returned to your family," she said and almost fled from the room.

Jaimy sat in confusion. "What in the world?" he said to himself. He wanted to go after her, though he was not sure where she had gone. Something stopped him. *She feels something for me,* he thought. *Flames!* Yet even that realization would not let him go in pursuit.

Sometime, late in the night, the countess reappeared. The gentlemen were suddenly aware that she sat in the corner.

"Have you learned anything new?"

"Only that 'buoh' is the root of 'book' and perhaps the name of the fifth book of lore," Valary said, clearly in his element.

Littel looked up from the text. "No, we have learned more than that. Mr. Valary has done much to make the purpose clear, and this has helped with my translation. This warding at the beginning, I now believe, has two purposes. *'The spoken flame burns before me, and at my back the cold fire seals the path.'* Mr. Valary has suggested that this somehow protects whoever performs the ritual as he advances forward—perhaps the advance is not actually physical. The word I have translated as 'path' is problematic. The original document was damaged in places, difficult to read. The word is, at best, a guess. It could also have been 'pattern' or even 'gathering,' for the ancient words were alike enough."

Valary was nodding as Littel talked. "And we are now almost certain that the text Mr. Wells was keeping to himself was part of this one. The more I study this, the more likely it seems that there was another section which fit on the end, for our text does not seem complete somehow—stops in mid-stride, as it were." Valary picked up a sheet of paper and gazed at it for a few seconds. "These are the lines and words Wells questioned Mr. Littel about, and we have little idea what they might mean. One phrase, though, does not bode well: *'the hidden world in all its terror.'*" He looked up at the countess. "I think we need to find this text Mr. Wells is so carefully hiding."

The countess nodded. "Yes. Do you think, Mr. Littel, that with the work you have done, Mr. Wells will manage to put the entire text together? Will he see the pattern you and Valary have discovered?"

The young man nodded grimly. "I would like to say that without me there is no hope of that, but I fear it is not so. They could have a translation sooner than we hope. It seems likely, now that I have thought about it, that Wells would keep the shortest and simplest section for himself. And we mustn't forget that Stedman Galton has come from Farrow. Wells spoke highly of the governor's skill."

The countess seemed to consider this. "'The way beneath the vaulted hill.' Is that not the line?" And then almost to herself. "How in the world did Erasmus know?"

ᓉ Twenty-Five

Tristam went ashore two hours before sunset, accompanied, against his will, by a somewhat recovered viscount. At Stern's insistence, they had dressed formally, and even though the sun was waning quickly, the clothes were unbearably hot.

A party of Varuans met them—six men dressed in their pareus with garlands of leaves about their heads. Special marks had been painted on their foreheads, and these looked disconcertingly like ghostly owls. They greeted Tristam with formality, ignored the viscount as though he were a lowly slave, and taking up positions around the naturalist, led off into the jungle.

They were soon on a track that twisted and crossed others so confusingly, that Tristam was certain he would never be able to find it again. The path led inevitably up, through a gap in the granite spires, crossed a falling stream, and then cut a diagonal line across the mountain's lower slopes. The Farrlanders removed their coats, waistcoats, and neck cloths, but even so they were soon dripping with sweat, and panting from exertion.

The Varuans stopped and waited silently while the two foreigners caught their breath, and then pushed on at exactly the same pace. Tristam had not expected the hiding place of the Varuans to be so far away. After an hour they came upon a tiny village, the inhabitants watching silently as the party passed through, and making Tristam feel like a condemned man on his last journey.

The track became less clear, but the Varuans never faltered or even stopped to consider which way it might go. Tristam, who believed himself skilled in the forest, could never hope to duplicate this feat.

A sudden downpour caught them, and the Varuans cut down massive leaves and gave one to each Farrlander as an umbrella, and the entire party continued, walking beneath their absurd parasols.

The sun was setting somewhere beyond the island's opposite shore when they came out into what, in Farrland, would have been called a hanging valley—a shallow valley slung between two shoulders of the mountain, and opening over a steep cliff. The valley looked out across the bay and lagoon, over the seemingly endless expanse of ocean, east to the distant horizon. A dark squall moved across the purple waters, like some hunting creature, Tristam thought.

He turned away from the view. A more beautiful setting was difficult to imagine. A stream wound through the glen, gathering momentum before it threw itself off the cliff. The trade wind picked up the spray from this cataract and spread it across the lip of the valley, so that leaves glistened and dripped as though in constant rain. The air was cooled by this continual drizzle, and Tristam stood breathing in the moist air, feeling the oddly cooled breeze slowly loosen his shirt from his sweating torso.

Tristam thought it was a beautiful fertile vale—a botanist's dream—but if the Varuans hid here, there were no signs. Only a single, somewhat dilapidated fale, half buried in the trees.

With a bow, the Varuans motioned Tristam forward, and then quickly faded back into the darkening forest.

The viscount gestured toward the fale, but waited to follow Tristam's lead. The dressing that encircled the viscount's wrist drew Tristam's eye, and he found himself hoping they were not alone in this place.

There is nothing to fear, he chided himself. At least so he had been told. Tristam started forward, not resolutely, but with a certain sense of inevitability. As though this place had long been awaiting him.

The quick twilight of the tropics came over the scene at that moment, like the shadow of a great wing, and as they came closer to the fale, a sudden light came to life within. It flickered desperately, like a butterfly set aflame, and then settled to a steady light, casting a shadow which moved slowly across the inner wall.

"Hel-lo," Tristam said quietly, and when this received no response he approached the nearly-open side of the house. It took a moment for his eyes to adjust, and then he realized that a ship's lantern hung from the ceiling, and before a rough plank table, a ragged man hunched, working at something in the shadow.

"Hello," Tristam tried again, and the man stopped, raising his head so that the light shone off his beard and hair, unkempt and streaked with gray.

"You're not Mr. Hobbes," the man croaked, his voice broken and distant, and deepened, Tristam immediately thought, by sorrow and regret. Tristam had heard that terrible voice before, in the palace arboretum. And this, too, was a Farr voice; here in the back country of this impossibly distant island.

"No. No, I'm not. I'm Tristam Flattery. And who might you be?" Tristam asked, the words sounding absurdly normal in this situation that was anything but normal.

This stopped the man for a second. "Some relation of Erasmus?" he said, then, nodding his head, went back to what he had been doing. "How did you find me?" the man asked, and Tristam realized that he struggled for each breath.

"The Varuans brought me up here . . . with the Viscount Elsworth. And who might you be, sir?"

The man paused to concentrate his efforts on grinding. "The Varuans . . . call me *Matea*."

Tristam thought he should know this word. "But you are Farr?"

"Was, long ago. I'm barely more than a ghost now." He waved a hand at a bench opposite him. "It is a long climb. Rest your legs. The descent is more difficult yet." Tristam stepped over the bench and sat down. The man continued his efforts, using a bone pestle, perhaps a rodent's femur, to crush some substance in a shell.

"Wallis has never mentioned you, sir," Tristam said. The man was either extremely eccentric or a little mad, Tristam could not decide which. Even across the wide table he could smell the man; sweat and smoke and mud and worse. His clothing was in ruin, and he was wrinkled and creased by what appeared to be several ages of men. This was unquestionably the man Tristam had seen the first night they had landed on Varua. A Farrlander . . . here, without the admiralty's knowledge.

"Wallis? Pankhurst's artist? The one they left here to die?" This produced what might have been a laugh—like a rasp being worked against a bone in the throat.

"You don't know him?"

"Nor does he me." He finished crushing whatever he had in the shell, and looked up at Tristam, his eyes squinting, head cocked to one side. The man was such a ruin Tristam could hardly bear to look at him.

"*Erasmus*," the castaway whispered, and shook his head in disbelief. He pushed himself up from the table and made his way to a door-sized opening in the back of the structure. Here Tristam could see him bend over to retrieve a kettle from a firepit built up with rocks. He shuffled back across the small room and found three rough pottery vessels which he brought with him to the table. He set himself down with obvious relief.

"If I may ask," Tristam began, thinking how absurd this politeness sounded here, "how have you come to be here?"

The man appeared to have fallen into a brief sleep, and jerked his head up when Tristam spoke.

"How? I was carried here by folly. Nothing more, nothing less. The folly of man." He turned away, and put his head in his hands for a moment. Quiet. Only the sounds of the small fire and the voices of insects and frogs. Water plunging over the cliff. Far off, the surf battered the reef without respite.

"There should be three for a tribunal," the man said softly, breaking the eerie quiet, "but then perhaps I shall be the third. I outrank both of you, that's certain." He looked up at Tristam, and then over at the viscount, who still stood, leaning against a post in the opening, the near-full moon rising behind him.

"Your shadow," the ragged man said, with some distaste. "Tried to murder Hobbes. . . ." He shook his head, and wiped his sleeve across his mouth. Sitting upright, he combed his fingers into his beard, as though aware suddenly of his appearance.

"You were on one of Gregory's voyages," Tristam said suddenly. "That is why you know Hobbes. That's how you got here."

The man looked at Tristam, then carefully picked up the shell he had been using as a mortar. With a tremulous hand he began shaking the powder, equally, into each vessel. It was a laborious process, and the man concentrated on it as though to misapportion would be a sin.

He poured the water from the kettle into the cups with the same exaggerated care, his shape distorting behind a cloud of steam. He leaned as far as he could to the right, managing to get his fingertips on a dagger, and with this he stirred each cup.

"You will join me?" he said, obviously an afterthought.

"What is it?" Tristam asked, his body reacting on its own to the smell.

"What you've come so far seeking, Tristam Flattery," the man said, pushing a cup across the table for Tristam, and then moving the other in the viscount's direction. Tristam closed his eyes, willing his body to be still. The odor alone wakened something within him and he thought of Faairi's star. Tried to focus on it. His right hand twitched as though some other will struggled to move it, and Tristam removed this hand from the table. With effort he opened his eyes.

"It is Kingfoil," Tristam said, regretting even inhaling the vapor.

"Kingfoil? Yes, that's it. King's leaf." The man raised his cup and sipped as though it were fine brandy. In the glow of the lantern he could see the man's eyelids flutter and then close.

"All right," he whispered, his breathing already eased, "I'm ready to begin."

"Your name; Matea," Tristam said, the cup still sitting before him like a taunt. "It means what?"

"*Death,*" the man said, drinking again.

Tristam closed his own eyes. Why had he been brought here?

"But I have not always been named thus. I was once known as 'Tommy boy,' to a mother who is long dead. And then 'Master Tomas.' 'Midshipman,' for a time. 'Lieutenant.' Then Captain Tomas Gregory, of the Royal Navy."

"*You aren't Gregory!*" Tristam said, the denial coming out in a burst of resentment.

The man half-opened his eyes, and his face changed, the mouth tightening a little. "No. I'm merely a half-mad castaway the Varuans do not speak of because they fear me. Because they call me 'the matea,' and leave offerings at the head of my valley. The valley of death."

Tristam almost rose from the table, unable to bear the man's presence. This was not Gregory! "Why did they bring me here?" Tristam asked, fearing the answer, and more than a little disturbed by the man's claim.

"Because they would like to be rid of me, but are too superstitious to do the deed themselves. It is a test. Let me see this mark on your hand."

"How do you know about my hand?" Tristam asked.

"Even death has his followers," the man said, sitting forward and opening his eyes. He sipped his drink again, gazing strangely at Tristam, as though he almost recognized him. Then his eyes darted to the left, and Tristam realized that the viscount had come up beside him.

Before he knew what he did, Tristam snatched up the cup that had been left for the viscount, just as Julian reached for it. Tristam glared up at the man, who stepped back quickly.

The old castaway was nodding his head as though now he understood. With effort Tristam set the cup back on the table, beside the other.

Tristam tried to control the surge of rage that had taken hold of him, and when he turned to find Julian, the man was no longer in his place, standing guard.

"Show me what was done to you," the castaway said again, his tone more insistent, edged with a little hysteria, Tristam thought.

Unsettled by his response, the naturalist hesitated, then drew his sleeve back and extended his arm, afraid to look himself.

The old man leaned forward, forcing his eyes open. He turned Tristam's hand over, the touch of his fingers like wood. "It disappears if you have not had the seed?" he said, and Tristam nodded.

Taking up a cup of the tea he splashed some of the physic over Tristam's wrist, the liquid still painfully hot. Tristam tried to jerk his hand back, but the old man proved to be stronger than he looked. He held Tristam's hand, apparently with little effort, staring at it as though his own future was to be revealed.

With each flicker of the lantern's light the snake became more distinct, its raptor head appearing as though it were rising up through murky water. And then it surfaced, welt-red, coiling out of the vein, and appearing to move in the inconstant light. Tristam closed his eyes, and the man released his hand.

"And what did they look like, these men who did this to you?"

"I didn't see them," Tristam said, drawing the hand back close to him. He opened his eyes and saw the surprise on the man's face.

"Didn't see them?"

"No."

The man sat back, reaching for his cup impulsively, appearing shaken. In that second Tristam could see the illness in him: habituation to the seed. The man was as much a ruin as this house that sagged around him, and almost as empty within.

Tristam turned so that he looked out over the vale toward the sea. A cluster of stars hung on the horizon, forming a pattern that Tristam felt he should know—like so much that occurred on this voyage.

"The ruin of my ship lies beyond the reef," the man said quietly, "in deep water. All hands . . . wandering with the dolphins now. They mutinied, you see. Tried to take the ship so that they could have the seed. Wanted to live forever: the dream of even humble men. A group forced their way into the armory and magazine. I was on the quarterdeck with my officers—those who had not joined the mutineers. I was killing my own crew. Putting them to the sword." He had closed his eyes again, and spoke in a near whisper, his voice oddly devoid of emotion, as though he could not tell the story any other way. "We'll never know what happened. Perhaps they broke a lantern. The explosion blew me clear and I landed in the dark water among a rain of debris. And there, bobbing on the sea, lay the ship's yawl boat, which had been towing astern, ready to sound the pass." Silence. He combed the fingers of both hands into his hair, pulling it hard back from his face. In the orange glow of the lamp the man's features contorted, as though he watched the entire scene again.

"I came ashore like a ghost," he hissed. "Farrelle bring them peace. The Varuans had never seen anything like it—a ship blown to hell in a blaze of flames. They have stories of fiery mountains exploding; caused by the gods, of course. They cannot imagine that such a violent end could have had any other source. Thus the Varuans fear me. And call me 'death'—although I alone lived. And so I sit here in my valley and watch the ships come and go, while something feeds on my soul. I don't know what: the cursed seed, or my own remorse. How can I know? Seventy-five men. . . . All dead. My command. *Mine.*" He looked at Tristam, the flame from the lamp flickering in his eye. "The most distinguished naval career of my time. And now I cannot even make an end of it." He looked down at the cup he cradled in one hand, a thin serpent of steam rising from its depths. "Denied even that. Robbed of one's will. Robbed of one's life."

"Tell me, truly," Tristam said. "Who were you?"

"Were?" The man shook his head. "No, you have it right. I was someone. Someone else. I am death, now. A walking corpse, with only memories circulating in my veins. Memories and this elixir I must have. I came back to Varua to have this seed for my own use. That is the truth. Trevelyan and the King had kept it for themselves, and I, who had gifted it to them, was left to death. A seaman without influence. Never mind that I had braved all the unknown terrors of the world. Never mind that I brought my crews back entire. 'Legend' they said of me. 'Hero' I was named then. But the word got out among the Jacks, many of whom had sailed with me before.

"The King was denying life to me, and I, in turn, was denying it to my pitiable crew. My own betrayal was to be secret, for it began with a mutiny in my heart, but the Jacks were not so cunning. They knew they could never bring the seed back to Farrland and hope to keep it. No, they would have to wrest it from the Varuans, and then find some island of their own to live out their long lives. What reason had they to return to Farrland and the lives of poor men?"

He sipped his physic, stopping to look into the steaming cup as he swallowed, as though realizing what he had just done. Then his eye fell on the cup that Tristam had refused. Again he looked up at the naturalist, something like wonder in that gaze. "Can you truly refuse it?" He reached out and raised Tristam's cup, tilting it precariously over the ground. "Say yea or nay."

"Spill it," Tristam said, forcing the words out. "I will have none of it."

The old man began to tilt the cup further, but when a drop escaped the lip and ran down onto his hand he relented, returning the cup gently to the table. As he did so, a sweat broke on the man's brow, as though simply raising a cup was exertion. For a moment he struggled to regain his breath.

"All around me on the dark sea, the body of my ship lay," he said, drawn back to the vision that clearly haunted him, his terrible voice echoing up from the emptiness within, "some of it aflame. Men floated nearby, staring down into the fathomless depths. Men who had dreamed of living forever. I stood in the rocking yawl boat, helpless, not a living soul to save. Left alive myself by some vengeful god who wished me an eternity of torment. And I knew why. Knew as though I had been told in words.

"Everywhere my ship had sailed I sowed the seeds of ruin. All of the peoples I had discovered were destined to be overwhelmed, their ways lost, their gods put aside. Replaced by the gods of the peoples of the Entide Sea: reason and commerce, progress, empiricism. Possessions and wealth. For this, the gods of the islands and the sea punished me.

"I think the gods fled, then, to some distant corner of the world. And now the Varuans sense the change. The King and his sorcerers have retreated up into the ancient city, hoping to call their gods back. Hoping to keep their people alive."

He stopped and looked at Tristam. "And they want me dead. They sense that the gods' disfavor has something to do with my presence here—little do they realize. But they cannot kill the bearers of the curse, those they have allowed to take the seed. It is tapu. But you. . . . What you do affects only yourself and the people of your own land. It is nothing to them."

"But I will not commit murder," Tristam said. *Especially one as pitiable as yourself,* he thought.

The old man, whom Tristam feared might actually be Gregory, drained his cup, staring down into its emptiness. Then he rose, standing more erect. "Let me show you," he said, and motioning for Tristam to follow, they stepped out into the moonlit valley.

The viscount was nowhere to be seen, which Tristam did not like. But he followed the old man, treading along a well-worn path that led into a copse of breadfruit trees. Here the man stopped before half a dozen neat rows of *regis* plants. Tristam could see their pale blossoms in the moonlight.

"My greatest victory," the man said, the irony clear.

"You take the *regis* physic," Tristam said, "but you are not young. How is that possible?"

The man stood staring at his plants with such a mixture of emotion that Tristam wondered how he remained even as sane as he did.

"If you have not the ways of the Old Men, the makings of a mage, I have come to believe, then the seed betrays you. Sooner or later. You require more and more, yet you age. Eventually, there is no amount of seed that will keep time at bay. And I have so little left. *Look at them.* As innocent seeming as children. Yet even this viscount was a child once. As sweet as any, I'm sure." He reached out and gently turned one of the flowers up, as though it were the face of a child. "This is what you came for?"

Tristam did not answer. Here it was. *Regis.* And not in the possession of the islanders. With only a few plants and some seed he could return to Farrland a hero. Wealth, a title, and the gratitude of the duchess.

A bat flitted over the garden, once, twice, its flight erratic. An owl hooted, causing Tristam to look up. Was this the owl he had seen? His owl?

The naturalist let the silence go on, afraid to speak. He wanted no more answers from this man. Nor did he want to consider any of his requests.

"Yours," the old man whispered hoarsely, "if you want it."

"I cannot do what you ask," Tristam said.

"But can you not help me?" the man said, suddenly turning on Tristam, pleading. "You are a relation of Erasmus. You understand these things. Will you not take pity on a sorry shell of a man? Help me regain what I have lost. The Old Men could do it, but they have changed toward me, and will do nothing to assist me, now. But you, Tristam Flattery, are my countryman, and I was once counted great among the citizens of Farrland. I do not wish to die ancient, and infirm, and without all honor. Was it such a terrible thing I did? Many a commander has lost a ship, yet retained his honor. Many who had accomplished less than I. Do I deserve such an end? Do I, sir?"

Tristam did not answer, but shook his arm free of the man's grip. "I am not your judge, Captain Gregory, or whoever you are. And, contrary to what you think, I understand almost nothing of these matters. I could not help you if I wanted to, and that's the truth of it."

The man turned back to his plants, his shoulders sagging. Again he reached out and caressed a blossom. "Even if what you say is true, Tristam Flattery, you could help me still. Would you not put a beast from its suffering? I am such a beast."

"*No*. You are speaking to the wrong man. Talk to my shadow. Did you know he cut a bird-serpent into his arm with the point of a knife, and slit his wrist as well?"

The man nodded. "*Despair*. He can never be you, so he attempted self-murder. You . . . you can live to thrice the age of men, have the love of his adored sister, and are free of his particular demons."

Clearly this man knew more than he claimed. "But what are these demons?" Tristam asked. "What drives him to be as he is?"

"I heard him speak with Hobbes. He believes he is the servant of death."

Tristam turned away, unable to bear it any more. *No more!*

If I accept the seed, the quest will be over and this madness will be done with, he told himself. But he could not—he believed now that it was a curse. Look at what it had done to this man. Could he truly have been Gregory?

Tristam walked back toward the fale, led by the flaming butterfly in the ship's lantern. A few steps into the shadow of the trees, he came upon the viscount, standing silent and still. Tristam almost stopped and spoke, but instead went on. They had a pact, these two: *Death* and his manservant.

Reaching the edge of the trees he stopped, morbid curiosity gaining the better of him. He saw the shadow of the larger man standing before the aged seaman, and then the viscount dropped to his knees. Tristam turned and fled toward the single light.

Tristam did not know how much time had passed. He sat, staring out toward the stars that lifted slowly above the sea, his mind in such confusion it was its own kind of emptiness. Finally a noise startled him, and the viscount stood in the door, bearing the limp form of Gregory in his arms.

Tristam rose from his seat, pulling back a step, staring at this horrifying sight: the viscount holding the man as tenderly as though he were his own dead father. In the faint light Tristam could see what appeared to be tears on the viscount's face.

"Lay him here, on the table," Tristam said, and the viscount did as he said, arranging the man's hands on his breast, brushing the strands of hair back from his face.

Tristam reached the lantern down. "Set it afire," he forced himself to say. He went out, crossing the vale to the stand of trees. Hanging the lantern from a branch, he stared at the plants a moment, the blossoms like tiny bells in the moonlight. "I have come for you," he whispered, and went quickly to work, removing each plant, taking care that no seeds fell to the ground. He imagined he could feel the plants exerting their primitive will toward him, trying to stop him. Tristam's longing for the physic grew, and his hands trembled, but he would not relent. Behind him the dry thatch of the fale caught, going up with a high, crackling hiss. The light of the blaze caused the shadows of the trees to battle around him, like enormous many-armed warriors.

The fale was an inferno when Tristam returned, and the viscount stood there, too close, as though paying honor to a dead hero. Daring the scorching heat, Tristam cast the *regis* plants on the flames, where they twisted and sizzled in the blaze.

The viscount pounced forward, trying to rescue the Kingfoil, but he pulled away, the heat too much for him. *"What have you done?"* he said, grabbing Tristam roughly by the front of his shirt.

The two men froze that way, their faces inches apart. *"Take your hands off me,"* Tristam said with controlled rage, feeling something stir within him, something frightening. And to his surprise, the viscount let him go, stepping back quickly. Tristam shrugged his shirt back into place. "It is a curse," he said, moving away from both the viscount and the heat of the fire. "I will have no part of it. Nor will I take it back to Farrland, King or no. I will risk prison before that."

The viscount stood glaring at him, and Tristam took another step back, suddenly afraid of this madman, unsure of the source of his apparent immunity. Gregory had suggested that the viscount was jealous of him. Jealousy caused madness to take hold of *sane* men.

But then the viscount nodded. "You understand these things, Tristam," Julian said, his tone almost subservient. He looked over his shoulder at the burning structure. "He was a father to me," the viscount said, his tone eminently reasonable, "demanding sometimes, but just and fair. . . ."

Tristam scooped the lantern up off the ground and fled, searching desperately for the path to the lagoon, wanting to hear no more. No more.

The darkness among the trees was so dense it resisted the moonlight, and Tristam was soon lost, finding himself on steep slopes, where he could barely make his way. For a long time he followed the flaming butterfly, but finally the lantern flickered out, empty, and Tristam sat down in the dark and tried to catch his breath. Was the viscount searching for him? Yes. Tristam was quite certain he was.

He lay back on the soft earth, listening, attuning his ear to the sounds of the forest—the running of a stream somewhere nearby, the sound of the wind among the leaves. Insects sang their high, strange songs, and occasionally came the sound of an owl, like a question. *Where? Where are you?*

For a long time Tristam listened, and then he heard the sound of the Tithy running outside his home in Locfal. His uncle walked there, by the brook, lost in thought. Tristam threw open the window of his room and cupped his hands to his mouth. *"What is it you want of me?"* he shouted. His uncle looked up, as though vaguely aware of a sound, and then went back to his musing. A falcon cried from the aviary.

Tristam awoke to first light, the sunrise smeared across the eastern sky like a swelling wound. For a moment he could not think where he was or how he had come there, and then he remembered. . . . The night in the valley. A man who made impossible claims.

"Blood and flames." He sat up quickly, and found that a dagger lay in his lap. Tristam cursed, snatching up the weapon, which was still stained with dried blood. He looked around, suddenly frightened, still half in the world of dreams. This was the dagger that belonged to the man who had claimed to be Gregory, and only Julian could have carried it down. Tristam shuddered at the thought of the viscount near him while he slept. He looked at the knife again, and found the letter 'G' engraved on the handle.

For a moment he shut his eyes, seeing the pathetic creature who huddled over his physic, having lost all sense of himself—all honor, all pride. The shell of Tomas Gregory, the greatest explorer in Farr history. This is what the seed wrought in men. Unless they had the talents of a mage—and then Tristam suspected the effects were even worse.

"I can deny myself anything," Tristam told himself, though his obsession with the duchess made this half a lie.

He staggered to his feet, and immediately set off along the hillside, feeling relief in movement. The events of the previous night seemed like a nightmare to him—the kind of nightmare you couldn't shake in the morning, and which left you feeling strange and tainted, somehow.

The terrain forced him up, and repeatedly he kept encountering slopes too steep to descend. Three hours found him looking over a bluff into a deep valley, not sure where he was or how he would get down.

He thought he heard his name echo across the valley, and he went out to the edge of the cliff, hoping to catch sight of his rescuers.

Again the call repeated up the valley, to be lost among the trees. Tristam answered, reminded immediately of his dream. *What is it you want of me?*

It was half of the hour before Tristam realized that it was Faairi searching for him, and longer than that before she managed to find him. She smiled with relief when she finally saw him, but there was some underlying anxiety that this smile could not erase.

"Tristam," she said, hurrying up through the trees. "You must hurry. There has been fighting on the ship."

⌒ Twenty-Six

Tumney paced the width of the arboretum, stopped, and stared out over the neat rows of plants. He removed his hat and turned it slowly in his hands, as though searching with his thumb for irregularities in the headband. He realized he was not comfortable here alone at night. These plants had always seemed strange to him. "Foreign" was what he thought of them. Peculiar. But tonight this did not seem an adequate explanation. "Aware" was much more what he thought, though he would never admit it to anyone. Brooding. Intent on a purpose he did not understand, he who knew plants well.

The waxy leaves of *regis* glistened dully in the lamplight, and the silence in the room almost felt like patience. They seemed a bit like murderous innocents to him; raised apart from others, never learning right from wrong. They had a purpose of their own, and like everything in nature but man, did not care how they achieved it. Perhaps it would be more true to say that some men cared.

Tumney shivered suddenly, and turned away, crossing to the small planting boxes, but he stopped a few feet short, keeping his distance. These were the seeds planted by that young naturalist months before. Tumney had tended them, as the duchess had asked, but nothing had happened. And now virtually every box had the beginnings of a Kingfoil seedling, erupting out of the earth like small green hands, reaching for light and air.

"Unnatural," he muttered. There was no explanation for it. None.

He heard a door open and turned expectantly. A moment later Princess Joelle arrived accompanied by the young prince and Teiho Ruau. The gardener bowed as best he could, gratified by the kind smile from the princess. She always called him 'Mr. Tumney,' and even, on occasion, 'sir,' which he liked more than a little, the princess being born to such a high station and all.

"Mr. Tumney," she said, nodding her head to him. "I do apologize for leaving you waiting. We came as soon as we were able."

He shook his head, not sure how to respond. Certainly the princess should not be apologizing to him. Not wanting to keep the princess so late at night, he led them immediately to the planting boxes. For a moment no one spoke and Ruau reached out and touched one of the emerging seedlings. He glanced up, sharing a look with the princess, and then took his hand away.

"These were all planted by Tristam Flattery?" the prince asked quietly.

"Yes. Just before high summer. Almost eight months past." The gardener took a step away. "There is something else." He gestured with his hat.

They followed him down the rows of Kingfoil, the princess waving off his expressed concern for her shoes. He crouched by a plant and took the end of a branch, lifting the flower that grew there. "It is a girl," he said. "The first female flower in months and months. There will be seed from this." He pointed to some other buds on the same plant, and others nearby as well. "All females," he said, a bit in awe. "And I take no credit. I can't begin to explain it," he said.

Again the Varuan and the princess shared a look.

"*Tristam Flattery*," the prince said, staring down at the flower. His mother looked at him sharply, and he said nothing more.

"You're certain, Mr. Tumney, that no one knows of this?"

Tumney nodded. "Sure as sure, ma'am."

She considered this for only a second before speaking. "Destroy the seedlings," the princess said firmly. "Cut every female bud and flower off and put everything into the fire. No one must know what has happened."

"But . . . we have hoped for so long!" The gardener didn't go on. The look on the princess' face told him that he had spoken out of place. "Excuse me, Your Highness. Old Tumney speaks before he thinks. Excuse me."

She reached out and put a hand on his shoulder, an easy gesture, for the princess was considerably taller than the old gardener. "I know it seems mad, Mr. Tumney, but you must do this for me. It is for everyone's good. Don't ask me more."

The gardener nodded. "I'll do it this night."

The princess mouthed the words, "Thank you," though no sound came. She took Ruau and her son in tow, and left Tumney alone in the arboretum.

For a few moments the old gardener stared at his charges, wondering how they would react to the coming assault, but he shook his head. "Don't be an old fool," he chided himself, and went to get his tools, though not without a feeling that he was being observed.

The prince looked over his sketch. He thought it might have been good fortune that had him born a prince, for he clearly didn't have the talent to be an artist. Though, to be fair, Averil Kent had said his own early sketches showed little promise. Of course, the artist might have been merely trying to encourage. One could not rely on others to be truthful about their abilities.

He wondered if the eyebrows should not really be so arched. He closed his eyes and tried to summon up a clear mental image of Alissa Somers, and though he was able to do this easily, when he tried to concentrate on specific features, the whole picture seemed to lose focus.

He thought her high forehead and eyebrows must represent perfection of form, the skin unmarred by even a hint of a line, as though she had never worried in her life. But then she had not been born into a royal family. When people spoke to her, it was likely that they felt no need to speak anything but the truth.

He opened his eyes and looked with some despair upon his creation. Perhaps she was not really so perfect, but he had made her so in his mind. People did this; he had seen it. As though the world of humans was created from their desires as much as their perception—an issue the empiricists tried to deal with in their natural philosophy.

Although he realized this was a trivial truth, still, trying to comprehend the reality of a situation was his constant activity. He could not necessarily trust the word of ministers, who all had their own purposes; nor what his mother might think, for her own perception was colored by her desire to see people in certain ways. One did not trust the periodicals, certainly, and pamphleteers were never disinterested. Everyone seemed to see the world and events a little differently, depending on their own personal mixture of desire and pragmatism. In history there were any number of rulers whose perception of events was so far removed from reality that it led to calamity. Prince Wilam did not want to be one of those—at any cost. Even if it meant giving up the world as he desired it to be.

He looked again at his drawing. Well, she might not be quite the paragon he wanted to believe, but Alissa was certainly more beautiful than his sketch indicated. That, at least, he knew for truth.

His mother's signature knock sounded on the door and he turned his drawing facedown before answering. It was late, but it seemed that both he and the princess were managing with limited sleep these days.

"Princess," he said, following the ritual they had long ago evolved— "Princess" was not a proper form of address.

"Prince." She entered his room with more assurance than last she had visited. The princess scanned her surroundings quickly, no doubt taking notice of his sketch, turned over on the desk. "Wilam, I have been torturing my brain trying to understand the significance of the *regis* flowering at this precise point in time, but I can arrive at no explanation. I am quite sure there is no empirical explanation. I think we need to consult with Averil Kent. Will you go to him in the morning?"

The prince nodded. "Yes. Of course."

The princess nodded, giving half a smile—worry obviously preyed upon her. "I have tried to find some explanation that does not rely on logic, but once the borders of rationality have been removed I cannot imagine what should take their place. How does one begin to measure? What standards should one apply?"

The prince understood what she meant. Once reason was no longer your guide, you were like a man stranded in a featureless landscape. There were no landmarks to use. One direction was as likely to yield results as any other. Even so, the prince found he had a hunch, though it was not more than that. Certainly he could not justify it. "I understand what you're saying. I don't know why, but I feel sure, somehow, that this sudden flowering has something to do with Tristam Flattery. It is not rational, I realize. Flattery has not set foot in the palace in months, but, still, I think it."

"Perhaps you are right. Intuition is not to be discounted; no matter that it is not empirical. Talk to Mr. Kent. He knows more than most realize."

The prince nodded. The two stood awkwardly for a moment, not knowing what to say.

"I have kept my word regarding Miss Somers," the prince began, trying to make his voice calm and adult. "But I find that I am concerned. It might give me some peace to know that she is well. Is that possible?"

The princess stopped in the middle of the room, gazing at her son with a serious look that he could not read. "I've received a note from Lady Galton, and will dine with her tomorrow. Afterward, we can speak." She reached out and put a hand on his shoulder, then kissed his cheek and left without another word.

The prince went back to his desk and flipped the drawing over. It was not only a poor likeness of Alissa Somers, but it was a poor representation of his own idealized image. And to think a real portraitist captured not only a person's likeness but something of their inner being as well. His sketch showed a woman stiff and wooden, perhaps a little apprehensive. This was not the Alissa he knew. Not even remotely like her.

Despite the return of his vitality, Kent was miserable. He could barely meet the eyes of his friends, and slumped in his chair with his hands jammed into the pockets of his frock coat. His meeting with Palle had left him feeling morally tainted. The man was a devil incarnate!

"If there was any way at all for us to see it," Valary said. "Though I am sure that Wells and Palle have taken every precaution to keep this away from prying eyes."

Kent could feel the countess look at him, even if he could not see her clearly. Her lifeless tones came out of the darkness. "What do you say, Averil? Is it possible?"

Kent found that this question robbed him of his desire for humor. "Possible. . . . Perhaps. There would be some risk involved. As things stand now, Galton will alert us if Palle and his group decide to attempt this ritual. I'm not quite sure what we will do, but at least we will know. But if Galton is found copying this text . . . Wells is distrustful in the extreme, and his experience with Mr. Littel will have only made that worse. I would dearly like to see this text myself, but to endanger Galton. . . . I'm not sure it is wise."

Silence. Kent thought he could hear a clock ticking.

"I think Averil is right in this. We have a man in Palle's inner circle, now, and that may prove to be the more valuable thing—at least for the time being.

If Palle suddenly decides that he must act. . . ." The countess looked around at the men present. "Well, then I am not sure what we shall do."

Kent rose out of his chair. "We have stronger allies than most realize. We need only prepare them. Which we must do rather quickly, for we cannot know when Palle and Wells will act. I will need the assistance of Lord Jaimas, if he will not mind being made a mere messenger."

When Smithers appeared at the door to his study, Kent hoped it would be to inform him that a young woman from the opera had come calling. It was relatively early in the morning, really too early for visitors, but then these were not normal times.

"There is a young gentleman to see you, Sir Averil."

"And what name might he go by?"

"He would not say, sir, but gave me this envelope, insisting that you would see him." A second of hesitation.

Kent took the envelope from the silver tray and slit it open. "Show him up immediately . . . and, Smithers? The proper form of address to use is 'Your Highness.'"

The servant hurried from the room.

Kent removed his spectacles and rose from his chair, stretching his arms to loosen his shoulders. He had been working on his sketch of the King, though when he would ever have the leisure to paint a portrait he did not know. A moment later a somberly dressed young prince was shown into the room.

"Your Highness," Kent said, making a leg. "It is a great honor."

The young man grinned a little self-consciously, as though he suspected Kent of making sport of him. "The princess has sent me to ask you a question, Sir Averil."

Kent gestured to a chair, and the two sat, Kent leaning forward, his hands on his knees, ready to offer whatever service he might to the princess.

"But before I speak further, we must reach an understanding. . . ." The prince gazed at him, turning his head slightly to one side. "Although the princess has the highest opinion of you, Sir Averil, as do I, we have had no formal declaration of your intent or loyalty."

Kent nodded, thinking immediately of his conversation with Palle. Everyone else trusted him so completely. Did they not know that there were things that could tempt even Averil Kent?

"It is my intention to see that knowledge thought lost for many years is not recovered. I am opposed to Roderick Palle and his colleagues."

"One of whom is my father," the prince said.

Kent hesitated barely half a beat. "One of whom is the prince. Yes," he said quietly, realizing that these words still seemed true to him, despite what he had been offered.

"And what are you prepared to do to stop these men from regaining the lost knowledge?"

"Whatever I must," Kent said without pause. And this seemed true as well.

The young man nodded. "Then we are of one mind, Sir Averil," he said, staring down at the floor for a moment, losing his focus. "Last summer," he began suddenly, as though remembering his purpose, "while staying in Avonel, Tristam Flattery planted *regis* seeds in the arboretum. On the instructions of the Duchess of Morland, the gardener watered these seeds but otherwise left them alone all these months. A few days ago they began to sprout."

Kent sat back in his chair.

"That is not all. The *regis* plants in the arboretum have begun to bloom: female blossoms."

"You're certain?"

The prince nodded, carefully gauging Kent's reaction.

"*My word,*" Kent muttered.

"What does it mean, Sir Averil?"

Kent rose from his chair and paced across the front of the hearth. "Simply started growing, you say? The gardener did nothing different?"

"According to him, nothing."

Kent dearly wanted to go and see this for himself, though he knew there would be no point. "What do Wells and company make of this?"

"They don't know. The princess had the seedlings destroyed. And all the female blossoms and buds were pinched off."

Kent stopped, staring down at the prince. "You're sure Palle doesn't know? Few things pass in the kingdom without his knowledge, and we're talking about the palace. Ostensibly his home."

"I'm certain he does not know. Even the King has not been told."

Kent reached back and put an elbow on the mantelpiece. "You may not be able to keep it secret for long. *Regis* seems to have a mind of its own, or nearly so."

"You have no idea what this might mean, then?"

"Mean? I dare say it means that the things we have struggled to keep from waking have begun to stir. It could be due to events here in Farrland, or it might even have some connection to Tristam Flattery, wherever he might be."

The prince nodded, as though this corroborated his own thinking. "Is there any way we might discover more certainly?"

Kent considered a moment. "There are several people who might cast light upon this. Two I will consult, but the third is Stedman Galton. You might tell the princess that I think she acted wisely," Kent added. "I think it is best to keep the plants from flowering. Anything that might give us an advantage over these others. Even the smallest thing."

Smithers knocked on the door, apologizing profusely. "A young lady to see you, sir. Shall I have her wait or send her on?"

Kent felt his heart rise, and then sink. She was an agent of the Entonne government, and the future King of Farrland sat in his study speaking openly about the most sensitive matters. Smithers must have understood his master's hesitation.

"It is Miss Alissa Somers, sir."

"Ah. Bring her up, Smithers. Send her along immediately."

Kent noticed that the prince's color changed, his face becoming a little bright.

"Perhaps I should . . ." the young man started to rise, but the sentence trailed off and he did not move. An awkward silence ensued, reminding Kent of what Sennet had told him.

Have they arranged an "accidental" meeting at my home?

A moment later Alissa Somers burst through the door and answered Kent's question; her face changed utterly when she saw the prince, and she faltered. Stopping self-consciously just inside the door.

"Your Highness," Kent said, "I believe you have met Miss Alissa Somers, the future Duchess of Blackwater."

Alissa curtsied quickly and the prince bowed more deeply than he strictly should have. The poor young man looked so out of sorts. Torn between wanting to leave and needing to stay.

"It is the greatest good fortune that I find you both here," Alissa began, then she looked at them in turn as she spoke. "Do you know the whereabouts of Jaimas? Is he truly well?"

The prince turned away at this, stricken with pain and remorse, Kent could see.

"Lord Jaimas is perfectly well."

She paused for a moment. "You are absolutely certain?"

"I have seen him with my own eyes, Miss Alissa. He might well be home to you this very day."

She put a hand to her face, and Kent saw her eyes brim with tears. The prince had turned and was staring at him in disbelief.

Kent felt himself floundering, wondering how he might save the situation. "Fortunately, Your Highness managed to spirit Lord Jaimas and Mr. Littel away, or who knows what might have happened. As it was, Palle's minions committed the foul murder of two young gentlemen by mistake, and believe that Lord Jaimas and Littel are dead."

Alissa turned her lovely eyes, still glistening with tears, on the prince.

"How terrible for these young men," she said. "I—I owe you a great debt, Your Highness."

This simple declaration melted Kent's heart entirely, and he could only imagine the effect on the prince. The poor young man looked as though he would never find words to answer.

"Certainly my part was very small," he managed.

The prince and Alissa stood on either edge of the rug, as though it were a chasm between them, looking at each other, their eyes filled with questions.

"I am glad you have come, Miss Alissa," Kent said. "If you don't mind, I would have you carry a note to the duke."

Kent's words seemed to break the spell, and the two began a show of acting normally. Kent offered them tea, wondering if he was furthering a romance, feeling a bit sorry for Lord Jaimas—a bit guilty.

The prince's carriage stopped and rolled back a foot. Alissa glanced out at the facade of the Flatterys' Avonel residence—it seemed so grand, and it was not a palace. She looked back to her companion. She dearly hoped they would not be seen.

"Your Highness has been very kind," she said, looking down at her hands, which were clasped tightly on her knee. There had been only stilted conversation after the prince offered to return her from Averil Kent's. She had seldom felt so uncomfortable. A footman opened the door and lowered the step.

She forced a smile at her anxious looking companion, and then turned to go.

"Lady Alissa?" he said quickly, a hint of urgency in his voice. "I wanted to apologize for what happened at the iron bridge celebration."

She put on her most naive look and then caught herself. For some reason she could not make herself pretend that she didn't understand what he meant—the princess steering him away.

"No need to apologize," she said, warmth coming through.

"It won't happen again. I . . . It won't happen, I promise."

She nodded.

"My mother," he paused. "She is too perceptive sometimes." He meant to say more but could not choose among the endless possibilities, and he ended up shrugging foolishly.

"It's all right," she said softly, looking down so that her thick lashes hid her eyes. "My heart . . . it belongs to Jaimas, but if it did not. . . ." She met his eye. "*Thank you,*" she managed, and then reached out to squeeze his hand before leaving.

The prince raised her hand to his lips and kissed her fingers. "Thank you," he said.

She nodded, and stepped down to the ground, turning once to wave, conscious of his gaze as she mounted the steps.

He thinks he loves me, she thought. *Farrelle save us, he is a prince of Farrland!*

Inside the door she gave her cloak to a servant and then, looking up, she was greeted by the sight of Jaimas coming down the stairs. She did not wait but rushed up to meet him.

The story took some time in the telling, and Alissa clung to his hand through much of it. Although she had been certain that Lady Gallon's news was wrong, she had not slept that night for worry. And now here he was, returned to her, returned from the dead, almost.

"I can't imagine how you escaped," she said. "It was clever of you to set the dogs off after the fox."

Jaimas nodded his head, his look distracted. "You know, when that fox appeared, I had the strongest impression that it was not an accident."

"You're saying that it came to rescue you?" She poked him in the ribs with a finger, as she liked to do when they teased.

"Not quite, but I don't believe it was an accident either."

She laughed, she was just so overwhelmed with happiness to have him back. "You will become superstitious next."

"But I already am. I believe I found you when I was following a hooded crow that seemed to be carrying a silver ring, and hopping furtively from branch to branch."

She laughed. "Well, my life has been less eventful, I will say."

"Oh? And whose great carriage brought you home early this morning, my dear?"

"I was delivering a message to Mr. Kent," she said, trying not to sound too serious. "Prince Wilam happened to be there and kindly saved me from hiring a hack to get home."

"Accidental meetings with royalty? Hardly uneventful."

"I suppose," she said, more seriously. "I think the prince is lonely, you know. Perhaps lonely is not the right word." She turned a lock of Jaimy's hair around a finger. "He does not have what we have: people around us who care for us enough to be critical when needed. People whose reactions we trust."

"Yes," Jaimy said. "I need someone to be critical of me occasionally. Left to my own devices, I would make a perfect fool of myself." He thought of Angeline and closed his eyes, embarrassment and guilt causing that strange tightness, as though something inside him cringed.

"I hardly think that. Jaimas? I believe the prince is sweet on me." She paused for a beat. "Now don't laugh."

"I am not laughing. It's very likely true. We don't need to change our marriage plans, do we?"

She laughed and kissed his cheek, then turned his head and kissed him sweetly on the lips. "No. I think we can go ahead. At least I haven't had a better offer yet." Then more seriously, "I feel a little sorry for him, as absurd as it is to pity an heir to the throne."

Jaimas pulled her closer and she put her head against his shoulder.

"Isn't it odd, Jaimas, that your great-uncle had the portrait of the Countess of Chilton, and then Kent sends you to her home? I wish you had seen her. Imagine hiding away from the world for so many years!"

Jaimy shrugged. He dearly wanted to examine that portrait. Did the countess' niece really look so much like her? Almost too uncanny to believe.

The carriage moved quietly through the streets of Avonel, and the prince stared out the window at the people going about their daily business. A world so far removed from his that the glass he looked through might have been a magic mirror, showing scenes of another land.

The words of Alissa Somers echoed in his mind. *"My heart . . . it belongs to Jaimas, but if it did not. . . ."* And then she had thanked him. For what? Was it a compliment that he had paid her? Not by the standards of gentlemen— expressing one's feelings for another man's fiancée! But she had thanked him, and he was certain it was not just for escorting her home.

He wondered if that had been the moment he dreamed of? The moment when two people ignored all propriety, and spoke from their hearts. Yes, perhaps it was. And if the world did not seem overly changed by it, that did not matter. It was precious to him all the same.

"But if it did not," he whispered, and laid his head against the seat, curling up like a child, pressing his eyes closed as though he could shut out the coldness of world and somehow inhabit those five words.

◞ Twenty-Seven

The words on the page had begun to blur and Stedman Galton closed his eyes, feeling a mild burning sensation behind the lids. He had not slept enough these past nights, and his lung condition was not liking the dampness of the late Farr winter. The only good news had been the assurance of his wife that Lord Jaimas Flattery and Egar Littel were still alive—though who the two unfortunates in County Coombs had been was still a mystery.

It did not matter to Galton that it was not Lord Jaimas and Egar Littel who had been murdered. Palle had let his people commit this crime, and their intended victims had broken no laws. And then there were these poor young gentlemen who couldn't have had the slightest idea of why they were attacked.

No, Galton had no second thoughts—when he woke up to the truth of what was happening around him he had awakened completely. There was no rest for him now.

"Shall we give it a rest, Sir Stedman?" Wells asked solicitously.

Galton's eyes snapped open as though he had been startled as he dozed. "No. I can go on a bit longer yet. We are so close." He forced his eyes to focus on the text before him.

Wells leaned over the table as well, sighing a little as he moved. After a brief silence he said, "I still think that 'gwydd' will prove to be the root of 'wood.' The 'g' became silent, as we know, in words like 'gnarled' and 'gnat.' Consider the root of 'gnat': 'gnætt.' It is almost a perfect model. So 'gwyddhyll' is 'woodhill' or 'wooded hill.' 'Tree mount.' We know that Kent and this man Valary visited the abbey."

Galton nodded blankly, even the simplest things taking a moment to coalesce in his exhausted mind. They were debating a passage that described the ritual, written in a different tongue than the chant of the ritual itself. "That might be true, Wells, but Sir Roderick sent a man up there to search the place and he reported nothing out of the ordinary. It may not be the site we're searching for."

"Yes, but would this man have known what to look for? It might take more knowledge than he possessed."

Galton had been doing everything in his power to slow Wells' progress, but feared that his purpose would be perceived if he was not careful. There were times when he needed to agree, even make a small contribution so that he did not fall under suspicion, for Wells had become very suspicious, guarding the text as though it might walk off of its own accord.

"I take your point, but there must be five hundred 'wooded hills' or 'forest hills' or variants. Yes, Kent visited this one, but it might have been only coincidence. Knowing we look for a variant of 'forest hill' is about as exact as knowing we look for a town with a name ending in the suffix 'field' or 'bridge' or 'ford.' They are countless." He paused for a moment. He had been trying to put Wells off this inquiry all evening. "Do you think it important?"

Wells considered for a moment. "It depends entirely on how we interpret the writings on your Ruin, Stedman. If we must go to Farrow, as you think, perhaps it will not matter. The journey to Farrow this time of year, though, is many more days than to any place in the kingdom—assuming the 'gwyddhyll' is in Farrland. If Valary and Kent are involved with the Entonne, as Roderick insists, then it is possible that Massenet could make use of the abbey site while we were at sea on our way to Farrow. It is a risk."

They both heard the steps in the hallway, and paused, wondering who it might be. The door opened without a knock and Sir Roderick stopped in the opening. "*Littel is almost certainly still alive*," he said, and Galton half rose from his chair. It had happened sooner than he'd hoped.

"But how can that be?" Wells said. "Hawksmoor's men. . . ." He stopped, not liking to use the word "murdered" or "killed."

Roderick shook his head angrily. "I don't know who they were, but they were not Flattery and Littel." He looked up and caught Galton's eye. "Farrelle rest them," he added quickly.

"But where is he, then?" Galton asked, fearing the answer.

"Kent has him, I'm certain. Or will know where he is. I have Hawksmoor out now. We will apprehend Sir Averil and his driver, and whoever else is unlucky enough to be with him. That Entonne-loving historian, I hope. That will be a start." He began to pace across the room. "I can't arrest Massenet, but we can apprehend his agents. We will see." He looked up at his colleagues, something like alarm on his face. "What the duke will do when his son returns with his tale of being hunted by Hawksmoor's people, I don't know. If we are very fortunate, the duke will be satisfied with just Hawksmoor." Palle appeared to see the two men before him for the first time. "Have you both given up sleeping?"

Neither man answered.

"But there can be no rest for any of us now," Palle went on. "We might need to act immediately. Is it possible? Are we ready?"

Wells looked down at the pages spread across the table. "To be honest, Sir Roderick, we don't know. It isn't really a matter of translation at this point so much as interpretation. This is what I have been saying to Stedman. We must perform the ritual correctly: the language—the part that is spoken—is recited in the original tongue. That is not the problem. It is the other elements of the ritual that are not clear, and that is simply because the text is so . . . vague. It speaks in allegory and strange images. We are only guessing at what much of it means."

Palle collapsed in a chair, thinking. "If we perform the ritual incorrectly, what will result?"

Wells looked over at Galton, raising his eyebrows, and then back to Palle. "We are not sure. Perhaps nothing will occur. It's possible that the warding will protect those involved, even from their own mistakes—or it might have another purpose altogether."

"I would venture that there is substantial risk," Galton said quietly. "We are a bit like children playing with a water-driven loom—it is so powerful and our understanding of its mechanisms and purpose so imperfect. There is every chance that it will catch hold of us and drag us in, with tragic results, I fear."

Palle gripped the arms of the chair with his soft hands. "Even so, I don't think we dare delay, Stedman. If the second earth tremor on Farrow meant what we thought, then Tristam Flattery was well along the path we foresaw. Assuming that Llewellyn can do his part, how long could they be?"

Galton shook his head. "Augury is an inexact art, and we are only novices in its practice. I am concerned that we'll rush into action before we're truly prepared to do so. Even if Kent passes Littel's knowledge on to Massenet, are the Entonne better prepared than we? Would they dare perform this ritual so soon? Have they someone with adequate talent?"

"Have we someone with adequate talent?" Palle asked. "That is my fear, though I understand your concern. We might bring ourselves and our purpose to ruin, leaving Massenet the field. But what else can we do? If the Entonne gain this knowledge before we do. . . ."

Wells went to a sideboard and filled three glasses with wine from a decanter. Passing each man a glass, he said, "There are precautionary steps we could take. There is the Ruin on Farrow. Can we not place it under guard so that others cannot employ it?"

Galton shook his head. "Not without drawing great attention to ourselves. Farrow is so small—no matter how quietly this was done, people would soon know."

Wells was staring at a map hanging on the wall. "There must be several sites around the Entide Sea where the mages performed their rituals. After all, they were practicing their art long before Farrow was discovered." Wells looked back to his companions. "There is this other possibility we have been puzzling over," he added. "The 'gwyddhyll.' My wooded hill."

"You've not given up on the old abbey, then?" Palle asked.

Wells shook his head. "No."

Sir Roderick rose from his chair, gesturing with his glass. "Valary's servant claimed that Kent and his master were extremely excited by what they had discovered up there, but he was not absolutely clear about what it might have been. The man is thick, even for one in his position. I had Hawksmoor send someone up to look, but he reported nothing extraordinary."

"But as I have said to Galton, would they have known what to look for? It might take someone with the knowledge of Kent or Valary to understand what they were seeing." Wells pressed his fingers to his eyes as though he could not bear to have them open a second longer. He did not like to admit that this man Valary might be as knowledgeable as himself. He gave his head a shake, and turned his reddening gaze on each of his companions. "We should send someone to the abbey immediately," he said. "We need to know if something significant lies hidden there."

Palle stopped to consider this, staring into the bowl of his glass as though events were revealed to him in the blood-red light. "No," he said, his voice surprisingly soft. "There is no one we might send who has the knowledge necessary for a proper inquiry. We must travel there ourselves. It is impossible for me to believe that Kent and Valary journeyed so far in winter for no reason.

This servant of Valary's is no genius, but his eyesight is perfectly fine. He described a cellar where many carvings had been destroyed. 'A room like a temple apse,' were his words. Nothing left now but scars where its various elements once stood. A number of holes set in the floor, a wall with stones removed or chiseled clean of their design. Signs that a stream of water had once poured forth from an opening in the rocks and disappeared through the floor." He looked up, his face a bit drawn. "It is likely what we seek, don't you think, Sir Stedman?"

Galton tried to respond accordingly, though he wanted to weep with frustration. "It seems possible. I just don't want to see us wasting time. We know the Ruin on Farrow will suit our purpose."

Palle nodded agreement. "I am more concerned that the site in the abbey is no longer fit for use, if it is in ruins."

Wells shook his head vigorously. "I am sure that it will not prove a problem. It is the place, I think, not the decoration. The stage is the thing here, not the set. Do you think that Kent has told Massenet about this?"

"I fear it is likely. But I think we shall soon be able to ask Kent that very question. Don't be too concerned, Mr. Wells, at least for the moment. As of an hour ago Hawksmoor's people had our good ambassador under his watchful eye. But we must not rely on that continuing," he said. "We must proceed while others talk. Risk is hardly to be considered now. There are too many working against us." He looked pointedly at Galton and Wells. "We will know when Tristam Flattery has completed his task, will we not?"

Wells nodded, lost in thought himself. Then he stirred. "You are right, Roderick. We might wait years to gather all the information we feel we need. There comes a time when we must act or lose our advantage."

The door was not locked, but the two young guards stationed outside seemed more than capable of stopping an aging painter from escaping, even in his revitalized state. Kent paced back and forth, swinging his arms, and occasionally muttering in anger.

"I should be frightened," he said aloud. But he was not. Anger was what he felt. He stopped before the window and looked out over the grounds toward the lights of the palace. Occasionally a large carriage would sweep along the lighted carriageway to the main entrance, passing through the trees like the shadow of a hunting owl. There was a function at the palace tonight, but what was it? A ball he thought, though for the life of him he could not remember what had occasioned it.

Kent turned the cold bronze handle of the window and found that it was not locked. He swung it open and stared down. One floor—perhaps twice the height of a tall man. If the ground was soft. . . . But no, it was unlikely that his old bones would stand it. He must not let his temporary return to youth make him take foolish risks.

There was still a chance that Palle merely wanted to speak with him. Most likely he would demand Kent's response to his offer a bit earlier than he had arranged.

But then the guards who had apprehended him had taken Hawkins as well. Pushing the poor driver in with his master and putting their own man to drive. And then, when they arrived here, they had led Hawkins off in a different direction. It did not bode well. *Poor Hawkins*, Kent thought. He hoped he had not put the man in danger.

He crossed to a sideboard and poured himself two fingers of brandy. This was obviously the apartment of a senior officer in the palace guard. There were three badly painted miniatures on the mantelpiece depicting a stern looking woman, and two unremarkable children.

Kent began a thorough search of the room, wondering what he might find that could aid him. A cherrywood box on a small table was a sword case, but it contained no weapon. He pulled open cupboards and drawers and found nothing of import. The occupant of these rooms was apparently named Ceril Hampton, Colonel Ceril Hampton, though that knowledge did him no good. There were Hamptons to burn in Farrland.

Kent stood in the center of the room and glared around him. There were not even bed sheets to tie together to make his escape, as there would be in any good story.

The door opened at that moment, and Kent must have had such a look on his face that even the King's Man hesitated in the doorway. But the hesitation was brief. Palle was accompanied by Noyes, wearing one of his typically outlandish outfits, and two guards.

"Mr. Kent," Roderick nodded.

Kent said nothing but continued to glare. Noyes would not meet his eye.

"Why am I here?"

Palle gave a tight smile, as quick as a blink. "Let us not waste time, Sir Averil," the King's Man said, his voice showing no signs of anger. The guards took up positions to either side of the door. "Will you not sit?"

"I prefer to stand."

"Very well. I am looking for a young scholar named Egar Littel. Only a few days past you helped him escape from Merton. He is wanted for a terrible crime, Mr. Kent. It would give me confidence in your intentions if you would tell us where this man is hiding."

"Littel? I meet so many people, and the name is not uncommon."

A look of pained distaste registered on the face of the King's Man. "Mr.

Kent. No one knows where you are." He waved toward the door. "These men are entirely loyal to me. They would torture Princess Joelle if I commanded it. Will you tell me what I want to know, or will I resort to more extreme methods? And do not forget that I have your good driver as well. Perhaps he will be more willing to reveal where Mr. Littel is hiding."

"He does not know," Kent said quickly.

"Ah. . . . Then you do. Please, Kent, consider the heartache you will bring to others." Palle took a chair and folded his hands in his lap. "You should have taken my offer, Kent, rather than trying to continue in your path. It was an offer made in good faith."

Kent stared down at Palle for a few seconds, but the man's face remained impassive, registering nothing—like a page before it is written upon. "I could not ally myself with murderers," Kent said, turning toward Noyes, who looked away immediately.

Palle nodded, as though everything were clear now. "Recently a young Entonne opera singer was seen calling at your home, Sir Averil. This young woman is an agent of Count Massenet. I must say, she is being much more cooperative than you. Earlier, she told me that her sole reason for visiting you was to retrieve a certain letter that Count Massenet desired; which she did. What was the significance of this letter?"

Kent wondered if his alarm showed. He took a seat as casually as he could manage. "I cannot imagine."

Palle laughed softly. "What was it Massenet gave you that made you think you had acquired some form of *diplomatic protection?* Was this the 'root' that you said reached right to the heart of the palace? That would cause enough scandal to bring down the government?" Palle tilted his head as though encouraging an answer. "Massenet is entirely treacherous, Mr. Kent. Loyal only to his King and to his appetites. You see, you should have taken my generous offer." Palle traced a circle on the arm of his chair. "I will make you my final offer. Answer my questions, and I will let you retire honorably to your home in the country. In time you may even be allowed to return to Avonel. Refuse to cooperate with me, Mr. Kent, and I will deprive you of your physic. Consider the fate of poor Trevelyan." He looked up. "Where is this man Littel? Have you passed his knowledge on to Massenet?"

Kent looked over at Noyes, but the man still would not meet his eye, which told Kent only that he felt enormous guilt. Kent shifted in his chair, trying to look as little like a cornered beast as was possible. "Littel is in Locfal, at the home of Tristam Flattery."

Palle looked over at Noyes, then back to Kent. "I wonder if what we learn from your driver will corroborate this. And Massenet?"

"He knows nothing of Mr. Littel, I assure you."

Palle raised his eyebrows as though to say, *"really."* "Then what is the count planning?"

"I'm sure you know as well as I, Sir Roderick. It is you he despises and would thwart at any opportunity. He wishes to stop your *great endeavor,* obviously. But you say you have one of his agents: what does she tell you?"

"A great deal. It is remarkable how informative fear of beheading will make a person. Treason, Mr. Kent; we tolerate it no more than the Entonne."

Kent knew he should say nothing, but he could not help himself. "And what will you do with her once she has told you everything she knows?"

Palle met Kent's eye, but his look was not so unreadable now. There was amusement there. "That depends on how truthful you are with me, Mr. Kent. I place her life in your hands."

ᕧ Twenty-Eight

The Duke of Blackwater followed his servant to a small withdrawing room on the main floor.

"What is the hour?" he asked, more than a little irked by being wakened.

"Half twelve, sir."

"My word," the duke muttered.

The man awaiting him was a complete stranger, a servant, the duke realized immediately. Perhaps sixty, balding, utterly fastidious in his modest dress. The man seemed almost overcome with worry. As the duke entered, the man rose and made a leg.

"Sir, you are using the calling card of my friend, Sir Averil Kent. Can you explain this?"

"I am Sir Averil's manservant, Your Grace. I apologize profusely for waking Your Grace at this hour, but I am following Sir Averil's express instructions."

The duke nodded and waved the man back into his chair, taking a seat himself.

"My instructions from Sir Averil were precise. Whenever he leaves the house, he gives me an exact hour by which he will return or send a message. If at any time he fails to do so, I am to take a certain letter and bring it to Your Grace immediately."

"To me?" the duke said, caught by surprise.

"Yes, Your Grace."

"I see. Well, perhaps I should see this letter."

Smithers reached into his coat, a look of great distress on his face. "I retrieved the letter, as instructed, sir, but I could see immediately that the envelope contained nothing." He passed an envelope to the duke, who looked at it, still completely taken aback by what was happening—it was indeed empty. The envelope bore the name of Count Massenet, and the hand seemed vaguely familiar.

"How long is your master overdue?"

"I expected him some hours ago, sir. He has never failed to send a message in the past."

"What . . . what did Sir Averil expect of me?"

"I don't know," Smithers said, looking both embarrassed and deeply distressed. "He said that Your Grace would know."

The duke nodded, staring at the writing again. "Sir Averil disappeared not long ago, when he was visiting Merton, and then reappeared unharmed. Perhaps that will be the case again."

"I hope Your Grace is correct, but I think circumstances might be different. As I slipped out the back of our home, a group of men arrived. I stood in the shadows, not too far off, and watched them, trying to determine if they were friends of Sir Averil—perhaps bearing a message. When they finally managed to raise the housemaid, they thrust her aside and forced their way into the house. From the sounds, and what could be seen at the windows, these men appeared to be searching the house quite thoroughly. I slipped away then and came immediately here."

"And you did not know these men?"

"I did not, but if I had to guess, I would say they served the King's Man."

"Where had Sir Averil gone, do you know?"

"He seldom says, sir."

The duke nodded. "I think you should stay here for the rest of the night, Smithers. I will do what I can to locate your master."

The duke sat thinking after the manservant had been led away. For a moment he considered waking the duchess, but decided to let her rest.

When the servant returned, the duke considered a moment longer. "Wake Lord Jaimas and Miss Alissa," he instructed, and the servant backed from the room, exhibiting no surprise at this request.

A quarter of the hour went silently by before the two arrived, looking more anxious than sleepy.

"Is it Mother?" Jaimas asked immediately, making an effort to sound calm.

"No. No, the duchess is perfectly well. It is Kent." He related what had happened.

Alissa and Jaimy looked at each other, not liking what they heard, he could see.

"Where had Mr. Kent gone off to?" Alissa asked.

"The servant did not know. Kent wisely tells him little, I think."

Alissa bit her lip, lost in concentration. "When I visited him this morning, he said nothing that would indicate his plans." She looked at the duke. "Did the letter I brought offer any clues?"

The duke considered a moment. "He wrote to inform me that the plants the King keeps hidden in his arboretum had begun to flower. Do you know what I refer to?" Jaimy and Alissa nodded. "He indicated that Palle's group did not yet know of this, but once they did, he believed, it would set them on a course that would endanger all of Farrland. Kent is not known to be melodramatic. I'm sure what he says is true."

"Do you think the palace has taken him?" Jaimy asked.

For some reason the casualness with which this was said made the duke very sad. The statement spoke too much truth about Farrland at the present. "It is quite likely. I will find out. Better sooner than later." He picked up the empty envelope, glancing at it again. "This hand . . . it is familiar. . . ." He proffered the envelope to Jaimas, and he and Alissa bent over it.

"The princess," Alissa blurted out.

The duke looked at her, more questions in that gaze than anything. "You're certain?"

"Yes. The duchess could confirm it, but I'm quite sure."

The duke shook his head. It was not what he was expecting to hear. Kent had possessed a letter from the princess to Massenet. But the letter had been stolen, apparently, the envelope left in hopes that Kent would not notice the theft immediately. And this letter was to come to him if anything happened to Kent. It suggested innumerable possibilities.

"I should get a message to the Countess of Chilton immediately," Jaimy said, thinking aloud.

The duke nodded. "Yes. There is a ball at the palace," he said suddenly, "I will go see what I might learn."

Alissa rose from her chair. "I'll look like a country cousin, but I could be ready almost immediately."

The duke considered this a moment. "Yes. As quickly as you can. And Jaimas, you will accompany me, also. Let us see what effect that has on the King's Man."

Prince Wilam was trying to escape two very pleasant sisters, daughters of a marquess, who unfortunately bored him into somnolence. He kept trying to catch the eye of a young naval officer whose express duty that evening was to intervene as subtly as possible when such things occurred. Unfortunately the man was suffering a similar fate himself—the daughter of an admiral had his undivided attention—leaving the prince alternately furious and trying not to laugh at the absurdity of the situation.

The more he tried not to laugh, the more fragile his control became. The more fragile his control, the more animation the sisters forced into their conversation, looking distinctly uncomfortable at the prince's reddening face.

"Eh-xcuse me," the prince said, turning a laugh into something resembling a sneeze. It was at that moment that the Duke of Blackwater entered the room, accompanied by Alissa Somers and Lord Jaimas. All feelings of levity fled. Ignoring his companions, the prince began to search the room for Palle and spotted the King's Man just as one of his assistants brought the duke to Sir Roderick's attention.

Palle's face did not change when he turned his gaze on the duke and his, undeniably, living son, but it froze for just a moment, as though he had been stunned into immobility—like a man who has seen something horrific in the midst of battle. And then he turned away, speaking close to his assistant's ear as he swept out of the room. Noyes followed in his wake, looking back over his shoulder once, clearly frightened.

"He is wearing a sword," one of the sisters whispered, and the prince followed their gaze, realizing that they referred to the Duke of Blackwater. Since Beaumont had written his scathing attack on the barbarians who strode about bristling with weapons—and had not been challenged to a duel for it—the wearing of swords had fallen out of fashion, and the duel had almost disappeared. But here was a most civilized man wearing a rapier at his hip, and it did not appear to be a dress sword.

"Flames," the prince heard himself say.

Alissa and Jaimas made their way immediately toward Princess Joelle, and as the prince's eye followed them, he realized that his father, Prince Kori, had disappeared at the same time as the King's Man.

"I must congratulate Lord Jaimas on his coming marriage," the prince lied, and with a smile frozen in place, escaped his sleep fairies.

The prince could not make his way through the crowd quickly enough to reach his mother before Alissa and Jaimas, but he was only seconds behind them.

"Kent is gone," his mother whispered as soon as he was close enough.

Alissa did not meet his eye, but Jaimas' bow and the look on his face spoke of no animosity.

"If he is on the palace grounds, we know where they would keep him," the prince said. He looked quickly around the room and realized that several prominent lords had gathered around the Duke of Blackwater. "We should waste no time. Let me collect our loyal few," he said, and hurried off.

The guards were taken aback when they opened the door. Princess Joelle stood there, dressed for the ball and wearing a lord's fortune in precious stones. Beside her a young lord and the Duke of Blackwater stood silently, their stance determined: both carried swords.

"You will release Sir Averil Kent to me immediately," the princess said, her tone suggesting that compliance was not optional.

"Sir Averil?" the senior guard said, almost stuttering in his surprise.

The princess stepped aside so that the guard could see she was not without armed Palace Guards of her own. "Take these two men into custody. They have broken their oath and the laws of the Kingdom."

The sound of a sword being drawn hissed in the darkness. The lords of Blackwater pushed the door open and the guards on duty fell back, drawing their weapons. They may have been well trained in their duties, but their instructors had never imagined that they would be confronted by a member of the Royal Family. The two parties squared off, and, just when it seemed they would acquiesce, Palle's men chose which side they would back.

The struggle was brief, and the guards who came running to the clash of swords were so surprised by the situation that the building quickly fell to the princess and her supporters.

As soon as the fighting stopped, Princess Joelle entered the house, but was stopped by what she saw, color draining from her face. One guard lay unmoving on the floor, a small pool of blood forming slowly beneath him, and two others clutched wounds, anger written on their faces.

"It has begun," she said softly, and a single tear clung to her lashes, quivering there like a jewel taking form from the substance of human sadness and remorse.

They found Kent standing before an open window, staring down into the darkened garden. He spun quickly upon hearing the door, and for a second seemed disoriented, staring oddly at the rapiers, drawn and stained. His manner changed, becoming stiff and formal, his face grim with knowledge.

"Your Highness," he said, bowing formally, his voice laden with concern. "I prayed it would never come to this."

The princess seemed affected by Kent's reaction, and she stood for a moment as though overwhelmed by doubts. "We must hurry, Sir Averil," she said. "Nothing is settled. We may all be under armed guard before the night is over."

The ball continued, music drifting through the doors and into the myriad hallways of the palace like faint ghosts. No one was quite sure what would result from their actions, not even the princess. The unspoken rules that governed Farr politics were being broken by all sides. Palle and his supporters had attempted to murder the son of one of the kingdom's most powerful lords, and then they had abducted one of Farrland's most famed citizens—and all for their own purpose. And now the duke and a princess royal had risen against them, which would divide the government, at the very least. But everyone realized that they could not afford to lose their nerve now.

The princess gathered her supporters at the guard house and marched on the palace, armed almost entirely with the element of surprise. In consultation with the duke, they had agreed that immediate action was their only option. If Galton would side with them, and they could produce the King during a lucid period, they could then claim that Palle and Prince Kori had usurped power in the kingdom, keeping the King under the influence of a powerful physic. The regency could be dissolved and, at the very least, Palle brought down.

It was a dangerous gamble. Everyone understood that it could mean their own imprisonment, or even civil war. Their best chance lay in taking Palle and Prince Kori immediately, before they realized what was planned.

The Duke of Blackwater and guards loyal to the princess led the way into the palace through a little-used door. They swept into the larger hallways, surprising servants and guards as they went, taking them all in tow so that they could not sound the alarm.

They came into one of the main thoroughfares and saw, in the distance, a lone woman, dressed for the ball. She paused, shocked to see a band of armed men proceeding down the hallway, but just as she turned to flee, she hesitated. Wavered so that she almost lost balance.

"Lady Galton!" the duke called, and the woman's shoulders could be seen to sag with relief. She came hurrying down the hall as quickly as her elaborate gown would allow.

She was out of breath when she arrived. "They . . . have fled," she managed, and the princess and Alissa pushed through to take her arms, offering her support. Assisting her to sit in a chair.

She looked up at them, terribly distressed. "All of them . . ." she said. "The prince, Palle, Wells. . . . Gone. And they have Stedman with them."

"But where?" the duke asked, bending to one knee. "Where would they go?"

Lady Galton raised a hand, nodding, clearly indicating that she knew, but must catch her breath before speaking. She turned away from the group then, removing something from the bodice of her gown. She handed several folded sheets of thick paper to the princess, who opened them quickly.

"But what is this?" She showed the pages to the duke, who waved Kent forward.

The painter took one look and turned to Lady Galton. "The missing section of the text?"

She nodded, still unable to speak.

"But where has my husband gone?" the princess asked.

"*Tremont Abbey,*" Lady Galton whispered, barely managing to find enough breath.

*   *   *

Palle and his group had indeed fled. The princess and her followers secured the palace while most of the people in attendance at the ball had no idea that anything untoward occurred. Others, slightly more in the know, realized that something was happening and speculated endlessly in whispers. A third group knew that there was a struggle in the kingdom that had just broken out in actual hostilities, and they had slipped out of the palace quickly, and were desperately trying to gather information on what transpired.

No doubt, some of these were committed to one side or another, but many were waiting to see which way the struggle would go before declaring themselves. It was not important to them who won, as long as they were, in the end, aligned with the winners.

There was a very small fourth group who actually were players in the drama, and most of those had gathered in a state dining room on the ground floor. It was not a large gathering: Princess Joelle and her son; the Duke of Blackwater and Lord Jaimas; Kent and his rescued driver; Lady Galton; Alissa Somers; the Marquess of Sennet; several officers of the Palace Guard; the Sea Lord and his wife; and one Entonne opera singer, who looked decidedly frightened and out of place.

Sennet was sitting on the edge of his chair, shaking his head, not in disbelief so much as awe. "And I thought I knew what transpired in the Kingdom." He kept glancing up at Kent with something like admiration, a bemused smile spreading over his face.

A map lay on the table and the duke and Jaimy were leaning over it, occasionally tracing some significant line with a finger. Alissa sat with Lady Galton, who was recovering and trying not to be seen watching the beautiful young Entonne girl who sat by herself, looking entirely dejected. Kent had spoken to her earlier, not unkindly, but their conversation had been in Entonne— something about a letter—and Alissa had not caught it all. The woman had shown great difficulty meeting the painter's eye, and had been near to tears, Alissa thought. Very odd, but then everything about the situation was extraordinary. She was not sure that anyone really believed what had happened. In less than an hour their entire world had changed, and they were the agents of this change.

Alissa wondered if she would not have been better off staying in Merton and marrying some young scholar, as her father had wanted. She had enough knowledge of what went on to realize that if this rebellion failed she would likely be charged with treason. It was frightening knowledge to have.

In its absence, the powers of the Regency Council would normally devolve to Lord Harrington, the Chancellor of the Exchequer. Alissa remembered Kent pointing out Lord Harrington at the duchess' birthday celebration. He was a very small, dapper man, known for his brilliance. If he had a weakness as a politician, it was his alleged single-minded drive to increase his personal fortune—not that this was uncommon among ministers, Alissa was given to understand.

At the moment no one knew Lord Harrington's whereabouts. *"Probably plundering the treasury,"* someone had suggested, but it had sounded too much like gallows humor, and the laughter had been bitten off short. Alissa sensed that there was nothing that worried the people present so much at this moment, unless it was the sudden disappearance of Palle and his entire cabal.

Jaimy stood with his father speaking in low tones, both terribly serious, but there was something else in their manner.

She felt at that moment that these men were strangers to her. Men who discussed the fate of the kingdom as though it were not absurd to be doing so. As though it were not unnatural. She was overcome by a feeling that she did not belong in this room. Perhaps did not want to belong here. This was not the insular world of Merton where politics was another subject for discussion, like literature, or philosophy. In this room politics had ceased to be theory.

Jaimy's belief that he could avoid the responsibilities of his position was proven naive here, and this, she found, caused her great distress.

Alissa was also aware that the prince occasionally looked her way, as much as he tried not to. Oh, he did not stare, nor was he obvious about it, but he could not stop himself from glancing at her. Alissa sensed this more than saw it, for she would not meet his gaze. If this rebellion actually survived the night, the prince would be put forward to succeed the King, rather than Prince Kori. No one had said this, but it was obvious. Prince Kori would have to fall with Palle and the others—abdicate in favor of his son. This young man who was infatuated with her would be next in line for the throne.

The door opened and a woman was allowed to enter. Everyone turned toward her, but no one spoke or made any gesture of welcome.

"Lady Rawdon," Lady Galton whispered near Alissa's ear.

The woman who had stopped inside the door was not beautiful, but she had such bearing and poise that she drew the eye all the same. Alissa did not know Lady Rawdon, but had heard she had been very ill only the previous year. For some reason Alissa was interested to see the woman who had captured the heart of the royal physician, for Benjamin Rawdon was one of the most admired men in the kingdom, by the ladies at least. He was certainly one of the most handsome men Alissa had ever seen, though aloof and distracted in his manner.

The duke greeted her, acting as the princess' representative—a sort of Queen's Man.

Lady Rawdon did not speak, but stood looking about her, as though suddenly and uncharacteristically unsure of herself.

"I wish to speak with the princess. I beg your indulgence, Duke, but it is concerning a matter of some sensitivity."

The duke glanced at the princess, who nodded, and he waved Lady Rawdon forward. As she passed, Alissa saw that she had the most intelligent look. As though her mental acuity was so strong that it almost shone in her eyes, the way self-doubt did in others.

Lady Rawdon and the princess went to the far end of the long room, and spoke quietly before the hearth. The princess stood aloof from this woman—unquestionably a sovereign being petitioned by one of her subjects, and not necessarily one she felt any warmth or compassion toward.

Thinking that it was impolite to stare at this private interchange, Alissa looked away, but noticed that the duke stared openly, his manner intent. Alissa was certain that he could not be concerned for the princess' safety, and wondered what it was that caused him to act so.

Suddenly he turned and crossed to Lady Galton. Bending down close to her he whispered, "Did Rawdon cure his wife with this seed?"

Lady Galton's head snapped up at his question, and she met the duke's eye. "You would be wise not to pursue this," she said quietly, a slight quaver in her voice, her head shaking as she spoke.

"It is true, then?" the duke said, ignoring her admonition.

Lady Galton did not answer, but her eyes searched the duke's as though she were deciding what he might do with this information.

The princess left Lady Rawdon standing by the hearth and returned, walking directly toward the duke and Lady Galton, gesturing for her son to follow. Alissa stayed where she was, and realized she had not been so close to the prince all evening, even though he purposely stood on the opposite side of the circle.

"Do not rise, cousin," the princess said to Lady Galton, who held so tightly to Alissa's hand that she could not rise either, though no one seemed to notice. "Lady Rawdon claims that her husband is disillusioned with Sir Roderick and the prince. He is nearby, she will not say where, unwilling to leave the King, who is his charge. Rawdon is prepared to give his support to us, and Lady Rawdon has told me Roderick's destination to prove her good faith."

The duke cast his gaze toward the woman standing near the fireplace, but she had her back to them and stood hugging herself, her head to one side, staring down as though lost in sad memories. The duke turned back to the princess. "Lady Galton has already told us their destination. Why did Palle fly when he did, leaving only Rawdon behind? That is the information we require. If she will tell us that, I will look more kindly on their defection, for it is remarkably convenient that she has come to us now. If we carry the day, they will be safe, and if we do not, they will claim that they had no choice but to make concessions to preserve the King." The duke stopped to think for a moment. "I also fear that Rawdon will control the King's mental state with this physic, as Your Highness has suggested that he does. If we cannot prove His Majesty to be competent—our resistance will be treason."

The princess stood with an arm folded across her breast, the hand supporting the opposite elbow so that she could stroke her chin with the free hand. "Only Rawdon truly understands this physic. It has all been kept such a secret. I do not know what will happen to the King if we do not have Rawdon to attend him. I tend to think that Lady Rawdon is sincere. I have never known her to be otherwise. And if that is true, we could certainly use Rawdon's voice to support our claims."

"I have never thought anything but the best of Lady Rawdon," the duke conceded, "and before his support of Palle, I always thought highly of her husband. Will Rawdon sign documents that explain how the King has been kept in a state of near madness and dependence? Will he name Palle and Prince Kori as the instigators?"

"Yes," the princess said. "He will denounce the regents and swear that the King is competent still. My husband asked the doctor to stay to watch over the King. Say what you will against the prince, he has not allowed the King to suffer any accident, which would have been the easiest way to power. Apparently regicide is beyond even him."

The duke looked over at Lady Rawdon again. "I say we should accept their pledge of loyalty, but keep them under careful scrutiny. If we are to claim that Palle and the prince seized power from a competent King, then His Majesty must appear competent. That is the one certainty."

Both pain and exasperation were revealed in the princess' next words. "Then we cannot allow the King to continue this overindulgence in the seed. Palle and the prince fostered this dependence and now Rawdon must bring it under control, without endangering the King's life."

Alissa wondered immediately how much the duke's own interest in the seed had colored his judgment. It was obvious that his questioning of Lady Galton was not innocent.

The princess put her hands together. "Then we agree," she said. "But we mustn't forget that we are restoring power to the King. It is our only chance of survival. If Lord Harrington is confronted with a King restored in both mind and position, then he will be taking the greatest risk to not pledge his support. We must move quickly to legitimize our position and gain recognition from the senior ministers."

With that the princess crossed back to Lady Rawdon and took her hands, kissing her on both cheeks in the Entonne manner. They spoke for a moment, and then Lady Rawdon hurried out, leaving the princess to return to her supporters.

"Lady Rawdon says that Palle and his followers fled Avonel the moment they learned that Count Massenet and this Entonne doctor, Varese, had slipped away and gone north. Palle and the prince were convinced Massenet was making for Tremont Abbey, and they went in immediate pursuit. It was only coincidental that the duke arrived at the same moment."

Kent bobbed his head. "Yes. Yes. That makes sense. My own colleague, Mr. Valary, believes the abbey was once used by the mages for certain rituals, before it was destroyed by the Farrellites. . . . And maybe even after. I have seen it myself. In a hidden chamber in a deep cellar there was once a close copy of the Ruin of Farrow." Kent held up the pages that Lady Galton had given him. "Mr. Littel and Mr. Valary must see this. They are the authorities."

"And the Countess of Chilton, Lord Jaimas tells me," the duke added.

Kent nodded, obviously still unwilling to name the countess.

"We need their counsel, then," the princess said quickly. "Can you have them brought here?"

Kent nodded. "Though I cannot speak for the countess. She has remained aloof these thirty years. I don't think she will emerge, now, no matter what goes on in the kingdom."

"I will write the countess myself," the princess said. "We must draw upon all the wisdom we can in these matters. We have not a moment to waste. The struggle for the kingdom may be waged far away."

The dining room had been chosen because of its proximity to both the apartments of the King and to the arboretum where His Majesty spent much of his time. The princess and her followers could not risk having the King fall into the hands of their rivals, and so put this area under control of those Palace Guards who were most trusted.

Kent and Sennet had commandeered a separate table, and immediately set about gathering information on the state of the capital. A constant stream of supporters came and went, reporting everything they learned. Alissa was astonished by the number of informants the two gentlemen could call into service on such short notice. Every so often one or both of them would report something to the duke and the princess, and occasionally the duke would go to them with questions.

Alissa had the distinct impression that the individuals gathered in this room were like people walking in the dark, listening so intently that their own heartbeats were almost too loud, overwhelming the faint sounds they sought so desperately. She felt they attempted to sense vibrations, movements in the air, and even tried to look into the pitch-black night. The tension in the room was captured in this forced silence.

Somewhere in the city of Avonel, officers loyal to the Regency Council might be gathering an army. Lord Harrington could be plotting to take the palace, even now. The princess had secured the grounds, but at this point it was impossible to be sure of the loyalty of every guard. It would take only a single man opening a gate, and everyone in this room could find themselves in prison.

"You must turn your mind elsewhere," Lady Galton said, regaining her breath finally. "There is no profit in dwelling on what might happen, Lady Alissa. We have taken a leap into the darkness, unsure of where we will land. But there is no way to turn back in midair. We must land where we will land, and try to keep our feet. There is nothing else for it. That is all we can do." She squeezed Alissa's hand and smiled kindly at her, which touched the younger woman. At a moment that would be written in Farr history, this woman had taken time to comfort her. It showed a kindness and compassion that Alissa thought she would never equal.

An hour later Sir Benjamin Rawdon arrived in the company of his wife. The physician appeared troubled and more than a little apprehensive. He made a leg to the princess, and, very self-consciously, swore an oath of loyalty to the King, renouncing his allegiance to the Regency Council. After this formality, Prince Wilam and the duke accompanied the princess and Sir Benjamin to visit the King.

It was near to morning by this time and people were leaving the ball; most still completely unaware of what had gone on, which Alissa found astonishing. But then, only a year earlier she would not even have received an invitation, let alone known what transpired behind the closed doors of the palace. She was a little saddened to realize how far even the educated of Farrland were from the true workings of government.

Jaimy was sent as envoy to the Countess of Chilton, and Alissa accompanied Lady Galton, who had been summoned to the famous arboretum. Alissa thought she would never look pityingly at an elderly person again. The older generation in the persons of Lady Galton, Kent, and Sennet, seemed to be proving its mettle tonight.

A guard led them down a path that wound its way through dense jungle. Despite the season outside, beneath the glass it was almost hot, and quite humid. Alissa wondered if any of these plants were Kingfoil; but none seemed to fit the description Tristam had given Jaimy. The sound of water falling and then a sweet tenor floated through the branches, sounds as ethereal as the flight of a butterfly.

They found Rawdon seated on a stone bench, listening to Teiho Ruau, who stood by a small pond, singing as though his heart would break. The music touched Alissa immediately, though she could not understand a word. Her eyes adjusted to the poor light, and she realized that Prince Wilam sat beside someone slumped on a cushioned bench, almost hidden by the darkness. Close at hand the princess was seated in her own chair, and beside her the duke.

Rawdon gestured to them, and gave up his bench. For a few moments Alissa sat, transported by the singing. She had heard Ruau perform only once, and that had been Farr and Entonne music, but this was a sweet foreign tongue, a song of heartache, she was sure; of loss or parting. The staccato of falling water, and the sweet perfume of exotic flowers combined to make the situation seem entirely unreal. It was almost impossible to believe she was in Farrland in late winter.

The song ended, much to Alissa's regret, though it left an ache in her breast that would not be easily erased.

The Royal Physician escorted Lady Galton forward to take the prince's place. Prince Wilam bowed to his grandfather and turned toward Alissa. She realized that he was going to come and sit beside her—he simply could not help himself.

Neither of them spoke, though he motioned for her not to rise and curtsy, so they exchanged nods only. Above the sound of the tumbling water Alissa could hear the mumble of conversation between Lady Galton, the King, and the princess. His Majesty's voice was a deep, disconcerting rumble; a sound no human throat should have been capable of producing.

Rawdon caught Alissa's eye and whispered to her. "We will see Lady Galton safely returned."

Prince Wilam rose immediately. "It would be an honor to escort you back, Lady Alissa." He offered his hand, and she accepted it to rise but purposely did not take his arm as they left.

"I had not heard Teiho Ruau sing in his own tongue. Very beautiful," Alissa said as they passed into the jungle.

"Yes. I have found that not understanding the words is a small impediment— the sentiment is conveyed perfectly. Dr. Rawdon's associate, a man named Llewellyn, spent some time translating the lyrics, and though I found these of great interest, my appreciation of the songs was not greatly increased. It occurred to me that one could translate the words of our best Farr songs into an unknown tongue and they would affect the heart just as strongly. Music is a conduit for emotion." He cocked his head at her. "Do you play?"

"Not well, though I enjoy it a great deal. And you?"

"Poorly. I have often thought that I was born with the temperament of an artist, but none of the talents." She could see his smile in the poor light.

"Perhaps you have not found your talent, yet, Your Highness."

"I would like to think that is true, but I suspect it's not. I will have to learn to be a passable King, I'm afraid."

An awkward silence fell, as false as the conversation that had preceded it.

Alissa could not bear empty conversation, and wondered how she would survive as a duchess of Farrland.

The prince began to speak, but Alissa raised her hand. "Say nothing, please. Let us have silence that is true: like music without words."

The prince nodded his head, and they walked on in silence. Alissa knew what emotion this silence conveyed, and felt deep regret that she could not respond.

Lady Galton found that the arboretum had a surprisingly kind effect on her breathing. Heat and dampness hardly seemed a physic for improved breathing, but then perhaps it was really the soothing sounds of the falling water, the charm and serenity of the environment.

"I will die without it," the King said to the princess. "Look. Look what want of it has done to me already. I am living my death. Who can even bear to set eyes on me? NO! I must have more, not less. More!"

"But if the Ministers of the Government cannot be convinced that His Majesty is competent, then Prince Kori and Palle will return, and the seed will fall under their control again. They will let you slip back into your world of dreams, while stealing the kingdom."

"But I am old, old. What need have I to govern? Let me have my physic. Have I not earned my rest? A century I have labored. A *century*."

The princess was near to tears, Lady Galton thought. This terrible, willful old man would condemn them all to prison or worse if he would not cooperate. The princess had underestimated his desire for the seed. It was greater than his desire to do well by his kingdom. He had sacrificed everything to it, why not his daughter-in-law and grandson? Had he asked them to stage this rebellion?

"Your Majesty must remember that Palle would withhold the seed when he wanted to bend you to his will. Withhold it and make Your Majesty suffer. I ask only that you reduce your intake until we have proven your competence. Once there is a new King's Man and the succession is arranged to Your Majesty's satisfaction—the throne going to Wil—then you may do as you like."

"I will do as I like now!" he raged in his terrible voice.

"But they have set out to retrieve the knowledge of the mages," Lady Galton said suddenly. "What will we do if they accomplish that?"

The King shook his head, rubbing his brow gently. "Yes. I remember. Yes. That young Flattery came, and then they sent him on their errand. Has the time come? Has Elorin fulfilled her promise?"

"What promise?" the princess asked.

"Where have they gone?" he asked, suddenly calm, almost interested. "Palle and the others?"

"Tremont Abbey."

"I see. Yes. Then we must go as well. Bring my physic, and Ruau, and this treacherous doctor, too. He keeps my physic from me. Ready my carriage, bring a company of loyal guards. We must leave at first light, but don't forget my physic. And my portrait. Has Kent finished my portrait? There is no hope without him. There is nothing more certain than that."

"But, Your Majesty," Princess Joelle said soothingly, "we must convince the Ministers that you are lucid, and that the Regency Council is unnecessary."

The old man shifted on his bench so that he looked at his daughter-in-law in the darkness. "My dear Joelle," he said, a sudden clarity of thought apparent in those terrible tones, "if we do not arrive at the abbey before Sir Roderick; who controls the kingdom according to the law will be of no importance whatsoever. All will be lost. Ready my carriage. If we ruin a hundred horses, we must be at the abbey before Palle, or everything I have planned will be lost. Ready yourself in all haste. I leave in three hours."

Alissa sat by the window watching the sun rise through the mist, which hung in the garden like a thin wash of paint smeared across the air. An arrangement of purple iris and pale yellow roses stood before the window in a simple vase, catching the morning light. One particular rose had opened far beyond maturity, as though attempting to reveal its heart, and appeared almost languid, the largest outer petal falling away like the train of a lady's gown. She admired the way the light and shadow fell among the petals. How the fluted edges caught the sun and rippled through the shadows like movement on the surface of water. Astonishing that the flower had achieved this moment of intense beauty only an instant before its petals would fall. The slightest breeze would carry them away—a door opening too quickly, a child running near.

"Everything is so fragile," she whispered.

Jaimy found her there some time later. The morning sun had risen, like a ship's flare, and hung burning beyond the park, casting a golden light over Alissa, illuminating the straying strands of her auburn hair. She sat on a divan, her arms around her drawn-up knee, her skirt trailing like a fan to the floor. She cradled her head on her arms, and Jaimy thought he had never seen such dejection.

As he took a seat beside her, she raised her head: obviously she had not been sleeping, as he thought.

"You look very dejected, my love," he said softly.

"Dejected? No, I am merely adjusting to what I now perceive as the real world."

Jaimy reached out and put a hand gently on her back. "Yes. It has all changed in so few hours. Suddenly we are risking everything over this matter, though it is not entirely clear what it all means."

She looked at him closely for a moment, and then took his hand and wrapped his arm around her, turning away and pressing her back against him.

"That is not the reality I speak of," she said. "If we survive this, I will become a real duchess—not just one in name. We will be embroiled in the intrigues of the court, the social life of the aristocracy, the constant concern for power and place. We think we can avoid it and live quietly, but we cannot. Without your father, tonight, what would have happened? And it is the duke's place you take, with all its attendant responsibilities. Our lives will not be our own."

Jaimy put his cheek against her back and heard the slow measured beat of her heart, or was it his own? He could not be sure. "Although my heart would be broken, utterly, Alissa. . . ." For a second his nerve failed, but then he shut his eyes and continued in a whisper. "I would release you from your vow if you will not be happy in our life together." It was said. The heartbeat did not alter but continued to measure the endless silence.

"I will consider your offer," Alissa said in a small voice. "Jaimas?"

"Yes."

"I love only you."

The sun continued to wash them in the colors of a late winter morning, and they sat unmoving, not wanting to give up the other's presence. A petal fell from the rose, turning once slowly in the air, before landing without a sound.

* * *

Tier and Tarré draw near and far
While starlit gates await the hand
The moon shall sail o'er hidden realms
To seek the heart of mage and man.

Valary pushed ineffectually at his unruly hair, and stared down at the pages Lady Galton had delivered. "Tier and Tarré are the names of stars, I believe, but possibly names of places as well. There are other references to them, you see. Lapin mentioned Tier in the presence of Dunn, who recorded everything he could remember the mage saying, though he did not understand the reference. A star, a place—those were his guesses."

Littel sat massaging his temples, his excitement only somewhat blunted by his obvious exhaustion. "The translation is competent. I see a few things that I would dispute, but largely it is good." He placed his finger on one page. "This line is certainly open to argument, but then. . . . It is hard to be sure."

"But what do you think it means?" It was the princess speaking. The room had been cleared of everyone but the princess, Prince Wilam, the Duke of Blackwater, Kent, Lady Galton, and Sennet, and the countess, who sat in a corner of the purposely darkened room (her face hidden by a veil) where she was the object of deep fascination for everyone there.

Valary straightened up, rubbed his eyes for just a second, and then looked around the group. "My best guess is that it is a ritual for opening a portal—'the way beneath the vaulted hills.' I've now come to believe that Tier is the site beneath the ruin of Tremont Abbey. I have several reasons for this. . . ." He lifted a finger like a lecturer and then saw the look on Kent's face. "But I can explain another time. This text seems to imply that two such sites must be employed simultaneously." He pointed to the pages on the table. "It states several times that one must heed the words of Tarré. We might ask Lady Chilton, but I think this would mean the rite is performed turn about. The person performing the rite at one site taking his turn and then the other."

"But where is the other site?" Kent asked. "Farrow?"

"It seems most likely."

"I think you will find that the site is on Varua, Mr. Valary," the countess said, her flat tones catching everyone's attention so that they turned toward this apparition in the corner, intensely fascinated. The countess raised a gloved hand. "That is what the signs mean, I think. The *regis* blossoming. The appearance of the ghost boy to Sir Averil and Lord Jaimas. This earth tremor on Farrow. Tristam Flattery has begun the transformation from human to mage. This ritual will be the culmination of that process, or so I surmise."

"But what of all this talk of gates? To where do they lead?"

"Perhaps the question might be to what do they lead, Mr. Littel. Knowledge, I fear. The knowledge we thought lost."

"My uncle, Erasmus Flattery, believed that the mages were involved in a great undertaking," said the duke, causing Kent to turn suddenly. "An undertaking that absorbed almost all their efforts for some time. Decades, he thought. My uncle didn't know the precise nature of this endeavor, but Eldrich apparently referred to it as 'the grand exploration.' It was Erasmus' obsession, though I am not sure how much he actually learned in the end."

"Well," Sennet said, speaking for the first time since this group had gathered, "it seems clear that we cannot let Palle or Massenet have whatever knowledge there is to be found. We must have it first."

There was a moment of silence and then Kent said kindly, "No one must have it, Sennet, absolutely no one. Not even someone as kindly and honorable as yourself. That was what the mages learned in the end, though we have only suspicions of why. But rest assured, we do not race Palle and Massenet to gain the knowledge ourselves. We go to destroy it forever."

Sennet looked as though he would protest but finally nodded. If he was embarrassed at his mistake, he did not show it.

"Kent is absolutely right." Valary opened a small box that lay among the chaos of his papers. With great care he removed a yellowed scrap of paper from a stiff envelope. "I am absolutely certain that this is authentic. These are the words of Lucklow:

I have been a witness to this horror and can tell you that our colleague exaggerated nothing. Children armed with fearsome weapons roam the streets as brigands, killing man or woman for little gain—often enough for none at all. Sky choked with a yellowish pall, noxious and unwholesome to the lung, it blots out the blue by day and the stars by night. The poor starve on the paving stones, and citizens shut themselves up in homes that have casements barred and doors of iron. In our darkest times we have not known such calamity, and this is the common day in this benighted land! At all costs we must end this fool's endeavor! We are tainted enough as it is.

Valary looked up at those gathered around the table. There was a profound silence, broken only by Lady Galton's breathing.

"We believe that this 'fool's endeavor' Lucklow refers to is the same matter spoken of by the duke," Kent said quietly. "We may never know what it was the mages encountered, but by all accounts Lucklow was a man of considerable brilliance. If it frightened him, then it terrifies me. We would not easily make a decision to bring Farrland to an end, yet that is, in effect, what the mages chose to do. By refusing to train the generation to follow, they brought an end to their world. Imagine us choosing to bear no children, and letting the human race come to an end. That is what they did. And, as Valary has said, we may never know why. But this knowledge is enough for me."

"Where in the world did you come by that?" Littel asked, incredulous.

Kent looked directly at the princess as he answered. "It came from Count Massenet, though we are sure it is no forgery."

This brought a second silence, not quite as deep as the first. Everyone in the room wondered how in the world Kent had managed to come by this document, yet no one wanted to hear the answer. The name Massenet was used in the palace to conjure visions of betrayal and treason.

Jaimas broke the silence. "Sir Averil? Does Roderick have someone who can perform this ritual? I thought that was the role they had hoped Tristam would fulfill."

Kent shook his head. "I don't understand it either." He glanced at the princess, and then at Lady Galton. "I thought that they were seeking someone with talent as well. Perhaps they seek only to stop the Entonne."

"Baron Trevelyan," Lady Galton said. "He was their last resort if they could find no other."

"Trevelyan?" Kent said, shaking his head sadly. "No. The poor baron is quite mad."

"Not at all times, and Stedman thought that Palle could control his condition, at least for short periods of time. Rawdon would know."

"And the Entonne have Bertillon—and Varese filling in for Mr. Valary and Mr. Littel—though what they hope to accomplish, I cannot say." Kent looked down at the pages spread over the table. "Have they discovered some text we know nothing of, or did they manage to steal the work of Wells and Galton? I will ask this young Entonne singer, though it is unlikely that she will agree to answer." Kent closed his eyes for a second, as though fatigue had caught up with him as well.

"Perhaps they mean to damage the site at the abbey in some way. Make it unusable for others?" the duke suggested, and then turned to ask a question of the countess. "But where has Lady Chilton gone?"

Her chair was empty. The guard at the door reported that the woman in the veil had left several moments earlier, though no one in the room had noticed.

Kent immediately went in search of the countess and soon learned that she had left the palace, and, to his utter astonishment, taken Tenil with her. The painter sat down on a bench in an alcove, looking out over the gardens. The countess had gone without so much as a word, and taken with her Massenet's agent. He had never mentioned his dealings with Massenet to the countess, but she would soon know. Tenil would not be able to keep anything from Lady Chilton, he was sure of that. The countess would even learn that Kent and Tenil had spent the night together. She would realize that it was the first thing Kent had done with his restored vitality.

"*I felt betrayed,*" he whispered. But how would the countess feel when she found out? Likely she would feel nothing. Kent did not wish anyone pain, but could she not experience just a little?

The King proved determined to make the journey, and though no one thought it wise, especially the Royal Physician, even he had to concede that it was less dangerous for all involved to take the King with them—providing His Majesty survived.

In the end the princess pronounced. "If we are restoring power to the King, then we must abide by His Majesty's will in such matters."

And so the King's carriage took its place in the cavalcade. The princess and Lady Galton and Alissa traveled together. Kent, Valary, and Littel took another carriage. The King traveled with his doctor and Ruau, while various servants and functionaries followed, and Palace Guards went both before and behind. The duke, Jaimy and—after a heated battle with the princess—Prince Wilam, set out on horseback with a company of Palace Guards, in hope of overtaking the other parties and delaying them in the name of the King.

The Marquess of Sennet was appointed King's Man and left behind to deal with Lord Harrington and to spearhead the restoration of power to the King, something, the duke confided to his son, that should not be relegated such a minor part in the bigger scheme. Even with signed letters from the King, the Duke of Blackwater, and the princess, Sennet would be trying to garner support for the King while unable to explain the sovereign's absence.

If Massenet and Palle had left agents in the city, which certainly they had, they could not miss the parade of carriages leaving Avonel escorted by armed Palace Guards. Whether these agents could catch their masters to warn them was the question.

Kent worried that they would never make it to the abbey in time. This convoy would not travel quickly, despite the King apparently swearing they must not rest until they had overtaken their rivals.

"What do you think the King knows about these matters?" Kent asked his companions, not because they were likely to know more than he did, but because he could not bear to be alone with his questions any longer.

Littel shrugged. "You have spoken with His Majesty, Kent, you should know if anyone does."

"Yes, I should. But, unfortunately, I don't. I shall have to corner Rawdon. Despite his apparent defection, the good doctor is not being generous with his knowledge unless it is specifically asked for. I don't care for his attitude." Kent looked out at the passing scene. "I have often wondered if His Majesty sent the Duchess of Morland on this voyage of discovery, or if it was her own initiative. Certainly she would never have gone if she had not believed it was of the utmost importance. But was the King involved in the decision?"

Valary touched his arm, drawing his attention back from the passing scene. "According to Lady Galton, His Majesty has waking dreams. Portents of what is to come. The King has been taking this seed for some years now. Even if his talent is very small, I think this could well be true. Lady Galton assures me that Wells and company believe they have foreknowledge. Events were foreseen, and this led them to send Tristam Flattery to Oceana. And the King may have sent the duchess as a result of his own intuition. Palle certainly has people aboard the *Swallow* who plan to exploit the situation, just as the duchess must be hoping to do."

"Valary, what in the world are we heading into?" Kent said with feeling. "Even if we are able to stop Massenet and Palle, will it matter? The real threat may be this young Flattery. Did the countess not say he had begun the transformation from human to mage? Were those not her words? And that is exactly what we have struggled against. That fragment of Lucklow's letter . . . I have seldom read anything so ominous. And the countess, despite her tendency to secrecy, is convinced that a rediscovery of the arts will bring about a cataclysm. And she knows more than we."

Valary nodded. "Yes. And where has the countess gone? That is what I'm wondering. What was said that set her off so quickly?"

Kent wondered the same thing. And why had she taken Tenil? It seemed very odd. Had Tenil actually been watching Massenet for the countess all along? And watching Kent for both of them? He just did not know.

"You're our authority on Tremont Abbey, Valary; what do you think the mages used it for? Was it required for their arts in some way?"

Valary considered a moment, running through the countless details of the history in his mind. "It is difficult to answer, Kent. There were times when the abbey was not controlled by the mages—some quite long stretches—so it's impossible that it could have served for something so central as the rites of initiation, or some such thing. The discovery of the Ruin on Farrow was only four hundred or so years ago, and the mages certainly did not build that. It now appears that they were as fascinated by it as anyone. I'm beginning to believe that the purpose of the two ruins was realized after their discovery. Perhaps long after. It had something to do with their great endeavor, and then the fragment written by Lucklow. But what that great endeavor was, is still a mystery."

"Not to Lady Chilton," Littel said firmly, surprising the other two.

"Did she say something to you that I did not hear?" Valary asked.

"Not really, no. It is what she did not say, coupled with the strength of her conviction. I am certain she knows. Knows even more than Wells and company. More than this man Massenet. That is why she ran off. I'm sure she is on this road before us, journeying north with all speed. Faster than we will manage, that is certain. Only the duke and the others have a chance of catching her. No, we will arrive after it has all been decided, I'm afraid. And then, perhaps, we will find what this has all been about. I pray we have not done some terrible evil with our efforts, Valary. I could not live with that."

⤷ Twenty-Nine

Even with Faairi leading, it was not an easy hike down to the village on Gregory Bay. Tristam scrambled along after his Varuan maiden as best he could, but her legs were more accustomed to roaming the island than his, and he barely kept up. An ominous rumble, like thunder, tumbled up the slopes from the bay, and they both stopped in alarm.

"Was that your ship's guns?" she asked.

"I'm not sure," Tristam said, almost certain that it was. There was no thundercloud in the sky that he could see. They carried on, Tristam pushing himself now, and neither sparing breath to speak.

As they approached the abandoned village, Faairi took them off the path, and they crept quietly through a grove of trees. And here, hiding in dense bush, they found some of the *Swallow*'s crew. The viscount was there, standing near to his sister, and Stern was crouched down behind the foliage, staring intently out through the branches toward the bay.

"Tristam!" Some part of the duchess' apprehension disappeared as she noticed the naturalist. "I have been worried unto madness. You are well? You look exhausted." She eyed Tristam's companion dubiously.

"Perfectly well. What in the world has happened?"

"We've had a mutiny," the duchess said, placing a hand on his shoulder as though assuring herself he was real. "At first light. Somehow Llewellyn got word of it, and we were lucky to escape into the boats. We got ashore, but then they drove us away from the boats with cannon fire. We wait, now, to see what they will do."

Tristam looked around, making note of who had come ashore: Tobias Shuk; Jacel, of course; Beacham; Osier; Llewellyn, but not the ship's surgeon; a dozen Jacks; Pim; the captain's steward; a few others. Not quite half the crew, Tristam could see, and they were poorly armed. Only a few swords and short pikes among them. Some of the Jacks had made spears by sharpening poles, and this gave Tristam no confidence at all. Stern had been caught completely unawares, despite his confrontation with the Jacks.

Wallis caught Tristam's eye and nodded, looking more anxious and despairing than anyone present.

"Who was it led them?" Tristam asked. "Kreel?"

"*Hobbes!*" the duchess said, her own shock and sadness apparent.

Tristam sat down on the stump of a felled tree. "Hobbes?"

"Yes. We still cannot believe it. The master will have this seed for himself. That is what Stern thinks. They will take it by force from the Varuans, if need be, and with such women as they can tempt along, will set off to find an island of their own in unknown seas."

Faairi brought Tristam an opened drinking nut, receiving another strange look from the duchess, though the islander did not seem to much care. Tristam searched the group again, and found Julian standing near to Stern, now, the most dangerous position, without a doubt—as near to death as he could be. Everyone focused their attention on Stern and what was happening in the bay.

"Elorin," Tristam said, keeping his voice low. "Julian tried to murder Hobbes."

Her manner became suddenly guarded and stiff. "Did you see this?"

"No, but I spoke with another who did. I don't doubt his word. And it might explain things. After the deaths of Garvey and Chilsey, Hobbes intended self-murder, but could not go through with it. Julian attacked him. Now Hobbes must believe his life is in constant danger, and that we harbor a murderer." Tristam moved his head toward the viscount, almost without meaning to. "What little loyalty Hobbes might still have for Stern and the service has been destroyed utterly. He has chosen to live. And if he cannot go home to Farrland with honor, then by Farrelle, he will have this seed we seek and live long among the islands."

The duchess looked distant, as though she were barely able to contain her anger—but it seemed to Tristam that he was the focus of this rage, not Julian.

"They're coming ashore," Stern said, raising his voice enough to carry to his supporters. "Move back. Mr. Wallis, can you lead us to a safe place? We are outnumbered, and poorly armed."

"Yes. Certainly, yes. Come along quickly."

Stern began shepherding his charges back into the forest, glancing back over his shoulder. "They will take the ship's boats now," he said to Osler.

"There's nothing for it, sir. They will drive us back with cannon fire if we attempt the beach again."

Out on the lagoon Tristam caught a glimpse of a manned raft made of barrels. It bobbed precariously as the Jacks paddled toward shore. At the mention of danger, Tristam found that his exhaustion passed. He could easily have outpaced the others but followed up the rear of the party with Stern.

"Osler tells me you are a swordsman, Mr. Flattery?" Stern asked, his manner calm.

"Of sorts," Tristam said quickly.

"Doctor?" Stern called out. "Would you give Mr. Flattery your blade?"

Reluctantly, Llewellyn paused to let Tristam catch up. The man was obviously terrified. He pressed his sword into Tristam's hand and the naturalist realized that it was his own blade, from his cabin. And Llewellyn carried Tristam's canvas bag, as well.

"I managed to rescue a few thing from your cabin, Tristam," the doctor said matter-of-factly. "Shall I keep this safe for you for the time being?"

Tristam was too surprised to feel anger. What was the man up to? Certainly Llewellyn did nothing for anyone but himself. "Yes," Tristam managed, "do that, Doctor." And Llewellyn hurried up to the front of the group again, showing no signs of shortness of breath.

Stern looked back, exhibiting some reluctance to retreat. "Let us stop here, and watch what they do," he said suddenly. "Mr. Wallis. Take everyone on. I wish to see what they intend."

Tristam found himself in the company of the captain, Osler, Beacham, and an ominously silent viscount. They slipped back down the path toward the bay, keeping well to cover, catching occasional glimpses of the turquoise water.

"You haven't your glass, Mr. Flattery?" Stern said.

"Llewellyn might have it, sir."

"Mr. Beacham," Stern said, "run along to the doctor and fetch back Mr. Flattery's glass, if he has it."

Without a word, Beacham was off.

"They are in no hurry," Osler said. "Look at them."

"There is no officer present," Stern said, "so they take their time. Such laxity may prove to our advantage. We will see how they keep their watches."

Tristam moved to a position where he could see through the foliage, and, just as they stepped ashore, he spotted the mutineers. The word had such infamy attached to it that he half-expected to see some band of terrible cutthroats. But there, on the beach, were the men he had sailed with these past months, appearing no more treacherous or fierce than usual. Not one of them looked the part, he thought. Some were so young that they had only recently begun to shave. And others had families waiting back home. Yet every one of them faced hanging if they were captured, now. They had made an irretrievable step. There was no choice for them but to pursue their course with total commitment.

Beacham delivered Tristam's glass to the captain, and then bent double trying to catch his breath.

"There is Mr. Hobbes," Stern said, "standing on the quarterdeck. It is a hard way to come by a command," he said with feeling. "They are getting ready to push the boats out, now. Tell me, Mr. Osler; what would you do if you were in Hobbes' position?"

"Tie a pig of iron around my neck and step off the rail, sir," Osler answered, but there was no humor in his tone. "They want this herb. That is their goal. And the sooner they get their hands on it, the sooner they can make their escape. If I were the master, I would come ashore late tonight. The Varuans are superstitious about the darkness and do not like to be about. The crew could slip up to the Sacred City and find what they're after, or perhaps take some hostages they can use for trade. But if the King and the Old Men leave the city . . . well, there will be no finding the Varuans in the bush, Captain. I'm sure of that. The crew will have to come ashore this night."

Stern passed the glass to his lieutenant. "You're right in every way, Mr. Osler. If we can get Wallis to convince the Varuans to put aside their superstitions, we have a chance of taking the *Swallow* back. Otherwise we will be here until the Admiralty sends a ship to search for us."

Tristam sat in one of the abandoned fales, staring out at the *Swallow* with his Fromme glass. It was late afternoon, and there seemed to be every indication that Stern and Osler had predicted Hobbes' plans correctly. The crew were preparing arms on the deck—swords and bows and short pikes. But most frightening, they had lowered one of the small cannon into a boat, as though they meant to use it as a field piece.

Immediately Tristam had sent Beacham off to inform Stern, and while he sat waiting for the officer, the mutineers began climbing down into the boats.

Stern and Osler both came at a run, careful not to be seen by the men on the ship.

"Well, Hobbes will not waste a moment," Stern observed. "I sent Wallis up to warn the Varuans, but I do not know what they will choose to do. They might help us, but they have such a fear of our guns that it is just as likely that they will let us work this out ourselves." He borrowed Tristam's glass and focused on the mutineers as they pushed away from the ship.

"We might try to retake the ship while they are gone," Osler suggested.

"No, they've rigged boarding nets and left enough men aboard to man the guns. Even under cover of darkness I fear we would suffer great loss of life, and with little chance of success." Stern passed the glass to Osler. Tristam thought the redness of the captain's face was suppressed anger, but his manner was calm.

Stern seemed to be struggling with a decision, though Tristam was not sure what this might be.

"Though it seems the Varuans have abandoned us," the captain said finally, "we cannot abandon them to these men—we don't know what atrocities they might commit. If we are cunning, we might slow their advance to the upper city, and perhaps there is still a chance they might listen to reason. There must be a few among them who are having second thoughts about what they have done."

"Too late for second thoughts," Osler said. "You might offer them amnesty, Captain, but the Admiralty will not be so kind. They must realize that, if they surrender to you now, they will hang."

Stern nodded, not quite listening, Tristam thought. "Yes, but the duchess has offered to guarantee the King's pardon to any man who gives up this madness. And there could be a reward as well. Hobbes, of course, I cannot save, but he has long put the welfare of his shipmates above his own. I have hopes that he will do so again." Stern moved back out of sight, and stood to full height. "Come away. It will take them two trips to bring their party ashore. We must meet them at the stairs to the Sacred City, and make it known that they will pay dearly for every step."

They retreated back into the trees and found the rest of their party. It was in Stern's mind to separate those who could not fight, and send them up into the forest, but it was decided that the duchess must be present to make the King's pardon sound credible, and Llewellyn, to Tristam's surprise, would not be sent away. That left only Jacel, and a few of the men who had sustained slight injuries as they escaped the ship, and none of these wanted to be separated from their fellows.

Tristam had not yet seen the stair to the city. When they found it, he felt his heart sink a little, for it was stone, though not carved into the rock, but carefully built by master masons. Thankfully no water flowed down the steps.

Stern had his crew take up anything heavy that could be found—stones, lumps of wood, even fallen coconuts—and this debris he piled on the first landing where it could be thrown down upon any who advanced.

Tristam had one of the few bows in the group, though hardly enough arrows, and these were meant for taking small specimens and doing as little harm to the skin as possible. Not really the best weapon for repelling mutineers.

Tristam understood Stern's feeling of responsibility toward the islanders—this was, after all, his own crew advancing with both weapons of steel and a cannon—but there seemed little chance that the mutineers could be stopped by a party so poorly armed. Nor was anyone sure how the Varuans would react when they found the Farrlanders battling at the gate to their most sacred shrine.

The landing on which they made their stand was all of twenty feet square, and crowded once Stern's people had assembled there. The captain sent those less fit for battle up the next flight of stairs, gathering his strongest men around him.

Like everyone else, Tristam realized that they stood little chance. Their only hope lay in Wallis convincing the Varuans to come to their aid, but with the King cut off from what occurred, it seemed highly unlikely that the Varuans would come to a decision quickly enough to make any difference. And everyone knew that one shot from the mutineers' cannon would send an army of Varuans scrambling for cover. The islanders were said to be fierce warriors, but having once seen the devastation wrought by cannon, they would not stand against it again.

"There!" Beacham said suddenly, pointing. "To the left, in the trees."

A line of men could just be made out, advancing slowly but purposefully. Two Jacks appeared ahead of the others, scouting, and when they saw Stern's party on the stair, one set off at a run.

"The flag," Stern said, and Beacham passed him a staff bearing the remains of a white shirt. "Duchess. And Mr. Flattery. If you will."

Taking the duchess' arm, Tristam fell in behind Stern. He had to keep his eyes on his footing and did not see the mutineers draw up, a hundred feet from the base of the stair.

Tristam felt the duchess holding tight to his arm, her usual confidence apparently having abandoned her. This group of men she found unnerving—she who knew so much about the ways of men. Their eyes met once, and Tristam realized that he had never seen her look so frightened, not even when they had been pursued by corsairs.

She does not believe this will work, he realized. And this increased his own fear tenfold. If the duchess was frightened, then there was reason to fear.

Stern stopped without warning, a dozen steps remaining to the ground. He stood there, with one foot a step higher, half-turned a little to the side. Tristam thought he cut a fine but tragic figure there, with the tatters of a shirt in his hand, his uniform torn and dirty, and the light of late afternoon slanting down through the trees at his back. It would make a memorable painting. *"The final stand of Captain Josiah Stern."*

Hobbes stepped through the crowd of Jacks, his face grim, but his manner resolute.

"Mr. Hobbes," Stern said, nodding and the master nodded in return, though he said nothing, but stood sullenly waiting, a sword gripped in one powerful hand.

"Mr. Hobbes . . ." Stern began, "all of you. I implore you to reconsider this course you follow." He paused, looking over the group, his manner one of concern for their welfare. "The Varuans will never give up this herb. They have been warned by Wallis, and the King and the Old Men have fled into the forest. There is no point in going further." Again he paused, letting his lie sink in. "I know you believe you've gone too far to turn back now, but that is not so. The Duchess of Morland will guarantee the King's pardon to any man who will give up this madness now. The King's pardon. . . ." He paused again, but only for a second. "You will be able to go home again. You will have a country. But those who refuse will be pursued for the rest of their days. No land will be safe, for the navy will not rest until you are brought to justice. And you know what that justice will be." He paused again, looking the men over, gauging the effect of his words. "In all honesty, I cannot guarantee this pardon to you, Mr. Hobbes, but consider your shipmates. Consider the life you lead them to. It will be as brief as it is desperate. I know you don't wish to bring them to ruin, Mr. Hobbes. Let them make their own choice. Let them become citizens of Farrland again. Rescind the sentence of death that shall be decreed for each and every man."

The mutineers stood shoulder to shoulder, glaring darkly at the captain.

It is not working, Tristam thought, and he could not understand why. Had not the captain's claims been perfectly true and logical? Could it be that an appeal to their reason would not be listened to? It was madness.

Hobbes looked down for a few seconds at the sword in his hand. "You offer us pardon?" he said suddenly, his soft voice quivering with long-suppressed anger. "It should be you, Stern, and your precious Admiralty, who stand trial." He pointed his sword at the captain. "But you will feel the justice of the Admiralty soon enough, for they will come for you, Stern." Hobbes lowered his sword. *"You* bring a murderer among us," he said softly, waving his sword up the stairs. "A man who murdered Dakin, and tried to kill both me and Kreel.

And you dine with him evenings while your crew lives in fear of this monster." He paced to one side, agitated, enraged, filled with despair at the truth he spoke. "You carry this spawn of a mage, who will bring our souls to what kind of ruin we cannot imagine; and you speak to us of justice?" He stopped and looked up at Stern, such loathing in his eyes that the captain actually wavered. "We have all risked much to carry this herb back to the worthies of Farrland, who sit in their palaces and fine mansions, awaiting this gift, this elixir that will extend their days of pleasure, and keep them from the ravages of disease. And what will we gain? The men who risk their short, hard lives, and the ruin of their souls? The wages of poor men, and no hope for any better life. There is your justice, Stern! And it will be meted out to you, in your turn. Your career is ended, Captain. I know your masters well. I have felt their justice. You will pay a price for failing them. You will give all, Stern." He turned and looked at the men who stood behind, listening and nodding their agreement.

And then he looked back at Stern, his anger tempering to pity. "No, we will not take the *justice* you offer. We will make our own laws and trust that they will be fairer than those of your masters. And if the navy finds us one day, what of it? To live in our own way, among these beautiful islands, for even five short years, would provide us with more joy then we would find in three lifetimes in Farrland. That is the truth. And if they never find us . . . ? We both know the ocean is vast. Men have disappeared in it before." Hobbes stood, taking the blade of his sword in his free hand, standing with his legs apart, facing the captain squarely.

"Let me make an offer to you, Captain. It will not profit you to return to Farrland. Disgrace awaits you. No reward, no pension from the crown. You will find this much-vaunted justice you speak of, meted out by men who have never been to sea, and done at the bidding of others who have never known discomfort. Join with us," he said, raising his voice, to be certain that all of Stern's crew would hear. "Join with us and take the risk of living for a century in paradise. That is your real choice. Risk creating your own future, or return to the *life* prescribed for you by those who profit from your efforts and sacrifice. I extend this offer to everyone, but especially to those who have nothing to gain by returning to Farrland."

A long silence. Tristam could sense the men above them on the stairs reconsidering their choice. And now that he had heard the master speak, Tristam was not sure what he would choose for himself, if he were one of them.

"And if we do not join you, Mr. Hobbes?" Stern asked.

Hobbes stepped forward. "Do not stand between us and what we have come for, Captain Stern. We wish no one harm, and will leave everyone present untouched, unless we are forced to do otherwise. I will even say freely, that any man who so wishes may cross over and join you." He turned to the men behind him. "Any man who will accept this King's pardon, do so now. But do not stand against us, or I cannot guarantee your safety."

For a second there was no reaction, then men began shaking their heads and muttering their refusal. No one moved to cross the sea of sand.

"That is your answer, Stern. Now I will have mine."

The captain hesitated, as though desperately hoping for a way through this, but finally he shook his head. "We cannot do as you ask, Mr. Hobbes. I cannot stand by and let you bring harm to the islanders. I am sworn to protect them from the follies of my crew. We will stand against you, Hobbes, and may Farrelle forgive you for the souls you take."

It was said, and everyone present felt the impact of these words, as though the sentence had been passed down—death for some; though no one could predict who. The captain looked over his shoulder at the duchess, almost an appeal.

"There is something you don't know about this herb," Tristam heard himself say, his voice, though quiet, carrying in the terrible silence. "It will keep you young only if you have the knowledge and talent of a mage." He paused, trying to discern the impact of his words. The sun dipped behind the mountains then, plunging the scene into shadow, and it seemed as though a pall had fallen over the mood of the mutineers. "If you don't possess that knowledge, the physic will drive you into a terrible madness, and rob you of your will. Our own King is enslaved to this herb, and though he has lived long, he bears the burden of those years like a great weight. I swear, it will not profit you to take this seed from the Varuans. You can neither use it nor, in your situation, can you sell it. Your desire to possess it has already brought you to mutiny and sentence of death. And if you don't turn aside now, it will only become worse. This seed is a curse. If you will not accept the King's pardon, then at least save yourselves from this one fate. Sail away. Sail away this moment. Hide yourselves in some corner of the globe. But I will tell you, as surely as my uncle served a mage, if you continue this pursuit of the seed, it will bring about your ruin." Suddenly he raised a dagger up for all to see. "This blade belonged to Gregory. It bears his initial and crest. The islanders have always known his fate, but superstition kept them silent." Stern looked at him, eyes wide, as though he thought Tristam had taken leave of his senses. "His ship lies in deep water beyond the pass, where mutineers brought about its wreck. Mutineers who wanted this seed for themselves, not realizing it was cursed. That is the fate that awaits you." Tristam tossed the dagger into the sands before them, where it landed point first. No one moved to examine it.

These words had impact on the sailors. In the diminishing light, Tristam could see some making warding signs. Others were muttering, and they had begun to shrink back.

"And that is why you have traveled so far to have this herb, Mr. Flattery?"

Hobbes said, his tone mocking. "Gregory's dagger?" He laughed. "The King bears the burden of this seed so heavily that he has sent you to bring him more? And the Duchess of Morland has taken ship with a bunch of ragtag sailors because she feels this seed is of no value, that it is a curse?" He laughed, and Tristam could see the men at his back, nodding, the doubt he had sowed being stripped away like newly planted seed torn up by a storm. "Make your decision, all of you. Either join us, or step aside. Duchess, please. Do not stand with these men. If they do not surrender the stair to us now, the cost will be great."

Tristam saw the duchess shake her head minutely, and then turn her gaze down. Stern lifted his tattered flag, and pointed up the stair, sending Tristam and the duchess up before him. At his back Tristam heard Hobbes order the gun brought forward, the master's voice heavy with emotion.

Night was not far off, Tristam knew, and darkness would fall swiftly. Hobbes would want to climb to the stairhead while there was still light.

Tristam thought of Gregory. *Greed and folly,* he thought. The fire of the crew's resentment had been kindling long. Ignited by the injustice of being born the sons of the poor, fed by the knowledge of what they were deprived. Hobbes' words had contained much truth—that was the power of them. Justice was an illusion—a luxury of the educated classes.

They came up onto the landing, puffing from the exertion. Beacham and the viscount stood at the edge, peering down.

"Lie down," Stern said. "Lie facedown and cover your heads." The captain crawled to the edge of the landing so that he could see what transpired below. Tristam dropped down, and lay there, smelling the indescribable smells of stone and sand. Impossible that stone could have an odor.

He felt the duchess take his hand, and he looked over at her frightened face. *Madness,* he thought she mouthed, but could not be sure.

The sound of the cannon firing caused everyone to flinch and press themselves into the rock. An instant later stone exploded above them with an ear-splitting crack, and dust and pieces of shattered rock rained down on them.

"*Up!*" Stern yelled. And those who were not undone by fear grabbed up some of the rocks and lumps of wood and cast them down the stair toward the advancing mutineers.

Tristam jumped forward and loosed an arrow toward the men who cowered below, and then a second, and a third. He could see the mutineers had halted, and some were even falling back, and then Osler shouted for everyone to get down again.

The gun sounded before many were prostrate, and this time the ball struck lower down, whistling close over their heads, and impacting the stone with such force that it shook the landing. Tristam heard people moaning and crying out, and only half the number rose to meet the men advancing below.

The mutineers had gained more stairs than Tristam expected, and then crouched down, exposing only their backs to the rain of stone and debris. Tristam realized that, even with the stone broken by cannon fire, their supply of debris to throw down was almost at an end. Suddenly, Stern called for everyone to climb up, and they turned and fled up the stairs.

Ahead of Tristam, people stumbled and fell in the failing light, and others tripped over them, yet somehow they scrambled upward. When the cannon fired, fear propelled everyone up a few extra steps, and the stone exploded behind them, fragments knocking people to the stairs. Several struggled to rise and were left on the landing, no one stopping to tend to them or to help them go on. They were running for their lives before cannon fire, and Tristam thought their fear was no different from that of the poor Varuans who had encountered it for the first time.

They came to another landing and though Stern tried to muster them here to make another stand, many simply ran on.

"The trees will offer . . . some protection," Osler said, gasping for breath.

Only half a dozen had rallied on the landing, and Tristam looked down the stairs. Their pursuers were swarming up the steps now, but there were no shouts of triumph at this rout of their former shipmates. They came on grimly, determined to have it over with quickly.

The trees arching over the stairs hid much of what went on from those manning the cannon below, and they held their fire, lest they gun down their own shipmates.

Tristam sent two quick arrows into the ascending mutineers and those around him cast down their few stones and bits of the shattered stair, but the men below hardly slowed.

"What happens when we come to the city above?" Tristam heard Beacham ask, no doubt thinking of the fate of Chilsey and Garvey. No one had an answer.

The brief tropical twilight fell then, which meant darkness was only moments behind, and Tristam was not sure if this would be to their advantage or not. He leaned over the side of the stair to see if it was possible to escape. A man might climb down off the stairs, but it would be onto a steep slope, and even a ledge might not lead them to any kind of safety—though it might well be their only option.

"We'll keep going up until we meet the guards at the stairhead," Stern said. "Perhaps they will let us through, or stand with us. I don't believe they will allow mutineers into their most sacred site without resistance."

The cannon sounded just then, and everyone with presence of mind dropped to the stone. There was a crash in the trees to their left, and Tristam actually saw sparks where the iron ball struck stone. The island night had fallen.

There was a sound similar to arrows in the air, and the shouting and cursing of men. After a few seconds of confusion, Tristam rose and tried to make out what went on down the now darkened stair. In the gathering gloom he found the mutineers retreating desperately under a hail of stones which seemed to be coming out of the trees.

"Blood and flames!" Osler said. "The islanders have come to our rescue. They're using slings."

Even in the fading night Tristam could see men falling senseless to the stairs, some rolling limply down behind their fellows. The cannon had fallen silent, and Tristam wondered if it had been fired so erratically because the crew manning if had been attacked as well. The mutineers kept falling back, their numbers thinning rapidly. And there among them went Hobbes. He came to the rear and clambered down behind the others, as though he could shield them from the lethal missiles with his great frame. Tristam could see the master flinch and stumble as stones struck him, but he did not give way to panic and kept his place. Tristam saw the master's head driven forward suddenly, and then he toppled, arms outstretched like a wounded bird. He toppled into the darkness and the mass of falling bodies before him.

Stern stood looking down for the moment, rigid, like a man helpless to stop what he watched, though every muscle strained with his desire to act.

"We must gather up those who are left," Stern said, his voice thick and subdued, and then he turned away, motioning the others to go before him.

"But will they show them no mercy?" Osler cried out suddenly, still unable to see his former shipmates as enemies. He looked at Stern as though appealing for him to intervene.

"None, I fear," Stern answered, marshaling them up the stairs. So they turned away from the screams and curses of the Farrlanders and began to climb, unsure of what lay ahead for them.

"You must understand, Lieutenant," Stern said quietly, all signs of anger gone, "the so-called city above and this ritual are deeply sacred to the Varuans. They would die rather than see them desecrated. It seems they would even face darkness and cannon fire."

"And what of us?" Beacham said, glancing back over his shoulder.

"They have not turned on us thus far, so I hope that bodes well." Stern paused for a moment. "But I would be a liar to say that the islanders' actions are so easy to predict."

They found the other victims of the mutiny huddling on the landing before the final flight of stairs. They apparently already knew what had happened below and were now waiting to discover their own fate.

Stern stood before the remains of his crew, his clothes tattered, and his face bruised and bleeding. Tristam thought the captain looked like a man with little hope, yet he would not shirk his duty. Like Hobbes, Tristam was sure Stern would put himself between his crew and the missiles of the enemy. "I think our mutiny is over, though what will be done with us I am not sure. They have not attacked us yet, when they could easily have done so, and I hope this means they will leave us unharmed. Perhaps we will be returned to our ship this very night. I cannot say. If the Varuans come to us armed, remain calm. Show no anger at what they have done, but do not show them fear either. I will try to get us out of this. Dr. Llewellyn? We may have need of your linguistic skill. And where has that Varuan girl gone? Mr. Flattery?"

"I don't know, sir."

Apparently no one knew. She had disappeared not long after the first cannon shot.

"Where is Mr. Wallis?" Llewellyn said, coming forward with obvious reluctance.

"I wish I knew," Stern said, turning back to look down the stairs.

Night had fallen completely, and a net of stars appeared through the trees. The trade began its nightly abatement, and the surf, beating down upon the reef, could almost be felt, like the heartbeat of this exotic island. No sounds of fighting came up from below, and most of the crew crowded to the back of the landing, where they remained uncommonly silent. Everyone strained to hear, wondering what went on in the dark. No one even dared whisper lest they miss some warning sound.

A silvery glow spread across the eastern horizon, and then the full moon floated up, released into the sky by a giant whale.

"Captain," Beacham hissed. "I think I hear someone coming."

Stern went forward, with a terrified Llewellyn at his back. Tristam came up beside the captain, thinking that his own limited knowledge of the language might be needed if Llewellyn lost his nerve.

"Captain Stern?" came a man's voice out of the dark. "It is Madison Wallis."

"Mr. Wallis? What has happened? Are my men . . . ?"

The sound of footsteps on stone came softly up the stair and then the gangly form of Wallis appeared in the moonlight. He moved slowly, as though bearing the weight of what he had just witnessed. Instead of coming up onto the landing, he stopped several steps down, as though afraid the Farrlanders would not welcome his presence.

"I think they are all dead, but one, Captain Stern. I cannot be sure because of the darkness. One Jack had been rendered unconscious, and I think I managed to intervene when he was discovered alive. At least he was alive when I began to climb up." Wallis sat down heavily on a step and put his head in his hands.

Tristam heard muttering behind him, partly from relief that they had been delivered, partly from horror. Their former shipmates, all dead but one.

"What will they do with us, Mr. Wallis?" Stern asked. "Do they understand that we came up the stair only to keep the mutineers from entering the City of the Gods? Our intentions were to protect the Varuans."

"That is what I assumed, Captain, and is the case I have made, but I'm not certain what they believe, and the Varuans will not tell me what they intend. They have sent me only to instruct you to keep your people where they are. Do not, under any circumstances, try to go up into the city. Only stay where you are, and I will try to find out what they will do."

"We will not move, Mr. Wallis. Please, do everything you can on our behalf. I have no intention of allowing my people to desecrate their sacred sites. We want only to go about our business and then be gone. We wish the Varuans no harm."

"I will convey your message, Captain. But it is your business that is at issue. You may be forced to renounce your quest for this herb. That is what I think, at least."

The duchess came forward when she heard this, suddenly more concerned with what was being said than with their situation. Tristam did not think she would give up so easily.

∽ Thirty

Baron Trevelyan had not really slept, only dozed lightly between lurches of the carriage. But all the same he had dreamed. Dreamed he had been ascending a stairway, dressed in a white robe, a cold glittering stream flowing about his ankles. An owl had called in the darkness, its sound almost human. Then the carriage had swayed and cracked his head against the window frame.

His eyes focused on Roderick Palle, who sat staring at him with that same measuring gaze that he habitually turned on the poor, unsuspecting world. The carriage hit a pothole and the two men bounced several inches out of their seats. The pounding of hooves over the earth's drum was loud.

"Are you feeling more yourself, Lord Trevelyan?"

"Has my lunacy passed, do you mean? For the moment, it seems. But this state of grace will disappear the moment you deprive me of the seed again."

"We have no intention of depriving you of the seed ever again. Once you have performed your task for us, Lord Trevelyan, you shall have physic enough for the rest of your years, if that is what you choose."

Trevelyan was certain that his suspicion was not well masked. "I saw what happened to His Majesty. I require just enough to keep the madness at bay—no more. Overindulgence is a vice easily learned, and its effects are devastating."

"But what of your youth, Lord Trevelyan? Do you not want your vitality restored?"

The baron attempted to hide his disgust for Roderick. The King's Man was such a master at discovering men's weaknesses. But the baron would not be tempted again. Palle and his group had betrayed him once, and he was not sure they had any intention of honoring their bargain this time. "Tell me about this rite you wish performed."

Palle smiled at him, or tried to—the King's Man was famous for this grimace that he thought was a smile. "It is a simple enough thing. Mr. Wells will instruct you." He nodded to Wells, who lay unconscious in the corner. The man was either exhausted beyond measure, or could sleep through a cataclysm.

"I think it will be small service for your return to sanity. And then you may take up your work again, and every man in the Society will sing his praises for the great Trevelyan's return."

"You make it sound so easy, Roderick. And what will you gain from such a *simple* task?"

Roderick shrugged.

"Do you actually know what you possess? A text, I assume. Do you even understand its purpose? Let me see it."

"Soon enough, my dear baron, soon enough."

Trevelyan knew he would get no more from Roderick. The King's Man had spent his lifetime harboring secrets, rising through the court by trading what he knew to advantage. He was a merchant of secrecy, Trevelyan thought, keeping every bit of knowledge, no matter how inconsequential it seemed, increasing its value by its scarcity. Palle could have been rich beyond imagining if he had chosen the world of commerce, but the coin he valued was not gold.

"Why do we race on so, Roderick? Who is it we are hoping to best?"

Palle looked at the baron for a moment, never embarrassed to stare at a man's face for any length of time, though it was considered most impolite in Farr society. "Massenet," he said, finally, deciding it was not information that he could trade, and so gave it away, probably interested in Trevelyan's reaction to the news.

"Ah. I might have known." The baron pushed himself back up into his seat and gazed out the window. The day was clear and somewhat cool, with a harsh wind from the north. The carriage was as uncomfortable as a ship beating into a gale, and the wind whistled as though it blew through the rigging, moving the barren branches so that they clattered against one another horribly.

"He does not know we follow," Palle said. "It is to our advantage. With a little luck the count is not racing north as we do, but is taking his own good time. We might hope that he finds an inn where the serving girls are fair. That could slow him substantially."

Obviously the King's Man thought of this information as a peace offering. It was *information*—the most valuable commodity Palle could conceive of. Trevelyan should be honored; but the baron knew that if there was something he truly needed to know, Palle would certainly hold it back, for use later. The baron was not deceived. He had run afoul of the King's Man before, and paid a terrible price for it. He would not make that mistake again.

The carriage came to a halt, and the shouts of men up and down the line replaced the thrumming of horses' hooves. Palace Guards rode past, and then one stopped and dismounted by the carriage. Palle allowed the door to be opened.

"It is the ford, Sir Roderick. It has swollen." He looked a little abashed explaining this, as though, somehow, he were responsible for this setback.

Palle cast a look of annoyance at Wells, who sat up, rubbing his eyes. "Let us see what this is about."

No one protested, so the baron followed the others out of the carriage, stretching his great frame, stiff and bruised from their mad dash. The carriage of Galton and Noyes had stopped behind a farmer's wagon filled with grain. Guards on horseback were milling about ineffectually in an attempt to look as though they were doing something useful. One officer, more imaginative than the others, was coaxing his horse out into the current.

The river was certainly high, flooding back into the trees, running swiftly, catching the sunlight on its endlessly changing surface. A gathering of small gulls circled over the ford, calling and diving in the sunlight. Occasionally one would light upon the surface and bob along the small waves like a toy, making a mockery of the men standing timidly on the banks.

Trevelyan breathed in the fresh air, unable to express the relief he felt at finding himself released from the prison of his madness. With all of his heart he did not want to be serving these men, but the thought of returning to his cell of darkness terrified him utterly. *Better anything than that.* To think that he had possessed one of the most celebrated minds of his generation. He was sure that he could never perform at that level again, but just to be able to think clearly! To look around him and see the world for what it was! It was enough. He did not care if he would die in his own time. Just let him be sane for a few years. Let him have the dignity of that, and he would do whatever Roderick required.

The rider was struggling out in midstream, but managing. His mount was being swept somewhat downstream; apparently its natural buoyancy was having an effect and the beast was beginning to float, losing its footing. But then it passed the deepest point and found the earth again. A few more yards and the horse began to surge forward, gathering its powerful haunches, and driving toward the bank. The other guards cheered.

Roderick, Trevelyan realized, was paying no attention. Instead, he was walking around the farmer's wagon, examining it as though it were some innovative carriage he had discovered.

"The rider has crossed, Sir Roderick." said one of the guards.

"Proving only that a horse and rider can manage," Palle said without bothering to look at the man. "Mr. Hawksmoor!"

The minion of the King's Man stood nearby, ever attentive to his master's needs. "Sir?"

"This will serve nicely. Send it across."

The farmer who stood by suddenly realized what was in the wind. "But, Your Grace, it is the end of last season's grain, sir. For market. . . ."

Guards moved in on the man, and he fell silent with fear.

Palle raised his hand and the guards stopped as they were about to grab hold of the frightened farmer. "Pay this man for his rig and grain, Mr. Hawksmoor, and then get a driver aboard. We have no time to waste."

The farmer scrambled up into his wagon to rescue a few of his effects, while Hawksmoor counted out some coins. The baron was sure the farmer had been well compensated, but the man stopped and stroked the noses of each of the big draft horses, and spoke softly to them.

One of the guards removed his sword and hat, climbed up onto the loaded wagon, and started the horses forward.

"We might use this team to draw each wagon over, sir," Hawksmoor said, looking at the massive work horses.

Roderick nodded distractedly, his eyes fixed on the wagon as it rolled into the water. Two mounted guards, carrying coiled ropes at the ready, followed, prepared to cast a line to the driver if things did not go well. Like almost all Farrlanders, these men did not swim, and though the ford was not overly deep, the current was strong and could sweep a man off his feet.

"It is odd that the sky is clear, and the earth dry," Wells observed to Noyes. "There has been no rain here for several days, I would venture."

Roderick waved a hand vaguely upstream. "It is from the Camden Hills."

The wagon had rolled forward until its hubs disappeared; a moment more and the water reached to the wagon body. Without pause the draft horses kept pulling their burden forward. The water would not affect them so much, Trevelyan thought, for they each stood eighteen hands, he was certain.

The team reached the river's midpoint, where the current ran most swiftly, and still they plodded forward as though they were some great beasts of the river or the intertidal zone. Another two yards and they began to rise up the opposite slope, and the men watching all began to relax, suddenly aware of how intently they had been observing.

It was just then that the wheel broke, or perhaps the axle, and the rear of the wagon swung sharply downstream, sinking as it did so. The horses' rear quarters were swept to the side and they stumbled over each other and fell, struggling, the wagon dragging them in harness, spluttering and crying out, trying to keep their heads above the surface.

The driver tried for a moment to control the situation, but then realized what had happened, and managed to take hold of the rope thrown his way and jump clear of the flailing horses.

The rickety wagon began to break up, and as it did so, one horse shook itself free, suddenly surging toward the same shore it had left. Seconds later it pulled up onto the bank, where it stopped and whinnied to its trace mate, gone now into the deeper water beyond the ford, pulled under by the remains of the wagon and the harness wrapped about its limbs.

The horse came trotting along the bank, hanging its head, back to its former master, where it stood trembling and agitated. Trevelyan thought it looked at the men with reproach, perhaps anger, and the poor farmer could barely speak, his voice thick with emotion, as he tried to calm the beast.

"That answers our questions, I think," Palle said. "We must detour to the Tainsill Bridge, though we will lose much time." He turned to go back to his carriage when Hawksmoor stopped him.

"What about this horse, sir? We paid gold for it."

"Oh, let the poor man have it!" Galton said, raising his voice. "I will repay you the gold myself." And he went over to the farmer, who stood wretchedly by his horse, and gave him some coins. Trevelyan could not hear what the governor said, but his tone was kind. There was one among them, at least, who had not lost his compassion entirely. It was good to know.

The night was chill. A tear of molten silver had frozen on the icy sky, and as this near-full moon lifted above the surrounding hills it cast a faint light into the vale. People did not come to this place at night. The local shepherds would not even leave their herds to graze past sunset. There were terrible stories of those who had, by accident or bravado, defied this simple rule. Ghosts of the men lost in battle haunted the night, and mages on gray horses galloped silently across the hilltops. Green light was seen emanating from the ruin of the ancient keep, and beyond this the middens themselves lay, like the backs of green whales. It was said that no tree ever took root there, nor would burrowing animals make their homes in that terrible field.

Count Massenet was not frightened by the tales of shepherds, but he had learned too much of arcane matters these past years to discount everything. It was, he admitted, if only to himself, a disturbing place.

"Can we not draw the water from here?" Bertillon whispered. "It is the same water."

"No, it must come from the falls," Massenet said, purposely speaking in a normal tone. "Do not offer me an argument based on logic, Charl, it has nothing to do with logic. Or reason, for that matter. The text says it must come from the falls, and so it must come from the falls."

"The count is absolutely right, Mr. Bertillon," Varese added. "We must not deviate in the slightest from the instructions."

Bertillon shook his head. "I still can't see how this water could differ from the water a hundred paces downstream . . . but I bow to your superior knowledge." He tried not to make this last sound sarcastic, but didn't quite succeed. The count did not take offense. It was an unsettling place, and perhaps even more so for the musician. Bertillon's talent would lay him open to things others would not feel. The truth was, Massenet did not like this place either.

"Indulge us, Charl," Massenet chided him. "It won't take long."

They didn't carry a lamp, as Varese was sure that the light of stars and moon must be kept pure, so they picked their way through the darkness beneath the trees, stumbling occasionally. Bertillon wished that he had brought a blade from the carriage, but he had been afraid the others would laugh at this impulse. He would have felt better, however, to know he carried steel at his side.

Their path followed a small stream that ran through the forest like a black artery, carrying the vital fluids of the earth among the trees. Twisted roots emerged through the surface to trip the men who trespassed here, as though the interlopers could be kept at bay and the source of the forest's elixir protected.

A breeze like a chill breath would sigh through the wood occasionally, rattling the dried leaves that still clung to the branches.

"Do the leaves not fall here?" Bertillon asked.

"These are oaks, Mr. Bertillon," Varese answered. "They keep their dead leaves till spring. It is most common."

The musician had never noticed. *Oaks.*

Occasionally a bird would call—a soft, falling tone that would die without echo, as though absorbed by the darkness. Bertillon thought it a call of profound sadness.

The spattering of falling water began to distinguish itself from the other night sounds, and a small breeze stirred among the trees, the dried leaves scraping together in a most unsettling manner. Bertillon was surprised by a strange rattle, followed by a distinctive croak. A raven. Birds, at least, did not fear this place.

The trio plunged on, tripping as they stepped into shadow, then making good time as they crossed starlit glades. The path suddenly stepped upward among a jumble of large rocks where the stream dropped from one small pool to another. They were panting when the path leveled again, and the night seemed suddenly warm.

Again Massenet led them into the shadow of the twisted ancient oaks; trees that had stood in this place during the battle of the Midden Vale itself. Trees that had watched silently while Dunsenay rode out alone against the host of Farrelle. Witnessed the green sea-light form about the mage, and then the coming of the storm, summoned in strange tongues. Massenet had always thought the tale fanciful, but was no longer quite so sure. And this power that Dunsenay wielded was not lost! If only the count had more talent himself!

The air grew damp as they made their way further into the stand of oaks and young pines, where the scent of pine needles was fresh and fair, in contrast to the age of the forest. Beneath the trees the men progressed slowly, Massenet waving his hands before him, feeling carefully for each step. Bertillon held tight to his coattail and no doubt Varese had hold of the musician—like the three blind men of fables.

A dim light tempted them forward, and the sound of water rushing increased in volume. Perhaps a dozen paces would take them to the pool. Massenet felt some apprehension, as though they were engaged in an endeavor that was somehow deeply wrong. *Like thieves in the night,* he thought suddenly.

The pale light of stars and moon glittered on water, and Massenet caught a glimpse of the stream, erupting from an opening in a limestone cliff. It glittered like a column of liquid crystal.

They emerged from the shadow of the trees on the edge of a pool, and there, before the falls, knee-deep in water, stood a woman, ghostly pale. She half-raised her hands, and chanted as though standing before an altar. Dark curls fell down her naked back like a twisted vine.

Varese stumbled at the sight. *"A ghost!"* he hissed.

The woman whirled about, clutching her arms to her breasts. Massenet was transfixed. Certainly this woman was too perfectly formed to be anything but a vision. He heard Varese gasp and step back, fearful, but unwilling to bolt alone into the shadows.

The woman regarded them, saying nothing, but not frightened, now that she saw them. Shadows played across her face and her body, but even so Massenet could see the heart-shaped face was lovely, her lips full and sensuous. A large stone hung from a chain around her neck, and this seemed to be as full of starlight as the falling waters.

"Count Massenet," she said, surprising the count, who had half-expected her to vanish, or step back into the waterfall and disappear. "I think you do not understand what is taking place here," she continued, her voice lovely and melodious, but commanding all the same.

Massenet took a step forward. "I know you . . ." he said, certain he had seen this woman before. "You are Angeline Christophe," he said, a little triumphantly, but she did not seem to hear. The woman continued to stare at him, apparently unaware of the chill in the air and the water.

Massenet realized then that she held a small glass bottle that glittered as though many faceted. "What do you do here?"

She said nothing, though she did not look frightened into silence.

"Prince Kori has sent you," the count said. He moved forward again, about to step into the water.

She raised her hand quickly. "Do not sully the waters. They are pure, untouched by men." Angeline pushed the hair back from her face with one hand, lifting a breast enticingly, and then she cast her eyes down as though suddenly shy.

Massenet thought she was maddeningly beautiful. To a man who thrived on the new, the situation seemed charged with eroticism. A wraith of a woman, hiding none of her charms, here in this forbidden wood, alone. She was like a creature from a fable; a water nymph. He could barely take his eyes from her. But certainly this meant the prince and Palle were preparing to complete their plans. And this woman was somehow part of them.

She looked up, though only barely raising her head. "You have given in to the temptation, I see," she said quietly, and then nothing more.

"I could find no other way to stop the King's Man . . ." the count said, speaking before he realized that he had begun to justify his actions to this young woman who stood before him so immodestly.

She raised her head just a fraction of an inch, meeting his eyes, almost taking his breath away. "The temptation is great. Imagine; power, knowledge, youth. . . . I hardly blame you, though I had hoped you would be wiser."

"You presume to know a great deal," the count said, still not sure what to do.

She shrugged at this, apparently unconcerned that she might insult the ambassador of Entonne. Nor did she seem particularly afraid to be revealing herself as his adversary, as though meeting three men in a dark wood was not cause for alarm. "*Youth*," she almost whispered, "it holds such promise." Then she turned and took three graceful steps up onto the opposite bank. She turned and looked over her shoulder. "In the next village there is an inn. Perhaps we might continue this discussion there?"

Massenet knew that he should not let this woman escape, with her starwater and obvious knowledge of the arcane, but he was so used to women desiring him. He could not believe that her suggestion was anything but what it seemed. She would succumb to him—as other women had. Women with marriages and places in society. Women who had much to lose, but simply could not help themselves. He felt both his desire and his pride swell. Angeline Christophe was not indifferent to his charms after all.

He could see her now, half hidden by shadow, moonlight falling upon her through the branches. She took up a black shift and let it slide slowly down over her curls, so that darkness seemed to envelop her. The white of her face appeared and she shook her hair free.

"Count Massenet," she said, nodding her head. "Gentlemen." And she turned and walked into the shadows and shattered moonlight. For a second

Massenet thought he saw a child at her side, but he blinked and she was gone, disappearing into the shadow-wood.

"Prince Kori's mistress . . ." Bertillon said.

"That woman is no mistress of that fatuous little prince," Massenet said derisively.

"You—you shouldn't have let her escape," Varese said, finding his voice. "She was collecting water from the falls, as do we."

"But we will meet her in the next town, Doctor," Massenet said.

"She will never be there," Bertillon said firmly.

Massenet turned to the musician, whose skin appeared even paler in the moonlight—as though he were a ghost himself. "Of course she will be there, Charl. Of course she will."

Massenet sat in a large chair, sipping wine. His companions had been invited as well, to his disappointment, but he was sure that he would be alone with Angeline soon enough. If anything, it allowed him to savor the moment a little more. Both Bertillon and Varese were nearly speechless in the face of this woman's beauty, and this made Massenet smile. They were like boys. Massenet turned his gaze on Angeline, who stood at a side table pouring a glass of wine herself. There were no servants present. Massenet savored the sight for a moment, imagining what he would do to her once they were alone, imagining her response. Massenet had made the closest study of what gave women pleasure— it was one of his areas of vanity.

The shape of her bare shoulders attracted him, promising some strength. Her hair was pulled back from her face with silver combs, falling in thick dark curls. Massenet knew enough of such things to realize that she had done very little to prepare herself for this evening. Her black dress was simple, and her use of makeup so sparse that she might not have bothered. Yet she was as striking as any woman he had seen.

She passed a glass to Varese, who took it quickly, obviously uncomfortable. Raising her glass, Angeline met each gentleman's gaze for the briefest second. "To chance encounters," she said.

Massenet smiled broadly and drank. It was at that moment that he realized the stone Angeline still wore around her neck was the very diamond he had given to Kent. His smile disappeared. *Kent?*

For a moment his confidence wavered. What was her involvement with the old man? Obviously she had both talent and knowledge—but what did she intend to use them in pursuit of? He realized that his evening of much-anticipated pleasure might be extremely unwise. He was not about to allow anyone to endanger his purpose. Did she realize that?

"So," Angeline began, taking a seat opposite Massenet, "we are all on the same quest, it seems. No, I suppose that is not really true. You have decided that you will seek . . . what? Dominion, Count Massenet? Is that it? You will command whatever power your discovered text leads you to?"

"I seek only to retain the balance of power in the nations surrounding the Entide Sea, Lady Angeline," Massenet made an effort to sound casual. He refused to look as foolish as his companions simply because she was beautiful! "What is it that you and my friend, Mr. Kent, hope to gain?"

She did not look surprised, and he was happy to see she was not so easily thrown off. Massenet could not bear to win too easily.

"It is Kent's desire to find his lost muse, Count, if you must know. He would sacrifice much to this end." She held up her glass. "To the muse."

Massenet lifted his glass and stared into its dark center. A moment later he realized that Angeline stood before him and had just removed the glass from his fingers. She leaned over and placed a hand on his forehead, mumbling words he could not catch. He reached out for her and then realized that his hands had not obeyed the command. He felt cool lips brush his forehead, and then Angeline rose and moved away. He tried to turn his head to follow but found he could not, and his eyes were closing, as though gravity had suddenly chosen to increase its force at that moment.

From some distance Massenet heard more mumbling in a strange tongue. *I have been drugged,* he realized. He struggled to open his eyes, and force his head to turn. Despite blurred vision he could see that Angeline now sat speaking with Varese. They appeared to be examining something. Papers. Distorted vowels and sharp consonants reached him, as though the words had been broken as they passed through the air, and his mind could not put them right again. Sometimes the voice was soft and melodious, and at other times it was deeper, and the deeper voice went on at length.

He is telling her everything, the count thought, but he could not move nor even speak. His eyes closed, and the voices continued, like chanting. There were moments when he could almost make sense of what was said—almost. He forced his eyes open and found the blurred form of Angeline standing before him looking down upon him as though he could not see her in return—as though he were not really present.

He tried to force his lids to stay open. Angeline turned away, and in two steps she had gone out of his narrowing field of vision, and he could see only the shadows of someone moving. Then she reappeared to take her place on the divan, facing Bertillon. Massenet could see her smile—and still she ignored him. She was speaking earnestly with Bertillon, her hands moving. Occasionally she would touch his arm, and even in his drugged state the count could see the musician was affected. More and more frequently Bertillon would nod, reluctantly at first, but less so after a while.

Massenet's eyes closed and he fought to keep his focus, his mind slipping off into dream. He wakened to find a naked Angeline standing before him, but then his eyes opened and revealed a second truth. She still sat on the divan with Bertillon, but they were not speaking. The musician stared down at the cushions, in the grip of indecision. He looked up once at the count, his gaze cool, unreadable, and then he turned to Angeline and nodded. She leaned forward and kissed him on the corner of his mouth.

Massenet realized the grunt he heard was his own curse, and this caused the woman to raise her head and look his way. For a second she leaned toward him, but seemed to decide he was no threat and turned back to Bertillon. Massenet's world went dark again and anger fled like a winged creature. He fell.

"Count?" Massenet tried to stir, wondering who called him. *"Count Massenet?"* He forced one eye open, and found Varese bent over him, his manner filled with concern. "They've gone," he said, as though Massenet would know who he meant. "Gone. And taken the text with them."

The count sat up. "Who?"

"That young woman and Bertillon. And our text has disappeared with them," he said again.

Massenet put his face in his hands. Yes, he remembered. She had drugged him and then. . . . Had he dreamed everything else?

"Do you know what happened? Did she learn everything?" The look on Varese's face answered the question before it was out. Massenet stood, too quickly and sank back into his chair. *She made a fool of me,* he thought. *Made a fool of me!* "She drugged the wine."

"I think she did more than that." Varese shook his head, obviously unsettled. "I fear we have met someone who knows more about these matters than we can claim ourselves. It was a mistake to let her escape the pool, though perhaps we could not have stopped her." He shook his head again, as though he had just predicted the end of the world.

"You can ride, I assume," Massenet said, and it was not a question. Varese nodded. "Good. We'll catch them before they reach the abbey."

ᓚ Thirty-One

Jaimy wondered if their escort of out-of-uniform Palace Guards deceived any-one. Perhaps here, a day's ride from Avonel, people wouldn't recognize the soldiers so readily: Palace Guards, after all, tended to stay near to the palace. The lieutenant approached their table, stifling his automatic desire to salute and bow to the prince.

"Massenet took rooms here last night, Your. . . ." The guard cleared his throat. "He was entertained by two ladies who had arrived earlier—a woman who kept her face hidden behind a veil, and a young companion. Massenet left this morning, on horseback rather than in his carriage, but was not accompa-nied by the younger of the two Entonne gentlemen who traveled with him. No one was quite sure when this young man left the inn, though some are of the opinion that he went off with the two ladies."

"The Countess of Chilton and her niece," Jaimy said quietly.

"But who was the younger man?" the prince asked, keeping his voice low. The inn's common room was not empty and the locals exhibited some interest in the gentlemen traveling with their armed escort.

"Did Kent not mention Bertillon, the musician?" the duke asked, and Jaimy nodded agreement.

"So, they are ahead of us by several hours yet," the prince said. "And where are Palle and my father, I wonder?"

No one answered.

"Best that we continue," the duke said, wiping his mouth with a threadbare piece of linen. "Do we have fresh horses?"

The lieutenant nodded.

"Gentlemen . . ." the duke said, as though insisting they enter a door before him. Jaimy knew his father well, though, and this lightness of tone was meant only to raise spirits. The duke was more concerned than Jaimy had ever seen him.

They mounted horses, and as they waited for the guards to finish adjusting saddles, Jaimy caught his father's gaze. "Uncle Erasmus had something to do with this, didn't he? Were there writings, after all?"

The duke's temper, usually kept in close check, flared, but then subsided just as quickly. "If there is an opportunity, Jaimas, I will try to explain," he said softly, then looked off at the facade of the inn. "And apologize to Lady Alissa for ter-rorizing her unjustifiably." He nodded to his son, motioned to the lieutenant, made sure the prince was with him, and spurred his horse onto the road.

Jaimy followed, purposely riding alone. He wondered how much his father knew about this business. The portrait of that too-beautiful woman in the library was something of an obsession of the duke's, Jaimy was aware, and now perhaps he would learn why. He tried to remember if his father had spoken to the countess at all when she came to the palace. But other than the introductions, he could think of no instance—and his father's reaction to the woman had revealed nothing. Unless not speaking to her at all could be considered revelatory.

But they were not too far behind the countess now—only a few hours—and Massenet was somewhere in between. It was difficult to imagine that the countess was allied with the Entonne, but why else would Bertillon have accompanied her? If the countess was interfering in the affairs of the Entonne ambassador, Jaimy thought she was in some danger.

He carried a sword on his saddle—not a weapon designed for the duel, but a sword meant to take punishment without failing. He touched it quickly as he rode, but this did not bring the comfort he hoped.

Alissa worried constantly about Jaimy, though after what he had told her of his flight from Palle's men, she knew he was more capable than she had realized. And he was with the duke, of course, as well as a detachment of Palace Guards.

He would release me from my vow, she thought suddenly, and that thought came like sudden rush of fear, followed immediately by a feeling in her chest— a hollowness she could not adequately describe. She wondered about Jaimy's loyalty to her. He had seemed a bit distant since returning from his time with the countess. But he had been through a great deal. She should be a little more understanding. *But can I be a Duchess of Blackwater,* she asked herself. It was a question difficult to answer. She realized the few months of her engagement had changed her more than a little.

Just look at her situation at that very moment. She rode in a carriage with Princess Joelle and her cousin, Lady Galton. Even if Alissa had never aspired to such company, still she had to admit it was flattering. Perhaps more than flattering, she felt as though her relationship with the world had changed. After all those years of listening to endless discussion of politics, here she was, involved at the highest level. It was more than a little flattering, and seductive as well.

But was it truly the life she desired? Alissa remembered that she had rather quickly gone through the childhood phase of playing princess. Other things had interested her more.

Alissa gazed out at the passing road, realizing that Jaimy had ridden this way only a few hours earlier. How could she let him go? As mad as it sounded, she would be happier if he had been born to more humble circumstances. . . . But he had not, and she had not been born to this world in which she now found herself. *I am an outsider here,* she told herself, *and likely will always feel the same.*

Where was Jaimy now, she wondered. *Pray that he is safe,* she thought, though it was only a reflex: she could not pray.

Perhaps it was the young prince she should be worried about, though by the look of great distraction on the face of the princess, it seemed she had that area well under control. Unless she fretted about her husband? How in the world was the princess making peace with that situation? Or had that been done years before?

Alissa had no doubt that her party, those who accompanied the King, were bringing up the rear in this race to Tremont Abbey. It seemed rather futile. She could sit a horse—not with any grace, but she never fell or lost control of her mount. If only she had been allowed to go on with Jaimy and the duke. Occasionally she thought it something of a curse to have been born a woman.

The driver called out to his team, and the carriage swayed and rocked as it came to a halt. She pushed the window open quickly, wondering what had stopped them here, apparently near no human habitation.

She heard men talking, but no one came to the carriage to explain their situation.

"Let us see what goes on," the princess said suddenly. "Cousin?" she said to Lady Galton, the single word standing in for the entire question.

"Go along," Lady Galton said. "I'll sit quietly here. Go along."

A footman jumped down and lowered the step for the ladies, who quickly descended onto a dry, dirt road. Forty paces along, the track disappeared beneath a flowing river.

Kent came walking up from his own carriage, swinging his cane like a man about town, two ragtag boys running at his heels. "Brookford," he said smiling. "Apparently a wagon was swept away here just yesterday."

"Grand folk set it out into the flood," one of the boys piped up, looking at the two women with awe. "The King's own Man, they say. And you can see the wagon washed up on the bar, with Burnett's old Ned lying there, drownt."

"Goodness!" the princess said, looking down at these children as though they were pixies, so strange were the sons of farm laborers to her. "Someone died?"

"I believe he means a horse, Your Highness," Kent said kindly, causing the boys to step back a bit. They knew enough to realize that Kent's form of address indicated this woman was of very high birth.

"Can we not cross, then?" the princess asked.

"We're just trying to determine exactly that," Kent said, then bent down to speak with the boys. "Has anyone crossed since the wagon foundered?"

"Wha?" the boy said, fingers in his mouth.

"He means since the horse drowned yesterday," Alissa offered, thinking it her place, as resident commoner, to translate. "Has anyone crossed the river since then?"

"Just Burnett's Bill, and Foster's cattle, Yer Ladyship."

The princess smiled. "But any horses or carriages?"

"Burnett's Bill, Your Majesty," the boy managed.

"Let's go have a look for ourselves," Kent said. "Now tell me, lad, what happened with the King's own Man, yesterday? Jog your memory and I shall give you a coin for your troubles. I'll give you each a coin."

They walked to the edge of the river, the boys chattering away about the "grand folk" who had come to the ford the previous day, unaware that the woman who walked nearby was a princess, and inside the curtained carriage the King of Farrland slipped in and out of his waking dreams. As they passed the carriage of the King, Alissa thought she heard soft singing.

Alissa noted that a line of debris, leaves and twigs and seeds, no doubt deposited by the river, lay now far above the level of the waters. "It has gone down about two feet, I should think," she said, pointing to the evidence, and impressing the princess with her powers of observation. Her Highness might function at the highest level in the world of the palace, but apparently her experience of the real world was limited.

A guard was leading his horse out into the middle of the river. Downstream, Alissa saw the remains of a wagon stranded on a gravel bar. As the boys had said, a horse lay there, beneath a covering of crows, which moved like a feathered cape in the breeze. Each bird bobbing and moving like an automaton, an unfeeling machine, sun glinting off metallic feathers. For a second the birds interrupted their gluttony to look up, assessing the visitors with their dark glinting eyes.

Alissa turned away. All she could think of was the two young men who were murdered when mistaken for her own Jaimas and Egar. It could have been Jaimas, lying in some unknown field, left for the roving bands of cutthroat crows. It could be, yet.

"I think it is perfectly safe to cross today," Kent said, watching the guard walk easily to the other shore. "Palle will have been forced around to the bridge at Tainsill. They are not so far ahead of us now. If we can just keep moving. How fares the King?" he asked Rawdon, who had joined them.

"His Majesty is growing tired. He is not fit for such a journey." Rawdon looked a bit pale himself. Perhaps he was regretting his defection, considering that Palle was not so far ahead of them.

"We must find a place for the King to await our return . . ." the princess began.

"The King will not be left behind," the physician said firmly. "His Majesty has stressed this to me over and over. It is not just his wish to go on, he commands it. No matter what, His Majesty will go on."

Alissa saw Kent and the princess exchange a look, though she could not quite tell what it meant. Alarm, perhaps. Concern. But it may simply have been a question: *What is driving the King on like this?* Although Alissa believed that all parties were keeping their own secrets, apparently Kent and the princess didn't understand the motivation of the King.

"As pleasant as I am finding not being dashed against the hardest parts of my carriage," Kent said, "I think we must carry on."

Kent found Valary and Littel engaged in heated discussion by the roadside, and herded them back into the carriage. They had been studying Wells' text, and working on it as they could in the moving carriage.

"But if it is not the Midden Vale, then how do you explain it?" Valary was asking, his tone almost accusatory. Obviously being shut up in a carriage for hours on end was having its effect.

Littel shrugged, apparently tired of arguing.

"Kent," Valary said, turning to the painter. "You remember the sections of the text that dealt with the gathering of starlight and moonlight?"

"Captured in snow and water, I seem to remember."

"Well, not quite, but close enough. The text speaks of a spring where snow-melt and rain water meet. We have been puzzling over the location of that spring forever. But it occurred to us that the ancient word evolved into 'mog-dynge' in Old Farr, and that is midden. The Midden Vale, don't you see."

Kent glanced over at Littel, who shrugged. The young scholar may have been a genius with language, but Valary had been studying these matters longer than Littel had been alive. Kent had begun to think the old scholar's intuition in these matters was a bit uncanny.

"The road branches not too far off. If Palle has taken the fork to the Midden Vale, or even sent others in that direction, it would indicate something. But what are you suggesting we do, Valary?"

The man looked a bit surprised, as though it were merely academic debate— he expected no one to act on his discoveries. "I—I don't really know. I am merely trying to puzzle it out."

Kent nodded. The water would be necessary to perform the ritual. If he did not have it, he could not be tempted—not that they would ever be there in time. No, he had been offered his chance to keep his youth, and thrown it away. His thoughts turned immediately to the countess and the question that plagued him. *What had she been willing to do to stave off age, if indeed she was still young?*

The dried oak leaves scraped together like the carapaces of a cloud of insects. It was not the usual sound of a breeze passing through the forest. Galton, oddly enough, had the best vision in the dark and led the way, probing the trail with his cane like a blind man. As usual, the governor was breathing with difficulty, but their pace through the darkness was such that even Galton was not taxed overmuch.

Wells and Palle supported the baron, who made his slow way down the narrow path. A stream rushed along to their right, though the hollow sounds of water lapping and splashing over rocks did not seem to fit with the mood of the place. This water came from the spring in the Midden Vale, which would make it unwholesome by Galton's reckoning.

The prince and Noyes had remained with the guard at the carriages, as Palle was unwilling to allow the prince to participate in this endeavor. Despite great expressions of confidence, Galton knew that no one was really sure what would happen tonight. Up until now it had been all theory—no one had yet tried to apply what they'd learned. He was distinctly uneasy, himself.

The governor was not sure how he could thwart Palle now. He was beginning to realize that unless Lady Galton managed to send Kent and the others to his rescue, the governor would be forced to tip his hand at some point. And that could prove extremely dangerous. If he could only think of some way around this, but he was so fatigued from his endless efforts on the text that his poor mind did not even offer him possibilities to consider.

"Do you think it is far?" Trevelyan asked, his voice taking on the pitiful tone that had characterized his madness.

"Not too far," Palle said, making his voice kindly. "Do you have your part, Lord Trevelyan?"

The baron grunted.

"I hope this is really necessary," Galton managed.

"Utterly necessary, my dear fellow," Wells said. "Have no doubt of it."

They trudged on, saying nothing. The leaves scraped their dried bodies together again, and Galton gave an involuntary shudder. Bits of cloud drifted across the sky at intervals, increasing the shadow under the trees. A storm was in the air, Galton was certain. Tiny flashes of light, like sparks from a distant fire, punctured the darkness on the southern horizon. Lightning, the governor was sure, and though he could hear no thunder he could sense something deep and powerful approaching—like a hound seemed to hear thunder long before its master. The air had that feeling of odd dryness and gathering galvanic power that accompanied a lightning storm.

Like an agitated bull, Galton thought. The charge would come soon.

The path crossed a glade, faintly lit by starlight, and then was absorbed into the shadow of the wood again. A moment more of fumbling through total blackness and the path began to rise. Galton was forced to stop and catch his breath, giving poor Trevelyan a rest at the same time.

"Not far, I'm sure," Palle said.

"And we still have the holyoak to find," Galton said, and then regretted it. It would be better if they had forgotten.

"Don't worry, Stedman," Wells said. "It grows in several places along our road."

They felt their way up the last steps, crouching and feeling the path with their hands. The sound of falling water was loud.

A pool appeared through the trees, like the forest's dark eye, staring up, glittering with the tears of reflected stars. Galton glanced up and realized that cloud had covered the moon and stars, but that did not matter in this place. Their light had been captured, and spewed from a fissure in the cliff, down a pillar of water into the pool below.

Galton stood transfixed. It was like a column of glittering ice, turning slowly in the darkness.

Wells stopped beside Palle, staring at this scene, almost imperceptible in the darkness. He searched the sky for a moment. "Do you see? The starlight appears in the water even when the sky is blanketed with cloud! Natural philosophy will never explain this!"

"We must not tarry," Palle said quickly, unsettled by what he saw. "Lord Trevelyan."

"I am to climb naked into this pool of ice melt?" Trevelyan said, a little outrage creeping into his whimpering.

"Remember our bargain, Lord Trevelyan. The sooner you are done, the sooner we will be away from here and back to a warm carriage. There is an inn not too far off. We will stop there for a few hours. Help him, Wells, we haven't the entire night to wait."

Wells and Galton began assisting the baron with his clothes, coaching him in his part as they did so. The cloud opened a little, like a wound, revealing a scattering of stars, and bleeding a cool, brittle light into the pond. The oaks that leaned protectively over the water took on definition now, their leaves like remnants of dried skin on ancient bones.

"All right," Trevelyan said after a moment, "I'm ready. Flames, it is cold! Where is the jar?"

Wells passed him a glass jar, the stopper removed. Bending to touch the water with a finger, Trevelyan began to recite the lines he had memorized. He touched the finger to his lips, and spoke again, his voice gaining a bit of strength.

Galton thought the old man looked more than pathetic as he waded tentatively out into the pond, his massive bulk like an overgrown grub in the moonlight. He had barely gone three paces when a fox appeared at the water's edge. It stood with one delicate paw raised, as though surprised in mid step. Palle took a sharp breath, and Galton thought he was about to shout, but Wells touched his hand.

"It is all right. That will be Trevelyan's familiar. A good sign."

"But I thought nothing was to sully the waters?" Palle whispered.

"The fox is an extension of Trevelyan, in a way," Wells said, the excitement clear in his voice. "It will cause no harm."

The fox seemed to keep its eyes fixed on the strangers as it bent to the pool. A small tongue flicked out once or twice, and then the fox raised its head again. Trevelyan was not the object of its attention, but it eyed the others as though they were not to be trusted.

Trevelyan lumbered ungracefully across the pool, nearly falling with each uncertain step, dragging his feet beneath the water, slipping on submerged stones. He kept looking up at the falls as though it posed a threat. Galton saw the baron shiver, though he was not sure if it was from the cold or from fear. The fox seemed to become less sure as Trevelyan progressed, leaning more toward the shadowed wood, as though it might seek safety at any second.

Trevelyan finally came to the foot of the falls, where he stood, unmoving, his shoulders fallen like one who had lost confidence entirely. Galton thought the baron would not continue, but then Trevelyan raised his fatladen arms, his stance changing, and he called out in the strange tongue of the mages.

"*Tandre mal!*"

Galton heard Wells catch his breath. But nothing changed. The pale light of the almost full moon and the stars still fell into the glade, the falling water glittered as it had. The fox, though, bolted into darkness, and Galton wondered what that could mean.

A breeze caused the leaves to rasp together, like a shaman's rattle, and Galton felt his hair take on a charge, the strands clinging together unnaturally. Trevelyan's voice fell to a chant now as he continued with the ritual.

Reaching down into the pool, the baron brought up water to anoint his own shoulders and brow. It appeared to Galton that Trevelyan began to coalesce in the poor light, and he believed that direct moonlight had found its way through the trees to illuminate the scene. But when he looked up, he recoiled before he was able to control himself.

"*Sea fire,*" Wells whispered.

The light appeared to cling to the tips of branches like some luminescent green lichen. Slowly it grew, slipping down the branches, springing from one tree to the next.

Trevelyan droned on, apparently so caught up in the rite that he saw nothing else. The sea fire continued its descent, the three men watching with fear and fascination.

Trevelyan stepped forward and filled his jar from the falls, still reciting the words of the rite.

A deep rumble of thunder boomed somewhere beyond the vale, and Galton felt an echo in his own chest. The three men watching this scene had all moved closer together, their shoulders touching. The sea light spread down to the forest floor, and suddenly touched the baron where he stood completing his ritual.

"*Impossible,*" Wells whispered.

The baron continued, as though unaware that he had been enveloped in pale green light. Another rumble, closer this time, and a gust of wind rattled through the trees like hail.

Trevelyan finished then, and lightning stabbed the forest not far off, thunder booming through the wood like cannon exploding. The sea fire intensified, flaring up, jumping from treetop to treetop, then blinked out, leaving darkness but for the glitter from the pool. Clouds had covered the stars, plunging the wood into renewed darkness.

The baron seemed stronger and less hesitant as he waded back across the pool. Galton threw a blanket around the man, who seemed dazed, not quite aware of what went on around him. Wells could not pry the jar from his grasp and was forced to stopper it while still in Trevelyan's hand.

"The fire is gone," Wells said. "It touched you, Lord Trevelyan. Did you feel it?"

"What?"

"The sea fire. Did you not see it?"

"Yes, I saw," the baron said, covering his face with his free hand. "The dreams. . . . The dreams of my madness. Not dreams at all," he whispered, horrified. He began to shake, and Galton thought he would collapse. Lightning flared again, so close that they all flinched. Palle managed to take the jar from the baron and stepped away from the others.

"Come, Trevelyan," Wells said. "Dress quickly. We must get away from this place. The sea fire. The storm. It is too much like the battle of the Midden Vale. The spirit of Dunsenay is said to ride the hilltops at such times." He began helping the frightened baron into his clothes.

Again lightning struck, so close that they were nearly blinded by its flash. Their courage gave way then, terror taking hold. The baron had begun to weep, falling to his knees. Wells and Galton pulled the man to his feet, throwing his coat over the blanket, and leading the poor baron away, barefoot.

He whimpered as they made their way through the dark, flinching occasionally as though warding off a blow. But even worse; Galton realized that not all the words mumbled were from familiar languages, nor were they all from the ritual the baron had memorized.

Galton began to feel his own fear taking hold of him, overcoming his reason. The darkness seemed frightening, and each time the lightning flashed he expected to see some terrible spectacle—an army of ghostly warriors surrounding them silently. Or something even worse.

Trevelyan fell repeatedly, and cried and whimpered in his fear, making no sense now at all. The wind whipped the branches in frantic circles so that they creaked and moaned, the dried leaves almost hissing as they moved.

The path had begun to seem endless, and at times they lost it completely. When a flash of lightning revealed them on it again, Galton thought it nothing short of a miracle. A light flickered in the trees ahead, like a flame brought to life by a lightning strike. It appeared to waver and then disappear as though floating through the trees.

"Is it a lantern?" Galton wondered aloud, hoping it was nothing unnatural.

A moment later, in a lull in the storm, they heard Noyes shout, and they all answered in unison. Prince Kori and Noyes appeared, looking distinctly disturbed in the light of their storm lantern. The fury of the storm was such that no one tried to speak when they met, but Noyes turned and led the way back through the trees. A branch split with a crack and fell across the path twenty feet ahead, and the air was full of the dried leaves of oaks, torn free by the storm, battering against the men like a plague of insects.

Finally, they came out of the trees, and the night was revealed in all of its horror and glory. Lightning flashed continuously, far off on the horizon, and close by. A fire seemed to be flickering on the hillside, and the men could not look into the wind, which hurled bits of the valley floor against them.

"Fire writing!" Trevelyan shouted, pointing at the lightning filled sky, and then he stopped as though transfixed, his eyes wide.

The drivers and guards struggled with the horses, though they seemed hardly less frightened themselves. Rain fell, propelled by the wind so that it struck man and beast like gravel. Galton and Wells managed to push a struggling Trevelyan into the rocking carriage, and then crawl up behind him. Palle went to his own coach, and the drivers sent their charges forward, and as soon as they were given leave to move, the horses bolted in terror.

The darkness inside the carriage was held at bay by the continual lightning, and over the sound of the rain and his own breathing Galton could hear Trevelyan muttering—some of it in the strange tongue of the ritual.

The governor of Farrow was deeply distressed by what had happened. Surely they could not go on. . . . It was completely clear that they did not understand in the slightest what they were involved in or what forces might be involved. Had Trevelyan somehow unleashed this storm and the sea light?

"Lord Trevelyan," Wells said, shouting over the cacophony of nature, the mad drumming of horse's hooves. "You must take hold of yourself, sir. We are not finished, yet."

"*Oh, we are finished, Roderick,*" Trevelyan said, his voice strange. "We are quite finished. *Lachevé.*"

*　　　*　　　*

Massenet pulled his horse up at the top of the hill, and sat waiting for the others. He could see the road ahead in sections: usually where it climbed a hill between hedges and rows of trees. The hills would then hide the track for a stretch, and it would appear again, brown against the emerald fields and gray woods, a light strip of green up the road's center like the stripe on a snake's back. For the most part the road was empty, though the low light of late afternoon created dense areas of shadow that hid much.

They were not far behind Angeline Christophe and Bertillon now, but they were narrowing the gap at a maddingly slow pace, despite pushing their horses cruelly. Varese, of course, was not the best horseman, but he was doing all he could, and not complaining. He said little each time they stopped, though he did not hide his growing pain.

The count looked up at the sun, and realized that he would have to give up his hope of catching Lady Angeline and Bertillon before nightfall. All of the things he had considered doing and saying when finally he faced the woman would have to wait. He wondered if they would stop for the night, and the thought that she might spend the night with Bertillon caused his anger to surge. He tried to calm himself. This was a time when he needed to think clearly, though he still felt his anger burning slowly beneath the surface. He did not know exactly what this woman intended, but clearly he could not let her arrive at the abbey before him. He could not understand why he was not gaining more ground in this race, and it unsettled him. Riders were faster than carriages, after all.

Varese and the others came up then, and Massenet nodded to the doctor.

"Why do you think she took Bertillon?" he asked Varese suddenly.

"To stop us," Varese said quickly, obviously having considered the same question.

"Yes, but why take him with her? Could she not have poisoned us all, or just Bertillon, for that matter?"

"Perhaps she is not so mad, Count Massenet. Not everyone is capable of murder."

"No. Surely. But is there some other explanation? Does she need Bertillon? Are we missing something obvious?"

Varese shrugged.

Far off, on the most distant curve of road, a carriage appeared, accompanied by horsemen. Even at a distance they could be seen to be making good time.

Massenet said nothing, but spurred his horse forward, determined to resolve this situation. He was not used to being made to look a fool.

Bertillon realized that the dark objects he stared at were women in veils. He shut his eyes tightly and wondered how, exactly, one forced one's eyes to focus when they refused to cooperate. Opening them again revealed the scene a little more clearly.

"Can you hear me, Mr. Bertillon?" said one of the women. Her tone was musical and pleasant, and somewhat familiar. He found it stirred him in an odd way.

"Yes." His voice came out as a whisper. "What has happened? Where is Massenet?"

"Be at peace, Mr. Bertillon. Your mind will clear in a few moments. Do not be alarmed."

He tried to nod his head but was unsuccessful.

A carriage. He was in a moving carriage. The blinds were drawn almost completely, and light found its way into the coach only when the curtains swayed. Parts of the interior were illuminated by quick moving javelins of light that appeared and disappeared abruptly. It was as though reality had been shattered into fragments, and all the normal relations of time and substance no longer existed. His confused mind struggled to pull these fragments into a coherent pattern. Two women, dressed in dark clothing, wearing black veils and gloves.

They are like visions of death, he thought suddenly, and felt fear flash through him. Angels of death, and the final journey to the underworld. He felt sudden nausea.

"You do not look well, Mr. Bertillon. We could stop, though only for a moment."

He nodded. "Please."

The light outside the carriage was blinding, the late afternoon sun casting long shadows. Two men appeared and supported Bertillon while he urinated. For a moment he thought he would be ill, but when he appeared to recover, the men helped him back to the carriage.

"A moment more," he said drinking in the pure spring air.

"We have not a moment to squander, Mr. Bertillon," the woman said again, and the two men helped him up into the carriage against his will, though he had not the strength to resist.

"Do you feel better?"

He nodded, laying his head back against the swaying seat. "Am I ill?"

"No, Mr. Bertillon, you took the physic. More than you have in the past. You don't remember?"

"Massenet . . . ? We left him at the inn?"

"Yes, he is not far behind us, now."

That seemed to be correct, though Bertillon was not sure why he thought that. "We're going to the abbey?"

"Yes, it is not far off. I think we should be there by morning."

"The count. . . . It seems unlikely that he will let us escape. He is a skilled rider."

This statement caused brief laughter, though he could not imagine why. "So I have heard. He will not overtake us, do not worry. Do you remember our agreement, Mr. Bertillon?"

"I—I don't." *Agreement?* What had been done to him? He could remember nothing.

"Wait a few moments, and it will all be clear. Breathe deeply. Be at peace. Sleep if you are so inclined. You are quite safe. I will wake you when it is time."

Time? the musician thought. Time? What had he agreed to? When he shut his eyes, the strangest visions appeared before them. A persistent scene of him having love with a strikingly beautiful woman, which was powerfully erotic even in his present state. The vision seemed to draw him in a manner he could not describe, as though it had significance he could not quite grasp—it seemed more a ritual than a night of pleasure.

They had stopped again, and Kent could not bear it. If only he had gone with the duke and his son. But, despite his feelings of vitality, that might have been tempting fate. Better not to have taken the chance of slowing the duke's progress. Horses were being replaced and people were seeing to their necessities. Kent had wolfed down some food earlier, not wanting to be responsible for slowing their progress.

"Sir Averil?"

Kent turned to find Princess Joelle approaching him. In the golden sun of late afternoon she looked years younger, as though human concerns could not stand up to such light. "Your Highness," he said.

She nodded in a way that seemed to speak familiarity, though was no less regal for all that. Beside Kent she stopped, shaded her eyes with one hand, and looked off down the road. "What do you think Massenet intends?" she asked quietly.

Kent shook his head. "I was hoping Your Highness would know that."

She looked down at the ground, and then up again at the road, as though following it from her feet into the distance, ascertaining that there was no trick to this route. "Men are commonly more predictable."

"I am not sure how to broach this subject, Your Highness." Kent paused, looking for a sign that she knew what he referred to, but she kept her gaze fixed on the distance. "Massenet gave me a letter. A letter that I thought indicated he had the trust of someone . . . someone in the palace."

She nodded, but Kent was not sure what that gesture might acknowledge. "And where is this letter now?"

"It was taken from my home, by an agent of the count's, or so I assume."

"He has a way of winning people's confidence, but his true intentions are never revealed. If he arrives at the abbey first, is there some way that he can render the site unusable?"

"Valary does not think so."

She raised her hand to shade her eyes again, hiding her reaction to what Kent had said. "Then one would be inclined to believe that the count has every hope of recovering this knowledge for his own use, or the use of his government."

"I'm afraid I must agree."

"We must pray that the duke arrives first. May Farrelle speed them."

Kent nodded. She did not mention her concern for her only son, and that touched the painter strongly.

The princess nodded to Kent and went off to see to her party, leaving Kent wondering what she had meant exactly. *"He has a way of winning people's confidence, but his true intentions are never revealed."* It would appear to be a lesson learned at first hand.

Kent could see Alissa sitting alone on a bench beneath a tree, lost in thought, probably thankful to have a moment alone. Kent decided not to interrupt. Being shut up in a carriage for so long was affecting everyone.

Valary waved to him then and came striding across the open yard before the small inn. "Kent, I've been thinking. I am more and more convinced that I'm right about the Midden Vale, do you see? I don't think I'm merely being pigheaded."

"Well, it seems that Palle and his followers went that way. I take that as a fairly strong indication that you are right."

Valary nodded, suddenly distracted, as though he had forgotten why he had come to speak with the painter. He stood struggling for a moment and then picked up the thread of his thought. "I think we may have made a mistake, Averil. We should have gone to the vale ourselves. If there is no way to stop the others from recovering the lost knowledge, it might be better that we possess it ourselves. Do you see? Better us than Palle or Massenet."

Kent did not respond for a second. "It hardly matters, Valary. We shall be there long after everyone else. We must pin our hopes on the duke, or perhaps the countess. I have begun to wonder why we make this journey at all. Perhaps the King truly is mad. What in the world does he hope to accomplish?"

Valary looked thoughtful for a moment. "It is not inconceivable, Kent, that the others will fail. You must realize that we are not at all sure we can perform this ritual in a manner that will yield results. We can't, of course, be sure what Massenet might know, but from what Littel has told me, I would give Wells and company no better than even odds. We might not be there first, but we might be the ones to succeed. If only we had gone through the Midden Vale. We would need water from the spring and certain herbs that grow there. And there is something else. . . . The more I look at the text that Wells had, the more I am convinced that it is not complete. Could they be holding back a section of the text? Something neither Galton nor Mr. Littel knew anything of?"

"Why would they do that, Valary?" Kent asked, a little alarmed at the suggestion.

"I don't know, but I have the worst feeling about this. I have developed quite a sense for these things, Kent, and if I am right about there being a missing section, I don't like to think what its purpose might be."

Kent found Valary's reaction deeply disturbing. The only one who might be able to tell if the text was complete was the countess, and she had run off without explanation—not for the first time.

People were beginning to board their respective carriages, and Kent motioned Valary back to their own horse-drawn cell, as he was beginning to think of it. He went to climb up behind the scholar, but his leg gave way as he put his weight on the step. If not for the quickness of the guard holding the door, he would have fallen. Mounting more carefully, he sat heavily on the seat and broke into a sudden sweat.

Was the countess' enchantment weakening so quickly? Was the disease of age about to invade his body again? He shut his eyes for a moment, but could not bear the darkness.

∽ Thirty-Two

Bertillon was still feeling at a remove from the world of common perception, as though his awareness had sunk deeper into his skull and peered out at the world through narrow tunnels. Despite all the assurances he had received from Massenet, the musician now regretted his decision extremely. If not for Angeline, he was not certain that he could have dealt with the effects of the physic—especially in the quantities this endeavor was to require. Either Massenet had not known, or he had not been completely honest with Bertillon, and the musician would not have been surprised to find it was the latter. He had been drawn in by a promise that he would be able to extend his years—his productive years—but now he was not so confident of his decision.

He paced purposefully across the grass and scrub before the abbey, stepping carefully among the sheep droppings. He stopped and searched the horizon, assessing the weather the sea would send that afternoon. It was best to keep moving, and try to focus his mind on something, otherwise he would drift into the unsettling, waking dreams that the seed generated.

"There is no road back," he whispered, as though addressing the distant gulls

that rode the breeze. Perhaps one of these would be his familiar. Angeline had said to be on the watch for such a thing, but so far any animals he had seen seemed perfectly natural.

Massenet would arrive soon. He could not get over how little concern Angeline displayed over this—her mind seemed to be on other matters. Bertillon was not sure whether this was a display of confidence or a measure of her nerve. Did she actually have the cards or was she merely bluffing? Bertillon did not know her well enough to guess. There was no doubt in his mind that there was far more to Angeline Christophe than his few hours of observation would reveal.

The count would be in a rage when he arrived—a controlled rage, perhaps even silent, but it would be a rage nonetheless. She had stolen Bertillon away, and perhaps even worse, had done it by suggesting she was available to the count. Massenet's great vanity in this one area would make him now very dangerous. It was not a good idea to make a fool of Count Massenet.

If at all possible, the count would have his revenge for this affront. Bertillon could not return his support to Massenet now, even if he wanted to.

Angeline claimed that Bertillon was under no enchantment and that he had made his decision freely. In fact, she claimed that the ritual could not be performed successfully by someone who was doing so under duress—but he wondered if this were true. He was not sure what it felt like to be bespelled, so he was not sure if he were making his own decisions or not. But then, there was more than one type of spell that such a woman could cast, he was sure of that.

A gust of wind made his coat flap, and he felt for a moment like a scarecrow, standing guard over the ruined abbey, keeping at bay all the humans who flocked there, drawn by its strange promise.

"*Already you are thinking of them as human,*" he said aloud. It was an odd feeling. *I will not be a true mage,* he reminded himself, and that was some comfort.

He turned away from the view to find Angeline staring at him, her gaze measuring him disinterestedly. She had shed her veil and gathered her hair in a ribbon of black velvet. She was dressed simply, and Bertillon saw grime from her forays into the abbey had left a stain on her shawl. The wind colored her face, making the blue of her eyes even more striking, and Bertillon found he could not easily pull his gaze away.

"They are nearby," she said, and Bertillon did not need to ask who she meant. "You don't need to speak with him, Charl, if you would rather not."

"No. I will stand with you, if you will let me."

She smiled as though the seriousness of his tone or perhaps his choice of words amused her. "We'll make our stand together, then," she said, though it was not mockery. "Come." She inclined her head toward the spot where the road emerged through the trees.

They walked silently to the top of the track, and waited expectantly. Bertillon did not bother to ask how she knew "they" were arriving now. He had learned that Angeline knew many things that could not be readily explained.

It did not take long. As Bertillon expected, Massenet was ahead of the others—incautious when it came to his own safety, as usual. He was leading a horse that looked like it might not manage the last few yards. Even Massenet looked filthy and fatigued—a sight Bertillon had never seen before. By contrast, Angeline appeared as though she had merely stepped from the front door of her home.

"Count Massenet," she said, her tone perfectly warm, "we have been awaiting you."

The Entonne Ambassador stopped, his legs spread as though to keep his balance, and regarded the pair before him with obvious disdain. Bertillon did not like finding himself facing that glare.

"Are you happy in your new country, Charl?" the count asked softly.

Bertillon did not know what to answer, but found he could not continue to endure that terrible stare, and looked away, feeling a quick flush of shame.

"There is more at stake than you realize, Count Massenet," Angeline said, her voice still calm. "More at stake than our vanity." She smiled charmingly as she said this.

But Massenet did not rise to the challenge. Bertillon knew the count loved a strong woman—one with wit and confidence—but Massenet's look of anger and disdain did not change.

"I have not come this far to banter with traitors and girls. I have every intention of completing my task," he turned to Bertillon, "and you will help me, Charl."

Bertillon hesitated only a second, then shook his head. "I cannot," he said quietly.

Angeline spoke just as Massenet opened his mouth, his temper flaring. "Allow me to explain, Count Massenet," she said, her voice infinitely reasonable, and still showing no signs of concern about Massenet's threats. "And Mr. Varese; you must hear this as well."

The Entonne doctor had struggled up the path, looking far worse for his journey than the count. He sat down heavily on the ground, staring up at Bertillon and this woman before him, his mouth open and his lungs drawing in great heaving draughts of air.

"I have seen the text that you posses, and the text of Roderick Palle's group, and they are not the same." Angeline crossed her arms, a stance of complete defiance, Bertillon thought. "These texts cannot be employed independently. You were not meant to have this power you dream of, Count Massenet. Even if Charl agreed to cooperate, you would succeed in accomplishing nothing but

Charl's own horrible ruin. I believe I can convince Doctor Varese that what I claim is true, if you will allow me to do so."

Massenet looked over at Varese, who considered a moment and then shrugged, as though passing the decision back to the count. "We have some hours before the ritual can be performed," Massenet said, "but I warn you, Lady Angeline, if I suspect you are attempting to subdue us again, by any means, my response will be immediate and extreme."

To this threat she merely smiled sweetly, and then motioned the count toward the abbey, as though inviting them into her manor house.

In one corner of the ruined building shepherds had thatched over a frame of poles before an ancient hearth, providing rough shelter. A bench, a low table of old planks, and a few rough stools were scattered about, and a kettle hung from a rusted hook over the fire. The servants and horsemen who had accompanied Angeline left immediately, the riders taking up stations not far off, like well-trained guards, Bertillon thought. The other lady, the one who did not speak, was not to be seen.

Massenet took a stool at the table, across from Angeline, and Varese sat just at his shoulder, like an advisor. It was impressive to see how quickly everyone learned his place in Massenet's scheme of things. Bertillon thought it must make his own apparent betrayal all the harder to accept. Men who were used to subordinating others to their wills were invariably surprised by rebellion—as though this imaginary prison that they created was, in fact, real.

"You are not innocent of the mage's arts," Massenet said, going immediately on the offensive. "Where did you learn them?"

Angeline smiled as though the count had said something witty, and that was too much for Massenet. He half-rose, pulling back his hand to strike her, but something dove at the count's face, causing him to pull back.

Massenet put a hand to his cheek and came away with a jewel of blood on his finger. Bertillon glanced up at the stone wall and caught sight of a small bird, almost invisible in the shadows.

"Please sit down, Count Massenet," Angeline said. "You are far from your lair in Avonel and have come here with little strength and nothing to bargain with. It is an unusual position for you, I realize, and therefore, I will forgive you this one indiscretion. If you attempt violence against me or anyone in my party again, one of my guards will put an arrow in your heart. Do you understand? You are present at my sufferance only. I have absolutely no need of you."

Massenet lowered himself back to his stool but said nothing, his face revealing even less. Bertillon wondered if Angeline had any idea what she had just done. She had better have every bit of power that her manner claimed, or Bertillon did not want to contemplate what awaited her.

She rose from her chair, turning her back unconcernedly on the count, and poured water from the kettle into a battered teapot. "I don't suppose I can interest you in tea?"

"I've had your wine," Massenet said, eliciting only a shrug from her.

As she returned to her seat, Angeline began to speak. "It will come as something of a surprise to you, I think, but this text that you have come to possess—you were intended to find it. Oh, not you, necessarily. Let me try again. The discovery of the text suited another purpose, but it was not meant to serve yours. Nor could it, I must tell you."

Varese leaned forward to speak, but Massenet silenced him with a gesture.

Was I like that, Bertillon found himself wondering, *so utterly subservient?*

"And whose purpose is this all in service of, may I ask?"

Angeline shrugged. "I will tell you honestly that I am not absolutely sure myself."

Massenet leaned back from the table. "But you. . . . You did not acquire your skills by some accident of nature. Where did you learn them? You asked me here to listen to an explanation, but I begin to think you are merely wasting time. Whose purpose does the Lady Angeline serve? And who are you? Why is it that no one can name your parents or family?"

She looked up and met his gaze without blinking. "Some of these things will become clear to you in time," she said quietly. "Who do I serve? That fragment you gave to Averil Kent, Count Massenet: I serve those who understood what that vision meant."

Bertillon watched Massenet closely. He could not help himself. It was fascinating. Like watching a predator realize that it was being hunted. He had shifted almost imperceptibly back from the table, as though suddenly wary of the woman who sat across from him.

"I see. And what will you do?"

"We will seal the power away, forever if we can. And I think we can."

"What do you want from me?"

"Your cooperation, Count Massenet. Others will arrive soon. There is nothing we can do until everything is in place. But I appeal to your reason. Better no one have the lost knowledge than it fall into the hands of Palle or some other. I think you will agree. I want nothing for myself but to complete a task begun long ago. If you threaten my purpose, you increase the chances that this power will come into someone's possession. Quite likely someone you would rather see without it."

"Why do you not merely render me obedient? You could do that, could you not? Is it because you need Bertillon's willing participation? Are you afraid that you will lose it if you act against me?" He turned suddenly to Bertillon, his manner determined as only Massenet could be determined. "Charl, do you see?

We are being manipulated by a master; an enchantress. She is a loyal Farr-lander. Do not doubt it. We await others, she admits, and we know who those others will be: Palle and his prince. We are being duped, Charl. Made fools of. Palle will arrive, and she will surrender the arts to him. It will mean the ruin of Entonne. She claims that this is not so, but are you willing to take such a risk?"

Bertillon struggled for a moment. He had not realized how difficult it would be to break free of this man. How much he wanted to please him. "I think Angeline tells the truth, Count Massenet. There is much more to what goes on than we ever suspected. Let Angeline and Doctor Varese speak and I think you will see."

"She has influenced you, Charl. We were all drugged. . . ."

He did not finish, for the sound of horses and men's voices caused them all to stop. The count cast an accusatory glance at Bertillon. "She has delayed long enough," he said.

A moment later the Duke of Blackwater appeared around the end of a stone wall, and Bertillon heard the woman beside him sigh with apparent relief, causing Massenet to shift his gaze back to her.

The duke stopped, observing the scene, and his son and Prince Wilam appeared at his side.

"Lady Angeline," Jaimy said, bowing quickly, "it is a pleasure to see you again so soon."

The duke nodded to Massenet, and then turned to Angeline, his gaze searching. "We arrived before Palle and the others." It was half a statement of the obvious, and half a question, for nothing could be sure in this matter.

"They are behind you, though not so far."

"And the countess?"

"She is preparing for the ritual."

Bertillon thought this duke looked more like Massenet than not, and though his bearing was less haughty, his mannerisms were not so different. *Two powerful men*, the musician thought, *and neither is entirely sure why they are here, nor what is about to occur. Drawn, almost instinctively, to a struggle over power.* The duke kept his gaze fixed on Angeline, ignoring Massenet, although Bertillon knew this did not necessarily indicate the duke's interests or concerns.

"I have been ordered to secure the abbey until the King arrives, and I will use my guards to insure this."

"You will receive no opposition from the countess, Duke. We await the King, as well. It is the King's Man and Prince Kori who are the threat. I understand they travel with a guard."

Bertillon had made a study of the count's most subtle mannerisms, and he could tell now, simply by the stiffness of his body and the position of his hands, that the count was near to exploding with frustration. Bertillon almost smiled.

Not only was Massenet not in control of the situation, but he did not even fully understand what was going on. It must be driving him mad.

"And Count Massenet? What is the ambassador's intention?" the duke asked.

"The Count can do nothing without my cooperation, Duke," Bertillon offered, "and I have agreed to assist Lady Angeline." And the countess, he thought. Whoever she was.

The duke glanced at Massenet, as though assessing his reaction, and then turned back to Angeline. "I will post guards in the abbey, then."

Everyone stayed in their place for a moment, all the unasked questions struggling to take form, and then the duke turned away and began giving orders to the palace guards. Angeline rose to show him the entrance to the lower levels, and Bertillon found himself alone with the count.

The second the others were out of hearing Massenet turned to him. "I can do nothing without you, Charl?" he said, cocking his head to one side. "I had not realized your opinion of me was so low." He rose and walked out from under the shelter with what Bertillon knew was a tightly controlled fury.

It was probably nothing more than a boast, an attempt to make Bertillon worry, but he would warn the duke and Angeline. Better to underestimate anyone but Massenet—many would attest to that.

Kent emerged from the woods, his spirits raised a little by the signs of spring, the buds on trees and bushes, the buzz of insects, the scent of newly emerged flowers, and the excited songs of birds. *The power of the earth reawakening,* he thought.

They had stopped at a roadside spring to water the horses, and the carriages were drawn up haphazardly, the teams led away. Guards and drivers were busy with their charges and the passengers lounged about or, as Kent had done, answered the call of nature.

A guard officer approached Kent.

"His Majesty requests you attend him, Sir Averil." The man inclined his head away from everyone, not looking in that direction himself. One did not look at the King.

Under the spreading branches of a cherry tree that was just coming into blossom, sat the King on a stone bench. His back was to everyone, and he wore a heavy coat thrown over his shoulders, but there was no doubt of who it was. The sovereign of Farrland was bent over, as though the weight of the coat was more than he could bear.

Kent approached, making as much noise as he could, as there seemed to be no one at hand to announce him.

"Your Majesty?"

There was no reaction for a few seconds, and then the King lifted his head, turning it slightly from side to side.

"*Your Majesty?*" Kent said, louder this time.

The King raised a hand and motioned the painter to come around before him. "Is it Mr. Kent?" His voice did not seem quite so unearthly, though Kent wondered if it was the setting.

"Yes, sir." Kent made a leg before the King, who squinted at him in the bright sunlight.

"Imagine coming to a point in one's existence," the King said, "where one shunned the light of the sun."

Kent nodded, not sure what to say.

"Well, I am a little more myself, though I suffer terribly for want of my physic. You know about my physic?"

"I do, sir."

The King looked sour. "It seems everyone knows. Secrets are not what they once were, Kent, I'll tell you that. In my day I knew men who could keep secrets! But they are all gone now. I'm the only one left. Once I'm gone there will be no one who can keep a secret, and everyone will know everything." The King looked up at Kent, and a terrible smile appeared on the ruined face. "Don't look so, man; I jest. You have the painting?"

"I have only a sketch, Your Majesty. I could show it to you."

The King raised his hand quickly and shut his eyes, turning his head away. "No. No, I don't need to see it. It will do, I'm sure."

Kent stood in silence—one waited to be addressed by the King—but the silence stretched on so that Kent wondered if His Majesty had slipped off into one of his waking dreams.

"Kent?"

"Your Majesty?"

"Do you fear death?"

He had asked this same question of Kent before. "I do, sir."

The King nodded, his head shaking just perceptibly, as though he were palsied. "Is there anything you would not do to evade it?" he said quietly, as though he would be ashamed to have anyone hear.

"One can never know until faced with the choice," Kent said, thinking of Palle's offer.

The King nodded his head again, keeping his eyes shut, agonizing over his choice, Kent thought. "*Yes,*" he whispered. "Do you think our 'age of reason' is an improvement, Kent?"

The painter considered for a moment, wondering what this conversation was really about. "I think it promises more than it will deliver, but, in balance, I think it will lead to a better world, a fairer world."

"Fairer? I wonder if the mages would agree," the King said. "But then you mean more equitable and just, don't you? Not 'beautiful.' I sometimes think, Kent, that I will be looked upon as the last of the Farr Kings before the 'age of reason.' The last unreasonable King. Do you think history will deal kindly with me?"

"I am sure that historians will deal with you very kindly, Your Majesty."

"Perhaps," the King said softly. He opened his eyes suddenly, and nodded up at the tree. "Is this a hawk?"

Kent followed his King's gaze. "A kestrel, sir."

"It appears to be watching me," he said, and Kent could not tell if this were another jest. The King closed his eyes and turned his face up, something like a look of peace on his horrible features. "The caress of the sun, Kent. The sounds and perfumes of spring. These are the things I could not bear to lose—yet my craving for the seed, in the end, saw me shut up in the darkness. My world reduced to a mere imitation. Think of all the years I have lost—though I believed I had gained those years. Well, we are only hours away now. Not too long. Thank you, Kent. Keep my portrait at hand. Thank you."

Kent bowed, though the King's eyes were closed, and then backed away. This audience, he felt, was only slightly less disconcerting than the last. Just the man's appearance was horrifying! But the terrible voice had lost some of its hollowness and strange distance—a result of Rawdon controlling the physic, no doubt. Kent was now quite sure that the enchantment of the countess was wearing off, but any temptation he felt to accept Palle's offer of the physic was erased by his meeting with the King. What could be worse than ending up like that? Even if it was years off.

Had the countess enough talent or training to avoid the King's fate? The question never went unasked for long, and now that they drew near to their destination, Kent's curiosity seemed to be increasing—as his vitality ebbed. *Soon,* he thought. *Tomorrow before sunset. We will see what has transpired in our absence. If the duke was swift enough. And I will see the countess again, and have an answer to my question.*

"Sir Averil?"

Kent turned to find Alissa Somers standing behind him, her lovely brow creased with worry. "Lady Alissa, you look positively distressed. Will you tell me what an old man might do to help?"

This brought some response, not a smile, but a softening of her appearance, as though muscles had relaxed. "Sir Averil, I must confess that my life has become more complex than I ever anticipated. It has become impossible to make any decisions at all. I am no longer sure even who I am. People constantly refer to me as 'Lady Alissa,' yet even if I am to marry, I shall never feel that anyone could be addressing me in this manner." She looked up at Kent and bit her lip.

Kent noted the words she used—'even if I am to marry'—and thought this did not bode well for poor Lord Jaimas. And Alissa looked almost overwhelmed with distress, which touched him in some way he could not explain. "Although we are taught that certain kinds of promises are inviolate," he said, "I think it is too much to expect that someone sacrifice their happiness for the sake of a promise." He thought of the countess' decision, all those years ago. "If you really cannot go on, Alissa, be honest with your young man, but treat him as kindly as you can. You will be glad of it in the future, and so will he. I myself. . . ." He found he must close his eyes for a moment.

"Mr. Kent?"

He opened his eyes and smiled as best he could, blinking back a tear. "This may sound rather foolish and overly romantic, but do you love this young man?"

"Without question," she said solemnly.

"Well, then you know something for certain. One must predicate one's decisions on something. Of course, there are many who have made their decisions on just such a foundation and will tell you that they brought their lives to ruin. But I can tell you without a doubt—if you decide that other factors are more important than what you feel for Lord Jaimas, at the very least you will always wonder if you have made the right decision. When you grow old, such questions will plague you, like repeating nightmares. Be sure you know what is important to you, before you decide."

Alissa nodded and looked away from Kent's gaze. "I'm sure you're right. I am to tell you the princess would like to speak with you."

Kent found the princess in her carriage, the door open to the spring air. She was making a lunch of bread and cheese, apparently not too concerned that she wasn't surrounded by a bevy of servants.

"Ah, Mr. Kent," she said as he appeared in the open doorway. "You have spoken to His Majesty?"

"Yes, just now. Remarkable to find him outside, out where others might see him."

The princess nodded. "It is more than remarkable. Doctor Rawdon tells me that His Majesty is hardly less morbid, however, and still speaks constantly of death. Can you tell me if anything was said of which I should be aware?"

"The King was concerned that I brought the sketch I had made. Otherwise I think the conversation was of little consequence."

"I wish I understood what the King hopes to accomplish, Mr. Kent. I dearly wish I did.

"I am told that, if all goes well, we may arrive at the abbey tomorrow afternoon. Do you think the duke has managed to stop Palle?"

"I hope so, Your Highness. If Roderick and the others have managed to win through and perform their ritual. . . . Well, the world seems little changed to me."

"The world has a history of such deceptions. Many a ruler has sat, unaware, in his palace while outside the world changed irrevocably. King Ambray had been deposed for three days before anyone bothered to inform him. He was playing the pianum for his grandchildren at the time. But who is it that plays on, foolishly, here? Is it my husband? Or is it me?"

Kent wondered the same thing himself. "The Duke of Blackwater is a resourceful man. He traveled with loyal guards. I think that the day seems innocent because that is the truth of it. What has happened at the abbey I cannot say, but I suspect if anything arcane had occurred, the King would have sensed it. His Majesty gave no indication to me of having done so."

"I hope you're right." The princess looked at Kent suddenly, squinting a little in the light, and then she shut her eyes briefly. He realized she was near to tears, from constant anxiety, no doubt. "That fragment from Lucklow," she said, looking away; "what did it mean? What was this a vision of?"

Kent touched a hand to his cheek. "I have wondered long over this same question. Valary believes that the mages had a limited skill at augury—some were likely more able than others. Perhaps it is the future—or a possible future. Though it is worded in such a way as to make one believe it is another land that Lucklow spoke of. As though he had traveled there himself, and seen it with his own eyes. Whatever the case, clearly he feared that this same tragedy could come to pass here."

The princess considered a moment. "It is too altruistic," she said firmly. "The mages were not known for their concern for others." She shook her head, with resignation, Kent thought. "There is more hidden here than we guess, Averil. Does the countess not tell you her thoughts?"

"The countess tells no one her thoughts, Your Highness," Kent said, again surprised by the bitterness that crept into his voice when he spoke of the countess.

The princess did not respond to this, as though he had not spoken, but in truth he had revealed something too personal. One should not presume such familiarity with the princess.

"When can we get underway?" she asked suddenly. "These constant delays will be our ruin."

"I will see to it," Kent said, bowing stiffly, and making quick his escape. *No one understands*, he thought. *Has there ever been such an occurrence in known history? The powerful of two nations racing toward a ruined abbey for a purpose that no one can articulate. It is like a madness.*

↜ Thirty-Three

Jaimy had never been to a military staff meeting, but even so he was quite sure this one deviated from the pattern. The senior ranking officer was a lieutenant of the guards with a mustache like the bottom two inches of a broom. The man had every sign of being a fop, but Jaimy knew that there was a tradition among the guards: they were the best riders and most skilled swordsmen in the kingdom. Their training was said to be so demanding as to be just short of brutal, and the guards were renowned for courage and toughness. It was no wonder that over the years they had been instrumental in deciding several struggles over the throne.

Colonel Townes sat on his stool, leaning over the low table as though a map had been laid there. His uniform jacket was open at the collar—the only concession he made to their exhausting ride, for though he had ridden as far as everyone else, the miles did not leave the same mark on him. His shoulders did not sag, his gestures were precise and strong, and his wit did not seem to have been dulled by lack of rest.

Like many military men Jaimy had met, Colonel Townes seemed to believe that hesitation of any kind was a sign of weakness. Only an inferior man had to stop and "think," a good officer simply "knew." Despite this, the man did not seem a fool. Perhaps his experience and training had better prepared him to meet such situations.

But then Jaimy was quite certain there was nothing in the officer's manual that would cover what was about to occur here. The members of the legally constituted Regency Council were about to meet a force representing a King whose supporters claimed he was fit to rule, as well as reign. And all parties had gathered in this out-of-the-way corner of the kingdom to perform an arcane ritual of indeterminate purpose. Under the circumstances he was performing his duties with elan.

"If we do not take Prince Kori's party, Your Grace," the colonel said to the Duke of Blackwater, "then what will stop them from simply retreating and gathering reinforcements? We have the element of surprise, and it seems imprudent to squander it."

"I don't think they will surrender the abbey to us so easily, Colonel Townes," Lady Angeline interjected. Her manner was patient, as though she were practiced at dealing with men whose grasp of events was inferior to her own, and this had the effect of heightening the color of the officer's face.

"But if they do, they can gather any kind of ragtag army and easily overrun our position here," he said, his voice remaining calm and reasonable. He was too much of a gentleman, and too impressed with this woman's beauty, to disregard what she said, though, clearly, he thought her understanding of military matters imperfect.

"Not before we have completed our task," Angeline answered quickly, as though even her patience could wear thin.

"But we will lose the kingdom to Sir Roderick if we do not take this opportunity to arrest him. Is what you do here more important than the kingdom?"

"Yes," she said without hesitation.

That brought a moment of silence. The colonel cast a glance at the two officers who accompanied him. They knew what awaited them if this rebellion against the Regents failed. He then turned his eye on the duke, perhaps hoping a man would better understand their position.

The duke did not appear to be worried by the officer's concerns. "My instructions from Princess Joelle were to secure the abbey until the arrival of the King. 'Secure the abbey at all costs.' That, Colonel, is the will of the King. It is your duty to consider all possibilities, Colonel Townes, but trust that securing the abbey is of ultimate importance. I would lay down my own life to stop these others from wresting control of this site."

"Then I can do no less, sir," the colonel said quickly. "I would still suggest that we can best secure the abbey by arresting the King's Man and his followers."

"Something that cannot be done without some risk," the duke said, "especially as we do not know the precise size of their party. We are few, Colonel. I think it would be better to continue to barricade the abbey as best we can, and hold it. I will try to reason with Prince Kori; after all, he has a kingdom to lose, and little of real worth to gain. If reason does not work, we will do everything within our power to hold the abbey for the King, who, I believe, travels with enough troops to deal with Palle."

The colonel looked down and tapped a finger on the table, as though pointing out something crucial on a map displaying the arrangement of armies. "Accepting your argument that holding the abbey for thirty-six hours is our primary function, Your Grace, then I would agree. I fear what will happen to the kingdom of Farrland, but I will put my guards to work again, as tired as they are, and we'll finish doing what we can to fortify the abbey. And that is very little, I fear. We should be prepared to retreat down into the cellars to defend the critical chamber."

The colonel bowed, and retreated with his officers, leaving the prince, Jaimy, his father, and Lady Angeline to wonder if they had made the right decisions.

The three sat, saying nothing, the last light of the evening soft and warm on their careworn faces. To all appearances it was a situation where, all having been said, people sought comfort in each other's company, but Jaimy knew this was not so. He wanted desperately to speak privately with Angeline, and was certain she must sense this.

He remembered the night at the countess' house. *"You mustn't do this,"* she had said. *"It is futile even to begin."* Now this admission of her feelings seemed to lay between them like the map Townes had imagined—it was etched with the beginning of a path that they could choose to pursue or abandon. Jaimy wished his father would leave them alone, even for a moment. When he thought he could bear the silence no longer and had decided he must speak, Angeline rose, bid a hurried good night, and slipped away, though not before Jaimy saw the blush of red that colored her cheeks.

He watched her go, his eye following until she disappeared around the end of a wall. And then Jaimy realized that his father was staring at him. "I'll help the guards barricade the abbey," he said quickly.

"No need, Jaimas. There is little that can be done, and all of that is near complete. I expect we shall see Palle before the night is over, and there is something that we need to discuss before then." The duke moved closer to his son, his manner changing. He met Jaimy's eye, his look suggesting that he was surprised to find himself speaking with a man and not a boy. "If fighting breaks out, one of us must try to bring down Prince Kori; it may cost us dearly, but it has to be done. Do you understand?"

Jaimy nodded, hardly believing what he heard, but realizing the utter, cold logic of it.

"It is unlikely that the prince will expose himself to danger, but one never knows. I will attempt to do what must be done, but should I fail. . . ." The duke looked down at the table, lost in thought and concern. "Anything can happen in battle, Jaimas. One can never predict. If the fighting goes against us, you must escape with the prince. No one is more important." He looked up at his son. "Do you understand? No one."

Jaimy felt that distancing from reality that one experienced upon receiving bad news. "That is not true for me, but I understand, and will do as you say."

The duke gripped his son's shoulder, but it turned almost to a caress, the hand suddenly resting lightly. "Sennet will bring forces to Prince Wilam's banner, if it comes to that. Even if Kori is brought down, war might still come. If Palle can seize the King, he will have a chance, don't doubt it. We must hope for the best, but plan for the worst." The duke tried to smile.

"I want to protect you from this," he said suddenly, "but you are a duke's son. . . ." He gave Jaimy's arm a last squeeze and then withdrew his hand. "I will tell you my secret hope, in case things do not go as we wish." He lowered his voice to something just above a whisper. "I believe Rawdon cured his wife from a terrible illness using this seed. My uncle, Erasmus, had a similar theory about the Countess of Chilton. This physic—it might restore your mother to health. She has been so ill for so long. . . ." He fell silent as though he had lost his train of thought. "A cure for your mother. . . . Imagine," he almost whispered.

"If circumstances require," Jaimy said, not liking even the sounds of this phrase, "I will pursue this matter."

A soft smile appeared on the duke's face. "I rest easier knowing that. And seeing the man you have grown to be. You make us proud, Jaimas. You make us proud."

To the east the moon, one day shy of full, floated free of the ocean, casting a path of porcelain shards toward the Farr shore. In the west, the very last light of a warm day fled over the horizon. The wind fell silent, then would speak in syllabic gusts, muttering like an old man in his sleep.

Jaimy paced back and forth across the ridge top beyond the abbey and its surrounding trees. The vista was spectacular, and occasionally he would tear his focus away from his concerns and gaze out at the distant coastline, the shimmering ocean, and the strands of cloud illuminated at their edges by the newly risen moon.

How quickly and surely it floats heavenward, Jaimy thought, *like the pendulum of a celestial clock.* The only thing of which we can be sure—time passes— everything else is vanity.

The smell of smoke reached him, and then the odors of cooking. There were no more sounds of guards at work. Earlier they had felled trees and hauled them into place with teams. Rocks had been skidded on makeshift stone-boats, and all the gaps in the small building had been roughly closed. All was in readiness—as ready as could be made under the circumstances. Everyone still expected to retreat to the lower chambers, and there they thought they might hold out for some time, for the openings and hallways were narrow.

The area around the abbey had begun to take on the appearance of a military bivouac, though a small and somewhat odd encampment. There were no tents or pavilions or machines of war, but there were men gathered about fires, guards posted, horses tethered, weapons being tended. Here, in this somewhat forsaken district of Farrland, assembled the oddest collection of scholars, nobles, reclusive legends, foreigners, and renegades. It would become a story told over and over down through the years; and Jaimy was here, part of it.

"*If I do not hang,*" he whispered.

Palle and Prince Kori could not be too far off now. If they didn't stop for darkness, they would likely arrive this night.

Jaimy was not sure what his father could say that would sway Prince Kori or Sir Roderick Palle. These were not men used to being thwarted in their desires. And after Jaimy's brush with Palle's followers, he realized there was little the man would not do to achieve his ends.

He stared out over the sea, and thought of Tristam, sent to gather more of this plant that was so valued. The countess had said that Tristam had begun the transformation from man to mage. What did that mean for poor Tristam?

My brother, he thought.

Tristam was to have gone off on an adventure and Jaimy was to have remained quietly at home to marry. But it had all gone wrong somehow.

Jaimy wondered if he was still about to marry. He had offered to free Alissa from her vow, and she had agreed to consider his offer. He closed his eyes. Had he done this because he had met another? Was this truly what he wanted? The idea that Alissa would spurn him and find another caused his eyes to suddenly burn. How could he possibly want that?

His thoughts returned to Angeline Christophe. Their paths kept crossing, yet never ran together for any distance. What was this man Bertillon to her? The duke was certain that Bertillon was, or had been, an agent of Count Massenet. How had she convinced him to change his allegiance? Anger and jealousy boiled up in him as his imagination took hold.

I am still betrothed to another! It was almost a cry of anguish. This was how the Countess of Chilton had affected men in her day. Men whose names she did not even know would abandon their wives for love of her. And now the niece had brought out this madness in him.

I am hardly worthy of Alissa, he told himself angrily. If she knew.... This thought brought despair. He could not bear the idea of bringing Alissa pain. *Perhaps, after we are married, we should go abroad for a time, to allow this madness to work its way out of my blood—if we are married at all.*

"Lord Jaimas?"

Jaimy spun around to find Bertillon standing a few feet away, ghostlike in the moonlight.

"Mr. Bertillon."

They stood for a moment like that, eyeing each other, somewhat less than politely.

"Warn the duke that Massenet is not to be trusted," the musician said quickly, as though once he had decided to speak he wanted it over with as soon as possible. "He would never passively accept being bested. It is not in his nature."

Jaimy considered these words for a moment, keeping his eyes fixed on the man. "Massenet thought he would gain this power through you.... But how was he planning to insure your allegiance?"

Bertillon looked at Jaimy oddly, as though searching for mockery in the question. "Count Massenet does not admit the possibility of independent will.

The world is full of people who do not yet realize that they long to subject themselves to the will of Massenet. His vanity is unimaginable. But that is no longer my concern. I believe that Lady Angeline is right—this knowledge is best left hidden, destroyed if at all possible. You must warn the duke."

"Why don't you speak to my father yourself?"

Bertillon hesitated for a moment, and then jerked his head toward the trees. "I saw a child prowling through the trees a few moments ago and followed him. He came and stood at the edge of the wood, as though watching something. When the moon rose, I realized it was you he watched, Lord Jaimas. As I slipped closer, he became aware of me and looked my way. Light did not seem to reflect from him as it should, and then I saw that he cast no shadow. He slipped back into the darkness, more cunning than any wild animal—became part of it, really. But he had been watching you, is probably doing so at this moment. I thought you should know, in case you were unaware." The Entonne bowed as though he had just finished a recital, and acknowledged the chorus of applause. He walked back into the wood like a man who had no fear of ghosts.

Jaimy stood a moment, staring at the dark line of trees, the deep blue of the shadows, but once Bertillon had been absorbed into that liquid darkness, he could see nothing. No eyes staring out.

But we are so far from Merton, he thought. *It couldn't be the same specter following me.*

There was a shout, and he heard a horse coming up the track from the valley below. Forcing the thoughts of ghosts from his mind, he found the footpath through the woods and plunged into the pool of shadow, somewhat apprehensive of what might lurk there. A moment later he emerged gratefully from the wood and found the camp alive.

"My father is here," Prince Wilam said as Jaimy appeared, and the young royal seemed truly dismayed. Jaimy thought everyone else was equally alarmed, but even so, there was no chaos. The duke and the colonel had been preparing for this eventuality. Jaimy scrambled up a rough ladder to take his place on the wall, throwing aside his coat so that his sword was easily reached. The guards wore helmets and swords, and some took up pikes. Horses were quickly saddled and mounted, and the group of riders faded quietly into the trees. The colonel wanted to maintain some element of surprise, Jaimy guessed, but perhaps these men had some specific purpose.

He wondered how much strength Palle's followers would have when they arrived. They had been racing across the Kingdom themselves. Apparently Palle had set out with a small party, preferring speed over numbers, but the precise size of the party was unknown.

Jaimy knew this was a decisive moment, and not just because it would tell who controlled the abbey, but because it could mark the beginning of civil war. It was not a moment of normal life, but an instant in history, and he wondered how he would acquit himself, and whether his name would one day appear in history books.

If the Regency Council retreated, claiming the King had been abducted by parties wishing to usurp the legal right of the Council, many would support them. It was, as the colonel had pointed out, a terrible gamble. The duke was counting on a stand-off, betting that Palle would be unwilling to surrender the abbey, and would, therefore, take up a position nearby. Before Palle could find reinforcements, the King would arrive, and whatever needed to be done would be quickly concluded. It was the ragged end of a plan, cobbled together, as everyone realized, but fortunately Palle would have had no way to prepare a counter plan—completely unaware as he was of what went on at the abbey.

Jaimy found the prince at his side, holding a sword slightly away from him as though he feared it, or what he might do with it. No doubt the prince had fenced at the university, as everyone did, but this was not the practice floor. The two young men locked gazes briefly: some strange unspoken acknowledgment, and then the prince nodded.

He is in love with Alissa, Jaimy realized, the thought stabbing into his consciousness like a blade. But there was far more to it. Prince Wilam did not wish him ill. No, they were here, cast together by their common cause, their fear of the coming confrontation, and apparently by the love of the same woman. The possibility of losing Alissa became real for the first time and almost overwhelmed his fear of the coming confrontation.

The sounds of horses came up the track from below, refocusing Jaimy's mind on the present events. Fear. Jaimy felt some, there was no doubt. Men had tried to kill him before. It was no longer beyond imagining, as it might still be for the prince. But Jaimy had also learned an invaluable lesson during that cross-country chase: he knew that survival would depend on keeping his wits about him.

Jaimy also knew that the prince was about to face a situation he could hardly imagine. Prince Wilam's father was about to become his rival.

My father and I stand side by side, Jaimy thought. *The prince's father will ride up this trail, and realize the betrayal.* Jaimy offered up a silent prayer thanking whatever gods there might be that he was not forced to this same experience. Halden had written that all young men must vanquish their fathers, but he had not meant it so literally. Would Prince Kori send troops against his own son, Jaimy wondered? If the moment came, could the son raise the sword to the father?

"Will you fight, if that is what comes about?" Jaimy asked suddenly, keeping his voice low.

The prince nodded, his look sad. "Anyone but my father. But I hope it will not come to that."

"I know these men," Jaimy said. "They tried to murder me once. They are more determined and less concerned about lives than we might imagine. If you find yourself crossing swords with a man you recognize, do not count on him respecting your royal person. Take whatever advantage is offered, and strike with all force. But for now put your sword in its sheath until we see what occurs."

The prince looked down at his sword with some misgivings, and then returned it to its sheath.

The first horseman, a Palace Guard, appeared at the top of the road, riding bent over, sore and tired. Seeing armed guards of his own company before him he pulled up, dazed. The third man to appear took one look at the situation, wheeled his exhausted mount, and tore off down the trail. Jaimy heard the horse stumble and fall, but all the same, Roderick and the prince would know the situation in moments. There was a madding quarter hour during which the sounds of horses and occasionally men could be heard, though no one appeared.

Jaimy had been given a bow, a weapon he had been forced to master by his cousin Tristam. He stood atop the trunk of a tree that had been braced up against the wall at such a height as to allow a man to look over. The abbey roof had fallen in decades before, leaving the structure much like a walled keep, though with the gable ends still in place, their glassless rose windows, complete with stone traceries, still intact.

"Imagine that we defend such a place with our lives," Jaimy whispered to the prince, wanting to hear someone speak.

The young royal looked over at him, perhaps a little relieved to hear a voice. "Yes, but we are not the first to do so. Over the centuries countless lives have been squandered to control this site. Whatever is here does not go away—the attraction always returns."

Jaimy looked down the line of men at the wall, their faces illuminated by moonlight. They stared out at the shadows, searching for attackers, desperately wondering what Palle's men were preparing. Even Jaimy found himself hunkering down, exposing less of himself, imagining an arrow coming out of the darkness to pierce his face.

At that moment a rider on a gray horse appeared, an officer of the Palace Guard. He did not even bother with a flag of truce, but came out into the open, holding his head high and his back straight. Even his horse held itself proudly, as though mimicking its master's mood.

The officer stopped his horse in the open area, and for a moment stared at the abbey, using the opportunity to assess the situation.

"I am Ceril Hampton, Colonel of the Palace Guards," he called out, his voice confident and filled with authority. "I accompany Prince Kori, and members of the Council of Regents. You were once my fellows, my brothers in both arms and purpose, but if you do not lay down your weapons and surrender this site to us, you will become nothing more than criminals—failed mutineers—who bring dishonor to your uniform and your oath."

"You have said enough!" the duke called out suddenly. "The Regency Council has been dissolved, and the King rules again in Farrland. Sir Roderick Palle is the King's Man no more, and it is you in danger of being named 'mutineer.' I am Edward Flattery, Duke of Blackwater, and I stand beside Prince Wilam of Farrland, sent by the King to represent His Majesty's will in this matter. A loyal army will reach this place within hours. You have no choice but to surrender. No Palace Guards will be held responsible for their actions until this moment, for you have opposed the King's will unwittingly. But now you have been warned. The powers of the King have been restored. Continue to support the members of the dissolved council, and you will be rebels. The palace guards are sworn to guard the King—not those who would usurp His Majesty's throne. You have sworn fealty to the King. Act according to that oath, or declare yourself this moment."

Jaimas could sense the officer wavering. His silence was caused by doubt. The Duke of Blackwater was known as a man of honor. Not a man who haunted the halls of the palace, seeking power for himself.

"And who has appointed you abbot, Duke?"

Jaimy knew that voice. It was Palle. And then he appeared, mostly obscured by the rider and his mount, for he was protecting himself from bow shot. Obviously the King's Man hadn't guessed there were mounted guards in the wood.

"Have you really the prince with you?" he said a bit mockingly, "Come down, Your Highness, your father awaits you."

"I will not come down," Prince Wilam called out, barely hesitating. "I follow the orders of the King, whom you formerly served. You are no longer a Regent of Farrland, Roderick, nor are you King's Man. Surrender yourself now, before you are branded a rebel and lose more than your position."

Palle said nothing. Jaimy was almost certain he heard men speaking in the dark.

"But I know the voice of my prince," Palle said, as though this were friendly banter. "Know it well. That is not Prince Wilam. What lie will you threaten the King's Man with next, Blackwater? Will you tell me the King rides at the head of this phantom army? *Give this up!*" he shouted, his voice suddenly harsh. "I have come with a force of my own. You are no match for us. Many lives could be lost. Perhaps you have your own son with you? Do you really wish to endanger his life so pointlessly?"

"He survived your first attempt at his murder, Roderick. Do not think we Flatterys are so easily murdered."

The King's Man may have been about to answer when suddenly a woman appeared in the moonlight, walking calmly to the center of the open area. She stopped before a fire that had burned down to coals. Jaimy could see her silhouetted against the dull red, an almost invisible plume of smoke rising before her.

"Do not look so, Roderick," the countess said, for Jaimy recognized her voice immediately. "Let us end this charade. Come out from behind your brave knight, *Sir Roderick,* and speak with me. I shall not hurt you."

"Who are you, lady?" Palle said, his voice suddenly quiet.

The countess reached up to her veil and pulled it free, folding it back over the rim of her hat. Her back was to the abbey, but even so, Jaimy felt himself lean forward as though he might catch a glimpse of this legendary face.

Palle emerged gingerly from behind the rider. *"Lady Chilton?"*

Jaimy saw her head nod once. "You are no fool, Roderick, you must guess why I am here."

Roderick neither spoke nor moved. Clearly, even the King's Man could be shocked into silence.

"You cannot have what you've come to claim," she went on, as though instructing a child who would be terribly disappointed. "Even if I were to step aside, you could not have it. But no one else will possess it either. I will seal it off, Roderick. Seal it off from anyone's reach." The fire at her feet roused itself, coming back to life with a sound like an exhalation. A narrow tongue of flame wove up, licking the air as though tasting the night. "You have Trevelyan with you. Bring him to me, and I will save his mind. Take pity on the poor man, he has served you as best he could."

Palle reached out and put his hand on the horse's flank, as though he would steady himself, but instead the hand reappeared holding a sword, and the King's Man backed quickly in behind the rider.

"You are the one Eldrich left. Not Erasmus," Palle said, his voice rising. "Stay back from me! I saw you gesture and the fire come to life. I know what you can do with fire." He was retreating quickly now, and the rider was backing up his mount, protecting his master from this unarmed woman before them. At that moment armed men rushed out of the shadows, coming to Palle's aid.

"Protect the countess!" the duke shouted, and Jaimy let an arrow fly into the midst of Palle's men, unsure of the result.

Horses erupted out of the wood, but before they could engage the opposing guards, the fire before the countess blazed up once and a thick black smoke spread across the meadow like an advancing wave. Before it men fled, though the smoke was so thick Jaimy could see nothing more.

A hand gripped Jaimy's shoulder, and he found his father beside him.

"Massenet has disappeared down into the abbey. I can't leave the wall. Go after him, but be careful."

Jaimy jumped down to the ground and quickly gathered the three others his father detailed to him, one of whom was the prince, and sprinted for the stair down into the cellars. Behind them they could hear horses galloping, and the shouts of men.

They took a single lantern, turning the flame low so that it did not make them such a target, and made their way down the stairs into a narrow passageway. Jaimy had been down here once, only as far as the door to the crucial chamber, but the route was not difficult to remember.

He wondered what the Entonne count was up to. Without Bertillon, Jaimy thought the Entonne were effectively neutralized. But then Bertillon had warned him. Trust an old tactician like Massenet to wait quietly until such a moment to move.

At a turning in the hall Jaimy stopped, not sure if he heard a sound beyond, or if he was listening to his imagination.

"Did you hear that?"

The prince nodded. A guard brought up the rear, hovering over the prince, obviously not happy to find a member of the family he was sworn to protect in such a position.

Jaimy realized the lantern cast their shadows on the wall, so that anyone ahead could see their every movement. He made his shadow move as though he were leaping out into the hallway, and an arrow shattered against the stone, bits of wood striking Jaimy.

"Stay back," the guard cautioned unnecessarily. "If they block the opening to the chamber, I think it could be held for some time. Even to get near enough to force our way in we will need to fashion shields, or lose many men to arrows. We can do nothing," he cautioned. "We are only three."

Jaimas considered for a moment. As much as he would like to report that he had retaken the chamber from Massenet, he believed the guard was right. Massenet was no fool. "Then go up to my father and tell him what has happened. I do not know if Massenet can make use of the chamber on his own, but if not, the count will want to negotiate. Tell the duke that."

Jaimy and the prince crouched down, keeping their swords ready. They both strained to hear the smallest sound on the stairs below. Though the silence was tangible, the silence between them was greater.

Almost as though the presence of Alissa could be felt, as though she had come and sat between them.

"Do you think, Lord Jaimas," the prince whispered suddenly, "that you will be happy in your future life?"

To Jaimas, to whom happiness never seemed to be in doubt, the question sounded very odd. "I have always assumed so. And Your Highness?"

"I . . . I do not make that assumption." The prince kept his gaze fixed on the stairs below. "I have often thought that if I find a bride, she will merely share my unhappiness—a terrible fate, I think."

Jaimas nodded. Alissa. The prince wanted her to be happy. In his awkward way, that is what he was saying.

"I would not want my bride to be unhappy either," Jaimas said quietly. "I would rather she change her mind than be unhappy."

The prince nodded once. "My feelings as well."

And the silence returned. Not quite so filled with things unspoken.

⌒ Thirty-Four

The moon lifted up above the distant sea, but overhead a tattered cloud rained a constant drizzle down upon the party in the valley. Palle stood beneath a tarp that had been suspended between the prince's carriage and three saplings freshly cut for the purpose. Just beyond the shelter, a fire sputtered pathetically, sizzling as the rain fell into the flames, and smoking terribly. In this situation the Regents of Farrland met to discuss the future of their nation. Not quite what they were used to.

Stedman Galton was cold to the bone, damp, and only slightly relieved that the duke had arrived first. He looked around at the others, wondering what they would do. Palle especially worried him. The man was resourceful in the extreme, and especially so when threatened.

"How long has the countess been involved in this matter?" Prince Kori asked, his tone clearly accusatory. "I thought you had agents, Roderick. I thought you knew what transpired in my Kingdom."

Palle did not seem overly intimidated by the prince's manner, however. He stood, unmoving, his hands jammed into pockets, his features almost hidden in the collar of his greatcoat, though they were hardly less expressive for this. He was obviously lost in thought, hardly paying attention to what was said.

"Is it a bluff, do you think?" he asked suddenly. "This army the duke claimed?"

This thought seemed to unnerve the prince enough that he dropped his accusations, and fell to thinking himself. "It would make sense," he said after a moment. "Obviously my traitorous wife has joined the duke in this—that is why the prince is here, doing his mother's foolish bidding. But it would be reasonable to assume that, as the duke outraced us here, the princess raised an army to send to his aid. Perhaps we should not be so complacent, Roderick." The prince looked over at Galton. "Perhaps we should be about raising a force of our own?"

Galton nodded. "It would mean civil war, of course, but if the princess and

Blackwater have the King, and have managed to delude Prince Wilam. . . . I agree with the Prince. We cannot afford to be made prisoners." Anything to get them away from the abbey. He was concerned about what the countess had said about Trevelyan, though. Was the baron's mind in danger? Or did she have some other purpose?

Palle reached a hand out beyond their shelter to gauge the severity of the rainfall. "Mud always slows armies. Real armies. But if there are reinforcements on the way, I am quite sure they are only a light mounted force. Speed is of the essence, here. Less than a hundred men, would be my guess. Soldiers, Your Highness. Men trained not to think for themselves." He looked over at the prince. "Confronted with the heir to the throne, I feel quite sure they would easily be convinced that they have, through no fault of their own, made a grave error."

"Well, that is a gamble you are suggesting! No doubt they have orders to arrest us, all three," the prince said, his voice rising just a little. "Why don't *you* confront them, Roderick? You are the King's Man and a regent, too. They are just as likely to listen to you."

Roderick stared impassively at the prince from the shadow of his greatcoat. "Shall I leave Your Highness here to deal with the situation? With the Duke of Blackwater and this unnatural countess? I saw her, Your Highness. I saw what she did. There can be no doubt that she has been following the arts of the mages."

This silenced the prince for a moment, and made Galton wonder again what Palle would do.

"What will you do against such an adversary, Roderick?" the prince asked, voicing Galton's question.

Palle looked up at the ridge above them. "I am not sure, but there is something I find odd." He turned to Hawksmoor, who stood just outside the shelter. "Bring me the baron," he said.

Galton rode occasionally on Farrow, but there it was a pleasant occupation, done only in the best weather and over soft ground. The horse he rode this night had a terrible gait—though he had no doubt that it had speed bred into it like nothing else—and he jarred along the dark road in the continuing and worsening rain, cursing Roderick silently.

Palle was so sure the duke and his party were utterly determined to hold the abbey, and therefore would not venture out, that the King's Man had detailed almost all of their guards to support the prince and Galton. It was like Roderick to be so sure of himself—of his understanding of others—and Galton had to admit that Roderick was seldom wrong.

It had been decided that Galton would accompany the prince, the reasoning being that two members of the Regency Council would add legitimacy to their words, though Galton was almost sure Roderick had sent him to bolster the prince's resolve. The farther from the palace they went, the less confident the prince seemed, as though the source of his actual power really did lay in the physical symbols of it: the throne and crown, the great seal and staff.

No one spoke as they rode along in the darkness, the wind rushing past them, sweeping the chaotic sky with clouds. Occasionally the moon emerged, appearing itself to race as the clouds passed over it, and then the road would be illuminated for a moment. An empty road, filled with only the sounds of their horses, the voice of the wind, and the spattering of rain on their coats, and on the moving river.

Galton was not sure what he should do if they really did meet troops sent to reinforce the duke. If they outnumbered their own party at all, Galton might try to convince the prince to surrender; to cast Roderick adrift and swear allegiance to the King. The Prince could claim ignorance of what Rawdon and Palle had done to the King—keeping His Majesty in thrall to the seed, driving him into madness. Prince Kori might even retain his place in the succession—not an appealing prospect.

It was difficult to know what to do. Best to prepare himself to act, though; consider all possibilities, or at least all he could imagine.

He wondered if the prince actually could manage to sway any troops they might meet. Certainly Kori did not seem too confident of his place at the moment. Any guards sent north would, undoubtedly, be led by officers loyal to Princess Joelle, if not the King. But this far from the princess herself they may have begun to wonder about their choice, about what else went on in the kingdom in their absence. If the prince could regain his customary aplomb, he might well carry it off, and that would likely give Palle all the troops he would need to storm the abbey. Astonishing that matters of such import could be decided by a mere handful of armed men.

Better keep the prince from getting too confident, he decided.

"What if Rawdon has gone over?" Galton said suddenly, casting his voice over the sounds of wind and rain.

"What?" the prince said, clearly in bad humor.

"What if Rawdon has gone over to the princess? If they could produce a lucid King. . . ." He let the statement hang in the air. For a moment the prince did not answer, and Galton began to think that he would not.

"I have thought the same thing," the prince said suddenly. "It is the greatest danger to our endeavors. And Rawdon . . . well, he has been none too stable these past months."

"My thoughts exactly," Galton said, a bit relieved to hear the prince might be easily convinced this was true.

"But do not underestimate Roderick, Stedman," the prince said suddenly.

"He is the most formidable statesman in the Kingdom, and I include myself in this assessment. And we mustn't forget, if Rawdon really has gone over, and the King is found to be even reasonably lucid . . . well, what we are engaged in here will be even more important. We will never regain the throne but through this power that we seek. Have no doubt of that. We dare not fail, Stedman. We dare not fail."

A light appeared around the corner ahead, and then another. A large party was on the road—in this remote corner of the kingdom.

The Entonne messenger was a small man, entirely begrimed, and soaked to the very skin. He stood before Roderick and Wells, shivering uncontrollably, but no one offered him so much as a blanket, or even suggested he stand near to the fire. He had come out of the darkness and been snared by two of Roderick's guards. The King's Man was not convinced the man was actually a messenger to him from Massenet at all, but may have simply made that claim once he found himself a captive.

"You say Count Massenet has taken control of this chamber in the abbey?"

The man nodded. "Yes, sir. And I came out through a tunnel we found in a lower chamber."

"Convenient. So, what does the count want of me?"

"He says, sir, that it would be better that you and he form an alliance than to let the arts fall to your enemies. The duke and the countess: they are bent on taking this power for their own. But the count will not surrender the lower chamber, and he has Mr. Bertillon, whom the countess needs to gain her ends."

Roderick was alarmed now. Did Massenet really have the chamber and this man Bertillon? What was stopping him from gaining the power for himself? Roderick glanced at Wells, but he was not looking.

"But what does the count want of me?"

"I am to tell you that to achieve the countess' goal she needs another with talent to perform the rites. That is what the countess told Bertillon. Under no circumstances should you allow Trevelyan to fall into her hands. Under no circumstances.

"At this moment no one has an advantage. The count controls the chamber. The countess and the Duke of Blackwater control the approach, and you, Sir Roderick, control access to the outside world. As things are, no one can win. Unless the duke can take the chamber from the Entonne, and there is another with talent, unknown to us. But time works against us. I can take you down to the chamber: yourself, and the baron, and a few others." The man looked quickly over at Wells, then back to Palle. "We each have a part of the text, and one with talent. The count believes we can bring this power to light, and share it equally. Neither with an advantage—as is the case now between our two nations." The man shifted from one foot to the other, shivering. "I will tell you something the count has learned. Your King comes. He cannot be far off. He comes in the company of an army, his intentions unclear. But why else would His Majesty journey so far but to have this power for his own, and to extend his already-long life? The duke need only wait. Time will win his campaign for him.

"Bring Trevelyan down to the chamber. With what you have learned, and what the Entonne know, the count believes we can succeed. Who knows what might be learned? A world of knowledge, Sir Roderick. The arts so long hidden."

Silence. The rain continued to drum on the tarpaulin and hiss in the fire. Roderick looked over at Wells, then back to the shivering messenger. "We shall discuss your proposal." Roderick nodded at the guard who took the messenger away.

"What do you make of this, Wells?"

The empiricist bent his head, looking down at the puddles forming around their feet. "I distrust Massenet in the extreme, but I suspect there is some truth buried in what he says. I agree that we should not allow Trevelyan to fall into their hands. The countess seemed all too interested in the baron for my liking. But I would not want the baron to fall into Massenet's hands either."

"Yes, I felt the countess' interest was odd as well, but Trevelyan claims he knows no reason for this. I spoke with him earlier. Do you think Massenet realizes that we have two who do our bidding?"

"No," Wells said quickly. "No, I'm quite sure he does not. I think we should find out how this messenger got in and out of the abbey, if indeed that is what happened. That would be useful to us." He looked up, trying to read Roderick's face in the darkness. "This news of the King? Do you think it is possible?"

Roderick shook his head. It was so implausible as to almost be true. "Only if Rawdon has betrayed us," he said with finality.

"If it is true. . . ." Wells did not finish.

"All the more reason that we must gain access to the chamber. Do you think this Entonne would know Trevelyan to see him?"

Wells shrugged. "I can't imagine why he would."

"Who shall play the baron, then? Noyes looks the part, don't you think?"

Moonlight glinted off helmets and lances, creating shadow armies on the narrow road. Both parties held their positions nervously. Banners were unfurled, though remained unrecognizable at a distance. Horses pranced nervously, sniffing the air and tossing their heads.

And then the colonel who had ridden out before the abbey and confronted the Duke of Blackwater went forward again. He stopped his horse in the center of the neutral ground between the two parties, and stared into the poor light with appropriate arrogance.

"The Regents of Farrland and His Royal Highness, Prince Kori, demand to know by whose orders you are on this road."

There was no answer while around the prince swords were drawn and helmet straps tightened. And then a horseman rode out to meet their own.

"I know your voice, Hampton," the rider said, "but you are mistaken. The Regency Council is no more. It has been dissolved and the powers of the King restored. We are here on the orders of the King, and we shall bring all of those who conspired to usurp his powers to justice. Lay down your sword, Colonel, and tell your men to do likewise. You will have the King's mercy, for you have been misled and shall not be held responsible for what you have done."

"How many are there?" Prince Kori whispered to Galton. "Can you tell?"

Galton had no idea, fewer than he hoped was his fear. "It is difficult to tell, but their numbers are greater than our own, I think."

No one broke the silence for a moment, and then, having worked up his nerve, Prince Kori spurred his horse forward. He pulled up beside Colonel Hampton, and peered into the darkness.

"I am Prince Kori," he said with admirable calm. "Who is in command here? Bring him to me."

"I have been given the King's trust, Your Highness," the rider said.

The prince maintained the confidence in his voice. "The King is not well, and any who claim to represent his will are but opportunists attempting to seize power in the absence of the legally constituted council. It is you who have been misled. There are some within our Kingdom who would risk civil war so that they might seize power, and they are using you to achieve this end. Do not allow the peace of our nation to fall victim to such ambitions. Lay down your weapons and join with us. I am the heir to the throne, and a Regent of the council. I have no interests but the welfare of the people and the well-being of my father, the King. Do not bring my people to war, I beseech you. Join with us, and preserve the peace and the rule of law."

"It was a pretty speech, Your Highness," a voice came out of the darkness. "As sweet a lie as I have heard in recent years, and I have heard many."

"Kent? Is that you?"

"Yes, it is Averil Kent. Do not waste more words for our benefit. We have seen the King with our own eyes. Spoken to His Majesty at length. Not just me, but these good officers whom you attempt to sway." The dark form of Kent appeared out of the gloom, sitting astride a horse. He rode forward where the moonlight fell upon him, and Galton could see the old-fashioned tricorn, and could not help but smile. If anyone could convince the prince to surrender, it would be Kent. No one was more trusted.

"Rawdon has admitted what he and Palle did, Your Highness. The ministers of government know how these two plotted to keep the King in ignorance and near madness, but the King is returned to his senses, and to his rightful place. Tell these men to lay down their arms so that there will be no bloodshed. The King awaits your return, and we shall be most happy to make up your honor guard, Your Highness, for your return to Avonel. There is no question but that you have been the victim of the plotting of Roderick Palle, and the former King's Man shall pay the price."

Galton moved his horse forward slowly, trying to miss nothing, expecting the next conversation to take place between the prince and Kent alone. *Surrender,* Galton willed the prince. He spurred his horse forward to offer his council, but the prince wheeled his mount at that instant and set it to gallop, almost directly at Galton.

"Do not let them pass!" the prince shouted. "Galton!" he called as he thundered by.

Horses surged past Galton at that instant, and a guard grabbed his horse's bridle, pulling him quickly around and sending him off after the prince. Unwillingly, Galton retreated, then realized that battle had been engaged, and spurred his horse lest he be caught up in the midst of it, unarmed, and unrecognizable to either side.

Suddenly two guards came up beside him, hurrying him along, and any thoughts of defecting were put to rest. The sounds of fighting became more and more muffled as they galloped along the road, and after a moment the noise of their passing drowned out everything else. They came upon the prince and two guards in a moment.

"What has happened?" the prince asked, panting.

"We could not tell," Galton answered. "Let us wait here a moment, and send a man back to see." He wanted to stall, perhaps convince the prince that they were making a terrible mistake, but he was afraid that the prince's faith in Palle was unshakable.

One of the guards spurred his horse back along the road, and they all sat silently, straining to hear.

Suddenly the prince turned to him. Even in the dark Galton could see the despair written on the man's face. "Do you think it is possible?" he asked. "Have they managed to return that terrible old man to some semblance of sanity? Don't they realize that he would send them all to be hanged for a single draught of his physic?"

Galton did not know what to answer. But here it was: the prince would clearly take his chances as a rebel rather than submit to the will of the King. The tone in his voice suggested that he might rather face death. There was no chance that Galton could sway him now.

A horse galloped around the curve in the road, causing them to start. But the man called out as he came and they recognized him as one of their own.

"The fighting has broken off," he said, as he reined in his horse, "and the two sides face each other, waiting. We cannot be sure how large their party is, nor can they determine the size of ours. They'll wait for morning, I'm certain. Wait until they can judge the risk."

"But are their numbers great? Greater than ours?"

"We cannot be sure, Your Highness. We cannot be sure."

The prince turned to Galton, as though seeking council, but when Galton did not speak, he turned his attention back to the officer. "Send a rider to tell Sir Roderick what has happened. I cannot be sure if we should stand here and hope to delay these riders, or retreat back toward the abbey."

"If I may, Your Highness?" the officer said.

"Yes. Yes, of course. Speak up."

"If we retreat just beyond this point and fell trees over the road, we might delay even a much larger force for some time. The river is high and cannot be crossed, and there is no track up to the ridge above."

"That is what we will do. Tell the colonel to fall back as quietly as possible. We must delay Kent and his army. Even a day will make all the difference. Even half of the day."

Kent stood in the rain, staring into the dark interior of the King's carriage, waiting. Perhaps Rawdon had not managed to keep the King's lust for his physic under control—or worse, the physician had betrayed them. For some minutes now the painter had been waiting for the King to answer his question.

In the light of the coach lamp, the princess appeared, holding up the hems of her cape and gown. Lady Galton hurried along behind her. They stopped suddenly when they realized that Kent waited for the King to speak.

"Kent?" The terrible voice emanated from the dark carriage, though it was weak and unfocused.

"Your Majesty."

"We must find a way up. We must not be delayed."

"But it is a steep embankment, Your Majesty. I have seen it in the daylight. Perhaps young men might find a way up on foot, but there is no track for a carriage, or a horse either."

"There is always a track," the King said. "Find a shepherd or a huntsman. A good poacher would do. There will be a track up. But we cannot delay. My hour is near, Kent. My hour. Have you my portrait?"

"I—I have, sir," Kent said, answering the question for perhaps the dozenth time on this journey. He glanced over at the careworn face of the princess, who stood silently awaiting the King's words. A fine rain began to drizzle down again.

"Kent?"

"Sir?"

"Do you fear death?"

*   *   *

Kent was more than slightly in fear of his life. The path they followed was narrow, and though it was not properly a cliff they traversed, the drop to one side was steep enough that he was sure no horse could stop itself if it began to slide. Guards with lanterns were spaced evenly among the party, but these lights were not strong enough to matter. It was morning, or at least that is what Kent's timepiece claimed. But a fog had drifted in from the sea, and they made their slow way through this clinging haze. Kent thought the world seemed ominous, trees looming up almost like threats.

Ahead of him the King went, hunched over his mount's neck, immobile beneath his cape and hood. Kent had a memory of the King as a powerful man, and an excellent horseman, yet this figure he could barely see in the gloom ahead seemed shrunken and fragile, not really human at all.

Somewhere up in the mist, a shepherd and his son led the way, picking their way along the path. The man kept flocks up on the abbey ridge in the summer months.

The dull thud of a horse's hoof striking a root came out of the gray and his own horse pricked up its ears. Kent patted the gelding's neck, and looked again down the steep bank to his left.

He wondered how Lady Galton and the princess were managing, though he seemed to remember that both had been keen riders in their youth. They were likely faring better than he.

Kent was forced to admit that the countess' spell of rejuvenation, or whatever it was called, was losing its power. He had begun to ache as he had before the miracle had been performed. His back was causing him some distress as they rode, and he did not expect it to stop until he could lie down on a proper bed—and he expected that to be some time off, if ever.

Bear up, he told himself. He wondered again how he had refused Palle's offer. The memory of his tryst with Tenil came back to him. And it seemed impossible that this cell of pain in which he was imprisoned—his body—could have known such pleasure. If nothing else he had a memory recent enough that it might not fade so quickly. It still had . . . texture and substance, and evoked strong feeling. Something to take into the final infirmity of old age. Kent was like a man who felt an illness returning. Some dread disease that he had miraculously escaped, and then, without warning, the symptoms began to return. And this was an illness that, sooner or later, would see his end.

He looked up at the King on his horse, like a strange creature who guided him on a last journey.

Having come so far, Kent was unsure, now, of what use he would be. They simply didn't know what they would find when they reached the abbey, though somehow the King was not in doubt. His Majesty either did not believe that

Palle held the abbey, or he simply did not care. They blundered on in the darkness, skirting Prince Kori's troops on the road, but perhaps riding into an even more hostile situation.

Several guards were at the head of the long line, and Kent had made certain that they would stop and reconnoiter the abbey. Whether they would be able to get the King to wait was another issue. His Majesty did not seem to care but kept saying that his hour was near and asking Kent if he had remembered his portrait.

And asking if Kent feared death.

Why does he ask only me, the painter wondered, overcome with a sudden wash of fear. Did the King have some premonition? Flames, but he wished he were still in Avonel.

Yet something drew him on. Somewhere ahead in the fog, he was sure the countess waited. He did not know exactly why he believed this, but he did. She waited, and there were things that must be resolved between them, once and for ever. Kent could not go on without a heart, and she had held it in her keeping long enough. Kept it in snow, perhaps, for it had not known warmth now for many a year. He simply could not go on like this.

⤳ Thirty-Five

Noyes crawled out of the Farrelle-forsaken tunnel into a small damp chamber. Once he stood straight, he began to wipe at the dirt on his clothing but stopped, dismayed. Even in the poor light of the lamp he could see that it was futile. The wiry Entonne nodded to him and tried to smile encouragingly, and Noyes was sure he responded with a look of rage.

He wondered if the real Trevelyan would ever make it through such narrow openings. Noyes had barely done so himself. He hoped that Palle's men had managed to follow him to the entrance to this bloody hole.

"Shall we go on, Lord Trevelyan?" the Entonne asked.

"Yes, yes. Lead on." Noyes glanced around. It was a small room, the walls wet with seeping water but clear of any growth whatsoever, which meant no light found its way to this chamber, in any season.

He followed the ridiculously dim light from the tin lamp, up a few steps and through an arch, then left, he memorized. Through a larger room, then left again. He scuffed his shoe in the mud, marking the way in case Palle's men followed. Up a longer flight of stairs. The place was clearly a labyrinth. Through a door, and suddenly the man in front of him recoiled in fear, flailing with his arms so that the flame in the lantern sputtered. At the end of the chamber, just touched by the light, a woman in a dark gown disappeared around a corner, followed by her fleeing shadow.

The Entonne started to retreat, but Noyes grabbed hold of the man's jacket. "No. She ran from us. Take me on."

"But that is the countess," the man said nervously. "The mage countess."

"Yes, and I am a large baron with a dagger. Take me on." He pushed the man forward. In truth he was not so confident, but could not imagine going back to that twisting, narrow tunnel. He'd rather face the countess, whom he was sure was not really so formidable. She had managed to make a fire come to life and spread a thick smoke. Noyes had seen conjurers do much the same, and they were no more mages than he was.

The Entonne crept forward reluctantly, looking about a bit wildly. Noyes was not sure what the man expected, but then the tales of mages were part of the fabric of Entonne culture—and the Entonne were more apt to believe.

Noyes concentrated on memorizing the path. Finally they came to the bottom of a stair that circled up into the darkness.

"You must wait here, baron," the Entonne said, "I will go ahead to be sure that it is safe."

"I shall do no such thing," Noyes answered. Did this man really think he would be allowed to go ahead and alert Massenet? Noyes took the dagger out of his belt. "Go ahead. I hope there is no treachery planned, for your sake."

The man put his foot to the step, going even more slowly now. He swung the lantern before him, so that shadows wavered across the walls and steps. When they had gone up for a few minutes, he stopped and whistled softly. "It is George," he whispered. "I have brought the baron. Just the baron."

They heard a scraping sound, and then a whisper echoed down the stairwell. "Come up, but quickly."

The Entonne turned to Noyes. "There is a hole in the wall up ahead, to the left. We must pass through quickly. The duke's men are not far above." He turned and went up, holding the lantern before him so that Noyes could barely see his footing. The two raced up, and then the man passed his lantern into a hole in the stone. As he went through, hands took him and pulled him out of sight. Noyes sheathed his dagger and ducked through as the man's feet disappeared, and hands took hold of him, passing him inside to a dimly lit chamber.

He was helped to his feet, and there before him stood the Entonne Ambassador.

"Mr. Noyes," the count said, showing no surprise.

"Count," Noyes said, bobbing his head. His guide turned on him with a look of distress.

Massenet did not speak immediately, but stood staring as though wondering what he would do with this intruder.

"You have a message from Sir Roderick?" the count said at last.

"I am the ambassador of His Highness, Prince Kori, and the King's Man, yes."

"Can you tell me what goes on above? I have sent out men, but they have not yet returned."

"The countess is in the chambers below," Noyes' Entonne guide said quickly. "We saw her as we came."

"The countess, you say?"

The man nodded, but Massenet did not look overly impressed with this news. He turned his attention back to Noyes. "I assume Roderick will want some assurance of my intentions before he will bring the baron?"

"That is what we discussed before I came to you, but now that I have come through your tunnel, I am not sure that Trevelyan could follow. It is small, and the baron is old and weak, and far too large."

Massenet shook his head. "Fat old fool," he said almost beneath his breath. "Your King is coming, Noyes, and then there will be a reckoning. Unless you have an army racing to your rescue, your opportunity is about to be lost. I cannot hold this chamber forever. We are few, as you see, and poorly armed. Tell Roderick that we have no time to waste in negotiation. We must put aside our differences and seize what we may. We can retain the balance we have now, between Entonne and your own faction here in Farrland. But we must push Trevelyan down here even if we have to squeeze him like a stopper through a bottle."

"I have tried to tell the count that it will not work," a man said, and Noyes turned to find Bertillon, the Entonne virtuoso, sitting dejectedly on a stone. He wore a dressing torn from a shirt about his arm, as though he had been injured, and his look was tired and dejected. "He will not listen to me. All parts of the text are needed. But there is more. There is knowledge not contained in the writings. You would bring disaster upon yourself and more if you were to proceed with what you have now, and despite all threats, I will not cooperate. Only the countess can succeed. And she will ensure that no one comes to possess this knowledge."

Count Massenet rolled his eyes. "Charl has fallen victim to a woman's sorcery, but I'm still hoping he will come to his senses."

Noyes realized at that moment that Massenet was beaten—Bertillon would not do his bidding. The only card the count held was his control of the chamber, which he could not hold against a determined assault, Noyes was sure. Attempting to make a deal with Palle was a last, pathetic attempt to remain in the game. But the plans of Noyes' own group were in danger. Especially if the King really was near.

"Perhaps, Count Massenet, we can still manage without Mr. Bertillon's cooperation," Noyes said. "We know more, perhaps, than you realize."

"Count Massenet?" came a distant voice, echoing down the stairwell. Everyone in the chamber stopped where they stood.

"Count Massenet? It is Lady Chilton. We must speak. It is imperative."

The count motioned to Varese and moved toward the opening into the stairwell.

"What is it you want, Lady Chilton?" Massenet shouted.

"An end to this foolish struggle. Only I have all the pieces of the puzzle, Count Massenet. You gave the Lucklow fragment to Kent: you must realize what is at risk? The arts of the mages were never meant for the untrained. You cannot practice their arts, and master your enemies without terrible cost to the world at large. You would bring ruin upon yourself and your nation more quickly than you would gain mastery over others. It took fifty years to make a mage, Count Massenet. Half a century. And that was to allow them to practice their arts without bringing ruin to the world around them. And in the end even they failed, and realized that their arts must pass from knowledge. Consider what is at risk, Count Massenet. Give up your aspirations for the greater good."

Varese reached over and touched Massenet's arm. "I am not sure that she is not telling the truth, Count," he said, and then shook his head, obviously troubled. "The Lucklow fragment was ominous in the extreme."

Massenet considered for a moment, his face unreadable. "Why would I trust you, Lady Chilton? Once you have entrance to the chamber, how would I know your actions will do what you promise?"

Suddenly a figure shot through the opening, knocking the count back so that he slid down the pile of rock and dirt. Palace Guards began to pour into the chamber, with swords in their hands. Massenet was up immediately, tearing his rapier from its sheath, and Noyes took that opportunity to step forward and push the count from behind with all his strength. Noyes was not a swordsman of note, but he was large, and weight counted for a lot.

Massenet sprawled on the floor and one of the guards put a boot on the blade of the count's rapier, and the point of his own weapon to Massenet's throat. The fight was over in that instant.

A moment later Roderick Palle scrambled through the opening, followed by Prince Kori, and finally Baron Trevelyan, who whimpered and moaned like a man who had been beaten. He immediately collapsed on the floor, gasping for breath.

"Well, here we all are," Massenet said, shaking his head, "like rats in a trap. But you still have only one with talent, Palle, and that is one too few. You need me yet."

Palle looked around the chamber, and then back to the count. "But we have two, Count Massenet. Two. And a third who does our bidding. Your part will be to witness," Palle said with some delight. "Yes, you can record the moment for history."

Thirty-Six

The moon continued to float heavenward, etching a brittle path across the sea. Tristam sat at the landing's edge looking out, thinking that he had sailed along that very path. Journeyed along it unknowingly, to this place: this very step.

It did not seem possible that he had come so far to suffer the fate of his shipmates below, but then it was he the Varuans distrusted. Tristam glanced down at his wrist in the dark, but the bird-viper had drawn back again to lurk somewhere in the vein—perhaps even in his heart.

For a moment he wondered if the crew of this expedition would suffer the same fate as Gregory's—disappearing mysteriously, so that no one would ever know their fate: no one in Farrland, at least.

Tristam turned his head, and found the viscount shrunk back into a tree's shadow, watching Tristam. The naturalist almost shuddered, and turned away. Everyone else was huddled close to the center of the landing, silent in their fear, but this macabre viscount could sense death. Could sense it below, where the mutineers had fallen, and perhaps sensed it coming, as well.

No one knew what the Varuans would do with them. The friendly islanders seemed suddenly unpredictable, capable of anything. Tristam was certain that the stories of human sacrifice had surfaced from everyone's memory.

"Captain Stern?" came a voice up the stair.

"Captain?" Tristam almost whispered, "it is Wallis."

Stern, who had been trying to reassure his people, came forward, crouching next to Tristam. "Mr. Wallis?"

The painter appeared out of a shadow, looking up, the moonlight turning his tanned face pale. "The Varuans are willing to let you go free, Captain, but they will only do so if you agree to cooperate."

Stern motioned to Wallis to come up. "I'm sure we can reach an agreement, Mr. Wallis," Stern said. "What is it they want?"

The duchess appeared at Stern's side. "Take care what you agree to, Captain," she cautioned, and Tristam saw Stern tense in anger.

"We are in no position to negotiate, Duchess," Stern said shortly. "Come up, Mr. Wallis. Tell us what the islanders want."

Wallis could be seen to turn and look down the stair, and suddenly a woman appeared. It was Anua, Tristam realized. Wallis followed obediently at her heels. Neither stepped up onto the landing but stopped some few steps down, so that they were eye-to-eye with the crouching Stern.

Anua looked at the Farrlanders, her manner not unfriendly but reserved. "You must agree to two things, Captain Stern," Anua said.

Stern nodded, but said nothing.

"You must depart as soon as you can ready your ship," Anua went on. "And Mr. Flattery and Dr. Llewellyn must agree to lend their skills to the King. If you will do these things, you will be given seed to take back to your King."

Tristam closed his eyes for a second, not believing what he heard. Better to leave this seed behind. He had seen Gregory and knew what desire for this seed would do.

"We will do as you ask," Stern said with finality, looking triumphantly at the duchess as he spoke. He turned back to Anua and Wallis. "What is it you want of my people?"

Wallis met Tristam's eye. "The ritual has not gone well. The King requires the help of Mr. Flattery and Dr. Llewellyn."

"*No*," Tristam said, "I will have nothing to do with it!" He rose from the step, starting to back away. He felt the duchess take his arm and shoulder, attempting to check his retreat.

"Tristam," she implored, "think what you say."

"No! Wallis was right; this seed is a curse. I will have nothing to do with it. They think I can perform necromancy." He thrust out his hand so that the scar could be seen. "They believe this means something. They will want me to take the physic again, but you can't understand what this would mean. I will become enslaved to it. Mad."

He tore his arm free of the duchess, and glared at Wallis and Anua, who stood silently watching. Anua spoke quickly to the painter in her own language, and then turned and began to descend the stair with great dignity, though her shoulders were stiff with anger.

"Mr. Flattery. . . ." Wallis said, "think what you do. The Varuan people ask your help, sir. And for this they will give you the seed you have journeyed half-way around the world to find. Though, in truth, it should be *you* offering to help them in their time of need. They have held back nothing from you; not food, not drink, not the favors of their women, not even this seed your King so desires." Wallis glanced down the stair. "Anua will return shortly to hear your answer. I will tell you honestly, Captain Stern, I don't know what the Varuans will do if you refuse to grant your assistance. Talk to Mr. Flattery." He looked back at Tristam. "There are more lives than his involved in this decision."

Tristam turned away, walking to the corner of the landing, separating himself from the others as much as possible. He saw Llewellyn talking to the duchess and Stern, glancing occasionally at Tristam. Out in the bay, Tristam could just make out the lamps of the *Swallow*. Did the men left aboard realize what had happened to their shipmates?

If we could only get to the ship, Tristam thought, though he could not imagine that there was any way down but the stair, and the Varuans waited at the foot.

Llewellyn appeared beside him, his lung affliction apparently vanished.

"Have things worked out as you planned, Dr. Llewellyn?" Tristam asked. Out of the corner of his eye, Tristam could see Llewellyn pull back a little to look at him in the poor light.

"Very closely, yes," the doctor admitted, surprising Tristam by not offering a denial. "We had not planned on the mutiny, but I soon realized we could not do without it."

Tristam met the man's gaze, which was cool and objective, bearing no animosity.

"Now you will have no choice," the doctor went on. "The safety of the ship's company depends on you, Tristam, and you are a compassionate man."

"And this will complete the transformation?" Tristam said. "Is that the plan? Did you foresee this?"

"More or less," Llewellyn said. "Your transformation will draw the power back. You are like a wick, Tristam, it will come up through you, as it has done to a degree for some time. Do not be downcast," he said, his tone almost consoling. "We will have no use for you after. You will have completed your part, and may live as you wish."

"But I do not get to choose who I will be? I will be transformed, a slave to the seed."

Llewellyn shook his head. "And you can live, perhaps two centuries, even if you choose not to explore this new world that will be opened up for you. But can you truly do that, Tristam? Will you not want to learn what you might do? To discover the secrets that have so long been hidden? You are a young man of great natural curiosity. Can you really resist?"

Tristam thought of Gregory threatening to spill the physic. "Yes," he said.

Llewellyn looked at him a moment longer, then turned to walk away.

"Dr. Llewellyn?"

The physician stopped.

"Do you fear death?" Tristam asked.

The man hesitated before answering, as though wondering if Tristam mocked him, as men were wont to do. "Every man fears death," he answered.

Tristam turned and stared at the doctor. "Well, death is here, on this island, waiting. He will take one of us before we leave. Mark this. I have dreamed it, and it will come true."

Llewellyn began to turn but stopped as though held by Tristam's vision. Finally, he forced himself away, though much shaken, Tristam was sure. It was small satisfaction—in return for the price he would have to pay.

Tristam sat down on the edge of the landing, staring out over Gregory Bay, watching the full moon rise up like a bubble through water, leaving a trail of luminescence across the surface of the sea.

"Tristam?" It was the duchess. She sat beside him, and for a moment said nothing.

There was a movement in the air before them, and a small owl landed on a branch not five feet away. It seemed to regard Tristam a little nervously.

"But this is not a falcon," the duchess said. "Is it drawn to you?"

"I created it," Tristam answered, his voice so devoid of emotion that it surprised him. "It is the symbol of my death."

"What are you saying, Tristam?" She put a hand on his arm, but he did not respond.

"The transformation. I will be gone," he whispered. "Like transmutation. I shall be something else entire. There will be little or nothing of Tristam left."

She put her cheek to his shoulder, apparently not caring what the others thought, and searched for his hand. "How do you know this?"

"I know. I felt the beginnings of it in the Lost City. Say good-bye to me, Elorin, for you shall not see me again."

She held his hand, almost desperately hard. As though she would not let go. But then the pressure eased.

The owl made a soft sound, as though in sympathy.

"Tell me why you have come, Elorin," Tristam said suddenly. "No more evasions. I must know."

She hesitated. "I was sent by the King to retrieve this seed. That is the truth. And I hoped to save my place at court by bringing *regis* back. If that did not come to be, then it was my hope, Tristam, that I might find here a way to preserve my appearance, my youth—even for a few years—without suffering as the King suffers. It is vanity, Tristam, I know, but I could see the way my life was progressing—and I had the Countess of Chilton's example before me. That is the truth; I swear. I was sent by the King, and I was to bring Julian. The King would not say more." Silence slipped in between them. For a moment the tropical night seemed to be listening. "The King dreams," she said, her voice falling very low, "and some of these dreams he believes are visions. *I* believe they are visions. What we do here has, in some way, bearing on his visions. Or at least that is my guess. That is all I know, Tristam. His Majesty does not tell me all that is in his mind. . . ."

"Anua is here." It was Stern, standing back a few paces, as though he would not intrude on their privacy.

The duchess met Tristam's eye, clearly anxious, then she embraced him and rose, drawing him up by the hand.

"Will you help the islanders, Mr. Flattery?" Stern asked.

Tristam nodded, not meeting Stern's eye. Anua came up onto the stair with Wallis and several men who brought a captive Jack with them. *Kreel.*

Tristam stopped, staring at the man, who looked sullenly back. "What will be done with him?" Tristam asked.

Anua motioned for Tristam to go on. "That is for the King to decide," she said.

Tristam did not move but stood staring at the Jack. "I saved you twice, Kreel. I do not know if I can do it again."

The man said nothing, only continued to stare. "That is likely so, Mr. Flattery," he said slowly, "but I would still rather be me than you, for who is it will save you, that is what I wonder?"

Tristam shook his head, but it was not denial. He did not know who would save him.

He mounted the last flight of stairs that led to the Varuans' sacred city. Wallis and Anua behind him, followed by the duchess and Stern, and then the others.

Ahead of him, perhaps ten feet above, the owl landed for a second, looked back, almost expectantly, and then disappeared up the stairs.

My course, Tristam thought. *Unavoidable, as I suspected.*

Burning Gregory's *regis* had not worked as he'd hoped. The Kingfoil was not the reason he was here. That was clear, if nothing else was.

Guards wearing elaborate feathered headdresses stood on the final stair, and they crossed their spears before Tristam, allowing him to go no further. Anua came up then, speaking to the two men, though what she said Tristam was sure was ritual, like requesting admittance to the palace to be knighted. They bowed to her and swept their lances back, inviting Tristam to proceed.

On the landing stood one of the Old Men Tristam had seen the night of the dance of transformation. Transformation from bird to man—a man who pursued a ghost, who gave him the *regis* blossom. Somewhere in the darkness Tristam heard the soft call of his owl, and it spoke to him so directly that he felt a chill, almost as though he understood.

The Old Man waved a talking stick around Tristam, chanting as he did so. A young girl delivered a half coconut to the Old Man, who formally presented it to Tristam, after Anua had instructed him to clap his hands loudly.

Tristam drank, emptying the kava, the metallic taste of root and soil seeming to cling to his teeth and causing a slight numbness in tongue and lips.

"You must remove your shirt, Mr. Flattery," Wallis whispered from behind, and Tristam did as instructed. A man came forward with a crude brush and a shell filled with dark liquid. Quickly, he began brushing a design across Tristam's torso and upper arms. Marks were added to his cheeks, and finally some small ornamentation was carefully applied to the center of his forehead.

Around his wrist a girl wove a bracelet of *regis* blossoms, covering the scar. Into his hand they put a polished, leafless branch, with one short limb projecting at right angles near the top. This, he was shown, should be carried upright.

The Old Man chanted over him again, and Tristam was brought forward to wait for the others to be purified so that they might enter the city. This took little time for they were not treated to such elaborate preparations.

Tristam looked out at the City of the Gods, lit dimly by moonlight and torches. He could see several large fales scattered about in no apparent pattern, and here and there man-high standing stones cast shadows in the moonlight. These were carved like the faces of Old Men, and faced east, looking out over the endless sea toward the rising moon and sun.

A jumble of stone rose from the center of the open area, and it was crowned with what might have been a platform—Tristam could not be sure. Palm trees and the sacred *aito* tree were planted here and there, as were the flowering shrubs most admired by the Varuans. The trade wind whispered languidly through their branches. Stern had been right; there was little here that resembled the Lost City, but even so Tristam found the mystery of the place unsettled him.

Some race had dwelt here before the present inhabitants, as had been the case on Farrow. A mysterious race; and just as it was clear that the race that had built the Lost City had some connection to the Ruin of Farrow, Tristam was certain that this site was associated with them as well. Associated with them—and to mages and their arts.

The Old Man finished his rites, and Wallis motioned for Tristam to follow, the others taking up the same positions as before.

They passed by a standing stone, the strange, elongated face staring empty-eyed, but its gaze somehow more penetrating for that. The jumble of broken stone in the center of the "city" loomed up, and Tristam could see that this was the ruin of a structure—the one building that had been left behind by the mysterious race who had once dwelt here. Some of the stones had been carved and carefully shaped, but now they lay in ruin, like the remains of his father's theater in Avonel. It made the entire moment doubly disquieting for Tristam, as though his father's ghost lurked even here half the globe distant from Avonel.

The Old Man led them on, the entire group passing from the ruddy light of one torch, into the cool moonlight, to torchlight again, as though they journeyed from one island of firelight to the next. Tristam glanced over his shoulder and found that everyone had been treated as he had, and were stripped to the waist: even the duchess, and her maid, and Stern.

It was the custom of Varua that the islanders wore no clothing above the waist before their King, but Farrlanders had always been exempt from this practice.

The duchess did not seem embarrassed or concerned by her state of undress, though even the lowly Jacks could see parts of her body that, all her life, had barely been touched by a breeze.

A moment's walk brought them to the largest fale that Tristam had yet seen. This one had the most elaborately carved columns of stone supporting its corners and a magnificent and gracefully curving roof of thatch. A torch was thrust into the ground a few feet before either post, and these smoked in the small trade that blew, casting wavering shadows.

In the light of these torches, but standing respectfully back from the structure, Old Men had gathered. Seven in all, each wearing a headdress like the first, and an ancient and faded red-feathered cape. They stood silently, ignoring the Farrlanders, their attention fixed on the opening to the fale.

Tristam looked back at his own people again. They all appeared grim and frightened, but they were enduring in silence, hoping, no doubt, that it would be over soon, and they would be returned to their ship. Jacel sobbed suddenly, and Tristam saw the duchess take her softly by the shoulder, and hush her like a frightened child. The gesture touched him somehow, for it seemed so genuine. The heart was revealed when no one was thought to be watching.

But will I have a heart come morning, Tristam wondered.

Llewellyn was standing near the duchess, shifting the weight of the canvas bag on his shoulder. What had the doctor rescued from Tristam's cabin? Nothing of import to Tristam, the naturalist guessed. Things needed by Llewellyn, he was sure. And how was it that only Llewellyn had time to collect any belongings before the mutineers struck?

If Tristam could have felt anger in the state he was in, he realized he would have felt rage toward the doctor. Palle's minion. One of the group so casually using Tristam to further their interests. And Tristam was not sure there was anything he could do about it.

Suddenly the Old Men clapped their hands loudly in unison, and out of the fale emerged a man Tristam was certain must be the King. He was small by Varuan standards, shriveled and old, and he walked ever so slowly, as though each movement took concentrated effort. "Ancient" was what Tristam thought. The King paused before the building for a moment, the moonlight and wavering torchlight seeming to do battle over him, struggling across his crimson cape of feathers and his headdress, more grand than all the others. Tristam thought he was watching a battle between a light so ancient that it burned to coolness, and the brief, ambitious fire of man.

The King came forward and stepped into a small canoe that was set on the ground, taking a seat on red tapa cloth spread over a thwart. Around the King's feet, Tristam could see baskets, and small packages wrapped in leaves or tapa cloth, tools, and plants that had been carefully prepared for a journey.

Four young men came forward and lifted the canoe by two cross pieces that had been lashed to the gunnels, and laying these across their shoulders, walked forward following the procession of Old Men.

Tristam fell in behind the canoe, looking up occasionally at the man bent over beneath the weight of feathers. In that light and from that angle he appeared almost birdlike. Some ancient flightless species, that had come down from the air to live on the land, its crest trembling with each step. And here was the last of the race, ravaged and ill, going quietly to its end in pathetic dignity.

They came to the edge of the City of the Gods and went in under the trees, shaded from moonlight, where the bloody glow of the torches seemed to grow brighter, casting wavering shadows around them. A wide sand path curved up the side of the mountain, turning occasionally, and cutting diagonally back, like the path of a snake.

Tristam felt his wrist begin to itch under the bracelet of *regis* flowers, but he dared not touch it, afraid of what might be revealed.

They went up for almost an hour, their pace slow, almost stately. Finally the path leveled for a short distance. Tristam wondered if they were arriving at their destination when he realized that the Old Men had disappeared up into the trees, and the men bearing the King were preparing to follow.

Stairs, Tristam realized by the way the men moved. They had come to more stairs. Under the moonlight he found a broad flight of even stairs lifting up into the jungle. The stone was pale, almost white, and Tristam knew immediately that it was not indigenous rock. From what distance had it been carried?

He set a foot on the first tread and hesitated, staring up into the dark where two torches swayed beneath the trees, so that he appeared to be looking into a great columned hall.

"Don't falter, Mr. Flattery," Llewellyn whispered. "Think of the others." Whatever irony the doctor intended was buried beneath his tone of excitement. This was what the man had sailed halfway round the world for. He could barely contain himself.

Tristam thought about his dream of death. *Who will he chose,* Tristam wondered, more than a little disturbed at how much the question sounded like the ramblings of the viscount. Wind hissed in the trees, and Tristam closed his eyes for a second, feeling the distant pounding of the surf, beating always in the background.

He started up the steps, moving slowly in the wake of the King's canoe. The stairway passed up through the trees and into a deep ravine cut into the mountainside. The moon had lifted just high enough that its light flooded down on this section of the stair. *Like water,* Tristam thought. On the walls above, he could see ferns and flowering shrubs growing from every ledge and niche, and they, too, cast their moving shadows down the walls of stone. Tristam wondered if Beacham was experiencing similar feelings to his own. They had climbed such a stair before, led by an owl.

What awaited them atop this staircase? Would they be captured by dreams again? Tristam was reminded of his recurrent dream—the dream of being paralyzed in sleep, unable to wake. Helpless. That was what he felt now. As though he had been caught in a nightmare that would not let him free.

Above, the Old Men began a musical chant, their voices low though devoid of warmth. It seemed a song of sorrow, and then Tristam realized it was the same song he had heard Teiho Ruau sing before they set out on their journey. And then it had been sung by the Varuans who brought the bodies of Chilsey and Garvey down to the beach. What had Wallis said? It was sung at the outset of a journey, and for the dead, for death was thought to be a journey to an island—the Faraway Paradise. And here went the King before him, borne in a small boat, Tristam swept along in its wake.

The stair snaked up between the high cliffs, small gusts of wind accompanying them, like words almost forgotten, spoken just as one said farewell. *"Remember me,"* Tristam thought they were saying, the lament of ghosts and spirits.

Suddenly the owl fluttered soundlessly down and landed on the branch Tristam carried. It blinked at him with its yellow eyes, turning its head almost fully around.

Up they went until Llewellyn began to falter, and the stair ended at a high arched door, perfectly carved into the cliff. They stopped here, and the old men spoke and beat their staffs upon the stair. They chanted and Tristam smelled something being burned that gave a fair perfume to the air.

Ahead of him the Old Men passed in, and Tristam followed the King, wondering where they had brought him and what the Varuans kept hidden in this cave that they spoke of to no one.

The same white stone that had been used to build the stair made a short walkway in, and in the torchlight Tristam could see that it was laid over the natural rock. At first Tristam thought he had entered a passage cut into the cliff by the efforts of men, but as they went deeper, the cave became larger and less regular in shape, and Tristam realized it had once been a natural fissure in the volcano.

All of a piece, he thought.

They continued up a broad stair, perhaps a dozen steps, the torchlight glittering off the walls, then they passed along a landing and the cavern opened up before them. Tristam could see the stair curving down, perhaps half a hundred feet, and there against the end of the cavern, he saw seven pillars carved like the trunks of trees, set in a semicircle: the two outermost to either side were white, the next two were rose, the next pair were green marble, and the central column was black.

Water ran into a fount from the head of serpent, set upon the body of a raptor, and above, a small landing was borne upon the shoulders of a naked man and woman who hid their faces in shame.

Tristam lowered his weight heavily onto each stair, as stiffly as an automaton, unable to look away, or even to blink. *The race that had gone before,* he thought. A race that girdled the globe, seeking places to build their temples. Had the first mages been remnants of that race? Or had they somehow discovered their arts, for Tristam realized that the magic struggled to be reborn when the knowledge was lost.

The owl took to wing and circled once around the floor inside the columns, and then alighted on the lintel. A lintel scribed with characters that Tristam had seen before.

He glanced over at Llewellyn, who stood rapt, his eyes consuming the sight. *He does not understand what is happening here,* Tristam thought. *Llewellyn believes that he and his fellows arranged all of this, but it is not so. We play out some other's design, and cannot know if it is for good or ill.*

"*Evil is done by those who mean only well,*" Lady Galton had said. Tristam looked back at the others, still standing awestruck on the stair. Would history say he had made a fool's bargain? That these few lives would have been better forfeit, and the arts kept from knowledge? Did he trust men like Palle and Llewellyn to act out of wisdom?

But it is I who will be a mage, or so Llewellyn inferred. What will I do with this power? Can I limit the harm these others might do? Will I be forced to learn the arts to stop these others? Or will it be me who is performing evil deeds, with the best of intentions?

"There is little time," Llewellyn said suddenly. "We must begin. In an hour you must learn your part, Tristam, though I shall be here to guide you."

Tristam half-hoped that the Old Men would wave Llewellyn aside and take control of what was to come, but they stood expectantly, waiting for the Farrlanders to lead.

Llewellyn set Tristam's bag down in the center of the design, and out of it took a portfolio of worn paper. He looked up at the naturalist. "Come, there is no time to be wasted. Much depends on you, Mr. Flattery. More than you know. Think of these good people." He waved a hand at the frightened Farrlanders. Tristam looked back at his shipmates—the duchess standing among them, her torso bared—and thought that he could do nothing but try to save them. *The best intentions.*

⟿ Thirty-Seven

Jaimas and the prince emerged from the abbey floor not far behind the countess, who immediately began walking slowly across the expanse, staring down as though she could see through stone, right down into the heart of the earth. He stopped, letting the prince go on, and waited for her to notice him. After a moment he was forced to clear his throat. She did not look up.

"Is Massenet holding Lady Angeline and Bertillon?" he asked, chagrined that he had not been able to dislodge the Entonne from the chamber. But even more, he wished that he had been able to rescue the countess' niece—thinking of her gratitude.

The countess did not seem to hear the question. "It is part of the whole," she said, as though that was what they had been discussing, "but . . . it is hard to know where it fits."

Jaimy was taken aback by how unconcerned she seemed with her niece's safety. She continued to search the floor, as though it were the most important activity in the world.

It was quiet now; morning not far off. The moon had swung across the sky and floated above the eastern horizon. It cast long, indistinct shadows through the ruin that seemed somehow to evoke the past in Jaimy's mind. What had transpired here over the centuries? What secret history had Eldrich taken to his grave, or remained hidden away in the unread books of the Farrellite Church? It did not take much imagination to see mages at work here, and armies gathering to contest ownership of this sacred site.

A guard came up, bowing to the countess. "The duke has need of you, Lady Chilton."

She looked up, confused for a moment, as though she had been dwelling in that same past that Jaimy could see, and then she nodded. In the chamber where the hearth burned they found a small group standing around the table, while only one man sat, hunched over on a stool.

The countess immediately curtsied deeply.

"Your Majesty," she said.

"Lady Chilton?" the King responded in a voice that Jaimas could not believe came from the mouth of a man. "All is in readiness?"

"You intend to go through with this?" she said, surprising more people present than just Jaimy.

The King did not answer, but his head fell forward and then lifted slowly in a tired nod of ascent.

"There is something that must be done before we can proceed."

The King nodded again, his hood falling a little farther over his face.

The countess motioned to the duke, who stepped closer so that she might speak privately.

"Palle and the prince have gained control of the chamber," she whispered, surprising Jaimy again. They had reported odd sounds of men moving but had never made this claim.

"How?"

"We might ask Mr. Kent and Valary. There must be some entrance we knew nothing of."

Princess Joelle came into the circle of light, followed by Lady Galton, who was supported by Alissa.

Jaimy's gaze found hers, and she tried to smile, but failed, and he thought in that instant that the decision had been reached. She would accept his release from her vow. He closed his eyes, and was swept by a wave of grief and guilt. He had allowed this to happen, through his foolish infatuation with Angeline Christophe. Why had he ever made such an offer? But it was impossible to retract it now.

His father, the duchess, and a few others went out of the chamber; rather than stay and hear Alissa's decision put into words, Jaimy attached himself to this group. Kent and Valary nodded to him as he joined them.

They stopped in the central hall of the old abbey, the walls and columns casting soft shadows in the moonlight, mist seeming to float through the windows.

"We will have to take the chamber by force," the duke said.

"No," the countess said firmly. "It is too late for that. They already have Trevelyan, and if they can press Mr. Bertillon into their service, great harm could be done here." The countess was looking over the chamber, gazing down at the uneven stones of the floor. "I shall have to chase them out on my own."

Two guards appeared, escorting a woman between them, and Jaimy felt a wash of hope, for it was Angeline, covered in mud, her dress torn. Then, as she was brought into the light of the lamp, Jaimy realized it was not Angeline at all but the Entonne singer he had seen at the palace!

He looked over quickly at the countess, her face hidden behind the veil.

"How in the world did you escape?" the countess said.

The woman looked frightened beyond measure and utterly exhausted. When the guards released her arms, she almost collapsed to the floor.

"I was not in the chamber when the count took it," she said in Entonne. "I had gone out into the stairwell and down—to obey the call of nature. I had a lantern, and hid in the cellars below. Eventually the oil was gone, and I was left in darkness, until one of Massenet's men came by with a lamp. I tried to follow him, but, afraid of being heard, I stayed too far back and lost sight of him. What seemed like hours later he returned with another. And then more men came. Palle and others. I found the tunnel they had used and, in the darkness crawled up until I saw a tiny point of light—a star. And I came out on the surface in the wood behind the abbey."

The countess nodded. "Take her to Lady Galton, and ask that she treat her kindly," the countess said. She turned back to contemplating the floor, and though she passed by Jaimy, he could not tell if she met his gaze.

They are one and the same, Jaimy thought. She has chosen the path of the mages, and has hidden herself away, not because she is old and vain and has lost her beauty, but because she is *young.* Angeline was old enough to be his grandmother.

"I will need candles and ash from the hearth," she said suddenly. "Lord Jaimas, if you please? But bring no others here."

She slipped off her shoes and walked slowly across the stones as though searching them with the soles of her feet. Sensing vibrations, perhaps.

Jaimy rushed off to do her bidding and, when he returned, discovered that she stood facing the moon, her face buried in her hands, speaking softly.

"Put out the lamp," she said quietly, "and stand away. If you will stay, say nothing, and be still."

She took up a double handful of ash and began to sprinkle it in a line along the floor, muttering to herself as she did so. Jaimy crouched down near his father and Kent, all three in awed silence, fascinated, unsure of what they witnessed.

She scribed a ten-foot circle with the ash and then began careful lines of intersection. Jaimy counted them as she went. Seven. Taking up the largest candle, she began dripping wax along the pattern—evenly spaced drops—and then, in the center, she set the three candles, chanting over them for a moment.

Jaimy thought he felt a charge in the air, like a gathering lightning storm. He half expected his hair to stand on end.

But Angeline, he thought suddenly, she was not the woman who modeled for the portrait in their library. Oh, there were undeniable similarities, but they were not the same woman, there was no doubt of that. It made no sense.

The countess finished dripping wax on her pattern, and stood on the intersection of two lines. She began to chant now, in the language of the text. He glanced over at Valary, who was more alert than Jaimy had ever thought the scholar could be. Jaimy could see him memorizing every detail of what was done.

The countess raised her hands stiffly, twisting them strangely, as though they were not fully under her control. She seemed to be in a trance, unaware of what went on around her. Her voice changed, taking on the hollow sound of the King's, the alien words requiring an alien tone.

Three dark plumes of smoke rose from the candles, twisted about one another once, then joined into one. The smoke bent in a short arc and almost flowed like a stream of water, though inches above the stone, following one line from the center. It curved sharply along the outer line of the circle, and then suddenly turned down, to disappear through some fissure in the floor.

The duke rose slowly, and slipped back into the darkness. Jaimy heard him take several quiet steps, then break into a run.

For several minutes the smoke streamed from the candles and followed its unnatural course, then suddenly the candles began to gutter and then flickered madly, as though something were caught in the flames and struggling to escape. And then they went out, faint smoke now rising vertically in the moonlight.

The countess stood, embracing herself, fingers stroking her upper arms reflexively, and she rocked back and forth like some did who had lost their reason. No one dared approach her.

Jaimy saw the duke and a group of guards pass among the columns, their pace determined.

"Where does he go?" Jaimy asked.

"To intercept Prince Kori and the others when they are forced up from below," Valary whispered.

Jaimy rose, stepping back into the shadow of a column, avoiding the others. He found a fallen stone in a dark corner, and sat there, overcome with remorse and sadness. "What a terrible betrayal," he whispered. "And it was all illusion."

The globe of the moon seemed, at that moment, as desolate as he felt. Alissa was gone and the woman who had caused him such confusion was not what she seemed. Not at all.

"What do you see in the face of the moon?"

Jaimy turned his head and found the countess perched on another stone a few feet away.

He turned back to his view. "A simple face, almost innocent in its beauty. And though it remains untouched by the years, feels no need to hide this."

"But even the moon changes, Jaimas: goes through its phases, disappears altogether at times, or is hidden by clouds."

"As you are hidden by a veil, Lady Angeline?"

"It is not the same, I think," she said softly.

Jaimy shook his head, he looked back at this woman, hidden by her mask. "No? Why do you hide your face from me? I've learned the truth now."

"No," she said. "You haven't begun to learn the truth."

Jaimy turned so that he was close enough to whisper. "What is the truth, then? You remain young. Is that not so?"

"*I am ancient,*" she said harshly.

"But I have seen you, a beautiful woman, with all the excitement and yearning of youth."

"No. I am able to embody those things. That is all the difference between me and any other old woman. The old say that they are young in their hearts, though their bodies are aged. But I am old in my heart, and young in my form. I cannot see the world as I once did. It is impossible for another to understand, for it is unnatural and common only to those who practice the arts."

"You are a mage, then?"

She laughed bitterly. "I am not even an apprentice, as the mages reckoned such things. Even Eldrich was barely a mage at all. No, they have passed. Gone," she whispered. "*Gone.*"

"Then what is it we do here? What do Palle and Massenet hope to accomplish? What will these texts do, and where did they come from?"

She sat silently, her hands around one knee, rocking back and forth, her manner giving lie to her claims of age. "They were hidden long ago. Before Lucklow and the others had made their pact. The mages could sometimes sense events in the future, as we see forms in the mist, perhaps. Hardly clear visions, but some were skilled in their interpretation. The texts were hidden so that they could not be located, even by a mage. It must have taken decades to accomplish this one act. Hidden away, to await certain events." She shifted her hands to the other knee and continued to rock. "Like the darkness calling forth the owl." She gestured down. "Their mark was above the door. The vale rose, and the falcon. It is their chamber."

"Whose mark?"

She shook her head. "The mages never spoke their names." She lowered her head, and was still for a long moment. In the moonlight Jaimas could almost see her silhouette beneath the veil. She seemed old at that moment. Old and in pain.

"But what do Palle and Massenet expect to find here?" Jaimas asked again, softly.

"Ascendancy, for themselves, for their countries. They fear others—that is why they sought positions of power. Their greatest dream is to have a King who dances when they move the threads: and for Massenet, to marry his child to the heir of Entonne, and sit his grandson upon the throne. The ordinary desires of those who rise to such positions. In their appetites, they are not men of great originality. Though they will do enormous harm in spite of that."

There was a scuffing noise and they both looked up to see Kent standing a few feet away, such a look of unhappiness on his face that Jaimy felt deep pity for the old man.

He has suffered so much longer than I, Jaimy thought.

"Will you leave us?" the countess asked softly.

Jaimy nodded and rose, but as he passed the countess reached out and pressed his hand as though she could not quite bear to let him go. "Tell the duke we must begin in one hour." And then she did let him go—Jaimy felt it—released him as much as she was able. It was up to him now.

Kent stood looking at the woman in the moonlight. He wanted to ask her to lift her veil, but it was far too late. He had made no demands on her all these years, and now the habit could not be broken.

"You have every right to feel as you do," the countess said suddenly.

"You know what I feel?"

"Resentment. Anger. Bitterness."

Kent shook his head. "No, that is not what I feel." He looked up at the moon. "*Loss.* That is what I feel. All the years we have lost. Why did you hide yourself away from me?"

She had clasped her hands in her lap, so tight Kent could see the veins stand out, even in the moonlight. "My heart belonged to another, Averil," she said, as though the words hurt her.

"Gone, how many years?" Kent said, before he thought, for he knew the futility of debating past decisions, or of attempting to change someone who could not change.

She took a long, deep breath of frustration.

"But then, I am old," Kent said, wistfully.

"And I am changed," she said. "Not as you remember me. The spell is gone."

Kent looked at her quizzically as though she had ceased to make sense or he was not understanding the allusion.

The countess began to pull back her veil, removing it altogether. She turned away from Kent as she did this, facing the setting moon.

"Come around, Averil," she said, her voice taking on a little warmth.

Kent moved slowly, keeping his distance, suddenly unsure of what might be revealed. And there, in the soft light of the moon, was the woman he had painted often from memory, yet it was not her—not quite.

"Am I as you remember?" her voice no longer flat.

Kent hesitated. "The light is poor."

"No. It is not the light," she said. "The form is little changed. But something is gone. Is that not so? I was bespelled, Averil. Or perhaps it was my mother or grandmother who was so unfortunate. But in the womb I was formed in no common way. And about me, all my days there was some unnatural attraction. Look at this face. I am still beautiful—and I say this without vanity. But would men I had not spoken a word to, duel over me? Would flocks of young gallants be reduced to fool's tears because I spurned them? You know the answer. The spell is gone, its purpose served.

"I was a trap for Eldrich, though I did not know it—nor did he. But he could not resist me, nor could the spell be detected, for it was wrought by men whose powers far exceeded Eldrich's own. He could not bear to see me age. And so he passed some knowledge on to me, against all his oaths and judgment, so that I should not lose my beauty. So that he would not lose it.

"And I have been the one keeping the magic alive in this world. I drew it, like a lodestone draws iron. And set in motion all that has come about. Though only slowly did I become aware of it. Me, Averil. I have caused all of this. Someone long ago, through augury, saw what might come, and set the stones in place. Laid the foundation of all that happens this night." She rose from her stone, and took Kent's hands in both of hers. They were so warm and soft, denying all that she said, for the flame of youth seemed strong in her. "And you were bespelled, Averil, like so many others. Bespelled, and I am sorry for it."

Kent's mind could not accept this. "There was more to it than that," he managed. "What of my feelings now? The spell is gone, you say?"

She raised one of his hands to her soft lips. "I cannot explain your feelings now, for I have not been kind to you. Decades of silence, and then I set you this impossible task. You should despise me. It is what I deserve." She looked up at him, searching his eyes. "But here we are, so many years later. Tell me honestly, Kent, do you think you love me? Love me a little?"

"I have loved you through all the years of silence," Kent said, almost robbed of his voice by emotion. "How could I stop now that I hear your beautiful voice again?"

She stood up on her toes and kissed the corner of his mouth. "Then if I live beyond this night, we will speak again. There might be a few years left to us. I have no skill at augury, but it is not impossible. Though I will tell you true, Averil, that it will be a miracle if I survive what is to come, and miracles have become rare in our age."

"Then I shall pray for a miracle."

She squeezed his hands, as though what he said had not pleased her. "I have need of you one last time. May I impose upon you again? I will warn you, there might be some danger, even to you."

Kent shook his head. "I have come this far. I could not shirk my duties now."

"Then come down with me," she said releasing his hands, her manner suddenly deeply serious. "I will ask a few others to accompany us."

She replaced her veil and then turned to go. "Kent?" she whispered.

"Yes?"

"I am afraid."

Knowing there was nothing he could say, Kent reached out his hand. She took it in her own and they set off in the last light of the moon.

A bird fluttered above, flitting from a window to the top of a column, and then to the head of the stairs that led to the rooms below.

*   *   *

They found Prince Kori, Stedman Galton, Palle, and Massenet gathered before
the King, silent, as though judgment were being passed. The duke stood at the
King's right hand, and Kent could not remember seeing the man so troubled.

"Why do you bother me with this?" the King asked peevishly. "Do you not
see that my hour is here? I have no care for such trivialities! Let the succession
fall where it will. Only a fool cannot see it is a curse! Let he that wants to, be
cursed, and damn them for it." The King rose awkwardly. "Wil?" he called, looking around.

"I am here," the prince said, hurrying forward, clearly unsettled by what he
had just witnessed.

"Take me down to this cellar."

Massenet took a step forward. "As the representative of His Holy Entonne
Majesty, I demand to be present at this rite. Myself and Mr. Varese." Massenet
did not quite know who to address with his demand, for clearly the King would
not care, so he spoke to the larger group. "We want to be reassured that the
countess keeps her word."

The King gestured impatiently as though giving permission.

"I will be present as well," Prince Kori said, "with Wells, and Sir Roderick.
I will be sure that nothing goes amiss in my Kingdom." He looked over at the
duke, something like triumph in his manner.

"He is a willful old man," Kent whispered to the countess.

"It does not matter," the countess said. "It is time, Your Majesty. Mr. Bertillon? Are you still prepared to carry this through?"

The musician stood as far from Massenet as the small room would allow.
He nodded, though he could not hide his apprehension with silence.

"Lord Trevelyan?"

The baron had collapsed on a stool, where he leaned heavily on a cane. "Yes.
Yes. Only let it be over. . . . No. Do not caution me. I understand the risk. But
let us get on with it."

"I will need the help of others as well. The prince, Lord Jaimas, and Alissa.
No. I meant Prince Kori," she said as Prince Wilam nodded his assent.

"I will have no part in this!" Kori said quickly.

The King paused, half-turning toward his son. "Of course you will. Would
I leave my throne to a coward? Bring him," he said to a guard. The prince
looked over at Palle, who, for once, offered no counsel. A guard stepped forward, and the prince went on, his moment of triumph dimmed, and more
frightened than angry.

They descended slowly by lamplight, no one but the countess aware of what
they went to do. *"To seal off this knowledge,"* she had said.

Teiho Ruau began to sing in his native tongue, his fair voice lifting up above all the apprehension and fear. Jaimy found the music calmed him a little, though he had no idea what the words might mean.

Lady Galton caught up with him, leaving her husband behind for a moment.

"Did the King bring us here only to abandon us?" Jaimy said to her. "What will happen to us?"

Lady Galton shook her head, struggling a bit to breathe. "I do not know. But if the worst should occur, do not let silence be your final word." She moved her head indicating Alissa, who went before them.

"Alissa has chosen not to become a duchess," Jaimy said sadly.

"She told you this?"

"No, but I am quite sure."

"And I am quite sure you are having a misunderstanding common to youth. Be sure of nothing until you have heard it spoken. Spoken from her heart, mind you." She put a hand on his arm and pressed him gently forward.

At the bottom of a stair the party was held up while others made their way through some narrow opening, and Jaimy dared to whisper. "Alissa?"

She looked up quickly upon hearing his voice, a flash of desperate hope crossing her face.

"If it is possible, might we speak later?"

"*Yes,*" she said. "Indeed, yes."

In the poor light he found her hand, and clasped it for a second. Despite their situation, he found his hopes rise. Alissa mouthed the words, *"Be careful,"* and then went on.

The entrance to the chamber had been cleared of stone by guards, and the group struggled in. A large, damp cellar, Jaimy thought, half-expecting the place to have been transformed.

"There is no time for discussion," the countess announced, turning to address the gathering. "Please do as I say, and ask no questions." She waved a hand at the crowd. "All of you, back."

She went to the opening in the floor, farthest to the right, and nearest to the wall. "Mr. Bertillon, you will be here. You are confident of your part, I hope? Lord Trevelyan, you will take this next place. There was once a column here; stand as though it were at your back. Mr. Ruau?" she called, motioning the Varuan forward. "You know your place, I'm sure. To the right of the King. Your Majesty, please. You will have to leave him, Prince Wilam. Averil. You will be to the King's left."

"Have you my portrait?" the King asked, and Kent waved the roll of paper.

"Give that to me, Kent," the countess said, taking the sketch from the painter. "Lord Jaimas. You will be here, next to Kent. And finally, Prince Kori." She addressed the last three to be placed on the pattern. "You have no part of your own in what is to come, but you represent others who are distant. You will feel them inhabit you, and you will lose control of your ability to move or speak. Do not struggle. They will not harm you. I cannot say, 'don't be afraid'; it is a frightening experience, but it will prove easier if you do not resist." She turned away, time too short now to offer reassurance.

"Lord Trevelyan, you have learned your part? Good. Lady Alissa?" she called, and Jaimy saw Alissa squeeze Lady Galton's hand, and come out onto the floor. The countess pulled back her veil enough that she could reach into the collar of her gown, and she drew out a glittering stone on a silver chain, which she clasped around Alissa's neck.

"If this site had not been destroyed, your place would be on a small platform, here," the countess pointed to the wall that had been effaced. "But you will have to stand here, next to the font. When the ritual begins, you must put your hand upon this stone and fix its image in your mind. Imagine it a star burning bright in the sky above our heads. Then speak my name, over and over. Do not falter, no matter what occurs. This is of the utmost importance. I am trusting my life to you, my dear, because you are true of heart." She kissed Alissa on each cheek, and whispered something in her ear. "Where is my servant?" she asked, turning back to the others.

A manservant came forward with a leather bag, and from it the countess began to remove odd objects and small parcels. She glanced up at the servant. "You may extinguish the lanterns."

The chamber became darker as each lantern died, and finally it was entirely black, as only a cavern that sees no daylight can be black. Jaimy felt his heart pounding in the forced silence. All he could hear was the trickle of water and Alissa chanting softly, a name he could not catch. *Do not falter,* he thought, *and I will not falter again.*

The countess produced what appeared to be a glass jar filled with a pale, luminescent liquid. She set the jar on the floor, where it cast a weak light around the room. Directly across from him, Jaimy could see Trevelyan, bent over, leaning with both hands on his cane. The baron appeared to be in pain. Jaimy hoped that not too much was to be asked of the old man, and that his own safety did not depend on the baron.

The countess removed her veil in one unconscious motion, as though all the years she had hidden her features were now of no consequence. Angeline Christophe stood before him—the woman in his father's portrait, but not quite. She went to the opening in the floor against the wall—the fount—and here she spoke quietly for several minutes, though to no one. Two feet away, Alissa chanted, her face determined, though a little pale.

The trickle of water increased, and the countess reached out and filled her cupped hands. She sipped some of the water, and then went to Bertillon, who tilted back his head and took a few drops on his tongue. She did this for each of them in turn, and Jaimy was surprised to find that it was only water, unremarkable in every way.

By some means that Jaimy could not see, the countess lit a short candle, and on this flame she cast some herbs that smelled sweet and fair when they burned. Jaimy almost felt a sense of calm inhabit him at that moment, as though nothing were amiss. He looked over at Alissa, but she was lost in her task, and did not notice him. *"Because you are true of heart,"* the countess had said. Unlike Jaimy, who had fallen to confusion the moment he had met this woman of beauty and mystery.

The countess took up her jar of luminescent fluid, and with great concentration, began sprinkling it over the floor, drawing lines, as earlier she had with ash. But each line glowed faintly, and here and there were little orbs of concentrated light that seemed to create a pattern across the floor; like constellations, Jaimy thought, though none that he knew.

From each person in the semicircle, lines were etched to the fount, and these the countess crossed with arcs. For a moment she studied her pattern, examining all the elements, and then nodded as though satisfied. Immediately she began to pour some seeds from a small bag into a mortar—*regis,* Jaimy realized, surprised at how benign they appeared, like peppercorns. She ground the seed methodically. A second bottle, though this one of darkened glass, was produced and she poured some inky liquid into the mortar, mixing as she did so, until a thick broth was made. She took this up, stepped to the center of the pattern, spoke a few foreign words, and drank the mortar dry, casting it into the opening that had once been a fount. She hung her head then, as though already exhausted, and Jaimy saw her waver and he almost stepped forward to catch her if she fell.

But she raised her head and stared at the fount for a moment, as though in prayer. She let out a long breath, and began to unfasten the cuffs of her sleeves. Though the light was poor, Jaimy was certain that she bore an ugly scar upon her right wrist.

She nodded to Ruau, who came forward, careful to step between the glowing lines, and coiled his belt of snake-skin around her right arm, so that the head of the snake was at the back of her hand. He then retreated, and the countess looked up once more at the wall, held up her unencumbered hand, and a small falcon, a kestrel, lit upon her wrist. Jaimy saw the bird dig its talons into the soft skin beneath her wrist, and tears of blood appeared, running slowly across the marble-white skin until a drop or two fell to the stone floor.

The countess stamped her foot, so that it echoed in the chamber. *"Curre d' Efeu!"* she said strongly, and let the words die. *"Curre d' Emone!"* Then in Farr. "Heart of flame! Heart of the world. *Vere viteur aupel e' loscure.*"

"Your servant calls out in darkness," Jaimy heard Egar whisper to Valary.

"Vau d' Efeu. Ivanté!"

"Voice of flame. Come forth!"

"Par d' embou vere fant!"

"Speak from the mouth of your child."

Jaimy could not swallow, and his heart began a wild erratic pounding. Cold sweat dripped down his brow and stung his eyes. He felt himself gasping for breath, and speaking strange words.

Only Tristam's skill with languages and trained memory allowed him to make use of Llewellyn's hurried instruction. As Tristam went over the text once again, Llewellyn began organizing the others. Before the first column on the right, he placed Beacham. Before the next pillar, to her utter surprise, the duchess was positioned. Then the viscount. The Varuans had placed the King in his canoe before the black column, and next came Wallis, standing before a column of green. An Old Man took up position before the rose column on the left, and the final position was left vacant.

"Are you ready, Tristam?" Llewellyn asked.

"Ready? As much as one can be with an hour to prepare. Do you know what will happen if I do not manage to do it right?"

"Once the ritual has begun, you will remember what is needed. Do not fear." He gestured to gain the attention of the Farrlanders. "Do not move from your place no matter what happens. No flame can burn you, no thing can harm you—if you stay in your appointed position. You shall feel the will of another, do not resist, but let yourself relax. Breathe slowly, and concentrate on breathing. Everyone else . . ." he said to the Farrlanders who remained on the stair. "It would cost your life to set foot on the septogram. Stay well clear. Look to your people, Stern." Llewellyn glanced around the circle to see that everything was in place, then took up his own position at the first column on the left. "Mr. Wallis," he said, and the painter crossed the few steps to the canoe and removed an object wrapped in tapa cloth. Quickly he unwound the wrapping, and unrolled the canvas within, revealing a portrait of the Varuan King. He laid it at Tristam's feet.

Faairi crossed the floor to Tristam, and taking his hand, placed it on her star tattoo. "Look for my star," she said, then kissed him on both cheeks. She went to the fount and climbed up quickly to the platform above, where she sat, holding one hand to her star, and began to chant his name, over and over.

It has come, Tristam thought, *as it does for every man. The hour of my death.* He glanced around quickly at all the others—the living. Those who would leave this chamber and resume their lives, while Tristam Flattery would be gone. His horror was that he might still be within, conscious, but submerged, unable to move or speak, while the *other* emerged into the world. Would that not be worse than oblivion? He thought of Dandish, suddenly—the kindly old don puttering in his garden—and he felt a tear wash his eye and cling to the lid. Dandish had held such hopes for Tristam, but in all his days the professor could never have imagined this. Jaimy came to mind; no doubt blissfully married by now, and Tristam felt a spark of jealousy, though this was quickly overcome by love. *Let him live in happiness,* he thought. *Let one of us live so.*

He glanced at the duchess; unsure, even now, of his feelings for her. Not even sure that he knew why she had come, despite all that had been said.

Beacham was staring at him, frightened, Tristam could see, wondering if he would be saved. Wondering if Tristam would suddenly refuse his part. *Young,* Tristam thought. *He is so young.*

The Farrlanders looked completely out of place and helpless, as though they were children. And like children, understood far less than they believed, yet blundered on with misplaced confidence. *It is the story of our race,* Tristam thought. *Their race.* But the mages, and the race that had gone before—the practitioners of magic—they had disappeared. Like species whose forms were preserved only in stone.

We built our most important city of such stone, Tristam thought, *built it out of their bodies.* All the species that had mysteriously vanished—as Tristam would vanish, to become something else. *Transmutation.*

"Mr. Flattery," Llewellyn's voice came. "It is time."

The torches were extinguished, and Tristam watched the light die, as though it were his last sunset; and then darkness. The earth sang its ancient song in moving water, and Faairi droned his name.

"Farewell," Tristam whispered, and then bent to begin his part.

He opened an earthenware jar, which emitted a glow, like luminescence—the star-water that Faairi and he had collected. By this pale light Tristam went to the fount, and began to speak the strange words he had so hurriedly studied. At first they came awkwardly, but with each word he seemed to gain confidence, as though he could see the text in his mind and read the words. He filled his hands with water from the serpent's mouth, and drank, then went to Llewellyn and let a few drops escape onto the man's tongue, and then to each of the others in turn.

The most frightening thing was how natural it all felt, as though he had done it before, and Tristam had a nagging feeling that he had, or perhaps that he had done this in a dream. It was like a dance he had not performed in decades, but somehow his body remembered every step.

At one point he glanced over at the duchess, who kept her hands on her shoulders, so that her arms covered her breasts. She bit her lip in concentration, and Tristam saw her shiver, as though it were cool in the chamber. After that he had no thought of the others.

He sprinkled water carefully along the lines of the pattern on the marble floor, and they began to glow with a ghostly light. Overhead, on the dome of the ceiling, stars seemed to glitter.

From a bag of leather, Tristam poured seed into a stone mortar, and this he crushed to fine powder with a pestle made of bone. From the box he removed his uncle's wine—the blood of his ancestor—and mixed the fluid into the seed so that a thin paste was made. Standing to stare at the fount, Tristam closed his eyes and downed the bitter mixture, casting the bowl into the fount, where the water turned to crimson.

For a moment he was overcome, and felt the other move within him. He thought of Faairi's star, and then heard her voice, *"tamtristamtristamtris. . . ."* He raised his head and tried to focus but could not. The chamber had grown dark and was filled with shadows that moved and changed. Before him, the serpent tasted the air with its tongue.

Someone came forward and coiled the skin of the viper around Tristam's arm—the viper he had killed in the Archipelago. He held up his left hand and the owl dug its talons into his wrist, drawing tears of blood that fell to the center of the pattern.

Let us begin, Tristam thought, and opened his mouth to call out.

"Curre d' Efeu!" and then almost the same words he had heard Bertillon use that night at the house of the duchess. *"Curre d' Emonde! Vere viteur aupel e' loscure. Vau d' Efeu. Ivante! Par d' embou vere fant!"*

There was a moment of stillness, and the air seemed to crackle with gathering lightning, and then a blossom of flame rose up from the water of the fount and consumed Faairi on her perch above.

Jaimy began to jump forward, but something checked his movement, and his arms and legs would not quite obey. The pillar of flame rolled across the ceiling with a strangled shriek, and then he heard the drone of Alissa chanting the name he could not quite hear. She was there in the fire, unharmed he prayed. But the flame did not subside. It boiled from the fount, rising up like molten liquid, but spreading no farther, and smoked not at all.

The countess began what Littel had described as a chant of warding, pushing her hands first before her, as though they were pressed against glass, and then behind. It almost seemed that the flame flattened somewhat against the wall.

"Ivanté!" she called out, spreading her arms.

Jaimy felt suddenly as though his vision swam. As though he had taken far too much wine. Stars appeared before him, and areas of spiraling darkness. For a second he thought the countess was a man, stripped to the waist, a white owl on his wrist. Vertigo took him, and he felt the floor tilting. Then his hands found something solid at his back. Stone. And he leaned back, grasping the rock.

He dared to open his eyes, and across the glowing pattern he saw others standing before pillars of stone; white, rose, and green. And there was a fount where flame boiled up from water, and above it, on a ledge that seemed to be supported by a column of fire, he saw Alissa, her right hand grasping something at her breast. And she was saying Tristam's name again and again, like a litany of love.

Voices seemed to speak in his mind, strange words he did not know, and they echoed and reverberated as though spoken by many at once.

Suddenly fire spread around the circle, burning in a thin line beyond the columns, casting shadows and strange patterns of light.

". . . *loginé*," voices were saying, and Jaimy realized that he was part of this chorus.

Jaimy tried to force his eyes to focus, but the form of the countess had become insubstantial. He turned his head and among the moving shadows, saw grim-faced men in tall headdresses, who wore capes of feathers. He was speaking again, chanting the language of the mages, and then he extended his hands and discovered they were covered in strange tattoos.

I am safe, he told himself. *I must not fear.* Desperately he listened for Alissa's voice, even though it was not his name she chanted, and again he heard a woman saying, *"Tristamtristamtristam."*

Tristam finished the chant of warding, and felt something like exhilaration, like he had known after surviving his first action at sea.

Before he could consider what would come next, the flame before him rose up, hissing, and in response he felt the viper skin come suddenly to life, twisting quickly around his arm. The owl spread its wings as though it would take flight, and Tristam felt himself falling, slowly falling. And the snake and the falcon met in the air, striking, the viper twisting itself around its prey, and the talons of the falcon grasping. They fell, locked in battle. Fell through a lightless sky, through the net of stars.

Tristam felt the stab of the razor-sharp bill in his side, and writhed in agony. Then the hot fangs of the viper sank into his flank, and a burning poison spread. He fell. The scream of the falcon in his ears, the hiss of the viper.

"Tristamtristamtristam," someone said, and something inside him answered, *"Yes, I am Tristam."* And then they crashed to earth, pain overwhelming him, so that he screamed, the sound more like an animal than even the falcon's cry.

"I am Tristam," he said rising in the ruins of the darkened city. A small boy scuttled off into a hole, and Tristam followed. Someone whispered his name and he remembered, looking up until he found the star he sought. He let the boy go his own way, to follow or not, and went seeking the bright star.

Once he stopped when he found his reflection staring back at him from a shallow slick of water on the stone, though it was the face of a woman, at once young and old. *"I am Tristam,"* he repeated and went on.

The sound of water splashing drew him, and when he found the source— water pouring, like a scream, from the mouth of a stone bust—he drank.

Then he felt himself swell with power and pride and anger, and the shriek of a bird filled his ears, and they fought again, high in the air. And fell again.

Seven times they struggled, and seven times they crashed to the earth. And some small part of Tristam crawled away from the death throes of the viper and raptor.

I cannot win, he thought, *I am Tristam. Yet I cannot master the other inside of me.*

"But what uneasy peace shall this be?" the countess sobbed, and Jaimy saw that she did not return to the fount to drink again, but lay writhing on the floor, her clothing torn, her hair in dark, wet ribbons across her face. Shadow swept over her, like the silhouettes of fleet birds. And she twisted as though in agony, as though she had fallen from a great height, to be broken upon the stone.

"You shall not master me!" Jaimy heard a voice call out, and he thought he should know that voice. Before him the countess rose, sobbing in rage, and defeat, and sorrow. A small bird fluttered past her, and then went skyward. She stood breathing as though she had not had air in uncounted time. Breathing like a beast in battle.

"Tandre vere viteur!" she called in her anger. "Hear me!" She wavered as she stood, as though she had lost what she would say. And then quietly, almost with resignation, she said, *"Ci's m'curre."* From the bodice of her gown she took a pale blossom and cast it toward the fire, but the kestrel swooped down and took it on the wing. It circled the chamber twice, then with great speed, plunged into the flame, which vanished with the sound of a dying wave.

Darkness, and Jaimy felt himself spinning. He clung to the stone pillar until he felt the vertigo subside, and then opened his eyes. They seemed to be in very high place surrounded by stars. A faint, cool breeze moved in his hair and the feathers of his cape. It was silent, but for a distant tinkling, like chimes. Before him the countess lay in a heap of dark clothing.

"Where are you?" a terrible voice whispered.

"I am here," the countess answered, her voice small and devoid of all pretension. "Alone. With the alone. Among the stars."

"What do you hear?"

"The voices . . . of constellations."

"Then tell me your true name."

"Elaural," she breathed.

"Then you may scribe it here, among the stars."

Slowly, the countess rose, like a woman aged from a long struggle. When she got to her knees, she reached out and began to move her hand across the floor, and the pattern of light changed.

"Will you open the way, so that we may pass through?" the voice asked.

The countess nodded, raised her hands and began to speak. Jaimy felt the floor tilt, and his knees and hands strike hard stone. He moaned, and slipped into darkness.

"J?"

Jaimas felt that if he moved or spoke he would certainly retch.

"J? You're all right."

"Tristam?"

"Rise up, lad, you're not done yet. Come out of it now."

Jaimy lifted his head or, rather, felt that it was lifted for him, yet from within, somehow. The countess knelt before him, her arms outstretched, her head thrown back, and she chanted too rapidly for him to discern words.

They were back in the chamber now, though not quite the chamber he had first seen. The columns still rose around the circle, and the play of shadow and light was swift and confusing to the eye.

He managed to get to his feet.

On the floor, before the countess, Jaimy could see a portrait etched onto the stone. It appeared almost to ripple, as though it floated on the surface of some liquid. As he watched, the background of the picture changed, from the blue of a lagoon, to a sky filled with stars. She ran her finger around the edge of the canvas several times, and the last time, a thin line of red flame followed the gesture. And slowly the frame of fire began to advance, consuming the portrait.

The countess glanced over her right shoulder, and Jaimy saw the Varuan singer, Ruau, nod once, and then step carefully forward.

He crossed the few paces to the King, who was slumped down on the floor, unmoving beneath his cape and hood. Gently Ruau lifted the man in his arms, bore him up as though he were no greater burden than a child. Placing his feet as though he crossed a stream on stepping stones, the Varuan passed by the countess toward the flame.

Very gradually, as though it resisted, the column of flame began to part, almost trembling as it did so. Finally a passage opened in its center, beyond which Jaimy could not see stone, but only darkness. And then points of light. Unknown stars. A warm breeze touched him, and seemed to bear the scent of flowers and the sea. He heard a sound like distant waves. The portrait continued to burn, more quickly now, and the flame around the opening trembled. Ruau paused for a heartbeat, and then went quickly through. Jaimy saw him step into knee-deep water, and then heard his pure tenor lift in song. And though the words were in no language he knew, Jaimy understood them all the same.

"The mother wind carries us
Into the distant west
The great whale appears
With the sun's last rays.
And stars light to mark our way
Like islands cast upon the sea.

Suddenly the scene changed, the stars wavering like reflections in disturbed water, then they were gone. In their place Jaimy could see three curving structures, bridges he realized, that crossed over each other high in the air, supported so infrequently that they seemed to defy the forces of gravity. Behind them, painfully bright against the night sky, stood towers of brittle glass and light. As he drew in his breath in amazement, a noxious odor of unwholesome burning gagged him, and he saw that the air was an unnatural brown, and the stars had been blotted from the sky leaving only a stained moon, drifting in the pall.

Beneath the bridges men and women moved, but Jaimy could see that they were ragged and shuffled along with the slow pitiful steps of those utterly discouraged or ill beyond hope. A few stunted trees grew in the shadow of the great city, but their foliage was so sparse they seemed to be winter trees, despite the warmth Jaimy could feel in this filthy air.

It is the world that we build, a sudden intuition told him. *The world of empiricism and commerce—but not the world of men.*

A sallow boy darted across the opening behind the flame, and Jaimy saw lights moving, both on land and in the darkened sky. And then this scene changed as well.

They looked out through the branches of a forest, barren of leaves and blackened, as though it had been fired. On the horizon hung the slender crescent of a waning moon. For a moment it seemed that he looked into a world devoid of life, but then, on the darkened hillside beyond the wood, creatures moved. They were *men,* he realized, on a terrible field of battle. The stench of death was carried to him, and he felt bile rise in his throat. And then he saw the armies, or their ragged remains, drawn up upon opposing hills. About one hill lightning flickered from a cloudless sky, and the green sea-flame spread like a tide of light, while about the other he saw flames erupt while terrible explosions drove men screaming in terror. Faint cries of anguish reached him. Jaimy knew that this was the final battle of men: the forces of empiricism against the forces of magic. He felt all hope was lost, and then a cry went up from the gathered armies, like a note of grief and horror, and they charged once more across the field of the dead.

And, mercifully, the scene changed.

A moon floated over distant mountains. Peaks that rose out of calm water. From a mountainside, a single light flickered, and then the countess spoke out strongly in the tongue of the mages, and this flame guttered and died.

Jaimy was overwhelmed with distress by this sight, and then realized that these were the feelings of another within him. But was there only one? The flame within the chamber began to waver, and the countess spoke again, and then cried out. The other's distress turned to fear.

Wallis could feel the others that were somehow with, rather than in him. Two, men, he thought, and one of his counterparts in this ceremony was a man of such kindness and refined sensibilities that his fear was assuaged. Like Wallis, this man had prepared the portrait of a King, and so was an artist. The castaway watched his portrait float within a burning frame, and somehow felt that he had some part in this magic.

"You must take him through," a voice said, its tone reasonable, but commanding all the same.

Wallis was not sure who this was speaking, and if it were here, or in the other locations where his counterparts dwelt. He saw Mr. Flattery, who slumped upon the floor, shake his head in denial, and the portal of flame wavered.

"You must! The lives of your people are dependent on you!"

Still Tristam refused, and Wallis felt a wash of fear. The speaker was right, the Varuans would be enraged if Tristam were to back out now.

"I will not," Tristam said. "I have scribed my name in the secret place, and now I will not conveniently disappear, Doctor. Take him through yourself."

There was a moment of silence. Wallis could feel the breeze touch him. He could smell the perfume of the Faraway Paradise. Almost he wanted to go through himself. To pass through without dying! Only gods had done this before. Only gods and now this half-mad King.

Wallis could see the King struggling in his canoe, where he slumped on the seat, his aged hands grasping the gunwales, the plumes of his crested hat moving as he sobbed. His moment was here, and no one would bear him through. Wallis turned to see what happened to his portrait and realized that it burned away quickly now. The moment would pass, pass utterly. Never to come again.

Out of the corner of his eye he saw someone move toward the King.

"*Julian!*" a voice called out in horror, but said only that one word.

Wallis watched the viscount bend, and with a show of strength lift the canoe, King and all, onto his shoulder. Stepping deliberately between the glowing lines, he crossed the pattern, speaking to Tristam as he passed, words Wallis could not hear.

As he went, the duchess reached out to touch him, but could not reach, and she dared not move from her place.

"No! This is wrong!" The voice of Llewellyn screamed. "It was not foreseen."

"Not by you, Doctor," Tristam said simply, his voice dry and sad.

The viscount bent to pass through the gate of fire, and stepped into knee-deep water. He lowered the canoe to the surface, and pulled it on, toward the distant shore. The Varuan song of farewell could be heard, far off, and then the gate wavered, and the King had passed from this world.

"*Ju-li-an . . .*" a voice whispered, though it was as close to a wail of sadness and loss as a whisper could be. The duchess buried her face in her hands and wept. And Wallis thought she wept, not from loss, but at what her brother had become, and for the things he had done in this world.

May he find peace in the next world, Wallis thought. *May we all.*

With great effort Tristam raised himself to his knees, every motion seeming to take minutes, as though he were exhausted beyond human endurance.

"What are you doing?"

"Searching, Doctor. And then we will seal the portal, seal it so that it cannot be opened until the stars align again."

"You cannot, Tristam! You do not know how." And then more desperately. "Think of the knowledge that will be lost!"

"Yes, far too much knowledge, and not nearly enough wisdom," Tristam said, his voice seeming to come from a man half-sunk in sleep.

With the cooperation of his other, for there seemed to be only one now, Wallis managed to turn his head to the left, to find Llewellyn, contorted in rage, shaking his small fists at the man in the center of the pattern.

A shadow flitted among the flames, and then Tristam began to chant, moving his hands in strange, intricate motions. The gate of flame wavered, and began to draw closed.

"Now is the time," Llewellyn said. "It must be done." And immediately he started toward Tristam, walking in odd jerky steps. He drew a blade from his coat, and raised it high.

"Tristam!" the Old Man beside Wallis called out, in a voice not his own, but the mage could not hear, caught in the midst of his labors.

Llewellyn cast a handful of white feathers before him and spoke in the tongue of the mages. The feathers caught fire, and floated, burning, to the floor—and still Tristam chanted and moved his hands, his eyes closed.

Llewellyn stopped, put both hands to the raised blade, and called out. *"Elé y'alin!"*

Wallis would have shut his eyes, but he could not. At that instant a Jack bounded onto the pattern, flames erupting at his feet so that he caught fire. The man's hands were tied at his back, but his speed and size were such that when he collided with Llewellyn, both were carried several feet, flailing—then into the flame.

There was no scream. Barely a hiss escaped, and Tristam continued as if unaware that death had brushed by him so closely that its breath had been upon him.

The gate turned to a column of writhing flame, and then subsided into the fount, which bubbled for a moment, and then was still.

Voices began to sing, the Varuan song of farewell. Tristam lay prostrate on the floor, unmoving, as though death had not missed him after all. Wallis wanted to move, but found he could not. He wanted to sleep, it seemed, for darkness called out to him. He let his eyes close and fell into dream.

ᔰ Thirty-Eight

"Auralelauralelauralel . . ." the voice droned on without pause. One star seemed, somehow, brighter than the others, brighter and more beautiful. Almost, it had a voice, like far off chimes sounding in the wind. *"Elaural,"* it rang in an unknown scale, and she followed.

Wind. She could hear wind in the branches of trees, and smell grass and blossoms.

"Lady Chilton?" a voice said with infinite tenderness.

That is not my name, she thought. But perhaps it was, in some odd way.

She opened her eyes and discovered that she lay upon grass, and a small, pale blossom was almost beneath her nose.

"Where?"

"I do not know," Kent said, his voice sounding terribly old. He laid his hand gently on her shoulder. "We are in a bower of seven trees, where a small spring bubbles up from the base of a short cliff, but whether we are in Locfal, or Farrland, or some other land or place, I cannot say. It is the morning of a fine day. The trees, the likes of which I have never seen, are in blossom, and even now rain their petals down upon us."

The countess rolled to her side with difficulty and lay still for a moment.

Her head spun and she pressed a hand to her brow. When she took it away, she realized her skin was lined and spotted and was devoid of all its luster. For a moment she simply stared in shock.

"Yes," Kent said softly, "I'm afraid it's true, though I'm sure you need not remain so, now. You can be as young as any mage," he said a bit sadly.

"No," she said, her mouth almost too dry for words to flow. "I shall not be tempted again. This time I shall not weaken," she whispered. "I will wean myself of the seed, and grow old and pass on, as I should."

She saw Kent's shadow, on the grass beside her, nod in sad agreement.

"Are you injured?"

"Yes," she said, "but not in body." She felt pains, and stiffness, and aches, but they were nothing to her anguish. "Did you see, Kent? The vision? The vision of the mages?"

"I saw, but I did not understand. A great battle on a bleak landscape devoid of all trees, of all hope. And then a great darkened city, sinking in a pall of noxious fumes."

The countess nodded her head, and felt sharp pain in her neck. "Our two futures. The war between the forces of magic and the forces of reason. A war that would wound the world beyond recovery. I know now why the mages did not love men, though they bore a deep love of the earth right to the end."

"Is there no hope, then?" Kent asked.

"There is hope, but it is small. We have sealed the magic away again, so there shall be no final war. That was their choice. The mages knew that empiricism was understood by many, and the spread of it could not be stopped. But the arts—they were ever in the hands of a few, and therefore they believed it possible to avoid this war by bringing the knowledge of their arts to an end. That is my guess, at least." She paused, visions of what she had been through coming to the fore. "This world that empiricism will build, Kent—you read what Lucklow wrote. That was his vision, and it was hardly less dark than the alternative. But perhaps there is some hope there, though it is not great. If men were only as wise as they are clever. . . ."

She lay listening to the sound of the breeze, feeling entirely empty inside. Closing her eyes again, she tried to generate some response to the warmth of Kent's hand upon her—though the hand itself was not warm. Nothing. A tear streaked down her cheek. "The others?" she forced herself to ask.

"They sleep. But the prince, the King, Mr. Ruau, and Trevelyan are not here. Near the end Prince Kori came forward to strike you with a knife. I tried to move, to stop him . . . but I could not. And then, I don't know how, he stumbled and fell into the fire. Your doing, I think?"

She shook her head. "No," she said, but did not explain.

"What happened to him?"

"They are ghosts now," she managed.

This brought a moment's silence. She watched Kent's shadow move, as they surveyed their surroundings. "I have seen a small boy about; very furtive and quiet is he."

"Has he a shadow?"

"I believe he does."

She nodded. "Good. Kent?"

"Yes?"

"He is gone. . . . I believed with all my heart that I would find him, but he is gone. All these years . . . and he was truly gone."

The shadow put a hand to its face, and the hand bent a moment.

"Kent?" she tried to work some saliva into her mouth, to moisten the words, to soften them. *"I'm sorry. . . ."*

Kent did not answer, but she felt his hand almost tremble, and then be still.

"One of the lessons of age," he said softly. "Do not waste what time you have in regret." Kent brushed the hair away from her face—gray hair, and not so thick as it once had been.

With Kent's help, the countess sat up, then suffered a wave of nausea. Kent supported her, rubbing her back gently.

"I'm all right. We must collect the others, for we may have some distance to go."

"Do you know where we are?"

"Not exactly, though not far from the abbey, I think." She looked around at the bower of seven trees.

"Are you thirsty?" Kent asked.

"Yes. We must all drink from this fount," she said. "It will bring you luck, and health, and love, and. . . . Well, it is a long list, or so legends say." She waved a hand around the bower. "Look upon it, Averil, for you will not find it again, though you spend three lifetimes searching." She noticed Alissa lying on the grass, and crossed slowly to her, bending down too quickly.

The countess brushed the long tresses from Alissa's face, and found she clutched the diamond still. Softly she kissed the young woman's cheek, and gave her shoulder a gentle shake. "She was my star," the countess said to Kent. "I would not be here but for her. Alissa?"

Alissa opened her eyes to slits, wrinkling up her nose. "What has happened?"

"You have aided me, and all others immeasurably. And now you are safe and unharmed, and you shall soon be on your way home. Wherever that may be. But try to rise now, and quench your thirst at the spring. Then help me rouse the others."

Alissa sat up, staring at the countess for a moment, and then she looked away, realizing what she saw.

"Do not be embarrassed," the countess said to her. "I shall have to get used to people's stares."

Alissa put her hand to her throat quickly, found the diamond still there, and reached back for the clasp.

"No, no. It is yours, my dear, for guiding me home." Then she turned to Kent, thinking that he might be hurt by what she did, but he nodded.

"It is too small a fee, in fact," he agreed.

Alissa thanked them both, and went to the spring and washed her face, and drank. She realized that Jaimy lay unmoving against the bole of a tree, and she ran over to him, and found that he only slept, and it was a quiet untroubled sleep at that.

She shook him gently, and then kissed his brow. His eyes darted open.

"Have we survived?" he asked, and she nodded in answer. "Then will you, yet, marry me, Alissa Somers?"

She sat back, regarding him as though she would finally take his measure, now. "There is not another you love more?"

He shook his head.

"And there is no way to give up this title you will inherit?"

"Only through death, I understand."

"That seems a bit extreme. Then the answer, I suppose, is yes. Though you must swear that you will give up gallivanting across the country and visiting the homes of strange women."

"I swear."

"Then get up, you lazy thing, and see where we are. Not in the abbey at all."

Jaimy sat up and looked about, but he was clearly troubled. "Alissa, I thought Tristam spoke to me during the ritual. It was the strongest impression. Though it must have been a dream."

"Perhaps not. I heard another—or perhaps felt another who chanted his name, and called to him, as I called to the countess. We will ask her."

The countess and Kent roused Bertillon, who lay for a moment trying to gather his wits. Surprised to find this elderly woman with the youthful voice.

"Lady Chilton?" he said after a moment.

"Yes, Charl," she said, surprised at how much his shock hurt her. She turned away and went to the fount to drink.

Jaimas and Alissa stood back a little from her, perhaps frightened by how she had changed, or perhaps they merely sensed her pain.

The water was so cold it almost hurt to drink it, but she splashed some on her face, and shivered.

"Lady Chilton?" Jaimy asked tentatively. "I thought my cousin Tristam spoke to me in the midst of the ritual . . ."

"Perhaps he did. He survived the rite, Lord Jaimas, but I know no more than that." She could not in honesty offer more, though the look of disappointment and concern on the young man's face touched her.

Bertillon came up, looking around, still mystified. "But where are we?" he asked.

The countess shrugged. "It is a hidden place. . . ." She looked around hoping to find a clue to an answer. "Perhaps it is like the places reached through the gate of fire—very near, yet out of reach. The mages called this place the *fantime valone*. The 'phantom glen.'" She poked into her memory to find how it had been affected by the transformation. "These trees are the *valonemme*, called 'evermore' by the mages, for they are said to be always in flower." The countess realized that everyone was looking at her in wonder. "And that is all I shall tell you, for now," she said, oddly self-conscious.

Something caught her eye and she rose stiffly. "Drink from the spring and rest a little, but we must leave this place soon. Events go on without us, and I am concerned."

She turned away and beckoned Alissa and Jaimy. "We must coax a small boy to come out, but I have no sweets." She turned and stared into the surrounding wood. "Though perhaps it would be a mistake to pursue him. We will watch and see that he follows."

They gathered themselves together, and the countess led them reluctantly out of the bower, for no one wanted to rush from that place, which felt so tranquil and removed from the worries of the world. They all felt that nothing evil could ever befall them while they stayed within that arbor.

Along a grassy path they walked, between beautiful trees that none could name, through a plain stone arch that stood alone without wall or structure, then down a stairway of flat stones set into the earth. When Kent thought to look back, he saw nothing but familiar trees—holyoaks and linden—but no archway or stair. A small boy darted between two trees, watching them as they went.

"We are back," Kent said, "and draw a small boy in our wake." And the countess nodded and took his arm.

The sun had risen to the surface, and bobbed on the eastern horizon, the clouds that lay too close catching fire. Tristam sat with his back against the trunk of a tree and stared out over the endless ocean.

He had regained the world before the others and stumbled down the steps from the cavern, stopping here, somewhere above the Varuans' Sacred City.

He heard the steps of others coming down the pathway from the cave above. Varuans, he thought, by their pace.

"Tristam?" came a softly accented voice.

"Thank you for guiding me back, Faairi," Tristam said as she settled on the ground near him. "If you go down to your fale, I think you will find your sister returned from her journeys."

She put her hand to her mouth, and tears appeared on her cheeks. "How? Did you carry her with you?"

Tristam nodded.

She leaned forward to kiss his cheek but stopped, and then rose, backing away as though he were another forbidding Old Man, or perhaps a spirit that one did not trust.

I do not blame her, Tristam thought as he heard her steps on the pathway.

The sun lifted clear of the water, burning through thin cloud as it rose.

The duchess roused to the sound of whispers and opened her eyes quickly. It was dark, though a thin light seemed to find its way into the chamber. People were moving about and speaking in hushed voices, both Varuan and Farr.

She sat up, realizing as she did that she was unclothed from the waist up, and quickly she began pulling her dress into order. And then, suddenly, she stopped as the memories of the night came back. She staggered to her feet, her eyes searching the room, and then she stared at the stone wall where the gate of fire had opened.

Julian was gone. He had taken Tristam's place, and gone into the fire—or whatever lay beyond.

May he pass out of torment, she thought. *For all that he has done, I cannot fault him or feel less for him. Poor Julian, he was born thus, just as Tristam was born with his talent.* And she lowered herself awkwardly to the floor behind the column, and there she wept. Wept silently and long, for what had come to pass, and for what might have been.

After a long while she realized Tristam was not in the chamber.

She looked again but could not find him. Beacham lay quite near her, unmoving yet, and she was sure those were Wallis' long limbs across the floor. That left only Llewellyn . . . and then she remembered that he had gone into the fire as well—pushed in by a Jack as he had tried to murder Tristam.

Upon the stairs and the sloping rock others stirred—Stern and the crew—but she did not want to speak with them now. She wanted to be alone with her grief. Alone to consider what had happened.

She rose and went quickly off the pattern and onto the stair. A Jack stood by his crewmates, as though guarding them while they slept. It was young Pim, she realized; the cabin boy.

"Mr. Flattery?" she whispered.

"Gone out, Your Grace, some moments ago," he said, his voice hushed with awe at what he had seen. "Is . . . is he all right, ma'am?"

"That is my hope," she said, and laid a hand upon his arm as she passed. She could not help it; the boy looked so frightened.

The light grew as the duchess climbed the stairs, and she realized, as she emerged from the cavern, that it was early morning. She had no idea how long she had been asleep, or how long the ritual had taken. It might not have even been the previous night.

She went slowly down the stairs, surprised at how fatigued she was, both in body and in mind. It seemed that her thoughts floated in a great hollow chamber in which there was an unnatural silence, and that it was from there that she looked out, vaguely distant from the world.

At the bottom of the stair she found Tristam, off the path on the edge of a high cliff, gazing out over the ocean.

As she approached, he glanced over his shoulder, and then turned away. She hesitated, not sure what this meant, but certain it did not bode well.

"Are you yourself?" she asked from three paces distant.

Tristam shook his head, but did not look up at her. Overcome with fatigue and loss, the duchess sank to the ground.

"Should I be frightened?"

He considered for a moment. "I am not sure."

She stared out at the ocean, trying to get her mind to work as it should. "This is never what I expected to happen," she said, almost to herself. "Where has he gone?"

"Julian? The Varuans call it the Faraway Paradise."

"Then he is alive?" she said hopefully.

"If you will never see or know of him again, is he then alive?"

"Yes," she said, "somehow I think he is, though I'm certain it is not reasonable." She looked at Tristam, his face in profile to her. He seemed much the same, though overcome with sadness, perhaps. "You do not care if he lives or dies," she said suddenly, not quite sure why.

Tristam shrugged.

"He took your place, Tristam. Grant him that."

"Yes, but I will not take his."

"I'm not sure what you're suggesting, Mr. Flattery."

"Beware, Elorin. I am now more powerful than you imagine, and less patient."

She almost moved back then, her fear ignited by how coldly he spoke. "Shall I go?"

He seemed almost to struggle within for a moment. "No. Stay." Neither spoke for some time. "I am sorry for your brother, Elorin," Tristam said. "Sorry for what he was, and what he did. But a man owes no debt to his shadow, and

I cannot mourn his passing." Again he struggled, as though speaking had become difficult. "The Varuans believe regicide to be a crime that can never be erased. The family, the village, and the island of the murderer bear the stigma of it forever. It is an offense against the gods, and can never be atoned for. But an outsider . . . they have no concern for what befalls an outsider or his people. Passing into the Faraway Paradise, without first dying, has never been done by mortal man. Until last night. It is a sign that the gods' favor will return, they think, for the King and his servant will search for the gods. But no Varuan could take the King through into the other world, for that would be, to them, regicide."

"*That* is why we came halfway round the world?" the duchess asked.

"So the Varuans believe."

"And is it the truth?"

"A small part of it, perhaps. The design was infinitely complex, and I do not pretend to understand it all. Though perhaps I see more now." He stretched out his legs, such a common motion that it gave the duchess hope that Tristam was not completely gone. "The design was drawn long ago by men of enormous skill and patience. They sought to keep the arts from passing from this world. That was their intention. And you, and me, and Stern, and Averil Kent, and the Varuan King, and many others have taken part in this design. But I think it has been thwarted. Others perceived the intentions of these men, and worked against them. My uncle Erasmus, I believe, was one, for without him I could not have performed my part."

She watched him brush his fingers through his hair, pulling it back harshly from his face. He looked like a haunted man.

"But you, Tristam. You performed the ritual. Are you not one of them now? Are you not a mage, in fact?"

Tristam laughed, but joylessly. "By some miracle I survived—another came to my aid. . . . But I have not a thousandth the knowledge of a mage, nor do I have the least intention of exploring this *gift*. I saw the vision of the mages, Elorin. I know what they feared. I will take what I know to the grave. I swear. I will not be tempted."

"And the struggle between the viper and falcon. I saw it Tristam, saw you writhe upon the floor and cry out in strange tongues. It was a struggle inside of you, wasn't it? I sensed it."

Tristam covered his eyes for a moment, pressing the heels of his palms to his face as though he would keep something in. "*Yes,*" he whispered.

"The victory went to whom, Tristam?" she asked, afraid of the answer.

"There is no victory, only an uneasy peace. I have no words to explain it." He took his hands from his face and looked out over the sea. "I have been transformed, as though I aged half a century in one night, with all the unexpected changes that the years bring. I am not so different, and yet I am entirely changed. Do you see the waves crashing on the reef? They travel thousands of miles, and minute by minute they are transformed. The wave that dies here on the coral is the same wave that left the Archipelago so many leagues away, and yet it is unrecognizable. That is what has happened to me. I do not feel as though I have lost myself, only that I have changed, Elorin. Changed utterly."

Saying this he put his head on his knee and wept.

ᔰ Thirty-Nine

Although the sun in the phantom glade had indicated morning, it was afternoon in the world they returned to. They came out of a small wood up the ridge from the abbey and made their way across open pasture, then through the trees that surrounded the ruin.

Palace Guards were drawn up outside the abbey, looking tense and confused. Those who had supported the regents and those who supported the princess and the King were separated by open ground, watching each other warily.

As the countess and the others appeared, both groups fell silent, but no one moved to stop them from entering the abbey. Even before they found the others, they heard raised voices.

"I do not think my King will quickly recognize a regency led by Roderick Palle. Not after what I have seen," Count Massenet was saying.

Jaimy followed Kent and the countess into the chamber where the hearth stood and there found the others locked in heated argument.

"Where is the King?" Roderick said as soon as he saw the countess, as though he was not surprised to find her so changed. "Where is my prince, the rightful heir?"

The countess stopped and looked once around the group, giving a tight smile to Lady Galton. Then she turned her attention to Palle. "The King has passed through, as His Majesty chose to do. Prince Kori . . ." she looked sadly at Princess Joelle and the prince who stood by her side, "stumbled into the fire. He is gone, gone from this world."

"But you do not say the prince is dead," Palle said. "I demand you bring him back."

The countess stared at Palle as though he were a servant who had forgotten his place. "I regret to say that His Highness, Prince Kori, is dead. I am sorry, Your Highness," she said to Princess Joelle, and then to the prince. "My heartfelt condolences, Your Majesty."

Others in the circle doffed hats and bowed to the prince, echoing the countess and her form of address.

"I will not accept it!" Palle shouted. "I demand this woman be taken before a court of law!"

"Have a care how you speak of Lady Chilton, Sir Roderick," the princess said, and then turned her attention to the countess and Kent. "We have been waiting anxiously for you. You have all returned unharmed?"

"Unharmed," the countess said, "if not unchanged."

But Roderick stepped forward, still not done, his usual demeanor subverted by anger. Jaimy thought the King's Man looked desperate at the thought that his power might slip away. "I might remind Your Highness that the countess murdered your husband."

"That is your claim, Roderick, but who here will support it but for your minions? Not I." She looked around the group, but none offered their support to Palle. He was alone, and realized it for the first time.

"Your Highness," Doctor Rawdon said. "Sir Averil is here. I think we should proceed."

Palle glared at Rawdon, not needing to speak the word: *"traitor."*

She nodded, then turned to Kent. "The King left a will with Sir Benjamin, with instructions that it was to be opened and read by you, Sir Averil."

Kent showed his surprise. "Me?"

"It seems you are the one His Majesty trusted."

Rawdon handed Kent a sealed envelope. "We have all examined the seal, Kent, but be sure of it yourself."

Kent located his spectacles and then turned the envelope over, finding a simple design pressed into sealing wax. "It is only the King's signet ring," he said, "not the Great Seal of Farrland."

Rawdon nodded. "His Majesty wrote the will in his own hand as we traveled. But it is witnessed, and properly so."

Kent broke the seal and opened the document. The writing was indeed that of the King, for it was a hand not soon forgotten; elongated and extremely old-fashioned. Jaimy watched the painter run his eye over the pages of the document. "But it is so brief!" he exclaimed. "Barely two pages. And who are these witnesses, Doctor? I don't know these names."

"The King's footmen, Sir Averil."

"Footmen?!" Palle exclaimed, for once speaking for everyone.

Kent shook his head. "His Majesty leaves all of his property and estate to his heir, Prince Wilam." Which surprised all present. Was this some mistake, Jaimy wondered, or did the King have a premonition about Prince Kori's death?

Kent ran his finger down the page. "There are some special arrangements for servants and others—a house for Mr. Tumney, for instance. And His Majesty names the Duke of Blackwater to the Regency Council. Clearly he was not lucid," Kent said. "There is no council. It had been dissolved."

Palle looked at Wells, his face changing with the realization of what this might mean. "Was it dissolved in law?" he asked quickly.

The query was met with silence.

Palle's face suddenly lost its unaccustomed edge of desperation. "Then Sir Stedman and I are still Regents of Farrland." Then he looked over at Galton, who stood beside his wife, near to the Princess. "Though, perhaps, Sir Stedman will be returning to Farrow soon. . . ."

"No, Roderick," Galton said firmly. "Do not deceive yourself. Things have changed utterly. I shall stay for the course of the Regency. Two short years. If that is His Majesty's will?"

The prince looked over at Galton, his young face pale with grief and shock. He nodded his assent, then turned to the duke. "And I would like to begin by having these two mysterious deaths in County Coombs investigated. Perhaps, Duke, you might take charge of this?"

The duke gave a small bow of acquiescence, and Palle fell silent.

"Then we can mourn our losses," the princess said softly, "and celebrate the new King."

"Long live King Wilam," an officer of the guard called out, and everyone present responded in kind, and then an echo came from beyond the walls as the message was relayed to the waiting guards. The prince glanced once at Alissa, standing near to Jaimy, and then he turned quickly away.

"I shall begin my reign by exonerating the Palace Guards of any wrongdoing, for all involved believed they supported the rightful government." Prince Wilam turned to the duke. "Do you agree, Duke? Sir Stedman?" And when each had nodded, he looked at Palle, who also nodded stiffly.

"But where is Trevelyan?" Kent asked, suddenly aware that someone was missing.

"We have laid him here," the duke said, motioning through an archway.

Immediately Kent went through, and the others followed.

He found the body of Trevelyan lying on a window ledge beneath a deep crimson cover. It fluttered a little in the breeze. A fox darted out of a shadow, disappearing as the people approached, and the countess followed it with her eyes, almost starting to reach toward the beast.

"Look what ruin this seed brings," Kent said, his voice low and nearly breaking. He laid his hand on Trevelyan's breast. Jaimy had never seen Kent so affected. "One of the great minds of our time," he said, then turned to Palle, who hung back behind the others. "And what do you say now, Roderick? 'That he served his country well'? Have you brought enough evil among us?"

"You know me, Kent," Roderick said quickly. "My intentions were never to do harm. . . . I thought only of Farrland. At all times I put my nation's interests above my own well-being."

Kent shook his head. "You believe what you say, that is the saddest part. Did Farrland ask you to bring our great Trevelyan to ruin? Did her people ask that you murder two innocent young men in County Coombs?"

"*Kent*," the princess cautioned, for the painter was making accusations that might never be proven.

Roderick did not look cowed by Kent's attack, nor did it seem that remorse touched him. Doubt, perhaps, crossed his mind—self-doubt—but it was not his way, and Roderick hardly knew what to do with such feelings. *Doubt?*

Wells tugged at Palle's sleeve, and though the former King's Man pulled his arm free, he reluctantly turned to follow, looking as though he felt he should not retreat—one should never retreat.

"We must be gone," the princess said. "We might make the next town before it is too late. And there is much to do elsewhere."

Carriages were drawn up, and the assorted parties began to climb aboard. Jaimy saw the prince turn and cast his gaze toward Alissa, almost in appeal, and then he nodded to both she and Jaimy, his face contorting as he attempted a smile. The carriage door swung closed, and the driver pulled away.

Alissa squeezed Jaimy's arm. "I am glad we are not going off alone," she said.

Jaimy turned and found her face very serious as she watched the carriage pass from view. "Yes," he said, squeezing her hand. "It is enough to one day be a duke—I am grateful I will never be a King. But at least I shall not be a duke alone." He turned and looked back at the ruined abbey. "I shall not soon forget what happened here."

Alissa smiled. "And I shall not soon forget the setting you chose to ask for my hand. Many claim that such a moment carries a little magic, but not so much as ours, I think."

Tristam sat upon the bench Tobias Shuk had built for the pleasure of the duchess, and stared out over the bay toward the open sea. Stern and Osler were still examining the ship, as though during the twenty-four hours she was not under their command, something terrible had been done to her. The crew wandered about the deck, unable to keep their minds on their duties, for they had been witness to things that only happened in old tales, and their minds were not able to easily make peace with this.

Beacham roamed about the deck as aimlessly as any Jack, constantly distracted from his duties. Tristam kept noticing him staring off into the distance, though he knew that it was into his memory that Beacham stared.

I am little better off, myself, he thought. Pim came by to light the ship's lanterns as the sun disappeared, and Tristam thought that there was perhaps some truth to the old saw that the young were more resilient. Pim's step was light, and he sang quietly to himself as he passed, nodding to Tristam with a little bit of awe. The fact that the boy did not seem to be afraid of him was gratifying to Tristam. At least someone aboard could treat him as though he were not an object of fear and perhaps even horror. But they were now all polite in the extreme. Tristam had saved their lives, after all, and in the process had changed, becoming something they could not comprehend.

Stern came to inspect the shrouds of the mizzen mast, testing the tension of the lanyards, examining the dead-eyes. And then even Stern lost his focus, and stood for a moment like a man so aged that he had forgotten where he went, and why.

The captain turned slowly, noticed Tristam, and broke out in an embarrassed smile. "Ah, Mr. Flattery. She will carry us back," he pronounced, patting the rail. "I have no doubt of it, though we shall be desperately short of crew."

"I am at your disposal, Captain," Tristam said.

"And I shall have to take you up on your kind offer, Mr. Flattery. I think I shall have the duchess' maidservant standing tricks at the wheel before we are home." And then Stern's face became terribly serious, and a little of his usual confidence slipped away. "What you said last night . . . about Gregory." His eyes narrowed. "Was it true?"

Tristam looked up at the face of poor Stern, a man whose illusions had suffered enough on this voyage. "No," Tristam said. "I hoped only to save the mutineers from what they would do. And save us as well. No, Captain Stern, it was a lie. I. . . . You may tell the crew it was a lie."

An islander had brought Tristam the dagger that morning, but Tristam did not think anyone knew.

Stern looked relieved, but still he stood there, something else on his mind. Something he did not quite know how to say. "Can you see a bit ahead, Mr. Flattery? Do you know what will become of us?"

Tristam shook his head. "I cannot, but even short of able seamen, I trust you will get us home, Captain Stern. I do not doubt it."

Wrinkles appeared at the corners of the captain's eyes, as though he tried to not grimace from some pain. "I was thinking of afterward, Mr. Flattery," he said, embarrassed by the admission.

Tristam realized what was meant. Poor Stern, he thought. "I have little influence myself, Captain Stern, but I shall certainly do everything I can on your behalf. I'm sure the duchess will do the same."

Stern nodded, not terribly reassured. He was certain that with all that had happened on the voyage—all the arcane occurrences—the Admiralty would want no word of it to get out. And with the King dead, as Tristam assured Stern he was, there would now be no recognition of his service from the palace. The mutiny would not be forgotten, though; he could count on that, at least. The already-stalled career of Josiah Stern did not look promising.

Osler sent a Jack from the bow to draw the captain's attention, and Stern went off to see to what he believed would be his last command. Stern, who had circled the globe with Gregory.

Jacel appeared to have been waiting in the companionway for the men to end their conversation, and she came quickly out now, curtsying to Tristam.

"I have some concern for the duchess," she said in Entonne.

"No one aboard is acting as you would expect, Jacel."

"But the duchess. . . . Well, it would be good for her to speak with someone, I think."

"You are suggesting me, I take it?" Tristam said.

She nodded.

"I will come along in a moment."

With a last look at the light dying across the bay, Tristam went below. He found the duchess sitting at the windows, staring out, apparently as unable to function as everyone else.

"I thought you might have a cup of tea left for a weary naturalist," Tristam said.

She looked up at him as though she had not registered the meaning of his words. "I think Jacel has some still hidden away. If it was not all consumed by mutineers."

Tristam took a seat near her, resting his elbow on the ledge of the open window. "You look lost in thought, Elorin." Terns called across the bay, diving desperately before the tropical day came to its abrupt end.

"Yes," she pulled at a loose thread on a cushion. "We will bury the mutineers at first light—bury them at sea that is—and I was thinking of Hobbes. I cannot help but feel pity for the man. Was he not driven to his actions by injustice? Was he not a victim of the greed in the Navy Board that sent him to sea in a rotten ship? And when he stood before us on the stair, did he not say many things that were true?—Or at least partly so?"

"I thought he did, as well," Tristam said, surprised that "fairness" was ever a concern of the duchess, who seemed much too self-interested. "One of the finest seamen in the navy, Stern called him, and he was ever kind to me when the Jacks were most hostile. I am not even sure that Llewellyn did not have something to do with the mutiny of Hobbes, though we shall never know now. It was a tragedy, the life of Mr. Hobbes, and I feel for him. But even so, he made his choices, and he was a man who would suffer the consequences. I don't think you saw, but in the end, when the islanders caught them on the stair, Hobbes went down last, as though he might shield his men from the stones.

"Odd, is it not? A mutineer. A man who would have faced hanging for his crime, yet he cared so for his Jacks that he let himself be battered to death by stones in a vain attempt to protect them. Not a simple man, our poor Hobbes, and I suspect that, at least in the eyes of the Jacks, his mutiny will not diminish him. There will be songs about him, and they will not be all lies."

The countess looked out the window again, thinking. "But perhaps he was only playing his part, as we all seem to have been on this voyage. Perhaps the mutiny of Hobbes was foreordained, just as the Duchess of Morland taking ship was fated—the duchess and her mad brother. . . ." she whispered. "I feel, Tristam, as though I have become lost among the endless reefs and islands of Oceana. Lost without charts or instruments. The King is dead, you tell me, so I no longer have a place at court. And what do I return to? Will the amusements of Avonel seem as bright now that I have sailed across the oceans and seen how people live on these beautiful islands?" She gestured out the window. "Will the splendor of the opera equal the beauties of a tropical lagoon in the day's last light? Will the theater even mimic the drama we have lived? I feel as though I have only recently come to life, for the first time since. . . . Well, for a very long time. And now I go back to my walking death in Avonel—the 'ghost duchess.' I will be dead soon enough, I have no desire to hurry it. And this. . . ." She raised her hands to her face and delicately traced her fingers down, across her lips and neck to her breasts. "My precious youth will be gone. Suitors will begin to seek me for my wealth." She almost wailed at the thought, and raised her hands to her face as though this were the greatest horror of all. "Have I wasted my years, do you think, Tristam? Will I squander the time that is left? The few years while I am still young? But how shall I use them wisely? If I renounce the games of courtiers, what shall I do? I cannot bear the thought that I will come to the end of my days and think I have wasted my short life. Wasted all that I was given. But what shall I do? How shall I choose to live my life, knowing what I know—having seen what I have seen—for the world of Farrland tolerates so very little.

"Think of poor Wallis. I do not blame him for what he did. What would he have returned to? The life of a little-known artist, struggling for recognition, for enough coins to rent a room in which he would not have even wanted to live." She stopped, as though suddenly realizing that Farrland was not her true home. She had no home. No place in which she could be herself and not cause whispers and odd looks of disapproval. "I have been transformed," she said quietly, as though it were both impossible to believe, and a tragedy of the greatest order—Elorin, the Duchess of Morland, could not be a victim of circumstances. Other people had things happen to them that were beyond their control, but not she. "And you, Tristam, have suffered this same fate—so much more than I. What will you do now?" She reached out and took his hand, and Tristam felt his breath catch—but she touched only his hand, not his heart.

He shrugged.

"But you can remain as you are, untouched by age, and Tristam, I could remain young as well. Could you not do that? We would, at least, have each other. And we could have love. Endless nights and years of love. I do not know what else remains, for it seems everything else has been taken from me. Everything but you. Could you not be happy with me?"

Tristam did not answer, but looked into her large, soft eyes, filled it seemed with desperation, and wondered what such a life would be. Filled with pleasure, no doubt, but desperate pleasure. He remembered his night at the duchess' home.

"I will not keep myself from aging. You saw the vision of the war. . . . The arts must dissipate, disappear. I will not take such risks. I'm sorry, Elorin, but you must age as you will, though I do not think it will be so terrible for you. There is more to your beauty than smooth skin and lustrous hair, though you do not know it yet." Tristam looked out across the bay as the first stars began to appear. "But there is magic still. It is in the earth, and all the living things. I can feel it now, though perhaps I was aware of it before. That is the true magic and treasure of our world, Elorin. Greater than any work of man, magic enough for me, at least, if I can but learn to live simply in it. Perhaps I will try to take up residence on Farrow, and learn the art of growing grapes, perhaps even making wines. Though I do not know if I can live in the shadow of the Ruin. It has haunted me enough."

The duchess moved closer to him, nuzzling into the crook of his neck so that her hair tickled his face. "You are telling me that you will let me age, and become like every old crone?"

"Precisely."

"And my offer of endless pleasure does not tempt you at all?"

"More than I can say; but I shall engage all my will to resist."

"Small recompense." She was still for a moment. The darkness seemed to slip in and settle around them. "I do not know if I could live on Farrow," she said suddenly.

"Would an offer of nights of pleasure—though not endless—tempt you?"

"You know my particular weakness, Tristam," she whispered. "It is not fair." She pressed closer to him. "I cannot promise that I shall completely relent in my efforts to have you keep me young, if for no other reason than I do rather like getting my own way."

"I know." Quiet. Perhaps, far off, Tristam heard the call of an owl. "Elorin? I no longer know who I am. I . . . I do not know if I am capable of happiness, of kindness even, let alone love."

"I make no promises either. We have been transformed, Tristam, suffered far more than a sea change. I do not know who we will become, but who else would even begin to understand what we have suffered?"

"Yes. Who, indeed."

*   *   *

Tristam stood at the rail watching the distant shadows of dancers, as the Varuans began to celebrate the miracle of their King entering the Faraway Paradise without first passing through death in this life. And there was a new King as well—a boy of perhaps six years.

The night seemed very beautiful to him, almost imbued with enchantment. *It is inside me,* Tristam thought with some pleasure, *the night is no different.* At the same time he felt an ache. A sure knowledge that such beauty, and his experience of it, would be so brief.

There was a sound of some large fish in the water, or perhaps a dolphin.

"Tristam?" someone whispered from below.

"Faairi?" Tristam scrambled down the side of the ship into the yawl boat. "Are you not afraid to be in the water at night? There are sharks and eels and barracuda."

"I am wearing a charm that protects me," she said.

Tristam felt her soft hands, dripping with water, take hold of his own. But she remained in the water. Starlight touched her, and he could just barely make her out, long hair floating on the surface of the water, and at the center of this darkness, her eyes. "I brought you a gift of parting, Tristam," she said, her voice sad. "Give to me your hand."

Tristam did as he was told, not having to ask which hand, and felt her fasten something over the scar on his wrist.

There, dangling from a woven leather thong, was a small carved head of stone. "It is a guardian," she said, "and will watch over you, keeping despair away. 'Despair,' is that right? The deepest sadness?"

"That is right."

"And it will help you in times of pain." She said nothing for a moment. "I thank you for finding my sister and guiding her back."

Tristam gripped her hand suddenly. "I have a message for Wallis. No. I know that he is alive. Tell him that if a Farr ship comes again they must never find out he is here. This is very important. Will you tell him?"

She pulled herself up so that she was half out of the water, and embraced him strongly. "Fare well, Tristam. May you find peace in your heart."

"And may you find peace in yours," Tristam whispered.

She slipped back into the water as though it were her natural element. It was all Tristam could do to release her hands.

"You need never worry for me," she said. "And if our child is a boy, I will name him Tristam."

Tristam was taken aback, and then realized it had been only days since they had had love—she could not know. "I think it is unlikely you shall bear a child of mine," he said.

"Oh, the Old Men do not agree. If she is a girl, I shall call her Elaural."

"Where did you hear that name?"

"When I was your star. I heard another, chanting a name: Elaural." She said something in Varuan that Tristam did not understand, and then set out for the shore. He stayed in the yawl boat a long time, hoping perhaps that she would come back, and even considering going after her, though he knew he should not. *I have done what I am to do here,* he thought. *The Varuans have no more need of me. Faairi has no more need of me.* He fingered the carving at his wrist, and the words of Averil Kent came back to him.

"Isollae," he whispered to the night, but the night seemed not to hear.

∽ Forty

The survey vessel *Swallow* slipped into Avonel Harbor on a warm day near summer's end. It was early morning, just light, and the whitestone of the city seemed somehow faded and cool beneath the clinging vines and late flowers. Among the walls of stone and slate roofs, trees moved slowly in the breeze, some already burnishing to copper.

Tristam Flattery was aloft, furling sail with the topmen, but when the Jacks had finished their task and clambered down, eager to get ashore, Tristam remained, staring out over the city. He searched inside himself for a response to his return.

Is this a homecoming? he asked himself. But in truth, nothing inside of him said that it was.

"You are home," he whispered to see if the words would arouse the proper emotions, but they were only sounds, devoid of meaning.

Boats were being lifted clear of the deck and lowered over the side, but Tristam continued to sit in his aerie, staring out over the city. Below him on the deck even the Jacks were subdued, speaking in hushed tones. There was no laughter or song, no celebration of their arrival. It was a voyage all wished they had never made, and the events had left their mark on every memeber of the crew.

The young face of Pim appeared suddenly between the futtock shrouds. "Captain bids you come down, Mr. Flattery," the boy said with his usual exaggerated respect.

"Does he, indeed?" Tristam answered, making no move to comply with the captain's wishes.

"Yes, sir. There's been a signal from the tower," he said, pointing off toward a tall structure festooned with flags of various colors. "I don't know, Mr. Flattery, but it has the captain and Lieutenant Osler whispering, and looking none too happy."

"I'd better come down, then," Tristam said. He reached out and took hold of the backstay and slid down to the deck like a man with saltwater in his veins.

"We've been placed under quarantine, Mr. Flattery," Stern said quietly as Tristam arrived on the quarterdeck. The duchess stood nearby searching along the quay, then casting odd glances at Stern and Tristam. There was, Tristam realized, no one on the shore to meet her. Once the favorite of the King, now shunned. He thought she would slink below to hide her pain and humiliation. Tristam wanted to take her in his arms, but thought it would be little compensation. It was the admiration of the courtiers that she wanted, he was sure.

"We have no disease aboard," Tristam said, to Stern. "Is there some plague about that we know nothing of?"

He glanced around the harbor, and though there were ships of all nations he saw no quarantine flags flying, or any sign that men did not pass freely between shore and ship.

"A boat has put out toward us, captain," Osler said.

Beacham was standing by with a field glass, and examining the approaching cutter.

"It appears to be Admiral Gage, sir," he said, handing the glass to Stern.

"In a cutter? With no pennant flying?" Stern lifted the glass. "Flames! Prepare to pipe the admiral aboard." He looked around. "We are not ready for this," he said.

But before anything could be done, the cutter came alongside, and the old admiral clambered over the bulwark without even waiting for a proper boarding stair.

"No. No, stay your crew, Captain Burns," the admiral said, raising his hands. He bowed to the duchess, then looked around suddenly, aware of the men forming up on the deck. "This is not your entire crew, surely?" he said, turning to gaze at Stern as though to be sure he was the right man.

"All that's left," Stern said softly.

Gage looked around like a man disoriented. "But did you not have Hobbes aboard, and one of the King's physicians? And Viscount Elsworth?"

Stern nodded. "I have written a full report, Sir Jonathan."

"Well, don't deliver it to me," the admiral said, unable to hide his reaction. "Responsibility for the entire voyage has been taken from my hands. The palace will send a carriage for you at eight this evening. You, your officers, and guests. No one else is to go ashore or have contact with anyone at all who is not a member of your crew. You'll shift your berth to the quarantine anchorage and fly the quarantine flag as well." He paused to look at Stern closely, obviously wanting to ask but knowing that he could not. "I don't know what in the world you've been up to, Burns, but you have the palace in a flap such as I have not seen since the last war. I hope you have done nothing that will reflect on the service. . . ." It was almost a question, but not quite.

Stern did not respond. Not even the smallest shrug or shake of his head. "There's a bit of wind, Sir Jonathan," he said, "we should shift our berth while it holds. And Admiral? It's Stern. Lieutenant Stern."

Tristam was only halfheartedly working at packing his specimens. He had commandeered the 'tween decks mess and spread his hoard out there. Not so large a collection compared with other voyages, but not so small either. He sat on a stool and stared at the mementos of his journey—round the entire globe—having forgotten precisely what it was he had been doing.

"You look a bit distracted, my dear Tristam."

He looked up to find the duchess surveying the numerous vials and jars and boxes of skins and feathers and bones.

"Is it not utterly frustrating to be this close to the comforts of Avonel and forced to remain aboard?" she said. The duchess looked at Tristam, her gaze as penetrating as always.

"I seem to be in no hurry to go ashore," he said, a bit surprised by this statement.

The duchess' face softened suddenly, and she shook her head, coming to take a seat near him on a wooden box. "For almost four months we have had but one goal," she said, her manner earnest: "Bring this great ship home with less than half a crew. That has taken up all of our energies both day and night. But we have been suspended between the things that occurred on Varua and our return to Farrland. During all this time, Tristam, we could both put off thinking about the future—what we would do when we reached Farrland. Who we would be. It has been like any journey, a respite, a time when no decisions need be made—as though time itself paused and would resume only when our feet touched the soil of Farrland. So we cling to this moment; or at least I do. Our cramped little *Swallow* suddenly seems a place of refuge, and I am loath to leave it, if you can believe that. My old life is past, Tristam, and I cannot imagine trying to build a new one. What effort it took to build the one I had!"

She took Tristam's hand. "So here we sit, among all your dead beetles and birds and dried leaves and plants, and we do not want the clock to begin measuring time again." She tried a weak smile. "But surely we will make some kind of life ashore, people such as ourselves. After all, we are not without resources."

"No, we will make some kind of life, I have no doubt of it," Tristam said. "I am just in mourning. Do you remember the boy who arrived in Avonel to answer the summons of the King?"

The duchess smiled at this memory.

"I am mourning his passing, I think," Tristam said, a bit self-consciously.

The duchess cocked her head to one side, regarding him with some affection, he thought. "We all grieve for the passing of our idealistic young selves, at some point or another. You are doing it sooner than most, and for good reason, but it is something we all must do." She paused for only a second, barely a hint of a smile appearing. "I have been doing it myself these last ten years or more."

"The frost lays its hand upon the bloom,
For youth and beauty all must pass.
Each child is lost and never found,
And briefly wisdom's truce at last."

Tristam tried to smile.

She leaned forward and kissed his cheek. "Wisdom's truce," she said, but no more.

They were taken through a side gate to the palace and then in a small entrance. Ironically, this was the way that Roderick Palle had brought Tristam on his first trip to the palace. When they passed the spot where Tristam had first met the duchess, he looked over at her and saw that she remembered as well, which he found gratifying in some way.

As on that earlier trip, they were taken to the arboretum, though not to the place where *regis* grew. They passed through the transplanted jungle of Oceana, in single file, until they heard the sounds of water splashing into a pool. The smells of the place, and the sounds of the water tugged at Tristam's heart, and he remembered Faairi, and felt the languid tropical heat.

If only I could have done as Wallis did, Tristam found himself thinking.

They came out into the grotto and here they were greeted by familiar faces. Jaimy was there, with Alissa Somers—perhaps a Somers no more—the Duke of Blackwater, Averil Kent, Princess Joelle, Sir Stedman and Lady Galton, and Prince Wilam.

The Duke of Blackwater stood immediately. "King Wilam would like to bid you welcome, but first let me apologize for treating you so abysmally. Rumors are spreading of what happened at the abbey and on Varua, and the Farrellite Church as well as others are in a great panic. The nations around the Entide Sea fear that mages are among us again and that this power might be turned against them. We must have secrecy at all costs, as you will see when all has been told and all heard." He turned to the King, bowing, perhaps not realizing how surprised the *Swallow*'s officers and guests were not to find Prince Kori upon the throne.

Prince Wilam—King Wilam now—rose from his seat, smiling at the gathered voyagers. Tristam had only seen the young monarch once before, and he was surprised at what effect so few years had accomplished. Though he still had the youthful face of a scholar, his manner was that of one much older. Slower, more deliberate, more thoughtful of one's impact on the world around. "I am happy to see you returned safely," he began, "though saddened to hear of your losses. With all that could have befallen your ship and crew, Captain Stern, I am amazed that you were able to bring so many back, for you were sent off with so little knowledge of your voyage's true intent." He took three paces toward the pool, gathering his thoughts. "So much has happened in your absence. Much of it so extraordinary that if I had not been witness to the events myself, I would never have believed the reports of others." He shook his head as he said this, clearly not exaggerating. "But perhaps tonight we will make some sense of it, when all the stories have been recounted. There is a great deal that is still not clear to us." He looked over at Kent. "And Lady Chilton is not inclined to say more, for reasons of her own—which I feel we must respect." He paused, looking around the seated guests, holding each person's gaze for just a few seconds, and Tristam was touched by the warmth and concern in that look. "But I feel we must speak openly so that we might come to an understanding of what has happened, and form our future policy from knowledge not prejudice. We should speak of these matters, as well, for the peace of mind of those who have been involved, often against their will, in these strange matters." He gestured beyond the trees. "There will be a table set for all, but right now I think we are hungry for knowledge. Captain Stern, might I call upon you to begin, and others may add and fill in as needed? No, no. Sit. Be at your ease. It is a long tale, I imagine, and may need a glass of ale or two to help its telling."

Stern returned to his seat, more than a little self-conscious, and began his tale with being assigned the voyage of discovery, and the interview with Admiral Gage, the Sea Lord. By the time he had related the appearance of the falcon at sea, he had the full attention of his listeners.

It was, as the prince had guessed, a long tale, and occasionally it was interrupted by others. When Stern told of the Entonne ship, playing the part of a corsair, demanding Tristam be turned over to them, Kent was heard to curse the treachery of Count Massenet.

The escape into the Archipelago was overshadowed by the discovery of the Lost City, and here many questions were asked, and descriptions called for, astounding all those present. Tristam could see Jaimy looking at Alissa occasionally and raising his eyebrows in amazement, and the prince looked ready to take ship himself to see this wonder.

After this, servants brought food and drink to everyone, and Averil Kent, now the Earl of Sandhurst, took up the story, beginning with a letter from the

Countess of Chilton, from whom he had not heard for many years. Tristam was surprised to learn that Kent had seen the locked room in Dandish's home where the plants had grown, and that he had suspected the death of Baron Ipsword had related to the baron's continual attacks on Dandish.

The duchess sat rigidly still during this, but Kent tactfully did not name the person Dandish had grown the seed for, nor did he describe in much detail the evening at the duchess' home when Tristam had set the rose aflame.

It was a complex story, with many players, and the voyagers were as amazed by the revelations as the others had been by their exploits. The replica of the Ruin of Farrow in the cellar of Tremont Abbey was almost as much a surprise as the Lost City.

It was past the night's middle hour when the story was told and everyone sat in silence, still not quite able to believe that they had lived the story they had just heard, for it seemed too extraordinary to have involved real people.

A table was set there on the sand beside the speaking pool, and everyone found a place. Tristam beside Jaimy and Alissa, across from Kent and the duchess. Stern was seated to the King's left, and the princess to the right, and the captain was questioned carefully about all that he had said.

"You see now why all must be kept in confidence," the King said at one point. "And, Captain Stern, we must be absolutely sure your crew understand this, though I shall leave that to you and the duke to manage."

"But what was the purpose of this attack on our people in the Lost City?" the princess asked. She glanced at Tristam as she said this, but when he did not offer to answer, she looked quickly away.

"Like the Varuan King and Palle's group," Kent said, saving the moment, "this race in the Archipelago had some foreknowledge, and it was their hope to retrieve the arts that had been lost to them. That is what the countess believes. And they were part of the final ritual, adding their voices to our own, but Lady Chilton made sure their efforts bore no fruit. Sadly for these poor people, the knowledge was not regained. Sad for them, but better for the world at large, I think."

Tristam thought his uncle was unusually subdued, and there seemed to be some underlying sorrow in the Duke of Blackwater, though Tristam could not recognize its cause. He worried that it was the duchess, who had been so ill these past years. The man looked tired and deeply melancholy, though he struggled to be sure his manner and voice revealed none of this.

"Could you feel Trevelyan's presence, Duchess? Was he your counterpart here?" Kent asked.

She nodded, her manner solemn, and placed a hand on her heart. "I could. I felt his pain all through the ritual, and when his heart gave out, I knew his fear and then final resignation. At the last I felt him reach out toward death, as though he would embrace it and escape finally from life's suffering and sorrow. I felt him die, as though it were my own death, as indeed for a moment I thought it was." She looked very serious, as though it were her own death she spoke of. "I know now what that final moment is like; the utter horror one feels as the realization strikes, and then the resignation. It comes to us all—why struggle anymore? And we slip our life off like a robe, and go into the darkness, like a swimmer diving into the sea." She shook her head, as though trying to forget what she had experienced, then looked up at the others. "It was peaceful for him in the end, almost his last thought was that he had been the great Trevelyan, and he was proud of that."

"As he should have been," Kent said in the silence that followed the duchess' words.

For a moment everyone turned to their food, but there was too much curiosity and the questions began again.

Jaimy wanted to know if Tristam had spoken to him during the ritual, and Tristam admitted that he had. The Phantom Glen was the subject of much speculation, as were the other worlds that they had seen.

Kent was questioned about these, hoping the countess had given him some insight. "I'm afraid I know little about this," the painter said. "The war between the forces of magic and the forces of reason—that seemed to be a vision, such as the mages were able to call up. The possible world we saw, filled with squares of light and astounding machines, and squalor and terrible crime. . . . I am not sure if that is a vision or another world, like the one entered by the King. 'A world near to ours, yet infinitely distant,' Lady Chilton said." He shrugged, gesturing with his hands to indicate it was speculation. He turned to Tristam. "But you saw the same visions, or very similar. Did you think them real?"

"I am no more sure than you, Lord Sandhurst. They were real in the way that the future is real, or the past is real. We are separated from them utterly, but just because you cannot visit a land does not mean it does not exist. Two Kings chose to pass through the portal into one such world—the Faraway Paradise, the Varuans call it, so that, at least, seemed real. I could smell the flowers, and hear the sea. I saw Viscount Elsworth step into water, and I heard Ruau singing. But perhaps some of these worlds have substance in a different way." He smiled awkwardly. "Without the writings of the mages we cannot know. Perhaps even they did not know."

"Do you think then that the Varuan King sent Mr. Ruau here for that purpose?" the princess asked Tristam. "So the gate would be opened and they could pass from this life into this promised land?"

Tristam nodded. "That is what I think, though I don't believe that is the function all of this served. They were but players, performing their part, as were Mr. Ruau and the viscount. Somehow they were needed. They were almost sacrificial. But the countess knew that everything that had been planned by these others, whoever they really were, could be used to seal the way, though where she learned that part of the ritual I do not know. But I could hear it in my mind as though she spoke it to me, and together we were able to perform the rite. The rite that would avoid the war which would so gravely wound our world, as difficult as that is for us to imagine."

"Yes," the Duke of Blackwater said, "the world is so vast, and the strength and vigor of nature so ultimately powerful. Still . . . I do not doubt what was seen, nor what it meant."

Tristam was aware that people looked at him oddly, and when he met their eyes they would look away quickly—even Jaimy did this. And when Tristam spoke, other conversations would fall silent so that the speakers might listen. *They think I am a mage,* Tristam knew. *It is as though Eldrich had come to sit at their table.*

Tristam also noted that the new King did not look at Alissa unless she spoke, except once he glanced her way quickly, as though afraid he would be caught. There was another story there, Tristam was sure.

"May I make a toast to my cousin, Lord Jaimas, and his bride Lady Alissa?" Tristam asked suddenly, and his words produced smiles all around. "I know it is months late, but I could not be present at the wedding and missed my opportunity then." Tristam stood and raised his glass. "May life be kind, and friends loyal. Ventures profitable, children plentiful, and age like a slow turning of the leaves in autumn; grand, beautiful, and tranquil."

Glasses were raised to the obviously happy couple and Tristam could not help but notice brief looks of pain on the face of the young King, and the Duchess of Morland.

Galton caught Tristam's eye. "I still do not understand how Llewellyn thought that he could attack you. Have I completely misunderstood things? Did you not perform a rite of warding?"

"I do not understand it myself, Sir Stedman," Tristam said, "nor was I aware of his attempt on my life."

"I think I have an answer there," Kent said. "The countess told me that, after the struggle with the emerging mage, there is a point in the ritual where the new mage can be slain. It was always thus, for some lost the struggle entire, and would have become something even the mages feared. But they had ways of knowing this at the time, and ways of dealing with it. This was in the text that Llewellyn and Wells had held back, even from some of their own people. They were afraid to show it to Sir Stedman or Dr. Rawdon—afraid they would alienate them—but I think they might have planned to use it all along to rid themselves of Tristam, once the portals were opened. This Jack who leaped onto the stage . . . He did not save just Tristam, I think."

The meal ended and the duke, as a member of the Council of Regents, swore everyone present to secrecy regarding certain aspects of the voyage, and a plausible story of the voyage was agreed upon by all present.

"I'm sure that word of this will get out to Massenet," Galton said, "even if we were to jail every Jack from the *Swallow* for the rest of their natural lives. That cannot be helped, I'm afraid."

"Even more reason to send a ship back to this Lost City," the King said. "We must get there before the Entonne and make certain nothing remains that will lead them to these lost arts. Even with this portal sealed, it is yet possible that some of the arts might be recovered, perhaps not the power the mages once knew, but some part of it. No, we must send a ship to the Archipelago as early in the spring as we can manage to make contact with this secretive race, and to explore the Lost City." He turned to Stern. "Captain Stern, I would most like to see you in command of this voyage, if you can be ready for such an undertaking in so few months."

Stern nodded his head in deference. "I go where the Admiralty sends me, Your Majesty," the captain said evenly.

"And poorly they have rewarded you for it, Lieutenant," the duchess interjected. "Excuse me for bringing up this matter at such a time, Your Majesty, but an officer with such an exemplary career as Lieutenant Stern should have been made Post Captain long ago. The Admiralty have not repaid his service and loyalty in kind, that is certain."

Stern appeared mortified by the duchess' outburst, and the King turned to look at both Galton and the Duke of Blackwater, clearly irate. "It is a grave problem in the King's Navy," he said, as though he were not the king. "A man must have a patron to advance, no matter what his record of service. It shall be the ruin of Farrland, one day." He turned back to Stern. "But it shall be made up to you, Captain Stern. You shall have your post and more. In fact, you shall have a knighthood for your service to the crown, and the disservice you have suffered at the hands of my admirals."

Both Galton and the duke started forward as though they would protest, but a look from the young King stopped them. "A knighthood," he repeated. "And then the admirals can vie for your favor!" he said with more than a little glee. "The Sea Lord shall have you to dinner fortnightly, and the sons of peers will compete to serve under the great Stern, who sailed with Gregory!" The King exhibited a certain boyish delight at making waves in the Admiralty.

Galton glanced over at the duke and the two men smiled.

The duchess raised her glass, then motioned with it in the smallest way to Tristam; a toast to her still undiminished skills and timing, or so he thought.

The King rose at his place and lifted a glass. "And to you all for your efforts, those who journeyed to strange and distant lands, and those who entered the secret struggle here on our own shores. There will be rewards for all, and none shall be overlooked. Especially those who have crossed over—a saying that now has real meaning. The great Trevelyan, and even this poor officer, Hobbes, who was a victim of our corrupt service and the treachery of Dr. Llewellyn, I suspect. This mutineer Kreel who lost his life to save Mr. Flattery might have a family. All will be remembered. And some I have asked to name their reward must speak soon or I shall have to decide on my own." He looked pointedly at the Duke of Blackwater, who would not meet his young sovereign's gaze.

"We must remember, Your Majesty," Stedman Galton said, "that if we are to keep so much secret, conspicuous rewards that cannot be justified in other ways will only start people asking questions."

The young King nodded, breaking into a smile. "Much can be attributed to the capriciousness of a young king, though I take your point, Sir Stedman."

The King retired then, asking for private audiences with a few of those present. Tristam went to him first.

The King had taken a seat in a glade filled with the flowers of Varua, and Tristam stood before him. He thought Wilam looked a serious young man, perhaps a little strained by his new responsibilities, for it was clear he was not sitting back and allowing the Council of Regents to run his nation. Knowing at least two of the regents, Tristam was certain they were not trying to marginalize this young ruler, but train him in his duties, and involve him in the running of his nation.

"I have been assured by your uncle, the duke," the King began, "that you will swear never to use these powers you have gained. Lady Chilton has said that the use of magic sustains it somehow, that it always remains a danger while even one practitioner lives. I do not know how the duke can presume to speak for you, Mr. Flattery, so I should like to hear what you have to say for yourself."

Tristam knew this moment would come, but he had long since made his decision. "Lady Chilton and the duke both spoke the truth. The arts cannot be practiced or all we have accomplished will be endangered. I will swear never to use these powers, and not to pass them on to another."

The young sovereign stared up at Tristam, his gaze filled with questions. "I know what price you will pay for this, Mr. Flattery," he said, "but I think it will ask even more of your uncle, the duke, and his fair wife. He had hoped to cure the duchess with the seed, for she lies wasting away from some mysterious ailment that no physician can even name, let alone cure. That is the price they will pay to see that the arts are not reborn, and I am deeply sorry for it."

Tristam nodded. He should have realized. Perhaps Llewellyn's story about Rawdon curing his wife had not been fabrication.

"Have you seed in your possession still?" the King asked.

"Some small amount that Dr. Llewellyn had. I have almost weaned myself of it now, though I am not quite done."

The King bit his lip for a second. "Well, keep it safe, Mr. Flattery. Let none of it escape, or it might find some way to propagate even at these latitudes. This seed is unnatural and strange; almost 'aware,' our own gardener claims."

"I will be sure it falls into no one's hands, sir," Tristam said, reminded of old Tumney by the King's words, and the day he had come to the palace for the first time. "No one has bothered to explain what happened to Sir Roderick Palle?"

The King blew out a long breath, looking down at the ground. "We have his man Hawksmoor and some others in prison, as we speak, but none will incriminate their master. He is, if you can believe it, still a Regent, clinging to power with a tenacity that can hardly be believed. And on top of that he has made himself enormously useful. The man has a cunning that one cannot help but admire—even if there is little else admirable about him. But it will not profit him in the end. The regency will end too soon, and I will not have forgotten what he did. Lord Jaimas told me the tale of how he and his companion were hunted up and down the length of County Coombs. Palle may not have ordered it, and I suspect he did not, but his flexible morality and ability to look away at just the right moment fostered it. I will see him end his life in such obscurity that he will begin to wonder if he was ever actually the King's Man at all." He looked up, impressing Tristam with his resolve. Palle's tenacity had met its match, Tristam thought.

The young King's gaze softened then. "And what can an inexperienced King do for you Mr. Flattery, for we are all in your debt—those who know what went on and the thousands who will never know? Few could resist what you will swear to renounce: long life, vitality, power, knowledge. I am not so sure I could deny myself these so easily."

"I saw the vision of the mages, Your Majesty. I am not so far removed from other men that I could allow that, nor could I allow the world to be brought to ruin. We have all given up something, sir," Tristam said, thinking of the look the King had given Alissa. "I deserve no more than any other."

"But what will you do now? Where does a near-mage make his life? You will suffer from want of this seed, I know. I saw what it did to my grandfather. It will be a torment, even to you. Is there nothing at all that I might do?"

"There is one thing," Tristam said, having already considered this possibility.

"Name it."

"I know this will be difficult because of the feelings of Princess Joelle, but if Your Majesty could bring the Duchess of Morland into the life of the court, I would be grateful."

The King looked up at him, a little surprised by this request. "I will do it if that is what you truly want."

Tristam nodded, suddenly unable to speak.

The King gazed at him a moment, eyes narrowing, perhaps feeling that this gesture bound them together. "The King left an envelope for the Duchess of Morland. I don't know what it contains, but Galton will give it to her. His Majesty cared for her, I know, and in her turn the duchess protected him and brought him no small measure of joy—the daughter he never had, I think. I will do as you ask, for you and for the sake of my late grandfather. The princess will simply have to accept it. There is nothing I might do for Tristam Flattery?"

"Nothing, but I thank you for granting my request."

Tristam stood there, unable to retire until he had been given leave, but feeling the interview was over.

"This talisman on your wrist, Mr. Flattery . . . what is it?"

"It was given to me by the Varuans, to help me in times of pain."

The King took a long breath, absorbing the statement. "And does it?" he asked softly.

Tristam shrugged. "Perhaps."

The King considered for a moment, his young face so very serious. "Good fortune to you, Mr. Flattery," he said. "Call upon me if ever you have a need. You have not asked nearly enough of me and I will not forget it."

Alissa had retired to bed, leaving Jaimy and Tristam alone in the library of the newlyweds' Avonel home. It was near to morning. Tristam could hear the carriages of tradesmen passing already, though the light was still two hours off.

"I hope you will stay with us a while," Jaimy said, "though I'm sure you are anxious to see your home in Locfal again, after all that has happened. Though I will tell you, I wish you would find a place in Avonel so that you won't be so far away. After all, you might be an uncle one day, and one cannot perform one's avuncular duties from such a distance."

Tristam smiled. "I do want to make a trip to Locfal, though I am of a mind to spend the winter months on Farrow, perhaps even longer." Tristam could see Jaimy's disappointment at this news.

"Will you take after Uncle Erasmus and withdraw from friends and family? Become the recluse of our generation?"

"I find it difficult to be in society now, J. Oh, I do not include yourself or your bride in that, of course, but I am not as I once was, and the company of others seems only to succeed in making me feel even more odd, more isolated. I need to get away. I need to come to grips with what has happened, and with what I have become. And I need to rest. Perhaps it is a result of weaning myself from the seed, but I seem to be in desperate need of rest, of sleep, of time to contemplate. The duke has promised to give me Erasmus' journals and papers, and I would like to sit on the terrace, gaze out over the shoreless sea, and read. It is a chance to get to know this man who was my guardian, for he always kept himself a stranger."

"So I cannot manage a match for you with one of Alissa's sisters and convince you to buy a home nearby?" Jaimy said, a bit resignedly.

Tristam reached out and touched his cousin's arm. "There is nothing I would like more, but I'm not fit to be a husband to a young woman raised in the lovely world of Merton. I am haunted, Jaimas. I cannot begin to explain, but I am haunted. . . . I have not the words," he said, closing his eyes wearily.

Jaimy nodded, his look infinitely sad. "The countess told me that she was young in her form but ancient in her heart. I suspect this has happened to you, Tristam, and if there is anything at all that I can do to help, just tell me and I will do it."

Tristam was struck by what the countess had said, and touched by his cousin's concern. "You brought me into the fold when we attended Merton, Jaimy. Made me one of the gang. I would have been miserable there without you. But I don't think you can do that now. The problem is different. I knew immediately what the countess meant. In some inexplicable way, I feel ancient." Tristam shook his head, desperately wishing he could make his cousin understand, so that he might understand himself.

"I worry about you going off to Farrow, Tristam. I. . . ." He considered his next words. Tristam saw the skin around his eyes tighten, as though there were tears not far off. "I worry that you will slip into melancholia, and I will not know, for I am so far away."

"You need not worry, Jaimy. I think I will be all right. I don't think I am destined to follow my father's course. And I will write. There is monthly mail, even in winter. I will visit, I promise. And you might even visit me, and see the famous ruin."

Jaimy shook his head, almost a shudder. "I would be afraid to even glimpse it, Tristam. I have had enough of all that. I want to turn away from the visions I saw through the portal. I want to live in the world of the daylight and blue skies."

"And so do I, Jaimy," Tristam said softly. "And so do I."

Tristam sat alone in the library, unable to sleep. He clasped Faairi's talisman in his hand, rubbing it as though something might be absorbed through the skin—something that would dull pain.

"Tristam?"

He looked up to find Alissa standing in the doorway, wrapped in a warm robe, her hair in disarray.

"Can you not sleep?" she asked.

"I am not tired," he lied, and tried to smile. "This stone the countess gave you, Alissa; might I see it?"

She looked at him quizzically, clearly surprised by his request. "Yes. Certainly." She half-turned in the door. "Shall I fetch it now?"

"Please."

A moment later she returned bearing a small silver box. She opened the clasp and took out a perfect stone, the size of which Tristam had never seen. He took it by the chain and held it up to the light, turning it slowly, and then he dropped it on his palm and closed his hand over it for a few seconds.

"You wore this during the ritual?" Tristam asked, and Alissa nodded. "And held it with which hand? May I see?"

She offered Tristam her hand, looking a little confused, but clearly showing her trust of him.

Tristam turned her hand over and seemed to stare at it, but then she realized that his eyes were pressed tightly closed. He released her hand, and sat back in his chair, his eyes opened but focused somewhere beyond the room. He still held the stone in his closed fist.

After a moment he looked up and smiled, opening his hand to reveal the glittering diamond. "This stone, Alissa, I am surprised the countess did not realize. It has some residue of the ritual in it still, for it was an instrument in what was done."

"You are saying it is magical?" Alissa asked, suddenly looking fully awake.

"More or less, yes. It has some residue of the power that was touched. Do you see? It will fade in time, I'm sure, but I can feel it strongly now. And your hand is the same, through to a lesser degree. You have some residue of the power there as well, though it will fade even more quickly. But while it lasts you will be able to perform some astonishing feats, I think."

"Such as?" Alissa said, raising her hand and looking at it.

"Has Jaimy not told you that I could flip a coin and have it land heads an impossible number of times?"

She nodded.

"Well, certainly you can do that, so you will be a terror at the gambling tables. But more important, you will be able to give people a blessing such as no priest of Farrelle ever managed."

"What are you saying?" she asked, suddenly a bit alarmed.

"Place your hand upon someone's brow and see what will happen in their lives. They will have good fortune in the extreme. And you will be able to heal. Oh, not terrible diseases, perhaps, but take away pain and heal minor hurts, I'm sure."

Alissa looked at him, suddenly wary, as though she wondered if he were practicing on her.

"I swear I am speaking true," Tristam said.

"Are you saying I might cure the duchess?"

Tristam shook his head. "No, you have not enough power or skill. But the diamond, Alissa. . . . Give it to the duchess. Have her wear it night and day, and I think you will see a difference. More than that perhaps."

"But Tristam, is this not dangerous? Did you not swear to never use the power you have gained?"

"I did, but I will not do it. This stone, its power cannot be taken away but by the arts. Perhaps the countess could do that, but she would have to use the arts. Do you see? The best thing is to let its power fade, as it will in time. But I think it will do no harm if it is kept safe around the neck of the duchess, for a while. Then have it delivered to me, and I will keep it safe. In a dozen years, perhaps, you shall have it back."

Tristam could see that the thought of a cure for the duchess brought Alissa close to tears. "But what of my hand? I cannot send that to you."

Tristam laughed. "No, but you shall do no ill, I'm certain. And it will fade soon. In a few months, I think. A year at the most. But tell no one, Alissa. Best even the duchess does not know. If word got out. . . ."

Alissa nodded, and touched her hand to her heart. "Do you know, Averil Kent once said he thought I had the power to heal in my hands. If he had only known."

"And perhaps he did. Never underestimate our good Kent," Tristam said offering the stone back to Alissa. She took it carefully, as though to drop it would be to condemn the duchess to a brief life of pain and suffering. Then she leaned forward, kissed Tristam on the cheek, and went silently out.

The stars were sinking beneath the surface of the morning sky when Kent arrived at the countess' Avonel home. She could not quite change the habit of the past decades and remained for the most part in seclusion within her own walls. Kent was not sure that would ever change—not within his lifetime anyway. But he stayed with her now most nights, and she accepted the occasional visitor.

Despite the hour Kent found the countess sitting on the terrace, a coffee serving on a small table at her side. She turned her face up to the growing light, as though the caress of the breeze gave her immeasurable pleasure. She had regained some of her youthful appearance since they had returned to Avonel, though as she slowly deprived herself of the physic, this was waning. He thought she had the appearance of a well preserved woman of perhaps sixty years. Her hair was very fine and pure white, lines drew a pattern across her once perfect skin, and her lips were bordered with the tiniest wrinkles. But Kent did not care, she was still beautiful to him. Just standing there looking at her he felt his heart swell. He was not sure what would become of them, but these last months he had felt a contentment like he had never known in all his life, and the countess seemed happier as well.

She smiled when she heard Kent arrive, but did not open her eyes. "Lord Sandhurst," she said, and the warmth and color in her voice caused a little surge of joy within him.

"Lady Chilton," he answered, equally formal.

"You have seen our voyagers?"

"Yes . . . the few that returned," Kent said, his voice serious now.

She nodded, the look of pleasure disappearing. Her eyes opened, and she turned to Kent. "Come and sit by me," she said softly, "and tell me their tale." She poured coffee into a second cup as though she had been expecting his arrival, which she very likely had. Kent was quite sure she knew and could predict things in a way that was not natural.

"You spoke with Tristam Flattery?" she asked.

"Yes, and he seemed little changed. Oh, he has grown up a great deal and become more serious, if not a bit grim, but he did not seem utterly transformed as I expected." He looked over the countess, as though expecting an explanation.

She nodded. "Perhaps he has come through it better than I had hoped. And he swore never to use his new-gained knowledge?"

Kent nodded.

"I would like to meet this young man. Will you arrange that, Averil?"

"Gladly. And the Duchess of Morland would like to visit you as well."

"Good. I have a few words to say to her, too. Bring them both, but separately." She smiled at the painter and reached out and took his hand. "Do you need sleep? You have been up all night."

"No, I am surprisingly filled with energy these days." He saw the concern in her face, and it touched him. "Perhaps I will sleep a little later. But let me begin this tale, it is long and involved."

The countess settled back in her chair but did not release his hand. "Then let us begin, and then you shall sleep for a while and later this evening perhaps I would like to see the view from the high road to Brigham Head. Can one still walk there beneath the elms? It has not been spoiled?"

"No, there is a park there yet. Very pretty in the evening light." Kent sipped his coffee, and then began the tale as he had heard it from the voyagers. All the while he felt the warmth from the countess' hand in his, as though it gave him strength and more than that, happiness. As he spoke a small boy appeared in the shade of a tree, curling up against the bole to listen.

"Do you see, Kent?" the countess whispered, "he likes you. Almost always he appears when you are here. And he takes food now when I leave it on the table, and does not always hide when I come into the garden. I have hope for him yet, poor thing. Imagine, lost in time, wandering in a dream all those years. How I want to learn how this happened, if the poor boy even knows. But your story first, my dear. And then we shall rest. Rest and take our leisure. We have no reason to hurry. No reason at all."

Autumn had come down off the northern hills and spread like a tide of copper and crimson and gold across the woods and meadows of Farrland. It flowed slowly, day by day, through gardens and along hedges until it came at last to the city of Avonel, where the reflections of the turning trees cast their dying colors on the waters of the harbor, where they looked like the wavering reflections of flames. And the tide turned and swept this fire silently out to sea.

Tristam stood at the rail of the mail ship, looking across the water to the city spread across the hill in the warm sunlight.

"I'm sure the duchess has been detained," Jaimy said, looking at his watch.

Tristam nodded. "Perhaps."

They stood in awkward silence, staring out toward the quay. An officer came up behind Tristam and cleared his throat quietly.

"The captain says we're going to lose the tide, sir," the man said.

Tristam nodded, then turned to Jaimy. "I guess you should be going, J," he said, masking all emotion in his voice.

Jaimy's look was filled with compassion. "You procured her a place at court," he said quietly. "I'm sure it's not that she doesn't have feelings for you. . . . But the duchess is a creature of the court, Tris, and well, Farrow. . . ." He did not finish.

Tristam nodded. "Your boat is about to leave."

Jaimy looked over the rail and then back at his cousin. "It seems so wrong, that you have sacrificed so much, and now I feel like you are going into exile. And going alone. But I cannot accompany you, Tristam."

"Your place is here, Jaimas. And don't forget, I have never had such a need for the company of others. My love to Alissa, and to you, J."

The two cousins embraced, and then Jaimy went quickly down the stair into the boat. He looked up at Tristam and tried to smile as they pulled away, and then took his place, and sat staring back at his cousin as the oarsmen pulled across the harbor.

Jacks began to labor at the capstan and the topmen scrambled aloft.

Tristam turned away as Jaimy's boat disappeared behind a ship. He looked out to sea, to the white clouds floating on the horizon, like clouds gathered above a distant island. He thought of Varua and Faairi, and closed his eyes, caressing her talisman between his fingers.

There was a shout from behind, and Tristam turned, searching for the source. Then he saw a boat making its way through the maze of ships, the oarsmen bent to their work. And there, among the Jacks, he saw the duchess. She raised a hand and waved, though not with enthusiasm.

She has come to bid me farewell, Tristam thought immediately. As the boat drew closer he was even more sure, for the duchess bore such a look of sadness—as though she were about to break his heart and did not know how to do it gently. A breeze caught a stray strand of her hair and it fluttered slowly in the wind and Tristam remembered the first time he had laid eyes on her. She had seemed so impossibly remote and beautiful to him then. But now he knew her face better than he did his own. Knew there was a tiny mole hidden in her hairline above her right ear. He could read her moods in her eyes and on her mouth. Knew that when she was truly joyous, her smile revealed too much of the upper gum—something she struggled never to do—but he loved to see it.

As the boat came alongside, he could see her perfect soft lips were pressed hard together, and she looked so filled with regret and unhappiness that Tristam thought his heart would break.

The duchess lifted up her skirts and came up the stair, watching every step so that Tristam could no longer see her face. When she reached the deck, she looked up and a smile that was forming dissolved.

"My dear Tristam, are you unwell?" she asked. "You look like a man lost in melancholia."

Tristam shrugged, not sure what to say.

She came up then and kissed his cheek, and took his arm, standing close beside him, and looking out at the city of Avonel. She sighed. "Well, have I passed your little test? Choosing you over the court?"

Tristam found her hand, and she squeezed his hand as though she were angry with him, but then this subsided and she caressed it gently. "I should never have doubted it," he said. "The countess predicted you would come."

"Did she?" the duchess said, genuinely interested. "She said something of it to me." She fell silent for a few seconds, lost in thought. "All she said to me, Tristam, was, 'be sure you have someone who can see past your beauty, otherwise you will find one day that you have become invisible.' You do care for me for what is in my mind and heart, don't you, Tristam?"

Tristam squeezed her hand. "Though your lovely lips and eyes have not lost their allure, to me at least."

The duchess was quiet again. The ship had begun to make way, heeling just slightly to the breeze, gathering way. "Did you see how she was with Kent?" the duchess asked suddenly. Tristam did not need to ask who "she" was.

"I saw."

"She does not expect to keep him with her for very long, does she?"

Tristam shook his head, thinking of how kind and generous Averil Kent was, and all that the artist had done in his years. "No," Tristam said, his voice almost a whisper. "I think we have seen the last painting from Averil Kent."

"Well, at least he shall have his heart's desire for a short time," the duchess said. "Not everyone can say that."

"Only a very few," Tristam said, squeezing her hand. He turned and met her gaze. For a second she seemed almost disoriented by the intensity of that look, but then her face lit in a mischievous smile.

"I must tell you, Tristam, the court is not what it once was. Everyone seems to possess half my years and a third of my wit." She shook her head. "It makes even Farrow sound enticing." But then, in the midst of her words, her mask of mocking good humor fell away, and she looked suddenly anguished. Tristam put his arm around her, and they did not speak for a while. When the duchess broke the silence, her voice was very small. "Do you remember setting out aboard the *Swallow*? You took your Fromme glass and showed me my home as we left the harbor?"

Tristam nodded.

"But where is my home now?" she whispered.

"I don't know," Tristam said, "but perhaps we will find it yet."

Jaimy appeared from behind a ship. He stood on the quay, and waved his hat, looking almost like a schoolboy at that distance.

Tristam lifted up his arm to wave in return, and a bird cried somewhere high overhead where it rose on a fair wind, at home among the clouds.

ACKNOWLEDGMENTS

For *World Without End*:
As always this book wouldn't have come into being without the input and support of many. Thanks go to Karen, of course; Jill, Walter and Chris at White Dwarf Books; Ian Dennis; my agent, Bella Pomer; my editor, Betsy Wollheim, and all the folks at DAW; Sean Stewart; Stephen and Petra; Margo; Rory MacIntosh for geological information; Elizabeth Towers and Mark Hobson for their help with the natural history; Don and Michael; and John Harland and Mark Myers for writing their impressive *Seamanship in the Age of Sail.*

For *Sea Without a Shore*:
Sean Stewart actually moved to Texas to avoid reading this one, but my usual readers were up to the task. Thanks to Karen, naturally; Jill, Walter, and Chris at White Dwarf Books. I also want to thank Rose and Brian Klinkenberg for answering all of my botanical and zoological questions not only graciously but promptly!